Dust
of Dreams

STEVEN ERIKSON

Dust of Dreams

BOOK NINE OF
THE MALAZAN
BOOK OF THE FALLEN

A TOM DOHERTY ASSOCIATES BOOK
NEW YORK

DUST OF DREAMS: BOOK NINE OF THE MALAZAN BOOK OF THE FALLEN

Copyright © 2009 by Steven Erikson

First published in Great Britain by Bantam Press, a division of Transworld Publishers

Map by Neil Gower

A Tor Book
Published by Tom Doherty Associates, LLC
175 Fifth Avenue
New York, NY 10010

www.tor-forge.com

Tor® is a registered trademark of Tom Doherty Associates, LLC.

Library of Congress Cataloging-in-Publication Data

Erikson, Steven.
    Dust of dreams / Steven Erikson. — 1st ed.
        p. cm. — (The Malazan book of the fallen ; bk. 9)
    "A Tom Doherty Associates book."
    ISBN 978-0-7653-1009-5 (hardcover)
    ISBN 978-0-7653-1655-4 (trade paperback)
    I. Title.
  PR9199.4.E745D87 2010
  813'.6—dc22

                                  2009040411

First U.S. Edition: January 2010

Printed in the United States of America

0 9 8 7 6 5 4 3 2 1

Ten years ago I received an endorsement from a most
unexpected source, from a writer I respected and admired.
The friendship born in that moment is one I deeply treasure.
With love and gratitude, I dedicate this novel
to Stephen R. Donaldson.

Contents

Acknowledgments

Commenting on the first half of a very long, two-volume novel is not an easy task. My thanks (and sympathy) go to William Hunter, Hazel Kendall, Bowen Thomas-Lundin, and Aidan-Paul Canavan for their percipience and forbearance. Appreciation also goes to the staff at The Black Stilt and Café Macchiato in Victoria who were very understanding in my surrender to caffeine-free coffee. Thanks too to Clare Thomas; and special gratitude goes to my students in the writing workshop I have been conducting for the past few months. Shannon, Margaret, Shigenori, Brenda, Jade, and Lenore: you have helped remind me what fiction writing is all about.

Author's Note

While I am, of course, not known for writing door-stopper tomes, the conclusion of 'The Malazan Book of the Fallen' was, to my mind, always going to demand something more than modern bookbinding technology could accommodate. To date, I have avoided writing cliff-hangers, principally because as a reader I always hated having to wait to find out what happens. Alas, *Dust of Dreams* is the first half of a two-volume novel, to be concluded with *The Crippled God*. Accordingly, if you're looking for resolutions to various story-threads, you won't find them. Also, do note that there is no epilogue and, structurally, *Dust of Dreams* does not follow the traditional arc for a novel. To this, all I can ask of you is, please be patient. I know you can do it: after all, you have waited this long, haven't you?

Steven Erikson
Victoria, B.C.

The EMPIRE of LETHER
and its neighbours...

CALASH SEA

Reach Inlet

The Reach · Fent Reach

Tiste

Katter Bight

Old Katter

Saltsong's Reach

Dresh

First Reach

Three Maidens Forts

Awl

Tulamesh

Rennis

Brous

Letheras

Miner Sluice

Bridle

Harness

Lether River

EMPIRE of LETHER

Old Gedure

Roster

Sadon

Gedry

DOMAIN OCEAN

Lenth

OUSTER SEA

Trails

Gress

Obertull

Gress Bay

Rance

Deselen

Deepwaters

Beller

East Bay

Truce

Brys

DRACONS SEA

Tallis

Mawkesh

DRACONS

Mawkesh Strait

TRUCE

The Preserve

Ridge Island

Reef Strait

KARN

Karn

Peckface Islands

Karyx

Blueglow Point

Hyacinth Passage

Moon Bay

Peaks Bay

Fire

Twill

Ender

Port

Hyacinth Reach

PILOTT ISTHMUS

Korshenn

Peck

KORSHENN

Goss

DESCENT T'ROOS

SEA IBAN

D'ALIBAN

Dramatis Personae

The Malazans

Adjunct Tavore
High Mage Quick Ben
Fist Keneb
Fist Blistig
Captain Lostara Yil
Banaschar
Captain Kindly
Captain Skanarow
Captain Faradan Sort
Captain Ruthan Gudd
Captain Fast
Captain Untilly Rum
Lieutenant Pores
Lieutenant Raband
Sinn
Grub

The Squads

Sergeant Fiddler
Corporal Tarr
Koryk
Smiles
Bottle
Corabb Bhilan Thenu'alas
Cuttle

Sergeant Gesler
Corporal Stormy
Shortnose
Flashwit
Mayfly
Sergeant Cord
Corporal Shard
Limp
Ebron
Crump (Jamber Bole)
Sergeant Hellian
Corporal Touchy
Corporal Brethless
Balgrid
Maybe
Sergeant Balm
Corporal Deadsmell
Throatslitter
Galt
Lobe
Widdershins
Sergeant Thom Tissy
Tulip
Gullstream
Sergeant Urb
Corporal Reem
Masan Gilani
Saltlick
Scant

Sergeant Sinter
Corporal Pravalak Rim
Honey
Strap Mull
Shoaly
Lookback
Sergeant Badan Gruk
Corporal Ruffle
Skim
Nep Furrow
Reliko
Vastly Blank
Sergeant Primly
Corporal Kisswhere
Hunt
Mulvan Dreader
Neller
Skulldeath
Drawfirst

Dead Hedge
Alchemist Bavedict
Sergeant Sunrise
Sergeant Nose Stream
Corporal Sweetlard
Corporal Rumjugs

The Khundryl

Warleader Gall
Hanavat (Gall's wife)
Jarabb
Shelemasa
Vedith

The Perish Grey Helms

Mortal Sword Krughava
Shield Anvil Tanakalian
Destriant Run'Thurvian

The Letherii

King Tehol
Queen Janath
Chancellor Bugg
Ceda Bugg
Treasurer Bugg
Yan Tovis (Twilight)
Yedan Derryg (the Watch)
Brys Beddict
Atri-Ceda Aranict
Shurq Elalle
Skorgen Kaban
Ublala Pung
Witch Pully
Witch Skwish
Brevity
Pithy
Rucket
Ursto Hoobutt
Pinosel

The Barghast

Warleader Onos Toolan
Hetan
Stavi
Storii
Warchief Stolmen
Warlock Cafal
Strahl
Bakal
Warchief Maral Eb
Skincut Ralata
Awl Torrent
Setoc of the Wolves

The Snake

Rutt
Held
Badalle

Saddic
Brayderal

Imass

Onrack
Kilava
Ulshun Pral

T'lan Imass

Lera Epar
Kalt Urmanal
Rystalle Ev
Brolos Haran
Ilm Absinos
Ulag Togtil
Nom Kala
Inistral Ovan

K'Chain Che'malle

Matron Gunth'an Acyl
J'an Sentinel Bre'nigan
K'ell Hunter Sag'Churok
One Daughter Gunth Mach
K'ell Hunter Kor Thuran
K'ell Hunter Rythok
Shi'Gal Assassin Gu'Rull
Sulkit
Destriant Kalyth (Elan)

Others

Silchas Ruin
Rud Elalle
Telorast
Curdle
The Errant (Errastas)
Knuckles (Sechul Lath)
Kilmandaros
Mael
Olar Ethil
Udinaas

Sheb
Taxilian
Veed
Asane
Breath
Last
Nappet
Rautos

Sandalath Drukorlat
Withal
Mape
Rind
Pule
Bent
Roach

Dust
of Dreams

Prologue

Elan Plain, west of Kolanse

There was light, and then there was heat.

He knelt, carefully taking each brittle fold in his hands, ensuring that every crease was perfect, that nothing of the baby was exposed to the sun. He drew the hood in until little more than a fist-sized hole was left for her face, her features grey smudges in the darkness, and then he gently picked her up and settled her into the fold of his left arm. There was no hardship in this.

They'd camped near the only tree in any direction, but not under it. The tree was a gamleh tree and the gamlehs were angry with people. In the dusk of the night before, its branches had been thick with fluttering masses of grey leaves, at least until they drew closer. This morning the branches were bare.

Facing west, Rutt stood holding the baby he had named Held. The grasses were colourless. In places they had been scoured away by the dry wind, wind that had then carved the dust out round their roots to expose the pale bulbs so the plants withered and died. After the dust and bulbs had gone, sometimes gravel was left. Other times it was just bedrock, black and gnarled. Elan Plain was losing its hair, but that was something Badalle might say, her green eyes fixed on the words in her head. There was no question she had a gift, but some gifts, Rutt knew, were curses in disguise.

Badalle walked up to him now, her sun-charred arms thin as stork necks, the hands hanging at her sides coated in dust and looking oversized beside her skinny thighs. She blew to scatter the flies crusting her mouth and intoned:

> 'Rutt he holds Held
> Wraps her good
> In the morning
> And then up he stands—'

'Badalle,' he said, knowing she was not finished with her poem but knowing, as well, that she would not be rushed, 'we still live.'

She nodded.

These few words of his had become a ritual between them, although the ritual never lost its taint of surprise, its faint disbelief. The ribbers had been especially hard on them last night, but the good news was that maybe they had finally left the Fathers behind.

Rutt adjusted the baby he'd named Held in his arm, and then he set out, hobbling on swollen feet. Westward, into the heart of the Elan.

He did not need to look back to see that the others were following. Those who could, did. The ribbers would come for the rest. He'd not asked to be the head of the snake. He'd not asked for anything, but he was the tallest and might be he was the oldest. Might be he was thirteen, could be he was fourteen.

Behind him Badalle said,

> *'And walks he starts*
> *Out of that morning*
> *With Held in his arms*
> *And his ribby tail*
> *It snakes out*
> *Like a tongue*
> *From the sun.*
> *You need the longest*
> *Tongue*
> *When searching for*
> *Water*
> *Like the sun likes to do . . .'*

Badalle watched him for a time, watched as the others fell into his wake. She would join the ribby snake soon enough. She blew at the flies, but of course they came right back, clustering round the sores puffing her lips, hopping up to lick at the corners of her eyes. She had been a beauty once, with these green eyes and her long fair hair like tresses of gold. But beauty bought smiles for only so long. *When the larder gapes empty, beauty gets smudged.* 'And the flies,' she whispered, 'make patterns of suffering. And suffering is ugly.'

She watched Rutt. He was the head of the snake. He was the fangs, too, but that last bit was for her alone, her private joke.

This snake had forgotten how to eat.

She'd been among the ones who'd come up from the south, from the husks of homes in Korbanse, Krosis and Kanros. Even the isles of Otpelas. Some, like her, had walked along the coast of the Pelasiar Sea, and then to the western edge of Stet which had once been a great forest, and there they found the wooden road, Stump Road they sometimes called it. Trees cut on end to make flat circles, pounded into rows that went on and on. Other children then arrived from Stet itself, having walked the old stream beds wending through the grey tangle of shattered tree-fall and diseased shrubs. There were signs that Stet had once been a forest to match its old name which was Forest Stet, but Badalle was not entirely convinced—all she could see was a gouged wasteland, ruined and ravaged. There were no trees standing anywhere. They called it Stump Road, but other times it was Forest Road, and that too was a private joke.

Of course, someone had needed lots of trees to make the road, so maybe there really had once been a forest there. But it was gone now.

At the northern edge of Stet, facing out on to the Elan Plain, they had come upon another column of children, and a day later yet another one joined them, down from the north, from Kolanse itself, and at the head of this one there had been Rutt. Carrying Held. Tall, his shoulders, elbows, knees and ankles protruding and the skin round them slack and stretched. He had large, luminous eyes. He still had all his teeth, and when the morning arrived, each morning, he was there, at the head. The fangs, and the rest just followed.

They all believed he knew where he was going, but they didn't ask him since the belief was more important than the truth, which was that he was just as lost as all the rest.

> 'All day Rutt holds Held
> And keeps her
> Wrapped
> In his shadow.
> It's hard
> Not to love Rutt
> But Held doesn't
> And no one loves Held
> But Rutt.'

Visto had come from Okan. When the starvers and the bone-skinned inquisitors marched on the city his mother had sent him running, hand in hand with his sister who was two years older than he was, and they'd run down streets between burning buildings and screams filled the night and the starvers kicked in doors and dragged people out and did terrible things to them, while the bone-skins watched on and said it was necessary, everything here was necessary.

They'd pulled his sister out of his grip, and it was her scream that still echoed in his skull. Each night since then, he had ridden it on the road of sleep, from the moment his exhaustion took him until the moment he awoke to the dawn's pale face.

He ran for what seemed forever, westward and away from the starvers. Eating what he could, savaged by thirst, and when he'd outdistanced the starvers the ribbers showed up, huge packs of gaunt dogs with red-rimmed eyes and no fear of anything. And then the Fathers, all wrapped in black, who plunged into the ragged camps on the roads and stole children away, and once he and a few others had come upon one of their old night-holds and had seen for themselves the small split bones mottled blue and grey in the coals of the hearth, and so understood what the Fathers did to the children they took.

Visto remembered his first sight of Forest Stet, a range of denuded hills filled with torn-up stumps, roots reminding him of one of the bone-yards that ringed the city that had been his home, left after the last of the livestock had been slaughtered. And at that moment, looking upon what had once been a forest, Visto had realized that the entire world was now dead. There was nothing left and nowhere to go.

Yet onward he trudged, now just one among what must be tens of thousands, maybe even more, a road of children leagues long, and for all that died along the way, others arrived to take their place. He had not imagined that so many children existed. They were like a great herd, the last great herd, the sole source of food and nourishment for the world's last, desperate hunters.

Visto was fourteen years old. He had not yet begun his growth-spurt and now never would. His belly was round and rock hard, protruding so that his spine curved deep just above his hips. He walked like a pregnant woman, feet splayed, bones aching. He was full of Satra Riders, the worms inside his body endlessly swimming and getting bigger by the day. When they were ready—soon—they would pour out of him. From his nostrils, from the corners of his eyes, from his ears, from his belly button, his penis and his anus, and from his mouth. And to those who witnessed, he would seem to deflate, skin crinkling and collapsing down into weaving furrows running the length of his body. He would seem to instantly turn into an old man. And then he would die.

Visto was almost impatient for that. He hoped ribbers would eat his body and so take in the eggs the Satra Riders had left behind, so that they too would die. Better yet, Fathers—but they weren't that stupid, he was sure—no, they wouldn't touch him and that was too bad.

The Snake was leaving behind Forest Stet, and the wooden road gave way to a trader's track of dusty, rutted dirt, wending out into the Elan. So, he would die on the plain, and his spirit would pull away from the shrunken thing that had been its body, and begin the long journey back home. To find his sister. To find his mother.

And already, his spirit was tired, so tired, of walking.

At day's end, Badalle forced herself to climb an old Elan longbarrow with its ancient tree at the far end—grey leaves fluttering—from which she could turn and look back along the road, eastward, as far as her eyes could retrace the day's interminable journey. Beyond the mass of the sprawled camp, she saw a wavy line of bodies stretching to the horizon. This had been an especially bad day, too hot, too dry, the lone waterhole a slough of foul, vermin-ridden mud filled with rotting insect carcasses that tasted like dead fish.

She stood, looking for a long time on the ribby length of the Snake. Those that fell on the track had not been pushed aside, simply trampled on or stepped over, and so the road was now a road of flesh and bone, fluttering threads of hair, and, she knew, staring eyes. The Snake of Ribs. Chal Managal in the Elan tongue.

She blew flies from her lips.

And voiced another poem.

> 'On this morning
> We saw a tree
> With leaves of grey

And when we got closer
The leaves flew away.

At noon the nameless boy
With the eaten nose
Fell and did not move
And down came the leaves
To feed.

At dusk there was another tree
Grey fluttering leaves
Settling in for the night
Come the morning
They'll fly again.'

Ampelas Rooted, the Wastelands

The machinery was coated in oily dust that gleamed in the darkness as the faint glow of the lantern light slid across it, conveying motion where none existed, the illusion of silent slippage, as of reptilian scales that seemed, as ever, cruelly appropriate. She was breathing hard as she hurried down the narrow corridor, ducking every now and then to avoid the lumpy black cables slung along from the ceiling. Her nose and throat stung with the rank metal reek of the close, motionless air. Surrounded by the exposed guts of Root, she felt besieged by the unknowable, the illimitable mystery of dire arcana. Yet, she had made these unlit, abandoned passageways her favoured haunt, knowing full well the host of self-recriminating motivations that had guided her to such choices.

The Root invited the lost, and Kalyth was indeed lost. It was not that she could not find her way among the countless twisting corridors, or through the vast chambers of silent, frozen machines, evading the pits in the floors over which flagstones had never been installed, and staying clear of the chaos of metal and cables spilling out from unpanelled walls—no, she knew her way round, now, after months of wandering. This curse of helpless, hopeless bewilderment belonged to her spirit. She was not who they wanted her to be, and nothing she said could convince them of that.

She had been born in a tribe on the Elan Plain. She had grown into adulthood there, from child to girl, from girl to woman, and there had been nothing to set her apart, nothing to reveal her as unique, or gifted with unexpected talents. She had married a month after her first blooding. She had borne three children. She had almost loved her husband, and had learned to live with his faint disappointment in her, as her youthful beauty gave way to weary motherhood. She had, in truth, lived a life no different from that of her own mother, and so had seen clearly—without any special talent—the path of her life ahead, year after year, the slow decay of her body, the loss of suppleness, deepening lines upon her face, the sag of her breasts, the miserable weakening of her bladder. And one day she would find herself unable to walk, and the tribe would leave her where she was. To die in solitude, as dying was always a thing of solitude, as it must ever be. For the Elan knew better than the settled peoples of Kolanse, with their crypts and treasure troves for the dead, with the family servants and advisors all throat-cut and packed in the corridor to the sepulchre, servants beyond life itself, servants for ever.

Everyone died in solitude, after all. A simple enough truth. A truth no one need fear. The spirits waited before they cast judgement upon a soul, waited for that soul—in its dying isolation—to set judgement upon itself, upon the life it had lived, and if peace came of that, then the spirits would show mercy. If torment rode the Wild Mare, why, then, the spirits knew to match it. When the soul faced itself, after all, it was impossible to lie. Deceiving arguments rang loud with falsehood, their facile weakness too obvious to ignore.

It had been a life. Far from perfect, but only vaguely unhappy. A life one could whittle down into something like contentment, even should the result prove shapeless, devoid of meaning.

She had been no witch. She had not possessed the breath of a shaman, and so would never be a Rider of the Spotted Horse. And when the end of that life had come for her and her people, on a morning of horror and violence, all that she had revealed then was a damning selfishness—in refusing to die, in fleeing all that she had known.

These were not virtues.

She possessed no virtues.

Reaching the central, spiral staircase—each step too shallow, too broad for human strides—she set off, her gasps becoming shallower and quicker with the exertion as she ascended level after level, up and out from Root, into the lower chambers of Feed, where she made use of the counterweighted ramp that lifted her by way of a vertical shaft past the seething vats of fungi, the stacked pens of orthen and grishol, drawing to a grating, shivering halt on the base level of Womb. Here, the cacophony of the young assailed her, the hissing shrieks of pain as the dread surgeries were performed—as destinies were decreed in bitter flavours—and, having regained some measure of her wind, she hastened to ascend past the levels of terrible outrage, the stench of wastes and panic that shone like oil on soft hides among shapes writhing on all sides—shapes she was careful to avoid with her eyes, hurrying with her hands clapped over her ears.

From Womb to Heart, where she now passed among towering figures that paid her no heed, and from whose paths she had to duck and dodge lest they simply trample her underclaw. Ve'Gath Soldiers stood flanking the central ramp, twice her height and in their arcane armour resembling the vast machinery of Root far below. Ornate grilled visors hid their faces save their fanged snouts, and the line of their jaws gave them ghastly grins, as if the implicit purpose of their breed delighted them. More so than the J'an or the K'ell, the true soldiers of the K'Chain Che'Malle frightened Kalyth to the very core of her being. The Matron was producing them in vast numbers.

No further proof was needed—war was coming.

That the Ve'Gath gave the Matron terrible pain, each one thrust out from her in a welter of blood and pungent fluid, had become irrelevant. Necessity, Kalyth well knew, was the cruellest master of all.

Neither soldier guarding the ramp impeded her as she strode on to it, the flat stone underfoot pitted with holes designed to hold claws, and from which cold air flowed up around her—the plunge in ambient temperature on the ramp evidently served somehow to quell the instinctive fear the K'Chain experienced as the conveyance lifted with squeals and groans up past the levels of Heart, ending at Eyes, the Inner Keep, Acyl Nest and home of the Matron herself. Riding the ramp alone, however, the strain of the mechanism was less pronounced, and she heard little more than the rush of air that ever disoriented her with a sense of falling even as she raced upward, and the sweat on her limbs and upon her brow quickly cooled. She was shivering by the time the ramp slowed and then halted at the base level of Eyes.

J'an Sentinels observed her arrival from the foot of the half-spiral stairs that led to the Nest. As with the Ve'Gath, they were seemingly indifferent to her—no doubt aware that she had been summoned, but even were that not so they would see in her no threat whatsoever to the Matron they had been bred to protect. Kalyth was not simply harmless; she was useless.

The hot, rank air engulfed her, cloying as a damp cloak, as she made her way to the stairs and began the awkward climb to the Matron's demesne.

At the landing one last sentinel stood guard. At least a thousand years old, Bre'nigan was gaunt and tall—taller even than a Ve'Gath—and his multilayered scales bore a silvered patina that made the creature seem ghostly, as if hewn from sun-bleached mica. Neither pupil nor iris was visible in his slitted eyes, simply a murky yellow, misshapen with cataracts. She suspected the bodyguard was blind, but in truth there was no way to tell, for when Bre'nigan moved, the J'an displayed perfect sureness, indeed, grace and liquid elegance. The long, vaguely curved sword slung through a brass ring at his hip—a ring half embedded in the creature's hide—was as tall as Kalyth, the blade a kind of ceramic bearing a faint magenta hue, although the flawless edge gleamed silver.

She greeted Bre'nigan with a nod that elicited no reaction whatsoever, and then stepped past the sentinel.

Kalyth had hoped—no, she had *prayed*—and when she set eyes upon the two K'Chain standing before the Matron, and saw that they were unaccompanied, her spirits plummeted. Despair welled up, threatened to consume her. She fought to draw breath into her tight chest.

Beyond the newcomers and huge on the raised dais, Gunth'an Acyl, the Matron, emanated agony in waves—and in this she was unchanged and unchanging, but now Kalyth felt from the enormous queen a bitter undercurrent of . . . something.

Unbalanced, distraught, Kalyth only then discerned the state of the two K'Chain Che'Malle, the grievous wounds half-healed, the chaotic skeins of scars on their flanks, necks and hips. The two creatures looked starved, driven to appalling extremes of deprivation and violence, and she felt an answering pang in her heart.

But such empathy was shortlived. The truth remained: the K'ell Hunter Sag'Churok and the One Daughter Gunth Mach had failed.

The Matron spoke in Kalyth's mind, although it was not speech of any sort, simply the irrevocable imposition of knowledge and meaning. '*Destriant Kalyth, an error in choice. We remain broken. I remain broken. You cannot mend, not alone, you cannot mend.*'

Neither knowledge nor meaning proved gifts to Kalyth. For she could sense Gunth'an Acyl's madness beneath the words. The Matron was undeniably insane. So too the course of action she had forced upon her children, and upon Kalyth herself. No persuasion was possible.

It was likely that Gunth'an Acyl comprehended Kalyth's convictions—her belief that the Matron was mad—but this too made no difference. Within the ancient queen, there was naught but pain and the torment of desperate need.

'*Destriant Kalyth, they shall try again. What is broken must be mended.*'

Kalyth did not believe Sag'Churok and the One Daughter could survive another quest. And that was another truth that failed in swaying Acyl's imperative.

'*Destriant Kalyth, you shall accompany this Seeking. K'Chain Che'Malle are blind to recognition.*'

And so, at last, they had reached what she had known to be inevitable, despite her hopes, her prayers. 'I cannot,' she whispered.

'*You shall. Guardians are chosen. K'ell Sag'Churok, Rythok, Kor Thuran. Shi'gal Gu'Rull. One Daughter Gunth Mach.*'

'I cannot,' Kalyth said again. 'I have no . . . talents. I am no Destriant—I am blind to whatever it is a Destriant needs. I cannot find a Mortal Sword, Matron. Nor a Shield Anvil. I am sorry.'

The enormous reptile shifted her massive weight, and the sound was as of boulders settling in gravel. Lambent eyes fixed upon Kalyth, radiating waves of stricture.

'*I have chosen you, Destriant Kalyth. It is my children who are blind. The failure is theirs, and mine. We have failed every war. I am the last Matron. The enemy seeks me. The enemy will destroy me. Your kind thrives in this world— to that not even my children are blind. Among you, I shall find new champions. My Destriant must find them. My Destriant leaves with the dawn.*'

Kalyth said no more, knowing any response was useless. After a moment, she bowed and then walked, feebly, as if numb with drink, from the Nest.

A Shi'gal would accompany them. The significance of this was plain. There would be no failure this time. To fail was to receive the Matron's displeasure. Her judgement. Three K'ell Hunters and the One Daughter, and Kalyth herself. If they failed . . . against the deadly wrath of a Shi'gal Assassin, they would not survive long.

Come the dawn, she knew, she would begin her last journey.

Out into the wastelands, to find Champions that did not even exist.

And this, she now understood, was the penance set upon her soul. She must be made to suffer for her cowardice. *I should have died with the rest. With my husband. My children. I should not have run away. I now must pay for my selfishness.*

The one mercy was that, when the final judgement arrived, it would come quickly. She would not even feel, much less see, the killing blow from the Shi'gal.

A Matron never produced more than three assassins at any one time, and their flavours were anathema, preventing any manner of alliance. And should one of them decide that the Matron must be expunged, the remaining two, by their very natures, would oppose it. Thus, each Shi'gal warded the Matron against the others. Sending one with the Seeking was a grave risk, for now there would be only two assassins defending her at any time.

Further proof of the Matron's madness. To so endanger herself, whilst at the same time sending away her One Daughter—her only child with the potential to breed—was beyond all common sense.

But then, Kalyth was about to march to her own death. What did she care about these terrifying creatures? Let the war come. Let the mysterious enemy descend upon Ampelas Rooted and all the other Rooted, and cut down every last one of these K'Chain Che'Malle. The world would not miss them.

Besides, she knew all about extinction. *The only real curse is when you find yourself the last of your kind.* Yes, she well understood such a fate, and she knew the true depth of loneliness—no, not that paltry, shallow, self-pitying game played out by people everywhere—but the cruel comprehension of a solitude without cure, without hope of salvation.

Yes, everyone dies alone. And there may be regrets. There may be sorrows. But these are as nothing to what comes to the last of a breed. For then there can be no evading the truth of failure. Absolute, crushing failure. The failure of one's own kind, sweeping in from all sides, finding this last set of shoulders to settle upon, with a weight no single soul can withstand.

There had been a residual gift of sorts with the language of the K'Chain Che'Malle, and it now tortured Kalyth. Her mind had awakened, far beyond what she had known in her life before now. Knowledge was no blessing; awareness was a disease that stained the entire spirit. She could gouge out her own eyes and still see too much.

Did the shamans of her tribe feel such crushing guilt, when recognition of the end finally arrived? She remembered anew the bleakness in their eyes, and understood it in ways she had not comprehended before, in the life she had once lived. No, she could do naught but curse the deadly blessings of these K'Chain Che'Malle. Curse them with all her heart, all her hate.

Kalyth began her descent. She needed the closeness of Root; she needed the decrepit machinery on all sides, the drip of viscid oils and the foul, close air. The world was broken. She was the last of the Elan, and now her sole remaining task on this earth was to oversee the annihilation of the last Matron of the K'Chain Che'Malle. Was there satisfaction in that? If so, it was an evil kind of satisfaction, making its taste all the more alluring.

Among her people, death arrived winging across the face of the setting sun, a black, tattered omen low in the sky. She would be that dread vision, that shred of the murdered moon. Driven to the earth as all things were, eventually.

This is all true.

See the bleakness in my eyes.

Shi'gal Gu'Rull stood upon the very edge of Brow, the night winds howling round his tall, lean form. Eldest among the Shi'gal, the assassin had fought and defeated seven other Shi'gal in his long service to Acyl. He had survived sixty-one centuries of life, of growth, and was twice the height of a full-grown K'ell Hunter, for unlike the Hunters—who were flavoured with mortality's sudden end at the close of ten centuries—the Shi'gal possessed no such flaw in their making. They could, potentially, outlive the Matron herself.

Bred for cunning, Gu'Rull held no illusions regarding the sanity of Mother Acyl. Her awkward assumption of godly structures of faith ill fitted both her and all the K'Chain Che'Malle. The matron sought human worshippers, human servants, but humans were too frail, too weak to be of any real value. The woman Kalyth was proof enough of that, despite the flavour of percipience Acyl had given her—a percipience that should have delivered certitude and strength, yet had been twisted by a weak mind into new instruments of self-recrimination and self-pity.

That flavour would fade in the course of the Seeking, as Kalyth's swift blood ever thinned Acyl's gift, with no daily replenishment possible. The Destriant would revert to her innate intelligence, and that was a meagre one by any standard. She was already useless, as far as Gu'Rull was concerned. And upon this meaningless quest, she would become a burden, a liability.

Better to kill her as soon as possible, but alas, Mother Acyl's command permitted no such flexibility. The Destriant must choose a Mortal Sword and a Shield Anvil from among her own kind.

Sag'Churok had recounted the failure of their first selection. The mass of flaws that had been their chosen one: Redmask of the Awl. Gu'Rull did not believe the Destriant would fare any better. Humans might well have thrived in the world beyond, but they did so as would feral orthen, simply by virtue of profligate breeding. They possessed no other talents.

The Shi'gal lifted his foreshortened snout and opened his nostril slits to scent the chill night air. The wind came from the east and, as usual, it stank of death.

Gu'Rull had plundered the pathetic memories of the Destriant, and therefore knew that no salvation would be found to the east, on the plains known as the Elan. Sag'Churok and Gunth Mach had set out westward, into the Awl'dan, and there too they found only failure. The north was a forbidding, lifeless realm of ice, tortured seas and bitter cold.

Thus, they must journey south.

The Shi'gal had not ventured outside Ampelas Rooted in eight centuries. In that short span of time, it was likely that little had changed in the region known to humans as the Wastelands. Nonetheless, some advance scouting was tactically sound.

With this in mind, Gu'Rull unfolded his month-old wings, spreading the elongated feather-scales so that they could flatten and fill out under the pressure of the wind.

And then the assassin dropped over the sheer edge of Brow, wings snapping out to their fullest extent, and there arose the song of flight, a low, moaning whistle that was, for the Shi'gal, the music of freedom.

Leaving Ampelas Rooted . . . it had been too long since Gu'Rull felt this . . . this exhilaration.

The two new eyes beneath the lines of his jaw now opened for the first time, and the compounded vision—of the sky ahead and the ground below—momentarily confused the assassin, but after a time Gu'Rull was able to enforce the necessary separation, so that the vistas found their proper relationship to one another, creating a vast panorama of the world beyond.

Acyl's new flavours were ambitious, indeed, brilliant. Was such creativity implicit in madness? Perhaps.

Did that possibility engender hope in Gu'Rull? No. Hope was not possible.

The assassin soared through the night, high above a blasted, virtually lifeless landscape. Like a shred of the murdered moon.

The Wastelands

He was not alone. Indeed, he had no memory of ever having been alone. The notion was impossible, in fact, and that much he understood. As far as he could tell, he was incorporeal, and possessed of the quaint privilege of being able to move from one companion to another almost at will. If they were to die, or somehow find a means of rejecting him, why, he believed he would cease to exist. And he so wanted to stay alive, floating as he did in the euphoric wonder of his friends, his bizarre, disjointed family.

They traversed a wilderness ragged and forlorn, a place of broken rock, wind-rippled fans of grey sand, screes of volcanic glass that began and ended with random indifference. Hills and ridges clashed in wayward confusion, and not a single tree broke the undulating horizon. The sun overhead was a blurred eye that smeared a path through thin clouds. The air was hot, the wind constant.

The only nourishment the group had been able to find came from the strange swarms of scaled rodents—their stringy meat tasting of dust—and an oversized breed of rhizan that possessed pouches under their wings swollen with milky water. Day and night capemoths tracked them, waiting ever patient for one to fall and not rise, but this did not seem likely. Flitting from one person to the next, he could sense their innate resolve, their unfailing strength.

Such fortitude, alas, could not prevent the seemingly endless litany of misery that seemed to comprise the bulk of their conversation.

'What a waste,' Sheb was saying, clawing at his itching beard. 'Sink a few wells, pile these stones into houses and shops and whatnot. Then you'd have something worth something. Empty land is useless. I long for the day when it's all put to use, everything, right over the surface of the world. Cities merging into one—'

'There'd be no farms,' objected Last, but as always it was a mild, diffident objection. 'Without farms, nobody eats—'

'Don't be an idiot,' snapped Sheb. 'Of course there'd be farms. Just none of this kind of useless land, where nothing lives but damned rats. Rats in the ground, rats in the air, and bugs, and bones—can you believe all the bones?'

'But I—'

'Be quiet, Last,' said Sheb. 'You never got nothing useful to say, ever.'

Asane then spoke in her frail, quavering voice. 'No fighting, please. It's horrible enough without you picking fights, Sheb—'

'Careful, hag, or you're next.'

'Care to try *me*, Sheb?' Nappet asked. He spat. 'Didn't think so. You talk, Sheb, and that's all you do. One of these nights, when you're asleep, I'm gonna cut out your tongue and feed it to the fuckin' capemoths. Who'd complain? Asane? Breath? Last? Taxilian? Rautos? Nobody, Sheb, we'd all be dancing.'

'Leave me out of this,' said Rautos. 'I suffered enough for a lifetime when I was living with my wife and, needless to say, I don't miss her.'

'Here goes Rautos again,' snarled Breath. 'My wife did this, my wife said that. I'm sick of hearing about your wife. She ain't here, is she? You probably drowned her, and that's why you're on the run. You drowned her in your fancy fountain, just held her down, watching as her eyes went wide, her mouth opened and she screamed through the water. You watched and smiled, that's what you did. I don't forget, I can't forget, it was awful. You're a murderer, Rautos.'

'There *she* goes,' said Sheb, 'talking about drowning again.'

'Might cut out *her* tongue, too,' said Nappet, grinning. 'Rautos's, too. No more shit about drowning or wives or complainin'—the rest of you are fine. Last, you don't say nothing and when you do, it don't rile nobody. Asane, you mostly know when to keep your mouth shut. And Taxilian hardly ever says nothing anyway. Just us, and that'd be—'

'I see something,' said Rautos.

He felt their attentions shift, find focus, and he saw with their eyes a vague smudge on the horizon, something thrusting skyward, too narrow to be a mountain, too massive to be a tree. Still leagues away, rising like a tooth.

'I want to see that,' announced Taxilian.

'Shit,' said Nappet, 'ain't nowhere else to go.'

The others silently agreed. They had been walking for what seemed forever, and the arguments about where they should go had long since withered away. None of them had any answers, none of them even knew where they were.

And so they set out for that distant, mysterious edifice.

He was content with that, content to go with them, and he found himself sharing Taxilian's curiosity, which grew in strength and if challenged would easily overwhelm Asane's fears and the host of obsessions plaguing the others—Breath's drowning, Rautos's miserable marriage, Last's meaningless life of diffidence, Sheb's hatred and Nappet's delight in viciousness. And now the conversations fell away, leaving naught but the crunch and thud of bare feet on the rough ground, and the low moan of the ceaseless wind.

High above, a score of capemoths tracked the lone figure walking across the Wastelands. They had been drawn by the sound of voices, only to find this solitary, gaunt figure. Skin of dusty green, tusks framing its mouth. Carrying a sword but otherwise naked. A lone wanderer, who spoke in seven voices, who knew himself by seven names. He was many, but he was one. They were all lost, and so was he.

The capemoths hungered for his life to end. But it had been weeks. Months. In the meantime, they just hungered.

There were patterns and they demanded consideration. The elements remained disarticulated, however, in floating tendrils, in smears of loose black like stains swimming in his vision. But at least he could now see, and that was something. The rotted cloth had pulled away from his eyes, tugged by currents he could not feel.

The key to unlocking everything would be found in the patterns. He was certain of that. If only he could draw them together, he would understand; he would know all he needed to know. He would be able to make sense of the visions that tore through him.

The strange two-legged lizard, all clad in black gleaming armour, its tail nothing more than a stub, standing on a stone landing of some sort, whilst rivers of blood flowed down gutters to each side. Its unhuman eyes fixed unblinking on the source of all that blood—a dragon, nailed to a latticework of enormous wooden beams, the spikes rust-hued and dripping with condensation. Suffering roiled down from this creature, a death denied, a life transformed into an eternity of pain. And from the standing lizard, cold satisfaction rose in a cruel penumbra.

In another, two wolves seemed to be watching him from a weathered ridge of grasses and bony outcrops. Guarded, uneasy, as if measuring a rival. Behind them, rain slanted down from heavy clouds. And he found himself turning away, as if indifferent to their regard, to walk across a denuded plain. In the distance, dolmens of some sort rose from the ground, scores of them, arranged without any discernible order, and yet all seemed identical—perhaps statues, then. He drew closer, frowning at the shapes, so oddly surmounted by jutting cowls, their hunched, narrow backs to him, tails curled round. The ground they crouched on glittered as if strewn with diamonds or crushed glass.

Even as he closed in on these silent, motionless sentinels, moments from reaching the nearest one, a heavy shadow slipped over him and the air was suddenly frigid. In wrought despair, he halted, looked up.

Nothing but stars, each one drifting as if snapped from its tether, like motes of dust on a slowly draining pool. Faint voices sinking down, touching his brow like flecks of snow, melting in the instant, all meaning lost. Arguments in the Abyss, but he understood none of them. To stare upward was to reel, unbalanced, and he felt his feet lift from the earth until he floated. Twisting round, he looked down.

More stars, but emerging from their midst a dozen raging suns of green fire, slashing through the black fabric of space, fissures of light bleeding through. The closer they came, the more massive they grew, blinding him to all else, and the maelstrom of voices rose to a clamour, and what had once felt like flakes of snow, quickly melting upon his heated brow, now burned like fire.

If he could but draw close the fragments, make the mosaic whole, and so comprehend the truth of the patterns. If he could—

Swirls. Yes, they are that. The motion does not deceive, the motion reveals the shape beneath.

Swirls, in curls of fur.

Tattoos—see them now—see them!

All at once, as the tattoos settled into place, he knew himself.

I am Heboric Ghost Hands. Destriant to a cast-down god. I see him—

I see you, Fener.

The shape, so massive, so lost. Unable to move.

His god was trapped, and, like Heboric, was mute witness to the blazing jade suns as they bore down. He and his god were in their path, and these were forces that could not be pushed aside. No shield existed solid enough to block what was coming.

The Abyss cares nothing for us. The Abyss comes to deliver its own arguments, against which we cannot stand.

Fener, I have doomed you. And you, old god, you have doomed me.

Yet, I no longer regret. For this is as it should be. After all, war knows no other language. In war we invite our own destruction. In war we punish our children with a broken legacy of blood.

He understood now. The gods of war and what they meant, what their very existence signified. And as he stared upon those jade suns searing ever closer, he was overwhelmed by the futility hiding behind all this arrogance, this mindless conceit.

See us wave our banners of hate.

See where it gets us.

A final war had begun. Facing an enemy against whom no defence was possible. Neither words nor deeds could fool this clear-eyed arbiter. Immune to lies, indifferent to excuses and vapid discourses on necessity, on the weighing of two evils and the facile righteousness of choosing the lesser one—and yes, these were the arguments he was hearing, empty as the ether they travelled.

We stood tall in paradise. And then called forth the gods of war, to bring destruction down upon ourselves, our world, the very earth, its air, its water, its myriad life. No, show me no surprise, no innocent bewilderment. I see now with the eyes of the Abyss. I see now with my enemy's eyes, and so I shall speak with its voice.

Behold, my friends, I am justice.

And when at last we meet, you will not like it.

And if irony awakens in you at the end, see me weep with these tears of jade, and answer with a smile.

If you've the courage.

Have you, my friends, the courage?

Book One

The Sea Does Not Dream of You

I will walk the path forever walked
One step ahead of you
And one step behind
I will choke in the dust of your passing
And skirl more into your face
It all tastes the same
Even when you feign otherwise

But here on the path forever walked
The old will lie itself anew
We can sigh like kings
Like empresses on gift-carts
Resplendent in imagined worth.

I will walk the path forever walked
Though my time is short
As if the stars belong
Cupped here in my hands
Showering out these pleasures
That so sparkle in the sun
When down they drift settling flat

To make this path forever walked
Behind you behind me
Between the step past, the step to come
Look up look up once
Before I am gone

TELLER OF TALES
FASSTAN OF KOLANSE

Chapter One

Abject misery lies not in what the blanket reveals, but in what it hides.

KING TEHOL THE ONLY OF LETHER

War had come to the tangled, overgrown grounds of the dead Azath tower in the city of Letheras. Swarms of lizards had invaded from the river's shoreline. Discovering a plethora of strange insects, they began a feeding frenzy.

Oddest among the arcane bugs was a species of two-headed beetle. Four lizards spied one such creature and closed in, surrounding it. The insect noted threats from two directions and made a careful half-turn, only to find two additional threats, whereupon it crouched down and played dead.

This didn't work. One of the lizards, a wall-scampering breed with a broad mouth and gold-flecked eyes, lunged forward and gobbled up the insect.

This scene was played out throughout the grounds, a terrible slaughter, a rush to extinction. The fates, this evening, did not appear kind to the two-headed beetles.

Not all prey, however, was as helpless as it might initially seem. The role of the victim in nature is ephemeral, and that which is fed upon might in time feed upon the feeders in the eternal drama of survival.

A lone owl, already engorged on lizards, was the sole witness to the sudden wave of writhing deaths on the rumpled earth below, as from the mouths of dying lizards, grotesque shapes emerged. The extinction of the two-headed beetles proved not as imminent a threat as it had seemed only moments earlier.

But owls, being among the least clever of birds, are unmindful of such lessons. This one watched, wide-eyed and empty. Until it felt a strange stirring in its own gut, sufficient to distract it from the wretched dying below, that array of pale lizard bellies blotting the dark ground. It did not think of the lizards it had eaten. It did not take note, even in retrospect, of the sluggish efforts some of them had displayed at escaping its swooping talons.

The owl was in for a long night of excruciating regurgitation. Dimwitted as it was, from that moment on and for ever more, lizards were off its menu.

The world delivers its lessons in manners subtle or, if required, cruel and blunt, so that even the thickest of subjects will comprehend. Failing that, they die. For the smart ones, of course, incomprehension is inexcusable.

———

A night of heat in Letheras. Stone dripped sweat. The canals looked viscid, motionless, the surface strangely flattened and opaque with swirls of dust and rubbish. Insects danced over the water as if seeking their reflections, but this smooth patina yielded nothing, swallowing up the span of stars, devouring the lurid torchlight of the street patrols, and so the winged insects spun without surcease, as though crazed with fever.

Beneath a bridge, on stepped banks buried in darkness, crickets crawled like droplets of oozing oil, glistening, turgid, haplessly crunched underfoot as two figures drew together and huddled in the gloom.

'He never would've went in,' one of them said in a hoarse whisper. 'The water reeks, and look, no ripples, no nothing. He's scarpered to the other side, somewhere in the night market where he can get lost fast.'

'Lost,' grunted the other, a woman, lifting up the dagger in one gloved hand and examining the edge, 'that's a good one. Like he could get lost. Like any of us could.'

'You think he can't wrap himself up like we done?'

'No time for that. He bolted. He's on the run. Panicked.'

'Looked like panic, didn't it,' agreed her companion, and then he shook his head. 'Never seen anything so . . . disappointing.'

The woman sheathed her dagger. 'They'll flush him out. He'll come back across, and we jump him then.'

'Stupid, thinking he could get away.'

After a few moments, Smiles unsheathed her dagger again, peered at the edge. Beside her, Throatslitter rolled his eyes but said nothing.

Bottle straightened, gestured for Koryk to join him, then watched, amused, as the broad-shouldered half-blood Seti shoved and elbowed his way through the crowd, leaving a wake of dark glares and bitten-off curses—there was little risk of trouble, of course, since clearly the damned foreigner was looking for just that, and instincts being what they were the world over, no one was of a mind to take on Koryk.

Too bad. It'd be a thing worth seeing, Bottle smiled to himself, if a mob of irate Letherii shoppers descended on the glowering barbarian, pummelling him into the ground with loaves of crusty bread and bulbous root-crops.

Then again, such distractions wouldn't do. Not right now, anyway, when they'd found their quarry, with Tarr and Corabb moving round back of the tavern to cover the alley bolt-hole, and Maybe and Masan Gilani up on the roof by now, in case their target got imaginative.

Koryk arrived, in a sweat, scowling and grinding his teeth. 'Miserable turds,' he muttered. 'What's with this lust to spend coin? Markets are stupid.'

'Keeps people happy,' said Bottle, 'or if not exactly happy, then . . . temporarily satiated. Which serves the same function.'

'Which is?'

'Keeping them outa trouble. The disruptive kind of trouble,' he added, seeing Koryk's knotted forehead, his darting eyes. 'The kind that comes when a population finds the time to think, really think, I mean—when they start realizing what a piece of shit all this is.'

'Sounds like one of the King's speeches—they put me to sleep, like you're doing right now, Bottle. Where exactly is he, then?'

'One of my rats is crouching at the foot of a banister—'

'Which one?'

'Baby Smiles—she's the best for this. Anyway, she's got her beady eyes fixed right on him. He's at a table in the corner, just under a shuttered window—but it doesn't look like the kind anyone could actually climb through. Basically,' Bottle concluded, 'he's cornered.'

Koryk's frown deepened. 'That's too easy, isn't it?'

Bottle scratched at his stubble, shifted from one foot to the other, and then sighed. 'Aye, way too easy.'

'Here come Balm and Gesler.'

The two sergeants arrived.

'What are we doing here?' Balm asked, eyes wide.

Gesler said, 'He's in his funk again, never mind him. We got us a fight ahead, I figure. A nasty one. He won't go down easy.'

'What's the plan, then?' Koryk asked.

'Stormy leads the way. He's going to spring him loose—if he heads for the back door your friends will take him down. Same for if he goes up. My guess is, he'll dodge round Stormy and try for the front door—that's what I'd do. Stormy's huge and mean but he ain't fast. And that's what we're counting on. The four of us will be waiting for the bastard—we'll take him down. With Stormy coming up behind him and holding the doorway to stop any retreat.'

'He's looking nervous and in a bad mood in there,' Bottle said. 'Warn Stormy—he just might stand and fight.'

'We hear a scrap start and in we go,' said Gesler.

The gold-hued sergeant went off to brief Stormy. Balm stood beside Koryk, looking bewildered.

People were rolling in and out of the tavern like it was a fast brothel. Stormy then appeared, looming over almost everyone else, his visage red and his beard even redder, as if his entire face was aflame. He tugged loose the peace-strap on his sword as he lumbered towards the door. Seeing him, people scattered aside. He met one more customer at the threshold and took hold of the man by the front of his shirt, then threw him into his own wake—the poor fool yelped as he landed face first on the cobbles not three paces from the three Malazans, where he writhed, hands up at his bloodied chin.

As Stormy plunged into the tavern, Gesler arrived, stepping over the fallen citizen, and hissed, 'To the door now, all of us, quick!'

Bottle let Koryk take the lead, and held back even for Balm who almost started walking the other way—before Gesler yanked the man back. If there was going to be a scrap, Bottle preferred to leave most of the nasty work to the others. He'd done his job, after all, in tracking and finding the quarry.

Chaos erupted in the tavern, furniture crashing, startled shouts and terrified screams. Then something went *thump*! And all at once white smoke was billowing out from the doorway. More splintering furniture, a heavy crash, and then a figure sprinted out from the smoke.

An elbow cracked hard on Koryk's jaw and he toppled like a tree.

Gesler ducked a lashing fist, just in time to meet an upthrust knee, and the sound the impact made was of two coconuts in collision. The quarry's leg spun round, taking the rest of the man with it in a wild pirouette, whilst Gesler rocked back to promptly sit down on the cobbles, his eyes glazed.

Shrieking, Balm back-stepped, reaching for his short sword—and Bottle leapt forward to pin the sergeant's arm—as the target lunged past them all, running hard but unevenly for the bridge.

Stormy stumbled out from the tavern, his nose streaming blood. 'You didn't get him? You damned idiots—look at my face! I took this for nothing!'

Other customers pushed out round the huge Falari, eyes streaming and coughing.

Gesler was climbing upright, wobbly, shaking his head. 'Come on,' he mumbled, 'let's get after him, and hope Throatslitter and Smiles can slow him down some.'

Tarr and Corabb showed up and surveyed the scene. 'Corabb,' said Tarr, 'stay with Koryk and try bringing him round.' And then he joined Bottle, Gesler, Stormy and Balm as they set out after their target.

Balm glared across at Bottle. 'I coulda had him!'

'We need the fool alive, you idiot,' snapped Bottle.

The sergeant gaped. 'We do?'

'Look at that,' hissed Throatslitter. 'Here he comes!'

'Limping bad, too,' observed Smiles, sheathing her dagger once more. 'We come up both sides and go for his ankles.'

'Good idea.'

Throatslitter went left, Smiles went right, and they crouched at either end of the landing on this side of the bridge. They listened to the *step-scruff* of the limping fugitive as he reached the span, drawing ever closer. From the edge of the market street on the opposite side, shouts rang through the air. The scuffling run on the bridge picked up pace.

At the proper moment, as the target reached the end and stepped out on to the street's cobbles, the two Malazan marines leapt out from their hiding places, converging, each wrapping arms round one of the man's legs.

The three went down in a heap.

Moments later, amidst a flurry of snarled curses, gouging thumbs and frantic kicking, the rest of the hunters arrived, and finally succeeded in pinning down their quarry.

Bottle edged closer to gaze down at their victim's bruised, flushed visage. 'Really, Sergeant, you had to know it was hopeless.'

Fiddler glared.

'Look what you did to my nose!' Stormy said, gripping one of Fiddler's arms and apparently contemplating breaking it in two.

'You used a smoker in the tavern, didn't you?' Bottle asked. 'What a waste.'

'You'll all pay for this,' said Fiddler. 'You have no idea—'

'He's probably right,' said Gesler. 'So, Fid, we gonna have to hold you down here for ever, or will you come peacefully now? What the Adjunct wants, the Adjunct gets.'

'Easy for you,' hissed Fiddler. 'Just look at Bottle there. Does he look happy?'

Bottle scowled. 'No, I'm not happy, but orders are orders, Sergeant. You can't just run away.'

'Wish I'd brought a sharper or two,' Fiddler said, 'that would've settled it just fine. All right now, you can all let me up—I think my knee's busted anyway. Gesler, you got a granite jaw, did you know that?'

'And it cuts me a fine profile besides,' said Gesler.

'We was hunting Fiddler?' Balm suddenly asked. 'Gods below, he mutiny or something?'

Throatslitter patted his sergeant on the shoulder. 'It's all right now, Sergeant. Adjunct wants Fiddler to do a reading, that's all.'

Bottle winced. *That's all. Sure, nothing to it. I can't wait.*

They dragged Fiddler to his feet, and wisely held on to the man as they marched him back to the barracks.

Grey and ghostly, the oblong shape hung beneath the lintel over the dead Azath's doorway. It looked lifeless, but of course it wasn't.

'We could throw stones,' said Sinn. 'They sleep at night, don't they?'

'Mostly,' replied Grub.

'Maybe if we're quiet.'

'Maybe.'

Sinn fidgeted. 'Stones?'

'Hit it and they'll wake up, and then out they'll come, in a black swarm.'

'I've always hated wasps. For as long as I can remember—I must've been bad stung once, do you think?'

'Who hasn't?' Grub said, shrugging.

'I could just set it on fire.'

'No sorcery, Sinn, not here.'

'I thought you said the house was dead.'

'It is . . . I think. But maybe the yard isn't.'

She glanced round. 'People been digging here.'

'You ever gonna talk to anybody but me?' Grub asked.

'No.' The single word was absolute, immutable, and it did not invite any further discussion on that issue.

He eyed her. 'You know what's happening tonight, don't you?'

'I don't care. I'm not going anywhere near that.'

'Doesn't matter.'

'Maybe, if we hide inside the house, it won't reach us.'

'Maybe,' Grub allowed. 'But I doubt the Deck works like that.'

'How do you know?'

'Well, I don't. Only, Uncle Keneb told me Fiddler talked about me last time, and I was jumping into the sea around then—I wasn't in the cabin. But he just knew, he knew exactly what I was doing.'

'What *were* you doing?'

'I went to find the Nachts.'

'But how did you know they were there? You don't make sense, Grub. And anyway, what use are they? They just follow Withal around.'

'When they're not hunting little lizards,' Grub said, smiling.

But Sinn was not in the mood for easy distraction. 'I look at you and I think . . . *Mockra*.'

To that, Grub made no reply. Instead, he crept forward on the path's uneven pavestones, eyes fixed on the wasp nest.

Sinn followed. 'You're what's coming, aren't you?'

He snorted. 'And you aren't?'

They reached the threshold, halted. 'Do you think it's locked?'

'Shh.'

Grub crouched down and edged forward beneath the huge nest. Once past it, he slowly straightened and reached for the door's latch. It came off in his hand, raising a puff of sawdust. Grub glanced back at Sinn, but said nothing. Facing the door again, he gave it a light push.

It crumpled like wafer where his fingers had prodded. More sawdust sifted down.

Grub raised both hands and pushed against the door.

The barrier disintegrated in clouds and frail splinters. Metal clunked on the floor just beyond, and a moment later the clouds were swept inward as if on an indrawn breath.

Grub stepped over the heap of rotted wood and vanished in the gloom beyond.

After a moment, Sinn followed, ducking low and moving quickly.

From the gloom beneath a nearly dead tree in the grounds of the Azath, Lieutenant Pores grunted. He supposed he should have called them back, but to do so would have revealed his presence, and though he could never be sure when it came to Captain Kindly's orders—designed and delivered as they were with deliberate vagueness, like flimsy fronds over a spike-filled pit—he suspected that he was supposed to maintain some sort of subterfuge when following the two runts around.

Besides, he'd made some discoveries. Sinn wasn't mute at all. Just a stubborn little cow. What a shock. And she had a crush on Grub, how sweet—sweet as tree sap, twigs and trapped insects included—why, it could make a grown man melt, and then run down a drain into that depthless sea of sentimentality where children played, and, occasionally, got away with murder.

Well, the difference was Pores had a very good memory. He recalled in great detail his own childhood, and could he have reached back, into his own past, he'd give that snot-faced jerk a solid clout to the head. And then look down at that stunned, hurt expression, and say something like 'Get used to it, little Pores. One day you'll meet a man named Kindly . . .'

Anyway, the mice had scurried into the Azath House. Maybe something would take care of them in there, bringing to a satisfying conclusion this stupid assignment. A giant, ten-thousand-year-old foot, stomping down, once, twice. Splat, splot, like stinkberries, Grub a smear, Sinn a stain.

Gods no, I'd get blamed! Growling under his breath, he set out after them.

In retrospect, he supposed he should have remembered that damned wasp nest. At the very least, it should have caught his attention as he leapt for the doorway. Instead, it caught his forehead.

Sudden flurry of enraged buzzing, as the nest rocked out and then back, butting his head a second time.

Recognition, comprehension, and then, appropriately enough, blind panic.

Pores whirled and ran.

A thousand or so angry black wasps provided escort.

Six stings could drop a horse. He shrieked as a fire ignited on the back of his neck. And then again, as another stinger stabbed, this time on his right ear.

He whirled his arms. There was a canal somewhere ahead—they'd crossed a bridge, he recalled, off to the left.

Another explosion of agony, this time on the back of his right hand.

Never mind the canal! I need a healer—fast!

He could no longer hear any buzzing, but the scene before him had begun to tilt, darkness bleeding out from the shadows, and the lights of lanterns through windows blurred, lurid and painful in his eyes. His legs weren't working too well, either.

There, the Malazan Barracks.

Deadsmell. Or Ebron.

Staggering now, struggling to fix his gaze on the compound gate—trying to shout to the two soldiers standing guard, but his tongue was swelling up, filling his mouth. He was having trouble breathing. Running . . .

Running out of time—

'Who was that?'

Grub came back from the hallway and shook his head. 'Someone. Woke up the wasps.'

'Glad they didn't come in here.'

They were standing in a main chamber of some sort, a stone fireplace dominating one wall, framed by two deep-cushioned chairs. Trunks and chests squatted against two other walls, and in front of the last one, opposite the cold hearth, there was an ornate couch, above it a large faded tapestry. All were little more than vague, grainy shapes in the gloom.

'We need a candle or a lantern,' said Sinn. 'Since,' she added with an edge to her tone, 'I can't use sorcery—'

'You probably can,' said Grub, 'now that we're nowhere near the yard. There's no one here, no, um, presence, I mean. It really is dead.'

With a triumphant gesture Sinn awakened the coals in the fireplace, although the flames flaring to life there were strangely lurid, spun through with green and blue tendrils.

'That's too easy for you,' Grub said. 'I didn't even feel a warren.'

She said nothing, walking up to study the tapestry.

Grub followed.

A battle scene was depicted, which for such things was typical enough. It seemed heroes only existed in the midst of death. Barely discernible in the faded weave, armoured reptiles of some sort warred with Tiste Edur and Tiste Andii. The smoke-shrouded sky overhead was crowded with both floating mountains—most of them burning—and dragons, and some of these dragons seemed enormous, five, six times the size of the others even though they were clearly more distant. Fire wreathed the scene, as fragments of the aerial fortresses broke apart and plunged down into the midst of the warring factions. Everywhere was slaughter and harrowing destruction.

'Pretty,' murmured Sinn.

'Let's check the tower,' said Grub. All the fires in the scene reminded him of Y'Ghatan, and his vision of Sinn, marching through the flames—she could have walked into this ancient battle. He feared that if he looked closely enough he'd see her, among the hundreds of seething figures, a contented expression on her round-cheeked face, her dark eyes satiated and shining.

They set off for the square tower.

Into the gloom of the corridor once more, where Grub paused, waiting for his eyes to adjust. A moment later green flames licked out from the chamber they had just quit, slithering across the stone floor, drawing closer.

In the ghoulish glow, Sinn smiled.

The fire followed them up the saddled stairs to the upper landing, which was bare of all furnishings. Beneath a shuttered, web-slung window was slumped a desiccated corpse. Leathery strips of skin here and there were all that held the carcass together, and Grub could see the oddity of the thing's limbs, the extra joints at knee, elbow, wrist and ankle. The very sternum seemed horizontally hinged midway down, as were the prominent, birdlike collarbones.

He crept forward for a closer look. The face was frontally flattened, sharpening the angle where the cheekbones swept back, almost all the way to the ear-holes. Every bone he could see seemed designed to fold or collapse—not just the cheeks but the mandibles and brow-ridges as well. It was a face that in life, Grub suspected, could manage a bizarre array of expressions—far beyond what a human face could achieve.

The skin was bleached white, hairless, and Grub knew that if he so much as touched the corpse, it would fall to dust.

'Forkrul Assail,' he whispered.

Sinn rounded on him. 'How do you know that? How do you know anything about anything?'

'On the tapestry below,' he said, 'those lizards. I think they were K'Chain Che'Malle.' He glanced at her, and then shrugged. 'This Azath House didn't die,' he said. 'It just . . . *left*.'

'Left? How?'

'I think it just walked out of here, that's what I think.'

'But you don't know anything! How can you say things like that?'

'I bet Quick Ben knows, too.'

'*Knows what?*' she hissed in exasperation.

'This. The truth of it all.'

'Grub—'

He met her gaze, studied the fury in her eyes. 'You, me, the Azath. It's all changing, Sinn. Everything—it's all changing.'

Her small hands made fists at her sides. The flames dancing from the stone floor climbed the frame of the chamber's entranceway, snapping and sparking.

Grub snorted, 'The way you make it talk . . .'

'It can shout, too, Grub.'

He nodded. 'Loud enough to break the world, Sinn.'

'I would, you know,' she said with sudden vehemence, 'just to see what it can do. What *I* can do.'

'What's stopping you?'

She grimaced as she turned away. 'You might shout back.'

Tehol the Only, King of Lether, stepped into the room and, arms out to the sides, spun in a circle. Then beamed at Bugg. 'What do you think?'

The manservant held a bronze pot in his battered, blunt hands. 'You've had dancing lessons?'

'No, look at my blanket! My beloved wife has begun embroidering it—see, there at the hem, above my left knee.'

Bugg leaned forward slightly. 'Ah, I see. Very nice.'

'Very nice?'

'Well, I can't quite make out what it's supposed to be.'

'Me neither.' He paused. 'She's not very good, is she?'

'No, she's terrible. Of course, she's an academic.'

'Precisely,' Tehol agreed.

'After all,' said Bugg, 'if she had any skill at sewing and the like—'

'She'd never have settled for the scholarly route?'

'Generally speaking, people useless at everything else become academics.'

'My thoughts inexactly, Bugg. Now, I must ask, what's wrong?'

'Wrong?'

'We've known each other for a long time,' said Tehol. 'My senses are exquisitely honed for reading the finest nuances in your mood. I have few talents but I do assert, howsoever immodestly, that I possess exceptional ability in taking your measure.'

'Well,' sighed Bugg, 'I am impressed. How could you tell I'm upset?'

'Apart from besmirching my wife, you mean?'

'Yes, apart from that.'

Tehol nodded towards the pot Bugg was holding, and so he looked down, only to discover that it was no longer a pot, but a mangled heap of tortured metal. Sighing again, he let it drop to the floor. The thud echoed in the chamber.

'It's the subtle details,' said Tehol, smoothing out the creases in his Royal Blanket. 'Something worth saying to my wife . . . casually, of course, in passing. Swift passing, as in headlong flight, since she'll be armed with vicious fishbone needles.'

'The Malazans,' said Bugg. 'Or, rather, one Malazan. With a version of the Tiles in his sweaty hands. A potent version, and this man is no charlatan. He's an adept. Terrifyingly so.'

'And he's about to cast the Tiles?'

'Wooden cards. The rest of the world's moved on from Tiles, sire. They call it the Deck of Dragons.'

'Dragons? What dragons?'

'Don't ask.'

'Well, is there nowhere you can, um, hide, O wretched and miserable Elder God?'

Bugg made a sour face. 'Not likely. I'm not the only problem, however. There's the Errant.'

'He's still here? He's not been seen for months—'

'The Deck poses a threat to him. He may object to its unveiling. He may do something . . . precipitous.'

'Hmm. The Malazans are our guests, and accordingly if they are at risk, it behoves us to protect them or, failing that, warn them. If that doesn't work, we can always run away.'

'Yes, sire, that might be wise.'

'Running away?'

'No, a warning.'

'I shall send Brys.'

'Poor Brys.'

'Now, that's not my fault, is it? Poor Brys, exactly. It's high time he started earning his title, whatever it is, which at the moment escapes me. It's that bureaucratic mindset of his that's so infuriating. He hides in the very obscurity of his office. A faceless peon, dodging this way and that whenever responsibility comes a-knocking at his door. Yes, I've had my fill of the man, brother or not—'

'Sire, you put Brys in charge of the army.'

'Did I? Of course I did. Let's see him hide now!'

'He's waiting for you in the throne room.'

'Well, he's no fool. He knows when he's cornered.'

'Rucket is there, too,' said Bugg, 'with a petition from the Rat Catchers' Guild.'

'A petition? For what, more rats? On your feet, old friend, the time has come to meet our public. This whole kingship thing is a real bother. Spectacles, parades, tens of thousands of adoring subjects—'

'You've not had any spectacles or parades, sire.'

'And still they adore me.'

Bugg rose and preceded King Tehol across the chamber, through the door, and into the throne room.

The only people awaiting them were Brys, Rucket and Queen Janath. Tehol edged closer to Bugg as they ascended the dais. 'See Rucket? See the adoration? What did I tell you?'

The King sat down on the throne, smiled at the Queen who was already seated in a matching throne to his left, and then leaned back and stretched out his legs—

'Don't do that, brother,' advised Brys. 'The view from here . . .'

Tehol straightened. 'Oops, most royally.'

'About that,' said Rucket.

'I see with relief that you've shed countless stones of weight, Rucket. Most becoming. About what?'

'That adoration bit you whispered to Bugg.'

'I thought you had a petition?'

'I want to sleep with you. I want you to cheat on your wife, Tehol. With me.'

'That's your petition?'

'What's wrong with it?'

Queen Janath spoke. 'It can't be cheating. Cheating would be behind my back. Deceit, deception, betrayal. I happen to be sitting right here, Rucket.'

'Precisely,' Rucket replied, 'let's do without such grim details. Free love for all,' and she smiled up at Tehol. 'Specifically, you and me, sire. Well, not entirely free, since I expect you to buy me dinner.'

'I can't,' said Tehol. 'Nobody wants my money any more, now that I actually have some, and isn't that always the way? Besides, a public dalliance by the King? What sort of example would that set?'

'You wear a blanket,' Rucket pointed out. 'What kind of example is that?'

'Why, one of airy aplomb.'

Her brows lifted. 'Most would view your aired aplomb with horror, sire. But not,' she added with a winning smile, 'me.'

'Gods below,' Janath sighed, rubbing at her brow.

'What sort of petition is this?' Tehol demanded. 'You're not here representing the Rat Catchers' Guild at all, are you?'

'Actually, I am. To further cement our ties. As everyone knows, sex is the glue that holds society together, so I figured—'

'Sex? Glue?' Tehol sat forward. 'Now I'm intrigued. But let's put that aside for the moment. Bugg, prepare a proclamation. The King shall have sex with every powerful woman in the city, assuming she can be definitively determined to actually be a woman—we'll need to devise some sort of gauge, get the Royal Engineers on it.'

'Why stop with powerful women?' Janath asked her husband. 'Don't forget the power that exists in a household, after all. And what about a similar proclamation for the Queen?'

Bugg said, 'There was a tribe once where the chief and his wife had the privilege of bedding imminent brides and grooms the night before the marriage.'

'Really?'

'No, sire,' admitted Bugg, 'I just made that up.'

'I can write it into our histories if you like,' said Janath in barely concealed excitement.

Tehol made a face. 'My wife becomes unseemly.'

'Just tossing my coin into this treasure trove of sordid idiocy, beloved. Rucket, you and I need to sit down and have a little talk.'

'I never talk with the other woman,' pronounced Rucket, standing straighter and lifting her chin.

Tehol slapped his hands. 'Well, another meeting done! What shall we do now? I'm for bed.' And then, with a quick glance at Janath, 'In the company of my dearest wife, of course.'

'We haven't even had supper yet, husband.'

'Supper in bed! We can invite—oh, scratch that.'

Brys stepped forward. 'About the army.'

'Oh, it's always about the army with you. Order more boots.'

'That's just it—I need more money.'

'Bugg, give him more money.'

'How much, sire?'

'Whatever he needs for the boots and whatnot.'

'It's not boots,' said Brys. 'It's training.'

'They're going to train without boots? Extraordinary.'

'I want to make use of these Malazans quartered in our city. These "marines." And their tactics. I want to reinvent the entire Letherii military. I want to hire the Malazan sergeants.'

'And does their Adjunct find this acceptable?'

'She does. Her soldiers are getting bored and that's not good.'

'I imagine not. Do we know when they're leaving?'

Brys frowned. 'You're asking me? Why not ask her?'

'Ah, the agenda is set for the next meeting, then.'

'Shall I inform the Adjunct?' Bugg asked.

Tehol rubbed his chin, and then nodded. 'That would be wise, yes, Bugg. Very wise. Well done.'

'What about my petition?' demanded Rucket. 'I got dressed up and everything!'

'I will take it under advisement.'

'Great. How about a Royal Kiss in the meantime?'

Tehol fidgeted on his throne.

'Airy aplomb shrinking, husband? Clearly, it knows better than you that there are limits to my forbearance.'

'Well,' said Rucket, 'what about a Royal Squeeze?'

'There's an idea,' said Bugg, 'raise the taxes. On guilds.'

'Fine,' snapped Rucket, 'I'm leaving. Another petition rejected by the King. Making the mob ever more restive.'

'What mob?' Tehol asked.

'The one I'm about to assemble.'

'You wouldn't.'

'A woman scorned, 'tis a dangerous thing, sire.'

'Oh, give her a kiss and squeeze, husband. I'll avert my eyes.'

Tehol leapt to his feet, and then quickly sat back down. 'In a moment,' he gasped.

'Gives a new meaning to regal bearing,' commented Bugg.

But Rucket was smiling. 'Let's just take that as a promissory note.'

'And the mob?' asked Bugg.

'Miraculously dispersed in a dreamy sigh, O Chancellor, or whatever you are.'

'I'm the Royal Engineers—yes, all of them. Oh, and Treasurer.'

'And Spittoon Mangler,' Tehol added.

The others frowned.

Bugg scowled at Tehol. 'I'd been pleasantly distracted until you said that.'

'Is something wrong?' Brys asked.

'Ah, brother,' Tehol said, 'we need to send you to the Adjunct—with a warning.'

'Oh?'

'Bugg?'

'I'll walk you out, Brys.'

After the two had left, Tehol glanced at Janath, and then at Rucket, and found them both still frowning. 'What?'

'Something we should know?' Janath asked.

'Yes,' added Rucket, 'on behalf of the Rat Catchers' Guild, I mean.'

'Not really,' Tehol replied. 'A minor matter, I assure you. Something to do with threatened gods and devastating divinations. Now, I'm ready to try for my kiss and squeeze—no, wait. Some deep breathing first. Give me a moment—yes, no, wait.'

'Shall I talk about my embroidery?' Janath asked.

'Yes, that sounds perfect. Do proceed. Be right there, Rucket.'

Lieutenant Pores opened his eyes. Or tried to, only to find them mostly swollen shut. But through the blurry slits he made out a figure hovering over him. A Nathii face, looking thoughtful.

'You recognize me?' the Nathii asked.

Pores tried to speak, but someone had bound his jaw tight. He nodded, only to find his neck was twice the normal size. Either that, he considered, or his head had shrunk.

'Mulvan Dreader,' the Nathii said. 'Squad healer. You'll live.' He leaned back and said to someone else, 'He'll live, sir. Won't be much use for a few days, though.'

Captain Kindly loomed into view, his face—consisting entirely of pinched features—its usual expressionless self. 'For this, Lieutenant Pores, you're going up on report. Criminal stupidity unbecoming to an officer.'

'Bet there's a stack a those,' muttered the healer as he moved to depart.

'Did you say something, soldier?'

'No, sir.'

'Must be my poor hearing, then.'

'Yes, sir.'

'Are you suggesting I have poor hearing, soldier?'

'No, sir!'

'I am certain you did.'

'Your hearing is perfect, Captain, I'm sure of it. And that's, uh, a healer's assessment.'

'Tell me,' said Captain Kindly, 'is there a cure for thinning hair?'

'Sir? Well, of course.'

'What is it?'

'Shave your head. Sir.'

'It looks to me as though you don't have enough things to do, Healer. Therefore, proceed through the squads of your company to mend any and every ailment they describe. Oh, delouse the lot besides, and check for blood blisters on the testicles of the men—I am certain that's a dread sign of something awry.'

'Blood blisters, sir? On the testicles?'

'The flaw in hearing seems to be yours, not mine.'

'Uh, nothing dread or awry, sir. Just don't pop 'em, they bleed like demons. Comes with too much riding, sir.'

'Indeed.'

. . .

'Healer, why are you still standing there?'

'Sorry, sir, on my way!'

'I shall expect a detailed report on the condition of your fellow soldiers.'

'Aye, sir! Testicular inspection, here I go.'

Kindly leaned forward again and studied Pores. 'You can't even talk, can you? Unexpected mercy there. Six black wasp stings. You should be dead. Why aren't you? Never mind. Presumably, you've lost the two runts. Now I'll need to unchain that cattle-dog to find them. Tonight of all nights. Recover quickly, Lieutenant, so I can thrash your hide.'

Outside the dormitory, Mulvan Dreader paused for a moment, and then set off at a swift pace to rejoin his companions in an adjoining dorm. He entered the chamber, scanned the various soldiers lounging on cots or tossing knuckles, until he spied the wizened black face of Nep Furrow barely visible between two cots, whereupon he marched up to the Dal Honese shaman, who was sitting cross-legged with a nasty smile on his lips.

'I know what you done, Nep!'

'Eh? Eggit'way fra meen!'

'You've been cursin' Kindly, haven't you? Blood blisters on his balls!'

Nep Furrow cackled. 'Black blibbery spoots, hah!'

'Stop it—stop what you're doing, damn you!'

'Too laber! Dey doan gee'way!'

'Maybe he should find out who's behind it—'

'Doan deedat! Pig! Nathii frup pahl! Voo booth voo booth!'

Mulvan Dreader stared down at the man, uncomprehending. He cast a be-seeching glance over at Strap Mull the next cot along. 'What did he just say?'

The other Dal Honese was lying on his back, hands behind his head. 'Hood knows, some shaman tongue, I expect.' And then added, 'Curses, I'd wager.'

The Nathii glared back down at Nep Furrow. 'Curse me and I'll boil your bones, y'damned prune. Now, leave off Kindly, or I'll tell Badan.'

'Beedan nar'ere, izzee?'

'When he gets back.'

'Pahl!'

No one could claim that Preda Norlo Trumb was the most perceptive of individ-uals, and the half-dozen Letherii guards under his command, who stood in a twitching clump behind the Preda, were now faced with the very real possibility that Trumb's stupidity was going to cost them their lives.

Norlo was scowling belligerently at the dozen or so riders. 'War is war,' he in-sisted, 'and we were at war. People died, didn't they? That kind of thing doesn't go unpunished.'

The black-skinned sergeant made some small gesture with one gloved hand and crossbows were levelled. In rough Letherii he said, 'One more time. Last time. They alive?'

'Of course they're alive,' Norlo Trumb said with a snort. 'We do things prop-erly here. But they've been sentenced, you see. To death. We've just been waiting for an officer of the Royal Advocate to come by and stamp the seal on the orders.'

'No seal,' said the sergeant. 'No death. Let them go. We take now.'

'Even if their crimes were commuted,' the Preda replied, 'I'd still need a seal to release them.'

'Let them go now. Or we kill you all.'

The Preda stared, and then turned back to his unit. 'Draw your weapons,' he snapped.

'Not a chance,' said gate-guard Fifid. 'Sir. We even twitch towards our swords and we're dead.'

Norlo Trumb's face darkened in the lantern light. 'You've just earned a court-martial, Fifid—'

'At least I'll be breathing, sir.'

'And the rest of you?'

None of the other guards spoke. Nor did they draw their swords.

'Get them,' growled the sergeant from where he sat slouched on his horse. 'No more nice.'

'Listen to this confounded ignorant foreigner!' Norlo Trumb turned back to the Malazan sergeant. 'I intend to make an official protest straight to the Royal Court,' he said. 'And you will answer to the charges—'

'Get.'

And to the left of the sergeant a young, oddly effeminate warrior slipped down from his horse and settled hands on the grips of two enormous falchions of some sort. His languid, dark eyes looked almost sleepy.

At last, something shivered up Trumb's spine to curl worm-like on the back of his neck. He licked suddenly dry lips. 'Spanserd, guide this Malazan, uh, warrior, to the cells.'

'And?' the guard asked.

'And release the prisoners, of course!'

'Yes, sir!'

Sergeant Badan Gruk allowed himself the barest of sighs—not enough to be visible to anyone—and watched with relief as the Letherii guard led Skulldeath towards the gaol-block lining one wall of the garrison compound.

The other marines sat motionless on their horses, but their tension was a stink in Badan's nostrils, and under his hauberk sweat ran in streams. No, he'd not wanted any sort of trouble. Especially not a bloodbath. But this damned shrew-brained Preda had made it close. His heart thumped loud in his chest and he forced himself to glance back at his soldiers. Ruffle's round face was pink and damp, but she offered him a wink before angling her crossbow upward and resting the stock's butt on one soft thigh. Reliko was cradling his own crossbow in one arm while the other arm was stretched out to stay Vastly Blank, who'd evidently realized—finally —that there'd been trouble here in the compound, and now looked ready to start killing Letherii—once he was pointed in the right direction. Skim and Honey were side by side, their heavy assault crossbows aimed with unwavering precision at the Preda's chest—a detail the man seemed too stupid to comprehend. The other heavies remained in the background, in ill mood for having been rousted from another drunken night in Letheras.

Badan Gruk's scan ended on the face of Corporal Pravalak Rim, and sure enough, he saw in that young man's features something of what he himself felt. A damned miracle. Something that'd seemed impossible to ever have believed— they'd all seen—

A heavy door clunked from the direction of the gaol.

Everyone—Malazan and Letherii—now fixed gazes on the four figures slowly approaching. Skulldeath was half-carrying his charge, and the same was true of the Letherii guard, Spanserd. The prisoners they'd just helped from their cells were in bad shape.

'Easy, Blank,' muttered Reliko.

'But that's—they—but I know them two!'

'Aye,' the heavy infantryman sighed. 'We all do, Vastly.'

Neither prisoner showed any signs of having been beaten or tortured. What left them on the edge of death was simple neglect. The most effective torture of all.

'Preda,' said Badan Gruk, in a low voice.

Norlo Trumb turned to face him. 'What is it now?'

'You don't feed them?'

'The condemned received reduced rations, I am afraid—'

'How long?'

'Well, as I said, Sergeant, we have been awaiting the officer of the Royal Advocate for some time. Months and—'

Two quarrels skimmed past the Preda's head, one on either side, and both sliced the man's ears. He shrieked in sudden shock and fell back, landing heavily on his behind.

Badan pointed at the now cowering garrison guards. 'No move now.' And then he twisted in his saddle to glare at Honey and Skim. In Malazan he said, 'Don't even think about reloading! Shit-brained sappers!'

'Sorry,' said Skim, 'I guess we both just sort've . . . twitched.' And she shrugged.

Honey handed her his crossbow and dropped down from his horse. 'I'll retrieve the quarrels—anybody see where they ended up?'

'Bounced and skittered between them two buildings there,' Reliko said, pointing with his chin.

The Preda's shock had shifted into fury. Ears streaming blood, he now staggered to his feet. 'Attempted murder! I will see those two arrested! You'll swim the canal for this!'

'No understand,' said Badan Gruk. 'Pravalak, bring up the spare horses. We should've brought Dreader. I don't think they can even ride. Flank 'em close on the way back—we'll take it slow.'

He studied the stumbling figures leaning on their escorts. Sergeant Sinter and her sister, Kisswhere. Looking like Hood's own soiled loincloth. But alive. 'Gods below,' he whispered. *They are alive.*

'Aaii! My leg's fallen off!'

Banaschar sat motionless in the chair and watched the small skeletal lizard lying on its side and spinning now in circles on the floor, one leg kicking.

'Telorast! Help me!'

The other reptile perched on the window sill and looked down, head tilting from one side to the other, as if seeking the perfect angle of regard. 'It's no use, Curdle,' it finally replied. 'You can't get anywhere like that.'

'I need to get away!'

'From what?'

'From the fact that my leg's fallen off!'

Telorast scampered along the sill until it was as close as it could get to

Banaschar. 'Sodden priest of wine, hssst! Look over here—the window! It's me, the clever one. Stupid one's down on the floor there, see her? She needs your help. No, of course you can't make her any less stupid—we're not discussing that here. Rather, it's one of her legs, yes? The gut binding or whatever has broken. She's crippled, helpless, useless. She's spinning in circles and that's far too poignant for us. Do you understand? O Wormlet of the Worm Goddess, O scurrier of the worship-slayer eyeless bitch of the earth! Banaschar the Drunk, Banaschar the Wise, the Wisely Drunk. Please be so kind and nimble as to repair my companion, my dear sister, the stupid one.'

'You might know the answer to this,' said Banaschar. 'Listen, if life is a joke, what kind of joke? The funny ha ha kind? Or the "I'm going to puke" kind? Is it a clever joke or a stupid one that's repeated over and over again so that even if it was funny to begin with it's not funny any more? Is it the kind of joke to make you laugh or make you cry? How many other ways can I ask this simple question?'

'I'm confident you can think of a few hundred more, good sir. Defrocked, detached, essentially castrated priest. Now, see those strands there? Near the unhinged leg—oh, Curdle, will you stop that spinning?'

'I used to laugh,' said Banaschar. 'A lot. Long before I decided on becoming a priest, of course. Nothing amusing in that decision, alas. Nor in the life that followed. Years and years of miserable study, rituals, ceremonies, the rigorous exercises of magery. And the Worm of Autumn, well, she did abide, did she not? Delivered our just reward—too bad I missed out on the fun.'

'Pitiful wretch of pointless pedantry, would you be so kind—yes, reach out and down, out and down, a little further, ah! You have it! The twine! The leg! Curdle, listen—see—stop, right there, no, there, yes, see? Salvation is in hand!'

'I can't! Everything's sideways! The world pitches into the Abyss!'

'Never mind that—see? He's got your leg. He's eyeing the twine. His brain stirs!'

'There used to be drains,' said Banaschar, holding up the skeletal leg. 'Under the altar. To collect the blood, you see, down into amphorae—we'd sell that, you know. Amazing the stuff people will pay for, isn't it?'

'What's he doing with my leg?'

'Nothing—so far,' replied Telorast. 'Looking, I think. And thinking. He lacks all cleverness, it's true. Not-Apsalar Apsalar's left earlobe possessed more cleverness than this pickled grub. But never mind that! Curdle, use your forelimbs, your arms, I mean, and crawl closer to him—stop kicking in circles! Stop it!'

'I can't!' came the tiny shriek.

And round and round Curdle went.

'Old blood out, shiny coins in. We'd laugh at that, but it wasn't the happy kind of laugh. More like disbelief, and yes, more than a little cynicism regarding the inherent stupidity of people. Anyway, we ended up with chests and chests of riches—more than you could even imagine. Vaults filled to bursting. You could buy a lot of laughs with that, I'm sure. And the blood? Well, as any priest will tell you, blood is cheap.'

'Please oh please, show the mercy your ex-goddess so despised. Spit in her face with a gesture of goodwill! You'll be amply rewarded, yes, amply!'

'Riches,' Banaschar said. 'Worthless.'

'Different reward, we assure you. Substantial, meaningful, valuable, timely.'

He looked up from his study of the leg and eyed Telorast. 'Like what?'

The reptile's skeleton head bobbed. 'Power, my friend. More power than you can imagine—'

'I doubt that most sincerely.'

'Power to do as you please, to whomever or whatever you please! Power gushing out, spilling down, bubbling up and leaving potent wet spots! Worthy reward, yes!'

'And if I hold you to that?'

'As surely as you hold that lovely leg, and the twine, as surely as that!'

'The pact is sealed,' said Banaschar.

'Curdle! You hear that!'

'I heard. Are you mad? We don't share! We never share!'

'Shhh! He'll hear you!'

'Sealed,' repeated Banaschar, sitting up.

'Ohhh,' wailed Curdle, spinning faster and faster. 'You've done it now! Telorast, you've done it now! Ohhh, look, I can't get away!'

'Empty promises, Curdle, I swear it!'

'Sealed,' said Banaschar again.

'Aaii! Thrice sealed! We're doomed!'

'Relax, lizard,' said Banaschar, leaning over and reaching down for the whirling creature, 'soon you'll dance again. And,' he added as he snatched up Curdle, 'so will I.'

Holding the bony reptile in one hand, the leg in the other, Banaschar glanced over at his silent guest—who sat in shadows, lone eye glittering. 'All right,' said Banaschar, 'I'll listen to you now.'

'I am pleased,' murmured the Errant, 'for we have very little time.'

Lostara Yil sat on the edge of her cot, a bowl filled with sand on her lap. She dipped her knife's blade into the topped gourd to her right, to coat the iron in the pulp's oil, and then slid the blade into the sand, and resumed scouring the iron.

She had been working on this one weapon for two bells now, and there had been other sessions before this one. More than she could count. Others swore that the dagger's iron could not be cleaner, could not be more flawless, but she could still see the stains.

Her fingers were rubbed raw, red and cracked. The bones of her hands ached. They felt heavier these days, as if the sand had imparted something to her skin, flesh and bones, beginning the process of turning them to stone. There might come a time when she lost all feeling in them, and they would hang from her wrists like mauls. But not useless, no. With them she could well batter down the world—if that would do any good.

The pommel of a weapon thumped on her door and a moment later it was pushed open. Faradan Sort leaned in, eyes searching until she found Lostara Yil. 'Adjunct wants you,' she said tonelessly.

So, it was time. Lostara collected a cloth and wiped down the knife-blade. The captain stood in the doorway, watching without expression.

She rose, sheathed the weapon, and then collected her cloak. 'Are you my escort?' she asked as she approached the door.

'We've had one run away already this night,' Faradan replied, falling in step beside Lostara as they made their way up the corridor.

'You can't be serious.'

'Not really, but I am to accompany you this evening.'

'Why?'

Faradan Sort did not reply. They'd reached the pair of ornate, red-stained double doors that marked the end of the corridor, and the captain drew them open.

Lostara Yil strode into the chamber beyond. The ceiling of the Adjunct's quarters—the command centre in addition to her residence—was a chaotic collection of corbels, vaults and curved beams. Consequently it was enwreathed in cobwebs from which shrivelled moths dangled down, mocking flight in the vague draughts. Beneath a central, oddly misshapen miniature dome stood a huge rectangular table with a dozen high-backed chairs. A series of high windows ran across the wall opposite the door, reached by a raised platform that was lined with a balustrade. In all, to Lostara's eyes, one of the strangest rooms she had ever seen. The Letherii called it the Grand Lecture Medix, and it was the largest chamber in the college building that temporarily served as the officers' quarters and HQ.

Adjunct Tavore stood on the raised walkway, intent on something beyond one of the thick-glassed windows.

'You requested me, Adjunct.'

Tavore did not turn round as she said, 'There is a tablet on the table, Captain. On it you will find the names of those who will attend the reading. As there may be some resistance from some of them, Captain Faradan Sort will accompany you to the barracks.'

'Very well.' Lostara walked over and collected the tablet, scanned the names scribed into the golden wax. Her brows rose. 'Adjunct? This list—'

'Refusals not permitted, Captain. Dismissed.'

Out in the corridor once again, the two women paused upon seeing a Letherii approaching. Plainly dressed, an unadorned long, thin-bladed sword scabbarded at his hip, Brys Beddict possessed no extraordinary physical qualities, and yet neither Lostara nor Faradan Sort could take their eyes off him. Even a casual glance would slide past only to draw inexorably back, captured by something ineffable but undeniable.

They parted to let him by.

He halted to deliver a deferential half-bow. 'Excuse me,' he said, addressing Lostara, 'I would speak with the Adjunct, if that is possible.'

'Of course,' she replied, reaching to open one of the double doors. 'Just step inside and announce yourself.'

'Thank you.' A brief smile, and then he entered the chamber, closing the door behind him.

Lostara sighed.

'Yes,' agreed Faradan Sort.

After a moment they set out once more.

As soon as the Adjunct turned to face him, Brys Beddict bowed, and then said, 'Adjunct Tavore, greetings and salutations from the King.'

'Be sure to return the sentiments, sir,' she replied.

'I shall. I have been instructed to deliver a caution, Adjunct, with respect to this session of divination you intend this night.'

'What manner of caution, and from whom, if I may ask?'

'There is an Elder God,' said Brys. 'One who traditionally chose to make the court of Letheras his temple, if you will, and did so for an unknown number of generations. He acted, more often than not, as consort to the Queen, and was known to most as Turudal Brizad. Generally, of course, his true identity was not known, but there can be no doubt that he is the Elder God known as the Errant, Master of the Tiles, which, as you know, is the Letherii corollary to your Deck of Dragons.'

'Ah, I begin to comprehend.'

'Indeed, Adjunct.'

'The Errant would view the divination—and the Deck—as an imposition, a trespass.'

'Adjunct, the response of an Elder God cannot be predicted, and this is especially true of the Errant, whose relationship with fate and chance is rather intense, as well as complicated.'

'May I speak with this Turudal Brizad?'

'The Elder God has not resumed that persona since before the Emperor's reign; nor has he been seen in the palace. Yet I am assured that once more he has drawn close—probably stirred awake by your intentions.'

'I am curious, who in the court of your king is capable of discerning such things?'

Brys shifted uneasily. 'That would be Bugg, Adjunct.'

'The Chancellor?'

'If that is the capacity in which you know him, then yes, the Chancellor.'

Through all of this she had remained standing on the platform, but now she descended the four steps at one end and walked closer, colourless eyes searching Brys's face. 'Bugg. One of my High Mages finds him . . . how did he put it? Yes. "*Adorable.*" But then, Quick Ben is unusual and prone to peculiar, often sardonic assessments. Is the Chancellor a Ceda—if that is the proper term for High Mage?'

'It would be best to view him as such, yes, Adjunct.'

She seemed to consider the matter for a time, and then she said, 'While I am confident in the abilities of my mages to defend against most threats . . . that of an Elder God is likely well beyond their capacities. What of your Ceda?'

'Bugg? Uh, no, I do not think he's much frightened by the Errant. Alas, he intends to take refuge tonight should you proceed with the reading. As I stated earlier, I am here to give caution and convey King Tehol's genuine concern for your safety.'

She seemed to find his words discomforting, for she turned away and walked slowly round to halt at one end of the rectangular table, whereupon she faced him once more. 'Thank you, Brys Beddict,' she said with stilted formality. 'Unfortunately, I have delayed this reading too long as it is. Guidance is necessary and, indeed, pressing.'

He cocked his head. What were these Malazans up to? A question often voiced in the Royal Court, and no doubt everywhere else in the city, for that matter. 'I understand, Adjunct. Is there any other way we can assist?'

She frowned. 'I am not sure how, given your Ceda's aversion to attending, even as a spectator.'

'He does not wish his presence to deliver undue influence on the divination, I suspect.'

The Adjunct opened her mouth to say something, stopped, closed it again. And it was possible her eyes widened a fraction before she looked away. 'What other form of assistance is possible, then?'

'I am prepared to volunteer myself, as the King's Sword.'

She shot him a glance, clearly startled. 'The Errant would hesitate in crossing you, sir?'

He shrugged. 'At the very least, Adjunct, I can negotiate with him from a position of some knowledge—with respect to his history among my people, and so on.'

'And you would risk this for us?'

Brys hesitated, never adept at lying. 'It is no risk, Adjunct,' he managed.

And saw his abysmal failure in her narrowed gaze. 'Courtesy and decency demand that I reject your generous offer. However,' she added, 'I must descend to rudeness and say to you that your presence would be most appreciated.'

He bowed again.

'If you need to report back to your king,' said the Adjunct, 'there is still time—not much time, but sufficient for a brief account, I should think.'

'That will not be necessary,' said Brys.

'Then please, help yourself to some wine.'

He grimaced. 'Thank you, but I have given up wine, Adjunct.'

'There is a jug of ale, there, under that side table. Falari, I believe—a decent brew, I'm told.'

He smiled and saw her start, and wondered, although not for long, as women often reacted that way when he smiled. 'Yes, I would like to give that a try, thank you.'

'What I can't tolerate,' he said, 'is the very fact of your existence.'

The man sitting opposite him looked up. 'So it's mutual.'

The tavern was crowded, the clientele decidedly upscale, smug with privilege. Coins in heaps, dusty bottles and glittering glass goblets, and an eye-dazzling array of ostentatious attire—most of which suggested some version of the Royal Blanket, although this generally involved only a narrow wrap swathing the hips and groin. Here and there, some overscented young man also wore woollen pants with one trouser leg ending halfway down.

In a cage near the table where the two Malazans sat, two strange birds exchanged guttural comments every now and then, in tones singularly unimpressed. Short-beaked, yellow-plumed and grey-hooded, they were the size of starlings.

'Maybe it is,' the first man said after taking a mouthful of the heady wine, 'but it's still different.'

'That's what you think.'

'It is, you ear-flapped idiot. For one thing, you were dead. You hatched a damned cusser under your butt. Those clothes you're wearing right now, they were in shreds. Fragments. Flecks of ash. I don't care how good Hood's seamstresses might be—or even how many millions of 'em he's got by now, *nobody* could have stitched all that back together—of course, there are no stitches, not where they're not supposed to be, I mean. So, your clothes are intact. Just like you.'

'What's your point, Quick? I put myself back together in Hood's cellar, right? I even helped out Ganoes Paran, and rode with a Trygalle troupe for a time. When you're dead you can do . . . stuff—'

'That depends on your will-power, actually—'

'The Bridgeburners ascended,' Hedge pointed out. 'Blame Fid for that—nothing to do with me.'

'And you're their messenger, are you?'

'Could be. It's not like I was taking orders from anybody—'

'Whiskeyjack?'

Hedge shifted uneasily, glanced away, and then shrugged. 'Funny, that.'

'What?'

The sapper nodded towards the two caged birds. 'Those are jaraks, aren't they?'

Quick Ben tilted his head downward and knuckled his brow with both hands. 'Some kind of geas, maybe? Some curse of evasiveness? Or just the usual obstinate stupidity we all knew so well?'

'There you go,' said Hedge, reaching for his ale, 'talkin' to yourself again.'

'You're shying from certain topics, Hedge. There's secrets you don't want to spill, and that makes me nervous. And not just me—'

'Fid always gets nervous round me. You all do. It's just my stunning looks and charm, I figure.'

'Nice try,' drawled Quick Ben. 'I was actually talking about the Adjunct.'

'What reason's she got to be nervous about me?' Hedge demanded. 'In fact, it's the other damned way round! There's no making sense of that woman—you've said so yourself often enough, Quick.' He leaned forward, eyes narrowing. 'You heard something new? About where we're going? About what in Hood's name we're doing next?'

The wizard simply stared.

Hedge reached under a flap and scratched above his ear, and then settled back, looking pleased with himself.

A moment later two people arrived to halt at their table. Glancing up, Hedge started guiltily.

'High Mage, sapper,' said Lostara Yil, 'the Adjunct requests your immediate presence. If you will follow us.'

'Me?' asked Hedge, his voice almost a squeal.

'First name on the list,' said Faradan Sort with a hard smile.

'Now you've done it,' hissed Quick Ben.

As the four foreigners left, one of the jarak birds said, 'I smell death.'

'No you don't,' croaked the other.

'I smell death,' the first one insisted.

'No. You smell *dead*.'

After a moment, the first bird lifted a wing and thrust its head underneath, and then withdrew and settled once more. 'Sorry.'

The matted wicker bars of the pen wall between them, Captain Kindly and the Wickan cattle-dog Bent glared at each other with bared teeth.

'Listen to me, dog,' said Kindly, 'I want you to find Sinn, and Grub. Any funny business, like trying to rip out my throat, and I'll stick you. Mouth to butt, straight through. Then I'll saw off your head and sink it in the river. I'll chop off your paws and sell 'em to ugly witches. I'll strip your hide and get it cut up and made into codpieces for penitent sex-addicts-turned-priests, the ones with certain items hidden under their cots. And I'll do all this while you're still alive. Am I understood?'

The lips on the beast's scarred, twisted muzzle had if anything curled back even further, revealing blood-red lacerations from the splintered fangs. Crimson froth bubbled out between the gaps. Above that smashed mouth, Bent's eyes burned like two tunnels into a demon lord's brain, swirling with enraged madness. At the dog's back end, the stub of the tail wagged in fits and starts, as if particularly pleasing thoughts spasmed through the beast.

Kindly stood, holding a braided leather leash with one end tied into a noose. 'I'm going to slip this over your head, dog. Make a fuss and I'll hang you high and laugh at every twitch. In fact, I'll devise a hundred new ways of killing you and I'll use every one of them.' He lifted the noose into view.

A matted ball of twigs, hair and clumps of mud that had been lying off to one side of the pen—a heap that had been doing its own growling—suddenly launched itself forward in a flurry of bounds until it drew close enough to fling itself into the air—sharp, tiny teeth aiming for the captain's neck.

He lashed out his left fist, intercepting the lapdog in mid-air. A muted crunching sound, and the clack of jaws snapping shut on nothing, as the Hengese lapdog named Roach abruptly altered course, landing and bouncing a few times behind Bent, where it lay stunned, small chest heaving, pink tongue lolling.

The gazes of Kindly and the cattle-dog had remained locked through all of this.

'Oh, never mind the damned leash,' said the captain after a moment. 'Never mind Grub and Sinn. Let's make this as simple as possible. I am going to draw my sword and chop you to pieces, dog.'

'Don't do that!' said a voice behind him.

Kindly turned to see Grub and, behind the boy, Sinn. Both stood just inside the stable entrance, wearing innocent expressions. 'Convenient,' he said. 'The Adjunct wants you both.'

'The reading?' Grub asked. 'No, we can't do that.'

'But you will.'

'We thought we could hide in the old Azath,' said Grub, 'but that won't work—'

'Why?' Kindly demanded.

Grub shook his head. 'We don't want to go. It'd be . . . bad.'

The captain held up the leash with its noose. 'One way or the other, maggots.'

'Sinn will burn you to a crisp!'

Kindly snorted. 'Her? Probably just wet herself, from the look on her face. Now, will this be nice or will it be *my* way? Aye, you can guess which way I'm leaning, can't you?'

'It's the Azath—' began Grub.

'Not my problem,' cut in Kindly. 'You want to whine, save it for the Adjunct.' They set out.

'Everyone hates you, you know,' Grub said.

'Seems fair,' Kindly replied.

She rose from her chair, wincing at the ache in her lower back, and then waddled towards the door. She had few acquaintances, barring a titchy midwife who stumbled in every now and then, inside a cloud of eye-watering d'bayang fumes, and the old woman down the lane who'd baked her something virtually every day since she started showing. And it was late, which made the heavy knock at her door somewhat unusual.

Seren Pedac, who had once been an Acquitor, opened the door.

'Oh,' she said, 'hello.'

The old man bowed. 'Lady, are you well?'

'Well, I've no need for any masonry work, sir—'

'Acquitor—'

'I am no longer—'

'Your title remains on the kingdom's tolls,' he said, 'and you continue to receive your stipend.'

'And twice I have requested that both be terminated.' And then she paused and cocked her head. 'I'm sorry, but how do you know about that?'

'My apologies, Acquitor. I am named Bugg, and my present responsibilities include those of Chancellor of the Realm, among, uh, other things. Your requests were noted and filed and subsequently rejected by me.' He held up a hand. 'Be at ease, you will not be dragged from your home to resume work. You are essentially retired, and will receive your full pension for the rest of your life, Acquitor. In any case,' he added, 'I am not visiting this night in that capacity.'

'Oh? Then, sir, what is it you want?'

'May I enter?'

She stepped back, and once he'd come inside she shut the door, edged past him in the narrow corridor, and led him into the sparsely furnished main room. 'Please sit, Chancellor. Having never seen you, I'm afraid I made no connection with the kind gentleman who helped me move a few stones.' She paused, and then said, 'If rumours are correct, you were once the King's manservant, yes?'

'Indeed I was.' He waited until she'd settled into her chair before seating himself in the only other chair. 'Acquitor, you are in your sixth month?'

She started. 'Yes. And which file did you read to discover that?'

'Forgive me,' he said, 'I am feeling unusually clumsy tonight. In, uh, your company, I mean.'

'It has been some time since I last intimidated anyone, Chancellor.'

'Yes, well, perhaps . . . well, it's not quite you, Acquitor.'

'Should I be relieved that you have retracted your compliment?'

'Now you play with me.'

'I do. Chancellor, please, what is all this about?'

'I think it best you think of me in a different capacity, Acquitor. Rather than "chancellor", may I suggest "Ceda".'

Her eyes slowly widened. 'Ah. Very well. Tehol Beddict had quite the manservant, it seems.'

'I am here,' said Bugg, eyes dropping momentarily to the swell of her belly, 'to provide a measure of . . . protection.'

She felt a faint twist of fear inside. 'For me, or my baby? Protection from what?'

He leaned forward, hands entwined. 'Seren Pedac, your child's father was Trull Sengar. A Tiste Edur and brother to Emperor Rhulad. He was, however, somewhat *more* than that.'

'Yes,' she said, 'he was my love.'

His gaze shied away and he nodded. 'There is a version of the Tiles, consisting of Houses, a kind of formal structure imposed on various forces at work in the universe. It is called the Deck of Dragons. Within this Deck, the House of Shadow is ruled, for the moment, not by the Tiste Edur who founded that realm, but by new entities. In the House, there is a King, no Queen as yet, and below the King of High House Shadow there are sundry, uh, servants. Such roles find new faces every now and then. Mortal faces.'

She watched him, her mouth dry as sun-baked stone. She watched as he wrung his hands, as his eyes shifted away again and again. 'Mortal faces,' she said.

'Yes, Acquitor.'

'Trull Sengar.'

'The Knight of Shadow.'

'Cruelly abandoned, it would seem.'

'Not by choice, nor neglect, Acquitor. These Houses, they are engaged in war, and this war escalates—'

'Trull did not choose that title, did he?'

'No. Choice plays little part in such things. Perhaps even the Lords and Ladies of the Houses are in truth less omnipotent than they would like to believe. The same, of course, can be said for the gods and goddesses. Control is an illusion, a deceptive one that salves thin-skinned bluster.'

'Trull is dead,' Seren said.

'But the Knight of Shadow lives on,' Bugg replied.

The dread had been building within her, an icy tide rising to flood every space within her, between her thoughts, drowning them one by one, and now cold fear engulfed her. 'Our child,' she whispered.

Bugg's eyes hardened. 'The Errant invited the murder of Trull Sengar. Tonight, Acquitor, the Deck of Dragons will be awakened, in this very city. This awakening is in truth a challenge to the Errant, an invitation to battle. Is he ready? Is he of sufficient strength to counter-attack? Will this night end awash in mortal blood? I cannot say. One thing I mean to prevent, Seren Pedac, is the Errant striking his enemies through the child you carry.'

'That's not good enough,' she whispered.

His brows rose. 'Acquitor?'

'I said it's not good enough! Who is this King of High House Shadow? How dare he claim my child! Summon him, Ceda! Here! Now!'

'Summon? Acquitor, even if I could, that would be . . . please, you must understand. To summon a god—even if naught but a fragment of its spirit—will be to set afire the brightest beacon—one that will be seen by not just the Errant, but other forces as well. On this night, Acquitor, we must do nothing to draw attention to ourselves.'

'It is you who needs to understand, Ceda. If the Errant wants to harm my child . . . you may well be a Ceda, but the Errant is a *god*. Who has already murdered the man I loved—a Knight of Shadow. You may not be *enough*. My child is to be the new Knight of Shadow? Then the High King of Shadow will come here— tonight—*and he will protect his Knight!*'

'Acquitor—'

'Summon him!'

'Seren—I am enough. Against the Errant. Against any damned fool who dares to come close, *I am enough*.'

'That makes no sense.'

'Nevertheless.'

She stared at him, unable to disguise her disbelief, her terror.

'Acquitor, there are other forces in the city. Ancient, benign ones, yet power-ful nonetheless. Would it ease your concern if I summon *them* on your behalf? On your unborn son's behalf?'

Son. The red-eyed midwife was right, then. 'They will listen to you?'

'I believe so.'

After a moment, she nodded. 'Very well. But Ceda, after tonight—I will speak to this King of Shadow.'

He flinched. 'I fear you will find the meeting unsatisfactory, Acquitor.'

'I will decide that for myself.'

Bugg sighed. 'So you shall, Seren Pedac.'

'When will you summon your friends, Ceda?'

'I already have.'

Lostara Yil had said there'd be eleven in all not counting Fiddler himself. That was madness. Eleven players for the reading. Bottle glanced across at Fiddler as they marched up the street in the wake of the two women. The man looked sick, rings under his eyes, mouth twisted in a grimace. The darker roots of his hair and beard made the silvered ends seem to hover like an aura, a hint of chaos.

Gesler and Stormy clumped along behind them. Too cowed for their usual argu-ing with each other about virtually everything. As bad as a married couple, they were. Maybe they sensed the trouble on the way—Bottle was sure those two marines had more than just gold-hued skin setting them apart from everyone else. Clearly, whatever fates existed displayed a serious lack of discrimination when choosing to single out certain people from the herd. Gesler and Stormy barely had one brain between them.

Bottle tried to guess who else would be there. The Adjunct and Lostara Yil, of course, along with Fiddler himself, and Gesler and Stormy. Maybe Keneb—he'd been at the last one, hadn't he? Hard to remember—most of that night was a blur now. Quick Ben? Probably. Blistig? Well, one sour, miserable bastard might settle things out some. Or just make everything worse. Sinn? Gods forbid.

'This is a mistake,' muttered Fiddler. 'Bottle—what're you sensing? Truth now.'

'You want the truth? Really?'

'Bottle.'

'Fine, I'm too scared to edge out there—this is an old city, Sergeant. There's . . . things. Mostly sleeping up until now. I mean, for as long as we've been here.'

'But now they're awake.'

'Aye. Noses in the air. This reading, Sergeant, it's about as bad an idea as voic-ing a curse in Oponn's name while sitting in Hood's lap.'

'You think I don't know that?'

'Can you spike the whole thing, Sergeant? Just say it won't go, you're all closed up inside or something?'

'Not likely. It just . . . takes over.'

'And then there's no stopping it.'

'No.'

'Sergeant.'

'What?'

'We're going to be exposed, horribly exposed. Like offering our throats to who-ever—and they're probably not merciful types. So, how do we defend ourselves?'

Fiddler glanced across at him, and then edged closer. Ahead was the HQ—they were running out of time. 'I can't do nothing, Bottle. Except take the head off, and with luck some of those nasties will go down with it.'

'You're going to be sitting on a cusser, aren't you?'

Fiddler shifted the leather satchel slung from one shoulder, and that was con-firmation enough for Bottle.

'Sergeant, when we get into the room, let me try one last time to talk her out of it.'

'Let's hope she at least holds to the number.'

'What do you mean?'

'Eleven is bad, twelve is worse. But thirteen would be a disaster. Thirteen's a bad number for a reading. We don't want thirteen, anything but—'

'Lostara said eleven, Sergeant. Eleven.'

'Aye.' And Fiddler sighed.

When another knock sounded at the door, Bugg raised a hand. 'Permit me, please, Acquitor.' And he rose at her nod and went to let in their new guests.

She heard voices, and looked up to see the Ccda appear with two bedraggled fig-ures: a man, a woman, dressed in rags. They halted just inside the main room and a roiling stink of grime, sweat and alcohol wafted towards Seren Pedac. She strug-gled against an impulse to recoil as the pungent aroma swept over her. The man grinned with greenish teeth beneath a massive, red-veined, bulbous nose. 'Greet-ings, Mahybe! Whachoo got t'drink? Ne'er mind,' and he flourished a clay flask in one blackened hand. 'Lovey dear moogins, find us all some cups, willya?'

Bugg was grimacing. 'Acquitor, these are Ursto Hoobutt and Pinosel.'

'I don't need a cup,' Seren said to the woman who was rummaging through a cupboard.

'As you like,' replied Pinosel. 'But you won't be no fun at this party. Tha's typ-ical. Pregnant women ain't no fun at all—always struttin' around like a god's gift. Smug cow—'

'I don't need this rubbish. Bugg, get them out of here. Now.'

Ursto walked up to Pinosel and clopped her on the side of the head. 'Behave, you!' Then he smiled again at Seren. 'She's jealous, y'see. We bin tryin and, uh, tryin. Only, she's this wrinkled up bag and I ain't no better. Soft as a teat, I am, and no amount a lust makes no diff'rence. All I do is dribble dribble dribble.' He winked. 'O'course, iffin it wuz you now, well—'

Pinosel snorted. 'Now that's an invitation that'd make any woman abort. Pregnant or not!'

Seren glared at the Ceda. 'You cannot be serious.'

'Acquitor, these two are the remnants of an ancient pantheon, worshipped by the original inhabitants of the settlement buried in the silts beneath Letheras. In fact, Ursto and Pinosel are the first two, the Lord and the Lady of Wine and Beer. They came into being as a consequence of the birth of agriculture. Beer preceded bread as the very first product of domesticated plants. Cleaner than water, and very nutritious. The first making of wine employed wild grapes. These two creations are elemental forces in the history of humanity. Others include such things as animal husbandry, the first tools of stone, bone and antler, the birth of music and dance and the telling of tales. Art, on stone walls and on skin. Crucial, profound moments one and all.'

'So,' she asked, 'what's happened to them?'

'Mindful and respectful partaking of their aspects have given way to dissolute, careless excess. Respect for their gifts has vanished, Acquitor. The more sordid the use of those gifts, the more befouled become the gift-givers.'

Ursto belched. 'We don't mind,' he said. 'Far worse if we wuz outlawed, becuz that'd make us evil and we don't wanna be evil, do we, sweet porridge?'

'We's unber attack alla time,' snarled Pinosel. 'Here, les fill these cups. Elder?'

'Half measure, please,' said Bugg.

'Excuse me,' said Seren Pedac. 'Ceda, you have just described these two drunks as the earliest gods of all. But Pinosel just called you "Elder".'

Ursto cackled. 'Ceda? Mealyoats, y'hear that? Ceda!' He reeled a step closer to Seren Pedac. 'O round one, blessed Mahybe, we may be old, me and Pinosel, compared to the likes a you. But against this one 'ere, we're just babies! Elder, yes, Elder, as in *Elder God*!'

'Time to party!' crowed Pinosel.

Fiddler halted just within the entrance. And stared at the Letherii warrior standing near the huge table. 'Adjunct, is this one a new invite?'

'Excuse me, Sergeant?'

He pointed. 'The King's Sword, Adjunct. Was he on your list?'

'No. Nonetheless, he will stay.'

Fiddler turned a bleak look on Bottle, but said nothing.

Bottle scanned the group awaiting them, did a quick head count. 'Who's missing?' he asked.

'Banaschar,' Lostara Yil said.

'He is on his way,' said the Adjunct.

'Thirteen,' muttered Fiddler. 'Gods below. *Thirteen*.'

Banaschar paused in the alley, lifted his gaze skyward. Faint seepage of light from various buildings and lantern-poled streets, but that did not reach high enough to devour the spray of stars. He so wanted to get out of this city. Find a hilltop in the countryside, soft grass to lie on, wax tablet in his hands. The moon, when it showed, was troubling enough. But that new span of stars made him far more nervous, a swath like sword blades, faintly green, that had risen from the south to slash through the old familiar constellations of Reacher's Span. He could not be certain, but he thought those swords were getting bigger. Coming closer.

Thirteen in all—at least that was the number he could make out. Perhaps there were more, still too faint to burn through the city's glow. He suspected the actual number was important. Significant.

Back in Malaz City, the celestial swords would not even be visible, Banaschar surmised. Not yet, anyway.

Swords in the sky, do you seek an earthly throat?

He glanced over at the Errant. If anyone could answer that, it would be this one. This self-proclaimed Master of the Tiles. God of mischance, player of fates. A despicable creature. But no doubt powerful. 'Something wrong?' Banaschar asked, for the Errant's face was ghostly white, slick with sweat.

The one eye fixed his gaze for a moment and then slid away. 'Your allies do not concern me,' he said. 'But another has come, and now awaits us.'

'Who?'

The Errant grimaced. 'Change of plans. You go in ahead of me. I will await the full awakening of this Deck.'

'We agreed you would simply stop it before it can begin. That was all.'

'I cannot. Not now.'

'You assured me there would be no violence this night.'

'And that would have been true,' the god replied.

'But now someone stands in your way. You have been outmanoeuvred, Errant.'

A flash of anger in the god's lone eye. 'Not for long.'

'I will accept no innocent blood spilled—not my comrades'. Take down your enemy if you like, but no one else, do you understand me?'

The Errant bared his teeth. 'Then just keep them out of my way.'

After a moment, Banaschar resumed his journey, emerging along one side of the building and then walking towards the entrance. Ten paces away he halted once more, for a final few mouthfuls of wine, before continuing on.

But that's the problem with the Bonehunters, isn't it?

Nobody can keep them out of anyone's way.

Standing motionless in the shadows of the alley—after the ex-priest had gone inside—waited the Errant.

The thirteenth player in this night's game.

Had he known that—had he been able to pierce the fog now thickening within that dread chamber and so make full count of those present—he would have turned round, discarding all his plans. No, he would have run for the hills.

Instead, the god waited, with murder in his heart.

As the city's sand clocks and banded wicks—insensate and indifferent to aught but the inevitable progression of time—approached the sounding of the bells.

To announce the arrival of midnight.

Chapter Two

Do not come here old friend
If you bring bad weather
I was down where the river ran
Running no more
Recall that span of bridge?
Gone now the fragments grey
And scattered on the sand
Nothing to cross
You can walk the water's flow
Wending slow into the basin
And find the last place where
Weather goes to die
If I see you hove into view
I'll know your resurrection's come
In tears rising to drown my feet
In darkening sky
You walk like a man burned blind
Groping hands out to the sides
I'd guide you but this river
Will not wait
Rushing me to the swallowing sea
Beneath fleeing birds of white
Do not come here old friend
If you bring bad weather

BRIDGE OF THE SUN
FISHER KEL TATH

He stood amidst the rotted remnants of ship timbers, tall yet hunched, and if not for his tattered clothes and long, wind-tugged hair, he could have been a statue, a thing of bleached marble, toppled from the Meckros city behind him to land miraculously upright on the colourless loess. For as long as Udinaas had been watching, the distant figure had not moved.

A scrabble of pebbles announced the arrival of someone else coming up from the village, and a moment later Onrack T'emlava stepped up beside him. The warrior said nothing for a time, a silent, solid presence.

This was not a world to be rushed through, Udinaas had come to realize; not that he'd ever been particularly headlong in the course of his life. For a long time since his arrival here in the Refugium, he had felt as if he were dragging chains, or wading through water. The slow measure of time in this place resisted hectic presumptions, forcing humility, and, Udinaas well knew, humility always arrived uninvited, kicking down doors, shattering walls. It announced itself with a punch to the head, a knee in the groin. Not literally, of course, but the result was the same. Driven to one's knees, struggling for breath, weak as a sickly child. With the world standing, looming over the fool, slowly wagging one finger.

There really should be more of that. Why, if I was the god of all gods, it's the only lesson I would ever deliver, as many times as necessary.

Then again, that'd make me one busy bastard, wouldn't it just.

The sun overhead was cool, presaging the winter to come. The shoulder-women said there would be deep snow in the months ahead. Desiccated leaves, caught in the tawny grasses of the hilltop, fluttered and trembled as if shivering in dread anticipation. He'd never much liked the cold—the slightest chill and his hands went numb.

'What does he want?' Onrack asked.

Udinaas shrugged.

'Must we drive him off?'

'No, Onrack, I doubt that will be necessary. For the moment, I think, there's no fight left in him.'

'You know more of this than me, Udinaas. Even so, did he not murder a child? Did he not seek to kill Trull Sengar?'

'He crossed weapons with Trull?' Udinaas asked. 'My memories of that are vague. I was preoccupied getting smothered by a wraith at the time. Well, then, friend, I can understand how you might want to see the last of him. As for Kettle, I don't think any of that was as simple as it looked. The girl was already dead, long dead, before the Azath seeded her. All Silchas Ruin did was crack the shell so the House could send down its roots. In the right place and at the right time, thus ensuring the survival of this realm.'

The Imass was studying him, his soft, brown eyes nested in lines of sorrow, in lines that proved that he felt things too deeply. This fierce warrior who had—apparently—once been naught but leathery skin and bones was now as vulnerable as a child. This trait seemed true of all the Imass. 'You knew, then, all along, Udinaas? The fate awaiting Kettle?'

'Knew? No. Guessed, mostly.'

Onrack grunted. 'You rarely err in your guesses, Udinaas. Very well, go then. Speak with him.'

Udinaas smiled wryly. 'Not bad at guessing yourself, Onrack. Will you wait here?'

'Yes.'

He was glad of that, for despite his conviction that Silchas Ruin did not intend violence, with the White Crow there was no telling. If Udinaas ended up cut down by one of those keening swords, at least his death would be witnessed, and unlike his son, Rud Elalle, Onrack was not so foolish as to charge out seeking vengeance.

As he drew closer to the albino Tiste Andii, it became increasingly evident that Silchas Ruin had not fared well since his sudden departure from this realm. Most of his armour was shorn away, leaving his arms bare. Old blood stained the braided leather collar of his scorched gambeson. He bore new, barely healed gashes and cuts, and mottled bruises showed below skin like muddy water beneath ice.

His eyes, alas, remained hard, unyielding, red as fresh blood in their shadowed sockets.

'Longing for that old Azath barrow?' Udinaas asked as he halted ten paces from the gaunt warrior.

Silchas Ruin sighed. 'Udinaas. I had forgotten your bright gift with words.'

'I can't recall anyone ever calling it a gift,' he replied, deciding to let the sarcasm pass, as if his stay in this place had withered his natural acuity. 'A curse, yes, all the time. It's amazing I'm still breathing, in fact.'

'Yes,' the Tiste Andii agreed, 'it is.'

'What do you want, Silchas Ruin?'

'We travelled together for a long time, Udinaas.'

'Running in circles, yes. What of it?'

The Tiste Andii glanced away. 'I was . . . misled. By all that I saw. An absence of sophistication. I imagined the rest of that world was no different from Lether . . . until that world arrived.'

'The Letherii version of sophistication is rather narcissistic, granted. Comes with being the biggest lump of turd on the heap. Locally speaking.'

Ruin's expression soured. 'A turd thoroughly crushed under heel, now.'

Udinaas shrugged. 'Comes to us all, sooner or later.'

'Yes.'

Silence stretched between them, and still Ruin would not meet his gaze. Udinaas understood well enough, and knew too that it would be unseemly to show any pleasure at the White Crow's humbling.

'She will be Queen,' Silchas Ruin said abruptly.

'Who?'

The warrior blinked, as if startled by the question, and then fixed his unhuman attention once more upon Udinaas. 'Your son is in grave danger.'

'Is he now?'

'I thought, in coming here, that I would speak to him. To offer what meagre advice of any worth I might possess.' He gestured at the place where he stood. 'This is as far as I could manage.'

'What's holding you back?'

Ruin's expression soured. 'To the Blood of the Eleint, Udinaas, any notion of community is anathema. Or of alliance. If in spirit the Letherii possess an ascendant, it is the Eleint.'

'Ah, I see. Which was why Quick Ben managed to defeat Sukul Ankhadu, Sheltatha Lore and Menandore.'

Silchas Ruin nodded. 'Each intended to betray the others. It is the flaw in the blood. More often than not, a fatal one.' He paused, and then said, 'So it proved with me and my brother Anomander. Once the Draconic blood took hold of us, we were driven apart. Andarist stood between us, reaching with both hands, seeking to hold us close, but our newfound arrogance surpassed him. We ceased to be brothers. Is it any wonder that we—'

'Silchas Ruin,' Udinaas cut in, 'why is my son in danger?'

The warrior's eyes flashed. 'My lesson in humility very nearly killed me. But I survived. When Rud Elalle's own lesson arrives, he may not be so fortunate.'

'Ever had a child, Silchas? I thought not. Giving advice to a child is like flinging sand at an obsidian wall. Nothing sticks. The brutal truth is that we each suffer our own lessons—they can't be danced round. They can't be slipped past. You cannot gift a child with your scars—they arrive like webs, constricting, suffocating, and that child will struggle and strain until they break. No matter how noble your intent, the only scars that teach them anything are the ones they earn themselves.'

'Then I must ask you, as his father, for a boon.'

'Are you serious?'

'I am, Udinaas.'

Fear Sengar had tried to stab this Tiste Andii in the back, had tried to step into Scabandari Bloodeye's shadow. Fear had been a difficult man, but Udinaas, for all his jibes and mockery, his bitter memories of slavery, had not truly disliked him. Nobility could be admired even when not met eye to eye. And he had seen Trull Sengar's grief. 'What would you ask of me, then?'

'Give him to me.'

'*What!*'

The Tiste Andii held up a hand. 'Make no answer yet. I will explain the necessity. I will tell you what is coming, Udinaas, and when I am done, I believe you will understand.'

Udinaas found he was trembling. And as Silchas Ruin continued to speak, he felt the once-solid ground inexorably shifting beneath his feet.

The seemingly turgid pace of this world was proved an illusion, a quaint conceit.

The truth was, everything was pitching headlong, a hundred thousand boulders sliding down a mountainside. The truth was, quite simply, terrifying.

Onrack stood watching the two figures. The conversation had stretched on much longer than the Imass had anticipated, and his worry was burgeoning along with it. Little good was going to come of this, he was certain. He heard a coughing grunt behind him and turned to see the two emlava crossing his trail a hundred or so paces back. They swung their massive, fanged heads in his direction and eyed him warily, as if seeking permission—but he could see by their loping gait and ducked tail-stubs that they were setting out on a hunt. The guilt beneath their intent seemed instinctive, as did their wide-eyed belligerence. They might be gone a day, or weeks. In need of a major kill, with winter fast approaching.

Onrack turned his attention back to Udinaas and Silchas Ruin, and saw that they were now walking towards him, side by side, and the Imass could read well enough Udinaas's battered spirit, his fugue of despair.

No, nothing good was on its way here.

He heard the scrabble behind him as the emlava reached the point where the trail they'd taken would move them out of Onrack's line of sight, and both animals bolted to escape his imagined attention. But he had no interest in calling them back. He never did. The beasts were simply too stupid to take note of that.

Intruders into this realm rode an ill tide, arriving like vanguards to legions of chaos. Change stained the world the hue of fresh blood more often than not. When the truth was, the one thing all Imass desired was peace, affirmed in the ritual of living, secure and stable and exquisitely predictable. Heat and smoke from the hearths, the aromas of cooking meats, tubers, melted marrow. The nasal voices of the women singing as they went about their day's modest demands. The grunts and gasps of love-making, the chants of children. Someone might be working an antler tine, the spiral edge of a split long-bone, or a core of flint. Another kneeling by the stream, scraping down a hide with polished blades and thumbnail scrapers, and nearby there was the faint depression marking a pit of sand where other skins had been buried. When anyone needed to urinate they would squat over the pit to send their stream down. To cure the hides.

Elders sat on boulders and watched the camp and all their kin going about their tasks, and they dreamed of the hidden places and the pathways that opened in the fever of droning voices and drumming and swirling scenes painted on torch-lit stone, deep in the seethe of night when spirits blossomed before the eyes in myriad colours, when the patterns rose to the surface and floated and flowed in the smoky air.

The hunt and the feast, the gathering and the shaping. Days and nights, births and deaths, laughter and grief, tales told and retold, the mind within unfolding to reveal itself like a gift to every kin, every warm, familiar face.

This, Onrack knew, was all that mattered. Every appeasement of the spirits sought the protection of that precious peace, that perfect continuity. The ghosts of ancestors hovered close to stand sentinel over the living. Memories wove strands that bound everyone together, and when those memories were shared, that binding grew ever stronger.

In the camp behind him, his beloved mate, Kilava, reclined on heaps of soft furs, only days away from giving birth to their second child. Shoulder-women brought her wooden bowls filled with fat, delicious grubs still steaming from the hot flatrocks lining the hearths. And cones of honey and pungent teas of berry and bark. They fed her continuously and would do so until her labour pains began, to give her the strength and reserves she would need.

He recalled the night he and Kilava went to the home of Seren Pedac, in that strange, damaged city of Letheras. To hear of Trull Sengar's death had been one of the hardest moments of Onrack's life. But to find himself standing before his friend's widow had proved even more devastating. Setting eyes upon her, he had felt himself collapse inside and he had wept, beyond any consolation, and he had—some time later—wondered at Seren's fortitude, her preternatural calm, and he had told himself that she must have gone through her own grief in the days and nights immediately following her love's murder. She had watched him weep with sorrow in her eyes but no tears. She'd made tea, then, methodical in its preparation, while Onrack huddled inside the embrace of Kilava's arms.

Only later would he rail at the injustice, the appalling senselessness of his friend's death. And for the duration of that night, as he struggled to speak to her of Trull—of the things they had shared since that moment of frail sympathy when Onrack elected to free the warrior from his Shorning—he was reminded again and again of fierce battles, defiant stands, acts of breathtaking courage, any one of which would have marked a worthy end, a death swollen with meaning, shining with sacrifice. And yet Trull Sengar had survived those, every one of them, fashioning a kind of triumph in the midst of pain and loss.

Had Onrack been there, in the blood-splashed arena of sand, Trull's back would not have been unguarded. The murderer would never have succeeded in his act of brutal treachery. And Trull Sengar would have lived to see his own child growing in Seren Pedac's belly, would have witnessed, in awe and wonder, that glow of focused inwardness in the expression of the Acquitor. No male could know such a sense of completeness, of course, for she had become a vessel of that continuity, an icon of hope and optimism for the future world.

Oh, if Trull could have witnessed that—no one deserved it more, after all the battles, the wounds, the ordeals and the vast solitude that Onrack could never pierce—so many betrayals and yet he had stood unbowed and had given of himself all that he could. No, there had been nothing fair in this.

Seren Pedac had been kind and gracious. She had permitted Kilava's ritual ensuring a safe birth. But she had also made it clear that she desired nothing else, that this journey would be her own, and indeed, she was strong enough to make it.

Yes, women could be frightening. In their strengths, their capacity to endure.

As much as Onrack would have treasured being close to Kilava now, to treat her with gifts and morsels, any such attempt would have been met with ridicule from the shoulder-women and a warning snarl from Kilava herself. He had learned to keep his distance, now that the birthing was imminent.

In any case, he had grown fond of Udinaas. True, a man far more inclined to edged commentary than Trull had been, prone to irony and sarcasm, since these were the only weapons Udinaas could wield with skill. Yet Onrack had come to appreciate his wry wit, and more than that, the man had displayed unexpected virtues in his newfound role as father—ones that Onrack noted and resolved to emulate when his time arrived.

He had missed such an opportunity the first time round, and the man who was his first son, Ulshun Pral, had been raised by others, by adopted uncles, brothers, aunts. Even Kilava had been absent more often than not. And so, while Ulshun was indeed of their shared blood, he belonged more to his people than he did to his parents. There was only faint sorrow in this, Onrack told himself, fragments of regret that could find no fit in his memories of the Ritual's deathless existence.

So much had changed. This world seemed to rush past, ephemeral and elusive, days and nights slipping through his hands. Time and again he was almost paralysed by a sense of loss, overwhelmed with anguish at the thought of another moment gone, another instant dwindling in his wake. He struggled to remain mindful, senses bristling to every blessed arrival, to absorb and devour and luxuriate in its taste, and then would come a moment when everything flooded over him and he would be engulfed, flailing in the blinding, deafening deluge.

Too many feelings, and it seemed weeping was his answer to so much in this mortal life—in joy, in sorrow, in gifts received and in the losses suffered. Perhaps he had forgotten all the other possible ways of responding. Perhaps they were the first to go once time became meaningless, cruel as a curse, leaving tears as the last thing to dry up.

Udinaas and Silchas Ruin drew closer.

And once more, Onrack felt like weeping.

The D'rhasilhani coast looked gnawed and rotted, with murky silt-laden rollers thrashing amidst pitted limestone outcrops and submerged sandbars overgrown with mangroves. Heaps of foam the hue of pale flesh lifted and sagged with every breaker, and through the eyeglass Shield Anvil Tanakalian could see, above the tideline where crescent pockets of sand and gravel were visible, mounds of dead fish, swarmed by gulls and something else—long, low and possibly reptilian—that heaved and bulled through the slaughter every now and then, sending the gulls flapping and screeching.

He was relieved he was not standing on that shore, so alien from the coast he had known almost all of his life—where the water was deep, clear and deathly cold; where every inlet and reach was shrouded in the gloom of black cliffs and thick forests of pine and fir. He had not imagined that such shorelines as he was seeing now even existed. Squalid, fetid, like some overripe pig slough. Northeastward along the coastline, at the base of a young range of mountains angling south, what must be a huge river emptied out into this vast bay, filling the waters with its silts. The constant inflow of fresh water, thick and milky-white, had poisoned most of the bay, as far as Tanakalian could determine. And this did not seem right. He felt as if he was looking upon the scene of a vast crime of some sort, a fundamental *wrongness* spreading like sepsis.

'What is your wish, sir?'

The Shield Anvil lowered the eyeglass and frowned at the coast filling the view to the north. 'Make for the river mouth, Captain. I gauge the outflow channel lies upon the other side, closest to that eastern shore—the cliffs seem sheer.'

'Even from here, sir,' said the captain, 'the barely submerged banks upon this side are plain to our sight.' He hesitated. 'It is the ones we cannot see that concern me, Shield Anvil. I am not even appeased should we await the tide.'

'Can we not withdraw, further out to sea, and then make our approach closer to the eastern coastline?'

'Into the head of the river's current? Possibly, although in the clash with the tide, that current will be treacherous. Shield Anvil, this delegation we seek—not a seafaring people, I assume?'

Tanakalian smiled. 'A range of virtually impassable mountains blocks the kingdom from the coast, and even on the landward side of that range a strip of territory is claimed by pastoral tribes—there is peace between them and the Bolkando. Nonetheless, to answer you, sir, no, the Bolkando are not a seafaring people.'

'Thus, this river mouth . . .'

'Yes, Captain. By gracious agreement with the D'rhasilhani, the Bolkando delegation is permitted an encampment on the east side of the river.'

'The threat of invasion can make lifelong enemies into the closest allies,' observed the captain.

'So it seems,' agreed Tanakalian. 'What is extraordinary is that the alliances seem to be holding, even now when there will be no invasion from the Lether Empire. I suspect certain benefits from peace became evident.'

'Profitable, you mean.'

'Mutually so, yes, Captain.'

'I must attend to the ship now, sir, if we are to revise our approach to the place of landing.'

The Shield Anvil nodded and, as the captain departed, Tanakalian raised the eyeglass once more, leaning for support against the starboard figurehead as he steadied himself. The seas were not especially rough this far inside the nameless bay, but in moments the Throne of War would begin to come about, and he was intent on making use of the hard pitch to scan further along the sheer cliffs of the eastern shoreline.

The Mortal Sword Krughava remained in her cabin. Since his return from visiting the Adjunct, Destriant Run'Thurvian had elected to begin an extended period of secluded meditation, and was also below decks. The presence of either one would have imposed a degree of formality that Tanakalian found increasingly chafing. He understood the necessity for propriety, and the burden of tradition that ensured meaning to all that they did—and all that they were—but he had spent time on the command ship of the Adjunct, in the company of Malazans. They displayed an ease in shared hardship that had at first shocked the Shield Anvil, until he comprehended the value of such behaviour. There could be no challenging the discipline of the Bonehunters when battle was summoned. But the force that truly held them together was found in the camaraderie they displayed during those interminably long periods of inactivity, such as all armies were forced to endure. Indeed, Tanakalian had come to delight in their brash lack of decorum, their open irreverence and their strange penchant for revelling in the absurd.

Perhaps an ill influence, as Run'Thurvian's faintly disapproving frowns implied, whenever Tanakalian attempted his own ironic commentary. Of course, the Destriant possessed no shortage in his list of disappointments regarding the Order's new Shield Anvil. Too young, woefully inexperienced, and dismayingly inclined to rash judgement—this last flaw simply unacceptable in one bearing the title of Shield Anvil.

'Your mind is too active, sir,' the Destriant had said once. 'It is not for the Shield Anvil to make judgement. Not for you to decide who is worthy of your embrace. No, sir, but you have never disguised your predilections. I give you that.'

Generous of the man, all things considered.

As the ship lost headway in its long, creaking coming-about, Tanakalian studied that forbidding coast, the tortured mountains—many of them with cones shrouded in smoke and foul gases. It would not do to find themselves thrown against that deadly shoreline, although given the natural inclination of outflow currents, the risk was very real. Leading the Shield Anvil to one of those ghastly judgements, and in this case, even the Destriant could not find fault.

With a faint smile, Tanakalian lowered the eyeglass once more and returned it to its sealskin sheath slung beneath his left arm. He descended from the forecastle and made his way below decks. They would require Run'Thurvian and his sorcery to ensure safe passage into the river mouth, and this, Tanakalian concluded, was fair justification for interrupting the Destriant's meditation, which had been going on for days now. Run'Thurvian might well cherish his privilege of solitude and unmitigated isolation, but certain necessities could not be avoided even by the Order's Destriant. The old man could do with the fresh air, besides.

The command ship was alone in this bay. The remaining twenty-four serviceable Thrones of War held position far out to sea, more than capable of weathering whatever the southern ocean could muster, barring a typhoon, of course, and that season had passed, according to local pilots.

Since they had relinquished the *Froth Wolf* to the Adjunct, the *Listral* now served as the Order's flagship. The oldest ship in the fleet—almost four decades since the laying of the keels—the *Listral* was the last survivor of the first line of trimarans, bearing antiquated details in style and decoration. This lent the ship a ferocious aspect, with every visible span of ironwood carved into the semblance of a snarling wolf's head, and the centre hull was entirely shaped as a lunging wolf, three-quarters submerged so that the crest of foam at the bow churned from the beast's gaping, fanged mouth.

Tanakalian loved this ship, even the archaic row of inside-facing cabins lining the corridor of the first level below deck. *Listral* could manage but half as many passengers as could the second and third lines of Thrones of War. At the same time, each cabin was comparatively spacious, indeed, almost luxurious.

The Destriant's abode encompassed the last two cabins of this, the starboard hull. The wall between them now bore a narrow, low door. The stern chamber served as Run'Thurvian's private residence, whilst the forward cabin had been sanctified as a temple of the Wolves. As expected, Tanakalian found the Destriant kneeling, head bowed, before the twin-headed altar. Yet something was wrong—the air reeked of charred flesh, burnt hair, and Run'Thurvian, his back to Tanakalian, remained motionless as the Shield Anvil swung in through the corridor hatch.

'Destriant?'

'Come no closer,' croaked Run'Thurvian, his voice almost unrecognizable, and Tanakalian now heard the old man's desperate wheezing of breath. 'There is not much time, Shield Anvil. I had . . . concluded . . . that none would disturb me after all, no matter how overlong my absence.' A hacking, bitter laugh. 'I had forgotten your . . . temerity, sir.'

Tanakalian drew a step closer. 'Sir, what has happened?'

'*Stay back, I beg you!*' gasped the Destriant. 'You must take my words to the Mortal Sword.'

Something glittered on the polished wooden floor around the kneeling form, as if the man had leaked out on all sides—but the smell was not one of urine, and the liquid, while thick as blood, seemed almost golden in the faint lantern light. Real fear flowed through Tanakalian upon seeing it, and the Destriant's words barely reached him over the thumping of his own heart. 'Destriant—'

'I travelled far,' Run'Thurvian said. 'Doubts . . . a growing unease. Listen! She is not as we believed. There will be . . . betrayal. Tell Krughava! The vow—*we have made a mistake!*'

The puddle was spreading, thick as honey, and it seemed the robed shape of the Destriant was diminishing, collapsing into itself.

He is dying. By the Wolves, he is dying. 'Destriant,' Tanakalian said, forcing his terror down, swallowing against the horror of what he was witnessing, 'will you accept my embrace?'

The laugh that made its way out sounded as if it had bubbled up through mud. 'No. I do not.'

Stunned, the Shield Anvil staggered back.

'You . . . you are . . . *insufficient*. You always were—another one of Krughava's errors in . . . in judgement. You fail me, and so you shall fail her. The Wolves shall abandon us. The vow betrays them, do you understand? I have seen our deaths—this one here before you, and the ones to come. You, Tanakalian. The Mortal Sword too, and every brother and sister of the Grey Helms.' He coughed, and something gushed out in the convulsion, spraying the altar with liquid and shapeless gobbets that slid down into the folds of stone fur, traversing the necks of the Wolves.

The kneeling figure slumped, folded in the middle at an impossible angle. The sound made when Run'Thurvian's forehead struck the floor was that of a hen's egg breaking, and that span of bone offered little resistance, so that the man's face collapsed as well.

As Tanakalian stared, drawn forward once more, he saw watery streams leaking out from the Destriant's ruined head.

The man had simply . . . *melted*. He could see that greyish pulp boiling, thinning down into clear streams of fat.

And he so wanted to scream, to unleash his horror, but a deeper dread had claimed him. *He would not accept my embrace. I have failed him, he said. I will fail them all, he said.*

Betrayal?

No, that I cannot believe.

I will not.

Although he knew Run'Thurvian was dead, Tanakalian spoke to him nonetheless. 'The failure, Destriant, was yours, not mine. You journeyed far, did you? I suggest . . . not far enough.' He paused, struggling to quell the trembling that had come to him. 'Destriant. Sir. It pleases me that you rejected my embrace. For I see now that you did not deserve it.'

No, he was not simply a Shield Anvil, in the manner of all those who had come before, all those who had lived and died beneath the burden of that title. He was not interested in passive acceptance. He would take upon himself mortal pain, yes, but not indiscriminately.

I too am mortal, after all. It is my essence that I am able to weigh my judgement. Of what is worthy. And what is not.

No, I shall not be as other Shield Anvils. The world has changed—we must change with it. We must change to meet it. He stared down at the heaped mess that was all that remained of Destriant Run'Thurvian.

There would be shock. Dismay and faces twisted into distraught fear. The Order would be flung into disarray, and it would fall to the Mortal Sword, and to the Shield Anvil, to steady the rudder, until such time as a new Destriant was raised among the brothers and sisters.

Of more immediate concern, however, as far as Tanakalian was concerned, was that there would be no sorcerous protection in traversing the channel. In his assessment—shaky as it might be at the moment—he judged that news to be paramount.

The Mortal Sword would have to wait.

He had nothing to tell her in any case.

'Did you embrace our brother, Shield Anvil?'

'Of course, Mortal Sword. His pain is with me, now, as is his salvation.'

The mind shaped its habits and habits reshaped the body. A lifelong rider walked with bowed legs, a seafarer stood wide no matter how sure the purchase. Women who twirled strands of their hair would in time come to sit with heads tilted to one side. Some people prone to worry might grind their teeth, and years of this would thicken the muscles of the jaws and file the molars down to smooth lumps, bereft of spurs and crowns.

Yedan Derryg, the Watch, wandered down to the water's edge. The night sky, so familiar to one who had wrapped his life about this late stretch of time preceding the sun's rise, was now revealed to him as strange, jarred free of the predictable, the known, and the muscles of his jaw worked in steady, unceasing rhythm.

The reflected smear of vaguely green comets rode the calm surface of the inlet, like slashes of luminous glow-spirits, as were wont to gather in the wake of ships. There were strangers in the sky. Drawing closer night after night, as if summoned. The blurred moon had set, which was something of a relief, but Yedan could still observe the troubled behaviour of the tide—the things that had once been certain were certain no longer. He was right to worry.

Suffering was coming to the shore, and the Shake would not be spared. This was a knowledge he shared with Twilight, and he had seen the growing fear in the rheumy eyes of the witches and warlocks, leading him to suspect that they too had sensed the approach of something vast and terrible. Alas, shared fears did not forge any renewed commitment to co-operation—for them the political struggle remained, had indeed intensified.

Fools.

Yedan Derryg was not a loquacious man. He might well possess a hundred thousand words in his head, open to virtually infinite rearrangement, but that did not mean he laboured under the need to give them voice. There seemed to be little point in that, and in his experience comprehension diminished as complexity deepened—this was not a failing of skills in communication, he believed, but one of investment and capacity. People dwelt in a swamp of feelings that stuck like gobs of mud to every thought, slowing those thoughts down, making them almost shapeless. The inner discipline demanded in order to cleanse such maladroit tendencies was usually too fierce, too trying, just too damned hard. This, then, marked the unwillingness to make the necessary investment. The other issue was a far crueller judgement, in that it had to do with the recognition that in the world there were numerically far more stupid people than there were smart ones. The difficulty was in the innate cleverness of the stupid in disguising their own stupidity. The truth was rarely displayed in an honest frown or a sincere knotting of the brow. Instead, it was revealed in a flash of suspicion, the hint of diffidence in an offhand dismissal, or, perversely, muteness offered up to convey a level of thoughtful consideration which, in truth, did not exist.

Yedan Derryg had little time for such games. He could smell an idiot from fifty paces off. He watched their sly evasions, listened to their bluster, and wondered again and again why they could never reach that essential realization, which was that the amount of effort engaged in hiding their own stupidity would serve them better used in cogent exercise of what little wits they possessed. Assuming, of course, that improvement was even possible.

There were too many mechanisms in society designed to hide and indeed coddle its myriad fools, particularly since fools generally held the majority. In addition to such mechanisms, one could also find various snares and traps and ambushes, one and all fashioned with the aim of isolating and then destroying smart people. No argument, no matter how brilliant, can defeat a knife in the groin, after all. Nor an executioner's axe. And the bloodlust of a mob was always louder than a lone, reasonable voice.

The true danger, Yedan Derryg understood, was to be found in the hidden deceivers—those who could play the fool yet possessed a kind of cunning that, while narrowly confined to the immediate satisfaction of their own position, proved of great skill in exploiting the stupid and the brilliant alike. These were the ones who hungered for power and more often than not succeeded in acquiring it. No genius would willingly accept true power, of course, in full knowledge of its deadly invitations. And fools could never succeed in holding on to it for very long, unless they were content as figureheads, in which case the power they held was an illusion.

Gather a modest horde of such hidden deceivers—those of middling intelligence and clever malice and avaricious ambition—and serious trouble was pretty much assured. A singular example of this was found in the coven of witches and warlocks who, until recently, had ruled the Shake—inasmuch as a scattered, dissolute and depressed people could be ruled.

Jaws bunching, Yedan Derryg crouched down. Ripples from the faint waves rolled round the toes of his boots, gurgled into the pits they made in the soft sand. His arms trembled, every muscle aching with exhaustion. The brine from the shoreline could not wash the stench from his nostrils.

Behind him, in the squalid huddle of huts beyond the berm, voices had awakened. He heard someone come on to the shore, staggering it seemed, drawing closer in fits and starts.

Yedan Derryg reached down his hands until the cold water flowed over them, and what was clear suddenly clouded in dark blooms. He watched as the waves, sweeping out so gently, tugged away the stains, and in his mind uttered a prayer.

> *This to the sea*
> *This from the shore*
> *This I give freely*
> *Until the waters run clear*

She came up behind him. 'In the name of the Empty Throne, Yedan, *what have you done?*'

'Why,' he replied to his sister's horrified disbelief, 'I have killed all of them but two, my Queen.'

She stepped round, splashed into the water until she faced him, and then set a palm against his forehead and pushed until she could see his face, until she could stare into his eyes. 'But . . . *why*? Did you think I could not handle them? That *we* couldn't?'

He shrugged. 'They wanted a king. One to control you. One they could control in turn.'

'And so you murdered them? Yedan, the longhouse has become an abattoir! And you truly think you can just wash your hands of what you have done? You've just butchered twenty-eight people. Shake. *My people!* Old men and old women! You slaughtered them!'

He frowned up at her. 'My Queen, I am the Watch.'

She stared down at him, and he could read her expression well enough. She believed her brother had become a madman. She was recoiling in horror.

'When Pully and Skwish return,' he said, 'I will kill them, too.'

'You will not.'

He could see that a reasonable conversation with his sister was not possible, not at this moment, with the cries of shock and grief rising ever higher in the village. 'My Queen—'

'Yedan,' she gasped. 'Don't you see what you have done to me? Don't you realize the wound you have delivered—that you would do such a thing in my name . . .' She seemed unable to finish the statement, and he saw tears in her eyes now. And then that gaze iced over and her tone hardened as she said, 'You have two choices left, Yedan Derryg. Stay and be given to the sea. Or accept banishment.'

'I am the Watch—'

'Then we will be blind to the night.'

'That cannot be permitted,' he replied.

'You fool—you've left me no choice!'

He slowly straightened. 'Then I shall accept the sea—'

She turned round, faced the dark waters. Her shoulders shook as she lowered her head. 'No,' she managed in a grating voice. 'Get out of here, Yedan. Go north, into the old Edur lands. I will not accept one more death in my name—not one. No matter how deserved it is. You are my brother. Go.'

She was not one of the deceivers, he knew. Nor was she a fool. Given the endless opposition from the coven, she had possessed less power than her title proclaimed. And perhaps, intelligent as Yan Tovis was, she had been content to accept that limitation. Had the witches and warlocks been as wise and sober in their recognition of the deadly lure of ambition, he could well have left things as they were. But they had not been interested in a balance. They wanted what they had lost. They had not shown the intelligence demanded by the situation.

And so he had removed them, and now his sister's power was absolute. Understandable, then, that she was so distraught. Eventually, he told himself, she would come to comprehend what was now necessary. Namely, his return, as the Watch, as the balance to her potentially unchecked power.

He would need to be patient.

'I shall do as you say,' he said to her.

She would not turn round, and so, with a nod, Yedan Derryg set out, northward along the shoreline. He'd left his horse and pack-mount tethered two hundred paces along, just above the high-water mark. One sure measure of intelligence, after all, was in the accurate anticipation of consequences. Emotions stung to life could drown one as easily as a riptide, and he had no desire to deepen her straits.

Soon the sun would rise, although with rain on the way its single glaring eye would likely not be visible for long, and that too was well. Leave the cloud's tears to wash away all the blood, and before too long the absence of over a score of brazen, incipient tyrants would rush in among the Shake like a sudden fresh and bracing wind.

Strangers rode the night sky, and if the Shake had any hope of surviving what was coming, the politics of betrayal must be swept away. With finality.

It was his responsibility, after all. Perhaps his sister had forgotten the oldest vows that bound the Watch. But he had not. And so he had done what was necessary.

There was no pleasure in the act. Satisfaction, yes, as would be felt by any wise, intelligent person who succeeds in sweeping aside a multitude of short-sighted sharks, thus clearing the water. But no pleasure.

To his right, as he walked the shoreline, the land was growing light.

But the sea to his left remained dark.

Sometimes the verge between the two grew very narrow indeed.

Shifting weight from one foot to the other, Pully stared down into the pit. Snakes swarmed by the hundred in that hole, sluggish at first but now, as the day warmed, they writhed like worms in an open wound. She tugged at her nose, which had a tendency to tingle whenever she fell back into the habit of chewing her lips, but the tingling wouldn't leave. Which meant, of course, that she was gnawing away at those wrinkled flaps covering what was left of her teeth.

Getting old was a misery. First the skin sagged. Then aches settled into every place and places that didn't even exist. Pangs and twinges and spasms, and all the while the skin kept sagging, lines deepening, folds folding, and all beauty going away. The lilt of upright buttocks, the innocence of wide, shallow tits. The face still able to brave the weather, and lips still sweet and soft as pouches of rendered fat. All gone. What was left was a mind that still imagined itself young, its future stretching out, trapped inside a sack of loose meat and brittle bones. It wasn't fair.

She yanked at her nose again, trying to get the feeling back. And that was another thing. The wrong parts kept on growing. Ears and nose, warts and moles, hairs sprouting everywhere. The body forgot its own rules, the flesh went senile and the bright mind within could wail all it wanted, but nothing that was real ever changed except for the worse.

She widened her stance and sent a stream of piss down into the stony earth. Even simple things got less predictable. Oh, what a misery ageing was.

Skwish's head popped up amidst seething snakes, eyes blinking.

'Yah,' said Pully, 'I'm still here.'

'How long?'

'Day and a night and now it's morning. Y'amby get what yer needed? I got aches.'

'An' I got reck'lections I ain't ever wanted.' Skwish started working herself free of the heaps of serpents, none of which minded much or even noticed, busy as they were, breeding in a frenzy that seemed to last for ever.

'T'which we might want, iyerplease?'

'Mebee.'

Skwish reached up and, grunting, Pully helped her friend out of the pit. 'Yee, y'smell ripe, woman. Snake piss and white smear, there'll be onward eggs in yer ears.'

'It's a cold spirit t'travel on, Pully, an' I ain't ever doin it agin, so's if I rank it's the leese of our perbems. Gaf, I need a dunk in the sea.'

They set off for the village, a half day's journey coastward.

'An ya tervilled afar, Skwish, did yee?'

'It's bad an' it's bad, Pully. Cold blood t'the east no sun could warm. I seen solid black clouds rollin down, an' iron rain an gashes in th'geround. I see the stars go away an' nothing but green glows, an' them green glows they is cold, too, cold as th'east blooding. All stems but one branch, y'see. One branch.'

'So's we guessed right, an' next time Twilight goes an' seal barks on 'bout a marchin' the Shake away from the shore, you can talk up an' cut er down and down. An' then we vote and get er gone. Er and the Watch, too.'

Skwish nodded, trying to work globs of snake sperm out of her hair, without much success. 'Comes to what's d'served, Pully. The Shake did ever 'ave clear eyes. Y'can't freck on an' on thinkin' th'world won't push back. It'll push awright. Till the shore breaks an' breaks it will an' when it does, we ever do drown. I saw dust, Pully, but it wasn't no puffy earth. T'was specks a bone an' skin an' dreams an' motes a surprise, hah! We's so freckered, sister, it's all we can do is laughter an prance into the sea.'

'Goo' anough fra me,' Pully grumbled. 'I got so many aches I might be the def'nition a ache irrself.'

The two Shake witches—the last left alive, as they were soon to learn—set out for the village.

Take a scintillating, flaring arm of the sun's fire, give it form, a life of its own, and upon the faint cooling of the apparition, a man such as Rud Elalle might emerge, blinking with innocence, unaware that all he touched could well explode into destructive flames—had he been of such mind. And to teach, to guide him into adulthood, the singular aversion remained: *no matter what you do, do not awaken him to his anger.*

Sometimes, Udinaas had come to realize, potential was a force best avoided, for the potential he sensed in his son was not a thing for celebration.

No doubt every father felt that flash of blinding, burning truth—the moment when he sensed his son's imminent domination, be it physical or something less overtly violent in its promise. Or perhaps such a thing was in fact rare, conjured from the specific. After all, not every father's son could veer into the shape of a dragon. Not every father's son held the dawn's golden immanence in his eyes.

Rud Elalle's gentle innocence was a soft cloak hiding a monstrous nature, and that was an unavoidable fact, the burning script of his son's blood. Silchas Ruin had spoken to that, with knowing, with the pained truth in his face. The ripening harvest of the Eleint, a fecund brutality that sought only to appease itself—that saw the world (any world, every world) as a feeding ground, and the promise of satisfaction waited in the bloated glut of power.

Rare the blood-fouled who managed to overcome that innate megalomania. '*Ah, Udinaas,*' Silchas Ruin had said. '*My brother, perhaps, Anomander. Osserc? Maybe, maybe not. There was a Bonecaster, once . . . and a Soletaken Jaghut. A handful of others—when the Eleint blood within them was thinner—and that is why I have hope for Rud Elalle, Udinaas. He is third-generation—did he not clash with his mother's will?*'

Well, it was said that he had.

Udinaas rubbed his face. He glanced again at the tusk-framed hut, wondering if he should march inside, put an end to that parley right now. Silchas Ruin, after all, had not included himself among those who had mastered their Draconean blood. A sliver of honesty from the White Crow, plucked from that wound of humility, no doubt. It was all that was holding Udinaas back.

Crouched beside him, shrouded by gusts of smoke from the hearth, Onrack released a long sigh that whistled from his nostrils—break a nose enough times and every breath was tortured music. At least it was so with this warrior. 'He will take him, I think.'

Udinaas nodded, not trusting himself to speak.

'I am . . . confused, my friend. That you would permit this . . . meeting. That you would excuse yourself and so provide no counter to the Tiste Andii's invitation. That hut, Udinaas, may be a place filled with lies. What is to stop the White Crow from offering your son the sweet sip of terrible power?'

There was genuine worry in Onrack's tone, deserving more than bludgeoning silence. Udinaas rubbed again at his face, unable to determine which was the more insensate: his features or his hands; and wondering why an answer seemed to important to him. 'I have walked in the realm of Starvald Demelain, Onrack. Among the bones of countless dead dragons. At the gate itself, the corpses were heaped like glitter flies along a window sill.'

'If it is indeed in the nature of the Eleint to lust for self-destruction,' ventured Onrack, 'would it not be better to guide Rud away from such a flaw?'

'I doubt that would work,' Udinaas said. 'Can you turn nature aside, Onrack? Every season the salmon return from the seas and heave their dying bodies upstream, to find where they were born. Ancient tenag leave the herds to die amid the bones of kin. Bhederin migrate into the heart of the plains every summer, and return to forest fringes every winter—'

'Simpler creatures one and all—'

'And I knew slaves in the Hiroth village—ones who'd been soldiers once, and they withered with the anguish of knowing that there were places of battle—places of their first blooding—that they would never again see. They longed to return, to walk those old killing grounds, to stand before the barrows filled with the bones of fallen friends, comrades. To remember, and to weep.' Udinaas shook his head. 'We are not much different from the beasts sharing our world, Onrack. The only thing that truly sets us apart is our talent for rejecting the truth—and we're damned good at that. The salmon does not question its need. The tenag and the bhederin do not doubt what compels them.'

'Then you would doom your son to his fate?'

Udinaas bared his teeth. 'The choice isn't mine to make.'

'Is it Silchas Ruin's?'

'It may seem, Onrack, that we are protected here, but that's an illusion. The Refugium is a rejection of so many truths it leaves me breathless. Ulshun Pral, you, all your people—you have willed yourself this life, this world. And the Azath at the gate—it holds you to your convictions. This place, wondrous as it is, remains a prison.' He snorted. 'Should I chain him here? Can I? Dare I? You forget, I was a slave.'

'My friend,' said Onrack, 'I am free to travel the other realms. I am made flesh. Made whole. This is a truth, is it not?'

'If this place is destroyed, you will become a T'lan Imass once more. That's the name for it, isn't it? That immortality of bones and dried flesh? The tribe here will fall to dust.'

Onrack was staring at him with horror-filled eyes. 'How do you know this?'

'I do not believe Silchas Ruin is lying. Ask Kilava—I have seen a certain look in her eyes, especially when Ulshun Pral visits, or when she sits beside you at the fire. She knows. She cannot protect this world. Not even the Azath will prevail against what is coming.'

'Then it is we who are doomed.'

No. There is Rud Elalle. There is my son.

'And so,' said Onrack after a long pause, 'you will send your son away, so that he may live.'

No, friend. I send him away . . . to save you all. But he could not say that, could not reveal that. For he knew Onrack well now; and he knew Ulshun Pral and all the others here. And they would not accept such a potential sacrifice—they would not see Rud Elalle risk his life in their name. No, they would accept their own annihilation, without a second thought. Yes, Udinaas knew these Imass. It was not pride that made them what they were. It was compassion. The tragic kind of compassion, the kind that sacrifices itself and sees that sacrifice as the only choice and thus no choice at all, one that must be accepted without hesitation.

Better to take the fear and the hope and all the rest and hold it inside. What could he give Onrack now, at this moment? He did not know.

Another pause, and then the Imass continued, 'It is well, then. I understand, and approve. There is no reason that he must die with us. No reason, indeed, that he must witness such a thing when it comes to pass. You would spare him the grief, as much as such a thing is possible. But, Udinaas, it is not acceptable that *you* share our fate. You too must depart this realm.'

'No, friend. That I will not do.'

'Your son's need for you remains.'

Oh, Rud loves you all, Onrack. Almost as much as he seems to love me. I will stay nonetheless, to remind him of what he fights to preserve. 'Where he and Silchas Ruin will go, I cannot follow,' he said. And then he grunted and managed to offer Onrack a wry smile. 'Besides, here and only here, in your company—in the company of all the Imass—I am almost content. I'll not willingly surrender that.' So many truths could hide inside glib lies. While the reason was a deceit, the sentiments stacked so carefully within it were not.

So much easier, he told himself, to think like a tenag, or a bhederin. Truth from surface to core, solid and pure. Yes, that would indeed be easier than this.

Rud Elalle emerged from the hut, followed a moment later by Silchas Ruin.

Udinaas could see in his son's face that any formal parting would prove too fraught. Best this was done with as little gravitas as possible. He rose, and Onrack did the same.

Others stood nearby, watchful, instincts awakened that something grave and portentous was happening. Respect and courtesy held them back one and all.

'We should keep this . . . casual,' Udinaas said under his breath.

Onrack nodded. 'I shall try, my friend.'

He is no dissembler, oh no. Less human than he looks, then. They all are, damn them. 'You feel too much,' Udinaas said, as warmly as he could manage, for he did not want the observation to sting.

But Onrack wiped at his cheeks and nodded, saying nothing.

So much for making this casual. 'Oh, come with me, friend. Even Rud cannot withstand your gifts.'

And together, they approached Rud Elalle.

Silchas Ruin moved off to await his new charge, and observed the emotional farewells with eyes like knuckles of blood.

Mortal Sword Krughava reminded Tanakalian of his childhood. She could have stridden out from any of a dozen tales of legend he had listened to curled up beneath skins and furs, all those breathtaking adventures of great heroes pure of heart, bold and stalwart, who always knew who deserved the sharp end of their sword, and who only ever erred in their faith in others—until such time, at the tale's dramatic climax, when the truth of betrayal and whatnot was revealed, and punishment soundly delivered. His grandfather always knew when to thicken the timbre of his voice, where to pause to stretch out suspense, when to whisper some awful revelation. All to delight the wide-eyed child as night drew in.

Her hair was the hue of iron. Her eyes blazed like clear winter skies, and her face could have been carved from the raw cliffs of Perish. Her physical strength was bound to a matching strength of will and neither seemed assailable by any force in the mortal world. It was said that, even though she was now in her fifth decade of life, no brother or sister of the Order could best her in any of a score of weapons: from skinning knife to mattock.

When Destriant Run'Thurvian had come to her, speaking of fraught dreams and fierce visions, it was as tinder-dry kindling to the furnace of Krughava's inviolate sense of purpose, and, it turned out, her belief in her own imminent elevation to heroic status.

Few childhood convictions survived the grisly details of an adult's sensibilities, and although Tanakalian accounted himself still young, still awaiting the temper of wisdom, he had already seen enough to comprehend the true horror waiting beneath the shining surface of the self-avowed hero known to all as the Mortal Sword of the Grey Helms of Perish. Indeed, he had come to suspect that no hero, no matter what the time or the circumstance, was anything like the tales told him so many years ago. Or perhaps it was his growing realization that so many so-called virtues, touted as worthy aspirations, possessed a darker side. Purity of heart also meant vicious intransigence. Unfaltering courage saw no sacrifice as too great, even if that meant leading ten thousand soldiers to their deaths. Honour betrayed could plunge into intractable insanity in the pursuit of satisfaction. Noble vows could drown a kingdom in blood, or crush an empire into dust. No, the true nature of heroism was a messy thing, a confused thing of innumerable sides, many of them ugly, and almost all of them terrifying.

So the Destriant, in his last breaths, had made a grim discovery. The Grey Helms were betrayed. If not now, then soon. Words of warning to awaken in the Mortal Sword all those blistering fires of outrage and indignation. And Run'Thurvian had expected the Shield Anvil to rush into Krughava's cabin to repeat the dire message, to see the fires alight in her bright blue eyes.

Brothers and sisters! Draw your swords! The streams must run crimson in answer to our besmirched honour! Fight! The enemy is on all sides!

Well.

Not only had Tanakalian found himself unwilling to embrace the Destriant and his mortal pain, he was reluctant to launch such devastating frenzy upon the Grey Helms. The old man's explanations, his reasons—the details—had been virtually non-existent. Essential information was lacking. A hero without purpose was like a blinded cat in a pit of hounds. Who could predict the direction of Krughava's charge?

No, this needed sober contemplation. The private, meditative kind.

The Mortal Sword had greeted the dreadful news of the Destriant's horrid death in pretty much the expected manner. A hardening of already hard features, eyes glaring like ice, the slow, building rise of questions that Tanakalian either could not hope to answer, or, as it turned out, was unwilling to answer. Questions and unknowns were the deadliest foes for one such as Mortal Sword Krughava, who thrived on certainty regardless of its relationship to reality. He could see how she was rocked, all purchase suddenly uncertain beneath her boots; and the way her left hand twitched—as if eager for the grip of her sword, the sure promise of the heavy iron blade; and the way she instinctively straightened—as if awaiting the weight of her chain surcoat—for this surely was news that demanded she wear armour. But he had struck her unawares, in her vulnerability, and this might well constitute its own version of betrayal, and he knew to be careful at that moment, to display for her a greater helplessness than she herself might be feeling; to unveil in his eyes and in his seemingly unconscious gestures enormous measures of need and need for reassurance. To, in short, fling himself like a child upon her stolid majesty.

If this made him into something despicable, a dissembler, a creature of intrigue and cunning manipulation, well, these were dire charges indeed. He would have to consider them, as objectively as possible, and withhold no judgement no matter how self-damning, no matter how condign.

The Shield Anvils of old, of course, would not have bothered. But absence of judgement in others could only emerge from absence of judgement in oneself, a refusal to challenge one's own assumptions and beliefs. Imagine the atrocities such inhuman postures invited! No, that was a most presumptuous game and not one he would play.

Besides, giving the Mortal Sword what she needed most at that moment—all his apparently instinctive nudges to remind her of her noble responsibilities—was in fact the proper thing to do. It would serve no one to have Krughava display extreme distress or, Wolves forbid, outright panic. They were sailing into war, and they had lost their Destriant. Matters were fraught enough in bare facts alone.

She needed to steel herself, and she needed to be seen doing so by her Shield Anvil in this moment of privacy, and in the wake of presumed success she would then find the necessary confidence to repeat the stern ritual before the brothers and sisters of the Order.

But that latter scene must wait, for the time had come to greet the Bolkando emissaries, and Tanakalian was comforted in the solid crunch of his and her boots on the strand of crushed coral that served as a beach in this place of landing. One pace behind the Mortal Sword—and while curiosity and wonder at the Destriant's absence might trouble the crew of the skiff and the captain and all the others aboard the *Listral*, now firmly anchored in the broad disc of a slow eddy in the river mouth, neither Krughava nor her Shield Anvil seemed to be displaying anything untoward as they set out for the elaborate field tent of the Bolkando. And such was their faith in their commanders that minds settled back into peaceful repose.

Could such observations be seen as cynical? He thought not. Comportment had value at times like these. There was no point in distressing the members of the Order, only to pointedly delay resolution until after this parley.

The air was sultry, heat seething up from the blinding white strand. The shattered carapaces of crabs were baked red by the sun, forming a ragged row at the fringe of the high-water line. Even the gulls looked beaten half-senseless where they perched on the bones of uprooted mangrove trunks.

The two Perish worked their way up the verge and set out across a silted floodplain that spread away in a broad fan from the river on their left. Bright green tufts of seasonal grasses dotted the expanse. A long column of Bolkando sentries stood lining the bank of the river, about twenty paces back from row upon row of short, tapering logs stacked in the mud. Oddly, those sentries, tall, dark-skinned and barbaric in their spotted hide cloaks, were all facing the river and so presenting their backs to the two Perish guests.

A moment later Tanakalian was startled to see some of those logs explode into thrashing motion. He tugged the eyeglass from its holster and slowed to examine the river bank through the magnifying lenses. *Lizards. Enormous lizards— no wonder the Bolkando warriors have their backs to us!*

If Krughava had noticed anything of the scene at the river bank, she gave no sign.

The Bolkando pavilion sprawled vast enough to encompass scores of rooms. The flaps of the main entrance were drawn back and bound to ornate wooden poles with gilt crow-hook clasps. The sunlight, filtering in through the weave of the canopy, transformed the spaces within into a cool, soft world of cream and gold, and both Tanakalian and Krughava halted once inside, startled by the blessed drop in temperature. The air, fanning across their faces, carried the scents of exotic, unknown spices.

Awaiting them was a functionary of some sort, dressed in deerskin and silvered mail so fine it wouldn't stop a child's dagger. The man, his face veiled, bowed from the waist and then gestured the two Perish through a corridor walled in silks. At the far end, perhaps fifteen paces along, stood two guards, again bedecked in long surcoats of the same ephemeral chain. Tucked into narrow belts were throwing knives, two on each hip. Leather sheaths, trimmed in slivers of bone, slung under the left arm, indicated larger weapons, cutlasses perhaps, but these were pointedly empty. The soldiers wore skullcap helms but no face-guards, and as he drew closer, Tanakalian was startled to see a complex skein of scarification on those grim faces, every etched seam stained with deep red dye.

Both guards stood at attention, and neither seemed to take any notice of the two guests. Tanakalian followed a step behind Krughava as she passed between them.

The chamber beyond was spacious. All the furniture within sight—and there was plenty of it—appeared to consist of articulating segments, as if capable of being folded flat or dismantled, yet this did nothing to diminish their delicate beauty. No wood within sight was bare of a glossy cream lacquer that made the Shield Anvil think of polished bone or ivory.

Two dignitaries awaited them, both seated along one side of a rectangular table on which wrought silver goblets had been arrayed, three before each chair. Servants stood behind the two figures, and two more were positioned beside the seats intended for the Perish.

The walls to the right and left held tapestries, each one bound to a wooden frame, although not tightly. Tanakalian's attention was caught when he saw how the scenes depicted—intimate gardens devoid of people—seemed to flow with motion, and he realized that the tapestries were of the finest silks and the images themselves had been designed to awaken to currents of air. And so, to either side as they walked to the chairs, water flowed in stony beds, flower-heads wavered in gentle, unfelt breaths of wind, leaves fluttered, and now all the pungent scents riding the air brought to him in greater force this illusion of a garden. Even the light reaching down through the canopy was artfully dappled.

One such as Mortal Sword Krughava, of course, was inured, perhaps even indifferent, to these subtleties, and he was reminded, uncharitably, of a boar crashing through the brush as he followed her to the waiting seats.

The dignitaries both rose, the gesture of respect exquisitely timed to coincide with the arrival of their armoured, clanking guests.

Krughava was the first to speak, employing the trader tongue. 'I am Krughava, Mortal Sword of the Grey Helms.' Saying this, she tugged off her heavy gauntlets. 'With me is Shield Anvil Tanakalian.'

The servants were all pouring a dark liquid from one of three decanters. When the two Bolkando representatives picked up their filled goblets, Krughava and Tanakalian followed suit.

The man on the left, likely in his seventh decade, his dark face etched with jewel-studded scars on brow and cheeks, replied in the same language. 'Welcome, Mortal Sword and Shield Anvil. I am Chancellor Rava of Bolkando Kingdom, and I speak for King Tarkulf in this parley.' He then indicated the much younger man at his side. 'This is Conquestor Avalt, who commands the King's Army.'

Avalt's martial profession was plain to see. In addition to the same chain surcoat as worn by the guards in the corridor, he wore scaled vambraces and greaves.

His brace of throwing knives, plain-handled and polishéd by long use, was accompanied by a short sword scabbarded under his right arm and a sheathed cutlass under his left. Strips of articulated iron spanned his hands from wrist to knuckle, and then continued on down the length of all four fingers, while an oblong piece of rippled iron protected the upper half of his thumbs. The Conquestor's helm rested on the table, the skullcap sporting flared cheek-guards as well as a nose-bridge wrought in the likeness of a serpent with a strangely broad head. A plethora of scars adorned the warrior's face, the pattern ruined by an old sword slash running diagonally down his right cheek, ending at the corner of his thin-lipped mouth. That the blow had been a vicious one was indicated by the visible dent in his cheekbone.

Once the introductions and acknowledgements had been made, the Bolkando raised their goblets, and everyone drank.

The liquid was foul and Tanakalian fought down a gag.

Seeing their expressions, the Chancellor smiled. 'Yes, it is atrocious, is it not? Blood of the King's fourteenth daughter, mixed with the sap of the Royal Hava tree—the very tree that yielded the spike thorn that opened her neck vein.' He paused, and then added, 'It is the Bolkando custom, in honour of a formal parley, that he sacrifice a child of his own to give proof to his commitment to the proceedings.'

Krughava set the goblet down with more force than was necessary, but said nothing.

Clearing his throat, Tanakalian said, 'While we are honoured by the sacrifice, Chancellor, our custom holds that we must now grieve for the death of the King's fourteenth child. We Perish do not let blood before parley, but I assure you, our word, when given, is similarly honour-bound. If you now seek some gesture of proof of that, then we are at a loss.'

'None is necessary, my friends.' Rava smiled. 'The virgin child's blood is within us now, is it not?'

When the servants filled the second of the three goblets arrayed before each of them, Tanakalian could sense Krughava stiffening. This time, however, the liquid ran clear, and from it wafted a delicate scent of blossoms.

The Chancellor, who could not have been blind to the sudden awkwardness in the reactions of the Perish, renewed his smile. 'Nectar of the sharada flowers from the Royal Garden. You will find it most cleansing of palate.'

They drank and, indeed, the rush of sweet, crisp wine was a palpable relief.

'The sharada,' continued the Chancellor, 'is fed exclusively from the still-births of the wives of the King, generation upon generation. The practice has not been interrupted in seven generations.'

Tanakalian made a soft sound of warning, sensing that Krughava—her comportment in blazing ruins—was moments from flinging the silver goblet into the Chancellor's face. Quickly setting his own goblet down he reached for hers and, with only a little effort, pried it from her hand and carefully returned it to the tabletop.

The servants poured the last offering, which to Tanakalian's eyes looked like simple water, although of course by now that observation was not as reassuring as he would have preferred. *A final cleansing, yes, from the Royal Well that holds the bones of a hundred mouldering kings! Delicious!*

'Spring water,' said the Chancellor, his gentle tones somewhat strained, 'lest in our many words we should grow thirsty. Please, now, let us take our seats. Once our words are completed, we shall dine on the finest foods the kingdom has to offer.'

Sixth son's testicles! Third daughter's left breast!

Tanakalian could almost hear Krughava's inner groan.

The sun was low when the final farewells were uttered and the two barbarians marched back down to their launch. Chancellor Rava and Conquestor Avalt escorted the Perish for precisely half the distance, where they waited until that clumsy skiff was pushed off the sands where it wallowed about before the rowers found their rhythm, and then the two dignitaries turned about and walked casually back towards the pavilion.

'Curious, wasn't it?' Rava murmured. 'This mad need of theirs to venture east.'

'All warnings unheeded,' Avalt said, shaking his head.

'What will you say to old Tarkulf?' the Chancellor asked.

The Conquestor shrugged. 'To give the fools whatever they need, of course, with a minimum of haggling on price. I will also advise we hire a salvage fleet from Deal, to follow in the wake of their ships. At least as far as the edge of the Pelasiar Sea.'

Rava grunted. 'Excellent notion, Avalt.'

They strolled into the pavilion, made their way down the corridor and returned to the main chamber, secure once more in the presence of servants whose eardrums had been punctured and tongues carved out—although there was always the chance of lip-reading spies, meaning of course that these four hapless creatures would have to die before the sun had set.

'This land-based force of theirs to cross the kingdom with,' Rava said, sitting down once more, 'do you foresee any problem?'

Avalt collected the second decanter and poured some more wine. 'No. These Perish place much value in honour. They will stay true to their word, at least on the march out. Those that make it back from the Wastelands—assuming any do— will be in no position to do much besides submitting to our will. We will strip the survivors of any valuables and sell them on as castrated slaves to the D'rhesh.'

Rava made a face. 'So long as Tarkulf never finds out. We were caught completely unawares when those allies of the Perish ran headlong into our forces.'

Avalt nodded, recalling the sudden encounter during the long march towards the border of the Lether Empire. If the Perish were barbaric, then the Khundryl Burned Tears were barely human. But Tarkulf—damn his scaly crocodile hide— had taken a liking to them, and that was when this entire nightmare began. Nothing worse, in Avalt's opinion, than a king deciding to lead his own army. Every night scores of spies and assassins had waged a vicious but mostly silent war in the camps. Every morning the nearby swamps were filled with corpses and squalling carrion birds. And there stood Tarkulf, breathing deep the night-chilled air and smiling at the cloudless sky—the raving, blessedly thick-headed fool.

Well, thank the nine-headed goddess the King was back in his palace, sucking the bones of frog legs, and the Burned Tears were encamped across the river-bed just beyond the northeast marches, dying of marsh fever and whatnot.

Rava drained his wine and then poured some more. 'Did you see her face, Avalt?'

The Conquestor nodded. 'Still-births . . . fourteenth daughter's blood . . . you always had a fertile, if vaguely nasty imagination, Rava.'

'Belt juice is an acquired taste, Avalt. Strangers rarely take to it. I admit, I was reluctantly impressed that neither one actually gagged on the vile stuff.'

'Wait until it shows up in any new scars they happen to suffer.'

'That reminds me—where was their Destriant? I fully expected their High Priest would have accompanied them.'

Rava shrugged. 'For the moment, we cannot infiltrate their ranks, so that question cannot yet be answered. Once they come ashore and enter our kingdom, we'll have plenty of camp followers and bearers and we will glean all we need to know.'

Avalt leaned back, and then shot the Chancellor a glance. 'The fourteenth? Felash, yes? Why her, Rava?'

'The bitch spurned my advances.'

'Why didn't you just steal her?'

Rava's wrinkled face twisted. 'I tried. Heed this warning, Conquestor, do not try getting past a Royal blood's handmaidens—the cruellest assassins this world has ever seen. Word got back to me, of course . . . three days and four nights of the most despicable torture of my agents. And the bitches had the temerity to send me a bottle of their pickled eyeballs. Brazen!'

'Have you retaliated?' Avalt asked, taking a drink to disguise his shiver of horror.

'Of course not. I overreached, casting my lust upon her. Lesson succinctly delivered. Heed that as well, my young warrior. Not every slap of the hand should ignite a messy feud.'

'I heed everything you say, my friend.'

They drank again, each with his own thoughts.

Which was just as well.

The servant standing behind and to the right of the Chancellor was making peace with his personal god, having worked hard at exchanging the blink code with his fellow spy across the table from him, and well knowing that he was about to have his throat slit wide open. In the interval when the two snakes were escorting the Perish down to their boat, he had passed on to a plate-bearer a cogent account of everything that had been said in the chamber, and that woman was now preparing to set out this very night on her perilous return journey to the capital.

Perhaps Chancellor Rava, having overreached, was content to accept the grisly lesson of his temerity, as delivered by Lady Felash's torturers upon his clumsy agents. The Lady, alas, was not.

It was said that Rava's penis had all the lure of an eviscerated snake belly. The very thought of that worm creeping up her thigh was enough to send the fourteenth daughter of the King into a sizzling rage of indignation. No, she had only begun delivering her lessons to the hoary old Chancellor.

In the tiny kingdom of Bolkando, life was an adventure.

Yan Tovis was of a mind to complete the ghastly slaughter her brother had begun, although it was questionable whether she'd succeed, given the blistering, frantic fury of Pully and Skwish as they spat and cursed and danced out fragments of murder steps, sending streams of piss in every direction until the hide walls of the hut were wine-dark with the deluge. Twilight's own riding boots were similarly splashed, although better suited to shed such effrontery. Her patience, however, was not so immune.

'Enough of this!'

Two twisted faces snapped round to glare at her. 'We must hunt him down!' snarled Pully. 'Blood curses! Rat poisons, thorn fish. Nine nights in pain! Nine an' nine amore!'

'He is banished,' said Yan Tovis. 'The matter is closed.'

Skwish coughed up phlegm and, snapping her head round, sent it splatting against the wall just to the left of Twilight. Growling, Yan Tovis reached for her sword.

'Accident!' shrieked Pully, lunging to collide with her sister, and then pushing the suddenly pale witch back.

Yan Tovis struggled against unsheathing the weapon. She hated getting angry, hated that loss of control, especially since once it was awakened in her, it was almost impossible to rein in. At this moment, she was at the very edge of rage. One more insult—by the Errant, an unguarded expression—and she would kill them both.

Pully had wits enough to recognize the threat, it was clear, since she continued pushing Skwish back, until they were both against the far wall, and then she pitched round, head bobbing. 'R'grets, Queen, umbeliss r'grets. Grief, an' I'm sure, grief, Highness, an' it may be that shock has the sting a venom in these old veins. Pologies, fra me and Skwish. Terrible tale, terrible tale!'

Yan Tovis managed to release the grip of her longsword. In bleak tones she said, 'We have no time for all this. The Shake has lost its coven, barring you two. And it has lost its Watch. There are but the three of us now. A queen and two witches. We need to discuss what we must do.'

'An' it says,' said Pully, vigorously nodding, 'an' it says the sea is blind t'the shore an' as blind to the Shake, and the sea, it does rises. It does rises, Highness. The sixth prophecy—'

'Sixth prophecy!' hissed Skwish, pushing her way round her sister and glaring at Yan Tovis. 'What of th'fifteenth prophecy? The Night of Kin's Blood! "And it rises and the shore will drown, all in a night tears into water and the world runs red! Kin upon kin, slaughter marks the Shake and the Shake shall drown! In the unbreathing air." And what could be more unbreathing than the sea? Your brother has killed us all an us all!'

'Banished,' said Twilight, her tone flat. 'I have no brother.'

'We need a king!' wailed Skwish, pulling at her hair.

We do not!

The two witches froze, frightened by her ferocity, shocked by her words.

Yan Tovis drew a deep breath—there was no hiding the tremble in her hands, the extremity of her fury. 'I am not blind to the sea,' she said. 'No—listen to me, both of you! Be silent and just listen! The water is indeed rising. That fact is undeniable. The shore drowns—even as half the prophecies proclaim. I am not so foolish as to ignore the wisdom of the ancient seers. The Shake are in trouble. It falls to us, to me, to you, to find a way through. For our people. Our feuding must end— but if you cannot set aside all that has happened, and do it now, then you leave me no choice but to banish you both.' Even as she uttered the word 'banish' she saw— with no little satisfaction—that both witches had heard something different, something far more savage and final.

Skwish licked her withered lips, and then seemed to sag against the hut's wall. 'We muss flee th'shore, Queen.'

'I know.'

'We muss leave. Pu'a'call out t'the island, gather all the Shake. We muss an' again we muss begin our last journey.'

'As prophesized,' whispered Pully. 'Our lass journey.'

'Yes. Now the villagers are burying the bodies—they need you to speak the closing prayers. And then I shall see to the ships—I will go myself back out to Third Maiden Isle—we need to arrange an evacuation.'

'Of the Shake only y'mean!'

'No, Pully. That damned island is going to be inundated. We take everyone with us.'

'Scummy prizzners!'

'Murderers, slackers, dirt-spitters, hole-plungers!'

Yan Tovis glared at the two hags. 'Nonetheless.'

Neither one could hold her gaze, and after a moment Skwish started edging towards the doorway. 'Prayers an' yes, prayers. Fra th'dead coven, fra all th'Shake an' th'shore.'

Once Skwish had darted out of sight, Pully sketched a ghastly curtsy and then hastened after her sister.

Alone once more, Yan Tovis collapsed down into the saddle-stool that passed for her throne. She so wanted to weep. In frustration, in outrage and in anguish. No, she wanted to weep for herself. The loss of a brother—again—*again*.

Oh. Damn you, Yedan.

Even more distressing, she thought she understood his motivations. In one blood-drenched night, the Watch had obliterated a dozen deadly conspiracies, each one intended to bring her down. How could she hate him for that?

But I can. For you no longer stand at my side, brother. Now, when the Shore drowns. Now, when I need you most.

Well, it served no one for the Queen to weep. True twilight was not a time for pity, after all. Regrets, perhaps, but not pity.

And if all the ancient prophecies were true?

Then her Shake, broken, decimated and lost, were destined to change the world.

And I must lead them. Flanked by two treacherous witches. I must lead my people—away from the shore.

With the arrival of darkness, two dragons lifted into the night sky, one bone-white, the other seeming to blaze with some unquenchable fire beneath its gilt scales. They circled once round the scatter of flickering hearths that marked the Imass encampment, and then winged eastward.

In their wake a man stood on a hill, watching until they were lost to his sight. After a time a second figure joined him.

If they wept the darkness held that truth close to its heart.

From somewhere in the hills an emlava coughed in triumph, announcing to the world that it had made a kill. Hot blood soaked the ground, eyes glazed over, and something that had lived free lived no more.

Chapter Three

On this the last day the tyrant told the truth
His child who had walked from the dark world
Now rose as a banner before his father's walls
And flames mocked like celebrants from every window
A thousand thousand handfuls of ash upon the scene
It is said that blood holds neither memory nor loyalty
On this the last day the tyrant thus beheld a truth
The son was born in a dark room to womanly cries
And walked a dark keep along halls echoing pain
Only to flee on a moonless night beneath the cowl
Of his master's weighted fist and ravaging face
The beget proved to all that a shadow stretches far
Only to march back to its dire maker ever deepening
Its matching desire and this truth is plain as it is blind
Tyrants and saints alike must fall to the ground
In their last breaths taken in turn by the shadow
Of their final repose where truth holds them fast
On a bed of stone.

The Sun Walks Far
Restlo Faran

Your kisses make my lips numb.'

'It's the cloves,' Shurq Elalle replied, sitting up on the edge of the bed.

'Got a toothache?'

'Not that I'm aware of.' Scanning the clothing littering the floor, she spied her leggings and reached over to collect them. 'You marching soon?'

'We are? I suppose so. The Adjunct's not one to let us know her plans.'

'Commander's privilege.' She rose to tug the leggings up, frowning as she wriggled—was she getting fat? Was that even possible?

'Now there's a sweet dance. I'm of a mind to just lean forward here and—'

'I wouldn't do that, love.'

'Why not?'

You'll get yourself a numb face. 'Ah, a woman needs her secrets.' *Well, this one does, at least.*

'I'm also of a mind to stay right here,' the Malazan said.

Leaning far over to lace up her boots, Shurq scowled. 'It's not even midnight, Captain. I wasn't planning on a quiet evening at home.'

'You're insatiable. Why, if I was half the man I'd like to be . . .'

She smiled. It was hard being annoyed with this one. She'd even grown used to that broad waxed moustache beneath his misshapen nose. But he was right about her in ways even he couldn't imagine. Insatiable indeed. She tugged on the deer-hide jerkin and tightened the straps beneath her breasts.

'Careful, you don't want to constrict your breathing, Shurq. Hood knows, the fashions hereabouts all seem designed to emasculate women—would that be the right word? Emasculate? Everything seems designed to imprison you, your spirit, as if a woman's freedom was some kind of threat.'

'All self-imposed, sweetie,' she replied, clasping her weapon belt and then collecting her cape from where it lay in a heap on the floor. She shook it out. 'Take ten women, all best friends. Watch one get married. Before you know it she's top of the pile, sitting smug and superior on her marital throne. And before long every woman in that gaggle's on the hunt for a husband.' She swung the cape behind her and fastened the clasps at her shoulders. 'And Queen Perfect Bitch sits up there nodding her approval.'

'History? My my. Anyway, that doesn't last.'

'Oh?'

'Sure. It's sweet blossoms until her husband runs off with one of those best friends.'

She snorted and then cursed. 'Damn you, I told you not to make me laugh.'

'Nothing will crack the perfection of your face, Shurq Elalle.'

'You know what they say—age stalks us all, Ruthan Gudd.'

'Some old hag hunting you down? No sign of that.'

She made her way to the door. 'You're lovely, Ruthan, even when you're full of crap. My point was, most women don't like each other. Not really, not in the general sense. If one ends up wearing chains, she'll paint them gold and exhaust herself scheming to see chains on every other woman. It's our innate nasty streak. Lock up when you leave.'

'As I said—I intend staying the night.'

Something in his tone made her turn round. Her immediate reaction was to simply kick him out, if only to emphasize the fact that he was a guest, not an Errant-damned member of the household. But she'd heard a whisper of iron beneath the man's words. 'Problems in the Malazan compound, Captain?'

'There's an adept in the marines . . .'

'Adept at what? Should you introduce him to me?'

His gaze flicked away, and he slowly edged up in the bed to rest his back against the headboard. 'Our version of a caster of the Tiles. Anyway, the Adjunct has ordered a . . . a casting. Tonight. Starting about now.'

'And?'

The man shrugged. 'Maybe I'm just superstitious, but the idea's given me a state of the nerves.'

No wonder you were so energetic. 'And you want to stay as far away as possible.'

'Aye.'

'All right, Ruthan. I should be back before dawn, I hope. We can breakfast together.'

'Thanks, Shurq. Oh, have fun and don't wear yourself out.'

Little chance of that, love. 'Get your rest,' she said, opening the door. 'Come the morning you'll need it.'

Always give them something before leaving. Something to feed anticipation, since anticipation so well served to blind a man to certain obvious discrepancies in, uh, appetite. She descended the stairs. *Cloves. Ridiculous.* Another visit to Selush was required. Shurq Elalle's present level of maintenance was proving increasingly complicated, not to mention egregiously expensive.

Stepping outside, she was startled as a huge figure loomed out from the shadows of an alcove. 'Ublala! Shades of the Empty Throne, you startled me. What are you doing here?'

'Who is he?' the giant demanded. 'I'll kill him for you if you like.'

'No, I don't like. Have you been following me around again? Listen, I've explained all this before, haven't I?'

Ublala Pung's gaze dropped to his feet. He mumbled something inaudible.

'What?'

'Yes. I said "yes", Captain. Oh, I want to run away!'

'I thought Tehol had you inducted into the Palace Guard,' she said, hoping to distract him.

'I don't like polishing boots.'

'Ublala, you only have to do that once every few days—or you can hire someone—'

'Not my boots. Everyone else's.'

'The other guards'?'

He nodded glumly.

'Ublala, walk with me—I will buy you a drink. Or three.' They set off up the street towards the canal bridge. 'Listen, those guards are just taking advantage of your kindness. You don't have to polish their boots.'

'I don't?'

'No. You're a guardsman. If Tehol knew about it . . . well, you should probably tell your comrades in the Guard that you're going to have a word with your best friend, the King.'

'He is my best friend, isn't he? He gave me chicken.'

They crossed the bridge, waving at swarming sludge flies, and made their way on to an avenue flanking one of the night markets. More than the usual number of Malazan soldiers wandering about, she noted. 'Exactly. Chicken. And a man like Tehol won't share chicken with just anyone, will he?'

'I don't know. Maybe.'

'No no, Ublala, trust me on this. You've got friends in high places. The King, the Chancellor, the Ceda, the Queen, the King's Sword. Any one of them would be delighted to share chicken with you, and you can bet they wouldn't be so generous with any of your fellow guards.'

'So I don't have to polish boots?'

'Just your own, or you can hire someone to do that.'

'What about stitching tears in their uniforms? Sharpening their knives and swords? And what about washing their underclothes—'

'Stop! None of that—and now especially I want you to promise to talk to your friends. Any one of them. Tehol, Bugg, Brys, Janath. Will you do that for me? Will you tell them what the other guards are making you do?'

'All right.'

'Good, those bastard comrades of yours in the Guard are in for some serious trouble. Now, here's a suitable bar—they use benches instead of chairs, so you won't be getting stuck like last time.'

'Good. I'm thirsty. You're a good friend, Shurq. I want to sex you.'

'How sweet. But just so you understand, lots of men sex me and you can't let that bother you, all right?'

'All right.'

'Ublala—'

'Yes, all right, I promise.'

Kisswhere sat slumped in the saddle as the troop rode at a slow trot towards the city of Letheras. She would not glance across to her sister, Sinter, lest the guilt she was feeling simply overwhelm her, a clawing, stabbing clutch at her soul, dragging it into oblivion.

She'd known all along Sinter would follow her anywhere, and when the recruiter train rolled into their village in the jungles of Dal Hon, well, it had been just one more test of that secret conviction. The worst of it was, joining the marines had been little more than a damned whim. Spurred by a bit of a local mess, the spiralling inward of suspicions that would find at its heart none other than Kisswhere herself—the cursed 'other' woman who dwelt like a smiling shadow unseen on the edge of a family—oh, she could have weathered the scandal, with just one more toss of her head and a few careless gestures. It wasn't that she'd loved the man—all the forest spirits well knew that an adulterous man wasn't worth a woman's love, for he lived only for himself and would make no sacrifice in the name of his wife's honour, nor that of their children. No, her motives had been rather less romantic.

Boredom proved a cruel shepherd—the switch never stopped snapping. A hunger for the forbidden added yet another dark shade to the cast of her impulses. She'd known all along that there would come a time when they'd drive her from the village, when she'd be outcast for the rest of her life. Such banishment was no longer a death sentence—the vast world beyond the jungle now opened a multitude of escape routes. The Malazan Empire was vast, holding millions of citizens on three continents. Yes, she knew she would have no difficulty vanishing within that blessed anonymity. And besides, she knew she'd always have company.

Sinter—so capable, so practical—was the perfect companion for all her adventures. And oh, the White Jackal well knew, her sister was a beauty and together they'd never have to fear an absence of male company.

The recruiters seemed to offer a quick escape, fortuitous in its timing, and were happy to pay all travel expenses. So she'd grasped hold of the hyena's tail.

And sure enough, sister Sinter was quick to follow.

It should have ended there. But Badan Gruk was whipped into the rushing current of their wake. The fool had fallen for Sinter.

If she'd bothered putting any thought behind her decisions, she would have comprehended the terrible disaster she had dragged them all into. The Malazan marines demanded a service of ten years, and Kisswhere had simply smiled and shrugged and then had signed on for the long count, telling herself that, as soon as she tired of the game, she'd just desert the ranks and, once more, vanish into anonymity.

Alas, Sinter's nature was a far tighter weave. What she took inside she kept, and a vow once made was held to, right down to her dying breath.

It did not take long for Kisswhere to realize the mistake she'd made. She couldn't very well run off and abandon her sister, who'd then gone and showed enough of her talents to be made a sergeant. And although Kisswhere was more or less indifferent to Badan Gruk's fate—the man so wretchedly ill cast as a soldier, still more so as a squad sergeant—it had become clear to her that Sinter had tightened some knots between them. Just as Sinter had followed Kisswhere, so Badan Gruk had followed Sinter. But the grisly yoke of responsibility proved not at the core of the ties between Sinter and Badan Gruk. There was something else going on. Did her sister in fact love the fool? Maybe.

Life had been so much easier back in the village, despite all the sneaking round and frantic hip-locking in the bushes up from the river—at least then Kisswhere was on her own, and no matter what happened to her, her sister would have been free of it. And safe.

Could she take it all back . . .

This jaunt among the marines was likely to kill them all. It had stopped being fun long ago. The horrid voyage on those foul transports, all the way to Seven Cities. The march. Y'Ghatan. More sea voyages. Malaz City. The coastal invasion on this continent—the night on the river—chains, darkness, rotting cells and no food—

No, Kisswhere could not look across at Sinter, and so witness her broken state. Nor could she meet Badan Gruk's tortured eyes, all that raw grief and anguish.

She wished she had died in that cell.

She wished they had taken the Adjunct's offer of discharge once the outlawing was official. But Sinter would have none of that. Of course not.

They were riding in darkness, but Kisswhere sensed when her sister suddenly pulled up. Soldiers immediately behind them veered aside to avoid the horses colliding. Grunts, curses, and then Badan Gruk's worried voice. 'Sinter? What's wrong?'

Sinter twisted in her saddle. 'Is Nep with us? Nep Furrow?'

'No,' Badan replied.

Kisswhere saw real fear sizzle awake in her sister, and her own heart started pounding in answer. Sinter had sensitivities—

'In the city! We need to hurry—'

'Wait,' croaked Kisswhere. 'Sinter, please—if there's trouble there, let them handle it—'

'No—*we have to ride!*'

And suddenly she drove heels into her horse's flanks and the beast lunged forward. A moment later and everyone was following, Kisswhere in their company. Her head spun—she thought she might well be flung from her mount—too weak, too weary—

But her sister. Sinter. Her damned sister, she was a marine, now. She was one of the Adjunct's very own—and though that bitch had no idea, it was soldiers like Sinter—the quiet ones, the insanely loyal ones—who were the iron spine of the Bonehunters.

Malice flashed through Kisswhere, ragged as a flag at midnight. *Badan knows it. I know it. Tavore—you've stolen my sister. And that, you cold bitch, I will not accept!*

I want her back, damn you.

I want my sister back.

'So where is the fool?'

Fist Keneb shrugged. 'Arbin prefers the company of heavies. The soldiers with dirt on their noses and dust storms in their skulls. The Fist plays knuckles with them, gets drunk with them, probably sleeps with some of them, for that matter.'

Blistig grunted as he sat down. 'And this is the proper way to earn respect?'

'That depends, I suppose,' Keneb said. 'If Arbin wins at knuckles, drinks everyone else under the table, and wears out every lover brave enough to share a bed, then maybe it works.'

'Don't be a fool, Keneb. A Fist needs to keep distant. Bigger than life, and meaner besides.' He poured himself another tankard of the foamy local beer. 'Glad you're sitting here, I'd imagine.'

'I didn't even belong at the last reading. I was there in Grub's place, that's all.'

'Now the boy's got to swallow his own troubles.' Blistig leaned forward—they had found an upscale tavern, overpriced and so not likely to draw any Malazan soldiers below the rank of captain, and for a time over the past weeks the Fists had gathered here, mostly to drink and complain. 'What's one of those readings like? Y'hear all sorts of rumours. People spitting up newts or snakes slithering out of their ears, and woe betide any baby born at that moment anywhere in the district—three eyes and forked tongues.' He shook his head, drank down three quick mouthfuls, and then wiped at his mouth. 'It's said that whatever happened at that last one—it made up the Adjunct's mind, about everything that followed. The whole night in Malaz City. All skirling out with the cards. Even Kalam's murder—'

'We don't know he was murdered,' cut in Keneb.

'You were there, in that cabin,' Blistig insisted. 'What happened?'

Keneb glanced away, suddenly wanting something stronger than beer. He found that he was unaccountably chilled, clammy as if fevered. 'It's about to begin,' he muttered. 'Touched once . . .'

'Anybody with neck hairs has left the barracks, did you know that? The whole damned army has scattered into the city tonight. You're scaring me, Keneb.'

'Relax,' he heard himself reply. 'I spat up only one newt, as I recall. Here comes Madan.'

Deadsmell had hired a room for the night, fourth floor with a balcony and quick access to the roof. A damned month's wages, but he had a view of the temporary headquarters—well, its squat dome at any rate, and at the far end of the inn's roof it was a short drop to an adjoining building, a quick sprint across its length and down to an alley not three streets from the river. Best he could do, all things considered.

Masan Gilani had arrived with a cask of ale and a loaf of bread, though the only function Deadsmell could foresee for the bread was to be used to soak up vomit— gods knew he wasn't hungry. Ebron, Shard, Cord, Limp and Crump then crowded in, arms loaded with dusty bottles of wine. The mage was deathly pale and shaky. Cord, Shard and Limp looked frightened, while Crump was grinning like a man struck senseless by a fallen tree branch.

Scowling at them all, Deadsmell lifted his own knapsack from the floor and set it with a thump on the lone table. At the sound Ebron's head snapped round.

'Hood take you, necromancer, you and your stinking magics. If I'd a known—'

'You weren't even invited,' Deadsmell said in a growl, 'and you can leave any time. And what's that ex-Irregular doing with that driftwood?'

'I'm going to carve something!' Crump said with a bright toothy smile, like a horse begging an apple. 'Maybe a big fish! Or a troop of horse-soldiers! Or a giant salamander—though that could be dangerous, oh, too dangerous, unless'n I give its tail a plug so you can pull it off—and a hinged jaw that goes up and down and makes laughing sounds. Why I could—'

'Stuff it in your mouth, is what you could do,' Deadsmell cut in. 'Better yet, I'll do it for you, sapper.'

The smile faltered. 'No need to be mean and all. We all come here to do stuff. Sergeant Cord and Corporal Shard are gonna drink, they said, and pray to the Queen of Dreams. Limp's gonna sleep and Ebron's gonna make protection magics and all.' His equine eyes swivelled to Masan Gilani—who was slumped in the lone cushy chair, legs outstretched, lids lowered, fingers laced together on her lap—and Crump's long jaw slowly sagged. 'And she's gonna be beautiful,' he whispered.

Sighing, Deadsmell untied the pack's leather strings and began lifting out various small dead creatures. A flicker bird, a black-furred rat, an iguana, and a strange blue-skinned, big-eyed thing that might be a bat or a shell-less turtle—he'd found the fox-sized creature hanging by its three-tipped tail on a stall in the market. The old woman had cackled when he'd purchased it, a rather ominous reaction, as far as Deadsmell was concerned. Even so, he had a decent enough—

Glancing up, he saw that everyone was staring at him. 'What?'

Crump's frown was darkening his normally insipid face into something . . . alarming. 'You,' he said. 'You're not, by any chance, you're not a . . . a . . . a *necromancer*? Are you?'

'I didn't invite you here, Crump!'

Ebron was sweating. 'Listen, sapper—you, Crump Bole or whatever your name is. You're not a Mott Irregular no longer, remember that. You're a soldier. A Bonehunter. You take orders from Cord, Sergeant Cord, right?'

Clearing his throat, Cord spoke up, 'That's right, Crump. And, uh, I'm ordering you to, uh, to carve.'

Crump blinked, licked his lips, and then nodded at his sergeant. 'Carve, right. What do you want me to carve, Sergeant? Go on, anything! Except'n not no necromancers, all right?'

'Sure. How about everybody here in this room, except Deadsmell, of course. But everyone else. Uhm, riding horses, galloping horses. Horses galloping over flames.'

Crump wiped at his lips and shot Masan Gilani a shy glance. 'Her, too, Sergeant?'

'Go ahead,' Masan Gilani drawled. 'Can't wait to see it. Don't forget to include yourself, Crump. On the biggest horse.'

'Yah, with a giant sword in one hand and a cusser in the other!'

'Perfect.'

Deadsmell returned to his menagerie of dead animals, arranging them in a circle, head to tail, on the tabletop.

'Gods, those stink,' Limp said. 'Can't you dip 'em in scented oils or something?'

'No, I can't. Now shut up everyone. This is about saving all our skins, right? Even yours, Ebron, as if Rashan's going to help one whit tonight. To keep Hood from this room is down to me. So, no more interruptions, unless you want to kill me—'

Crump's head bobbed up. 'That sounds perfect—'

'And everyone else, too, including you, Crump.'

'That doesn't sound so perfect.'

'Carve,' Cord ordered.

The sapper bent his head back down to the task once more, the tip of his tongue poking out like a botfly grub coming up for air.

Deadsmell fixed his attention on the array of carcasses. The fox-sized bat turtle thing seemed to be staring up at him with one giant doe eye. He fought down a shiver, the motion becoming a flinch when the dead iguana languidly blinked. 'Gods below,' he moaned. 'High House Death has arrived.'

Corks started popping.

———

'We're being followed.'

'Wha? Now Urb, tha's your shadow, is all. We're the ones doin' th'folloan, right? I ain't 'lowing no two-faced corporal a mine t'go awol—now, we turn leff 'ere—'

'Right, Hellian. You just turned right.'

'Tha's only cos we're side by side, meanin' you see it diffren. It was leff for me and if it's right for you tha's your probbem. Now look, izzat a broffle? He went up a broffle? Wha kinda corporal o' mine iz he? Whas wrong wi' Mlazan women, hey? We get 'im an' I wan you t'cut off his balls, okay? Put an end t'this onct and ferawl.'

When they arrived at the narrow stairs tucked between two broad, antiquated entrances, Hellian reached out with both hands, as if to grasp the rails. But there were no rails and so she fell flat on to the steps, audibly cracking her chin. 'Ow! Damn reels broke right off in my hands!' And she groped and clutched with her fingers. 'Turned t'dust too, see?'

Urb leaned closer to make sure her sodden brains weren't leaking out—not that Hellian would notice—and was relieved to see nothing more than a minor scrape on the underside of her chin. While she struggled to her feet, patting at her bleached hair, he glanced back once more up the street they had just come down. 'It's Skulldeath doing the lurking, Hellian—'

She reeled round, blinking owlishly. 'Squealdeath? Him agin?' She made more ineffectual adjustments to her hair. 'Oh, he's a darling thing, izzn't he? Wants to climb inta my knickers—'

'Hellian,' Urb groaned. 'He's made that desire plain enough—he wants to marry you—'

She glared. 'No no, ijit. He wants to wear 'em. All th'rest he don't know nuffin about. He's only done it wi'boys, y'see. Kept trying t'get on his stomach under me or me doin' th'same under 'im wi' the wrong 'ole showin' an' we end up wrasslin' instead a other more fun stuff. Anyway, les go an' get our corporal, affore he d'scends into cruption.'

Frowning to hide his discomfiture, Urb followed Hellian's swaying behind up the stairs. 'Soldiers use whores all the time, Hellian—'

'It's their innocence, Urb, that a right an' proper sergeant needs t'concern 'erself wiff.'

'They're grown men, Hellian—they ain't so innocent—'

'Who? I wuz talkin' bout my corporal, bout Touchy Breffless. The way he's always talking wi'imself no woman's gong go near 'im. Bein' insane ain't a quality women look for, y'know. In their men, I mean.' She waved vaguely at the door in front of her. 'Which iz why they's now tryin' whores, an' I ain't gonna allow it.' She tried a few times to grasp the latch, finally succeeded, and then twisted it in both directions, up and down, up and down. 'Gor b'low! Who invented this piece a crud?'

Urb reached past her and pushed open the door.

Hellian stepped in, still trying to work the latch. 'Don't worry, Urb, I'll get it right—jus' watch an' learn.'

He edged past her and paused in the narrow hallway, impressed by the extraordinary wallpaper, which seemed to consist of gold leaf, poppy-red velvet and swaths of piebald rabbit skins all in a crazed pattern that unaccountably made him want to empty his coin purse. And the black wooden floor, polished and waxed until it seemed almost liquid, as if they were walking upon glass beneath which waited the torment of unending oblivion—he wondered if the whole thing weren't ensorcelled.

'Where you goin?' Hellian demanded.

'You opened the door,' Urb said. 'And asked me to take point.'

'I did? I did? Take point—in a broffle?'

'That's right.'

'Okay, then get your weapon out, Urb, in case we get jumped.'

He hesitated, and then said, 'I'm a fast draw, Hellian.'

'Not what I seen,' she said behind him.

Confused, he paused again. 'What do you mean?'

'Meanin' you need some lessons in cruption, I'd say.' She straightened up, but that wasn't so straight, since she used a wall to manage the posture. 'Unless o'course it's Squatdeath y'want. Not that you'd fit in my knickers, though. Hey, are these baby pelts?'

'Rabbit. I ain't interested in Skulldeath, Hellian. And no, I don't want to wear your knickers—'

'Listen you two—' someone snapped from behind a door to one side, 'quit that foreign jabbering and find a room!'

Face darkening, Hellian reached for her sword, but the scabbard was empty. 'Who stole—you, Urb, gimme your sword, damn you! Or bust down this door—yah, this one 'ere. Bust it down the middle. Use your head—smash it!'

Instead of attempting any of that, Urb took Hellian's arm and guided her farther down the corridor. 'They're not in that one,' he said, 'that man was speaking Letherii.'

'That was Letherii? That foreign jabber? No wonder this city's fulla ijits, talking like that.'

Urb moved up alongside another door and leaned close to listen. He grunted. 'Voices. Negotiating. This could be the one.'

'Kick it down, bash it, find us a battering ram or a cusser or an angry Napan—'

Urb flipped the latch and shoved the door back and then he stepped inside.

Two corporals, mostly undressed, and two women, one stick thin, the other grossly fat, all staring at him with wide eyes. Urb pointed at Brethless and then at Touchy. 'You two, get your clothes on. Your sergeant's in the corridor—'

'No I ain't!' and Hellian reeled into the room, eyes blazing. 'He hired two of 'em! Cruption! Scat, hags, afore I cut my leg off!'

The thin one spat something and suddenly had a knife in a hand, waving it threateningly as she advanced on Hellian. The fat prostitute picked up a chair and lumbered forward a step behind her.

Urb chopped one hand down to crack on the knife-wielder's wrist—sending the weapon clattering on the floor—and used his other to grasp the fat woman's face and push her back. Squealing, the monstrous whore fell on to her ample backside—the room shook with the impact. Clutching her bruised forearm, the skinny one darted past and out the door, shrieking.

The corporals were scrambling with their clothes, faces frantic with worry.

'Get a refund!' Hellian bellowed. 'Those two should be paying *you*! Not t'other way round! Hey, who called in the army?'

The army, as it turned out, was the establishment's six pleasure guards, armed with clubs, but the fight in the room only turned nasty when the fat woman waded back in, chair swinging.

Standing near the long table, Brys Beddict took a cautious sip of the foreign ale, bemused at the motley appearance of the reading's participants, the last of whom arrived half-drunk with a skittish look to his eyes. An ex-priest of some sort, he surmised.

They were a serious, peculiar lot, these Malazans. With a talent for combining offhand casual rapport with the grimmest of subject matter, a careless repose and loose discipline with savage professionalism. He was, he admitted, oddly charmed.

At the same time, the Adjunct was somewhat more challenging in that respect. Tavore Paran seemed virtually devoid of social graces, despite her noble ancestry—which should have schooled her in basic decorum; as indeed her high military rank should have smoothed all the jagged edges of her nature. The Adjunct was awkward in command and clumsy in courtesy, as if consistently distracted by some insurmountable obstacle.

Brys could imagine that such an obstacle might well be found in the unruliness of her legions. And yet her officers and soldiers displayed not a flicker of insubordination, not a single eye-roll behind her back, nor the glare of daggers cast sidelong. There was loyalty, yes, but it was strangely flavoured and Brys was still unable to determine its nature.

Whatever the source of the Adjunct's distraction, she was clearly finding no release from its strictures, and Brys thought that the burden was slowly overwhelming her.

Most of the others were strangers to him, or at best vaguely familiar faces attesting to some past incidental encounter. He knew the High Mage, Ben Adaephon Delat, known to the other Malazans as Quick Ben—although to Brys that name seemed a version lacking in the respect a Ceda surely deserved. He knew Hedge and Fiddler as well, both of whom had been among the soldiers first into the palace.

Others in the group startled him. Two children, a boy and a girl, and a Tiste Andii woman, mature in years and manner and clearly put out by her inclusion in this ragged assembly. All the rest, with the exception of the ex-priest, were officers or soldiers in the Adjunct's army. Two gold-skinned, fair-haired marines—neither young—named Gesler and Stormy. A nondescript man named Bottle who couldn't be much older than two decades; and Tavore's aide, the startlingly beautiful, tattooed officer, Lostara Yil, who moved with a dancer's grace and whose exotic features were only tempered by an air of ineffable sorrow.

Soldiers lived difficult lives, Brys well knew. Friends lost in horrible, sudden ways. Scars hardening over the years, ambitions crushed and dreams set aside. The world of possibilities diminished and betrayals threatened from every shadow. A soldier must place his or her trust in the one who commands, and by extension in that which the commander serves in turn. In the case of these Bonehunters, Brys understood that they and their Adjunct had been betrayed by their empire's ruler. They were adrift, and it was all Tavore could do to hold the army together: that they had launched an invasion of Lether was in itself extraordinary. Divisions and brigades—in his own kingdom's history—had mutinied in response to commands nowhere near as extreme. For this reason alone, Brys held the Adjunct in true respect, and he was convinced that she possessed some hidden quality, a secret virtue, that her soldiers well recognized and responded to—and Brys wondered if he would come to see it for himself, perhaps this very night.

Although he stood at ease, curious and moderately attentive, sipping his ale, he could well sense the burgeoning tension in the room. No one was happy, least of all the sergeant who would awaken the cards—the poor man looked as bedraggled as a dog that had just swum the breadth of River Lether, his eyes red-shot and bleak, his face battered as if he had been in a brawl.

The young soldier named Bottle was hovering close to Fiddler, and, employing—perhaps for Brys's benefit—the trader tongue, he spoke to the sergeant in a low tone. 'Time for a Rusty Gauntlet?'

'What? A what?'

'That drink you invented last reading—'

'No, no alcohol. Not this time. Leave me alone. Until I'm ready.'

'How will we know when you're ready?' Lostara Yil asked him.

'Just sit down, in any order, Captain. You'll know.' He shot the Adjunct a beseeching look. 'There's too much power here. Way too much. I've no idea what I'll bring down. This is a mistake.'

Tavore's pinched features somehow managed to tauten. 'Sometimes, Sergeant, mistakes are necessary.'

Hedge coughed abruptly, and then waved a hand. 'Sorry, Adjunct, but you're talking to a sapper there. Mistakes mean we turn into red mist. I take it you're referring to other kinds, maybe? I hope?'

The Adjunct swung to Gesler's oversized companion. 'Adjutant Stormy, how does one turn an ambush?'

'I ain't no adjutant any more,' the bearded man growled.

'Answer my question.'

The huge man glared, then, seeing as it elicited no reaction whatsoever from the Adjunct, he grunted and then said, 'You spring it and then charge 'em, hard and fast. Y'climb down the bastards' throats.'

'But first the ambush must be sprung.'

'Unless y'can sniff 'em out beforehand, aye.' His small eyes fixed on her. 'We gonna sniff or charge tonight, Adjunct?'

Tavore made no reply to that, facing the Tiste Andii woman instead. 'Sandalath Drukorlat, please sit. I understand your reluctance—'

'I don't know why I'm here,' Sandalath snapped.

'History,' muttered the ex-priest.

A long moment of silence, and then the girl named Sinn giggled, and everyone jumped. Seeing this, Brys frowned. 'Excuse me for interrupting, but is this the place for children?'

Quick Ben snorted. 'The girl's a High Mage, Brys. And the boy's . . . well, he's different.'

'Different?'

'Touched,' said Banaschar. 'And not in a good way, either. Please, Adjunct, call it off. Send Fiddler back to the barracks. There's too many here—the safest readings involve a few people, not a mob like this one. Your poor reader's gonna start bleeding from the ears halfway through.'

'He's right,' said Quick Ben, shifting uneasily in his chair. 'Fid's ugly enough without earrings of blood and whatnot.'

The Adjunct faced Fiddler. 'Sergeant, you know my desire in this—more than anyone else here, you also know my reasons. Speak now honestly, are you capable of this?'

All eyes fixed on the sapper, and Brys could see how everyone—excepting perhaps Sinn—was silently imploring Fiddler to snap shut the lid on this dread box. Instead, he grimaced, staring at the floor, and said, 'I can do it, Adjunct. That's not the problem. It's . . . unexpected guests.'

Brys saw the ex-priest flinch at that, and a sudden, hot flood of alarm rose through the King's Sword. He stepped forward—

But the Deck was in Fiddler's hands and he was standing at one end of the table—even though not everyone had taken seats—and three cards clattered and slid on the polished surface.

The reading had begun.

Standing in the gloom outside the building, the Errant staggered back, as if buffeted by invisible fists. He tasted blood in his mouth, and hissed in fury.

In the main room of her small home, Seren Pedac's eyes widened and then she shouted in alarm as Pinosel and Ursto Hoobutt ignited into flames where they sat—and she would have lunged forward if not for Bugg's staying hand. A hand sheathed in sweat.

'Do not move,' the old man gasped. 'Those fires burn nothing but them—'

'Nothing but *them*? What does that mean?'

It was clear that the two ancient gods had ceased being aware of their surroundings—she could see their eyes staring out through the blue flames, fixed upon nothing.

'Their essence,' Bugg whispered. 'They are being devoured . . . by the power—the power awakened.' He was trembling as if close to incapacitation, sweat streaming like oil down his face.

Seren Pedac edged back and placed her hands upon her swollen belly. Her mouth was dry, her heart pounding hard. 'Who assails them?'

'They stand between your child and that power—as do I, Acquitor. We . . . we can withstand. We must—'

'*Who is doing this?*'

'Not malign—just vast. *Abyss below, this is no ordinary caster of the Tiles!*'

She sat, terrified now, her fear for her unborn son white-hot in her soul, and stared at Pinosel and Ursto Hoobutt—who burned and burned, and beneath the flames they were *melting like wax.*

In a crowded room on the top floor of an inn, a flurry of once-dead beasts now scampered, snarled and snapped jaws. The black-furred rat, trailing entrails, had suddenly fallen *upward* to land on the ceiling, claws digging into the plaster, intestines dangling like tiny sausages in a smoke-house. The blue bat-turtle had bitten off the iguana's tail and that creature escaped in a slithering dash and was now butting at the window's shutters as if desperate to get out. The flicker bird, shedding oily feathers, flapped in frantic circles over the heads of everyone—none of whom had time to notice, as bottles smashed down, wine spilling like thinned blood, and the barely begun carving of riders on charging horses now writhed and reared on Crump's lap, whilst he stared bug-eyed, mouth gaping—and moments later the first tiny horse dragged itself free and leapt down from the sapper's thigh, wooden hoofs clopping across the floor, misshapen lump of rider waving a splinter.

Bellowing, shouts, shrieks—Ebron vomited violently, and, ducking to avoid that gush, Limp slipped in a puddle of wine and shattered his left knee. He howled.

Deadsmell started crawling for a corner. He saw Masan Gilani roll under the fancy bed as the flicker bird cracked headlong into a bedpost, exploding in a cloud of rank feathers.

Smart woman. Now, if only there was room under there for me, too.

In another section of the city, witnesses would swear in the Errant's name, swear indeed on the Empty Throne and on the graves of loved ones, that two dragons burst from the heart of an inn, wreckage sailing out in a deadly rain of bricks, splinters, dust and fragments of sundered bodies that cascaded down into streets as far as fifty paces away—and even in the aftermath the next morning no other possible explanation sufficed to justify that shattered ruin of an entire building, from which no survivors were pulled.

The entire room trembled, and even as Hellian drove her elbow into a bearded face and heard a satisfying crunch, the wall opposite her cracked like fine glass and then toppled into the room, burying the figures thrashing about in pointless clinches on the floor. Women screamed—well, the fat one did, and she was loud enough and repetitive enough in those shrieks to fill in for everyone else—all of whom were too busy scrabbling out from the wreckage.

Hellian staggered back a step, and then, as the floor suddenly heaved, she found herself running although she could not be sure of her precise direction, but it seemed wise to find the door wherever that might be.

When she found it, she frowned, since it was lying flat on the floor, and so she paused and stared down for a time.

Until Urb stumbled into her. 'Something just went up across the street!' he gasped, spitting blood. 'We got to get out of here—'

'Where's my corporal?'

'Already down the stairs—let's go!'

But, no, it was time for a drink—

'Hellian! Not now!'

'Gare away! If not now, when?'

'Spinner of Death, Knight of Shadow, Master of the Deck.' Fiddler's voice was a cold, almost inhuman growl. 'Table holds them, but not the rest.' And he started flinging cards, and each one he threw shot like a plate of iron to a lodestone, striking one person after another—hard against their chests, staggering them back a step, and with each impact—as Brys stared in horror—the victim was lifted off the floor, chair tumbling away, and slammed against the wall behind them no matter the distance.

The collisions cracked bones. Backs of heads crunched bloodily on the walls.

It was all happening too fast, with Fiddler standing as if in the heart of a maelstrom, solid as a deep-rooted tree.

The first struck was the girl, Sinn. 'Virgin of Death.' As the card smacked into her chest it heaved her, limbs flailing, up to a section of wall just beneath the ceiling. The sound she made when she hit was sickening, and she went limp, hanging like a spiked rag doll.

'Sceptre.'

Grub shrieked, seeking to fling himself to one side, and the card deftly slid beneath him, fixing on to his chest and shoving him bodily across the floor, up against the wall just left of the door.

Quick Ben's expression was one of stunned disbelief as Fiddler's third card slapped against his sternum. 'Magus of Dark.' He was thrown into the wall behind him with enough force to send cracks through the plaster and he hung there, motionless as a corpse on a spike.

'Mason of Death.' Hedge bleated and made the mistake of turning round.

The card struck his back and hammered him face first into the wall, whereupon the card began pushing him upward, leaving a red streak below the unconscious man.

The others followed, quick as a handful of flung stones. In each, the effect was the same. Violent impact, walls that shook. Sandalath Drukorlat, *Queen of Dark*. Lostara Yil, *Champion of Life*.

'Obelisk.' Bottle.

Gesler, *Orb*.

Stormy, *Throne*.

And then Fiddler faced Brys. 'King of Life.'

The card flashed out from his hand, glittering like a dagger, and Brys snatched a breath the instant before it struck, eyes closing—he felt the blow, but nowhere near as viciously as had the others, and nothing touched his breast. He opened his eyes to see the card hovering, shivering, in the air before him.

Above it, he met Fiddler's flat eyes.

The sapper nodded. 'You're needed.'

What?

Two remained untouched, and Fiddler turned to the first and nearest of these. 'Banaschar,' he said. 'You keep poor company. Fool in Chains.' He drew a card and snapped out his hand. The ex-priest grunted and was flung back over his chair, whereupon he shot upward to the domed ceiling. Dust engulfed the man at the impact.

Fiddler now faced the Adjunct. 'You knew, didn't you?'

Staring, pale as snow, she said nothing.

'For you, Tavore Paran . . . *nothing*.'

She flinched.

The door suddenly opened, hinges squealing in the frozen silence.

Turudal Brizad stepped into the chamber and then halted. *Turudal . . . no, of course not. The Errant. Who stands unseen behind the Empty Throne. I wondered when you would show yourself.* Brys realized he had drawn his sword; realized, too, that the Errant was here to kill him—a deed without reason, a desire without motive—at least none fathomable to anyone but the Errant himself.

He will kill me.

And then Fiddler—for his audacity.

And then everyone else here, so that there be no witnesses.

Fiddler slowly turned to study the Errant. The Malazan's smile was chilling. 'If that card was for you,' he said, 'it would have left the table the moment you opened the door. I know, you think it belongs to you. You think it's yours. You are wrong.'

The Errant's lone eye seemed to flare. 'I am the Master of the Tiles—'

'And I don't care. Go on then. Play with your tiles, Elder. You cannot stand against the Master of the Deck—your time, Errant, is past.'

'*I have returned!*'

As the Errant, raw power building round him, took another stride into the chamber, Fiddler's low words cut into his path. 'I wouldn't do that.'

The Elder God sneered. 'Do you think Brys Beddict can stop me? Can stop what I intend here?'

Fiddler's brows lifted. 'I have no idea. But if you take one more step, Errant, the Master of the Deck will *come through*. Here, now. Will you face him? Are you ready for that?'

And Brys glanced to that card lying on the table. Inanimate, motionless. It seemed to yawn like the mouth of the Abyss itself, and he suddenly shivered.

Fiddler's quiet challenge had halted the Errant, and Brys saw uncertainty stirred to life on the once-handsome features of Turudal Brizad.

'For what it is worth,' Brys Beddict said then, 'you would not have made it past me anyway, Errant.'

The single eye flicked to him. 'Ridiculous.'

'I have lived in stone, Elder One. I am written with names beyond counting. The man who died in the throne room is not the man who has returned, no matter what you see.'

'You tempt me to crush you,' the Errant said in a half-snarl.

Fiddler swung round, stared down at the card on the table. 'He is awakened.' He faced the Elder God. 'It may be too late . . . for you.'

And Brys saw the Errant suddenly step back, once, twice, the third time taking him through the doorway. A moment later and he vanished from sight.

Bodies were sliding slowly towards the floor. As far as Brys could see, not one was conscious. Something eased in the chamber like the release of a breath held far too long.

'Adjunct.'

Tavore's attention snapped from the empty doorway back to the sapper.

Spring the ambush. Find your enemy.

'This wasn't a reading,' Fiddler said. 'No one here was found. No one was claimed. Adjunct, they were *marked*. Do you understand?'

'I do,' she whispered.

'I think,' Fiddler said, as grief clenched his face, 'I think I can see the end.'

She nodded.

'Tavore,' said Fiddler, his voice now ragged. 'I am so sorry.'

To that, the Adjunct simply shook her head.

And Brys knew that, while he did not understand everything here, he understood enough. And if it could have meant anything, anything at all, he would have repeated Fiddler's words to her. To this Adjunct, this Tavore Paran, this wretchedly lonely woman.

At that moment, the limp form of Banaschar settled on to the tabletop, like a corpse being lowered on a noose. As he came to rest, he groaned.

Fiddler walked over and collected the card called the Master of the Deck. He studied it for a moment, and then returned it to the deck in his hands. Glancing over at Brys, he winked.

'Nicely played, Sergeant.'

'Felt so lifeless . . . still does. I'm kind of worried.'

Brys nodded. 'Even so, the role did not feel . . . vacant.'

'That's true. Thanks.'

'You know this Master?'

'Aye.'

'Sergeant, had the Errant called your bluff—'

Fiddler grinned. 'You would've been on your own, sir. Still, you sounded confident enough.'

'Malazans aren't the only ones capable of bluffing.'

And, as they shared a true smile, the Adjunct simply stared on, from one man to the other, and said nothing.

Bugg stood at the back window, looking out on Seren Pedac's modest garden that was now softly brushed with the silvery tones reflected down from the dusty, smoky clouds hanging over the city. There had been damage done this night, far beyond one or two knocked-down buildings. The room had been silent behind him for some time now, from the moment that the reading had ended a short while ago. He still felt . . . fragile, almost fractured.

He heard her stir into motion behind him, the soft grunt as she climbed upright, and then she was beside him. 'Are they dead, Bugg?'

He turned and glanced at the now conjoined, colourless puddles on the floor beneath the two chairs. 'I don't know,' he admitted, and then added, 'I think so.'

'Th-that was not . . . expected—please tell me, Ceda, that such a fate was not in the plans tonight.'

'No, Acquitor.'

'Then . . . *what happened?*'

He rubbed at the bristles on his chin, and then sighed and shook his head. 'She chooses a narrow path—gods, the audacity of it! I must speak with the King. And with Brys—we need to decide—'

'Ceda! Who killed Pinosel and Ursto?'

He faced her, blinked. 'Death but passed through. Even the Errant was . . . dismissed.' He snorted. 'Yes. *Dismissed.* There is so much power in this Deck of Dragons. In the right hands, it could drain us all dry. Every god, new and elder. Every ascendant cast into a role. Every mortal doomed to become a face on a card.' He resumed his gaze out the window. 'He dropped one on to the table. Your son's. The table would hold it, he said. Thus, he made no effort to claim your son. He let it be. He let *him* be.' And then he shivered. 'Pinosel and Ursto—they just sat too close to the fire.'

'They . . . what?'

'*The caster held back, Acquitor.* No one attacked Ursto and Pinosel. Even your unborn son's card did not try for *him.* The caster locked it down. As would a carpenter driving a nail through a plank of wood. Abyss take me, the sheer *brazen* power to do that leaves me breathless. Acquitor, Ursto and Pinosel were here to defend you from the Errant. And yes, we felt him. We felt his murderous desire. But then he was thrown back, his power scattered. What arrived in its place was like the face of the sun, ever growing, becoming so vast as to fill the world—they were pinned there, trapped in those chairs, unable to move . . .' He shook himself. 'We all were.' He looked down at the puddles. 'Acquitor, I truly do not know if they are dead. The Lord of Death fed on no one this night, beyond a few hapless souls in a destroyed inn. They may be simply . . . reduced . . . and after a time they will reconstitute themselves, find their shapes—their flesh and bone—once more. I do not know, yet I will hope.'

He saw her studying his face, and wondered if he'd managed to hide any of his anxiety, his grief. The look in her eyes spoke of his failure.

'Speak with this caster,' she said. 'And . . . ask him . . . to refrain. Never again in this city. Please.'

'He was unwilling, Acquitor. He did what he could. To protect . . . everyone.' *Except, I think, himself.* 'I do not think there will be another reading.'

She stared out the window. 'What awaits him? My . . . son,' she asked in a whisper.

He understood her question. 'He will have you, Seren Pedac. Mothers possess a strength, vast and strange—'

'Strange?'

Bugg smiled. 'Strange to us. Unfathomable. Also, your son's father was much loved. There will be those among his friends who would not hesitate—'

'Onrack T'emlava,' she said.

Bugg nodded. 'An Imass.'

'Whatever that is.'

'Acquitor, the Imass are many things, and among those things, one virtue stands above all the others. Their loyalty cannot be sundered. They feel such forces with a depth vast and—'

'Strange?'

Bugg said nothing for a moment, knowing that he could, if he so chose, be offended by the implication in that lone word she had added to his sentence. Instead, he smiled. 'Even so.'

'I am sorry, Ceda. You are right. Onrack was . . . remarkable, and a great comfort to me. Still, I do not expect him to visit again.'

'He will, when your son is born.'

'How will he know when that happens?'

'Because his bonecaster wife, Kilava, set a blessing upon you and your child. By this means she remains aware of you and your condition.'

'Oh. Would she have sensed tonight, then? The risk? The danger?'

'Perhaps,' Bugg replied. 'She would have been . . . attentive. And had some form of breach occurred to directly threaten you, then I suspect that yes, she would have . . . intervened.'

'How could she have hoped to defend me,' Seren said, 'if three ancient gods had already failed?'

Bugg sighed. 'A conviction I am slowly coming to accept. People do not understand power. They view it exclusively as a contest, this against that; which is the greater? Which wins, which fails? Power is less about actual conflict—recognizing as it does the mutual damage conflict entails, with such damage making one vulnerable—less about actual conflict, then, than it is about statements. *Presence*, Acquitor, is power's truest expression. And presence is, at its core, the occupation of space. An assertion, if you will. One that must be acknowledged by other powers, lesser or greater, it matters not.'

'I am not sure I understand you.'

'Kilava would have invoked her presence, Acquitor. One that embraced you. Now, if you still insist on simplistic comparisons, then I tell you, she would have been as a stone in a stream. The water may dream of victory, may even yearn for it, but it had best learn patience, yes? Consider every dried stream bed you have seen, Acquitor, and judge who was the ultimate victor in that war of patience.'

The woman sighed, and Bugg heard her exhaustion.

He bowed to her. 'I shall leave—matters remain pressing for me—but the danger to you and your unborn son has passed.'

She glanced back at the puddles. 'Do I just . . . mop that up?'

'Leave it for the morning—it may be that you will find little more than a stain by then.'

'I can point to it when I have guests and say: "This is where two gods melted."'

Yes, she had need to defend herself against the events of this night. No room in her thoughts, for the moment, for anything but the child within her. Despite her words, she was not indifferent to the sundering of Pinosel and Ursto. Everything right now was about control—and this, Bugg understood, came from that ineffable strength within a woman who was or would be a mother. 'They are stubborn, those two. I would not discount them quite yet.'

'I hope you are right. Thank you, Ceda—even if the threat did not come to pass, I do appreciate your willingness to protect us. Please do not be offended if I add that I hope I never experience another night like this.'

'I take no offence. Goodnight, Acquitor.'

Beyond the moment's heat, in the cool trickle that was the aftermath of a confrontation, bleak realizations shook free in the mind of the Errant. While he did not know if indeed the Master of the Deck had awakened—as the Malazan had claimed—the risk of such a premature clash had been too great. As for Brys Beddict and his bold arrogance, ah, that was a different matter.

The Errant stood in an alley, not far from the Malazan headquarters, and he trembled with rage and something else, something that tasted delicious. The promise of vengeance. No, Brys Beddict would not survive his return journey to the palace. It did not matter the fool's skills with a sword. Against the raw assault of the Errant's sorcery, no flickering blade could defend.

True, this would be no gentle, unseen nudge. But old habits, by their very predictability, could be exploited. Defended against. Besides, at times, the subtle did not satisfy. He recalled, with a rush of pleasure, holding Feather Witch's head under the water, until her feeble struggles ceased. Yes, there was glory in being so forceful, so direct in the implementation of one's own will.

It could become addictive, and indeed, he welcomed the invitation.

So much gnawed at him at the moment, however, that he was anxious and wary about doing much of anything. The caster had been . . . frightening. The ones who were made miserable by the use of their own power ever disturbed the Errant, for he could not fathom such creatures, did not understand their reluctance, the self-imposed rules governing their behaviour. Motives were essential—one could not understand one's enemy without a sense of what they wanted, what they hungered for. But that caster, all he had hungered for was to be left alone.

Perhaps that in itself could be exploited. Except that, clearly, when the caster was pushed, he did not hesitate to push back. Unblinking, smiling, appallingly confident. *Leave him for now. Think of the others—any threats to me?*

The Acquitor's child had guardians assembled to defend it. Those squalid drunks. Mael. Other presences, as well. Something ancient, black-furred with glowing eyes—he'd heard its warning growl, like a rumble of thunder—and that had been enough to discourage the Errant's approach.

Well, the child could wait.

Oh, this was a vicious war indeed. But he had potential allies. Banaschar. A weak man, one he could use again. And Fener, the cowering god of war—yes, he could feed on the fool's power. He could take what he wanted, all in exchange for the sanctuary he offered. Finally, there were other forces, far to the east, who might well value his alliance.

Much still to do. But for now, this night, he would have his vengeance against that miserable heap of armour, Brys Beddict.

And so he waited for the fool to depart the headquarters. No nudge this time. No, only his hands on the bastard's throat would appease the depth of the Errant's malice. True enough, the man who had died was not the same man who returned. More to Brys Beddict than just an interminable skein of names written into the stone of his soul. There was something else. As if the man cast more than one shadow. If Brys was destined for something else, for something more than he was now, then it behoved the Errant to quell the threat immediately.

Remove him from the game, and this time make certain he stayed dead.

Nothing could be worse than to walk into a room in a middling inn, stride up to the bed, and fling back the woollen blanket, only to find a dragon. Or two. All unwillingly unveiled. And in a single miserable instant, the illusions of essential, mutual protection, are cast off. Violent transformation and lo, it turns out, one small room in an inn cannot hold two dragons.

It is the conviction of serving staff the world over that they have seen everything. The hapless maid working at the inn in question could now make claim to such an achievement. Alas, it was a shortlived triumph.

Telorast and Curdle, sembled once more into their quaint, tiny skeletal forms—which had become so much a part of them, so preciously adorable, that neither could bear to part with the lovely lizards—were now on a hilltop a few leagues north of the city. Once past the indignity of the unexpected event and their panicked flight from Letheras, they had spent the last bell or so howling in laughter.

The expression on the maid's face was truly unforgettable, and when Curdle's draconic head had smashed through the wall to fill the corridor, why, every resident guest had then popped out from their rooms for a look at the source of the terrible ruckus, my, such consternation—Curdle squealed in gut-busting hilarity, or would have, had she a gut.

Telorast's tiny fangs still glistened with blood, although when she'd last used them they had been much, much larger. An instinctive snap—no one could blame her, not really—had collected up a fat merchant in the street below, a moment before she herself landed to fill it amidst crashing bricks and quarried limestone, and was it not essential among carnivores to indulge in blubber on occasion? It must be so, for some scholar had said it, once, somewhere. In any case, he had been delicious!

Could one blame the shark that takes a swimmer's leg? The coiling serpent that devours a toddler? The wolves that run down an old woman? Of course not. One might decry the deed and weep for the slain victims, but to then track and hunt the killer down—as if it was some kind of evil murderer—was simply ridiculous. Indeed, it was hubris of the worst sort. 'It's the way of the world that there are hunters and the hunted, Curdle. And to live in the world is to accept that as a truth. Beasts eat other beasts, and the same is true for all these precious humans—do they not thrive and preen as hunters? Of course they do. But sometimes the hunter becomes the hunted, yes? Consider if you will and you will: some bow-legged yokel traps a hare for supper—should the rest of the hares all gather and incite themselves into deadly vengeance against that yokel? Would this be proper and just?'

'I dare say the hares would think so!' cried Curdle, spiny tail lashing the short grasses.

'No doubt, no doubt, but think of the outrage among the yokel's family and friends! Why, there'd be a war, a feud! Soldiers would be called in, slit-eyed scouts and master hunters wearing green floppy hats, the king would raise taxes and a thousand whores would follow in the baggage train! Poets would sing rousing ballads to fan the flames of righteousness! Entire epics would be penned to recount the venal escapades!'

'They're just puffed up on themselves, Telorast. That's all. They're all emperors and empresses in their own puny minds, don't you see? With all in the domain theirs to do with as they will. How dare some dumb beast bite back!'

'We'll get them in the end, Curdle.'

'Us and the hares!'

'Exactly! Rule the domain, will you? No, my friends, the domain rules you!'

Telorast fell silent then, as grim thoughts whispered through her. 'Curdle,' she ventured, lifting her small reptilian skull. 'We'll need to act soon.'

'I know. It's awful!'

'Someone in the city's causing trouble. We don't like trouble, do we? At least, I don't think we do.'

'Unless it's ours, Telorast. If we're the ones causing trouble, that's just fine. Perfect, in fact.'

'Until it all goes wrong, like last time. And wasn't that your fault? That's how I remember it, Curdle. All your fault. This time round, watch yourself. Do as I say, everything I say.'

'Should we tear him apart then?'

'Who?'

'The one who likes keeping the throne empty. In out in out in out, just shuffle them through. Nobody get comfortable! Chaos and confusion, civil wars and betrayals and blood everywhere! What a creep!'

'You think we should tear him apart, Curdle?'

'I thought I was supposed to be following your lead. So lead, Telorast! Do we rend him into little messy pieces or don't we?'

'That depends.' Telorast leapt to her taloned feet and began pacing, tiny forearms twitching. 'Is he the enemy?'

'Is he—what? Sweetness, aren't they *all* our enemies?'

'Agh! You're right! What got into me?'

'Simple, he just thought to ignore us. We don't like being ignored. People who ignore us die. That's the rule we've always lived by. Snub us and we'll chew you into mangled flaps of skin and hair! Chips of bone, things that drip and leak!'

'Should we go and kill him then?'

'Maybe.'

'Oh, tell me what to do! I can't tell you to follow my lead unless I get guidance from you first!'

'It's a partnership all right,' agreed Curdle. 'Let me think.'

Telorast paused, head lifting yet higher. 'Gah! What's those green blobs in the sky?'

'Don't come near me.'

Withal eyed his wife, decided he'd seen this before, and so kept his distance. 'Why did she want you there at all? That's what I can't figure.'

Sandalath sat down, the effort a protracted procedure measured in winces, grunts and cautious sighs. 'I didn't anticipate a physical assault, that's for sure.'

Withal almost stepped forward then, but managed to restrain his instinctive gesture. 'She beat you up? Gods below, I knew the Adjunct was a hard woman, but that's going too far!'

'Oh, be quiet. Of course she didn't beat me up. Let's just say the cards were assigned with some, uh, force. As if that would convince us of anything. The whole sorcery surrounding the Deck of Dragons is an affront to sensible creatures—like me.'

Sensible? *Well, I suppose.* 'The caster found you a card, then. Which one?'

He watched as she weighed the value of answering him. 'It threw me into a wall.'

'What did?'

'The card, you idiot! Queen of Dark! As if I could be anything like that—stupid deck, what does it know of High House Dark? The past is dead, the thrones abandoned. There is no King and certainly no Queen! It's senseless—how can Quick Ben be Magus of Dark? He's not even Tiste Andii. Bah, all nonsense, all of it—gods, I think my ribs are cracked. Make some tea, love, be useful.'

'Glad I waited up for you,' Withal muttered, setting off to brew a pot. 'Any preferences?'

'No, but add a drop of d'bayang oil, will you? Next time, I'll wear armour. Is it cold in here? Feed the hearth, I don't want to get a chill. Throw me those furs. Is that water pipe just ornamental? Do we have any durhang? Gods, it hurts to talk.'

News to me, darling.

The dead iguana's last animate act had been to clamp its jaws on Limp's right ear. The soldier was weeping softly as Deadsmell knelt beside him and tried to prise loose the lizard's savage grip. Blood flowed and it looked as if Limp was going to be left with half an ear on that side.

Ebron was sitting on the bed, head in his hands. 'It'll be all right, Limp. We'll get the knee fixed up. Maybe sew that bit of ear back on—'

'No we won't,' said Deadsmell. 'That'll go septic for sure and then spread out. Iguana saliva, especially a dead iguana's saliva, is bound to be nasty stuff. As it is, I'll need to work a ritual to purge whatever toxins have already slipped into him.' He paused. 'Masan, you can crawl out from under the bed now.'

'So you say,' the woman replied, then coughed. 'Hood-damned hairballs—I'll never be clean again.'

Limp squealed when Deadsmell worked a knife-blade between the iguana's jaws and, failing to open them, simply started cutting at the tendons and muscle tissue at the hinges. A moment later and the creature fell away, startling everyone when it whistled an exhalation through its slitted nostrils.

'I thought you said it was dead!' Cord accused, walking over to slam his boot heel down on the iguana's head. Things splatted out to the sides.

'Now it is,' Deadsmell affirmed. 'Lie still, Limp. Let's get the healing started—'

'You should never let necromancers heal people,' Crump complained, glowering from the corner of the room. The various components of his wood carving, shapeless riders on shapeless horses, had all vanished out into the corridor after breaching the door, which seemed to have been achieved by a combination of chewing and hacking and who knew what else.

Deadsmell scowled over at the sapper. 'You wouldn't be saying that if you were dying of some wound and I was your only hope.'

'Yes I would.'

The necromancer offered him a nasty smile. 'We'll see some day, won't we?'

'No we won't. I'll kill you first before I get wounded.'

'And then we'd both be dead.'

'That's right, so there! Just what I was saying—nothing good comes of no necromancers no how!'

The flicker bird was a mashed heap of feathers on the floor. The bat-turtle had fled through the hole in the door, possibly in pursuit of the wooden troop. The black-furred rat still clung on all fours to the ceiling.

Shard moved to stand opposite Ebron. 'Was Deadsmell right, mage? Did the Lord of Death show up here?'

'No. Not as such. Why don't you ask him yourself—'

'Because he's busy healing. I want to hear from you, Ebron.'

'More like all the warrens woke up all at once. Corporal, I don't know what the Adjunct's playing at, but it won't be fun. We're gonna march soon—I think tonight's decided it. The roles are set, only I doubt anybody—even Tavore—knows all the players. Noses are gonna get bloodied.'

Deadsmell had of course been listening. Working on the wreck that was Limp's knee had become rote for the healer—as it was for virtually every healer in the company, not one of whom had escaped delivering ministrations to the hapless fool. 'Ebron's right. I don't envy your squad, if you end up as Sinn's escort again— she's right in the middle of it.'

'I don't like her neither,' said Crump.

Ebron sneered at Deadsmell. 'How close we happen to be with anybody won't make any difference. We're all in trouble.'

An odd, frothy, bubbling sound drew everyone's attention, and all eyes fixed on the crushed head of the iguana, as it exhaled yet again.

A snort came from under the bed. 'I ain't leaving here until the sun comes up.'

The others had left, their departure more a headlong flight than a solemn dismissal, until only the Adjunct, Lostara Yil and Brys Beddict remained. Plaster dust hazed the light from the lanterns, and the floor ground and crunched underfoot.

Brys watched as the Adjunct slowly sat down in the chair at the head of the table, and it was hard to determine which woman was more shaken or distraught. Whatever sorrow was buried within Lostara Yil now seemed much closer to the surface, and she had said not a word since Fiddler's exit, standing with arms crossed—a gesture that likely had as much to do with aching ribs as anything else.

'Thank you,' said the Adjunct, 'for being here, sir.'

Startled, Brys frowned. 'I may well have been the reason for the Errant's attention, Adjunct. You would perhaps be more justified in cursing me instead.'

'I do not believe that,' she replied. 'We are in the habit of acquiring enemies.'

'This is the Errant's back yard,' Brys pointed out. 'Naturally, he resents intruders. But even more, he despises the other residents who happen to share it with him. People like me, Adjunct.'

She glanced up at him. 'You were dead, once. Or so I understand. Resurrected.'

He nodded. 'It is extraordinary how little choice one has in such matters. If I mull on that overlong I become despondent. I do not appreciate the notion of being so easily manipulated. I would prefer to think of my soul as my own.'

She looked away, and then settled her hands flat on the table before her—a strange gesture—whereupon she seemed to study them. 'Fiddler spoke of the Errant's . . . rival. The Master of the Deck of Dragons.' She hesitated, and then added, 'That man is my brother, Ganoes Paran.'

'Ah. I see.'

She shook her head but would not look up, intent on her hands. 'I doubt that. We may share blood, but in so far as I know, we are not allies. Not . . . close. There are old issues between us. Matters that cannot be salved, not by deed, not by word.'

'Sometimes,' Brys ventured, 'when nothing can be shared except regret, then regret must serve as the place to begin. Reconciliation does not demand that one side surrender to the other. The simple, mutual recognition that mistakes were made is in itself a closing of the divide.'

She managed a half-smile. 'Brys Beddict, your words, however wise, presume communication between the parties involved. Alas, this has not been the case.'

'Perhaps, then, you might have welcomed the Master's attention this night. Yet, if I did indeed understand Fiddler, no such contact was in truth forthcoming. Your soldier bluffed. Tell me, if you would, is your brother aware of your . . . predicament?'

She shot him a look, sharp, searching. 'I do not recall sharing any details of my predicament.'

Brys was silent. Wondering what secret web he had just set trembling.

She rose, frowned over at Lostara for a moment, as if surprised to find her still there, and then said, 'Inform the King that we intend to depart soon. We will be rendezvousing with allies at the border to the Wastelands, whereupon we shall march east.' She paused. 'Naturally, we must ensure that we are well supplied with all necessities—of course, we shall pay in silver and gold for said materiel.'

'We would seek to dissuade you, Adjunct,' said Brys. 'The Wastelands are aptly named, and as for the lands east of them, what little we hear has not been promising.'

'We're not looking for promises,' the Adjunct replied.

Brys Beddict bowed. 'I shall take my leave now, Adjunct.'

'Do you wish an escort?'

He shook his head. 'That will not be necessary. Thank you for the offer.'

The roof would have to do. He'd wanted a tower, something ridiculously high. Or a pinnacle and some tottering, ragged keep moments from plunging off the cliff into the thrashing seas below. Or perhaps a cliff-side fastness on some raw mountain, slick with ice and drifts of snow. An abbey atop a mesa, with the only access through a rope and pulley system with a wicker basket to ride in. But this roof would have to do.

Quick Ben glared at the greenish smear in the south sky, that troop of celestial riders not one of whom had any good news to deliver, no doubt. *Magus of Dark. The bastard! You got a nasty nose, Fid, haven't you just. And don't even try it with that innocent look. One more disarming shrug from you and I'll ram ten warrens down your throat.*

Magus of Dark.

There was a throne once . . . no, never mind.

Just stay away from Sandalath, that's all. Stay away, ducked out of sight. It was just a reading, after all. Fiddler's usual mumbo jumbo. Means nothing. Meant nothing. Don't bother me, I'm busy.

Magus of Dark.

Fiddler was now drunk, along with Stormy and Gesler, badly singing old Napan pirate songs, not one of which was remotely clever. Bottle, sporting three fractured ribs, had shuffled off to find a healer he could bribe awake. Sinn and Grub had run away, like a couple of rats whose tails had just been chopped off by the world's biggest cleaver. And Hedge . . . Hedge was creeping up behind him right now, worse than an addled assassin.

'Go away.'

'Not a chance, Quick. We got to talk.'

'No we don't.'

'He said I was the Mason of Death.'

'So build a crypt and climb inside, Hedge. I'll be happy to seal it for you with every ward I can think of.'

'The thing is, Fid's probably right.'

Eyes narrowing, Quick Ben faced the sapper. 'Hood's been busy of late.'

'You'd know more of that than me, and don't deny it.'

'It's got nothing to do with us.'

'You sure?'

Quick Ben nodded.

'*Then why am I the Mason of Death?*'

The shout echoed from the nearby rooftops and Quick Ben flinched. 'Because you're needed,' he said after a moment.

'To do what?'

'You're needed,' Quick Ben snarled, '*to build us a road.*'

Hedge stared. 'Gods below, where are we going?'

'The real question is whether we'll ever get there. Listen, Hedge, she's nothing like you think. She's nothing like any of us thinks. I can't explain—I can't get any closer than that. Don't try anticipating. Or second-guessing—she'll confound you at every turn. Just look at this reading—'

'That was Fid's doing—'

'You think so? You're dead wrong. He knows because she told him. Him and no one else. Now, you can try to twist Fiddler for details all you like—it won't work. The truth as much as cut out his tongue.'

'So what's made you the Magus of Dark? What miserable piss-sour secret you holding back on now, Quick?'

The wizard turned away once more, stared out over the city, and then stiffened. 'Shit, what now?'

The sorcery erupted from an alley mouth, striking Brys Beddict from his left side. The impact sent him sprawling, grey tendrils writhing like serpents about his body. In the span of a single heartbeat, the magic had bound him tight, arms trapped. The coils began constricting.

Lying on his back, staring up at the night sky—that had at last begun to pale—Brys heard footsteps and a moment later the Errant stepped into the range of his vision. The god's single eye gleamed like a star burning through mist.

'I warned you, Brys Beddict. This time, there will be no mistakes. Yes, it was me who nudged you to take that mouthful of poisoned wine—oh, the Chancellor had not anticipated such a thing, but he can be forgiven that. After all, how could I have imagined that you'd found a guardian among Mael's minions?' He paused, and then said, 'No matter. I am done with subtlety—this is much better. I can look into your eyes and watch you die, and what could be more satisfying than that?'

The sorcery tautened, forcing Brys's breath from his lungs. Darkness closed in round his vision until all he could see was the Errant's face, a visage that had lost all grace as avid hunger twisted the features. He watched as the god lifted one hand and slowly clenched the fingers—and the pressure around Brys's chest built until his ribs creaked.

The new fist that arrived hammered like a maul against the side of the Errant's head, snapping it far over. The gleaming eye seemed to wink out and the god crumpled, vanishing from Brys's dwindling vision.

All at once the coils weakened, and then frayed into dissolving threads.

Brys drew a ragged, delicious breath of chill night air.

He heard horse hoofs, a half dozen beasts, maybe more, approaching at a canter from up the street. Blinking sweat from his eyes, Brys rolled on to his stomach and then forced himself to his knees.

A hand closed on his harness and lifted him to his feet.

He found himself staring up at a Tarthenal—a familiar face, the heavy, robust features knotted absurdly into a fierce frown.

'I got a question for you. It was for your brother and I was on my way but then I saw you.'

The riders arrived, horses skidding on the dew-slick cobbles—a Malazan troop, Brys saw, weapons unsheathed. One of them, a dark-skinned woman, pointed with a sword. 'He crawled into that alley—come on, let's chop the bastard into stewing meat!' She made to dismount and then seemed to sag and an instant later she collapsed on to the street, weapon clattering.

Other soldiers dropped down from their mounts. Three of them converged on the unconscious woman, while the others fanned out and advanced into the alley.

Brys was still having difficulty staying upright. He found himself leaning with one forearm against the Tarthenal. 'Ublala Pung,' he sighed, 'thank you.'

'I got a question.'

Brys nodded. 'All right, let's hear it.'

'But that's the problem. I forgot what it was.'

One of the Malazans crowded round the woman now straightened and faced them. 'Sinter said there was trouble,' he said in heavily accented trader tongue. 'Said we needed to hurry—to here, to save someone.'

'I believe,' Brys said, 'the danger has passed. Is she all right, sir?'

'I'm a sergeant—people don't "sir" me . . . sir. She's just done in. Both her and her sister.' He scowled. 'But we'll escort you just the same, sir—she'd never forgive us if something happened to you now. So, wherever you're going . . .'

The other soldiers emerged from the alley, and one said something in Malazan, although Brys needed no translation to understand that they'd found no one—the Errant's survival instincts were ever strong, even when he'd been knocked silly by a Tarthenal's fist.

'It seems,' Brys said, 'I shall have an escort after all.'

'It is not an offer you can refuse, sir,' said the sergeant.

Nor will I. Lesson learned, Adjunct.

The soldiers were attempting to heave the woman named Sinter back into her saddle. Ublala Pung stepped up to them. 'I will carry her,' he said. 'She's pretty.'

'Do as the Toblakai says,' said the sergeant.

'She's pretty,' Ublala Pung said again, as he took her limp form in his arms. 'Pretty smelly, too, but that's okay.'

'Perimeter escort,' snapped the sergeant, 'crossbows cocked. Anybody steps out, nail 'em.'

Brys prayed there would be no early risers between here and the palace. 'Best we hurry,' he ventured.

On a rooftop not far away, Quick Ben sighed and then relaxed.

'What was all that about?' Hedge asked beside him.

'Damned Toblakai . . . but that's not the interesting bit, though, is it? No, it's that Dal Honese woman. Well, that can all wait.'

'You're babbling, wizard.'

Magus of Dark. Gods below.

Alone in the cellar beneath the dormitories, Fiddler stared down at the card in his hand. The lacquered wood glistened, dripped as if slick with sweat. The smell rising from it was of humus, rich and dark, a scent of the raw earth.

'Tartheno Toblakai,' he whispered.

Herald of Life.

Well, just so.

He set it down and then squinted at the second card he had withdrawn to close this dread night. *Unaligned.* Chain. *Aye, we all know about those, my dear. Fret naught, it's the price of living.*

Now, if only you weren't so . . . strong. If only you were weaker. If only your chains didn't reach right into the heart of the Bonehunters—if only I knew who was dragging who, why, I might have reason to hope.

But he didn't, and so there wasn't.

Chapter Four

Behold these joyful devourers
The land laid out skewered in silver
Candlesticks of softest pewter
Rolling the logs down cut on end
To make roads through the forest
That once was—before the logs
(Were rolled down cut on end)—
We called it stump road and we
Called it forest road when
Our imaginations starved
You can make fans with ribs
Of sheep and pouches for baubles
By pounding flat the ears
Of old women and old men—
Older is best for the ear grows
For ever it's said, even when
There's not a scrap anywhere to eat
So we carried our wealth
In pendulum pouches wrinkled
And hairy, diamonds and gems
Enough to buy a forest or a road
But maybe not both
Enough even for slippers of
Supplest skin feathered in down
Like a baby's cheek
There is a secret we know
When nothing else is left
And the sky stops its tears
A belly can bulge full
On diamonds and gems
And a forest can make a road
Through what once was
You just won't find any shade

PENDULUMS WERE ONCE TOYS
BADALLE OF KORBANSE SNAKE

To journey into the other worlds, a shaman or witch of the Elan would ride the Spotted Horse. Seven herbs, softened with beeswax and rolled into a ball and then flattened into an oblong disc that was taken into the mouth and held between lip and gum. Coolness slowly numbing and saliva rising as if the throat was the mouth of a spring, a tingling sensation lifting to gather behind the eyes in coalescing colours and then, in a blinding flash, the veil between worlds vanished. Patterns swirled in the air; complex geometries played across the landscape—a landscape that could be the limitless wall of a hide tent, or the rolling plains of a cave wall where ran the beasts—until the heart-stains emerged, pulsing, blotting the scene in undulating rows, sweet as waves and tasting of mother's milk.

So arrived the Spotted Horse, a cascade of heart-stains rippling across the beast, down its long neck, sweeping along its withers, flowing like seed-heads from its mane and tail.

Ride into the alien world. Ride among the ancestors and the not-yet-born, among the tall men with their eternally swollen members, the women with their forever-filled wombs. Through forests of black threads, the touch or brush of any one of them an invitation to endless torment, for this was the path of return for all life, and to be born was to pass through and find the soul's fated thread—the tale of a future death that could not be escaped. To ride the other way, however, demanded a supple traverse, evading such threads, lest one's own birth-fate become entangled, knotted, and so doom the soul to eternal prison, snared within the web of conflicted fates.

Prophecies could be found among the black threads, but the world beyond that forest was the greatest gift. Timeless, home to all the souls that ever existed; this was where grief was shed, where sorrow dried up and blew away like dust, where scars vanished. To journey into this realm was to be cleansed, made whole, purged of all regrets and dark desires.

Riding the Spotted Horse and then returning was to be reborn, guiltless, guileless.

Kalyth knew all this, but only second-hand. The riders among her people passed on the truths, generation upon generation. Any one of the seven herbs, if taken alone, would kill. The seven mixed in wrong proportions delivered madness. And, finally, only those chosen as worthy by the shamans and witches would ever know the gift of the journey.

For one such as Kalyth, mired in the necessary mediocrity so vital to the maintenance of family, village and the Elan way of living, to take upon herself such a ritual—to even so much as taste the seven herbs—was a sentence to death and damnation.

Of course, the Elan were gone. No more shamans or witches to be found. No families, no villages, no clans, no herds—every ring of tipi stones, spanning the rises tucked at the foot of yet higher hilltops, now marked the motionless remnant of a final camp, a camp never to be returned to, the stones destined to sink slowly where they lay, the lichen on their undersides dying, the grasses so indifferently crushed beneath them turning white as bone. Such boulder rings were now maps of extinction and death. They held no promises, only the sorrow of endings.

She had suffered her own damnation, one devoid of any crime, any real culpability beyond her cowardly flight: her appalling abandonment of her family. There had been no shamans left to utter the curse, but that hardly mattered, did it?

She sat, as the sun withered in the west and the grasses surrounding her grew wiry and grey, staring down at the disc lying in the palm of her hand.

Elan magic. As foreign to her world now as the Che'Malle machines in Ampelas Rooted had been when she'd first set eyes upon them. To ride the Spotted Horse through the ashes of her people invited . . . what? She did not know, could not know. Would she find the spirits of her kin—would they truly look upon her with love and forgiveness? Was this her secret desire? Not a quest into the realms of prophecy seeking hidden knowledge; not searching for a Mortal Sword and a Shield Anvil for the K'Chain Che'Malle?

Dire confusion—her motivations were suspect—*hah, rotted through and through!*

And might there not be another kind of salvation she was seeking here? The invitation into madness, into death itself? Possibly.

'Beware the leader who has nothing to lose.'

Her people were proud of their wise sayings. And yet now, in their mortal silence, wisdom and pride proved a perfect match in value. Namely: worthless.

The Che'Malle were camped—if one could call it that—behind the rise at her back. They had built a fire inviting Kalyth's comfort, but this night she was not interested in comfort.

The Shi'gal Assassin still circled high in the darkening sky above them—their nightly sentinel who never tired and never spoke and yet was known to all (she suspected) as their potential slayer, should they fail. Blessings of the spirits, that was a ghastly creature, a demon to beggar her worst nightmares. Oh, how it sailed the night winds, a cold-eyed raptor, a conjuration of singular purpose.

Kalyth shivered. Then, squeezing shut her eyes as the sun's sickle of fire dipped below the horizon, she slid the disc into her mouth.

Stinging like a snake's bite, and then numbness, spreading, spreading . . .

'Never trust a leader who has nothing to lose.'

At these muttered words from the human female, drifting over the hummock down to where stood the K'Chain Che'Malle, the K'ell Hunter Sag'Churok swung round his massive, scarred head. Over his eyes, three distinct lids blinked in succession, reawakening the camp's reflected firelight in a wet gleam. The Matron's daughter, Gunth Mach, seemed to flinch, but she remained closed to Sag'Churok's tentative query.

The other two K'ell Hunters, indifferent to anything the human might say, were half-crouched and facing away from the ring of stones that surrounded a half-dozen bricks of burning bhederin dung, away from the flames that could steal their night vision. The enormous cutlasses at the ends of their wrists rested point-down, their arms stretched out to the sides. By nature, K'ell disliked such menial tasks as sentry duty. They existed to pursue quarry, after all. But the Matron had elected to send them out without J'an Sentinels; further proof that in keeping all her guardians close, Gunth'an Acyl feared for her own life.

Senior among these K'ell, Sag'Churok was Gunth Mach's protector, and should the time come when the Destriant found a Mortal Sword and a Shield Anvil, then he would also assume the task of escorting them on the return to Acyl Nest.

Errors in judgement plagued Ampelas Rooted. A flawed Matron produced flawed spawn. This was a known truth. It was not a thing that could be defeated or circumvented. The spawn must follow. Even so, Sag'Churok knew an abiding sense of failure, a dull, persistent anguish.

Beware the leader . . .

Yes. The one they had chosen, known as Redmask, had proved as flawed as any K'Chain Che'Malle of the Hive, and the cruel logic of that still stung. Perhaps the Matron was correct in electing a human to undertake the search this time.

Visions bound with intent whispered through Sag'Churok. The Shi'gal Assassin, wheeling in the darkness far above them, had thrust a sending into the brain of the K'ell Hunter. Cold, rough-skinned, careless of the pain the sending delivered—indeed, it was of such power that Gunth Mach's head snapped up, eyes fixing on Sag'Churok as ripples overflowed to brush her senses.

Intruders in vast herd, countless fires.

'*Perhaps, then, among these ones?*' Sag'Churok sent in return.

The one who leads is not for us.

A bestial scent followed that statement, one that Sag'Churok recognized. Glands awakened beneath the heavy armoured scales along the K'ell's spine, the first of the instinctive preparations for hunting, for battle, and as those scales seemed to lift and float on the thickening layer of oil, the innermost lids closed over his eyes, rising from below to entirely sheathe his vision. Boulders on a distant hill suddenly glowed, still bearing the heat of the sun. Small creatures moved in the grasses, revealed by their breaths, their rapidly beating hearts.

K'ell Rythok and Kor Thuran both caught the bitter signature of the oil, and they straightened from their crouches, swinging free their swords.

A final thought reached Sag'Churok. *Too many to slay. Best avoid.*

'*How do we avoid, Shi'gal Gu'Rull? Do they bestride our chosen path?*'

But the Assassin did not deem such questions worth an answer, and Sag'Churok felt the Shi'gal's contempt.

Gunth Mach sent her guardian a private thought. *He wishes that we fail.*

'*If he so hungers to slay, then why not these strangers?*'

It is not for me to say, she replied. *Gu'Rull spoke not to me, after all, but to you. He would admit to nothing, but he holds you in respect. You have Hunted and like me you have borne wounds and tasted your own blood and in that taste we both saw our mortality. This, Gu'Rull shares with you, while Rythok and Kor Thuran do not.*

'*And yet in his careless power his thoughts leak to you—*'

Does he know of my growth? I think not. Only you know the truth, Sag'Churok. To all others I reveal nothing. They believe me still little more than a drone, a promise, a possibility. I am close, first love, so very close.

Yes, he had known, or thought he had. Now, shock threatened to reveal itself and the K'ell struggled to contain it. *'Gunth'an Acyl?'*

She cannot see past her suffering.

Sag'Churok was not certain of that, but he sent nothing. It was not for him to counsel Gunth Mach, after all. Also, the notion that the Shi'gal Assassin sought to share anything with him was troubling. The taste of mortality was the birth of weakness, after all.

Rythok addressed him suddenly, gruffly pushing through his inner turmoil. *'You waken to threat, yet we sense nothing. Even so, should we not quench this useless fire?'*

Yes, Rythok. The Destriant sleeps and we have no need.

'Do you hunt?'

No. But we are not alone in this land—human herds move to the south.

'Is this not what Acyl desires? Is this not what the Destriant must find?'

Not these ones, Rythok. Yet, we shall pass through this herd . . . you will, I think, taste your own blood soon. You and Kor Thuran. Prepare yourselves.

And, with faint dismay, Sag'Churok saw that they were pleased.

The air thickened, clear as the humour of an eye, and all that Kalyth could see through it shimmered and shifted, swam and blurred. The sweep of stars flowed in discordant motion; the grasses of the undulating hills wavered, as if startled by wayward winds. Motes of detritus drifted about, shapeless and faintly pulsing crimson, some descending to roll across the ground, others wandering skyward as if on rising currents.

Every place held every memory of what it had once been. A plain that had been the bottom of a lake, the floor of a shallow sea, the lightless depths of a vast ocean. A hill that had been the peak of a young mountain, one of a chain of islands, the jagged fang of the earth buried in glacial ice. Dust that had been plants, sand that had been stone, stains that had been bone and flesh. Most memories, Kalyth understood, remain hidden, unseen and beneath the regard of flickering life. Yet, once the eyes were awakened, every memory was then unveiled, a fragment here, a hint there, a host of truths whispering of eternity.

Such knowledge could crush a soul with its immensity, or drown it beneath a deluge of unbearable futility. As soon as the distinction was made, that separation of self from all the rest, from the entire world beyond—its ceaseless measure of time, its whimsical game with change played out in slow siege and in sudden catastrophe—then the self became an orphan, bereft of all security, and face to face with a world now become at best a stranger, at worst an implacable, heartless foe.

In arrogance we orphan ourselves, and then rail at the awful solitude we find on the road to death.

But how could one step back into the world? How could one learn to swim such currents? In self-proclamation, the soul decided what it was that lay within in opposition to all that lay beyond. Inside, outside, familiar, strange, that which is possessed, that which is coveted, all that is within grasp and all that is forever beyond reach. The distinction was a deep, vicious cut of a knife, severing tendons and muscles, arteries and nerves.

A knife?

No, that was the wrong weapon, a pathetic construct from her limited imagination. Indeed, the force that divided was something . . . other.

It was, she now believed, maybe even alive.

The multilayered vista before her was suddenly transformed. Grasses withered and blew away. High dunes of sand humped the horizon, and in a basin just ahead of her she saw a figure, its back to her as it knelt in the hard-edged shadow of a monolith of some sort. The stone—if that was what it was—was patinated with rust, the mottled stains looking raw, almost fresh against the green-black rock.

She found herself drawing closer. The figure was not simply kneeling in worship or obeisance, she realized. It was digging, hands thrust deep into the sands, almost up to the elbows.

He was an old man, his skin blue-black. Bald, the skin covering the skull scarred. If he heard her approaching, he gave no sign.

Was this some moment of the past? Millennia unfolding as all those layers fleeted away? Was she now witness to a memory of the Wastelands?

The monolith, Kalyth suddenly comprehended, was carved in the likeness of a finger. And the stone that she had first seen as green and black was growing translucent, serpentine green, revealing inner flaws and facets. She saw seams like veins of deep emerald, and masses that might be bone, the colour of true jade, deep within the edifice.

The old man—whose skin was not blue and black as she had first believed, but so thickly tattooed in swirling fur that nothing of its natural tone remained—now spoke, though he did not cease thrusting his hands into the sand at the base of the monolith. 'There is a tribe in the Sanimon,' he said, 'that claims it was the first to master the forging of iron. They still make tools and weapons in the traditional manner—quenching blades in sand, just as I'm doing right now, do you see?'

Though she did not know his language, she understood him, and at his question she squinted once more at his arms—if his hands gripped weapons, then he had pushed them deep into the sands indeed.

Yet she saw no forge—not even a firepit—anywhere in sight.

'I do not think,' the man continued, gasping every now and then, as if in pain, 'I do not think, however, that I have it exactly right. There must be some other secrets involved. Quenching in water or manure piles—I have no experience in such things.' He paused. 'At least, I don't think I do. So much . . . forgotten.'

'You are not Elan,' Kalyth said.

He smiled at her words, although instead of looking at her he fixed his gaze on the monolith. 'But here is a thing,' he said. 'I can name, oh, a hundred different tribes. Seven Cities tribes, Quon Talian tribes, Korel tribes, Genabackan—and they all share one thing and one thing only and do you know what that is?'

He waited, as if he had addressed the monolith rather than Kalyth, who stood beside him, close enough to reach out and touch. 'I will tell you,' he then said. 'Every one of them is or is about to be extinct. Melted away, in the fashion of all peoples, eventually. Sometimes some semblance of their blood lives on, finds new homes, watered down, forgetful. Or they're nothing but dust, even their names gone, for ever gone. No one to mourn the loss . . . and all that.'

'I am the last Elan,' she told him.

He resumed pushing his hands deep into the sand, as deep as he could manage. 'I am readying myself . . . to wield a most formidable weapon. They thought to hide it from me. They failed. Weapons must be tempered and tempered well, of course. They even thought to kill it. As if such a thing is remotely possible'—he paused—'then again, perhaps it is. The key to everything, you see, is to cut clean, down the middle. A clean cut—that's what I dream of.'

'I dream of . . . this,' she said. 'I have ridden the Spotted Horse. I have found you in the realms beyond—why? Have you summoned me? What am I to you? What are you to me?'

He laughed. 'Now that amuses me! I see where you're pointing—you think I don't? You think I am blind to this, too?'

'I ride the—'

'Oh, enough of that! You took something. That's how you get here, that's how everyone gets here. Or they dance and dance until they fall into and out from their bodies. Whatever you took just eased you back into the rhythm that exists in all things—the pulse of the universe, if you like. With enough discipline you don't need to take anything at all—which is a good thing, since after ten or twenty years of eating herbs or whatever, most shamans are inured to their effects anyway. So the ingesting serves only as ritual, as permission to journey.' He suddenly halted all motions. 'Spotted Horse . . . yes, visual hallucinations, patterns floating in front of the eyes. The Bivik called it Wound Drumming—like blossoming blood-stains, I suppose they meant. *Thump thump thump* . . . And the Fenn—'

'The Matron looks to our kind,' she cut in. 'The old ways have failed.'

'The old ways ever fail,' the old man said. 'So too the new ways, more often than not.'

'She is desperate—'

'Desperation delivers poison counsel.'

'*Have you nothing worthwhile to tell me?*'

'The secret lies in the tempering,' he said. 'That is a worthwhile thing to tell you. Your weapon must be well tempered. Soundly forged, ingeniously annealed, the edges honed with surety. The finger points straight towards them, you see— well, if this were a proper sky, you'd see.' His broad face split in a smile that was more a grimace than a signature of pleasure—and she thought that, despite his words suggesting otherwise, he might be blind.

'It is a flaw,' he continued, 'to view mortals and gods as if they were on opposite sides. A flaw. An error most fundamental. Because then, when the blade comes down, why, they are for ever lost to each other. Now, does she understand? Possibly, but if so, then she terrifies me—for such wisdom seems almost . . . inhuman.' He shook himself and leaned back, withdrawing his arms from the sand.

She stared, curious and wondering at the weapons he held—only to find he held none. And that his hands, the hue of rust, gleamed as if polished.

He held them up. 'Expected green, did you? Green jade, yes, and glowing. But not this time, not for this, oh no. Are they ready? Ready to grasp that most deadly weapon? I think not.'

And down went those hands, plunging into the sands once more.

A foot troop of human scouts, ranging well north of the main herd, had caught sight of the lone campfire. They now moved towards it—even as the distant flickering flames winked out—and, spreading out into a crescent formation, they displayed great skill in stealth, moving virtually unseen across the plain.

One of the scouts, white-painted face covered in dark cloth, came near a motionless hare and the creature sensed nothing of the warrior edging past, no more than five paces away.

Few plains were truly flat or featureless. Dips and rises flowed on all sides; stretches tilted and in so doing mocked all sense of distance and perspective; burrow mounds hid beneath tufts of grass; gullies ran in narrow, treacherous channels that one could not see until one stumbled into them. To move unseen across this landscape was to travel as did the four-legged hunters and prey, from scant cover to scant cover, in fits and starts, eloquent as shadows. Even so, the Wastelands were aptly named, for much of the natural plain had been scoured away, and spans of little more than broken rock and windblown sand challenged any measure of skill.

Despite such restrictions, these scouts, eighteen in number, betrayed not a breath as they closed in on where that campfire had been. Although all bore weapons—javelins and odd single-edged cutlasses—the former remained slung across their broad backs, while the swords were strapped tight, bound and muffled at their sides.

Clearly, then, curiosity drove them to seek out the lone camp, to discover with whom they shared this land.

Two thousand paces and closing, the scouts slipped into a broad basin, and all that lit them now was the pale jade glow of the mysterious travellers in the night sky.

The crescent formation slowly inverted, the central scout moving ahead to form its apex. When the troop reached a certain distance, the lead scout would venture closer on his own.

Gu'Rull stood awaiting him. The towering K'Chain Che'Malle should have been clearly visible, but not a single human saw him. When it was time to kill, the Shi'gal Assassin could cloud the minds of his victims, although this was generally only effective while such targets were unsuspecting; and against other

Shi'gal, J'an Sentinels and senior Ve'Gath Soldiers, no such confusion was possible.

These humans, of course, were feeble, and for all their stealth, the heat of their bodies made them blaze like beacons in Gu'Rull's eyes.

The lead scout padded directly towards the Assassin, who waited, wings folded and retracted. The hinged claws on his narrow, long fingers slowly emerged from their membrane sheaths, slick with neural venom—although in the case of these soft-skinned humans, poison was not necessary.

When the warrior came into range, Gu'Rull saw the man hesitate—as if some instinct had awakened within him—but it was too late. The Assassin lashed out one hand. Claws sliced into the man's head from one side, through flesh and bone, and the strength of the blow half tore the scout's head from his neck.

Long before the first victim fell, Gu'Rull was on the move, an arching scythe of night rushing to the next warrior. Claws plunged into the man's midsection, hooked beneath the rib cage, and the assassin lifted him from his feet and then flung the flailing, blood-spewing body away.

Daggers flashed in the air as the rest of the scouts converged. Two of the thrown weapons struck Gu'Rull, both skidding off his thick, sleek scales. Javelins were readied, poised for the throw—but the Shi'gal was already amongst them, batting aside panicked thrusts, claws raking through bodies, head snapping out on its long neck, jaws crushing skulls, chests, biting through shoulders. Blood spattered like sleet on the rough, stony ground, and burst in dark mists in the wake of the Assassin's deadly blows.

Two scouts pulled back, sought to flee, and for the moment Gu'Rull let them go, occupied as he was with the last warriors surrounding him. He understood that they were not cowards—the two now running as fast as they could southward, each choosing his own path—no, they sought to bring word of the slaughter, the new foe, to the ruler of the herd.

This was unacceptable, of course.

Moments later and the Assassin stood alone, tail lashing, hands shedding long threads of blood. He drew a breath into his shallow lungs, and then into his deep lungs, restoring strength and vigour to his muscles.

He unfolded his wings.

The last two needed to die.

Gu'Rull launched himself into the air, wings flapping, feather-scales whistling a droning dirge.

Once aloft, the bright forms of the two scouts shone like pyres on the dark plain. While, in the Assassin's wake as he swept towards the nearer of the two, sixteen corpses slowly cooled, dimming like fading embers from a scattered hearth.

Sag'Churok could smell blood in the air. He heard, as well, the frustrated snorts from the two unblooded Hunters who stood, limbs quivering with the sweet flood of the Nectar of Slaying that now coursed through their veins and arteries, their tails lashing the air. They had indeed lost control of their fight glands, a sign of their inexperience, their raw youth, and Sag'Churok was both amused and disgusted.

Although, in truth, he himself struggled against unleashing the full flow of the nectar, forcing open his sleep glands to counteract the ferocious fires within.

The Shi'gal had hunted this night, and in so doing, he had mocked the K'ell, stealing their glory, denying them the pleasure they sought, the pleasure they had been born to pursue.

Come the dawn, Sag'Churok would lead the Seeking well away from that scene of slaughter. Destriant Kalyth need not know anything of it—the frame of her mind was weak enough as it was. The Seeking would work eastward, further out into the wastes, where no food could be found for the strangers. Of course, this caution would likely fail, if the herd was as vast as Gu'Rull had intimated.

And so Sag'Churok knew that his fellow Hunters would find their blood before too long.

They hissed and snorted, quivered and yawned with their jaws. The heavy blades thumped and grated over the ground.

It did not occur to Gu'Rull that the scores upon scores of dogs plaguing the human herd were anything but scavengers, such as the beasts that had once tracked the K'Chain Che'Malle Furies in times of war. And so the Assassin paid no attention whatsoever to the six beasts that had moved parallel to the scouts, and had made no effort to cloud their senses. And even as these beasts now fled south, clearly making for the human herd, Gu'Rull attributed no special significance to their peregrinations. Scavengers were commonplace, their needs singular and far from complex.

The Assassin killed the scouts, both times descending from above, tearing their heads from their shoulders when they each halted upon hearing the moan of Gu'Rull's wings. Task completed, the Shi'gal rose high into the dark sky, seeking the strong flows of air that he would ride through the course of the day to come— air cold enough to keep him from overheating, for he had discovered that during the day his wings, when fully outstretched, absorbed vast amounts of heat, which in turn strained his equanimity and naturally calm repose.

And that would not do.

Kalyth watched the scene before her fragment and then vanish as if blown away in a gust of wind she could not feel. The old man, the monolith, his polished hands and all his words—they had been a distraction, proof of her ignorance that she had so easily been snared by something—and someone—not meant for her.

But it seemed that willpower alone was not enough, particularly when she had no real destination in mind—she had but mentally reached out for a notion, a vague feeling of the familiar—was it any wonder she stumbled about, aimless, lost, pathetically vulnerable?

Faintly, as if from the ether, she heard the old man say, 'It ever appears dead, spiked so cruelly and no, you will see no motion, not a twitch. Even the blood does not drip. Do not be deceived. She will be freed. She must. It is necessary.'

She thought he might have said something more, but his voice dwindled, and the landscape before her found a new shape. Wreckage or pyres burned across an unnaturally flat plain. Smoke rolled black and hot, stinging her eyes. She could make no sense of what she saw; the horizons seethed, as if armies contended on all sides but nowhere close.

Heavy shadows scudded over the littered ground and she looked up, but beyond the columns of smoke rising from the pyres, the sky was empty, colourless. Something about those untethered shadows frightened Kalyth, the way they seemed to be converging, gathering speed, and she could feel herself drawn after them, swept into their wake.

It seemed then that she truly left her body behind, and now sailed on the same currents, casting her own paltry, shapeless shadow, and she saw that the wreckage looked familiar—not pyres as such, after all, but crushed and twisted pieces of the kinds of mechanism she had seen in Ampelas Rooted. Her unease deepened. Was this a vision of the future? Or some frayed remnant of the distant past? She suspected that the K'Chain Che'Malle had fought vast wars centuries ago, yet she also knew that a new war was coming.

The horizon drew closer, at a point where the massive shadows seemed destined to converge. Its seething edge was indeed armies locked in battle, yet she could make out little detail. Humans? K'Chain Che'Malle? She could not tell, and even as she swept towards them, they grew indistinct, as if swallowed in dust.

There would be nothing easy in any of this, Kalyth realized. No gifts delivered with simple clarity, with unambiguous meaning. She floundered in sudden panic, trying to pull herself back as the shadows swarmed to a single point, only to vanish, as if plunging through a gate—she did not want to follow. She wanted none of this.

Twin suns blazed to life, blinding her. Searing heat washed over her, building, and she screamed as she withered in the firestorm—but it was too late—

She awoke lying on the damp grasses, lids fluttering open, to find herself staring up at a paling sky. Dull motes still drifted across her vision, but she could feel their loss of strength. Kalyth had returned, no wiser, no surer of the path ahead.

Groaning, she rolled on to her side, and then to her hands and knees. Every bone in her body ached; twinges speared every muscle, and she shivered, chilled right down to the roots of her soul. Lifting her head, she saw that Sag'Churok stood beside her, the Hunter's terrible eyes fixed on her as if contemplating a hare trapped under his talons.

She looked away and then climbed to her feet. The thin odour of dung smoke reached her and she turned to see Gunth Mach hunkered down before the campfire, her huge hands deftly turning skewers of dripping meat.

The damned creatures had been obsessed with meat from the moment they departed the Nest—on this journey she'd yet to see them unwrap a single root crop or lump of bread (or what passed for bread, for although on the tongue it possessed the consistency of a fresh mushroom, she had seen loaves in countless shapes and sizes). Meat to break the night's fast, meat at the mid-morning rest stop, meat whilst on the move at afternoon's waning, and meat at the final meal well after the sun's setting. She suspected that, if not for her, it would have been eaten raw. The Wastelands offered little else, she had discovered—even the grasses, berries and tubers that had once been common on the plains of the Elan were entirely absent here.

Feeling miserable, and terribly alone, she went over to collect her breakfast.

Stavi looked to her sister and saw, as ever, her own face, although the expression was never a match to her own. Twins they might be, but they were also two sides of a coin, and took turns in what they offered to the world. Hetan knew as much, and had observed more than once how, when one of her first daughters set eyes upon the other, there grew a look of surprise and something like guilt in the child's face—as if in seeing an unexpected attitude displayed in her other self, she had perhaps ambushed her own innermost feelings.

Not surprisingly, Stavi and Storii were in the habit of avoiding one another's regard, as much as was possible, as if neither welcomed that flash of confusion. They much preferred to sow confusion in everyone else, particularly, Hetan noted yet again, their adopted father.

Although not within hearing range of the conversation, Hetan could well see how it was proceeding. The girls had stalked the poor man, wicked as a pair of hunting cats, and whatever it was that they wanted from him, they would get. Without fail.

Or so it would be, each and every time, if not for their cruel and clever mother, who, when she took it upon herself, could stride into the midst of the ambush and, with a bare word or gesture, send the two little witches scampering. Knowing this, of course, at least one of the twins would have her attention fixed on Hetan's location, measuring distances and the intensity of their mother's attention. Hetan knew that, should she so much as turn towards them, the girls would break off the wheedling, crassly manipulative assault on their father, and, flicking dark, sharp glares her way, scuttle off in the manner of frustrated evil imps the world over.

Oh, they could be lovable enough, when it suited them, and, in sly gift from their true father, both possessed a natural talent for conveying innocence, so pure and so absolute it verged on the autistic, guaranteed to produce nausea in their mother, and other mothers besides. Why, Hetan had seen great-aunts—normally indulgent as befitted their remote roles—narrow their gazes when witnessing the display.

Of course, it was no easy thing to measure evil, or even to be certain that the assignation was appropriate. Was it not a woman's gift to excel in the entirely essential guidance of every aspect of her chosen man's life? It most certainly was. Accordingly, Hetan pitied the future husbands of Storii and Stavi. At the same time, however, she was not about to see her own man savaged by the two creatures. The issue was down to simple possession. And the older the twins grew, the more brazen their efforts at stealing him away from her.

Yes, she understood all of this. It was not anything direct, or even conscious on the part of the girls. They were simply trying out their skills at capturing, rending and devouring. And it was also natural that they would decide upon their own mother as competition. There were times, Hetan reflected, when she wished she could track down their distant, wayward and diabolical father, and thrust both rotters on to his plump lap—yes, Kruppe of Darujhistan was indeed welcome to his inadvertent get.

Alas, she could well see that the man who now stood in Kruppe's stead would not have accepted such a gesture, no matter how just Hetan might deem it. Such were the myriad miseries of parenthood. And her bad luck in choosing an honourable mate.

He was vulnerable, apt to descend into indulgence, and the twins knew it and like piranhas they had closed in. It wasn't that Stavi and Storii were uniquely insensitive—like all girls of their age, they just didn't care. They wanted whatever they wanted and would do whatever was necessary to get it.

Long before their coming of age, of course, tribal life among the White Face Barghast would beat that out of them, or at least repress its more vicious impulses, all of which were necessary to a proper life.

Storii was the first to note Hetan's approach, and the dark intent in her mother's eyes was reflected in a sudden flash of terror and malice in the girl's sweet, rounded face. She flicked her fingertips against her sister's shoulder and Stavi flinched at the stinging snap and then caught sight of Hetan. In a heartbeat the twins were in full flight, bounding away like a pair of stoats, and their adopted father stared after them in surprise.

Hetan arrived. 'Beloved, you have all the wit of a bhederin when it comes to those two.'

Onos Toolan blinked at her, and then he sighed. 'I am afraid I was frustrating them nonetheless. It is difficult to concentrate—they speak too fast, so breathless—I lose all sense of what they mean, or want.'

'You can be certain that whatever it was, its function was to spoil them yet further. But I have broken their siege, Tool, to tell you that the clan chiefs are assembling—well, those who managed to heed the summons.' She hesitated. 'They are troubled, husband.'

Even this did little to penetrate the sorrow that he had folded round him since the brutal death of Toc the Younger. 'How many clans sent no one?' he asked.

'Almost a third.'

He frowned at that, but said nothing.

'Mostly from the southern extremes,' Hetan said. 'That is why those here are now saying that they must have mutinied—lost their way, their will. That they have broken up and wandered into the kingdoms, the warriors hiring on as bodyguards and such to the Saphin and the Bolkando.'

'You said "mostly", Hetan. What of the others?'

'All outlying clans, those who travelled farthest in the dispersal—except for one. Gadra, which had found a decent bhederin herd in a pocket between the Akryn and the Awl'dan, enough to sustain them for a time—'

'The Gadra warchief—Stolmen, yes? I sensed no disloyalty in him. Also, what chance of mutiny in that region? They would have nowhere to go—that makes no sense.'

'You are right, it doesn't. We should have heard from them. You must speak to the clan chiefs, Tool. They need to be reminded why we are here.' She studied his soft brown eyes for a moment, and then looked away. The crisis, she knew, dwelt not just in the minds of the Barghast clan chiefs, but also in the man standing beside her. Her husband, her love.

'I do not know,' said Tool, slowly, as if searching for the right words, 'if I can help them. The shoulder-seers were bold in their first prophecies, igniting the fires that have brought us here, but with each passing day it seems their tongues wither yet more, their words dry up, and all I can see in them is the fear in their eyes.'

She took him by the arm and tugged until he followed her out from the edge of the vast encampment. They walked beyond the pickets and then the ring-trench dry-latrines, and still further, on to the hard uneven ground where the herds had tracked not so long ago, in the season of rains.

'We were meant to wage war against the Tiste Edur,' Tool said as they drew up atop a ridge and stared northward at distant dust-clouds. 'The shoulder-seers rushed their rituals in finding pathways through the warrens. The entire White Face Barghast impoverished itself to purchase transports and grain. We hurried after the Grey Swords.' He was silent for a moment longer, and then he said, 'We sought the wrong enemy.'

'No glory to be found in crushing a crushed people,' Hetan observed, tasting the bitterness of her own words.

'Nor a people terrorized by one of their own.'

There had been fierce clashes over this. Despite his ascension to Warchief, a unanimous proclamation following the tragic death of her father, Onos Toolan had almost immediately found himself at odds with all the clan chiefs. War against the Lether Empire would be an unjust war, the Edur hegemony notwithstanding. Not only were the Letherii not their enemy, even these Tiste Edur, crouching in the terrible shadow of their emperor, likely bore no relationship whatsoever to those ancient Edur who had preyed upon the Barghast so many generations past. The entire notion of vengeance, or that of a war resumed, suddenly tasted sour, and for Tool, an Imass who felt nothing of the old festering wounds in the psyche of the Barghast—who was indeed deaf to the fury of the awakened Barghast gods . . . well, he'd shown no patience with those so eager to shed blood.

The shoulder-seers had by this time lost all unity of vision. The prophecy, which had seemed so simple and clear, was all at once mired in ambiguity, seeding such discord among the seers that even their putative leader, Cafal, brother to Hetan, failed in his efforts to quell the schisms among the shamans. Thus, they had been no help in the battle of wills between Tool and the chiefs; and they were no help now.

Cafal persisted in travelling from tribe to tribe—she had not seen her brother in months. If he had succeeded in repairing any damage, she'd not heard of it; even among the shoulder-seers in this camp, she sensed a pervasive unease, and a sour reluctance to speak with anyone.

Onos Toolan had been unwilling to unleash the White Faces upon the Lether Empire—and his will had prevailed, until that one fated day, when the last of the Awl fell—when Toc the Younger had died. Not only had Hetan's own clan, the Senan, been unleashed, so too had the dark hunger of Tool's own sister, Kilava.

Hetan missed that woman, and knew that her husband's grief was complicated by her departure—a departure that he might well see as her abandoning him in the moment of his greatest need. Hetan suspected, however, that in witnessing Toc's death—and the effect it had had upon her brother, Kilava had been brutally reminded of the ephemeral nature of love and friendship—and so she had set out to rediscover her own life. A selfish impulse, perhaps, and an unfair wounding of a brother already reeling from loss.

Yes, Kilava deserved a good hard slap to the side of that shapely head, and Hetan vowed that she would be the one to deliver it, when next they met.

'I see no enemy,' her husband said now.

She nodded. Yes, this was the crisis afflicting her people, and so they looked to their Warchief. In need of a direction, a purpose. Yet he gave them nothing. 'We have too many young warriors,' she said. 'Trained in the ancient ways of fighting, eager to see their swords drink blood—slaughtering a half-broken, exhausted Letherii army did little to whet the appetites of those in our own clan—yet it was enough to ignite envy and feuding with virtually everyone else.'

'Things were simpler among the Imass,' said Tool.

'Oh, rubbish!'

He shot her a glare, and then looked away once more, shoulders slumping. 'Well, we had purpose.'

'You had a ridiculous war against a foe that had no real desire to fight you. And so, instead of facing the injustice you were committing, you went and invoked the Ritual of Tellann. Clever evasion, I suppose, if rather *insane*. What's so frightening about facing your own mistakes?'

'Dear wife, you should not ask that question.'

'Why not?'

He met her eyes again, not with anger this time, but bleak despair. 'You may find that mistakes are all you have.'

She grew very still, chilled despite the burgeoning heat of the morning. 'Oh, and for you, does that include me?'

'No, I speak to help you understand an Imass who was once a T'lan.' He hesitated, and then said, 'With you, with our children, I had grown to believe that such things were at last behind me—those dread errors and the burden of all they yielded. And then, in an instant . . . I am reminded of my own stupidity. It does no good to ignore one's own flaws, Hetan. The delusion comforts, but it can prove fatal.'

'You're not dead.'

'Am I not?'

She snorted and turned away. 'You're just as bad as your sister!' Then wheeled back to him. 'Wake up! Your twenty-seven clans are down to nineteen—how many more will you lose because you can't be bothered to make a decision?'

His eyes narrowed on her. 'What would you have me decide?' he asked quietly.

'We are White Face Barghast! *Find us an enemy!*'

The privilege of being so close to home was proving too painful, even as Torrent—the last warrior of the Awl—sought to exult in the anguish. Punishment for surviving, for persisting, like one last drop of blood refusing to soak into the red mud; he did not know what held him upright, breathing, heart pounding on and on, thoughts clawing through endless curtains of dust. Somewhere, deep inside, he prayed he would find his single, pure truth, squeezed down into a knucklebone, polished by all the senseless winds, the pointless rains, the spiralling collapse of season upon season. A little knot of something like bone, to stumble over, to roll across, to send him sprawling.

He might find it, but he suspected not. He did not possess the wit. He was not sharp in the way of Toc Anaster, the Mezla who haunted his dreams. Thundering hoofs, a storm-wracked night sky, winds howling like wolves, and the dead warrior's single eye fixed like an opal in its shadowed socket. A face horrifying in its red, glistening ruin—the skin cut away, smeared teeth exposed in a feral grin—oh, perhaps indeed the Mezla rode into Torrent's dreams, a harbinger of nightmares, a mocker of his precious, fragile truth. One thing seemed clear—the dead archer was *hunting* Torrent, fired by hatred for the last Awl warrior, and the pursuit was relentless, Torrent's steps dragging even as he ran for his life, gasping, shrieking—until with a start he would awaken, sheathed in sweat and shivering.

It seemed that Toc Anaster was in no hurry to bring the hunt to its grisly conclusion. The ghost's pleasure was in the chase. Night after night after night.

The Awl warrior no longer wore a copper mask. The irritating rash that had mottled his face was now gone. He had elected to deliver himself and the children into the care of the Gadra clan, camped as they were at the very edge of the Awl'dan. He had not wished to witness the devastating grief of the strange warrior named Tool, over Toc Anaster's death.

Shortly after joining the clan, and with the fading of his rash, Gadra women had taken an interest in him, and they were not coy, displaying a boldness that almost frightened Torrent—he had fled a woman's advance more than once—but of late the dozen or so intent on stalking and trapping him had begun cooperating with one another.

And so he took to his horse, riding hard out from the camp, spending the entire span of the sun's arc well away from their predations. Red-eyed with exhaustion, miserable in his solitude, and at war with himself. He had never lain with a woman, after all. He had no idea what it involved, beyond those shocking childhood memories of seeing, through the open doorways of huts, adults clamped round one another grunting and moaning and sighing. But they had been Awl—

not these savage, terrifying Barghast who coupled with shouts and barks of laughter, the men bellowing like bears and the women clawing and scratching and biting.

No, none of it made any sense. For, even as he endeavoured to escape these mad women with their painted faces and bright eyes, he wanted what they offered. He fled his own desire, and each time he did so the torture he inflicted upon himself stung all the worse.

Such misery as no man deserves!

He should have rejoiced in his freedom, here on the vast plains so close to the Awl'dan. To see the herds of bhederin—which his own people had never thought to tame—and the scattering of rodara, too, that the surviving children of the Awl now cared for—and to know that the cursed Letherii were not hunting them, not slaughtering them . . . he should be exulting in the moment.

Was he not alive? Safe? And was he not the Clan Leader of the Awl? Undisputed ruler of a vast tribe of a few score children, some of whom had already forgotten their own language, and now spoke the barbaric foreign tongue of the Barghast, and had taken to painting their bodies with red and yellow ochre and braiding their hair?

He rode his horse at a slow canter, already two or more leagues from the Gadra encampment. The herds had swung round to the southeast the night before, so he had seen no one on his journey out. When he first caught sight of the Barghast dogs, he thought they might be wolves, but upon seeing Torrent they altered their route straight towards him—something no pack of wolves would do—and as they drew closer he could see their short-haired, mottled hides, their shortened muzzles and small ears. Larger than any Awl or Letherii breed, the beasts were singularly savage. Until this moment, they had ignored Torrent, beyond the occasional baring of fangs as they trotted past in the camp.

He slipped his lance from its sling and anchored it in the stirrup step just inside his right foot. Six dogs, loping closer—they were, he realized, exhausted.

Torrent reined in to await them, curious.

The beasts slowed, and then encircled the warrior and his horse. He watched as they sank down on to their bellies, jaws hanging, tongues lolling and slick with thick threads of saliva.

Confused, Torrent settled back in the saddle. Could he just ride through this strange circle, continue on his way?

If these were Awl dogs, what would their behaviour signify? He shook his head— maybe if they were drays, then he would imagine that an enemy had drawn near. Frowning, Torrent stood in his stirrups and squinted to the north, whence the dogs had come. Nothing . . . and then he shaded his eyes. Yes, nothing on the horizon, but above that horizon—circling birds? Possibly.

What to do? Return to the camp, find a warrior and tell him or her of what he had seen? *Your dogs found me. They laid themselves down. Far to the north . . . some birds.* Torrent snorted. He gathered the reins and nudged his mount between two of the prone dogs, and then swung his horse northward. Birds were not worth reporting—he needed to see what had drawn them.

Of the six dogs he left behind him, two fell into his wake, trotting. The remaining four rose and set out for the camp to the south.

In the time of Redmask, Torrent had known something close to contentment. The Awl had found someone to follow. A true leader, a saviour. And when the great victories had come—the death of hundreds of Letherii invaders in fierce, triumphant battles—they were proof of Redmask's destiny. He could not be certain when things began to go wrong, but he recalled the look in Toc Anaster's eye, the cynical set of his foreign face, and with every comment the man uttered, the solid foundations of Torrent's faith seemed to reverberate, as if struck deadly blows . . . until the first cracks arrived, until Torrent's very zeal was turned upon itself, jaded and mocking, and what had been a strength became a weakness.

Such was the power of scepticism. A handful of words to dismantle certainty, like seeds flung at a stone wall—tender greens and tiny roots, yes, but in time they would take down that wall.

Contentment alone should have made Torrent suspicious, but it had reared up before him like a god of purity and willingly he had knelt, head bowed, to take comfort in its shadow. In any other age, Redmask could not have succeeded in commanding the Awl. Without the desperation, without the succession of defeats and mounting losses, without extinction itself looming before them like a cliff's edge, the tribes would have driven him away—as they had done once before. Yes, they had been wiser, then.

Some forces could not be defeated, and so it was with the Letherii. Their hunger for land, their need to possess and rule over all that they possessed—these were terrible desires that spread like the plague, poisoning the souls of the enemy. Once the fever of seeing the world as they did erupted like fire in one's brain, the war was over, the defeat absolute and irreversible.

Even these Barghast—his barbaric saviours—were doomed. Akrynnai traders set up camps up against the picket lines. D'rhasilhani horse sellers drove herd after herd in a mostly futile parade past the encampment, and every now and then a Barghast warrior would select one of the larger animals, examine it for a time, and then, with a dismissive bark of laughter, send it back to the herd. Before too long, Torrent believed, a breed of sufficient height and girth would arrive, and that would be that.

Invaders did not stay invaders for ever. Eventually, they became no different from every other tribe or people in a land. Languages muddied, blended, surrendered. Habits were exchanged like currency, and before too long everyone saw the world the same way as everyone else. And if that way was wrong, then misery was assured, for virtually everyone, for virtually ever.

The Awl should have bowed to the Letherii. They would be alive now, instead of lying in jumbled heaps of mouldering bones in the mud of a dead sea.

Redmask had sought to stop time itself. Of course he failed.

Sometimes, belief was suicide.

Torrent had cast away his faiths, his certainties, his precious beliefs. He did nothing to resist the young ones losing their language. He saw the ochre paint on

their faces, the spiked hair, and was indifferent to it. Yes, he was the leader of the
Awl, the last there would ever be, and it was his task to oversee the peaceful
obliteration of his culture. Ways will pass. He vowed he would not miss them.

No, Torrent wore no copper mask. Not any more. And his face was clear as his
eyes.

He slowed his horse's canter as soon as he made out the corpses, the bodies
scattered about. Crows and gold-beaked vultures moved here and there in the
carrion dance, whilst rhinazan flapped about, disturbing capemoths into flight—
sudden blossoms of white petals that settled almost as quickly as they appeared.
A scene of the plains that Torrent knew well.

A troop of Barghast had been ambushed. Slaughtered.

He rode closer.

No obvious tracks, neither foot nor hoof, led away from the killing ground. He
saw how the Barghast had been in close formation—and that was odd, contrary to
what Torrent had seen of their patrols. Perhaps, he thought, they had contracted
defensively, which suggested an enemy in overwhelming numbers. But then . . .
there was no sign of that. And whoever had murdered these warriors must have
taken their own dead with them—he walked his horse in a circuit round the
bodies—saw no trailing smears of blood, no swaths through the grasses to mark
dragged heels.

The bodies, he realized then, had not been looted. Their beautiful weapons
were scattered about, the blades devoid of blood.

Torrent felt his nerves awaken, as if brushed by something unholy. He looked
once more at the corpses—not a contraction, but a converging . . . upon a single
foe. And the wounds—despite the efforts of the scavengers—displayed nothing of
what one would expect. *As if they closed upon a beast, and see how the blows
struck downward upon them. A plains bear? No, there are none left. The last surviving skin of one of those beasts—among my people—was said to be seven generations old.* He remembered the thing, vast, yes, but tattered. And the claws had
been removed and since lost. Still . . .

Torrent glanced at the two dogs as they trotted up. The beasts looked preter-
naturally cowed, stubby tails ducked, the glances they sent him beseeching and
frightened. If they had been Awl drays, they would now be moving on to the enemy's trail, eager, hackles raised. He scowled down at the quivering beasts.

He swung his horse back round and set off for the Gadra camp. The dogs hurried after him.

A beast, yet one that left no trail whatsoever. A ghost creature.

Perhaps his solitary rides had come to an end. He would have to surrender to
those eager women. They could take away his unease, he hoped.

*Leave the hunt to the Barghast. Give their shamans something worthwhile to
do, instead of getting drunk on D'ras beer every night. Report to the chief, and
then be done with it.*

He already regretted riding out to find the bodies. For all he knew the ghost
creature was close, had in fact been watching him. Or something of its foul sorcery

lingered upon the scene, and now he was marked, and it would find him no matter where he went. He could almost smell that sorcery, clinging to his clothes. Acrid, bitter as a snake's belly.

Setoc, who had once been named Stayandi, and who in her dreams was witness to strange scenes of familiar faces speaking in strange tongues, of laughter and love and tenderness—an age in the time before her beasthood—stood facing the empty north.

She had seen the four dogs come into the camp, in itself an event unworthy of much attention, and if the patrol was late in returning, well, perhaps they had surprised a mule deer and made a kill, thus explaining the absence of two dogs from the pack, as the beasts would have been strapped to a travois to carry back the meat. Explanations such as these served for the moment, despite the obvious flaws in logic (these four would have remained with the patrol in such a case, feeding on the butchered carcass and its offal and whatnot); although the truth of it was Setoc spared few thoughts for what interpretations the nearby Barghast might kick up in small swirls of agitated dust, as they tracked with their eyes the sweat-lathered beasts, or for their growing alarm when the dogs then sank down on to their bellies.

So, she watched as a dozen or so warriors gathered weapons and slowly converged on the exhausted beasts, and then returned her attention to the north.

Yes, the animals stank of death.

And the wild wolves in the emptiness beyond, who had given her life, had howled with the dawn their tale of terror.

Yes, her first family ever remained close by, accorded a kind of holy protection in the legend that was the girl's finding—no Barghast would hunt the animals, and now even the Akrynnai had been told the story of her birth among the pack, of the lone warrior's discovery of her. Spirit-blessed, they now all said when looking upon her. The holder of a thousand hearts.

At first, that last title had confused Setoc, but her memories slowly awakened, with each day that she grew older, taller, sharper-eyed. Yes, she held within herself a thousand hearts, even more. Wolf gifts. Milk she had suckled, milk of blood, milk of a thousand slain brothers and sisters. And did she not recall a night of terror and slaughter? A night fleeing in the darkness?

They spoke of her legend, and even the shoulder-seers made her offerings and would come up and touch her to ease their troubled expressions.

And now the Great Warlock, the Finder of the Barghast Gods, the one named Cafal, had come to the Gadra, to speak with her, to search her soul if she so permitted it.

The wild wolves cried out to her, their minds a confused tumult of fear and worry. Anxious for their child, yes, and for a future time when storms gathered from every horizon. They understood that she would be at the very heart of that celestial conflagration. They begged to sacrifice their own lives so that she might live. And that, she would not permit.

If she was spirit-blessed, then the wolves were the spirits that had so blessed her. If she was a thing to be worshipped here among the Barghast, then she was but a symbol of the wild and it was this wild that must be worshipped—if only they could see that.

She glanced back at the cowering dogs, and felt a rush of sorrowful regret at what such beasts could have been, if their wildness was not so chained, so bound and muzzled.

God, my children, does not await us in the wilderness. God, my children, is the wilderness.

Witness its laws and be humbled.

In humility, find peace.

But know this: peace is not always life. Sometimes, peace is death. In the face of this, how can one not be humble?

The wild laws are the only laws.

She would give these words to Cafal. She would see in his face their effect.

And then she would tell him that the Gadra clan was going to die, and that many other Barghast clans would follow. She would warn him to look to the skies, for from the skies death was coming. She would warn him against further journeys—he must return to his own clan. He must make peace with the spirit of his own kin. The peace of life, before the arrival of the peace of death.

Warriors had gathered round the dogs, readying weapons and such. Tension flowed out from them in ripples, spreading through the camp. In moments a war-leader would be selected from among the score or so milling about. Setoc pitied them all, but especially that doomed leader.

A wind was blowing in from the east, scratching loose her long sun-bleached hair until it whispered across her face like withered grass. And still the stench of death filled her senses.

Cafal's heavy features had broadened, grown more robust since his youth, and there were deeply etched lines of stress between his brows and framing his mouth. Years ago, in a pit beneath a temple floor, he had spoken with the One Who Blesses, with the Malazan captain, Ganoes Paran. And, seeking to impress the man—seeking to prove that, somehow, his wisdom belied his few years—he had uttered words he had heard his father use, claiming them as his own.

'A man possessing power must act decisively . . . else it trickle away through his fingers.'

The observation, while undoubtedly true, now echoed sourly. The voice that made that pronouncement, back then, was all wrong. It had no right to the words. Cafal could not believe his own pretensions uttered by that younger self, that bold, clear-eyed fool.

A pointless, stupid accident had stolen away his father, Humbrall Taur. For all that the huge, wise warrior had wielded his power, neither wisdom nor that power availed him against blind chance. The lesson was plain, the message bleak and humbling. Power was proof against nothing, and *that* was the only wisdom worth recognizing.

He wondered what had happened to that miserable Malazan captain, chosen and cursed (and was there any real difference between the two?), and he wondered, too, why he now longed to speak with Ganoes Paran, to exchange a new set of words, these ones more honest, more measured, more *knowing*. Yes, the young were quick with judgement, quick to chastise their torpid elders. The young understood nothing about the value of sober contemplation.

Ganoes Paran had been indecisive, in Cafal's eyes back then. Pitifully, frustratingly so. But to the Cafal of this day, here on this foreign plain under foreign skies, that Malazan of years ago had been rightly cautious, measured by a wisdom to which young Cafal had been woefully blind. *And this is how we gauge a life, this is how we build the bridge from what we were to what we are. Ganoes Paran, do you ever look down? Do you ever stand frozen in place by that depthless chasm below?*

Do you ever dream of jumping?

Onos Toolan had been given all the power Cafal's own father had once commanded, and there was nothing undeserved in that. And now, slowly, inexorably, it was trickling away through the fingers of that ancient warrior. Cafal could do nothing to stop it—he was as helpless as Tool himself. Once again, blind chance had conspired against the Barghast.

When word reached him that wardogs had returned to the camp—beasts bereft of escort and therefore mutely announcing that something ill had befallen a scouting troop—and that a war-party was forming to set out on the back-trail, Cafal drew on his bhederin-hide cloak, grunting beneath its weight, and kicked at the ragged, tufted doll crumpled on the tent floor near the foot of his cot. 'Wake up.'

The sticksnare spat and snarled as it scrambled upright. 'Very funny. Respect your elders, O Great Warlock.'

The irony oozing like pine sap from the title made Cafal wince, and then he cursed himself when Talamandas snorted in amusement upon seeing the effect of his mockery. He paused at the entrance. 'We should have burned you on a pyre long ago, sticksnare.'

'Too many value me to let you do that. I travel the warrens. I deliver messages and treat with foreign gods. We speak of matters of vast importance. War, betrayals, alliances, betrayals—'

'You're repeating yourself.'

'—and war.'

'And are the Barghast gods pleased with your efforts, Talamandas? Or do they snarl with fury as you flit this way and that at the behest of *human* gods?'

'They cannot live in isolation! *We* cannot! They are stubborn! They lack all sophistication! They *embarrass* me!'

Sighing, Cafal stepped outside.

The sticksnare scrambled after him, skittish as a stoat. 'If we fight alone, we will all die. We need allies!'

Cafal paused and looked down, wondering if Talamandas was, perhaps, insane. How many times could they repeat this same conversation? 'Allies against whom?' he asked, as he had done countless times before.

'Against what comes!'

And there, the same meaningless answer, the kind of answer neither Cafal nor Tool could use. Hissing under his breath, the Great Warlock set off once more, ignoring Talamandas who scrambled in his wake.

The war-party had left the camp. At a trot, the warriors were already reaching the north ridge. Once over the crest, they would vanish from sight.

Cafal saw the wolf-child, Setoc, standing at the camp's edge, evidently watching the warriors, and something in her stance suggested she longed to lope after them, teeth bared and hackles raised, eager to join in the hunt.

He set out in that direction.

There was no doubt that she was Letherii, but that legacy existed only on the surface—her skin, her features, the traits of whatever parents had given her birth and then lost her. But that nascent impression of civilization had since faded, eroded away. She had been given back to the wild, a virgin sacrifice whose soul had been devoured whole. She belonged to the wolves, and, perhaps, to the Wolf God and Goddess, the Lord and Lady of the Beast Throne.

The Barghast had come to find the Grey Swords, to fight at their side—believing that Toc Anaster and his army knew the enemy awaiting them. The Barghast gods had been eager to serve Togg and Fanderay, to run with the bold pack in search of blood and glory. They had been, Cafal now understood, worse than children.

The Grey Swords were little more than rotting meat when the first scouts found them.

So much for glory.

Was Setoc the inheritor of the blessing once bestowed upon the Grey Swords? Was she now the child of Togg and Fanderay?

Even Talamandas did not know.

'Not her!' the sticksnare now snarled behind him. 'Cast her out, Cafal! Banish her to the wastes where she belongs!'

But he continued on. When he was a dozen paces away, she briefly glanced back at him before returning her attention upon the empty lands to the north. Moments later, he reached her side.

'They are going to die,' she said.

'What? Who?'

'The warriors who just left. They will die as did the scout troop. You have found the enemy, Great Warlock . . . but it is the wrong enemy. Again.'

Cafal swung round. He saw Talamandas squatting in the grasses five paces back. 'Chase them down,' he told the sticksnare. 'Bring them back.'

'Believe nothing she says!'

'This is not a request, Talamandas.'

With a mocking cackle the sticksnare darted past, bounding like a bee-stung hare on to the trail of the war-party.

'There is no use in doing that,' Setoc said. 'This entire clan is doomed.'

'Such pronouncements weary me,' Cafal replied. 'You are like a poison thorn in this clan's heart, stealing its strength, its pride.'

'Is that why you've come?' she asked. 'To . . . pluck out this thorn?'

'If I must.'

'Then why are you waiting?'

'I would know the source of your pronouncements, Setoc. Are you plagued with visions? Do spirits visit your dreams? What have you seen? What do you know?'

'The rhinazan whisper in my ear,' she said.

Was she taunting him? 'Winged lizards do not whisper anything, Setoc.'

'No?'

'No. Is nonsense all you can give me? Am I to be nothing but the object of your contempt?'

'The Awl warrior, the one so aptly named Torrent, has found the war-party. He adds to your doll's exhortations. But . . . the warleader is young. Fearless. Why do the fools choose one such as that?'

'When older warriors see a pack of wardogs drag themselves into the camp,' said Cafal, 'they hold a meeting to discuss matters. The young ones clutch their weapons and leap to their feet, eyes blazing.'

'It is a wonder,' she observed, 'that any warrior ever manages to get old.'

Yes. It is.

'The Awl has convinced them.'

'Not Talamandas?'

'No. They say dead warlocks never have anything good to say. They say your sticksnare kneels at the foot of the Death Reaper. They call it a Malazan puppet.'

By the spirits, I cannot argue against any of that!

'You sense all that takes place on these plains, Setoc. What do you know of the enemy that killed the scouts?'

'Only what the rhinazan whisper, Great Warlock.'

Winged lizards again . . . spirits below! 'In our homeland, on the high desert mesas, there are smaller versions that are called rhizan.'

'Smaller, yes.'

He frowned. 'Meaning?'

She shrugged. 'Just that. Smaller.'

He wanted to shake her, rattle loose her secrets. 'Who killed our scouts?'

She bared her teeth but did not face him. 'I have already told you, Great Warlock. Tell me, have you seen the green spears in the sky at night?'

'Of course.'

'What are they?'

'I don't know. Things have been known to fall from the sky, whilst others simply pass by like wagons set ablaze, crossing the firmament night after night for weeks or months . . . and then vanishing as mysteriously as they arrived.'

'Uncaring of the world below.'

'Yes. The firmament is speckled with countless worlds no different from ours. To the stars and to the great burning wagons, we are as motes of dust.'

She turned to study him as he spoke these words. 'That is . . . interesting. This is what the Barghast believe?'

'What do the wolves believe, Setoc?'

'Tell me,' she said, 'when a hunter throws a javelin at a fleeing antelope, does the hunter aim at the beast?'

'Yes and no. To strike true, the hunter must throw into the space in front of the antelope—into the path it will take.' He studied her. 'Are you saying that these spears of green fire are the javelins of a hunter, and that we are the antelope?'

'And if the antelope darts this way, dodges that?'

'A good hunter will not miss.'

The war-party had reappeared on the ridge, and accompanying it was the Awl warrior on his horse, along with two more dogs.

Cafal said, 'I will find Stolmen, now. He will want to speak with you, Setoc.' He hesitated, and then added, 'Perhaps the Gadra warchief can glean clearer answers from you, for in that I have surely failed.'

'The wolves are clear enough,' she replied, 'when speaking of war. All else confuses them.'

'So you indeed serve the Lady and Lord of the Beast Throne. As would a priestess.'

She shrugged.

'Who,' Cafal asked again, 'is the enemy?'

Setoc looked at him. 'The enemy, Great Warlock, is peace.' And she smiled.

The ribbers had dragged Visto's body a dozen or so paces out into the flat, until something warned them against eating the wrinkled, leathery flesh of the dead boy. With the dawn, Badalle and a few others walked out to stand round the shrunken, stomach-burst thing that had once been Visto.

The others waited for Badalle to find her words.

Rutt was late in arriving as he had to check on Held and make adjustments to the baby's wrap. By the time he joined them, Badalle was ready. 'Hear me, then,' she said, 'at Visto's deading.'

She blew flies from her lips and then scanned the faces arrayed round her. There was an expression she wanted to find, but couldn't. Even remembering what it looked like was hard, no, impossible. She'd lost it, truth be told. But wanted it, and she knew she would recognize it as soon as she saw it again. An expression . . . some kind of expression . . . what was it? After a moment, she spoke,

> 'We all come from some place
> And Visto was no different
> He come
> From some
> Place
> And it was different and
> It was the same no different
> If you know what I mean
> And you do
> You have to

All you standing here
The point is that Visto
He couldn't remember
Anything about that place
Except that he come from it
And that's like lots of you
So let's say now
He's gone back there
To that place
Where he come from
And everything he sees
He remembers
And everything he remembers
Is new'

They always waited, never knowing if she was finished until it became obvious that she was, and in that time Badalle looked down at Visto. The eggs of the Satra Riders clung like crumbs to Visto's lips, as if he had been gobbling down cake. The adult riders had chewed out through his stomach and no one knew where they went, maybe into the ground—they did all that at night.

Maybe some of the ribbers had been careless, with their eager jaws and all, which was good since then there'd be fewer of them strong enough to launch attacks on the ribby snake. It wasn't as bad having them totter along in the distance, keeping pace, getting weaker just as the children did, until they lay down and weren't trouble any more. You could live with that, no different from the crows and vultures overhead. Animals showed, didn't they, how to believe in patience.

She lifted her head and as if that was a signal the others turned away and walked slowly back to the trail where the ones who could were standing, getting ready for the day's march.

Rutt said, 'I liked Visto.'

'We all liked Visto.'

'We shouldn't have.'

'No.'

'Because that makes it harder.'

'The Satra Riders liked Visto too, even more than we did.'

Rutt shifted Held from the crook of his right arm into the crook of his left arm. 'I'm mad at Visto now.'

Brayderal, who had showed up to walk at the snake's head only two days ago—maybe coming from back down the snake's body, maybe coming from somewhere else—walked out to stand close to them, as if she wanted to be part of something. Something made up of Rutt and Held and Badalle. But whatever that something was, it had no room for Brayderal. Visto's deading didn't leave a hole. The space just closed up.

Besides, something about the tall, bony girl made Badalle uneasy. Her face was too white beneath all this sun. She reminded Badalle of the bone-skins—

what were they called again? Quisiters? Quitters? Could be, yes, the Quitters, the bone-skins who stood taller than anyone else and from that height they saw everything and commanded everyone and when they said *Starve and die*, why, that's just what everyone did.

If they knew about the Chal Managal, they would be angry. They might even chase after it and find the head, find Rutt and Badalle, and then do that quitting thing with the hands, the thing that broke the necks of people like Rutt and Badalle.

'We would be . . . quitted unto deading.'

'Badalle?'

She looked at Rutt, blew flies from her lips, and then—ignoring Brayderal as if she wasn't there—set off to rejoin the ribby snake.

The track stretched westward, straight like an insult to nature, and at the distant end of the stony, lifeless ground, the horizon glittered as if crusted with crushed glass. She heard Rutt's scrabbling steps coming up behind her, and then veering slightly as he made for the front of the column. She might be his second but Badalle wouldn't walk with him. Rutt had Held. That was enough for Rutt.

Badalle had her words, and that was almost too much.

She saw Brayderal follow Rutt. They were almost the same height, but Rutt looked the weaker, closer to deading than Brayderal, and seeing that, Badalle felt a flash of anger. It should have been the other way round. They needed Rutt. They didn't need Brayderal.

Unless she was planning on stepping into Rutt's place when Rutt finally broke, planning on being the snake's new head, its slithery tongue, its scaly jaws. Yes, that might be what Badalle was seeing. And Brayderal would take up Held all wrapped tight and safe from the sun, and they'd all set out on another day, with her instead of Rutt leading them.

That made a kind of sense. No different than with the ribber packs—when the leader got sick or lame or just wasn't strong enough any more, why, that other ribber that showed up and started trotting alongside it, it was there just for this moment. To take over. To keep things going.

No different from what sons did to fathers and daughters did to mothers, and princes to kings and princesses to queens.

Brayderal walked almost at Rutt's side, up there at the head. Maybe she talked with Rutt, maybe she didn't. Some things didn't need talking about, and besides, Rutt wasn't one to say much anyway.

'I don't like Brayderal.'

If anyone nearby heard her, they gave no sign.

Badalle blew to scatter the flies. They needed to find water. Even half a day without it and the snake would get too ribby, especially in this heat.

On this morning, she did as she always did. Eating her fill of words, drinking deep the spaces in between, and mad—so mad—that none of it gave her any strength.

Saddic had been Rutt's second follower, the first being Held. He now walked among the four or so moving in a loose clump a few paces behind Rutt and the new girl. Badalle was a little way back, in the next clump. Saddic worshipped her, but he would not draw close to her, not yet, because there would be no point. He had few words of his own—he'd lost most of them early on in this journey. So long as he was in hearing range of Badalle, he was content.

She fed him. With her sayings and her seeings. She kept Saddic alive.

He thought about what she had said for Visto's deading. About how some of it wasn't true, the bit about Visto not remembering anything about where he'd come from. He'd remembered too much, in fact. So, Badalle had knowingly told an un-truth about Visto. At his deading. Why had she done that?

Because Visto was gone. Her words weren't for him because he was gone. They were for us. She was telling us to give up remembering. Give it up so when we find it again it all feels new. Not the remembering itself but the things we re-membered. The cities and villages and the families and the laughing. The water and the food and full stomachs. Is that what she was telling us?

Well, he had his meal for the day, didn't he? She was generous that way.

The feet at the ends of his legs were like wads of leather. They didn't feel much and that was a relief since the stones on the track were sharp and so many others had bleeding feet making it hard to walk. The ground was even worse to either side of the trail.

Badalle was smart. She was the brain behind the jaws, the tongue. She took what the snake's eyes saw. She made sense of what the tongue tasted. She gave names to the things of this new world. The moths that pretended to be leaves and the trees that invited the moths to be leaves so that five trees shared one set of leaves between them, and when the trees got hungry off went the leaves, looking for food. No other tree could do that, and so no other tree lived on the Elan.

She talked about the jhaval, the carrion birds no bigger than sparrows, that were the first to swarm a body when it fell, using their sharp beaks to stab and drink. Sometimes the jhaval didn't even wait for the body to fall. Saddic had seen them attacking a wounded ribber, even vultures and crows. Sometimes each other, too, when the frenzy was on them.

Satra Riders, as what did in poor Visto, and flow-worms that moved in a seething carpet, pushing beneath a corpse to squirm in the shade. They bit and drenched themselves in whatever seeped down and as the ground softened down they went, finally able to pierce the skin of the blistered earth.

Saddic looked in wonder at this new world, listened in awe as Badalle gave the strange things names and made for them all a new language.

Close to noon they found a waterhole. The crumbled foundations of makeshift corrals surrounded the shallow, muddy pit.

The snake halted, and then began a slow, tortured crawl into and out of the churned-up mud. The wait alone killed scores, and even as children emerged from the morass, slathered black, some fell to convulsions, curling round mud-filled guts. Some spilled out their bowels, fouling things for everyone that came after.

It was another bad day for the Chal Managal.

Later in the afternoon, during the worst of the heat, they spied a greyish cloud on the horizon ahead. The ribbers began howling, dancing in terror, and as the cloud rushed closer, the dogs finally fled.

What looked like rain wasn't rain. What looked like a cloud wasn't a cloud.

These were locusts, but not the normal kind of locusts.

Wings glittering, the swarm filling half the sky, and then all the sky, the sound a clicking roar—the rasp of wings, the snapping open of jaws—each creature a finger long. Out from within the cloud, as it engulfed the column, lunged buzzing knots where the insects massed almost solid. When one of these hammered into a huddle of children, shrieks of pain and horror erupted—the flash of red meat, and then bone—and then the horde swept on, leaving behind clumps of hair and heaps of gleaming bone.

These locusts ate meat.

This was the first day of the Shards.

Chapter Five

The painter must be mute
The sculptor deaf
Talents are passed out
Singly
As everyone knows
Oh let them dabble
We smile our indulgence
No end to our talent
For allowances
But talents are passed out
Singly
We permit you one
Worth lauding
The rest may do service
In serviceable fashion
But greatness?
That is a title passed out
Singly
Don't be greedy
Over trying our indulgence
Permission
Belongs to us
Behind the makeshift wall—
The bricks of our
Reasonable scepticism.

A Poem That Serves
Astattle Pohm

Corporal Tarr's memory of his father could be entirely summed up inside a single recollected quote, ringing like Talian death bells across the breadth of Tarr's childhood. A raw, stentorian pronouncement battering down on the flinching son. 'Sympathy? Aye, I have sympathy—for the dead and no one else! Ain't nobody in this world deserves sympathy unless they're dead! You understanding me, son?'

'*You understanding me, son?*'

Yes, sir. Good words for making a soldier. Kept the brain from getting too . . . cluttered. With things that might get in the way of holding his shield just so, stabbing out with his short sword right *there*. It was a kind of discipline, what others might call obstinate stupidity, but that simply showed that lots of people didn't understand soldiering.

Teaching people to be disciplined, he was discovering, wasn't easy. He walked the length of Letherii soldiers—and aye, that description was a sorry stretch—who stood at what passed for attention for these locals. A row of red faces in the blazing sunlight, dripping like melting wax.

'Harridict Brigade,' Tarr said in a snarl, 'what kind of name is that? Who in Hood's name was Harridict—no, don't *answer* me, you damned fool! Some useless general, I'd imagine, or worse, some merchant house happy to kit you all in its house colours. Merchants! Businesses got no place in the military. We built an empire across three continents by keeping 'em outa things! Businesses are the vultures of war, and maybe those beaks look like smiles, but take it from me, they're just beaks.'

He halted then, his repertoire of words exhausted, and gestured to Cuttle, who stepped up with a hard grin—the idiot loved this Braven role, as it was being called now ('Letherii got master sergeants; we Malazans got Braven Sergeants, and say it toothy when you say it, lads, and be sure to keep the joke private'—so said Ruthan Gudd and *that*, Tarr had decided then and there, was a *soldier*).

Cuttle was wide and solid, a perfect fit to the role. Wider than Tarr but shorter by half a head, which meant that Tarr was an even better fit. Not one of these miserable excuses for soldiers could stand toe to toe with either Malazan for anything past twenty heartbeats, and that was the awful truth. They were soft. 'This brigade,' Cuttle now said, loud and contemptuous, 'is a waste of space!' He paused to glare at the faces, which were slowly hardening under the assault.

About time. Tarr watched on, thumbs hooked now in his weapon belt.

'Aye,' Cuttle went on, 'I've listened to your drunken stories—' and his tone invited them to sit at his table: knowing and wise and damned near . . . sympathetic. 'And aye, I've seen for myself that raw, ugly pig you call magic hereabouts. Undisciplined—no finesse—brutal power but nothing clever. So, for you lot, battle means eating dirt, and a battlefield is where hundreds die for no good reason. Your mages have made war a miserable, useless joke—' and he spun round and stepped up to one soldier, nose to nose. 'You! How many times has this brigade taken fifty per cent or more losses in a single battle?'

The soldier—and Cuttle had chosen well—almost bared his teeth. 'Seven times, Braven Sergeant!'

'Seventy-five per cent losses?'

'Four, Braven Sergeant!'

'Losses at ninety?'

'Once, Braven Sergeant, but not ninety—one hundred per cent, Braven Sergeant.'

Cuttle let his jaw drop. 'One hundred?'

'Yes, Braven Sergeant!'

'Wiped out to the last soldier?'

'Yes, Braven Sergeant!'

And Cuttle leaned even closer, his face turning crimson. In a bellowing shout, he said, 'And has it not *once* occurred to you—any of you—that you might do better by murdering all your mages at the very start of the battle?'

'Then the other side would—'

'You parley with 'em first, of course—you *all* agree to *butcher the bastards*!' He reeled back and threw up his hands. 'You don't fight wars! You don't fight battles! You just all form up and make new cemeteries!' He wheeled on them. '*Are you all idiots?*'

On a balcony overlooking the parade grounds, Brys Beddict winced. Beside him, standing in the shade, Queen Janath grunted and then said, 'You know, he has a point.'

'It is, for the moment,' Brys said, 'almost irrelevant. We have few mages of any stature left, and even those ones have gone to ground—it seems there is a quiet revolution under way, and I suspect that when the dust has settled, the entire discipline of sorcery will be transformed.' He hesitated, and then said, 'In any case, that wasn't what alarmed me—listening to that soldier down there. It's their notion of taking matters into their own hands.'

'An invitation to mutiny,' Janath was nodding, 'but you could look at it another way. Their kind of thinking in turn keeps their commanders in check—following orders is one thing, but if those orders are suicidal or just plain stupid . . .'

'The thought of my soldiers second-guessing me at every turn hardly inspires confidence. I am beginning to regret employing these Malazans in the reshaping of the Letherii military. Perhaps the way they do things works for them, but it does not necessarily follow that it will work for us.'

'You may be right, Brys. There is something unusual about the Malazans. I find them fascinating. Imagine, an entire civilization that does not suffer fools.'

'From what I have heard,' Brys pointed out, 'that did not protect them from betrayal—their very own Empress was prepared to sacrifice them all.'

'But they did not kneel to the axe, did they?'

'I see your point.'

'There exists an exchange of trust between the ruler and the ruled. Abuse that from either direction and all mutual agreements are nullified.'

'Civil war.'

'Unless one of the aggrieved parties has the option of simply leaving. Assuming it's not interested in retribution or vengeance.'

Brys thought about that for a time, watching the relentless bullying of his Letherii soldiers by those two Bonehunters in the yard below. 'Perhaps they have things to teach us after all,' he mused.

Cuttle stepped close to Tarr and hissed, 'Gods below, Corporal, they're worse than sheep!'

'Been thrashed too many times, that's their problem.'

'So what do we do with them?'

Tarr shrugged. 'All I can think of is thrash 'em again.'

Cuttle's small eyes narrowed on his corporal. 'Somehow, that don't sound right.'

Grimacing, Tarr looked away. 'I know. But it's all I've got. If you've a better idea, feel free, sapper.'

'I'll get 'em marching round—that'll give us time to think.'

'There must be some clever strategy at work down there,' Brys concluded after a time, and then he turned to the Queen. 'We should probably attend to Tehol—he said something about a meeting in advance of the meeting with the Adjunct.'

'Actually, that was Bugg. Tehol proposed a meeting to discuss Bugg's idea of the meeting in advance—oh, listen to me! That man is like an infection! Yes, let us march with solemn purpose upon my husband—your brother—and at least find out whatever needs finding out before the Malazans descend upon us. What must they think? Our King wears a blanket!'

Lostara Yil's hand crept to the knife at her hip and then drew back once more. A muttering whisper in her head was telling her the blade needed cleaning, but she had just cleaned and honed it not a bell ago, and even the sheath was new. None of this was logical. None of this made sense. Yes, she understood the reasons for her obsession. Twisted, pathetic reasons, but then, driving a knife through the heart of the man she loved was bound to leave an indelible stain on her soul. The knife had become a symbol—she'd be a fool not to see that.

Still, her hand itched, desperate to draw forth the knife.

She sought to distract herself by watching Fist Blistig pacing along the far wall, measuring out a cage no one else could see—yet she knew its dimensions. Six paces in length, about two wide, the ceiling low enough to make the man hunch over, the floor worn smooth, almost polished. She understood that kind of invention, all the effort in making certain the bars fit tightly, that the lock was solid and the key flung into the sea.

Fist Keneb was watching the man as well, doing an admirable job of keeping his thoughts to himself. He was the only one seated at the table, seemingly relaxed, although Lostara well knew that he was probably as bruised and battered as she was—Fiddler's cursed reading had left them all in rough shape. Being bludgeoned unconscious was never a pleasant experience.

The three of them looked over as Quick Ben walked into the chamber. The High Mage carried an air of culpability about him, which was nothing new. For all his bravado, accusations clung to him like gnats on a web. Of course he was hiding secrets. Of course he was playing unseen games. He was Quick Ben, the last surviving wizard of the Bridgeburners. He thought outwitting gods was fun. But even he had taken a beating at Fiddler's reading, which should have humbled the man.

She squinted as he sauntered up to the table, pulled out the chair beside Keneb, and sat, whereupon he began drumming his fingers on the varnished surface.

No, not much humility there.

'Where is she?' Quick Ben asked. 'We're seeing the King in a bell's time—we need to settle on what we're doing.'

Blistig had resumed pacing, and at the wizard's words he snorted and then said, 'She's settled already. This is just a courtesy.'

'Since when is the Adjunct interested in decorum?' Quick Ben retorted. 'No, we need to discuss strategies. Everything has changed—'

Keneb straightened at that. 'What has, High Mage? Since the reading? Can you be specific?'

The wizard grinned. 'I can, but maybe she doesn't want me to.'

'Then the rest of us should just leave you and her to it,' said Blistig, his blunt features twisting with disgust. 'Unless your egos demand an audience, in which case, why, we wouldn't want *those* bruised, would we?'

'Got a doghouse in there, Blistig? You could always take a nap.'

Lostara made sure to glance away, amused. She had none of their concerns on her mind. In fact, she didn't care where this pointless army ended up. Maybe the Adjunct would simply dissolve the miserable thing, cashier them all out. Letheras was a nice enough city, although a little too humid for her tastes—it was probably drier inland, away from this sluggish river.

She knew that such an outcome was unlikely, of course. Impossible, in fact. Maybe Tavore Paran didn't possess the nobility's addiction to material possessions. The Bonehunters were the exception. This was her army. And she didn't want it sitting pretty on a shelf like some prized bauble. No, she wanted to use it. *Maybe even use it up.*

Which was where everyone else came in. Blistig and Keneb, Quick Ben and Sinn. Ruthan Gudd—not that he ever bothered attending briefings—and Arbin and Lostara herself. Add to that eight and a half thousand soldiers in Tavore's own command, along with the Burned Tears and the Perish, and that, Lostara supposed, more than satisfied whatever noble acquisitiveness the Adjunct might harbour.

It was no wonder these men here were nervous. Something was driving the Adjunct, her very own fierce, cruel obsession. Quick Ben might have some idea about it, but she suspected the man was mostly bluff and bluster. The one soldier who might well know wasn't even here. *Thank the gods above and below for that one mercy.*

'We're marching into the Wastelands,' said Keneb. 'We know that much, I suppose. Just not the reasons why.'

Lostara Yil cleared her throat. 'That is a rumour, Fist.'

His brows lifted. 'I understood it to be more certain than that.'

'Well,' said Quick Ben, 'it's imprecise, as most rumours turn out to be. More specifically, it's incomplete. Which is why most of the speculation thus far has been useless.'

'Go on,' said Keneb.

The wizard drummed the tabletop once more, and then said, 'We're not marching into the Wastelands, my friends. We're marching *through* them.' He smiled but it wasn't a real smile. 'See how that added detail makes all the difference? Because now the rumours can chew hard on possibilities. The notion of goals, right? Her goals. What she needs us to do to meet them.' He paused and then added, 'What we need to do to convince ourselves and our soldiers that meeting them is even worth it.'

Well, that was said plainly enough. *Here, chew hard on this mouthful of glass.*

'Unwitnessed,' Keneb muttered.

Quick Ben fluttered a hand dismissively. 'I don't think we have a problem with that. She's already said what she needed to say on that subject. It's settled. Her next challenge will come when she finally spills out precisely what she's planning.'

'But you think you've already figured that out.'

Lostara wasn't fooled by the High Mage's coy smile. *The idiot hasn't a clue. He's just like the rest of us.*

Adjunct Tavore made her entrance then, dragging Sinn by one skinny arm—and the expression on the girl's face was a dark storm of indignation and fury. The older woman pulled out the chair opposite Keneb and sat Sinn down in it, then walked to position herself at one end, where she remained standing. When she spoke, her tone was uncharacteristically harsh, as if rage seethed just beneath the surface. 'The gods can have their war. We will not be used, not by them, not by anyone. I do not care how history judges us—I hope that's well understood.'

Lostara found herself captivated; she could not take her eyes off the Adjunct, seeing at last a side of her that had remained hidden for so long—that indeed might never before have revealed itself. It was clear that the others were equally shocked, as not one spoke to fill the silence when Tavore paused—showing them all the cold iron of her eyes.

'Fiddler's reading made it plain,' she resumed. 'That reading was an *insult*. To all of us.' She began drawing off her leather gloves with a kind of ferocious precision. 'No one owns our minds. Not Empress Laseen, not the gods themselves. In a short time we will speak with King Tehol of Lether. We will formalize our intention to depart this kingdom, marching east.' She slapped the first glove down. 'We will request the necessary permissions to ensure our peaceful passage through the petty kingdoms beyond the Letherii border. If this cannot be achieved, then we will cut our way through.' Down thumped the second glove.

If there was any doubt in this chamber that this woman commanded the Bonehunters, it had been obliterated. Succinctly.

'Presumably,' she went on, her voice a rasp, 'you wish to learn of our destination. We are marching to war. We are marching to an enemy that does not know we even exist.' Her icy gaze fixed on Quick Ben and it was a measure of the man's courage that he did not flinch. 'High Mage, your dissembling is at an end. Know that I value your penchant for consorting with the gods. You will now report to me what you believe is coming.'

Quick Ben licked his lips. 'Shall I be specific or will a summary suffice, Adjunct?'

She said nothing.

The High Mage shrugged. 'It will be war, yes, but a messy one. The Crippled God's been busy, but his efforts have been, without exception, defensive, for the Fallen One also happens to know what is coming. The bastard's desperate, probably terrified, and thus far, he has failed more often than succeeded.'

'Why?'

He blinked. 'Well, people have been getting in the way—'

'People, yes. Mortals.'

Quick Ben nodded, eyes narrowing. 'We have been the weapons of the gods.'

'Tell me, High Mage, how does it feel?'

Her questions struck from unanticipated directions, Lostara could see, and it was clear that Quick Ben was mentally reeling. This was a sharp talent, a surprising one, and it told Lostara that Adjunct Tavore possessed traits that made her a formidable tactician—but why had none of them seen this before?

'Adjunct,' the wizard ventured, 'the gods have inevitably regretted using me.'

The answer evidently satisfied her. 'Go on, High Mage.'

'They will chain him again. This time it will be absolute, and once chained, they will suck everything out of him—like bloodflies—'

'Are the gods united on this?'

'Of course not—excuse me, Adjunct. Rather, the gods are never united, even when in agreement. Betrayals are virtually guaranteed—which is why I cannot fathom Shadowthrone's thinking. He's not that stupid—he can't be that stupid—'

'He has outwitted you,' Tavore said. 'You "cannot fathom" his innermost intentions. High Mage, the first god you have mentioned here is one that most of us wouldn't expect to be at the forefront of all of this. Hood, yes. Togg, Fanderay—even Fener. Or Oponn. And what of the Elder Gods? Mael, K'rul, Kilmandaros. No. Instead, you speak of Shadowthrone, the upstart—'

'The once Emperor of the Malazan Empire,' cut in Keneb.

Quick Ben scowled. 'Aye, even back then—and it's not easy to admit this—he was a wily bastard. The times I thought I'd worked round him, beat him clean, it turned out he had been playing me all along. He was the ruler of shadows long before he even ascended to that title. Dancer gave him the civilized face, that mask of honest morality—just as Cotillion does now. But don't be fooled, those two are ruthless—none of us mortals are worth a damned thing, except as a means to an end—'

'And what, High Mage, would that end be?'

Quick Ben threw up his hands and leaned back. 'I have little more than rude guesses, Adjunct.'

But Lostara saw something shining in the wizard's eyes, as if he had been stirred into wakefulness from a long, long sleep. She wondered if this was how he had been with Whiskeyjack, with Dujek Onearm. No wonder they saw him as their shaved knuckle in the hole.

'I would hear those guesses,' the Adjunct said.

'The pantheon comes crashing down—and what emerges from the dust and ashes is almost unrecognizable. The same for sorcery—the warrens—the realm of K'rul. All fundamentally changed.'

'Yet, one assumes, at the pinnacle . . . Shadowthrone and Cotillion.'

'A safe assumption,' Quick Ben admitted, 'which is why I don't trust it.'

Tavore looked startled. 'Altruism from those two?'

'I don't even believe in altruism, Adjunct.'

'Thus,' she observed, 'your confusion.'

The wizard's ascetic face was pinched, as if he was tasting something unbearably foul. 'Who's to say that the changes create something better, something more equitable? Who's to say that what emerges isn't even worse than what we have right now? Yes, it might seem a good move—driving that mob of miserable gods off some cliff, or some other place that puts them out of reach, that puts *us* out of *their* reach.' He was musing now, as if unaware of his audience. 'But consider that eventuality. Without the gods, we're on our own. And with us on our own— Abyss fend!—what mischief we might do! What grotesque invention to plague the world!'

'But . . . not entirely on our own.'

'The fun would pall,' Quick Ben said, as if irritated with the objection. 'Shadowthrone has to realize that. Who would he have left to play with? And with K'rul a corpse, sorcery will rot, grow septic—it will kill whoever dares use it.'

'Perhaps,' said Tavore with a certain remorselessness, 'it is not Shadowthrone's intent to reshape anything. Rather, to end it once and for all. To wipe the world clean.'

'I doubt that. Kallor tried it and the lesson wasn't lost on anyone—how could it be? Gods know, Kellanved then went and *claimed* that destroyed warren for the empire, so he couldn't be blind . . .' His words fell away, but Lostara saw how his thoughts suddenly raced down a new, treacherous track, destination unknown.

Yes, they claimed Kallor's legacy. But . . . what does that signify?

No one spoke for a time. Blistig stood rooted—he had not moved from the moment the Adjunct began speaking, and what should have been a confused expression was nowhere to be seen on his rough features. Instead, he was closed up with a kind of obstinate belligerence, as if everything he had heard thus far wasn't relevant, could not rattle the cage—for even as the cage imprisoned him within it, so it kept everything else at a safe distance.

Sinn sat perched on the oversized chair, glowering at the tabletop, pretending not to listen to anything being said here, but she was paler than usual.

Keneb leaned forward on his elbows, his hands against the sides of his face: the pose of a man wishing to be elsewhere.

'It comes down to gates,' Quick Ben muttered. 'I don't know how, or even why, but my gut tells me it comes down to gates. Kurald Emurlahn, Kurald Galain, Starvald Demelain—the old ones—and the Azath. No one has plumbed the secrets of the Houses as they have, not even Gothos. Windows on to the past, into the future, paths leading to places no mortal has ever visited. They have crawled up and down the skeleton of existence, eager as bone-grubs—'

'Too many assumptions,' Tavore said. 'Rein yourself in, High Mage. Tell me, have you seen the face of our enemy to the east?'

The look he shot her was bleak, wretched. 'Justice is a sweet notion. Too bad its practice ends up awash in innocent blood. Honest judgement is cruel, Adjunct, so very cruel. And what makes it a disaster is the way it spreads outward, swallowing everything in its path. Allow me to quote Imperial Historian Duiker: "The object of justice is to drain the world of colour." '

'Some would see it that way—'

Quick Ben snorted. 'Some? Those cold-eyed arbiters *can't see it any other way*!'

'Nature insists on a balance—'

'Nature is blind.'

'Thus favouring the notion that justice too is blind.'

'Blinkered, not blind. The whole notion is founded on a deceit: that truths are reducible—'

'Wait!' barked Keneb. 'Wait—wait! You're leaving me behind, both of you! Adjunct, are you saying that *justice* is our enemy? Making us what, the champions of injustice? How can justice be an enemy—how can you expect to wage war against it? How can a simple soldier cut down an idea?' His chair rocked back as he suddenly rose. 'Have you lost your minds? I don't understand—'

'Sit down, Fist!'

Shocked by the order, he sank back, looking defeated, bewildered.

Hood knew, Lostara Yil sympathized.

'Kolanse,' said Tavore. 'According to Letherii writings, an isolated confederation of kingdoms. Nothing special, nothing particularly unique, barring a penchant for monotheism. For the past decade, suffering a terrible drought, sufficient to cripple the civilization.' She paused. 'High Mage?'

Quick Ben rubbed vigorously at his face, and then said, 'The Crippled God came down in pieces. Everyone knows that. Most of him, it's said, fell on Korel, which is what gave that continent its other name: Fist. Other bits fell . . . elsewhere. Despite the damage done to Korel, that was not where the true heart of the god landed. No, it spun away from the rest of him. It found its very own continent . . .'

'Kolanse,' said Keneb. 'It landed in Kolanse.'

Tavore said, 'I mentioned that penchant for monotheism—it is hardly surprising, given what must have been a most traumatic visitation by a god—the visitor who never went away.'

'So,' said Keneb through clenched teeth, 'we are marching to where the gods are converging. Gods that intend to chain the Crippled God one final time. But we refuse to be anyone's weapon. If that is so, then what in Hood's name will we be doing there?'

'I think,' Quick Ben croaked, 'we will have the answer to that when we get there.'

Keneb groaned and slumped back down, burying his face in his hands.

'Kolanse has been usurped,' said Tavore. 'Not in the name of the Crippled God, but in the name of justice. Justice of a most terrible kind.'

Quick Ben said, 'Ahkrast Korvalain.'

Sinn jumped as if stung, then huddled down once more.

Keneb's hands dropped away, though the impressions of his fingertips remained, mottling his face. 'I'm sorry, what?'

'The Elder Warren, Fist,' said the Adjunct, 'of the Forkrul Assail.'

'They are preparing the gate,' Quick Ben said, 'and for that, they need lots of blood. Lots.'

Lostara finally spoke. She could not help it. She knew more about the cult of Shadow than anyone here, possibly excepting Quick Ben. 'Adjunct, you say we march at the behest of no god. Yet, I suspect, Shadowthrone will be most pleased when we strike for Kolanse, when we set out to destroy that unholy gate.'

'Thank you,' Tavore said. 'I take it we now comprehend High Mage Quick Ben's angst. His fear that, somehow, we are playing into Shadowthrone's hands.'

I think we are.

'Even when he was Emperor,' said Keneb, 'he learned to flinch from the sting of justice.'

'The T'lan Imass occupation of Aren,' said Blistig, nodding.

Tavore flicked a glance at Blistig, and then said, 'Though we may share an enemy it does not mean we are allies.'

Adjunct, that is too brazen. Fiddler's reading was anything but subtle. But she was awestruck. By what Tavore had done here. Something blistered in this chamber now, touching like fire everyone present—even Blistig. Even that whelp of nightmare, Sinn. If a god showed its face in this chamber at this moment, six fists would vie to greet it.

'What is the gate for?' Lostara asked. 'Adjunct? Do you know that gate's purpose?'

'The delivery of justice,' Quick Ben offered in answer. 'Or so one presumes.'

'Justice against whom?'

The High Mage shrugged. 'Us? The gods? Kings and queens, priests, emperors and tyrants?'

'The Crippled God?'

Quick Ben's grin was feral. 'They're sitting right on top of him.'

'Then the gods might well stand back and let the Forkrul Assail do their work for them.'

'Not likely—you can't suck power from a dead god, can you?'

'So, we could either find ourselves the weapon in the hands of the gods after all, or, if we don't cooperate, trapped between two bloodthirsty foes.' Even as she spoke those words, Lostara regretted them. *Because, once said, everything points to . . . points to the worst thing imaginable. Oh, Tavore, now I understand your defiance when it comes to how history will judge us. And your words that what we will do will be unwitnessed—that was less a promise, I think now. More like a prayer.*

'It is time,' the Adjunct said, collecting her gloves, 'to speak with the King. You can run away now, Sinn. The rest of you are with me.'

———

Brys Beddict needed a moment alone, and so he held back when the Queen entered the throne room, and moved a few paces away from the two helmed guards flanking the entrance. The Errant was on his mind, a one-eyed nemesis clutching a thousand daggers. He could almost feel the god's cold smile, icy and chilling as a winter breath on the back of his neck. Inside and outside, in front of him and behind him, it made no difference. The Errant passed through every door, stood on both sides of every barrier. The thirst for blood was pervasive, and Brys felt trapped like a fly in amber.

If not for a Tarthenal's mallet fist, Brys Beddict would be dead.

He was still shaken.

Since his return to the mortal world, he had felt strangely weightless, as if nothing in this place could hold him down, could keep him firmly rooted to the earth. The palace, which had once been the very heart of his life, his only future, now seemed but a temporary respite. This was why he had petitioned his brother to be given command of the Letherii army—even in the absence of enemies he could justify travelling out from the city, to wander to the very border marches of the kingdom.

What was he looking for? He did not know. Would he—could he—find it in the reaches beyond the city's walls? Was something out there awaiting him? Such thoughts were like body-blows to his soul, for they sent him reeling back—*into brother Hull's shadow.*

Perhaps he haunts me now. His dreams, his needs, slipping like veils in front of my eyes. Perhaps he has cursed me with his own thirst—too vast to be appeased in a single life—no, he will now use mine.

Ungracious fears, these. Hull Beddict was dead. The only thing that haunted Brys now was his memories of the man, and they belonged to no one else, did they?

Let me lead the army. Let us march into unknown lands—leave me free, brother, to try again, to deliver unto strangers a new meaning to the name 'Letherii'—not one foul with treachery, not one to become a curse word to every nation we encounter.

Let me heal Hull's wounds.

He wondered if Tehol would understand any of that, and then snorted—the sound startling both guards, their eyes shifting to him and then away again. Of course Tehol would understand. All too well, in fact, on levels far surpassing Brys's paltry, shallow efforts. And he would say something offhand, that would cut deep enough to bite bone—or he might not—Tehol was never as cruel as Brys dreaded. *And what odd dynamic is that? Only that he's too smart for me . . . and if I had his wits, why, I would use them with all the deadly skill I use when wielding a sword.*

Hull had been the dreamer, and his dreams were the kind that fed on his own conscience before all else. *And see how that blinded him? See how that destroyed him?*

Tehol tempered whatever dream he held. It helped having an Elder God at his side, and a wife who was probably a match to Tehol's own genius. *It helps, too, I suppose, that he's half mad.*

What of Brys, then? This brother least of the three? Taking hold of a sword and making it a standard, an icon of adjudication. A weapon master stood before two worlds: the complex one within the weapon's reach and the simplified one beyond it. *I am Hull's opposite, in all things.*

So why do I now yearn to follow in his steps?

He had been interred within stone upon the unlit floor of an ocean. His soul had been a single thread woven into a skein of forgotten and abandoned gods. How could that not have changed him? Perhaps his new thirst was *their* thirst. Perhaps it had nothing whatsoever to do with Hull Beddict.

Perhaps, indeed, this was the Errant's nudge.

Sighing, he faced the doors to the throne room, adjusted his weapon belt, and then strode into the chamber.

Brother Tehol, King of Lether, was in the midst of a coughing fit. Janath was at his side, thumping on his back. Bugg was pouring water into a goblet, which he then held at the ready.

Ublala Pung stood before the throne. He swung round at Brys's approach, revealing an expression of profound distress. 'Preda! Thank the spirits you're here! Now you can arrest and execute me!'

'Ublala, why would I do that?'

'Look, I have killed the King!'

But Tehol was finally recovering, sufficiently to take the goblet Bugg proffered. He drank down a mouthful, gasped, and then sat back on the throne. In a rasp he said, 'It's all right, Ublala, you've not killed me . . . yet. But that was a close one.'

The Tarthenal whimpered and Brys could see that the huge man was moments from running away.

'The King exaggerates,' said Janath. 'Be at ease, Ublala Pung. Welcome, Brys, I was wondering where you'd got to, since I could have sworn you were on my heels only a few moments ago.'

'What have I missed?'

Bugg said, 'Ublala Pung was just informing us of, among other things, something he had forgotten. A matter most, well, extraordinary. Relating to the Toblakai warrior, Karsa Orlong.'

'The slayer of Rhulad Sengar has returned?'

'No, we are blessedly spared that, Brys.' And then Bugg hesitated.

'It turns out,' explained Janath—as Tehol quickly drank down a few more mouthfuls of water—'that Karsa Orlong set a charge upon Ublala Pung, one that he had until today entirely forgotten, distracted as he has been of late by the abuses heaped upon him by his fellow guards.'

'I'm sorry—what abuses?'

Tehol finally spoke. 'We can get to that later. The matter may no longer be relevant, in any case, since it seems Ublala must leave us soon.'

Brys squinted at the abject Tarthenal. 'Where are you going?'

'To the islands, Preda.'

'The islands?'

Ublala nodded solemnly. 'I must gather all the Tarthenal and make an army. And then we have to go to find Karsa Orlong.'

'An army? Why would Karsa Orlong want an army of Tarthenal?'

'To destroy the world!'

'Of course,' interjected Bugg, 'by my last census there are fourteen hundred and fifty-one Tarthenal now settled on the islands. One half of them not yet adults—under seventy years of age by Tarthenal reckoning. Ublala's potential "army" will amount to around five hundred adults of reasonable maturity and dubious martial prowess.'

'To destroy the world!' Ublala shouted again. 'I need a boat! A big one!'

'These sound like heady matters,' Brys said after a moment, 'which require more discussion. For the moment—forgive me, Ublala—we are soon to entertain the Malazan high command. Should we not begin discussing that impending meeting?'

'What's to discuss?' Tehol asked. He scowled suddenly down at his cup. 'Gods below, I've been drinking *water*! Bugg, are you trying to poison me or something? Wine, man, wine! Oops, sorry, Brys, that was insensitive of me. Beer, man, beer!'

'The Malazans will probably petition us,' Brys said. 'For some unfathomable reason, they intend to march into the Wastelands. They will seek to purchase writs of passage—which will involve diplomatic efforts on our part—as well as sufficient supplies to satisfy their troops. King Tehol, I admit to having little confidence with respect to those writs of passage—we all know the inherent duplicity of the Bolkando and the Saphii—'

'You want to provide the Malazans with an escort,' said Janath.

'A big one!' shouted Ublala, as if unaware that the conversation in the throne room had moved on. 'I want Captain Shurq Elalle. Because she's friendly and she likes sex. Oh, and I need money for food and chickens, too, and boot polish to make my army. Can I get all that?'

'Of course you can!' replied Tehol with a bright smile. 'Chancellor, see to it, won't you?'

'This very day, King,' said Bugg.

'Can I go now?' Ublala asked.

'If you like.'

'Sire,' began Brys, in growing exasperation, 'I think—'

'Can I stay?' Ublala asked.

'Naturally!'

'Sire—'

'Dear brother,' said Tehol, 'have you gleaned no hint of my equanimity? Of course you can escort the Malazans, although I think your chances with the Adjunct are pretty minimal, but who am I to crush hopeless optimism under heel? I mean, would I even be married to this lovely woman at my side here, if not for her seemingly unrealistic hopes?' Bugg delivered a new mug to the King, this one filled with beer. 'Bugg, thank you! Do you think Ublala's worked up a thirst?'

'Undoubtedly, sire.'

'Then pour away!'

'Not away!' cried Ublala. 'I want some!'

'It would give me an opportunity to observe the Malazan military in the field, sire,' explained Brys, 'and to learn what I can—'

'Nobody's objecting, Brys!'

'I am simply stating the accurate reasons justifying my desire—'

'Desires should never be justified,' Tehol said, wagging a finger. 'All you end up doing is illuminating the hidden reasons by virtue of their obvious absence. Now, brother, you happen to be the most eligible Beddict—legitimately eligible, I mean—so why *not* cast wide your amorous net? Even if, by some peculiar quirk on your part, the Adjunct is not to your tastes, there is always her aide—what was that foreign-sounding name again, Bugg?'

'Blistig.'

Tehol frowned. 'Really?'

Brys rubbed at his brow, and at an odd splashing sound glanced over at Ublala and saw the man guzzling from an enormous pitcher, a brown pool spreading round his bare feet. 'Her name is Lostara Yil,' he said, unaccountably weary, almost despondent.

'Then,' demanded Tehol, 'who is Blistig, Bugg?'

'Sorry, one of the Fists—uhm, Atri-Predas—in her command. My mistake.'

'Is he pretty?'

'I'm sure someone exists in the world who might think so, sire.'

'Tehol,' said Brys, 'we need to discuss the motivations of these Malazans. Why the Wastelands? What are they looking for? What do they hope to achieve? They are an army, after all, and armies exist to wage wars. Against whom? The Wastelands are empty.'

'It's no use,' said Janath. 'I've already tried addressing this with my husband.'

'A most enlightening discussion, dear wife, I assure you.'

She regarded him with raised brows. 'Oh? That hardly describes my conclusions.'

'Isn't it obvious?' Tehol asked, gaze flicking from Janath to Brys, to Bugg and hence to Ublala, and then back to Brys once more—and then, with a slight widening of his eyes, back again to the Tarthenal who had just consumed most of the contents of the pitcher and was belching golden froth that ran down his chin. Noting the King's attention, Ublala Pung wiped his chin and smiled.

'Isn't what obvious?' Janath asked.

'Huh? Oh, they're not going to the Wastelands, my Queen, they're going to Kolanse. They're just passing through the Wastelands since they no longer have the transports to get to Kolanse by sea. Nor have we the ships to accommodate them, alas.'

'What do they seek in Kolanse?' Brys asked.

Tehol shrugged. 'How should I know? Do you think, maybe, we should ask them?'

'I would wager,' said Bugg, 'they'll rightly tell us it's none of our business.'

'Is it?'

'Sire, your question encourages me to dissemble, and I'd rather not do that.' .

'Entirely understandable, Bugg. Let's leave it there, then. Are you unwell, Ublala Pung?'

The giant was frowning down at his feet. 'Did I piddle myself?'

'No, that's beer.'

'Oh. That's good, then. But . . .'

'Yes, Ublala?'

'Where are my boots?'

Janath reached out and stayed her husband's hand as he was lifting his goblet to drink. 'Not again, husband. Ublala, you informed us earlier that you fed your boots to the other guards in your billet.'

'Oh.' Ublala belched, wiped foam from his nose, and then smiled again. 'I remember now.'

Tehol blessed his wife with a grateful look and then said, 'That reminds me, did we send healers to the palace barracks?'

'Yes, sire.'

'Well done, Bugg. Now then, since I hear the Malazan entourage on its way in the hallway beyond: Brys, how big do you want to make your escort?'

'Two brigades and two battalions, sire.'

'Is that reasonable?' Tehol asked, looking round.

'I have no idea,' Janath replied. 'Bugg?'

'I'm no general, my Queen.'

'We need an expert opinion, then,' said Tehol. 'Brys?'

Nothing good was going to come of this, Bottle knew, but he also recognized the necessity and so walked uncomplaining in Ebron's company as they cut across the round with its heaving, shouting throng locked in a frenzy of buying and selling and consuming—like seabirds flocking to a single rock day after day, reliving the same rituals that built up a life in layers of . . . *well, don't hedge now . . . of guano*. Of course, one man's shit was another man's . . . whatever.

There was a hidden privilege in being a soldier, he decided. He had been pushed outside normal life, protected from the rigours of meeting most basic needs—food, drink, clothes, shelter: all of these were provided to him in some form or other. *And family—don't forget that.* All in exchange for the task of delivering terrible violence; only every now and then to be sure, for such things could not be sustained over long periods of time without crushing the capacity for feeling, without devouring a mortal's humanity.

In that context, Bottle reconsidered—with a dull spasm of anguish deep inside— maybe the exchange wasn't that reasonable after all. Less a privilege than a burden, a curse. Seeing the faces in this crowd flashing past, a spinning, whirling cascade of masks—each a faintly stunning alternative to his own—he felt himself not simply pushed outside, but estranged. Leaving him bemused, even perturbed, as he witnessed their seemingly mindless, pointless activities, only to find himself envious of these shallow, undramatic lives—wherein the only need was satiation. Possessions, stuffed bellies, expanding heaps of coin.

What do any of you know about life? he wanted to ask. *Try stumbling through a burning city. Try cradling a dying friend with blood like tattered shrouds on all sides. Try glancing to an animated face beside you, only to glance a second time and find it empty, lifeless.*

A soldier knew what was real and what was ephemeral. A soldier understood how thin, how fragile, was the fabric of life.

Could one feel envy when looking upon the protected, ignorant lives of others—those people whose cloistered faith saw strength in weakness, who found hope in the false assurance of routine? *Yes, because once you become aware of that fragility, there is no going back. You lose a thousand masks and are left with but one, with its faint lines of contempt, its downturned mouth only a comment away from a sneer, its promise of cold indifference.*

Gods, we're just going for a walk here. I don't need to be thinking any of this.

Ebron tugged at his arm and they edged into a narrow, high-walled alley. Twenty paces down, the well-swept corridor broadened out into a secluded open-air tavern shaded by four centuries-old fig trees, one at each corner.

Deadsmell was already sitting at one of the tables, scraping chunks of meat and vegetable from copper skewers with his dagger and with a stab lifting morsels to his grease-stained mouth, a tall cup of chilled wine within reach.

Leave it to necromancers to find pleasure in everything.

He looked up as they arrived. 'You're late.'

'See how you suffered for it?' Ebron snapped, dragging out a chair.

'Yes, well, one must make do. I recommend these things—they're like Seven Cities tapu, though not as spicy.'

'What's the meat?' Bottle asked, sitting down.

'Something called orthen. A delicacy, I'm told. Delicious.'

'Well, we might as well eat and drink,' said Ebron, 'while we discuss the miserable extinction of sorcery and the beginning of our soon-to-be-useless lives.'

Deadsmell leaned back, eyes narrowing on the mage. 'If you're going to steal my appetite, you're paying for it first.'

'It was the reading,' Bottle said, and oh, how that snared their attention, not to mention demolished the incipient argument between the two men. 'What the reading revealed goes back to the day we breached the city wall and struck for the palace—do you recall those conflagrations? That damned earthquake?'

'It was the dragon that showed up,' said Deadsmell.

'It was munitions,' countered Ebron.

'It was neither. It was Icarium Lifestealer. He was here, waiting in line to cross blades with the Emperor, but he never got to him, because of that Toblakai—who was none other than Leoman of the Flails' old friend back in Raraku, by the way. Anyway, Icarium did something, right here in Letheras.' Bottle paused and eyed Ebron. 'What are you getting when you awaken your warren?'

'Confusion, powers spitting at each other, nothing you can grasp tight, nothing you can use.'

'And it's got worse since the reading, hasn't it?'

'It has,' confirmed Deadsmell. 'Ebron will tell you about the madhouse we unleashed the night of the reading—I could have sworn Hood stepped right into our room. But the truth was, the Reaper was nowhere even close. If anything, he was sent sprawling the other way. And now, it's all . . . jumpy, twisty. You take hold and everything shudders until it squirms loose.'

Bottle was nodding. 'That's the real reason Fid was so reluctant. His reading fed into what Icarium made here all those months back.'

'Made?' Ebron demanded. 'Made what?'

'I'm not sure—'

'Liar.'

'No, Ebron, I'm *really* not sure . . . but I have an idea. Do you want to hear it or not?'

'No, yes. Go on, I need to finish my list of reasons to commit suicide.'

A server arrived, a man older than a Jaghut's stockings, and the next few moments were spent shouting at the deaf codger—fruitlessly—until Ebron stumbled on to the bright notion of pointing at Deadsmell's plate and goblet and showing two fingers.

As the man set off, wilful as a snail, Bottle said, 'It might not be that bad, Ebron. I think what we're dealing with here is the imposition of a new pattern on to the old, familiar one.'

'Pattern? What pattern?'

'The warrens. *That* pattern.'

Deadsmell dropped his last skewer—scraped clean—on the plate and leaned forward. 'You're saying Icarium went and made a *new set* of warrens?'

'Swallow what's in your mouth before you gape, please. Yes, that's my idea. I'm telling you, Fiddler's game was insane with power. Almost as bad as if someone tried a reading while sitting in K'rul's lap. Well, not quite, since this new pattern is young, the blood still fresh—'

'Blood?' demanded Ebron. 'What blood?'

'Icarium's blood,' Bottle said.

'Is he dead then?'

'Is he? How should I know? Is K'rul dead?'

'Of course not,' Deadsmell answered. 'If he was, the warrens would have died— that's assuming all your theories about K'rul and the warrens are even true—'

'They are. It was blood magic. That's how the Elder Gods did things—when we use sorcery we're feeding on K'rul's blood.'

No one spoke for a time. The server approached with a heavy tray. It was like watching the tide come in.

'So,' ventured Ebron once the tray clunked down and the plates and wine and goblets were randomly arrayed on the table by a quivering hand, 'are things going to settle out, Bottle?'

'I don't know,' he admitted, pouring out some wine as the waiter shuffled away. 'We may have to do some exploring.'

'Of what?'

'The new warrens, of course.'

'How can they be any different?' Ebron asked. 'It's the fact that they're mostly the same that's got things confused—has to be. If they were completely different, there wouldn't be this kind of trouble.'

'Good point. Well, we should see if we can nudge things together, until the overlap is precise.'

Deadsmell snorted. 'Bottle, we're squad mages, for Hood's sake. We're like midges feeding on a herd of bhederin—and here you're suggesting we try and drive that herd. It's not going to happen. We haven't the power—even if we put ourselves together on this.'

'That's why I'm thinking we should involve Quick Ben, maybe even Sinn—'

'Don't even think that,' Ebron said, eyes wide. 'You don't want her anywhere close, Bottle. I still can't believe the Adjunct made her High Mage—'

'Well,' cut in Deadsmell, 'since she's mute she'll be the only High Mage in history who never complains.'

'Just Quick Ben, then.'

'He'll complain enough for both of them,' Deadsmell nodded.

'Just how nasty is he?' Ebron asked Bottle.

'Quick? Well, he gave a dragon a bloody nose.'

'A real dragon or a Soletaken dragon?'

'It makes no difference, Ebron—you pretty much can't tell just from looking at them. You'll only know a Soletaken when it veers. Anyway, don't forget, he faced down the Edur mages once we quit Seven Cities.'

'That was illusion.'

'Ebron, I was in on that—a lot closer than you. Sure, maybe it was illusion, but maybe not.' He paused, then said, 'That's another thing to consider. The local mages. They used raw sorcery, pretty much Chaotic and nothing else. No warrens. But now there's warrens here. The local mages are in worse shape than we are.'

'I still don't like the idea of some kind of collective ritual,' Deadsmell said. 'When you're under siege you don't pop your head up over the parapet, do you? Unless you want feather eyelashes.'

'Well, Fiddler went and did just that with the reading, didn't he? Nobody died—'

'Rubbish. A whole building went crashing down!'

'Nothing new there, Ebron. This whole city is on shaky ground.'

'People died, is what I'm telling you, Bottle. And if that's not bad enough, there were plenty of witnesses claiming to see two dragons rise out of the rubble.' He ducked his head and looked round. 'I don't like dragons. I don't like places where dragons show up all the time. Say we try some ritual—what if fifty dragons come blasting down out of the sky, splatting right on top of us? What then, hey?'

'Well, I don't know, Ebron. It depends. I mean, are they real or Soletaken?'

Sinn held Grub's hand in a tight, sweaty grip. They were edging once more on to the grounds of the old Azath tower. The day was hot, steamy, the air above the tortured mounds glittering with whirling insects. 'Can you smell it?' she asked.

He didn't want to reply.

She shot him a wild look, and then tugged him on to the winding stone path. 'It's all new, Grub. You can drink it like water. It tastes sweet—'

'It tastes dangerous, Sinn.'

'I can almost see it. New patterns, getting stronger—it's running roots right through this place. This is all new,' she said again, almost breathless. 'Just like us—you and me, Grub, we're going to leave all the old people behind. Feel this power! With it we can do anything! We can knock down gods!'

'I don't want to knock anything down, especially gods!'

'You didn't have to listen to Tavore, Grub. And Quick Ben.'

'We can't just *play* with this stuff, Sinn.'

'Why not? No one else is.'

'Because it's broken, that's why. It doesn't feel right at all—these new warrens, they feel *wrong*, Sinn. The pattern is broken.'

They halted just outside the tower's now gaping doorway and its seemingly lifeless wasp nest. She faced him, eyes bright. 'So let's fix it.'

He stared at her. 'How?'

'Come on,' she said, pulling him into the gloom of the Azath tower.

Feet crunching on dead wasps, she led him without hesitation to the stairs. They climbed to the empty chamber that had once been the nexus of the Azath's power.

It was empty no longer.

Blood-red threads sizzled within, forming a knotted, chaotic web that spanned the entire chamber. The air tasted metallic, bitter.

They stood side by side at the threshold.

'It uses what it finds,' Sinn whispered.

'So now what?'

'Now, we step inside.'

'They march in circles any longer and they'll drop.'

Corporal Tarr squinted at the gasping, foot-dragging soldiers. 'They're out of shape, all right. Pathetic. Of course, we were supposed to think of something.'

Cuttle scratched at his jaw. 'So we ended up thrashing them after all. Look, here comes Fid, thank the gods.'

The sergeant scowled upon seeing his two soldiers and almost turned round before Cuttle's frantic beckoning beat down his defences, or at least elicited the man's pity. Raking fingers through his red and grey beard, he walked over. 'What are you two doing to those poor bastards?'

'We run out of things to make them do,' Cuttle said.

'Well, stumbling round inside a compound only takes it so far. You need to get them out of the city. Get them practising entrenchments, redoubts and berms. You need to turn their penchant for wholesale rout into something like an organized withdrawal. You need to stretch their chain of command and see who's got the guts to step up when it snaps. You need to make those ones squad-leaders. War games, too—set them against one of the other brigades or battalions being trained by our marines. They need to win a few times before they can learn how to avoid losing. Now, if Hedge comes by, you ain't seen me, right?'

They watched him head off down the length of the colonnade.

'That's depressing,' Cuttle muttered.

'I'll never make sergeant,' Tarr said, 'not in a thousand years. Damn.'

'Good point, you just lifted my mood, Corporal. Thanks.'

Hedge pounced on his old friend at the end of the colonnade. 'What're you bothering with them for, Fid? These Bonehunters ain't Bridgeburners and those Letherii ain't soldiers. You're wasting your time.'

'Gods below, stop stalking me!'

Hedge's expression fell. 'It's not that, Fid. Only, we were friends—'

'And then you died. So I went and got over you. And now you show up all over again. If you were just a ghost then maybe I could deal with it—aye, I know you whispered in my ear every now and then, and saved my skin and all that and it's not that I ain't grateful either. But . . . well, we ain't squad mates any more, are we? You came back when you weren't supposed to, and in your head you're still a Bridgeburner and you think the same of me. Which is why you keep slagging off these Bonehunters, like it was some rival division. But it isn't, because the Bridgeburners are finished, Hedge. Dust and ashes. Gone.'

'All right all right! So maybe I need to make some adjustments, too. I can do that! Easy. Watch me! First thing—I'll get the captain to give me a squad—'

'What makes you think you deserve to lead a squad?'

'Because I was a—'

'Exactly. A damned Bridgeburner! Hedge, you're a sapper—'

'So are you!'

'Mostly I leave that to Cuttle these days—'

'You did the drum! Without me!'

'You weren't there—'

'That makes no difference!'

'How can it not make a difference?'

'Let me work on that. The point is, you were doing sapping stuff, Fid. In fact, the point is, you and me need to get drunk and find us some whores—'

'Only works the other way round, Hedge.'

'Now you're talking! And listen, I'll get a finger-bone nose-ring so I can fit right in with these bloodthirsty Bonehunters you're so proud of, how does that sound?'

Fiddler stared at the man. His ridiculous leather cap with its earflaps, his hopeful grin. 'Get a nose-ring and I'll kill you myself, Hedge. Fine, then, let's stir things up. Just don't even think about asking for a squad, all right?'

'So what am I supposed to do instead?'

'Tag along with Gesler's squad—I think it's short of a body.' And then he snorted a laugh. 'A body. You. Good one.'

'I told you I wasn't dead no more, Fid.'

'If you say so.'

Lieutenant Pores sat in the captain's chair behind the captain's desk, and held his hands folded together on the surface before him as he regarded the two women who had, until recently, been rotting in cells in some Letherii fort. 'Sisters, right?'

When neither replied, Pores nodded. 'Some advice, then. Should either of you one day achieve higher rank—say, captain—you too will learn the art of stating the obvious. In the meantime, you are stuck with the absurd requirement of answering stupid questions with honest answers, all the while keeping a straight face. You will need to do a lot of this with me.'

The woman on the right said, 'Aye, sir, we're sisters.'

'Thank you, Sergeant Sinter. Wasn't that satisfying? I'm sure it was. What I will find even more satisfying is watching you two washing down the barracks' latrines for the next two weeks. Consider it your reward for being so incompetent as to be captured by these local fools. And then failing to escape.' He scowled. 'Look at you two—nothing but skin and bones! Those uniforms look like shrouds. I order you to regain your lost weight, in all the right places, within the same fortnight. Failure to do will result in a month on half-rations. Furthermore, I want you both to get your hair cut, down to the scalp, and to deposit said sheared hair on this desk precisely at the eighth bell this evening. Not earlier, not later. Understood?'

'Yes, sir!' barked Sergeant Sinter.

'Very good,' nodded Pores. 'Now get out of here, and if you see Lieutenant Pores in the corridor remind him that he has been ordered to a posting on Second Maiden Fort, and the damned idiot should be on his way by now. Dismissed!'

As soon as the two women were gone, Pores leapt up from behind the captain's desk, scanned the surface to ensure nothing had been knocked askew, and then carefully repositioned the chair just so. With a nervous glance out the window, he hurried out into the reception room and sat down behind his own, much smaller desk. Hearing heavy boots in the corridor he began shuffling the scrolls and wax tablets on the surface in front of him, planting a studious frown on his features in time for his captain's portentous arrival.

As soon as the door opened, Pores leapt to attention. 'Good morning, sir!'

'It's mid-afternoon, Lieutenant. Those wasp stings clearly rotted what's left of your brain.'

'Yes, sir!'

'Have those two Dal Honese sisters reported yet?'

'No, sir, not hide nor . . . hair, sir. We should be seeing one or both any time now—'

'Oh, and is that because you intend to physically hunt them down, Lieutenant?'

'As soon as I've done this paperwork, sir, I will do just that, even if it takes me all the way to Second Maiden Fort, sir.'

Kindly scowled. 'What paperwork?'

'Why, sir,' Pores gestured, 'this paperwork, sir.'

'Well, don't dally, Lieutenant. As you know, I need to attend a briefing at half seventh bell, and I want them in my office before then.'

'Yes, sir!'.

Kindly walked past and went inside. Where, Pores imagined, he would spend the rest of the afternoon looking at his collection of combs.

'Everyone's right,' Kisswhere muttered as she and her sister made their back to the dormitory, 'Captain Kindly is not only a bastard, but insane. What was all that about our hair?'

Sinter shrugged. 'No idea.'

'Well, there's no regulations about our hair. We can complain to the Fist—'

'No we won't,' Sinter cut in. 'Kindly wants hair on his desk, we give him hair on his desk.'

'Not mine!'

'Nor mine, Kisswhere, nor mine.'

'Then whose?'

'Not whose. What's.'

Corporal Pravalak Rim was waiting at the entrance. 'Did you get commendations then?' he asked.

'Oh love,' said Kisswhere, 'Kindly doesn't give out commendations. Just punishments.'

'What?'

Sinter said, 'The captain ordered us to put on weight,' and then she stepped past him, 'among other things.' And then she paused and turned back to Pravalak. 'Corporal, find us some shears, and a large burlap sack.'

'Aye, Sergeant. Shears—how big?'

'I don't care, just find some.'

Kisswhere offered the young man a broad smile as he hurried off, and then she went inside, marching halfway down the length of the dormitory. She halted at the foot of a cot where the bedding had been twisted into something resembling a nest. Squatting in the centre of this nest was a wrinkled, scarified, tattooed bad dream with small glittering eyes. 'Nep Furrow, I need a curse.'

'Eh? Geen way! Groblet! Coo!'

'Captain Kindly. I was thinking hives, the real itchy kind. No, wait, that'll just make him even meaner. Make him cross-eyed—but not so he notices, just everyone else. Can you do that, Nep?'

'War butt wod i'meen, eh?'

'How about a massage?'

'Kissands?'

'My very own, yes.'

'Urble ong eh? Urble ong?'

'Bell to bell, Nep.'

'Nikked?'

'Who, you or me?'

'Bat!'

'Fine, but we'll need to rent a room, unless of course you want an audience?'

Nep Furrow was getting excited, in all the wrong ways, she saw. He jumped round, squirmed, his skin glistening with sweat. 'Blether squids, Kiss, blether squids!'

'With the door barred,' she said. 'I won't have any strangers walking in.'

'Hep haw! Curseed?'

'Aye, cross-eyed, but he can't know it—'

'Impable, lees in glusion.'

'Illusion? A glamour? Oh, that's very good. Get on it, then, thanks.'

Badan Gruk rubbed at his face as Sinter collapsed on to the cot beside him. 'What in Hood's name are we doing here?' he asked.

Her dark eyes flicked to his—the momentary contact sweet as a caress—and then she looked away. 'You're the only kind of soldier a body can trust, Badan, did you know that?'

'What? No, I—'

'You're reluctant. You're not cut out for violence and so you don't go looking for it. You use your wits first and that silly bonekisser as a last resort. The dangerous ones do it the other way round and that costs lives every time. Every time.' She paused. 'Did I hear right? Some drunk marine sergeant crossed this damned empire from tavern to tavern?'

He nodded. 'And left a trail of local sympathizers, too. But she wasn't afraid of spilling blood, Sinter, she just picked out the right targets—people nobody liked. Tax collectors, provosts, advocates.'

'But she's a drunk?'

'Aye.'

Shaking her head, Sinter fell back on to the cot. She stared at the ceiling. 'How come *she* doesn't get busted down?'

'Because she's one of the Y'Ghatan Stormcrawlers, that's why. Them that went under.'

'Oh, right.' A moment's consideration, and then: 'Well, we're marching soon.'

Badan rubbed at his face again. 'But nobody knows where, or even why. It's a mess, Sinter.' He hesitated, and then asked, 'You got any bad feelings about it?'

'Got no feelings at all, Badan. About anything. And no, I don't know what took me by the throat the night of Fid's reading, either. In fact, I don't even remember much of that night, not the ride, nor what followed.'

'Nothing followed. Mostly, you just passed out. Some Fenn had already stepped in, anyway. Punched a god in the side of the head.'

'Good.'

'That's it? That's all you're going to say?'

'Well, like the one-eyed hag says, there's all kinds of worship in the world, Badan.'

'I don't . . .' but the look she shot him ground the words down to dust in his mouth. He flinched and glanced away. 'That thing you said about wits, Sinter, was that a joke, too?'

She sighed, closing her eyes. 'No, Badan. No. Wake me when Rim gets back, will you?'

Trailed by Lostara Yil, Keneb, Blistig and Quick Ben, the Adjunct Tavore strode down the length of the throne room and halted ten paces from the two thrones.

'Welcome to you all,' said King Tehol. 'Adjunct, my Chancellor here informs me that you have a list of requests, most of which will contribute to a happy burgeoning of the royal coffers. Now, if I was the venal sort I would say let's get right to that. But I am no such sort and so I would like to broach an entirely different matter, one of immense importance.'

'Of course, sire,' said Tavore. 'We are at your disposal and will assist in any way we can.'

The King beamed.

Lostara wondered at the Queen's sigh, but not for long.

'Wonderful! Now, as soon as I recall the specific details of what I wanted to ask, why, I will. In the meantime, my Ceda tells me that you have stirred awake a sorcerous nest of trouble. My Chancellor, alas, assures me that the confusion is exaggerated—which of the two am I to believe? Please, if you can, break asunder this dreadful deadlock.'

Frowning, Tavore turned and said, 'High Mage, can you address this matter, please?'

Quick Ben moved to stand beside the Adjunct. 'Sire, both your Chancellor and your Ceda are, essentially, correct.'

Lostara saw Bugg smile, and then scowl from where he stood to the right of Tehol's throne.

'How fascinating,' the King murmured, leaning forward to settle his chin in one hand. 'Can you elaborate, High Mage?'

'Probably not, but I will try. The situation, terrifying as it is, is probably temporary. The reading of the Deck of Dragons, which Preda Brys Beddict attended, seems to have illuminated a structural flaw in the . . . uhm . . . fabric of reality, a wounding of sorts. It seems, sire, that someone—someone very powerful—attempted to impose a new structure upon the already existing warrens of sorcery.'

Brys Beddict, positioned to the left of the Queen, asked, 'High Mage, can you explain these "warrens" which seem so central to your notions of magic?'

'Unlike the sorcery that prevailed on this continent until recently, Preda, magic everywhere else exists in a more formalized state. The power, so raw here, is elsewhere refined, aspected, organized into something like themes, and these themes are what we call warrens. Many are accessible to mortals and gods alike; others are'—and he glanced at Bugg—'Elder. Some are virtually extinct, or inaccessible due to ignorance or deliberate rituals of sealing. Some, in addition, are claimed and ruled over by elements either native to those warrens, or so fundamentally related to them as to make the distinction meaningless.'

King Tehol lifted a finger. 'A moment, whilst I blink the glaze from my eyes. Now, let's mull on what has been said thus far—I'm good at mulling, by the way. If I understand you, High Mage, the realm the Tiste Edur called Kurald Emurlahn represents one of these warrens, yes?'

'Aye,' Quick Ben responded, and then hastily added, 'sire. The Tiste warrens—and there are three that we know of—are all Elder. Two of them, by the way, are no longer ruled by the Tiste. One is virtually sealed. The other has been usurped.'

'And how do these warrens relate to your Deck of Dragons?'

The High Mage flinched. 'Not my Deck, sire, I assure you. There is no simple answer to your question—'

'It's about time! I was beginning to feel very stupid. Please understand, I have no problem about being stupid. *Feeling* stupid is entirely another matter.'

'Ah, yes, sire. Well, the Deck of Dragons probably originated as a means of divination—less awkward than tiles, burnt bones, silt patterns, random knots, knucklebones, puke, faeces—'

'Understood! Please, there are ladies present, good sir!'

'Forgive me, sire. In some obvious ways, the High Houses of the Deck relate to certain warrens and as such they present a kind of window looking in on those warrens—conversely, of course, things can in turn look out from the other side, which is what makes a reading so . . . risky. The Deck is indifferent to barriers—in the right hands it can reveal patterns and relationships hidden to mortal eyes.'

'Even what you describe,' said Brys, 'hardly matches what happened at that reading, High Mage.'

'Aye, Preda, which brings us back to the wound that is this city. Someone drew a knife and carved a new pattern here. New, and yet ancient beyond belief. There was an attempt at a reawakening, but what awoke was broken.'

'And do you know who that "someone" might have been?' King Tehol asked.

'Icarium Lifestealer, sire. A Champion intended to cross blades with Emperor Rhulad Sengar.'

Tehol leaned back and said, 'Ceda, do you have anything to add at this moment?'

Bugg started and then winced. 'The High Mage's knowledge is most impressive, sire. Uncannily so.'

Queen Janath asked, 'Can this wound be healed, Ceda? And if not, what is the threat to Letheras should it continue to . . . bleed?'

The old man made a face that suggested he'd just tasted something unpleasant. 'Letheras is now like a pool of water with all the silts stirred up. We are blinded, groping, and none of us can draw more than a thin, shallow handful of magic. The effect ripples outward and will soon incapacitate the mages throughout the kingdom.'

'High Mage,' Janath then said, 'you said earlier that the effect is temporary. Does this presume a healing is imminent?'

'Most wounds heal themselves, over time, Highness. I expect that will begin . . . as soon as we Malazans get the Hood out of here. The reading gave that wound a sharp poke. Blood flowed out, and in this instance, *blood is power*.'

'Well now,' mused the King. 'How fascinating, how curious, how alarming. I think we had best proceed with haste to the matter of filling the royal coffers. Adjunct Tavore, you wish to supply a baggage train sufficient to see you into and, presumably, across the Wastelands. This we are happy to provide, at a complimentary, reduced rate—to show our appreciation of your exemplary efforts in ousting the Edur tyranny. Now, my Chancellor has already begun arranging matters from our end, and he informs me that his projected estimate to meet your needs is substantial. It will take us approximately four weeks to assemble such a train and hopefully only moments for you to pay for it. Of course, Brys will arrange his escort's resupply, so you need not worry about that.'

He paused then, noting the Adjunct's involuntary start. 'Ah, your escort. Yes, my brother insists that he accompany you through the neighbouring kingdoms. Quite simply, neither Saphinand nor Bolkando can be trusted to do anything but betray and undermine you at every turn. Depressing neighbours—but then, so were we to them not so long ago. I am considering announcing a Royal Project to construct the world's highest fence for ever separating our respective territories, with some fine hedging to soften the effect. Yes yes, dear wife, I am now rambling and yes, it was fun!'

'Sire,' said Tavore, 'thank you for the offer of an escort, but I assure you, there is no need. Those kingdoms we seek to pass through may well be treacherous, but I doubt they can succeed in surprising us.' Her tone was flat and though she couldn't see, Lostara was certain that the Adjunct's eyes were if anything even flatter.

'They are thieves,' said Brys Beddict. 'Your baggage train, Adjunct, will be enormous—the lands you seek are bereft—it may be that even Kolanse itself is unable to accommodate you.'

'Excuse me,' said Tavore. 'I do not recall stating our intended destination.'

'There's little else out there,' said Brys, shrugging.

The Adjunct said nothing and all at once the atmosphere was tense.

'Preda Brys,' said the King, 'will be assisting in policing your train as you pass through two entire nations of pickpockets.'

Still Tavore hesitated. 'Sire, we have no desire to embroil your kingdom in a war, should Saphinand or Bolkando attempt to betray the passage agreements.'

'It will be our very presence,' said Brys, 'that will ensure nothing so overt on their part, Adjunct. Please understand, if we do not escort you and you subsequently find yourselves in a vicious war with no retreat possible, then we in turn will have no choice but to march to your rescue.'

'Just so,' agreed the King. 'So accept the escort, Adjunct, or I shall hold my breath until I achieve a most royal shade of purple.'

Tavore bowed her head in acquiescence. 'I withdraw all objections, sire. Thank you for the escort.'

'That's better. Now, I must now seek reassurance from my staff on three distinct issues. Chancellor, are you content with everything pertaining to outfitting the Adjunct's forces?'

'I am, sire,' said Bugg.

'Excellent. Royal Treasurer, are you confident that the Malazans have sufficient funds for this enterprise?'

'So I am assured, sire,' said Bugg.

'Good. Ceda, do you concur that the departure of the Malazans will hasten the healing that has befallen the city?'

'I do, sire,' said Bugg.

'Consensus at last! How delightful! Now what should we do?'

Queen Janath stood. 'Food and wine awaits us in the dining hall. Allow me to lead our guests.' And she stepped down from the dais.

'Darling wife,' said Tehol, 'for you I make all manner of allowances.'

'I am relieved that you so willingly assume such a burden, husband.'

'So am I,' he replied.

Chapter Six

The beetle that walks slowly has nothing to fear.

SAPHII SAYING

Coated in dust-spattered blood, Vedith rode out of the billowing smoke, in his wake piteous screams and the raucous roar of flames as they engulfed the three-storey government building in the town's centre. Most of the other structures lining the main street were already gutted, although fires still licked the blackened frames and the foul smoke lifted pillars skyward.

Four other riders emerged behind Vedith, scimitars unsheathed, the Aren steel blades streaked with gore.

Hearing their wild whoops, Vedith scowled. The mangled round shield strapped to his right forearm had driven splinters through the wrist and that hand could not grip the reins. In his left hand he held his own scimitar, the blade snapped a hand's-width above the hilt—he would have thrown it away but he valued the hilt, grip and pommel too much to part with it.

His horse's reins dragged between the beast's front legs and at any moment the galloping mount, in her fear and pain, might slam a hoof down on them, which would snap her neck down and send her rider tumbling.

He rose in his stirrups, leaned forward—pounded by the horse's pitching neck—and bit the animal's left ear, tugging backwards. Squealing, the beast's head lifted, her plunging hoofs slowing, drawing up. This gave Vedith time to sheathe what was left of his father's sword and then slip his arm round the horse's neck, easing the pressure of his teeth.

Moments later, the wounded mare pitched and wobbled down off the cobbled road into the high grasses of the ditch and clumped to a halt, body trembling.

Murmuring calming words, the warrior released the animal's ear and settled back on the saddle, collecting the reins with his one usable hand.

His four companions rode up and, beasts jostling on the road, they held their swords high in triumph, even as they spat dust and blood from their mouths.

Vedith felt sick. But he understood. The growing list of proscriptions, the ever-dwindling freedom, the indignities and undisguised contempt. Each day in the past week more Bolkando soldiers had arrived, fortlets springing up round the Khundryl encampment like mushroom knuckles on dung. And tensions twisted ever tighter. Arguments burst to life like spotfires, and then, all at once—

He guided his horse back on to the road and glared back at the burning town.

And then scanned the horizons to either side. Columns of coiling black smoke rose everywhere like crooked spears—yes, the patience of the Burned Tears was at an end, and he knew that a dozen villages, twice as many hamlets, scores of farms and, now, one town, had felt the wrath of the Khundryl.

Vedith's raiding party, thirty warriors—most of them barely into their third decade—had clashed with a garrison. The fighting had been ferocious. He'd lost most of his troop, and this had been fuel enough to set ablaze the Khundryl fury, inflicting wrathful vengeance upon wounded soldiers and the civilian inhabitants of the town.

The taste of that slaughter left a bitter, toxic stain, inside and out.

His horse could not hold still. Her slashed flank still bled freely. She circled, head tossing, kicking with the wounded hind leg.

They'd left scores of corpses in that nameless town. This very morning it had been a peaceful place, life awakening and crawling on to the old familiar trails, a slow beating heart. Now it was ruin and charred meat—they'd not even bothered looting, so fierce upon them was the lust for slaughter.

To a proud people, the contempt of others drives the deepest wound. These Bolkando had thought the Khundryl knives were dull. Dull knives, dull minds. They had thought they could cheat the savages, mock them, ply them with foul liquor and steal their wealth.

We are Seven Cities—did you think you were the first to try to play such games with us?

Stragglers were still emerging—three, two, a lone wounded warrior slumped over his saddle, two more.

The soldiers of the garrison had not understood how to meet a cavalry charge. It was as if they had never before seen such a thing, gaping at the precise execution, the deadly timing of the javelins launched when the two sides were but a dozen paces apart. The Bolkando line—formed up across the main street—had crumpled as the barbed javelins punched through shield and scale armour, as figures reeled, buckled and fouled others.

The Khundryl warhorses and their howling, scimitar-slashing riders then smashed into that tattered formation.

A slaughter. Until the rear sections of the Bolkando dispersed, scattering into clumps, pelting into the side avenues, the alleys, the sheltered mouths of stone-faced shops. The battle broke up then, knots spinning away. Khundryl warriors were forced to dismount, unable to press into the narrower alleys, or draw back out into the open soldiers crouched behind drawn-up shields in the niches of doorways. Still outnumbered, warriors of the Burned Tears began falling.

It had taken most of the morning to hunt down and butcher the last garrison soldier. And barely a bell to murder the townsfolk who had not fled—who had, presumably, imagined that seventy-five soldiers would prevail against a mere thirty savages—and then set fire to the town, roasting alive the few who had successfully hidden themselves.

Such scenes, Vedith knew, were raging across the entire countryside now. No one was spared, and to deliver the message in the clearest way imaginable, every Bolkando farm was being stripped of anything and everything edible or otherwise useful. The revolt had been ignited by the latest Bolkando price hike—a hundred per cent, applicable only to the Khundryl—on all necessities, including fodder for the horses. *Revile us, yes, even as you take our silver and gold.*

He had a dozen warriors with him now, one of them likely to die soon—well before they reached the encampment. And thick splinters rode up his forearm like extra longbones, pain throbbing.

Yes, the losses had been high. But then, what other troop had attacked a garrisoned town?

Still, he wondered if, perhaps, the Burned Tears had kicked awake the wrong nest.

'Bind Sidab's wounds,' he now said in a growl. 'Has he his sword?'

'He has, Vedith.'

'Give it to me—mine broke.'

Although he was dying and knew it, Sidab lifted his head at this and showed Vedith a red smile.

'It shall weight my hand as did my father's sword,' Vedith said. 'I shall wield it with pride, Sidab.'

The man nodded, smile fading. He coughed out a gout of blood and then slid out of his saddle, thumping heavily on to the cobbled road.

'Sidab stays behind.'

The others nodded and spat to make a circle round the corpse, thus sanctifying the ground, completing the only funeral ceremony needed for Khundryl warriors on the path of war. Vedith reached out and took up the reins of Sidab's horse. He would take the beast as well, and ride it, to ease his own mount's discomfort. 'We return to Warleader Gall. Our words shall make his eyes shine.'

Warleader Gall sagged back into his antler and rope throne, the knots creaking. 'Coltaine's sweet breath,' he sighed, squeezing shut his eyes.

Jarabb, Tear Runner to the warleader and the only other occupant of Gall's tent, removed his helmet, and then the padded doeskin cap, and raked thick fingers through his hair, before stepping forward and dropping to one knee. 'Command me,' he said.

Gall groaned. 'Not now, Jarabb. The time for play's over—my Fall-damned young braves have given us a war. Twenty raids have howled back into camp, sacks filled with hens and pups and whatnot. I'd wager nigh on a thousand innocent farmers and villagers already dead—'

'And hundreds of soldiers, Warleader,' reminded Jarabb. 'The fortlets burn—'

'And I've been coughing from the smoke all morning—we didn't need to torch them—that timber would have been useful. So we spit and snarl like a desert lynx in her lair, and what do you think King Tarkulf is going to do? Wait, never mind him—the man's got fungi for brains—it's the Chancellor and his cute Conquestor we have to worry about. Let me tell you what they'll do, Jarabb. They won't demand we return to this camp. They won't insist on reparations and blood-coin. No, they'll raise an army and march straight for us.'

'Warleader,' Jarabb said, straightening, 'wildlands beckon us north and east—once out on the plains, no one can catch us.'

'All very well, but these Bolkando aren't our enemy. They were supplying us—'

'We loot all we can before fleeing.'

'And won't the Adjunct be thrilled by how we've smoothed the sand before her. This is a mess, Jarabb. A mess.'

'What, then, will you do, Warleader?'

Gall finally opened his eyes, blinked, and then coughed. After a moment he said, 'I won't try to mend what cannot be undone. This aids the Adjunct nothing. No, we need to seize the bull's cock.' He surged to his feet, collected up his crow-feather cloak. 'Break this camp—kill all livestock and start curing the meat. It will be weeks before the Bolkando muster the numbers they need against us. To ensure safe passage of the Bonehunters—not to mention the Grey Helms—we're going to march on the capital. We're going to pose such a threat that Tarkulf voids his bladder and overrules his advisors—I want the King thinking he might be facing a three-pronged invasion of his piss-ass latrine pit of a kingdom.'

Jarabb smiled. He could see the embers glowing in his warleader's dark eyes. Which meant that, once all the orders were barked and all the other runners were scrambling dust-trails, Gall's mood would be much improved.

Sufficient, perhaps, to once more invite some . . . play.

All he need do was make sure the old man's wife was nowhere close.

Shield Anvil Tanakalian shifted uncomfortably beneath his chain surcoat. The quilted underpadding had worn through on his right shoulder—he should have patched it this morning and would have done so had he not been so eager to witness the landing of the first cohort of Grey Helms on this wretched ground.

For all his haste he found Mortal Sword Krughava already positioned on the rise overlooking the shoreline, red-faced beneath her heavy helm. Though the sun was barely above the mountain peaks to the east, the air was stifling, oppressive, swarming with sand flies. As he approached he could see in her eyes the doom of countless epic poems, as if she had devoted her life to absorbing the tragedies of a thousand years' worth of fallen civilizations, finding the taste savagely pleasing.

Yes, she was a holy terror, this hard, iron woman.

Upon arriving at her side, he bowed in greeting. 'Mortal Sword. This is a portentous occasion.'

'Yet but two of us stand here, sir,' she rumbled in reply, 'when there should be three.'

He nodded. 'A new Destriant must be chosen. Who among the elders have you considered, Mortal Sword?'

Four squat, broad-beamed avars—the landing craft of the Thrones of War—were fast closing on the channel wending through the mud flats, oar blades flashing. The tide wasn't cooperating at all. The bay should be swelling with inflow; instead the water churned, as if confused. Tanakalian squinted at the lead avar, expecting it to run aground at any moment. The heavily burdened brothers and sisters would have to disembark and then slog on foot—he wondered how deep the mud was out there.

'I am undecided,' Krughava finally admitted. 'None of our elders happens to be very old.'

True enough. This long sea voyage had worn through the lives of a score or more of the most ancient brothers and sisters. Tanakalian swung round to study the two encampments situated two thousand paces inland, one on this side of the river and the other on the opposite, west side. As yet there had been no direct contact with the Akrynnai delegation—if the mob of spike-haired, endlessly singing, spear-waving barbarians truly justified such an honorific. So long as they stayed on the other side of the river, the Akrynnai could sing until the mountains sank into the sea.

The Bolkando camp, an ever burgeoning city of gaudy tents, was already aswarm—as if the imminent landing of the Perish had sent them into a frenzy. Strange people, these Bolkando. Scar-faced yet effete, polite yet clearly bloodthirsty. Tanakalian did not trust them, and it looked as if their escort through the mountain passes and into the kingdom amounted to an entire army—three or four thousand strong—and though he didn't think the average Bolkando soldier could hope to match a Grey Helm, still their sheer numbers were cause for concern. 'Mortal Sword,' he said, facing her once more, 'do we march into betrayal?'

'This journey must be considered one through hostile territory, Shield Anvil. We will march in armour, weapons at hand. Should the Bolkando escort precede us into the pass, then I shall have no cause for worry. Should they divide to form advance and rear elements, I will be forced to take measure of the strength of that rearguard. If it is modest then we need have little concern. If it is overstrength relative to the advance element, then one must consider the possibility that a second army awaits us at the far end of the pass. Given,' she added, 'that we must travel in column, such an ambush would put us at a disadvantage, initially at least.'

'We had best hope,' observed Tanakalian, 'that they intend treating with us honourably.'

'If not, they will regret their temerity, sir.'

Three legions, eighteen cohorts and three supply companies. Five thousand brothers and sisters in the land force. The remaining legions would accompany the Thrones of War on the ill-mapped sea-lanes south of the coast, seeking the Pelasiar Sea. It had been the judgement of both the Adjunct and Krughava that the Burned Tears needed support. Given the reported scarcity of resources in the Wastelands, the Bonehunters would travel independent of the more southerly forces consisting of the Khundryl mounted and the Perish foot legions. The two elements would march eastward on parallel tracks, with perhaps twenty leagues between them, until reaching the borders of the first kingdom beyond the Wastelands.

In Krughava's mind, Tanakalian well knew, a holy war awaited them, the singular purpose of their existence, and upon that foreign soil the Grey Helms would find their glory, their heroic triumph in service to the Wolves of Winter. He shared with her that sense of purpose, fate's bold promise, and like her he did not fear war. They were trained in the ways of violence, sworn to those cusps of history hacked into shape on battlefields. With sword and will, they could change the world. Such was the truth of war, for all that soft fools might wish otherwise, might dream of peace and harmony between strangers.

Romantics with their wishful notions invariably delivered the asp's bite, whether they sought to or not. Hope and faith seeped through like the sweetest nectar, only to sour into vile poison. Most virtues, Tanakalian well knew, were defenceless. Abused and corrupted with ease, ever made to turn in the wielder's hand. It took a self-deluded mind to force justice upon a world when that world cared for nothing; when all reality mocked the righteous with its indifference.

War swept such games aside. It was pure, unapologetic in its brutality. Justice arrived with the taste of blood, both sweet and bitter and that too was as it should be.

No, he would tell the Mortal Sword nothing of the Destriant's final words of terror, of his unmanned panic, the shrill clangour of his warnings. Such failings served no one, after all.

Even so, Tanakalian vowed to remain watchful, wary, trusting nothing and expecting betrayal from every stranger.

Run'Thurvian was too old for war. Fear took his life—I could see that clearly enough. He was blind, driven to madness. Babbling. It was all so . . . undignified.

The avars had run aground over a hundred paces from the high-tide mark. Burdened soldiers stumbled shin-deep in fly-swarmed mud, whilst the crews struggled to drag the boats free to retrace their route back to the anchored Thrones.

They were in for a long day.

'Well now,' muttered Chancellor Rava as he perused the coded missive, 'our dear King seems to have led our precious kingdom into a royal mess.'

Avalt paced in front of the old man, from one side of the tent's shrouded chamber to the other. He could guess at most of the details hidden on the parchment in Rava's hands. The Chancellor's comment was, if the truth was laid bare, entirely inaccurate. The 'mess' didn't come from King Tarkulf. In fact, it was without question the product of certain excesses among servants of the Chancellor and, indeed, of Conquestor Avalt himself. 'What we now need to determine,' he said, his voice still cracking from the tirade he had delivered a short time earlier to a select company of merchant agents and spies, 'is the nature of the relationship between our Perish friends and these Khundryl bandits.'

'True,' Rava replied. 'However, do recall that the Perish seem to hold to an absurdly elevated notion of honour. Once we present to them our version of the Khundryl's sudden, inexplicable rampage . . . once we speak of the atrocities and the slaughter of hundreds, if not thousands of innocents . . .' he smiled, 'I believe we shall see, to our blessed relief, a most stern disavowal from the Mortal Sword.'

Avalt's nod was sharp. 'Which will permit me to concentrate my forces on crushing the Khundryl without having to worry about the Perish.'

Rava's watery eyes seemed to slide from Avalt as he asked, 'Is there cause for worry, Conquestor? Do we not possess the military might to obliterate both forces if necessary?'

Avalt stiffened. 'Of course, Chancellor. But have you forgotten our latest intelligence from Lether? The third element in this foreign alliance intends to march through our kingdom. Perhaps, even then, we could crush all three forces. But at a dreadful cost. Furthermore, we do not know yet what agreements have been fashioned between the Letherii and these Malazans—we could well end up with the very war we did everything we could to avoid—'

'Resulting in the exposure of our deceptions with regard to our putative allies, the Saphii and the Akrynnai.'

'Said deceptions making obvious the betrayals we intended—yet with us suddenly incapable of backing them with force. It is one thing to make promises only to abandon our allies in the field—if we cannot then occupy the lands of those allies once their armies have been annihilated, then the entire enterprise fails.'

'Let us assume, for the moment,' said Rava, 'that the Letherii threat no longer exists, and so the great Bolkando Alliance need never show its paper fangs. What we presently face, at its worst, is three disconnected armies marching every which way across our kingdom. One of those has now given us a bloody nose, but it is likely that the Khundryl will beat a hasty retreat, now that they've satisfied their bloodlust. They will take their loot and flee into the Wastelands. Naturally, that will be a fatal error—we need only move a few legions of your Third Regulars to occupy the border forts and trenchworks—so that whatever remnants of the Khundryl come crawling back will not present any sort of threat.' He raised a finger. 'We must be sure to have our own commanders in charge, to profit from enslaving the Khundryl refugees.'

'Of course.'

'To continue, then, we are left with the Perish and the Malazans, and both, by all counts, appear eminently civilized. Of a sort to deplore the Khundryl excesses, and indeed they may end up feeling somewhat responsible. They may, in fact, offer reparations.'

Avalt had ceased pacing and he now stood, staring down at the Chancellor. 'What, then, of the ambush we were planning in the pass?'

'I would advise that it remain in place, for the moment, Conquestor. At least until we are able to gauge the Mortal Sword's reaction when we deliver the news of the Khundryl and their unwarranted depredations.'

'I assume you will assure the Mortal Sword of our faith in her and her Grey Helms,' said Avalt. 'And that we recognize that the actions of barbarians—allies or not—cannot be predicted, and that we in no way hold the Perish responsible.'

Rava was nodding. 'And so, having said just that, the fact that we are observed to array our escort in a defensive posture will simply indicate our . . . cautious natures.'

'Thus encouraging the Mortal Sword to make allowances, in her desire to alleviate our newfound uncertainty.'

'Precisely. Well said, Conquestor.'

Avalt resumed pacing. 'So, we drive the Khundryl into the Wastelands, and then enslave whoever makes it back. We ambush the Perish, resulting in a treasure trove of exquisite weaponry and armour—sufficient to outfit a new elite element—'

'Two units,' Rava reminded him. 'Your private guard and one for me as well.'

'As agreed, Chancellor. To resume, we are then facing one remaining army. The Malazans.'

'We must assume that word will reach them of the fate of their allies.'

'To which they will react, either with a perception of sudden vulnerability, in which case they will beat a retreat, or with anger, inciting aggression on their part.'

'Less than ten thousand of the fools,' observed Rava. 'If we invite our allies among the Akrynnai and Saphii, we can divide the spoils—'

'I want those crossbows of theirs,' Avalt said. 'I cannot tell you how frustrating it has been to fail again and again in stealing one thus far. With a legion or two armed with those weapons I could overrun Saphinand in a month.'

'All in due course,' Rava said.

'All of this assumes the Letherii do not get involved.'

The Chancellor sighed, and then made a face. 'My finest spies fall one after another in that court, and those few who have managed to escape are convinced that King Tehol is even worse than Tarkulf. A useless, bumbling idiot.'

'But you are not convinced, Chancellor?'

'Of course not.' He paused, and then said, 'most of the time. We may be dealing with a situation there uncannily identical to our own.'

Avalt caught his breath, frozen in place once again. 'Errant's nudge, can it be, Rava?'

'I wish I knew. Tehol Beddict's wife remains an unknown entity.'

'But surely not in a position to match Queen Abrastal?'

Rava shrugged. 'On the face of it, it seems unlikely. She possesses no private army. No elite units like Abrastal's Evertine Legion or anything comparable. If she has spies—and what queen doesn't—they seem to be engaged in intelligence gathering only, rather than active sabotage.'

'Yet,' said Avalt, 'someone is clearly hunting down *your* spies—'

'Even there, I cannot be certain. Each has died in mysterious circumstances—well, ones that I find mysterious. Tragic mishaps, each and every one. As if the Errant himself was giving each one his personal . . . attention.'

'Now that is an alarming thought, Chancellor.'

'Well, blessedly, not one has been exposed or captured. The accidents that have befallen them invariably resulted in sudden death.'

Avalt frowned. 'The only situation I can imagine that fits the situation, Chancellor, is that our own networks have been so compromised by the Letherii that neither public exposure nor torture is deemed necessary. Such a notion chills me to the bone.'

'You assume the Letherii have managed that infiltration,' said Rava. 'Is it not more likely that the compromise originates from within our own kingdom?'

'Surely not Tarkulf's spies—'

'No, we have them all in hand. No, my friend, is it truly inconceivable that the Queen has her own agents ensconced in Tehol's palace?'

'Actively eliminating rivals, yes, that seems terrifyingly possible,' conceded Avalt. 'Then, what is she planning?'

'I wish I knew.' And Rava sat forward, fixing Avalt with a hard stare. 'Assure me, Conquestor, that at no time will this situation force the Queen into the fore— at no time, Avalt, will we give her reason to shove her useless husband aside and sound the call.'

Avalt was suddenly trembling. The thought of the Evertine Legion stirred awake, actually on the march to clean up whatever mess the kingdom had been plunged into . . . no, that must not be. 'Surely,' he said, voice breaking, 'this present game is too small to concern Queen Abrastal.'

Rava's face was grave. He lifted the parchment note and fluttered it like a tiny white flag. 'An addendum informs me, Conquestor, that the King's fourteenth daughter and her handmaiden are no longer resident in the palace.'

'What? Where have they gone?'

To that, the Chancellor had no answer.

And that silence filled Avalt with dread.

The Bolkando commanders took their time to emerge from their encampment and ascend, with great ceremony, to the rise where Tanakalian and the Mortal Sword stood. It was late afternoon. The Perish legions, in full kit, had formed up and were now marching to the floodplain a thousand paces inland, where the supply units had already begun staking out the tent rows and service blocks. The insects swarming over the brothers and sisters formed sunlit, glittering clouds that spun and whirled even as orange-winged martins flickered through them.

The river lizards that had been basking on the banks for most of the day had begun rising up on their stubby legs and slinking their way into the water, warily eyed by the herons and storks stalking the reedy shallows.

Nights in this country, Tanakalian suspected, would not be pleasant. He could imagine all manner of horrid, poisonous creatures creeping, crawling and flying in the sweltering, steamy darkness. The sooner they climbed into the mountain passes the better he would feel. This notion of insanely inimical nature was new to him, and most unwelcome.

His attention was drawn back to Chancellor Rava and Conquestor Avalt as the unlikely pair—both riding chairs affixed to the saddled shoulders of four burly slaves slowly climbing the slope—rocked back and forth, like kings on shaky thrones. Others flanked them with feather fans, keeping insects at bay. A train of a dozen more trailed the two men. This time, at least, there were no armoured guards—nothing so obvious, although Tanakalian suspected that more than a few of those supposed slaves were in fact bodyguards.

'Solemn greetings!' called the Chancellor, waving one limp hand. He then snapped something to his porters and they set down his chair. He stepped daintily on to the ground, adjusting his silken robes, and was joined moments later by Avalt. They strode up to the Perish.

'A flawlessly executed landing—congratulations, Mortal Sword. Your soldiers are indeed superbly trained.'

'Kind words, Chancellor,' Krughava rumbled in reply. 'Strictly speaking, however, they are not my soldiers. They are my brothers and sisters. We are as much a priesthood as we are a military company.'

'Of course,' murmured Rava, 'and this is certainly what makes you unique on this continent.'

'Oh?'

Conquestor Avalt smiled and provided explanation, 'You arrive possessing a code of conduct unmatched by any native military force. We seek to learn much from you—matters of discipline and behaviour that we can apply to our own people to the benefit of all.'

'It distresses me,' said Krughava, 'that you hold your own soldiers in such low opinion, Conquestor.'

Tanakalian squinted as if he'd caught a glare of sunlight from some distant weapon, and hoped that this seemingly unconscious expression hid his smile.

When he looked back he saw Avalt's own eyes widening within their cage of dyed scars, and then thinning. 'You misunderstand, Mortal Sword.'

Rava said, 'You have perchance already sensed something of the incessant intrigue compounding alliances and agreements of mutual protection between the border nations, Mortal Sword. Such things, while regrettable, are necessary. The Saphii do not trust the Akrynnai. The Akrynnai do not trust the Awl nor the D'rhasilhani. And the Bolkando trust none of them. Foreign armies, we have all long since learned, cannot be held to the same high comportment as one holds one's own forces.' He spread his hands. 'Conquestor Avalt was simply expressing our unexpected pleasure in finding in *you* such unimpeachable honour.'

'Ah,' said Krughava, with all the percipient wit of a cliff goat.

Avalt was struggling to master his anger, and Tanakalian knew that the Mortal Sword—for all her seemingly oblivious insensitivity—was well taking note of this interesting flaw in the commander overseeing Bolkando Kingdom's combined military might. A commander with a temper and, evidently, poor discipline in mastering it—particularly in front of strangers and potential enemies—was one who would squander his soldiers to answer some insult, real or imagined. He was, therefore, both more dangerous and less threatening, the former for the risk of his doing the unexpected, the precipitous; and the latter for what would likely be a blunt, unsubtle execution, fuelled by an overwhelming need for satisfaction.

Tanakalian ran through these details in his mind, forcing himself to inwardly articulate the lessons that he knew Krughava had comprehended in an instant.

Now that the Destriant was gone, it fell to the Shield Anvil to seek a path as close as possible to the Mortal Sword, to find a way into her mind, to how she thought and those duties that drove her.

During these moments of reflection, Chancellor Rava had been speaking: '. . . unexpected tragedies, Mortal Sword, which have put us in a most awkward position. It is necessary, therefore, that we take measured pause here, whilst your formidable forces are poised outside the kingdom's boundaries.'

Krughava had cocked her head. 'Since you have not yet described these tragedies, Chancellor, I can only observe that, from my experience, most tragedies are unexpected, and invariably lead to awkwardness. Since it seems that the fact that we have not yet crossed into your kingdom is, for you, a salient point, am I to assume that your "unexpected tragedies" have in some way jeopardized our agreement?'

Now it was the Chancellor's turn to fail in disguising his irritation. 'You Perish,' he now said, tone brittle, 'have acknowledged a binding alliance with the Khundryl Burned Tears who are guests of the kingdom at the moment—guests who have ceased to behave in a civilized fashion.'

'Indeed? What leads you to this assessment, Chancellor?'

'This—this *assessment*?'

As Rava spluttered, speechless, Conquestor Avalt spoke sardonically: 'How might you assess the following, Mortal Sword? The Khundryl have broken out of their settlement and are now raiding throughout the countryside. Burning and looting farms, stealing herds, putting to the torch forts and hamlets and indeed an entire town. But I am remiss in speaking only of material depredations. I forgot to mention scores of murdered soldiers and thousands of slaughtered civilians. I failed in citing the rapes and butchering of children—'

'Enough!' Krughava's bellow sent all the Bolkando flinching back.

The Chancellor was first to recover. 'Is this to be the manner of your vaunted honour, Mortal Sword?' he demanded, red-faced, eyes bright. 'Can you not comprehend our newfound caution—nay, our distrust? Have we been led to expect such treachery—'

'You go too far,' said Krughava, and Tanakalian saw the faint curl of a smile on her lips—a detail that took his breath away.

It seemed to exert a similar effect upon the Bolkando dignitaries, as Rava paled and Avalt settled a mailed hand on his sword.

'What,' demanded Rava in a rasp, 'does that mean?'

'You describe a local history of internecine treachery and incessant betrayal, sirs, so much so as to be part of your very natures, and then you express horror and outrage at the supposed betrayal of the Khundryl. Your protestations are melodramatic, sirs. False in their extremity. I begin to see in you Bolkando a serpent delighting in the cleverness of its own forked tongue.' She paused in the shocked silence, and then added, 'When I invited you into the illusion of my ignorance, sirs, you slithered with eager glee. Who here among us, then, is the greater fool?'

Tanakalian gave credit to both men as he saw the rapid reassessment betrayed in their features. After a tense moment, Krughava continued in a quieter tone,

'Sirs, I have known Warleader Gall of the Khundryl Burned Tears for some time now. In the course of a long ocean voyage, no duplicities of character remain hidden. You assert the uniqueness of the Grey Helms, and in this you clearly reveal to me your lack of understanding with respect to the Khundryl. The Burned Tears, sirs, are in fact a warrior cult. Devoted to the very heart of their souls to a legendary warleader. This warleader, Coltaine, was of such stature, such honour, that he earned worship not among his allies, but among his putative enemies. Such as the Khundryl Burned Tears.' She paused, and then said, 'I am assured, therefore, that Warleader Gall and his people were provoked. Possessed of admirable forbearance, as I know him to be, Gall would have bowed as a sapling to the wind. Until such time as the insults demanded answer.

'They have raided and conducted wholesale looting? From this detail I conclude Bolkando merchants and the King's agents sought to take advantage of the Khundryl, imposing usurious increases in the price of essential supplies. Furthermore, you state that they broke out of their settlement. What manner of settlement requires a violent exit? The only one that comes to mind is one under siege. Accordingly, and in consideration of such provocation, I reaffirm the alliance between the Khundryl Burned Tears and the Grey Helms. If enemies to us you choose to be, sirs, then we must consider that we are now at war. Attend to your brigade, Conquestor—it is tactically imperative that we obliterate your presence here prior to invading your kingdom.'

For all his doubt and suspicions and, indeed, fears, Tanakalian was not averse to revelling in pride at this moment; seeing the effect of the Mortal Sword's words upon the Chancellor and the Conquestor he felt savage pleasure. *Play games with us, will you? The Khundryl may sting, but the Perish shall rend and tear.*

They would not call Krughava's bluff, for it was no bluff, and they both clearly knew it.

Nor, Tanakalian knew, would they accede to a state of war—not here against the Perish, and not, by extension, against the Burned Tears. The fools had miscalculated, badly miscalculated.

And now would begin the desperate renewal of negotiations, and the footing that had heretofore been on a matching level—as courtesy demanded—was level no longer.

After all, you may at this moment face two bridling, angry armies, my friends, and find yourselves shaking with terror.

Wait until you meet the Bonehunters.

He watched as, following hasty reiterations of a desire to work things through peacefully, the Chancellor and the Conquestor retreated back down the slope—not even bothering with the ridiculous chairs. The slaves stumbled after them in a fan-waving mob.

Beside him, Krughava sighed, and then said, 'It occurs to me, sir, that the Bolkando expected the Khundryl to prove little more than a minor irritant, confined to the region surrounding their settlement. Easily contained, or, indeed, quickly driven over the border into the Wastelands. That notion led, inevitably, to the conceit that we here could be isolated and dealt with at their leisure.'

'Then an ambush was intended all along?'

'Or the threat thereof, to win further concessions.'

'Well,' said Tanakalian, 'if the Khundryl will neither remain close to their settlement nor retreat over the border, then it follows that but one course remains.'

She nodded. 'As a barbed spear,' she said, 'Gall will lead his people into the very heart of the kingdom.' She rolled her shoulders in a rustle of chain and buckles. 'Shield Anvil, inform the legion commands that we are to march two bells before dawn—'

'Even if that means we are pursued by the Bolkando escort?'

She bared her teeth. 'Have you gauged those troops, sir? They could be naked and not keep up with us. Their baggage train alone is thrice the size of their combatants in column. That,' she pronounced, 'is an army used to going nowhere.'

She set off, then, to beat down the two Bolkando delegates, from flickering daggers to misshapen lumps of lead.

Tanakalian, on the other hand, made his way to the Perish camp.

The insects were maddening, and from the rushes lining the river birds screamed.

The rain thrashed down, making the world grey and turning the stony track into a foaming stream. The tall black boles of the trees to either side loomed into view and then receded in rippling waves as Yan Tovis guided her horse down the now treacherous trail. Her waxed cloak was drawn tight about her, the hood pulled over her helm. Two days and three nights of this and she was chilled and soaked through. Ever since she had departed the Cities Road, five leagues from Dresh, cutting northward to where she had left her people, league after league of this forest had begun to weigh upon her. Her descent to the coast was also a journey into the past, civilization fading into ghostly hopes in her wake. Patches of clear-cut meadow, bordered by snarled bomas of cut branches, hacked brush and root stumps, the triple ruts of log-tracks wending in and out; the rubbish of old camps and the ash heaps and trenches of charcoal makers: these marked the brutal imposition of Dresh's hunger and need.

As with the islands of Katter Bight, desolation was the promise. As she had ridden through the old timber camps, she had seen the soil erosion, the deep rocky channels cutting through every clearing. And when in Dresh, resigning her commission, she had noted the nervousness among the garrison troops. Following a royal decree halting logging operations, there had been riots—much of the city's wealth came from the forest, after all, and while the prohibition was a temporary one, during which the King's agents set about devising a new system—one centred on sustainability—the stink of panic clogged the city streets.

Yan Tovis was not surprised that King Tehol had begun challenging the fundamental principles and practices of Lether, but she suspected that he would soon find himself a solitary, beleaguered voice of reason. Even common sense was an enemy to the harvesters of the future. The beast that was civilization ever faced forward, and in making its present world it devoured the world to come. It was an appalling truth that one's own children could be so callously sacrificed to immediate comforts, yet this was so and it had always been so.

Dreamers were among the first to turn their backs on historical truths. King Tehol would be swept aside, drowned in the inexorable tide of unmitigated growth. No one, after all, can stand between the glutton and the feast.

She wished him well, even as she knew he would fail.

In the midst of pelting rain she had left the camps behind, taking one of the old wood-bison migration routes through virgin forest. The mud of the ancient track swarmed with leeches and she was forced to dismount every bell or so to tug the mottled black and brown creatures from her horse's legs, until the path led down on to a sinkhole basin that proved to be a salt-trap—the plague of leeches ended abruptly and, as she continued down-slope, did not return.

Signs of the old dwellers began to appear—perhaps they were Shake remnants, perhaps they belonged to a people now forgotten. She saw the slumping humps of round huts covered in wax-leaved vines. She saw on the massive trunks of the most ancient trees crumbled visages, carved by hands long since rotted to nothing. The wooden faces were smeared in black-slime, moss and lumps of sickly fungi. She halted her mount beside one such creation and stared at it through the rain for a long time. She could think of no finer symbol of impermanence. The blunted expression, its pits of sorrow that passed for eyes: these things haunted her long after she had left the ruined settlement.

The track eventually merged with a Shake road that had once joined two coastal villages, and this was the path she now took.

The rain had become a deluge, and its hissing rose to a roar on her hood, a curtain of water sheeting down in front of her eyes.

Her horse halted suddenly and she lifted her head to see a lone rider blocking her path.

He seemed a figure sculpted in flowing water. 'Listen to me,' she said, loud, unexpectedly harsh. 'Do you truly imagine that you can follow us, brother?'

Yedan Derryg made no reply—his typical statement of obstinacy.

She wanted to curse him, but knew that even that would be useless. 'You killed the witches and warlocks. Pully and Skwish are not enough. Do you understand what you have forced upon me, Yedan?'

He straightened in his saddle at that. Even in the gloom she saw his jaws bunching as he chewed for a time on his reply, before saying, 'You cannot. You must not. Make the journey, sister, upon the mortal path.'

'Because it is the only one you can follow, banished as you are.'

But he shook his head. 'The road you seek is but a promise. Never attempted. A promise, Yan Tovis. Will you risk the lives of our people upon such a thing?'

'You have left me no choice.'

'Take the mortal path, as you said you would. Eastward to Bluerose and thence across the sea—'

She wanted to scream at him. Instead, she bared her teeth. 'You damned fool,

Yedan. Have you seen the camp of our—my—people? The population of the whole island—old prisoners and their families, merchants and hawkers, cut-throats and pirates—*everyone* joined us! Not even including the Shake, there are close to ten thousand Letherii refugees in my camp! What am I to do with them all? How do I feed them?'

'They are not your responsibility, Twilight. Disperse them—the islands are very nearly under water now—this crisis belongs to King Tehol—to Lether.'

'You forget,' she snapped, 'Second Maiden proclaimed its independence. And made me Queen. The moment we arrived on the mainland, we became *invaders*.'

He cocked his head. 'It is said the King is a compassionate man—'

'He may well be, but how will everyone else think—all those people whose lands we must cross? When we beg for food and shelter? When our hunger grasps tight our souls, so that begging becomes demands? The northern territories have not yet recovered from the Edur War—fields lie fallow; the places where sorcery was unleashed now seethe with nightmare creatures and poisonous plants. I will not descend upon King Tehol's most fragile subjects with fifteen thousand desperate trespassers!'

'Take me back, then,' Yedan said. 'Your need for me—'

'I cannot! You are a Witchslayer! You would be torn to pieces!'

'Then find a worthy mate—a king—'

'Yedan Derryg, move aside. I will speak with you no longer.'

He collected his reins and made way for her to pass. 'The mortal path, sister. Please.'

Coming alongside, she raised a gloved hand as if to strike him, then lowered it and kicked her horse forward. Feeling his gaze upon her back was not enough to twist her round in her saddle. The weight of his disapproval settled on her shoulders, and with a faint shock she discovered that it was not entirely unfamiliar. Perhaps, as a child . . . well, some traits refused to go away, no matter the span of years. The notion made her even more miserable.

A short time later she caught the rank smell of cookfires dying in the rain.

My people, my realm, I am home.

Pithy and Brevity sat on a rolled-up, half-buried log at what used to be the high-water mark, their bare feet in the lukewarm water of the sea's edge. The story went that this precious, magical mix of fresh rain and salty surf was a cure for all manner of foot ailments, including bad choices that sent one walking in entirely the wrong direction. Of course, life being what it is, you can't cure what you ain't done yet, though it never hurts to try.

'Besides,' said Brevity, her short dark hair flattened on to her round cheeks, 'if we didn't swing the vote, you and me, why, we'd be swimming to the nearest tavern right about now.'

'Praying that there's still some beer on tap,' Pithy added.

'It was the ice melt, dearie, that done in the island, and sure, maybe it would've subsided some, maybe even enough, but who wanted to hold their breaths waiting for that?' She pulled a sodden rustleaf stick from some fold in her cloak and jammed it in the corner of her mouth. 'Anyway, we got us a Queen now and a government—'

'A divided government, Brevity. Shake on one side, Forters on the other, and the Queen hogtied and stretched in between—I can hear her creaking day and night. What we're looking at here is an impasse and it won't hold that way for much longer.'

'Well, with only two witches left, it's not like the Shake can do nothing but wave a bony fist our way.' Pithy kicked her feet, making desultory splashes quickly beaten down by the rain. 'We need to make our move soon. We need to swing the Queen over to our side. You and me, Brev, we should be leading the contingent to King Tehol, with a tidy resettlement scheme that includes at least three chests heaped with coins.'

'One for you, one for me, and one for Twilight's treasury.'

'Precisely.'

'Think she'll go for it?'

'Why not? We can't stay here on this rotten coast much longer, can we?'

'Good point. She saved us from drowning on the island, didn't she? No point in then having us drown here in the Errant's endless piss. Fent's Toes, what a miserable place this is.'

'You know,' said Pithy after a time, 'you and me, we could just abandon 'em all. Make our way to Letheras. How long do you think it'd take us to get re-established?'

Brevity shook her head. 'We'd get recognized, dearie. Worse, our scheme ain't going to work a second time—people will see the signs and know it for what it is.'

'Bah, every five years by my count you can find another crop of fools with too much money. Happy to hand it over.'

'Maybe, but it's not the marks I was thinking about—it's the authorities. I ain't in no mood to get arrested all over again. Twice offending means the Drownings for sure.'

Pithy shivered. 'Got a point there. All right, then we go the honest politician route, we climb the ladder of, uh, secular power. We soak and scam legitimately.'

Brevity sucked on the stick and then nodded. 'We can do that. Popularity contest. We divide up our rivals in the Putative Assembly. You bed one half, I bed the other, we set ourselves up as bitter rivals and make up two camps. Get voted as the Assembly's official representatives to the court of the Queen.'

'And then we become the choke-point.'

'Information and wealth, up and down, down and up. Neither side knowing anything but what we decide to tell 'em.'

'Precisely. No real difference from being the lying, cheating brokers we once were.'

'Right, only even more crooked.'

'But with a smile.'

'With a smile, always, dearie.'

Yan Tovis rode down into the camp. The place stank. Figures stumbled in the mud and rain. The entire shallow bay offshore was brown with churned-up run-off. They were short of food. All the boats anchored in the bay sat low, wallowing in the rolling waves.

The mortal path. Twilight shook her head.

Unmindful of the countless eyes finding her as she rode into the makeshift town, she continued on until she reached the Witch's Tent. Dismounting, she stepped over the drainage trench and ducked inside.

'We's in turble,' croaked Skwish from the far end. 'People getting sick now—we's running outa herbs and was'not.' She fixed baleful eyes on Twilight.

At her side, Pully smacked her gums for a moment, and then asked, 'What you going t'do, Queenie? Nafore everone dies?'

She did not hesitate. 'We must journey. But not on the mortal path.'

Could two ancient women be shocked?

Seemed they could.

'By my Royal Blood,' Twilight said, 'I will open the Road to Gallan.' She stared down at the witches, their gaping mouths, their wide eyes. 'To the Dark Shore. I am taking us home.'

He wished he could remember his own name. He wished for some kind of understanding. How could such a disparate collection of people find themselves stumbling across this ravaged landscape? Had the world ended? Were they the last ones left?.

But no, not quite, not quite accurate. While none of his companions, bickering and cursing, showed any inclination to glance back on their own trail, he found his attention drawn again and again to that hazy horizon whence they had come.

Someone was there.

Someone was after them.

If he could find out all the important things, he might have less reason to fear. He might even discover that he knew who hunted them. He might find a moment of peace.

Instead, the others looked ahead, as if they had no choice, no will to do otherwise. The edifice they had set out towards—what seemed weeks ago—was finally drawing near. Its immensity had mocked their sense of distance and perspective, but even that was not enough to account for the length of their trek. He had begun to suspect that his sense of time was awry, that the others measured the journey in a way fundamentally different from him—for was he not a ghost? He could only slip into and through them like a shadow. He felt nothing of the weight of each step they took. Even their suffering eluded him.

And yet, by all manner of reason, should he not be the one to have found time compacted, condensed to a thing of ephemeral ease? Why then the torture in his soul? The exhaustion? This fevered sense of crawling along every increment inside each of these bodies, one after another, round and round and round? When he first awoke among them, he had felt himself blessed. Now he felt trapped.

The edifice reared into the scoured blue sky. Grey and black, carved scales possibly rent by fractures and mottled with rusty stains, it was a tower of immense, alien artistry. At first, it had seemed little more than wreckage, a looming, rotted fang rendered almost shapeless by centuries of abandonment. But the closing of distance had, perversely, altered that perception. Even so . . . on the flat land spreading out from its base, there was no sign of settlement, no ancient, blunted furrows betraying once-planted fields, no tracks, no roads.

They could discern the nature of the monument now. Perhaps a thousand reaches tall, it stood alone, empty-eyed, a dragon of stone balanced on its hind limbs and curling tail. One of its forelimbs reached down to sink talons into the ground; the other was drawn up and angled slightly outward, as if poised to swipe some enemy from its path. Even its hind limbs were asymmetrically positioned, tensed, coiled.

No real dragon could match its size, and yet as they edged closer—mute now, diminished—they could see the astonishing detail of the creation. The iridescence of the whorls in each scale, lightly coated in dust; the folded-back skin encircling the talons—talons which were at least half again as tall as a man, their polished, laminated surfaces scarred and chipped. They could see creases in the hide that they had first taken to be fractures; the weight of muscles hanging slack; the seams and blood vessels in the folded, arching wings. A grainy haze obscured the edifice above its chest height, as if it was enwreathed in a ring of suspended dust.

'No,' whispered Taxilian, 'not suspended. That ring is *moving* . . . round and round it swirls, do you see?'

'Sorcery,' said Breath, her tone oddly flat.

'As might a million moons orbit a dead sun,' Rautos observed. 'Countless lifeless worlds, each one no bigger than a grain of sand—you say magic holds it in place, Breath—are you certain?'

'What else?' she snapped, dismissive. 'All we ever get from you. Theories. About this and that. As if explanations meant anything. What difference does knowing make, you fat oaf?'

'It eases the fire in my soul, witch,' Rautos replied.

'The fire is the reason for living.'

'Until it burns you up.'

'Oh, stop it, you two,' moaned Asane.

Breath wheeled on her. 'I'm going to drown you,' she pronounced. 'I don't even need water to do it. I'll use sand. I'll hold you under and feel your every struggle, your every twitch—'

'It's not just a statue,' said Taxilian.

'Someone carved down a mountain,' said Nappet. 'Means nothing. It's just stupid, useless. We've walked for days and days. For this. Stupid. I'm of a mind to kick you bloody, Taxilian. For wasting my time.'

'Wasting your time? Why, Nappet, what else were you planning to do?'

'We need water. Now we're going to die out here, just so you could look at this piece of stone.' Nappet lifted a battered fist. 'If I kill you, we can drink your blood—that'll hold us for a time.'

'It will kill you in turn,' Rautos said. 'You will die in great pain.'

'What do you know about it? We'll cook you down and drink all that melted fat.'

'It's not just a statue,' Taxilian repeated.

Last, who was not much for talking, surprised everyone when he said, 'He's right. It was alive, once, this dragon.'

Sheb snorted. 'Errant save us, you're an idiot, Last. This thing was never anything but a mountain.'

'It was no mountain,' Last insisted, brow darkening. 'There are no mountains here and there never were—anybody can see that. No, it was alive.'

'He's right, I think,' said Taxilian, 'only maybe not in the way you think, Sheb. This was built, and then it was lived in.' He spread his hands. 'It is a city. And we're going to find a way inside.'

The ghost, who had been hovering, swept this way and that, impatient and fearful, anxious and excited, now wanted to cry out with joy, and would have, had he a voice.

'A city?' Sheb stared at Taxilian for a long moment, and then spat. 'But abandoned now, right? Dead, right?'

'I would say so,' Taxilian replied. 'Long dead.'

'So,' and Sheb licked his lips, 'there might be . . . loot. Forgotten treasure— after all, who else has ever come out here? The Wastelands promise nothing but death. Everyone knows that. We're probably the first people to have ever seen this—'

'Barring its inhabitants,' murmured Rautos. 'Taxilian, can you see a way inside?'

'No, not yet. But come, we'll find one, I'm certain of it.'

Breath stepped in front of the others as if to block their way. 'This place is cursed, can't you feel that? It doesn't belong to people—people like you and me— we don't belong here. Listen to me! If we go inside, we'll never leave!'

Asane whimpered, shrinking back. 'I don't like it either. We should just go, like she says.'

'We can't!' barked Sheb. 'We need water! How do you think a city this size can survive here? It's sitting on a source of water—'

'Which probably dried up and that's why they left!'

'Dried up, maybe, for ten thousand thirsty souls. Not seven. And who knows how long ago? No, you don't understand—if we don't find water in there, we're all going to die.'

The ghost was oddly baffled by all this. They had found a spring only two evenings back. They all carried waterskins that still sloshed—although, come to think of it, he could not recall where they had found them—did his companions always have those skins? And what about the broad hats they wore, shielding them from the bright, hard sunlight? The walking sticks? Taxilian's rope-handled scribe box? Rautos's map-case that folded out into a desktop? Breath's cloak of sewn pockets, each pocket carrying a Tile? Nappet and his knotted skull-breaker tucked into his belt? Sheb's brace of daggers? Asane's spindle and the bag of raw wool from which she spun out her lacy webs? Last's iron pot and fire kit; his hand-sickle and collection of cooking knives—where, the ghost wondered—in faint horror—had all these things come from?

'No food, no water,' Nappet was saying, 'Sheb's right. But, most importantly, if we find a door, we can defend it.'

The words hung in the silence that followed, momentarily suspended and then slowly rising like grit—the ghost could see them, the way they lost shape but not meaning, definition but not dread import. Yes, Nappet had spoken aloud the secret knowledge. The words that terror had carved bloody on their souls.

Someone was hunting them.

Asane began weeping, softly, sodden hitches catching in her throat.

Sheb's hands closed into fists as he stared at her.

But Nappet had turned to face Last, and was eyeing the huge man speculatively. 'I know,' he said, 'you're a thick-skulled farmer, Last, but you look strong. Can you handle a sword? If we need someone to hold the portal, can you do that?'

The man frowned, and then nodded. 'Maybe I ain't never used a sword, but nobody will get past. I swear it. Nobody gets past me.'

And Nappet was holding a sheathed sword, which he now offered to Last.

The ghost recoiled upon seeing that weapon. He knew it, yet knew it not. A strange, frightening weapon. He watched as Last drew the sword from its sheath. Single-edged, dark, mottled iron, its tip weighted and slightly flaring. The deep ferule running the length of the blade was a black, nightmarish streak, like an etching of the Abyss itself. It stank of death—the whole weapon, this terrible instrument of destruction.

Last hefted the sword in his hand. 'I would rather a spear,' he said.

'We don't like spears,' Nappet hissed. 'Do we?'

'No,' the others chorused.

Last's frown deepened. 'No, me neither. I don't know why I . . . why I . . . wanted one. An imp's whisper in my head, I guess.' And he made a warding gesture.

Sheb spat to seal the fend.

'We don't like spears,' Rautos whispered. 'They're . . . dangerous.'

The ghost agreed. Fleshless and yet chilled, shivering. There had been a spear in his past—yes? Perhaps? A dreadful thing, lunging at his face, his chest, slicing the muscles of his arms. Reverberations, shivering up through his bones, rocking him back, one step, then another—

Gods, he did not like spears!

'Come on,' Taxilian said. 'It is time to find a way in.'

There *was* a way in. The ghost knew that. There was always a way in. The challenge was in finding it, in seeing it and knowing it for what it was. The important doors stayed hidden, disguised, shaped in ways to deceive. The important doors opened from one side only, and once you were through they closed in a gust of cold air against the back of the neck. And could never be opened again.

Such was the door he sought, the ghost realized.

Did it wait in this dead city?

He would have to find it soon. Before the hunter found him—found them all. *Spear Wielder, slayer, the One who does not retreat, who mocks in silence, who would not flinch—no, he's not done with me, with us, with me, with us.*

We need to find the door.

The way in.

They reached the dragon's stone forelimb with its claws that stood arrayed like massive, tapering pillars of marble, tips sunk deep into the hard earth. Everywhere surrounding the foundations the ground was fissured, fraught with cracks that tracked outward. Rautos grunted as he crouched down to peer into one such rent. 'Deep,' he muttered. 'The city is settling, suggesting that it has indeed sucked out the water beneath it.'

Taxilian was scanning the massive tower that comprised the limb in front of them, tilting his head back, and back. After a moment he staggered, cursing. 'Too much,' he gasped. 'This one leg could encompass a half-dozen Ehrlii spires—if it is indeed hollow, it could hold a thousand inhabitants all by itself.'

'And yet,' Rautos said, coming up alongside him, 'look at the artistry—the genius of the sculptors—have you ever seen such skill, on such a scale, Taxilian?'

'No, it surpasses . . . it surpasses.'

Sheb stepped in between two of the talons, slipped into shadows and out of sight.

There were no obvious entranceways, no formal portals or ramps, no gates; no windows or apertures higher up.

'It seems entirely self-contained,' said Taxilian. 'Did you notice—no evidence of outlying farms or pasture land.'

'None that survived the interval of abandonment,' Rautos replied. 'For all we know, after all, this could be a hundred thousand years old.'

'That would surprise me—yes, the surface is eroded, worn down, but if it was as old as you suggest, why, it would be little more than a shapeless lump, a giant termite tower.'

'Are you certain of that?'

'No,' Taxilian admitted. 'But I recall once, in a scriptorium in Erhlitan, seeing a map dating from the First Empire. It showed a line of rugged hills inland of the city. They ran like a spine parallel to the coast. Elevations had been noted here and there. Well, those hills are still there, but not as bold or as high as what was noted on the map.'

'And how old was the map?' Rautos asked.

Taxilian shrugged. 'Twenty thousand? Fifty? Five? Scholars make a career of not agreeing on anything.'

'Was the map on hide? Surely, no hide could last so long, not even five thousand years—'

'Hide, yes, but treated in some arcane way. In any case, it had been found in a wax-sealed container. Seven Cities is mostly desert. Without moisture, nothing decays. It just shrinks, dries up.' He gestured with one hand at the stone façade before them. 'Anyway, this should be much more weathered if it was so old as to outlast signs of farming.'

Rautos nodded, convinced by Taxilian's reasoning.

'Haunted,' said Breath. 'You're going to get us all killed, Taxilian. So I now curse your name, your soul. I will make you pay for killing me.'

He glanced at her, said nothing.

Rautos spoke. 'See that hind foot, Taxilian? It is the only one on a pedestal.'

The two men headed off in that direction.

Breath walked up to Asane. 'Spin that cocoon, woman, make yourself somewhere you can hide inside. Until you're nothing but a rotted husk. Don't think you can crawl back out. Don't think you can show us all your bright, painted wings. Your hopes, Asane, your dreams and secrets—all hollow.' She held up a thin spidery hand. 'I can crush it all, so easily—'

Last stepped up to her, then pushed her back so that she stumbled. 'I grow tired of listening to you,' he said. 'Leave her alone.'

Breath cackled and danced away.

'Thank you,' said Asane. 'She is so . . . hurtful.'

But Last faced her and said, 'This is not a place for fears, Asane. Conquer yours, and do it soon.'

Nearby, Nappet snickered. 'Dumb farmer's maybe not so dumb after all. Doesn't make him any less ugly though, does it?' He laughed.

As Rautos and Taxilian drew closer to the hind limb they could see that the pedestal was rectangular, like the foundation of a temple. The vertical wall facing them, as tall as they were, bore the faint remnants of a frieze, framed in an elaborate border. All too eroded to interpret. But no sign of an entranceway.

'We are confounded again,' Rautos said.

'I do not think so,' Taxilian replied. 'You look wrongly, friend. You search out what rises in front of you. You scan right and left, you crane your sight upward. Yes, the city encourages such deception. The dragon *invites* it, perched as it is. And yet . . .' He pointed.

Rautos followed the line of that lone finger, and grunted in surprise. At the base of the pedestal, wind-blown sands formed a hollow. 'The way in is *downward*.'

Sheb joined them. 'We need to dig.'

'I think so,' agreed Taxilian. 'Call the others, Sheb.'

'I don't take orders from you. Errant piss on you highborn bastards.'

'I'm not highborn,' said Taxilian.

Sheb sneered. 'You make like you are, which is just as bad. Get back down where you belong, Taxilian, and if you can't manage on your own then I'll help and that's a promise.'

'I just have some learning, Sheb—why does that threaten you so?'

Sheb rested a hand on one of his daggers. 'I don't like pretenders and that's what you are. You think big words make you smarter, better. You like the way Rautos here respects you, you think he sees you as an equal. But you're wrong in that—you ain't his equal. He's just humouring you, Taxilian. You're a clever pet.'

'This is how Letherii think,' said Rautos, sighing. 'It's what keeps everyone in their place, upward, downward—even as people claim they despise the system they end up doing all they can to keep it in place.'

Taxilian sighed in turn. 'I do understand that, Rautos. Stability helps remind you of where you stand. Affirms you've got a legitimate place in society, for good or ill.'

'Listen to you two shit-eaters.'

By this time the others had arrived. Taxilian pointed at the depression. 'We think we've found a way in, but we'll have to dig.'

Last approached with a shovel in his hands. 'I'll start.'

The ghost hovered, watching. Off to the west, the sun was settling into horizon's lurid vein. When Last needed a rest, Taxilian took his place. Then Nappet, followed by Sheb. Rautos tried then, but by this point the pit was deep and he had difficulty making his way down, and an even harder time flinging the sand high enough to keep it from sifting back. His stint did not last long before, with a snarl, Sheb told him to get out and leave the task to the lowborns who knew this business. Last and Taxilian struggled to lift Rautos out of the pit.

In the dusty gloom below, the excavation had revealed one edge of stone facing, the huge blocks set without mortar.

The argument from earlier disturbed the ghost, although he was not sure why it was so. He was past such silly things, after all. The games of station, so bitter, so self-destructive—it all seemed such a waste of time and energy, the curse of people who could look outward but never inward. Was that a measure of intelligence? Were such hapless victims simply dimwitted, incapable of introspection and honest self-judgement? Or was it a quality of low intelligence that its possessor instinctively fled the potentially deadly turmoil of knowing too many truths about oneself?

Yes, it was this notion—of self-delusion—that left him feeling strangely anxious, exposed and vulnerable. He could see its worth, after all. When the self was a monster—who wouldn't hide from such a thing? Who wouldn't run when it loomed close? Close enough to smell, to taste? Yes, even the lowest beast knew the value of not knowing itself *too* well.

'I've reached the floor,' announced Sheb, straightening. When the others crowded to the uncertain edge, he snarled, 'Keep your distance, fools! You want to bury me?'

'Tempting,' said Nappet. 'But then we'd have to dig out your miserable corpse.'

The shovel scraped on flagstones. After a time Sheb said, 'Got the top of the doorway here in front of me—it's low . . . but wide. There's a ramp, no steps.'

Yes, thought the ghost, *that is as it should be.*

Sheb wasn't interested in handing off the task, now that he could see the way in. He dug swiftly, grunting with every upward heave of heavy, damp sand. 'I can smell the water,' he gasped. 'Could be the tunnel's flooded—but at least we won't die of thirst, will we?'

'I'm not going down there,' said Breath, 'if there's water in the tunnel. I'm not. You'll all drown.'

The ramp angled downward for another six or seven paces, enough to leave Sheb exhausted. Nappet took over and a short time later, with dusk gathering at their backs, a thrust of the shovel plunged into empty space. They were through.

The tunnel beyond was damp, the air sweet with rotting mould and sour with something fouler. The water pooled on the floor was less than a finger's width deep, slippery underfoot. The darkness was absolute.

Everyone lit lanterns. Watching this, the ghost found himself frightened yet again. As with all the other accoutrements; as with the sudden appearance of the shovel, he was missing essential details—they could not simply veer into existence as needed, after all. Reality didn't work that way. No, it must be that he was blind to things, a vision cursed to be selective, yielding only that which was needed, that which was relevant to the moment. For all he knew, he suddenly realized, there might be a train of wagons accompanying this group. There might be servants. Bodyguards. An army. The real world, he comprehended with a shock, was not what he saw, not what he interacted with instant by instant. The real world was *unknowable.*

He thought he might howl. He thought he might give voice to his horror, his abject revelation. For, if indeed the world was unknowable, then so too were the forces acting upon him, and how could one guard against that?

Frozen, unable to move. Until the group descended into the tunnel, and then yet another discovery assailed him, as chains dragged him down into the pit, pulling him—shrieking now—into the passageway.

He was not free.

He was bound to the lives of these strange people, not one of whom knew he even existed. He was their slave, yet rendered so useless that he had no voice, no body, no identity beyond this fragile mockery of self—and how long could such a entity survive, when it was invisible to everyone else? When even the stone walls and pools of slimy water did not acknowledge his arrival?

Was this, then, the torment of all ghosts?

The possibility was so terrible, so awful, that he recoiled. How could mortal souls deserve such eternal penitence? What vast crime did the mere act of living commit? Or had he been personally consigned to this fate? By some god or goddess cruel in judgement, devoid of all mercy?

At that thought, even as he flailed about in the wake of his masters, he felt a sudden rage. A blast of indignation. *What god or goddess dares to presume the right to judge me? That is arrogance too vast to have been earned.*

Whoever you are, I will find you. I swear it. I will find you and I will cut you down. Humble you. Down to your knees. How dare you! How dare you judge anyone, when you ever hide your face? When you strip away all possible truth of your existence? Your wilful presence?

Hiding from me, whoever—whatever—you are, is a childish game. An unworthy game. Face your child. Face all your children. Show me the veracity of your right to cast judgement upon me.

Do this, and I will accept you.

Remain hidden, even as you consign my soul to suffering, and I will hunt you down.

I will hunt you down.

The ramp climbed until it reached a broad, low-ceilinged chamber.

Crowded with reptilian corpses. Rotting, reeking, in pools of thick ichor and rank blood. Twenty, perhaps more.

K'Chain Che'Malle. The makers of this city.

Each one throat-cut. Executed like goats on an altar.

Beyond them, a spiralling ramp climbed steeply upward. No one said a thing as they picked careful, independent paths through the slaughter. Taxilian in the lead, they began the ascent.

The ghost watched as Breath paused to bend down and run a finger through decaying blood. She slipped that finger into her mouth, and smiled.

Book Two

Eaters of Diamonds and Gems

I heard a story
Of a river
Which is where water flows over the ground
    glistening in the sun
It's a legend
And untrue
In the story the water is clear and that's why
    it's untrue
We all know
Water
Is the colour
Of blood
People make up legends
To teach lessons
So I think
The story is about us
About a river of blood
And one day
We'll run clear

OF A RIVER
BADALLE

Chapter Seven

The horrid creatures jostle in their line
A row of shields and a row of painted faces
They marched out of my mouth
As slayers are wont to do
When no one was looking busy as they were
With their precious banners and standards
And with the music of stepping in time
As the righteous are wont to do
Now see all these shiny weapons so eager
To clash in the discord of stunned agreement
Blind as millipedes in the mud
As between lovers words may do
In the murky depths swans slip like seals
Scaling the ice walls of cold's prison
All we dream is without tether

CONFESSIONS OF THE CONDEMNED
BANATHOS OF BLUEROSE

The errant walked the flooded tunnel, remembering the bodies that had once drifted there, shifting like logs, flesh turning to jelly. Now on occasion, in pushing a foot forward, he kicked aside unseen bones. Darkness promised no solitude, no true abandonment, no final resting place. Darkness was nothing more than a home for the forgotten. Which was why sarcophagi had lids and crypts were sealed under stone and barrows beneath heaped earth. Darkness was the vision behind shuttered eyes, little more than the dismissal of light when details ceased to be relevant.

He could find such a world. All he needed to do was close his one remaining eye. It should work. He did not understand why it didn't. The water, bitter cold, lapped round his thighs. He welcomed its gift of numbness. The air was foul, but he was used to that. There should be nothing to hold him here, chaining him to this moment.

Events were unfolding, so many events, and not all of them shifting to his touch, twisting to his will. Anger was giving way to fear. He had sought out the altar Feather Witch had consecrated in his name. He had expected to find her soul, her fleshless will curling in sinew currents round the submerged rubble, but there had been nothing, no one. Where had she gone?

He could still feel her hair beneath his hand, the muted struggles as some remnant of her sanity groped for air, for one more moment of life. His palm tingled with the echo of her faint convulsions beginning in that moment when she surrendered and filled her lungs with water, once, twice, like a newborn trying out the gifts of an unknown world, only to retreat, fade away, and slide like an eel back into the darkness, where the first thing forgotten was oneself.

This should not be haunting him. His act had been one of mercy. Gangrenous, insane, she'd had little time left. It had been the gentlest of nudges, not at all motivated by vengeance or disgust. Still, she might well have cursed him in that last exhaled, soured breath.

Her soul should be swimming these black waters. But the Errant knew that he had been alone. The altar chamber had offered him little more than desolation.

Wading, the tunnel's slimy floor descending with each step, his feet suddenly lost all grip and the water rose yet higher, past his chest, closing over his shoulders and lapping at his throat. The top of his head brushed the gritty stone of the tunnel's ceiling, and then he was under, blinking the sting from his eye.

He pushed onward through the murk, until the water turned salty, and light, reflecting down from a vague surface fathoms overhead, flashed like dulled, smeared memories of lightning. He could feel the heavy tugs of wayward currents and he knew that a storm did indeed rage, there upon the ceiling of this world, but it could do little to him down here. Scraping through thick mud, he walked the ocean floor.

Nothing decayed in this place, and all that had not been crushed to dust by the immense pressures now lay scattered beneath monochrome draperies of silt, like furniture in a vast, abandoned room. Everything about this realm invited horror. Time lost its way here, wandering until the ceaseless rain of detritus weighed it down, brought it to its knees, and then buried it. Anything—anyone—could fall to the same fate. The danger, the risk, was very real. No creature of sentience could withstand this place for long. Futility delivered its crushing symphony and the dread music was eternal.

He found himself walking down the length of a vast skeleton, jagged uneven ribs rising like the columns of a colonnade to either side, a roofless temple sagging under its own senseless burden. He passed the snaking line of boulders that was the immense creature's spine. Four scapulae formed broad concave platforms just ahead, from which bizarre long bones radiated out like toppled pillars. He could just make out, in the gloom, the massive crown of the back of the monster's skull. Here, then, awaited another kind of temple. Precious store of self, a space insisting on its occupation, an existence that demanded acknowledgement of its own presence.

The Errant sympathized with the notion. Such delicate conceits assembled the bones of the soul, after all. He moved past the last of the scapulae, noting the effect of some crushing, no doubt crippling impact. The bone looked like a giant broken plate.

Coming alongside the skull, he saw that the cave of its nearest orbital socket was shattered, above and behind an elongated, partly collapsed snout crowded with serrated teeth. The Elder God paused and studied that damage for some time. He could not imagine what this beast had been; he suspected it was a child of these deep currents, a swimmer through ancient ages, entirely uncomprehending that its time was past. He wondered if mercy had delivered that death blow.

Ah, but he could not fight his own nature, could he? Most of his nudges were fatal ones, after all. The impetus might find many justifications, and clearly mercy numbered among them. This was, he told himself, a momentary obsession. The feel of her hair under his hand . . . a lapse of conscience, then, this tremor of remorse. It would pass.

He pushed on, knowing that at last, he'd found the right trail.

There were places that could only be found by invitation, by the fickle generosity of the forces that gave them shape, that made them what they were. Such barriers defied the hungers and needs of most seekers. But he had learned the secret paths long, long ago. He required no invitations, and no force could stand in the way of his hunger.

The dull gleam of the light in the tower reached him before he could make out anything else, and he flinched at seeing that single mocking eye floating in the gloom. Currents swept fiercely around him as he drew closer, buffeting his body as if desperate to turn him aside. Silts swirled up, seeking to blind him. But he fixed his gaze on that fitful glow, and before long he could make out the squat, blockish house, the black, gnarled branches of the trees in the yard, and then the low stone wall.

Dunes of silt were heaped up against the tower side of the Azath. The mounds in the yard were sculpted, half-devoured, exposing the roots of the leaning trees. As the Errant stepped on to the snaking flagstones of the path, he could see bones scattered out from those sundered barrows. Yes, they had escaped their prisons at long last, but death had arrived first.

Patience was the curse of longevity. It could lure its ageless victim into somnolence, until flesh itself rotted off, and the skull rolled free.

He reached the door. Pushed it open.

The currents within the narrow entranceway swept over him warm as tears. As the portal closed behind him, the Errant gestured. A moment later he was standing on dry stone. Hovering faint on the air around him was the smell of wood-smoke. A wavering globe of lantern light approached from the corridor beyond.

The threadbare figure that stepped into view sent a pang through the Errant. Memories murky as the sea-bottom spun up to momentarily blind him. The gaunt Forkrul Assail was hunched at the shoulders, as if every proof of justice had bowed him down, left him broken. His pallid face was a mass of wrinkles, like crushed leather. Tortured eyes fixed on the Errant for a moment, and then the Assail turned away. 'Fire and wine await us, Errastas—come, you know the way.'

They walked through the double doors at the conjunction of the corridors, into the dry heat of the hearth room. The Assail gestured at a sideboard as he hobbled to one of the chairs flanking the fireplace. Ignoring the invitation to drink—for the moment—the Errant walked to the other chair and settled into it.

They sat facing one another.

'You have suffered some,' said the Assail, 'since I last saw you, Errastas.'

'Laughter from the Abyss, Setch, have you seen yourself lately?'

'The forgotten must never complain.' He'd found a crystal goblet and he now held it up and studied the flickering flames trapped in the amber wine. 'When I look at myself, I see . . . embers. They dim, they die. It is,' he added, 'well.' And he drank.

The Errant bared his teeth. 'Pathetic. Your hiding is at an end, Knuckles.'

Sechul Lath smiled at the old title, but it was a bitter smile. 'Our time is past.'

'It was, yes. But now it shall be reborn.'

Sechul shook his head. 'You were right to surrender the first time—'

'That was no surrender! I was driven out!'

'You were forced to relinquish all that you no longer deserved.' The haunted eyes lifted to trap the Errant's glare. 'Why the resentment?'

'We were allies!'

'So we were.'

'We shall be again, Knuckles. You were the Elder God who stood closest to my throne—'

'Your Empty Throne, yes.'

'A battle is coming—listen to me! We can cast aside all these pathetic new gods. We can drown them in blood!' The Errant leaned forward. 'Do you fear that it will be you and me alone against them? I assure you, old friend, we shall not be alone.' He settled back once more, stared into the fire. 'Your mortal kin have found new power, made new alliances.'

Knuckles snorted. 'You would trust to the peace and justice of the Forkrul Assail? After all they once did to you?'

'I trust the necessity they have recognized.'

'Errastas, my time is at an end.' He made a rippling gesture with his fingers. 'I leave it to the Twins.' He smiled. 'They were my finest cast.'

'I refuse to accept that. You will not stand aside in what is to come. I have forgotten nothing. Remember the power we once wielded?'

'I remember—why do you think I'm here?'

'I want that power again. I will have it.'

'Why?' Knuckles asked softly. 'What is it you seek?'

'Everything that I have lost!'

'Ah, old friend, then you do not remember everything.'

'No?'

'No. You have forgotten why you lost it in the first place.'

A long moment of silence.

The Errant rose and went over to pour himself a goblet of wine. He returned and stood looking down upon his fellow Elder God. 'I am not here,' he said, 'for you alone.'

Knuckles winced.

'I intend, as well, to summon the Clan of Elders—all who have survived. I am Master of the Tiles. They cannot deny me.'

'No,' Knuckles muttered, 'that we cannot do.'

'Where is she?'

'Sleeping.'

The Errant grimaced. 'I already knew that, Setch.'

'Sit down, Errastas. For now, please. Let us just . . . sit here. Let us drink in remembrance of friendship. And innocence.'

'When our goblets are empty, Knuckles.'

He closed his eyes and nodded. 'So be it.'

'It pains me to see you so,' the Errant said as he sat back down. 'We shall return you to what you once were.'

'Dear Errastas, have you not learned? Time cares nothing for our wants, and no god that has ever existed can be as cruel as time.'

The Errant half-closed his remaining eye. 'Wait until you see the world I shall make, Setch. Once more, you shall stand beside the Empty Throne. Once more, you shall know the pleasure of mischance, striking down hopeful mortals one by one.'

'I do remember,' Knuckles murmured, 'how they railed at misfortune.'

'And sought to appease ill fate with ever more blood. Upon the altars. Upon the fields of battle.'

'And in the dark bargains of the soul.'

The Errant nodded. Pleased. Relieved. Yes, he could wait for this time, this brief healing span. It served and served well.

He could grant her a few more moments of rest.

'So tell me,' ventured Knuckles, 'the tale.'

'What tale?'

'The one that took your eye.'

The Errant scowled and looked away, his good mood evaporating. 'Mortals,' he said, 'will eat anything.'

In the tower of the Azath, within a chamber that was an entire realm, she slept and she dreamed. And since dreams existed outside of time, she was walking anew a landscape that had been dead for millennia. But the air was sharp still, the sky overhead as pure in its quicksilver brilliance as the day of its violent birth. On all sides buildings, reduced to rubble, formed steep-sided, jagged mounds. Passing floods had caked mud on everything to a height level with her hips. She walked, curious, half-disbelieving.

Was this all that remained? It was hard to believe.

The mounds looked strangely orderly, the chunks of stone almost uniform in size. No detritus had drifted down into the streets or lanes. Even the flood silts had settled smooth on every surface.

'Nostalgia,' a voice called down.

She halted, looked up to see a white-skinned figure perched atop one of the mounds. Gold hair hanging long, loose, hinting of deep shades of crimson. A white-bladed two-handed sword leaned against one side of his chest, the multifaceted crystal pommel flashing in the brightness. He took many forms, this creature. Some pleasant, others—like this one—like a spit of acid in her eyes.

'This is your work, isn't it?'

One of his hands stroked the sword's enamel blade, the sensuality of the gesture making her shiver. He said, 'I deplore your messiness, Kilmandaros.'

'While you make death seem so . . . tidy.'

He shrugged. 'Tell me, if on your very last day—day or night, it makes no difference—you find yourself in a room, on a bed, even. Too weak to move, but able to look around—that's all. Tell me, Kilmandaros, will you not be comforted by the orderliness of all that you see? By the knowledge that it will persist beyond you, unchanged, bound to its own slow, so slow measure of decay?'

'You ask if I will be what, Osserc? Nostalgic about a room I'm still in?'

'Is that not the final gift of dying?'

She held up her hands and showed him her fists. 'Come down here and receive just such a gift, Osserc. I know this body—this face that you show me now. I know the seducer and know him too well. Come down—do you not miss my embrace?'

And in the dread truths of dreams, Osserc then chuckled. The kind of laugh that cut into its victim, that shocked tight the throat. Dismissive, devoid of empathy. A laugh that said: *You no longer matter to me. I see your hurt and it amuses me. I see how you cannot let go of the very thing I have so easily flung away: the conceit that we still matter to each other.*

So much, yes, in a dream's laugh.

'Emurlahn is in pieces,' he said. 'And most of them are now as dead as this one. Would you blame me? Anomander? Scabandari?'

'I'm not interested in your stupid finger-pointing. The one who accuses has nothing to lose and everything to hide.'

'Yet you joined with Anomander—'

'He too was not interested in blame. We joined together, yes, to save what we could.'

'Too bad, then,' Osserc said, 'that I got here first.'

'Where have the people gone, Osserc? Now that you've destroyed their city.'

His brows lifted. 'Why, nowhere.' He gestured, a broad sweep of one hand, encompassing the rows of mounds around them. 'I denied them their moment of . . . nostalgia.'

She found herself trembling. 'Come down here,' she said in a rasp, 'your death is long overdue.'

'Others concur,' he admitted. 'In fact, it's why I'm, uh, lingering here. Only one portal survives. No, not the one you came through—that one has since crumbled.'

'And who waits for you there, Osserc?'

'Edgewalker.'

Kilmandaros bared her massive fangs in a broad smile. And then threw a laugh back at him. She moved on.

His voice sounded surprised as he called out behind her. 'What are you doing? He is angry. Do you not understand? He is *angry!*'

'And this is my dream,' she whispered. 'Where all that has been is yet to be.'
And still, she wondered. She had no recollection, after all, of this particular place.
Nor of meeting Osserc among the shattered remnants of Kurald Emurlahn.

Sometimes it is true, she told herself, that dreams prove troubling.

'Clouds on the horizon. Black, advancing in broken lines.' Stormy knuckled his
eyes and then glared across at Gesler from a momentarily reddened face. 'What
kind of stupid dream is that?'

'How should I know? There are cheats who make fortunes interpreting the
dreams of fools. Why not try one of those?'

'You calling me a fool?'

'Only if you follow my advice, Stormy.'

'Anyway, that's why I howled.'

Gesler leaned forward, clearing tankards and whatnot to make room for his
thick, scarred forearms. 'Falling asleep in the middle of a drinking session is unfor-
givable enough. Waking up screaming, why, that's just obnoxious. Had half the
idiots in here clutching at their chests.'

'We shouldn't've skipped out on the war-game, Ges.'

'Not again. It wasn't like that. We volunteered to go and find Hellian.' He nodded to the third occupant of the table, although only the top of her head was visible, the hair sodden along one side where it had soaked up spilled ale. Her snores
droned through the wood of the table like a hundred pine beetles devouring a sick
tree. 'And look, we found her, only she was in no shape to lead her squad. In fact,
she's in no shape for anything. She could get mugged, raped, even murdered. We
needed to stand guard.'

Stormy belched and scratched at his beard. 'It wasn't a fun dream, that's all.'

'When was the last fun dream you remember having?'

'Don't know. Been some time, I think. But maybe we just forget those ones.
Maybe we only remember the bad ones.'

Gesler refilled their tankards. 'So there's a storm coming. Impressive subtlety,
your dreams. Prophetic, even. You sleep to the whispers of the gods, Stormy.'

'Now ain't you in a good mood, Ges. Remind me not to talk about my dreams
no more.'

'I didn't want you talking about them this time round. It was the scream.'

'Not a scream, like I told you. It was a howl.'

'What's the difference?'

Scowling, Stormy reached for his tankard. 'Only, sometimes, maybe, gods
don't whisper.'

'*Furry women still haunting your dreams?*'

Bottle opened his eyes and contemplated throwing a knife into her face. Instead, he slowly winked. 'Good afternoon, Captain. I'm surprised you're not—'

'Excuse me, soldier, but did you just *wink* at me?'

He sat up on his cot. 'Was that a wink, Captain? Are you sure?'

Faradan Sort turned away, muttering under her breath as she marched towards the barracks door.

Once the door shut behind her, Bottle sat back, frowning. Now, messing with an officer's head was just, well, second nature. No, what disturbed him was the fact that he was suddenly unsure if she'd spoken at all. As a question, it didn't seem a likely fit, not coming from Faradan Sort. In fact, he doubted she even knew any-thing about his particular curse—how could she? There wasn't a fool alive who confided in an officer. Especially ones who viciously killed talented, happily mar-ried scorpions for no good reason. And if she did indeed know something, then it meant someone had traded that bit of information in exchange for something else. A favour, a deal, which was nothing less than a behind-the-back betrayal of every common soldier in the legion.

Who was vile enough to do that?

He opened his eyes and looked around. He was alone in the barracks. Fiddler had taken the squad out for that field exercise, the war-game against Brys Bed-dict's newly assembled battalions. Complaining of a bad stomach, Bottle had whined and groaned his way out of it. Not for him some useless trudging through bush and farmland; besides, it hadn't been so long ago that they were killing Letherii for real. There was a good chance someone—on either side—would for-get that everyone was friends now. The point was, he'd been the first one quick enough with the bad-stomach complaint, so no one else could take it up—he'd caught the vicious glare from Smiles, which of course he'd long got used to since he was always faster off the mark than she was.

Smiles. Bottle fixed his gaze on her cot, studied it through a suspicious squint. Behind-the-back shit was her forte, wasn't it? Aye, and who else had it in for him?

He swung his feet to the floor and—gods, that stone was cold!—padded over to her berth.

It paid to approach these things cautiously. If anyone was in the habit of rigging booby traps to just about everything they didn't want anyone else to touch, it was that spitting half-mad kitten with the sharp eye-stickers. Bottle drew his eating knife and began probing under the thin mattress, leaning close to peer at seams and seemingly random projections of tick straw—any one of which could be coated in poison—projections which, he discovered, turned out to be, uh, random projec-tions of tick straw. *Trying to lull me into something . . . I can smell it.*

He knelt and peeked under the frame. Nothing obvious, and that made him even more suspicious. Muttering, Bottle crawled round to kneel in front of her lockbox. Letherii issue—not something they'd be taking with them. She'd not have had much time to rig it, not deviously, anyway. No, the needles and blades would be poorly hidden.

She'd sold him out, but she would learn to regret doing that.

Finding nothing on the outside of the trunk, he slipped his knife point into the lock and began working the mechanism.

Discovering that the lockbox wasn't even locked froze him into a long moment of terror, breath held, sudden sweat beading his forehead. *A snare for sure. A killer snare. Smiles doesn't invite people in, oh no, not her. If I just lift this lid, I'm a dead man.*

He whirled upon hearing the scrape of boots, and found himself looking up at Corabb Bhilan Thenu'alas. 'Hood's breath, soldier, stop sneaking up on me like that!'

'What're you doing?' Corabb asked.

'Me? What're *you* doing? Don't tell me the scrap's already over—'

'No. I lost my new sword. Sergeant got mad and sent me home.'

'Bad luck, Corabb. No glory for you.'

'Wasn't looking for any—wasn't real fighting, Bottle. I don't see the point in that. They'd only learn anything if we could use our weapons and kill a few hundred of them.'

'Right. That makes sense. Bring it up with Fiddler—'

'I did. Just before he sent me back.'

'He's getting more unreasonable by the day.'

'Funny,' Corabb said, 'that's exactly what I said to him. Anyway, what're you doing? This isn't your bunk.'

'You're a sharp one all right, Corabb. See, it's like this. Smiles is trying to murder me.'

'Is she? Why?'

'Women like her don't need reasons, Corabb. She's set booby traps. Poison, is my guess. Because I was staying behind, you see? She's set a trap to kill me.'

'Oh,' said Corabb. 'That's clever.'

'Not clever enough, friend. Because now you're here.'

'I am, yes.'

Bottle edged back from the lockbox. 'It's unlocked,' he said, 'so I want you to lift the lid.'

Corabb stepped past and flung the lid back.

After he'd recovered from his flinch, Bottle crawled up for a look inside.

'Now what?' Corabb asked behind him. 'Was that practice?'

'Practice?'

'Aye.'

'No, Corabb—gods, this is strange—look at this gear! Those clothes.'

'Well, what I meant was, do you want me to open Smiles's box next?'

'What?'

'That's Cuttle's. You're at Cuttle's bunk, Bottle.' He pointed. 'Hers is right there.'

'Well,' Bottle muttered as he stood up and dropped the lid on the lockbox. 'That explains the codpiece.'

'Oh . . . does it?'

They stared at each other.

'So, just how many bastards do you think you've sired by now?'

'What?'

'What?'

'You just say something, Corabb?'

'What?'

'Before that.'

'Before what?'

'Something about bastards.'

'Are you calling me a bastard?' Corabb demanded, his face darkening.

'No, of course not. How would I know?'

'How—'

'It's none of my business, right?' Bottle slapped the man on one solid shoulder and set off to find his boots. 'I'm going out.'

'Thought you were sick.'

'Better now.'

Once he'd made his escape—in all likelihood narrowly avoiding being beaten to death by the squad's biggest fist over some pathetic misunderstanding—Bottle glared up at the mid-afternoon sun for a moment, and then set off. *All right, you parasite, I'm paying attention now. Where to?*

'It's about time. I was having doubts—'

Quick Ben! Since when were you playing around with Mockra? And do you have any idea how our skulls will ache by this evening?

'Relax, I got something for that. Bottle, I need you to go to the Old Palace. I'm down in the crypts.'

Where you belong.

'First time anybody's expressed that particular sentiment, Bottle. Tell me when you get to the grounds.'

What are you doing in the crypts, Quick Ben?

'I'm at the Cedance. You need to see this, Bottle.'

Did you find them, then?

'Who?'

Sinn and Grub. Heard they went missing.

'No, they're not here, and no sign that anyone's been down here in some time. As I've already told the Adjunct, the two imps are gone.'

Gone? Gone where?

'No idea. But they're gone.'

Bad news for the Adjunct—she's losing her mages—

'She's got me. She doesn't need anyone else.'

And all my fears are laid to rest.

'You may not have realized, Bottle, but I was asking you about your furry lover for a reason.'

Jealousy?

'Hurry up and get here so I can throttle you. No, not jealousy. Although, come to think on it, I can't even recall the last time—'

You said you had a reason, Quick Ben. Let's hear it.

'What's Deadsmell been telling you?'

What? Nothing. Well.

'Hah, I knew it! Don't believe him, Bottle. He hasn't any idea—any idea at all—about what's in the works.'

You know, Quick Ben, oh . . . never mind. So, I'm on the grounds. Where to now?

'Anybody see you?'

You didn't tell me to do this sneakily!

'Anybody in sight?'

Bottle looked round. Wings of the Old Palace were settled deep in mud, plaster cracking or simply gone, to reveal fissured, slumping brick walls. Snarls of grasses swallowed up old flagstone pathways. A plaza of some sort off to his left was now a shallow pond. The air was filled with spinning insects. No.

'Good. Now, follow my instructions precisely, Bottle.'

You sure? I mean, I was planning on ignoring every third direction you gave me.

'Fiddler needs to have a few words with you, soldier. About rules of conduct when it comes to High Mages.'

Look, Quick Ben, if you want me to find this Cedance, leave me to it. I have a nose for those kinds of things.

'I knew it!'

You knew what? I'm just saying—

'She's been whispering in your ear—'

Gods below, Quick Ben! The noises she makes aren't whispers. They're not even words. I don't—

'She gives you visions, doesn't she? Flashes of her own memories. Scenes.'

How do you know that?

'Tell me some.'

Why do you think it's any of your business?

'Choose one, damn you.'

He slapped at a mosquito. Some would be easier than others, he knew. Easier because they were empty of meaning. Most memories were, he suspected. Frozen scenes. Jungle trails, the bark of four-legged monkeys from cliff-sides. Huddled warmth in the night as hunting beasts coughed in the darkness. But there was one that returned again and again, in innumerable variations.

The sudden blossoming of blue sky, an opening ahead, the smell of salt. Soft rush of gentle waves on white coral beach. Padding breathless on to the strand in a chorus of excited cries and chatter. Culmination of terrifying journeys overland where it seemed home would never again find them. And then, in sudden gift . . . Shorelines, Quick. Bright sun, hot sand underfoot. Coming home . . . even when the home has never been visited before. And, all at once, they gather to begin building boats.

'Boats?'

Always boats. Islands. Places where the tawny hunters do not stalk the night. Places, where they can be . . . safe.

'The Eres—'

Lived for the seas. The oceans. Coming from the great continents, they existed in a state of flight. Shorelines fed them. The vast emptiness beyond the reefs called to them.

'Boats? What kind of boats?'

It varies—I don't always travel with the same group. Dug-outs. Reed boats and bamboo rafts. Skins, baskets bridged by saplings—like nests in toppled trees. Quick Ben, the Eres'al—they were smart, smarter than you might think. They weren't as different from us as they might seem. They conquered the entire world.

'So what happened to them?'

Bottle shrugged. *I don't know. I think, maybe, we happened to them.*

He had found a sundered doorway. Walking the length of dark, damp corridors and following the narrow staircases spiralling downward to landings ankle-deep in water. Sloshing this way and that, drawing unerringly closer to that pulsing residue of ancient power. *Houses, Tiles, Holds, Wandering—that all sounds simple enough, doesn't it, Quick Ben? Logical. But what about the roads of the sea? Where do they fit in? Or the siren calls of the wind? The point is, we see ourselves as the great trekkers, the bold travellers and explorers. But the Eres'al, High Mage, they did it first. There isn't a place we step anywhere in this world that they haven't stepped first. Humbling thought, isn't it?* He reached a narrow tunnel with an uneven floor that formed islands between pools. A massive portal with a leaning lintel stone beckoned. He stepped through and saw the causeway, and the broader platform at the end, where stood Quick Ben.

'All right, I'm here, Quick Ben. With soaked feet.'

The vast chamber was bathed in golden light that rose like mist from the Tiles spreading out from the disc. Quick Ben, head tilted to one side, watched Bottle approach up the causeway, an odd look in his eyes.

'What?'

He blinked, and then gestured. 'Look around, Bottle. The Cedance is *alive*.'

'Signifying what?'

'I was hoping you could tell me. The magic here should be waning. We've unleashed the warrens, after all. We've brought the Deck of Dragons. We've slammed the door on Chaos. It's like bringing the wheel to a tribe that has only used sleds and travois—there's been a revolution among this kingdom's mages. Even the priests are finding everything upside down—it'd be nice to sneak a spy into the cult of the Errant. Anyway, this place should be dying, Bottle.'

Bottle looked round. One Tile close by displayed a scatter of bones carved like impressions into the stone surface, impressions that glowed as if filled with embers. Nearby was another showing an empty throne. But the brightest Tile of all lifted its own image above the flat surface, so that it floated, swirling, in three dimensions. A dragon, wings spread wide, jaws open. 'Hood's breath,' he muttered, repressing a shiver.

'Your roads of the sea, Bottle,' said Quick Ben. 'They make me think about Mael.'

'Well, hard not to think about Mael in this city, High Mage.'

'You know, then.'

Bottle nodded.

'That's not nearly as worrisome as what was happening back in the Malazan Empire. The ascension of Mallick Rel, the Jhistal.'

Bottle frowned at Quick Ben. 'How can that be more worrying than finding an Elder God standing next to the Letherii throne?'

'It's not the *throne* he's standing beside. It's Tehol. From what I gather, that relationship has been there for some time. Mael's hiding here, trying to keep his head down. But he hasn't much say when some mortal manages to grasp some of his power, and starts forcing concessions.'

'The Elder God of the Seas,' said Bottle, 'was ever a thirsty god. And his daughter isn't much better.'

'Beru?'

'Who else? The Lady of Fair Seas is an ironic title. It pays,' he added, eyeing the dragon Tile, 'not to take things so literally.'

'I'm thinking,' said Quick Ben, 'of asking the Adjunct to elevate you to High Mage.'

'Don't do that,' snapped Bottle.

'Give me a reason not to. And not one of those pathetic ones about comradeship and how you're so needed in Fid's squad.'

'All right. See what you think of this one, then. Keep me where I am . . . as your shaved knuckle in the hole.'

The High Mage's glittering eyes narrowed, and then he smiled. 'I may not like you much, Bottle, but sometimes . . . I like what you say.'

'Lucky you. Now, can we get out of this place?'

'I think it is time,' she said, 'for us to leave.'

Withal squinted at her, and then rubbed at the bristle on his chin. 'You want better accommodation, love?'

'No, you idiot. I mean *leave*. The Bonehunters, this city, all of it. You did what you had to do. I did what I had to do—my miserable family of Rake's runts are gone, now. Nothing holds us here any more. Besides,' she added, 'I don't like where things are going.'

'That reading—'

'Meaningless.' She fixed a level gaze on him. 'Do I look like the Queen of High House Dark?'

Withal hesitated.

'Do you value your life, husband?'

'If you want us to leave, why, I don't expect anyone will try to stop us. We can book passage . . . somewhere.' And then he frowned. 'Hold on, Sand. Where will we go?'

Scowling, she rose and began pacing round their small, sparsely furnished room. 'Remember the Shake? On that prison island?'

'Aye. The ones that used old Andii words for some things.'

'Who worship the shore, yes.'

'Well?' he asked.

'Who also seemed to think that the shore was dying.'

'Maybe the one they knew—I mean, there's always some kind of shore.'

'Rising sea levels.'

'Aye.'

'Those sea levels,' she continued, now facing the window and looking out over the city, 'have been kept unnaturally low . . . for a long time.'

'They have?'

'Omtose Phellack. The rituals of ice. The Jaghut and their war with the T'lan Imass. The vast ice fields are melting, Withal.' She faced him. 'You're Meckros—you've seen for yourself the storms—we saw it again at Fent Reach—the oceans are in chaos. Seasons are awry. Floods, droughts, infestations. And where does the Adjunct want to take her army? East. To Kolanse. But it's a common opinion here in Lether that Kolanse is suffering a terrible drought.' Her dark eyes hardened. 'Have you ever seen an entire people starving, dying of thirst?'

'No. Have you?'

'I am *old*, husband. I remember the Saelen Gara, an offshoot Andii people in my home world. They lived in the forests. Until the forests died. We begged them, then, to come to Kharkanas. To the cities of the realm. They refused. Their hearts were broken, they said. Their world had died, and so they elected to die with it. Andarist begged . . .' Her gaze clouded then and she turned away, back to the window. 'Yes, Withal, to answer you. Yes, I have. And I will not see it again.'

'Very well. Where to, then?'

'We will begin,' she said, 'with a visit to the Shake.'

'What have they to tell you, Sand? Garbled memories. Ignorant superstitions.'

'Withal. I fell in battle. We warred with the K'Chain Che'Malle. Until the Tiste Edur betrayed us, slaughtered us. Clearly, they were not as thorough as they perhaps should have been. Some Andii survived. And it seems that there were more than just K'Chain Che'Malle dwelling in that region. There were humans.'

'The Shake.'

'People who would become the Shake, once they took in the surviving Andii. Once the myths and legends of both groups knitted together and became indistinguishable.' She paused, and then said, 'But even then, there must have been a schism of some sort. Unless, of course, the Tiste Andii of Bluerose were an earlier population, a migration distinct from our own. But my thinking is this: some of the Shake, with Tiste Andii among them, split away, travelled inland. They were the ones who created Bluerose, a theocracy centred on the worship of the Black-Winged Lord. On Anomander Rake, Son of Darkness.'

'Is it not equally possible,' ventured Withal, 'that *all* the Tiste Andii left? Leaving just the Shake, weakly blood-mixed here and there, perhaps, but otherwise just human, yet now possessing that knitted skein of myths and such?'

She glanced at him, frowned. 'That's a thought, husband. The Tiste Andii survivors used the humans, to begin with, to regain their strength—to stay alive on this unknown world—even to hide them from Edur hunting parties. And then, when at last they judged they were ready, and it was safe, they all left.'

'But wouldn't the Shake have then rejected them? Their stories? Their words? After all, they certainly didn't worship the Tiste Andii, did they? They worshipped the shore—and you have to admit, that's one strange religion they have. Praying to a strip of beach and whatnot.'

'And that is what interests me more than those surviving Tiste Andii. And that is why I wish to speak with their elders, their witches and warlocks.'

'Deadsmell described the horrid skeletons his squad and Sinn found on the north end of the island. Half reptilian, half human. Misbegotten—'

'That were quickly killed, disposed of. The taint, Withal, of K'Chain Che'Malle. And so, before we Tiste even arrived, they lived in the shadow of the Che'Malle. And it was not in isolation. No, there was some form of contact, some kind of relationship. There must have been.'

He thought about that, still uncertain as to where her thoughts were taking her. Why it had become so important that she uncover the secrets of the Shake. 'Sandalath, why did you Tiste war against the K'Chain Che'Malle?'

She looked startled. 'Why? Because they were different.'

'I see. And they fought against you in turn. Because you were different, or because you were invading their world?'

She reached up and closed the shutters, blocking out the cityscape and sky beyond. The sudden gloom was like a shroud on their conversation. 'I'm going out now,' she said. 'Start packing.'

With delicate precision, Telorast nipped at the eyelid, clasping it and lifting it away from the eye. Curdle leaned in for a closer look, then pulled back, hind claws scrabbling to maintain their grip on the front of Banaschar's tunic.

'He's piss drunk, all right. Snuffed candle. Doused fire, gutted lamp, the reeking dead.'

Telorast released the lid, watched it sink back down. Banaschar sighed wetly, groaned and shifted in the chair, head lolling.

The two skeletal creatures scrambled down and rendezvoused on the window sill on the other side of the small room. They tilted their heads closer together.

'What now?' Curdle whispered.

'What kind of question is that? What now? What now? Have you lost your mind?'

'Well, what now, Telorast?'

'How should I know! But listen, we need to do something! That Errant—he's . . . he's—well, I hate him, is what! And worse, he's using Banaschar, our very own ex-priest.'

'Our pet.'

'That's right. *Our* pet—not his!'

'We should kill him.'

'Who? Banaschar or the Errant?'

'If we kill Banaschar, then nobody has a pet. If we kill the Errant, then we can keep Banaschar all to ourselves.'

'Right, Curdle,' Telorast said, nodding, 'but which one would make the Errant angrier?'

'Good question. We need something to make him go mad, completely mad—that's the best revenge for stealing our pet.'

'And then we kill him.'

'Who?'

'It doesn't matter! Why are you being so thick? Oh, what a ridiculous question! Listen, Curdle, now we got ourselves a plan and that's good. It's a start. So let's think some more. Vengeance against the Errant.'

'The Elder God.'

'Right.'

'Who's still around.'

'Right.'

'Stealing pets.'

'Curdle—'

'I'm just thinking out loud, that's all!'

'You call that thinking? No wonder we ended up torn to pieces and dead and worse than dead!'

'Oh, and what are *you* thinking, then?'

'I didn't have any time to, since I had to answer all your questions!'

'You always got an excuse, Telorast, did you know that? Always.'

'And you're it, Curdle, did you know *that*?'

A voice croaked from the other side of the room, 'What are you two whispering about over there?'

The two skeletons flinched. Then, tail lashing about, Telorast ducked a head in Banaschar's direction. 'Absolutely nothing, and that's a fact. In fact, beloved pet, that's the problem! Every time! It's Curdle. She's an idiot! She drives me mad! Drives you to drink, too, I bet.'

'The Errant's game is one of fate,' Banaschar said, rubbing at his face. 'He uses—abuses—proclivities, tendencies. He nudges, pushes over the edge.' He blinked blearily at the two skeletons. 'To take him down, you need to take advantage of that selfsame obsession. You need to set a trap.'

Telorast and Curdle hopped down from the sill and advanced on the seated man, tails flicking, heads low. 'A trap,' whispered Telorast. 'That's good. We thought you'd switched gods, that's what we thought—'

'Don't tell him what we thought!' Curdle hissed.

'It doesn't matter now—he's on our side! Weren't you listening?'

'The Errant wants all he once had,' said Banaschar. 'Temples, worshippers, domination. Power. To do that, he needs to take down the gods. The High Houses . . . all in ruins. Smouldering heaps. This coming war with the Crippled God presents him with his chance—a few nudges on the battlefield—who'd notice? He wants spilled blood, my friends, that's what he wants.'

'Who doesn't?' asked Curdle.

The two creatures had reached Banaschar's scuffed boots and were now bobbing and fawning. 'The chaos of battle,' murmured Telorast, 'yes, that would be ideal.'

'For us,' nodded Curdle.

'Precisely. Our chance.'

'To do what?' Banaschar asked. 'Find yourselves a couple of thrones?' He snorted. Ignoring them as they prostrated themselves at his feet, he held up his hands and stared at them. 'See this tremble, friends? What does it truly signify? I will tell you. I am the last living priest of D'rek. Why was I spared? I lost all the privileges of worship within a temple. I lost a secular game of influence and power, diminished in the eyes of my brothers and sisters. In the eyes of everyone, I imagine. But I never gave up worshipping my god.' He squinted. 'I should be dead. Was I simply forgotten? Has it taken longer than D'rek thought? To hunt us all down? When will my god find me?' After a moment longer he lowered his hands on to his thighs. 'I just . . . wait.'

'Our pet's disenchanted,' whispered Telorast.

'That's bad,' Curdle whispered back.

'We need to find him a woman.'

'Or a child to eat.'

'They don't eat children, Curdle.'

'Well, some other kind of treat, then.'

'A bottle!'

'A bottle, yes, that's good!'

They went hunting.

Banaschar waited.

Koryk trained his crossbow on the back of the scout's helmed head. His finger edged down to the iron press.

The point of a knife hovered into view opposite his right eye. 'I got orders,' whispered Smiles, 'to kill you if you kill anyone.'

He drew his finger back. 'Like Hood you have. Besides, it might be an accident.'

'Oh, I saw that for sure, Koryk. Your trigger finger just accidentally slipping down like that. And then, oh, in went my knife point—another accident. Tragedies! We'll burn you on a pyre Seti style and that's a promise.'

He lowered the crossbow and rolled on to his side, out of sight of the clumsy scout on the track below. 'Right, that makes perfect sense, Smiles. A pyre for the people who live on the grasslands. We like our funerals to involve, why, everyone. We burn down whole villages and scorch the ground for leagues in every direction.'

She blinked at him, and then shrugged. 'Whatever you do with your dead, then.'

He worked his way down the slope, Smiles following.

'My turn,' she said when they reached the draw. 'Get back up there.'

'You waited till we got down here to say that?'

She grinned.

Leaving him to scrabble back into position, Smiles set off through the brush. It wasn't that the Letherii scouts were especially bad. It was more the case that their tradition of warfare kept them trapped in the idea of huge armies clashing on open fields. Where scouts were employed simply to find the enemy encamp-ments. The notion of a foe that could melt into the landscape the way the Malazans could, or even the idea that the enemy might split its forces, avoid direct clashes, and whittle the Letherii down with raids, ambushes and disrupted supply lines—none of that was part of their military thinking.

The Tiste Edur had been tougher by far. Their fighting style was much closer to the Malazan one, which probably explained why the Edur conquered the Letherii the first time round.

Of course, the Malazans could stand firm in a big scrap, but it made sense to have spent some time demoralizing and weakening their foe beforehand.

These Letherii had a lot still to learn. After all, one day the Malazans might be back. Not the Bonehunters, but the imperial armies of the Empress. A new king-dom to conquer, a new continent to subjugate. If King Tehol wanted to hold on to what he had, his brother had better be commanding a savvy, nasty army that knew how to face down Malazan marines, heavies, squad mages, sappers with munitions, and decent cavalry.

She quietly grunted as she approached the hidden camp. *Poor Brys Beddict. They might as well surrender now.*

'If you was any less ugly,' a voice said, 'I'd a killed you for sure.'

She halted, scowling. 'Took your time announcing yourself, picket.'

The soldier that edged into view was dark-skinned, barring a piebald blotch of pink disfiguring half his face and most of his forehead. The heavy crossbow in his hands was cocked but no quarrel rested in the slot.

Smiles pushed past him. 'Talk about ugly—you live in my nightmares, Gull-stream, you know that?'

The man stepped in behind her. 'Can't help being so popular with the ladies,' he said. 'Especially the Letherii ones.'

Despite the blotch, there was indeed something about Gullstream that made women take a second and third look. She suspected he might have some Tiste Andii blood in his veins. The almond-shaped eyes that never seemed to settle on any one colour; his way of moving—as if he had all the time in the world—and the fact that he was, according to rumour, well-hung. Shaking her head to clear away stupid thoughts, she said, 'Their scouts have gone right past—staying on the track mostly. So the Fist can move us all up. We'll fall on the main column screaming our lungs out and that will be that.'

As she was saying this, they entered the camp—a few hundred soldiers sitting or lying quietly amidst the trees, stumps and brush.

Seeing Keneb, Smiles headed over to make her report.

The Fist was sitting on a folding camp stool, using the point of his dagger to scrape mud from the soles of his boots. A cup of steaming herbal tea rested on a stump beside him. Sprawled on the ground a few paces away was Sergeant Fiddler, and just beyond him Sergeant Balm sat crosslegged, studying the short sword he was holding, his expression confused. A dozen heavies waited nearby, grouped to-gether and seeming to be engaged in comparing their outthrust hands—*counting knuckle hairs, I bet.*

'Fist, Scout Smiles reporting, sir.'

Keneb glanced up. 'As predicted?'

'Aye, sir. Can we go kill 'em all now?'

The Fist looked over at Fiddler, 'Looks like you lost your bet, Sergeant.'

Eyes still closed, Fiddler grunted, then said, 'We ain't done any killing yet, sir. Brys Beddict's been fishin in our brains for some time now, he's bound to have snagged a fin or gill or two. Smiles, how many scouts on the track?'

'Just the one, Sergeant. Picking his nose.'

Fiddler opened his eyes and squinted over at Keneb. 'Like that, Fist. Beddict's re-configured his scouting patrols—they pair up. If Smiles and Koryk saw only one, then where was the other one?' He shifted to get more comfortable and closed his eyes again. 'And he runs five units—five pairs—in advance of his main body. So.'

'So,' repeated Keneb, frowning. He rose, slipped the dagger into his scabbard. 'If he's sent one or two down the track, they were meant to be seen. Sergeant Balm, find me that map.'

'Map, sir? What map?'

Muttering under his breath, Keneb walked over to the heavies. 'You there— yes, you—name?'

'Reliko, sir.'

'What are you doing with those heavies, Reliko?'

'Why, cos I am one, sir.'

Watching this, Smiles snorted. The top of Reliko's gnarly head barely reached her shoulder. The man looked like a prune with arms and legs.

'Who's your sergeant?' Keneb asked the Dal Honese soldier.

'Badan Gruk, sir. But he stayed back sick, sir, along with Sergeant Sinter and Kisswhere. Me and Vastly Blank here, we squadding up with Drawfirst and Shoaly, under Sergeant Primly, sir.'

'Very well. Go into the command tent and bring me the map.'

'Aye sir. You want the table with it?'

'No, that won't be necessary.'

As the soldier walked off, Fiddler said, 'Coulda been there and back by now, sir. All by yourself.'

'I could have, yes. And just for that observation, Sergeant, go and get that map-table for me.'

'Thought it wasn't necessary, sir?'

'I changed my mind. On your feet.'

Groaning, Fiddler sat up, nudged Balm and said, 'You and me, we got work to do.'

Blinking, Balm stared at him a moment. Then he leapt upright, sword in his hand. 'Where are they, then?'

'Follow me,' Fiddler said, climbing to his feet. 'And put that thing away before you poke me with it.'

'Why would I stab you? I mean, I know you, right? I think. Aye, I know you.'

They passed Reliko on their way to the tent.

As the soldier stepped up, Keneb took the rolled-up hide. 'Thank you. Reliko, before you go, a question—why are all the heavies examining their hands?'

'We was adding up lost bits, sir, t'see if it made up a whole hand.'

'Does it?'

'We're missing a thumb, but we heard there's a heavy without any thumbs—might be over in Blistig's legion.'

'Indeed, and what would his name be?'

'Nefarias Bredd, sir.'

'And how would this soldier be able to wield any weapons, without thumbs?'

Reliko shrugged. 'Can't say, sir, as I only seen 'im once, and that was from too far away. I expect he ties 'em up sort of, somehow.'

'Perhaps,' ventured Keneb, 'he's missing only one thumb. Shield hand, perhaps.'

'Might be, sir, might be, in which case as soon as we find a thumb, why, we'll let him know.' Reliko returned to his companions.

Keneb stared after the soldier, frowning.

'Kingdoms toppled one by one,' said Smiles, 'because of soldiers like him, sir. Keep telling yourself that—that's how I do it.'

'Do what, scout?'

'Stay sane, sir. He's the one, you know.'

'Who, what?'

'The shortest heavy in the history of the Malazan Empire, sir.'

'Really? Are you certain of that, scout?'

'Sir?'

But he'd unfurled the map and was now studying it.

Fiddler and Balm were approaching, a heavy table between them. As soon as they arrived, Keneb rolled up the map and set it on the tabletop. 'You can take that back now, Sergeants. Thank you.'

Smiles jogged her way back to where Koryk was hidden along the ridge. Behind her clunked Corporal Tarr, sounding like a damned tinker's cart. She shot him a glare over one shoulder. 'You shoulda strapped down, you know that, don't you?'

'This is a damned feint,' said Tarr, 'what difference does it make?'

They reached the base of the ridge.

'I'll wait here. Go collect the fool, Smiles, and be quick about it.'

Biting back a retort, she set off up the slope. It'd be different, she knew, if she was the corporal. And this was a perfect example. If she was corporal, it'd be Tarr doing this climb and that was a fact.

Koryk heard her coming and worked his way down to meet her. 'No column, huh?'

'No, how'd you guess?'

'Didn't have to. I waited. And . . . no column.'

They descended the slope side by side to where Tarr waited.

'We lost the enemy, Corporal?'

'Something like that, Koryk. And now the Fist's got us on the move—we're going to be buggered trying catch-up, too. He's now thinking we've stuck our heads in a wasp nest.'

'These Letherii couldn't turn an ambush on us,' Koryk pronounced. 'We would've sniffed it out by now.'

'But we didn't,' Smiles pointed out. 'We been flushed, Koryk.'

'Lazy,' pronounced Tarr. 'Overconfident. Fiddler was right.'

'Of course he was,' said Smiles. 'He's Fiddler. It's always the problem, the people in charge never listen to the people in the know. It's like two different worlds, two different languages.'

She stopped when she noticed both men looking at her. 'What?'

'Nothing,' said Tarr, 'except, well, that was a sharp observation there, Smiles.'

'Oh, and did that shock you two?'

'Shocked me,' admitted Koryk.

She scowled at him.

But secretly, she was pleased. *That's right. I ain't the fool you think I am. I ain't the fool nobody thinks I am. Everybody, I mean. Well, they're the real fools, anyway.*

They hurried on, but long before they caught up to the company, it was all over.

The Letherii ambush caught Keneb's mob coming down a forested slope that funnelled before reaching the basin. Enemy ranks rose up on both sides from fast-dug foxholes and loosed a few hundred un-fletched arrows with soft clay balls instead of barbed iron points. If the flights had been real, half the Malazans would have been downed, dead or wounded. A few more salvos and most of the rest would be out of commission.

Brys Beddict made an appearance in the midst of Letherii catcalls and cheering, walking up to Fist Keneb and painting with one dripping finger a red slash across his boiled-leather cuirass.

'Sorry, Fist, but you have just been wiped out.'

'Indeed, Commander,' Keneb acknowledged. 'Three hundred dead Bonehunters, cut down in a pocket. Very well done, although I suspect it highlights a lesson as yet undiscovered.'

The smile on Brys's face faded slightly. 'Fist? I'm afraid I don't understand you.'

'Sometimes, one's tactics must prove brutal in the execution, Commander. Especially when the timing's off and nothing can be done for it.'

'I'm sorry?'

Horns sounded suddenly, from the ridge lines beyond the Letherii units—on all sides, in fact.

Keneb said, 'Three hundred dead Bonehunters, Commander, and eight hundred dead Letherii, including their supreme commander. Not an ideal exchange for either side, but in a war, probably one the Adjunct could stomach.'

Brys sighed, his expression wry. 'Lesson delivered, Fist Keneb. My compliments to the Adjunct.'

At that moment, Fiddler walked up to them. 'Fist, you owe me and my squad two nights' leave, sir.'

Keneb grinned at Brys Beddict. 'As much as the Adjunct would appreciate the compliments, Commander, they in fact belong to this sergeant here.'

'Ah, I see.'

'That's another lesson to mull over,' Keneb said, 'the one about listening to your veterans, regardless of rank.'

'Well,' mused Brys, 'I may have to go hunting for my few surviving veterans, then. None the less, Fist, the sacrifice of three hundred of your soldiers strikes me as a loss you can ill afford, regardless of the battle's outcome.'

'True. Hence my comment about timing, Commander. I sent a rider to Fist Blistig but we could not respond in time to your ambush. Obviously, I would rather have avoided all contact with your troops. But since I know we'd all prefer to sleep in real beds tonight, I thought it more instructive to invite the engagement. Now,' he added, smiling, 'we can all march back to Letheras.'

Brys drew out a handkerchief, wetted it from his canteen, and then stepped up to Fist Keneb, and carefully cleaned off the streak of red paint.

Captain Faradan Sort entered Kindly's office to find her counterpart standing to one side of his desk and staring down at an enormous mound of what looked like hair heaped on the desktop.

'Gods below, what is that?'

Kindly glanced over. 'What does it look like?'

'Hair.'

'Correct. Animal hair, as best as I can determine. A variety of domestic beasts.'

'It reeks. What is it doing on your desk?'

'Good question. Tell me, was Lieutenant Pores in the outer office?'

She shook her head. 'No one there, I'm afraid.'

He grunted. 'Hiding, I expect.'

'I doubt he'd do something like this, Kindly—'

'Oh, never directly. No, but I would wager a wagonload of imperials he's had a hand in it. He imagines himself very clever, does my lieutenant.'

'If he owns anything he values greatly,' she said, 'crush it under a heel. That's how I took care of the one I sensed was going to give me trouble. That was back in Seven Cities, and to this day he looks at me with hurt in his eyes.'

He glanced at her. 'Hurt? Truly?'

'Truly.'

'That's . . . exceptional advice, Faradan. Thank you.'

'You're welcome. Anyway, I was coming by to see if you'd had any better luck finding our two wayward mages.'

'No. We need to get High Mage Quick Ben involved in the search, I believe. Assuming,' he added, 'they're worth finding.'

She turned away, walked to the window. 'Kindly, Sinn saved many, many lives at Y'Ghatan. She did so the night of the assault and again with the survivors under the city. Her brother, Corporal Shard, is beside himself with worry. She is precipitous, yes, but I do not consider that necessarily a fault.'

'And the Adjunct has, it seems, desperate need for mages,' said Kindly. 'Why is that?'

She shrugged. 'I know as little as you, Kindly. We will march soon, away from the comforts of Letheras.'

The man grunted. 'Never let a soldier get too comfortable. Leads to trouble every time. She's right in kicking us into motion. Still, it'd be a comfort to know what we're heading into.'

'And a greater comfort to have more than one half-mad High Mage to support eight thousand soldiers.' She paused, and then said, 'We won't find ourselves another Beak hiding among the squads. We've had our miracle, Kindly.'

'You're starting to sound as grim as Blistig.'

She shook herself. 'You're right. Apologies. I'm just worried about Sinn, that's all.'

'Then find Quick Ben. Get him looking into those closets or whatever they're called—'

'Warrens.'

'Right.'

Sighing, she swung round and went to the door. 'I'll send Pores to you if I see him.'

'You won't,' Kindly said. 'He'll come up for air sooner or later, Faradan. Leave the lieutenant to me.'

Sergeant Sinter and her sister sat playing the Dal Honese version of bones with Badan Gruk. The human finger bones were polished with use, gleaming amber. The legend was that they'd belonged to three Li Heng traders who'd come to the village, only to be caught thieving. They'd lost more than their hands, naturally. Dal Honese weren't much interested in delivering lessons; they preferred something more succinct and, besides, executing the fools just left the path open for more to come wandering in, and everyone liked a good torture session.

That was before things got civilized, of course. Kellanved had put an end to torture. 'A state that employs torture invites barbarism and deserves nothing better than to suffer the harvest of its own excesses.' That was said to have been from the Emperor himself, although Sinter had her doubts. Sounded too . . . literate, especially for a damned Dal Honese thief.

Anyway, life stopped being much fun once civilization arrived, or so the old ones muttered. But then, they were always muttering. It was the last career to take up before dying of oldness, the reward for living so long, she supposed. She didn't expect to survive her career as a soldier. It was interesting to see how it was the green, fresh ones who did all the complaining. The veterans just stayed quiet. So maybe all that bitching was at both ends of life, the young and the old trapped inside chronic dissatisfaction.

Kisswhere collected up the bones and tossed them again. 'Hah! Poor Badan Gruk—you won't ever match that, let's see you try!'

It was a pretty good cast, Sinter had to acknowledge. Four of the core patterns with only a couple of spars missing and one true bridge. Badan would need a near perfect throw to top Kisswhere's run.

'I'll stop there, I said. Toss 'em, Badan. And no cheating.'

'I don't cheat,' he said as he collected up the bones.

'Then what's that you just palmed?'

Badan opened his hand and scowled. 'This one's gummed! No wonder you got those casts!'

'If it was gummed,' Kisswhere retorted, 'then it was from my sister's last throw!'

'Hood's breath,' sighed Sinter. 'Look, you fools, we're all cheating. It's in our blood. So now we've got to accept the fact that none of us is going to admit they were the one using the gum to get a stick. Clean the thing off and let's get on with it.'

The others subsided and Sinter was careful to hide her relief. That damned gum had been in her pouch too long, making it dirty, and she could feel the stuff on her fingers. She surreptitiously brought her hands down to her thighs and rubbed as if trying to warm up.

Kisswhere shot her a jaded look. The damned barracks was hot as a head-shrinker's oven.

They made a point of ignoring the clump of boots as someone marched up to their table. Badan Gruk threw the bones—and achieved six out of six in the core.

'Did you see that! Look!' Badan's smile was huge and hugely fake. 'Look, you two, look at that cast!'

But they were looking at him instead, because cheaters couldn't stand that for long—they'd twitch, they'd bead up, they'd squirrel on the chair.

'Look!' he said again, pointing, but the command sounded more like a plea, and all at once he sagged back and raised his hands. 'Fingers clean, darlings—'

'That would be a first,' said the man standing now at their table.

Badan Gruk's expression displayed hurt and innocence, with just a touch of in-dignation. 'That wasn't called for, sir. You saw my throw—you can see my fin-gers, too. Clean as clean can be. No gum, no tar, no wax. Soldiers can't be smelly or dirty—it's bad for morale.'

'You sure about that?'

Sinter twisted in her chair. 'Can we help you, Lieutenant Pores?'

The man's eyes flickered in surprise. 'You mistake me, Sergeant Sinter. I am Captain—'

'Kindly was pointed out to us, sir.'

'I thought I ordered you to cut your hair.'

'We did,' said Kisswhere. 'It grew back. It's a trait among Dal Honese, right in the blood, an aversion—is that the word, Sint? Sure it is. Aversion. To bad haircuts. We get them and our hair insists on growing back to what looks better. Happens overnight, sir.'

'You might be comfortable,' said Pores, 'believing that I'm not Captain Kindly; that I'm not, in fact, the man who was pointed out to you. But can you be certain that the right one was pointed out to you? If Lieutenant Pores was doing the pointing, for example. He's one for jokes in bad taste. Infamous for it, in fact. He could have elected to take advantage of you—it's a trait of his, one suspects. In the blood, as it were.'

'So,' asked Sinter, 'who might he have pointed to, sir?'

'Why, anyone at all.'

'But Lieutenant Pores isn't a woman now, is she?'

'Of course not, but—'

'It was a woman,' continued Sinter, 'who did the pointing out.'

'Ah, but she might have been pointing to Lieutenant Pores, since you asked about whoever was your immediate superior. Well,' said Pores, 'now that that's cleared up, I need to check if you two women have put on the weight you were ordered to.'

Kisswhere and Sinter both leaned back to regard him.

The man gave them a bright smile.

'Sir,' said Sinter, 'how precisely do you intend to do that?'

The smile was replaced by an expression of shock. 'Do you imagine your captain to be some dirty old codger, Sergeant? I certainly hope not! No, you will come to my office at the ninth bell tonight. You will strip down to your undergarments in the outer office. When you are ready, you are to knock and upon hearing my voice you are to enter immediately. Am I understood, soldiers?'

'Yes sir,' said Sinter.

'Until then.'

The officer marched off.

'How long,' asked Kisswhere after he'd left the barracks, 'are we going to run with this, Sint?'

'Early days yet,' she smiled, collecting the bones. 'Badan, since you're out of the game for being too obvious, I need you to do a chore for me—well, not much of a chore—anyway, I need you to go out into the city and find me two of the fattest, ugliest whores you can.'

'I don't like where this is all going,' Badan Gruk muttered.

'Listen to you,' chided Sinter, 'you're getting old.'

'What did she say?'

Sandalath Drukorlat scowled. 'She wondered why we'd waited so long.'

Withal grunted. 'That woman, Sand . . .'

'Yes.' She paused just inside the doorway and glared at the three Nachts huddled beneath the window sill. Their long black, muscled arms were wrapped about one another, forming a clump of limbs and torsos from which three blunt heads made an uneven row, eyes thinned and darting with suspicion. 'What's with them?'

'I think they're coming with us,' Withal replied. 'Only, of course, they don't know where we're going.'

'Tie them up. Lock them up—do something. Just keep them here, husband. They're grotesque.'

'They're not my pets,' he said.

She crossed her arms. 'Really? Then why do they spend all their time under your feet?'

'Honestly, I have no idea.'

'Who do they belong to?'

He studied them for a long moment. Not one of the Nachts would meet his eyes. It was pathetic.

'Withal.'

'All right. I think they're Mael's pets.'

'*Mael!?*'

'Aye. I was praying to him, you see. And they showed up. On the island. Or maybe they showed up before I started praying—I can't recall. But they got me off that island, and that was Mael's doing.'

'Then send them back to him!'

'That doesn't seem to be the way praying works, Sand.'

'Mother bless us,' she sighed, striding forward. 'Pack up—we're leaving tonight.'

'Tonight? It'll be dark, Sand!'

She gave him the same glare she'd given Rind, Pule and Mape.

Dark, aye. Never mind.

The worst of it was, in turning away, he caught the looks of sympathy in the Nachts' beady eyes, tracking him like mourners at a funeral.

Well, a man learns to take sympathy where he can get it.

'If this is a new warren,' whispered Grub, 'then I think I'd rather we kept the old ones.'

Sinn was quiet, as she had been for most of what must have been an entire day, maybe longer, as they wandered this terrible world.

Windswept desert stretched out in all directions. The road they walked cut across it straight as a spear. Here and there, off to one side, they spied fields of stones that might have once been dwellings, and the remnants of sun-fired mud-brick pen or garden walls, but nothing grew here, nothing at all. The air was acrid, smelling of burning pitch—and that was not too surprising, as black pillars of smoke stalked the horizons.

On the road itself, constructed of crushed rock and, possibly, glass, they came upon scenes of devastation. Burnt-out hulks of carriages and wagons, scorched clothing and shattered furniture. Fire-blackened corpses, limbs curled like tree roots and hands like bird feet, mouths agape and hollow sockets staring at the empty sky. Twisted pieces of metal lay scattered about, none remotely identifiable to Grub.

Breathing made his throat sore, and the bitter chill of the morning had given way to blistering heat. Eyes stinging, feet dragging, he followed in Sinn's wake until her shadow lengthened to a stretched-out shape painted in pitch, and to his eyes it was as if he was looking down upon the woman she would one day become. He realized that his fear of her was growing—and her silence was making it worse.

'Will you now be mute to me as well?' he asked her.

She glanced back over her shoulder. Momentarily.

It would soon grow cold again—he'd lost too much fluid to survive a night of shivering. 'We need to camp, Sinn. Make a fire—'

She barked a laugh, but did not turn round. 'Fire,' she said. 'Yes. *Fire*. Tell me, Grub, what do you believe in?'

'What?'

'Some things are more real than others. For everyone. Each one, different, always different. What's the most real to you?'

'We can't survive this place, that's what's most real, Sinn. We need water. Food. Shelter.'

He saw her nod. 'That's what this warren is telling us, Grub. Just that. What you believe has to do with surviving. It doesn't go any further, does it? What if I told you that it used to be that for almost everybody? Before the cities, before people invented being rich.'

'Being rich? I don't know what you're talking about.'

'Before some people found other things to believe in. Before they made those things more real than anything else. Before they decided it was all right even to kill for them. Or enslave people. Or keep them stupid and poor.' She shot him a look. 'Did you know I had a Tanno tutor? A Spiritwalker.'

'I don't know anything about them. Seven Cities priests, right?'

'He once told me that an untethered soul can drown in wisdom.'

'What?'

'Wisdom grows by stripping away beliefs, until the last tether is cut, and suddenly you float free. Only, because your eyes are wide open, you see right away that you can't float in what you're in. You can only sink. That's why the meanest religions work so hard at keeping their followers ignorant. Knowledge is poison. Wisdom is depthless. Staying ignorant keeps you in the shallows. Every Tanno one day takes a final spiritwalk. They cut the last tether, and the soul can't go back. When that happens, the other Tannos mourn, because they know that the spiritwalker has drowned.'

His mouth was too dry, his throat too sore, but even if that had been otherwise, he knew he would have nothing to say to any of that. He knew, after all, about his own ignorance.

'Look around, Grub. See? There are no gifts here. Look at these stupid bodies and their stupid wagonloads of furniture. The last thing that was real for them, the only thing, was *fire*.'

His attention was drawn to a dust-cloud, rising in a slanted shroud of gold. Something was on a track that would converge with this road. A herd? An army?

'Fire is not the gift you think it is, Grub.'

'We'll die tonight without it.'

'We need to stay on this road.'

'Why?'

'To find out where it leads.'

'We'll die here, then.'

'This land, Grub,' she said, 'has generous memories.'

The sun was low by the time the army arrived. Horse-drawn chariots and massive wagons burdened with plunder. The warriors were dark-skinned, tall and thin, bedecked in bronze armour. Grub thought there might be a thousand of them, maybe more. He saw spearmen, archers, and what must be the equivalent of heavy infantry, armed with sickle-bladed axes and short curved swords.

They cut across the track of the road as if blind to it, and as Grub stared he was startled to realize that the figures and their horses and chariots were vaguely transparent. *They are ghosts.* 'These,' he said to Sinn who stood beside him, 'are this land's memories?'

'Yes.'

'Can they see us?'

She pointed at one chariot that had thundered past only to turn round at the urging of the man behind the driver, and was now drawing up opposite them. 'See him—he's a priest. He can't see us, but he senses us. Holiness isn't always in a place, Grub. Sometimes it's what's passing through.'

He shivered, hugged himself. 'Stop this, Sinn. We're not gods.'

'No, we're not. We're'—and she laughed—'more like divine messengers.'

The priest had leapt down from the chariot—Grub could now see the old blood splashed across the spokes of the high wheels, and saw where blades were fitted in times of battle, projecting out from the hubs. A mass charge by such instruments of war would deliver terrible slaughter.

The hawk-faced man was edging closer, groping like a blind man.

Grub made to step back but Sinn caught him by the arm and held him fast.

'Don't,' she murmured. 'Let him touch the divine, Grub. Let him receive his gift of wisdom.'

The priest had raised his hands. Beyond, the entire army had halted, and Grub saw what must be a king or commander—perched on a huge, ornate chariot—drawing up to observe the strange antics of his priest.

'We can give him no wisdom,' Grub said. 'Sinn—'

'Don't be a fool. Just stand here. Wait. We don't have to do anything.'

Those two outstretched hands came closer. The palms were speckled with dried blood. There were, however, no calluses upon them. Grub hissed, 'He is no warrior.'

'No,' Sinn agreed, 'but he so likes the blood.'

The palms hovered, slipped forward, and unerringly settled upon their brows.

Grub saw the priest's eyes widen, and he knew at once that the man was seeing through—through to this road and its litter of destruction—to an age either long before or yet to come: the age in which Grub and Sinn existed, solid and real:

The priest lurched back and howled.

Sinn's laughter was harsh. 'He saw what was real! He saw!' She spun to face

Grub, her eyes bright. 'The future is a desert! And a road! And no end to the stupid wars, the insane slaughter—' She whirled back and jabbed a finger at the wailing priest who was staggering back to his chariot. 'He believed in the sun god! He believed in immortality—of glory, of wealth—golden fields, lush gardens, sweet rains and sweet rivers flowing without cease! He believed his people are—hah!—*chosen! They all do, don't you see? They do, we do, everyone does!* See our gift, Grub? See what knowledge yields him? The sanctuary of ignorance—is shattered! Garden into wilderness, cast out into the seas of wisdom! Is not our message *divine?*'

Grub did not think he had any tears left in him. He was wrong.

The army and its priest and its king all fled, wild as the wind. But, before they did, slaves appeared and raised a cairn of stones. Which they then surrounded with offerings: jars of beer and wine and honey, dates, figs, loaves of bread and two throat-cut goats spilling blood into the sand.

The feast was ghostly, but Sinn assured Grub that it would sustain them. Divine gifts, she said, were not gifts at all. The receiver must pay for them.

'And he has done that, has he not, Grub? Oh, he has done that.'

The Errant stepped into the vast, impossible chamber. Gone now the leisure of reminiscences, the satisfied stirring of brighter days long since withered colourless, almost dead. Knuckles trailed a step behind him, as befitted his role of old and his role to come.

She was awake, hunched over a scattering of bones. Trapped in games of chance and mischance, the brilliant, confounding offerings of Sechul Lath, Lord of the Hold of Chance—the Toppler, the Conniver, the Wastrel of Ruin. Too foolish to realize that she was challenging, in the Lord's cast, the very laws of the universe which were, in truth, far less predictable than any mortal might believe.

The Errant walked up and with one boot kicked the ineffable pattern aside.

Her face stretched into a mask of rage. She reared, hands lifting—and then froze as she fixed her eyes upon the Errant.

'Kilmandaros.'

He saw the flicker of fear in her gaze.

'I have come,' he said to her, 'to speak of dragons.'

Chapter Eight

In my lifelong study of the scores of species of ants to be found in the tropical forests of Dal Hon, I am led to the conviction that all forms of life are engaged in a struggle to survive, and that within each species there exists a range of natural but variable proclivities, of physical condition and of behaviour, which in turn weighs for or against in the battle to survive and procreate. Further, it is my suspicion that in the act of procreation, such traits are passed on. By extension, one can see that ill traits reduce the likelihood of both survival and procreation. On the basis of these notions, I wish to propose to my fellow scholars at this noble gathering a law of survival that pertains to all forms of life. But before I do so, I must add one more caveat, drawn from the undeniable behavioural characteristics of, in my instance of speciality, ants. To whit, success of one form of life more often than not initiates devastating population collapse among competitors, and indeed, sometimes outright extinction. And that such annihilation of rivals may in fact be a *defining feature of success*.

Thus, my colleagues, I wish to propose a mode of operation among all forms of life, which I humbly call—in my four-volume treatise—'The Betrayal of the Fittest'.

Obsessional Scrolls
Sixth Day Proceedings
Address of Skavat Gill
Unta, Malazan Empire, 1097 Burn's Sleep

As if riding a scent on the wind; or through the tremble in the ground underfoot; or perhaps the air itself carried alien thoughts, thoughts angry, malign—whatever the cause, the K'Chain Che'Malle knew they were now being hunted. They had no patience for Kalyth and her paltry pace, and it was Gunth Mach whose posture slowly shifted, spine drawing almost horizontal to the ground—as if in the course of a single morning some force reshaped her skeleton, muscles and joints—and before the sun stood high she had gathered up the Destriant and set her down behind the humped shoulder-blades, where the dorsal spikes had flattened and where the thick hide had formed something like a saddle seat. And Kalyth found herself riding a K'Chain Che'Malle, the sensation far more fluid than that she recalled of sitting on the back of a horse, so that it seemed they flowed over the broken scrubland, at a speed somewhere between a canter and a gallop. Gunth Mach made use of her forelimbs only as they skirted slopes or ascended the occasional low hill; mostly the scarred, scale-armoured arms remained drawn up like the pincers of a mantis.

The K'ell Hunters Rythok and Kor Thuran flanked her, with Sag'Churok almost a third of a league ahead—even from her vantage point atop Gunth Mach, Kalyth rarely caught sight of the huge creature, a speck of motion betrayed only by its shadow. All of the K'Chain Che'Malle now bore on their scaled hides the mottled hues of the ground and its scant plant cover.

And yet . . . *and yet . . .* they were afraid.

Not of those human warriors who pursued them—that was little more than an inconvenience, an obstacle to their mission. No, instead, the fear within these terrible demons was deeper, visceral. It rode out from Gunth'an Acyl, the Matron, in ice-laden ripples, crowding up against each and every one of her children. The pressure built, grinding, thunderous.

A war is coming. We all know this. But as to the face of this enemy, I alone am blind.

Destriant—what does it mean to be one? To these creatures? What faith am I supposed to shape? I have no history to draw from, no knowledge of K'Chain Che'Malle legends or myths—assuming they have any. Gunth'an Acyl has fixed her eyes upon humankind. She would pillage the beliefs of my kind.

She is indeed mad! I can give them nothing!

She would pluck not a single fragment from her own people. They were all dead, after all. Betrayed by their own faiths—that the rains would always come; that the land would ever provide; that children would be born and mothers and aunts would raise them; that there would be campfires and singing and dancing and loves and passions and laughter. All lies, delusions, false hopes—there was no point in stirring those ashes.

What else was left to her, then, to make this glorious new religion? When countless thousands of lizard eyes fixed unblinking on her, what could she offer them?

They had travelled east for the morning but were now angling southward once more, and Kalyth sensed a gradual slowing of pace, and as they slipped over a low rise she caught sight of Sag'Churok, stationary and apparently watching their approach.

Something had happened. Something had changed.

A gleam of weathered white—the trunk of a fallen tree?—amidst the low grasses directly ahead, and for the first time Kalyth was jolted as Gunth Mach leapt to one side to avoid it. As they passed the object, the Destriant saw that it was a long bone. Whatever it had belonged to, she realized, must have been enormous.

The other K'Chain Che'Malle were reacting in a like manner as each came upon another skeletal remnant, dancing away as if the splintered bones exuded some poison aura that assailed their senses. Kalyth saw that the K'ell's flanks glistened, dripping with oil from their glands, and so she knew that they were all afflicted by an extremity of emotion—terror, rage? She had no means of reading such things.

Was this yet another killing field? She wasn't sure, but something whispered to her that all of these broken bones belonged to a single, gargantuan beast. *A dragon? Think of the Nests, the Rooted. Carved in the likeness of dragons . . . dawn's breath, can this be the religion of the K'Chain Che'Malle? The worship of dragons?*

It made a kind of sense—were these reptiles not physically similar to such mythical beasts? Though she had never seen a dragon, even among her own people there were legends, and in fact she recalled one tale told to her as a child—a fragmented, confused story, which made its recounting rare since it possessed little entertainment value. *'Dragons swim the sky. Fangs slash and blood rains down. The dragons warred with one another, scores upon scores, and the earth below, and all things that dwelt upon it, could do naught but cower. The breath of the dragons made a conflagration of the sky . . .'*

They arrived where waited Sag'Churok. As soon as Gunth Mach halted, Kalyth slipped down, her legs almost folding under her. Righting herself, she looked around.

Skull fragments. Massive fangs chipped and split. It was as if the creature had simply blown apart.

Kalyth looked upward and saw, directly overhead, a dark speck, wheeling, circling. *He shows himself. This, here, this is important.* She finally understood what had so agitated the K'Chain Che'Malle. Not fear. Not rage. *Anticipation. They expect something from me.*

She fought down a moment of panic. Mouth dry, feeling strangely displaced inside her own body, she wandered into the midst of the bone-field. There were gouges scored into the shattered plates of the dragon's skull, the tracks of bites or talons. She found a dislodged tooth and pulled it up from its web of grasses, heavy as a club in her hands. Sun-bleached and polished on one side, pitted and stained amber on the other. She thought she might laugh—a part of her had never even believed in dragons.

The K'Chain Che'Malle remained at a respectful distance, watching her. *What do you want of me? Should I pray? Raise a cairn from these bones? Let blood?* Her searching gaze caught something—a large fragment of the back of the skull, and embedded in it . . . she walked closer, crouched down.

A fang, much like the one she still carried, only larger, and strangely discoloured. The sun had failed to bleach this one. The wind and the grit it carried had not pitted its enamel. The rain had not polished its surface. It had been torn from its root, so deeply had it impaled the dragon's skull. And it was the hue of rust.

She set down the tooth she had brought over, and knelt. Reaching out, she ran her fingers along the reddish fang. Cold as metal, a chill defying the sun and its blistering heat. Its texture reminded Kalyth of petrified wood. She wondered what creature this could have belonged to—*an iron dragon? But how can that be?* She attempted to remove the tooth, but it would not budge.

Sag'Churok spoke in her mind, in a voice strangely faint. '*Destriant, in this place it is difficult to reach you. Your mind. The otataral would deny us.*'

'The what?'

'*There is no single god. There can never be a single god. For there to be one face, there must be another. The Nah'ruk did not see it in such terms, of course. They spoke of forces in opposition, of the necessity of tension. All that binds must be bound to two foci, at the minimum. Even should a god exist alone, isolated in its perfection, it will come to comprehend the need for a force outside itself, beyond its omniscience. If all remains within, Destriant—exclusively within, that is— then there is no reason for anything to exist, no reason for creation itself. If all is ordered, untouched by chaos, then the universe that was, is and will ever be, is without meaning. Without value. The god would quickly comprehend, then, that its own existence is also without meaning, and so it would cease. It would succumb to the logic of despair.*'

She was studying the rusty fang as Sag'Churok's words whispered through her head. 'I'm sorry,' she sighed, 'I don't understand.' But then, maybe she did.

The K'Chain Che'Malle resumed: '*In its knowledge, the god would understand the necessity for that which lies outside itself, beyond its direct control. In that tension meaning will be found. In that struggle value is born. If it suits you and your kind, Destriant, fill the ether with gods, goddesses, First Heroes, spirits and demons. Kneel to one or many, but never—never, Kalyth—hold to a belief that but one god exists, that all that is resides within that god. Should you hold such a belief, then by every path of reasoning that follows, you cannot but conclude that your one god is cursed, a thing of impossible aspirations and deafening injustice, whimsical in its cruelty, blind to mercy and devoid of pity. Do not misunderstand me. Choose to live within one god as you like, but in so doing be certain to acknowledge that there is an "other", an existence beyond your god. And if your god has a face, then so too does that other. In such comprehension, Destriant, will you come to grasp the freedom that lies at the heart of all life; that choice is the singular moral act and all one chooses can only be considered in a moral context if that choice is free.*'

Freedom. That notion mocked her. 'What—what is this "otataral" you spoke of, Sag'Churok?'

'*We are reviled for revealing the face of that other god—that god of negation. Your kind have a flawed notion of magic. You cut the veins of other worlds and drink of the blood, and this is your sorcery. But you do not understand. All life is sorcery. In its very essence, the soul is magical, and each process of chemistry, of obeisance and cooperation, of surrender and of struggle—at every scale conceivable—is a consort of sorcery. Destroy magic and you destroy life.*' There was a long pause, and then a flood of bitter amusement flowed through Kalyth. '*When we kill, we kill magic. Consider the magnitude of that crime, if you dare.*

'*What is otataral, you ask? Otataral is the opposite of magic. Negation to creation, absence to presence. If life is your god, then otataral is the other god, and* that god is death. But, please understand, it is not an enemy. It is the necessary manifestation of a force in opposition. Both are essential, and together they are bound in the nature of existence itself. We are reviled for revealing the truth.

'The lesser creatures of this and every other world do not question any of this. Their comprehension is implicit. When we kill the beasts living on this plain, when we close our jaws about the back of the neck. When we grip hard to choke off the wind pipe. When we do all this, we watch, with intimate compassion, with profound understanding, the light of life leave our victim's eyes. We see the struggle give way to acceptance, and in our souls, Destriant, we weep.'

Still she knelt, but now there were tears streaming down her face, as all that Sag'Churok felt was channelled through her, cruel as sepsis, sinking deep into her own soul.

'The slayer, the Otataral Dragon, has been bound. But it will be freed. They will free it. For they believe that they can control it. They cannot. Destriant, will you now give us the face of our god?'

She whirled round. 'How am I supposed to do that?' she demanded. 'Is this Otataral Dragon your god?'

'No, Destriant,' Sag'Churok replied in sorrow, 'it is the other.'

She ran her hands through the brittle tangles of her hair. 'What you want . . . that face.' She shook her head. 'It can't be dead. It must be alive, a living thing. You built keeps in the shape of dragons, but that faith is ruined, destroyed by failure. You were betrayed, Sag'Churok. You all were.' She gestured, encompassing this killing field. 'Look here—the "other" killed your god.'

All of the K'Chain Che'Malle were facing her now.

'My own people were betrayed as well. It seems,' she added wryly, 'we share something after all. It's a beginning, of sorts.' She scanned the area once more. 'There is nothing here, for us.'

'You misunderstand, Destriant. It is here. It is all here.'

'What do you want me to do?' She was close to tears yet again, but this time from helplessness. 'They're just . . . bones.'

She started as Rythok stepped forward, massive blades lifting threateningly.

Some silent command visibly battered the Hunter and he halted, trembling, jaws half agape.

If she failed, she realized, they might well kill her. Cut her down as they had done Redmask, the poor fool. These creatures managed failure no better than humans. 'I'm sorry,' she whispered. 'But I don't believe in anything. Not gods, not anything. Oh, they might exist, but about us they don't care. Why should they? We destroy to create. But we deny the value of everything we destroy, which serves to make its destruction easier on our consciences. All that we reshape to suit us is diminished, its original beauty for ever lost. We have no value system that does not beggar the world, that does not slaughter the beasts we share it with—as if we are the gods.' She sank back down on to her knees and clutched the sides of her head. 'Where are these thoughts coming from? It was all so much simpler, once, here—in my mind—so much simpler. Spirits below, I so want to go back!'

She only realized she had been beating at her temples when two massive hands grasped her wrists and pulled down her arms. She stared up into Gunth Mach's emerald eyes.

And for the first time, the Daughter spoke inside her mind. *'Release, now. Breathe deep my breath, Destriant.'*

Kalyth's desperate gasping now caught a strange, pungent scent, emanating from Gunth Mach.

The world spun. She sagged back, sprawled to the ground. As something unfolded in her skull like an alien flower, virulent, beguiling—she lost grip of her own body, was whipped away.

And found herself standing on cold, damp stone, nostrils filling with a pungent, rank stench. Her eyes adjusted to the gloom, and she cried out and staggered back.

A dragon reared above her, its slick scales the colour of rust. Enormous spikes pinned its forelimbs, holding the creature up against a massive, gnarled tree. Other spikes had been driven into it but the dragon's immense weight had pulled them loose. Its wedge-shaped head, big as a migrant's wagon, hung down, streaming drool. The wings were crumpled like storm-battered caravan tents. Fresh blood surrounded the base of the tree, so that it seemed that the entire edifice rose from a gleaming pool.

'The slayer, the Otataral Dragon, has been bound. But it will be freed . . . ' Sag'Churok's words echoed in her mind. *'They will free it.'* Who? No matter, she realized. It would be done. This Otataral Dragon would be loosed upon the world, upon every world. A force of negation, a slayer of magic. And they would lose control of it—only mad fools could believe they could enslave such an entity.

'Wait,' she hissed, thoughts racing, *'wait.* Forces in opposition. Take away one— spike it to a tree—and the other is lost. It cannot exist, cannot survive looking across the Abyss and seeing nothing, no one, no *foe.* This is why you have lost your god, Sag'Churok. Or, if it still lives, it has been driven into the oblivion of insanity. Too alone. An orphan . . . just like me.'

A revelation, of sorts. What could she make of it?

Kalyth stared up at the dragon. 'When you are finally freed, then perhaps your "other" will return, to engage with you once more. In that eternal battle.' But even then, this scheme had failed before. It would fail again, because it was flawed— something was wrong, something was . . . broken. *'Forces in opposition, yes, that I do understand. And we each play our roles. We each fashion our "others" and chart the course of our lives as that eternal campaign, seasons of gain, seasons of loss. Battles and wounds and triumphs and bitter defeats. In comforts we fashion our strongholds. In convictions we occupy our fortifications. In violence we forge our peace. In peace, we win desolation.'*

Somewhere far behind her, Kalyth's body was lying on half-dead grasses, cast down on to the heart-stone of the Wastelands. *'It is here. It is all here.'*

'We are broken indeed. We are . . . fallen.'

What do to, then, when the battle cannot be won? No answers burgeoned before her. The only truth rearing to confront her was this blood-soaked sacrifice, destined to be un-done. 'Is it true, then, that a world without magic is a dead world? Is this what you promise? Is this to be your future? But no, for when you are at last freed, then your enemy will awaken once more, and the war will resume.'

There was no place in that scheme for mortals. A new course for the future was needed. For the K'Chain Che'Malle. For all humans in every empire, every tribe. If nothing changed in the mortal world, then there would be no end to the conflicts, to the interminable forces in opposition, be they cultures, religions, whatever.

She had no idea that intelligent life could be so stupid.

'They want a faith from me. A religion. They want to return to the vanity of the righteous. I can't do it. I can't. Rythok had better kill me, for I will offer them nothing they want to hear.'

Abruptly, she was staring up at a cloudless blue sky, heat rustling across her bare limbs, her face, the tracks of dried tears tight on her cheeks. She sat up. Her muscles ached. A sour taste thickened her tongue.

Still the K'Chain Che'Malle faced her.

'Very well,' she said, rising to her feet. 'I give you this. Find your faith in each other. Look no further. The gods will war, and all that we do will remain beneath their notice. Stay low. Move quietly. Out of sight. We are ants in the grass, lizards among the rocks.' She paused. 'Somewhere, out there, you will find the purest essence of that philosophy. Perhaps in one person, perhaps in ten thousand. Looking to no other entity, no other force, no other will. Bound solely in comradeship, in loyalty honed absolute. Yet devoid of all arrogance. Wise in humility. And that one, or ten thousand, is on a path. Unerring, it readies itself, not to shake a fist at the heavens. But to lift a lone hand, a hand filled with tears.' She found she was glaring at the giant reptiles. 'You want a faith? You want someone or something to believe in? No, do not worship the one or the ten thousand. Worship the sacrifice they will make, for they make it in the name of compassion—the only cause worth fighting and dying for.'

Suddenly exhausted, she turned away, kicked aside the bleached fang at her feet. 'Now, let us go find our champions.'

She led the way, and the K'Chain Che'Malle were content with that. Sag'Churok watched the frail, puny human taking her meagre strides, leaving behind the rise where two dragons had done battle.

And the K'ell Hunter was well pleased.

He sensed, in a sweet wave, Gunth Mach's pride.

Pride in their Destriant.

Drawn by four oxen the large wagon rolled into the camp, mobbed by mothers, husbands, wives and children who raised their voices in ululating grief. Arms reached out as if to grab hold of their dead loved ones who lay stacked like felled boles on the flat bed, as the burden of the slain rocked to a halt. The mob churned. Dogs howled.

On a nearby hill, Setoc stood watching the bedlam in the camp, the only motion from her the stirring of her weathered hair. Warriors were running back to their yurts to ready themselves for war, although none knew the enemy's face, and there was no trail to track. Would-be war leaders shouted and bellowed, beating on their own chests or waving weapons in the air. For all the grief and anger, there was something pathetic to the whole scene, something that made her turn away, suddenly weary.

No one liked being a victim of the unknown. They were driven to lash out, driven to deliver indiscriminate violence upon whoever happened to be close. She could hear some of those warriors vowing vengeance upon the Akrynnai, the D'rhasilhani, even the Letherii.

The Gadra Clan was going to war. Warchief Stolmen was under siege in his own tent, and to deny the murderous hunger of his warriors would see him deposed, bloodily. No, he would need to stand tall, drawing his bhederin cloak about his broad shoulders, and take up his twin-bladed axe. His wife, if anything fiercer than Stolmen himself, would begin painting the white mask of death, the slayer's bone-grin, upon her husband's scarred features. Her own mother, a wrinkled hatchet-faced hag, would do the same to her. Edges singing on whetstones, the Barghast were going to war.

She saw Cafal emerging from Stolmen's tent. Even at this distance, she could read his frustration as he marched towards the largest crowd of warriors. And when his steps slowed and he finally halted, Setoc understood him well enough. He had lost the Gadra. She watched as he looked round until he caught sight of yet another solitary figure.

Torrent was already saddling his horse. Not to join in this madness. But to leave.

As Cafal set out towards the Awl warrior, Setoc went down to meet them.

Whatever words they exchanged before she arrived were terse, unsatisfying to the Great Warlock. He noted her approach and faced her. 'You too?' he asked.

'I will go with you,' she said. 'The wolves will join none of this. It is empty.'

'The Gadra mean to wage war against the Akrynnai,' said Cafal. 'But the Akrynnai have done nothing.'

She nodded, reaching up to pull her long fair hair from her face as the hot wind gusted.

Torrent was lifting himself on to his horse. His face was bleak, haunted. He had the look of a man who did not sleep well at night. He gathered his reins.

Cafal turned to him. 'Wait! Please, Torrent, wait.'

The man grimaced. 'Is this to be my life? Dragged from one woman's tent to the next? Am I to rut my days away? Or do I choose instead to fight at your side? Why would I do that? You Barghast—you are no different from my own people, and you will share their fate.' He nodded towards Setoc. 'The wolf-child is right. The scavengers of this land will grow fat.'

Setoc caught a flash of something crouched behind a tuft of grass—a hare, no, Talamandas, that thing of twine and sticks. Child of the mad Barghast gods, child of children. Spying on them. She sneered.

'But,' asked Cafal, 'where will you go, Torrent?'

'I shall ride to Tool, and beg my leave of him. I shall ask for his forgiveness, for I should have been the warrior to fall against the Letherii, in defence of the Awl children. Not his friend. Not the Mezla.'

Cafal's eyes had widened at Torrent's words, and after a moment he seemed to sag. 'Ah, Torrent. Malazans have a way . . .' He lifted a sad smile to the Awl. 'They do humble us all. Tool will reject your words—there is nothing to forgive. There is no crime set against you. It was the Mezla's way, his choice.'

'He rode out in my place—'

The Great Warlock straightened. 'And could you have fared as well as he did, Torrent?'

That was a cruel question and Setoc saw how it stung the young warrior. 'That is not the—'

'But it is,' Cafal snapped. 'If Toc had judged you his superior in battle he would have exhorted you to ride against the Letherii. He would have taken the children away. And if it was that Malazan sitting here on his horse before me right now, he would not be moaning about forgiveness. Do you understand me, Torrent?'

The man looked cruelly bludgeoned by Cafal's words. 'Even if it is so, I ride to Tool, and then I shall set off, on my own. I have chosen. Tie no strands to my fate, Great Warlock.'

Setoc barked a laugh. 'He is not the one to do that, Torrent.'

His eyes narrowed on her. She thought he might retort—accusations, anger, bridling indignation. Instead, he said nothing, simply drawing up his reins. A last glance back to Cafal. 'You walk, but I ride. I am not interested in slowing my pace to suit you—'

'And what if I told you I could travel in such a way as to reach Tool long before you will?'

'You cannot.'

Setoc saw the Great Warlock lick dry lips; saw the sweat that had appeared upon his broad, flat brow, and her heart began thudding hard in her chest. 'Cafal,' she said, her voice flat, 'this is not your land. The warrens you people speak of are weak here—I doubt you can even reach them. Your gods are not ready—'

'Speak not of the Barghast gods!' squealed a voice. Talamandas, the sticksnare, scrambled out from cover and came closer in fits and starts. 'You know nothing, witch—'

'I know enough,' she replied. 'Yes, your kind once walked these plains, but how long ago was that? You warred with the Tiste Edur. You were driven from this place. A thousand years ago? Ten thousand? So now you return, to avenge your ancestors—but you found the Edur nothing like your legends. Unlike you Barghast, they had moved on—'

'As the victorious ever do,' the sticksnare hissed. 'Their wounds heal quickly, yes. Nothing festers, nothing rots, there is no bitterness on their tongues.'

She spat in disbelief. 'How can you say that? Their Emperor is dead. They are driven from all the lands they conquered!'

'*But not by our hands!*'

The shriek snatched heads round. Warriors drew closer. Cafal remained silent, his expression suddenly closed, while Torrent leaned forward on the saddle, squinting down at the sticksnare as if doubting his own sanity.

Setoc smiled at Talamandas. 'Yes, that is what galls, isn't it? So. Now,' and she turned to face the score or so warriors half-encircling them, 'now, yes, you would deliver such defeat upon the Akrynnai. Wounds that will fester, rot that sinks deep into the soul, that cruel taste riding every breath.'

Her tirade seemed to buffet them. She spat again. 'They did not kill your scouts. You all know this. And you do not even care.' She pointed at Cafal. 'And so the Great Warlock now goes to Tool, and he will say to him: War Master, yet another clan has broken away. They wage senseless war upon the wrong enemy, and so it will come to pass that, by the actions of the Gadra Clan, every people in this land will rise up against the Barghast. Akrynnai, D'rhasilhani, Keryn, Saphinand, Bolkando. You will be assailed from all sides. And those of you not killed in battle will be driven into the Wastelands, that vast ocean of nothing, and there you will vanish, your bones turning to dust.'

There was movement in the crowd, and warriors stepped aside as a scowling Warchief Stolmen lumbered forward, his wife a step behind him. That woman's eyes were dark, savage with hatred as she fixed her glare upon Setoc.

'This is what you do, witch,' she said in a rasp. 'You weaken us. Again and again, you seek to weaken us!'

'Are you so eager to see your children die?' Setoc asked her.

'Eager to see them win glory!'

'For themselves or for you, Sekara?'

Sekara would have flung herself at Setoc then, but Stolmen held out a staying arm, knocking her back. Though he could not see it, his wife then shot him a look of venomous malice.

Torrent spoke quietly to Setoc. 'Come with me, wolf-child. We will ride out of this madness.' He reached down with one hand.

She grasped hold of his forearm and he swung her easily on to the horse's back. As she closed her arms round his waist he said, 'Do you need to collect anything, Setoc? From your tent?'

'No.'

'Send them off!' snarled Sekara. 'Go, you foreign liars! Akrynnai spies! Go and poison your own kind! With terror—tell them, we are coming! The White Face Barghast! And we shall make of this land our home once again! Tell them, witch! *They* are the invaders, not us!'

Setoc had long sensed the animosity building among the women in this clan. She drew too many eyes among the men. Her wildness made them hungry, curious— she was not blind to any of this. Even so, this burst of spite startled her, frightened her. She forced herself to meet Sekara's blazing eyes. 'I am the holder of a thousand hearts.' Saying this, she looked to Sekara's husband and smiled a knowing smile.

Stolmen was forced to restrain his wife as she sought to lunge forward, a knife in one hand.

Torrent backed his horse, and she could feel how he tensed. 'Enough of that!' he snapped over his shoulder. 'Do you want us skinned alive?'

The mob had grown and now surrounded them. And, she saw at last, there were far more women than men in it. She felt herself withering beneath the hateful stares fixed upon her. Not just wives, either. That she was sitting snug against Torrent was setting fires in the eyes of the younger women, the maidens.

Cafal stepped closer, his face pale in dread mockery of the white paint of the warriors. 'I am going to open a warren,' he said in a low voice. 'With the help of Talamandas. We leave together, or you will be killed here, do you understand? It's too late for the Gadra—your words, Setoc, held too many truths. They are *shamed*.'

'Be quick, then,' Torrent said in a growl.

He swung round. 'Talamandas.'

'Leave them to their fate,' muttered the sticksnare, crouched like a miniature ghoul. It seemed to be twitching as if plucked and prodded by unseen hands.

'No. All of us.'

'You will regret your generosity, Cafal.'

'The warren, Talamandas.'

The sticksnare snarled wordlessly and then straightened, spreading wide its scrawny twig arms.

'Cafal!' hissed Setoc. 'Wait! There is a sickness—'

White fire erupted around them in a sudden deafening roar. The horse screamed, reared. Setoc's grip broke and she tumbled back. Searing heat, stunning cold. As quickly as the flames arrived, they vanished with a thunderous clap that reverberated in her skull. A kick from a hoof sent her skidding, pain throbbing from a bruised thigh. There was darkness now—or, she thought with a shock—she was blind. Her eyes curdled in their sockets, cooked like eggs—

Then she caught a glimmer, something smeared, a reflected blade. Torrent's horse was backing, twisting from side to side—the Awl warrior still rode the beast and she could hear him cursing as he fought to steady the animal. He had drawn his scimitar.

'Gods below!'

That cry had come from Cafal. Setoc sat up. Stony, damp earth, clumps of mould or guano squishing beneath her. She smelled burning grasses. Crawling to the vague blot in the gloom whence came the Warlock's voice, she struggled against waves of nausea. 'You fool,' she croaked. 'You should have listened. Cafal—'

'Talamandas. He's . . . he's destroyed.'

The stench of something smouldering was stronger now, and she caught the gleam of scattered embers. 'He burned? He burned, didn't he? The wrong warren—it ate him, devoured him—I warned you, Cafal. Something has infected your warrens—'

'No, Setoc,' Cafal cut in. 'It is not like that, not like what you say—we knew of that poison. We were warded against it. This was . . . different. Spirits fend, we have lost our greatest shaman—'

'You did not know it, did you? That gate? It was unlike anything you've ever known, wasn't it? Listen to me! It is what I have been trying to tell you!'

They heard Torrent dismount, his moccasins thudding on the yielding, strangely soft ground. 'Be quiet, both of you. Argue what happened later. Listen to the echoes—I think we are trapped inside a cavern.'

'Well,' said Setoc, carefully climbing to her feet. 'There must be a way out.'

'How do you know that?'

'Because, there's bats.'

'But I have my damned horse! Cafal—take us somewhere else!'

'I cannot.'

'What?'

'The power belonged to Talamandas. A binding of agreements, promises, with countless human gods. With Hood, Lord of Death. The Barghast gods are young, too young. I—I cannot even sense them. I am sorry, I do not know where we are.'

'I am cursed to follow fools!'

Setoc flinched at the anguish in that shout. *Poor Torrent. You just wanted to leave there, to ride out. Away. Your stupid sense of honour demanded you visit Tool. And now look . . .*

No one spoke for a time, the only sounds their breathing and anxious snorts from the horse. Setoc sought to sense some flow of air, but there was nothing. Her thigh aching, she sank back down. She then chose a direction at random and crawled. The guano thickened so that her hands plunged through up to her wrists, and then she found a stone barrier. Wiping the mess from her hands, she tracked with her fingers. 'Wait! These stones are set—I've found a wall.'

Scrabbling sounds behind her, and then the scratch of flint and iron. Sparks, actinic flashes, and then a burgeoning glow. Moments later Torrent had a taper lit and was setting the flame to the wick of a small camp lantern. The chamber took shape around them.

The entire cavern was constructed of set stones, the ones overhead massive, wedged in place in seemingly precipitous disorder. In seething patches here and there clung bats, chittering and squeaking now in agitation.

'Look, there!' Cafal pointed.

The bats were converging on a conjoining of ill-set stones, wriggling into cracks.

'There's the way out.'

Torrent's laugh was bitter. 'We are entombed. One day, looters will break in, find the bones of two men, a child, and a damned horse. For us to ride into the death-world, or so they might think. Then again, they might wonder at the gnaw marks on all but one set of bones, and at the scratchings and gougings on the stone. Tiny bat bones and heaps of dried-out scat . . .'

'Crush that imagination of yours, Torrent,' advised Cafal. 'Though the way out is nothing but cracks, we know the world outside is close. We need only dig our way out.'

'This is a stone barrow or something much like it, Cafal. If we start dragging stones loose the whole thing is likely to come down on us.'

'We have no choice.' He walked over to the wall where the bats had swarmed through moments earlier. Drawing a dagger, he began probing. A short time later, Torrent joined him, using his hunter's knife.

To the sounds of scraping and sifting earth, Setoc sat down closer to the lantern. Memories of that white fire haunted her. Her head ached as if the heat had seared parts of her brain, leaving blank patches that pulsed behind her eyes. She could hear no muted howls—the Wolves were lost to her in this place. *What world have we found? What waits beyond these stone walls? Does a sun shine out there? Does it blaze with death, or is this a realm for ever dark, lifeless?*

Well, someone built this place. But . . . if this is indeed a barrow, where are the bones? She picked up the lantern, wincing at the hot handle which had not been tilted to one side. Gingerly rising, she played the light over the damp, mottled ground at her feet. Guano, a few stones dislodged from above. If there had ever been a body interred in this place, it had long since rotted down to crumbs. And it had not been adorned with jewellery; no buckles nor clasps to evince clothing of any sort. 'This,' she ventured, 'is probably thousands of years old. There's nothing left of whoever was buried here.'

A muted mutter from Torrent, answered by a grunt from Cafal, who then glanced back at her. 'Where we're digging, Setoc—someone has been through this way before. If this is a barrow, it's been long since looted, emptied out.'

'Since when does loot include the corpse itself?'

'The guano is probably acidic,' Cafal said. 'It probably dissolved the bones. The point is, we can dig our way out and it's not likely everything will collapse down on us—'

'Don't be so certain of that,' Torrent said. 'We need to make a hole big enough to get my horse out. The looters had no need to be so ambitious.'

'You had best prepare yourself for the notion of killing your mount,' Cafal said.

'No. She is an Awl horse. The last Awl horse, and she is mine—no, we belong to each other. Both alone. If she must die, then I will die with her. Let this barrow be our home in the deathworld.'

'You have a morbid cast of mind,' Cafal said.

'He has earned the right,' Setoc murmured, still scanning the ground as she walked a slow circuit. 'Ah!' She bent down, retrieved a small, half-encrusted object. 'A coin. Copper.' She scraped the green disk clean and held it close to the lantern. 'I recognize nothing—not Letherii, nor Bolkando.'

Cafal joined her. 'Permit me, Setoc. My clan was in the habit of collecting coins to make our armour. It was his damned hauberk of coins that dragged my father to the sea bottom.'

She handed it to him.

He studied it for a long time, one side, then the other, over and over. And finally sighed and handed it back. 'No. Some empress, I imagine, looking so regal. The crossed swords on the other side could be Seven Cities, but the writing is all wrong. This is not our world, Setoc.'

'I didn't think it was.'

'Done with that, Cafal?' Torrent asked from where he worked at the wall, impatience giving an edge to his tone.

Cafal offered her a wry smile and then returned to Torrent's side.

A loud scrape followed by a heavy thud, and cool dew-heavy air flowed into the chamber.

'Smell that? It's a damned forest.'

At Cafal's words, Setoc joined them. She held up the lantern. *Night, cool . . . cooler than the Awl'dan.* 'Trees,' she said, peering at the ragged boles faintly visible in the light.

There was possibly a bog out there—she could hear frogs.

'If it was night,' Torrent wondered, 'what were the bats doing inside here?'

'Perhaps it was only nearing dusk when we arrived. Or dawn is but moments away.' Cafal tugged at another stone. 'Help me with this one,' he said to Torrent. 'It's too heavy for one man—Setoc, please, stand back, give us room.'

As they dragged the huge stone free, other rough-hewn boulders tumbled down. A large lintel stone ground its way loose and both men leapt back as it crashed on to the rubble. Clouds of dust billowed and a terrible grating groan sounded from the barrow's ceiling.

Coughing, Cafal waved at Setoc. 'Quickly! Out!'

She scrambled over the stones, eyes stinging, and staggered outside. Three paces and then she turned about. She heard the thump of stones from the ceiling. The horse shrilled in pain. From the gaping entrance Cafal appeared, followed a moment later by Torrent, who had somehow brought his mount down on to its knees. He held the reins and with rapid twitches on them he urged his horse forward. Its head thrust into view, eyes flashing in the reflected lantern light.

Setoc had never before seen a horse crawl—she had not thought it even possible, but here this mare was lurching through the gap, sheathed in dust and streaks of sweat. More rocks tumbled behind the beast and she squealed in pain, lunging, forelimbs scrabbling as she lifted herself up from the front end.

Moments after the animal finally lumbered clear the moss-humped roof of the barrow collapsed in thunder and dust. Decades-old trees that had grown upon it toppled in a thrash of branches and leaves. Wood splintered.

Blood streamed from the mare's haunches. Torrent had calmed the beast once more and was tending to the gashes. 'Not so bad,' he muttered. 'Had she broken a hip . . .'

Setoc saw that the warrior was trembling. This bond he had forged with his hapless mare stood in place of all those ties that had been so cruelly severed from his young life, and it was fast becoming something monstrous. *'If she must die, then I will die with her.'* Madness, Torrent. It's a damned horse, a dumb beast with its spirit broken by bit and rein. If she'd a broken hip or leg, we'd eat well this day.

She watched Cafal observing the Awl for a time, before he turned away and scanned the forest surrounding them. Then he lifted his eyes to the heavens. 'No moons,' he said. 'And the stars seem . . . hazy—there's not enough of them. No constellations I recognize.'

'There are no wolves here.'

He faced her.

'Their ghosts, yes. But . . . none living. They last ran here centuries past. Centuries.'

'Well, there's deer scat and trails—so they didn't starve to death.'

'No. Hunted.' She hugged herself. 'Tell me the mind of those who would kill every last wolf, who would choose to never again hear their mournful howls, or to see—with a shiver—a pack standing proud on a rise. Great Warlock, explain this to me, for I do not understand.'

He shrugged. 'We hate rivals, Setoc. We hate seeing the knowing burn in their eyes. You have not seen civilized lands. The animals go away. And they never return. They leave silence, and that silence is filled with the chatter of our kind. Given the ability, we kill even the night.' His eyes fell to the lantern in her hand.

Scowling, she doused it.

In the sudden darkness, Torrent cursed. 'That does not help, wolf-child. We light fires, but the darkness remains—in our minds. Cast light within and you will not like what you see.'

A part of her wanted to weep. For the ghosts. For herself. 'We need to find a way home.'

Cafal sighed. 'There is power here. Unfamiliar. Even so, perhaps I can make use of it. I sense it . . . fragmented, shredded. It has, I think, not been used in a long, long time.' He looked round. 'I must clear a space. Sanctify it.'

'Even without Talamandas?' Torrent asked.

'He would have been of little help here,' Cafal replied. 'His bindings all severed.' He glanced at Setoc. 'You, wolf-child, can help.'

'How?'

'Summon the wolf ghosts.'

'No.' The thought made her feel wretched. 'I can give them nothing in return.'

'Perhaps, a way through. Into another world, even our own, where they will find living kin, where they will run unseen shoulder to shoulder with them, and remember the hunt, old loyalties, sparks of love.'

She eyed him. 'Is such a thing possible?'

'I don't know. But, let us try. I do not like this world. Even in this forest, the air is tainted. Foul. We have most of the night ahead of us. Let us do what we can to be gone before the sun rises. Before we are discovered.'

'Sanctify your ground, then,' Setoc said.

She walked off into the wood, sat down upon the mossy trunk of a fallen tree—no, a tree that had been cut down, cleanly—no axe could have managed such level precision. Why then had it been simply left here? 'There is madness here,' she whispered. Closing her eyes, she sought to drive the bleak thoughts away.

Ghosts! Wolves! Listen to my mind's howl! Hear the sorrow, the anger! Hear my promise—I will guide you from this infernal realm. I will find you kin. Kin of hot blood, warm fur, the cry of newborn pups, the snarl of rival males—I will show you grasslands, my children. Vistas unending!

And she felt them, the beasts that had fallen in pain and grief here in this very forest, so long, long ago. The first to come to her was the last survivor of that time, the last to be cornered and viciously slain. She heard the echo of snarling hounds, the cries of human voices. She felt the wolf's terror, its despair, its helpless be-musement. She felt, as well, as the beast's lifeblood spilled into the churned-up soil, its surrender, its understanding—in that final moment—that its terrible loneliness was at last coming to an end.

And her mind howled anew, a silent cry that nevertheless sent rooks thrashing from tree branches in raucous flight. That froze deer and hares in their tracks, as some ancient terror within them was stirred to life.

Howls answered her. Closing from all sides.

Come to me! Gather all that remains of your power!

She could hear thrashing in the brush, as will and memory alone bulled through the bracken. And she sensed, with a shock, more than one species. Some dark, black-furred and low to the ground, eyes blazing yellow; others tall at the shoulders, rangy, with ebon-tipped silver fur. And she saw their ancestors, even larger beasts, short-nosed, massively muscled.

They came in multitudes beyond comprehension, and each bore their death wounds, the shafts of spears jutting from throat and flank, blood-gushing punctures streaming from chest. Snares and traps clanking and dragging from broken limbs. Bloated from poison—she saw, with mounting horror, a legacy of such hateful, spiteful slaughter that she cried out, a shriek tearing at her own throat.

Torrent was shouting, fighting to control his panicked horse as wolf ghosts flooded in, thousands, hundreds of thousands—this was an old world, and here, before her, crowding close with need, was the toll amassed by its insane victors, its triumphant tyrants.

Oh, there were other creatures as well, caught in the rushing tide, beasts long since crumbled to dust. She saw stags, bhederin, large cats. She saw huge furred beasts with broad heads and horns jutting from black snouts—*so many, gods, so many*—

'Setoc! Stop! The power—it is too great—it *overwhelms*!'

But she had lost all control. She had not expected anything like this. The pressure, crushing in from all sides now, threatened to destroy her. She wept like the last child on earth, the last living thing, sole witness to the legacy of all that her kind had achieved. This desolation. This suicidal victory over nature itself.

'Setoc!'

All at once she saw something glowing before her: a portal, pathetically small, nothing more than a bolt-hole. She raised a trembling hand and pointed towards it. 'My loved ones,' she whispered, 'the way through. *Make it bigger.*'

They had wandered far beyond the chamber of slaughter, where scores of K'Chain Che'Malle had seemingly been sacrificed. Lanterns cast fitful light against metal entrails embedded in niches along the walls of the corridors, and from the ceiling thick cables sagged, dripping some kind of viscous oil. The air was rank with acidic vapours, making their eyes water. Side passages opened to rooms crowded with strange, incomprehensible machinery, the floor slick with spilled oils.

Taxilian led the others in their exploration, wending ever deeper into the maze of wide, low-ceilinged corridors. Moving a step behind him, Rautos could hear the man muttering, but he could not make out the words—he feared Taxilian might be going mad. This was an alien world, shaped by alien minds. Sense and understanding eluded them all, and from this was born fear.

Behind Rautos, almost on his heels, was Breath, coughing, gasping, as if her endless talk of drowning had thickened the air around her.

'Tunnels!' she hissed. 'I hate tunnels. Pits, caves. Dark—always dark—rooms. Where is he leading us? We've passed countless ramps leading to higher levels—what is the fool looking for?'

Rautos had no answers, so he said nothing.

Behind Breath, Sheb and Nappet were bickering. Those two would come to blows soon; they were too much alike. Both vicious, both fundamentally amoral, both born betrayers. Rautos wished they would kill each other—they would not be missed.

'Ah!' cried Taxilian. 'Found it!'

Rautos moved up to the man's side. They stood at the threshold of a vast eight-walled chamber. A narrow ledge encircled it level with the passage they had just traversed. The actual floor was lost in darkness below. Taxilian edged out to the right, lifting his lantern.

The monstrous mechanism filling the centre of the expanse towered past level after level—only a few with balconies to match the one they were on—until it vanished high overhead. It seemed to be constructed entirely of metal, gleaming like brass and the purest iron, eight cylinders each the size of a city tower. Spigots jutted out from bolted collars that fastened the segments every second level, and attached to these were black, pliant ropes of some sort that reached out like the strands of an abandoned spider's web, converging on huge boxes of metal affixed to the walls. Peering downward, Rautos could just make out a change in the configuration of the towers, as if each one sat upon a beehive dome.

His gaze caught and held upon one piece of metal, bent so perfectly between two fittings, and he frowned as if silts had been brushed from some deeply submerged memory. He groped towards it, fighting back a whimper, and then the blinding clouds returned, and he was swept away once more. He reeled and would have fallen from the ledge had not Breath roughly pulled him back.

'Idiot! Do you want to kill yourself?'

He shook his head. 'Sorry. Thank you.'

'Don't bother. I acted on instinct. If I'd thought about it, I probably would have let you go. You're nothing to me, fat old man. Nothing. No one is, not here, not one of you.'

She had raised her voice to make certain everyone else heard her last words.

Sheb snorted. 'Bitch needs a lesson or two, I think.'

Breath spun to face him. 'Hungry for a curse, are you? What part of your body do you want to rot off first? Maybe I'll do the choosing—'

'Set your magic on me, woman, and I will throttle you.'

She laughed, turned away. 'Play with Asane if you have the need.'

Rautos, after a few deep, calming breaths, set out after Taxilian, who had begun walking round the ledge, eyes fixed on the edifice.

'It's an engine,' he said when Rautos drew close.

'A what? As in a mill? But I see nothing like gears or—'

'Like that, yes. You can hide gears and levers inside, in housings to keep them clean of grit and whatnot. Even more relevantly, you can seal things and make use of alternating pressures, and so move things from one place to another. It's a common practice in alchemy, especially if one conjures such pressures using heat and cold. I once saw a sorcerous invention that could draw the ether out of a glass jar, thus quenching the lit candle within it. A pump bound in wards was used to draw out the life force that exists in the air.' He waved one hand at the towers. 'Heat, cold—I think these are vast pressure chambers of some sort.'

'For what purpose?'

Taxilian looked at him with glittering eyes. 'That's what I mean to find out.'

There were no ladders or bridges across to the towers. Taxilian led him back to the entranceway. 'We're going up now,' he said.

'We need food,' said Last, his expression worried, frightened. 'We could get lost in here—'

'Stop whimpering,' growled Nappet. 'I could walk us out of here in no time.'

'None of you,' cut in Asane, startling everyone, 'wants to talk about what we found in the first room. That's what you're all running from. Those—those monsters—they were all slaughtered.' She glared at them, diffident, and rushed on. 'What killed them could still be here! We don't know anything about any of this—'

'Those monsters didn't die in battle,' said Sheb. 'That was a ritual killing we saw. Sacrifices, that's what they were.'

'Maybe they had no choice.'

Sheb snorted. 'I can't think of many beasts choosing to be sacrificed. Of course they had no choice. This place is abandoned—you can feel it. Smell it in the stale air.'

'When we climb higher,' said Last, 'we'll get out of the wet, and we can see if there's tracks in the dust.'

'Gods below, the farmer's good for something after all,' said Nappet with a hard grin.

'Let's go, then,' said Taxilian, and he set off. Once more the others fell in behind him.

Drifting between all of them, voiceless, half-blinded with sorrow that swept down like curtains of rain, the ghost yearned to reach through. To Taxilian, Rautos, even stolid, slow-thinking Last. In their journey through the bowels of the Dragon Keep, knowledge had erupted, thunderous, pounding concussions that sent him reeling.

He knew this place. He knew its name. Kalse Rooted. A demesne of the

K'Chain Che'Malle, a border keep. A vast body now drained of all life, a corpse standing empty-eyed on the plain. And he knew that a Shi'gal Assassin had slain those K'ell Hunters. To seal the failure of this fortress.

Defeat was approaching. The whispering chant, the song of scales. The great army sent out from here had been annihilated. Naught but a pathetic rearguard left behind. The J'an Sentinels would have taken the Matron away, to the field of the fallen, there to entomb her for evermore.

Taxilian! Hear me. What is lifeless is not necessarily dead. That which falls can rise again. Take care—take great care—in this place . . .

But his cries were not heard. He was trapped outside, made helpless with all that he understood, with this cascade of secrets that could do little more than tumble into an abyss of ignorance.

He knew how Asane railed in her own mind, how she longed to escape her own flesh. She wanted out from all that had failed her. Her damned flesh, her dying organs, her very mind. She had been awakened to the comprehension that the body was a prison, but one prone to terrible, inexorable decay. Oh, there was always that final flight, when the corroded bars ceased to pose a barrier; when the soul was free to fly, to wing out in search of unseen shores. But with that release—for all she knew—all that she called herself would be lost. Asane would *end.* Cease, and that which was born from the ashes held no regard for the living left behind, no regard for that world of aches, pain, and suffering. It was transformed into indifference, and all that was past—all that belonged to the mortal life now done—meant nothing to it; she could not comprehend such a cruel rebirth.

She longed for death none the less. Longed to escape her withered husk with all its advancing decrepitude, its sundering into the pathos of the broken. Fear alone held her back—back from that ledge in the eight-sided chamber, back from that fatal drop to some unseen floor far below. And that same fear clawed at her now. Demons stalked this keep. She dreaded what was coming.

Walking a step behind her was Last, aptly choosing a rearguard position. His shoulders were hunched, head ducked as if the corridor's ceiling were much lower than it was. He was a man born to open spaces, boundless skies overhead, the sweep of vistas. Within this haunted maze, he felt diminished, almost crippled. Vertigo lunged at him with each turn and twist. He saw how the walls closed in. He felt the mass looming over them all, the unbearable weight of countless storeys overhead.

He had a sudden memory of his childhood. He had been helping his father—before the debts arrived, before everything was taken away that meant anything at all—he had been helping his father, he recalled, dismantle a shed behind the stables. They had prised loose the warped planks and were stacking them in a dis-ordered heap this side of the pen's fence. Finishing a task begun months earlier, before the planting. By late afternoon the shed was down, and his father had told him to rearrange the boards, sorting them by length and condition.

He had set to the task. Recollection grew hazy then, up until the moment he lifted a grey, weathered plank—one from last season's work—and saw how its re-cent shifting from the day's work just done had crushed a nest of mice, the woven bundle of grasses flattened, smeared in a tangle of blood and tiny entrails. Hairless, pink pups scattered about, crushed, each one yielding up their single drop of lifeblood. Both parents suffocated beneath the weight of the overburden.

Kneeling before this tableau, his presence looming like a god come too late, he stared down at this destroyed family. Silly to weep, of course. There were plenty of other mice—Errant knew the yard's cats stayed fat. So, foolish, these tears.

Yes, he'd been just a child. A sensitive age, no doubt. And later that night his father took him by the hand and led him out to the modest barrow on the old plot, continuing what had been their the post-supper ritual ever since his mother was put into the ground, and they burned knotted hoops of wrinkle grass with their dried blossoms that flared bright the instant flames touched them. Bursts of fire that blotted the eyes with pulsing afterglows. And when his father saw the tears on his son's cheeks he drew him close and said, 'I've been waiting for that.'

Yes, the levels above seemed well built, the walls solid and sturdy. No reason to think it would all come down at the careless toss of some child god. These kinds of thoughts, well, they could only make a man angry. In ways every child would understand.

He walked with his huge hands balled into fists.

Sheb was fairly certain that he had died in prison, or come close enough to dead that the cell cutter simply ordered the bearers to carry him out to the lime pits, and they spilled him down on to a bed of dusted corpses. Searing pain from the lime had roused him from his fevered oblivion, and he must have climbed his way out, pushed through the bodies that had been dumped on top of him.

He recalled struggling. Vast, unshifting weights. He recalled even thinking that he had failed. That he was too weak, that he would never get free. He even remembered seeing swaths of red, blistered skin on his arms, sloughing away in his frenzied thrashing. And a nightmare instant where he gouged out his own burning eyes to bring an end to their agony.

Mad delusions, of course. He had won free. Had he not, would he be alive now? Walking at Nappet's side? No, he had cheated them all. Those Hivanar agents who brought the embezzlement charges against him, the advocates who bribed him out of the Drownings (where, he knew, he would have survived), seeing him instead sent to the work camps. Ten years' hard labour—no one survived that.

Except me. Sheb the unkillable. And one day, Xaranthos Hivanar, I will come back to steal the rest of your wealth. I still know what I know, don't I? And you will pay to keep me quiet. And this time round I won't get careless. I'll see your corpse lying in a pauper's pit. I swear it before the Errant himself. I swear it!

Walking at Sheb's side, Nappet held on to his cold, hard grin. He knew Sheb wanted to be the bully in this crowd. The man had a viper's heart, a stony knuckle of a thing, beating out venom in turgid spurts. One of these nights, he vowed, he'd throw the fool on his back and give him the old snake-head where it counted.

Sheb had been in a Letherii prison—Nappet was certain of it. His habits, his manners, his skittish way of moving—they told him all he needed to know about ratty little Sheb. He'd been used and used well in those cells. Calluses on the knees. Fish Breath. Slick cheeks. There were plenty of names for men like him.

Sheb had got it enough to start liking it, and all this bitching back and forth between Nappet and Sheb, well, that was just seeing who'd be the first one doing the old cat stretch.

Four years' back-breaking quarrying up near Bluerose. That had been Nappet's sentence for that little gory mess back in Letheras, the sister's husband who'd liked throwing the frail thing around—well, no brother was going to let that just sidle past. No brother worth anything.

The only damned shame was that he hadn't managed to kill the bastard. Close, though. Enough broken bones so that the man had trouble sitting up, never mind stalking the house breaking things and hitting defenceless women.

Not that she'd been grateful. Family loyalty only went one way, it turned out. He forgave her quick enough for ratting on him. She'd walked in on a messy scene, after all. Screams aplenty. Her poor mind was confused—she'd never been very sharp to begin with. If she had been, why, she'd never have married that nub-nosed swaggering turd in the first place.

Anyway, Nappet knew he'd get Sheb sooner or later. So long as Sheb understood that between them he was the man in charge. And he knew that Sheb would want it rough, at least to start with, so he could look outraged, wounded and all that. The two of them, they'd played in the same yard, after all.

Breath stumbled and Nappet shoved her forward. 'Stupid woman. Frail and stupid, that's what you are, like every other woman. Almost as bad as the hag back there. You got a swamp drying out in that blonde hair, did you know that? You stink of the swamp—not that we been through one.'

She shot him a glare, before hurrying on.

Breath could smell mud. Its stench seemed to ooze from her pores. Nappet was right in that, but that didn't stop her thinking about ways to kill him. If not for Taxilian, and maybe Last, he and Sheb would have raped her by now. Once or twice, to convince her about who was in charge. After that, she knew, they'd be happy enough with each other.

She'd been told a story, once, although she could not recall who had told it to her, or where they had been. It was a tale about a girl who was a witch, though she didn't know it yet. She was a seer of the Tiles long before she saw her first Tile. A gift no one thought to even look for in this small, wheat-haired child.

Even before her first bloodflow, men had been after her. Not the tall grey-skinned ones, though the girl feared them the most—for reasons never explained—but men living in the same place as her. Letherii. Slaves, yes, slaves, just like she'd been. That girl. That witch.

And there was one man, maybe the only one among them all, who did not look on her with hunger. No, in his eyes there had been love. That real thing, that genuine thing that girls dreamed of finding. But he was lowborn. He was nothing. A mender of nets, a man whose red hands shed fish scales when he returned from his day's work.

The tragedy was this, then. The girl had not yet found her Tiles. Had she done so early enough, she would have taken that man to her bed. She would have

made him her first man. So that what was born between her legs was not born in
pain. So that it would not become so dark in its delicious desires.

Before the Tiles, then, she had given herself to other men, unloving men.
She'd given herself over to be used.

The same men who then in turn gave her a new name, one born of the legend
of the White Crow, who once offered the gift of flight to humans, in the form of a
single feather. And, urged on by promises, men would grasp hold of that feather
and seek to fly. Only to fall to their deaths. With the crow laughing as they fell.
Crows needed to eat just like everything else, after all.

'I am the White Crow, and I will feed on your dreams. And feed well.'

They called her Feather, for the promise she offered, and never delivered. Had
she found the Tiles, Breath was certain, she would have been given a different
name. That little blonde girl. Whoever she was.

Rautos, who had yet to discover his family name, was thinking of his wife.
Trying to recall something of their lives together, something other than the disgusting misery of their last years.

A man does not marry a girl, nor a woman. He marries a promise, and it shines
with a bright purity that is ageless. It shines, in other words, with the glory of
lies. The deception is self-inflicted. The promise was simple in its form, as befitted the thick-headedness of young men, and in its essence it offered the delusion
that the present moment was eternal; that nothing would change; not the fires of
desire, not the flesh itself, not the intense look in the eye.

Now here he was, at the far end of a marriage—where she was at this moment
he had no idea. Perhaps he'd murdered her. Perhaps, as was more likely given the
cowardice in his soul, he had simply fled her. No matter. He could look back with
appalling clarity now, and see how her dissolution had matched his own. They
had each settled like a lump of wax, melting season by season, descending into
something shapeless, something not even hinting at the forms they had once possessed. Smeared, sagging, two heaps of sour smells, chafed skin, groans born of fitful motion. Fools that they both were, they had not moved through the years hand
in hand—no, they'd not possessed that wisdom, that ironic recognition of the inevitable.

Neither had mitigated their youthful desires with the limits imposed so cruelly by age. He had dreamed of finding a younger woman, someone nubile, soft,
unblemished. She had longed for a tall, sturdy benefactor to soften her bedding
with romance and delight her with the zealotry of the enchanted.

They had won nothing for all their desires except misery and loneliness. *Like
two burlap sacks filled with tarnished baubles, each squatting alone in its own
room. In dust and cobwebs.*

*We stopped talking—no, be truthful, we never talked. Oh, past each other of-
ten enough in those early years. Yes, we talked past each other, avid and sharp,
too humourless to be wry—fools that we were. Could we have learned how to
laugh back then? So much might have turned out differently. So much . . .*

Regrets and coin, the debt ever mounts.

This nightmarish keep was the perfect match to the frightening chaos in his mind. Incomprehensible workings, gargantuan machines, corridors and strange ramps leading upward to the next levels, mysteries on all sides. As if . . . as if Rautos was losing his sense of himself, was losing talents he had long taken for granted. How could knowledge collapse so quickly? What was happening to him? Could the mind sink into a formless, unstructured thing to match the flesh that held it?

Perhaps, he thought with a start, he had not fled at all. Instead, he was lying on his soft bed, eyes open but seeing nothing of the truth, whilst his soul wandered the maze of a broken brain. The thought horrified Rautos and he physically picked up his pursuit of Taxilian, until he trod on the man's heel.

A glance back, brows raised.

Rautos mumbled an apology, wiped sweat from his jowly face.

Taxilian returned his attention to this steep ramp before him, and the landing he could now see ahead and above. The air was growing unbearably warm. He suspected there were chutes and vents that moved currents of warmth and cold throughout this alien city, but as yet he'd found none, not a single grated opening—and there were no draughts flowing past. If currents flowed in this air, they were so muted, so constrained, that human skin could not sense their whispering touch.

The city was dead, and yet it lived, it breathed, and somewhere a heart beat a slow syncopation, a heart of iron and brass, of copper and acrid oil. Valves and gears, rods and hinges, collars and rivets. He had found the lungs, and he knew that in one of the levels still awaiting them he would find the heart. Then, higher still, into the dragon's skull, where slept the massive mind.

All his life, dreams had filled his thoughts, his inner world, that played as would a god, maker of impossible inventions, machines so complex, so vast, they would strike like bolts of lightning should a mortal mind suddenly comprehend them. Creations to carry people across great distances, swifter than any horse or ship. Others that could surround a human soul, preserve its every thought and sense, its very knowledge of itself—and keep it all safe beyond the failing of mortal flesh. Creations to end all hunger, all poverty, to crush avarice before it was born, to cast out cruelty and indifference, to defy every inequity and deny the lure of sadistic pleasure.

Moral constructs—oh, they were a madman's dreams, to be sure. Humans insisted on others behaving properly, but rarely forced the same standards upon themselves. Justifications dispensed with logic, thriving on opportunism and delusions of pious propriety.

As a child he had heard tales of heroes, tall, stern-faced adventurers who claimed the banners of honour and loyalty, of truthfulness and integrity. And yet, as the tales spun out, Taxilian would find himself assailed by a growing horror, as the great hero slashed and murdered his way through countless victims, all in pursuit of whatever he (and the world) deemed a righteous goal. His justice was sharp, but it bore but one edge, and the effort of the victims to preserve their lives was somehow made sordid, even evil.

But a moral machine, ah, would it not be forced by mechanics alone to hold itself to the same standard it set upon every other sentient entity? Immune to hypocrisy, its rule would be absolute and absolutely just.

A young man's dreams, assuredly. Such a machine, he now knew, would quickly conclude that the only truly just act was the thorough annihilation of every form of intelligent life in every realm known to it. Intelligence was incomplete—perhaps it always would be—it was flawed. It could not distinguish its own lies from its own truths. Upon the scale of the self, they often weighed the same. Mistakes and malice were arguments of intent alone, not effect.

There would always be violence, catastrophe, shortsighted stupidity, incompetence and belligerence. The meat of history, after all, was the flyblown legacy of such things.

And yet. *And yet. The dragon is home to a city, the city that lives when not even echoes survive to walk its streets. Its very existence is a salutation.*

Taxilian believed—well, he so wanted to believe—that he would discover an ancient truth in this place. He would come, yes, face to face with a moral construct. And as for Asane's words earlier, her fretting on the slaughtered K'Chain Che'Malle in the first chamber, such a scene made sense now to Taxilian. The machine mind had come to its inevitable conclusion. It had delivered the only possible justice.

If only he could awaken it once more, perfection would return to the world.

Taxilian could sense nothing, of course, of the ghost's horror at such notions. Justice without compassion was the destroyer of morality, a slayer blind to empathy.

Leave such things to nature, to the forces not even the gods can control. If you must hold to a faith, Taxilian, then hold to that one. Nature may be slow to act, but it will find a balance—and that is a process not one of us can stop, for it belongs to time itself.

And, the ghost now knew, he had a thing about *time*.

They came upon vast chambers crowded with vats in which grew fungi and a host of alien plants that seemed to need no light. They stumbled upon seething nests of scaled rats—orthen—that scattered squealing from the lantern's harsh light.

Dormitories in rows upon rows, assembly halls and places of worship. Work stalls and low-ceilinged expanses given over to arcane manufacture—stacks of metal, each one identical, proof of frightening precision. Armouries bearing ranks of strange weapons, warehouses with stacked packages of foodstuffs, ice-rooms filled with butchered, frozen meat hanging from hooks. Niches in which were stored bolts of cloth, leather, and scaled hides. Rooms cluttered with gourds arranged on shelves.

A city indeed, awaiting them.

And still, Taxilian led them ever upward. Like a man possessed.

A riot had erupted. Armed camps of islanders raged back and forth along the shoreline, while mobs plunged into the forests, weapons slick and dripping, into the makeshift settlements, conducting pathetic looting and worse among the poorest refugees. Murder, rapes, and everywhere, flames lifting orange light into the air. Before dawn, the fires had ignited the forest, and hundreds more died in smoke and heat.

Yan Tovis had drawn her Shake down on to the stony shoreline, where numbers alone kept the worst of the killers at bay.

The ex-prisoners of Second Maiden Fort had not taken well the rumour—sadly accurate—that the Queen of Twilight was preparing to lead them into an unknown world, a realm of darkness, a road without end. That, if she failed and lost her way, would find them all abandoned, trapped for ever in a wasteland that had never known a sun's light, a sun's blessed warmth.

A few thousand islanders had taken refuge among the Shake. The rest, she knew, were busy dying or killing each other amidst grey smoke and raging flames. Standing facing the ravaged slope with its morbid tree-stumps and destroyed huts, her face smeared with ash and sweat, her eyes streaming from the smoke, Yan Tovis struggled to find her courage, her will to take command once more. She was exhausted, in her bones and in her soul. Waves of ash-filled heat gusted against her. Distant screams drifted through the air, cutting through the surly growl of the motley rabble edging ever closer.

Someone was pushing through the crowd behind her, snarling curses and dire warnings. A moment later, Skwish scrambled forward. 'There's near a thousand gulpin' down o'er there, Queen. When they get their nerve, they're gonna carve inta us—we got a line a ex-guards an' the like betwixt 'em an' us. You better do somethin' and do it fast . . . Highness.'

She could hear renewed fighting, somewhere down the beach. Twilight frowned. Something about that sound . . . 'Do you hear that?' she asked the witch cowering at her side.

'Wha?'

'That's an organized advance, Skwish.' And she pushed past the old woman, making her way towards that steady clash of iron, the shouts of commands being given, the shrieks and cries of dying looters. Even in the uncertain flickering light from the forest fire, she could see how the mob was curling back—a wedge of Letherii soldiers was pushing through, drawing ever closer.

Twilight halted. *Yedan Derryg. And his troop. My brother—damn him!*

She saw her ex-guards shift uneasily as the wedge cut through the last looters. They did not know if the newcomers would attack them next—if they did, the poorly armed islanders would be cut to pieces. Twilight hurried, determined to throw herself between the two forces.

She heard Yedan snap an order, and saw the perfect precision of his thirty or so soldiers wheeling round, the wedge dispersing, flattening out to form a new line facing the churning crowd of looters, locking shields, drawing up their weapons.

The threat from that direction was now over. Actual numbers were irrelevant. Discipline among a few could defeat a multitude—that was Letherii doctrine, borne out in countless battles against wild tribes on the borderlands. Yan Tovis knew it as did her brother.

She pushed through her island guard, seeing the loose relief on the faces that swung to her, the sudden deliverance from certain death.

Yedan, blackened with soot and spatters of blood, must have seen her before she spied him, for he stepped into her path, lifting his helm's cheek-guards, revealing his black beard, the bunching muscles of his jaw. 'My Queen,' he said. 'Dawn fast approaches—the moment of the Watch is almost past—you will lose the darkness.' He hesitated, and then said, 'I do not believe we can survive another day in this uprising.'

'Of course we can't, you infuriating bastard!'

'The Road to Gallan, my Queen. If you will open the way, it must be now.' He gestured with a gauntleted hand. 'When they see the portal born, they will try for it—to escape the flames. To escape the retribution of the kingdom. You will have two thousand criminals rushing on your heels.'

'And what is there to do about it?' Even as she asked, she knew how he would answer. Knew, and wanted to scream.

'Queen, my soldiers will hold the portal.'

'And be slaughtered!'

He said nothing. Muscles knotted rhythmically beneath his beard.

'Damn you! *Damn you!*'

'Unveil the Road, my Queen.'

She spun to her two captains among the ex-prison guards. 'Pithy. Brevity. Support Yedan Derryg's soldiers—for as long as you can—but be sure not to get so entangled that your people cannot withdraw—I want you through the gate, do you understand?'

'We shall do as you say, Highness,' Brevity replied.

Yan Tovis studied the two women, wondering yet again why the others had elected them as their captains. They'd never been soldiers—anyone could see that. Damned criminals, in fact. Yet they could command. Shaking her head, she faced her brother once more.

'Will you follow us?'

'If we can, my Queen. But we must be certain to hold until we see the portal-way failing.' He paused, and then added with his usual terseness, 'It will be close.'

Yan Tovis wanted to tear at her hair. 'Then I begin—and,' she hesitated, 'I will talk to Pully and Skwish. I will—'

'Do not defend what I have done, sister. The time to lead is now. Go, do what must be done.'

Gods, you pompous idiot.

Don't die, damn you. Don't you dare die!

She did not know if he heard her sob as she rushed away. He'd dropped his cheek-guards once more. Besides, those helms blunted all but the sharpest sounds.

The Road to Gallan. The road home. Ever leading me to wonder, why did we leave in the first place? What drove us from Gallan? The first shoreline? What so fouled the water that we could no longer live there?

She reached the ancient shell midden where she and the witches had sancti-fied the ground, climbed, achingly, raw with desperation, to join the pair of old witches.

Their eyes glittered, with madness or terror—she could never tell with these two hags.

'Now?' asked Pully.

'Yes. Now.'

And Yan Tovis turned round. From her vantage point, she looked upon her cow-ering followers. Her people, crowded along the length of beach. Behind them the forest was a wall of fire. Ashes and smoke, a conflagration. *This—this is what we leave. Remember that.* From where she stood, she could not even see her brother.

No one need ever ask why we fled this world.

She whirled round, drawing her blessed daggers. And laid open her forearms. The gift of royal blood. To the shore.

Pully and Skwish screamed the Words of Sundering, their twisted hands grasp-ing her wrists, soaking in her blood like leeches.

They should not complain. That but two remain. They will learn, I think, to thank my brother. When they see what royal blood gives them. When they see.

Darkness yawned. Impenetrable, a portal immune to the water that its lower end carved into.

The road home.

Weeping, Yan Tovis, Twilight, Queen of the Shake, pulled her arms loose from the witches' grip, and lunged forward. Into the cold past.

Where none could hear her screams of grief.

The mob hesitated longer than Yedan expected, hundreds of voices crying out upon witnessing the birth of the portal, those cries turning to need and then anger as the Shake and the islanders among them plunged into the gate, vanishing—escaping this madness.

He stood with his troop, gauging the nearest of the rioters. 'Captain Brevity,' he called over a shoulder.

'Watch.'

'Do not tarry here. We will do what needs doing.'

'We got our orders.'

'I said we will hold.'

'Sorry,' the woman snapped. 'We ain't in the mood to watch you go all heroic here.'

'Asides,' added Pithy, 'our lads couldn't live with themselves if they just left you to it.'

A half-dozen voices loudly objected to her claim, to which both captains laughed.

Biting back a smile, Yedan said nothing. The mob was moments from rushing them—they were being pushed from behind. It was always this way, he knew. Someone else's courage, so boisterous in its refuge among walls of flesh, so easy with someone else's life. He could see, in heaving eddies, the worst of them, and set their details in his mind, to test their courage when at last he came face to face with each one.

'Wake up, soldiers,' he shouted. 'Here they come.'

The first task in driving back a charging mob was two quick steps forward, right into the faces of the foremost attackers. Cut them down, pull back a single stride, and hold fast. As the survivors were thrust forward once more, repeat the aggression, messy and brutal, and this time advance into the teeth of the crowd, blades chopping, stabbing, shield rims slamming into bodies, studded heels crunching down on those that fell underfoot.

The nearest ranks recoiled from the assault.

Then retaliated, rising like a wave.

Yedan and his troop delivered fierce slaughter. Held for twenty frantic heartbeats, and then were driven back one step, and then another. Better-armed looters began appearing, thrust to the forefront. The first Letherii soldier fell, stabbed through a thigh. Two of Brevity's guards hurried forward and pulled the man from the line, a cutter rushing in to staunch the wound with clumps of spider's web.

Pithy shouted from a position directly behind Yedan: '*More than half through, Watch!*'

The armed foes that fell to his soldiers either reeled back or collapsed at their feet. These latter ones gave up the weapons they held to more of the two captains' guards, who reached through quick as cats to snatch them away before the attackers could recover them. The two women were busy arming others to bolster their rearguard—Yedan could imagine no other reason for the risky—and, truth be told, irritating—tactic.

His soldiers were tiring—it had been some time since they'd last worn full armour. He'd been slack in keeping them fit. Too much riding, not enough marching. When had any of them last drawn blood? The Edur invasion for most of them.

They were paying for it now. Ragged gasps, slowing arms, stumbles.

'Back one step!'

The line edged back—

'Now forward! Hard!'

The mob had seen that retreat as a victory, the beginnings of a rout. The sudden attack into their faces shocked them, their weapons unreadied, their minds on everything but defence. That front line melted, as did the one behind it, and then a third. Yedan and his soldiers—knowing that this was their last push—fought like snarling beasts.

And all at once, the hundreds crowding before them suddenly scattered—the rough ranks shattering. Weapons thrown aside, fleeing as fast as legs could carry them, down the strand, out into the shallows. Scores were trampled, driven into mud or stones or water. Fighting broke out in desperate efforts to clear paths through.

Yedan withdrew his troop. They staggered back to the waiting rearguard— who looked upon them in silence, perhaps disbelieving.

'Attend to the wounded,' barked Yedan, lifting his cheek grilles to cool his throbbing face, snatching in deep breaths.

'We can get moving now,' Brevity said, tugging at his shield arm. 'We can just walk on through to . . . wherever. You, Watch, you need to be in charge of the Shake army, did you know that?'

'The Shake have no army—'

'They better get one and soon.'

'Besides, I am an outlaw—I slaughtered—'

'We know what you did. You're an Errant-damned up-the-wall madman, Yedan Derryg. Best kinda commander an army could have.'

Pithy said, 'Leave the petitioning to us, sweetie.' And she smiled.

He looked round. One wounded. None dead. None dead that counted, anyway. Screams of pain rose from the killing field. He paid that no attention, simply sheathed his sword.

When Yedan Derryg walked into the fading portalway—the last of them all—he did not look back. Not once.

There was great joy in discarding useless words. Although one could not help but measure each day by the sun's fiery passage through the empty sky, and each night by the rise and set of a haze-shrouded moon and the jade slashes cutting across the starscape, the essential meaning of time had vanished from Badalle's mind. Days and nights were a tumbling cavort, round and round with no beginning and no end. Jaws to tail. They rolled on and left nothing but a scattering of motionless small figures collapsed on to the plain. Even the ribbers had abandoned them.

Here, at the very edge of the Glass, there were only the opals—fat carrion beetles migrating in from the blasted, lifeless flanks to either side of the trail. And the diamonds—glittering spiked lizards that sucked blood from the fingertips their jaws clamped tight round every night—diamonds becoming rubies as they grew engorged. And there were the Shards, the devouring locusts sweeping down in glittering storms, stripping children almost where they stood, leaving behind snarls of rags, tufts of hair and pink bones.

Insects and lizards ruled this scorched realm. Children were interlopers, invaders. Food.

Rutt had tried to lead them round the Glass, but there was no way around that vast blinding desert. A few of them gathered after the second night. They had been walking south, and at this day's end they had found a sinkhole filled with bright green water. It tasted of limestone dust and made many children writhe in pain, clutching their stomachs. It made a few of them die.

Rutt sat holding Held, and to his left crouched Brayderal—the tall bony girl who reminded Badalle of the Quitters. She had pushed her way in, and for that Badalle did not like her, did not trust her, but Rutt turned no one away. Saddic was there as well, a boy who looked upon Badalle with abject adoration. It was disgusting, but he listened best to her poems, her sayings, and he could repeat them back to her, word for word. He said he was collecting them all. To one day make a book. A book of this journey. He believed, therefore, that they were going to survive this, and that made him a fool.

The four of them had sat, and in the silences that stretched out and round and in and through and sometimes between them all, they pondered what to do next. Words weren't needed for that kind of conversation. And no one had the strength for gestures, either. Badalle thought that Saddic's book should hold vast numbers of blank pages, to mark such silences and all they contained. The truths and the lies, the needs and the wants. The nows and the thens, the theres and the heres. If she saw such pages, and could crisp back each one, one after another, she would nod, remembering how it was. How it was.

It was Brayderal who stained the first blank page. 'We got to go back.'

Rutt lifted his bloodshot eyes. He drew Held tighter against his chest. Adjusted the tattered hood, reached in a lone finger to stroke an unseen cheek.

That was his answer, and Badalle agreed with him. Yes she did. Stupid, dangerous Brayderal.

Who scratched a bit at the sores encrusting her nostrils. 'We can't go round it. We can only cross it. But crossing it means we all die and die bad. I've heard of this Glass Desert. Never crossed. No one ever crosses it. It goes on for ever, straight down the throat of the setting sun.'

Oh, Badalle liked that one. That was a good scene to keep alive in her head. Down the throat, a diamond throat, a throat of glass, sharp, so very sharp glass. And they were the snake. 'We got thick skin,' she said, since the page was already ruined. 'We go down the throat. We go down it, because that's what snakes do.'

'Then we die.'

They all gave her silence for that. To say such things! To blot the page that way! They gave her silence. For that.

Rutt turned his head. Rutt set his eyes upon the Glass Desert. He stared that way a long, long time, as darkness quenched the glittering flats. And then he finished his looking, and he leaned forward and rocked Held to sleep. Rocked and rocked.

So it was decided. They were going into the Glass Desert.

Brayderal took a blank page for herself. She had thousands to choose from.

Badalle crawled off, trailed by Saddic, and she sat staring into the night. She threw away words. There. Here. Then. Now. When. Everybody had to cut what they carried, to cross this desert. Toss away what wasn't needed. Even poets.

'You have a poem,' Saddic said, a dark shape beside her. 'I want to hear it.'

> 'I am throwing away
> Words. You and me
> Is a good place to start
> Yesterday I woke up
> With five lizards
> Sucking my fingers
> Like tiny pigs or rat pups
> They drank down

You and me
I killed two of them
And ate what they took
But that wasn't taking back .
The words stayed gone
We got to lighten the load
Cut down on what we carry
Today I stop carrying
You
Tomorrow I stop carrying
Me.'

After a time of no words, Saddic stirred. 'I've got it, Badalle.'

'To go with the silent pages.'

'The what?'

'The blank ones. The ones that hold everything that's true. The ones that don't lie about anything. The silent pages, Saddic.'

'Is that another poem?'

'Just don't put it on a blank page.'

'I won't.'

He seemed strangely satisfied, and he curled up tight against her hip, like a ribber when ribbers weren't ribbers but pets, and he went to sleep. She looked down on him, and thought about eating his arms.

Chapter Nine

Down past the wind-groomed grasses
In the sultry curl of the stream
There was a pool set aside
In calm interlude away from the rushes
Where not even the reeds waver
Nature takes no time to harbour our needs
For depthless contemplation
Every shelter is a shallow thing
The sly sand grips hard no manner
Of anchor or even footfall
Past the bend the currents run thin
In wet chuckle where a faded tunic
Drapes the shoulders of a broken branch
These are the dangers I might see
Leaning forward if the effort did not prove
So taxing but that ragged collar
Covers no pale breast with tapping pulse
This shirt wears the river in birth foam
And languid streaming tatters
Soon I gave up the difficult rest
And floated down in search of boots
Filled with pebbles as every man needs
Somewhere to stand.

CLOTHES REMAIN
FISHER

'm stuffed,' said King Tehol, and then, with a glance at his guest, added, 'Sorry.'

Captain Shurq Elalle regarded him with her crystal goblet halfway to her well-padded, exquisitely painted lips. 'Yet another swollen member at my table.'

'Actually,' observed Bugg, 'this is the King's table.'

'I wasn't being literal,' she replied.

'Which is a good thing,' cried Tehol, 'since my wife happens to be sitting right here beside me. And though she has no need to diet, we'd all best stay figurative.' And his eyes shifted nervously before he hid himself behind his own goblet.

'Just like old times,' said Shurq. 'Barring the awkward pauses, the absurd opulence, and the weight of an entire kingdom pressing down upon us. Remind me to decline the next invitation.'

'Longing for a swaying deck under your feet?' Tehol asked. 'Oh, how I miss the sea—'

'How can you miss what you've never experienced?'

'Well, good point. I should have been more precise. I miss the false memory of missing a life on the sea. It was, at the risk of being coarse, my gesture of empathy.'

'I don't really think the captain's longings should be the subject of conversation, husband,' Queen Janath said, mostly under her breath.

Shurq heard her none the less. 'Highness, this night has made it grossly obvious that you hold to an unreasonable prejudice against the dead. If I was still alive I'd be offended.'

'No you wouldn't.'

'In a gesture of empathy, indeed I would!'

'Well, I do apologize,' said the Queen. 'I just find your, uh, excessively overt invitations to be somewhat off-putting—'

'My excessively overt *what*? It's called make-up! And clothes!'

'More like dressing the feast,' murmured Janath.

Tehol and Bugg shared a wince.

Shurq Elalle smirked. 'Jealousy does not become a queen—'

'Jealousy? Are you mad?'

The volume of the exchange was escalating. 'Yes, jealousy! I'm not getting any older and that fact alone—'

'Not any older, true enough, just more and more . . . putrid.'

'No less putrid than your unseemly bigotry! And all I need do by way of remedy is a bag full of fresh herbs!'

'That's what you think.'

'Not a single man's ever complained. I bet you can't say the same.'

'What's that supposed to mean?'

Shurq Elalle then chose the most vicious reply of all. She said nothing. And took another delicate mouthful of wine.

Janath stared, and then turned on her husband.

Who flinched.

In a tight, low voice, Janath asked, 'Dear husband, do I fail in pleasing you?'

'Of course not!'

'Am I the subject of private conversations between you and this—this creature?'

'Private? You, her? Not at all!'

'Oh, so what then is the subject of those conversations?'

'No subject—'

'Too busy to talk, then, is it? You two—'

'What? No!'

'Oh, there's always time for a few explicit instructions. Naturally.'

'I don't—we don't—'

'This is insane,' snapped Shurq Elalle. 'When I can get a man like Ublala Pung why should I bother with Tehol here?'

The King vigorously nodded, and then frowned.

Janath narrowed her gaze on the undead captain. 'Am I to understand that my husband is not good enough for you?'

Bugg clapped his hands and rose. 'Think I'll take a walk in the garden. By your leave, sire—'

'No! Not for a moment! Not unless I can go with you!'

'Don't even think it,' hissed Janath. 'I'm defending your honour here!'

'Bah!' barked Shurq Elalle. 'You're defending your choice in men! That's different.'

Tehol straightened, pushing his chair back and mustering the few remaining tatters of his dignity. 'We can only conclude,' he intoned loftily, 'that nostalgic nights of reminiscences are best contemplated in the abstract—'

'The figurative,' suggested Bugg.

'Rather than the literal, yes. Precisely. And now, my Chancellor and I will take the night air for a time. Court musicians—you! Over there! Wax up those instruments or whatever you have to do. Music! Something friendly!'

'Forgiving.'

'And forgiving!'

'Pacifying.'

'Pacifying!'

'But not patronizing—'

'But not— All right, that will do, Bugg.'

'Of course, sire.'

Shurq watched the two cowards flee the dining hall. Once the door had closed, and the dozen or so musicians had finally settled on the same song, the captain leaned back in her chair and contemplated the Queen for a moment, and then said, 'So, what's all this about?'

'I had some guests last night, ones that I think you should meet.'

'All right. In what capacity?'

'They may have need of you and your ship. It's complicated.'

'No doubt.'

Janath waved a handmaiden over and muttered some instructions. The short, overweight woman with the pimply face waddled off.

'You really don't trust Tehol, do you?' Shurq asked, watching the handmaiden depart.

'It's not a matter of trust. More a question of eliminating temptation.'

She snorted. 'Never works. You know that, don't you? Besides, he's a king. He has royal leave to exercise kingly excesses. It's a well-established rule. Your only reasonable response is to exercise in kind.'

'Shurq, I'm a scholar and not much else. It's not my way—'

'Make it your way, Highness. And then the pressure's off both of you. No suspicions, no jealousies, no unreasonable expectations. No unworkable prohibitions.'

'Such liberating philosophy you have, Captain.'

'So it is.'

'And doomed to sink into a most grisly mire of spite, betrayal and loneliness.'

'That's the problem with you living. You're all stuck on seeing only the bad things. If you were dead like me you'd see how pointless all that is. A waste of precious energy. I recommend your very own ootooloo—that'll put your thoughts in the right place.'

'Between my legs, you mean.'

'Exactly. Our very own treasure chest, our pleasure box, the gift most women lock up and swallow the key to, and then call themselves virtuous. What value in denying the gift and all it offers? Madness! What's the value of a virtue that makes you miserable and wretched?'

'There are other kinds of pleasure, Shurq—'

'But none so readily at hand for each and every one of us. You don't need coin. Errant fend, you don't even need a partner! I tell you, excess is the path to contentment.'

'And have you found it? Contentment, I mean, since your excesses are not in question.'

'I have indeed.'

'What if you could live again?'

'I've thought about it. A lot, lately, in fact, since there's a necromancer among the Malazans who says he can attempt a ritual that might return me to life.'

'And?'

'I'm undecided. Vanity.'

'Your ageless countenance.'

'The prospect of unending pleasure, actually.'

'Don't you think you might tire of it someday?'

'I doubt it.'

Queen Janath pursed her lips. 'Interesting,' she murmured.

Tehol plucked a globe of pinkfruit from the tree beside the fountain. He studied it. 'That was harsh,' he said.

'They wanted to make it convincing,' said Bugg. 'Are you going to eat that?'

'What? Well, I thought it made a nice gesture, holding it just so, peering at it so thoughtfully.'

'I figured as much.'

Tehol handed him the fruit. 'Go ahead, ruin the prosaic beauty of the scene.'

Squishy, wet sounds competed with the fountain's modest trickle.

'Spies and secret handshakes,' said Tehol. 'They're worse than the Rat Catchers' Guild.'

Bugg swallowed, licked his lips. 'Who?'

'Women? Lovers and ex-lovers? Old acquaintances, I don't know. Them. They.'

'This is a court, sire. The court plots and schemes with the same need that we—uh, you—breathe. A necessity. It's healthy, in fact.'

'Oh now, really.'

'All right, not healthy, unless of course one can achieve a perfect equilibrium, each faction played off against the others. The true measure of success for a king's Intelligence Wing.'

Tehol frowned. 'Who's flapping that, by the way?'

'Your Intelligence Wing?'

'That's the one.'

'I am.'

'Oh. How goes it?'

'I fly in circles, sire.'

'Lame, Bugg.'

'As it must be.'

'We need to invent another wing, I think.'

'Do we now?'

Tehol nodded, plucking another fruit and studying it contemplatively. 'To fly true, yes. A counter-balance. We could call it the King's Stupidity Wing.'

Bugg took the fruit and regarded it. 'No need, we already have it.'

'We do?'

'Yes, sire.'

'Hah hah.'

Bugg bit into the globe and then spat it out. 'Unripe! You did that on purpose!'

'How stupid of me.'

Bugg glared.

The two women who followed the spotty handmaiden back into the dining room were an odd study in contrast. The short, curvy one dripped and dangled an astonishing assortment of gaudy jewellery. The clothing she wore stretched the definition of the word. Shurq suspected it had taken half the night to squeeze into the studded leggings, and the upper garment seemed to consist of little more than a mass of thin straps that turned her torso into a symmetrical display of dimples and pouts. Her plumpness was, perhaps, a sign of her youth as much as of soft living, although there was plenty of indolence in her rump-swaying, overly affected manner of walking—as if through a crowd of invisible but audibly gasping admirers—perched so perfectly atop high spike-heeled shoes, with one hand delicately raised. Her petite features reminded Shurq of the painted exaggeration employed by stage actors and weeping orators, with ferociously dark eye liner flaring to glittering purple below the plucked line of her eyebrows; white dust and false bloom to the rounded plump cheeks; pink and amber gloss on the full lips in diagonal barbs converging on the corners of her faintly downturned mouth. Her hair, silky black, was bound up in a frenzied array of braided knots speared with dozens of porcupine quills, each one tipped with pearls.

It was likely Shurq gaped for a moment, sufficient to earn an indulgent smile from the haughty little creature as she flounced closer.

A step behind this two-legged tome of fashion travesty walked the handmaiden —at least, that's what the captain assumed she was. A head taller than most men, burly as a stevedore, the woman was dressed in an embroidered pink gown of some sort, shrieking femininity with a desperate air, and utterly failing to render the wearer any sort of elegance whatsoever. Diamond studs glinted high on her cheeks—and Shurq frowned, realizing with a start that the handmaiden's face was surprisingly attractive: even features, the eyes deep, the lips full and naturally sultry. Her hair was cut close to the scalp, so blonde as to be very nearly white.

The curtsy the highborn girl presented before Queen Janath was elaborate and perfectly executed. 'Highness, at your service.'

Janath cleared her throat. 'Princess Felash, welcome. May I present Shurq Elalle, captain of *Undying Gratitude*, a seaworthy vessel engaged in independent trade. Captain, Princess Felash is the fourteenth daughter to King Tarkulf of Bolkando.'

Shurq rose and then curtsied. 'Princess, may I compliment you on your attire. I cannot think of many women who could so exquisitely present such a vast assembly of styles.'

The handmaiden's dark eyes flicked to Shurq and then away.

Felash preened, one hand returning to hover an artful distance to one side of her head. 'Most kind, Captain. Few, even among my father's court, possess the necessary sophistication to appreciate my unique tastes.'

'I have no doubt of that, Highness.'

Another quick regard from the handmaiden.

Janath spoke hastily, 'Forgive me, please, do sit with us, Princess. Share some wine, some dainties.'

'Thank you, Queen Janath. You are most kind. Wine sounds wonderful, although I must regretfully decline partaking of any sweets. Must watch my weight, you know.'

Well, that's good, since everyone else has to.

'Oh,' Felash then amended as soon her veiled eyes fixed upon the nearest plate heaped with desserts, 'since this is a most special occasion, why not indulge?' And she reached for a honey-drenched cake that mocked the notion of dainty, veritably exuding its invitation to obesity. Devouring such a trifle challenged the princess's command of decorum, but she was quick, and in moments was carefully licking her fingertips. 'Wonderful.'

'Your handmaiden is welcome—'

'Oh no, Highness! She is on the strictest diet—why, just look at the poor child!'

'Princess Felash,' cut in Shurq Elalle—although the handmaiden's unchanged expression suggested she was well inured to her mistress's callous rudeness—'I must admit I have heard nothing of your visit to Lether—'

'Ah, but that is because I'm not here at all, Captain. Officially, that is.'

'Oh. I see.'

'Do you?' And the painted brat had the audacity to send her a sly wink. Felash then nodded towards Janath, even as she collected another sweetcake. 'Your Malazan allies are about to march into a viper's nest, you see. There is, in fact, the very real risk of a war. The more reasonable servants of the crown in Bolkando, of course, do not wish such a thing to come to pass. After all, should such conflict erupt, there is the chance that Lether will become embroiled, and then no one will be happy!'

'So your father has sent you here on a secret mission, with appropriate assurances.'

'My mother, actually, Captain,' Felash corrected. She smacked her lips. 'Alas, more than assurances were required, but all that has been taken care of, and now I wish to return home.'

Shurq thought about that for a moment. 'Princess, the sea lanes that can draw us close to your kingdom are not particularly safe. Areas are either uncharted or inaccurately charted. And then there are the pirates—'

'How better to confound such pirates than have one of them commanding our ship?'

Shurq Elalle started. 'Princess, I'm not—'

'Tush! Now you're being silly. And no, Queen Janath has not babbled any secrets. We are quite capable of gathering our own intelligence—'

'Alarmingly capable,' muttered Janath, 'as it turns out.'

'Even if I am a pirate,' Shurq said, 'that is no guarantee against being set upon. The corsairs from Deal—who ply those waters—acknowledge no rules of honour when it comes to rivals. In any case, I am in fact committed to transport a cargo which, unfortunately, will take me in the opposite direction—'

'Would that cargo be one Ublala Pung?' Janath asked.

'Yes.'

'And has he a destination in mind?'

'Well, admittedly, it's rather vague at the moment.'

'So,' continued the Queen thoughtfully, 'if you posed to him an alternative route to wherever it is he's going, would he object?'

'Object? He wouldn't even understand, Highness. He'd just smile and nod and try and tweak one of my—'

'Then it is possible you can accommodate Princess Felash even with Ublala Pung aboard, yes?'

Shurq frowned at the Queen, and then at Felash. 'Is this a royal command, Highness?'

'Let's just say we would be most pleased.'

'Then let me just say that the pleasure of however many of you exist isn't good enough, Highness. Pay me and pay well. And we agree on a contract. And I want it in writing—from either you, Queen, or you, Princess.'

'But the whole point of this is that it must remain unofficial. Really, Shurq—'

'Really nothing, Janath.'

Felash waved one sticky crumb-dusted hand. 'Agreed! I will have a contract written up. There is no problem with the captain's conditions. None at all. Well! I am delighted that everything's now arranged to everyone's satisfaction!'

Janath blinked.

'Well. That's fine, then,' said Shurq Elalle.

'Oh, these sweets are a terror! I must not—oh, one more perhaps—'

A short time later and the two Bolkando guests were given leave to depart. As soon as the door closed behind them, Shurq Elalle fixed a level gaze upon Janath. 'So, O Queen, what precisely is the situation in Bolkando?'

'Errant knows,' Janath sighed, refilling her goblet. 'A mess. There are so many factions in that court it makes a college faculty look like a neighbourhood sandbox. And you may not know it, but that is saying something.'

'A sandbox?'

'You know, in the better-off streets, the community commons—there's always a box of sand for children to play in, where all the feral cats go to defecate.'

'You privileged folk have strange notions of what your children should play with.'

'Ever get hit on the head by a gritty sausage of scat? Well then, enough of that attitude, Shurq. We were as vicious as any rags-gang you ran with, let me tell you.'

'All right, sorry. Have you warned the Malazans that Bolkando is seething and about to go up in their faces?'

'They know. Their allies are in the midst of it right now, in fact.'

'So what was that princess doing here in Letheras?'

Janath made a face. 'As far as I can tell, annihilating rival spy networks—the ones Bugg left dangling out of indifference, I suppose.'

Shurq grunted. 'Felash? She's no killer.'

'No, but I'd wager her handmaiden is.'

'How old is this fourteenth daughter, anyway? Sixteen, seventeen—'

'Fourteen, actually.'

'Abyss below! I can't say I'm looking forward to transporting that puffed-up pastry-mauler all the way to the Akrynnai Range.'

'Just go light on ballast.'

Shurq's eyes widened.

Janath scowled. 'The pilot charts we possess indicate shallow reefs, Captain. What did you think I was referring to?'

'No idea, Highness. Honest.'

Janath rose. 'Let's go pounce on the men in the garden, shall we?'

Departing the palace unseen was enabled by the Queen's silent servants leading the two Bolkando women down a maze of unused corridors and passageways, until at last they were ushered out into the night through a recessed postern gate.

They walked to a nearby street and there awaited the modest carriage that would take them back to their rooms in a hostel of passing quality down near the harbourfront.

Felash held one hand in the air, fingers moving in slow, sinuous rhythm—an affectation of which she seemed entirely unaware. 'A contract! Ridiculous!'

Her handmaiden said nothing.

'Well,' said Felash, 'if the captain proves too troublesome—' and into that uplifted hand snapped a wedge-bladed dagger, appearing so suddenly it might well have been conjured out of the thin night air.

'Mistress,' said the handmaiden in a low, smooth and stunningly beautiful voice, 'that will not work.'

Felash frowned. 'Oh, grow up, you silly girl. We can leave no trail—no evidence at all.'

'I mean, mistress, that the captain cannot be killed, for I believe she is already dead.'

'That's ridiculous.'

'Even so, mistress. Furthermore, she is enlivened by an ootooloo.'

'Oh, now that's interesting! And exciting!' The dagger vanished as quickly as it had appeared. 'Fix me a bowl, will you? I need to think.'

'Here they come,' murmured Bugg.

Tehol turned. 'Ah, see how they've made up and everything. How sweet. My darlings, so refreshing this night air, don't you think?'

'I'm not your darling,' said Shurq Elalle. 'She is.'

'And isn't she just? Am I not the luckiest man alive?'

'Errant knows, it's not talent.'

'Or looks,' added Janath, observing her husband with gauging regard.

'It was better,' Tehol said to Bugg, 'when they weren't allies.'

'Divide to conquer the divide, sire, that's my motto.'

'And a most curious one at that. Has it ever worked for you, Bugg?'

'I'll be sure to let you know as soon as it does.'

Thirty leagues north of Li Heng on the Quon Talian mainland was the village of Gethran, an unremarkable clump of middling drystone homes, workshops, a dilapidated church devoted to a handful of local spirits, a bar and a gaol blockhouse where the tax-collector lived in one of the cells and was in the habit of arresting himself when he got too drunk, which was just about every night.

Behind the squat temple with its thirty-two rooms was a tiered cemetery that matched the three most obvious levels of class in the village. The highest and furthest from the building was reserved for the wealthier families—the tradesfolk and skilled draft workers whose lineages could claim a presence in the town for more than three generations. Their graves were marked by ornate sepulchres, tombs constructed in the fashion of miniature temples, and the occasional tholos bricked tomb—a style of the region that reached back centuries.

The second level belonged to residents who were not particularly well-off, but generally solvent and upstanding. The burials here were naturally more modest, yet generally well maintained by relatives and offspring, characterized by flat-topped shrines and capped, stone-lined pits.

Closest to the temple, and level with its foundations, resided the dead in most need of spiritual protection and, perhaps, pity. The drunks, wastrels, addicts and criminals, their bodies stacked in elongated trenches with pits reopened in a migratory pattern, up and down the row, to allow sufficient time for the corpses to decompose before a new one was deposited.

A village no different from countless others scattered throughout the Malazan Empire. Entire lives spent in isolation from the affairs of imperial ambition, from the marching armies of conquest and magic-ravaged battles. Lives crowded with local dramas and every face a familiar one, every life known from blood-slick birth to blood-drained death.

Hounded by four older sisters, the grubby, half-wild boy who would one day be named Deadsmell was in the habit of hiding out with Old Scez, who might have been an uncle or maybe just one of his mother's lovers before his father came back from the war. Scez was the village dresser of the dead, digger of the graves, and occasional mason for standing stones. With hands like dusty mallets, wrists as big around as a grown man's calf, and a face that had been pushed hard to one side by a tumbling lintel stone decades back, he was not a man to draw admiring looks, but neither was he short of friends. Scez did right by the dead, after all. And he had something—every woman said as much—he had something, all right. A look in his eye that gave comfort, that promised more if more was needed. Yes, he was adored, and in the habit of making breakfasts for women all over the village, a detail young Deadsmell was slow to understand.

Naturally, a husband one day went and murdered Old Scez, and though the law said he was justified in doing it, well, that fool sickened and died a week later, and few came out to mourn the blue-faced, bloated corpse—by that time, Deadsmell had taken over as keeper of the dead, a seventeen-year-old lad everybody said never would have followed his own father—who was a lame ex-soldier who'd fought in the Quon Talian civil war but never talked about his experiences, even as he drank himself stupid with one red eye fixed on one of those trench graves behind the temple.

Young Deadsmell, who'd yet to find that name, had been pretty sure of his future once he had taken over Scez's responsibilities. It was respectable enough, all things considered. A worthy profession, a worthy life.

In his nineteenth year, he was well settled into the half-sunken flat-roofed stone house just outside the cemetery—a house that Scez had built with his own hands—when word arrived that Hester Vill, the temple's priest, had fallen with a stroke and was soon to enter the embrace of the spirits. It was long in coming. Hester was nearly a century old, after all, a frail thing who—it was said—had once been a hulk of a man. Boar tusks rode his ears, pierced through the lobes that had stretched over the decades until the curved yellow tusks rested on the man's bony shoulders. Waves of fur tattoos framed Vill's face—there had never been any doubt that Hester Vill was a priest of Fener; that he looked upon the local spirits with amused condescension, though he was ever proper in his observances on behalf of the villagers.

The priest's approaching death was a momentous one for the village. The last acolyte had run off with a month's worth of tithings a few years previously (Deadsmell remembered the little shit—he and Scez had once caught the brat pissing on a high-tier tomb—they'd beaten the boy and had taken pleasure in doing so). Once Vill was gone, the temple would stand abandoned, the spirits unappeased. Someone would have to be found, perhaps even a stranger, a foreigner—word would have to be sent out that Gethran Village was in need.

It was the keeper's task to sit with the one sliding into death, if no family was available, and so the young man had thrown on Old Scez's Greyman's cloak, and taken in one hand his wooden box of herbs, elixirs, knives and brain-scoop, and crossed the graveyard to the refectory attached to one side of the temple.

He could not recall the last time he'd visited Vill's home, but what he found on this night was a chamber transformed. The lone centre hearth raged, casting bizarre, frightening shadows upon all the lime-coated walls—shadows that inscribed nothing visible in the room, but skeletal branches wavering as if rattled by fierce winter winds. Half-paralysed, Hester Vill had dragged himself into his house—refusing anyone else's assistance—and Deadsmell found the old priest lying on the floor beside the cot. He'd not the strength to lift himself to his bed and had been there for most of a day.

Death waited in the hot, dry air, pulsed from the walls and swirled round the high flames. It was drawn close with every wheezing gasp from Vill's wrinkled mouth, feebly pushed away again in shallow, whispery exhalations.

Deadsmell lifted the frail body to the bed, tugged the threadbare blanket over Vill's emaciated form, and he then sat, sweating, feeling half-feverish, staring down at Vill's face. The strike was drawn heavily across the left side of the priest's visage, sagging the withered skin and ropy muscles beneath it, plucking at the lids of the eye.

Trickling water into Vill's gaping mouth did not even trigger a reflex swallow, telling Deadsmell that very little time remained to the man.

The hearth's fire did not abate, and after a time that detail reached through to Deadsmell and he turned to regard the stone-lined pit. He saw no wood at the roots of the flames. Not even glowing dusty coals or embers. Despite the raging heat, a chill crept through him.

Something had arrived, deep inside that conflagration. Was it Fener? He thought that it might be. Hester Vill had been a true priest, an honourable man—insofar as anyone knew—of course his god had come to collect his soul. This was the reward for a lifetime of service and sacrifice.

Of course, the very notion of reward was exclusively human in origin, bound inside precious beliefs in efforts noted, recognized, attributed value. That it was a language understood by the gods was not just given, but incumbent—why else kneel before them?

The god that reached out from the flames to take Vill's breath, however, was not Fener. It was Hood, with taloned hands of dusty green and fingertips stained black with putrescence, and that reach seemed halfhearted, groping as if the Lord of the Slain was blind, reluctant, weary of this pathetic necessity.

Hood's attention brushed Deadsmell's mind, alien in every respect but a deep, almost shapeless sorrow rising like bitter mist from the god's own soul—a sorrow that the young mortal recognized. It was the grief one felt, at times, for the dying when those doing the dying were unknown, were in effect strangers; when their fate was almost abstract. Impersonal grief, a ghost cloak one tried on only to stand motionless, pensive, trying to convince oneself of its weight, and how that weight— when it ceased being ghostly—might feel some time in the future. When death became personal, when one could not shrug out from beneath its weight. When grief ceased being an idea and became an entire world of suffocating darkness.

Cold, alien eyes fixed momentarily upon Deadsmell, and a voice drifted into his skull. '*You thought they cared.*'

'But—he is Fener's very own . . .'

'*There is no bargain when only one side pays attention. There is no contract when only one party sets a seal of blood. I am the harvester of the deluded, mortal.*'

'And this is why you grieve, isn't it? I can feel it—your sorrow—'

'*So you can. Perhaps, then, you are one of my own.*'

'I dress the dead—'

'*Appeasing their delusions, yes. But that does not serve me. I say you are one of my own, but what does that mean? Do not ask me, mortal. I am not one to bargain with. I promise nothing but loss and failure, dust and hungry earth. You are one of my own. We begin a game, you and me. The game of evasion.*'

'I have seen death—it doesn't haunt me.'

'*That is irrelevant. The game is this: steal their lives—snatch them away from my reach. Curse these hands you now see, the nails black with death's touch. Spit into this lifeless breath of mine. Cheat me at every turn. Heed this truth: there is no other form of service as honest as the one I offer you. To do battle against me, you must acknowledge my power. Even as I acknowledge yours. You must respect the fact that I always win, that you cannot help but fail. In turn, I must give to you my respect. For your courage. For the stubborn refusal that is a mortal's greatest strength.*'

'*For all that, mortal, give me a good game.*'

'And what do I get in return? Never mind respect, either. What do I get back?'

'*Only that which you find. Undeniable truths. Unwavering regard of the sorrows that plague a life. The sigh of acceptance. The end of fear.*'

The end of fear. Even for such a young man, such an inexperienced man, Deadsmell understood the value of such a gift. The end of fear.

'Do not be cruel with Hester Vill, I beg you.'

'*I am not one for wilful cruelty, mortal. Yet his soul will feel sorely abused, and for that I can do nothing.*'

'I understand. It is Fener who should be made to answer for that betrayal.'

He sensed wry amusement in Hood. '*One day, even the gods will answer to death.*'

Deadsmell blinked in the sudden gloom as the fire ebbed, flickered, vanished. He peered at Vill and saw that the old man breathed no more. His expression was frozen in a distraught, broken mask. Four black spots had burned his brow.

The world didn't give much. And what it did give it usually took back way too soon. And the hands stung with absence, the eyes that looked out were as hollow as the places they found. Sunlight wept down through drifts of dust, and a man could sit waiting to see his god, when waiting was all he had left.

Deadsmell was kicking through his memories, a task best done in solitude. Drawn to this overgrown, abandoned ruin in the heart of Letheras, with its otherworldly insects, its gaping pits and its root-bound humps of rotted earth, he wandered as if lost. The Lord of Death was reaching into this world once again, swirling a finger through pools of mortal blood. But Deadsmell remained blind to the patterns so inscribed, this intricate elaboration on the old game.

He found that he feared for his god. For Hood, his foe, his friend. The only damned god he respected.

The necromancer's game was one that others could not understand. To them it was the old rat dodging the barn cat, a one-sided hunt bound in mutual hatred. It was nothing like that, of course. Hood didn't despise necromancers—the god knew that no one else truly understood him and his last-of-last worlds. Ducking the black touch, stealing back souls, mocking life with the animation of corpses—they were the vestments of true worship. Because true worship was, in its very essence, a *game*.

" 'There is no bargain when only one side pays attention.' "

Moments after voicing that quote, Deadsmell grunted in sour amusement. Too much irony in saying such a thing to ghosts, especially in a place so crowded with them as here, less than a dozen paces from the gate to the Azath House.

He had learned that Brys Beddict had been slain, once, only to be dragged back. A most bitter gift, it was a wonder the King's brother hadn't gone mad. When a soul leaves the path, a belated return has the fool stumbling again and again. Every step settling awkwardly, as if the imprint of one's own foot no longer fit it, as if the soul no longer matched the vessel of its flesh and bone and was left jarred, displaced.

And now he had heard about a woman cursed undead. Ruthan Gudd had gone so far as to hint that he'd bedded the woman—and how sick was that? Deadsmell shook his head. As bad as sheep, cows, dogs, goats and fat bhokarala. No, even worse. And did she want the curse unravelled? No—at least with that he had to agree. It does no good to come back. One gets used to things staying the same, more used to that than how a living soul felt about its own sagging, decaying body. Besides, the dead never come back all the way. 'It's like knowing the secret to a trick, the wonder goes away. They've lost all the delusions that once comforted them.'

'Deadsmell!'

He turned to see Bottle picking his way round the heaps and holes.

'Heard you saying something—ghosts never got anything good to say, why bother talking with them?'

'I wasn't.'

The young mage reached him and then stood, staring at the old Jaghut tower. 'Did you see the baggage train forming up outside the city? Gods, we've got enough stuff to handle an army five times our size.'

'Maybe, maybe not.'

Bottle grunted. 'That's what Fiddler said.'

'We'll be marching into nowhere. Resupply will be hard to manage, maybe impossible.'

'Into nowhere, that seems about right.'

Deadsmell pointed at the Azath House. 'They went in there, I think.'

'Sinn and Grub?'

'Aye.'

'Something snatch them?'

'I don't think so. I think they went through, the way Kellanved and Dancer learned how to do.'

'Where?'

'No idea, and no, I have no plans to follow them. We have to consider them lost. Permanently.'

Bottle glanced at him. 'You throw that at the Adjunct yet?'

'I did. She wasn't happy.'

'I bet she wasn't.' He scratched at the scraggy beard he seemed intent on growing. 'So tell me why you think they went in there.'

Deadsmell grimaced. 'I remember the day I left my home. A damned ram had got on to the roof of my house—the house I inherited, I mean. A big white bastard, eager to hump anything with legs. The look it gave me was empty and full, if you know what I mean—'

'No. All right, yes. When winter's broken—the season, and those eyes.'

'Empty and full, and from its perch up there it had a damned good view of the graveyard, all three tiers, from paupers to the local version of nobility. I'd just gone and buried the village priest—'

'Hope he was dead when you did it.'

'Some people die looking peaceful. Others die all too knowing. Empty and full. He didn't know until he did his dying, and that kind of face is the worst kind to look down on.' He scowled. 'The worst kind, Bottle.'

'Go on.'

'What have you got to be impatient about, soldier?'

Bottle flinched. 'Sorry. Nothing.'

'Most impatient people I meet are just like that, once you kick through all the attitude. They're in a lather, in a hurry about nothing. The rush is in their heads, and they expect everyone else to up the pace and get the fuck on with it. I got no time for such shits.'

'They make you impatient, do they?'

'No time, I said. Meaning the more they push, the longer I take.'

Bottle flashed a grin. 'I hear you.'

'Good.' Deadsmell paused, working back round to his thoughts. 'That ram, looming up there, well, it just hit me, those eyes. We all got them, I think, some worse than others. For the priest, they came late—but the promise was there, all his life. Same for everyone. You see that it's empty, and that revelation fills you up.'

'Wait—what's empty?'

'The whole Hood-forsaken mess, Bottle. All of it.'

'Well now, aren't you a miserable crudge, Deadsmell.'

'I'll grant you, this particular place eats on me, chews up memories I'd figured were long buried. Anyway, there I was, standing. Ram on one side, the priest's tomb on the other—high ridge, highest I could find—and the highborn locals were going to howl when they saw that. But I didn't care any longer.'

'Because you left that day.'

'Aye. Down to Li Heng, first in line at the recruiting office. A soldier leaves the dead behind and the ones a soldier does bury, well, most of the time they're people that soldier knows.'

'We don't raise battlefield barrows for just our own dead.'

'That's not what I mean by "knowing", Bottle. Ever look down on an enemy's face, a dead one, I mean?'

'A few times, aye.'

'What did you see?'

Bottle shifted uneasily, squinted at the tower again. 'Point taken.'

'No better place to piss on Hood's face than in an army. When piss is all you got, and let's face it, it's all any of us has got.'

'I'm waiting—patiently—to see how all this comes back to Sinn and Grub and the Azath.'

'Last night, I went to the kennels and got out Bent and Roach—the lapdog's the one of them with the real vicious streak, you know. Old Bent, he's just a damned cattle-dog. Pretty simple, straightforward. I mean, you know what he really wants to do is rip out your throat. But no games, right? Not Roach, the simpering fanged demon. Well, I thumped Bent on the head which told him who's boss. Roach gave me a tail wag and then went for my ankle—I had to near strangle it to work its jaws loose from my boot.'

'You collected the dogs.'

'Then I unleashed them both. They shot like siege bolts—up streets, down alleys, round buildings and right through screaming crowds—right up to that door over there. The Azath.'

'How'd you keep up with them?'

'I didn't. I set a geas on them both and just followed that. By the time I got here, Roach had been throwing itself at the door so often it was lying stunned on the path. And Bent was trying to dig through the flagstones.'

'So why didn't any of us think of doing something like that?'

'Because you're all stupid, that's why.'

'What did you do then?' Bottle asked.

'I opened the door. In they went. I heard them racing up the stairs—and then . . . nothing. Silence. The dogs went after Sinn and Grub, through a portal of some sort.'

'You know,' said Bottle, 'if you'd come to me, I could have ridden the souls of one of them, and got maybe an idea of where that portal opened out. But then, since you're a genius, Deadsmell, I'm sure you've got a good reason for not doing that.'

'Hood's breath. All right, so I messed up. Even geniuses can get stupid on occasion.'

'It was Crump who delivered your message—I could barely make any sense of it. You wanted to meet me here, and here I am. But this tale of yours you could have told me over a tankard at Gosling's Tavern.'

'I chose Crump because I knew that as soon as he delivered the message he'd forget all about it. He'd even forget I talked to him, and that he then talked to you. He is, in fact, the thickest man I have ever known.'

'So we meet in secret. How mysterious. What do you want with me, Deadsmell?'

'I want to know about your nightly visitor, to start with. I figured it'd be something best done in private.'

Bottle stared at him.

Deadsmell frowned. 'What?'

'I'm waiting to see the leer.'

'I don't want those kind of details, idiot! Do you ever see her eyes? Do you ever look into them, Bottle?'

'Aye, and every time I wish I didn't.'

'Why?'

'There's so much . . . *need* in them.'

'Is that it? Nothing else?'

'Plenty else, Deadsmell. Pleasure, maybe even love—I don't know. Everything I see in her eyes . . . it's in the "now." I don't know how else to explain it. There's no past, no future, only the present.'

'Empty and full.'

Bottle's gaze narrowed. 'Like the ram, aye, the animal side of her. It freezes me in my tracks, I admit, as if I was looking into a mirror and seeing my own eyes, but in a way no one else can see them. My eyes with . . .' he shivered, 'nobody behind them. Nobody I know.'

'Nobody anyone knows,' Deadsmell said, nodding. 'Bottle, I once looked into Hood's own eyes, and I saw the same thing—I even felt what you just described. Me, but not me. Me, but really, *nobody*. And I think I know what I saw—what you keep seeing in her, as well. I think I finally understand it—those eyes, the empty and full, the solid *absence* in them.' He faced Bottle. 'It's our eyes in death. Our eyes when our souls have fled them.'

Bottle was suddenly pale. 'Gods below, Deadsmell! You just poured cold worms down my spine. That—that's just horrible. Is that what comes of looking into the eyes of too many dead people? Now I know to keep my own eyes averted when I walk a killing field—gods!'

'The ram was full of seed,' said Deadsmell, studying the Azath once more, 'and needed to get it out. Was it the beast's last season? Did it know it? Does it believe it *every* spring? No past and no future. Full and empty. Just that. Always that. For ever that.' He rubbed at his face. 'I'm out of moves, Bottle. I can feel it. I'm out of moves.'

'Listen,' she said, 'me puttin' my finiger—my finger—in there does nothing for me. Don't you get that? Bah!' And she rolled away from him, thinking to swing her feet down and then maybe stand up, but someone had cut the cot down the middle and she thumped on to the filthy floor. 'Ow. I think.'

Skulldeath popped up for a look, his huge liquid woman's eyes gleaming beneath his ragged fringe of inky black hair.

Hellian had a sudden bizarre memory, bizarre in that it reached her at all since few ever did. She'd been a child, only a little drunk (hah hah), stumbling down a grassy bank to a trickling creek, and in the shallows she'd found this slip of a minnow, dead but fresh dead. Taking the limp thing into her hand, she peered down at it. A trout of some kind, a flash of the most stunning red she'd ever seen, and along its tiny back ran a band of dark iridescent green, the colour of wet pine boughs.

Why Skulldeath reminded her of that dead minnow she had no idea. Wasn't the colours, because he wasn't red or even green. Wasn't the deadness because he didn't look very dead, blinking like that. The slippiness? Could be. That liquid glisten, aye, that minnow in the bowl of her hand, in its paltry pool of water wrapping it like a coffin or a cocoon. She remembered now, suddenly, the deep sorrow she'd felt. Young ones struggled so. Lots of them died, sometimes for no good reason. What was the name of that stream? Where the Hood was it?

'Where did I grow up?' she whispered, still lying on the floor. 'Who was I? In a city? Outside a city? Farm? Quarry?'

Skulldeath slithered to the cot's edge and watched her in confused hunger.

Hellian scowled. 'Who am I? Damned if I know. And does it even matter? Gods, I'm sober. Who did that to me?' She glared at Skulldeath. 'You? Bastard!'

'Not bastard,' he said. 'Prince! King in waiting! Me. You . . . you Queen. My Queen. King and Queen, we. Two tribes now together, make one great tribe. I rule. You rule. People kneel and bring gifts.'

She bared her teeth at him. 'Listen, idiot, if I never knelt to nobody in *my* life, there's no way I'll make anybody kneel to *me*, unless,' she added, 'we both got something else in mind. Piss on kings and queens, piss on 'em! All that pomp is pure shit, all that . . .' she scowled, searching for the word, '. . . all that def'rence! Listen! I'll salute an orficer, cos that crap's needed in an army, right? But that's because somebody needs to be in charge. Don't mean they're better. Not purer of blood, not even smarter, you unnerstand me? It's just—between that orficer and me—it's just something we agree between us. We agree to it, right? To make it work! Highborn, they're different. They got expectations. Piss on that! Who says they're better? Don't care how fuckin' rich they are—they can shit gold bricks, it's still shit, right?' She jabbed a finger up at Skulldeath. 'You're a hood-damned soldier and that's all you are. Prince! Hah!' And then she rolled over and threw up.

Cuttle and Fiddler stood watching the row of heavily padded wagons slowly wend through the supply camp to the tree-lined commons where they would be stored, well away from everything else. Dust filled the air above the massive sprawl of tents, carts, pens, and parked wagons, and now as the day was ending, thin grey smoke lifted lazily skyward from countless cookfires.

'Y'know,' said Cuttle, his eyes on the last of the Moranth munitions, 'this is stupid. We done what we could—either they make it or they don't, and even this far away, if they go up, we're probably finished.'

'They'll make it,' said Fiddler.

'Hardly matters, Sergeant. Fourteen cussers for a whole damned army. A hundred sharpers? Two hundred? It's nothing. If we get into trouble out there, it's going to be bad.'

'These Letherii have decent ballistae and onagers, Cuttle. Expensive, but lack of coin doesn't seem to be one of Tavore's shortcomings.' He was silent for a moment, and then he grunted. 'Let's not talk about anyone's shortcomings. Sorry I said it.'

'We got no idea what we're going to find, Fid. But we can all feel it. There's a dread, settling down on all of us like a sky full of ashes. Makes my skin crawl. We crossed Seven Cities. We took on this empire. So what's so different this time?' He shook himself. 'Our landings here, they were pretty much a blind assault—and what information we had was mostly wrong. But it didn't matter. Not knowing ain't enough to drag us down s'far as we been dragged down right now. I don't get it.'

Fiddler scratched at his beard, adjusted the strap beneath his chin. 'Hot and sticky, isn't it? Not dry like Seven Cities. Sucks all the energy away, especially when you're wearing armour.'

'We need that armour to guard against the Hood-damned mosquitoes,' said Cuttle. 'Without it we'd be wrinkled sacks filled with bones. And those bugs carry diseases—the healers been treating twenty soldiers a day who come down with that sweating ague.'

'The mosquitoes are the cause?'

'So I heard.'

'Well then, as soon as we get deeper into the wastelands, we won't have to worry about that any longer.'

'How's that?'

'Mosquitoes need water to breed. Anyway, these local ones, they're small. We hit swarms in Blackdog you'd swear were flocks of hummingbirds.'

Blackdog. Still a name that could send chills through a Malazan soldier, whether they'd been in it or not. Cuttle wondered how a place—a happening now years and years old—could sink into a people, like scars passed from parents to child. Scars, aye, and stains, and the sour taste of horror and misery—was it even possible? Or was it the stories—stories like the one Fiddler just told? Not even a story, was it? Just a detail. Exaggerated, aye, but still a detail. Enough details, muttered here and there, every now and then, and something started clumping up inside, like a ball of wet clay, smearing everything. And before too long, there it is, compacted and hard as a damned rock, perfect to rattle around inside a man's head, knocking about his thoughts and confusing him.

And confusion was what hid behind fear, after all. Every soldier knew it, and knew how deadly it could be, especially in the storm of battle. Confusion led to mistakes, bad judgements, and sure enough, blind panic was the first stinking flower confusion plucked when it was time to dance in the fields.

'Looking way too thoughtful there, sapper,' said Fiddler. 'Bad for your health.'

'Was thinking about dancing in the fields.'

'Hood's breath, it's been years since I heard that phrase. No reason to dredge that up just yet, Cuttle. Besides, the Bonehunters haven't shown any inclination to break and run—'

'I know it makes sense to keep us all dumb and ignorant, Sergeant, but sometimes that can go too far.'

'Our great unknown purpose.'

Cuttle nodded sharply. 'If we're mercenaries now we should be for hire. But we aren't, and even if we were, there's nobody around wants to hire us, is there? And not likely anybody out in the Wastelands or even beyond. And now I caught them rumours of scraps in Bolkando. The Burned Tears, and maybe even the Perish. Now, going in and extricating our allies is a good cause, a decent one—'

'Waves all the right banners.'

'Exactly. But it wouldn't be our reasons for being here in the first place, would it?'

'We kicked down a mad emperor, sapper. And delivered to the Letherii a message about preying on foreign shores—'

'They didn't need it. The Tiste Edur did—'

'And don't you think we humbled them enough, Cuttle?'

'So now what? We're really getting nothing here, Fid, and less than nothing.'

'Give it up,' drawled Fiddler. 'You wasn't invited to the reading. Nothing that happened then was for you—I've already told you so.'

'Plenty for Tavore, though, and hey, look! We just happen to be following her around!'

The last of the wagons reached the makeshift depot, and the oxen were being unhitched. Sighing, Fiddler unclipped his helm and drew it off. 'Let's go look in on Koryk.'

Cuttle frowned as he fell in beside his sergeant. 'Our squad's all over the place these days.'

'Bottle likes wandering off. Nobody else. You can't count Koryk, can you? It's not like he camped out in the infirmary because of the décor.'

'Bottle's your problem, Sergeant. Ducking out of stuff, disappearing for days on end—'

'He's just bored.'

'Who ain't? I just got this feeling we're going to fit badly for a week or two once we start marching.'

Fiddler snorted. 'We've never fit well, Cuttle. You telling me you've never noticed?'

'We done good in that Letherii village—'

'No we didn't. If it wasn't for Hellian's and Gesler's squads—and then Badan Gruk's, why, our fingernails would be riding flower buds right about now, like cute hats. We were all over the place, Cuttle. Koryk and Smiles running off like two lovestruck hares—turned out Corabb was my best fist.'

'You're looking at it bad, Fiddler. All that. Edur were coming in on all sides—we had to split 'em up.'

Fiddler shrugged. 'Maybe so. And granted, we did better in Y'Ghatan. I guess I can't help comparing, 'times. A useless habit, I know—stop looking at me like that, sapper.'

'So you had Hedge and Quick Ben. And that assassin—what was his name again?'

'Kalam.'

'Aye, that boar with knives. Stupid, him getting killed in Malaz City. Anyway, my point is—'

'We had a Barghast for a squad fist, and then there was Sorry—never mind her—and Whiskeyjack and Hood knows, I'm no Whiskeyjack.' Noticing that Cuttle was laughing, Fiddler's scowl deepened. 'What's so damned funny?'

'Only that it sounds like your old Bridgeburner squad was probably just as bad fitting as this one is. Maybe even worse. Look. Corabb's a solid fist, with the Lady's hand down the front of his trousers; and if he drops then Tarr steps in, and if Tarr goes, then Koryk. You had Sorry—we got Smiles.'

'And instead of Hedge,' said Fiddler, 'I got you, which is a damned improvement, come to think on it.'

'I can't sap the way he can—'

'Gods, I'm thankful for that.'

Cuttle squinted at his sergeant as they approached the enormous hospital tent. 'You really got something to pick with Hedge, don't you? The legend goes that you two were close, as nasty in your own way as Quick Ben and Kalam. What happened between you two?'

'When a friend dies you got to put them away, and that's what I did.'

'Only he's back.'

'Back and yet, not back. I can't say it any better.'

'So, if it can't be what it was, make it something new.'

'It's worse than you think. I see his face, and I think about all the people now dead. Our friends. All dead now. It was—I hate saying this—it was easier when it was just me. Even Quick Ben and Kalam showing up sort've left me out of sorts—but we were all the survivors, right? The ones who made it through, to that point. It was natural, I guess, and that was good enough. Now there's still Quick but the Adjunct's got him and that's fine. It was back to me, you understand? Back to just me.'

'Until Hedge shows up.'

'Comes down to what fits and what's supposed to fit, I suppose.' They had paused outside the tent entrance. Fiddler scratched at his sweaty, thinning hair. 'Maybe in time . . .'

'Aye, that's how I'd see it. In time.'

They entered the ward.

Cots creaked and trembled with soldiers rattling about beneath sodden woollen blankets, soldiers delirious and soaked in sweat as they thrashed and shivered. Cutters stumbled from bed to bed with dripping cloths. The air stank of urine.

'Hood's breath!' hissed Cuttle. 'It's looking pretty bad, ain't it?'

There were at least two hundred cots, each and every one occupied by a gnat-bit victim. The drenched cloths, Cuttle saw, were being pushed against mouths in an effort to get some water into the stricken soldiers.

Fiddler pointed. 'There. No, don't bother, he wouldn't even recognize us right now.' He reached out and snagged a passing cutter. 'Where's our Denul healers?'

'The last one collapsed this morning. Exhaustion, Sergeant. All worn out—now, I got to keep getting water in 'em, all right?'

Fiddler let go of the man's arm.

They retreated outside once more. 'Let's go find Brys Beddict.'

'He's no healer, Sergeant—'

'I know that, idiot. But, did you see any Letherii carters or support staff lying on cots in there?'

'No—'

'Meaning there must be a local treatment against this ague.'

'Sometimes local people are immune to most of what can get at 'em, Fid—'

'That's rubbish. What can get at them kills most of them so us foreigners don't ever see them in the first place. And most of the time it's the usual sources of contagion—leaking latrines, standing water, spoiled foods.'

'Oh. So how come you know so much about all that?'

'Before Moranth munitions, Cuttle, us sappers did a lot of rebuilding work, following occupations. Built sewage systems, dug deep wells, cold-pits—made the people we were killing a month before into smiling happy healthy citizens of the Malazan Empire. I'm surprised you didn't do any of that yourself.'

'I did, but I could never figure out why we was doing it in the first place.'

Fiddler halted. 'What you said earlier about not knowing anything . . .'

'Aye?'

'Has it ever occurred to you, Cuttle, that maybe not knowing anything has more to do with you than with anyone else?'

'No.'

Fiddler stared at Cuttle, who stared back, and then they continued on, in search of Brys Beddict.

The Malazan army was slowly decamping from the city, squads and half-squads trickling in to the company forts that now occupied what had once been killing fields. A lot of soldiers, after a few nights in the tents, were falling sick—like Koryk—and had to be carted off to the hospital compound set up between the army and the baggage camp.

The war-games were over, but they'd done their damage. So many soldiers had found ways out of them, ended up scattered all over the city, that the army's cohesion—already weakened by the invasion where the marines saw most of the messy work—was in a bad state.

Sitting on a camp stool outside the squad tent, Corporal Tarr uncoiled another reach of iron wire and, using an ingenious clipper some Malazan blacksmith had invented a few decades back, began cutting it into short lengths. Chain armour took a lot of work to maintain. He could have sent it off to the armourers but he preferred doing his own repairs, not that he didn't trust—well, aye, he didn't trust the bastards, especially when harried and overworked as they were these days. No, he'd use the tugger to wrap the length round a spar, shuck it off and close up the gaps one by one. Used to be they'd work a longer length, coiled right up the spar, and then swirl-cut across all the links, but that ruined whatever blade was used to do the cutting, and files made the gaps too wide and left ragged edges that cut an underpad to ribbons. Miserable, frustrating work. No, this was easier, working each link, pinching the gaps to check that the crimping hadn't left any spurs, and then using the tugger to fix each link in place. And then—

'Your obsessions drive me mad, Tarr, did you know that?'

'Go find something to do, Smiles. And you keep forgetting, I'm your corporal.'

'Proving just how messed-up the command structure's got to.'

'Bleat that to the sergeant, why don't you?'

'Where's Corabb gone?'

Tarr shrugged, adjusting the chain hauberk draped across his thighs. 'Went off to requisition a new weapon.'

'He lost another one?'

'Broke it, actually, and before you ask, I'm not telling you how.'

'Why not?'

Tarr said nothing for a moment, and then he looked up to see Smiles scowling down at him, her hands anchored on her hips. 'What shape's your kit in, soldier?'

'It's fine.'

'Restocked on quarrels?'

'Got one with your name on it. Got plenty others besides.'

Corabb Bhilan Thenu'alas was coming up the track, his gait peculiar, each step cautious—as if he was testing thin ice—and pitched slightly to the outside, as if he were straddling a barrel. Slung over one shoulder was a Letherii-made longsword in a scabbard still caked in burlap-patterned wax. Tucked under an arm was a feather-stuffed pillow.

Arriving at the cookfire, he set the pillow down on a stool and then gingerly settled on to it.

'What the Hood did you do?' Smiles demanded. 'Pick your hole with it?'

Corabb scowled. 'It's personal.' He brought his new sword round and set it across his thighs, and in his face was an expression Tarr had seen only on the faces of children on the Queen of Dreams's Gift-Day, a brightness, flushed, eyes eager to see what waited beneath the dyed snakeskin wrappings.

'It's just a sword, Corabb,' said Smiles. 'Really.'

Tarr saw that wondrous expression in Corabb's face fall away suddenly, slapped back into hiding. The corporal fixed hard eyes on Smiles. 'Soldier, go fill up enough travel sacks for each one of us in the squad. You'll need to requisition a mule and cart, unless you're planning on more than one trip.'

She bridled. 'Why me?'

Because you cut people out of boredom. 'Just get out of my sight. Now.'

'Ain't you the friendly one,' she muttered, setting off.

Tarr set down his tools. 'Letherii? Well, Corabb, let's see the thing, shall we?'

And the man's eyes lit up.

They had days before the official mustering for the march. Tarr's orders were premature. And if she was corporal, she'd have known that and not made her go off for no good reason. Why, if she was corporal, she'd dump stupid tasks all over Tarr every time he irritated her, which would probably be all the time. Anyway, she decided she'd let herself be distracted, maybe until late tonight. Tarr was in the habit of bedding down early.

If Koryk weren't sweating like a fish-trader in a soak-hole, she'd have some decent company right now. Instead, she wandered towards a huddle of heavies gathered round some sort of game. The usual crowd, she saw. Mayfly and Tulip, Flashwit, Shortnose, Saltlick, and some from a different company that she remembered from that village scrap—Drawfirst, Lookback and Vastly Blank. Threading through the smelly press, she made her way to the edge of the ring.

No game. A huge bootprint in the dust. 'What's going on?' Smiles demanded. 'It's a footprint, for Hood's sake!'

Huge faces peered at her from all sides, and then Mayfly said, in a tone of stunned reverence, 'It's from *him*.'

'Who?'

'Him, like she said,' said Shortnose.

Smiles looked back down at the print. 'Really? Not a chance. How can you tell?'

Flashwit wiped at her nose—which had been dripping ever since they arrived on this continent. 'It ain't none of ours. See that heel? That's a marine heel, them iron studs in a half ring like that.'

Smiles snorted. 'You idiots. Half the army wears those!' She looked round. 'Gods below, you're all wearing those!'

'Exactly,' said Flashwit.

And everyone nodded.

'So, let's just follow the tracks and get a real good look at him, then.'

'We thought of that,' said Shortnose. 'Only there's only the one, see?'

'What do you mean? One print? Just one? But that's ridiculous! You must've scuffed up the others—'

'No,' said Lookback, thick fingers twisting greasy hair beside a cabbage ear. 'I was the first to come on it, right, and it was all alone. Just like that. All alone. Who else coulda done something like that, but *him*?'

'You're all idiots. I don't think Nefarias Bredd even exists.'

'That's because you're stupid!' shouted Vastly Blank. 'You're a stupid, a stupid, uh, a stupid, you're just stupid. And I don't like you. Drawfirst, that's right, isn't it? I don't like her, do I? Do I?'

'Do you know her, Vastly? Know who she is?'

'No, Drawfirst. I don't. Not even that.'

'Well, then it's got to be you don't like her, then. It's got to be. You're right, Vastly.'

'I knew it.'

'Listen,' said Smiles, 'who wants to play bones?'

'With what?' Mayfly asked.

'With bones, of course!'

'We ain't got none.'

'But I do.'

'You do what?'

Smiles gave everyone a bright, happy smile, and even that made her face hurt. She drew out a small leather pouch. 'Lay your bets down, soldiers, and let's have us a game. Now listen carefully while I explain the rules—'

'We know the rules,' said Shortnose.

'Not my rules you don't. Mine are different.' She scanned the suddenly interested faces and all those tiny eyes fixed on her. 'Listen now, and listen carefully, because they're kind of complicated. Vastly, you come stand beside me, right here, the way best friends do, right?'

Vastly Blank nodded. 'Right!' And, chest swelling, he pushed through the others.

'A word with you, Lieutenant.'

Pores snapped to his feet. 'Aye, sir!'

'Follow me.' Captain Kindly walked sharply out from the headquarters, and soldiers busy packing equipment ducked desperately out of the man's path, furtive as cats underfoot. There was a certain carelessness when it came to getting out of Lieutenant Pores's way, however, forcing him to kick a few shins as he hastened after the captain.

They emerged into the parade square and halted before a ragged row of what looked like civilians with nowhere to go but up, an even dozen in all. Seeing the two at the far end, Pores's spirits sank.

'I am promoting you sideways,' Kindly said to him. 'Master Sergeant.'

'Thank you, sir.'

'I do this out of recognition of your true talents, Master Sergeant Pores, in the area of recruiting from the local population.'

'Ah, sir, I assure you again that I had nothing to do with those two whores'—

and he gestured at the pair of immensely obese women at the end of the row—
'showing up unannounced in your office.'

'Your modesty impresses me, Master Sergeant. As you can see now, however,
what we have before us here are Letherii recruits. Indebted, mostly, and, as you
observed, two now retired from a most noble and altruistic profession.' His tone
hardened. 'And as every Malazan soldier knows, a life before joining the ranks
has no bearing once the vows are sworn and the kit is issued. There exist no barriers to advancement beyond competence—'

'And sometimes not even that, sir.'

'Even confessions are insufficient cause to interrupt me, Master Sergeant.
Now, these venerable recruits belong to you. Kit them out and then take them
for a long hike—they clearly need to be worked into fighting trim. We march in
two days, Master Sergeant.'

'Fighting trim in just two days, sir?'

'Your recruits rely upon your competence, as do I,' said Kindly, looking nau-
seatingly satisfied. 'Might I suggest that your first task lies in sobering them up.
Now, I leave you to it, Master Sergeant.'

'Thank you, sir.' And he saluted.

Captain Kindly marched back into the headquarters.

Pores stared after him. 'This,' he whispered, 'is war.'

The nearest recruit, a scrawny man of forty or so with a huge stained moustache, suddenly brightened. 'Can't wait, sir!'

Pores wheeled on him. 'I'm no "sir", dung beetle! I am Master Sergeant!'

'Sorry, Master Sergeant!'

'You don't think, I trust, that my sideways promotion is not a bold announce-
ment of Captain Kindly's confidence in me?'

'Absolutely not, Master Sergeant!'

Pores strode down to the far end of the row and glared at the two whores.
'Gods below, what are you two doing here?'

The blonde one, her face glowing in the manner of overweight people the world
over, when made to stand for any length of time, belched and said, 'Master Sergeant, look at us!'

'I am looking.'

'We ain't had no luck cuttin' the lard, y'see. But in a army, well, we got no
choice, do we?'

'You're both drunk.'

'We give up that, too,' said the black-haired one.

'And the whoring?'

'Aw, Master Sergeant, leave us a little fun!'

'You're both standing here out of breath—kitting you out and running you
will kill you both.'

'We don't mind, Master Sergeant. Whatever works!'

'Tell me the name of the soldier who hired you to visit the captain.'

The women exchanged sly looks, and then the blonde said, 'Never gave it
to us.'

'Man or woman?'

'Never said either way, Master Sergeant.'

'It was dark that day,' added the black-haired woman. 'Anyway, Big Kindly said—'

'I'm sorry, what did you say?'

'Oh, uhm. Captain Kindly is what I meant, now that he's back in uniform, I mean—'

'And it's a nice uniform,' chimed in the blonde.

'And he said that you was the best and the hardest working, most fit, like, and healthy soldier in the whole Miserable Army—'

'That's *Malazan* Army.'

'Right. Sorry, Master Sergeant, it's all the foreign names done us in.'

'And the jug of rum, I'd wager.'

She nodded. 'And the jugs of rum.'

At the plural Pores's two eyes found a pernicious will of their own, and fell slightly down from the woman's face. He coughed and turned to study all the other recruits. 'Running from debt I understand,' he said. 'Same for armies the world over. Indebted, criminal, misfit, pervert, patriot and insane, and that list's from my very own military application. And look at me, promoted up to Lieutenant and sideways to Master Sergeant. So, dear recruits,' and Pores slapped on a broad smile, which was answered by everyone in the line, 'nobody knows better where you're coming from, and nobody knows better where you're going to end up, which is probably in either the infirmary or the stockade. And I mean to get you there in no time flat!'

'Yes, Master Sergeant!' shouted the moustached idiot.

Pores stamped up to the man, whose grin suddenly wavered. 'In the Malazan Army,' he said, 'old names are tossed. They were bad names anyway, every one of them. You, you are now Twit, and you're my first squad leader.'

'Yes, Master Sergeant! Thank you, Master Sergeant!'

'Now,' Pores continued, hands behind his back as he began strolling up and down the row, 'two days to turn you earwigs into soldiers—even for me—is simply impossible. No, what I need to do is attach you to a real squad, and I have the perfect squad in mind.' And then he halted and wheeled to face them. 'But first, we're all going to march to the privy, where each and every one of you is going to—in perfect unison as befits soldiers—shove a finger down your throat and vomit into the trough. And then we're going to collect uniforms from the quartermaster, and your training kits. Now, Sergeant Twit, fall 'em in behind you and follow me.'

'Yes, Master Sergeant! We're off to war!'

And the others cheered.

The cookfires were coal-bedded and simmering pots hung over them by the time Master Sergeant Pores led his sickly, gasping crew up to the squad tents of the 3rd Company. 'Third Company Sergeants!' he bellowed. 'Front and forward this instant!'

Watched by a score of faces half-lit by firelight, Badan Gruk, Sinter, and Primly slowly converged to stand in front of Pores.

'I am Master Sergeant Pores and this—'

'Thought you was Captain Kindly,' said Sinter.

'No, that would be my twin, who sadly drowned in a bucket of his own puke yesterday. Interrupt me again, Sergeant, and I've got a whole trough of puke waiting just for you.'

Badan Gruk grunted. 'But I thought he was Lieutenant Pores—'

Pores scowled at him. 'My other twin, now detached from the Bonehunters and serving as bodyguard and consort to Queen Frapalava of the Kidgestool Empire. Now, enough yabbering. As you can see behind me, we have new recruits who need to be ready to march in two days—'

'March where, Master Sergeant?'

Pores sighed. 'Why, with the rest of us, Sergeant Sinter. In fact, right beside your three squads, as they are now your responsibilities.' He turned and gestured at his row. Two recruits stepped out on cue. 'Acting Sergeants Twit and Nose Stream.' He gestured again and two more emerged. 'Acting Corporals Rumjugs and Sweetlard— I suggest Corporal Kisswhere take them under her personal care. Now, you will note that they've brought tents. Unfortunately, none of the recruits know how to put them up. Get them to it. Any questions? Good. Dismissed.'

A short time later, Pores sighted one of the newer tents in the camp and, after eyeing the three soldiers squatting round the nearest cookfire, he drew himself up and marched up to them.

'Soldiers—at ease. Is there a partition at the back of that tent? I thought so.'

'Sergeant Urb's commandeered that bit, Lieutenant—'

'Commendable. Alas, my friends—and I know this is miserable news—but Captain Kindly is now requisitioning it on my behalf. I argued against it—I mean, the injustice of such a thing, but, well, you all know about Captain Kindly, don't you?' And he was pleased to see the sullen nods. Pores patted a satchel at his hip. 'Supply lists—I need somewhere private, and now that the HQ's been shut down, well, you're to provide me with my office. But listen, friends—and be sure to tell this to Sergeant Urb—since I'm working on supplies, materiel and—did I mention?— foodstuffs for the officers, which of course includes wines of passing vintage—well, even one as perfect as me can't help but lose a crate or two from the inventory.' And see how they smiled.

'All yours, Lieutenant.'

'Excellent. Now, be sure not to disturb me.'

'Aye, Lieutenant.'

Pores made his way in, stepping over the bedrolls and kits, and through the curtain where he found a decent camp cot, clean blankets and a well-maintained pillow. Kicking his boots off, he settled down on the cot, turned the lantern down, and drew out from his satchel the first of the five flasks he'd confiscated from his recruits.

One could learn a lot about a man or woman by their alcohol or drug of choice. Time to look more closely at the Bonehunters' latest members, maybe work up something like a profile of their gumption. He tugged loose the first stopper.

'He made us puke,' said Rumjugs.

'He makes all of us do that,' Kisswhere replied. 'Now, angle that peg out a bit before your sister starts pounding it.'

'She ain't my sister.'

'Yes she is. We all are, now. That's what being a soldier is all about. Sisters, brothers.'

Sweetlard hefted the wooden mallet. 'So the officers, they're like, parents?'

'Depends.'

'On what?'

'Well, if your parents were demented, deluded, corrupt, useless or sadistic, or any combination of those, then yes, officers are just like them.'

'That's not always so,' said Corporal Pravalak Rim, arriving with a bundle of groundsheets. 'Some officers know what they're about.'

'It's got nothing to do with knowing what they're about, Rim,' said Kisswhere.

'You're right, Kiss, it comes down to do you take their orders when things get nasty? That's what it comes down to.' He dropped two of the rolled-up canvas sheets. 'Put these inside, laid out nice and flat. Oh, and check out if there's any slope in the ground—you want your heads higher than your feet or your dreams will get wild and you'll wake up with an exploding headache—'

'They're going to do that anyway,' observed Kisswhere. 'Can't you smell 'em?'

Rim scowled and pulled the mallet from Sweetlard's hands. 'You lost your mind, Kiss? She swings this and she'll crush the other one's hands.'

'Well, but then, one less dragging us down on the march.'

'You can't be serious.'

'Not really. So I wasn't thinking. I'm no good being in charge of people. Here, you take over. I'm going into the city to drag Skulldeath back out here, out of Hellian's clutches, I mean.'

As she walked off, Rumjugs licked her plump lips. 'Corporal Rim?'

'Aye?'

'You got a soldier in your squad named Skulldeath?'

Rim smiled. 'Oh yeah, and wait till you meet him.'

'I don't like the name he gave me,' muttered Twit. 'I mean, I tried looking at all this in the right spirit, you know? So it feels less like a death sentence. Made myself look all eager, and what does he do? He calls me Twit.'

Ruffle patted him on an arm. 'Don't like your name? That's fine. Next time Captain Lieutenant Master Sergeant Kindly Pores comes by, we'll tell him that Sergeant Twit drowned in a sop bucket, but his brother showed up and his name is . . . well? What name do you want?'

Twit frowned. He scratched his head. He stroked his moustache. He squinted. He shrugged. 'I have t'think on it, I think.'

Ruffle smiled sweetly. 'Let's see if I can help you some. You an Indebted?'

'I am. And it wasn't fair at all, Ruffle. I was doing fine, you see, living good, even. Had a pretty wife who I always figured was on the thick side, thicker than me, I mean, which was perfect, since it put me in charge and I like being in charge—'

'Don't let anybody know that. Not here.'

'Oh, so I already messed up, then.'

'No you didn't. That was your drowned brother.'

'What? By the Errant he's drowned—but, how did you hear about that? Hold on, wait! Oh, I get it. Right. Hah, that's perfect.'

'So you was doing fine.'

'Huh? Yes, that's just it. I was doing good. In fact, business was good enough so that I made some investments—first time in my life, some real investments. Construction. Not my area, but—'

'Which was? Your area, I mean?'

'Made and sold oil lamps, the big temple ones. Mostly bronze or copper, sometimes glazed clay.'

'And then you invested in the building trade.'

'And it all went down. Just before you all arrived. All went down. I lost everything. And my wife, why, she told me she'd only been waiting around until somebody better and richer showed up. So off she went, too.' He wiped at his face. 'Thought about killing myself, but I couldn't figure out the best way. And then it hit me—join the army! But not the Letherii army, since the new King's not looking to start any wars, is he? Besides, I'd probably get stationed here in the city and there I'd be, seeing all the people I once knew and thought my friends, and they'd be pretending I wasn't even there. And then I heard you Malazans was marching into a war—'

'Really? First I've heard of that.'

'Well, something like that. The thing was, it hit me then that maybe it wasn't a place to just up and get myself killed. No, it was a place where I could start over. Only'—and he pounded his thigh—'first thing I do is mess up. Some new beginning!'

'You're fine,' said Ruffle, grunting softly as she climbed to her feet. 'Twit was the one who messed up, right?'

'What? Oh, that's right!'

'I think maybe I come up with a new name for you,' she said, looking down at him where he squatted behind his bundled kit. 'How does Sunrise sound to you?'

'Sunrise?'

'Aye. Sergeant Sunrise. New beginnings, just like dawn breaking on the horizon. And every time you hear it out loud, you'll be reminded of how you've begun again. Fresh. No debts, no disloyal friends, no cut-and-run wives.'

He suddenly straightened and impulsively hugged her. 'Thanks, Ruffle. I won't forget this. I mean it. I won't.'

'That's nice. Now, spill out your bowl and spoon. Supper beckons.'

They found Brys Beddict standing on one of the canal bridges, the one closest to the river. He was leaning on the stone railing, eyes on the water flowing beneath the span.

Cuttle tugged on Fiddler's arm as they were about to step on to the bridge. 'What's he doing?' he whispered. 'Looks like—'

'I know what it looks like,' Fiddler replied, grimacing. 'But I don't think it's that. Come on.'

Brys glanced over as they approached, and straightened. 'Good evening to you, soldiers.'

'Commander Beddict,' said Fiddler, nodding. 'We've got ourselves a problem out in the camp, sir. That sweating ague, from the mosquitoes—got people falling ill everywhere, and our healers are dropping from exhaustion and making no headway.'

'The Shivers, we call it,' said Brys. 'There's a well, an imperial well, about half a league north of your camp. The water is drawn up by a sort of pump based on a mill. One of Bugg's inventions. In any case, that water is filled with bubbles and rather tart to the taste, and it is the local treatment for the Shivers. I will dispatch teams to deliver casks to your camp. How many of your fellow soldiers have sickened?'

'Two, maybe three hundred. With more every day, sir.'

'We'll start with five hundred casks—you need to get everyone drinking from them, as it may also possess some preventative properties, although no one has been able to prove that. I will also dispatch our military healers to assist your own.'

'Thank you, sir. It's been our experience that most of the time it's the locals who get sick when foreigners arrive from across the seas. This time it's proved the other way round.'

Brys nodded. 'I gather that the Malazan Empire was predicated on expansion, the conquering of distant territories.'

'Just a bit more rabid than your own Letherii expansion, sir.'

'Yes. We proceeded on the principle of creep and crawl—that's how our brother Hull described it, anyway. Spreading like a slow stain, until someone in the beleaguered tribe stood up and took notice of just what was happening, and then there'd be war. A war we justified at that point by claiming we were simply protecting our pioneering citizens, our economic interests, our need for security.' His smile was sour. 'The usual lies.'

Fiddler leaned on the railing beside Brys, and after a moment Cuttle did the same. 'I remember a landing on one of the more remote of the Strike Islands. We weren't assaulting, just making contact—the big island had capitulated by then. Anyway, the locals could muster about two hundred warriors, and there they were, looking out on a fleet of transports groaning with five thousand hardened marines. The old Emperor preferred to win without bloodshed, when he could. Besides, all of us, standing at the rails—sort of like we're doing right now—well, we just pitied them.'

'What happened?' Cuttle asked.

'The local chief gathered together a heap of trinkets on the beach, basically making himself look rich while at the same time buying our goodwill. It was a brave gesture, because it impoverished him. I don't think he was expecting any reciprocal gesture from Admiral Nok. He just wanted us to take it and then go away.' Fiddler paused, scratching at his beard, remembering those times. Neither Brys nor Cuttle prodded him to resume, but, with a sigh, he went on. 'Nok had his orders. He accepts the gift. And then has us deliver on to that beach a golden throne for the chief, and enough silks, linens and wool to clothe every living person on that island— he gave the chief enough to turn around and be generous to his people. I still remember his face, the look on it . . .' When he wiped at his eyes, only Brys held his gaze on Fiddler. Cuttle looked away, as if embarrassed.

'That was a fine thing to do,' said Brys.

'Seemed that way. Until the locals started getting sick. Something in the wool, maybe. Fleas, a contagion. We didn't even find out, not for days—we stayed away, giving the chief time and all that, and the village was mostly behind a fringe of thick mangroves. And then, one afternoon, a lookout spied a lone villager, a girl, staggering out on to the beach. She was covered in sores—that sweet, once smooth skin—' He stopped, shoulders hunching. 'Nok moved fast. He threw every Denul healer we had on to that island. We saved about two-thirds of them. But not the chief. To this day, I wonder what he thought as he lay dying—if an instant of calm spread out to flatten the storm of his fever, a single instant, when he thought that he had been betrayed, deliberately poisoned. I wondered if he cursed us all with his last breath. Had I been him, I know I would have. Whether we meant to or not—I mean, our intentions didn't mean a damned thing. Offered no absolution. They rang hollow then and they still do.'

After a long moment, Brys returned his attention to the canal waters below. 'This all flows out to the river, and the river into the sea, and out in the sea, the silts collected back here end up raining down to the bottom, down on to the valleys and plains that know no light. Sometimes,' he added, 'souls take the same journey, and they rain down, silent, blind. Lost.'

'You two keep this up,' Cuttle said in a growl, 'and I'll do the jumping.'

Fiddler snorted. 'Sapper, listen to me. It's easy to listen and even easier to hear wrongly, so pay attention. I'm no wise man, but in my life I've learned that knowing something—seeing it clearly—offers no real excuse for giving up on it. And when you put what you see into words, give 'em to somebody else, that ain't no invitation neither. Being optimistic's worthless if it means ignoring the suffering of this world. Worse than worthless. It's bloody evil. And being pessimistic, well, that's just the first step on the path, and it's a path that might take you down Hood's road, or it takes you to a place where you can settle into doing what you can, hold fast in your fight against that suffering. And that's an honest place, Cuttle.'

'It's the place, Fiddler,' said Brys, 'where heroes are found.'

But the sergeant shook his head. 'That don't matter one way or the other. It might end up being as dark as the deepest valley at the bottom of your ocean, Commander Beddict. You do what you do, because seeing true doesn't always arrive in a burst of light. Sometimes what you see is black as a pit, and it just fools you into thinking that you're blind. You're not. You're the opposite of blind.' And he stopped then, as he saw that he'd made both hands into fists, the knuckles pale blooms in the gathering night.

Brys Beddict stirred. 'I will see the crews sent out to the imperial well tonight, and I will roust my healers at once.' He paused, and then added, 'Sergeant Fiddler. Thank you.'

But Fiddler could find nothing to be thanked for. Not in his memories, not in the words he had spoken to these two men.

When Brys had left, he swung round to Cuttle. 'There you have it, soldier. Now maybe you'll stop worshipping the Hood-damned ground I walk on.' And then he marched off.

Cuttle stared after him, and then, with a faint shake of his head, followed his sergeant.

Chapter Ten

Is there anything more worthless than excuses?

EMPEROR KELLANVED

It was the task of a pregnant woman's sister or, if there were none, the nearest woman by blood, to fashion from clay a small figurine, its form a composite of spheres, and to hold it in waiting for the child's birth. Bathed in the blood and fluids of the issue, the human-shaped vessel was then ritually bound to the newborn, and that binding would remain until death.

Fire was the Brother and Husband Life-Giver of the Elan, the spirit-god with its precious gifts of light, warmth and protection. Upon dying, the Elan's figurine—now the sole haven of his or her soul—was carried to the flames of the family hearth. The vessel, in its making, had been left faceless, because fire greeted every soul in the same manner; when choosing, it favoured not by blunt features—which were ever a mask to truth—but upon the weighing of a life's deeds. When the clay figurine—born of Water, Sister and Wife Life-Giver—finally shattered in the heat, thus conjoining the spirit-gods, the soul was embraced by the Life-Giver, now the Life-Taker. If the figurine did not break, then the soul had been rejected, and no one would ever again touch that scorched vessel. Mourning would cease. All memory of the fallen would be expunged.

Kalyth had lost her figurine—a crime so vast that she should have died of shame long ago. It was lying somewhere, half-buried in grasses, perhaps, or swallowed up beneath drifts of dust or ashes. It was probably broken, the binding snapped—and so her soul would find no haven when she died. Malign spirits would close in on her and devour her piece by piece. There would be no refuge. No judgement by the Life-Giver.

Her people, she had since realized, had possessed grand notions of their own importance. But then, she was sure it was the same for every people, every tribe, every nation. An elevation of self, blistering in its conceit. Believers in their own immortality, their own eternal abiding, until came the moment of sudden, crushing revelation. Seeing the end of one's own people. Identity crumbling, language and belief and comfort withering away. Mortality arriving like a knife to the heart. A moment of humbling, the anguish of humility, all the truths once thought unassailable now proved to be fragile delusions.

Kneeling in the dust. Sinking still lower. Lying prostrate in that dust, pallid taste on the tongue, a smell of desiccated decay stinging the nostrils. Was it any wonder that all manner of beasts enacted the mission of surrender by lying prone on the ground, in a posture of vulnerability, beseeching mercy from a merciless nature: the throat-bared submission to knives and fangs dancing with the sun's light? Playing out the act of the victim—she recalled once seeing a bull bhederin, javelin-pierced half a dozen times, the shafts clattering and trailing, the enormous creature fighting to remain standing. As if to stand was all that mattered, all that defined it as being still alive, as being worthy of life, and in its red-rimmed eyes such stubborn defiance. It knew that as soon as it fell, its life was over.

And so it stood, weeping blood, on a crest of land, encircled by hunters who understood enough to keep their distance, to simply wait, but it refused them, refused the inevitable, for an extraordinary length of time—the hunters would tell this tale often round the flickering flames, they would leap upright to mimic its wounded defiance, wide of stance, shoulders hunched, eyes glaring.

Half a day, and then the evening, and come the next dawn and there the beast remained, upright but finally, at last, lifeless.

There was triumph in that beast's struggle, something that made its death almost irrelevant, a desultory, diminished arrival—no capering glee this time.

She thought she might weep now, for that bhederin, for the power of its soul so cruelly drained from its proud flesh. Even the hunters had been silent, crowding close in the chill dawn light to reach out and touch that matted hide; and the gaggle of children who waited to help with the butchering, why, like Kalyth herself, they sat round-eyed, strangely frightened, maybe a little stained with guilt, too, come to that. Or, more likely, Kalyth was alone in feeling that sentiment— or had she felt it at all? Was it not more probable that this guilt, this shame, belonged to her now—decades and decades later? And, in fact, that the beast had come to symbolize something else, something new and exclusively her own?

The death of a people.

And still she stood.

Still she stood.

Yet at this moment they were all sunk down into the grasses, up against boulders, and her face was pressed to the ground, smelling dust and her own sweat. The K'Chain Che'Malle seemed to have virtually vanished. Motionless, reminding her of coiled serpents or lizards basking on flat rocks, their hides growing mottled to mimic their immediate surroundings.

They were all hiding.

From what? What on this useless, lifeless ruin of a landscape could drive them to such caution?

Nothing. Nothing on the land at all. No . . . *we are hiding from clouds.*

Clouds, a dozen thunderheads arrayed in a row on the horizon to the southwest, five or more leagues distant.

Kalyth did not understand. So vast was her incomprehension that she could not even conjure any questions for her companions, nothing to send skirling up from her pit of fears and anxieties. What she could see of those distant storms told her of lightning, hail and walls of impenetrable dust—but the front edged no closer, not in all this time of waiting, of hiding. She felt broken by her own ignorance.

Clouds.

She wondered if the winged Assassin drifted somewhere high overhead. Exposed, vulnerable to rushing winds—but down here, the calm was uncanny. The very air seemed to be cowering, breath held, and even the insects had taken to the ground.

The earth trembled beneath her, a sudden barrage rolling in waves. She could not be certain if she was hearing that thunder, or simply feeling it. The shock set her heart hammering—she had never before heard such unceasing violence. Prairie storms were swift runners, knots of rage racing across the landscape, flattening grasses and hide tents, whipping flaring embers into the air, buffeting the humped walls of yurts. The howl rose to a shriek, and then died as quickly as it had come, and outside the lumps of hail glistened grey in the strange light as they melted. The storms of her memory were nothing like this, and the metallic taste of fear bit down on her tongue.

The K'Chain Che'Malle, her terrifying guardians, clung to the ground like rush-beaten curs.

And the thunder shook the earth again and again. Teeth clenched, Kalyth forced herself to tilt up her head. Dust had lifted like mists over the land. Through the brown veil she could make out incessant argent flashes beneath the bruised storm front, but the clouds themselves remained dark, like blind motes staining her eyes. Where were the spikes of lightning? Every blossom seemed to erupt from the ground, and now she could see the sickly glow of fires—the blasted plain was alight.

Gasping, Kalyth buried her head in her arms. A part of her sank back, like a bemused, faintly disgusted witness, as the rest of her trembled in terror—were these feelings her own? Or waves emanating from the K'Chain Che'Malle, from Gunth Mach and Sag'Churok and the others? But no, it was more likely that she was but witness to simple caution, bizarre, yes, and extreme—but they did not shiver or claw at the ground, did they? They were so still they might have been dead. As perfect in their repose as she—

Taloned hands snatched her up. She shrieked—the K'Chain Che'Malle were suddenly running, low, faster than she had thought possible—and she hung in the grip of Gunth Mach like a bhederin flank torn from a kill.

They fled the storm. North and east. For Kalyth, a blurred passage, nightmarish in her helplessness. Tufts of yellow grass spun past like tumbled balls of dull fire. Sweeps of bedded cobbles, sinkholes of water-worn gravel, and then low, flattened hills of layered slate. Stunted, leafless trees, a scattered knee-high forest, dead and every branch and twig spun with spider's webs. And then through, on to a pan of parched clay crusted with ridged knuckles of salt. The heavy thump of three-toed reptilian feet, the heave and drumming creak of breaths drawn and then hissed loose in whistling gusts.

A sudden skidding halt—K'ell Hunters weaving outward, pace falling off—they had ascended a hill, and had come face to face with the Shi'gal Assassin. Towering, wings folded like spiked, barbed shoulders framing the wide-snouted head—the glisten of eyes above and below that needle-fanged mouth.

Kalyth's breath caught—she could feel its rage, its contempt.

Gunth Mach's arms sagged down, and the Destriant twisted to find purchase with her feet.

Kor Thuran and Rythok stood to either side, ten or more paces distant, heads lowered and chests heaving, swords dug point-first into the hard stony earth. Positioned directly before Gu'Rull was Sag'Churok, standing motionless, almost defiant. Unashamed, hide gleaming with exuded oils.

The bitter reek of violence swirled in the air.

Gu'Rull tilted his head, as if amused by Sag'Churok, but his four eyes held unwavering on the huge K'ell Hunter, as if not too proud to admit to a measure of respect. This was, to Kalyth, a startling concession. The Shi'gal Assassin was almost twice Sag'Churok's height, and even without swords in his hands his reach matched that of the K'ell Hunter's weapon-extended arms.

This thing was bred to kill, born to an intensity of intention that beggared the K'ell Hunters', that would make the Ve'Gath Soldiers appear clumsy and thick.

She knew he could kill them all, here, now, with barely a lone drip of oil to mar his sleek, glistening hide. She knew it in her soul.

Gunth Mach released Kalyth, and she stumbled, needing both hands before she managed to regain her feet. 'Listen,' she said, surprised to find that her own voice was steady, if a little raw, 'I knew a camp dog, once. Could face down an okral. But at the first rise of wind, or the mutter of thunder, it was transformed into a quivering wreck.' She paused, and then said, 'Assassin. They took me away from that storm, at my command.' She forced herself closer, and coming up alongside Sag'Churok she reached out and set a hand against the Hunter's flank.

Sag'Churok need not have moved to the shove she gave him—she did not possess the strength for that—but he stepped aside none the less, so that she now stood directly in front of Gu'Rull. 'Be the okral, then.'

The head tilted further as the Assassin regarded her.

She flinched when his huge wings snapped open, and staggered back a step as they swept down to buffet the air—a minor thunder as if mocking what lay far behind them now—before he launched himself skyward, tail snaking in his wake.

Swearing under her breath, Kalyth turned to Gunth Mach. 'It's almost dusk. Let us camp here—every one of my bones feels rattled loose and my head aches.' *And that was not true fear, was it? Not blind terror. So I tell myself, words that give comfort.*

And we know how useful those ones are.

Zaravow of the Snakehunter, a minor sub-clan of the Gadra, was a huge man, a warrior of twenty-four years, and for all his bulk he was known to be quick, lithe in battle. The Snakehunter had once been among the most powerful political forces, not just among the Gadra, but throughout all the White Face Clans, until the war with the Malazans. Zaravow's own mother had died to a Bridgeburner's quarrel in the One Eye Cat Mountains, in the chaos of a turned ambush. The death had broken his father, dragged him down to a trader town where he wallowed for six months, drinking himself into a state of such bedraggled pathos that Zaravow had with his own hands suffocated the wretch.

The Malazans had assailed the Snakehunter, until, its power among the Barghast shattered, its encampment was forced to fend on its own, leagues from Stolmen's own. Snakehunter warriors lost mates to other clans, an incessant bleeding away that nothing could stem. Even Zaravow, who had once claimed three wives from rivals he'd slain, was now down to one, and she had proved barren and spent all her time with widows complaining about Zaravow and every other warrior who had failed the Snakehunter.

Rubbish littered the paths between rows of tents. The herds were scrawny and ill-kempt. Bitterness and misery were a plague. Young warriors were getting drunk every night on D'ras beer, and in the mornings they huddled round smouldering hearths, shivering in the aftermath of the yellow bitterroot they'd become addicted to. Even now, when the word had gone out that the Gadra would soon unleash war upon the liars and cheaters of this land, the mood remained sour and sickly.

This great journey across the ocean, through foul warrens with all those lost years heaving up one upon another, had been a mistake. A terrible, grievous mistake.

Zaravow knew that Warleader Tool had once been an ally of the Malazans, and if he had possessed greater influence in the council, he would have insisted that Tool be rejected—and more, flayed alive. His beget throat-slit. His wife raped and the toes clipped from her feet, so making her a Hobbler, lower than a camp cur, forced to lift her backside to any man at any time and in any place. And all of that, well, even then it would not be enough.

He had been forced to apply his own deathmask this day—his damned wife was nowhere to be found among the five hundred yurts in the Snakehunter camp—and he was crouched in front of the cookfire, face thrust to the rising heat to hasten the hardening of the paint, when he saw her appear up on the goat trail of the hill to the north, walking loosely—maybe she was drunk, but no, that gait recalled to him something else—in the mornings long ago now, after a night of sex—as if in spreading her legs she untied all the knots inside her.

And a moment later he saw, farther up the trail, Benden Ledag, that scrawny young warrior with the quick smile that always made Zaravow want to smash his even white teeth into bloody stumps. Tall, thin, awkward, with hands big as the wooden paddles used to pattern grain pots.

And, in a flash, Zaravow knew what those hands had been doing a short time earlier. And he knew, as well, the mocking secret behind the smile he offered Zaravow every time their paths crossed.

Not widows after all, for his wife. She'd moved past complaining about her husband. She'd decided to shame him.

He would make the shame hers.

This day, then, he would challenge Benden. He would cut the bastard to pieces, with his wife right there in the crowd, a witness, and she would know—everyone would know—that her punishment would follow. He'd take the front half of her feet, a single merciful chop of his cutlass, once, twice. And then he'd rape her. And then he'd throw her out and all his friends would take their turn. They'd fill her. Her mouth, the places between her thighs and cheeks. Three could take her all at once—

Breath hissed from his nostrils. He was growing hard.

No, there would be time for that later. Zaravow unsheathed his cutlass and worked a thumb crossways, back and forth down the cutting edge. The iron lived for the blood it would soon drink. He'd never liked Benden anyway.

He rose, adjusting his patchy bhederin half-cloak with a rippling shrug of his broad shoulders, and leaned the cutlass against the side of his right leg as he worked the chain gauntlets on to his hands.

His wife, he saw from the corner of his eye, had seen him, had halted at the last low ridge girdling the hill, and was watching. With sudden, icy comprehension. Hearing her shout back up the hill, he collected his cutlass and, mind blackening with rage, wheeled round—no, that rutting shit wasn't going to get away—

But her screams were not being flung back at Benden. And she was still facing the camp, and even at this distance Zaravow could see her terror.

Behind him, other voices rose in scattered alarm.

Zaravow spun.

The bank of storm clouds filled half the sky—he had not even seen their approach—why, he could have sworn—

Dust descended like the boles of enormous columns beneath each of at least a dozen distinct thunderheads, and those grey, impenetrable pillars formed a cordon that was marching straight for the camp.

Zaravow stared, mouth suddenly dry.

As the base of those pillars began to dissolve, revealing—

Some titles were worthy of pride, and Sekara, wife to Warchief Stolmen and known to all as Sekara the Vile, was proud of hers. She would burn to the touch and everyone knew it, knew the acid of her sweat, the vitriol of her breath. Wherever she walked, the path was clear, and when the sun's light cut upon her, someone would always move to stand so that blessed shade settled over her. The tough gristle that would make her gums bleed was chewed first by someone else. The paint she used to awaken her husband's Face of Slaying was ground from the finest pigments—by someone else's hand—and all of this was what her vileness had won her.

Sekara's mother had taught her daughter well. The most rewarding ways of living—rewarding in the sense of personal gain, which was all that truly counted—demanded a ruthlessness in the manipulation of others. All that was needed was a honed intelligence and an eye that saw clearly every weakness, every possible advantage to exploit. And a hand that did not hesitate, ever, to deliver pain, to render punishment for offences real or fabricated.

By how she was seen, by all that she had made of herself, she was a presence that could now slink into the heads of every Gadran, vicious as a wardog patrolling the perimeter of the camp, cruel as an adder in the bedding. And this was power.

Her husband's power was less subtle, and because it was less subtle, it was not nearly as efficient as her own. It could not work the language of silent threat and deadly promise. Besides, he was as a child in her hands; he had always been, from the very first, and that would never change.

She was regal in her attire, bedecked in gifts from the most talented among the tribe's weavers, spinners, seamstresses, bone and antler carvers, jewel-smiths and tanners—gifts that were given to win favour, or deflect Sekara's envy. When one had power, after all, envy ceased to be a flaw of character; instead, it became a weapon, a threat; and Sekara worked it well, so that now she was counted among the wealthiest of all the White Face Barghast.

She walked, back straight, head held high, reminding all who saw her that the role of Barghast Queen belonged to her, though that bitch Hetan might hold to that title—one that she refused, stupid woman. No, Sekara was known to all as its rightful bearer. By virtue of breeding, and by the brilliance of her cruelty. And were her husband not a pathetic oaf, why, they would have long since wrested control away from that bestial Tool and his insatiable slut of a wife.

The cape of sewn hides she wore trailed in the dust behind her as she traversed the stony path, slipping in and out of the shadows cast by the X-shaped crucifixes lining the ridge. It would not do to glance up at the skinless lumps hanging from the crosses—the now lifeless Akrynnai, D'ras and Saphii traders, the merchants and horsemongers, their stupid, useless guards, their fat mates and dough-fleshed children. In this stately promenade, Sekara was simply laying claim to the expression of her power. To walk this path, eyes fixed straight ahead, was enough proof of possession. Yes, she owned the tortured deaths of these foreigners.

She was Sekara the Vile.

Soon, she would see the same done to Tool, Hetan and their spoiled runts. So much had already been achieved, her allies in place and waiting for her command.

She thought back to her husband, and the soft ache between her legs throbbed with the memory of his mouth, his tongue, that made obvious his abject servility. Yes, she made him work, scabbing his knees, and gave him nothing in return. The insides of her thighs were caked in white paint, and she had slyly revealed that detail to her handmaidens when they dressed her—and now word would be out once again among all the women. Chatter and giggles, snorts of contempt. She'd left her husband hastily reapplying the paint on his face.

She noted the storm clouds to the west, but they were too distant to be of any concern, once she had determined that they were not drawing any closer. And through the thick soles of her beaded bhederin moccasins, she felt nothing of the thunder. And when a pack of camp dogs cut across just ahead, she saw in their cowering gaits nothing more than their natural fear of her, and was content.

Hetan lounged in the yurt, watching her fat imp of a son scrabbling about on the huge wardog lying on the cheap Akryn rug they had traded for when it finally became obvious that child and dog had adopted each other. She was ever amazed at the dog's forbearance beneath the siege of grubby, tugging, poking and yanking hands—the beast was big even by Barghast standards, eight or nine years old and scarred with the vicious scraps for dominance among the pack—no other dog risked its ire these days. Even so, permitting the rank creature into the confines of the yurt was virtually unheard of—another one of her husband's strange indulgences. Well, it could foul up that ugly foreign rug, and it seemed it knew the range of this unnatural gift and would push things no further.

'Yes,' she muttered to it, and saw how its ears tilted in her direction, 'a fist to your damned head if you try for any real bedding.' Of course, if she raised a hand to the dog, her son would be the one doing all the howling.

Hetan glanced over as the hide flap was tugged aside and Tool, ducking to clear the entrance, entered the yurt. 'Look at your son,' she accused. 'He's going to poke out the damn thing's eyes. And get a hand bitten off, or worse.'

Her husband squinted down at the squirming toddler, but it was clear he was too distracted to offer anything in the way of comment. Instead, he crossed the chamber and collected up his fur-bound flint sword.

Hetan sat straighter. 'What's happened?'

'I am not sure,' he replied. 'On this day, Barghast blood has been spilled.'

She was on her feet—noting that the hound lifted its head at the sudden tension—and, taking her scabbarded cutlasses, she followed Tool outside.

She saw nothing awry, barring the growing attention her husband garnered as he set out purposefully up the main avenue that bisected the encampment, heading westward. He still possessed some of the sensitivities of the T'lan Imass he had once been—Hetan did not doubt his assertion. Moving up alongside him, acutely aware of other warriors falling into their wake, she shot him a searching look, saw his sorrow stung afresh, his weariness furrowing deep lines on his brow and face.

'One of the outlying clans?'

He grimaced. 'There is no place on this earth, Hetan, where the Imass have not walked. That presence greets my eyes thick as fog, a reminder of ancient things, no matter where I look.'

'Does it blind you?'

'It is my belief,' he replied, 'that it blinds all of us.'

She frowned, unsure of his meaning. 'To what?'

'That we were not the first to do so.'

His response chilled her down in her bones. 'Tool, have we found our enemy?'

The question seemed to startle him. 'Perhaps. But . . .'

'What?'

'I hope not.'

By the time they reached the encampment's western edge, at least three hundred warriors were following them, silent and expectant, perhaps even eager although they could know nothing of their Warleader's intent. The sword in Tool's hands had been transformed into a standard, a brandished sigil held so loosely, in

a manner suggesting careless indifference, that it acquired the gravity of an icon
—Onos Toolan's deadly slayer, drawn forth with such reluctance—the promise
of blood and war.

The far horizon was a black band soon to swallow the sun.

Tool stood staring at it.

Behind them the crowd waited amidst the rustle of weapons, but no one spoke
a word.

'That storm,' she asked him quietly, 'is it sorcery, husband?'

He was long in replying. 'No, Hetan.'

'And yet . . .'

'Yes. And yet.'

'Will you tell me nothing?'

He glanced at her and she was shocked at his ravaged expression. 'What shall
I say?' he demanded in sudden anger. 'Half a thousand Barghast are dead. Killed
in twenty heartbeats. What do you want me to say to you?'

She almost recoiled at his tone. Trembling, she broke contact with his hard
glare. 'You have seen this before, haven't you? Onos Toolan—say it plain!'

'I will not.'

So many bonds forged between them, years of passion and the deepest of loves,
all snapped with his denial. She reeled inside, felt tears spring to her eyes. 'All
that we have—you and me—all of it, does it mean nothing, then?'

'It means everything. And so if I must, I will cut my tongue from my mouth,
rather than reveal to you what I now know.'

'We have our war, then.'

'Beloved.' His voice cracked on the word and he shook his head. 'Dearest wife,
forge of my heart, I want to *run*. With you, with our children. *Run*, do you hear me?
An end to this rule—I do not want to be the one to lead the Barghast into this—do
you understand?' The sword fell at his feet and a shocked groan erupted from the
mob behind them.

She so wanted to take him into her arms. To protect him, from all this, from the
knowledge devouring him from the inside out. But he gave her no opening, no
pathway back to him. 'I will stand with you,' she said, as the tears spilled loose and
tracked down her cheeks. 'I will always do so, husband, but you have taken away
all my strength. Give me something, please, anything. *Anything*.'

He reached up to his own face and seemed moments from clawing deep gouges
down its length. 'If—if I am to refuse them. Your people, Hetan. If I am to lead
them away from here, from this prophesied fate you are all so desperate to embrace, do you truly believe they will follow me?'

No. They will kill you. And our children. And for me, something far worse. In a
low whisper she then asked, 'Shall we flee, then? In the night, unseen by anyone?'

He lowered his hands and, eyes on the storm, offered up a bleak smile that
lanced her heart. 'I am to be the coward I so want to be? And I do, beloved, *I so
want to be a coward*. For you, for our children. Gods below, for myself.'

How many admissions could so crush a man like this? It seemed that in these
past few moments she had seen them all.

'What will you do?' she asked, for it seemed that her role in all of this had vanished.

'Select for me a hundred warriors, Hetan. My worst critics, my fiercest rivals.'

'If you will lead a war-party, why just a hundred? Why so few?'

'We will not find the enemy, only what they have left behind.'

'You will set fire to their rage. And so bind them to you.'

He flinched. 'Ah, beloved, you misunderstand. I mean to set fire not to rage, but fear.'

'Am I permitted to accompany you, husband?'

'And leave the children? No. Also, Cafal will return soon, with Talamandas. You must keep them here, to await our return.'

Without another word, she turned about and walked down to the throng. Rivals and critics, yes, there were plenty of those. She would have no difficulty in choosing a hundred. Or, indeed, a thousand.

With the smoke of cookfires spreading like grey shrouds through the dusk, Onos Toolan led a hundred warriors of the White Face Barghast out from the camp, the head of the column quickly disappearing in the darkness beyond.

Hetan had chosen a raised ridge to watch them leave. Off to her right a massive herd of bhederin milled, crowded together as was their habit when night descended. She could feel the heat from their bodies, saw the plume of their breaths drifting in streams. The herds had lost their caution with an ease that left Hetan faintly surprised. Perhaps some ancient memory had been stirred to life, the muddled comprehension that such proximity to the two-legged creatures kept away wolves and other predators. The Barghast knew to exercise tact in culling the herd, quietly separating the beasts they would slay from all the others.

So too, she realized, were the Barghast scattered, pulled apart, but not by the malevolent intent of some outside force. No, they had done this to themselves. Peace delivered a most virulent poison to those trained as warriors. Some fell into indolence; others found enemies closer to hand. 'Warrior, fix your gaze outward.' An ancient saying among the Barghast. An admonition born of bitter experience, no doubt. Reminding her that little had changed among her people.

She looked away from the bhederin—but the column was well and truly gone, swallowed by the night. Tool had not waited long to set the league-devouring pace that made Barghast war-parties so dangerous to complacent enemies. Even in that, she knew her husband could run those warriors into the ground. Now that would humble those rivals.

Her thoughts about her own people, as the two thousand or so bhederin stood massed and motionless a stone's throw away, had left her depressed, and the squabbling of the twins in the yurt only awaited her return before commencing once again, since the girls adored an audience. She was not quite ready for them. Too fragile with the battering she had received.

She missed the company of her brother with an intensity that ached in her chest.

The faintly lurid glow of the Jade Slashes drew her eyes to the south horizon. Lifting skyward to claw furrows across the breadth of the night—too easy to find omens beneath such heavenly violence; the elders had been bleating warnings for months now—and she suddenly wondered, with a faint catch of breath, if it had been too convenient to dismiss their dire mutterings as the usual disgruntled rubbish voiced by aching old men the world over. Change as the harbinger of disaster was an attitude destined to live for ever, feeding off the inevitable as it did and woefully blind to its own irony.

But some omens were just that. True omens. And some changes proved to be genuine disasters, and to stir sands already settled yielded shallow satisfaction.

When ruin is coming, we choose not to see it. We shift our focus, blurring the facts, the evidence before us. And we ready our masks of surprise, along with those of suffering and self-pity, and keep our fingers nimble for that oh-so-predictable cascade of innocence, that victim's charade.

Before reaching for the sword. *Because someone's to blame. Someone is always to blame.*

She spat into the gloom. She wanted to lie with a man this night. It almost did not matter who that man might be. She wanted her own method of escaping grim realities.

One thing she would never play, however, was that game of masks. No, she would meet the future with a knowing look in her eye, unapologetic, yet defying the prospect of her own innocence. No, be as guilty as everyone else, but announce the admission with bold courage. She would point no fingers. She would not reach for her weapons blazing with the lie of retribution.

Hetan found she was glaring at those celestial tears in the sky.

Her husband wanted to be a coward. So weakened by his love for her, for the children they shared, he would break himself to save them. He had, she realized, virtually begged her for permission to do just that. She had not been ready for him. She had failed in understanding what he sought from her.

Instead, I just kept asking stupid questions. Not understanding how each one tore out the ground beneath him. How he stumbled, how he fell again and again. My idiotic questions, my own selfish need to find something solid under my own feet—before deciding, before making bold judgement.

She had unknowingly cornered him. Refused his cowardice. She had, in fact, forced him out into that darkness, into leading his warriors to a place of truths—where he would seek to frighten them but already knowing—as she did—that he would fail.

And so we have our wish. We go to war.

And our Warleader stands alone in the knowledge that we will lose. That victory is impossible. Will he command with any less vigour? Will he slow the sword in his hands, knowing all that he knows?

Hetan bared her teeth with fierce, savage pride, and spoke to the jade talons in the sky. 'He will not.'

————

They emerged in darkness, and a moment later relief flooded through Setoc. The blurred, swollen moon, the faint green taint limning the features of Torrent and Cafal, casting that now familiar sickly sheen on the metal fittings of the horse's bit and saddle. Yet the skirl of stars overhead seemed twisted, subtly pushed— and it was a few heartbeats before she recognized constellations.

'We are far to the north and east,' said Cafal. 'But not insurmountably so.'

The ghosts from the other realm had flooded the plain, flowing outward and growing ever more ephemeral, finally vanishing entirely from her senses. She felt that absence with a deepening anguish, a sense of loss warring with pleasure at their salvation. Living kin awaited many of them, but not, she was certain, all. There had been creatures in that other world's past unlike anything she had seen or even heard of—limited as her experience was, to be sure—and they would find themselves as lost in this world as in the one they had fled.

A vast empty plain surrounded them, flat as an ancient seabed.

Torrent swung himself back into the saddle. She heard him sigh. 'Tell me, Cafal, what do you see?'

'It's night—I can't see much. We are on the northern edge of the Wastelands, I think. And so, around us, there is nothing.'

Torrent grunted, clearly amused by something in the Barghast's reply.

Cafal nosed the bait. 'What makes you laugh? What do you see, Torrent?'

'At the risk of melodrama,' he said, 'I see the landscape of my soul.'

'It is an ancient one,' Setoc mused, 'which makes you old inside, Torrent.'

'The Awl dwelt here hundreds of generations ago. My ancestors looked out upon this very plain, beneath these same stars.'

'I am sure they did,' acknowledged Cafal. 'As did mine.'

'We have no memory of you Barghast, but no matter, I will not gainsay your claims.' He paused for a time, and then spoke again, 'it would not have been so empty back then, I imagine. More animals, wandering about. Great beasts that trembled the ground.' He laughed again, but this time it was bitter. 'We emptied it and called that success. Fucking unbelievable.'

With that he reached down to Setoc.

She hesitated. 'Torrent, where will you ride from here?'

'Does it matter?'

'It didn't before. But I believe it does now.'

'Why?'

She shook her head. 'Not for you—I see nothing of the path awaiting you. No. For me. For the ghosts I have brought to this world. I am not yet quit of them. Their journey remains incomplete.'

He lowered his hand and studied her in the gloom. 'You hold yourself responsible for their fate.'

She nodded.

'I will miss you, I think.'

'Hold a moment,' said Cafal, 'both of you. Setoc, you cannot wander off all alone—'

'Have no fear,' she cut in, 'for I will accompany you.'

'But I must return to my people.'

'Yes.' But she would say no more. She was home to a thousand hearts, and that blood still ran sizzling like acid in her soul.

'I shall run at a pace you cannot hope to match—'

Setoc laughed. 'Let us play this game, Cafal. When you catch up to me, we shall rest.' She turned to Torrent. 'I shall miss you as well, warrior, last of the Awl. Tell me, of all the women who hunted you, was there one you would have let snare Torrent of the Awl?'

'None other than you, Setoc . . . in about five years from now.'

Flashing a bright smile at Cafal, she set off, fleet as a hare.

The Barghast grunted. 'She cannot maintain such a pace for long.'

Torrent gathered his reins. 'The wolves howl for her, Warlock. Chase her down, if you can.'

Cafal eyed the warrior. 'Your last words to her,' he said in a low voice, and then shook his head. 'No matter, I should not have asked.'

'But you didn't,' Torrent replied.

He watched Cafal find his loping jog, long legs taking him swiftly into Setoc's wake.

The city seethed. Unseen armies struggled against the ravages of decay, gathered in unimaginable numbers to wage pitched battles with neglect. Leaderless and desperate, legions massing barely a mote of dust sent out scouts ranging far from the well-travelled tracks, into the narrowest of capillaries threading senseless stone. One such scout found a Sleeper, curled and motionless—almost lifeless— in a long abandoned rest chamber in the beneath-the-floor level of Feed. A drone, forgotten, mind so somnolent that the Shi'gal Assassin that had last stalked Kalse Rooted had not sensed its presence, thus sparing it from the slaughter that had drenched so many other levels.

The scout summoned kin and in a short time a hundred thousand soldiers swarmed the drone, forming sheets of glistening oil upon its scaled hide, seeping potent nectars into the creature's body.

A drone was a paltry construct, difficult to work with, an appalling challenge to physically transform, to awaken with the necessary intelligence required to take command. A hundred thousand quickly became a million, and then a hundred million, soldiers dying once used up, hastily devoured by kin that then birthed anew, in new shapes with altered functions.

The drone's original purpose had been as an excretor, producing an array of flavours to feed newborn Ve'Gath to increase muscle mass and bone density. It was fed in turn by armies serving the Matron as they delivered her commands— but this Matron had been late in the breeding of Ve'Gath. She had produced fewer than three hundred before the enemy manifested and battle was joined. The drone, therefore, was far from exhausted. This potential alone gave purpose to the efforts of the unseen armies, but the desperation belonged to another cause—exotic flavours now marred Kalse Rooted. Strangers had invaded and had thus far proved insensible to all efforts at conjoining.

At long last the drone stirred. Two newborn eyes opened, seven distinct lids peeling back in each one, and a mind that had known only darkness—for excretors had no need for sight—suddenly looked upon a realm both familiar and unknown. Old senses merged with the new ones, quickly reconfiguring the world. Lids flickered up and down, constructing an ever more complete comprehension—heat, current, charge, composition—and many more, few of which the ghost understood beyond vague, almost formless notions.

The ghost, who did not even know his own name, had been drawn away from his mortal companions, swept along on currents that none of them could sense—currents that defied his own efforts at description. In helpless frustration, he settled upon the familiar concepts of armies, legions, scouts, battles and war, though he knew that none of these was correct. Even to attribute life to such minuscule entities was quite probably wrong; and yet they conveyed meaning to him, or perhaps he was simply capable of stealing knowledge from the clamouring host of instructions that raced through all of Kalse Rooted in a humming buzz too faint for mortal ears.

And now he found himself looking down upon a drone, a K'Chain Che'Malle unlike any he had ever seen before. No taller than a grown male human, thin-limbed, with a mass of tentacles instead of fingers at the ends of those arms. The broad head bulged behind the eyes, and at the base of the skull. The slash of a mouth was that of a lizard, lined with multiple rows of fine, sharp fangs. The colour of the two large, oversized eyes was a soft brown.

He watched it twitch for a time, knowing the creature was simply exploring the extent of its transformation, unfurling its ungainly limbs, turning its head from side to side in rapid flickers as it caught new and strange flavours. He saw then its growing agitation, its fear.

The smell of unknown invaders. The drone was able to gather, enclose and then discard the information that belonged to feral orthen and grishol; and this permitted it to isolate the location of the invaders. Alive, yes. Distant, discordant sounds, multiple breaths, soft feet on the floor, fingers brushing mechanisms.

The flavours the drone had once fed to Ve'Gath were now turned upon itself. In time, it would increase in size and strength. If the strangers had not departed by then, the drone would have to kill them.

The ghost struggled against panic. He could not warn them. This creature, so flush now with necessities and enormous tasks—the great war against the deterioration of Kalse Rooted, the ghost assumed—could not but see the clumsy explorations of Taxilian, Rautos and the others as a threat. To be eradicated.

The drone, named Sulkit—this being a name derived from birth-month and status, indeed a name once shared by two hundred identical drones—now rose on its hind limbs, thin, prehensile tail slithering across the floor. Oils dripped from its slate-grey hide, pooled and then quickly vanished as the unseen army, emboldened, purified and enlivened by the commander it had itself created, dispersed to renew its war.

And the ghost withdrew, raced back to his companions.

'If this was a mind,' said Taxilian, 'it has died.' He ran his hand along the sleek carapace, frowning at the ribbons of flexible, clear glass rippling out from the iron dome. Was something flowing through that glass? He could not be certain.

Rautos rubbed his chin. 'Truly, I do not see how you can tell,' he said.

'There should be heat, vibration. Something.'

'Why?'

Taxilian scowled. 'Because that would tell us it's working.'

Breath barked a laugh behind them. 'Does a knife talk? Does a shield drum? You've lost your mind, Taxilian. A city only lives when people are in it, and even then it's the people doing the living, not the city.'

In the chamber they had just left, Sheb and Nappet bickered as they cleared rubbish from the floor, making room for everyone to sleep. They had climbed level after level and, even now, still more waited above them. But everyone was exhausted. A dozen levels below, Last had managed to kill a nest of orthen, which he had skinned and gutted, and he was now arranging the six scrawny carcasses on skewers, while off to one side bhederin dung burned in a stone quern, the fire's heat slowly driving back the chilly, lifeless air. Asane was preparing herbs to feed into a tin pot filled with fresh water.

Bewildered, the ghost drifted among them.

Breath strode back into the chamber, eyes scanning the floor. 'Time,' she said, 'for a casting of the Tiles.'

Anticipation fluttered through the ghost, or perhaps it was terror. He felt himself drawn closer, staring avidly as she drew out her collection of Tiles. Polished bone? Ivory? Glazed clay? All kinds, he realized, shifting before his eyes.

Breath whispered, 'See? Still young. So much, so much to decide.' She licked her lips, her hands twitching.

The others drew closer, barring Taxilian who had remained in the other room. 'I don't recognize none of them,' said Sheb.

'Because they're new,' snapped Breath. 'The old ones are dead. Useless. These'— she gestured—'they belong to us, just us. For now. And the time has come to give them their names.' She raked them together in a clatter, scooped them up and held the Tiles in the enclosed bowl of her hands.

The ghost could see her flushed face, the sudden colour making her skin almost translucent, so that he could discern the faint cage of bones beneath. He saw her pulse through the finest vessels in her flesh, the rush and swish of blood in their eager circuit. He saw the sweat beading on her high brow, and the creatures swimming within it.

'First,' she said, 'I need to remake some old ones. Give them new faces. The names may sound like ones you've heard before, but these are new anyway.'

'How?' demanded Sheb, still scowling. 'How are they new?'

'They just are.' She sent the Tiles on to the floor. 'No Holds, you see? Each one is unaligned, all of them are unaligned. That's the first difference.' She pointed. 'Chance—Knuckles—but see how it's at war with itself? That's the truth of Chance right there. Fortune and Misfortune are mortal enemies. And that one: Rule—no throne, thrones are too obvious.' She flipped that Tile. 'And Ambition on the other side—they kill each other, you see?' She began flipping more Tiles. 'Life and Death, Light and Dark, Fire and Water, Air and Stone. Those are the old ones, remade.' She swept those aside, leaving three remaining Tiles. 'These are the most potent. Fury, and on its opposite side, Starwheel. Fury is just what it says. Blind, a destroyer of everything. Starwheel, that's Time, but unravelled—'

'Meaning what?' Rautos asked, his voice strangely tight, his face pale.

Breath shrugged. 'Before and after are meaningless. Ahead and behind, then and soon, none of them mean anything. All those words that try to force order and, uh, sequence.' She shrugged again. 'You won't see Starwheel in the castings. You'll just see Fury.'

'How do you know?'

Her smile was chilling. 'I just do.' She pointed at the second to last Tile. 'Root, and on the other side, Ice Haunt—they both seek the same thing. You get one or the other, never both. This last one, Blueiron there, that's the sorcery that gives life to machines—it's still strong in this place, I can feel it.' She turned the Tile on to its other side. 'Oblivion. Ware this one, it's a curse. A demon. It eats you from the inside out. Your memories, your self.' She licked her lips once more, this time nervously. 'It's very strong right now. And getting stronger . . . someone's coming, someone's coming to find us.' She hissed suddenly and swept up the last Tiles. 'We need—we need to feed Blueiron. Feed it!'

Taxilian spoke from the doorway. 'I know, Breath. It is what I am trying to do.'

She faced him, teeth bared. 'Can you taste this place?'

'I can.'

From one side Asane whimpered, and then flinched as Nappet lashed out a foot to kick her. He would have done more but Last interposed himself between the two, arms crossed, eyes flat. Nappet sneered and turned away.

'I don't understand,' said Rautos. 'I taste nothing—nothing but dust.'

'It wants our help,' Taxilian announced.

Breath nodded.

'Only I don't know how.'

Breath held up a knife. 'Open your flesh. Let the taste inside, Taxilian. Let it inside.'

Was this madness, or the only path to salvation? The ghost did not know. But he sensed a new flavour in the air. Excitement? Hunger? He could not be certain.

But Sulkit was on its way. Still gaunt, still weak. On its way, then, not to deliver slaughter.

The flavour, the ghost realized, was hope.

———

Some roads, once set out upon, reveal no possible path but forward. Every other track is blocked by snarls of thorns, steaming fissures or rearing walls of stone. What waits at the far end of the forward path is unknown, and since knowledge itself may prove a curse, the best course is simply to place one foot in front of the other, and think not at all of fate or the cruel currents of destiny.

The seven or eight thousand refugees trudging in Twilight's wake were content with ignorance, even as darkness closed in as inexorable as a tide, even as the world to either side of the Road of Gallan seemed to lose all substance, fragments drifting away like discarded memories. Linked one to another by ropes, strands of netting, torn strips of cloth and hide—exhausted but still alive, far from terrible flames and coils of smoke—they need only follow their Queen.

Most faith was born of desperation, Yan Tovis understood that much. Let them see her bold, sure strides on this stony road. Let them believe she had walked this path before, or that by virtue of noble birth and title, she was cloaked with warm, comforting knowledge of the journey they had all begun, this flowing river of blood. *My blood.*

She would give them that comfort. And hold tight to the truth that was her growing terror, her surges of panic that left her undergarments soaked with chill sweat, her heart pounding like the hoofs of a fleeing horse—no, they would see none of that. Nothing to drive stark fear into them, lest in blind horror the human river spill out, pushed off the road, and in screams of agony find itself shredded apart by the cold claws of oblivion.

No, best they know nothing.

She was lost. The notion of finding a way off this road, of returning to their own world, now struck her as pathetically naïve. Her blood had created a gate, and now its power was thinning; with each step she grew weaker, mind wandering as if stained with fever, and even the babble of Pully and Skwish behind her was drifting away—their wonder, their pleasure at the gifts of Twilight's blood had grown too bitter to bear.

Old hags no longer. Youth snatched back, the sloughing away of wrinkles, dread aches, frail bones—the last two witches of the Shake danced and sung as if snake-bitten, too filled with life to even take note of the dissolution closing in on all sides, nor their Queen's slowing pace, her drunken weaving on the road. They were too busy drinking her sweet blood.

Forward. Just walk. Yedan warned you, but you were too proud to listen. You thought only of your shame. Your brother, Witchslayer. And, do not forget, your guilt. At the brutal reprieve he gave you. His perfect, logical solution to all of your problems.

The Watch is as he must be. Yet see how you hated his strength—but it was nothing more than hating your own weakness. Nothing more than that.

Walk, Yan Tovis. It's all you need do—

With the sound of a sundered sail, the world tore itself wide open. The road dropped from beneath the two witches, then thundered and cracked like a massive spine as it slammed down atop rolling hills. Dust shot skyward, and sudden sunlight blazed down with blinding fire.

Pully staggered to where Twilight had collapsed, seeing the spatters of blood brown and dull on the road's cracked, broken surface. 'Skwish, y'damned fool! We was drunk! Drunk on 'er an now ye look!'

Skwish dragged herself loose from the half-dozen Shake who had tumbled into her. 'Oh's we in turble now—this anna Gallan! It's the unnerside a Gallan! The unnerside! Iz she yor an dead, Pully? Iz she?'

'Nearby, Skwish, nearby—she went on too long—we shoulda paid attention. Kept an eye on 'er.'

'Get 'er back, Pully! We can't be 'ere. We can't!'

As the two now young women knelt by Yan Tovis, the mass of refugees was embroiled in its own chaotic recovery. Broken limbs, scattered bundles of possessions, panicked beasts. The hills flanking the road were denuded, studded with sharp outcrops. Not a tree in sight. Through the haze of dust, now drifting on the wind, the sky was cloudless—and there were three suns.

Yedan Derryg scanned his troop of soldiers, was satisfied that none had suffered more than bruises and scrapes. 'Sergeant, attend to the wounded—and stay on the road—no one is to leave it.'

'Sir.'

He then set out, picking his way round huddled refugees—wide-eyed islanders silent with fear, heads lifting and turning to track his passage. Yedan found the two captains, Pithy and Brevity, directing one of their makeshift squads in the righting of a toppled cart.

'Captains, pass on the command for everyone to stay on the road—not a single step off it, understood?'

The two women exchanged glances, and then Pithy shrugged. 'We can do that. What's happened?'

'It was already looking bad,' Brevity said, 'wasn't it?'

'And now,' added Pithy, 'it's even worse. Three suns, for Errant's sake!'

Yedan grimaced. 'I must make my way to the front of the column. I must speak with my sister. I will know more when I return.'

He continued on.

The journey was cruel, as the Watch could not help but observe the wretched state of the refugees, islanders and Shake alike. He well comprehended the necessity of leaving the shore, and the islands. The sea respected them no longer, not the land, not the people clinging to it. His sister had no choice but to take them away. But she was also *leading* them. Ancient prophecies haunted her, demanding dread sacrifices—but her Shake were poor creatures for the most part. They did not belong in legends, in tales of hard courage and resolute defiance—he'd seen as much in the faces of the witches and warlocks he'd cut down. And he saw the same here, as he threaded through the crowds. The Shake were a diminished people, in numbers, in spirit. Generation upon generation, they had made themselves *small*, as if meekness was the only survival strategy they understood.

Yedan Derryg did not know if they were capable of rising again.

The islanders, he mused, might well prove more competent than the Shake, if Pithy and Brevity were any measure. He could use them. Letherii understood the value of adaptability, after all. And since these were the ones who had chosen Yan Tovis as their Queen, he could exploit that loyalty.

They needed an army. The two captains were right. And they were looking to him to lead it. That seemed plain enough. His task now was to convince his sister.

Of course, their paramount need at the moment was to leave this place. Before its residents found them.

Pushing clear of the last huddle of refugees he saw that a perimeter of sorts had been established by—he noted with a frown—two young women and a half-dozen Shake youths armed with fishing spears. The women were busy scratching furrows in the road with antler picks, spirals and wavy circles—fashioning wards, Yedan realized with a start—in the gap between the guards and a small tent surrounded by a rough palisade of carved poles.

Witching poles. Yedan Derryg walked up to the guards, who parted to let him pass—saving him the effort of beating the fools senseless—and halted before the women. 'Do you know what you're doing?' he demanded. 'Such rituals belong to Elder Witches, not their apprentices—where is my sister? In the tent? Why?'

The woman closest to him, curvaceous beneath her rags, her black hair glistening in the sunlight, placed two fingers beneath her large, dark eyes, and then smiled. 'The Watch sees but remains blind, an yer blind an blind.' Then she laughed.

Yedan narrowed his gaze, and then shot the other woman a second look.

This one straightened from etching the road. She lifted her arms as if to display herself—the tears and holes in her shirt revealing smooth flesh, the round fullness of her breasts. 'Hungry, Witchslayer?' She ran a hand through her auburn hair and then smiled invitingly.

'See what her blood done t'us?' the first one exclaimed. 'Ya didn't nearby kill us. Leff the two a us, an that made us rich wi' 'er power, and see what it done?'

Yedan Derryg slowly scowled. 'Pully. Skwish.'

Both women pranced the opening steps to the Shake Maiden Dance.

Growling under his breath, he walked between them, taking care not to scrape the patterns cut into the packed earth of the road.

The one he took to be Pully hurried up to his side. 'Careful, ya fat walrus, these are highest—'

'Wards. Yes. You've surrounded my sister with them. Why?'

'She's sleepin—don't asturb 'er.'

'I am the Watch. We need to speak.'

'Sleeps!'

He halted, stared at the witch. 'Do you know where we are?'

'Do you?'

Yedan stared at her. Saw the tremor behind her eyes. 'If not,' he said, 'the hold of the Liosan, then a neighbouring realm within their demesne.'

Pully flinched. 'The Watch sees and is not blind,' she whispered.

As he moved to continue to the tent the witch snapped out a hand to stay him. 'Lissen. Not sleep. Nearby a coma—she didn't know to slow 'er own blood, just let it pour out—nearby killt 'er.'

He ground his teeth, chewed silently for a moment, and then asked, 'You bound her wounds?'

'We did,' answered Skwish behind them. 'But mebbe we was too late—'

'Too busy dancing.'

Neither woman replied.

'I will look upon my sister.'

'An then stay close,' said Pully, 'an bring up your soljers.'

Yedan pointed to one of the Shake guards. 'Send that one back to Captains Pithy and Brevity. They are to take command of the rearguard with their company. Then have your lad lead my troop back here.'

Skwish turned away to comply with his commands.

They were flush, yes, these two witches. And frightened. Two forces he could use to ensure their cooperation. That and the guilt they must now be feeling, having drunk deep when—if not for Yedan's slaying of the others—they would have but managed a sip with the rest shared out among scores of parched rivals. He would keep them down from now on, he vowed. Serving the Royal Family. 'Pully,' he now said. 'If I discover you ever again withholding information from me—or my sister— I will see you burned alive. Am I understood?'

She paled and almost stepped back.

He stepped closer, permitting her no retreat. 'I am the Watch.'

'Aye. You are the Watch.'

'And until the Queen recovers, I command this column—including you and Skwish.'

She nodded.

'Make certain your sister witch understands.'

'I will.'

He turned and made his way to the tent. Crouched at the entrance. He hesitated, thinking, and then reached out to tug aside the hide flap—enough to give him a view inside. Hot, pungent air gusted out. She was lying like a corpse, arms at her sides, palms up. He could just make out the black-gut stitchwork seaming the knife cuts. Reaching in, he took one of her bare feet in his hand. Cold, but he could detect the faintest of pulses. He set the foot down, closed the flap, and straightened.

'Pully.'

She was standing where he'd left her. 'Yes.'

'She might not recover left just as she is.'

'Na, she might not.'

'She needs sustenance. Wine, meat. Can you force that into her without choking her?'

Pully nodded. 'Need us a snake tube.'

'Find one.'

'Skwish!'

'I heard.'

Yedan made his way back through the wards. Four horses were tethered to his sister's supply wagon. He selected the biggest one, a black gelding with a white blaze on its forehead. The beast was unsaddled but bridled. He drew it out from the others and then vaulted on to its back.

Pully was watching him. 'Can't ride through the wards!'

'I don't mean to,' he replied, gathering the reins.

The witch stared, baffled. 'Then where?'

Yedan chewed for a time, and then brought his horse round to face the nearest hills.

Pully shrieked and then leapt to block his path. 'Not off the road, ya fool!'

'When I return,' he said, 'you will have her awake.'

'Don't be stupid! They might not find us at all!'

He thought about dismounting, walking up and cuffing her. Instead, he simply stared down at her, and then said in a low voice, 'Now who is being the fool, witch? I go to meet them, and if need be, I will slow them down. Long enough for you to get my sister back on her feet.'

'And then we wait for you?'

'No. As soon as she is able, you will leave this realm. This time,' he added, 'you will help her. You and Skwish.'

'Of course! We was just careless.'

'When my troop arrives, inform my sergeant that they are to defend the Queen. Detail them to surround the tent—do not overcrowd them with your wards, witch.'

'Hold to yourself, Witchslayer,' said Pully. 'Hold tight—if your mind wanders, for e'en an instant—'

'I know,' Yedan replied.

She moved to one side, then stepped close and set a hand upon the gelding's head. 'This one should do,' she muttered with eyes closed. 'Wilful, fearless. Keep it collected—'

'Of that I know far more than you, witch.'

Sighing, she edged back. 'A commander does not leave his command. A prince does not leave his people.'

'This one does.'

He kicked his horse into motion. Hoofs thumped on to the hard-packed ground beyond the road.

This was dependent on his sister reviving—enough to lead them away from this infernal place—a prince must choose when he is expendable. Yedan understood the risk. If she did not awaken. If she died, then well and truly his leaving had damned his people—but then, if his sister did not recover, and quickly, then the entire column was doomed anyway. Yes, he could let his own blood, and the witches could take hold of it and do what must be done—but they would also try to enslave him—they could not help it, he knew. He was a man and they were women. Such things simply were. The greater danger was that they would lose control of the power in their hands—two witches, even ancient, formidable ones, were not enough. Ten or twenty were needed in the absence of a Queen to fashion a simulacrum of the necessary focus demanded upon the Road of Gallan. No, he could not rely on Pully and Skwish.

Skwish came up alongside her sister witch. They watched Yedan Derryg riding up the slope of the first hill. 'That's bad, Pully. A prince does not—'

'This one does. Listen, Skwish, we got to be careful now.'

Skwish held up the snake tube. 'If we left her t' jus live or die like we planned afirst—'

'He'll know—he will cut her open an check.'

'He ain't comin' back—'

'Then we do need 'er alive, don we? We can't use 'im like we planned—he's too ken—he won't let us take 'im—I lookt up inta his eyes, him on that 'orse, Skwish. His eyes an his eyes, an so I tell ya, he's gonna be bad turble if he comes back.'

'He won't. An' we can keep 'er weak, weak enough, I mean—'

'Too risky. She needs t'get us out. We can try something later, once we're all safe—we can take 'em down then. The one left or e'en both. But not this time, Skwish. Now, best go an feed 'er something. Start with wine, that'll loosen 'er throat.'

'I know what I'm about, Pully, leave off.'

The gelding had a broad back, making for a comfortable ride. Yedan rode at a canter. Ahead, the hills thickened with scrub, and beyond was a forest of white trees, branches like twisted bones, leaves so dark as to be almost black. Just before them and running the length of the wooded fringe rose dolmens of grey granite, their edges grooved and faces pitted with cup-shaped, ground-out depressions. Each stone was massive, twice the height of a grown man, and crowding the foot of each one that he could see were skulls.

He slowed his mount, reined in a half-dozen paces from the nearest standing stone. Sat motionless, flies buzzing round the horse's flickering ears, and studied those grisly offerings. Cold judgement was never short of pilgrims. Alas, true justice had no reason to respect secrets, as those close-fisted pilgrims had clearly discovered. A final and fatal revelation.

Minute popping sounds in the air announced the approach of dread power, as the buzzing flies ignited in mid-flight, black bodies bursting like acorns in a fire. The horse shied slightly, muscles growing taut beneath Yedan, and then snorted in sudden fear.

'Hold,' Yedan murmured, his voice calming the beast.

Those of the royal line among the Shake possessed ancient knowledge, memories thick as blood. Tales of ancient foes, sworn enemies of the uncertain Shore. More perhaps than most, the Shake rulers understood that a thing could be both one and the other, or indeed neither. Sides possessed undersides and even those terms were suspect. Language itself stuttered in the face of such complexities, such rampant subtleties of nature.

In this place, however, the blended flavours of compassion were anathema to the powers that ruled.

Yet the lone figure that strode out from the forest was so unexpected that Yedan Derryg grunted as if he had been punched in the chest. 'This realm is not yours,' he said, fighting to control his horse.

'This land is consecrated for adjudication,' the Forkrul Assail said. 'I am named Repose. Give me your name, seeker, that I may know you—'

'Before delivering judgement upon me?'

The tall, ungainly creature, naked and weaponless, cocked his head. 'You are not alone. You and your followers have brought discord to this land. Do not delay me—you cannot evade what hides within you. I shall be your truth.'

'I am Yedan Derryg.'

The Forkrul Assail frowned. 'This yields me no ingress—why is that? How is it you block me, mortal?'

'I will give you that answer,' Yedan replied, slipping down from the horse. He drew his sword.

Repose stared at him. 'Your defiance is useless.'

Yedan advanced on him. 'Is it? But, how can you know for certain? My name yields you no purchase upon my soul. Why is that?'

'Explain this, mortal.'

'My name is meaningless. It is my title that holds my truth. My title, and my blood.'

The Forkrul Assail shifted his stance, lifting his hands. 'One way or another, I will know you, mortal.'

'Yes, you will.'

Repose attacked, his hands a blur. But those deadly weapons cut empty air, as Yedan was suddenly behind the Forkrul Assail, sword chopping into the back of the creature's elongated legs, the iron edge cutting between each leg's two hinged knees, severing the buried tendons—Repose toppled forward, arms flailing.

Yedan chopped down a second time, cutting off the Assail's left arm. Blue, thin blood sprayed on to the ground.

'I am Shake,' Yedan said, raising his sword once more. 'I am the Watch.'

The sudden hiss from Repose was shortlived, as Yedan's sword took off the top of the Forkrul Assail's head.

He wasted little time. He could hear the pounding of hoofs. Vaulting on to his horse's back, he collected the reins in one hand and, still, gripping his blue-stained sword, wheeled the beast round.

Five Tiste Liosan were charging towards him, lances levelled.

Yedan Derryg drove his horse straight for them.

These were scouts, he knew. They would take him down and then send one rider back to gather a punitive army—they would then ride to the column. Where they would slaughter everyone. These were the ones he had been expecting.

The line of standing stones lay to Yedan's left. At the last moment before the gap between him and the Tiste Liosan closed, Yedan dragged his horse in between two of the stones. He heard a lance shatter and then snarls of frustration as the troop thundered past. The gelding responded with alacrity as he guided it back through the line, wheeling to come up behind the nearest Tiste Liosan—the one who'd snapped his lance on one of the dolmens and who was now reaching for his sword even as he reined in.

Yedan's sword caught beneath the rim of his enamelled helm, slicing clean through his neck. The decapitated head spun to one side, cracking against a dolmen.

The Watch slapped the flat of his blade on the white horse's rump, launching it forward in a lunge, and then, driving his heels into his own horse's flanks, he pulled into the other horse's wake.

The remaining four Liosan had wheeled in formation, out and away from the standing stones, and were now gathering for a second charge.

Their fallen comrade's horse galloped straight for them, forcing the riders to scatter once more.

Yedan chose the Liosan nearest the dolmens, catching the man before he could right his lance. A crossways slash severed the scout's right arm halfway between the shoulder and elbow, the edge cutting into and snapping ribs as Yedan's horse carried him past the shrieking warrior.

A savage yank on the reins brought him up alongside another scout. He saw the woman's eyes as she twisted round in her saddle, heard her snarled curse, before he drove the point of his sword into the small of her back, punching between the armour's plates along the laced seam.

His arm was twisted painfully as in her death roll she momentarily trapped his sword, but he managed to tear the weapon free.

The other two riders were shouting to each other, and one pulled hard away from the fight, setting heels to his horse. The last warrior brought his mount round and lowered his lance.

Yedan urged his gelding into a thundering charge, but at an angle away from his attacker—in the direction of the fleeing scout. An instant's assessment told him he would not catch the man. Instead he lifted himself upward, knees anchored tight to either side of the gelding's spine. Drew back his arm and threw his sword.

The point slammed up and under the rider's right arm, driven a hand's breadth between his ribs, deep enough to sink into the lung. He toppled from his horse.

The last rider arrived, coming at Yedan from an angle. Yedan twisted to hammer aside the lashing blade of the lance, feeling it cleave through his vambrace and then score deep into the bones of his wrist. Pain seared up his arm.

He dragged his horse into the rider's wake—the Liosan was pulling up. A mistake. Yedan caught up to him and flung himself on to the man's back, dragging him from the saddle.

There was a satisfying snap of a bone as the Watch landed atop the warrior. He brought his good hand up and round to the Liosan's face, thumb digging into one eye socket and fingers closing like talons on the upper lip and nose. He jammed his wounded arm with its loosened vambrace into the man's mouth, forcing open the jaws.

Hands tore at him, but feebly, as Yedan forced his thumb deeper, in as far as it could go, then angled it upwards—but he failed to reach the brain. He got on to his knees, lifting the Liosan's head by hooking his embedded thumb under the ridge of the brow. And then he forced it round, twisting even as he pressed down with his bloodied, armoured arm jammed across the man's mouth. Joints popped, the jaw swung loose, and then, as the Liosan's body thrashed in a frenzy, the vertebrae parted and the warrior went limp beneath him.

Yedan struggled to his feet.

He saw the scout with the punctured lung attempting to clamber back on to his horse. Collecting a lance, Yedan strode over. He used the haft to knock the warrior away from the horse, sending the man sprawling, and then stepped up and set the point against the Liosan's chest. Staring down into the man's terror-filled eyes, he pushed down on the lance, using all his weight. The armour's enamel surface crazed, and then the point punched through.

Yedan pushed harder, twisting and grinding the serrated blade into the Liosan's chest.

Until he saw the light leave the warrior's eyes.

After making certain the others were dead, he bound his wounded arm, retrieved his sword and then the surviving lances and long-knives from the corpses, along with the helms. Rounding up the horses and tying them to a staggered lead, he set out at a canter back the way he had come.

He was a prince of the Shake, with memories in the blood.

Yan Tovis opened her eyes. Shadowed figures slid back and forth above her and to the sides—she could make no sense of them, nor of the muted voices surrounding her—voices that seemed to come from the still air itself. She was sheathed in sweat.

Tent walls—ah, and the shadows were nothing more than silhouettes. The voices came from outside. She struggled to sit up, the wounds on her wrists stinging as the sutures stretched. She frowned down at them, trying to recall . . . things. Important things.

The taste of blood, stale, the smell of fever—she was weak, lightheaded, and there was . . . danger.

Heart thudding, she forced her way through the entrance, on her hands and knees, the world spinning round her. Bright, blinding sunlight, scorching fires in the sky—two, three, four—*four suns!*

'Highness!'

She sat back on her haunches, squinted up as a figure loomed close. 'Who?'

'Sergeant Trope, Highness, in Yedan's company. Please, crawl no further, the witches—there're wards, all round, Highness. All round you. A moment, the witches are on their way.'

'Help me up. Where's my brother?'

'He rode out, Highness. Some time ago. Before the fourth sun rose—and now we're burning alive—'

She took his proffered arm and pulled herself on to her feet. 'Not suns, Sergeant. *Attacks*.'

He was a scarred man, face bludgeoned by decades of hard living. 'Highness?'

'We are under attack—we need to leave here. We need to leave now!'

'O Queen!' Pully was dancing her way closer, evading the scored lines of the wards encircling the tent. 'He's coming back! Witchslayer! We must ready ourselves—drip drip drip some blood, Highness. We brought ya back, me an Skwish an we did. Leave off her, you oaf, let 'er stand!'

But Yan Tovis held on to the sergeant's wrist—solid as a rooted tree, and she needed that. She glared at Pully. 'Drank deep, I see.'

The witch flinched. 'Careless, an us all, Queen. But see, the Watch comes—with spare horses, white horses!'

Yan Tovis said to Trope, 'Guide me out of these wards, Sergeant.' *And get this pretty witch out of my face.*

She could hear the horses drawing closer, and, from the road, the suffering of thousands of people swept over her in an inundating tide—she almost gagged beneath that deluge.

'Clear, Highness—'

She straightened. A fifth sun was flaring to life on the horizon. The iron fastenings of Trope's armour were searing hot and she winced at their touch, but still would not let go of his arm. She felt her skin tightening—*We're being roasted alive.*

Her brother, one arm bound in blood-soaked rags, reined in at the side of the road. Yan Tovis stared at the trailing horses. Liosan horses, yes. That clutch of lances, the sheathed long-knives and cluster of helms. Liosan.

Skwish and Pully were suddenly there, on the very edge of the road. Pully cackled a laugh.

Yan Tovis studied her brother's face. 'How soon?' she asked.

She watched his bearded jaw bunch as he chewed on his answer, before squinting and saying, 'We have time, Queen.'

'Good,' she snapped. 'Witches, attend to me. We begin—not in haste, but we begin.'

Two young women, scampering and bobbing their heads like the hags they once were. New ambitions, yes, but old, old fears.

Yan Tovis met Yedan's eyes once more, and saw that he knew. And was prepared. *Witchslayer, mayhap you're not done with that, before this is all over.*

Chapter Eleven

In the first five years of King Tehol the Only's reign, there were no assassination attempts, no insurrections, no conspiracies of such magnitude as to endanger the crown; no conflicts with neighbouring realms or border tribes. The kingdom was wealthy, justice prevailed, the common people found prosperity and unprecedented mobility.

That all of this was achieved with but a handful of modest proclamations and edicts makes the situation all the more remarkable.

Needless to say, dissatisfaction haunted Lether. Misery spread like a plague. No one was happy, the list of complaints as heard on the crowded, bustling streets grew longer with each day that passed.

Clearly, something had to be done . . .

LIFE OF TEHOL
JANATH

Clearly,' said King Tehol, 'there's nothing to be done.' he held up the Akrynnai gift and peered at it for a time, and then sighed.

'No suggestions, sire?' Bugg asked.

'I'm at a loss. I give up. I keep trying, but I must admit: it's hopeless. Darling wife?'

'Don't ask me.'

'Some help you are. Where's Brys?'

'With his legions, husband. Preparing to march.'

'The man's priorities are a mess. I remember how our mother despaired.'

'Of Brys?' Janath asked, surprised.

'Well, no. Me, mostly. Never mind. The issue here is that we're facing a disaster. One that could scar this nation for generations to come. I need help, and see how none of you here can manage a single useful suggestion. My advisors are even more pathetic than the man they purport to advise. The situation is intolerable.' He paused, and then frowned over at Bugg. 'What's the protocol? Find me that diplomat so I can chase him out of here again—no, wait, send for the emissary.'

'Are you sure, sire?'

'Why wouldn't I be?'

Bugg gestured at the gift in the King's hands. 'Because we're no closer to finding a suitable gift in reciprocation.'

Tehol leaned forward. 'And why, dear Chancellor, is that?'

'Because none of us has a clue what that thing is, sire.'

Tehol grimaced. 'How can this thing defeat the greatest minds of the kingdom?'

'I didn't know we'd tried them yet,' murmured Janath.

'It's bone, antler, inlaid pearl and it has two handles.' Tehol waited, but no one had anything to add to that succinct description. 'At least, I think they're handles . . .'

Janath's breath caught, and then she said, 'Oh.'

King Tehol scratched his jaw. 'Best the emissary wait a little longer, I think.'

'Sound decision, sire.'

'Such opinions, Bugg, are invaluable. Now, dear wife, shall we retire to our private chambers to further our exploration of this, uhm, offering?'

'You must be mad. Find Shurq Elalle. Or Rucket.'

'Finally, proper advice!'

'And I'll buy myself a new dagger.'

'That hints of high emotions, my beloved. Jealous rage does not become you.'

'It doesn't become anyone, husband. You didn't really think I wanted you to follow my suggestion?'

'Well, it's true that it's easy to make suggestions when you know they won't be heeded.'

'Yes it is. Now, you will find a small room with a stout door and multiple locks, and once the emissary has departed, in goes that gift, never again to see the light of day.' And she settled back on the throne, arms crossed.

Tehol eyed the gift forlornly, and then sighed once more. 'Send for the emissary, Bugg.'

'At once, sire.' He gestured to a servant waiting at the far end of the throne room.

'While we're waiting, is there any kingly business we need to mull over?'

'Your repatriation proclamation, sire—that's going to cause trouble.'

Tehol thumped the arm of his throne with a fist. 'And trouble is precisely what I want! Indignation! Outrage! Protests! Let the people rail and shake their knobby fists! Let us, yes, stir this steaming stew, wave the ladle about, spattering all the walls and worse.'

Janath turned to eye him speculatively.

Bugg grunted. 'Should work. I mean, you're taking land away from some very wealthy families. You could well foment a general insurrection. Assuming that would be useful.'

'Useful?' demanded Janath. 'In what context could insurrection be useful? Tehol, I warned you about that edict—'

'Proclamation—'

'—and the rage you'll incite. But did you listen?'

'I most certainly did, my Queen. But let me ask you, are my reasons any less just?'

'No, it was stolen land to begin with, but that's beside the point. The losers won't see it that way.'

'And that, my love, is precisely *my* point. Justice bites. With snippy sharp teeth. If it doesn't, then the common folk will perceive it as unbalanced, forever favouring the wealthy and influential. When robbed, the rich cry out for protection and prosecution. When stealing, they expect the judiciary to look the other way. Well, consider this a royal punch in the face. Let them smart.'

'You truly expect to purge cynicism from the common people, Tehol?'

'Well, wife, in this instance it's more the sweet taste of vengeance, but a deeper lesson is being delivered, I assure you. Ah, enough prattling about inconsequential things—the noble Akrynnai emissary arrives! Approach, my friend!'

The huge man with the wolf-skin cloak strode forward, showing his fiercest scowl.

Smiling, King Tehol said, 'We delight in this wondrous gift and please do convey our pleasure to Sceptre Irkullas, and assure him we will endeavour to make use of it as soon as an opportunity . . . arises.'

The warrior's scowl deepened. 'Make use? What kind of use? It's a damned piece of art, sire. Stick it on a damned wall and forget about it—that's what I would do were I you. A closet wall, in fact.'

'Ah, I see. Forgive me.' Tehol frowned down at the object. 'Art, yes. Of course.'

'It wasn't even the Sceptre's idea,' the emissary grumbled. 'Some ancient agreement, wasn't it? Between our peoples? An exchange of meaningless objects. Irkullas has a whole wagon stuffed with similar rubbish from you Letherii. Trundles around after us like an arthritic dog.'

'The wagon's pulled by an arthritic dog?'

The man grunted. 'I wish. Now, I have something to discuss. Can we get on with it?'

Tehol smiled. 'By all means. This has proved most fascinating.'

'What has? I haven't started yet.'

'Just so. Proceed, then, sir.'

'We think our traders have been murdered by the Barghast. In fact, we think the painted savages have declared war on us. And so we call upon our loyal neighbours, the Letherii, for assistance in this unwanted war.' And he crossed his arms, glowering.

'Is there precedent for our assistance in such conflicts?' Tehol asked, settling his chin in one hand.

'There is. We ask, you say "no", and we go home. Sometimes,' he added, 'you say, "Of course, but first let us have half a thousand brokes of pasture land and twenty ranks of tanned hides, oh, and renounce sovereignty of the Kryn Freetrade Lands and maybe a royal hostage or two." To which we make a rude gesture and march home.'

'Are there no other alternatives?' Tehol asked. 'Chancellor, what has so irritated the—what are they called again—the Barnasties?'

'Barghast,' corrected Bugg. 'White Face Clans—they claim most of the plains as their ancestral homeland. I suspect this is the reason for their setting out to conquer the Akrynnai.'

Tehol turned to Janath and raised an eyebrow. 'Repatriation issues, see how they plague peoples? Bugg, are these Barghast in truth from those lands?'

The Chancellor shrugged.

'What kind of answer is that?' Tehol demanded.

'The only honest kind, sire. The problem is this: migratory tribes move around, that's what makes them migratory. They flow in waves, this way and that. The Barghast may well have dwelt on the plains and much of the Wastelands once, long, long ago. But what of it? Tarthenal once lived there, too, and Imass, and Jheck—a well-trammelled land, by any count. Who's to say which claim is more legitimate than the next?'

The emissary barked a laugh. 'But who lives there now? We do. The only answer that matters. We will destroy these Barghast. Irkullas calls to the Kryn and their mercenary Warleader Zavast. He calls to Saphinand and to the D'rhasilhani. And he sends me to you Letherii, to take the measure of your new King.'

'If you will crush the Barghast with the assistance of your allies,' said Tehol, 'why come here at all? What measure do you seek from me?'

'Will you pounce when our backs are turned? Our spies tell us your commander is in the field with an army—'

'*We* can tell you that,' Tehol said. 'There's no need for spies—'

'We prefer spies.'

'Right. Well. Yes, Brys Beddict leads a Letherii army—'

'Into the Wastelands—through our territory, in fact.'

'Actually,' said Bugg, 'we will be mostly skirting your territories, sir.'

'And what of these foreigners you march with?' the emissary asked, adding an impressive snarl after the question.

Tehol held up a hand. 'A moment, before this paranoia gets out of hand. Deliver the following message to Sceptre Irkullas, from King Tehol of Lether. He is free to prosecute his war against the Barghast—in defence of his territory and such—without fear of Letherii aggression. Nor, I add, that of the Malazans, the foreigners, I mean.'

'You cannot speak for the foreigners.'

'No, but Brys Beddict and his army will be escorting them, and so guarantee that nothing treacherous will take place—'

'Hah! Bolkando is already warring with the foreigners' allies!'

Bugg snorted. 'Thus revealing to you that the much acclaimed Bolkando Alliance has a straw spine,' he pointed out. 'Leave the Bolkando to sort out their own mess. As for the Malazans, assure Irkullas, they are not interested in you or your lands.'

The emissary's eyes had narrowed, his expression one of deep, probably pathological suspicion. 'I shall convey your words. Now, what gift must I take back to Irkullas?'

Tehol rubbed his chin. 'How does a wagonload of silks, linens, quality iron bars and a hundred or so silver ingots sound, sir?'

The man blinked.

'Outmoded traditions are best left behind, I'm sure Sceptre Irkullas will agree. Go, then, with our blessing.'

The man bowed and then walked off, weaving as if drunk.

Tehol turned to Janath and smiled.

She rolled her eyes. 'Now the poor bastard has to reciprocate in kind—which will likely impoverish him. Those old traditions survived for a reason, husband.'

'He won't be impoverished with the haul I just sent his way.'

'But he'll need to divide it up among his warleaders, to buy their loyalty.'

'He would have done that anyway,' said Tehol. 'And where did this insane notion of buying loyalty come from? It's a contradiction in terms.'

'The currency is obligation,' said Bugg. 'Gifts force honour upon the receiver. Sire, I must speak with you now as the Ceda. The journey Brys intends is more fraught than we had initially thought. I fear for his fate and that of his legions.'

'This relates, I assume,' said Janath, 'to the unknown motives of the Malazans. But Brys is not compelled to accompany them beyond the Wastelands, is he? Indeed, is it not his intention to return once that expanse is successfully crossed?'

Bugg nodded. 'Alas, I now believe that the Wastelands are where the greatest peril waits.' He hesitated, and then said, 'Blood has been spilled on those ancient soils. There will be more to come.'

Tehol rose from the throne, the Akrynnai gift in his hands. He held it out to one side and a servant hurried forward to take it. 'I do not believe my brother is as unaware of such dangers as you think, Bugg. His sojourn in the realm of the dead—or wherever it was—has changed him. Not surprising, I suppose. In any case, I don't think he returned to the realm of the living just to keep me company.'

'I suspect you are right,' said Bugg. 'But I can tell you nothing of the path he has taken. In a sense, he stands outside of . . . well, everything. As a force, one might view him as unaligned, and therefore unpredictable.'

'Which is why the Errant sought to kill him,' said Janath.

'Yes,' replied Bugg. 'One thing I can say: while in close company with the Malazans, Brys is perhaps safer from the Errant than he would be anywhere else.'

'And on the return journey?' Tehol asked.

'I expect the Errant to be rather preoccupied by then, sire.'

'Why is that?'

Bugg was long in replying, and on his blunt face could be seen a reluctant weighing of risks, ending in a grimace and then a sigh. 'He compels me. In my most ancient capacity, he compels me. Sire, by the time Brys begins his return to the kingdom, the Errant will be busy . . . contending with me.'

The iron beneath Bugg's words silenced the two others in the throne room, for a time.

Tehol then spoke, looking at neither his wife nor his closest friend. 'I will take a walk in the garden.'

They watched him leave.

Janath said, 'Brys is his brother, after all. And to have lost him once . . .'

Bugg nodded.

'Is there anything more you can do?' she asked him. 'To protect him?'

'Who, Brys or Tehol?'

'In this matter, I think, they are one and the same.'

'Some possibilities exist,' Bugg allowed. 'Unfortunately, in such circumstances as these, often the gesture proves deadlier than the original threat.' He held up a hand to forestall her. 'Of course I will do what I can.'

She looked away. 'I know you will. So, friend, you are compelled—when will you leave us?'

'Soon. Some things cannot be resisted for long—I am making him sweat.' He then grunted and added, 'and that's making me sweat.'

'Is this a "binding of blood"?' she asked.

He started, eyed her curiously. 'I keep forgetting you are a scholar, my Queen. That ancient phrase holds many layers of meaning, and almost as many secrets. Every family begins with a birth, but there can never be just one, can there?'

'Solitude is simple. Society isn't.'

'Just so, Janath.' He studied her for a moment. She sat on the throne, leaning to one side, head resting on one hand. 'Did you know you are with child?'

'Of course.'

'Does Tehol?'

'Probably not. It's early yet—Bugg, I suffered greatly in the hands of the Patriotists, didn't I? I see scars on my body but have no memory of how they came to be there. I feel pains inside and so I believe there are scars within, as well. I suspect your hand in my strange ignorance—you have scoured away the worst of what I experienced. I don't know if I should thank you or curse you.'

'An even measure of both, I should think.'

She regarded him levelly. 'Yes, you understand the necessity of balance, don't you? Well, I think I will give it a few more weeks before I terrify my husband.'

'The child is healthy, Janath, and I sense no risks—those pains are phantom ones—I was thorough in my healing.'

'That's a relief.' She rose. 'Tell me, was it simply a question of my twisted imagination, or did that Akrynnai artist have something disreputable in mind?'

'My Queen, neither mortal nor immortal can fathom the mind of an artist. But as a general rule, between two possible answers, choose the more sordid one.'

'Of course. How silly of me.'

'Draconus is lost within Dragnipur. Nightchill's soul is scattered to the winds. Grizzin Farl vanished millennia ago. And Edgewalker might well deny any compulsion out of sheer obstinacy or, possibly, a righteous claim to disassociation.' Knuckles managed a twisted smile, and then shrugged. 'If there is one presence I would find unwelcome above all others, Errastas, it is Olar Ethil.'

'She is dead—'

'And supremely indifferent to that condition—she embraced the Ritual of Tellann without hesitation, the opportunistic bitch—'

'And so bound herself to the fate of the T'lan Imass,' said the Errant, as he eyed Kilmandaros. The huge creature had dragged a massive trunk to the centre of the chamber, snapping the lock with one hand and then flinging back the lid; and now she was pulling out various pieces of green-stained armour, muttering under her breath. On the walls on all sides, seawater was streaming in through widening cracks, swirling ankle-deep and rising to engulf the fire in the hearth. The air was growing bitter cold.

'Not as bound as you might hope for,' said Sechul Lath. 'We have discussed K'rul, but there is one other, Errastas. An entity most skilled at remaining a mystery to us all—'

'Ardata. But she is not the only one. I always sensed, Setch, that there were more of us than any of us imagined. Even with my power, my command of the Tiles, I was convinced there were ghosts, hovering at the edge of my vision, my awareness. Ghosts, as ancient and as formidable as any of us.'

'Defying your rule,' said Sechul slyly, swirling the amber wine in his crystal goblet.

'Afraid to commit themselves,' the Errant said, sneering. 'Hiding from each other too, no doubt. Singly, not one poses a threat. In any case, it is different now.'

'Is it?'

'Yes. The rewards we can reap are vast—whatever has gone before is as nothing. Think on it. All that was stolen from us returned once more into our hands. The ghosts, the ones in hiding—they would be fools to hesitate. No, the wise course is to step out from the shadows.'

Knuckles took a mouthful of wine. The water was soaking the seat of the chair beneath him. 'The House is eager to wash us out.'

Kilmandaros had shrugged her way into a sopping hauberk of chain. She reached down to the submerged floor and lifted from the foaming swirl a huge gauntlet through which water gushed in a deluge. She dragged the gauntlet over one gnarled fist, and then reached down to find the other one.

'She's pleased,' said Errastas.

'No she isn't,' countered Knuckles. 'You have awakened her anger, and now she must find an enemy worthy of it. Sometimes—even for you—control is a delusion, a conceit. What you unleash here—'

'Is long overdue. Cease your efforts to undermine me, Setch—you only reveal your own weaknesses.'

'Weaknesses I have never run from, Errastas. Can you say the same?'

The Errant bared his teeth. 'You are cast. It cannot be undone. We must take our fate into our own hands—look to Kilmandaros—she will show us how it must be. Discard your fears—they sting like poison.'

'*I am ready.*'

At her words both men turned. She was clad for war and stood like a bestial statue, a hoary apparition enwreathed in seaweed. Algae mottled her hauberk. Verdigris mapped her helm's skullcap. The broad, low-slung, grilled cheek-guards looked like iron chelae, the bridge gleaming like a scorpion's pincer. Her gauntleted hands were closed into fists, like giant mauls at the ends of her apish, multi-jointed arms.

'So you are,' said Errastas, smiling.

'I have never trusted you,' Kilmandaros said in a growl.

He rose, still smiling. 'Why should I be unique? Now, who among us will open the portal? Knuckles, show us your power.'

The gaunt man flinched.

The water had reached hip-level—not Kilmandaros's hips, of course. The Errant gestured in Sechul Lath's direction. 'Let us see you as you should be. This is my first gift, Setch.' Power blossomed.

The ancient figure blurred, straightened, revealing at last a tall, youthful Forkrul Assail—who reeled, face darkening. He flung away his goblet. 'How dare you! Leave me as I was, damn you!'

'My gift,' snapped Errastas. 'To be accepted in the spirit in which it is given.'

Sechul held his elongated hands up over his face. 'How could you think,' he rasped, 'I ever regretted what I left behind?' He pulled his hands away, glaring. 'Give me back all that I have earned!'

'You are a fool—'

'*We will leave now,*' cut in Kilmandaros, loud enough to thunder in the chamber.

'Errastas!'

'No! It is done!'

A second gesture, and a portal opened, swallowing an entire wall of the House. Kilmandaros lumbered through, vanishing from sight.

The Errant faced Knuckles.

His old friend's eyes were filled with such wretched distress that Errastas snarled, 'Oh, have it your way, then—' and cruelly tore the blessing from the man, watched with satisfaction as the man bowed, gasping in sudden pain.

'There, wear your pathos, Setch, since it fits so damned well. What is this? You do not welcome its return?'

'It pleases you to deliver pain, does it? I see that you are unchanged . . . in the essential details of your nature.' Groaning, Sechul conjured a staff and leaned heavily upon it. 'Lead on then, Errastas.'

'Why must you sour this moment of triumph?'

'Perhaps I but remind you of what awaits us all.'

The Errant struggled not to strike Knuckles, not to knock that staff away with a kick and watch the old creature totter, possibly even fall. A shortlived pleasure. Unworthy to be sure. He faced the portal. 'Stay close—this gate will slam shut behind us, I suspect.'

'It's had its fill, aye.'

Moments later, water roared in to reclaim the chamber, darkness devoured every room, every hall. Currents rushed, and then settled, until all was motionless once more.

The House was at peace.

For a time.

Captain Ruthan Gudd was in the habit of grooming his beard with his fingers, an affectation that Shurq Elalle found irritating. Thoughtful repose was all very well, as far as poses went, but the man was so terse she had begun to suspect his genius was of the ineffable kind; in other words, it might be the man was thick but just clever enough to assume the guise of wisdom and depth. The silly thing was how damned successful and alluring the whole thing was—that hint of mystery, the dark veil of his eyes, his potent silences.

'Errant's sake, get out of here.'

He started, and then reached for his sword belt. 'I will miss you.'

'Everyone says that to me sooner or later.'

'A curious observation.'

'Is it? The simple truth is, I wear men out. In any case, I'm about to sail, so all in all it's just as well.'

He grunted. 'I'd rather be standing on a deck, letting the sails do all the work, than marching.'

'Then why did you become a soldier?'

He raked through his beard, frowned, and then said, 'Habit.' As he made his way to the door he paused, and squinted down at an urn sitting against one wall. 'Where did you get this?'

'That thing? I'm a pirate, Ruthan. I come by things.'

'Not purchased at a market stall in the city, then.'

'Of course not. Why?'

'The crows caught my eye. Seven Cities, that pot.'

'It's an urn, not a pot.'

'Fall of Coltaine. You preyed on a Malazan ship—' he turned and eyed her. 'Has to have been recently. Did you pounce on one of our ships? There were storms, the fleet was scattered more than once. A few were lost, in fact.'

She returned his stare flatly. 'And what if I had? It's not like I knew anything about you, is it?'

He shrugged. 'I suppose not. Though the idea that you put some fellow Malazans to the sword doesn't sit well.'

'I didn't,' she replied. 'I pounced on a Tiste Edur ship.'

After a moment he nodded. 'That makes sense. We first encountered them outside Ehrlitan.'

'Well, that's a relief.'

His eyes hardened. 'You are a cold woman, Shurq Elalle.'

'I've heard that before, too.'

He left without another word. It was always better this way, find something annoying to sour the moment, a brief exchange of lashing words, and then it was done with. Yearning goodbyes, dripping with soppy sentimentalities, were never quite as satisfying as one would like.

She quickly collected the last of her gear—most of her stuff was already stowed aboard *Undying Gratitude*. Skorgen Kaban the Pretty had taken charge of things, more or less, down at the harbour. Clearing up berth fees, sobering up the crew and whatnot. Her two Bolkando guests were safely stowed in the main cabin; and if Ublala Pung still hadn't shown up by the time she arrived, that was just too bad—the oaf had the memory of a moth.

He probably got confused and tried to walk to the islands.

She buckled her rapier to her hip, slung a modest duffel bag over one shoulder, and left, not bothering to lock the door—the room was rented and besides, the first thief inside was welcome to everything, especially that stupid urn.

A pleasant and promising offshore breeze accompanied her down to the docks. She was satisfied to see plenty of activity aboard her ship as she strode to the gang-plank. Stevedores were loading the last of the supplies, suffering under cruel commentary from the gaggle of whores who'd come down to send off the crew, said whores shooting her withering looks as she swept past them. Hardly deserved, she felt, since she hadn't been competing with them for months and besides, wasn't she now leaving?

She stepped down on to the main deck. 'Pretty, where did you get that nose?'

Her First Mate clumped over. 'Snapper beak,' he said, 'stuffed with cotton to hold back on the drip, Captain. I bought it at the Tides Market.'

She squinted at him. The strings holding the beak in place looked painfully tight. 'Best loosen it up some,' she advised, dropping the bag down to one side and then setting her fists on her hips as she surveyed the others on deck. 'No Pung?'

'Not yet.'

'Well, I want to take advantage of this wind.'

'Good, Captain, the giant's an ill omen besides—'

'None of that,' she snapped. 'He made a fine pirate in his days with us, and there was nothing ill-omened about him.' Kaban was jealous, of course. But the nose looked ridiculous. 'Get these dock rats off my ship and crew the lines.'

'Aye, Captain.'

She watched him limp off, nodded severely when he roared into the ear of a lounging sailor. Walking to the landward rail up near the bow, she scanned the crowds on the waterfront. No sign of Ublala Pung. 'Idiot.'

Captain Ruthan Gudd collected his horse at the stables and set out northward along the main avenue running partway alongside the central canal. He saw no other Malazans among the crowds—he could well be the last left in the city. This suited him fine, and better still if Tavore and her Bonehunters were to pull stakes before he arrived, leaving him behind.

He'd never wanted to be made a captain since it meant too many people paid attention to him. Given a choice, Ruthan would be pleased to spend his entire life not being noticed by anyone. Except for the occasional woman, of course. He had considered, rather often lately, deserting the army. If he had been a regular foot-soldier, he might well have done just that. But a missing officer meant mages joining in the search, and the last thing he wanted was to be sniffed down by a magicker. Of course Tavore wouldn't hold back on the army's march just to await his appearance—but there might well be a mage or two riding for him right now.

Either way, Fist Blistig was probably rehearsing the tongue-lashing he'd be delivering to Ruthan as soon as the captain showed.

Under normal circumstances, it was easy to hide in an army, even as an officer. Volunteer for nothing, offer no suggestions, stay in the back at briefings, or better still, miss them altogether. Most command structures made allowances for useless officers—no different from the allowances made for useless soldiers in the field. *'Take a thousand soldiers. Four hundred will stand in a fight but do nothing. Two hundred will run given the chance. Another hundred will get confused. That leaves three hundred you can count on. Your task in commanding that thousand is all down to knowing where to put that three hundred.'* Not Malazan doctrine, that. Some Theftian general, he suspected. Not Korelri, that was certain. Korelri would just keep the three hundred and execute the rest.

Greymane! No, don't be stupid, Ruthan. Be lucky to get five words a year out of that man. Then again, who needs words when you can fight like that! Hood keep you warm, Greymane.

In any case, Ruthan counted himself among the useless seven hundred, capable of doing nothing, getting confused, or routed at the first clash of weapons. Thus far, however, he'd not had a chance to attempt any of those options. The scraps he'd found himself in—relatively few, all things considered—had forced him to fight like a rabid wolf to stay alive. There was nothing worse in the world than being noticed by someone trying to kill you—seeing that sudden sharp focus in a stranger's eyes—

The captain shook himself. The north gate waited ahead.

Back into the army. Done with the soft bed and soft but oddly cool feminine flesh; with the decent (if rather tart) Letherii wines. Done with the delicious ease of doing nothing. Attention was coming his way and there was nothing to be done about it.

You told me to keep my head low, Greymane. I've been trying. It's not working. But then, something in your eyes told me you knew it wouldn't, because it wasn't working for you either.

Ruthan Gudd clawed at his bead, reminding himself of the stranger's face he now wore.

Let's face it, old friend. In this world it's only the dead who don't get noticed.

The place of sacrifice held an air of something broken. Ruined. It was a misery being there, but Ublala Pung had no choice. Old Hunch Arbat's rasping voice was in his head, chasing him this way and that, and the thing about a skull—even one as big as his—was how it was never big enough to run all the way away, even when it was a dead old man doing the chasing.

'I did what you said,' he said. 'So leave me alone. I got to get to the ship. So Shurq and me can sex. You're just jealous.'

He was the only living thing in the cemetery. It wasn't being used much any more, ever since parts of it started sinking. Sepulchres tilted and sagged and then broke open. Big stone urns fell over. Trees got struck by lightning and marsh gases wandered round looking like floating heads. And all the bones were pushing up from the ground like stones in a farmer's field. He'd picked one up, a leg bone, to give his hands something to play with while he waited for Arbat's ghost.

Scuffling sounds behind him—Ublala turned. 'Oh, you. What do you want?'

'I was coming to scare you,' said the rotted, half-naked corpse, and it raised bony hands sporting long, jagged fingernails. 'Aaaagh!'

'You're stupid. Go away.'

Harlest Eberict sagged. 'Nothing's working any more. Look at me. I'm falling apart.'

'Go to Selush. She'll sew you back up.'

'I can't. This stupid ghost won't let me.'

'What ghost?'

Harlest tapped his head, breaking a nail in the process. 'Oh, see that? It's all going wrong!'

'What ghost?'

'The one that wants to talk to you, and give you stuff. The one you killed. Murderer. I wanted to be a murderer, too, you know. Tear people to pieces and then eat the pieces. But there's no point in having ambitions—it all comes to naught. I was reaching too high, asking for too much. I lost my head.'

'No you didn't. It's still there.'

'Listen, the sooner we get this done the sooner that ghost will leave me so I can get back to doing nothing. Follow me.'

Harlest led Ublala through the grounds until they came to a sunken pit, three paces across and twice as deep. Bones jutted from the sides all the way down. The corpse pointed. 'An underground stream shifted course, moved under this cemetery. That's why it's slumping everywhere. What are you doing with that bone?'

'Nothing.'

'Get rid of it—you're making me nervous.'

'I want to talk to the ghost. To Old Hunch.'

'You can't. Except in your head and the ghost isn't powerful enough to do that while it's using me. You're stuck with me. Now, right at the bottom there's Tarthenal bones, some of the oldest burials in the area. You want to clear all that away, until you get to a big stone slab. You then need to pull that up or push it to one side. What you need is under that.'

'I don't need anything.'

'Yes you do. You're not going to get back to your kin for a while. Sorry, I know you've got plans, but there's nothing to be done for it. Karsa Orlong will just have to wait.'

Ublala scowled into the pit. 'I'm going to miss my ship—Shurq's going to be so mad. And I'm supposed to collect all the Tarthenal—that's what Karsa wants me to do. Old Hunch, you're ruining everything!' He clutched his head, hitting himself with the bone in the process. 'Ow, see what you made me do?'

'That's only because you keep confusing things, Ublala Pung. Now get digging.'

'I should never have killed you. The ghost, I mean.'

'You had no choice.'

'I hate the way I never get no choice.'

'Just climb into the hole, Ublala Pung.'

Wiping his eyes, the Tarthenal clambered down into the pit and began tossing out clumps of earth and bones.

Some time later Harlest heard the grinding crunch of shifting stone and drew closer to the edge and looked down. 'Good, you found it. That's it, get your hands under that edge and tilt it up. Go on, put your back into it.'

For all his empty encouragement, Harlest was surprised to see that the giant oaf actually managed to lift that enormous slab of solid stone and push it against one of the pit's walls.

The body interred within the sarcophagus had once been as massive as Ublala's own, but it had mostly rotted away to dust, leaving nothing but the armour and weapons.

'The ghost says there's a name for that armour,' said Harlest, 'even as the mace is named. First Heroes were wont to such affectations. This particular one, a Thelomen, hailed from a region bordering the First Empire—in a land very distant—the same land the first Letherii came from, in fact. A belligerent bastard—his name is forgotten and best left that way. Take that armour, and the mace.'

'It smells,' complained Ublala Pung.

'Dragon scales sometimes do, especially those from the neck and flanges, where there are glands—and that's where those ones came from. This particular dragon was firstborn to Alkend. The armour's name is Dra Alkeleint—basically Thelomen for "I killed the dragon Dralk." He used that mace to do it, and its name is Rilk, which is Thelomen for "Crush". Or "Smash" or something similar.'

'I don't want any of this stuff,' said Ublala. 'I don't even know how to use a mace.'

Harlest examined his broken nail. 'Fear not—Rilk knows how to use you. Now, drag it all up here and I can help you get that armour on—provided you kneel, that is.'

Ublala brought up the mace first. Two-handed, the haft a thick, slightly bent shaft of bone, horn or antler, polished amber by antiquity. A gnarled socket of bronze capped its base. The head was vaguely shaped to form four battered bulbs—the ore was marled mercurial and deep blue.

'Skyfall,' said Harlest, 'that metal. Harder than iron. You held it easily, Ublala, while I doubt I could even lift the damned thing. Rilk is pleased.'

Ublala scowled up at him, and then ducked down once again.

The armour consisted of shoulder plates, with the chest and back pieces in separate halves. A thick belt joined the upper parts to a waisted skirt. Smaller dragon scales formed the thigh-guards, with knee bosses made of dew-claws forming deadly spikes. Beneath the knees, a single moulded scale protected each shin. Vambraces of matching construction protected the wrists, with suppler hide covering the upper arms. Gauntlets of bone strips sheathed the hands.

Time's assault had failed—the scales were solid, the gut ties and leather straps supple as if new. The armour probably weighed as much as a grown human.

Last came the helm. Hundreds of bone fragments—probably from the dragon's skull and jaws—had been drilled and fastened together to form an overlapping skull cap, brow- and cheek-guards, and articulated lobster tail covering the back of the neck. The effect was both ghastly and terrifying.

'Climb out and let's get you properly attired.'

'I don't want to.'

'You want to stay in that hole?'

'Yes.'

'Well, that's not allowed. The ghost insists.'

'I don't like Old Hunch any more. I'm glad I killed him.'

'So is he.'

'I change my mind then. I'm not glad. I wish I'd left him alive for ever.'

'Then he would be the one standing here talking to you instead of me. There's no winning, Ublala Pung. The ghost wants you in this stuff, carrying the mace. You can leave off the helm for now, at least until you're out of the city.'

'Where am I going?'

'The Wastelands.'

'I don't like the sound of that place.'

'You have a very important task, Ublala Pung. In fact, you'll like it, I suspect. No, you will. Come up here and I'll tell you all about it while we're getting that armour on you.'

'Tell me now.'

'No. It's a secret unless you climb out.'

'You're going to tell me it if I come up there?'

'And get into the armour, yes.'

'I like people telling me secrets,' said Ublala Pung.

'I know,' said Harlest.

'Okay.'

'Wonderful.' Harlest looked away. Maybe he'd go to Selush after all. Not until night arrived, though. The last time he'd attempted the city streets in daytime a mob of scrawny urchins threw stones at him. What was the world coming to? Why, if he was in better shape, he could run after them and rip limbs from bodies and that'd be the end of the teasing and laughing, wouldn't it?

Children needed lessons, yes they did. Why, when he was a child . . .

Brys Beddict dismissed his officers and then his aides, waiting until everyone had left the tent before sitting down on the camp stool. He leaned forward and stared at his hands. They felt cold, as they had done ever since his return, as if the memory of icy water and fierce pressure still haunted them. Gazing upon the eager faces of his officers was proving increasingly difficult—something was growing within him, a kind of abject sorrow that seemed to broaden the distance between himself and everyone else.

He had looked at these animated faces but had seen in each the shadow of death, a ghostly face just beneath the outward one. Had he simply gained some new, wretched, insight into mortality? Sanity was best served when one dealt with the here and now, with reality's physical presence—its hard insistence. That brush of otherness scratched at his self-control.

If consciousness was but a spark, doomed to go out, fade into oblivion, then what value all this struggle? He held within him the names of countless long-dead gods. He alone kept them alive, or at least as near alive as was possible for such forgotten entities. To what end?

There was, he decided, much to envy in his brother. No one delighted more in the blessed absurdity of human endeavours. What better answer to despair?

Of the legions accompanying him, he had restructured all but one, the Harridict, and he had only spared that brigade at the request of the Malazan soldiers who'd worked with them. Doing away with the old battalion and brigade organization, he'd created five distinct legions, four of them consisting of two thousand soldiers and support elements. The fifth legion encompassed the bulk of the supply train as well as the mobile hospital, livestock, drovers and sundry personnel, including five hundred horse troops that employed the new fixed stirrups and were swiftly gaining competence under the tutelage of the Malazans.

Each of the combat legions, including the Harridict, now housed its own kitchen, smithy, armourers, triage, mounted scouts and messengers, as well as heavy assault weapons. More than ever, there was greater reliance upon the legion commanders and their staff—Brys wanted competence and self-reliance and he had selected his officers based on these qualities. The disadvantage to such personalities was evinced in every staff briefing, as egos clashed. Once on the march, Brys suspected, the inherent rivalries would shift from internal belligerence to competition with the foreign army marching on their flank, and that was just as well. The Letherii had something to prove, or, if not prove, then reinvent—the Malazans had, quite simply, trashed them in the invasion.

For too long the Letherii military had faced less sophisticated enemies—even the Tiste Edur qualified, given their unstructured, barbaric approach to combat. The few battles with the Bolkando legions, a decade ago, had proved bloody and indecisive—but those potential lessons had been ignored.

Few military forces were by nature introspective. Conservatism was bound to tradition, like knots in a rope. Brys sought something new in his army. Malleable, quick to adapt, fearless in challenging old ways of doing things. At the same time, he understood the value of tradition, and the legion structure was in fact a return to the history of the First Empire.

He clenched his hands, watched the blood leave his knuckles.

This would be no simple, uneventful march.

He looked upon his soldiers and saw death in their faces. Prophecy or legacy? He wished he knew.

Reliko saw the Falari heavies, Lookback, Shoaly and Drawfirst—all of them closing up their kit bags near the six-squad wagon—and walked over. 'Listen,' he said.
Three dark faces lifted to squint at him, and they didn't have to lift much, even
though they were kneeling. 'It's this. That heavy, Shortnose—you know, the guy
missing most of his nose? Was married to Hanno who died.'

The three cousins exchanged glances. Drawfirst shrugged, wiped sweat from
her forehead and said, 'Him, yeah. Following Flashwit around these days—'

'That's the biggest woman I ever seen,' said Shoaly, licking his lips.

Lookback nodded. 'It's her green eyes—'

'No it ain't, Lookie,' retorted Shoaly. 'It's her big everything else.'

Drawfirst snorted. 'You want big 'uns, look at me, Shoaly. On second thoughts,
don't. I know you too good, don't I?'

Reliko scowled. 'I was talking about Shortnose, remember? Anyway, I seem to
recall he only had one ear that time he got into that scrap and got his other ear
bitten off.'

'Yeah,' said Drawfirst. 'What about it?'

'You look at him lately? He's still got one ear. So what happened? Did it grow
back?'

The three soldiers said nothing, their expressions blank. After a moment they
returned to readying their kits.

Muttering under his breath, Reliko stomped off. This army had secrets, that
it did. Shortnose and his damned ear. Nefarias Bredd and his one giant foot.
That squad mage and his pet rats. Vastly Blank who had no brain at all but could
fight like a demon. Lieutenant Pores and his evil, now dead, twin. Bald Kindly
and his comb collection—in fact, Reliko decided as he returned to his squad, just
about everyone here, barring maybe himself and his sergeant, was completely
mad.

It's what no one outside an army understood. They just saw the uniforms and
weapons, the helms and visors, the marching in time. And if they ever did realize
the truth, why, they'd be even more scared. They'd run screaming.

'Ee cham penuttle, Erlko.'

'Shut up, Nep. Where's Badan?'

'Ee'n ere, y'poffle floob!'

'I can see that—so where did he go is what I want to know?'

The mage's wrinkled prune of a face puckered into something indescribable.
'Anay, ijit.'

'Ruffle! You seen the sergeant?'

The squad corporal sat leaning against a wagon wheel, one of those fat rustleaf
rollers jammed between her fat lips, smoke puffing out from everywhere, maybe
even her ears.

'Doo sheen see inny ting tru at smick!' barked Nep Furrow.

Despite himself Reliko grunted a laugh. 'Y'got that one right, Nep—Ruffle,
you got something wrong with air?'

She lifted one hand languidly and plucked the thing from her mouth. 'You fool. This is keeping those nasty mosquitoes away.'

'Hey, now that's clever—where can I get me some?'

'I brought about a thousand of 'em. But I warn you, Reliko, they'll make you green the first few days. But pretty soon you start sweating it outa your pores and not a bug will want you.'

'Huh. Anyway, where's Badan?'

'Having a chat with some other sergeants, Fiddler and them.' Ruffle puffed some more, and then added, 'I think Badan's decided we should stick with them— we all worked good enough before.'

'I suppose.' But Reliko didn't like the idea. Those squads were lodestones to trouble. 'What's Sinter say about that?'

'Seems all right with it, I guess.'

'Hey, where's our useless recruits?'

'Some Letherii came by and scooped them up.'

'Who said he could do that?'

Ruffle shrugged. 'Didn't ask.'

Reliko rubbed the back of his neck—not much to rub, he didn't have much of a neck, but he liked rubbing it, especially along the ridge of calluses where his helm's flare usually rested. He saw Skim's booted feet sticking out from under the wagon, wondered if she was dead. 'I'm going to get Vastly. Squad should be together for when Badan gets back.'

'Aye, good idea,' said Ruffle.

'You're the laziest damned corporal I ever seen.'

'Privilege of rank,' she said around her roller.

'You won't last a day on the march,' observed Reliko. 'You're fatter than the last time I seen you.'

'No I'm not. In fact, I'm losing weight. I can feel it.'

'Kennai felp too?'

'Don't even think it, Nep, you dried-up toad,' drawled Ruffle.

Reliko set off to find Vastly Blank. Him and Badan and that was it. The rest . . . not even close.

Fiddler tugged free the stopper on the jug and then paused to survey the others. Gesler had caught a lizard by the tail and was letting it bite his thumb. Balm sat crosslegged, frowning at the furious lizard. Cord stood leaning against the bole of a tree—something he'd likely regret as it was leaking sap, but he was making such an effort with the pose no one was going to warn him off. Thom Tissy had brought up a salted slab of some local beast's flank and was carving it into slices. Hellian was staring fixedly at the jug in Fiddler's hands and Urb was staring fixedly at Hellian. The three others, the two South Dal Honese—Badan Gruk and Sinter—and Primly, were showing old loyalties by sitting close together on an old boom log and eyeing everyone else.

Fiddler wanted maybe five more sergeants here but finding anyone in the chaotic sprawl that was a camp about to march was just about impossible. He lifted the jug. 'Cups ready, everyone,' and he set out to make the round. 'You only get half, Hellian,' he said when he came opposite her, 'since I can see you're already well on your way.'

'On my way where? Fillitup and don' be cheap neither.'

Fiddler poured. 'You know, you ain't treating Beak's gift with much respect.'

'What giff? He never give me nothing but white hair and thank the gods that's gone.'

When he had filled the other cups he returned to the rotted tree-stump and sat down once more. Fifty paces directly opposite was the river, the air above it swirling with swallows. After a moment he dropped his gaze and studied the soldiers arrayed round the old fisher's campfire. 'Now,' he said, 'this is the kind of meeting sergeants used to do back in the days of the Bridgeburners. It was a useful tradition and I'm thinking it's time it was brought back. Next time we'll get the rest of the company's sergeants.'

'What's the point of it?' Sinter asked.

'Every squad has its own skills—we need to know what the others can do, and how they're likely to do it. We work through all this and hopefully there won't be any fatal surprises in a scrap.'

After a moment, Sinter nodded. 'Makes sense.'

Cord asked, 'You're expecting us to run into trouble any time soon, Fid? That what your deck told you? Has this trouble got a face?'

'He's not saying,' said Gesler. 'But it's a fair guess that we'll know it when we see it.'

'Bolkando,' suggested Badan Gruk. 'That's the rumour anyway.'

Fiddler nodded. 'Aye, we might have a bump or two with them, unless the Burned Tears and the Perish slap them into submission first. The Saphii seem to be the only ones happy to have us pay a visit.'

'It's pretty isolated, ringed in mountains,' said Cord, crossing his arms. 'Probably starving for a few fresh faces, even ones as ugly as ours.'

'Thing is, I don't know if we're even heading into Saphinand,' Fiddler pointed out. 'From the maps I've seen it's well to the north of the obvious route across the Wastelands.'

Cord grunted. 'Crossing any place named the Wastelands seems like a bad idea. What's in this Kolanse anyway? What's driving the Adjunct? Are we heading into another war to right some insult delivered on the Malazan Empire? Why not just leave it to Laseen—it's not like we owe the Empress a damned thing.'

Fiddler sighed. 'I'm not here to chew on the Adjunct's motives, Cord. Speculation's useless. We're her army. Where she leads, we follow—'

'Why?' Sinter almost barked the word. 'Listen. Me and my sister half starved in a Letherii cell waiting on execution. Now, maybe the rest of you thought it was all fucking worth it taking down these Tiste Edur and their mad Emperor, but a lot of marines died and the rest of us are lucky to be here. If it wasn't for that Beak you'd all be dead—but he's gone. And so is Sinn. We got one High Mage and that's it, and how good is he? Fiddler—can Quick Ben do what Beak did?'

Fiddler unstrapped his helm and drew it off. He scratched at his sweat-matted hair. 'Quick Ben doesn't work that way. Used to be he was more behind-the-scenes, but Hedge tells me it's been different lately, maybe ever since Black Coral—'

'Oh great,' cut in Cord, 'where the Bridgeburners were wiped out.'

'That wasn't his fault. Anyway, we all saw what he could do against the Edur mages off the coast of Seven Cities—he made them back down. And then, in Letheras, he chased off a damned dragon—'

'I'm sure the cussers stuffed up its nose helped,' Cord muttered.

Gesler grunted a sour laugh. 'Well, Fid, Bridgeburner sergeants we ain't, and I guess that's pretty obvious. Can you imagine Whiskeyjack and Brackle and Picker and the rest moaning over every damned thing the way you got here? I can't and I never even met them.'

Fiddler shrugged. 'I wasn't a sergeant back then, so I really can't say. But something tells me they did plenty of chewing. Don't forget from about Blackdog all the way down to Darujhistan somebody in the empire wanted them dead. Now, maybe they never had much to complain about when it came to Dujek Onearm, but at the same time it's not like they knew what their High Fist was up to—it wasn't their business.'

'Even when that business killed soldiers?' Sinter asked.

Fiddler's laugh was harsh and cutting. 'If that isn't a commander's business, what is? The Adjunct's not our Hood-damned mother, Sinter. She's the will behind the fist and we're the fist. And sometimes we get bloodied, but that's what comes when you're hammering an enemy in the face.'

'It's all those teeth,' added Gesler, 'and I should know.'

But Sinter wasn't letting go. 'If we know what we're getting into, we've got a better chance of surviving.'

Fiddler rose, his right hand slamming the helm on to the ground where it bounced and rolled into the firepit's ashes. 'Don't you get it? Surviving isn't what all this is about!'

As those words shot out bitter as a dying man's spit, the gathered sergeants flinched back. Even Gesler's eyes widened. The lizard took that moment to pull free and scamper away.

In the shocked silence Fiddler half-snarled and clawed at his beard, unwilling to meet anyone's eyes. *Hood's breath, Fid—you're a damned fool. You let her get to you. That look in her eyes—she's no natural soldier—what in Fener's name is she even doing here? And how many more like her are there in this army?*

'Well,' said Cord in a flat voice, 'that must have been one Hood's piss of a reading.'

Fiddler forced out a ragged breath. 'Not a piss, Cord, a fucking deluge.'

And then Sinter surprised them all. 'Glad that's cleared up. Now, let's talk about how we're going to work together to make us the meanest Hood-shitting fist the Adjunct's got.'

Lying flat behind a tangle of brush, Throatslitter struggled to swallow. His mouth and throat were suddenly so dry and hot he thought he might cough flames. He cursed himself for being so damned nosy. He spied to feed his curiosity and—he had to admit—to give himself an advantage on his fellow soldiers, reason for his sly expression and sardonic, knowing smile, and a man like him wasn't satisfied if it was all just for show.

Well, now he knew.

Fid's been dragged low. He says he doesn't know Tavore's business but he just showed them he was lying. He knows and he's not telling. Aye, he's not telling but he just told them anyway. Who needs details when we're all ending up crow meat?

He might cough flames, aye, or laugh out a cloud of ashes. He needed to talk to Deadsmell, and he needed to find that other Talon hiding among the marines—there'd been markers, every now and then, calls for contact only a fellow Talon would recognize. He'd done a few of his own, but it seemed they were dancing round each other—and that had been fine, until now. *If we're heading for Hood's grey gate, I want allies. Deadsmell for certain. And whoever my hidden dancer happens to be.*

The sergeants were talking back and forth now, cool and calm as if Fiddler hadn't just sentenced them all, and Throatslitter wasn't paying much attention until he heard his name.

'He can guard our backs if we need it,' Balm was saying, not a hint of confusion in his voice.

'I don't think we will,' Fiddler said. 'When I spoke of betrayal I wasn't meaning within our ranks.'

Betrayal? What betrayal? Gods, what have I missed?

'Our allies?' Cord asked. 'I can't believe it, not from the Perish or the Burned Tears. Who else is there?'

'There's the Letherii,' said Sinter. 'Our oversized escort.'

'I can't be any more specific,' Fiddler responded. 'Just make sure we keep our noses in the air. Badan Gruk, what's your mage capable of?'

'Nep Furrow? Well, he's a bush warlock, mostly. Good at curses.' He shrugged. 'I've not seen much else, though he once conjured up a seething ball of spiders and threw it at Skim—they looked real and bit hard enough to make Skim shriek.'

'Could still have been an illusion, though,' Sinter said. 'Sometimes, Dal Honese curses edge close to Mockra—that's how it sneaks into the victim's thoughts.'

'You seem to know something about all that,' observed Gesler.

'I'm not a mage,' she replied. 'But I can smell magics.'

'Who's our nastiest all-weapons-out fighter?' Cord asked.

'Skulldeath,' said Sinter and Badan Gruk simultaneously.

Fiddler grunted and added, 'Koryk and Smiles would agree with you. Maybe reluctantly from Koryk, but that's just jealousy.'

Hellian laughed. 'Glad t'hear he's good f'something,' and she drank from her cup and then wiped her mouth.

When it became obvious she wasn't going to elaborate, Fiddler resumed. 'We can throw forward a solid line of heavies if we need to. While we're not short on sappers we are on munitions, but there's nothing to be done for that. They're good for night work, though. And they can crew the heavier weapons we got from the Letherii.'

The discussion went on, but Throatslitter was distracted by a faint scuffling sound beside his head. He turned to find himself eye to eye with a rat.

One of Bottle's. That bastard.

But that's a point, isn't it? Fiddler's not talked about him. He's holding him back.

Now, that's interesting.

He bared his teeth at the rat.

It returned the favour.

Riding along the well-beaten track leading to the Bonehunter encampment, Ruthan Gudd saw five other captains, all mounted, cantering to a rise between the Malazan and Letherii contingents. Grimacing, he angled his horse to join them. Palavers of this sort always depressed him. Captains got stuck from both ends, not privy to what the Fists knew and despised by their underlings. Lieutenants were usually either ambitious backstabbers or butt-licking fools. The only exception he'd heard about was Pores. Kindly was lucky having a rival like that, someone to match wits with, someone with enough malicious evil going on in his head to keep his captain entertained. Ruthan's own lieutenant was a sullen Napan woman named Raband, who might be incompetent or potentially murderous. He'd lost his other two in Y'Ghatan.

The others had reined in and were eyeing Ruthan as he rode up, an array of expressions unified in their disapproval. Seniority put Kindly in charge. Below him was a black-haired Kanese, Skanarow, a woman of about forty, uncharacteristically tall and lean-limbed for a Kanese—probably from the southern shore-folk who had originally been a distinct tribe. Her features were harsh, seamed in scars as if she'd suckled among wildcats as a child.

Next was Faradan Sort, who'd served all over the place and maybe even stood the Stormwall—Ruthan, who knew more about that than most, suspected it was true. She held herself like someone who'd known the worst and never wanted to know it again. But there were experiences that a person could never leave behind, could never, ever forget. Besides, Ruthan had seen the etching on Sort's sword, and that kind of damage could only come from the deadly touch of wand-magic.

Ruthan was next, followed by the two in-field promotions, a Hengian named Fast who was already taking aim on a fisthood, and an island-born ferret of a man named Untilly Rum, who'd been busted over from the marines after his soldiers had set a deathmark on him—for reasons unknown to any but them. Despite his background, Untilly could ride a horse like a damned Wickan, and so he was now commanding the light lancers.

'Considerate of you to show up,' said Kindly.

'Thank you, Captain,' Ruthan replied, combing fingers through his beard as he studied the chaos that was the Malazan encampment. 'We'll be lucky to get away by tomorrow.'

'My company's ready,' said Fast.

'Maybe the last time you saw them,' Skanarow said with a tight smile. 'Probably scattered to a dozen whore tents by now.'

Fast's pinched face darkened. 'Sit and wait, was my order, so that's what they're doing. My lieutenants are making sure of it.'

'If they're any good then I doubt it,' Skanarow replied. 'They've been watching the soldiers getting bored, listening to the bickering get worse and worse, and maybe pulling a few off each other. If they got any wits in them, they'll have cut them loose by now.'

'Skanarow's point, Captain Fast,' said Faradan Sort, 'is this: it doesn't pay to get your squads up and ready too early. You'd do well to heed the advice of those of us with more experience.'

Fast bit down on a retort, managed a stiff nod.

Ruthan Gudd twisted in his saddle to observe the Letherii legions. Well-ordered bastards, that much was clear. Brys Beddict had them all close hobbled and waiting on the Malazans, patient as old women waiting for their husbands to die.

Kindly spoke: 'Skanarow, Fast, you and the rest of the officers under Fist Blistig's command must be seeing firsthand the problem we're all facing. Fist Keneb is being pulled every which way when he should be worrying about his own companies and nothing else. He's shouldering the logistics for Blistig's companies and we're suffering for it.'

'There's no lighting fires under Blistig these days,' said Skanarow.

'Can you take up the slack?'

She blinked. 'The only reason I'm a captain, Kindly, is that I know how to lead soldiers into battle and I know what to do with them once there. I've no head for organization.' She shrugged. 'I've a pair of decent lieutenants who keep the rows tallied and nobody issued two left boots to march in. Without them I'd be as bad as Blistig.'

'Logistics is no problem for me,' opined Fast.

No one responded to that.

Kindly arched his back and winced. 'It was said, back when he was commanding the Aren Garrison, that Blistig was a sharp, competent officer.'

'Witnessing the slaughter of the Seventh and then Pormqual's army broke him,' Faradan Sort said. 'I am surprised the Adjunct doesn't see that.'

'The one thing we can address,' said Kindly, 'is how we can help Keneb—we need the best Fist we have, captains, not exhausted, not overwhelmed.'

'We can't do a thing without the squad sergeants,' Faradan Sort said. 'I suggest we corral our respective noncoms into the effort.'

'Risky,' said Kindly.

Ruthan grunted—an unintentional response that drew unwelcome attention.

'Pray, explain that,' Kindly asked in a drawl.

He shrugged. 'Maybe it suits us officers to think we're the only ones capable of seeing how High Command is falling apart.' He met Kindly's gaze. 'The sergeants see better than we do. Pulling them in sacrifices nothing and may even relieve them, since it'll show we're not all a bunch of blind twits, which is probably what they're thinking right now.' Having said his piece he subsided once more.

'"Who speaks little says a lot,"' Faradan Sort said, presumably quoting someone.

Kindly collected his reins. 'It's decided, then. Draw in the sergeants. Get them to straighten out their squads—Hood knows what Brys must be thinking right now, but I'm damned sure it's not complimentary.'

As Kindly and the others rode away, Skanarow angled her mount in front of Ruthan's, forcing him to halt. He squinted at her.

She surprised him with a grin and it transformed her face. 'The old ones among my people say that sometimes you find a person with the roar of a sea squall in their eyes, and those ones, they say, have swum the deepest waters. In you, Ruthan Gudd, I now understand what they meant. But in you I see not a squall. I see a damned typhoon.'

He quickly looked away, ran fingers through his beard. 'Just a spell of gas, Skanarow.'

She barked a laugh. 'Have it your way, then. Avoid raw vegetables, Captain.'

He watched her ride off. *Fisherfolk. You, Skanarow with the lovely smile, I need to avoid. Too bad.*

Greymane, you always said that between the two of us I was the luckier one. Wrong, and if your ghost hearkens to its name, spare me any echo of laughter.

He paused, but all he could hear was the wind, and there was no humour in that moan.

'Walk on, horse.'

Koryk looked a mess, trembling and wild-eyed, as he tottered back to the squad camp. Tarr frowned. 'You remind me of a pathetic d'bayang addict, soldier.'

'If paranoia comes with them shakes,' said Cuttle, 'he might as well be just that. Sit down, Koryk. There's room in the wagon for ya come tomorrow.'

'I was just sick,' Koryk said in a weak growl. 'I seen d'bayang addicts at the trader forts and I don't like being compared to them. I made a vow, long ago, to never be that stupid. I was just sick. Give me a few days and I'll be right enough to stick my fist in the next face gabbling about d'bayang.'

'That sounds better,' said Smiles. 'Welcome back.'

Corabb appeared from a tent carrying Koryk's weapon belt. 'Honed and oiled your blade, Koryk. But it looks like the belt will need another notch. You need to get some meat back on your bones.'

'Thanks, Mother, just don't offer me a tit, all right?' Sitting down on an old munitions box, he stared at the fire. The walk, Tarr judged, had exhausted the man. That boded ill for all the other soldiers who'd come down with the same thing. The tart water had worked, but the victims who'd recovered were wasted one and all, with a haunted look in their eyes.

'Where's Fid?' Koryk asked.

Bottle stirred from where he had been lying, head on a bedroll and a cloth over his eyes. Blinking in the afternoon light he said, 'Fid's been listing all our faults. One of those secret meetings of all the sergeants.'

Tarr grunted. 'Glad to hear it's secret.'

'We ain't got any faults,' said Smiles. 'Except for you, Corporal. Hey Bottle, what else were they talking about?'

'Nothing.'

That snatched everyone's attention. Even Corabb looked up from the new hole he was driving through the thick leather belt—he'd jammed the awl into the palm of his left hand but didn't seem to have noticed yet.

'Hood knows you're the worst liar I ever heard,' said Cuttle.

'Fid's expecting a fight, and maybe soon. He's tightening the squads. All right? There. Chew on that for a while.'

'How hard is he working on that?' the sapper asked, eyes narrowed down to slits.

Bottle looked ready to spit out something foul. 'Hard.'

'Shit,' said Koryk. 'Look at me. Shit.'

'Take the wagon bed tomorrow and maybe the next day,' said Tarr. 'And then spell yourself for a few days after that. We've that long at least until we're into possibly hostile territory. And eat, Koryk. A lot.'

'Ow,' said Corabb, lifting the hand with the awl dangling from the palm.

'Pull it and see if you bleed,' said Smiles. 'If you don't, go see a healer quick.' Noticing the others looking at her she scowled. 'Fish hooks. The, uh, fisherfolk who used to work for my family—well, I've seen it go bad, is all. Punctures that don't bleed, I mean. Oh, piss off, then.'

'I'm going for a walk,' said Bottle.

Tarr watched the mage wander off, and then glanced over and found Cuttle staring at him. *Aye, it's looking bad.*

Corabb plucked out the awl and managed to squeeze out a few drops of blood. He gave Smiles a triumphant grin, then returned to working on the belt.

Bottle wandered through the encampment, avoiding the disorganized mobs besieging the quartermaster's HQ, the armourer compound, the leather and cordage workshops, and a host of other areas crowded with miserable, overworked specialists. Even outside the whore tents soldiers were getting into scraps. *Gods, where are all the officers? We need military police—this is what happens when there's no imperial oversight, no Claws, no adjutants or commissars.*

Adjunct, why aren't you doing anything about this? Hold on, Bottle—it ain't your problem. You've got other problems to worry about. He found he was standing in the centre of a throughway, one hand clutching his hair. A storm of images warred in his head—all his rats were out, crouched in hiding in strategic places—but the one in Tavore's command tent was being assailed by folds of burlap—someone had bagged it! He forced the other ones out of his head. *You! Little Koryk! Pay attention! Start chewing as if your life depended on it—because maybe it does—get out of that sack!*

'You. You're in Fiddler's squad, right?'

Blinking, Bottle focused on the man standing in front of him. 'Hedge. What do you want?'

The man smiled, and given the wayward glint in the man's mud-grey eyes that was a rather frightening expression. 'Quick Ben sent me to you.'

'Really? Why? What's he want?'

'Never could answer that one—but you're the one, Bottle, isn't it?'

'Look, I'm busy—'

Hedge lifted up a sack. 'This is for you.'

'Bastard!' Bottle snatched the bag. A quick look inside. *Oh, stop your chewing now, Koryk. Relax.*

'It was moving,' said Hedge.

'What?'

'The sack. Got something alive in there? It was jumping around in my hand—' He grunted then as someone collided with him.

An armoured regular, big as a bear, lumbered past.

'Watch where you're walking, y'damned ox!'

At Hedge's snarl, the man turned. His broad, flat face assumed the hue of a beet. He stomped back, lips twisting.

Seeing the man's huge hands closing into fists, Bottle stepped back in alarm.

Hedge simply laughed.

The beet looked ready to explode.

Even as the first fist flew, Hedge was ducking under it, closing tight up against the man. The sapper's hands shot between the soldier's legs, grabbed, squeezed and yanked.

With a piercing shriek, the soldier doubled over.

Hedge added a knee to his jaw, flinging the head back upward. Then he drove an elbow into a cheekbone, audibly shattering it.

The huge man crumpled. Hedge stood directly over him. 'You just went for the last living Bridgeburner. I'm guessing you won't do that again, huh?' Hedge then turned back to Bottle and smiled a second time. 'Quick Ben wants to talk with you. Follow me.'

A few paces along, Bottle said, 'You're not, you know.'

'Not what?'

'The last living Bridgeburner. There's Fiddler and Quick Ben, and I even heard about some survivors from Black Coral hiding out in Darujhistan—'

'Retired or moved on every one of them. Fid said I should do the same and I thought about it, I really did. A new start and all that.' He tugged at his leather cap. 'But then I thought, what for? What's so good about starting all over again? All that ground you covered the first time, why do it a second time, right? No—' and he tapped the Bridgeburner sigil sewn on to his ratty rain-cape. 'This is what I am, and it still means something.'

'I expect that regular back there agrees with you.'

'Aye, a good start. And even better, I had me a talk with Lieutenant Pores, and he's giving me command of a squad of new recruits. The Bridgeburners ain't dead after all. And I hooked up with a Letherii alchemist, to see if we can come up with replacements for the Moranth munitions—he's got this amazing powder, which I'm calling Blue. You mix it and then get it inside a clay ball which you seal right away. In about half a day the mix is seasoned and set.'

Bottle wasn't much interested, but he asked anyway. 'Burns good, does it?'

'Don't burn at all. That's the beauty of Blue, my friend.' Hedge laughed. 'Not a flicker of flame, not a whisper of smoke. We're working on others, too. Eaters, Sliders, Smarters. And I got two assault weapons—a local arbalest and an onager— we're fitting clay heads on the quarrels. And I got me a new lobber, too.' He was almost jumping with excitement as he led Bottle through the camp. 'My first squad's going to be all sappers along with whatever other talents they got. I was thinking—imagine a whole Bridgeburner army, say, five thousand, all trained as marines, of course. With heavies, mages, sneaks and healers, but every one of them is also trained as a sapper, an engineer, right?'

'Sounds terrifying.'

'Aye, doesn't it? There.' He pointed. 'That tent. Quick's in there. Or he said he would be, once he got back from the command tent. Anyway, I got to go collect my squad.'

Hedge walked off.

Bottle tried to imagine five thousand Hedges, with the real Hedge in charge. *Hood's breath, I'd want a continent between me and them. Maybe two.* He repressed a shiver, and then headed to the tent. 'Quick? You in there?'

The flap rippled.

Scowling, Bottle crouched and ducked inside.

'Stop spying on the Adjunct and me,' the wizard said. He was sitting at the far end, crosslegged. In front of him and crowding the earthen floor in the tent's centre was a heap of what looked like children's dolls.

Bottle sat down. 'Can I play?'

'Funny. Trust me, these things you don't want to play with.'

'Oh, I don't know. My grandmother—'

'I'm tying threads, Bottle. You want to get yourself tangled in that?'

Bottle shrank back. 'Ugh, no thanks.'

Quick Ben bared his smallish teeth, a neat white row. 'The mystery is, there's at least three in there I can't even identify. A woman, a girl and some bearded bastard who feels close enough to spit on.'

'Who are they tied to?'

The wizard nodded. 'Your granny taught you way too much, Bottle. I already told Fiddler to treat you as our shaved knuckle. Aye, I've been trying to work that out, but the skein's still a bit of a mess, as you can see.'

'You're rushing it too much,' Bottle said. 'Leave them to shake loose on their own.'

'Maybe so.'

'So, what have you and the Adjunct got to be so secret about? If I really am your shaved knuckle, I need to know things like that, so I know what to do when it needs doing.'

'Maybe it's her,' mused Quick Ben, 'or more likely it was T'amber. They've sniffed me out, Bottle. They've edged closer than anybody's ever done, and that includes Whiskeyjack.' He paused, frowning. 'Maybe Kallor. Maybe Rake—yes, Rake probably saw clear enough—was it any wonder I avoided him? Well, Gothos, sure, but—'

'High Mage,' cut in Bottle, 'what are you going on about?'

Quick Ben started, and then glared. 'Distracted, sorry. You don't need to spy on her—Lostara saw the rat and nearly chopped it in half. I managed to intervene, made up some story about using it for an augury. If anything vital comes up, I will let you know.'

'A whisper in my skull.'

'We're heading into a maze, Bottle. The Adjunct's ageing in front of my eyes, trying to figure out a way through the Wastelands. Have you tried soul-riding anything into it? It's a snarl of potent energies, massive blind-spots, and a thousand layers of warring rituals, sanctified grounds, curse-holes, blood-pits, skin-sinks. I try and just reel back, head ready to split, tasting blood in my mouth.'

'The ghost of a gate,' said Bottle.

Quick Ben's eyes glittered in the gloom. 'An area of influence, yes, but that ghost gate, it's wandered—it's not even there any more, in the Wastelands, I mean.'

'East of the Wastelands,' said Bottle. 'That's where we'll find it, and that's where we're going, isn't it?'

Quick Ben nodded. 'Better the ghost than the real thing.'

'Familiar with the real one, are you, High Mage?'

He glanced away. 'She's worked that one out all on her own. Too canny, too damned unknowable.'

'Do you think she's in communication with her brother?'

'I don't dare ask,' Quick Ben admitted. 'She's like Dujek that way. Some things you just don't bring up. But, you know, that might explain a lot of things.'

'But then ask yourself this,' said Bottle. 'What if she isn't?'

The wizard was silent for a long moment. Then he sighed. 'If not Paran, then who?'

'Right.'

'That's a nasty question.'

'I don't spy on the Adjunct just when she has you for company, Quick Ben. Most of the time I watch her, it's when she's alone.'

'That's pathetic—'

'Fuck the jokes, High Mage. Our Adjunct knows things. And I want to know how. I want to know if she has company none of us know a thing about. Now, if you want me to stop doing that, give me a solid reason. You say she's got close to you. Have you returned the favour?'

'I would, if I knew how. That otataral sword pushes me away—it's what they're made to do, isn't it.' Seeing the sceptical expression opposite him, he scowled. 'What?'

'It doesn't push you as hard as you like to pretend it does. The risk is that the harder and deeper you push through the otataral, the more of yourself you potentially expose—and if she catches sight of you, she won't just be close to knowing you, she'll be certain.' He jabbed a finger at Quick Ben. 'And that is what you don't want to happen, and it's the real reason why you don't dare push through. So, your only chance is me. Do I resume spying or not?'

'Lostara's suspicious—'

'When the Adjunct is presumably alone.'

The High Mage hesitated, and then nodded. 'Found anything yet?'

'No. She's not in the habit of thinking out loud, that much is obvious. She doesn't pray, and I've yet to hear a one-sided conversation.'

'Could you be blinded?'

'I could, yes, but I'd sense the gaps of awareness. I think. Depending on how good the geas is.'

'If it's a geas directed specifically at your extra eyes?'

'It would have to be. But you're right, something specific, Mockra maybe, that slips into the rat's tiny brain and paints a pretty picture of nothing happening. If that's the case, then I don't know how I could do anything about it, because with the local effect of the otataral, the source of that sorcery would be an appallingly high level—a damned god's level, I mean.'

'Or an Elder's.'

'These waters are too deep for a mortal like me, Quick Ben. My spying only works because it's passive. Strictly speaking, riding a soul isn't magic, not in the common sense.'

'Then seek out something on the Wastelands, Bottle. See what you can see, because I can't get close and neither, I think, can the Adjunct. Find a wolf, or a coyote—they like to hang round armies and such. Who's out there?'

'I'll try. But if it's that risky, you might lose me. I might lose me, which is even worse.'

Quick Ben smiled his little smile and reached into the heap of dolls. 'That's why I've tied this thread to this particular doll.'

Bottle hissed. 'You miserable shit.'

'Stop complaining. I'll pull you back if you get into trouble. That's a promise.'

'I'll think about it,' said Bottle, rising.

The High Mage looked up in surprise. 'What's to think about?'

'Quick Ben, if it's that dangerous in the Wastelands, hasn't it occurred to you that if I'm grabbed, you may not be the one doing the pulling on that thread? With you suddenly drooling and playing with dolls for real, the Adjunct and, more importantly, her army, are well and truly doomed.'

'I can hold my own,' Quick Ben growled.

'How do you know you can? You don't even know what's out there. And why would I want to put myself in the middle of a tugging contest? I might well get torn to pieces.'

'Since that wasn't the first thing you brought up,' said Quick Ben, with a sly look, 'I expect you have a few contingency plans to deal with the possibility.'

'I said I'd think about it.'

'Don't wait too long deciding, Bottle.'

'Two full crates of that smoked sausage, aye. Fist Keneb's orders.'

'Will do, Master Sergeant.'

'Strap them tight, remember,' Pores reminded the spotty-faced young man and was pleased at the eager nod. Quartermaster division always pulled in the soldiers who couldn't fight their way out of a school playground, and they had two ways of going once they'd got settled—either puppies who jumped at the snap of an officer's fingers or the ones who built impregnable fortresses out of regulations and then hoarded supplies somewhere inside—as if to give anything up drew blood and worse. Those ones Pores had made a career out of crushing; but at times like this, the puppies were the ones he wanted.

He cast a surreptitious glance around, but the chaos swirled unabated on all sides and no one was paying him any attention. And the puppy was happy at being collared, so when accosted he could shake his head, duck down and use the various lines Pores himself used. *'Fist Keneb's orders, take it up with him.'* And *'Master Sergeant's got recruits to outfit, fifty of 'em, and Captain Kindly said to do it quick.'* Keneb was safe enough since at the moment nobody apart from his personal adjutants could even get close to him; and as for Kindly, well, the name itself usually sucked the blood from even the heartiest faces.

It was a minor and mostly irrelevant detail that Pores had somehow lost his recruits. Snatched away from the marine squads by someone nobody knew anything about. If trouble arrived Pores could look innocent and point fingers at the squad sergeants. *Never make a roadblock of yourself on trouble's road. No, make yourself a bridge instead, with stones slick as grease.*

I should compose a mid-level officer's guide to continued health, indolence and undeserved prosperity. But then, if I did that, I'd have to be out of the battle, no longer in competition, as it were. Say, retired somewhere nice. Like a palace nobody was using. And that would be my crowning feat—requisitioning a palace.

'Queen Frabalav's orders, sir. If you got a problem, you can always discuss it with her one-eyed torturer.'

But for now, fine Letherii smoked sausages, three crates of excellent wine, a cask of cane syrup, all for Fist Keneb (not that he'd ever see any of that); and extra blankets, extra rations, officer boots including cavalry high-steppers, rank sigils and torcs for corporals, sergeants, and lieutenants, all for his fifty or was it sixty vanished recruits—which translated into Pores's very own private stock for those soldiers on the march who lost things but didn't want to be officially docked for replacements.

He'd already commandeered three wagons with decent teams, under guard at the moment by soldiers from Primly's squad. It occurred to him he might have to draw those three squads in as partners in his black-market operation, but that shouldn't be too hard. Envy diminished the more one shared the rewards, after all, and with something at stake those soldiers would have the proper incentive when it came to security and whatnot.

All in all, things were shaping up nicely.

'Hey there, what's in that box?'

'Combs, sir—'

'Ah, for Captain Kindly then.'

'Aye, sir. Personal requisition—'

'Excellent. I'll take those to him myself.'

'Well, uhm—'

'Not only is the captain my immediate superior, soldier, I also happen to be his barber.'

'Oh, right. Here you go, sir—just a signature here—that wax bar, yes sir, that's the one.'

Smiling, Pores drew out his reasonable counterfeit of Kindly's own seal and pressed it firmly down on the wax bar. 'Smart lad, keeping things proper is what makes an army work.'

'Yes, sir.'

Hedge's pleasure at seeing that his Letherii alchemist had rounded up the new recruits as he had ordered quickly drained away when he cast a gauging eye on the forty would-be soldiers sitting not fifteen paces from the company latrine trench. When he first approached the bivouac he'd thought they were waving at him, but turned out it was just the swarming flies.

'Bavedict!' he called to his alchemist, 'get 'em on their feet!'

The alchemist gathered up his long braid and with a practised twist spun it into a coil atop his head, where the grease held it fast, and then rose from the peculiar spike-stool he'd set up outside his hide tent. 'Captain Hedge, the last mix is ready to set and the special rain-capes were delivered by my brother half a bell ago. I have what I need to do some painting.'

'That's great. This is all of them?' he asked, nodding towards the recruits.

Bavedict's thin lips tightened in a grimace. 'Yes, sir.'

'How long have they been sitting in that stench?'

'A while. Not ready to do any thinking for themselves yet—but that's what's to be expected from us Letherii. Soldiers do what they're told to do and that's that.'

Hedge sighed.

'There's two acting sergeants,' Bavedict added. 'The ones with their backs to us.'

'Names?'

'Sunrise—he's the one with the moustache. And Nose Stream.'

'Well now,' Hedge said, 'who named them?'

'Some Master Sergeant named Pores.'

'I take it he wasn't around when you snatched them.'

'They'd been tied to some squads and those squads were none too pleased about it anyway. So it wasn't hard cutting them loose.'

'Good.' Hedge glanced over at Bavedict's carriage, a huge, solid-looking thing of black varnished wood and brass fittings; he then squinted at the four black horses waiting in their harnesses. 'You was making a good living, Bavedict, leading me to wonder all over again what you're doing here.'

'Like I said, I got too close a look at what one of those cussers of yours can do—to a damned dragon, no less. My shop's nothing but kindling.' He paused and balanced himself on one foot, the other one set against the leg just below the knee. 'But mostly professional curiosity, Captain, ever a boon and a bane both. So, you just keep telling me anything and everything you recall about the characteristics of the various Moranth alchemies, and I'll keep inventing my own brand of munitions for your sappers.'

'My sappers, aye. Now I better go and meet—'

'Here come two of 'em now, Captain.'

He turned and almost stepped back. Two enormous, sweaty women had fixed small eyes on him and were closing in.

They saluted and the blonde one said, 'Corporal Sweetlard, sir, and this is Corporal Rumjugs. We got a request, sir.'

'Go on.'

'We want to move from where we was put down. Too many flies, sir.'

'An army never marches or camps alone, Corporal,' said Hedge. 'We got rats, we got mice, we got capemoths and crows, ravens and rhizan. And we got flies.'

'That's true enough, sir,' said the black-haired one, Rumjugs, 'but even over here there ain't so many of 'em. Ten more paces between us and the trench there, sir, is all we're asking.'

'Your first lesson,' said Hedge. 'If the choice is between comfortable and miserable, choose comfortable—don't wait for any damned orders neither. Distracted and irritated makes you more tired. Tired gets you killed. If it's hot look for shade. If it's cold bundle t'gether when not on post. If you're in a bad spot for flies, find a better one close by and move. Now, I got a question for you two. Why are you bringing me this request and not your sergeants?'

'They was going to,' said Rumjugs, 'but then me and Sweet here, we pointed out that you're a man and we're whores or used to be, and you was more likely to be nice to us than to them. Assuming you prefer women an' not men.'

'Good assumption and smart thinking. Now, go back there and get everybody on their feet and over here.'

'Yes, sir.'

He returned their salute and watched them wheeze and waddle back to the others.

Bavedict moved up beside him. 'Maybe there's hope for them after all.'

'Just needs teasing out, that's all,' said Hedge. 'Now, find a wax tablet or something—I need a list of their names made up—my memory is bad these days, ever since I died and came back, in fact.'

The alchemist blinked, and then recovered. 'Right away, Captain.'

All in all, Hedge concluded, a decent start.

Lostara slammed the knife back into its sheath, then walked to examine an array of tribal trophies lining one wall of the presence chamber. 'Fist Keneb is not at his best,' she said. Behind her in the centre of the room, the Adjunct said nothing. After a moment Lostara went on. 'Grub's disappearance hit him hard. And the thought that he might have been swallowed up by an Azath is enough to curdle anyone's toes. It's not helping that Fist Blistig seems to have decided he's already good as dead.'

She turned to see the Adjunct slowly drawing off her gauntlets. Tavore's face was pale, a taut web of lines trapping her eyes. She'd lost weight, further reducing the few feminine traits she possessed. Beyond grief waited emptiness, a place where loneliness haunted in mocking company, and memories were entombed in cold stone. The woman that was the Adjunct had decided that no one would ever take T'amber's place. Tavore's last tie to the gentler gifts of humanity had been severed. Now there was nothing left. Nothing but her army, which looked ready to unravel all on its own—and even to this she seemed indifferent.

'It's not like the King to keep us waiting,' Lostara muttered, reaching to unsheathe her knife.

'Leave it,' the Adjunct snapped.

'Of course. My apologies, Adjunct.' She dropped her hand and resumed her uninterested examination of the artifacts. 'These Letherii devoured a lot of tribes.'

'Empires will, Lieutenant.'

'I imagine this Kolanse did the same. It is an empire, is it not?'

'I do not know,' the Adjunct replied, then added, 'it does not matter.'

'It doesn't?'

But with her next words it was clear that the Adjunct was not interested in elaborating. 'My predecessor, a woman named Lorn, was murdered in a street in Darujhistan. She had, by that point, completed her tasks, insofar as anyone can tell. Her death seemed to be little more than ill luck, a mugging or something similar. Her corpse was deposited in a pauper's pit.'

'Forgive me, Adjunct, but what is this story in aid of?'

'Legacies are never what one would hope for, are they, Captain? In the end, it does not matter what was achieved. Fate holds no tally of past triumphs, courageous deeds, or moments of profound integrity.'

'I suppose not, Adjunct.'

'Conversely, there is no grim list of failures, moments of cowardice or dishonour. The wax is smooth, the past melted away—if it ever existed at all.' Those snared eyes fixed briefly on Lostara before sliding away once more. 'She died on a street, just one more victim of mischance. A death devoid of magic.'

Lostara's attention dropped down to the sword strapped at Tavore's hip. 'Most deaths are, Adjunct.'

Tavore nodded. 'The wax melts. There is, I think, some comfort to be found in that. A small measure of . . . release.'

Is that the best you can hope for, Tavore? Gods below. 'Lorn was not there to gauge the worth of her legacy, if that is what you mean, Adjunct. Which was probably a mercy.'

'I sometimes think that fate and mercy are often one and the same.'

The notion chilled Lostara.

'The army,' continued the Adjunct, 'will sort itself out once on the march. I give them this touch of chaos, of near anarchy. As I do for Fists Keneb and Blistig. I have my reasons.'

'Yes, Adjunct.'

'In the King's presence, Captain, I expect you to refrain from any undue attention to the knife at your side.'

'As you command, Adjunct.'

Moments later an inner door swung open and King Tehol strode in, trailed by the Chancellor. 'My sincerest apologies, Adjunct. It's all my Ceda's fault, not that you need to know that, but then'—and he smiled as he sat down on the raised chair—'now you do, and I don't mind telling what a relief that is.'

'You summoned us, Majesty,' said Adjunct.

'Did I? Oh yes, so I did. Relax, there's no crisis—well, none that concerns you directly. Well, not in Letheras, anyway. Not at the moment, I mean. Ceda, step forward there now! Adjunct Tavore, we have a gift for you. In expression of our deepest gratitude.'

Queen Janath had arrived as well, moving up to stand to one side of her husband, one hand resting on the chair's high back.

Bugg was holding a small hand-polished wooden case, which he now set into the Adjunct's hands.

The chamber was silent as Tavore unlatched the lid and tilted it back to reveal a water-etched dagger. The grip and pommel were both plain, functional, and as far as Lostara could see, the blade itself, barring the etched swirls, was unspectacular. After a moment's examination, the Adjunct shut the lid and looked up at the King. 'Thank you, sire. I shall treasure this—'

'Hold on,' said Tehol, rising and walking over. 'Let's see that thing—' and he lifted the lid once more, and then faced Bugg. 'Couldn't you have selected something prettier than that, Ceda? Why, I imagine the Chancellor is mortified now that he's seen it!'

'He is, sire. Alas, the Ceda was under certain constraints—'

'Excuse me,' said the Adjunct, 'am I to understand that this weapon is ensorcelled? I am afraid that such piquancy will be lost in my presence.'

The old man smiled. 'I have done what I can, Tavore of House Paran. When you face your most dire necessity, look to this weapon.'

The Adjunct almost stepped back and Lostara saw what little colour there had been in her face suddenly drain away. 'My most . . . dire . . . necessity? Ceda—'

'As I said, Adjunct,' Bugg replied, his gaze unwavering. 'When blood is required. When blood is *needed*. In the name of survival, and in that name alone.'

Lostara saw that Tavore was at a loss for words—and she had no idea why. *Unless the Adjunct already knows what that necessity will be. Knows, and is horrified by this gift.* Bowing, Adjunct closed the lid a second time and stepped back.

Tehol was frowning at Bugg. After a moment he returned to the modest chair and sat down once more. 'Fare you well on your journey, Adjunct. And you as well, Lostara Yil. Do not neglect my brother, he has many talents. A lot more than me, that's for certain—' and at seeing Bugg's nod he scowled.

Janath reached down and patted his shoulder.

Tehol's scowl deepened. 'Look to Brys Beddict during your traverse of Bolkando Kingdom. We are very familiar with our neighbours, and his advice should prove valuable.'

'I shall, sire,' the Adjunct said.

And suddenly it was time to go.

Moments after the Malazans had departed, Tehol glanced over at Bugg. 'My, you look miserable.'

'I dislike departures, sire. There is ever a hint of . . . finality.'

Janath came round and sat on one of the flanking benches. 'You do not expect to see the Malazans again?'

He hesitated, and then said, 'No.'

'What of Brys?' Tehol asked.

Bugg blinked and opened his mouth to reply but the King raised a hand. 'No, that question should not have been asked. I'm sorry, old friend.'

'Sire, your brother possesses unexplored . . . depths. Fortitude, unassailable fidelity to honour—and, as you well know, he carries within him a certain legacy, and while I cannot gauge the measure of that legacy, I believe it has the potential to be vast.'

'You danced carefully there,' Janath observed.

'I did.'

Sighing, Tehol leaned back on the chair. 'This seems a messy conclusion to things, doesn't it? Little that amuses, even less that entertains. You must know I prefer to leap from one delightful absurdity to another. My last gesture on the Malazan stage should have been the highest of dramas is my feeling. Instead, I taste something very much like ashes in my mouth and that is most unpleasant.'

'Perhaps some wine will wash things clean,' suggested Bugg.

'Won't hurt. Pour us some, please. You, guard, come and join us—standing there doing nothing must be a dreadful bore. No need to gape like that, I assure you. Doff that helm and relax—there's another guard just like you on the other side of that door, after all. Let him bear the added burden of diligence. Tell us about yourself. Family, friends, hobbies, scandals—'

'Sire,' warned Bugg.

'Or just join us in a drink and feel under no pressure to say anything at all. This shall be one of those interludes swiftly glossed over in the portentous histories of great and mediocre kings. We sit in the desultory aftermath, oblivious to omens and whatever storm waits behind yonder horizon. Ah, thank you, Bugg—my Queen, accept that goblet and come sit on my knee—oh, don't make that kind of face, we need to compose the proper scene. I insist and since I'm King I can do that, or so I read somewhere. Now, let's see . . . yes, Bugg, stand right over there—oh, massaging your brow is the perfect pose. And you, dearest guard—how did you manage to hide all that hair? And how come I never knew you were a woman? Never mind, you're an unexpected delight—ow, calm down, wife—oh, that's me who needs to calm down. Sorry. Women in uniforms and all that. Guard, that dangling helm is exquisite by the way, take a mouthful and do pass judgement on the vintage, yes, like that, oh, most perfect!

'Now, it's just occurred to me that we're missing something crucial. Ah, yes, an artist. Bugg, have we a court artist? We need an artist! Find us an artist! Nobody move!'

Chapter Twelve

The sea is blind to the road
And the road is blind to the rain
The road welcomes no footfalls
The blind are an ocean's flood
On the road's shore

Walk then unseeing
Like children with hands outstretched
Down to valleys of blinding darkness
The road leads down through shadows
Of weeping gods

This sea knows but one tide flowing
Into sorrow's depthless chambers
The sea is shore to the road
And the road is the sea's river
To the blind

When I hear the first footfalls
I know the end has come
And the rain shall rise
Like children with hands
Outstretched

I am the road fleeing the sun
And the road is blind to the sea
And the sea is blind to the shore
And the shore is blind
To the sea

The sea is blind . . .

RIDDLE OF THE ROAD OF GALLAN
SHAKE CHANT

When leading his warriors, warchief maral eb of the Barahn White Face Barghast liked to imagine himself as the tip of a barbed spearhead, hungry to wound, unerring in its drive. Slashes of red ochre cut through the white paint of his death-face, ran jagged tracks down his arms. His bronze brigandine hauberk and scaled skirt bore the muted tones of blood long dead, and the red-tipped porcupine quills jutting from the spikes of his black, greased hair clattered as he trotted in front of four thousand seasoned warriors.

The stink from the severed heads swinging from the iron-sheathed standards crowding behind the warchief left a familiar sting in the back of his broad, flattened nose, a cloying presence at the close of his throat, and he was pleased. Pleased, especially, that his two younger brothers carried a pair of those standards.

They'd stumbled upon the Akrynnai caravan late yesterday afternoon. A pathetic half-dozen guards, five drovers, the merchant and her family. It had been quick work, yet no less delicious for its brevity, tainted only when the merchant took a knife to her daughters and then slit her own throat—gestures of impressive courage that cheated his warriors of their fun. The puny horses in the herd they had slaughtered and feasted upon that night.

Beneath a cloudless sky, the war-party was cutting westward. A week's travel would find it in the Kryn Freetrade, the centre of all eastern commerce with Lether. Maral Eb would slaughter everyone and then assume control of the caravanserai and all the trader forts. He would make himself rich and his people powerful. His triumph would elevate the Barahn to the position they rightfully deserved among the White Faces. Onos Toolan would be deposed and the other clans would flock to join Maral. He would carve out an empire, selling Akrynnai and D'ras slaves until the vast plains belonged to the Barghast and no one else. He would set heavy tariffs on the Saphii and Bolkando, and he would build a vast city in Kryn, raising a palace and establishing impregnable fortresses along the borderlands.

His allies among the Senan had already been instructed to steal for him the twin daughters of Hetan. He would bring them into his own household and when they reached blooding age he would take them as his wives. Hetan's fate he left to others. There was the young boy, the true son of the Imass, and he would have to be killed, of course. Along with Cafal, to end once and for all Humbrall Taur's line.

His musings on the glory awaiting him were interrupted by the sudden appearance ahead of two of his scouts, carrying a body between them.

Another Barghast—but not one of his own.

Maral Eb held up one hand, halting his war-party, and then jogged forward to meet the scouts.

The Barghast was a mess. His left arm was gone below the elbow and the stump seethed with maggots. Fires had melted away half his face and fragments of his armour of tin coinage glittered amidst the weltered ruin of skin and meat on his chest. By the fetishes dangling from his belt Maral knew him to be a Snake-hunter, one of the smaller clans.

He scowled and waved at the flies. 'Does he live?'

One of the scouts nodded and then added, 'Not for much longer, Warchief.'

'Set him down, gently now.' Maral Eb moved up and knelt beside the young warrior. He swallowed down his disgust and said, 'Snakehunter, open your eyes. I am Maral Eb of the Barahn. Speak to me, give me your last words. What has befallen you?'

The one surviving eye that opened was thick with mucus, a dirty yellow rimmed in cracked, swollen flesh. The mouth worked for a moment, and then raw words broke loose. 'I am Benden Ledag, son of Karavt and Elor. Remember me. I alone survived. I am the last Snakehunter, the last.'

'Does an Akrynnai army await me?'

'I do not know what awaits you, Maral Eb. But I know what awaits me— damnation.' The face twisted with pain.

'Open your eye—look at me, warrior! Speak to me of your slayer!'

'Damnation, yes. For I fled. I did not stand, did not die with my kin. I ran. A terrified hare, a leap-mouse in the grass.' Speech was drying out the last fluids within him and his breath grated. 'Run, Maral Eb. Show me how . . . how cowards live.'

Maral Eb made a fist to strike the babbling fool, and then forced himself to relax. 'The Barahn fear no enemy. We shall avenge you, Benden Ledag. We shall avenge the Snakehunter. And may the souls of your fallen kin hunt you down.'

The dying fool somehow managed a smile. 'I will wait for them. I will have a joke, yes, one that will make them smile—as was my way. Zaravow, though, he has no reason to laugh, for I stole his wife—I stole her pleasure—' he hacked out a laugh. 'It is what weak men do . . . have always done.' The eye suddenly sharpened, fixed on Maral Eb. 'And you, Barahn, I will wait for you, too.' The smile faltered, the face lost its clenched pain, and the wind's air flowed unclaimed through the gape of his mouth.

Maral Eb stared down into that unseeing eye for a moment. Then he cursed and straightened. 'Leave him to the crows,' he said. 'Sound the horns—draw in the forward scouts. We shall camp here and ready ourselves—there is vengeance in our future, and it shall be sweet.'

Two of the six women dragged what was left of the horsetrader to the gully cutting down the hillside and rolled him into it. Hearing snakes slithering in the thick brush of the gully, they quickly backed away and returned to the others.

Hessanrala, warleader of this troop of Skincuts, glanced over from the makeshift bridle she was fixing to her new horse, grinned as both women tugged fistfuls of grass to clean the blood and semen from their hands, and said, 'See to your horses.'

The one closest to her flung the stained grasses to one side. 'A nest of vipers,' she said. 'Every clump of sagebrush and rillfire swarms with them.'

'Such omens haunt us,' the other one muttered.

Hessanrala scowled. 'A knife to your words, Ralata.' She waved one hand. 'Look at this good fortune. Horses for each of us and three more to spare, a bag of coins and mint-soaked bhederin and three skins of water—and did we not amuse ourselves with the pathetic creature? Did we not teach him the gifts of pain?'

'This is all true,' said Ralata, 'but I have felt shadows in the night, and the whisper of dread wings. Something stalks us, Hessanrala.'

In reply the warleader snarled and turned away. She vaulted on to her horse. 'We are Ahkrata Barghast. Skincuts—and who does not fear the women slayers of the Ahkrata?' She glared at the others, as if seeking the proper acknowledgement, and seemed satisfied as they drew their mounts round to face her.

Ralata spat into her hands and took charge of the only saddled horse—the Akrynnai trader's very own, which she had claimed by right of being the first to touch her blade to the man's flesh. She set a boot into the stirrup and swung on to the beast's back. Hessanrala was young. This was her first time as warleader, and she was trying too hard. It was custom that a seasoned warrior volunteer to accompany a new warleader's troop, lest matters go awry. But Hessanrala was not interested in heeding Ralata, seeing wisdom as fear, caution as cowardice.

She adjusted the fragments of Moranth chitin that served as armour among the Ahkrata, and made sure the chest-plate of Gold was properly centred. Then took a moment to resettle into her nostrils the broad hollow bone plugs that made Ahkrata women the most beautiful among all the White Face Barghast. She swung her horse to face Hessanrala.

'This trader,' said the warleader with a faint snarl directed at Ralata, 'was returning to his kin as we all know, having chased him from our camp. We can see the ancient trail he was using. We shall follow it, find the Akrynnai huts, and kill everyone we find.'

'The path leads north,' said Ralata. 'We know nothing of what lies in that direction—we might ride into a camp of a thousand Akrynnai warriors.'

'Ralata bleats like a newborn kid, but I hear no pierce-cry of a hawk.' Hessanrala looked to the others. 'Do any of you hear the winged hunter? No, only Ralata.'

Sighing, Ralata made a gesture of release. 'I am done with you, Hessanrala. I return to our camp, and how many women will come to my Skincut cry? Not five. No, I shall be warleader to a hundred, perhaps more. You, Hessanrala, shall not live long—' and she looked to the others, was dismayed to see their expressions of disgust and contempt—but they too were young. 'Follow her into the north, warriors, and you may not return. Those who would join me, do so now.'

When none made a move, Ralata shrugged and swung her horse round. She set off, southward.

Once past a rise and out of sight of the troop—which had cantered off in the opposite direction—Ralata reined in. She would have the blood of five foolish girls on her hands. Most would understand her reasons for leaving. They knew Hessanrala, after all. But the families that lost daughters would turn away.

There was a hawk out there. She knew it with certainty. And the five kids had no shepherd, no hound to guard them. Well, she would be that hound, low in the grasses on their trail, ever watchful. And, should the hawk strike, she would save as many as she could.

She set out to follow them.

The low cairns set in a row across the hill's summit and leading down the slope were almost entirely overgrown. Windblown soils had heaped up along one side, providing purchase for rillfire trees, their gnarled, low branches spreading out in swaths of sharp thorns. High grasses knotted the other sides. But Tool knew the piles of stone for what they were—ancient blinds and runs built by Imass hunters—and so he was not surprised when they reached the end of the slope and found themselves at the edge of a precipice. Below was a sinkhole, its base thick with skalberry trees. Buried beneath that soil, he knew, there were bones, stacked thick, two or even three times the height of a grown man. In this place, Imass had driven herds to their deaths in great seasonal hunts. If one were to dig beneath the skalberry trees, one would find the remains of bhed and tenag: their bones and shattered horns, tusks, and embedded spear-points of grey chert; one would find, here and there, the skeletons of ay that had been dragged over the cliff's edge in their zeal—the wolves' canines filed down to mark them as pups found in the wild, too fierce to have their massive fangs left in place; and perhaps the occasional okral, for the plains bears often tracked the bhed herds and found themselves caught up in the stampedes, especially when fire was used.

Generation upon generation of deadly hunts mapped out in those layers, until all the tenag were gone, and with them the okral, and indeed the ay—and the wind was hollow and empty of life, no howls, no shrill trumpeting from bull tenag, and even the bhed had given way to their smaller cousins, the bhederin—who would have vanished too, had their two-legged hunters thrived.

But they did not thrive, and Onos T'oolan knew the reason for that.

He stood at the edge of the sinkhole, anguish deep in his soul, and he longed for the return of the great beasts of his youth. Eyes scanning the lie of the land to the sides of the pit, he could see where the harvest had been processed—the slabs of meat brought up to the women who waited beside smaller, skin-lined pits filled with water that steamed as heated stones built it to boiling—and yes, he could see the rumpled ground evincing those cooking pits, and clumps of greenery marking hearths—and there, to one side, a huge flattened boulder, its slightly concave surface pocked where longbones had been split to extract the marrow.

He could almost smell the reek, could almost hear the droning chants and buzzing insects. Coyotes out on the fringes, awaiting their turn. Carrion birds scolding in the sky overhead, the flit of rhizan and the whisper of capemoths. Drifts of smoke redolent with sizzling fat and scorched hair.

There had been a last hunt, a last season, a last night of contented songs round fires. The following year saw no one in this place. The wind wandered alone, the half-butchered carcasses grew tough as leather in the sinkhole, and flowers fluttered where blood had once pooled.

Did the wind mourn with no song to carry on its breath? Or did it hover, waiting in terror for the first cries of bestial pain and fear, only to find that they never came? Did the land yearn for the tremble of thousands of hoofs and the padded feet of tenag? Did it hunger for that flood of nutrients to feed its children? Or was the silence it found a blessed peace to its tortured skin?

There had been seasons when the herds came late. And then, with greater frequency, seasons when the herds did not come at all. And the Imass went hungry. Starved, forced into new lands in a desperate search for food.

The Ritual of Tellann had circumvented the natural, inevitable demise of the Imass. Had eluded the rightful consequences of their profligacy, their shortsightedness.

He wondered if, among the uppermost level of bones, one might find, here and there, the scattered skeletons of Imass. A handful that had come to this place to see what could be salvaged from the previous year's hunt, down beneath the picked carcasses—a few desiccated strips of meat and hide, the tacky gel of hoofs. Did they kneel in helpless confusion? Did the hollow in their bellies call out to the hollow wind outside, joined in the truth that the two empty silences belonged to one another?

If not for Tellann, the Imass would have known regret—not as a ghost memory—but as a cruel hunter tracking them down to their very last, staggering steps. And that, Tool told himself, would have been just.

'Vultures in the sky,' said the Barghast warrior at his side.

Tool grimaced. 'Yes, Bakal, we are close.'

'It is as you have said, then. Barghast have died.' The Senan paused, and then said, 'yet our shouldermen sensed nothing. You are not of our blood. How did you know, Onos Toolan?'

The suspicion never went away, Tool reflected. This gauging, uneasy regard of the foreigner who would lead the mighty White Faces to what all believed was a righteous, indeed a *holy* war. 'This is a place of endings, Bakal. Yet, if you know where to look—if you know how to see—you find that some endings never end. The very absence howls like a wounded beast.'

Bakal uttered a sceptical grunt, and then said, 'Every death-cry finds a place to die, until only silence waits beyond. You speak of echoes that cannot be.'

'And you speak with the conviction of a deaf man insisting that what you do not hear does not exist—in such thinking you will find yourself besieged, Bakal.' He finally faced the Barghast warrior. 'When will you people discover that your will does not rule the world?'

'I ask how you knew,' Bakal said, expression darkening, 'and you answer with insults?'

'It is curious what you choose to take offence to,' Tool replied.

'It is your cowardice that offends us, Warleader.'

'I refuse your challenge, Bakal. As I did that of Riggis, and as I will all others that come my way—until our return to our camp.'

'And once there? A hundred warriors shall vie to be first to spill your blood. A thousand. Do you imagine you can withstand them all?'

Tool was silent for a moment. 'Bakal, have you seen me fight?'

The warrior bared his filed teeth. 'None of us have. Again you evade my questions!'

Behind them, close to a hundred disgruntled Senan warriors listened to their every word. But Tool would not face them. He found he could not look away from the sinkhole. *I could have drawn my sword. With shouts and fierce faces, enough to terrify them all. And I could have driven them before me, chased them, shrieking at seeing them run, seeing their direction shift, as the ancient rows of cairns channelled them unwittingly on to the proper path—*

—and then see them tumble over the cliff's edge. Cries of fear, screams of pain— the snap of bones, the thunder of crushed bodies—oh, listen to the echoes of all that!

'I have a question for you, Bakal.'

'Ah! Yes, ask it and hear how a Barghast answers what is asked of him!'

'Can the Senan afford to lose a thousand warriors?'

Bakal snorted.

'Can the Warleader of the White Face Barghast justify killing a thousand of his own warriors? Just to make a point?'

'You will not survive one, never mind a thousand!'

Tool nodded. 'See how difficult it is, Bakal, to answer questions?'

He set out, skirting the sinkhole's edge, and made his way down the slope to the left—a much gentler descent into the valley, and had the beasts been clever, they would have used it. But fear drove them on, and on. Blinding them, deafening them. Fear led them to the cliff's edge. Fear chased them into death.

Look on, my warriors, and see me run.

But it is not you that I fear. A detail without relevance, because, you see, the cliff edge does not care.

'Which damned tribe is this one?' Sceptre Irkullas asked.

The scout frowned. 'The traders call them the Nith'rithal—the blue streaks in their white face paint distinguish them.'

The Akrynnai warleader twisted to ease the muscles of his lower back. He had thought such days were past him—a damned war! Had he not seen enough to earn some respite? When all he sought was a quiet life in his clan, playing bear to his grandchildren, growling as they swarmed all over him with squeals and leather knives stabbing everywhere they could reach. He so enjoyed his lengthy death-throes, always saving one last shocking lunge when all were convinced the giant bear was well and truly dead. They'd shriek and scatter and he would lie back, laughing until he struggled to catch his breath.

By the host of spirits, he had *earned* peace. Instead, he had . . . this. 'How many yurts did you say again?' His memory leaked like a worm-holed bladder these days.

'Six, maybe seven thousand, Sceptre.'

Irkullas grunted. 'No wonder they've devoured half that bhederin herd in the month since they corralled them.' He considered for a time, scratching the white bristles on his chin. 'Twenty thousand inhabitants then. Would you say that a fair count?'

'There's the track of a large war-party that headed out—eastward—a day or so ago.'

'Thus diminishing the number of combatants even more—tracks, you say? These Barghast have grown careless, then.'

'Arrogant, Sceptre—after all, they've slaughtered hundreds of Akrynnai already—'

'Poorly armed and ill-guarded merchants! And that makes them strut? Well, this time they shall face true warriors of the Akrynnai—descendants of warriors who crushed invaders from Awl, Lether and D'rhasilhani!' He collected his reins and twisted round towards his second in command. 'Gavat! Prepare the wings to the canter—as soon as their pickets see us, sound the Gathering. Upon sighting the encampment, we charge.'

There were enough warriors nearby to hear his commands and a low, ominous *hhunn* chant rumbled through the ranks.

Irkullas squinted at the scout. 'Ride back out to your wing, Ildas—ride down their pickets if you can.'

'It's said the Barghast women are as dangerous as the men.'

'No doubt. We kill every adult and every youth near blooding—the children we will make Akrynnai and those who resist we will sell as slaves to the Bolkando. Now, enough talking—loosen the arrows in your quiver, Ildas—we have kin to avenge!'

Sceptre Irkullas liked playing the bear to his grandchildren. He was well suited to the role. Stubborn, slow to anger, but as the Letherii and others had discovered, ware the flash of red in his eyes—he had led the warriors of the Akrynnai for three decades, at the head of the most-feared cavalry on the plains, and not once had he been defeated.

A commander needed more than ferocity, of course. A dozen dead Letherii generals had made the mistake of underestimating the Sceptre's cunning.

The Barghast had lashed out to slay traders and drovers. Irkullas was not interested in chasing the damned raiding parties this way and that—not yet, in any case. No, he would strike at the very homes of these White Face Barghast—and leave in his wake nothing but bones and ashes.

Twenty thousand. Seven to ten thousand combatants is probably a high estimate—although it's said they've few old and lame, for their journey into these lands was evidently a hard one.

These Barghast were formidable warriors; of that Irkullas had no doubt. But they thought like thieves and rapists, with the belligerence and arrogance of bullies. Eager for war, were they? *Then Sceptre Irkullas shall bring them war.*

Formidable warriors, yes, these White Faces.

He wondered how long they would last.

Kamz'tryld despised picket duty. Tripping over bhederin dung—and more than a few bones of late, as the slaughter to ready for winter had begun—while biting flies chased him about and the wind drove grit and sand into his face so that by day's end his white deathmask was somewhere between grey and brown. Besides, he was not so old that he could not have trotted out with Talt's war-party yesterday—not that Talt agreed, the one-fanged bastard.

Kamz was reaching an age when loot became less a luxury than a need. He had a legacy to build, something to leave his kin—he should not be wasting his last years of prowess here, so far from—

Thunder?

No. Horses.

He was on a ridge that faced a yet higher one just to the north—he probably should have walked out to that one, but he'd decided it was too far—and as he turned to squint in that direction he caught sight of the first outriders.

Akrynnai. A raid—ah, we shall have plenty of blood to spill after all! He snapped out a command and his three wardogs spun and bolted for the camp. Kamz voiced a cry and saw that his fellow sentinels, two off to his left, three to his right, had all seen and heard the enemy, and dogs were tearing down towards the camp— where he discerned a sudden flurry of activity—

Yes, these Akrynnai had made a terrible mistake.

He shifted grip on his lance, as he saw one of the riders charging directly for him. A fine horse: it would make his first trophy of this day.

And then, along the ridge behind the first scatter of riders, a mass of peaked helms—a blinding glare rising like the crest of an iron wave, and then the flash of scaled armour—

Kamz involuntarily stepped back, the rider closing on him forgotten in his shock.

He was a seasoned warrior. He could gauge numbers in an instant, and he counted as he watched the ranks roll down the slope. *Spirits below! Twenty—no, thirty thousand—and still more! I need to—*

The first arrow took him high between his neck and right shoulder. Staggered by the blow, he recovered and looked up only to greet the second arrow, tearing like fire into his throat.

As blood spurted down his chest, the biting flies rushed in.

Warleader Talt probed with his tongue his single remaining upper canine and then glared at the distant horse-warriors. 'They lead us ever on, and not once do they turn and fight! We are in a land of cowards!'

'So we must scrape it clean,' said Bedit in a growl.

Talt nodded. 'Your words ring like swords on shields, old friend. These Akrynnai start and dance away like antelope, but their villages are not so fleet, are they? When we are killing their children and raping their young ones, when we are burning their huts and slaughtering their puny horses, then they will fight us!'

'Or run in terror, Warleader. Torture kills them quick—we've seen that. They are spineless.' He pointed with the tip of his spear. 'We must choose our own path here, I think, for it is likely they seek to lead us away from their village.'

Talt studied the distant riders. No more than thirty—they had spied them at dawn, waiting, it seemed, on a distant rise. Talt had half-exhausted his warriors attempting to chase them down. A few scattered arrows sent their way was the extent of their belligerence. It was pathetic. The warleader glanced back at his warriors. Eight hundred men and women, their white paint streaked now with sweat, most of them sitting, hunched over in the heat. 'We shall rest for a time,' he said.

'I shall remain here,' Bedit said, lowering himself into a crouch.

'If they move sound the call.'

'Yes, Warleader.'

Talt hesitated, turning to squint at a mountainous mass of storm clouds to the southwest. Closer, yes.

Bedit must have followed his gaze. 'We are in its path. It will do much to cool us down, I think.'

'Be sure to leave this hilltop before it arrives,' Talt advised. 'And hold that spear to the ground.'

Nodding, Bedit grinned and tapped the side of his bone and horn helm. 'Tell the fools below who are wearing iron peaks.'

'I will, although it's the Akrynnai who should be worried.'

Bedit barked a laugh.

Talt turned and trotted back down to his warriors.

Inthalas, third daughter of Sceptre Irkullas, leaned forward on her saddle.

Beside her, Sagant shook himself and said, 'They're done, I think.'

She nodded, but somewhat distractedly. She had lived her entire life on these plains. She had weathered the fiercest prairie storms—she recalled, once, seeing a hundred dead bhederin on a slope, each one killed by lightning—but she had never before seen clouds like these ones.

Her horse was trembling beneath her.

Sagant gusted out a breath. 'We have time, I think, if we strike now. Get it over with quickly and then try to outride the storm.'

After a moment, Inthalas nodded.

Sagant laughed and swung his horse round, leaving the small troop of outriders to - ride down to where waited—unseen by any Barghast—three wings of Akrynnai horse-archers and lancers, along with nine hundred armoured, axe-wielding shock troops: in all, almost three thousand warriors. As he drew closer, he gestured with his free hand, saw with pleasure the alacrity with which his troops responded.

The Sceptre's great success had been founded, in part, on the clever adoption of the better qualities of the Letherii military—foot-soldiers capable of maintaining tight, disciplined ranks, for one, and an adherence to a doctrine of formations, as well as dictating the field of battle in situations of their own choosing.

Leading the Barghast ever onward, until they were exhausted—leading them straight to their waiting heavy infantry, to a battle in which the White Faces could not hope to triumph—Inthalas had learned well from her father.

This would be a fine day of slaughter. He laughed again.

Inthalas had done her part. Now it was time for Sagant. They would finish with these Barghast quickly—she glanced again at the storm-front—yes, it would have to be quickly. The blackened bellies of those clouds seemed to be scraping the ground, reminding her of smoke—but she could not smell anything like a grass fire— no, this was uncanny, troubling. Still a league or more distant, but fast closing.

She shook herself, faced her fellow outriders. 'We will ride to find a better vantage point once the battle is engaged—and should any Barghast break free, I give you leave to chase them down. You have done well—the fools are spent, unsuspecting, and even now the great village they left behind is likely burning to the Sceptre's touch.'

At that she saw cold smiles.

'Perhaps,' she added, 'we can capture a few here, and visit upon them the horrors they so callously delivered upon our innocent kin.'

This pleased them even more.

Bedit had watched one of the riders disappear down the other side of the ridge, and this struck him with a faint unease. What reason for that, except to join another troop—hidden in the hollow beyond? Then again, it might be that the entire village waited there, crowded with hundreds of terrified fools.

He slowly straightened—and then felt the first rumble beneath his feet.

Bedit turned to face the storm, and his eyes widened. The enormous, swollen clouds were suddenly churning, lifting. Walls of dust or rain spanned the distance between them and the ground, but not—as one would expect—a single front; rather, countless walls, shifting like curtains in a broken row of bizarre angles— and he could now see something like white foam tumbling out from the base of those walls.

Hail.

But if that was true, then those hailstones must be the size of fists—even larger— else he would not be able to see anything of them at this distance. The drumming beneath him shook the entire hill. He shot the Akrynnai a glance and saw them riding straight for him.

Beneath hail and lightning then! He tilted his head back and shrieked his warning to Talt and the others, then collected up his spear and ran down to join them.

He had just reached the ranks when Akrynnai horse-warriors appeared behind the Barghast, and then on both sides, reining up and closing at the ends to form a three-sided encirclement. Cursing, Bedit spun to face the hill he had just descended. The scouts were there, but well off to one side, and as he stared— half-hearing the shouts of dismay from his fellow warriors through the tumult of thunder—he saw the first ranks of foot-soldiers appear above the crest. Rectangular shields, spiked axes, iron helms with visors and nose-guards, presenting a solid line advancing in step. Rank after rank topped the rise.

We have the battle we so lusted after. But it shall be our last battle. He howled his defiance, and at his side—stunned, appalled, young Talt visibly flinched at Bedit's cry.

Then Talt straightened, drawing his sword. 'We shall show them how true warriors fight!' He pointed at the closing foot-soldiers. 'Nith'rithal! *Charge!*'

Inthalas gasped, eyes widening. The Barghast were rushing the foot-soldiers in a ragged mass, *uphill.* True, they were bigger, but against that disciplined line they would meet nothing but an iron wall and descending axe blades.

She expected them to break, reel back—and the Akrynnai ranks would then advance, pressing the savages until they routed—and as they fled, the cavalry would sweep in from the flanks, arrows sleeting, while at the far end of the basin the lancers would level their weapons and then roll down in a charge into the very face of those fleeing Barghast.

No one would escape.

Thunder, flashes of lightning, a terrible growing roar—yet her eyes held frozen on the charging Barghast.

They hammered into the Akryn ranks, and Inthalas shouted in shock as the first line seemed to simply vanish beneath a crazed flurry of huge Barghast warriors, swords slashing down. Shield edges crumpled. Fragments of shattered helms spat into the air. The three front rows were driven back by the concussion. The chop and clash rose amidst screams of pain and rage, and she saw the Akryn legion bow inward as the remainder of the Barghast pushed their own front ranks ever deeper into the formation. It was moments from being driven apart, split in half.

Sagant must have seen the same from where he waited with the lancers. In actual numbers, the Barghast almost matched the foot-soldiers, and their ferocity was appalling. Darkness was swallowing the day, and the flashes of lightning from the west provided moments of frozen clarity as the battle was joined now on all sides—arrows lashing into the Barghast flanks in wave after wave. The plunging descent of Sagant and his lancers closed fast on the rearmost enemy warriors—who seemed indifferent to the threat at their backs as they pushed their comrades in front of them, clawing forward in a frenzy.

But that made sense—carve apart the Akryn legion and a way would be suddenly open before the Barghast, and in the ensuing chaos of the breakout the lancers would end up snarled with the foot-soldiers, and the archers would hunt uselessly in the gloom to make out foe from friend. All order, and with it command, would be lost.

She stared, still half-disbelieving, as the legion buckled. The Barghast had now formed a wedge, and it drove ever deeper.

Should the enemy push through and come clear, momentarily uncontested, they could wheel round and set weapons—they could even counter-attack, slaughtering disordered foot-soldiers and tangled lancers.

Inthalas turned to her thirty-odd scouts. 'Ride with me!' And she led them down the back slope of the ridge, cantering and then galloping, to bring her troop round opposite the likely fissure in the legion.

'When the Barghast fight clear—we charge, do you understand? Arrows and then sabres—into the tip of the wedge. We tumble them, we slow them, we bind them—if with our own dead horses and our own dying bodies, we bind them!'

She could see a third of a wing of horse-archers pulling clear to the east—they were responding to the threat, but they might not be ready in time.

Damn these barbarians!

Inthalas, third daughter of the Sceptre, rose on her stirrups, gaze fixed on the writhing ranks of the legion. *My children, your mother will not be returning home. Never again to see your faces. Never—*

A sudden impact sent the horses staggering. The ground erupted—and she saw figures wheeling through the air, flung to one side as the storm struck the flank of the hills to the west, struck and tumbled over those hills, swallowing them whole. Inthalas, struggling to stay on her mount, stared in horror as a seething crest of enormous boulders and jagged rocks lifted over the nearest ridge—

Something huge and solid loomed within the nearest cloud—towering to fill half the sky. And its base was carving a bow-wave before it, as if tearing up the earth itself. The avalanche poured over the crest and down the slope of the basin in a roaring wave.

An entire wing of horse-archers was simply engulfed beneath the onslaught, and then the first of the broken boulders—many bigger than a trader's wagon—crashed into the milling mass of Barghast and Akryn. As the rocks rolled and bounced through the press, pieces of crushed, smeared bodies spun into the air.

At that moment the lightning struck. Lashing, actinic blades ripping out from the dark, heaving cloud, cutting blackened paths through Sagant's lancers and the clumps of reeling foot-soldiers. The air was filled with burning fragments—bodies lit like torches—men, women, horses—lightning danced from iron to iron in a crazed, terrifying web of charred destruction. Flesh burst in explosions of boiling fluid. Hair ignited like rushes—

Someone was shrieking in her ear. Inthalas turned, and then gestured—they had to get away. Away from the storm, away from the slaughter—they had to—

Deafening white light. Agony, and then—

As if a god's sword had slashed across the hills on the other side of the valley, not a single ridge remained. Something vast and inexorable had pushed those summits down into the valley, burying the Snakehunter camp in a mass of deadly rubble. Here and there, Tool could see, remnants were visible among the shattered boulders—torn sections of canvas and hide, snarled shreds of clothing, guy-rope fetishes and feather-bundles, splintered shafts of ridge-poles—and there had been mangled flesh once, too, although now only bleached bones remained, broken, crushed, jutting—yet worse, to Tool's mind, was the black hair, torn loose from flaps of scalp by the beaks of crows, and now wind-blown over the entire slope before them.

Riggis had shouldered aside a speechless Bakal and now glared down into that nightmarish scene. After a moment he shook his huge frame and spat. 'This is our enemy, Warleader? Bah! An earthquake! Shall we war against the rocks and soil, then? Stab the hills? Bleed the rivers? You have led us to this? Hoping for what? That we beg you to take us away from an angry earth?' He drew his tulwar. 'Enough wasting our time. Face me, Onos T'oolan—I challenge your right to lead the White Face Barghast!'

Tool sighed. 'Use your eyes, Riggis. What shifting of the earth leaves no cracks? Pushes to one side hilltops without touching their roots? Drives three—possibly more—furrows across the plain, each one converging on this valley, each one strik-ing for the heart of the Snakehunter camp?' He pointed to the north channel of the valley. 'What earthquake cuts down fleeing Barghast in the hundreds? See them, Riggis—that road of bones?'

'Akryn raiders, taking advantage of the broken state of the survivors. Answer my challenge, coward!'

Tool studied the enormous warrior. Not yet thirty, his belt crowded with tro-phies. He turned to the others and raised his voice, 'Do any of you challenge Rig-gis and his desire to be Warleader of the White Face Barghast?'

'He is not yet Warleader,' growled Bakal.

Tool nodded. 'And should I kill Riggis here, now, will you draw your weapon and voice your challenge to me, Bakal?' He scanned the others. 'How many of you will seek the same? Shall we stand here over the broken graveyard of the Snake-hunter clan and spill yet more Barghast blood? Is this how you will honour your fallen White Faces?'

'They will not follow you,' Riggis said, his eyes bright. 'Unless you answer my challenge.'

'Ah, and so, if I do answer you, Riggis, they will then follow me?'

The Senan warrior's laugh was derisive. 'I am not yet ready to speak for them—'

'You just did.'

'Spar no more with empty words, Onos Toolan.' He widened his stance and readied his heavy-bladed weapon, teeth gleaming amidst his braided beard.

'Were you Warleader, Riggis,' Tool said, still standing relaxed, hands at his sides, 'would you slay your best warriors simply to prove your right to rule?'

'Any who dared oppose me, yes!'

'Then, you would command out of a lust for power, not out of a duty to your people.'

'My finest warriors,' Riggis replied, 'would find no cause to challenge me in the first place.'

'They would, as soon as they decided to disagree with you, Riggis. And this would haunt you, in the back of your mind. With every decision you made, you would find yourself weighing the risks, and before long you would gather to your-self an entourage of cohorts—the ones whose loyalty you have purchased with favours—and you would sit like a spider in the centre of your web, starting at every tremble of the silk. How well can you trust your friends, knowing how you yourself bought them? How soon before you find yourself swaying to every gust of desire among your people? Suddenly, that power you so hungered for proves to be a prison. You seek to please everyone and so please no one. You search the eyes of those closest to you, wondering if you can trust them, wondering if their smiles are but lying masks, wondering what they say behind your back—'

'Enough!' Riggis roared, and then charged.

The flint sword appeared as if conjured in Tool's hands. It seemed to flicker.

Riggis staggered to one side, down on to one knee. His broken tulwar thumped to the ground four paces away, the warrior's hand still wrapped tight about the grip. He blinked down at his own chest, as if looking for something, and blood ran from the stump of his wrist—ran, but the flow was ebbing. With his remaining hand he reached up to touch an elongated slit in his boiled-leather hauberk, from which the faint glisten of blood slowly welled. A slit directly above his heart.

He looked up at Tool, perplexed, and then sat back.

A moment later, Riggis fell on to his side, and no further movement came from him.

Tool faced Bakal. 'Do you seek to be Warleader, Bakal? If so, you can have it. I yield command of the White Face Barghast. To you'—he turned to the others—'to any of you. I will be the coward you want me to be. For what now comes, someone else shall be responsible—not me, not any more. In my last words as Warleader, I say this: gather the White Face Barghast, gather all the clans, and march to the Lether Empire. Seek sanctuary. A deadly enemy has returned to these plains, an ancient enemy. You are in a war you cannot win. Leave this land and save your people. Or remain, and the White Faces shall all die.' He ran the tip of his sword through a tuft of grass, and then slung it back into the sheath beneath his left arm. 'A worthy warrior lies dead. The Senan has suffered a loss this day. The fault is mine. Now, Bakal, you and the others can squabble over the prize, and those who fall shall not have me to blame.'

'I do not challenge you, Onos Toolan,' said Bakal, licking dry lips.

Tool flinched.

In the silence following that, not one of the other warriors spoke.

Damn you, Bakal. I was almost . . . free.

Bakal spoke again, 'Warleader, I suggest we examine the dead at the end of the valley, to determine what manner of weapon cut them down.'

'I will lead the Barghast from this plain,' Tool said.

'Clans will break away, Warleader.'

'They already are doing so.'

'You will have only the Senan.'

'I will?'

Bakal shrugged. 'There is no value in you killing a thousand Senan warriors. There is no value in challenging you—I have never seen a blade sing so fast. We shall be furious with you, but we shall follow.'

'Even if I am a leader with no favours to grant, Bakal, no loyalty I would purchase from any of you?'

'Perhaps that has been true, Onos Toolan. In that, you have been . . . fair. But it need not remain so . . . empty. Please, you must tell us what you know of this enemy—who slays with rocks and dirt. We are not fools who will blindly oppose what we cannot hope to defeat—'

'What of the prophecies, Bakal?' Tool then smiled wryly at the warrior's scowl.

'Ever open to interpretation, Warleader. Will you speak to us now?'

Tool gestured at the valley below. 'Is this not eloquent enough?'

'Buy our loyalty with the truth, Onos Toolan. Gift us all with an even measure.'

Yes, this is how one leads. Anything else is suspect. Every other road proves a maze of deceit and cynicism. After a moment, he nodded. 'Let us look upon the fallen Snakehunters.'

The sun was low on the horizon when the two scouts were brought into Maral Eb's presence where he sat beside a dung fire over which skewers of horse meat sizzled. The scouts were both young and he did not know their names, but the excitement he observed in their faces awakened his attention. He pointed to one. 'You shall speak, and quickly now—I am about to eat.'

'A Senan war-party,' the scout said.

'Where?'

'We were the ones backtracking the Snakehunters' trail, Warchief. They are camped in a hollow not a league from here.'

'How many?'

'A hundred, no more than that. But, Warchief, there is something else—'

'Out with it!'

'Onos Toolan is with them.'

Maral Eb straightened. 'Are you certain? Escorted by a mere hundred? The fool!'

His two younger brothers came running at his words and Maral Eb grinned at them. 'Stir the warriors—we eat on the march.'

'Are you sure of this, Maral?' his youngest brother asked.

'We strike,' the warchief snarled. 'In darkness. We kill them all. But be certain every warrior understands—no one is to slay Tool. Wound him, yes, but not unto death—if anyone gets careless I will have him or her skinned alive and roasted over a fire. Now, quickly—the gods smile down upon us!'

The Barahn warchief led his four thousand warriors across the rolling plains at a ground-devouring trot. One of the two scouts padded twenty paces directly ahead, keeping them to the trail, whilst others ranged further out on the flanks. The moon had yet to rise, and even when it did, it would be weak, shrouded in perpetual haze—these nights, the brightest illumination came from the jade streaks to the south, and that was barely enough to cast shadows.

The perfect setting for an ambush. None of the other tribes would ever know the truth—after all, with Tool and a hundred no doubt elite warriors dead the Senan would be crippled, and the Barahn Clan would achieve swift ascendancy once Maral Eb attained the status of Warleader over all the White Face Barghast. And was it not in every Barahn warrior's interest to hide the truth? The situation was ideal.

Weapons and armour were bound, muffled against inadvertent noise, and the army moved in near silence. Before long, the lead scout hurried back to the main column. Maral Eb gestured and his warriors halted behind him.

'The hollow is two hundred paces ahead, Warchief. Fires are lit. There will be pickets—'

'Don't tell me my business,' Maral Eb growled. He drew his brothers closer. 'Sagal, take your Skullsplitters north. Kashat, you lead your thousand south. Stay a hundred paces back from the pickets, low to the ground, and form into a six-deep crescent. There is no way we can kill those sentinels silently, so the surprise will not be absolute, but we have overwhelming numbers, so that will not matter. I will lead my two thousand straight in. When you hear my war-cry, brothers, rise and close. No one must escape, so leave a half hundred spread wide in your wake. It may be we will drive them west for a time, so be sure to be ready to wheel your crescents to close that route.' He paused. 'Listen well to this. To-night, we break the most sacred law of the White Faces—but necessity forces our hand. Onos Toolan has betrayed the Barghast. He dishonours us. I hereby pledge to reunite the clans, to lead us to glory.'

The faces arrayed before him were sober, but he could see the gleam in their eyes. They were with him. 'This night shall stain our souls black, my brothers, but we will spend the rest of our lives cleansing them. Now, go!'

Onos Toolan sat beside the dying fire. The camp was quiet, as his words of truth now sank into hearts like the flames, flaring and winking out.

The stretch of ages could humble the greatest of peoples, once all the self-delusions were stripped away. Pride had its place, but not at the expense of sober truth. Even back on Genabackis, the White Faces had strutted about as if un-aware that their culture was drawing to an end; that they had been pushed into inhospitable lands; that farms and then cities rose upon ground they once held to be sacred, or rightly theirs as hunting grounds or pasture lands. All around them, the future showed faces ghastlier and more deadly than anything white paint could achieve—when Humbrall Taur had led them here, to this continent, he had done so in fullest comprehension of the extinction awaiting his Barghast should they remain on Genabackis, besieged by progress.

Prophecies never touched on such matters. By nature, they were proclama-tions of egotism, rife with pride and bold fates. Humbrall Taur had, however, managed a clever twist or two in making use of them.

Too bad he is gone—I would rather have stood at his side than in his place. I would rather—

Tool's breath caught and he lifted his head. He reached out and settled one hand down on the packed earth, and then slowly closed his eyes. *Ah, Hetan . . . my children . . . forgive me.*

The Imass rose, turned to the nearest other fire. 'Bakal.'

The warrior looked over. 'Warleader?'

'Draw your dagger, Bakal, and come to me.'

The warrior did not move for a moment, and then he rose, sliding the gutting knife from its scabbard. He walked over, cautious, uncertain.

My warriors . . . enough blood has been shed. 'Drive the knife deep, directly under my heart. When I fall, begin shouting these words—as loud as you can. Shout *"Tool is dead! Onos Toolan lies slain! Our Warleader lies dead!"* Do you understand me, Bakal?'

The warrior, eyes wide, slowly backed away. Others had caught the words and were now rising, converging.

Tool closed on Bakal once again. 'Be quick, Bakal—if you value your life and the lives of every one of your kin here. You must slay me—now!'

'Warleader! I will not—'

Tool's hands snapped out, closed on Bakal's right hand and wrist.

The warrior gasped, struggled to tug free, but against Tool's strength, he was helpless. The Imass pulled him close. 'Remember—shout out my death, it is your only hope—'

Bakal sought to loosen his grip on his knife, but Tool's huge, spatulate hand wrapped his own as would an adult's a child's. The other, closed round his wrist, dragged him inexorably forward.

The blade's tip touched Tool's leather armour.

Whimpering, Bakal sought to throw himself backward—but the imprisoned arm did not move. He tried to drop to his knees, and his elbow dislocated with a pop. He howled in pain.

The other warriors—who had stood frozen—suddenly rushed in.

But Tool gave them no time. He drove the dagger into his chest.

Sudden, blinding pain. Releasing Bakal's wrist, he staggered back, stared down at the knife buried to its hilt in his chest.

Hetan, my love, forgive me.

There was shouting all round him now—horror, terrible confusion, and then, on his knees, Bakal lifted his head and met Tool's gaze.

The Imass had lost his voice, but he sought to implore the man with his eyes. *Shout out my death! Spirits take me—shout it out loud!* He stumbled, lost his footing, and fell heavily on to his back.

Death—he had forgotten its bitter kiss. *So long . . . so long.*

But I knew a gift. I tasted the air in my lungs . . . after so long . . . after ages of dust. The sweet air of love . . . but now . . .

Night-stained faces crowded above him, paint white as bone.

Skulls? Ah, my brothers . . . we are dust—

Dust, and nothing but—

He could hear shouting, alarms rising from the Senan encampment. Cursing, Maral Eb straightened, saw the sentinels clearly now—all running back into the camp.

'Damn the gods! We must charge—'

'Listen!' cried the scout. 'Warchief—listen to the words!'

'What?'

And then he did. His eyes slowly widened. *Could it be true? Have the Senan taken matters into their own hands?*

Of course they have! They are Barghast! White Faces! He raised his sword high in the air. 'Barahn!' he roared. 'Hear the words of your warchief! Sheathe your weapons! The betrayer is slain! Onos Toolan is slain! Let us go down to meet our brothers!'

Voices howled in answer.

They will have someone to set forward—they will not relinquish dominance so easily—I might well draw blood this night after all. But none will stand long before me. I am Maral Eb, slayer of hundreds.

The way lies open.

It lies open.

The Barahn warchief led his warriors down into the hollow.

To claim his prize.

Hetan woke in the night. She stared upward, eyes wide but unseeing, until they filled with tears. The air in the yurt was stale, darkness heavy and suffocating as a shroud. *My husband, I dreamed the flight of your soul . . . I dreamed its brush upon my lips. A moment, only a moment, and then it was as if a vast wind swept you away.*

I heard your cry, husband.

Oh, such a cruel dream, beloved.

And now . . . I smell dust in the air. Rotted furs. The dry taste of ancient death.

Her heart pounded like a mourner's drum in her chest, loud, heavy, the beat stretching with each deep breath she took. *That taste, that smell.* She reached up to touch her own lips. And felt something like grit upon them.

O beloved, what has happened?

What has happened—

To my husband—to the father of my children—what has happened?

She let out a ragged sigh, forcing out the unseemly fear. Such a cruel dream.

From the outer room, the dog whined softly, and a moment later their son suddenly sobbed, and then bawled.

And she knew the truth. Such a cruel truth.

Ralata crouched in the high grasses and studied the figures gathered round the distant fire. None had stirred in the time she had been watching. But the horses were tugging at their stakes and even from here she could smell their terror—and she did not understand, for she could see nothing—no threat in any direction.

Even so, it was strange that none of her sisters had awakened. In fact, they did not move at all.

Her confusion was replaced by unease. Something was wrong.

She glanced back at the hollow where waited her horse. The animal seemed calm enough. Collecting her weapons, Ralata rose and padded forward.

Hessanrala might be a headstrong young fool, but she knew her trade as well as any Ahkrata warrior—she should be on her feet by now, drawing the others in with silent hand gestures—was it just a snake slithering among the horses' hoofs? A scent on the wind?

No, something was very wrong.

As she drew within ten paces, she could smell bile, spilled wastes, and blood.

Mouth dry, Ralata crept closer. They were dead. She knew that now. She had failed to protect them—but how? What manner of slayer could creep up on five Barghast warriors? As soon as night had fallen, she had drawn near enough to watch them preparing camp. She had watched them rub down the horses; had watched them eat and drink beer from Hessanrala's skin. They had set no watch among themselves, clearly relying upon the horses should danger draw near. But Ralata had remained wakeful, had even seen when the horses first wakened to alarm.

Beneath the stench of death there was something else, an oily bitterness reminding her of serpents. She studied the movements of the Akryn mounts—no, they were not shying from any snake in the grasses. Heads tossed, ears cocking in one direction after another, eyes rolling.

Ralata edged towards the firelight. Once lit, dried dung burned hot but not bright, quick to sink into bricks of pulsating ashes; in the low, lurid reflection, she could see fresh blood, glistening meat from split corpses.

No quick knife thrusts here. No, these were the wounds delivered by the talons of a huge beast. Bear? Barbed cat? If so, why not drag at least one body away . . . to feed upon? Why ignore the horses? And how was it that Ralata had seen nothing; that not one of her kin had managed to utter a death-cry?

Gutted, throat-slit, chests ripped open—she saw the stubs of ribs cut clean through. Talons sharp as swords—or swords in truth? All at once she recalled, years ago, on the distant continent they had once called home, visions of giant undead, two-legged lizards. K'Chain Che'Malle, arrayed in silent ranks in front of the city called Coral. Swords at the end of their wrists instead of hands—but no, the wounds she looked upon here were different. What then had triggered that memory?

Ralata slowly inhaled once more, deeply, steadily, running the acrid flavours through her. *Yes, the smell. Although, long ago, it was more . . . stale, rank with death.*

But the kiss upon the tongue—it is the same.

The horses ducked and fanned out, heads snapping back as they reached the ends of their tethers. A faint downdraught of wind—the whish of wings—

Ralata threw herself flat, rolled, making for the legs of the horses—anything to put between her and whatever hovered above.

Thuds in the air, leathery hissing—she stared up into the night, caught a vast winged silhouette that devoured a sweep of stars. A flash, and then it was gone.

Hoofs kicked at her, and then settled.

She heard laughter in her head—not her own, something cold, contemptuous, fading now into some inner distance, until even the echoes were gone.

Ralata rose to her feet. The thing had flown northeastward. Of course, there could be no tracking such a creature, but at least she had a direction.

She had failed to protect her kin. Perhaps, however, she could avenge them.

The Wastelands were well named, but Torrent had always known that. He had last found water two days past, and the skins strapped to his saddle would suffice him no more than another day. Travelling at night was the only option, now that the full heat of summer had arrived, but his horse was growing gaunt, and all that he could see before them beneath dull moonlight was a vast, flat stretch of sun-baked clay and shards of broken stone.

The first night following the gate and his parting ways with Cafal and Setoc, he had come upon a ruined tower, ragged as a rotten fang, the walls of which seemed to have melted under enormous heat. The destruction was so thorough not a single window or dressed facing survived, and much of the structure's skeleton was visible as sagging latticework snarled with twisted ropes of rusting metal wire. He had never before seen anything remotely like it, and superstitious fear kept him from riding closer.

Since then, Torrent had seen nothing of interest, nothing to break the monotony of the blasted landscape. No mounds, no hills, not even ancient remnants of myrid, rodara and goat pens, as one often found on the Awl'dan.

It was nearing dawn when he made out a humped shape ahead, directly in his path, barely rising above the cracked rock. The ripple of furs—a torn, frayed hide riding hunched, narrow shoulders. Thin, grey hair seeming to float up from the head in the faint, sighing wind. A girdled skirt of rotted strips of snakeskin flared out from the seated form. He drew closer. The figure's back was to Torrent, and beyond the wind-tugged hair and accoutrements, it remained motionless as he walked his horse up and halted five paces behind it.

A corpse? From the weathered pate beneath the sparse hair, it was likely. But who would have simply left one of their own out on this lifeless pan?

When the figure spoke, Torrent's horse started back, nostrils flaring. 'The fool. I needed him.'

The voice was rough as sand, hollow as a wind-sculpted cave. He could not tell if it belonged to a man or a woman.

It uttered something between a sigh and a hissing snarl, and then asked, 'What am I to do now?'

The Awl warrior hesitated, and then said, 'You speak the language of my people. Are you Awl? No, you cannot be. I am the last—and what you wear—'

'You have no answer, then. I am used to disappointment. Indeed, surprise is an emotion I have not known for so long, I believe I have forgotten its taste. Be on your way then—this world and its needs are too vast for one such as you. He would have fared better, of course, but now he's dead. I am so . . . irritated.'

Torrent dismounted, collecting one of his waterskins. 'You must be thirsty, old one.'

'Yes, my throat is parched, but there is nothing you can do for that.'

'I have some water—'

'Which you need more than I do. Still, it is a kind gesture. Foolish, but most kind gestures are.'

When he walked round to face the elder, he frowned. Much of the face was hidden in the shadow of protruding brows, but it seemed it was adorned in rough strings of beads or threads. He caught the dull gleam of teeth and a shiver whispered through him. Involuntarily he made a warding gesture with his free hand.

Rasping laughter. 'Your spirits of wind and earth, warrior, are my *children*. And you imagine such fends work on me? But wait, there is this, isn't there? The long thread of shared blood between us. I might be foolish, to think such things, but if anyone has earned the right to be a fool, it must surely be me. Thus yielding this . . . gesture.'

The figure rose in a clatter of bones grating in dry sockets. Torrent saw the long tubes of bare, withered breasts, the skin patched and rotted; a sagging belly cut and slashed, the edges of the wounds dry and hanging, and in the gashes themselves there was impenetrable darkness—as if this woman was as dried up inside as she was on the outside.

Torrent licked parched lips, struggled to swallow, and then spoke in a hushed tone, 'Woman, are you dead?'

'Life and death is such an old game. I'm too old to play. Did you know, these lips once touched those of the Son of Darkness? In our days of youth, in a world far from this one—far, yes, but little different in the end. But what value such grim lessons? We see and we do, but we know nothing.' A desiccated hand made a fluttering gesture. 'The fool presses a knife to his chest. He thinks it is done. He too knows nothing, because, you see, *I will not let go*.'

The words, confusing as they were, chilled Torrent nonetheless. The waterskin dangled in his hand, and its pathetic weight now mocked him.

The head lifted, and beneath those jutting brow ridges Torrent saw a face of dead skin stretched across prominent bones. Black pits regarded him above a permanent grin. The beaded threads he had thought he'd seen turned out to be strips of flesh—as if some clawed beast had raked talons down the old woman's face. 'You need water. Your horse needs fodder. Come, I will lead you and so save your useless lives. Then, if you are lucky, I will eventually find a reason to keep you alive.'

Something told Torrent that refusing her was impossible. 'I am named Torrent,' he said.

'I know your name. The one-eyed Herald begged me on your behalf.' She snorted. 'As if I am known for mercy.'

'The one-eyed Herald?'

'The Dead Rider, out from Hood's Hollow. He knows little respite of late. An omen harsh as a crow's laugh, thus comes Toc the Younger—but do I not cherish the privacy of my dreams? He is rude.'

'He haunts my dreams as well, Old One—'

'Stop calling me that. It is . . . inaccurate. Call me by my name, and that name is Olar Ethil.'

'Olar Ethil,' said Torrent, 'will he come again?'

She cocked her head, was silent a moment. 'As they shall, to their regret, soon discover, the answer is *yes*.'

Sunlight spilled over a grotesque scene. Cradling his injured arm, Bakal stood with a half-dozen other Senan. Behind them, the new self-acclaimed Warleader of the White Faces, Maral Eb, was cajoling his warriors to wakefulness. The night had been long. The air smelled of spilled beer and puke. The Barahn were rising rough and loud, unwilling to relinquish their abandon.

Before Bakal and the others was the flat where their encampment had been—not a tent remained, not a single cookfire still smouldered. The Senan, silent, grim-faced, were ready to begin the march back home. A reluctant escort to the new Warleader. They sat on the ground to one side, watching the Barahn.

Flies were awakening. Crows circled overhead and would soon land to feed.

Onos Toolan's body had been torn apart, the flesh deboned and pieces of him scattered everywhere. His bones had been systematically shattered, the fragments strewn about. His skull had been crushed. Eight Barahn warriors had tried to break the flint sword and had failed. In the end, it was pushed into a fire built from dung and Tool's furs and clothing, and then, when everything had burned down, scores of Barahn warriors pissed on the blackened stone, seeking to shatter it. They had failed, but the desecration was complete.

Deep inside Bakal, rage seethed black and biting as acid upon his soul. Yet for all its virulence, it could not destroy the knot of guilt at the very centre of his being. He could still feel the handle of his dagger in his hand, could swear that the wire impressions remained on his palm, seared like a brand. He felt sick.

'He has agents in our camp,' said the warrior beside him, his voice barely a murmur. 'Barahn women married into the Senan. And others. Stolmen's wife, her mother. We know what Hetan's fate will be—and Maral Eb will not permit us to travel ahead of him—he does not trust us.'

'Nor should he, Strahl,' replied Bakal.

'If there were more of us and less of them.'

'I know.'

'Bakal, do we tell the Warleader? Of the enemy Onos Toolan described?'

'No.'

'Then he will lead us all to our deaths.'

Bakal glared across at the warrior. '*Not the Senan.*' He studied the array of faces before him, gauging the effect of his words, and then nodded. 'We must cut ourselves loose.'

'Into the Lether Empire,' said Strahl, 'as Tool said. Negotiate settlement treaties, make peace with the Akrynnai.'

'Yes.'

They fell silent again, and, inevitably, eyes turned once more to the scene before them. Their rendered Warleader, the endless signs of vicious blasphemy.

This dull, discredited morning. This foul, accursed land. The crows had landed and were now hopping about, beaks darting down.

'They will hobble her and kill the spawn,' said Strahl, who then spat to clear the foulness of the words. 'Yesterday, Bakal, we would have joined in. We would have each taken her. One of our own knives might well have tasted the soft throats of the children. And now, look at us. Ashes in our mouths, dust in our hearts. What has happened? What has he done to us?'

'He showed us the burden of an honourable man, Strahl. And yes, it stings.'

'He used you cruelly, Bakal.'

The warrior stared down at his swollen hand, and then shook his head. 'I failed him. I did not understand.'

'If you failed him,' growled Strahl, 'then we all have.'

In Bakal's mind, there was no disputing that. 'To think,' he muttered, 'we called him coward.'

Before them and behind them, the crows danced.

Some roads were easier to leave than others. Many walked to seek the future, but found only the past. Others sought the past, to make it new once more, and discovered that the past was nothing like the one they'd imagined. One could walk in search of friends, and find naught but strangers. One could yearn for company but find little but cruel solitude.

A few roads offered the gift of pilgrimage, a place to find somewhere ahead and somewhere in the heart, both to be found at the road's end.

It was true, as well, that some roads never ended at all, and that pilgrimage could prove a flight from salvation, and all the burdens one carried one must now carry back to the place whence they came.

Drop by drop, the blood built worn stone and dirt. Drop by drop, the way of the Road to Gallan was opened. Weak, ever on the edge of fever, Yan Tovis, Queen of the Shake, commander of thousands of the dispirited and the lost, led the wretched fools ever onward. To the sides, shadows thickened to darkness, and still she walked.

Hunger assailed her people. Thirst haunted them. Livestock lowed in abject confusion, stumbled and then died. She had forgotten that this ancient path was one she had chosen to ease the journey, to slip unseen through the breadth of the Letherii Kingdom. She had forgotten that they must leave it—and now it was too late.

The road was more than a road. It was a river and its current was tightening, holding fast all that it carried, and the pace quickened, ever quickened. She could fight—they all could fight—and achieve nothing but drowning.

Drop by drop, she fed the river, and the road rushed them forward.

We are going home. Did I want this? Did I want to know all that we had abandoned? Did I want the truth, an end to the mysteries of our beginnings?

Was this a pilgrimage? A migration? Will we find salvation?

She had never even believed in such things. Sudden benediction, blessed release—these were momentary intoxications, as addictive as any drug, until one so hungered for the escape that the living, mindful world paled in comparison, bleached of all life, all wonder.

She was not a prophet. But they wanted a prophet. She was not holy. But they begged her blessing. Her path did not promise a road to glory. Yet they followed unquestioningly.

Her blood was not a river, but how it flowed!

No sense left for time. No passage of light to mark dawn, noon and dusk. Darkness all around them, before and behind, darkness breeding in swirls of stale air, the taste of ashes, the stench of charred wood and fire-cracked stone. How long? She had no idea.

But people behind her were falling. Dying.

Where is home? It lies ahead. Where is home? Lost far behind us.

Where is home? It is within, gutted and hollow, waiting to be filled once more.

Where is Gallan?

At this road's end.

What is Gallan's promise? It is home. I—I need to work through this. Round and round—madness to let it run, madness. Will the light never return? Is the joke this: that salvation is all around us, even as we remain for ever blind to it?

Because we believe . . . there must be a road. A journey, an ordeal, a place to find.

We believe in the road. And in believing we build it, stone by stone, drop by drop. We bleed for our belief, and as the blood flows, the darkness closes in—

'The Road to Gallan is not a road. Some roads . . . are not roads at all. Gallan's promise is not from here to there. It is from now to then. The darkness . . . the darkness comes from *within*.'

A truth, and most truths were revelations.

She opened her eyes.

Behind her, parched throats opened in a moaning chorus. Thousands, the sound rising to challenge the rush of black water on stony shores, to waft out and run between the charred tree-stumps climbing the hillsides to the left.

Yan Tovis stood at the shore, not seeing the river sweeping past the toes of her boots. Her gaze had lifted, vision cutting through the mottled atmosphere, to look upon the silent, unlit ruins of a vast city.

The city.

Kharkanas.

The Shake have come home.

Are we . . . are we home?

The air belonged in a tomb, a forgotten crypt.

And she could see, and she knew. *Kharkanas is dead.*

The city is dead.

Blind Gallan—you lied to us.

Yan Tovis howled. She fell to her knees, into the numbing water of River Eryn.

'You lied! *You lied!*' Tears ran from her eyes, streamed down her cheeks. Salty beads spun and glittered as they plunged into the lifeless river.

Drop by drop.

To feed the river.

Yedan Derryg led his horse forward, hoofs crunching on the stones, and relaxed the reins so that the beast could drink. He cradled his wounded arm and said nothing as he looked to the right and studied the kneeling, bent-over form of his sister.

The muscles of his jaw bunched beneath his beard, and he straightened to squint at the distant ruins.

Pully stumped up beside him. Her young face looked bruised with shock. 'We . . . walked . . . to this?'

'Blind Gallan gave us a road,' said Yedan Derryg. 'But what do the blind hold to more than anything else? Only that which was sweet in their eyes—the last visions they beheld. We followed the road into his memories.' After a moment, he shrugged, chewed for a time, and then said, 'What in the Errant's name did you expect, witch?'

His horse had drunk enough. Gathering up the reins, he backed the mount from the shore's edge and then wheeled it round. 'Sergeant! Spread the soldiers out—the journey has ended. See to the raising of a camp.' He faced the two witches. 'You two, bind Twilight's wounds and feed her. I will be back shortly—'

'Where are you going?'

Yedan Derryg stared at Pully for a time, and then he set heels to his horse and rode past the witch, downstream along the shoreline.

A thousand paces further on, a stone bridge spanned the river, and beyond it wound a solid, broad road leading to the city. Beneath that bridge, he saw, there was some kind of logjam, so solid as to form a latticed barrier sufficient to push the river out to the sides, creating elongated swampland skirting this side of the raised road.

As he drew closer he saw that most of the logjam seemed to consist of twisted metal bars and cables.

He was forced to slow his mount, picking his way across the silted channel, but at last managed to drive the beast up the bank and on to the road.

Hoofs kicked loose lumps of muck as he rode across the bridge. Downstream of the barrier the river ran still, slightly diminished and cutting a narrower, faster channel. On the flats to either side there was more rusted, unidentifiable wreckage.

Once on the road, he fixed his gaze on the towering gate ahead, but something in its strange, alien architecture made his head spin, so he studied the horizon to the right—where massive towers rose from sprawling, low buildings. He was not certain, but he thought he could detect thin, ragged streamers of smoke from the tops of those towers. After a time, he decided that what he was seeing was the effect of the wind and updraughts from those chimneys pulling loose ashes from deep pits at the base of the smokestacks.

On the road before him, here and there, he saw faint heaps of corroded metal, and the wink of jewellery—corpses had once crowded this approach, but the bones had long since crumbled to dust.

The mottled light cast sickly sheens on the outer walls of the city—and those stones, he could now see, were blackened with soot, a thick crust that glittered like obsidian.

Yedan Derryg halted before the gate. The way was open—no sign of barriers remained beyond torn hinges reduced to corroded lumps. He could see a broad street beyond the arch, and dust on the cobbles black as crushed coal.

'Walk on, horse.'

And Prince Yedan Derryg rode into Kharkanas.

Book Three

Only the Dust Will Dance

The dead have found me in my dreams
Fishing beside lakes and in strange houses
That could be homes for lost families
In all the pleasures of completeness
And I wander through their natural company
In the soft comforts of contentment.
The dead greet me with knowing ease
And regard nothing the forsaken awakening
That abandons me in this new solitude
Of eyes flickering open and curtains drawing.
When the dead find me in my dreams
I see them living in the hidden places
Unanchored in time and ageless as wishes.
The woman lying at my side hears my sigh
Following the morning chime and asks
After me as I lie in the wake of sorrow's concert,
But I will not speak of life's loneliness
Or the empty shorelines where fishermen belong
And the houses never lived in never again
That stand in necessary configurations
To build us familiar places for the dead.
One day I will journey into her dreams
But I say nothing of this behind my smile
And she will see me hunting the dark waters
For the flit of trout and we will travel
Strange landscapes in the forever instant
Until she leaves me for the living day
But as the dead well know the art of fishing
Finds its reward in brilliant joyous hope
And eternal loving patience, and it is my
Thought now that such gods that exist
Are the makers of dreams and this is their gift
This blessed river of sleep and dreams
Where in wonder we may greet our dead
And sages and priests are wise when they say
Death is but sleep and we are forever alive
In the dreams of the living, for I have seen
My dead on nightly journeys and I tell you this:
They are well.

SONG OF DREAMING
FISHER

Chapter Thirteen

They came late to the empty land and looked with bitterness upon the six wolves watching them from the horizon's rim. With them was a herd of goats and a dozen black sheep. They took no account of the wolves' possession of this place, for in their minds ownership was the human crown that none other had the right to wear. The beasts were content to share in survival's struggle, in hunt and quarry, and the braying goats and bawling sheep had soft throats and carelessness was a common enough flaw among herds; and they had not yet learned the manner of these two-legged intruders. Herds were fed upon by many creatures. Often the wolves shared their meals with crows and coyotes, and had occasion to argue with lumbering bears over a delectable prize.

When I came upon the herders and their longhouse on a flat above the valley, I found six wolf skulls spiked above the main door. In my travels as a minstrel I knew enough that I had no need to ask—this was a tale woven into our kind, after all. No words, either, for the bear skins on the walls, the antelope hides and elk racks. Not a brow lifted for the mound of bhederin bones in the refuse pit, or the vultures killed by the poison-baited meat left for the coyotes.

That night I sang and spun tales for my keep. Songs of heroes and great deeds and they were pleased enough and the beer was passing and the shank stew palatable.

Poets are sembling creatures, capable of shrugging into the skin of man, woman, child and beast. There are some among them secretly marked, sworn to the cults of the wilderness. And that night I shared out my poison and in the morning I left a lifeless house where not a dog remained to cry, and I sat upon a hill with my pipe, summoning once more the wild beasts. I defend their ownership when they cannot, and make no defence against the charge of murder; but temper your horror, friends: there is no universal law that places a greater value upon human life over that of a wild beast. Why would you ever imagine otherwise?

CONFESSIONS OF TWO HUNDRED
TWENTY-THREE COUNTS OF JUSTICE
WELTHAN THE MINSTREL (AKA SINGER MAD)

He came to us in the guise of a duke from an outlying border fastness—a place remote enough that none of us even thought to suspect him. And in his manner, his hard countenance and few words, he matched well our lazy preconceptions of such a man. None of us could argue that there was something about him, a kind of self-assurance rarely seen at court. In his eyes, like wolves straining at chains, there was a hint of the feral—the priestesses positively dripped.

'But, they would find, his was a most potent seed. And it was not Tiste Andii.'

Silchas Ruin poked at the fire with a stick, reawakening flames. Sparks fled up into the dark. Rud watched the warrior's cadaverous face, the mottled play of orange light that seemed to paint brief moments of life in it.

After a time, Silchas Ruin settled back and resumed. 'Power was drawn to him like slivers of iron to a lodestone . . . it all seemed so . . . natural. His distant origins invited the notion of neutrality, and one might argue, in hindsight, that Draconus was indeed neutral. He would use any and every Tiste Andii to further his ambitions, and how were we to imagine that, at the very core of his desire, there was *love*?'

Rud's gaze slid away from Silchas Ruin, up and over the Tiste Andii's right shoulder, to the terrible slashes of jade in the night sky. He tried to think of something to say, a comment of any sort: something wry, perhaps, or knowing, or cynical. But what did he know of the love such as Silchas Ruin was describing? What, indeed, did he know of anything in this or any other world?

'Consort to Mother Dark—he laid claim to that title, eventually, as if it was a role he had lost and had vowed to reacquire.' The white-skinned warrior snorted, eyes fixed on the flickering flames. 'Who were we to challenge that assertion? Mother's children had by then ceased to speak with her. No matter. What son would not challenge his mother's lover—new lover, old lover, whatever—' and he looked up, offering Rud a faint grin. 'Perhaps you've some understanding of that, at least. After all, Udinaas was not Menandore's first and only love.'

Rud looked away again. 'I am not certain love was involved.'

'Perhaps not. Do you wish more tea, Rud Elalle?'

'No, thank you. It is a potent brew.'

'Necessary, for the journey to come.'

Rud frowned. 'I do not understand.'

'This night, we shall travel. There are things you must see. It is not enough that I simply lead you this way and that—I do not expect a loyal hound at my heel, I expect a comrade standing at my side. To witness is to approach comprehension, and you will need that, when you decide.'

'Decide what?'

'The side you will take in the war awaiting us, among other things.'

'Other things. Such as?'

'Where to make your stand, and when. Your mother chose a mortal for your father for a good reason, Rud. Unexpected strengths come from such mating: the offspring often exhibit the best traits from both.'

Rud started as a stone cracked in the fire. 'You say you will lead me to places, Silchas Ruin, for you have no wish that I be naught but a loyal, mindless hound. Yet it may be that I shall not, in the end, choose to stand beside you at all. What then? What if I find myself opposite you in this war?'

'Then one of us will die.'

'My father left me in your care—and this is how you betray his trust?'

Silchas Ruin bared his teeth in a humourless smile. 'Rud Elalle, your father gave you to my care not out of trust—he knows me too well for that. Consider this your first lesson. He shares your love for the Imass of the Refugium. That realm—and every living thing within it—is in danger of annihilation, should the war be lost—'

'Starvald Demelain—but the gate was sealed!'

'No seal is perfect. Will and desire gnaw like acid. Well. Hunger and ambition are perhaps more accurate descriptions of that which assails the gate.' He collected the blackened pot from beside the coals and poured Rud's cup full once more. 'Drink. We have strayed from the path. I was speaking of the ancient forces—your kin, if you like. Among them, the Eleint. Was Draconus a true Eleint? Or was he something else? All I can say is, he wore the skin of a Tiste Andii for a time, perhaps as a sour joke, mocking our self-importance—who can know? In any case, it was inevitable that Anomander, my brother, would step into the Consort's path, and all those opportunities for knowledge and truth came to a swift end. To this day,' he added, sighing, 'I wonder if Anomander regrets killing Draconus.'

Rud started. His mind was awhirl. 'What of the Imass? This war—'

'I told you,' Silchas Ruin snapped, face betraying his irritation. 'Wars are indifferent to the choice of victims. Innocence, guilt, such notions are irrelevant. Grasp hold of your thoughts and catch up. I wondered if Anomander has regrets. I know that I do not. Draconus was a cold, cold bastard—and with the awakening of Father Light, ah, well, we saw then the truth of his jealous rage. The Consort cast aside, see the malice of the spurned ignite a black fire in his eyes! When we speak of ancient times, Rud Elalle, we find in our words things far nearer to hand, and all those emotions we imagined new, blazing with our own youth, we find to be ancient beyond imagining.' He spat into the coals. 'And this is why poets never starve for things to sing about, though rare is the one who grows fat upon them.'

'I will defend the Refugium,' said Rud, hands clenching into fists.

'We know that, and that is why you are here—'

'But that makes no sense! I should be *there*, standing before the gate!'

'Another lesson. Your father may love the Imass, but he loves you more.'

Rud surged to his feet. 'I will return—'

'No. Sit down. You have a better chance of saving them all by accompanying me.'

'How?'

Silchas Ruin leaned forward and reached into the fire. He scooped up two handfuls of coals and embers. He held them up. 'Tell me what you see, Rud Elalle, Ryadd Eleis—do you know those words, your true name? They are Tiste Andii—do you know what they mean?'

'No.'

Silchas Ruin studied the embers cupped in his hands. 'Just this. Your true name, Ryadd Eleis, means "Hands of Fire". Your mother looked into the soul of her son, and saw all there was to see. She may well have cherished you, but she also feared you.'

'She died because she chose betrayal.'

'She was true to the Eleint blood within her—but you also possess the blood of your father, a mortal, and he is a man I came to know well, to understand as much as anyone could. A man I came to respect. He was the first to comprehend the girl's purpose, the first to realize the task awaiting me—and he knew that I did not welcome the blood that would stain my hands. He chose not to stand in my way—I am not yet certain what happened at the gate, the clash with Wither, and poor Fear Sengar's misplaced need to stand in Scabandari's stead—but through it all, Kettle's fate was sealed. She was the seed of the Azath, and a seed must find fertile soil.' He dropped the embers—now cooled—back on to the fire. 'She is young yet. She needs time, and unless we stand against the chaos to come, she will not have that time—and the Imass will die. Your father will die. They will all die.' He rose and faced Rud. 'We leave now. Korabas awaits.'

'What is Korabas?'

'For this we must veer. Kallor's dead warren should suffice. Korabas is an Eleint, Ryadd. She is the Otataral Dragon. There is chaos in a human soul—it is your mortal gift, but be aware—like fire it can turn in your hands.'

'Even to one named "Hands of Fire"?'

The Tiste Andii's red eyes seemed to flatten. 'My warning was precise.'

'What do we seek in meeting this Korabas?'

Silchas slapped the ashes from his palms. 'They will free her, and that we cannot stop. I mean to convince you that we should not even try.'

Rud found his fists were still clenched tight, aching at the ends of his arms. 'You give me too little.'

'Better than too much, Ryadd.'

'Because like my mother, you fear me.'

'Yes.'

'Between you and your brothers, Silchas Ruin, who was the most honest?'

The Tiste Andii cocked his head, and then smiled.

A short time later, two dragons lifted into the darkness, one gleaming polished gold that slid in and out of the gloom in lurid smears; the other was bone white, the pallor of a corpse in the night—save for the twin embers of its eyes.

They rose high and higher still above the Wastelands, and then vanished from the world.

In their wake, in a nest of rocks, the small fire glowed fitfully in its bed of ashes, eating the last of itself. Until nothing was left.

Sandalath Drukorlat gave the hapless man one last shake that sent spittle whipping from his lips, and then threw him further up the shoreline. He scrambled to his feet, fell over, got up a second time and stumbled unsteadily away.

Withal cleared his throat. 'Sweetness, you seem a little short of temper lately.'

'Challenge yourself, husband. Find something to improve my mood.'

He glanced out at the crashing waves, licked salt from around his mouth. The three Nachts were sending the scrawny refugee off with hurled shells and dead crabs, although not a single missile managed to strike the fleeing man. 'The horses have recovered, at least.'

'Their misery has just begun.'

'I couldn't quite make out what happened, but I take it the Shake vanished through a gate. And, I suppose, we're going to chase after them.'

'And before they left, one of their own went and slaughtered almost all of the witches and warlocks—the very people I wanted to question!'

'We could always go to Bluerose.'

She stood straight, almost visibly quivering. He'd heard, once, that lightning went from the ground up and not the other way round. Sandalath looked ready to ignite and split the heavy clouds overhead. Or cut a devastating path through the ramshackle, stretched-out camp of those islanders Yan Tovis had left behind— the poor fools lived in squalid driftwood huts and wind-torn tents, all along the highwater line like so much wave-tossed detritus. And though the water was ever rising, so that the spray of the tumultuous seas now drenched them, not one had the wherewithal to move.

Not that they had anywhere to go. The forest was a blackened wasteland of stumps and ash for as far as he could see.

Just outside Letheras, Sandalath had cut open a way into a warren, a place she called Rashan, and the ride through it had begun in terrifying darkness that quickly dulled to torrid monotony. Until it began falling apart. *Chaos, she said. Inclusions, she said. Whatever that means.* And the horses went mad.

They had emerged into the proper world on the slope facing this strand, the horses' hoofs pounding up clouds of ash and cinders, his wife howling in frustration.

Things had eased up since then.

'What in Hood's name are you smiling about?'

Withal shook his head. 'Smiling? Not me, beloved.'

'Blind Gallan,' she said.

There had been more and more of this lately. Incomprehensible expostulations, invisible sources of irritation and blistering fury. *Face it, Withal, the honeymoon's over.*

'In the habit of popping up like a nefarious weed. Spouting arcane nonsense impressing the locals. Never trust a nostalgic old man—or old woman, I suppose. Every tale they spin has a hidden agenda, a secret malice for the present. They make the past—their version of it—into a kind of magic potion. "Sip this, friends, and return to the old times, when everything was perfect." Bah! If it'd been me doing the blinding, I wouldn't have stopped there. I would have scooped out his entire skull.'

'Wife, who is this Gallan?'

She bridled, jabbed a finger at him. 'Did you think I hadn't *lived* before meeting you? Oh, pity poor Gallan! And if he left a string of women in the wake of his wanderings, why, be so good as to indulge the sad creature—well, this is what comes of it, isn't it?'

Withal scratched his head. *See what happens when you marry an older woman? And face it, it doesn't take a Tiste Andii to have about a hundred thousand years of history behind her.* 'All right,' he said slowly, 'what now, then?'

She gestured after the refugee she'd sent scampering. 'He doesn't know if Nimander and the others were with the Shake—there were thousands—the only time he saw Yan Tovis was at the landing, and she was three thousand paces away. But, then, who else could have managed to open the gate? And then keep it open to admit ten thousand people? Only Andii blood can open the Road, and only *royal* Andii blood could *keep* it open! By the Abyss, they must have bled one of their own dry!'

'This road, Sand, where does it lead?'

'Nowhere. Oh, I should never have left Nimander and his kin! The Shake not only listened to Blind Gallan, they then went and *believed* him!' She stepped closer and raised a hand, as if to strike him.

Withal backed up a step.

'Oh, gods, just get the horses, Withal.'

As he set off, he glanced—with odd longing—after the still-running refugee.

A short time later they sat mounted, pack-horses behind them, while Sandalath, motionless, seemed to study something in front of them that only she could see. The waves thrashed to their left, the burnt forest stank on their right. The Nachts fought over a thick, massive length of driftwood that probably weighed more than all three put together. *That'd make a good club . . . for a damned Toblakai. Sink brace plugs, wrap the knobby end in hammered iron. Stud with beaten bronze rivets and maybe a spike or three. Draw wire down the length of the shaft, and then sink a deep and heavy counterweight butt—*

'It's healing, but the skin is thin.' She suddenly had a knife in her hand. 'I can get us through, I think.'

'Do you have royal blood then?'

'Snap shut that trap or I'll do it for you. I told you, it's a huge wound—barely mended. In fact, it seems weaker on the *other* side, which isn't good, isn't right, in fact. Did they stay on the Road? They must have known that much at least. Withal, listen well. Ready a weapon—'

'A weapon? What kind of weapon?'

'Wrong choice. Find another one.'

'What?'

'Stupidity won't work. Try that mace on your belt.'

'That's a smith's hammer—'

'And you're a smith, so presumably you know how to use it.'

'So long as my victim lays his head on an anvil, aye.'

'Can't you fight at all? What kind of husband are you? You Meckros—always fighting off pirates and such, or so you always said—' Her eyes narrowed. 'Unless they were just big fat lies, trying to impress your new woman.'

'I haven't used a weapon in decades—I just make the damned things! And why do I need to anyway? If you wanted a bodyguard you should have said so in the first place, and I could have hired on to the first ship out of Lether Harbour!'

'Abandon me, you mean! I knew it!'

He reached up to tear at his hair and then recalled that he didn't have enough of it. *Gods, life can be damned frustrating, can't it just?* 'Fine.' He tugged loose the hammer. 'I'm ready.'

'Now, remember, I died the first time because I don't know anything about fighting, and I don't want to die a second time—'

'What's all this talk about fighting and dying? It's just a gate, isn't it? What in Hood's name is on the other side?'

'I don't know, you idiot! Just be ready!'

'*For what?*'

'For anything!'

Withal slipped his left foot out of its stirrup and swung down to the littered sand.

Sandalath stared. 'What are you doing?'

'I'm going to piss, and maybe whatever else I can manage. If we're going to end up in a hoary mess, I don't want fouled breeches, not stuck in a saddle, not riding with a horde of shrieking demons on my tail. Besides, I probably only have a few moments of living left to me. When I go I plan on doing it clean.'

'Just blood and guts.'

'Right.'

'That's pathetic. As if you'll care.'

He went off to find somewhere private.

'Don't take too long!' she shouted after him.

There was a time, aye, when I could take as damned well long as I pleased.

He returned and would have climbed back into the saddle, but Sandalath insisted he wash his hands in the sea. Once this was done, he collected up the hammer, brushed sand from it, and then mounted the horse.

'Anything else needing doing?' she asked. 'A shave, perchance? Buff your boots, maybe?'

'Good suggestions. I'll just—'

With a snarl she slashed her left palm. The air split open before them, gaping red as the wound in her hand. 'Ride!' she yelled, kicking her horse into a lunge.

Cursing, Withal followed.

They emerged on to a blinding, blasted plain, the road beneath them glittering like crushed glass.

Sandalath's horse squealed, hoofs skidding, slewing sideways as she sawed on the reins. Withal's own beast made a strange grunting sound, then its head seemed to drop out of sight, front legs folding with sickening snaps—

Withal caught a glimpse of a pallid, overlong hand, slashing through the path where his horse's head had been a moment earlier, and then a curtain of blood lifted before him, wrapped hot and thick over his face, neck and chest. Blinded, flaying empty air with his mace, he pitched forward, leaving the saddle, and struck the road's savage surface. The cloth of his jerkin disintegrated, and the skin of his chest followed suit. The breath was knocked from his lungs. He vaguely heard the hammer bounce and skitter down the road.

Sudden bellowing roars, the impact of something huge against bare flesh and bone. Splintering blows drumming the road beneath him—the hot splash of something drenching his back—he clawed the blood from his eyes, managed to lift himself to his hands and knees—coughing, spewing vomit.

The thundering concussions continued, and then Sandalath was kneeling beside him. 'Withal! My love! Are you hurt—oh, Abyss take me! Too much blood—I'm sorry, oh, *I'm sorry, my love!*'

'My horse.'

'What?'

He spat to clear his mouth. 'Someone chopped off my horse's head. With his *hand.*'

'What? That's your horse's blood? All over you? You're not even hurt?' The hands that had been caressing him now shoved him away. 'Don't you dare do that again!'

Withal spat a second time, and then pushed himself to his feet, eyes fixing on Sandalath. 'This is enough.' As she opened her mouth for a retort he stepped close and set a filthy finger against her lips. 'If I was a different kind of man, I'd be beating you senseless right about now—no, don't give me that shocked look. I'm not here to be kicked around whenever your mood happens to turn foul. A little measure of respect—'

'But you can't even fight!'

'Maybe not, and neither can you. What I can do, though, is make things. And something else, too, I can decide, at any time, when I've had enough. And I will tell you this right now, I'm damned close.' He stepped back. 'Now, what in Hood's name just—*gods below!*'

This shout burst from him in shock—three enormous, hulking, black-skinned demons were on the road just beyond the dead horse. One of them held a club of driftwood that looked like a drummer's baton in its huge hands, and was using it to pound down some more on a mangled, crushed corpse. The other two followed the blows as if gauging the effects of each and every crushing impact. Bluish blood had sprayed out on the road, along with other less identifiable discharges from the pulped ruin of their victim's body.

In a low voice Sandalath said, 'Your Nachts—the Jaghut were inveterate jokers. Hah hah. That was a Forkrul Assail. It seems the Shake stirred things up somewhat—they're probably all dead, in fact, and this one was backtracking with the intention of cleaning up any stragglers—out through the gate, probably, to murder every refugee on that shoreline we've just left behind. Instead, he ran into us—and your Venath demons.'

Withal wiped blood from his eyes. 'I'm, uh, starting to see the resemblances—they were ensorcelled before?'

'In a manner of speaking. A geas, I suspect. They're Soletaken . . . or maybe D'ivers. Either way, this particular realm forced a veering—or a sembling—who can say which species is the original, after all?'

'Then what do the Jaghut have to do with any of this?'

'They created the Nachts. Or so I gathered—the mage Obo in Malaz City seemed to be certain of that. Of course, if he's right and they did, then what they managed to do was something no one else has ever managed—they found a way to chain the wild forces of Soletaken and D'ivers. Now, husband, get cleaned up and saddle a new horse—we can't stay here long. We ride as far as we need to on this road to confirm the slaughter of the Shake, and then we ride back out the way we came.' She paused. 'Even with these Venath, we'll be in danger—if there's one Forkrul Assail, there's bound to be more.'

The Venath demons had evidently decided they were done with the destruction of the Forkrul Assail, as they now bounded up the road a few paces to then huddle round the club and examine the damage to their lone weapon.

Gods, they're still stupid Nachts. Only bigger.

What a horrid thought.

'Withal.'

He faced her again.

'I'm sorry.'

Withal shrugged. 'It will be all right, Sand, if you don't expect me to be what I'm not.'

'I may have found them infuriating, but I fear for Nimander, Aranatha, Desra, all of them. I fear for them so.'

He grimaced, and then shook his head. 'You underestimate them, I think, Sand.' *And may Phaed's ghost forgive us all for that.*

'I hope so.'

He went to work loose the saddle, paused to pat the animal's gore-soaked neck. 'Should've given you a name, at least. You deserved that much.'

Her mind was free. It could slip down among the sharp knuckles of quartz studding the plain, where nothing lived on the surface. It could slide beneath the stone-hard clay to where the diamonds, rubies and opals hid from the cruel heat. All this land's wealth. And deep into the crumbling marrow of living bones wrapped in withered meat, crouched in fever worlds where blood boiled. In the moments before the very end, she could hover behind hot, bright eyes—the brightness that was the final looking upon all the surrounding things—all the precious vistas—that announced saying goodbye. That look, she now knew, did not shine forth solely among old people, though perhaps they were the only ones to whom it belonged. No, here, in this gaunt, slow, slithery snake, it was the beacon blazing in the eyes of children.

But she could fly away from such things. She could wing high and higher still, to ride the fuzzy backs of capemoths, or the feathered tips of vultures' wings. And look down wheeling round and round the crawling, dying worm far below, that red, scorched string winking with dull motion. Thread of food, knots of promise, the countless strands of salvation—and see all the bits and pieces falling off, left in its wake, and down and down low and lower still, to eat and pick at leather skin, pluck the brightness from eyes.

Her mind was free. Free to make beauty with a host of beautiful, terrible words. She could swim through the cool language of loss, rising to touch precious surfaces, diving into midnight depths where broken thoughts fluttered down, where the floor fashioned vast, intricate tales.

Tales, yes, of the fallen.

There was no pain in this place. Her untethered will recalled no aching joints, no crusting flies upon split, raw lips; no blackened, lacerated feet. It was free to float and then sing across hungry winds, and comfort was a most natural thing, reasonable, a proper state of being. Worries dwindled, the future threatened no alteration to what was and one could easily believe that what was would always be.

She could be an adult here, splashing water on to pretty flowers, dipping fingers into dreaming fountains, damming up rivers and devouring trees. Filling lakes and ponds with poison rubbish. Thickening the air with bitter smoke. And nothing would ever change and what changes came would never touch her adultness, her perfect preoccupation with petty extravagances and indulgences. The adults knew such a nice world, didn't they?

And if the bony snake of their children now wandered dying in a glass wilderness, what of it? The adults don't care. Even the moaners among them—their caring had sharp borders, not far, only a few steps away, patrolled borders with thick walls and bristling towers and on the outside there was agonizing sacrifice and inside there was convenience. Adults knew what to guard and they knew, too, how far to think, which wasn't far, not far, not far at all.

Even words, especially words, could not penetrate those walls, could not overwhelm those towers. Words bounced off obstinate stupidity, brainless stupidity, breathtaking, appalling stupidity. Against the blank gaze, words are useless.

Her mind was free to luxuriate in adulthood, knowing as it did that she would never in truth reach it. And this was her own preoccupation, a modest one, not very extravagant, not much of an indulgence, but her own which meant that she owned it.

She wondered what adults owned, these days. Apart from this murderous legacy, of course. Great inventions beneath layers of sand and dust. Proud monuments that not even spiders could map, palaces empty as caves, sculptures announcing immortality to grinning white skulls, tapestries displaying grand moments to fill the guts of moths. All this, such a bold, joyous legacy.

Flying high, among the capemoths and vultures and rhinazan and swarms of Shards, she was free. And to look down was to see the disordered patterns writ large across the glass plain. Ancient causeways, avenues, enclosures, all marked out by nothing more than faint stains—and the broken glass was all that remained of some unknown civilization's most wondrous chalice.

At the snake's head and in front of it, the tiny flickering tongue that was Rutt and the baby he named Held in his arms.

She could descend, plummeting like truth, to shake the tiny swaddled form in Rutt's twig-arms, force open the bright eyes to the glorious panorama of rotted cloth and layers of filtered sunlight, the blazing rippling heat from Rutt's chest. Final visions to take into death—this was the meaning behind that brightness, after all.

Words held the magic of the breathless. But adults turn away.

They have no room in their heads for a suffering column of dying children, nor the heroes among them.

'So many fallen,' she said to Saddic who remembered everything. 'I could list them. I could make them into a book ten thousand pages long. And people will read it, but only so far as their own private borders, and that's not far. Only a few steps. Only a few steps.'

Saddic, who remembered everything, he nodded and he said, 'One long scream of horror, Badalle. Ten thousand pages long. No one will hear it.'

'No,' she agreed. 'No one will hear it.'

'But you will write it anyway, won't you?'

'I am Badalle, and all I have is words.'

'May the world choke on them,' said Saddic, who remembered everything.

Her mind was free. Free to invent conversations. Free to assemble sharp knuckles of quartz into small boys walking beside her endless selves. Free to trap light and fold it in and in and in, until all the colours became one, and that one was so bright it blinded everyone and everything.

The last colour is the word. See it burn bright: that is what there is to see in a dying child's eyes.

'Badalle, your indulgence was too extravagant. They won't listen, they won't want to know.'

'Well, now, isn't that convenient?'

'Badalle, do you still feel free?'

'Saddic, I still feel free. Freer than ever before.'

'Rutt holds Held and he will deliver Held.'

'Yes, Saddic.'

'He will deliver Held into an adult's arms.'

'Yes, Saddic.'

The last colour is the word. See it burn bright in a dying child's eyes. See it, just this once, before you turn away.

'I will, Badalle, when I am grown up. But not until then.'

'No, Saddic, not until then.'

'When I've done away with these things.'

'When you've done away with these things.'

'And freedom ends, Badalle.'

'Yes, Saddic, when freedom ends.'

Kalyth dreamed she was in a place she had not yet reached. Overhead was a low ceiling of grey, turgid clouds, the kind that she had seen above the plains of the Elan, when the first snows came down from the north. The wind howled, cold as ice, but it was dry as a frozen tomb. Across the taiga, stunted trees rose from the permafrost like skeletal hands, and she could see sinkholes, here and there, in which dozens of some kind of four-legged beast had become mired, dying and freezing solid, and the wind tugged and tore at their matted hides, and frost painted white their curved horns and ringed the hollow pits of their eyes.

In the myths of the Elan, this vista belonged to the underworld of death; it was also the distant past, the very beginning place, where the heat of life first pushed back the bitter cold. The world began in darkness, devoid of warmth. It awakened, in time, to an ember that flared, ever so brief, before one day returning to where it had begun. And so, what she was seeing here before her could also belong to the future. Past or in the age to come, it was where life ceased.

But she was not alone.

A score of figures sat on gaunt horses along a ridge a hundred paces distant. Wrapped in black rain-capes, armoured and helmed, they seemed to be watching her, waiting for her. But terror held Kalyth rooted, as if knee-deep in frozen mud.

She wore a thin tunic, torn and half-rotted, and the cold was like the Reaper's own hand, closing about her from all sides. She could not move within its intransigent grip, even had she wanted to. She would will the strangers away; she would scream at them, unleash sorcery to send them scattering. She would banish them utterly. But no such powers belonged to her. Kalyth felt as useless here as she felt in her own world. A vessel empty, longing to be filled by a hero's bold fortitude.

The wind ripped at the grim figures, and now at last the snow came, cutting like shards of ice from the heavy clouds.

The riders stirred. The horses lifted their heads, and all at once they were descending the slope, hoofs cracking hard the frozen ground.

Kalyth huddled, arms tight about herself. The frost-rimed riders drew closer, and she could just make out that array of faces behind the serpentine nose-guards of their helms—deathly pale, bearing slashes gaping deep crimson but bloodless. They wore surcoats over chain, uniforms, she realized, to mark allegiance to some foreign army, grey and magenta beneath frozen bloodstains and crusted gore. One, she saw, was tattooed, bedecked with fetishes of claws, feathers and beads—huge, barbaric, perhaps not even human. But the others, they were of her own kind—she was certain of that.

They reined in before her and something drew Kalyth's wide stare to one rider in particular, grey-bearded beneath the dangling crystals of ice, his grey eyes, set deep in shadowed sockets, reminding her of a bird's fixed regard—cold and rapto-rial, bereft of all compassion.

When he spoke, in the language of the Elan, no breath plumed from his mouth. 'Your Reaper's time is coming to an end. Death shall surrender his face—'

'Never was a welcoming one,' cut in the heavy, round-faced soldier on the man's right.

'Enough of that, Mallet,' snapped another horseman, one-armed, hunched with age. 'You don't even belong here yet. We're waiting for the world to catch up—such are dreams and visions—they are indifferent to the ten thousand unerr-ing steps in any given mortal's life, much less the millions of useless ones. Learn patience, healer.'

'Where one yields,' continued the bearded soldier, 'we shall stand in his stead.'

'In times of war,' growled the barbaric warrior—who seemed preoccupied with braiding the ratty tatters of his dead horse's mane.

'Life itself is a war, one it is doomed to lose,' retorted the bearded man. 'Do not think, Trotts, that our rest will come soon.'

'He was a god!' barked another soldier, baring teeth above a jet-black forked beard. 'We're just a company of chewed-up marines!'

Trotts laughed. 'See how high you've climbed, Cage? At least you got your head back—I remember burying you in Black Dog—we looked for half the night and never found it.'

'Got ett by a frog,' another suggested.

The dead soldiers laughed, even Cage.

Kalyth saw the grey-bearded soldier's faint smile and it transformed his fal-con's eyes into something that seemed capable of holding, without flinching, the compassion of an entire world. He leaned forward on his saddle, the horn creak-ing as it bent on its hinge. 'Aye, we're no gods, and we're not going to attempt to replace him beneath that rotted cowl. We're Bridgeburners, and we've been posted to Hood's Gate—one last posting—'

'When did we agree to that?' Mallet demanded, eyes wide.

'It's coming. In any case, I was saying—and gods below you're all getting damned insubordinate in your hoary deadness—we're Bridgeburners. Why are any of you surprised to find that you're still saluting? Still taking orders? Still marching out in every miserable kind of weather you can imagine?' He glared left and right, but it was softened by the wry twist of his lips. 'Hood knows, it's what we do.'

Kalyth could hold back no longer. 'What do you want with me?'

The grey eyes settled on her once more. 'Destriant, by that title alone you must now consort with the likes of us—in Hood's—your Reaper's—stead. You see us as Guardians of the Gate, but we are more than that. We are—or will become—the new arbiters, for as long as is necessary. Among us there are fists, mailed gauntlets of hard violence. And healers, and mages. Assassins and skulkers, sappers and horse-archers, lancers and trackers. Cowards and brave, stolid warriors.' He hitched a half-smile. 'And we've found all manner of unexpected . . . allies. In all our guises, Destriant, we shall be more than the Reaper ever was. We are not distant. Not indifferent. You see, unlike Hood, we remember what it was to be alive. We remember each and every moment of yearning, of desperate need, the anguish that comes when no amount of beseeching earns a single instant's reprieve, no pleading yields a moment's mercy. We are here, Destriant. When no other choice remains, call upon us.'

The ice of this realm seemed to shatter all around Kalyth and she staggered as warmth flooded through her. Blessed—no, the *blessing* of warmth. Gasping, she stared up at the unnamed soldier as tears filled her eyes. 'This . . . this is not the death I imagined.'

'No, and I give you this. We are the Bridgeburners. We shall sustain. But not because we were greater in life than anyone else. Because, Destriant, *we were no different.* Now, answer me as a Destriant, Kalyth of Ampelas Rooted, do we suffice?'

Does anything *suffice? No, that is too easy. Think on your answer, woman. He deserves that much at least.* 'It is a natural thing to fear death,' she said.

'It is.'

'And so it should be,' grunted the one named Cage. 'It's miserable—look at my company—I can't get rid of these ugly dogs. The ones you leave behind, woman, they're waiting for you.'

'But without judgement,' said the grey-eyed soldier.

The one-armed one was nodding, and he added, 'Just don't expect any of 'em to have lost their bad habits—like Cage and his eternally sour bile. It's all what you knew—who you knew, I mean. It's all that and nothing more.'

Kalyth did not know these people, yet already they felt closer to her than anyone she had ever known. 'I am becoming a Destriant in truth,' she said in wonder. *And I no longer feel so . . . alone.* 'I fear death still, I think, but not as much as I once did.' *And I once flirted with suicide, but I have left that behind, for ever. I am not ready to embrace an end to things. I am the last Elan. And my people are waiting for me, not caring if I come now or a hundred years from now—it is no different to them.*

· *The dead—my dead—will indulge me.*

For as long as I need. For as long as I have.

The soldier gathered his reins. 'You shall find your Mortal Sword and your Shield Anvil, Kalyth. Against the cold that slays, you must answer with fire. There will come to you a moment when you must cease following the K'Chain Che'Malle; when you must lead them. In you lies their last hope for survival.'

But are they worth preserving?

'That judgement does not belong to you.'

'No—no, I'm sorry. They are so . . . alien—'

'As you are to them.'

'Of course. I am sorry.'

The warmth was fading, the snow closing in.

The riders wheeled their lifeless mounts.

She watched them ride off, watched them vanish in the swirling white.

The white, how it burns the eyes, how it insists—

Kalyth opened her eyes to bright, blinding sunlight. *I am having such strange dreams. But I still see their faces, each one. I see the barbarian with his filed teeth. I see scowling Cage, whom I adore because he could laugh at himself. And the one named Mallet, a healer, yes—it is easy to see the truth of that. The one-armed one, too.*

And the one with the falcon's eyes, my iron prophet, yes. I did not even learn his name. A Bridgeburner—such a strange name for soldiers, and yet . . . so perfect there in the chasm between the living and the dead.

Death's guardians. Human faces in place of the Reaper's shadowed skull. Oh, what a thought! What a relief!

She wiped her eyes and sat up. And a flood of memories returned. Her breath caught and she twisted about, finding the K'Chain Che'Malle. Sag'Churok, Rythok, Gunth Mach . . . 'O spirits bless us.'

Yes, she would not find Kor Thuran, the K'ell Hunter's stolid, impervious presence. The space beside Rythok howled its emptiness, shrieked his absence. The K'Chain Che'Malle was dead.

Scouting far to the west, out of sight—but they all felt the sudden explosive clash. Kor Thuran's snarls filled their skulls, his rage and baffled defiance—his *pain.* She found she was shivering, as bitter recollections assailed her. *He died. We could not see who killed him.*

Our winged Assassin has vanished. Was it Gu'Rull? Had Kor Thuran committed a transgression? Was the Hunter fleeing us all and did the Assassin punish him? No, Kor Thuran did not flee. He fought and he died guarding our flank.

Enemies now hunt us. They know we are close. They mean to find us.

She rubbed at her face, forced out a broken sigh, the echoes of the K'ell Hunter's terrible death still crowding her mind, leaving her feeling exhausted. *And this day has only begun.*

The K'Chain Che'Malle faced her, motionless, waiting. There would be no cookfire this morning. They had carried her through most of the night, and in her exhaustion she had slept like a fevered child in Gunth Mach's arms. She wondered why they had set her down, why they had not kept going. She could feel their nervous impatience to be off—away—the disaster of failure stalked this quest now, closer than ever before. As huge and imposing as they were, she now saw them as vulnerable, insufficient to this task.

There are deadlier things out there. They brought down a K'ell Hunter in a score of heartbeats.

Yet, as she rose to her feet, a new assurance filled her—gift of her dreams, and though they might be nothing more than fanciful conjurations, false benedictions, they seemed to give her something solid, and she could feel her frailty falling away from her soul like a cracked seed husk. Her eyes hardened as she regarded the three K'Chain Che'Malle.

'If they find us, they find us. We cannot run from . . . from ghosts. Nor can we trust in the protection of Gu'Rull. So, we drive south—straight as a lance. Gunth Mach, give me your back to ride. This will be a long day—there is so much, so much we must now leave behind us.' She looked to Rythok. 'Brother, I mean to honour Kor Thuran—we all must—by succeeding in our quest.'

The K'ell Hunter's reptilian eyes remained fixed on her, cold, unyielding.

Sag'Churok and Gunth Mach rarely spoke to her these days, and when they did it seemed their voices were more distant, harder to make out. She did not think the fault was theirs. *I am dwindling within myself. The world narrows—but how is it I even know this? What part within me is aware of its own measure?*

No matter. We must do this.

'It is time.'

Sag'Churok watched Gunth Mach force her own body into the configuration necessary to accommodate the Destriant. The heady, spice-drenched scents roiled from her in tendrils that spread like branches on the currents of air, and they carried to the K'ell Hunter echoes of Kor Thuran's last moments of agony.

When the hunter became the hunted, every retort was reduced to a defiant snarl, a few primitive threat postures, and the body existed to absorb damage—to weather and withstand all it could as the soul that dwelt within it sought, if not escape, then a kind of comprehension. A recognition. That even the hunter must know fear. No matter how powerful, no matter how superior, how supreme, sooner or later forces it could not defeat or flee from would find it.

Domination was an illusion. Its coherence could only hold for so long.

This lesson was a seared brand upon the memories of the K'Chain Che'Malle. Its bitter taste soured the dust of the Wastelands, and eastward, on the vast plain that had once known great cities and the whisper of hundreds of thousands of K'Chain Che'Malle, now there was nothing but melted and crushed fragments, and what the winds sought they could not find, and so wandered for ever lost.

Kor Thuran had been young. No other crime belonged to the K'ell Hunter. He had made no foolish decisions. Had not fallen victim to his own arrogance or sense of invulnerability. He had simply been in the wrong place at the wrong time. And now so much was lost. And for all the Destriant's noble words—her sudden, unwarranted confidence and determination—Sag'Churok, along with Rythok and Gunth Mach, knew that the quest had failed. Indeed, it was not likely that they would survive the day.

Sag'Churok shifted his gaze from Gunth Mach as she suffered her transformation in runnels of oil that dripped like blood.

Gu'Rull was gone, probably dead. Every effort to brush his thoughts had failed. Of course, the Shi'gal Assassin could shield his mind, but he had no reason to do so. No, two of the five protectors were gone. And still this puny human stood, her soft face set in an expression Sag'Churok had come to know as defiant, weak eyes fixed on the undulating horizon to the south as if her will alone could conjure into being her precious Shield Anvil and Mortal Sword. It was brave. It was . . . unexpected. For all that the Matron's gifts were fading from the woman, she had indeed found some kind of inner strength.

All for naught. They would die, and soon. Their torn and broken bodies would lie scattered, lost, their great ambitions unheralded.

Sag'Churok lifted his head, drank in the air, and caught the taint of the enemy. Close. Drawing closer. Threat oils rising between his scales, he scanned the horizon, and finally settled on the west—where Kor Thuran had fallen.

Rythok had done the same, and even Gunth Mach's head had swivelled round.

The Destriant was not blind to their sudden fixation. She bared her teeth. 'Guardians,' she said. 'It seems we need your help—not some time in the future, but now. What can you send to us? Who among you can stand against that which my companions will not let me even see?'

Sag'Churok did not understand her meaning. He did not know whom she was addressing. Was this the Matron's madness, or Kalyth's very own?

The Destriant's gait was stiff with fear as she walked up to Gunth Mach, who helped the woman on to the gnarled saddle of scales behind her shoulders.

Sag'Churok faced Rythok. *Hunter. Slow them down.*

Rythok stretched his jaws until they creaked, and then drew the edges of his blades against each other in a singing rasp. Tail lashing—spraying thick droplets of oil that pattered the ground—the K'ell Hunter set off at a run, head dipping in the attack posture. Westward.

'Where is he going?' Kalyth shouted. 'Call him back! Sag'Churok—'

But he and Gunth Mach sprang into motion, side by side, legs scything the air, taloned feet snapping as they kicked them forward, ever swifter, the pace building until the broken ground blurred beneath them. South.

The Destriant shrieked—her mask of determination shattered and in its place the raw truth of comprehension and all the horror that followed. Her puny fists beat at Gunth Mach's neck and shoulders, and for an instant it looked as if Kalyth would throw herself from the First Daughter's back—but their speed was too great, the risk of broken limbs, or indeed, a broken neck, defeated the impulse and forced her to hold tightly to Gunth Mach's neck.

They had gone a third of a league when Rythok's savage hiss burst into their skulls—the blistering acid of sudden, frenzied battle. Blades striking home, impacts reverberating like thunder. A crackling, terrifying sound, and all at once blood was gushing from the K'ell Hunter. A piercing cry, a weaving stagger, burning pain and then baffled anguish as Rythok's legs gave way.

Ribs cracked as he struck the ground. Sharp rocks tore and stabbed the softer hide of his belly as he skidded.

But Rythok was not yet done. Dying would have to wait.

He rolled, twisted round, blade lashing back into his wake. The edge struck armour, chopped through it, and bit deep into flesh.

Phlegm and blood spattered, stung like fire in Rythok's eyes—a sudden image, brutal in its clarity, as a massive axe swung down, filling the Hunter's vision on his left side.

An explosion of white.

And death made the two fleeing K'Chain Che'Malle stagger. A moment, and then, with unyielding will, they recovered. Glistening with grief, rank with battle oils.

The Destriant was weeping—shedding her own oil, thin, salty, all that she could muster.

She humbled Sag'Churok. Had his hide grown slick with sorrow when he killed Redmask? No, it had not. Bitter with disappointment, yes, he had known that. But greater the icy grip of intransigent judgement. He and Gunth Mach had been witness to humans slaughtering each other. The fire of battle had raged on all sides. Human life was, it was clear, of little value—even to the humans themselves. When the world is swarming with a hundred million orthen, what loss a few tens of thousands?

Yet, this frail alien creature wept. For Rythok.

In moments he would wheel. He would do as Rythok had done. But not precisely so. There was little point in attempting to kill. Maiming was a more useful tactic. He would wound as many as he could and so diminish the numbers capable of pursuing Gunth Mach and the Destriant.

He would employ skills Rythok had not yet learned and now never would. Sag'Churok might not be a Ve'Gath Soldier, but he would surprise them nonetheless.

Gunth Mach.

'Yes, beloved.'

Sag'Churok whetted his blades.

'*No!*' Kalyth shrieked. 'Do not dare leave us! Sag'Churok—I forbid it!'

Destriant. I shall succeed where Rythok failed. My life shall purchase you a day, perhaps two, and you must make it enough.

'Stop! I have prayed! Do you not understand? *They said they would answer!*'

I do not know of whom you speak, Destriant. Listen well to my words. Acyl Nest shall die. The Matron is doomed, and all those within the Rooted. Gunth Mach carries my seed. She shall be a new Matron. Find your Shield Anvil and your Mortal Sword—the three of you shall be Gunth Mach's J'an Sentinels, until such time as she breeds her own.

Then Gunth Mach shall free you.

This is not your war. This is not your end—it is ours.

'Stop!'

Sag'Churok prepared to speak to her once more, despite the growing effort it entailed. He would tell her of his admiration. And his faith in her—and of his own astonishment at feeling such emotions for a human. They were paltry things, too weak to be considered gifts of any sort, but he would—

Figures in the distance ahead. Not the enemy. Not born and bred of matrons either. And not, Sag'Churok realized, human.

Standing, readying an array of weapons.

Fourteen in all. Details assembling as Sag'Churok and Gunth Mach raced ever closer. Gaunt despite the blackened, gnarled armour encasing their torsos and limbs. Strange helms with down-swept cheek-guards that projected below their chins. Ragged camails of black chain. Thick, tattered and stained cloaks that had once been dyed an intense, deep yellow, trimmed in silver fur.

Sag'Churok saw that seven of the strangers held in their gauntleted hands long, narrow-bladed swords of blued steel, basket-hilted with half-moon knuckle-guards, and ornate bucklers. He saw two others with heavier single-edged axes and embossed round shields covered in mottled hides. Three with broad-headed, iron-sheathed spears. And two more, standing behind the rest, preparing slings.

And, surrounding them all, spreading down from the faint rise on which they waited, frost sparkled on earth and stone.

Disbelief struck Sag'Churok like a hammer-blow.

This was not possible. This was . . . without precedent. *Impossible—what cast these strangers? Foes or allies? But no, they cannot be allies.*

Besides, as all know, Jaghut stand alone.

'There!' shouted Kalyth, pointing. 'I prayed! There—run to them—quickly! Guardians of the Gate!'

Destriant—hear me. These ones will not help us. They will do nothing.

'You're wrong!'

Destriant. They are Jaghut. They are . . .

. . . impossible.

But Gunth Mach had altered her course, was closing directly upon the waiting warriors. Sag'Churok fell in beside her, still shocked, still confused, uncomprehending—

And then he and Gunth Mach caught the stench wafting from the Jaghut, gusting out from the frozen ground encircling them.

Destriant, beware! They are undead!

'I know what they are,' snapped Kalyth. 'Stop, Gunth Mach—stop retreating—right here, don't move.' And then she slipped down from the Daughter's back.

Destriant, we do not have time—

'We do. Tell me, how many pursue us? Tell me!'

A Caste. Fifty. Forty-nine now. Four wield Kep'rah, weapons of sorcery. A Crown commands them, they flow as one.

She looked to the northwest. 'How far away?'

Your eyes shall find them shortly. They are . . . mounted.

'On what?'

Sag'Churok would have sent her an image, but she was beyond such things now. She was closed and closing. *Wrought . . . legs. To match our own. Tireless.*

He watched as the Destriant absorbed this information, and then she faced the Jaghut.

'Guardians. I thought to see . . . familiar faces.'

One of the spear-wielders stepped forward. 'Hood would not want us.'

'If he had,' said the swordswoman beside him, 'he would have summoned us.'

'He would not choose that,' resumed the first Jaghut, 'for he knew we would not likely accede.'

'Hood abused our goodwill,' the swordswoman said, tusks gleaming with frost, 'at the first chaining. He knew enough to face away from us at the next one.' An iron-sheathed finger pointed at the Destriant. 'Instead, he abused you, child of the Imass. And made of one his deadliest enemy. We yield him no sorrow.'

'No commiseration,' said the spear-wielder.

'No sympathy,' added one of the slingers.

'He will stand alone,' the swordswoman said in a rasp. 'A Jaghut in solitude.'

Sag'Churok twisted round, studied the glint of metal to the northwest. Not long now.

The swordswoman continued. 'Human, you keep strange company. They will teach you nothing of value, these Che'Malle. It is their curse to repeat their mistakes, again and again, until they have destroyed themselves and everyone else. They have no gifts for you.'

'It seems,' said Kalyth of the Elan, 'we humans have already learned all they could teach us, whether we ever knew it or not.'

A chilling sound, the rattling laughter of fourteen undead Jaghut.

Then the spear-wielder spoke. 'Flee. Your hunters shall know the privilege of meeting the last soldiers of the only army the Jaghut ever possessed.'

'The last to die,' one added in a growl.

'And should you see Hood,' said the swordswoman, 'remind him of how his soldiers never faltered. Even in his moment of betrayal. We never faltered.'

More laughter.

Pale, trembling, the Destriant returned to Gunth Mach. 'We go. Leave them to this.'

Sag'Churok hesitated. *They are too few, Destriant. I will stay with them.*

Fourteen pairs of cold, lifeless eyes fixed on the K'ell Hunter, and, smiling, the swordswoman spoke. 'There are enough of us. Kep'rah never amounted to much of a threat against Omtose Phellack. Still, you may stay. We appreciate an audience, because we are an arrogant people.' The ghastly grin broadened. 'Almost as arrogant as you, Che'Malle.'

'I think,' observed the spear-wielder, 'this one is . . . humbled.'

His companion shrugged. 'Into the twilight of a species comes humility, like an old woman who has just remembered she's still a virgin. Too late to count for anything. I am not impressed.' And the swordswoman attempted to spit, failed, and quietly cursed.

'Sag'Churok,' said the Destriant from Gunth Mach's saddled back, 'do not die here. Do you understand me? I need you still. Watch, if you must. See what there is to be seen, and then return to us.'

Very well, Kalyth of the Elan.

The K'ell Hunter watched his beloved carry the human away.

Battered armour rustled and clanked as the Jaghut warriors readied themselves, fanning out along the crest of the hill. As they did so, the frigid air crackled around them.

Sag'Churok spoke: *Proud soldiers, do not fear they will pass you by. They pass by nothing they believe they can slay, or destroy.*

'We have observed your folly countless times,' replied the swordswoman. 'Nothing of what we are about to face will catch us unawares.' She turned to her companions. 'Is not Iskar Jarak a worthy leader?'

'He is,' answered a chorus of rough voices.

'And what did he say to us, before he sent us here?'

And thirteen Jaghut voices answered: " 'Pretend they are T'lan Imass.' "

The last survivors of the only army of the Jaghut, who had not survived at all, then laughed once more. And that laughter clattered on, to greet the Caste, and on, through the entire vicious, stunning battle that followed.

Sag'Churok, watching from a hundred paces away, felt the oil sheathing his hide thicken in the bitter gusts of Omtose Phellack, as the ancient Hold of Ice trembled to the impacts of Kep'rah, as it in turn lashed out—bursting flesh, sending frozen pieces and fragments flying.

In the midst of the conflagration, iron spoke with iron in that oldest of tongues.

Sag'Churok watched. And listened. And when he had seen and heard enough, he did as the Destriant commanded. He left the battle behind. Knowing the outcome, knowing a yet deeper, still sharper bite of humility.

Jaghut. Though we shared your world, we never saw you as our foe. Jaghut, the T'lan Imass never understood—some people are simply too noble to be rivals. But then, perhaps it was that very nobility they so despised.

Iskar Jarak, you who commanded them . . . what manner of thing are you? And how did you know? I wish you could answer me that one question. How did you know precisely what to say to your soldiers?

Sag'Churok would never forget that laughter. The sound was carved into his very hide; it rode the swirls of his soul, danced light on the heady flavours of his relief and wonder. Such knowing amusement, both wry and sweet, such a cruel, breathtaking sound.

I have heard the dead laugh.

He knew he would ride that laughter through the course of his life. It would hold him up. Give him strength.

Now I understand, Kalyth of the Elan, what made your eyes so bright on this day.

Behind him, the earth shook. And the song of laughter went on and on.

The swollen trunks of segmented trees rose from the shallows of the swamp, so bloated that Grub thought they might split open at any moment, disgorging . . . what? He had no idea, but considering the horrific creatures they had seen thus far—mercifully from a distance—it was likely to be so ghastly it would haunt his nightmares for the rest of his life. He swatted at a gnat chewing on his knee and crouched further down behind the bushes.

The buzz and whine of insects, the slow lap of water on the sodden shoreline, and the deep, even breathing of something massive, each exhalation a sharp whistle that went on . . . and on.

Grub licked sweat from his lips. 'It's big,' he whispered.

Kneeling at his side, Sinn had found a black leech and let each of its two suckers fasten on to the tip of a finger. She spread the fingers and watched how the slimy thing stretched. But it was getting fatter. 'It's a lizard,' she said.

'A dragon.'

'Dragons don't breathe, not like we do, anyway. That's why they can travel between worlds. No, it's a lizard.'

'We lost the path—'

'There never was a path, Grub,' Sinn replied. 'There was a trail, and we're still on it.'

'I preferred the desert.'

'Times change,' she said, and then grinned. 'That's a joke, by the way.'

'I don't get it.'

She made a face. 'Time doesn't change, Grub, just the things in it.'

'What does that mean?'

'This trail, of course. It's as if we're walking the track of someone's life, and it was a long life.' She waved with her free hand. 'All this, it's what's given shape to the mess at the far end—which was where we started from.'

'Then we're going back in time?'

'No. That would be the wrong direction, wouldn't it?'

'Get that thing off your fingers before it sucks you dry.'

She held it out and he tugged it loose, which wasn't as easy as he would have liked. The puckered wounds at the ends of Sinn's fingers bled freely. Grub tossed the creature away.

'Think he'll smell it?' Sinn asked.

'He who?'

'The lizard. My blood.'

'Gods below!'

Her eyes were bright. 'Do you like this place? The air, it makes you drunk, doesn't it? We're back in the age when everything was raw. Unsettled. But maybe not, maybe *we're* from the raw times. But here, I think, you could stay for ten thousand years and nothing would change, nothing at all. Long ago, time was slower.'

'I thought you said—'

'All right, *change* was slower. Not that anything living would sense that. Everything living just knows what it knows, and that *never* changes.'

She was easier when she never said anything, Grub decided, but he kept that thought to himself. Something was stirring, out in the swamp, and Grub's eyes widened when he studied the waterline and realized that it had crept up by a full hand's span. Whatever it was, it had just displaced a whole lot of water. 'It's coming,' he said.

'Which flickering eye,' Sinn mused, 'is *us*?'

'Sinn—we got to get out of here—'

'If we're not even here,' she continued, 'where did we come from, except from something that *is* here? You can't just say, "Oh, we come through a gate," because, then, the question just shows up all over again.'

The breathing had stopped.

'It's coming!'

'But you can breed horses—and you can see how they change—longer legs, even a different gait. Like turning a desert wolf into a hunting dog—it doesn't take as long as you'd think. Did someone breed us to make us like we are?'

'If they did,' hissed Grub, 'they should've given one of us more brains!' Snatching her by the arm, he pulled her upright.

She laughed as they ran.

Behind them, water exploded, enormous jaws snapped on empty air, breath shrieking, and the ground trembled.

Grub did not look behind them—he could hear the monstrous thrash and whip of the huge lizard as it surged through the undergrowth, closing fast.

Then Sinn tore herself free.

His heels skidded on wet clay. Spinning round, he caught an instant's glimpse of Sinn—her back to him—facing a lizard big as a Quon galley, its elongated jaws bristling with dagger-sized fangs. Opening wide and wider still.

Fire erupted. A conflagration that blinded Grub, made him reel away as a solid wall of heat struck him. He stumbled to his knees. It was raining—no, that was hail—no, *bits of flesh, hide and bone.* Blinking, gasping, he slowly lifted his head.

A crater gaped before Sinn, steaming.

He climbed to his feet and walked unevenly to her side. The pit was twenty or more paces across, deep as a man was tall. Murky water gurgled, filling the basin. In that basin, a piece of the lizard's tail thrashed and twitched. Mouth dry, Grub asked, 'Did you enjoy that, Sinn?'

'None of it's real, Grub.'

'Looked real enough to me!'

She snorted. 'Just a memory.'

'Whose?'

'Maybe mine.' Sinn shrugged. 'Maybe yours. Something buried so deep inside us, we would never have ever known about it, if we weren't here.'

'That makes no sense.'

Sinn held up her hands. The one that had been streaming blood looked scorched. 'My blood,' she whispered, 'is on *fire.*'

They skirted the swamp, watched by a herd of scaly, long-necked beasts with flattened snouts. Bigger than any bhederin, but with the same dull, bovine eyes. Tiny winged lizards patrolled their ridged backs, picking at ticks and lice.

Beyond the swamp the land sloped upward, festooned with snake-leafed trees with pebbled boles and feathery crowns. There was no obvious way around the strange forest, so they entered it. In the humid shade beneath the canopy, iridescent-winged moths fluttered about like bats, and the soft, damp ground was crawling with toads that could swallow a man's fist and seemed disinclined to move aside, forcing Grub to step carefully and Sinn to lash out with her bare feet, laughing with every meaty impact.

The slope levelled out and the trees grew denser, gloom closing in like a shroud. 'This was a mistake,' muttered Grub.

'What was?'

'All of it. The Azath House, the portal—Keneb must be worried sick. It wasn't fair, us just leaving like that, telling no one. If I'd known it was going to take this long to find whatever it was you think we need to find, I'd probably have said "no" to the whole idea.' He eyed the girl beside him. 'You knew from the very start, didn't you?'

'We're on the trail—we can't leave it now. Besides, I need an ally. I need someone who can guard my back.'

'With what, this stupid eat-knife in my belt?'

She made a face. 'Tell me the truth. Where did you come from?'

'I was a foundling in the Chain of Dogs. The Imperial Historian Duiker saved me. He picked me up outside Aren's gate and put me into Keneb's arms.'

'Do you actually remember all of that?'

'Of course.'

Her eyes had sharpened their study. 'You remember walking in the Chain of Dogs?'

He nodded. 'Walking, running. Being scared, hungry, thirsty. Seeing so many people die. I even remember seeing Coltaine once, although the only thing I can see in my head now, when I think of him, is crow-feathers. At least,' he added, 'I didn't see him die.'

'What city did you come from?'

'That I can't remember.' He shrugged. 'Anything before the Chain . . . is gone, like it never existed.'

'It didn't.'

'What?'

'The Chain of Dogs made you, Grub. It built you up out of dirt and sticks and rocks, and then it filled you with everything that happened. The heroes who fought and then died, the people who loved, then lost. The ones that starved and died of thirst. The ones whose hearts burst with terror. The ones that drowned, the ones that swallowed an arrow or a sword. The ones who rode spears. It took all of that and that became your soul.'

'That's ridiculous. There were lots of orphans. Some of us made it, some of us didn't. That's all.'

'You were what, three years old? Four? Nobody remembers much from when they were that young. A handful of scenes, maybe. That's it. But you remember the Chain of Dogs, Grub, because you're its get.'

'I had parents. A real father, a real mother!'

'But you can't remember them.'

'Because they died before the Chain even started!'

'How do you know?'

'Because what you're saying makes no sense!'

'Grub, I know because you're just like me.'

'What? You got a real family—you even got a brother!'

'Who looks at me and doesn't know who or what he's looking at. I'll tell you who made me. An assassin named Kalam. He found me hiding with a bunch of bandits who were pretending to be rebels. He carved things on to my soul, and then he left. And then I was made a second time—I was added on to. At Y'Ghatan, where I found the fire that I took inside me, that now burns on and on like my very own sun. And after, there was Captain Faradan Sort, because she knew that I knew they were still alive—and I knew because the fire never went out—it was under the city, burning and burning. I knew—I could feel it.' She stopped then, panting to catch her breath, her eyes wild as a wasp-stung cat's.

Grub stared at her, not knowing whether he wanted to hug her or hit her. 'You were born to a mother, just like I was.'

'*Then why are we so different?*'

Moths fled at her shout, and sounds fell away on all sides.

'I don't know,' he replied in a soft voice. 'Maybe . . . maybe you did find something in Y'Ghatan. But nothing like that ever happened to me—'

'Malaz City. You jumped ship. You went to find the Nachts. Why?'

'I don't know!'

She leapt away from him, rushed off into the wood. In moments he had lost sight of her. 'Sinn? What are you doing? Where are you going?'

The gloom vanished. Fifty paces away a seething sphere of flames blossomed. Trees exploded in its path as it rolled straight towards Grub.

He opened his mouth to scream, but no sound emerged.

The blistering ball of fire heaved closer, huge, bristling—

Grub gestured. The ground lifted suddenly into the fire's path, in a mass of roots, humus and mud, surging upward, toppling trees to the sides. A thousand twisted brown arms snaked out from the churning earth. The writhing wall engulfed the rolling sphere of fire, slapped it down as would a booted heel crush the life from a wayward ember. Thunder shook. The earth subsided, the arms vanishing, leaving nothing more than a slowly settling, chewed-up mound. Clouds of steam billowed and then drifted, thinning as the darkness returned once more.

He saw her walking calmly towards him, stepping over shattered trunks, brushing dirt from her plain tunic.

Sinn halted directly before him. 'It doesn't matter, Grub,' she said. 'You and me—*we're different.*'

She set off, and after a moment he stumbled after her.

Never argue with a girl.

It was a day for strangers. One was beyond his reach, the other he knew well. Taxilian and Rautos had prised loose a panel to reveal a confused mass of metal coils, tubes and wire-wrapped cables. Muttering about finding the necessary hinge spells needed to unleash sorcerous power, thus awakening the city's brain, Taxilian began poking and prodding the workings. Crowding behind him, sweat beading his brow, Rautos ran through a litany of cautions, none of which Taxilian heeded.

Last had devised a trap for the lizard-rats—the orthen—and had headed off to check it, Asane accompanying him.

At the top of a ramp and in a long but shallow antechamber, Nappet and Sheb had found a sealed door and were pounding at it with iron-headed sledges, each blow ringing like a tortured bell. Most of the damage they likely inflicted was to their ears, but since neither had anything to say to the other, they'd yet to discover it.

Breath was exploring the Nest itself, the now empty, abandoned abode of the Matron, finding nothing of interest, although unbeknownst to her residual flavours flowed in through her lungs and formed glistening minute droplets on her exposed skin. Vague dreams of producing children dogged her, successive scenes of labour and birth, tumbling one upon the next like a runaway nightmare. What had begun as a diffuse irritation was quickly building to an indefinable rage.

Breath had been living inside the Tiles since creating them, but even she could not find the meaning she sought in them. And now the outside world was seeping into her. Confusion swarmed.

And then there was the K'Chain Che'Malle drone. Climbing, drawing ever closer to this hapless collection of humans.

The ghost drifted amongst his family, haunted by a growing trepidation. His people were failing. In some ineffable, fundamental way, they were pulling apart. Even as he had wondered at their purpose, now each one—barring perhaps Taxilian—was doing the same. A crisis was upon them, and he could feel the growing turbulence. They would not be ready for Sulkit. They might even kill the drone. And then all would be lost.

He recalled—once, a thousand times?—standing on the deck of a ship, witness to the sea's surface spreading out smooth as vitreous glass on all sides, a strange quality suffusing the still air, the light becoming uncanny, febrile. And around him faceless sailors scrambling, pale as motes—bloody propitiations to the Elder God, the bawling bleat of goats brought up from the hold, the flash of sea-dipped blades and twisted blankets of blood floating on the seas—all around him, such rising fear. And in answer to all of this, he heard his own laughter. Cruel as a demon's, and wide eyes fixed on him, for they had found a monster in their midst. And he was that monster.

I called storms, didn't I? Just to see the violence, to draw it round me like the warmest cloak. And even the cries of drowning mortals could not break my amusement.

Are these memories mine? What manner of beast was I?

The blood tasted . . . good. Propitiation? The fools—they simply fed my power.

I remember a tribe, corpses cooling beneath furs and blankets, and the stains of spite on my hands. I remember the empty hole I found myself in, the pit that was my crime. Too late to howl at its depth, its lifeless air, the deadness inside.

Betrayed by a wife. Everyone laughing behind my back. For that, all would die. So it must be, and so it was. And I fled that place, the home I destroyed in the span of a single night. But some holes cannot be climbed out of. I ran and ran, and each night, lying exhausted, I fell back into that hole, and I looked up at that mouth of light far above, and I watched it ever recede. Until it winked out.

When you see my eyes now, all you see is that deadness. You see the black, smooth walls. And you know that, though I look back at you, I see nothing that makes me feel . . . anything.

I am walking still, alone on the empty plain, and the edifice I approach looms ever bigger, a thing of stone and dried blood, a thing eager to awaken once more.

Come find me.

Asane came staggering back into the chamber where Taxilian and Rautos still crouched at the gutted wall. Gasping, frightened, she struggled to find her breath, as Rautos turned round.

'Asane? What is it? Where is Last?'

'A demon! One lives! It found us!'

They could hear sounds now on the ramp, leather soles and something else—the click of claws, the flicking hiss of a tail brushing stone.

Asane backed to the far wall. Rautos hissed, 'Taxilian! Get Nappet and Sheb! Quickly!'

'What?' the man glanced back over his shoulder. 'What is it?'

Last appeared, looking faintly bewildered, but otherwise unharmed. Two dead orthen hung from a string at his belt. Moments later, the K'Chain Che'Malle loomed into view. Gaunt, but no taller than a man, thin-limbed, a tail that lashed about as if possessing its own will.

The ghost felt the fear, in Asane and Rautos. But in Taxilian, who slowly straightened from the exposed machinery, there was wonder, curiosity. And then . . . excitement. He stepped forward.

The drone was studying the chamber, as if searching for something. At the incessant clanging from above, it cocked its head. A moment later there were shouts of triumph from Nappet and Sheb—the door had opened, but the ghost knew that the surrender of that barrier had not come beneath their sledges. Sulkit had simply unlocked it. A moment later, he wondered how he knew this.

Breath reappeared from a side passage. 'Blueiron,' she whispered, staring at the drone. 'Like a . . . a Fulcrum. Taxilian, go to it—we need it.'

'I know,' he replied, licking dry lips. 'Rautos, go up to Sheb and Nappet—keep them occupied up there. I don't want them charging down here with swords out. Make them understand—'

'Understand what?' Rautos demanded.

'That we've found an ally.'

Rautos's eyes widened. He wiped sweat from his face. A moment later, he backed up, then turned and set off up the ramp.

Taxilian spoke to the drone. 'Can you understand me? Nothing works. We need to fix it. We need your help—no, perhaps it's the other way round. We'd like to help you bring all of this back to life.'

Silence. The K'Chain Che'Malle seemed to be ignoring everyone in the chamber, its tentacled fingers writhing like seagrass at the ends of its arms. The rows of fangs glistened in its broad slash of a mouth. After a moment, the drone blinked. Once, twice, three times, each lid distinct. Then it walked in a hitching gait to where Taxilian had been working. It picked up the panel and deftly replaced it. Straightening, it turned and faced the ghost, eyes fixing on his.

You can see me. The realization stunned him. And all at once he could feel something—*my own body*—and with it jarring pain in his hands, the ache of abuse. He could taste his own sweat, the acrid exhaustion of his muscles. And then it was gone.

He cried out.

Help me!

Sulkit's reptilian eyes blinked again, and then the drone set off, quickly crossing the room and vanishing down the ramp that led to the domed carapace—the chamber that housed this city's mind.

Taxilian barked a laugh. 'Follow it!' He hurried after the K'Chain Che'Malle. Breath fell in behind him.

Once the three were gone, Asane ran to Last and he took her in his arms.

Rautos, Sheb and Nappet arrived. 'We got the door open,' said Sheb, his voice overloud. 'It just slid to one side. It leads outside, to a balcony—gods, we're high up!'

'Never mind that,' growled Nappet. 'We saw someone, way out on the plain. Walking. Seems we've found another wanderer.'

'Maybe,' said Rautos, 'maybe he'll know.'

'Know what?' snapped Sheb, baring his teeth.

Rautos gestured helplessly.

Nappet was glaring round, hefting the sledge in his hands. 'So where's the fucking demon?'

'It means no harm,' said Last.

'Too bad for it.'

'Don't hurt it, Nappet.'

Nappet advanced on Last. 'Look at the stupid farmer—found an animal to pet, did you? She's not much—Breath looks a damned sight better.'

'The demon isn't even armed,' said Last.

'Then it's stupid. Because if I was it, I'd be swinging the biggest damned axe I could find. I'd start by killing you and that hag you're holding. Then fat, useless Rautos there, with the stupid questions.'

'The first one it'd kill would be you, Nappet,' laughed Sheb.

'Because I'm the most dangerous one here, aye, it'd try. But I'd smash its skull in.'

'Not the most dangerous,' corrected Sheb, 'just the stupidest. It'd kill you out of pity.'

'Let's go and prepare the meal,' Last said to Asane, still guarding her with one thick, muscled arm. 'Sorry, Nappet, there's not enough for you.'

The man stepped closer. 'Try and stop me—'

Last spun. His fist hammered into Nappet's face, shattering the man's nose. In a welter of blood he reeled back. Teeth bounced on the floor. The sledge fell from his hands. After a moment he fell down, and then curled up, covering his broken face.

The others stared at Last.

Then Sheb laughed, but it was a weak laugh.

'Come on,' said Last to Asane.

They left the chamber.

After a moment, Sheb said, 'I'm heading back up to the balcony.'

Rautos went to his pack and rummaged within it until he found some rags and a flask. He then went over to crouch, grunting, beside Nappet. 'Let's see what we can do here, Nappet.'

Betrayal could lie dead, a cold heap of ashes, only to blaze alight in an instant. What drove me to such slaughter? They were kin. Companions. Loved ones. How could I have done that to them? My wife, she wanted to hurt me—why? What had I done? Gorim's sister? That was nothing. Meaningless. Not worth all the screaming, she had to have seen that.

Hurting me like she did, but I won't ever forget the look in her eyes—her face—when I took her life. And I'll never understand why she looked like the one betrayed. Not me. Gorim's sister, that wasn't anything to do with her. I wasn't out to hurt her. It just happened. But what she did, that was like a knife stabbed into my heart.

She had to know I wasn't the kind of man to let that pass. I got my pride. And that's why they all had to die, all of them who knew and laughed behind my back. I needed to deliver a lesson, but then, after it was all done, why, there was no one left to heed it. Just me, which didn't work, because it made it into a different lesson. Didn't it?

The dragon waits on the plain. It doesn't even blink. It did, once, and everything disappeared. Everything and everyone. It won't ever do that again.

You blink, you lose that time for ever. You can't even be sure how long that blink lasted. A moment, a thousand years. You can't even know for sure that what you see now is the same as what you saw before. You can't. You think it is. You tell yourself that, convince yourself of that. Just a continuation of everything you knew before. What you see is still there. That's what you tell yourself. That's the game of reassurance your mind plays. To keep things sane.

But think on that one blink—you've all known it—when all that you thought was real suddenly changes. From one side of the blink to the other side. It comes with bad news. It comes with soul-plummeting horror and grief. How long was that blink?

Gods below, it was fucking eternity.

Chapter Fourteen

Turn this dark maddening charge
All you I once knew snagged like moths
In the still web of younger days
Rise up from the fresh white foam
In the face of my seaward plunge
Howl against my wild run and these wild
Blazing eyes—but I hear the call
Of how life once had been and such heat
In the crushed chirr of locusts rubbing
The high grasses of a child's road
And the summer was unending
The days refused to close and I played
Savage and warrior, the heroic nail
Upon which worlds pitched and wobbled
Blue as newborn iron and these salt-winds
Were yet to blow and sink corrosive teeth
Into my stolid spine and my stiffened ribs
That could take the golden weight
Of a thousand destinies
Where are you now, my unlined faces
On those rich sighing summers
When we gods ruled feral the wilding
World? Hollow husks turning on
Threads of tired silk so lost in my wake,
And you that run with me in the blind
Stampede—this charge we cannot turn
And the sea awaiting us waits with its
Promise of dissolution, the fraying of
Youthful days, the broken nails, the sagging
Ribs—the summers drifting away and away
And forever away.

Broken Nail's Lament
Fisher

Someone was screaming in agony, but that was a sound warleader Gall had grown used to. Eyes stinging in the drifting smoke, he swung his horse round on the dirt track and unleashed a stream of curses. At least three raids were swarming out from the village in the valley, lances held high, grisly trophies bobbing and weaving. 'Coltaine take those fools and crush them under his heel! Jarabb—ride down to that commander. He's to form up his troop and resume scouting to the south—no more attacks—tell the fool, I'll have his loot, his wives and his daughters, all of it, if he disobeys me again.'

Jarabb was squinting. 'That is Shelemasa, Warleader.'

'Fine. Her husband and her sons—I'll take them as slaves and then sell them to a D'ras. Bult's broken nose, she needs better control of her warriors!'

'They're just following her lead,' Jarabb said. 'She's worse than a rabid she-wolf.'

'Stop chewing my ear,' Gall said, wanting to pull a foot out of the stirrup and drive it into the man's chest—too familiar of late, too smug, too many Hood-damned words and too many knowing looks. After Shelemasa was dealt with, he'd send the pup yelping and turn a blind eye to all the wounded looks sure to follow.

Jarabb tried a smile which faltered as Gall's scowl deepened. A moment later the young Tear Runner kicked his horse into motion and rode hard for the shouting, yipping raids.

Above the sickly smears of smoke the sky was cloudless, a canopy of saturated blue and a baleful sun that seemed to boil in the sky. Flocks of long-tailed birds swooped and cut in erratic patterns, too terrified to land as Khundryl warriors swarmed the ground in all directions. Fat, finger-long locusts crawled through the ruined fields.

The advance scout troop was returning from up the road, and Gall was pleased to see their disciplined, collected canter, lances shod and upright. Which officer was that one? Making out the leather-wound hoop dangling from the man's weapon, he knew who it was. Vedith, who had crushed a town garrison early on in the campaign. Heavy losses to his raid, but then, hardly surprising. Young, in that stupid, foolhardy way, but worth taking note of—since he clearly had firm command of his warriors.

A gesture while they were still some distance away halted all the riders behind Vedith, who then rode up to Gall and reined in. 'Warleader. A Bolkando army awaits us, two leagues distant. Ten thousand, two full legions, with a supply camp crawling with three times that number. Every stand of trees within a league of them has been cut down. I'd wager they've been in place for three or four days.'

'Stupid Bolkando. What value fielding an army that crawls like a bhederin with its legs cut off? We could dance round it and strike straight for the capital. I could drag that King off his throne and plant myself in it sloppy as a drunk, and that would be that.' He snorted. 'Generals and commanders understand nothing. They think a battle answers everything, like fists in an alley. Coltaine knew better—war is the means, not the end—the goal is not to wage slaughter—it is to achieve domination in the bargaining that follows.'

Another scout was riding down from the north, her horse's hoofs kicking up clods of dirt from the trampled plough-furrows. Hares scattered from her path as she cut through the trampled crops. Gall squinted at her for a moment, and then shifted round in his saddle to glare southward. Yes, there, another rider, in foaming gallop, shouting as he wove through Shelemasa's whooping mob. The Warleader grunted.

Vedith had taken note of both riders. 'We are flanked,' he said.

'What of it?' Gall asked, eyes narrowing once more on this young, clever warrior.

The man shrugged. 'Even should a fourth element march up our backsides, Warleader, we can slip through the gaps—they're all on foot, after all.'

'Like a slink between the claws of a hawk. But nothing here can even hope to pluck our tail. Vedith, I give you command of a thousand—yes, fifty raids. Take the north army—they'll be on the march, dog-tired and choking on dust, likely in column. Give them no time. Sweep and cut, leave them in disarray, and then ride on to their baggage train. Take everything you can carry and burn the rest. Do not lose control of your warriors. Just cut off the enemy's toes and leave them there, am I understood?'

Grinning, Vedith nodded. 'I would hear from that scout,' he said after a moment.

'Of course you would.'

Gall saw that Jarabb had caught Shelemasa and both were now riding in the wake of the south scout. He spat to get the taste of the smoke out of his mouth. 'Duiker's eyes, what a sorry mess. No one ever learns, do they?'

'Warleader?'

'Would the Bolkando have been content if we had treated them as badly as they treated us? No. Of course not. So, how in their minds did they justify such abuse?'

'They thought they could get away with it.'

Gall nodded. 'Do you see the flaw in that thinking, warrior?'

'It's not hard, Warleader.'

'Have you noticed that it's the ones who think themselves so very clever that are the stupidest of the lot?' He tilted in his saddle and loosed a loud, gassy fart. 'Gods below, the spices they use round here have raised a typhoon in my bowels.'

The scout from the north arrived, the sweat on her face and forearms coated in dust. 'Warleader!'

Gall unslung his own waterskin and tossed it to her. 'How many and how far away?'

She paused to drink down a few mouthfuls, and then said above the heavy blows of her horse's breath, 'Perhaps two thousand, half of them levies, lightly armoured and ill-equipped. Two leagues away, in column on a too-narrow road.'

'Baggage train?'

She smiled through all the grit. 'Not in the middle and not flanked, Warleader. The rearguard's about three hundred, mixed infantry—looks like the ones with the worst blisters on their feet.'

'And they saw you?'

'No, Warleader, I don't think so. Their mounted scouts clung close, on the flat farmland to either side of the track. They know there's raids out in the countryside and don't want to get stung.'

'Very good. Change mounts and get yourself ready to lead Vedith and his wing to them.'

Her dark eyes flicked to Vedith in open appraisal.

'Something wrong?' Gall asked.

'No, Warleader.'

'But he's young, isn't he?'

She shrugged.

'Dismissed,' Gall said.

The scout tossed the waterskin back and then rode off.

Gall and Vedith now awaited the riders from the south.

Vedith twisted to ease his back, and then said, 'Warleader, who will lead the force against the southern jaw of this trap?'

'Shelemasa.'

Seeing the young warrior's brows lift, Gall said, 'She needs her chance to mend her reputation—or do you question my generosity?'

'I would not think to do that—'

'You should, Vedith. That's what the Malazans have taught us, if they've taught us anything. A smith's hammer in the hand, or a sword—it's all business, and each and every one of us is in it. The side with the most people using their brains is the side that wins.'

'Unless they are betrayed.'

Gall grimaced. 'Even then, Vedith, the crows—'

'—give answer,' Vedith finished. And both men made the gesture of the black wing, silently honouring Coltaine's name, his deeds and his resolute stand against the worst that humans could do.

A moment later, Gall swung his horse round to face the scout riding in from the south, and the two warriors pelting to catch up behind him. 'Shit of the Foolish Dog, look at those two.'

'Are you done with me, Warleader?'

'Yes. Go collect your raids.' And he leaned out one more time to make wind. 'Gods below.'

Still stinging from the Warleader's tirade, Shelemasa rode hard at the head of her wing. Shouts from behind her measured out the raid sergeants struggling to collect their warriors as the ground grew ever more uneven. Deep furrows scarred the stony hills, and many of those hills had been gouged out—the Bolkando had been mining here, for what Shelemasa had no idea. They skirted steep-sided pits half-filled with tepid water mottled with algae blooms, narrow edges thick with reeds and rushes. Bucket winches slumped above overgrown trenches, their wooden frames grey and bowing and strangled in vines. Hummingbirds darted above the lush crimson flowers dangling from those vines, and everywhere iridescent six-winged insects spun and whirled.

She hated this place. The cruel colours made her think of poisons—after all, on the Khundryl Odhan it was the brightest snakes and lizards that were the deadliest. She had seen a jet-black, purple-eyed spider as big as her damned foot only the day before. It had been eating a hare. Nekeh had woken to find the skin of one leg, hip to ankle, completely peeled away by huge amber ants—she hadn't felt a thing, and now she was raving with fever in the loot train. She'd heard that someone had smelled a flower only to have his nose rot off. No, they needed to be done with this, all of it. Marching with the Bonehunters was all very well, but the Adjunct wasn't Coltaine, was she? She wasn't Bult either, not even Duiker.

Shelemasa had heard about the goring the marines had suffered during the invasion. Like a desert cat thrown into a pit of starving wolves, if the tales were accurate. It was no wonder they'd been squatting in the capital for so long. The Adjunct had Mincer's luck, that she did, and Shelemasa wanted no part of it.

They were coming up out of the mining works, and to the south the land levelled out in a floodplain, broken up by blockish stands of bamboo bordered by water-filled ditches and raised tracks. Beyond this ran another row of serried hills, these ones flat-topped and fortified by stone-walled redoubts. Between the fortifications a Bolkando army was forming up, but in obvious disorganization. They'd expected to be one of the trap's jaws, arriving upon a battle already engaged, the Khundryl muzzle to muzzle with the main force. They'd been planning on driving into an exposed flank.

For all that, she could see they'd be hard to dislodge from those hills, especially with the enfilading forts. Even worse, she was outnumbered by at least two to one.

Shelemasa slowed her horse, and then reined in on the edge of the bamboo plantation. She waited for her officers to close on her.

Jarabb—who had been verbally flayed almost as fiercely as Shelemasa—was the first to arrive. 'Commander, we won't knock them off that, will we?'

Damned puffed-up messenger-boy. 'When did you last ride to battle?'

She saw him flinch.

'If you were my son,' she said, 'I would've dragged you out of the women's huts long ago. I've got no problem with you wearing whatever it is you wear under that armour, it's the fact that Gall cast a soft eye on you, Jarabb, and that's not served you well. We are at war, you simpering coodle-ape.' She turned as her six sub-wing captains rode up. 'Hanab,' she called to one, a veteran warrior whose bronze helm was a stylized crow's head, 'tell me what you see?'

'An old border is what I see,' the man said. 'But the forts got dismantled everywhere but on those tels there. So long as the army stays where they are, they're stuck like a knuckle under a rug. All we need to do is keep them put.'

Shelemasa looked to another captain, a tall, hunch-shouldered man with a vulpine face. 'And how, Kastra, do we do that?'

The man slowly blinked. 'We scare them so badly the hills they're on start running brown.'

'Draw up the horse-archers,' Shelemasa ordered. 'On to the slopes. Start bristling the fools. We'll spend the day harrying them and piling up wounded—until those forts are nothing more than hospitals. Come the night, we send raids into their baggage camps, and maybe a few to fire the forts since those roofs I see inside are thatched.' She scanned her officers. 'Is anyone here satisfied with just pinning the idiots in place?'

Jarabb cleared his throat. 'The Warleader wants the threat delayed long enough to stop being a threat, Commander.'

'Half the army up there are levies,' said Hanab. 'Skirmishers. Deploying them against light cavalry would be suicide. Yet,' he added with a sneer, 'look at how they're arrayed—five deep in front of the precious heavy infantry.'

'To absorb our arrows, yes,' Shelemasa said.

Kastra snorted. 'The heavies don't want to dirty their pretty armour.'

'Bloody those skirmishers enough and they'll break,' Hanab predicted. 'Then we can chew and nip the heavies for as long as we like.'

Shelemasa turned to regard Jarabb. 'You stay at my side. When we return to the Warleader, you will be carrying the Bolkando commander's head on your spear.'

Jarabb managed a sickly smile.

'Look down there,' Hanab pointed.

Sliming up from the ditch and on to the raised track was a yellow and black banded centipede, wide as a hand and as long as a sword. They watched it snake to the other side of the track and then vanish into the stand of bamboo.

Shelemasa spat and then said, 'Hood take this hole and shit in it.' After a moment she added, 'But only after we leave.'

A thousand warriors at his back, and Vedith did not want to lose a single one of them. Memories of the garrison attack still dogged him. A triumphant victory, yes, but now he had but a handful of companions left with whom he'd shared it, every blistering moment—and even now, should he meet the eyes of one of those warriors, he would see in them the perfect reflection of his own faint disbelief, his own sense of guilt.

The crows alone chose who lived and who fell. Prayers meant nothing, deeds and vows, honour and dignity, not one weighed more than a mote of dust on fate's scales. He even had his doubts about courage. Friends had fallen, one moment in his life and the next out of it, reduced to what memories he could conjure, all the incidental moments that had held little meaning until now.

Vedith didn't know what to make of it. But he now knew one thing. The warrior's life was in its essence a lonely one, and the loneliness only got worse, as one came to realize that it was best to hold back, to never draw too close to a companion. Yes, he would still give his life to save any one of them, whether he knew that warrior's face or not, but he would also simply walk away should one fall. He would move on, and in his eyes the barest hint of lost worlds.

A thousand warriors behind him. He would send them into battle, and some would die, and he hated that knowledge, he railed against it, but for all that he knew he would not hesitate. Among all warriors, the commander was the loneli-est by far, and he could feel that isolation thickening around him, hard as ar-mour, cold as iron.

Gall. Adjunct Tavore. Coltaine of the Crow Clan. Even that Bolkando fool lead-ing his or her unsuspecting column towards an afternoon of nightmarish horror. *This is what we share. And it tastes bitter as blood on the tongue.*

He wondered if the Bolkando King now regretted inviting this war. He won-dered if the bastard even cared that his subjects were dying. Or was it just the wound of lost revenues from wasted farms, devoured livestock and the stolen hoards of wealth that stung him now? And the next strangers to camp on his bor-ders? Would he treat them any differently? Would his successor heed the lessons carved out here in bone and flesh?

The Chain of Dogs had fallen at the foot of Aren. Pormqual's ten thousand danced on trees. Leoman's rebel army was destroyed at Y'Ghatan. It was clear—it could not be clearer—that for all there was to learn, no one ever bothered. Each new fool and tyrant to rise up from the mob simply set about repeating the whole fiasco, convinced that they were different, better, smarter. *Until the earth drinks deep again.*

He could see the scout riding back towards him.

It was about to begin. And, suddenly, each breath filling his lungs tasted sweeter than the last, and all that his eyes fixed upon seemed to throb with life. He looked upon things and thought that he had never before seen such colours, such textures—the world was made anew on all sides, but had he come too late to it? Only mo-ments left to savour this gift of glory?

The day's end would answer that question.

Vedith prepared to lead his first army into battle, and in that moment he hated Warleader Gall, who had forced this upon him. He did not want to command a thousand warriors. He did not want the weight of their gazes, the crushing aware-ness of their faith in him.

He wished he had the courage to flee.

But he did not.

For Gall had chosen well.

Parasols in their thousands, fan-wielding slaves in their tens of thousands, none of this could keep the sweat from the face of Chancellor Rava. He felt as if he was melting in the cauldron of history, one of his own making, alas, a realization that came to him again and again like a fresh heap of coals. He huddled shivering be-neath sodden silks as the palanquin he was in tipped precipitously, the bearers struggling to descend this confounded goat track.

Dust had seeped in to coat every surface, dulling all the ornate gilt edging and deadening the vibrant colours of the plush padding. Dust mingled with the taste of his own sweat in his mouth. He even pissed grit, and worse. 'Not there, you stupid woman,' he snapped.

The D'rhasilhani slave flinched back, ducking her head.

There would be no stirring awake down below, not today. He understood her desperation to please, and this knowledge made things all the more irritating. Whatever happened to proper, old-fashioned affection? But no, he'd done away with that long ago, as soon as he realized that, as much as he wanted it, he wasn't prepared to repay it with all that was expected in such an arrangement. Things such as loyalty, consideration, generosity. Those vile details that comprised the pathetic stupidity called reciprocity. He so disliked the notion of expectations—not the ones he held of others doing as they were supposed to do, but the expectations those others shackled upon Rava. Appalling, the nerve of some people.

The greatest skill one could achieve lay in evading such traps. He was Chancellor to the Realm, ostensibly in service to the King and (heavens forbid!) the Queen; but overriding even this, he stood to serve the kingdom itself, its myriad sources of wealth, prosperity and so on, not to mention its smelly, crab-faced masses of ignorant humanity. Of course, he knew that in truth such notions held all the gravity and import of a toddler's birthday celebration, when all the effort going into it wouldn't even be remembered by the child so indulged, and what of the mess afterward?

Never mind that Felash had made all the slaves drunk on suspiciously spiked punch, and that the chamber door's lock was jammed, and he—Chancellor of Bolkando!—found himself trapped inside with no choice but to clear up the mess— if only to find somewhere to stand. And never mind that—

Rava scowled. What had he been thinking about? Ah, yes, the paucity of sincerity that was, ultimately, at the very heart of political triumph. He had long ago discovered that brazen lies could be uttered with impunity, because nothing would come of exposure—should that unlikely consequence ever occur—for even when such lies were indeed exposed, why, in a month or two the finger-pointers would wander off, distracted by something or someone else worthy of their facile outrage. A mien of proper belligerence could weather virtually anything his accusers might throw at him. As with so many battles on a multitude of fields, it was all a matter of nerve.

And, dammit, here and now—against this monstrous woman Krughava—it was Rava's nerve that was failing, not hers.

Bested by a knuckle-browed barbarian! Outrageous!

But what had he been thinking about? His gaze fell on the slave woman who still crouched at his feet, wiping her chin, eyes downcast. Yes, love. And that obnoxious creature, Felash, to have so contemptuously spurned his advances, well now, she would pay for that. For the rest of her life, if Rava had his way—and, ultimately, he always did. Yes, he'd have her kneeling just the way this slave did, but the difference between the two would be the most delicious reward. Felash would not wear any visible shackles, after all. She would have enslaved herself. To him, to Rava, and she would find her only pleasure in servicing him, all his needs, every one of his desires. Now that was love.

Groans of relief from outside, and the palanquin levelled out. Rava drew a handkerchief and mopped at his face, and then tugged on the bell cord. The contrivance lurched to a merciful halt. 'Open the damned door! Be quick!' He tugged up his pantaloons and knotted the ties, and then half-rose, pushing the D'ras slave away.

Outside, he saw pretty much what he had expected to see. They were down from the pass. Before them spread somewhat more level land, strips and stands of deciduous forest broken up by meadows used for pasture by the local savages. This region had served as a buffer between the miserable hill tribes and Bolkando's civilized population, but the buffer was shrinking, as the locals drifted away in both directions, into the cities or taking up banditry among the rock-dwellers. There would come a time, Rava knew, when his kingdom would simply engulf the region, which meant establishing forts and border posts and maintaining garrisons and patrols to hold back the blue-skinned savages, all of which would devour yet more of the treasury. Well, Rava considered, there'd be income from cutting down all the trees, at least to begin with, and thereafter from whatever crops the soil could yield.

Such thoughts comforted him, righted the world beneath his pinched feet. Wiping sweat from his face again, he cast about for signs of Conquestor Avalt and his entourage of messengers, lackeys, and so-called advisors. The military was a miserable necessity, despite all its inherent pitfalls. Put a sword in a person's hands—and a few thousand others at their backs—and sooner or later the tip of that sword was going to lift to prick the necks of people like Rava. The Chancellor scowled, reminding himself to keep Avalt tightly bound to his belt, by way of that tangled skein of mutually rewarding interests he worked so hard to maintain.

Surrounding him, the column of the Bolkando Guard was spilling out, shaking loose over the swards to either side of the track. Oxen lowed, straining to reach the lush grasses, and from somewhere in the seething mob pigs were squealing. The air stank of human sweat and beastly dung and piss. This was worse than a D'ras trader camp.

After a moment Rava succeeded in picking out Avalt's pennon, two hundred or so paces down the trail. He beckoned to one of his servants, pointing to the wavering standard. 'I wish to speak with the Conquestor. Bring him to me.'

The old man plunged into the crowd.

This army was exhausted, desperate to camp right here though the day was barely two-thirds done. And as far as the Chancellor could tell, Avalt had halted the entire column. Rava craned but he could not even see the Perish legions— somewhere far ahead, marching brainless as millstones—they should have ambushed these fools after all—what army could fight after such a pace? In full armour barring shields, too, if that report held any truth. Ridiculous.

It was some time before he saw commotion in the crowd on the track, figures hastily shifting to either side; moments later Conquestor Avalt appeared, his face set in an uncharacteristic scowl. The gaze he fixed upon Rava as he drew nearer was something of a shock.

Even as the Chancellor opened his mouth to speak, Avalt stepped close and rasped, 'Do you think I exist only to scuttle at your beck and call, Chancellor? If you haven't noticed, my whole damned army here has fallen apart. I've had *officers* deserting, by the twenty pricks of Bellat. And now you want what? Another smug exchange of platitudes and reassurances?'

Rava's eyes narrowed. 'Careful, Conquestor. Be assured, when I summon you it is with good reason. I require an update, for as you can see my bearers were unable to maintain your vanguard's pace. And now you have halted the entire army, and I want to know why.'

Avalt blinked, as if disbelieving. 'Didn't you just hear me, Rava? Half my legions can barely walk—their boots fell apart under them. The under-rigging for their breastplates has sawn into their shoulders—the manufacturers didn't bother softening the leather. Bedrolls rot as soon as they get damp. Half the staples have gone foul and we're out of salt. And if all of that is not enough, then I should add this: we are at least five leagues behind the Perish, and as for the army we'd left here to greet them, one messenger remained—to inform me that the Khundryl Burned Tears are, as of three days ago, within seven leagues of the capital. Now,' he added in a snarl, 'how many other blithe assumptions we made weeks back are about to turn out fatally askew?' He pointed a gauntleted finger at the palanquin. 'Climb back inside, Chancellor, and leave me to my business—'

'A business you appear to be failing at, Conquestor,' snapped Rava.

'You want my resignation? You have it. Take over by all means, Chancellor. I'll ride back up into the mountains and toss in with the hill bandits—at least *they* don't pretend the world is just how they want it to be.'

'Calm down, Conquestor—you are understandably overwrought. I have no wish to assume the burden of your responsibility. I am not a military man, after all. Thus, I do not accept your resignation. Repair this army, Avalt, and take as long doing so as is needed. If the army we left here has departed, clearly it is to meet the threat of the Khundryl. Presumably the threat has by now been taken care of, and either way, we here are in no position to affect the outcome, are we?'

'I would imagine we've had enough of our *affecting* matters, don't you think, Chancellor?'

'Return to your command, Conquestor. We can speak again once safely ensconced in the palace.' *Where I can correct your misapprehensions about who serves whom.*

Avalt stared at him long enough to make plain his disrespect, and then turned to retrace his route.

Rava watched him march back into the crowd, and then gestured for his servant—who had unwisely stood less than half a dozen paces away during the course of the Chancellor's conversation with Avalt. 'Find us a place to camp. Raise the tent—the smaller one—tonight I will maintain the minimum number of providers, no more than twenty. And find me some new women from the train—and no D'ras, I am done with their haphazard attentions. Go, quickly—and get me some wine!'

Head bobbing, the servant scurried off. Rava looked round until he found one of his assassins. The man was staring directly at him. The Chancellor flicked his eyes in the direction of the servant. The assassin nodded.

See what you have done, Conquestor? You have killed the poor old man. And I shall send you his salted head, so that we clearly understand one another.

Shield Anvil Tanakalian stepped into the tent and drew off his gloves. 'I just took a look for myself, Mortal Sword. They are indeed done. I doubt they will even manage a march tomorrow, much less a fight any time in the next week or two.'

Krughava was intent on oiling her sword and did not look up from where she sat on the camp cot. 'That was easier than expected. There is water atop the chest—help yourself.'

Tanakalian stepped over to the salt-stained trunk. 'I have more news. We captured a Bolkando scout riding back through the dregs of the army that had been awaiting us. It would appear that Warleader Gall has done precisely what we anticipated, sir. He is probably even now within sight of the kingdom's capital.'

The woman grunted. 'Do we wait for the Chancellor to catch up, then, to inform him of the altered situation, or do we maintain our pace? As much as the Khundryl Warleader might wish to besiege the capital, he has but horse-soldiers at his disposal. One must assume that he will do nothing until we arrive. And that is at least three days from now.'

Tanakalian drank deep from the clay jug, then set it back down on the pitted lid of the chest. 'Do you expect a fight, Mortal Sword?'

She grimaced. 'Regardless of the unlikelihood that matters will deteriorate to that extreme, sir, we must anticipate every possibility. Even so,' and she rose, seeming to fill the confines of the tent, 'we will add a half-night march. There are times when achieving the unexpected well serves. I would rather we intimidate the King into submission. The very notion of losing a single brother or sister to this meaningless conflict with the Bolkando galls me. But we shall present to King Tarkulf a certain measure of short-tempered belligerence, as I am certain the Warleader has already done.'

Tanakalian considered her words, and then said, 'Khundryl warriors have no doubt fallen in this uninvited war, Mortal Sword.'

'Sometimes respect must be earned the hard way, Shield Anvil.'

'I expect the Bolkando have had little choice but to reassess their contempt for the Burned Tears.'

She faced him, teeth bared, 'Shield Anvil, they choke on it still. And we will ensure they continue to do so for a while longer. Tell me, have we availed ourselves of the supplies left behind by the fleeing army?'

'We have, Mortal Sword. Their haste is our gain.'

She sheathed her sword and strapped it on. 'Such are the spoils of war, sir. Now, let us make ourselves available to our sisters and brothers. They have done well and we should remind them of the measure of respect *we* hold for *them*.'

But Tanakalian hesitated. 'Mortal Sword, are you any closer to your selection of a new Destriant?'

Something flickered in her hard eyes before she turned to the tent-flap. 'Such matters will have to wait, Shield Anvil.'

He followed her out into the well-ordered, quiet camp. Cookfires were lit in rows, spaced between companies. Tents covered the clearings in precise, measured-out regularity. The heady scent of brewing tea filled the air.

As Tanakalian walked a step behind and to Krughava's left, he gave thought to the suspicions assembling in his mind. The Mortal Sword was, perhaps, content to stand virtually alone. The triumvirate of the Grey Helms' high command was, structurally, both incomplete and unbalanced. After all, Tanakalian was a very young Shield Anvil, and none would see him as the Mortal Sword's equal. In essence, his responsibility was passive, whilst hers was front and foremost. She was both fist and gauntlet, and he could do naught but trail in her wake—as he was physically doing here, now.

How could this not please her? Let the legends born of this mythic quest find sharpest focus upon Krughava; she could afford to be magnanimous to those she would permit to stand in her shadow. Standing tallest of them all, her face would be first to receive the sun's light, etching every detail of her heroic resolve.

But remember the words of Shield Anvil Exas a century ago. 'Even the fiercest mask can crack in the heat.' So, I will watch you, Mortal Sword Krughava, and yield you sole possession of this lofty dais. History waits for us, and all the creatures of our youth stand in our wake, to witness what their sacrifice has won.

And at that moment, it is the Shield Anvil who must stride to the fore, alone in the harsh glare of the sun, feeling the raw flames and flinching not. I shall be judgement's crucible, and even Krughava must step back and await my pronouncement.

She was generous with her time and attention this evening, addressing every sister and brother as equals, but Tanakalian could see the cold deliberation in all this. He could see her knitting every strand of her own personal epic, could see those threads trailing out in her wake as she moved from one knot of soldiers to the next. It took a thousand eyes to weave a hero, a thousand tongues to fill out the songs of worth. It took, in short, *the calculated gift of witnessing* to work every detail of every scene upon this vast, sprawling tapestry that was the Mortal Sword Krughava of the Perish Grey Helms.

And he walked a step behind her, playing his part.

Because we are all creators of private hangings, depicting our own heroic existences. Alas, only the maddest among us weave in nothing but gold thread—while others among us, unafraid of truth, will work the fullest palette, the darker skeins, the shadows, the places where the bright light can never reach, where grow all the incondite things.

It is tragic, indeed, how few we are, we who are unafraid of truth.

In any crowd, he suspected, no matter how large, how teeming, if he looked hard enough, he would see naught but golden fires on all sides, so bright, so blazing in self-deception and wildest ego, until he alone stood with eyes burned blind, sockets gaping.

But will any of you hear my warning? I am the Shield Anvil. Once, my kind were cursed to embrace all—the lies with the truth—but I shall not be as the ones before me. I will take your pain, yes, each and every one of you, but in so doing, I will drag you into this crucible with me, until the fires scour your souls clean. And consider this one truth . . . of iron, silver, bronze and gold, it is the gold that melts first.

She walked ahead of him, sharing laughter and jests, teasing and teased in the manner of all beloved commanders, and the legend took shape, step by step.

And he walked, silent, smiling, so generous of regard, so seemingly at peace, so content to share the rewards of her indulgence.

Some masks broke in the sun and the heat. But his mask was neither fierce nor hard. It could, in fact, take any shape he pleased, soft as clay, slick and clear as the finest of pressed oils. Some masks, indeed, broke, but his would not, for he understood the real meaning beneath that long-dead Shield Anvil's words.

It is not heat that breaks the mask, it is the face beneath it, when that mask no longer fits.

Remember well this day, Tanakalian. You are witness to the manufacture of delusion, the shaping of a time of heroes. Generations to come will sing of these lies built here, and there will be such fire in their eyes that all doubt is banished. They will hold up the masks of the past with dramatic fervour, and then bewail their present fallen state.

For this is the weapon of history when born of twisted roots. These are the lies that we are living, and they are all we will give to our children, to be passed down the generations, every catching edge of disbelief worn smooth as they move from hand to hand.

In the lie Krughava walks among her brothers and sisters, binding them with love to the fate awaiting them all. In the lie, this moment of history is pure, caged in the language of heroes. There is nothing to doubt here.

We heroes, after all, know when to don our masks. We know when the eyes of the unborn are upon us.

Show them the lies, all of you.

And so Shield Anvil Tanakalian smiled, and all the cynicism behind that smile stayed hidden from his brothers and sisters. It was not yet time for him. Not yet, but soon.

Warleader Gall drew his black feather cloak about his shoulders, and then strapped on his crow-beaked helm. He adjusted his over-weighted tulwar on to the point of his left hip as he strode to his horse. Insects whirred in the crepuscular air like flecks of winged dust. Gall hacked and spat out a lump of phlegm before swinging into the saddle.

'Why does war always bring smoke?'

The two young Tear Runners facing him exchanged looks of incomprehension.

'And not just regular smoke either,' the Warleader continued, kicking his mount forward to ride between the two warriors. 'No, it's the foul kind. Cloth. Hair. Sits like tar on the tongue, eats into the back of your throat. It's a Fall-damned mess, is what it is.'

Flanked now by the Tear Runners, Gall rode up the track. 'Yelk, you say there are Barghast among them?'

The scout on his left nodded. 'Two, maybe three legions, Warleader. They hold the left flank.'

Gall grunted. 'I've never fought Barghast before—there weren't many left in Seven Cities, and those ones were far to the north and east of our homelands, or so I recall. Do they seem formidable?'

'Undisciplined is what they seemed,' said Yelk. 'Squatter than I'd expected, and wearing armour that looks as if it's made of turtle shells. Their hair stands straight up, wedge-shaped, and with all the face paint they look half mad.'

Gall glanced over at the Tear Runner. 'Do you know why you two are accompanying me to this parley, and not any of my officers?'

Yelk nodded. 'We're expendable, Warleader.'

'As am I.'

'There we do not agree with you.'

'Glad to hear it. So, should they shit on the flag of peace, what will you and Ganap here do?'

'We shall offer our bodies between you and their weapons, Warleader, and fight until you can win clear.'

'Failing to save my life, what then?'

'We kill their commander.'

'Arrows?'

'Knives.'

'Good,' said Gall, well pleased. 'The young are fast. And you two are faster than most, which is why you're Tear Runners. Perhaps,' he added, 'they will think you two my children, eh?'

The track lifted and then wound down over the ridge to converge with a broad cobbled road. At the junction three squat, square granaries plumed columns of black smoke. A waste—the locals had lit their own harvest rather than yield it to the Khundryl. Pernicious attitudes annoyed Gall, as if war was an excuse for anything. He recalled a story he'd heard from a Malazan—Fist Keneb, he believed—about a company of royal guard in the city of Bloor on Quon Tali, who, surrounded in a square, had used children as shields against the Emperor's archers. Dassem Ultor's face had darkened with disgust, and he'd had siege weapons brought in to fling nets instead of bolts, and once all the soldiers were tangled and brought down, the First Sword had sent in troops to extricate the children from their clutches. Among all the enemies of the Empire during Dassem Ultor's command, those guards had been the only ones ever impaled and left to die slowly, in terrible agony. Some things were inexcusable. Gall would have skinned the bastards first.

Destroying perfectly good food wasn't quite as atrocious, but the sentiment behind the gesture was little different from that of those Bloorian guards, as far as he was concerned. Without the crimes that had launched this war, the Khundryl would have paid good gold for that grain. This was how things fell apart when stupidity stole the crown. War was the ultimate disintegration of civility, and, for that matter, simple logic.

At the far end of the plain, perhaps a fifth of a league distant, the Bolkando army was arrayed across a rumpled range of low hills. Commanding the centre, straddling the road, was a legion of perhaps three thousand heavy infantry, their armour black but glinting with gold, matching the facing on their rectangular shields. A small forest of standards rose from the centre of this legion.

'Ganap, your eyes are said to be sharpest among all Tear Runners—tell me what you see on those standards.'

The woman took a moment to dislodge the wad of rustleaf bulging one cheek, sent out a stream of brown juice, and then said, 'I see a crown.'

Gall nodded. 'So.'

The Barghast were presented on the left flank, as Yelk had noted. The ranks were uneven, with some of the mercenaries sitting, helms doffed and shields down. The tall standards rising above their companies were all adorned with human skulls and braids of hair.

Right of the centre legion earthworks mottled the crest and slope of the hills, and pikes were visible jutting above the trenches. Probably regulars, Gall surmised. Slippery discipline, ill-trained, but in numbers sufficient to fix any enemy they faced, long enough for the centre and left to wheel round after breaking whatever charge Gall might throw at them.

Behind all three elements and spilling out to the wings were archers and skirmishers.

'Yelk, tell me how you would engage what you see here.'

'I wouldn't, Warleader.'

Gall glanced over, his eyes brightening. 'Go on. Would you flap your tail in flight? Surrender? Cower in bulging breeches and sue for peace? Spill out endless concessions until the shackles close round the ankles of every living Khundryl?'

'I'd present our own wings and face them for most of a day, Warleader.'

'And then?'

'With dusk, we would retire from the field. Wait until the sun was fully down, and then peel out to either side and ride round the enemy army. We'd strike just before dawn, from behind, with flaming arrows and madness. We'd burn their baggage camp, scatter their archers, and then chew up the backsides of the legions. We'd attack in waves, with half a bell between them. By noon we would be gone.'

'Leaving them to crawl bloodied back to their city—'

'We would hit them again and again on that retreat—'

'And use up all your arrows?'

'Yes. As if we had millions of them, Warleader, an unending supply. And once we've chased them through the city gate, they would be ready to beg for peace.'

'The Khundryl are Coltaine's children indeed! Hah! Well done, Yelk! Now, let us meet this Bolkando King, and gauge well the chagrin in his eyes!'

Six slaves brought out the weapons and armour. The gold filigree on the black iron scales of the breastplate gleamed like runnels of sun-fire. The helm's matching bowl displayed writhing serpents with jaws stretched, while the elongated lobster tail was polished bright silver. The hinged cheek-guards, when swung forward, would click and lock against the iron nasal septum. The Bolkando Royal Crest adorned the vambraces, while the greaves were scaled black. The broad, straight-bladed, blunt-tipped sword rested in a lacquered scabbard of exquisite workmanship, belying the plain functionality of the weapon it embraced.

Every item was positioned with care upon a thick magenta carpet rolled out on the road, the slaves kneeling and waiting on three of the four sides.

Queen Abrastal walked up on the fourth side and stared down at the assemblage. After a moment she said, 'This is ridiculous. Give me the helm, sword-belt and those gauntlets—if I have to wear the rest I won't even be able to move, much less fight. Besides,' she added, with a glare to her cadre of pallid advisors, 'it hardly seems likely they're planning betrayal—the presumed warleader and two pups . . . against my bodyguard of ten. They'd have to be suicidal and they've not shown such failings thus far, have they?'

Hethry, her third daughter, stepped forward and said, 'It is your life that matters, Mother—'

'Oh, eat my shit. If you could pull off the perfect disguise of a Khundryl to get a knife in my back, there'd be four of 'em riding up to our parley, not three. Go play with your brother, and tell me nothing about what you get up to with him. I'd like to keep my food down for a change.' She held out her arms and slaves worked the gauntlets on. Another slave cinched the weapon belt round her solid, meaty hips, whilst a fourth one waited cradling the helm in gloved hands.

As Hethry retreated, after a few venomous darts at her mother, the Queen turned to the Gilk Warchief. 'You coming along to see if they make you a better offer, Spax?'

The Barghast grinned, revealed filed teeth. 'The Khundryl probably hold more of your treasury than you do, Firehair. But no, the Gilk are true to their word.'

Abastral grunted. 'I imagine the one you call Tool might piss in laughter at hearing that.'

The Gilk's broad, flat face lost all traces of humour. 'If you were not a queen, woman, I'd have you hobbled for that.'

She stepped up to the warrior and slapped him on one shell-armoured shoulder. 'Let's see those pointies again, Spax, while you walk beside me and tell me all about this hobbling thing. If it's as ugly as I suspect, I might adopt it for some of my daughters. Well, most of them, actually.'

Snagging the helm from the slave, she set out down the road, her bodyguard scrabbling to catch up and then flank her and Spax.

'Your daughters need a whipping,' the Gilk Warchief said. 'Those I have met, anyway.'

'Even Spultatha? You've been dimpling her thighs the last three nights straight—some kind of record for her, by the way. Must be she likes your barbarian ways.'

'Especially her, Firehair. Wilful, demanding—any Barghast but a Gilk would have died of exhaustion by now.' He barked a laugh. 'I like you, and so I would never want to see you hobbled.'

'But the wound that is named Tool is still raw, is it?'

He nodded. 'Disappointment is a cancer, Queen.'

'Tell me about it,' she responded, thinking of her husband, and a few other things besides.

'A woman hobbled has her feet chopped and can refuse no man or woman or, indeed, camp dog.'

'I see. Use that word in the same sentence as my name again, Spax, and I'll chop your cock off and feed it to my favourite corpse-rat.'

He grinned. 'See these teeth?'

'That's better.'

The three Khundryl were waiting on the road, still in their saddles, but as the Bolkando contingent approached, the feather-cloaked warrior in the centre swung down and left his horse behind him as he stepped forward three paces. A moment later his two companions did the same.

'Look at that,' Abrastal observed under her breath. 'Show me a Bolkando horse that just stands there once its reins are dropped.'

'Horse-warriors,' said Spax. 'They are closer to their horses than they are to their wives, husbands and children. They are infuriating to fight against, Queen. Why, I recall the Rhivi—'

'Not now, Spax. And stay back, among my soldiers. Watch. Listen. Say nothing.'

The Gilk shrugged. 'As you like, Firehair.'

Despite herself, Abrastal was forced to admit that her first impression of War-leader Gall of the Burned Tears left her uneasy. He had the sharp, avid eyes of a hunting bird. He was well into his sixth decade, she judged, but he had the physique of a blacksmith. The black tattoos of tears tracked down his gaunt cheeks, vanishing into an iron-shot beard. The vast crow-feather cape was too heavy to ride out behind him as he strode towards her, instead flaring to the sides until it seemed he was perpetually emerging from a cavern mouth. The scales of his black-stained hauberk were tear-shaped across his broad chest, elongating into layered feathers on his shoulders.

His two bodyguards looked barely out of their teens, but they had the same predatory glint in their dark eyes. Abrastal had a sudden vision of taking the young men to her bed, and something delicious squirmed below her rounded belly. The young ones were best, not yet sunk into self-serving habits and what-not, pliable to her domination, her measured techniques of training that some might call corruption. Well, her lovers never complained, did they?

The Queen blinked away the distraction and focused once more upon the War-leader. She had learned something of the cult binding these Khundryl. Struck to awe and then worship upon witnessing an enemy on the field of battle—an extra-ordinary notion, she had trouble believing it. So . . . foreign. In any case, whoever that commander was—who, in death, had found worshippers among his ene-mies—he must have possessed unusual virtues. One thing was undeniable, these savages had been fatally underestimated.

'Warleader Gall,' she said as the warrior halted two paces in front of her, 'I am Abrastal, commander of the Evertine Legion and Queen of the Bolkando.'

There was amusement in his eyes as they flicked to scan the heavily armoured legion bodyguards arrayed behind her. 'And these are the soldiers you command, Highness? These . . . tent-pegs. When the Khundryl whirlwind finds them, will they hold fast?'

'You are welcome to find out, Warleader.'

He grunted, and then said: 'They will hold, I'm sure, even as the tent you call a kingdom is torn to shreds behind them.' He shrugged. 'We'll take care not to stumble upon them when we leave. No matter, it pleases me that the first title you gave yourself was that of commander. That you are also the Queen had the flavour of an afterthought. By this, am I to assume that this parley is to be between commanders?'

'Not entirely,' Abrastal replied.

'So what you have to say this afternoon binds the kingdom itself, including your husband, the King?'

'It does.'

He nodded. 'Good.'

'I will hear from you your list of grievances, Warleader.'

His bushy brows lifted. 'Why? Are we to badger each other with matters of interpretation? Your merchants practised extortion on the Khundryl and clearly had the backing of the military. We took their contempt for us and rammed it up their backsides, and now we are but a day from the walls of your capital. And here you are, seeking to bar the way. Do we fight, or do you seek peace between us?'

Abrastal studied the man. 'The city behind me has walls and fortifications, Warleader. Your horse-warriors cannot hope to take it. What then is left to you? Why, to ravage the countryside until there is nothing left.'

'Easier to feed my warriors than for you to feed a city packed with tens of thousands of refugees.'

'You would seek to starve us out?'

Gall shrugged. 'Highness, Bolkando has lost this war. If we were so inclined, we could simply take over. Throw you and all of your bloodline into the nearest well and seal it up.'

Abrastal smiled. 'Oh, dear. Now you show your hut-dwelling roots, Warleader Gall. Before I tell you of the overwhelming logistics of ruling a kingdom whose citizens consider conspiracy a religion, I need to avail you of some other details. Yes, your fleet warriors have given us a great deal of trouble, but we are far from defeated. My Evertine Legion—yes, it belongs to me, not to the King, not to the kingdom—has never been defeated. Indeed, it has never retreated a single step in battle. By all means, fling your braves against our iron wall; we will heap the dead two storeys high around us. But I do not think you will have the chance, alas. Should we come to battle here, Warleader, you will be annihilated. The Khundryl Burned Tears shall have ceased to exist, reduced to a few thousand slaves with quaint tattoos.'

After a moment, Gall hacked up phlegm, turned and spat. Then he wiped his mouth and said, 'Highness, even as we stand here, your two flanking pincers are being filed down to stumps. Even should we lock jaws with your army, we'll hardly remain so locked until such time as any other relieving force you manage to cough up arrives.' He made a dismissive gesture with one scarred hand. 'This posturing is pointless. How many days away are the Perish? They will take your Evertine Legion and melt it down for all the fancy gold on that armour.' As she made to speak he held up his hand to forestall her. 'I have yet to mention the worst you will face—the Bonehunters. Among my people, arguments and opinions are unending as to who are the greatest soldiers the world has ever known—ah, I see in your face that you think we strut about as one of those two, but we do not. No, we speak of the Wickans of Coltaine, versus the marines of the Malazan Empire.' His teeth appeared in a hard smile. 'Lucky for you that there are no longer any Wickans among the Bonehunters, but alas, there are plenty of marines.'

A long moment of silence followed his words. Eventually, Abrastal sighed. 'What are your demands?'

'We already have enough loot, Highness, so now we're prepared to sell it back to you—for food, water, livestock and feed. But, for the cost of my warriors killed or maimed in this war, we will pay no more than a third of the true value of those supplies. Once these arrangements are completed to our satisfaction, and once we are reunited with the Perish Grey Helms, we shall leave your kingdom. For ever.'

'That is it?'

Gall made a face. 'We don't want your kingdom. We never did.'

She knew she should feel offended by that, but the time for such indulgences would have to wait. 'Warleader, understand. The pernicious acts of the merchant houses which led to this war were in themselves abuses of the King's official policy—'

'We made certain those thieves were the first to die, Highness.'

'The ones you killed were but the tip of the poisoned knife.' She half-turned and nodded to one of her guards. This officer led four other soldiers out from the squad, these ones carrying between them a leather satchel large enough to hold a Khundryl tipi. They set it down and untied the bound corners, and then pulled flat the edges.

A half-dozen bodies were revealed, although not much was left of them.

'These are the principal agents,' said Abrastal, 'believing themselves safely ensconced in the capital. As you can see, only their skins remain—our Punishers are skilled in such matters. Consider them evidence of our acknowledgement of the injustices set upon you. They are yours if you want them.'

Gall's raptor eyes fixed on her. 'I am tempted,' he said slowly, 'to renege on my avowed lack of interest in taking over your kingdom, if only out of compassion for your people, Highness.'

'We hold to justice,' Abrastal snapped, 'in our own way. I am frankly surprised at your sensitivity, Warleader. The stories I have heard about the habits of savages when it comes to inventing cruel tortures—'

'Do not apply to us,' Gall cut in, his voice hard as iron. After a moment he seemed to suddenly relax. 'Unless we happen to get very angry. In any case, you misunderstood me, Highness. That your kingdom is home to citizens of any stripe who know no self-constraint—no, even worse, that they would treat with foreigners unmindful of the fact that they stand as representatives of their own people— and their kingdom—speaks to me of your self-hatred.'

'Self-hatred. I see. And if you were the King of Bolkando, Warleader, what would you do?'

'I would make lying the greatest crime of all.'

'Interesting notion. Unfortunately, usually the biggest liars of all are the people at the top—it's how they stay there, after all.'

'Ah, then I am not to believe a word you say?'

'You can believe me, for I can think of no lies that would win me anything.'

'Because my sword hovers over your throat.'

'Precisely. But the lies I was speaking of are the ones the elite use to maintain the necessary distinctions, if you see my point.'

'I do,' and now he regarded her with keen interest. 'Highness, this has proved most interesting. But I must ask you one other thing—why are you here and not your husband the King?'

'The role of my Evertine Legion is to be arbiter of control within the kingdom—and its own populace—as much as to confront external threats.'

He nodded. 'Thus, your presence here serves dual purpose.'

'And the message presented to our rivals in the palace is—and do not be offended by this—the more important of the two.' And then she smiled and added, 'Unless, of course, you were seeking actual conquest.'

'Your husband holds great faith in you, Highness.'

He has no choice. 'He does, and with reason.'

'Do you accept our demands?'

'I do, Warleader, with some modifications.'

His eyes narrowed. 'Name them.'

'The water we provide you will be doubled, and it will be freely given. We shall also double the forage you require for your beasts, for we know far more about the Wastelands than you do, and we have no wish to make you into liars when you say you will never return to Bolkando.' She paused, cocked her head. 'Beyond the Wastelands you will find the dozen or so kingdoms of Kolanse. Warleader, I imagine you will not heed my advice, but I will give it anyway. You will find nothing of worth there. You will, in fact, find something terrible beyond imagining.'

'Will you tell me more, Highness?'

'If you like.'

'Then may I request that you do not do so until such time as either the Mortal Sword Krughava or the Adjunct Tavore is present.'

'Those you have named, they are both women, yes?'

'They are.'

'Will you feel . . . out of place, then?'

'I will, but not for the reasons you might think, Highness.'

'I shall then await this potent gathering with anticipation, Warleader.'

And for the first time, Gall bowed to her. 'Queen Abrastal, it has been a pleasure.'

'I am sure you feel so, and I do not begrudge you that. Are we now at peace?'

'We are.'

She glanced down at the skins on the leather tarp. 'And these?'

'Oh,' said Gall, 'we'll take them. My warriors will need to see them, to ease their rage. And for some, to soothe their grief over fallen kin.'

As he bowed again and turned away, Abrastal called out, 'Warleader.'

He faced her again, a question in his eyes.

The Queen hesitated, and then said, 'When you spoke of your people's opinions . . . of these marines of the Malazan Empire, was there truth to your words?'

He straightened. 'Highness, although the great Coltaine of the Crow Clan had many Wickans with him, he also possessed marines. Together, they escorted thirty thousand refugees across a third of a continent, and each step of the journey was *war*.'

'Have I misunderstood then, Warleader? Did not Coltaine fail? Did he not die? And everyone with him?'

The warrior's eyes were suddenly old. 'He did. They all died—the Wickans, the marines.'

'Then I do not—'

'They died, Highness, even as they delivered those thirty thousand refugees to safety. They died, but they *won*.'

When she had nothing more to say, Gall nodded and resumed his march back to his horse. The two young bodyguards moved to edge past her to help with the defleshed and de-boned merchants. Abrastal caught the eye of the boy and winked. If he had been a Bolkando, his eyes would have widened in return. Instead, he grinned.

That dark thing came alive in her once again.

Spax was suddenly at her side, watching as Gall swung himself on to his horse and then sat motionless, presumably waiting for his two charges and the legionaries. 'I well remember Malazan marines,' he muttered.

'And?'

'Gall spoke true. A more stubborn lot this world has never seen.'

Abrastal thought of Kolanse. 'They will need it.'

'Firehair, will you escort them to the border?'

'Who?'

'All of them. The Khundryl, the Perish, the Bonehunters.'

'I wasn't even aware the Bonehunters were entering our territory.'

'Perhaps they won't now that the need is gone.'

'The Evertine Legion shall accompany these Khundryl and the Perish. It seems, however, that some form of meeting of at least two of the three commanders is planned—and Gall seems to think it will be soon. I would like to speak with them. Accordingly, you and your Gilk will now attach to me—and if we have to march past the border, we shall.'

Spax showed his filed teeth. 'You can make a request to the Warleader, Queen.'

'I think I've already been invited—'

'Not that.' He jerked with his chin. 'The pup.'

She scowled.

The Gilk Warchief grunted a laugh. 'You told to me watch carefully, Firehair.'

Abrastal swung about and began marching back to her legion. 'Rava is going to pay for all of this.'

'He already has, I gather.'

'Not enough. I'll keep shaking him till he's old and grey and shedding teeth and whiskers.'

'Gall is disgusted by your people.'

'So am I, Spax.'

He laughed again.

'Stop sounding so smug,' she said. 'Hundreds, maybe thousands of Bolkando soldiers have died today. I had actually considered using your Gilk for one of the pincers—you would not be so pleased with yourself if I had.'

'We would have just kept on marching, Firehair.'

'Studded with arrows.'

'Oh, we'd leave a trail of our own, yes, but we would have arrived when we were supposed to, ready to deliver vengeance.'

She considered that, and concluded he was not simply full of himself. *We should have heeded what befell the Lether Empire. Dear Bolkando, the world beyond is very large indeed. And the sooner we send it on its way again the sooner we can get back to our orgy of sniping and backstabbing.*

'You've a nostalgic look in your eye, Firehair.'

'Stop seeing so much, Spax.'

His third laugh made her want to punch her fist through the man's ugly face.

Impatient, Gall left his two Tear Runners to deal with the gift of skins and rode back to the camp alone. A formidable woman, this Queen. Thick, long hair the hue of flames. Clever eyes, brown so deep as to be almost black. Stolid enough to give Krughava a tangle in the spit-circle with some lucky man the prize. *And I'd like to see that match—why, they're both enough to make me uncertain whether I was in bed with a woman or a man.* The thought enlivened him and he shifted in the saddle. *Bult's balls, never mind that, you old fool.*

They would not be quit of Abrastal and her Evertine Legion any time soon, he suspected. All the way to the border and perhaps even beyond. But he did not anticipate betrayal—the Khundryl had done enough to keep the fools honest—honest in that frightened, over-eager way that Gall so appreciated. Sometimes war did what was needed. Always easier—and lucrative—dealing with a reeling foe, after all.

He was well enough pleased with how the parley had played out, although some unease remained, like a yurt rat chewing on his toes. *Kolanse. What do you know, Adjunct? What is it you are not telling us?*

You're moaning like an old man shivering under furs, Gall. The Khundryl, the Perish Grey Helms and the Bonehunters. No army can hope to stand against the three of us combined. Bolkando is small. Queen Abrastal rules a tiny, insignificant realm. And the only empire she knows is the one the marines shattered.

No, we have nothing to fear. Still, it will be good to learn what the Queen knows.

A cadre of wing and sub-wing officers awaited him at the edge of the encampment. He scowled at them as he rode up. 'Seems they want to keep their kingdom after all. Send out word—hostilities are at an end. Recall all the raids.'

'What of the wings attacking the flanking armies?' one of the warriors asked.

'Too late to do anything about that, but send Runners in case they're still fighting. Order them to withdraw to the main camp—and no looting on the way!'

'Warleader,' said another warrior, 'your wife has arrived and awaits you in your tent.'

Gall grunted, kicking his horse onward.

He found her sprawled on his cot, naked and heavy as only a pregnant woman could be. Eyeing her as he drew off his cape, he said, 'Wife.'

She glanced up with lidded eyes. 'Husband. How goes the killing?'

'Over with, for now.'

'Oh. How sad for you.'

'I should have drowned you in a river long ago.'

'You'd rather have my ghost haunting you than this all too solid flesh?'

'Would you have? Haunted me?'

'Not for long. I'd get bored.'

Gall began unstrapping his armour. 'You still won't tell whose it is?'

'Does it matter?'

'So it could still be mine.'

She blinked, and a sharper focus came to her regard. 'Gall Inshikalan, you are fifty-six years old. You've been crushing your balls on a horse's back for four and a half decades—no Khundryl man your age can seed a woman.'

He sighed. 'That's the problem. Everyone knows that.'

'Are you humiliated, husband? I did not think that was possible.'

Humiliation. Well, though he'd never wanted it, he'd done his share of humiliating this woman, who had been his wife for most of his life. He had been fifteen. She had been ten. In the old days they would not lie together even when married, until she'd had her first bleed. He remembered the women's celebration when that time finally arrived for his wife—they bundled the pale girl away for a night of secret truths, and what had been a frightened child at the beginning of that night came back to him the following dawn with a look of such knowing in her eyes that he was left . . . uncertain, feeling foolish for no reason, and from that day onward, that he was five years older than her had ceased to be relevant; in fact, it seemed as if she was the elder between them. Wiser, sure of herself, and stronger in every way.

He had worshipped that truth in all the years they had been together. In fact, he realized with a sudden flush, he still did.

Gall stood, looking down at his wife, trying to think of the words he lacked to tell her this. And other things besides.

In her eyes, as she studied him in turn . . . something—

A shout from outside the tent.

She looked away. 'The Warleader is summoned.'

Just like that, the moment was gone, closed up tight. He turned away, stepped back outside.

The scout—the woman—he had sent with Vedith stood before him. Spattered in dried blood, dust, slick gore, stinking like a carcass. Gall frowned. 'So soon?'

'We crushed them, Warleader. But Vedith is dead.'

'Did you take command?'

'I did.'

He tried to recall her name, glancing away as she went on.

'Warleader, he was leading the first charge—we were arrayed perfectly. His horse stepped into a snake hole, went down. Vedith was thrown. He landed poorly, breaking his neck. We saw how his body flopped as he rolled and we knew.'

Gall was nodding. Such things happened, yes. Unexpected, impossible to plan around. That hoof, those shadows on the uneven ground, the eyes of the horse, that hole, all converging into a single fatal moment. To think too much of such things could drive one mad, could tip one into an all-consuming rage. At the games of chance, the cruel, bitter games.

'Warleader,' the scout continued after a moment, 'Vedith's command of the ambush was absolute. Every raid set about its task though we all knew he had fallen—we did this for him, to honour him **as** we must. The enemy was broken. Fourteen hundred dead Bolkando, the rest weaponless and in flight across the countryside. We have nineteen dead and fifty-one wounded.'

His gaze returned to her. 'Thank you, Rafala. The wing is now yours.'

'It shall be named Vedith.'

He nodded. 'See to your wounded.'

Gall stepped back inside the tent. He stood, not sure what to do next, where to go. Not sure why he was herc at all.

'I heard,' said his wife in a low tone. 'Vedith must have been a good warrior, a good commander.'

'He was young,' said Gall, as though that made a difference—as though saying it made a difference—but it didn't.

'Malak's cousin Tharat has a son named Vedith.'

'Not any more.'

'He used to play with our Kyth Anar.'

'Yes,' Gall said suddenly, eyes bright as he looked upon her. 'That is right. How could I have forgotten?'

'Because that was fifteen years ago, husband. Because Kyth did not live past his seventh birthday. Because we agreed to bury our memories of him, our wondrous first son.'

'I said no such thing and neither did you!'

'No. We didn't need to. An agreement? More like a blood vow.' She sighed. 'Warriors die. Children die—'

'Stop it!'

She sat up, groaning with the effort. Seeing the tears he could not wipe away she reached out one hand. 'Come here, husband.'

But he could not move. His legs were rooted tree-trunks beneath him.

She said, 'Something new comes squalling into the world every moment of every day. Opening eyes that can barely see. And as they come, other things leave.'

'I gave him that command. I did it myself.'.

'Such is a Warleader's burden, husband.'

He fought back a sob. 'I feel so alone.'

She was at his side, taking one of his hands. 'That is the truth we all face,' she said. 'I have had seven children since then, and yes, most of them are yours. Do you ever wonder why I cannot give up? What it is that drives women to suffer this time and again? Listen well to this secret, Gall, it is because to carry a child is to be not alone. And to lose a child is to be so wretchedly alone that no man can know the same . . . except perhaps the heart of a ruler, a leader of warriors, a Warleader.'

He found he could meet her eyes once again. 'You remind me,' he said, voice rough.

She understood. 'And you me, Gall. We forget too easily and too often these days.'

Yes. He felt her callused hand in his, and something of that loneliness crumbled away. Then he guided their hands down on to her rounded belly. 'What awaits this one?' he wondered aloud.

'That we cannot say, husband.'

'Tonight,' he said, 'we shall call all our children together. We shall eat as a family—what do you think?'

She laughed. 'I can almost see their faces, all around us—the looks so dumbfounded, so confused. What will they make of such a thing?'

Gall shrugged, a sudden looseness to his limbs, the tightness of his chest vanishing in a single breath. 'We call them not for them but for us; for you and me, Hanavat.'

'Tonight,' she said, nodding. 'Vedith plays with our son once more. I can hear them shouting and laughing, and the sky is before them and it does not end.'

With genuine feeling—the first time in years—Gall took his wife into his arms.

Chapter Fifteen

People will not know the guilt
they cannot deny, cannot escape.
Blind the gods and fix their scales
with binding chains and pull them
down like the truths we hate.
We puzzle over the bones of
strangers and wonder at the world
when they danced free of us
blessedly long ago and we are
different now, but even to speak
of the men and women we were
then, tempts the whirlwind ghosts
of our victims and this will not do
as we treasure the calm and the
smooth of pretend—what cruel
weapons of nature and time
struck down all these strangers
of long ago, when we were
witness in a hapless if smug way?
We dodged the spear-thrusts of
mischance where they stumbled
too oafish too clumsy and altogether
inferior—and their bones you will
find in mountain caves and river clay,
in white spider crevasses above
white beaches, in forest shelters of
rock and all the places in between,
so many that one slayer, we say,
cannot be responsible; but many
the weapons of nature—and the
skittish thing in our eyes as they
slide away, perhaps mutters, to a
sharp ear, the one constant shadow
behind all those deaths—why, that
would be us, silent in guilt, undeserving
recipients of the solitary gift
that leaves us nothing but the bones
of strangers to tumble and roll

beneath our arguments.
They are wordless in repose but
still unwelcome, for they speak
as only bones can, and still we will
not listen. Show me the bones of
strangers, and I become disconsolate.

UNWELCOME LAMENT
GEDESP, FIRST EMPIRE

He saw a different past. One that rolled out after choices not made. He saw the familiar trapped inside strangeness. Huddling round fires as winds howled and new things moved in the darkness beyond. The failure of opportunities haunted him and his kind. A dogged rival slipped serpent-like into the mossy cathedrals of needled forests, sliding along shadow streams, and life became a time of picking through long-dead kills, frowning at broken tools of stone different from anything ever seen before. This—all of this—he realized, was the slow failure that, in his own past, had been evaded.

By the Ritual of Tellann. The sealing of living souls inside lifeless bone and flesh, the trapping of sparks inside withered eyes.

Here, in this other past, in that other place, there had been no ritual. And the ice that was in his own realm the plaything of the Jaghut here lifted barriers unbidden. Everywhere the world shrank. Of course, such challenges had been faced before. People suffered, many died, but they struggled through and they survived. This time, however, it was different.

This time, there were strangers.

He did not know why he was being shown this. Some absurdly detailed false history to torment him? Too elaborate, too strained in its conceptualization. He had real wounds that could be torn open. Yes, the vision mocked him, but on a scale broader than that of his own personal failures. He was being shown the inherent weakness of his own kind—he was feeling the feelings of those last survivors in that other, bitter world, the muddy knowledge of things coming to an end. The end of families, the end of friends, the end of children. Nothing to follow.

The end, in fact, of the one thing never before questioned. *Continuation. We tell ourselves that each of us must pass, but that our kind will live on. This is the deeply buried taproot feeding our very will to live. Cut that root, and living fades. Bleeding dry and colourless, it fades.*

He was invited to weep one last time. To weep not for himself, but for his species.

When fell the last salty tear of the Imass? Did the soil that received it taste its difference from all those that came before? Was it bitterer? Was it sweeter? Did it sting the ground like acid?

He could see that tear, its deathly drop dragged into infinity, a journey too slow to measure. But he knew that what he was seeing was a conceit. The last to die had been dry-eyed—Onos Toolan had witnessed the moment here in this false past— the wretched brave lying bound and bleeding and awaiting the flint-toothed ivory blade in a stranger's hand. They too were hungry, desperate, those strangers. And they would kill the Imass, the last of his kind, and they would eat him. Leave his cracked and cut bones scattered on the floor of this cave, with all the others, and then, in sudden superstitious terror, the strangers would flee this place, leaving nothing behind of themselves, lest wronged ghosts find them on the paths of haunting.

In that other world, the end of Tool's kind came at the cut of a knife.

Someone was howling, flesh stretched to bursting by a surge of rage.

The children of the Imass, who were not children at all, but inheritors never-theless, had flooded the world with the taste of Imass blood on their tongues. Just one more quarry hunted into oblivion, with nothing more than a vague unease lodged deep inside, the mark of sin, the horror of a first crime.

The son devours the father, heart of a thousand myths, a thousand half-forgotten tales.

Empathy was excoriated from him. The howl he heard was rising from his own throat. The rage battered like fists inside his body, a demonic thing eager to get out.

They will pay—

But no. Onos Toolan staggered onward, hide-bound feet crunching on frozen moss and lichen. He would walk out of this damning, vicious fate. Back to his own world's paradise beyond death, where rituals delivered curse and salvation both. He would not turn. He was blind as a beast driven to the cliff's edge, but it did not matter, what awaited him was a death better than this death—

He saw a rider ahead, a figure hunched and cowled as it waited astride a gaunt, grey horse from which no breath plumed. He saw a recurved Rhivi bow gripped in one bony hand, and Onos Toolan realized that he knew this rider.

This inheritor.

Tool halted twenty paces away. 'You cannot be here.'

The head tilted slightly and the glitter of a single eye broke the blackness be-neath the cowl. 'Nor you, old friend, yet here we are.'

'Move aside, Toc the Younger. Let me pass. What waits beyond is what I have earned. What I will return to—it is mine. I will see the herds again, the great ay and the ranag, the okral and agkor. I will see my kin and run in the shadow of the tusked tenag. I will throw a laughing child upon my knee. I will show the children their future, and tell them how all that we are shall continue, unending, for here I will find an eternity of wishes, for ever fulfilled.

'Toc, my friend, do not take this from me. Do not take this, too, when you and your kind have taken everything else.'

'I cannot let you pass, Tool.'

Tool's scarred, battered hands closed into fists. 'For the love between us, Toc the Younger, do not do this.'

An arrow appeared in Toc's other hand, biting the bowstring and, faster than

Tool could register, the barbed missile flashed out and stabbed the ground at his feet.

'I am dead,' said Tool. 'You cannot hurt me.'

'We're both dead,' Toc replied, his voice cold as a stranger's. 'I will take your legs out from under you and the wounds will be real—I will leave you bleeding, crippled, in terrible pain. You will not pass.'

Tool took a step forward. *'Why?'*

'The rage burns bright within you, doesn't it?'

'Abyss take it—I am done with fighting! I am done with all of it!'

'On my tongue, Onos Toolan, is the taste of Imass blood.'

'You want me to fight you? I will—do you imagine your puny arrows can take down an Imass? I have snapped the neck of a bull ranag. I have been gored. Mauled by an okral. When my kind hunt, we bring down our quarry with our own hands, and that triumph is purchased in broken bones and pain.'

A second arrow thudded into the ground.

'Toc—why are you doing this?'

'You must not pass.'

'I—I gifted you with an Imass name. Did you not realize the measure of that honour? Did you not know that no other of your kind has ever been given such a thing? I called you *friend*. When you died, I *wept*.'

'I see you now, in flesh, all that once rode the bone.'

'You have seen this before, Toc the Younger.'

'I do not—'

'You did not recognize me. Outside the walls of Black Coral. I found you, but even your face was not your own. We were changed, the both of us. Could I go back . . .' He faltered, and then continued, 'Could I go back, I would not have let you pass me by. I would have made you realize.'

'It does not matter.'

Something broke inside Onos Toolan. He looked away. 'No, perhaps it doesn't.'

'On the Awl'dan plain, you saw me fall.'

Tool staggered back as if struck a blow. 'I did not know—'

'Nor me, Tool. And so truths come round, full circle, with all the elegance of a curse. I did not know you outside Black Coral. You did not know me on the plain. Fates have a way of . . . of *fitting together*.' Toc paused, and then hissed a bitter laugh. 'And do you recall when we met at the foot of Morn? Look upon us now. I am the withered corpse, and you—' He seemed to tremble, as if struck an invisible blow, and then recovered. 'On the plain, Onos Toolan. What did I give my life for? Do you recall?'

The bitterness in Tool's mouth was unbearable. He wanted to shriek, he wanted to tear out his own eyes. *'The lives of children.'*

'Can you do the same?'

Deeper than any arrows, Toc struck with his terrible words. 'You know I cannot,' Tool said in a rasp.

'You will not, you mean.'

'They are not my children!'

'You have found the rage of the Imass—the rage they escaped, Tool, with the Ritual. You have seen the truth of other pasts. And now you would flee—flee it all. Do you really believe, Onos Toolan, that you will find peace? Peace in self-deception? This world behind me, the one you so seek, you will infect with the lies you tell yourself. Every child's laugh will sound hollow, and the look in every beast's eye will tell you they see you truly.'

The third arrow struck his left shoulder, spun him round but did not knock him down. Righting himself, Tool reached to grip the shaft. He snapped it and drew out the fletched end. Behind him, the flint point and a hand's-width of shaft fell to the ground. 'What—what do you want of me?'

'You must not pass.'

'What do you want?'

'I want nothing, Tool. *I* want *nothing*.' And he nocked another arrow.

'Then kill me.'

'We're dead,' Toc said. 'That I cannot do. But I can stop you. Turn round, Onos Toolan. Go back.'

'To what?'

Toc the Younger hesitated, as if uncertain for the first time in this brutal meeting. 'We are guilty,' he said slowly, 'of so many pasts. Will we ever be made to answer for *any* of them? I wait, you see, for the fates to fit together. I wait for the poisonous beauty.'

'You want me to forgive you—your kind, Toc the Younger?'

'Once, in the city of Mott, I wandered into a market and found myself in front of row upon row of squall apes, the swamp dwellers. I looked into their eyes, Tool, and I saw their suffering, their longing, their terrible crime of living. And for all that, I knew that they were simply not intelligent enough. To refuse forgiveness. You Imass, you are. So. Do not forgive us. *Never* forgive us!'

'Am I to be the weapon of your self-hatred?'

'I wish I knew.'

In those four words, Tool heard his friend, a man trapped, struggling to recall himself.

Toc resumed. 'After the Ritual, well, you chose the wrong enemy for your endless war of vengeance. It would have been more just, don't you think, to proclaim a war against us humans. Perhaps, one day, Silverfox will come to realize that, and choose for her undead armies a new enemy.' He then shrugged. 'If I believed in justice, that is ... if I imagined that she was capable of seeing clearly enough. That you and you alone, T'lan Imass, are in the position to take on the necessary act of retribution—for those squall apes, for all the so-called lesser creatures that have fallen and ever fall to our slick desires.'

He speaks the words of the dead. His heart is cold. His single eye sees and does not shy away. He is ... tormented. 'Is this what you expected,' Tool asked, 'when you died? What of Hood's Gate?'

Teeth gleamed. 'Locked.'

'How can that be?'

The next arrow split his right knee-cap. Bellowing in agony, Tool collapsed. He writhed, fire tearing up his leg. Pain . . . in so many layers, folding round and round—the wound, the murder of a friendship, the death of love, history skirling up in a plume of ashes.

Horse hoofs slowly thumped closer.

Blinking tears from his eyes, Tool stared up at the ravaged, half-rotted face of his old friend.

'Onos Toolan, *I am the lock.*'

The pain was overwhelming. He could not speak. Sweat stung his eyes, more bitter than any tears. *My friend. The one thing left in me—it is slain. You have murdered it.*

'Go back,' said Toc in a tone of immeasurable weariness.

'I—I cannot walk—'

'That will ease, once you turn around. Once you retrace your route, the farther you get away . . . from me.'

With blood-smeared hands, Tool prised loose the arrow jutting from his knee. He almost passed out in the wave of agony that followed, and lay gasping.

'Find your children, Onos Toolan. Not of the blood. Of the spirit.'

There are none, you bastard. As you said, you and your kind killed them all. Weeping, he struggled to stand, twisting as he turned to face the way he had come. Rock-studded, rolling hills, a grey lowering sky. *You've taken it all—*

'And we're far from finished,' said Toc behind him.

I now cast away love. I embrace hate.

Toc said nothing to that.

Dragging his maimed leg, Tool set out.

Toc the Younger, who had once been Anaster First Born of the Dead Seed, who had once been a Malazan soldier, one-eyed and a son to a vanished father, sat on his undead horse and watched the broken warrior limp to the distant range of hills.

When, at long last, Tool edged over a ridge and then disappeared behind it, Toc dropped his gaze. His lone eye roved over the matted stains of blood on the dead grasses, the glistening arrows, one broken, the other not, and those jutting from the half-frozen earth. Arrows fashioned by Tool's own hands, so long ago on a distant plain.

He suddenly pitched forward, curling up like a gut-stabbed child. A moment later a wretched sob broke loose. His body trembled, bones creaking in dried sockets, as he wept, tearless, leaking nothing but the sounds pushing past his withered throat.

A voice broke through from a few paces away, 'Compelling you to such things, Herald, leaves me no pleasure.'

Collecting himself with a groan, Toc the Younger straightened in the saddle and fixed his eye upon the ancient bonecaster standing now in the place where Tool had been. He bared dull, dry teeth. 'Your hand was colder than Hood's own, witch. Do you imagine Hood is pleased at you stealing his Herald? At your using him as you will? This will not go unanswered—'

'I have no reason to fear Hood—'

'But you have reason to fear me, Olar Ethil!'

'And how will you find me, Dead Rider? I stand here, yet not here. No, in the living world I am huddled beneath furs, sleeping under bright stars—'

'You have no need of sleep.'

She laughed. 'Guarded well by a young warrior—one you knew well, yes? One you chase at night, there behind his eyes—and yes, when I saw the truth of that, why, he proved my path to you. And you spoke to me, begging for his life, which I accepted into my care. It has all led . . . to this.'

'And here,' Toc muttered, 'I'd given up believing in evil. How many others do you plan to abuse?'

'As many as I need, Herald.'

'I will find you. When my other tasks are finally done, I swear, I will find you.'

'To achieve what? Onos Toolan is severed from you. And, more importantly, from your kind.' She paused, and then added with a half-snarl, 'I don't know what you meant by that rubbish you managed to force out, about Tool finding his children. I need him for other things.'

'I was fighting free of you, bonecaster. He saw—he heard—'

'And failed to understand. Onos Toolan hates you now—think on that, think on the deepness of his love, and know that for an Imass hatred runs deeper still. Ask the Jaghut! It is done, and can never be mended. Ride away from this, Herald. I now release you.'

'I look forward,' said Toc, gathering the reins, 'to the next time we meet, Olar Ethil.'

Torrent's eyes snapped open. Stars in blurred, jade-tinged smears spun overhead. He drew a deep but ragged breath, shivered beneath his furs.

Olar Ethil's crackling voice cut through the darkness. 'Did he catch you?'

He was in no hurry to reply to that. Not this time. He could still smell the dry, musty aura of death, could still hear the drumbeat of hoofs.

The witch continued, 'Less than half the night is done. Sleep. I will keep him from you now.'

He sat up. 'Why would you do that, Olar Ethil? Besides,' he added, 'my dreams belong to me, not you.'

Rasping laughter drifted across to him. 'Do you see his lone eye? How it glitters in darkness like a star? Do you hear the howl of wolves echoing out from the empty pit of the one he lost? What do the beasts want with him? Perhaps he will tell you, when at last he rides you down.'

Torrent bit down one reply, chose another: 'I escape. I always do.'

She grunted. 'Good. He is filled with lies. He would use you, as the dead are wont to do to mortals.'

In the night Torrent bared his teeth. 'Like you?'

'Like me, yes. There is no reason to deny it. But listen well, I must leave your side for a time. Continue southward on your journey. I have awakened ancient springs—your horse will find them. I will return to you.'

'What is it you want, Olar Ethil? I am nothing. My people are gone. I wander without purpose, caring not if I live or die. And I will not serve you—nothing you can say can compel me.'

'Do you believe me a Tyrant? I am not. I am a bonecaster—do you know what that is?'

'No. A witch.'

'Yes, that will do, for a start. Tell me, do you know what a Soletaken is? A D'ivers?'

'No.'

'What do you know of Elder Gods?'

'Nothing.'

He heard something like a snarl, and then she said, 'How can your kind live, so steeped in ignorance? What is history to you, warrior of the Awl'dan? A host of lies to win you glory. Why do you so fear the truth of things? The darker moments of your past—you, your tribe, all of humanity? There were thousands of my people who did not join the Ritual of Tellann—what happened to them? Why, you did. No matter where they hid, you found them. Oh, on rare occasions there was breeding, a fell admixture of blood, but most of the time such meetings ended in slaughter. You saw in our faces the strange and the familiar—which of the two frightened you the most? When you cut us down, when you carved the meat from our bones?'

'You speak nonsense,' Torrent said. 'You tell me you are Imass, as if I should know what that means. I do not. Nor do I care. Peoples die. They vanish from the world. It is as it was and ever will be.'

'You are a fool. From my ancient blood ran every stream of Soletaken and D'ivers. And my blood, ah, it was but *half* Imass, perhaps even less. I am old beyond your imagining, warrior. Older than this world. I lived in darkness, I walked in purest light, I cast curses upon shadow. My hands were chipped stone, my eyes spawned the first fires to huddle round, my legs spread to the first mortal child. I am known by so many names even I have forgotten most of them.'

She rose, her squat frame dangling rotted furs, her hair lifting like an aura of madness to surround her withered face, and advanced to stand over him.

A sudden chill gripped Torrent. He could not move. He struggled to breathe.

She spoke. 'Parts of me sleep, tormented by sickness. Others rail in the fury of summer storms. I am the drinker of birth waters. And blood. And the rain of weeping and the oil of ordeal. I did not lie, mortal, when I told you that the spirits you worship are my children. I am the bringer of a land's bounty. I am the cruel thief of want, the sower of suffering.

'So many names . . . Eran'ishal, Mother to the Eres'al—my first and most sentimental of choices.' She seemed to flinch. 'Rath Evain to the Forkrul Assail. Stone Bitch to the Jaghut. I have had a face in darkness, a son in shadow, a bastard in light. I have been named the Mother Beneath the Mountain, Ayala Alalle who tends the Gardens of the Moon, for ever awaiting her lover. I am Burn the Sleeping Goddess, in whose dreams life flowers unending, even as those dreams twist into nightmares. I am scattered to the very edge of the Abyss, possessor of more faces than any other Elder.' She snapped out a withered, bony hand, the nails long and splintered, and slowly curled her fingers. 'And he thinks to hunt me down!' Her head tilted back to the sky. 'Chain down your servants, Hood!' She fixed him once more with her eyes. *'Tell me, mortal! Did he catch you?'*

Torrent stared up at her. An old hag crackling with venom and rage. Her dead breath reeked of serpents among the rocks. The onyx knuckles of her eyes glistened with the mockery of life. 'Perhaps,' he said, 'you were once all those things, Olar Ethil. But not any more. It's all torn away from you, isn't it? Scattered and lost, when you gave up life—when you chose to become this thing of bones—'

That hand lunged down, closed about his neck. He was lifted from the ground as if he weighed less than an orthen, flung away. Slamming hard down on one shoulder, breath whooshing from his lungs, half-blinded and unable to move.

She appeared above him, rotted teeth glittering like stumps of smoky quartz. 'I am promised! The Stone Bitch shall awaken once more, in plague winds and devouring locusts, in wildfires and drowning dust and sand! And you will fall upon each other, rending flesh with teeth and nails! You will choose evil in fullest knowledge of what you do—I am coming, mortal, the earth awakened to judgement! And you shall kneel, pleading, begging—your kind, human, shall make pathos your epitaph, for I will give you nothing, yield not a single instant of mercy!' She was gasping now, a pointless bellows of unwarmed breath. She trembled in terrible rage. *'Did he speak to you?'*

Torrent sat up. 'No,' he said through gritted teeth. He reached up to the swollen bruises on his throat.

'Good.' And Olar Ethil turned away. 'Sleep, then. You will awaken alone. But do not think you are rid of me, do not think that.' A pause, and then, 'He is filled with lies. Beware him.'

Torrent hunched forward, staring at the dew-speckled ground between his crooked legs. He closed his eyes. *I will do as you ask. When the time comes, I will do as you ask.*

She awoke to the howling of wolves. Setoc slowly sat up, ran a hand through the tangles of her matted hair, and then drew her bedroll closer about her body. False dawn was ebbing, almost drowned out by the glare of the jade slashes. As the echoes of those howls faded, Setoc cocked her head—had something else stirred her awake? She could not be certain. The stillness of night embraced them—she glanced across to the motionless form of Cafal. She'd run him into exhaustion. Each night since they'd begun this journey he'd fallen into deep sleep as soon as their paltry evening meal was done.

As her eyes adjusted, she could make out his face. It had grown gaunt, aged by deprivation. She knew he'd not yet reached his thirtieth year of life, but he seemed decades older. He lay like a dead man, yet she sensed from him troubled dreams. He was desperate to return to his tribe.

'Something terrible is about to happen.' These words had ground out from him again and again, a litany of dread, a chant riding out his tortured breaths as he ran.

She caught a scent, a sudden mustiness in the cool, dry air. Visions of strange fecundity fluttered across her eyes, as if the present was peeling away, revealing this landscape in ancient times.

An oasis, a natural garden rich with colour and life. Iridescent birds sang among palm fronds. Monkeys scampered, mouths stained with succulent fruit. A tiny world, but a complete one, seemingly changeless, untouched by her kind.

When she saw the grey cloud drifting closer, inexplicable bleak despair struck her and she gasped aloud. She saw the dust settling like rain, a dull patina coating the leaves, the globes of fruit, the once-clear pool of water. And everything began to die.

In moments there was nothing but blackened rot, dripping down the boles of the palms. The monkeys, covered in oozing sores, their hair falling away, curled up and died. The birds sought to flee but ended up on the grey ground, flapping and twitching, then falling still.

The oasis dried up. The winds blew away what was left and sands closed about the spring until it too vanished.

Setoc wept.

What had done this? Some natural force? Did some mountain erupt to fill the sky with poison ash? Or was it a god's bitter breath? Had some wretched city burned, spewing acidic alchemies into the air? Was this desecration an accident, or was it deliberate? She had no answer to such questions; she had only their cruel yield of grief.

Until a suspicion lifted from beneath her sorrow, grisly and ghastly. It . . . it was a weapon. But who wages war upon all living things? Upon the very earth itself? What could possibly be won? Was it just . . . stupidity? Setoc shook herself. She did not like such thoughts.

But this anger I feel, does it belong to the wolves? To the beasts on their forgotten thrones? No, not just them. It is the rage of every unintended victim. It is the fury of the innocents. The god whose face is not human, but life itself.

She is coming . . .

Setoc caught a host of vague shapes in the darkness now, circling, edging closer. Curious in the manner of all wolves, yet cautious. Old memories left scars upon their souls, and they knew what the presence of these two-legged intruders meant for them, for their kind.

They could smell her tears. Their child was in pain, and so the wolves spun their spiral ever tighter. Bringing their heat, the solid truth of their existence—and they would bare fangs to any and every threat. They would, if needed, die in her stead.

And she knew she deserved none of this.

How did you find me? After this long? I see you, grey-nosed mother—was I the last one to suckle from your teats? Did I drink in all your strength until you were left with aching bones, failing muscles? I see the clouds in your eyes, but they cannot hide your love—and it is that love that breaks my heart.

Still, she held out her hand.

Moments later she felt that broad head rise beneath it.

The warm, familiar smells of old assailed her, stinging her eyes. 'You must not stay,' she whispered. 'Where I go . . . you will be hunted down. Killed. Listen to me. Find the last of the wild places—hide there for ever more. Be free, my sweet ones . . .'

She heard Cafal awaken, heard his muffled grunt of shock. Seven wolves crowded their small camp, shy as uninvited children.

Her mother moved up closer, fur sliding the length of Setoc's arm. 'You must go,' she whispered to the beast. 'Please.'

'Setoc,' said Cafal. 'They bring magic.'

'What?'

'Can't you feel the power—so harsh, so untamed—but I think, yes, I can use it. A warren, close enough the barrier feels thin as a leaf. Listen, if we run within it, I think—'

'I know,' she said in a croak, leaning her weight against the she-wolf, so solid, so real, so sure. 'I know, Cafal, the gift they bring.'

'Perhaps,' he said in growing excitement as he tugged aside his blankets, 'we can get there in time. We can save—'

'Cafal, none of this is for you. Don't you understand *anything*? It's not for you!'

He met her glare unblinking—the dawn was finally paling the sky—and then nodded. 'Where will they lead you, then? Do you know?'

She turned away from his despair. 'Oh, Cafal, you really are a fool. Of course we're returning to your tribe's camp. No other path is possible, not any more.'

'I—I don't understand.'

'I know. Never mind. It's time to leave.'

Destriant Kalyth scanned the south horizon, the blasted, unrelieved emptiness revealed in the toneless light of the rising sun. 'Where then,' she muttered, 'are my hands of fire?' She turned to her two exhausted companions. 'You understand, don't you? I cannot do this alone. To lead your kind, I need my own kind. I need to look into eyes little different from my own. I need to see their aches come the dawn, the sleep still in their faces—spirits fend, I need to see them cough the night loose and then piss a steaming river!'

The K'Chain Che'Malle regarded her with their reptilian eyes, unblinking, unhuman.

Kalyth's beseeching frustration trickled away, and she fixed her attention on Sag'Churok, wondering what he had seen—those fourteen undead Jaghut, the battle that, it was now clear, completely eradicated their pursuers. This time, anyway.

Was there something different in the K'ell Hunter? Something that might be . . . unease?

'You wanted a Destriant,' she snapped. 'If you thought that meant a doe-eyed rodara, it must finally be clear just how wrong you were. What I am given, I intend to use—do you understand?' Still, for all the bravado, she wished she had the power to bind those Jaghut to her will. She wished they were with them right now. *Still not human, but, well, closer. Yes, getting closer.* She snorted and turned back to study the south.

'No point in waiting round here, is there? We continue on.'

'*Destriant,*' Sag'Churok whispered in her mind, '*we are running out of time. Our enemy draws ever closer—no, not hunting the three of us. They hunt the Rooted, our final refuge in this world.*'

'We're all the last of our kind,' she said, 'and you must have realized by now, in this world and in every other, there is no such thing as *refuge.*' *The world finds you. The world hunts you down.*

Time, once more, to ride Gunth Mach as if she were nothing more than a beast, Sag'Churok lumbering at their side, massive iron blades catching glares from the sun in blinding spasms. To watch small creatures start from the knotted grasses and bound away in panic. Plunging through clouds of midges driven apart by the prows of reptilian heads and broad heaving chests.

To feel the wind's touch as if it was a stranger's caress, startling in its unwelcome familiarity, reminding her again and again that she still lived, that she was part of the world's meat, forever fighting the decay dogging its trail. None of it seemed real, as if she was simply waiting for reality to catch up to her. Each day delivered the same message, and each day she met it with the same bemused confusion and diffident wariness.

These K'Chain Che'Malle felt none of that, she believed. They did not think as she did. Everything was a taste, a smell—thoughts and feelings, the sun's very light, all flowing in a swarm of currents. Existence was an ocean. One could skate upon the surface, clinging to the shallows, or one could plunge into the depths, until the skull creaked with the pressure. She knew they saw her and her kind as timid, frightened by the mystery of unplumbed depths. Creatures floundering in fears, terrified of drowning knee-deep in truths.

But your Matron wants you to slide into the shallows, to find my world of vulnerabilities—to find out what we do to defeat them. You seek new strategies for living, you seek our secret of success. But you don't understand, do you? Our secret is annihilation. We annihilate everyone else until none are left, and then we annihilate each other. Until we too are gone.

Such a wondrous secret. Well, she would give it to them, if she could. Her grand lessons of survival, and only she would hear the clamouring howl of the ghosts storming her soul.

Riding Gunth Mach's back, Kalyth's hands itched. Destinies were drawing close. *I will find my hands of fire, and we will use you, Sag'Churok. You and Gunth Mach and all your kind. We will show you the horrors of the modern world you so want to be a part of.*

She thought of their dread enemy, the faceless killers of the K'Chain Che'Malle. She wondered at this genocidal war, and suspected it was, in its essence, no different from the war humans had been engaged in for all time. *It is the same, but it is also different. It is . . . naïve.*

With what was coming, with what she would bring . . . Kalyth felt a deep, sickening stab.

Of pity.

In an unbroken line from each mother to every daughter, memory survived, perpetuating a continuous history of experience. Gunth Mach held in her mind generations of lives trapped in a succession of settings that portrayed the inexorable collapse, the decay, the failure of their civilization. This was unbearable. Knowledge was an unceasing scream in her soul.

Every Matron was eventually driven insane: no daughter, upon ascension to the role, could long withstand the deluge. Male K'Chain Che'Malle had no comprehension of this; their lives were perfectly contained, the flavours of their selves truncated and unsubtle. Their unswerving loyalty was sustained in ignorance.

She had sought to break this pattern, with Sag'Churok, and in so doing was betraying the inviolate isolation of the Matrons. But she did not care. All that had gone before had not worked.

She remembered half a continent pounded level and then made smooth as a frozen lake, on which cities sprawled in a scale distorted even to K'Chain Che'Malle eyes, as if grandeur and madness were one and the same. Domes large enough to swallow islands, curling towers and spires like the spikes riding the backs of dhenrabi. Buildings with single rooms so huge that clouds formed beneath the ceiling, and birds dwelt there in their thousands, oblivious to the cage that held them. She remembered entire mountain ranges preserved as if they were works of art, at least until their value as quarries for sky keeps was realized, in the times of the civil wars—when those mountains were carved down to stumps. She remembered looking upon her kind in league-wide columns twenty leagues long as they set out to found new colonies. She stood, creaking beneath her own weight, and watched as fifty legions of Ve'Gath Soldiers—each one five thousand strong—marched to wage war against the Tartheno Tel Akai. And she was there when they returned, decimated, leaving a trail of their own dead that stretched across the entire continent.

She recalled the birth pains of the Nah'ruk, and then the searing agony of their betrayal. Burning cities and corpses three-deep on vast fields of battle. Chaos and terror within the nests, the shriek of desperate births. And the sly mockery of the waves on the shores as a dying Matron loosed her eggs into the surf in the mad hope that something new would be made—a hybrid of virtues with all the flaws discarded.

And so much more . . . fleeing through darkness and blinding smoke . . . the slash of an Assassin's talons. Cold, sudden adjudication. Life draining away, the blessed relief that followed. Flavours awakening cruel and bitter in the daughter who followed—for nothing was lost, nothing was *ever* lost.

There *was* a goddess of the K'Chain Che'Malle. Immortal, omniscient as such things were supposed to be. The goddess was the Matron, mahybe of the eternal oil. Once, that oil had been of such strength and volume that hundreds of Matrons were needed as holy vessels.

Now there was but one.

She could remember the pride, the power of what had once been. And the futile wars waged to give proof to that pride and that power, until both had been utterly obliterated. Cities gone. The birth of wastelands across half the world.

Gunth Mach knew that Gu'Rull still lived. She knew, too, that the Shi'gal Assassin was her adjudicator. Beyond this quest, there waited the moment of inheritance, when Acyl finally surrendered to death. Was Gunth Mach a worthy successor? The Shi'gal would decide. Even the enemy upon the Rooted, slaughter unleashed in the corridors and chambers, would have no bearing upon matters. She would surge through the panicked crowds, seeking somewhere to hide, with three Assassins stalking her.

The will to live was the sweetest flavour of all.

She carried the Destriant on her back, a woman who weighed virtually nothing, and Gunth Mach could feel the tension in her small muscles, her frail frame of bones. Even an orthen bares its fangs in its last moments of life.

Failure in this quest was unacceptable, but in Gunth Mach's mind, it was also inevitable.

She would be the last Matron, and with her death so too would die the goddess of the K'Chain Che'Malle. The oil would drain into the dust, and all memory would be lost.

It was just as well.

Spirits of stone, what happened here?

Sceptre Irkullas slowly dismounted, staring aghast at the half-buried battlefield. As if the ground had lifted up to swallow them all, Barghast and Akrynnai both. Crushed bodies, broken limbs, faces scoured away as if blasted by a sandstorm. Others looked bloated, skin split and cracked open, as if the poor soldiers had been cooked from within.

Crows and vultures scampered about in frustrated cacophony, picking clean what wasn't buried, whilst Akrynnai warriors wandered the buried valley, tugging free the corpses of dead kin.

Irkullas knew his daughter's body was here, somewhere. The thought clenched in his stomach like a sickly knot leaching poison, weakening his limbs, tightening the breath in his throat. He dreaded the notion of sleep at this day's end, the stalking return of anguish and despair. He would lie chilled beneath furs, chest aching, rushes of nausea squirming through him, his every breath harsh and strained—close to the clutch of panic.

Something unexpected, something unknown, had come to this petty war. As if the spirits of the earth and rock were convulsing in rage and, perhaps, disgust. *Demanding peace. Yes, this is what the spirits have told me, with this here— this . . . horror. They have had enough of our stupid bloodletting.*

We must make peace with the Barghast.

He felt old, exhausted.

A day ago vengeance seemed bright and pure. Retribution was sharp as a freshly honed knife. Four major battles, four successive victories. The Barghast clans were scattered, fleeing. Indeed, only one remained, the southernmost, largest clan, the Senan. Ruled by the one named Onos Toolan. The Akrynnai had three armies converging upon the Warleader and his encampment.

We have wagons creaking beneath Barghast weapons and armour. Chests filled with foreign coins. Heaps of strange furs. Trinkets, jewellery, woven rugs, gourd bowls and clumsy pots of barely tempered clay. We have everything the Barghast possessed. Just the bodies that owned them have been removed. Barring a score of broken prisoners.

We are a travelling museum of a people about to become extinct.

And yet I will plead for peace.

Upon hearing this, his officers would frown behind his back, thinking him an old man with a broken heart, and they would be right to think that. They would accept his commands, but this would be the last time. Once they rode home Sceptre Irkullas would be seen—would be known to all—as a 'ruler in his grey dusk'. A man with no light of the future in his eyes, a man awaiting death. *But it comes to us all. Everything we fear comes to us all.*

Gafalk, who had been among the advance party, rode up and reined in near the Sceptre's own horse. The warrior dismounted and walked to stand in front of Irkullas. 'Sceptre, we have examined the western ridge of the valley—or what's left of it. Old Yara,' he continued, speaking of the Barghast spokesperson among the prisoners, 'says he once fought outside some place called One-Eye Cat. He says the craters remind him of something called Moranth munitions, but not when those munitions are dropped from the sky as was done by the Moranth. Instead, the craters look like those made when the munitions are used by the Malazans. Buried in the ground, arranged to ignite all at once. Thus lifting the ground itself. Some kind of grenado. He called them cussers—'

'We know there is a Malazan army in Lether,' Irkullas said, musing. Then he shook his head. 'Give me a reason for their being here—joining in a battle not of their making? Killing both Akrynnai and Barghast—'

'The Barghast were once enemies of these Malazans, Sceptre. So claims Yara.'

'Yet, have our scouts seen signs of their forces? Do any trails lead from this place? No. Are the Malazans *ghosts*, Gafalk?'

The warrior spread his hands in helpless dismay. 'Then what struck here, Sceptre?'

The rage of gods. 'Sorcery.'

A sudden flicker in Gafalk's eyes. 'Letherii—'

'Who might well be pleased to see the Akrynnai and Barghast destroy each other.'

'It is said the Malazans left them few mages, Sceptre. And their new Ceda is an old man who is also the Chancellor—not one to lead an army—'

But Irkullas was already shaking his head at his own suggestions. 'Even a Letherii Ceda cannot hide an entire army. You are right to be sceptical, Gafalk.'

A conversation doomed to circle round and devour its own tail. Irkullas stepped past the warrior and looked upon the obliterated valley once more. 'Dig out as many of our warriors as you can. At dusk we cease all such efforts—leaving the rest to the earth. We shall drive back the night with the pyre of our dead. And I shall stand vigil.'

'Yes, Sceptre.'

The warrior returned to his horse.

Vigil, yes, that will do. A night without sleep—he would let the bright flames drive back the sickness in his soul.

It would be best, he decided, if he did not survive to return home. An uncle or cousin could play the bear to his grandchildren—someone else, in any case. Better, indeed, if he was denied the chance of sleep until the very instant of his death.

One final battle—against the Senan camp? Kill them all, and then fall myself. Bleed out in the red mud. And once dead, I can make my peace . . . with their ghosts. Hardly worth continuing this damned war on the ash plains of death, this stupid thing.

Dear daughter, you will not wander alone for long. I swear it. I will find your ghost, and I will protect you for ever more. As penance for my failure, and as proof of my love.

He glared about, as if in the day's fading light he might see her floating spirit, a wraith with a dirt-smeared face and disbelieving eyes. No, eyes with the patience of the eternally freed. *Freed from all this. Freed . . . from everything. In a new place. Where no sickness grows inside, where the body does not clench and writhe, flinching at the siren calls of every twinge, every ache.*

Spirits of stone, give me peace!

Maral Eb's army had doubled in size, as survivors from shattered encampments staggered in from all directions—shame-faced at living when wives, husbands and children had died beneath the iron of the treacherous Akrynnai. Many arrived bearing no weapons, shorn of armour, proof that they had been routed, had fled in waves of wide-eyed cowardice. Cold waters were known to wash upon warriors in the midst of battle, even Barghast warriors, and the tug of currents could lift into a raging flood where all reason drowned, where escape was a need that overwhelmed duty and honour. Cold waters left the faces of the survivors grey and bloated, stinking of guilt.

But Maral Eb had been sobered enough by the news of the defeats to cast no righteous judgement upon these refugees with their skittish eyes. Clearly, he understood he would need every warrior he could muster, although Bakal knew as well as anyone how such warriors, once drowned beneath panic, were now broken inside—worse, in the instant when a battle tottered on the fulcrum's point, their terror could return. They could doom the battle, as their panic flooded out and infected everyone else.

No word had come from the Senan. It seemed that, thus far at least, the Akrynnai had yet to descend upon Bakal's own clan. Soon, Maral Eb would grasp hold of the Senan army and claim it for himself. And then he would lead them all against the deceitful Sceptre Irkullas.

A thousand curses rode the breaths of the mass of warriors. It was obvious now that the Akryn had been planning this war for some time, trickling in and out their so-called merchants as spies, working towards the perfect moment for betrayal. How else could the Sceptre assemble such forces so quickly? For every refugee insisted that the enemy numbered in the tens of thousands.

Bakal believed none of it. This was the war Onos Toolan did not want. The *wrong* war. Maral Eb walked flanked by his two brothers, and surrounding these three was a mob of strutting idiots, each one vying to find the perfect words to please their new Warleader and his two hood-eyed, murderous siblings. Arguments sending the arrow of blame winging away. Onos Toolan was no longer alive and so less useful as a target, although some murky residue remained, like handfuls of shit awaiting any rivals among the Senan. Now it was the Akrynnai—Irkullas and his lying, cheating, spying horsemongers.

By the time this army arrived at the Senan camp, they would be blazing with the righteous fury of innocent victims.

'*Whatever he needs,*' Strahl had said at the noon break. '*Falsehoods cease being false when enough people believe them, Bakal. Instead, they blaze like eternal truths, and woe to the fool who tries pissing a stream on that. They'll tear you to pieces.*'

Strahl's words were sound, ringing clear and true upon the anvil, leaving Bakal's disgust to chew him on the inside with no way out. That ache warred with the one in his barely mended elbow, making his stride stiff and awkward. But neither one could assail the shame and self-hatred that closed a fist round his soul. *Murderer of Onos Toolan. So fierce the thrust that he broke his arm. Look upon him, friends, and see a true White Face Barghast!* He had heard as much from Maral Eb's cronies. While behind him trudged his fellow Senan warriors, nothing like the triumphant slayers of Onos Toolan they pretended to be. Silent, grim as shoulderwomen at a funeral. *Because we share this crime. He made us kill him to save our own lives. He made us cowards. He made me a coward.*

Bakal felt like an old man, and each time his gaze caught upon those three broad backs arrayed like bonepicker birds at the head of the trail, it was another white-hot stone tossed into the cauldron. Soon to boil, yes, raging until the blackened pot boiled dry. *All that useless steam.*

What will you do with my people, Maral Eb? When Irkullas shatters us again, where will we run to? He needed to think. He needed to find a way out of this. Could he and his warriors convince the rest of the clan to refuse Maral Eb? Refuse this suicidal war? Teeth grating, Bakal began to understand the burdens under which Onos Toolan had laboured. The impossibility of things.

The real war is against stupidity. How could I not have understood that? Oh, an easy answer to that question. I was among the stupidest of the lot. And yet, Onos Toolan, you stood before me and met my eyes—you gave me what I did not deserve.

And look at me now. When Maral Eb stands before me, I choke at the very sight of him. His flush of triumph, his smirk, the drunken eyes. I am ready to spew into his face—and if I had any food in my guts I would probably do just that, unable to help myself.

Onos Toolan, you should have killed us—every warrior you brought with you. Be done with the stupid ones, be done with us all—instead, you leave us with the perfect legacy of our idiocy. Maral Eb. Precisely the leader we deserve.

And for our misplaced faith, he will kill everyone.

Bakal bared his teeth until the wind dried them like sun-baked stones. He would do nothing. He would defy even Strahl and his companions here. There would be justice after all. An ocean of it to feed the thirsty ground. So long as he did nothing, said nothing.

Lead us, Maral Eb—you are become the standard of Tool's truth. You are his warning to us, which we refused to heed. So, warrior of the Imass, you shall have your vengeance after all.

Strahl spoke at his side. 'I have seen such smiles, friend, upon the warrior I am about to slay—the brave ones who face their deaths unflinching. I see . . . crazed contempt, as if they say to me: "Do what you must. You cannot reach me—my flesh, yes, my life, but not my soul. Drive home your blade, warrior! The final joke is on you!" ' His laugh was a low snarl. 'And so it is, because it is a joke I will not get until I am in their place, facing down my own death.'

'Then,' said Bakal, 'you will have to wait.' *But not for long. And when the time comes I too will laugh at this perfect jest.*

The place belonged to Stolmen, but it was his wife who walked at the head of the Gadra column. And it was to Sekara the Vile that the scouts reported during the long march to the Senan encampment—which was now less than half a league away.

Her husband's face was set in a scowl as he trudged three paces behind her. The expression did not belong to offended fury, however. Confusion and fear were the sources of his anger, the befuddled misery of the unintelligent man. Things were moving too fast. Essential details were being kept from him. He did not understand and this made him frightened. He had right to be. Sekara was beginning to realize that his usefulness was coming to an end—oh, there were advantages to ruling through him, should that opportunity arise in the aftermath of the imminent power struggle, but better a husband who actually comprehended his titular function— assuming it was even necessary, since many a past warleader had been a woman. Although, truth be said, such women were invariably warriors, possessing the status of experienced campaigners.

Sekara had fought many battles, of course, in her own style. She had laid sieges, in tents and in yurts. She had drawn blood beneath the furs in the armour of night, had driven knives—figurative and literal—into the hearts of scores of lovers. She had unleashed precision ambushes with utter ruthlessness, and had stared down seemingly insurmountable odds. Her list of triumphs was well nigh unending. But few would countenance any of that. They held to out-of-fashion notions of prowess and glory, and for Sekara this had proved and would ever prove the greatest obstacle to her ascension.

No, for now, she would need a man to prop up in front of her. Not that anyone would be fooled, but so long as propriety was observed, they would abide.

There were challenges ahead. Stolmen was not ready to be the Warleader of the White Faces. Not while in the throes of a vicious war. No, at the moment, the greatest need was to ensure the survival of the Barghast, and that demanded a capable commander. Someone clever in the ways of tactics and whatnot. Someone swollen with ambition, eager to be quickly pushed to the fore, arriving breathless and flush—quickly, yes, so that he'd no opportunity to grow wary, to begin to recognize the flimsy supports beneath him, the clever traps awaiting his first misstep.

Sekara had long pondered prospective candidates. And she had to admit that she was not entirely satisfied with her final choice, but the bones were cast. Alone, in the chill night at that first secret meeting, in the wake of a tumultuous gathering of warchiefs, Maral Eb had seemed perfect. His contempt for Onos Toolan had filled him with hatred that she slyly fed until it became a kind of fevered madness. Nothing difficult there, and his willingness to bind himself to her conspiracy had struck her, at the time, as almost comical. Like a puppy eager to lick whatever she offered.

He had been alone. And perhaps, in that, she had been careless. She had not considered, for even an instant, Maral Eb's two brothers.

Three were harder to manage than one. Almost impossible, in fact. If they were left to consolidate their domination once the war was over, Sekara knew that her chance would be for ever lost. She knew, indeed, that Maral Eb would see her murdered, to silence all that she knew.

Well, his brothers would just have to die. In battle, to a stray arrow—these things, she had been told, happened all the time. Or some bad food, improperly cured, to strike with swift fever and terrible convulsions, until the heart burst. A lover's tryst gone awry, some enraged rival. Charges of rape, a trial of shaming and a sentence of castration. Oh, the possibilities were countless.

For the moment, of course, such delights would have to wait. The Akrynnai must be defeated first, or at least driven back—one more battle awaited them, and this time Sceptre Irkullas would be facing the combined might of the Senan, Barahn and Gadra clans.

Two Barahn scouts had found her three days past, carrying with them the stunning news of Onos Toolan's murder. The Gadra had already been on the march. Sekara had made certain that her people—a small clan, isolated and perilously close to Akryn lands—had not awaited the descent of thousands of enraged

Akrynnai horsewarriors. Instead, Stolmen had announced the breaking of camp and this fast-paced retreat to the safety of the Senan, almost as soon as news of the war reached them.

Since then, Gadra scouts had twice sighted distant riders observing them, but nothing more; and as Sekara learned from an alarmingly steady arrival of refugees from other clans, a half-dozen battles had left the Barghast reeling. The sudden coyness of the victorious Akrynnai was disturbing. Unless they too sought one final clash. One that they were content to let the Gadra lead them to at a steady dogtrot.

Stolmen complained that his warriors were weary, barely fit for battle. Their nerves were twisted into taut knots by constant vigilance and a sickening sense of vulnerability. They were a small clan, after all. It made no tactical sense for the Sceptre to let them reach the Senan. The Akrynnai horde should have washed over them by now.

Well, that was for Maral Eb to worry about. Sekara had just this morning sent her own agents ahead to the Senan. Onos Toolan was dead. But his wife was not, nor his children, bloodkin and otherwise. The time had come for Sekara to unleash her long-awaited vengeance.

The day's light was fading. Though she had exhorted her people with relentless impatience, they would not reach the Senan any time before midnight.

And by then the blood spilled would be as cold as the ground beneath it.

Stavi made a face. 'He has a secret name,' she said. 'An Imass name.'

Storii's brow knitted as she looked down upon the drooling toddler playing in the dirt. She twisted round on the stone she was sitting on. 'But we can't get it, can we? I mean, he doesn't know it, that name, how can he? He can't talk.'

'Not true! I heard him talk!'

'He says "blallablallablalla" and that's all he says. That doesn't sound Imass to me.'

Stavi tugged at the knots in her hair, unmindful of the midges swarming round her head. 'But I heard Father talking—'

Storii's head snapped up, eyes accusing. 'When? You snuck off to be with him—without me! I knew it!'

Stavi grinned. 'You were squatting over a hole. Besides, he wasn't talking to me. He was talking to himself. Praying, maybe—'

'Father never prays.'

'Who else would he be talking to, except some five-headed Imass god?'

'Really, which head?'

'What?'

'Which head was he talking to?'

'How should I know? The one listening. It had ears on stalks and they turned. And then it popped out one eye and swallowed it—'

Storii leapt to her feet. 'So it could look out its hole!'

'Only way gods know how to aim.'

Storii squealed with laughter.

The dirt-faced runt looked up from his playing, eyes wide, and then he smiled and said, 'Blallablallablalla!'

'That's the god's name!'

'But which head?' Stavi asked.

'The one with poop in his ears, of course. Listen, if we can really find out his secret name, we can curse him for ever and ever.'

'That's what I was saying. What kind of curses?'

'Good ones. He can only walk on his hands. He starts every sentence with blallablallablalla. Even when he's twenty years old! As old as that, and even older.'

'That's pretty old. That's grey-haired old. Let's think of more curses.'

Sitting oblivious on the ground, the son of Onos Toolan and Hetan made curling patterns in the soft dust with one finger. Four squiggles in one particular pattern, trying again and again to get it just right. It was getting dark. Shadows walked out from stones. The shadows were part of the pattern.

The Imass possessed no written language. Something far more ancient was buried deep within them. It was liquid. It was stain on skin. It was the magic of shadows cast by nothing—nothing real. It was the gift of discord, the deception of unnatural things slipped into a natural world. It was cause in search of effect. When the sun was gone from the sky, fire rose in its stead, and fire was the maker of shadows, revealer of secrets.

The child had a secret name, and it was written in elusive, impermanent games of light and dark, a thing that could flicker into and out of existence in the dancing of flames, or, as now, at the moment of the sun's death, with the air itself crumbling to grainy dust.

Absi Kire, a name gifted by a father struck with unexpected hope, long after the death of hopeful youth. It was a name striving for faith, when faith had departed the man's world. It whispered like a chill wind, rising up from the Cavern of the Worm. *Absi Kire*. Its breath was dry, plucking at eyes that had forgotten how to close. Born of love, it was a cry of desperation.

Patterns in the dirt, fast sinking into formless gloom.

Absi Kire.

Autumn Promise.

Storii held up a hand, cutting short a list of curses grown past breathless, and cocked her head. 'Some news,' she said.

Nodding, Stavi reached down and snatched up the boy. He struggled, tilting his head back until it pressed hard against her chest. She blew down, stirring the hair atop his slightly elongated head, and he instantly settled.

'Excited voices.'

'Not happy excited.'

'No,' Stavi agreed, turning to look in the direction of the camp—just beyond a sweep of tilted rock outcroppings. The glow of fires was rising beneath a layer of woodsmoke.

'We should get back.'

Hetan cursed under her breath. The girls had kidnapped their half-brother yet again, and no one had seen their escape. When they were out of her sight, the vast pit of her solitude opened its maw beneath her, and she could feel herself tumbling and spinning as she fell . . . and fell. So much darkness, so little hope that the plunge would end in a merciful snap of bones, the sudden bliss of oblivion.

Without her children, she was nothing. Sitting motionless, wandering inside her skull, dull-eyed and weaving like a hoof-kicked dog. Nose sniffing, claws scratching, but there was no way out. Without her children, the future vanished, a moth plunging into the fire. She blinked motes from her eyes, hands drawn together and thumbnails picking at the scabs and oozing slices left behind by the last assault on the ends of her fingers, the tender skin round the nails.

Frozen in place, sunken, in endless retreat.

Another bowl of rustleaf? Durhang? A resin bud of d'bayang? D'ras beer? Too much effort, every one of them. If she sat perfectly still, time would vanish.

Until the girls brought him back. Until she saw the twins pretending to smile but skittish and worried behind their eyes. And he would squirm in a girl's arms, reaching for Hetan, who would see those strangely large, wide hands with their stubby fingers, clutching, straining, and a howl would rise within her, lifting out of that black maw, blazing like a skystone returning to the sky.

She would take him into a suffocating embrace, desperate sparks igniting within her, forcing her into animation.

Strings on the ends of those pudgy fingers, plucking her to life.

And she howled and she howled.

Heavy footsteps rushed past the entrance to the tent. Voices, a few shouts. A runner had entered the camp. The word was delivered, and the word was *dead*.

How could imagination hope to achieve the wonders of reality? The broken, deathly landscape stretched out on all sides, but the vista was shrinking as the day's light faded. Yet more than darkness embraced the transformation. Domes of cracked bedrock appeared, skinned in lichen and moss. Shin-high trees with thick, twisted boles, branches fluttering with the last of the autumn leaves, like blackened layers of peeled skin. Bitter arctic wind rushing down from the northwest to herald winter's eager arrival.

Cafal and Setoc ran through this new world. The frigid air bit in their lungs, yet it was richer and sweeter than anything they had breathed in their own realm, their own time.

How to describe the noise of a hundred thousand wolves running across the land? It filled Cafal's skull with the immensity of an ocean. Padded footfalls delivered a pitch and rhythm unlike that of spaded hoofs. The brush of fur as shoulders rubbed was a seething whisper. The heat rising from bodies was thick as mist, the animal smell overwhelming—the smell of a world without cities, forges, charcoal burners, without battlefields, trenches filled with waste, without human sweat and perfumes, the smoke of rustleaf and durhang, the dust of frantic destruction.

Wolves. Before humans waged war upon them, before the millennia-long campaign of slaughter. Before the lands emptied.

He could almost see them. Every sense but sight was alive with the creatures. And he and Setoc were carried along on the ghostly tide.

All that was gone had returned. All this history, seeking a home.

They would not find it among his people. He did not understand why Setoc was leading them to the Barghast. He could hear her singing, but the words she used belonged to some other language. The tone was strangely fraught, as if warring forces were bound together. Curiosity and wariness, congress and terror—he could almost see the glint of bestial eyes as they watched the first band of humans from a distance. Did these two-legged strangers promise friendship? Cooperation? A recognition of brother- and sisterhood? Yes, to all of that. But this was no family at peace; this was a thing writhing with deceit, betrayal, black malice and cruelty.

The wolves were innocents. They stood no chance.

Flee the Barghast. Please, I beg you—

But his pleading rang hollow even to Cafal. He needed them—he needed this swift passage. Night had fallen. A wind was rising to tear at the torches and hearth-fires in the Senan camp. Rain spat with stinging fury and lightning ignited the horizon.

Eyes gleamed, iron licked the darkness—

The gods were showing him was what coming.

And he would not get there in time. Because, as has ever been known, the Barghast gods were bastards.

Heart thudding with anticipation, Sathand Gril slipped out from the light of the wind-whipped fires. He had watched the children and their furtive flight into the shattered hills northeast of the camp when the sun was still a hand's breadth above the horizon. This had been his singular responsibility for weeks now—spying on the horrid little creatures—all leading to this moment, this reward.

He had killed the boy's dog and now he would kill the boy. Plunging his knife into his belly with a hand over his mouth to stifle the shrieks. A large rock to crush the skull and destroy the face, because no one welcomed the face of a dead child, especially one frozen in twisted pain. He had no desire to look upon the half-lidded eyes that saw nothing, that had gone flat with the soul's absence. No, he would destroy the thing utterly, and then fling it into a defile.

The twins were destined for something far more elaborate. He'd break their legs. Then tie their hands. He'd blood them both, but not cruelly, for Sathand was not one of those who hungered to rape, not women, not children. But he would give them his seed to carry to the gods.

This night of murder, it was for the Barghast. The righting of wrongs. The end of the usurper's line and the eradication of Hetan's shame. Onos Toolan was not of the clans of the White Face. He was not even Barghast.

No matter. Word had come. Onos Toolan was dead—murdered by Bakal, who had broken his own arm with the force of the knife-thrust he had driven into the Warleader's heart. A power struggle was coming—Sathand Gril well knew that Sekara had decided on the Barahn warchief, Maral Eb. But to Sathand's eyes—and to those of many others among the Senan—Bakal could make a surer claim, and that was one Sathand would back. More blood to be spilled before things settled out. Most were agreed on that.

Sekara the Vile. Her idiot husband, Stolmen. Maral Eb and his vicious brothers. The new Warleader would be Senan—no other clan was as powerful, after all, not even the Barahn.

It would have to be quick—all of it. The cursed Akrynnai army was on its way.

Sathand Gril padded through the darkness—the brats should be on their way back by now. Even they weren't stupid enough to stay out once the sun set, what with both half-starved wolves and Akrynnai marauders on the hunt. So . . . where were they?

From the camp behind him, someone shrieked.

It had begun.

Three women entered the tent, and Hetan knew them all. She watched them advance on her, and suddenly everything became perfectly clear, perfectly understandable. Mysteries flitting away like veils of smoke on the wind. *Now I join you, husband.* She reached for her knife and found only the sheath at her hip—her eyes snapped to the flat-stone on which sat the remnants of her last meal, and there waited the knife—and Hetan lunged for the weapon.

She did not reach it in time. A knee slammed into her jaw, whipped her head round, blood spinning in threads. Hands snagged her wrists, dragged her round and pushed her to the ground.

Fists pummelled her face. Flares of light exploded behind her eyes. Stunned, suddenly too weak to struggle, she felt herself rolled on to her stomach. Rawhide bound her arms behind her. Fingers snarled a fist's worth of hair and lifted her head up.

Balamit's foul breath whispered across her cheek. 'No easy way for you, whore. No, it's hobbling for Hetan—and what's so different about that? You'd rut with a dog if it knew how to kiss! May you live a hundred years!'

She was thrown on to her back, and then lifted up from behind, Jayviss's nails digging deep into Hetan's armpits.

Hega, burly, miserable Hega, swung the hatchet down.

Hetan shrieked as the front half of her right foot was chopped off. The leg jumped, spraying blood. She tried to pull the other one away, but a crack of the hatchet's iron ball against her kneecap numbed the leg. The hatchet swung down again.

The pain rushed in a black flood. Balamit giggled.

Hetan passed out.

Krin, whose niece had married a Gadra warrior and was swollen with child, watched as Sekara's bitch dogs dragged Hetan out from the tent. The whore was unconscious. Her stumped feet trailed wet streaks that seemed to flare as lightning flashed in the night.

They brought her to the nearest hearth-fire. Little Yedin was tending to the flat blade and it was pale hot when she lifted it from the coals. Meat sizzled and popped as the blade was pushed against Hetan's left foot. The woman's body jerked, her eyes starting open in shock. A second shriek shattered the air.

Nine-year-old Yedin stared, and then at an impatient snap from one of the bitches, she flipped the blade and seared Hetan's other foot.

Krin hurried forward, scowling at the way Hetan's eyes had rolled up, head lolling. 'Wake her up, Hega. I'm first.'

His sister grinned, still holding the bloodied hatchet. 'Your son?'

Krin looked away, disgusted. He was barely half her age. Then he jerked a nod. 'Tonight's the night for it,' he said.

'Widow's gift!' Hega cried in glee.

Jayviss brought over a gourd of water and threw its contents into Hetan's bruised face.

She sputtered, coughed.

Krin advanced on her, mindful and delighted at how many people had gathered, and at how other men were arguing their place. 'Keep her hands tied,' he said. 'For the first dozen or so. After that, there won't be any need.'

It was true—no Barghast woman resisted by that point. And in a few days, she'd drop to her hands and knees at a glance, backside upthrust and ready.

'Might be two dozen,' someone in the crowd observed. 'Hetan was a warrior, after all.'

Hega stepped up and kicked Hetan in the ribs. Spittle flew from the widow's lips as she snarled and said, 'What's a warrior without a weapon? Bah, she'll be licking her lips after five or so, you'll see!'

Krin said nothing; nor did anyone else. The warriors knew their own, after all. Hega was an idiot, to think Hetan would break so easily. *I remember you, Hega. My sister, too fat to fight. And who was the one licking her lips five times a day? Oh, we see where your hate lives—gods, I am giving my son to this thing! Well, just for one night. And I'll give him my own knife, with leave to use it. No one will miss you, Hega. And no one will call out my boy, either.*

The wind was howling—a storm had found them on this fateful night—he could hear rain in the distance. Guy ropes quivered and hummed. Hide walls thumped and rippled—Barghast warriors were pouring into the encampment as if the wild drumming had summoned them, and Krin caught word that Maral Eb had arrived, along with the Senan warriors Tool had taken with him. Bakal among them. Slayer, liberator of all the Barghast. Who would forget this night?

Who would forget, too, that it was Krin, firstborn son of Humbrall Taur's own uncle, who was the first to fuck Hetan?

The thought hardened him. He stood above her, waiting until her wild eyes slanted across his own, and when that fevered gaze stuttered and then returned to lock with his, Krin smiled. He saw the shock, and then the hurt that was betrayal, and he nodded. 'Allies, Hetan? You lost them all. When you proclaimed him as your husband. When you championed your father's madness.'

Hega pushed back in. 'Where are your children, Hetan? Shall I tell you? Dead and cold in the darkness—'

Krin backhanded her across the face. 'Your time with her is over, widow! Go! Run and hide in your hut!'

Hega wiped blood from her lips, and then, eyes flashing, she wheeled, shouting, 'Bavalt son of Krin! Tonight you are mine!'

Krin almost sent a knife her way as she pushed through the crowd. *A knife, son, long before she wraps round you, long before you sink into that spider's hole.*

As the significance of Hega's words worked through, there was laughter, and Krin was stung by the contempt he heard all round him. He looked down at Hetan—she was still staring up at him, eyes unwavering.

Shame flooded through him, stealing his hardness fast as a mother's kiss.

'Don't think you can watch,' he said in a growl, crouching to pull her on to her stomach. As he tugged down her leathers, excitement returned—awakened by anger as much as anything else. Oh, and triumph, for many men among the Senan had looked upon her with lust and desire, and they were even now arguing their turn with her. *But I am the first. I will make you forget Onos Toolan. I will remind you of the manhood of the Barghast.* He knelt, pushing with his knees to splay wide her legs. 'Lift up to me, whore. Show them all how you accept your fate.'

Pain was a distant roar. Something cold and sharp now filled her skull, fixed like spears to her eyes, and every face she had looked upon since awakening once more had pierced her like lightning, arcing in from her eyes, igniting her brain. Faces—those expressions and all that they revealed—they were burned upon her soul now.

She had played with Hega's younger sister—they had been so close—but that woman was somewhere in the crowd now, flat-eyed, walled-off. Jayviss had spun a fine horse blanket as a wedding gift, and Hetan remembered her bright, proud smile when Hetan singled her out in giving public thanks. Balamit, daughter of a shoulderwoman, had been her keeper on the Night of First Blood, when Hetan was barely twelve years old. She'd sat awake, holding her hand, until sleep finally took the child now a woman.

Yedin often played with the twins—

Husband, I have betrayed you! In my misery, in my pathetic self-pity—I knew, I knew this was coming, how could it not? My children—I have abandoned them.

They killed them, husband. They killed our children!

'Lift up to meet me, whore.'

Krin, I used to laugh at your hunger for me, sick as it was. Does my father's ghost wait for you, Krin? Does he witness this, and what you demand of me?

Does he understand my shame?

Krin now punishes me. He is only the first, but no matter how many there are, the punishment will never be enough.

Now . . . now I understand the mind of a hobbled woman. I understand.

And she lifted up to meet him.

The wretches saw him before he saw them, and they saw, too, the heavy knife in his hand.

None would deny that the twins were clever, nasty creatures, in the manner of newborn snakes, and so when they spun round and fled, Sathand Gril was not surprised. But one of them was burdened with a child, and that child was now screaming.

Oh, they might silence him in the only way possible—a suffocating hand over his mouth and nose, thus sparing Sathand the blood on his own hands—and he waited for that as he plunged in pursuit, but the shrieks went on.

He could run them down, and so he would, eventually. He was sure they knew that they were already dead. Well, if they would make it a game, he would play. One last gesture of childhood, before he took childhood away. Would they squeal when he caught them? An interesting question. If not immediately, then later, yes, later they would squeal indeed.

Scrabbling sounds ahead, at the slumped end of a rock-walled defile, and Sathand lumbered forward—yes, there was one of them, with that boy in her arms, trying to climb up the scree—

The boulder very nearly killed him, dropping down to hammer into his shoulder. He howled in pain, stumbled—caught the flash of the other twin up on the edge of the wall to his left. 'You rotted piece of dung!' he snarled. 'You will pay for that!'

No longer a game. He would give them hurt for hurt, and then more. He would make them regret such stupid attempts.

Ahead, the girl with the boy had given up trying to climb the fan of sand and gravel, and had instead dropped down and to the right, vanishing into a crevasse. A moment later the other girl darted in after her sister.

The whole thing had been an act. A trap. So clever, weren't they?

Mind blackening with fury, he bolted after them.

Setoc was tugging at his arms. 'Cafal! Get up!'

It was too late. He was seeing all there was to see. Cursed by his own gods.

Could he close hands about their necks, one by one, and choke the life from them, he vowed he would.

His beloved sister—he had screamed as the hatchet chopped down. He had fallen to his knees when Krin stepped up to her, and now he sought to claw out his own eyes—although the visions behind them proved indifferent to the damage done to them. Blood ran with tears—he would dig and dig until never again would he look upon the world—but it seemed that blindness would for ever elude him.

He watched Krin rape his bloodkin. He heard the exhortations from the hundreds of warriors gathered round. He saw Bakal, gaunt and his eyes luminous, stumble into view, saw the man's horror as all the blood left his face, saw as the great slayer of Onos Toolan twisted round and fled, as if the Warleader's ghostly hand was reaching for him. But it was just the rape of a hobbled woman—not even considered rape, in fact. Just . . . *using*.

And Sathand Gril, whom he had hunted beside in years past, was now hunting Stavi and Storii, and Absi who flailed in Stavi's arms as if in full awareness that this new world he had found was crumbling around him, that death was coming to take him before he could as much as taste it. And the boy was outraged, indignant, defiant. Confused. Terrified.

Too much. No heart could withstand such visions.

Setoc tugged at his arms, fought to keep his hands from his face. 'We must keep going! The wolves—'

'Hood take the wolves!'

'But he won't, you fool! He won't—but someone will! We must hurry, Cafal—'

His hand lashed out, caught her flush on the side of her head. The way her neck twisted round as she fell horrified him. Crying out, he crawled to her.

The wolves were ghosts no longer. Blood clouded his eyes, dripped down in a mockery of tears. 'Setoc!' She was still a child, still so young, so thin—

The wolves howled, a chorus that deafened him, that drove him face-first into the frozen dirt. *Gods, my head! Stop! Stop, I beg you!* If he screamed, he could not hear it. The beasts surged on all sides, closing in and in—they wanted him.

They wanted his blood.

From somewhere sounded a hunter's horn.

Cafal leapt to his feet and ran. Ran from the world.

When her sister passed the wailing boy over, Stavi clutched him to her chest. Storii moved past her as they emerged from the fissure, grasping handfuls of tawny grasses to pull her way up the slope. This range of broken hills was narrow, an island of scoured limestone, and beyond it the land levelled out, flat, with nowhere to hide. She struggled up the tattered slope, gasping, the boy beating at her face with his tiny fists.

They were going to die. She knew that now. Their life in all its loose joy, its perfect security, was suddenly gone. She longed for yesterday, she longed for the solid presence that was her adopted father. Once more the sight of his face, a face wide and weathered, with every feature exaggerated, oversized, his soft eyes that had only ever looked upon his children with love—against the twins, it had seemed anger was impossible. Even disapproval wavered in a heartbeat. They had worked him like river clay, but they had known that beneath that clay there was a thing of iron, a thing of great power. He was a truth, resolute, unbreakable. They worked him because they knew that truth.

Where was he now? What had happened to their mother? Why was Sathand Gril hunting them? Why was he going to kill them?

Storii ran ahead, darting like a hare seeking cover, but there was none to be found. Ghoulish light painted the plain as the Slashes etched the night. A cruel wind cut into their faces, and the mass of storm clouds blotted out the north sky. The sight of her sister's panic was like a knife in Stavi's chest—the world was as broken as the hills behind them, as broken as the vicious look in Sathand's eyes. She could have dropped that rock on his skull—she should have—but the thought of hurting him that much had horrified her. A part of her had wanted to believe that if she could manage to break his shoulder, he would give up, he would return to the camp. She knew now, bleak with despair, that such faith—that all of this could be so easily righted—was ridiculous. Her error in judgement was going to see them all killed.

Hearing Sathand climb out of the fissure, Stavi cried out, running as fast as her legs could carry her. All at once the boy she held went quiet, and his arms wrapped tight round her neck, hands clutching her hair.

He understood as well. Motionless as a doe in the grasses not ten paces from a hunting cat, his eyes wide, his breath panting and hot against the side of her neck.

Tears streamed down her cheeks—he clutched her in the belief that she could protect him, that she could defend his life. But she knew she couldn't. She wasn't old enough. She wasn't fierce enough.

She saw Storii look back over a shoulder, saw her falter—

Sathand's heavy footfalls were closing fast.

'Go!' Stavi shrieked at her sister. '*Just go!*'

Instead, Storii bent down, scooped up a rock, and then sprinted back towards them.

Fierce sister, brave sister. You fool.

They would die together then.

Stavi stumbled, fell to her knees, skinning them on the grasses. The burning pain loosed more tears, and everything blurred. The boy kicked himself free—now he would run, fast as his short legs could take him—

Instead, he stood and faced the charging warrior. The man was not a stranger, was he? No, he was kin. And in the shadow of a kinsman there was safety.

Stavi whispered, 'Not this time.'

Sathand readied the knife in his hand, slowing now that the chase had come to an end—nowhere for them to go, was there?

His shoulder throbbed, and sharp bolts of pain shot out from his collar bone—he couldn't even lift that arm—she'd broken it.

But the warrior's rage was fading. *They did not choose their parents—who does? They're just . . . unlucky. But that is the way of the world. Spawn of rulers inherit more than power—they inherit what happens when that power collapses. When a night of blood is unleashed, and ambition floods black as locust ink.*

He saw the stone gripped by one of the girls and nodded, pleased with her defiance. Only half her blood was Barghast, but it had awakened for this. He would have to take her down first.

'What has happened?' asked the girl standing beside the boy. 'Sathand?'

He bared his teeth. The right words now could take the fight out of them. 'You are orphans,' he said. 'Your par—'

The stone was a blur, catching him a glancing blow above his left eye. He cursed in pain and surprise, and then shook his head. Blood ran down into the eye, blinding it. 'Spirits haunt you!' He laughed. 'I've taken fewer wounds in battle! But . . . one eye is enough. One working arm, too.' Sathand edged forward.

The boy's eyes were wide, uncomprehending. He suddenly smiled and held out his arms.

Sathand faltered. *Yes, I've taken you up and swung you in the air. I've tickled you until you shrieked. But that is done now.* He lifted the knife.

The twins stared, unmoving. Would they protect the boy? He suspected they would. With teeth and nails, they would.

We are as we are. 'I am proud of you,' he said. 'Proud of you all. But this must be.'

The boy cried out as if in joy.

Something slammed into his back. He staggered. The knife fell from his hand. Sathand frowned down at it. Why would he drop his weapon? Why was his strength draining away? On his knees, his lone eye finding the boy's, level at last. *No, he's not looking at me. He's looking past me.* Confusion, a roar of something rushing deep in his skull. The warrior twisted round.

The second arrow took him in the forehead, dead centre, punching through the bone and ploughing into the brain.

He never saw where it came from.

Stavi sank down on watery legs. Her sister ran to their brother and snatched him up. He yelped in delight.

In the greenish gloom, she could see the silhouette of a warrior astride a horse, sixty or more paces away. Something in that seemed unreal, and she struggled to track it down, and then gasped. *That arrow. Sathand was turning round—in motion—and yet . . . sixty paces away! In this wind!* Her gaze fell to Sathand's corpse. She squinted at that arrow. *I've seen the like before. I've—*Stavi moaned and crawled forward until she could close a hand about the arrow's shaft. 'Father made this.'

The rider was closing at a loose canter.

Behind Stavi, her sister said, 'That's not Father.'

'No—but look at the arrows!'

Storii set the boy down once more. 'I see them. I see them, Stavi.'

As the warrior drew closer, they could see that something was wrong with him— and with his horse. The beast was too gaunt, its hide worn away in patches, its long, stained teeth gleaming, the holes of its eyes lightless, lifeless.

The rider was no better. But he held a horn bow, and within a saddle quiver a dozen or so of Onos Toolan's arrows were visible. A cowl was draped over the warrior's head, hiding what was left of his face and seemingly impervious to the gale. He let his horse slow to a walk, and then halted it ten paces away with a twitch of the reins.

He seemed to study them, and Stavi caught an instant's blurred spark of a single eye. 'The boy, yes,' he said in Daru—but it was Daru with a Malazan accent. 'But not you two.'

A chill crept over Stavi, and she felt her twin's hand slip into hers.

'That,' he said after a moment, 'perhaps came out wrong. What I meant was, I see him in the boy, but not in you two.'

'You knew him,' Storii accused. She pointed at the quiver. 'He made those! You stole them!'

'He made them, yes, as a gift to me. But that was long ago. Before you were born.'

'Toc the Younger,' whispered Stavi.

'He spoke of me?'

That this warrior was undead did not matter. Both girls rushed forward, one to either side, to hug his withered thighs. At their touch, he might have flinched, but then he reached out with his hands. Hesitated, only to settle them on the heads of the girls.

As they wept in relief.

The son of Onos Toolan had not moved, but he watched, and he was still smiling.

Setoc's eyes fluttered open. The instant she moved her head, blinding agony lanced through her skull. She groaned. The night was luminous, the familiar green tinge of her own world. She could feel the wolves, no longer as solid beasts surrounding her, but as ghosts once more. Ephemeral, hovering, pensive.

A cold wind was blowing, lightning flashing to the north. Shivering, nauseated, Setoc forced herself on to her knees. The dark plain spun round her. She tried to recall what had happened. Had she fallen?

'Cafal?'

As if in answer thunder rumbled.

Blinking, she sat back on her haunches, looked round through bleared eyes. She found herself in the centre of a ring of half-buried boulders, the jade glow from the south adding a green hint to their silvery sheen. Whatever patterns had been carved upon them had long since weathered away to the barest of indentations.

But there was power here. Old. As old as anything on this plain. Whispering sorrow to the empty land as the wind curled between the bleached humps.

The wolf ghosts slowly circled, as if drawn inward to this ring of stones and its mournful dirge.

There was no sign of Cafal. Had he been lost in the realm of the Beast Hold? If so, then he was lost for ever, falling back and back through the centuries, into times so ancient not a single human walked the world, where no blood-line was drawn to divide the hunter from the hunted—animals all. He would fall victim eventually, prey to some sharp-eyed predator. His death would be a lonely one, so lonely she suspected he would welcome it.

Even the will of the wolves in their hundreds of thousands could barely brush the immensity of the lost Hold's power.

She huddled against the cold and the ache in her head.

The rain arrived with the rage of hornets.

Whipped by the wind and lashed by the rain, Cafal reached the edge of the encampment. Hearth-fires flared and dipped beneath the deluge, but even in the fitful light he could see huddled crowds and the smaller makeshift camps of the Barahn clustered round the edges. Figures hurried between the rows, hunched against the weather. He could see pickets here and there, haphazardly arranged with some of the posts abandoned.

When lightning lit the scene it seemed to seethe before his eyes.

Somewhere in there was his sister. Being used again and again. Warriors he had known all his life were pushing bloody paths into her, eager to join in the breaking of this once proud, beautiful and powerful woman. Cafal and Tool had spoken often of outlawing the tradition of hobbling, but too many resisted the casting away of traditions, even those as vicious as this one.

He could not change what had happened, all the damage already done, but he could steal her away, he could save her the months, even years, of horror that awaited her.

Cafal crouched, studying the Barghast camp.

Swathed in furs, Balamit made her way back to her yurt. Such a night! Too many years bowing to that bitch, too many years stepping from her path, eyes downcast as was demanded by Hetan's position as wife to the Warleader. Well, the whore was paying the soul's coin for that now, wasn't she?

Balamit ran through her mind once more the fateful moment when Hega's hatchet descended. The way Hetan's whole body contorted in pain and shock, the deafening shriek cutting like a knife in the air. Some people lived as if privilege was something they were born to, as if everyone else was a lesser being, as if their domination was a natural truth. Well, there were other truths in nature, weren't there? The gathering of the pack could bring down the fiercest wolf.

Balamit grinned as the rain spat icy against her face. Not just a pack, but a thousand of her kind! The pushed-down, the murky shapes that made up the common crowd, the ignored subjects of contempt. No, this was a worldly lesson, was it not? And, sweetest truth of all, *we are far from finished.*

Maral Eb was a fool, just another one of those superior bastards who thought their damned farts could buy a crown. Bakal was a much better choice—a Senan for one, and the Barahn were no match for her tribe—to think they could just step into the stirrup, when they'd not even had a hand in killing Onos Toolan, why, it was—

A huge shape stepped out from between two tarp-covered dung-piles, bulled into her hard enough to make her stagger. The figure reached out to right her even as she hissed a curse, and then the hand clutched tighter and snatched her close. A knife-blade sank between her ribs, the point slicing her heart in half.

Blinking in the sudden darkness, Balamit's legs gave out beneath her, and she fell to the mud.

Her killer left her there without a backward glance.

Jayviss finally rose from her place close to the fire, as the flames had at last guttered out beneath the rain. Her bones ached terribly when the weather turned cold, and the injustice of that galled her. She was barely into her fifth decade, after all—but now that she was among the powerful, she could demand a ritual of healing to scour clean the rot in her joints, and she would have to pay nothing, nothing at all.

Sekara had promised. And Sekara knew the importance of favouring her allies.

Life would be good once again, as it had been in her youth. She could take as many men as she wanted. She could take for herself the finest furs to stay warm at night. She might even buy a D'ras slave or two, to work oils into her skin and make her supple once more. She'd heard they could take away stretch marks and make sagging breasts taut. They could smooth the wrinkles from her face, even the deep bird-track between her brows, where had gathered a lifetime of injustice and anger.

Seeing the last of the coals blacken at her feet, she turned away.

Two warriors stood before her. Barahn—one of them Kashat, Maral Eb's brother. The other warrior she did not recognize.

'What do you want?' Jayviss demanded in sudden fear.

'Just this,' Kashat said, and he lashed out.

She caught the gleam of an etched blade. A sting against her throat, and suddenly heat poured down the front of her chest.

The ache in her bones vanished, and after a time the knot in her brow slowly relaxed, making her face, as the rain kissed it, almost young again.

Little Yedin crouched beside the body of Hega, staring at the pool of blood that still steamed even as raindrops pounded its surface. The nightmare would not end, and she could still feel the heat of the iron paddle she'd used to cauterize

Hetan's feet. It pulsed like fever up her arms, but could not reach the sickly chill wrapped about her heart.

So terrible a thing, and Hega had made her do it, because Hega had a way of making people do things, especially young people. She'd show them the danger-ous thing in her eyes and nothing more would be needed. But Hetan had never been mean, had never been anything but nice, gentle, always ready with a wink. And Stavi and Storii, too. Always making Yedin laugh, the acts they put on, all their crazy ideas and plans.

The world ahead was suddenly dark, unknowable. And look here, someone had gone and killed Hega. The dangerous thing in her eyes hadn't been enough, but then, what was?

What those men did to Hetan—

A hand grabbed the back of her collar and she was lifted from the ground.

A stranger's face stared at her own.

From one side another voice spoke, 'She won't remember much of this, Sagal.'

'One of Hega's imps.'

'Even so—'

Sagal set her down and she tottered on wobbly legs. He put his huge hands against the sides of her head. Their eyes met and Yedin saw a darkness come to life there, a dangerous thing—

Sagal snapped her neck, dropped the body on to Hega's. 'Find Befka. One more to go this night. For you.'

'What of Sekara and Stolmen?'

Sagal grinned. 'Kashat and me—we're saving the best for last. Now go, Corit.'

The warrior nodded. 'And then I get my turn with Hetan.'

'She's worth it, the way she squirms in the mud.'

Once Strahl had left, Bakal sat alone in his yurt. His wife would not return this night, he knew, and he admitted he would be not too upset if she did not return at all. Amazing, that surprises could come to a marriage after so many years. The skein of rules was torn apart this night, strands winging on the black wind. A thousand possibilities awakened in people's souls. Long-buried feuds clawed up out of the ground and knives dripped. A warrior could look into a friend's eyes and see a stranger, could look into a mate's eyes and see the flare of wicked desires.

She wanted another man but Bakal was in the way. That man wanted her in turn, but *his* wife was in the way. Bakal's wife had stood before him, a half-smile playing on her face, a living thing pleased to deliver pain—if pain was possible, which he'd found, to his own bemusement, it was not. The moment she'd real-ized that, her visage had transformed into hatred.

When she left, she was holding her knife. Between her and her new lover, a woman would die tonight.

Would he stop them?

He had not yet decided. Nothing raged inside him. Nothing smouldered an in-stant's breath from bursting into flame. Even the effort of thinking exhausted him.

'Blood runs down.' An ancient saying among the Barghast. When a ruler is murdered, a thousand blades are drawn, and the weak become savage. *We are in our night of madness. An enemy marches to find us, and we are locked in a frenzy of senseless slaughter, killing our own.* He could hear faint screams cutting through the howling wind.

The image of his wife's face, so ugly in its wants, rose before him.

No, I will not let it be. He rose, cast about until he found his coin-scaled hauberk. If he was too late to save the woman, he would kill both his wife and her lover. An act, he decided, devoid of madness.

'Find him!' exhorted Sekara. 'His brothers are out—killing our allies! Maral Eb is alone—'

'He is not,' said Stolmen. 'On this night, that would be insane.'

She glared at him. Huge in his armour, a heavy hook-knife in one gauntleted hand, a miserable look on his stolid face. 'Tell him you would discuss the alliance of the Gadra Clan—just find a reason. Once you cut his throat—'

'His brothers will hunt me down and kill me. Listen, woman, you told me you wanted Maral Eb to command the warriors—'

'I did not expect him to move on us this very night! Hega is dead! Jayviss is nowhere to be found. Nor is Balamit. Don't you understand what's happening?'

'It seems you don't. If they're all dead, then we are next.'

'He'll not dare touch us! I have a hundred slayers—I have spies in every clan! No, he still needs us—'

'He won't think that way when I try and kill him.'

'Don't just try, husband. Do it and be sure of it. Leave his fool brothers to me.'

The rain was hammering down on the thick hides humped over the sapling frame of the yurt's ceiling. Someone shrieked nearby. Stolmen's face was ashen. *Spirits below, he doesn't even need the paint tonight.* 'Must I do this, too? Are you worth *anything* to me?'

'Sekara, I stand here ready to give up my life—to protect you. Once this night is done, the madness will end. We need only survive—'

'I'm not interested in just surviving!'

He stared at her, as if seeing her for the first time. Something in that look, so strange on his face, sent a tendril of disquiet through Sekara. She stepped closer, set a hand on his scaled chest. 'I understand, husband. Know that I value what you are doing. I just don't think it's necessary, that's all. Please, do this for me. Find Maral Eb—and if you see that he is surrounded by bodyguards, then return here. We will know that he fears for his life—we will have struck our first blow against him without even raising a hand.'

He sighed, turned to the entrance.

The wind gusted round him when he pushed aside the flap and stepped outside. Sekara backed away from the chill.

A moment later she heard a heavy thump, and then something rolled into the tent wall before sliding to the ground.

Heart in her throat, hands to her mouth, Sekara froze.

Sagal was the first to enter the yurt. His brother Kashat came in behind him, a tulwar in one hand, the blade slick with watery blood.

'Sekara the Vile,' said Sagal, smiling. ''Tis a cruel night.'

'I'm glad he's dead,' she replied, nodding to the dripping blade. 'Useless. A burden upon my every ambition.'

'Ambitions, yes,' muttered Kashat, looking round. 'You've done yourself well, I see.'

'I have many, many friends.'

'We know,' said Sagal. 'We've met with some of them this night.'

'Maral Eb needs me—he needs what I know. My spies, my assassins. As a widow, I am no threat to you, any of you. Your brother shall be Warleader, and I will make certain he is unassailed.'

Sagal shrugged. 'We'll think on it.'

Licking her lips, she nodded. 'Tell Maral Eb, I will come to him tomorrow. We have much to discuss. There will be rivals—what of Bakal? Have you thought of him? I can lead you straight to his yurt, let me get my cloak—'

'No need for that,' Sagal said. 'Bakal is no longer a threat. A shame, the slayer of Onos Toolan dying so suddenly.' He glanced across at Kashat. 'Choked on something, wasn't it?'

'Something,' Kashat replied.

Sekara said, 'There will be others—ones that I know about that you don't. Among the Senan and even my own people.'

'Yes yes, you'll sell them all, woman.'

'I serve the Warleader.'

'We'll see, won't we?' At that Sagal swung round, left the yurt. Kashat paused to clean her husband's blood from his tulwar, using a priceless banner hanging from the ridge-pole. He paused at the entrance, grinned at her, and then followed his brother.

Sekara staggered back a step, sank down on to a travel chest. Shivering gripped her, shook her, rattled her very bones. She struggled to swallow, but her mouth and throat were too dry. She laced together her hands on her lap, but they slipped free of each other—she could not take hold . . . of anything.

The wind buffeted the hide walls, cold air lancing in from the entrance flap, which had not settled properly back into place. She should get up, fix that. Instead, she sat, shaking, fighting her slippery hands. 'Stolmen,' she whispered. 'Husband. You left me. Abandoned me. I almost'—she gasped—'I almost died!'

She looked to where he had been standing, so big, so solid, and her eyes strayed to the banner and its horrid, wet stain. 'Ruined it,' she said in a mutter. 'Ruined it.' She used to run it through her hands. That silk. Through and through, like a stream of wealth that never wetted her palms. But no more. She would feel the crust of his blood, the dust speckling her hands.

'He should have seen it coming. He should have.'

———

Bakal had just cinched on his weapon belt while sitting down, struggling one-handed with the clasp, when the two Barahn warriors rushed in. He surged up-right. The hookblade hissed free of its scabbard and he caught the heavy slash of a descending tulwar. His lighter weapon's blade snapped clean just above the hilt.

He leapt close and drove the jagged stub into the warrior's throat. Blood poured on to his hand.

The other was coming round the brazier.

Bakal back-stepped from the warrior drowning in his own blood. He had noth-ing with which to defend himself.

Wife, it seems you win—

A shape loomed behind the Barahn who was readying his tulwar for a decapi-tating cut. Hookblades licked both sides of his throat. The brazier hissed and crackled as spatters struck it. Reeling, the Barahn stumbled to one side, fell over the armour chest, leaving one twitching foot visible from where stood Bakal.

Gasping, his arm in agony, he swung his gaze to the newcomer.

'Cafal.'

'I dreamed it,' the priest said, face twisting. 'Your hand, your knife—into his heart—'

'Did you dream as well, Cafal, who delivered that blow?'

The burly warrior sagged, stepped clumsily away from the entrance, his eyes dropping to the weapons in his hands. 'I've come for her.'

'Not tonight.'

The hookblades snapped back into fighting position and Cafal made to ad-vance on him, but Bakal raised his hand.

'I will help you, but not tonight—she fell unconscious—two dozen men, maybe more, had used her. Any more and she would die and they won't let that hap-pen. The women have her, Cafal. They will tend to her, cackling like starlings—you know of what I speak. Until her flesh is healed—you cannot get into that hut. Those women will tear you to pieces. My—my wife went there first, before her other . . . tasks. To see, to join in—she, she laughed at me. At my horror. Cafal, she *laughed*.'

The priest's visage was furrowed in cuts—he had been clawing at his own face, Bakal realized. 'Your dreams,' he whispered, eyes widening. 'You saw.'

'I saw.'

'Cafal . . .'

'But it's not over. They don't know that—none of them know that. Our gods are howling. In terror.' He fixed wild eyes on Bakal. 'Did they think they could get away with that? Did they forget what he was? Where he came from? He will take them into his hands and he will *crush* them!' He bared his teeth. 'And I will stand back—do you hear me? I will stand back, Bakal, and do nothing.'

'Your sister—'

He started, as if Bakal had slapped him. 'Yes. I will wait—'

'You can't hide here, Cafal. More of Maral Eb's assassins will come for me—'

'This night is almost spent,' the priest said. 'The madness is already blowing itself out. Find your allies, Bakal, gather them close.'

'Come back in three days,' Bakal said. 'I will help you. We'll get her out—away. But . . . Cafal, you must know—'

The man flinched. 'It will be too late,' he said in a wretched tone. 'Yes, I know. I know.'

'Go with the last of the night,' Bakal said. He went to find one of his older weapons, and then paused, stared down at the two corpses crumpled on the floor. 'I must do something now. One last thing.' He lifted bleak eyes to the priest. 'It seems the madness is not quite blown out.'

The rider emerged from the night with a child before him on the saddle. Two young girls flanked the horse, staggering with exhaustion.

As the storm's ragged tail scudded south, taking the rain with it, Setoc watched the strangers approach. The man, she knew, was a revenant, an undead soldier of the Reaper. But, seated as she was in the centre of this ring of stones, she knew she had nothing to fear. This ancient power defied the hunger for blood—it was, she knew now, made for that very purpose. Against Elder Gods and their ceaseless thirst, it was a sanctuary, and was and would ever remain so.

He drew rein just outside the ring, as she knew he must.

Setoc rose to her feet, eyeing the girls. Dressed as Barghast, but neither was purely of that blood. Twins. Eyes dull with fading shock, and a kind of fearless calm rising in its place. The small boy, she saw, was smiling at her.

The revenant lifted the child with one hand, to which the boy clung like a Bolkando ape, and carefully set him down on the ground.

'Take them,' the revenant said to Setoc, and the undead eyes he fixed upon her blazed—one human and wrinkled in death, the other bright and amber—the eye of a wolf.

Setoc gasped. 'You are not the Reaper's servant!'

'It's my flaw,' he replied.

'What is?'

'Cursed by . . . indecision. Take them, camp within the circle. Wait.'

'For what?'

The rider collected the reins and drew the beast round. 'For his war to end, Destriant.' He hesitated, and then said, 'We leave when I return.'

She watched him ride away, westward, as if fleeing the rising sun. The two girls closed on the boy and each took one of his hands. They edged warily closer.

Setoc sighed. 'You are Hetan's get?'

Nods.

'I am a friend of your uncle. Cafal. No,' she added wearily, 'I do not know where he has gone. Perhaps,' she added, thinking of the revenant's last words, 'he will return. For now, come closer, I will make a fire. You can eat, and then rest.'

Once inside the circle, the boy pulled loose from his sisters' hands and walked to the southwestern edge of the ring, where he stared at seemingly nothing on the dark horizon, and then he began a strange, rhythmic babbling. Almost a song.

At the sound, Setoc shivered. When she turned to the twins, she saw that they had found her bedroll and were now wrapped together in its folds. Fast asleep.

Must have been a long walk.

The carrion eaters had picked away the last strip of meat. Jackals had chewed on the bones but found even their powerful jaws could not crush them sufficiently to swallow the splinters down, nor could they grind the ends as was their habit. In the end, they left the fragments scattered in the trampled grasses. Besides, there was more to be found, not only in this place, but in numerous others across the plain. It was proving a season for fly-swarmed muzzles and full bellies.

After a few days all the scavengers had left, abandoning the scene to the sun, wind and stars. The blades of grasses prickled free of dried-up blood, the roots thickened on enriched soil, and insects crawled like the teeth of the earth, devouring all they could.

On a night with a storm raging to the east and south, a night when foreign gods howled and ghost wolves raced like a tidal flood across an unseen landscape, when the campfires of armies whipped and stuttered, and the jackals ran first one way and then another, as the stench of spilled blood brushed them on all sides, the buried valley with its sprawl of boulders and bones and its ash heap of burnt remains began to move, here and there. Fragments drawing together. Forming into ribs, phalanges, leg bones, vertebrae—as if imbued with iron seeking a lodestone, they slid and rolled in fits and starts.

The wind that had begun in the southeast now rushed over the land, a gale like a hundred thousand voices rising, ever rising. Grasses whipped into frenzied motion. Dust swirled up and round and spun, filling the air with grit.

In the still cloudless sky overhead, the Slashes seemed to pulse and waver, as if seen through waves of heat.

Bones clattered together. From beneath the mass of boulders and crumpled armour in the valley, pieces of rotting flesh pulled free, tendons writhing like serpents, ligaments wriggling like worms, climbing free and crawling closer to the heap of bones—which were edging into a pattern, re-forming a recognizable shape— a skeleton, loosely assembled, but the bones were neither Akrynnai nor Barghast. These were thicker, with high ridges where heavy muscles once gripped tight. The skull that had been crushed was now complete once more, battered and scorched. It sat motionless, upper teeth on the ground, until the mandible clicked up against it, and then pushed beneath it, tilting the skull back, until the jaw's hinges slipped into their joints.

Flesh and desiccated skin, random clumps of filthy hair. Ligaments gripped long bones, ends fusing to join them into limbs. Twisted coils of muscle found tendons and were pulled flat as the tendons grew taut. An arm was knitted together, scores of finger bones clumping at the end of the wrist.

Rotting meat bound the vertebrae into a serpentine curl. Ribs sank into indentations on the sides of the sternum and lifted it clear of the ground.

When the Slashes were gouging the horizon to the southeast, and the wind was dying in fitful gusts, a body lay on the grasses. Fragments of skin joined to enclose it, each seam knitting like a scar. Strands of hair found root on the pate of the skull.

As the wind fell away, there was the distant sound of singing. An old woman's rough, enfeebled voice, and in the music of that song there were fists closed into tight knots, there was muscle building to terrible violence, and faces immune to the sun's heat and life's pity. The voice ensorcelled, drawing power from the land's deepest memories.

Dawn crept to the horizon, bled colour into the sky.

And a T'lan Imass rose from the ground. Walked, with slow, unsteady strides, to the fire-annealed flint sword left lying close to the Barghast pyre. A withered but oversized hand reached down and closed about the grip, lifting the weapon clear.

Onos T'oolan faced southeast. And then set out.

He had a people to kill.

Chapter Sixteen

Sower of words out from the hungry shade
The seeds in your wake drink the sun
And the roots burst from their shells—
This is a wilderness of your own making,
Green chaos too real to countenance
Your words unravel the paths and blind the trail
With crowding boles and the future is lost
To the world of possibilities you so nurtured
In that hungry shade—sower of words
Heed the truth they will make, for all they
Need is a rain of tears and the light of day

THE EASE OF SHADOWS (SIMPLE WORDS)
BEVELA DELIK

Desecration's gift was silence. the once-blessed boulder, massive as a wagon, was shattered. Nearby was a sinkhole at the base of which a spring struggled to feed a small pool of black water. The bones of gazelle and rodents studded the grasses and the stones of the old stream bed that stretched down from the sinkhole's edge, testament to the water's poison.

This silence was crowded with truths, most of them so horrid in nature as to leave Sechul Lath trembling. Shoulders hunched, arms wrapped about his torso, he stared at the rising sun. Kilmandaros was picking through the broken rock, as if pleased to examine her own handiwork of millennia past. Errastas had collected a handful of pebbles and was tossing them into the pool one by one—each stone vanished without a sound, leaving no ripples. These details seemed to amuse the Errant, if the half-smile on his face was any indication.

Sechul Lath knew enough to not trust appearances when it came to an Elder God infamous for misdirection. He might be contemplating his satisfaction at the undeniable imperative of his summons, or he might be anticipating crushing the throat of an upstart god. Or someone less deserving. He was the Errant, after all. His temple was betrayal, his altar mocking mischance, and in that temple and upon that altar he sacrificed mortal souls, motivated solely by whim. And, perhaps, boredom. It was the luxury of his power that he so cherished, that he so wanted back.

But it's done. Can't you see that? Our time is over with. We cannot play that game again. The children have inherited this world, and all the others we once terrorized. We squandered all we had—we believed in our own omnipotence. This world—Errastas, you cannot get back what no longer exists.

'I will have my throne,' you said. And the thousand faces laying claim to it, each one momentarily bright and then fading, they all just blur together. Entire lives lost in an instant's blink. If you win, you will have your throne, Errastas, and you will stand behind it, as you once did, and your presence will give the lie to mortal ambitions and dreams, to every aspiration of just rule, of equity. Of peace and prosperity.

You will turn it all into dust—every dream, nothing but dust, sifting down through their hands.

But, Elder God, these humans—they have left you behind. They don't need you to turn to dust all their dreams. They don't need anyone else to do that. 'This,' he said, facing Errastas, 'is what we should intend.'

The Errant's brows rose, his solitary eye bright. 'What, pray tell?'

'To stand before our children—the young gods—and tell them the truth.'

'Which is?'

'Everything they claim as their own can be found in the mortal soul. Those gods, Errastas, are not needed. Like us, they have no purpose. None at all. Like us, they are a waste of space. Irrelevant.'

The Errant's hands twitched. He flung away the pebbles. 'Is misery all we get from you, Knuckles? We have not yet launched our war and you've already surrendered.'

'I have,' agreed Sechul Lath, 'but that is a notion you do not fully understand. There is more than one kind of surrender—'

'Indeed,' snapped the Errant, 'yet the face of each one is the same—a coward's face!'

Knuckles eyed him, amused.

Errastas made a fist. 'What,' he said in a low rasp, 'is so funny?'

'The one who surrenders to his own delusions is, by your terms, no less a coward than any other.'

Kilmandaros straightened. She had taken upon herself the body of a Tel Akai, still towering above them but not quite as massively as before. She smiled without humour at the Errant. 'Play no games with this one, Errastas. Not bones, not words. He will tie your brain in knots and make your head ache.'

Errastas glared at her. 'Do you think me a simpleton?'

The smile vanished. 'Clearly, you think that of me.'

'When you think with your fists, don't complain when you appear to others as witless.'

'But I complain with my fists as well,' she replied. 'And when I do, even you have no choice but to listen, Errastas. Now, best be careful, for I feel in the mood for complaining. We have stood here all night, whilst the ether beyond this place has stirred something to life—my nerves are on fire, even here, where all lies in lifeless ruin. You say you have summoned the others. Where are they?'

'Coming,' the Errant replied.

'How many?'

'Enough.'

Knuckles started. 'Who defies you?'

'It is not defiance! Rather—must I explain myself?'

'It might help,' said Sechul Lath.

'I am not defied by choice. Draconus—within Dragnipur it's not likely he hears anything. Grizzin Farl is, I think, dead. His corporeal flesh is no more.' He hesitated, and then added with a scowl, 'Ardata alone has managed to evade me, but she was never of much use anyway, was she?'

'Then where—'

'I see one,' Kilmandaros said, pointing to the north. 'Taste of the blood, she was wise to take that shape! But oh, I can smell the stench of Eleint upon her!'

'Restrain yourself,' Errastas said. 'She's been dead too long for you to smell anything.'

'I said—'

'You imagine, nothing more. Tiam's daughter did not outlive her mother—this thing has embraced the Ritual of Tellann—she is less than she once was.'

'Less,' said Knuckles, 'and more, I think.'

Errastas snorted, unaware of Sechul Lath's deliberate mockery.

Kilmandaros was visibly shaking with her fury. 'It was *her*,' she hissed. 'Last night. That singing—*she awakened the ancient power! Olar Ethil!*'

Sechul Lath could see sudden worry on the Errant's face. Already, things were spiralling out of his control.

A voice spoke behind them. 'I too felt as much.'

They turned to see Mael standing beside the sinkhole. He had an old man's body and an old man's face and the watery eyes he fixed on the Errant were cold. 'This is already unravelling, Errant. War is like that—all the players lose control. "Chaos takes the sword."'

Errastas snorted a second time. 'Quoting Anomander Rake? Really, Mael. Besides he spoke that in prophecy. The other resonances came later.'

'Yes,' muttered Mael, 'about that prophecy . . .'

Sechul Lath waited for him to continue but Mael fell silent, squinting now at Olar Ethil. She had long ago chosen the body of an Imass woman, wide-hipped, heavy-breasted. When Knuckles had last seen her, he recalled, she was still mortal. He remembered the strange headgear she had worn, for all the world like a woven corded basket. With no holes for her eyes, or her mouth. Matron of all the bonecasters, mother to an entire race. *But even mothers have secrets.*

She no longer wore the mask. Nor much in the way of flesh. Desiccated, little more than sinews and bone. A T'lan Imass. Snakeskin webbing hung from her shoulders, to which various mysterious objects had been tied—holed pebbles, nuggets of uncut gems, bone tubes that might be whistles or curse-traps, soul-catchers of hollowed antler, a knotted bundle of tiny dead birds. A roughly made obsidian knife was tucked in her cord belt.

Her smile was an inadvertent thing, the teeth oversized and stained deep amber. Nothing glittered from the sockets of her eyes.

'How did it go again?' Sechul asked her. 'Your mother's lover and child both? Just how did you beget yourself, Olar Ethil?'

'Eleint!' growled Kilmandaros.

Olar Ethil spoke: 'I have travelled in the realm of birth-fires. I have sailed the dead sky of Kallor's Curse. I have seen all I needed to see.' Her neck creaked and made grinding noises as she turned her head until she faced the Errant. 'You were nowhere to be found. You hid behind your pathetic throne, ever proving the illusion of power—the world has long ago grasped your message, though by nature it will not ever heed it. You, Errastas, are wasting your time.'

Sechul Lath was startled that her words so closely matched his own thoughts. *Save it, Olar Ethil. He does not listen.*

She then turned to Mael. 'Your daughters run wild.'

The old man shrugged. 'Daughters will do that. Rather, they should do that. I would be disappointed otherwise. It's a poor father who does not nudge and then cut loose—as I am sure the Errant will eagerly chime, once he gathers what wits he has left. When that witch stole your eye, what else spilled out?'

Olar Ethil cackled.

Errastas straightened. 'I have summoned you. You could not deny me, not one of you!'

'Saved me hunting you down,' said Mael. 'You have much to answer for, Errant. Your eagerness to ruin mortal lives—'

'It is what I do! What I have always done—and you should talk, Mael! How many millions of souls have you drowned? Hundreds of millions, all to feed your power. No, old man, do not dare chide me.'

'What do you want?' Mael asked. 'You don't really think we can win this war, do you?'

'You have not been paying attention,' Errastas replied. 'The gods are gathering. Against the Fallen One—they don't want to share this world—'

'Nor, it seems, do you.'

'We never denied any ascendant a place in our pantheon, Mael.'

'Really?'

The Errant bared his teeth. 'Was there ever the risk of running out of mortal blood? Our children betrayed us, by turning away from that source of power, by accepting what K'rul offered them. And in turn, they *denied* us our rightful place.'

'So where is he, then?' Sechul asked. 'Brother K'rul? And the Sister of Cold Nights? What of the Wolves, who ruled this realm before humans even arrived? Errastas, did you reach some private decision to not invite them?'

'K'rul deserves the fate awaiting the gods—his was the cruellest betrayal of all.' The Errant gestured dismissively, 'One could never reason with the Wolves—I have long given up trying. Leave them the Beast Throne, it's where they belong.'

'And,' Mael added dryly, 'ambition does not beset them. Lucky for you.'

'For us.'

At the Errant's correction, Mael simply shrugged.

Olar Ethil cackled again, and then said, 'None of you understand anything. Too long hiding from the world. Things are coming back. Rising. The stupid humans have not even noticed.' She paused, now that she had everyone's attention, and something like breath rattled from her. 'Kallor understood—he saw Silverfox for what she was. Is. Do any of you really think the time of the T'lan Imass is over? And though she made a youthful error in releasing the First Sword, I have forgiven her. Indeed, I have seen to his return.

'And what of the Jaghut? Popping up like poison mushrooms! So comforting to believe they are incapable of working together—but then, lies can prove very comforting. What if I told you that in the Wastelands but a handful of days ago, *fourteen* undead Jaghut annihilated a hundred Nah'ruk? What if I told you that five thousand humans carrying the blood of the Tiste Andii have walked the Road of Gallan? That one with Royal Andiian blood has ridden through the gates of dead Kharkanas? And the Road of Gallan? Why, upon *that* path of blood hunt the Tiste Liosan. And,' her head creaked as she regarded Kilmandaros, 'something far worse. No, you are all blind. The Crippled God? He is nothing. Among the gods, his allies break and scatter. Among the mortals, corruption devours his cult, and his followers are the wasted and the lost—Kaminsod has no army to summon to his defence. His body lies in pieces scattered across seven continents. He is as good as dead.' She jabbed a bony finger at the Errant. 'Even the Deck of Dragons has a new Master, and I tell you this, Errastas. You cannot stand against him. You're *not enough*.'

The wind moaned in the wake of her words.

None spoke. Even Errastas stood as one stunned.

Bones clattering, Olar Ethil walked to the shattered boulder. 'Kilmandaros,' she said, 'you are a cow. A miserable, brainless cow. The Imass made this sanctuary in an act of love, as a place where not one of us could reach in to poison their souls.'

Kilmandaros clenched her fists, staring blankly at the old woman. 'I don't care,' she said.

'I can destroy the young gods,' Errastas suddenly said. 'Every one of them.'

'And have you told Kilmandaros about your secret killer?' Olar Ethil inquired. 'Oh yes, I knew you were there. I understand what you've done. What you intend.'

Sechul Lath frowned. He'd lost this trail. Too soon after Olar Ethil's speech, from which he still reeled. *Secret killer?*

'Tell her,' Olar Ethil went on, 'of the Eleint.'

'When the slayer has been unleashed, when it has done what it must,' Errastas smiled, 'then Kilmandaros shall receive a gift.'

'She slays the slayer.'

'So that, when all is done, we alone are left standing. Olar Ethil, all those things you spoke of, they are irrelevant. The Jaghut are too few, living or undead, to pose any sort of threat. The dust of the T'lan Imass has crossed the ocean and even now closes upon the shores of Assail, and we all know what awaits them there. And Kharkanas is dead, as you say. What matter that one of Royal Andiian blood has returned to it? Mother Dark is turned away from her children. As for the Tiste Liosan, they are leaderless and do any of us here actually think Osserc will go back to them?'

Sechul Lath hugged himself tighter. He would not look at Kilmandaros. Neither Olar Ethil nor Errastas had spoken of the Forkrul Assail. Were they ignorant?

Was the knowledge that Sechul held within him—that Kilmandaros possessed, as well—truly a secret? *Olar Ethil, we cannot trust you. Errastas should never have invited you here. You are worse than K'rul. More of a threat to us than Draconus, or Edgewalker. You are Eleint and you are T'lan Imass, and both were ever beyond our control.*

'The Master of the Deck,' said Mael, 'has an ally. One that even you, Olar Ethil, seem unaware of, and she is more of a wild knuckle than anything Sechul Lath was ever in the habit of casting.' His cold eyes settled upon the Errant. 'You would devour our children, but even that desire proves that you have lost touch, that you—we, all of us here—are nothing more than the spent forces of history. Errant, our children have grown up. Do you understand the significance of that?'

'What stupidity are you—'

'Old enough,' cut in Sechul Lath, all at once comprehending, 'to have children of their own.' *Abyss below!*

Errastas blinked, and then gathered himself, waving a hand in dismissal. 'Easily crushed once we have dealt with their parents, don't you think?'

'Crushed. As we were?'

Errastas glared at Mael.

Sechul Lath barked a wry laugh. 'I see your point, Mael. Our killing the gods could simply clear the way for their children.'

'This is ridiculous,' said Errastas. 'I have sensed nothing of . . . grandchildren. Nothing at all.'

'Hood summons the dead,' Olar Ethil said, as if Mael's words had launched her down a track only she could see. 'The fourteen undead Jaghut—they did not belong to him. He has no control over them. They were summoned by an ascendant who had been mortal only a few years ago.' She faced Mael. 'I have seen the dead. They march, not as some mindless mob, but as would an army. It is as if the world on the lifeless side of Hood's Gates has *changed*.'

Mael nodded. 'Prompting the question, what is Hood up to? He was once a Jaghut. Since when do Jaghut delegate? Olar Ethil, who was this recent ascendant?'

'Twice brought into the world of worship. Once, by a tribal people, and named Iskar Jarak. A bringer of wisdom, a saviour. And the other time, as the commander of a company of soldiers—promised to ascension by a song woven by a Tanno Spiritwalker. Yes, the entire company ascended upon death.'

'Soldiers?' Errastas was frowning. 'Ascended?' Confused. Frightened by the notion.

'And what name did he possess among these ascended soldiers?' Mael asked.

'Whiskeyjack. He was a Malazan.'

'A Malazan.' Mael nodded. 'So too is the Master of the Deck. And so too is the Master's unpredictable, unknowable ally—the Adjunct Tavore, who leads a Malazan army east, across the Wastelands. Leads them,' he turned to Sechul Lath, 'into Kolanse.'

The bastard knows! He understands the game we're playing! It was a struggle not to betray everything with a glance to Kilmandaros. Seeing the quiet knowledge in Mael's eyes chilled him.

Olar Ethil bestowed on them a third cackle, a gift no one welcomed.

Errastas was no fool. Suspicion glittered from his eye as he studied Sechul Lath. 'Well now,' he said in a low tone, 'all those nights tossing the bones for Kilmandaros here . . . I suppose you found plenty of things to talk about, killing time as it were. Some *plans*, perhaps, Setch? Foolish of me, I see now, to imagine you were content with simply wasting away, leaving it all behind. It seems,' and the smile he gave was dangerous, 'you played me. Using all of your most impressive talents.'

'This meeting,' drawled Mael, 'was premature. Errant, consider yourself banished from Letheras. If I sense your return, I will hunt you down and drown you as easily as you did Feather Witch.'

He walked to the spring, descended into the sinkhole and vanished from sight.

Olar Ethil pointed a finger at Kilmandaros, waggled it warningly, and then set off, northward. A miserable collection of skin and bones. The three remaining Elder Gods watched her walk away. When the T'lan Imass was perhaps fifty paces distant, she veered into her draconic form, dust billowing, and then lifted skyward.

A low growl came from Kilmandaros.

Sechul Lath rubbed at his face. He sighed. 'The power you seek to bleed dry, Errastas,' he said, facing the Errant, 'well, it turns out we were all working to similar ends.'

'You anticipated me.'

Sechul shrugged. 'We had no expectation that you would just show up at the door.'

'I do not appreciate being played, Setch. Do you see no value to my alliance?'

'You have irrevocably altered the strategy. As Mael pointed out, though perhaps for different reasons, this meeting was premature. Now our enemies are awakened to us.' He sighed again. 'Had you stayed away, stayed quiet, why, Mother and I— we'd have stolen that power from beneath their very noses.'

'To share solely between the two of you.'

'To the victors the spoils.' *But none of this mad usurpation, this desire to return to what once was.* 'But, I dare say, had you come begging, we might well have proved magnanimous . . . for old times' sake.'

'I see.'

Kilmandaros faced him. 'Do you, Master of the Holds? You summoned us here, only to find that you are the weakest, the most ignorant among us. You forced us all—Sechul, Mael, Olar Ethil, to put you in your place. To make you realize that you alone have been wallowing in self-pity and wasting away doing nothing. Perhaps Mael thinks our time is done, but then, why has he ensured that his worship is on the ascent? That a Jhistal Priest of Mael now rises to take the throne of the most powerful empire this world has seen since the time of Kallor and Dessimbelackis? Who among us has proved the witless one this day?'

With a snarl, Errastas swung away from them.

Sechul turned to his mother. 'Mael was warning us, I think. This Adjunct Tavore he spoke of. These infernal Malazans.'

'And the children of the gods. Yes, many warnings, Sechul. From Olar Ethil as well. Jaghut, T'lan Imass, Tiste Andii—bah!'

'All subtlety is lost,' agreed Sechul Lath. 'Errastas, return to us, we have much to discuss. Come now, I will tell you of the path we have already prepared. I will tell you just how close we are to achieving all that we desire. And you, in turn, can tell us how you intend to release the Otataral Eleint. Such exchanges are the heart of an alliance, yes?'

His poor friend had been humiliated. Well, there was value in lessons. *So long as it's someone else receiving them.*

Kilmandaros spoke: 'Time has come to build anew the bridge, Errastas. Let us ensure that it is strong, immune to fire and all manner of threat. Tell me of how I will kill the Otataral Eleint—for that promise alone I will stand with you.'

He returned to them, eventually, as they had known he would.

'They never burned the bridge behind them before finishing the one in front of them. But there then came a day when the bridges ran out. Nowhere ahead. The road's end.' Cuttle reached out and a clay jug was pressed into his hand. He drank down another mouthful, and would not look at the young soldiers with whom he shared the brazier. The rush of water under the flat-bottomed hull was an incessant wet scrape, far too close beneath the sapper for his liking. Silly, he reflected, being a marine who hated water. Rivers, lakes, seas and rain, he despised them all.

'Black Coral,' someone said in a low, almost reverent tone.

'Like the ten thousand veins in a hand,' Cuttle said sourly, 'stories spread out. Not a single Malazan army out there doesn't know about them. The Chain of Dogs, the Fall. The Aren Way. Blackdog. Pale. And . . . Black Coral, where died the Bridgeburners.'

'They didn't all die,' objected that same soldier.

It was too dark to make out the speaker, and Cuttle didn't recognize the voice. He shrugged. 'High Mage Quick Ben. Dead Hedge—but he died there and that's why we call him Dead Hedge, so that's one who didn't make it. Maybe a handful of others did. But the Bridgeburners were finished and that's how the histories will tell it. Destroyed at Black Coral, at the close of the Pannion War. The few who crawl out of such things, well, they vanish like the last wisps of smoke.' He drank down another mouthful. 'It's how things are.'

'It's said they were dropped into the city by the Black Moranth,' another soldier said. 'And they went and took the palace—went straight for the Pannion Domin himself. Was Whiskeyjack dead by then? Does anyone know? Why wasn't he leading them? If he'd done that, maybe they wouldn't have—'

'Stupid, that kind of thinking.' Cuttle shook his head. He could hear the faint sweeps from the other barges—the damned river was packed with them, with Letherii crews struggling day and night to avoid collisions and tangled lines. Bonehunters and Commander Brys's escort—almost twenty thousand soldiers, support elements, pack animals—the whole lot, riding this river south. Better than walking. Better, and worse, reminding him of past landings, marines struggling beneath the hail of arrows and slingstones, dying and drowning. Barges raging with flames, the shrieks of burning men and women.

Not that they would be landing under fire. Not this time. This was a leisurely journey, surrounded by allies. It was all so civilized, so peaceful, that Cuttle's nerves were shredded. 'It's just how it played out. Choices are made, accidents happen, the fates fall. Remember that, when our own falls on us.'

'Nobody's going to sing songs about us,' the hidden speaker said. 'We're not the Bridgeburners. Not the Grey Swords. Not Coltaine's Seventh. She said as much, the Adjunct did.'

'Open that last jug,' someone advised.

Cuttle finished the one in his hand. Three fast swallows. He sent the empty vessel over the side. ' "Bonehunters",' he said. 'Was that Fiddler's idea? Maybe. Can't really remember.' *I just remember the desperation. I remember the Adjunct. And Aren's quiet streets and empty walls. I remember being broken, and now I'm wondering if anything's changed, anything at all.* 'Histories, they're just what's survived. But they're not the whole story, because the whole story can never be known. Think of all the histories we've gone and lost. Not just kingdoms and empires, but the histories inside every one of us, every person who ever lived.' As the new jug of peach rum came within reach Cuttle's hand snapped out to snare it. 'What do you want? Any of you? You want the fame of the Bridgeburners? Why? They're all dead. You want a great cause to fight for? To die for? Show me something worth *that*.'

He finally looked up, glared at the half-circle of coal-lit faces, so young, so bleak now.

And from behind him, a new voice spoke. 'Showing's not enough, Cuttle. You need to see, you need to *know*. I'm standing here, listening to you, and I'm hearing the rum; it's running through a soldier who thinks he's at his end.'

Cuttle took another drink. 'Just talk, Sergeant Gesler. That's all.'

'Bad talk,' Gesler said, pushing in. Soldiers moved aside to make room as he settled down opposite the sapper. 'They wanted stories, Cuttle. Not a reason to throw themselves over the side. Those are the cheapest reasons of all—you should know that.'

'Speaking freely here, Sergeant, that's how it was.'

'I know. This ain't no official dressing down. That's for your own sergeant to do, and if he was here, he'd be tacking up your hide right about now. No, you and me, we're just two old soldiers here.'

Cuttle gave a sharp nod. 'Fine, then. I was just saying—'

'I know. I heard. Glory's expensive.'

'Exactly.'

'And it's not worth it.'

'Right.'

'But that's where you're wrong, Cuttle.'

There was speaking freely and that's what this was, but Cuttle wasn't a fool. 'If you say so.'

'All those choices you complained about, the ones that take you to the place you can't avoid, the place none of us can escape. You say it's not worth it, Cuttle, that's a choice, too. It's the one you've decided to make. And maybe you want company, and that's what all this is about. Personally, I think you're a damned liability—not because you ain't a good soldier. You are. And I know for a fact that when the iron sings, having you at my back makes no itch. But you keep pissing on the coals, Cuttle, and then complaining about the smell.'

'I'm a sapper with a handful of munitions, Gesler. When they're gone, then I step into the crossbow ranks, and I ain't as fast a loader as I used to be.'

'I already said it's not your soldiering that worries me. Maybe you reload slower, but your shots will count and don't try saying otherwise.'

Cuttle answered with a gruff nod. He'd asked for this, this dressing down that wasn't supposed to happen. This speaking freely that was now nailing him like a rusty nail to the wooden deck. In front of a bunch of pups.

'There were sappers,' Gesler continued, 'long before the munitions came along. In fact, the sappers will need veterans like you, the ones who remember those days.' He paused, and then said, 'I got you a question, Cuttle.'

'Go on.'

'Tell me the one thing that can rot an army.'

'Time with nothing to do.'

'Nothing to do but talk. Why is it the people with the least useful things to say do most of the talking?'

The unseen speaker from earlier spoke up behind Gesler, 'Because their pile of shit never gets smaller, Sergeant. In fact, just keeps getting bigger.'

Cuttle heard the relief in the laughter that followed. His face was burning, but that might just be the coals, or the rum, or both. Could be he was just drunk. 'All this talk of piss and shit,' he muttered, forcing himself upright. He weaved, managed to find his balance, and then turned about and stumbled off in the direction of the stern.

As the sapper staggered away, Gesler said, 'You that spoke, behind me—that you, Widdershins?'

'Aye, Sergeant. Was wandering past when I heard the bleating.'

'Go after him, make sure he doesn't topple o'er the rail.'

'Aye, Sergeant. And, uh, thanks, he was dragging even me down.'

Gesler rubbed at his face. His skin felt loose and slack, all suppleness long gone. Getting old, he decided, was miserable. 'Needs a shaking awake,' he said under his breath. 'And don't we all. Here, give me that jug, I've worked up a thirst.'

He didn't recognize any of the faces he could make out round the brazier. They were young, foot-soldiers, the ones who'd barely known a fight since joining up. They'd watched the marines assault Y'Ghatan, and fight on the landing in Malaz City. They'd watched those marines set off to invade the Letherii mainland. They'd done a lot of watching. And no amount of marching, or drilling, or war-games could make a young soldier hungrier for glory than did all that watching.

He knew how they looked upon the marines. He knew how they bandied the names back and forth, the legends in the making. Throatslitter, Deadsmell, Hellian, Masan Gilani, Crump, Mayfly and all the rest. He knew how they damn-near worshipped Sergeant Fiddler. *And gods forbid anything bad should happen to him.*

Maybe Cuttle had a point with all that pushing down. On things like glory, the making of legends. Maybe he was undermining all those romantic notions for a good reason. *Don't hold to any faith. Even legends die.* Gesler shivered, drank down a mouthful of rum.

Tasted like shit.

Bottle slipped away. He'd listened to Cuttle. He'd watched Gesler slide morosely into the sapper's place, settling in for a night of drinking.

The entire army lounged on the open decks. Getting bored and lazy. After the eastward trek from Letheras, they'd crossed River Lether and marched through the rich lands to the south, finally reaching this river, known as the Gress. No shortage of food, drink, or whores the whole damned way. A sidling pace, a march that barely raised a sweat. League upon league of bickering, nasty hangovers and nobody having a clue what they were up to, where they were going, and what was waiting for them.

A joke ran through the ranks that, after this river journey ended at the city of Gress on the Dracons Sea, the entire army would simply swing back westward, come up round to Letheras again, and start the whole thing over, round and round, and round. Nobody laughed much. It was the kind of joke that wouldn't go away, and when it no longer fitted the circumstances, why, it would twist a tad and start its run all over again. *Like dysentery.*

The forty-two barges that had been awaiting them south of the Bluerose Range, just beyond the Gress's cataracts, were all new, built specifically for transporting the army downstream. Once at the journey's end, with all the soldiers and supplies off-loaded, the barges would be dismantled and carried with the army overland to the West Kryn River, where they'd be rebuilt and sent on their way down to the Inside Hyacinth Reach, and from there on to the D'rhasilhani—who had purchased the wood. The Letherii were clever that way. If you could take something and make a profit from it once, why not twice? It was, Bottle supposed, an admirable trait. Maybe. He could imagine that such predilections could become a fever, a poison in the soul.

He walked to the nearest unoccupied rail and stared out over the jade-lit water. The hulk of another barge blocked the shoreline opposite. The night air was filled with flitting bats. He could make out a figure over there, doing what Bottle was doing, and he wondered if he knew him, or her. The squads were scattered. Probably someone's bright idea about knitting new ties and friendships among the soldiery. Or, the even brighter realization that the squads needed a break from staring at each other's ugly faces. Mix 'em up to keep 'em from killing each other. Hood knew, he wasn't missing Koryk or even Smiles. Just damned bad luck finding himself on the same deck as Cuttle.

The man was a walking plague of the spirit. Almost as bad as Fist Blistig. But then, what army didn't have them? Sour, stone-eyed, using their every breath to bitch. He used to admire soldiers like that, the ones who'd seen it all and were still waiting to be impressed. The ones who looked at a recruit's face as if studying a death-mask. Now, he realized, he despised such soldiers.

Could be that was unfair, though. The misery and horror that got them to that cold, lifeless place was nothing to long for in one's own life. Was it? What he and all the other younger soldiers had to live with, then, was the curse of the survivors, the veteran's brand leaking like a septic wound. It stained. It fouled. It killed dreams.

He wasn't one of them. Had no desire to join their ranks. And could not imagine an entire army consisting of such twisted, scarred creatures. *But that was the Bridgeburners. That was Coltaine's, by the end, anyway. Onearm's Host. Greymane's Stone. Dassem's First Sword. Nothing but the dead-eyed.* He shivered, drawing his rain-cape tighter. The Bonehunters was another army headed that way—if it didn't tear itself apart first.

But wait, Bottle. You've forgotten Fiddler. He's nothing like the rest. He still cares . . . doesn't he? Even the question troubled him. His sergeant had been growing ever more distant of late. A generational thing? Maybe. The burden of rank? Possibly, since when he'd been a Bridgeburner, he'd had no responsibilities beyond that of a regular soldier. A sapper, in fact, and sappers were notorious for the threat they presented to their own comrades, never mind the enemy. So, not just a regular but an irresponsible one at that. But now Fid was a sergeant, and a whole lot more. Reader of the Deck of Dragons. Legendary survivor of the Bridgeburners. He was the iron stake driven deep into the ground, and no matter how fierce the raging winds, he held fast—and everyone in turn clung to him, the whole damned army, it seemed. *We hold tight. Not to the Adjunct. Not to Quick Ben or Fist Keneb. We hold tight to Fiddler, a damned sergeant.*

Hood's breath. This sounds bad. I shouldn't be thinking of things this way. Fid deserves better. He deserves to have his life back.

No wonder he ran when she wanted the reading.

The black water swirled past, oblivious to the maelstrom of his thoughts, carrying what it could down to the distant sea. Cold with the memories of snow and ice in the high mountains, slowing with the silts of overturned earth and stones worn down to dust. Huge turtles slid through the muck far below. Blood-drinking eels— little more than jaws and tail—slithered in the currents, seeking the soft bellies of massive carp and catfish. Silt blooms billowed and rolled over rounded stones and gravel banks. Bedded in muck, amphorae of fired clay, fragments of corroded metal —tools, fittings, weapons—and the smooth, vaguely furry long bones of countless animals—the floor of this river was crowded indeed, unfurled like a scroll, writing a history down to the sea.

He had already freed his mind to wander, sliding from spark to spark among the multitude of creatures beneath the spinning surface. It had become something of a habit. Wherever he found himself, he sent out tendrils, spreading like roots to expand his skein of awareness. Without it, he felt lost. And yet, such sensitivity was not always a gift. Even as he came to comprehend the vast interconnectedness of things, so too grew the suspicion that each life possessed its circle, closed-in, virtually blind to all that lay outside. No matter the scale, no matter the pretensions of the things within that circle, no matter even their beliefs, they travelled in profound ignorance of the vastness of the universe beyond.

The mind could do no better. It wasn't built for profundity, and each time it touched upon the wondrous, it slid away, unable to find purchase. *No, we do fine with wood-chips flying from the axe's bite, the dowels we drive home, the seeds we scatter, the taste of ale in our mouths, the touch of love and desire at our fingertips. Comfort doesn't lie in the mystery of the unknown and the unknowable. It lies in the home we dwell in, the faces we recognize, the past in our wake and the future we want for ourselves.*

All this is what is solid. All this is what we grasp hold of. Even as we long for the other.

Was the definition of religion as simple as that? Longing for the other? Fuelling that wish with faith, emulating desires through rituals? *That what we wish to be therefore is. That what we seek in truth exists. That in believing we create, and in creating we find.*

By that argument, is not the opposite equally true? That what we reject ceases. That 'truth' is born in what we seek. That we create in order to believe. That we find only what we have created.

That wonder does not exist outside ourselves?

By our belief, we create the gods. And so, in turn, we can destroy them. With a single thought. A moment's refusal, an instant's denial.

Is this the real face of the war to come?

Chilled by the notion, Bottle contracted his senses, fled the indifferent sparks swirling through the river's depths. He needed something . . . closer. Something human. He needed his rats in the hold.

Deadsmell coughed, and then dropped two coins into the trough. 'You won't get your cage, Throatslitter. You watch as four comes back to me.' He looked up and scowled. 'What's wrong? Throw the bones, fool.'

'You must be kidding. Ebron?'

'Aye, he glamoured the trough.'

Throatslitter leaned forward. 'You got yourself a problem, Deadsmell—and heed this too, Ebron, since you're a mage and all—'

'Hey! I just told you—'

'And kindly, aye, you did. But listen anyway. Deadsmell, might be it's a safe thing to be magicking the casts and whatnot, so long as you're playing nitwits or fellow spooks or both. But, see, I'm Throatslitter, remember? I kill people for a living, in ways no reasonable, sane soldier could hope to imagine. Am I getting through here? You bring your talents to this game, maybe so will I.'

'Gods below,' Deadsmell said, 'no need to get all riled.'

'You cheated.'

'So?'

'With sorcery!'

'I'm not quick enough for the other stuff, not any more. So maybe I was desperate.'

'Maybe? Ebron—you got to agree here—a clean cheat, well, that's expected. But a magicked one, that's not acceptable. That's knife-kissing stuff, and if I wasn't so damned magnanimous, not to mention being sober enough to know that killing the squad healer's probably not a good idea, why, there'd be blood running a'tween the boards right now.'

'He's got a point, Deadsmell. Here I figured on joining this game all clean like—'

Deadsmell's snort cut him off. 'You threw a web over the whole field when you sat down, Ebron. I was just giving it a twist.'

Throatslitter stared, and then held up the first polished bone. 'See this, Ebron? Since you're so happy to magic everything, let's see how you do eating this. And the next one. In fact, how 'bout you eat them all?'

'Not a chance—'

Throatslitter lunged over the chalked-out field on the deck. Ebron shrieked.

Things got ugly, and Bottle's rat was lucky to escape unscathed.

Skulldeath sat huddled beneath blankets, staring morosely at the unconscious form of Hellian. She had passed out halfway through their love-making, which probably wasn't unusual. Another soldier was sitting nearby, studying the Seven Cities prince with a knowing expression on his face.

The young man's need for comfort and all the rest was not doomed this night, and in a short time he would slide over. It was a good thing that the only thing Hellian was possessive about was her rum and whatnot. She eyed a jug in someone else's hand with all the fiery jealousy of a jilted lover. In any case, a drunk she might be, but she was no fool when it came to Skulldeath's confused desires.

No, the real fool in the equation was sitting off to one side. Sergeant Urb, whose love for the woman glittered like the troubled waters of a spring, fed unceasingly from the bedrock of his childlike faith. A faith in the belief that one day her thoughts would clear, enough for her to see what was standing right in front of her. That the seduction of alcohol would suddenly sour.

The man was an idiot. But there were idiots aplenty in the world. An unending supply, in fact.

When Skulldeath finally stirred, Bottle edged out of the rat's mind. Watching things like that—love-making—was too creepy. Besides, hadn't his grandmother pounded into him the risk of deadly perversions offered by his talents? Oh, she had, she had indeed.

Skanarow moved up to stand alongside Captain Ruthan Gudd where he leaned on the rail.

'Dark waters,' she murmured.

'It's night.'

'You like keeping things simple, don't you?'

'It's because things are, Skanarow. All the complications we suffer through are hatched inside our own skulls.'

'Really? Doesn't make them any less real, though. Does it?'

He shrugged. 'Something you want?'

'Many things, Ruthan Gudd.'

He looked across at her—seemed startled to find how close she stood, almost as tall as he was, her Kanese eyes dark and gleaming—and then away again. 'And what makes you think I can help you with any of them?'

She smiled, though the captain was not paying attention, and it was a lovely smile. 'Who promoted you?' she asked.

'A raving lunatic.'

'Where?'

He raked fingers through his beard, scowled. 'And all this is in aid of what, precisely?'

'Kindly was right, you know. We need to work together. You, I want to know more about, Ruthan Gudd.'

'It's not worth it.'

She leaned on the railing. 'You're hiding, Captain. But that's all right. I'm good at finding things out. You were among the first list of officers for the Fourteenth. Meaning you were in Malaz City, already commissioned and awaiting attachment. Now, which armies washed up on Malaz Island too torn up to keep intact? The Eighth. The Thirteenth. Both from the Korelri Campaign. Now, the Eighth arrived at about the time the Fourteenth shipped out, but given the slow pace of the military ink-scratchers, it's not likely you were from the Eighth—besides, Faradan Sort was, and she doesn't know you. I asked. So, that leaves the Thirteenth. Which is rather . . . interesting. You served under Greymane—'

'I'm afraid you got it all wrong,' Ruthan Gudd cut in. 'I came in on a transfer from Nok's fleet, Skanarow. Wasn't even a marine—'

'Which ship did you serve on?'

'The *Dhenrabi*—'

'Which sank off the Strike Bight—'

'Aye—'

'About eighty years ago.'

He eyed her for a long moment. 'Now, that kind of recall verges on the obsessive, don't you think?'

'As opposed to pathological lying, Captain?'

'That was the first *Dhenrabi*. The second one slammed into the Wall at five knots. Of the two hundred and seventy-two on board, five of us were dragged out by the Stormguard.'

'You stood the Wall?'

'No, I was handed over in a prisoner exchange.'

'Into the Thirteenth?'

'Straight back to the fleet, Skanarow. We'd managed to capture four Mare triremes loaded with volunteers for the Wall—aye, hard to believe anyone would volunteer for that. In any case, the Stormguard were desperate for the new blood. So, you can put all your suspicions to rest, Captain. My history is dull and un-eventful and far from heroic. Some mysteries, Skanarow, aren't worth knowing.'

'All sounds very convincing, I'll grant you that.'

'But?'

She gave him another bright smile, and this one he saw. 'I still think you're a liar.'

He pushed himself away from the railing. 'Lots of rats on these barges, I've no-ticed.'

'We could go hunting.'

Ruthan Gudd paused, combed his beard, and then shrugged. 'Hardly worth the trouble, I should think.'

When he walked off, the Kanese woman hesitated, and then followed.

'Gods below,' Bottle muttered, 'everyone's getting it this night.' He felt a stab somewhere deep within him, an old, familiar one. He'd not been the kind of man that women chased down. He'd had friends who rolled from one bed to the next, every one of those beds soft and warm. He'd had no such fortune. The irony of the thing that visited him in his dreams was that much sharper, in how it mocked the truths of his life.

Not that she'd been appearing of late, not for a month. Maybe she'd grown tired of him. Maybe she'd taken all she needed, whatever that was. But those last few times had been frightening in their desperation, the fear in her unhuman eyes. He'd awaken to the stench of grass fires on the savannah, the sting of smoke in his eyes and the thunder of fleeing herds ringing in his skull. Sickened by the over-whelming sense of dislocation, he would lie shivering beneath his threadbare blan-kets like a fevered child.

A month of peace, but why then did her absence fill him with foreboding?

The barge opposite had slipped ahead, riding some vagary of the current, and he could now see the eastern shore of the river. A low bank of boulders and reeds and beyond that rolling plains lit a luminous green by the jade slashes in the southern sky. Those grasslands should have been teeming with wildlife. Instead, they were empty.

This continent felt older than Quon Tali, older than Seven Cities. It was a land that had been fed on for too long.

On the western shore, farmland formed narrow strips with one end reaching down to the river and the other, a third of a league inland, debouching on to the network of roads crisscrossing the region. Without these farms, the Letherii would starve. Yet Bottle was troubled by the dilapidated condition of many of the homesteads, the sagging barns and weed-ringed silos. Not a single stand of trees remained; even the stumps had been pulled from the withered earth. The alder and aspen windbreaks surrounding the farm buildings looked skeletal, not parched but perhaps diseased. Broad fans of topsoil formed muddy islands just beyond drainage channels, making that side of the river treacherous. The rich earth was drifting away.

Better indeed, then, to be facing the eastern shoreline, desolate as it was.

Some soldier had been making the circuit, pacing the barge as if it was a cage, and he'd heard the footsteps pass behind him twice since he'd first settled at the railing. This time, those boots came opposite him, hesitated, and then clumped closer.

A midnight-skinned woman arrived on his left, setting hands down on the rail.

Bottle searched frantically for her name, gave up and sighed. 'You're one of those Badan Gruk thought drowned, right?'

She glanced over. 'Sergeant Sinter.'

'With the beautiful sister—oh, not that you're not—'

'With the beautiful sister, aye. Her name's Kisswhere, which is a kind of knowing wink all on its own, isn't it? Sometimes names find you, not the other way round. So it was with my sister.'

'Not her original name, I take it.'

'You're Bottle. Fiddler's mage, the one he doesn't talk about—why's that?'

'Why doesn't he talk about me? How should I know? What all you sergeants yak about is no business of mine anyway—so if you're curious about something Fid's saying or not saying, why don't you just ask him?'

'I would, only he's not on this barge, is he?'

'Bad luck.'

'Bad luck, but then, there's you. When Fiddler lists his, uh, assets, it's like you don't even exist. So, I'm wondering, is it that he doesn't trust us? Or maybe it's you he doesn't trust? Two possibilities, two directions—unless you can think of another one?'

'Fid's been my only sergeant,' Bottle said. 'If he didn't trust me, he'd have long since got rid of me, don't you think?'

'So it's us he doesn't trust.'

'I don't think trust has anything to do with it, Sergeant.'

'Shaved knuckle, are you?'

'Not much of one, I'm afraid. But I suppose I'm all he's got. In his squad, I mean.'

She'd chopped short her hair, probably to cut down on the lice and whatnot—spending a few months in a foul cell had a way of making survivors neurotic about hygiene—and she now ran the fingers of both hands across her scalp. Her profile, Bottle noted with a start, was pretty much . . . perfect.

'Anyway,' Bottle said, even as his throat tightened, 'when you first showed up, I thought you were your sister.' And then he waited.

After a moment, she snorted. 'Well now, that took some work, I'd wager. Feeling lonely, huh?'

He tried to think of something to say that wouldn't sound pathetic. Came up with nothing. It all sounded pathetic.

Sinter leaned back down on the rail. She sighed. 'The first raiding parties us Dal Honese assembled—long before we were conquered—were always a mess. Suicidal, in fact. You see, no way was a woman going to give up the chance to join in, so it was always both men and women forming the group. But then, all the marriages and betrothals started making for trouble—husbands and wives didn't always join the same parties; sometimes one of them didn't even go. But a week or two on a raid, well, fighting and lust suckle from the same tit, right? So, rather than the whole village tearing itself apart in feuds, jealous rages and all that, it was decided that once a warrior—male or female, married or betrothed—left the village on a raid, all pre-existing ties no longer applied.'

'Ah. Seems a reasonable solution, I suppose.'

'That depends. Before you knew it, ten or twelve raiding parties would set out all at once. Leaving the village mostly empty. With the choice between living inside rules—even comfortable ones—and escaping them for a time, well, what would you choose? And even worse, once word reached the other tribes and they all adopted the same practice, well, all those raiding parties started bumping into each other. We had our first full-scale war on our hands. Why be a miserable farmer or herder with one wife or one husband, when you can be a warrior drumming a new partner every night? The entire Dal Hon confederacy almost self-destructed.'

'What saved it?'

'Two things. Exhaustion—oh, well, three things, now that I think on it. Exhaustion. Another was the ugly fact that even free stuff isn't for free. And finally, apart from imminent starvation, there were all those squalling babies showing up nine months later—a population explosion, in fact.'

Bottle was frowning. 'Sinter, you could have just said "no", you know. It's not the first time I've heard that word.'

'I gave up the Dal Honese life, Bottle, when I joined the Malazan marines.'

'Are you deliberately trying to confuse me?'

'No. Just saying that I'm being tugged two ways—I already got a man chasing me, but he's a bad swimmer and who knows which barge he's on right now. And I don't think I made any special promises. But then, back at the stern—where all the fun is—there's this soldier, a heavy, who looks like a marble statue—you know, the ones that show up at low tide off the Kanese coast. Like a god, but without all the seaweed—'

'All right, Sergeant, I see where you're going, or going back to, I mean. I'm no match for that, and if he's offering—'

'He is, but then, a drum with him might complicate things. I mean, I might get possessive.'

'But that's not likely with me.'

'Just my thinking.'

Bottle eyed the dark waters roiling past below, wondering how fast he'd sink, and how long it took to drown when one wasn't fighting it.

'Oh,' she murmured, 'I guess that was a rather deflating invitation, wasn't it?'

'Well put, Sergeant.'

'Okay, there's more.'

'More of what?' He could always open his wrists before plunging in. Cut down on the panic and such.

'I got senses about things, and sometimes people, too. Feelings. Curiosity. And I've learned it pays to follow up on that when I can. So, with you, I'm thinking it's worth my while to get to know you better. Because you're more than you first seem, and that's why Fid's not talking.'

'Very generous, Sergeant. Tell you what, how about we share a meal or two over the next few days, and leave it at that. At least for now.'

'I've made a mess of this, haven't I? All right, we've got lots of time. See you later, Bottle.'

Paralt poison, maybe a vial's worth, and then a knife to the heart to go with the slitted wrists, and then the drop over the side. Drowning? Nothing to it. He listened to the boots clump off, wondering if she'd pause at some point to wipe off what was left of him from her soles.

Some women were just out of reach. It was a fact. There were ones a man could get to, and then others he could only look at. And they in turn could do the calculations in the span of the barest flutter of an eye—walk up or walk over, or, if need be, run away from.

Apes did the same damned thing. And monkeys and parrots and flare snakes: the world was nothing but matches and mismatches, posturing and poses, the endless weighing of fitness. *It's a wonder the useless ones among us ever breed at all.*

A roofed enclosure provided accommodation for the Adjunct and her staff of one, Lostara Yil, as well as her dubious guest, the once-priest Banaschar. Screened from the insects, cool in the heat of the day and warm at night when the mists lifted from the water. One room functioned as a mobile headquarters, although in truth there was little need for administration whilst the army traversed the river. The single table bore the tacked maps—sketchy as they were—for the Wastelands and a few scraps marking out the scattered territories of Kolanse. These latter ones were renditions of coastlines for the most part, pilot surveys made in the interests of trade. The vast gap in knowledge lay between the Wastelands and those distant coasts.

Banaschar made a point of studying the maps when no one else was in the room. He wasn't interested in company, and conversations simply left him weary, often despondent. He could see the Adjunct's growing impatience, the flicker in her eyes that might be desperation. She was in a hurry, and Banaschar thought he knew why, but sympathy was too rich a sentiment to muster, even for her and the

Bonehunters who blindly followed her. Lostara Yil was perhaps more interesting. Certainly physically, not that he had any chance there. But it was the haunted shadow in her face that drew him to her, the stains of old guilt, the bitter flavours of regret and grievous loss. Such desires, of course, brought him face to face with his own perversions, his attraction to dissolution, the allure of the fallen. He would then tell himself that there was value in self-recognition. The challenge then was in measuring that value. A stack of gold coins? Three stacks? A handful of gems? A dusty burlap sack filled with dung? Value indeed, these unblinking eyes and their not-too-steady regard.

Fortunately, Lostara had little interest in him, relegating his hidden hungers to harmless imaginings, where the illusions served to gloss over the wretched realities. Dissolution palled in the details, even as blazing health and vigour could not but make a realist—like him—choke on irony. Death, after all, played against the odds with a cheating hand. It was a serious struggle to find righteous moralities in who lived and who died. He often thought of the bottle he reached for, and told himself: *Well, at least I know what will kill me. What about that paragon of perfect living, cut down by a mole on his back he couldn't even see? What about the glorious young giant who trips on his own sword in his first battle, bleeding out from a cut artery still thirty paces from the enemy? The idiot who falls down the stairs? Odds, don't talk to me about odds—take a good look at the Hounds' Toll if you don't believe me.*

Still, she wasn't eager for his company so that conversation would have to wait. Her aversion was disappointing and somewhat baffling. He was educated, wasn't he? And erudite, when sober and sometimes even when not sober. As capable of a good laugh as any defrocked priest with no future. And as for his own dissolution, well, he wasn't so far along as to have lost the roguish qualities that accompanied that dissolution, was he?

He could walk the decks, he supposed, but then he would have no choice but to let the miasma of the living swirl over him with all the rank insistence that too many sweaty, unwashed bodies could achieve. Not to mention the snatches of miserable conversation assailing him as he threaded through the prostrate, steaming forms—nothing was uglier, in fact, than soldiers at rest. Nothing was more insipid, more degenerate, or more honest. Who needed reminding that most people were either stupid, lazy or both?

No, ever since the sudden disappearance of Telorast and Curdle—almost a month ago, now—he was better off with these maps, especially the blank places that so beckoned him. They should be feeding his imagination, even his sense of wonder, but that wasn't why they so obsessed him. The unmarked spans of parchment and hide were like empty promises. The end of questions, the failure of the pursuit of knowledge. They were like forgotten dreams, ambitions abandoned to the pyres so long ago not a single fleck of ash remained.

He so wanted such blank spaces, spreading through the maps of his own history, the maps pinned to that curling table of bone that was the inside of his skull, the cave walls of his soul. *Here be thy failures.* Of resonance and mystery and truth. *Here be the mountains vanishing in the mists, never to return. Here*

*be the rivers sinking into the sands, and these are the sands that never rest. And
the sky that looks down and sees nothing. Here, aye, is the world behind me, for
I was never much of a map-maker, never much the surveyor of deeds.*

*Bleach out the faces, scour away the lives, scrape down the betrayals. Soak
these maps until all the inks blur and float and wash away.*

*It is the task of priests to offer absolution, after all. And I shall begin by ab-
solving myself.*

It's the lure, you see, of dissolution.

And so he studied the maps, all those empty spaces.

The river was a promise. That it could take the knife from Lostara's hand. A glimmering flash and gone, for ever gone. The silts could then swallow everything up,
making preservation and rot one and the same. The weight of the weapon would
defy the current—that was the important thing, the way it would refuse to be carried along. Some things could do that. Some things possessed the necessary weight
to acquire a will of their own.

She could follow the knife into the stream, but she knew she'd be tugged and
pulled, spun and rolled onward, because no one was a knife, no one could stay in
one place, no matter how hard they tried.

Lately, she had been thinking about the Red Blades, the faces and the life she
had once known. It was clear to her now that what was past had stopped moving,
but the sense of distance ever growing behind her was proving an illusion. Eddies
drew her back, and all those mired memories waited to catch her like hidden
snags.

A knife in hand, then, was sound wisdom. Best not surrender it to these troubled waters.

The Red Blades. She wondered if that elite company of fanatics still served the
Empress. Who would have taken command? Well, there were plenty, enough of
them to make the accession a bloody one. Had she been there, she too would have
made a try. A knife in hand, then, was an answer to many things. The Adjunct's irritation with it bordered on obsession, but she didn't understand. A weapon needs
to be maintained, after all. Honed, oiled, sliding quickly from the sheath. With that
knife, Lostara could cut herself loose whenever she liked.

A little earlier, she had sat at the evening meal with Tavore, a ritual of theirs
since leaving Letheras. Food and wine and not much in the way of conversation.
Every effort Lostara made to draw the Adjunct out, to come to know her better—
on a more personal level—had failed. For a long time, Lostara had concluded that
the woman in command of the Bonehunters was simply incapable of revealing
her vulnerable side. A flaw in her personality, as impossible to reject or change as
the colour of one's eyes. But Lostara was coming to believe that Tavore was afflicted with something else. She behaved as would a widow, the kind that then
made mourning a way of life, a ritualized assembly of habits. The light of day had
become a thing to turn away from. A gesture of invitation was answered with
muttered regrets. And the sorrowing mask never left her face.

A widow should not be commanding an army, and the thought of Adjunct Tavore leading that army into a war left Lostara both disturbed and frightened. To wear the mask of the widow was to reject life itself, scattering ashes into one's own path ahead, making the future as grey as the past. It was as if a pyre awaited them all, and at the moment of standing on the threshold of those murderous flames, she saw Tavore Paran stride forward, bold and resolute. And the army at her back would simply follow.

Two people seated across from one another, silent and trapped inside the world of their unspoken, private thoughts. The waters never blended, and the currents of the other were for ever strange and forbidding. There was no comfort in these suppers. They were, in fact, excruciating.

She quickly made her escape. Each night, retreating to the silk-walled chamber that was her bedroom. Where she sharpened and oiled her knife to drive away the red stain. Solitude could be an unwelcome place, but even the unwelcome could become habit.

Lostara had heard Banaschar's footsteps as he headed for his temple of maps. They were steady this night, those footsteps, which meant he was more or less sober. Not often the case, alas, which was too bad—or perhaps not. Sometimes—his clear, sober times—the bleak horror in his eyes could overwhelm. What had it been like, worshipping the Worm of Autumn, that pale bitch of decay? It would take a particular person to be drawn to such a thing. One for whom abject terror meant facing the nightmare. Or, conversely, one who hungered for what could not be avoided, the breaking down of flesh and dreams, the knowledge of the multitude of carrion eaters that waited for him at life's end.

But the Worm had cast him out. She had embraced all her other lovers, but not Banaschar. What did that mean to the man? The eaters would have to wait. The nightmare was not yet ready to meet his eyes. Obeisance to the inevitable was denied. Go away.

So, he would begin the rotting from the inside out. Spilling libations to drown the altar of his own soul. It was not desecration, it was worship.

The knife-edge went *snick* against the whetstone, steady as a heartbeat, each side in counter-beat as she flipped the blade in perfect rhythm. *Snick snick snick . . .*

Here in this cloth house, the others had their rituals. While she—she had her tasks of maintenance and preparedness. As befitted a soldier.

Stormy sat, back against the stepped rail that served as the barge's gunwale, positioned just so. Opposite, the jade slashes loomed in the south sky, fierce and ominous, and to his eyes it seemed the heavens were coming for him, a personal and most private vendetta. He tried to think of a guilt worthy of the magnitude. That pouch of coins he'd once lifted from a drunk noble in Falar? He'd been able to buy a decent knife with that. How old had he been? Ten? Twelve?

Maybe that passed-out woman he'd groped? That friend of his aunt's, easily twice his age—her tits had felt huge in his hands, heavy and wayward, and she'd moaned when he pinched her nipples, legs shifting and opening up—and what would a fifteen-year-old boy do with that? Well, the obvious, he supposed. In went his finger, and then a few more.

At some point she'd opened her eyes, frowned up at him, as if trying to place him. And then she'd sighed, the way a mother sighed when a wide-eyed son pressed her with awkward questions. And she took hold of that hand with all its probing fingers—he'd expected her to pull him out. Instead, she pushed the whole hand inside. He didn't even think that was possible.

Drunk women still held a certain fascination for Stormy, but he never went after them, in case he heard that sigh again, the one that could turn him back into a nervous, lip-licking fifteen-year-old. Guilt, aye, it was a terrible thing. The world tilted, came back, eager to crush him flat. Because doing something wrong pushed it the other way, didn't it? Keep pushing until you lose your footing and then wait for the sudden shadow, the huge thing blotting out the sky. Splat was another word for justice, as far as he was concerned. When it all comes back, aye.

He'd thrown his sister into a pond, once. But then, she'd been doing that to him for years, until that day when he realized he was bigger and stronger than she was. She'd hissed and spat her way back out, a look of outrage on her face. Recalling that, Stormy smiled. Justice by his own hand—no reason for feeling guilty about that one.

He'd killed plenty of people, of course, but only because they'd been trying to kill him and would have done just that if he'd let them. So that didn't count. It was the soldier's pact, after all, and for all the right decisions that kept one alive, a thousand things one could do nothing about could take a fool down. The enemy wasn't just the one in front of you—it was the uncertain ground underfoot, the stray arrow, the flash of blinding sunlight, the gust of grit in the eye, the sudden muscle cramp or the snapped blade. A soldier fought against a world of enemies each and every time, and walking free of that was a glory to make the gods jealous. Maybe the guilt showed up, but that was later, like an aftertaste when you can't even remember the taste itself. It was thin, not quite real, and to chew on it too long was just self-indulgence, as bad as probing a loose tooth.

He glared at the southern night sky. This celestial arbiter was indifferent to everything but the punishment it would deliver. Cut sharp as a gem, five jade swords were swinging down.

Of course they weren't all aiming at him. It just felt that way, on this steamy night with the river full of glinting eyes from those damned crocodiles—and they wanted him too. He'd heard from the barge hands about how they'd tip a boat if they could and then swarm the hapless victims, tearing them to pieces. He shivered.

'There's a glamour about you, Adjutant.'

Stormy looked up. 'I'm a corporal, High Mage.'

'And I'm a squad mage, aye.'

'You was a squad mage, just like I was maybe once an Adjutant, but now you're a High Mage and I'm a corporal.'

Quick Ben shrugged beneath his rain-cape, which he'd drawn tight. 'At first I thought it was just the Slashes, giving you that glow. But then, I saw how it flickered—like flames under your skin, Stormy.'

'You're seeing things. Go scare someone else.'

'Where's Gesler?'

'How should I know? On some other barge.'

'Fires are burning on the Wastelands.'

Stormy started, scowled up at Quick Ben. 'What's that?'

'Sorry?'

'What was that you were saying? About fires?'

'The ones under your skin?'

'No, the Wastelands.'

'No idea, Adjutant.' Quick Ben turned away, strangely ghostly, and then wandered off.

Stormy stared after him, chewing at his lower lip, and from the whiskers there he tasted bits of stew. His stomach rumbled.

They weren't on any official list, which meant no ink-stained clerk had a chance to break them up for this voyage. Sergeant Sunrise thrice-blessed the Errant for that. He lounged on a mass of spare bedrolls, feeling half-drunk with all this freedom. And the camaraderie. He already loved all the soldiers in this company, and the thought that it was a continuation of a famous Malazan company made him proud and eager to prove himself, and he knew he wasn't alone in that.

Dead Hedge was the perfect commander, as far as he was concerned. A man brimming with enthusiasm and boundless energy. Happy to be back, Sunrise surmised. From that dead place where the dead went after they were dead. It had been a long walk, or so Hedge had said when he'd been cajoling them all on the long march to the river. 'You think this is bad? Try walking on a plain of bones that stretches to the damned horizon! Try being chased by Deragoth'—whatever they were, they sounded bad—'and stalked by an evil T'lan Imass!' Sunrise wasn't sure what T'lan Imass were either, but Hedge had said they were evil so he was glad never to have met one.

'Death, dear soldiers, is just another warren. Any of you know what a warren is? . . . Gods, you might as well be living in mud huts! A warren, friends, is like a row of jugs on a shelf behind the bar. Pick one, pull the stopper, and drink. That's what mages do. Drink too much and it kills you. But just enough and you can use it to do magic. It's fuel, but each jug is different—tastes different, does different magic. Now, there's a few out there, like our High Mage, who can drink from 'em all, but that's because he's insane.'

Sunrise wondered where that bar was, because he'd like to try some of those jugs. But he was afraid to ask. You probably needed special permission to get in there. Of course, drinking always caused him trouble, so maybe it was just as well that the Warrens Bar was in some city in faraway Malaz. Besides, it'd be crowded with mages, and mages made Sunrise nervous. Especially High Mage Quick Ben, who seemed to be mad at Dead Hedge for some reason. Mad? More like furious.

But Dead Hedge just laughed it off, because nothing could put him in a bad mood for very long.

Corporal Rumjugs waddled into view, sighing heavily as she seated herself on a bale. 'What a workout! You'd think these soldiers never before held a decent woman.'

'A good night then?' Sunrise asked.

'My money purse is bulging, Sunny, and I'm leaking every which way.'

She'd lost some weight, just like her friend, Sweetlard. That march had almost done them both in. But they were still big, big in that way of swallowing a man up and it sure seemed there were lots of men who liked that just fine. For himself, he preferred to make out a bit more of an actual body under all that fat. Another few months of marching and they'd be perfect.

'I'm going to start charging them ones who like to watch, too. Why should that be free?'

'You're right in that, Rumjugs. Ain't nothing should be for free. But that's where us Letherii are different from the Malazans. We see the truth of that and it's no problem. Malazans, they just complain.'

'Worse is all the marriage offers I'm getting. They don't want me to stop work-ing, those ones, they just want to be married to me. Open-minded, I'll grant you that. With Malazans, pretty much anything goes. It's no wonder they conquered half the world.'

Sweetlard joined them from the other side of the deck. 'Errant's shrivelled cock, I can barely walk!'

'Rest the slabs, sweetie,' Rumjugs offered, waving a plump hand at a nearby bale close to the lantern.

'Where's Nose Stream?' Sweetlard asked. 'I'd heard he was going to talk to the Boss. About us trying some of them new missions—'

'Munitions,' corrected Rumjugs.

'Right, munitions. I mean, that sword I got, what am I supposed to do with it? I was collared to clear an overgrown lot once when I was little, and I took one look at them machetes and I threw up all over the Penal Mistress. Sharp edges give me the shakes—I got too much that looks too easy to cut, if you know what I mean.'

'We can't do nothing with the ones Bavedict's made up,' said Sunrise. 'Not un-til we're off these barges. And even then, we got to work in secret. Boss doesn't want anybody else knowing anything about them, you see?'

'But why?' Sweetlard demanded.

'Cos, love,' drawled Rumjugs, 'there's other sappers, right? In the Bonehunters. They see what Bavedict's come up with and everyone will want 'em, and before you know it, all the powders and potions are used up and we got us nothing.'

'The greedy bastards!'

'So make sure you say nothing, right? Even when you're working, I mean.'

'I hear you, Rummy Cups. No worries in that regard—I can't get a word in with all the marriage proposals.'

'You too? Why's they all so desperate, I wonder?'

'Children,' said Sunrise. 'They want children and they want 'em quick.'

'Why would they all want that?' Sweetlard asked.

The only answer that came to Sunrise was a grim one, and he hesitated.

After a moment Rumjugs gusted out a loud sigh. 'Errant's balls. They're all ex-pectin' to die.'

'Not the best attitude,' mused Sweetlard, as she pulled out a leaf stick and leaned in to the lantern slung close to her left shoulder. Once the end was smouldering, she drew it to a bright coal and then settled back. 'Spirits below, I'm chafing.'

'When did you last have a drink?' Rumjugs asked her.

'Weeks now. You?'

'Same. Funny how things kind of clear up.'

'Funny, aye.'

Sunrise smiled to himself at hearing Sweetlard try out that Malazan way of talking. *'Aye.' It's a good word, I think. More a whole attitude than a word, really. With lots of meaning in it, too. A bit of 'yes' and a bit of 'well, fuck' and maybe some 'we're all in this mess together'. So, a word to sum up the Malazans.* He uttered his own sigh and settled his head back. 'Aye,' he said.

And the others nodded. He knew they did, and he didn't even have to look.

We're tightening up. Just like Dead Hedge said we would. Just like that, aye.

'Idle hands, soldier. Take hold of that chest there and follow me.'

'I got an idea about what you can t-take hold of, Master Sergeant, and you don't n-need my help at all.'

Pores wheeled on the man. 'Impudence? Insubordination? Mutiny?'

'K-keep going, sir, and we can end on r-r-r-regicide.'

'Well now,' Pores said, advancing to stand in front of the solid, scowling bastard. 'I didn't take you for a mouthy one, Corporal. What squad and who's your sergeant?'

The man's right cheek bulged with something foul—the Malazans were picking up disgusting local habits—and he worked it for a moment before saying, 'Eighth Legion, Ninth c-c-c-company, Fourth su-su-squad. Sergeant F-F-F-Fiddler. Corporal Tarr, na-na-na-not at your service, Master Sergeant.'

'Think you got spine, Corporal?'

'Spine? I'm a f-f-f-fucking tree, and you ain't the wind to b-b-b-blow me down. Now, as you can s-s-s-see, I'm trying to wake up here, since I'm c-c-c-coming on my watch. You want some fool to t-t-tote your ill-gotten spoils, find someone else.'

'What's that in your mouth?'

'Rylig, it's c-c-c-called. D'ras. You use it to wake you up shuh-shuh-shuh-sharp.'

Pores studied the man's now glittering eyes, the sudden cascade of jumpy twitches on his face. 'You sure you're supposed to chew the whole wad, Corporal?'

'You m-may huh-huh-have a p-p-p-point theh-theh-there.'

'Spit that ow-ow-out, Corporal, before your head explodes.'

'Ccccandoat, Mas-Mas-mmmmfuckface. Spenspenspensive—'

The idiot was starting to pop like a seed on a hot rock. Pores took Tarr by the throat and forced him half over the rail. 'Spit it out, you fool!'

He heard gagging, and then ragged coughing. The corporal's knees gave out, and Pores pulled hard to keep the man upright. He stared a long moment into Tarr's eyes. 'Next time, Corporal, be sure to listen when the locals tell you how to use it, right?'

'H-H-Hood's B-B-Breath!'

Pores stepped back as Tarr straightened, the corporal's head snapping round at every sound. 'Go on, then, do your twenty rounds for every two your partner does. But before you do,' he added, 'why not carry that chest for me.'

'Aye sir, easy, easy. Watch.'

Fools who messed up their own heads, Pores reflected, were the easiest marks of all. Might be worth buying an interest in this Rylig stuff.

The two half-blood D'ras hands lounged near the starboard tiller.

'The whole load?' one asked, eyes wide with disbelief.

'The whole load,' the other confirmed. 'Just jammed it into his mouth and walked off.'

'So where is he now?'

'Probably bailing the barge with a tin cup. The leaks ain't got a hope of keeping up.'

They both laughed.

They were still laughing when Corporal Tarr found them. Coming up from behind. One hand to each man's belt. They wailed as they were yanked from their feet, and wailed a second time as they went over the stern rail. Loud splashes, followed by shrieking.

Clear to Tarr's unnaturally bright vision, the V wakes of maybe a dozen crocodiles fast closing in. He'd forgotten about those things. Too bad. He'd think about it later.

The alarms rang for a time, big brass bells that soon slowed their frantic call and settled into something more like a mourning dirge, before echoing to silence once again.

Life on the river was a nasty business, nasty as nasty could get but that's just how it was. The giant lizards were horrible enough with all those toothy jaws but then the local hands started talking about the river cows waiting downstream, not that river cows sounded particularly frightening as far as Tarr was concerned, even ones with huge tusks and pig eyes. He'd heard a score of confusing descriptions on his rounds, but only fragmentary ones, as he was quickly past and into the next bizarre, disjointed conversation, quick as breaths, quick as the blur of his boots drumming the deck. Vigilant patrol, aye, no time for lingering, no time for all that unimportant stuff. Walk the rail and walk the rail, round and round, and this was decent exercise but he should have worn his chain and kit bag and maybe his folding shovel, and double time might be required, just so he could get to know all these sudden faces jumping up in front of him, know them inside and out and their names, too, and whether they liked smoked fish and chilled beer or proper piss-warm ale and so many bare feet what if someone attacked right here and now? they'd all have nails stuck in their tender soles and he'd be all alone leading the charge but that'd be fine since he could kill anything right now, even bats because they weren't so fast were they? not as fast as those little burning sparks racing everywhere into his brain and back out again and in one ear out the other two and look at this! Marching on his knees, it was easy! Good thing since he'd worn his legs down to stumps and now the deck was coming up fast to knock on his nose and see if anyone was home but was anyone home? only the bats—

'He going to live?' Badan Gruk asked.

'Eh? Egit primbly so, lurky bhagger.'

'Good. Keep him under those blankets—I never seen a man sweat like that, he's bound to chill himself to the bone, and keep forcing water down him.'

'Dentellit meen bazness, Sornt! Eenit known eeler, eh?'

'Fine then, just make sure you heal him. Sergeant Fiddler will not be pleased to hear his corporal went and died in your care.'

'Fabbler kint shit ding! Ee nair feered im!'

'Really? Then you're an idiot, Nep.'

Badan Gruk frowned down at Tarr. Some new fever to chase them down? He hoped not. It looked particularly unpleasant, reminding him of the shaking fever, only worse. This place had almost as many miserable diseases and parasites as in the jungles of Dal Hon.

Feeling nostalgic, the sergeant left Tarr to Nep Furrow's ministrations. He would have been happier if he'd been on the same barge as Sinter, even Kisswhere. Corporal Ruffle was around, but she'd discovered a bones and trough game with a few heavies and was either heading for a sharp rise in her income or a serious beating. No matter what, she'd make enemies. Ruffle was like that.

He still didn't know what to make of this army, these Bonehunters. He could find nothing—no detail—that made them what they were. *What we are. I'm one of them now.* There were no great glories in the history of these legions—he'd been in the midst of the conquest of Lether and it had been a sordid thing. When the tooth's rotten right down to its root, it's no feat to tug it out. Maybe it was a just war. Maybe it wasn't. Did it make any difference? A soldier takes orders and a soldier fights. The enemy wore a thousand masks but they all turned out the same. Just people determined to stand in their way. This was supposed to be enough. Was it? He didn't know.

Surrounded by foreigners, friendly or otherwise, settled a kind of pressure on every Malazan soldier here. Demanding a shape to this army, and yet something was resisting it, something within the Bonehunters, as if hidden forces pushed back against that pressure. *We are and we aren't, we will and we won't. Are we just hollow at the core? Does it start and end with the Adjunct?* That notion felt uncharitable. People were just restless, uneasy with all this not knowing.

Who was the enemy awaiting them? What sort of mask would they see this time?

Badan Gruk could not remember ever knowing a person who deliberately chose to do the wrong thing, the evil thing—no doubt such people existed, the ones who simply didn't care, and ones who, for all he knew, enjoyed wearing the dark trappings of malice. Armies served and sometimes they served tyrants—bloodthirsty bastards—and they fought against decent, right-minded folk out of fear and in the interests of self-preservation, and out of greed, too, come to that. Did they see themselves as evil? How could they not? *But then, how many campaigns could you fight, if you were in that army? How many before you started feeling sick inside? In your gut. In your head. When the momentum of all those conquests starts to falter, aye, what then?*

Or when your tyrant Empress betrays you?

No one talked much about that, and yet Badan Gruk suspected it was the sliver of jagged iron lodged in the heart of the Bonehunters, and the bleeding never slowed. *We did everything she asked of us. The Adjunct followed her orders and got it done. The rebellion crushed, the leaders dead or scattered. Seven Cities brought under the imperial heel once again. In the name of order and law and smiling merchants. But none of it mattered. The Empress twitched a finger and the spikes were readied for our heads.*

Anger burned for only so long. Enough to cut a messy path through the Empire of Lether. And then it was done. That 'then' was now. What did they have to take anger's place? *We are to be Unwitnessed, she said. We must fight for each other and ourselves and no one else. We must fight for survival, but that cannot hold us together—it's just as likely to tear us apart.*

The Adjunct held to an irrational faith—in her soldiers, in their resolve. *We're a fragile army and there are enough reasons for that being true. That sliver needs to be pulled, the wound needs to knit.*

We're far from the Malazan Empire now, but we carry its name with us. It's even what we call ourselves. Malazans. Gods below, there's no way out of this, is there?

He turned away from the inky river carrying them along, scanned the huddled, sleeping forms of his fellow soldiers. Covering every available space on the deck, motionless as corpses.

Badan Gruk fought off a shiver and turned back to the river, where nothing could resist the current for long.

It was an old fancy, so old he'd almost forgotten it. A grandfather—it hardly mattered whether he'd been a real one or some old man who'd thrown on that hat for the duration of the memory—had taken him to the Malaz docks, where they'd spent a sunny afternoon fishing for collar-gills and blue-tube eels. *'Take a care on keeping the bait small, lad. There's a demon at the bottom of this harbour. Sometimes it gets hungry or maybe just annoyed. I heard of fishers snapped right off this dock, so keep the bait small and keep an eye on the water.'* Old men lived for stories like that. Putting the fright into wide-eyed runts who sat with their little legs dangling off the edge of the pier, runts with all the hopes children have and wasn't that what fishing was all about?

Fiddler couldn't remember if they'd caught anything that day. Hopes had a way of sinking fast once you stepped out of childhood. In any case, escaping this motley throng of soldiers, he'd scrounged a decent line and a catfish-spine hook. Using a sliver of salted bhederin for bait and a bent, holed coin buffed to flash, he trailed the line out behind the barge. There was always the chance of snagging something ugly, like one of those crocodiles, but he didn't think it likely. He did, however, make a point of not dangling his legs over the edge. Wrong bait.

Balm wandered up after a time and sat down beside him. 'Catch anything?'

'Make one of two guesses and you'll be there,' Fiddler replied.

'Funny though, Fid, seen plenty jumping earlier.'

'That was dusk—tomorrow round that time I'll float something looking like a fly. Find any of your squad?'

'No, not one. Feels like someone cut off my fingers. I'm actually looking forward to getting back on land.'

'You always were a lousy marine, Balm.'

The Dal Honese nodded. 'And a worse soldier.'

'Now I didn't say—'

'Oh but I am. I lose myself. I get confused.'

'You just need pointing in the right direction, and then you're fine, Balm. A mean scrapper, in fact.'

'Aye, fighting my way clear of all that fug. You was always lucky, Fid. You got that cold iron that makes thinking fast and clear easy for you. I ain't neither hot or cold, you see. I'm more like lead or something.'

'No one in your squad has ever complained, Balm.'

'Well, I like them and all, but I can't say that they're the smartest people I know.'

'Throatslitter? Deadsmell? They seem to have plenty of wits.'

'Wits, aye. Smart, no. I remember when I was a young boy. In the village there was another boy, about my age. Was always smiling, even when there was nothing to smile about. And always getting into trouble—couldn't keep his nose out of anything. Some of the older boys would pick on him—I saw him punched in the face once, and he stood there bleeding, that damned smile on his face. Anyway, one day he stuck his nose into the wrong thing—no one ever talked about what it was, but we found that boy lying dead behind a hut. Every bone broken. And on his face, all speckled in blood, there was that smile.'

'Ever see a caged ape, Balm? You must have. That smile you kept seeing was fear.'

'I know it now, Fid, you don't need to tell me. The point is, Throatslitter and Deadsmell, they make me think of that boy, the way he always got into things he shouldn't have. Wits enough to be curious, not smart enough to be cautious.'

Fiddler grunted. 'I'm trying to think of any soldier in my squad who fits that description. It occurs to me that wits might be hard to find among 'em, barring maybe Bottle—but he's smart enough to keep his head down. I think. So far, anyway. As for the rest of them, they like it simple and if it ain't simple, why, they just get mad and break something.'

'You got yourself a good squad there, Fid.'

'They'll do.'

A sudden tug. He began hitching the line back in. 'Not much of a fight, can't be very big.' Moments later he drew the hook into view. They stared down at a fish not much bigger than the bait, but it had lots of teeth.

Balm snorted. 'Look, it's smiling!'

It was late and Brys Beddict was ready for bed, but the aide's face was set, as if the young man had already weathered a tirade. 'Very well, send her in.'

The aide bowed and backed away with evident relief, turning smartly at the silk curtain, slipping past to make his way to the outer midship deck. A short time later Brys heard boots thumping from bare boards to the rug-strewn corridor leading to his private chamber. Sighing, he rose from his camp chair and adjusted his cloak.

Atri-Ceda Aranict edged aside the curtain and stepped within. She was tall, somewhere in her late thirties, though the deep creases framing her mouth—from a lifetime of rustleaf—made her look older; although something about those lines suited her well. Her sun-faded brown hair was straight and hung loose, down to either side of her breasts. The uniform of her rank seemed an ill fit, as if she was yet to become accustomed to this new career. Bugg had found her in the most recent troll for potential cedas. She had been employed as a midwife in a household in the city of Trate, which had suffered terribly at the beginning of the Edur invasion. Her greatest talents were in healing, although Bugg had assured Brys that she possessed the potential for other magics.

To date, his impression of her was as a singularly dour and uncommunicative woman, so despite the lateness he found himself regarding her with genuine interest. 'Atri-Ceda, what is it that is so urgent?'

She seemed momentarily at a loss, as if she had not expected to succeed in receiving this audience. She met his eyes in the briefest flicker, which seemed to fluster her even more, and then she cleared her throat. 'Commander, it is best—I mean, you need to see for yourself. Will you permit me, sir?'

Bemused, Brys nodded.

'I have been exploring the warrens—the Malazan way of sorcery. It's so much more . . . elegant.' As she was speaking she was rummaging inside the small leather pouch tied to her belt. She withdrew her hand and opened it, revealing a small amount of grainy dirt. 'Do you see, sir?'

Brys tilted forward. 'That would be dirt, Aranict?'

A quick frown of irritation that delighted him. 'Look more carefully, sir.'

He did. Watching it settle, and then settle some more—no, the soil was *in motion*. 'You have ensorcelled this handful of earth? Er, well done, Atri-Ceda.'

The woman snorted, and then her breath caught. 'My apologies, Commander. It's obvious I've not explained myself—'

'As of yet you've not explained anything.'

'Sorry sir. I thought, if I didn't show you, you'd have no reason to believe me—'

'Aranict, you are my Atri-Ceda. You would not serve me well if I viewed you with scepticism. Please, go on, and please relax—I did not mean to sound impatient. In truth, this restless soil is most remarkable.'

'No sir, not in itself. Any Malazan mage could manage this with barely the twitch of a finger. The fact is, I'm not the source of this.'

'Oh, then who is?'

'I don't know. Before we boarded, sir, I was standing down at the water's edge—there'd been a hatching of watersnakes, and I was watching the little ones slither into the reeds—creatures interest me, sir. And I noticed something in the mud where the serpents had crawled. Parts of it were moving, shifting about, as you see here. Naturally, I suspected that some insect or mollusc was beneath the surface, so I probed—'

'Bare-handed? Was that wise?'

'Probably not, as the whole bank was full of mud-urchins, but I could see that this was different. In any case, sir, I found nothing. But the mud in my hand fairly seethed, as if it possessed a life of its own.'

Brys peered at the dirt cupped in her palm once more. 'And is this the offending material?'

'Yes, sir. And that's where the Malazan warrens come into this. It's called sympathetic linkage. Rather, with this bit of dirt, I can find others just like it.'

'Along the river?'

Her eyes met his again, and once more they flitted away—and with a start Brys realized that Aranict was shy. The notion endeared her to him and he felt a wave of sympathy, warm as a caress. 'Sir, it started there—since I'm new to working this kind of magic—but then it spread, inland, and I could sense the places of its greatest manifestation—this swarming power in the ground, I mean. In mud, in sands, the range, sir, is vast. But where you'll find more than anywhere else, Commander, is in the Wastelands.'

'I see. What, do you think, do these modest disturbances signify?'

'That something's just beginning, sir. But, I need to talk to some Malazan mages—they know so much more than I do. They can take it farther than I have managed.'

'Atri-Ceda, you have only begun your explorations of the Malazan warrens, and yet you have extended your sensitivity all the way to the Wastelands. I see now why the Ceda held you in such high regard. However, come the morning we shall send you in a launch to a Malazan barge.'

'Perhaps the one where Ebron will be found, or Widdershins—'

'Squad mages? No, Atri-Ceda. Like it or not, you are my equivalent of High Mage. Accordingly, your appropriate contact among the Bonehunters is their High Mage, Adaephon Ben Delat.'

All colour drained from her face. Her knees buckled.

Brys had to move quickly to take her weight as she slumped in a dead faint. 'Granthos! Get me a healer!'

He heard some muffled response in reply from the outer chamber.

The dirt had scattered on to the rug and Brys caught motion from the corner of his eye. It was gathering together, forming a roiling heap. He thought he could almost make out shapes within it, before everything fell away, only to re-form once more.

She was heavier than he'd expected. He looked down at her face, the parted lips, and then away again. 'Granthos! Where in the Errant's name are you?'

Chapter Seventeen

I have reached an age when youth itself is beauty.

A Brief Assembly of Ugly Thoughts
(interlude)
Gothos' Folly

The bones of the rythen rested on a bed of glittering scales, as if in dying it had shed its carpet of reptilian skin, unfolding it upon the hard crystals of the Glass Desert's lifeless floor: a place to lie down, the last nest of its last night. The lizard-wolf had died alone, and the stars that looked down upon the scene of this solitary surrender did not blink. Not once.

No wind had come to scatter the scales, and the relentless sun had eaten away the toxic meat from around the bones, and had then bleached and polished those bones to a fine golden lustre. There was something dangerous about them, and Badalle stood staring down at the hapless remains for some time, her only movement coming when she blew the flies away from the sores clustering her mouth. Bones like gold, a treasure assuredly cursed. 'Greed invites death,' she whispered, but the voice broke up and the sounds that came out were likely unintelligible, even to Saddic who stood close by her side.

Her wings were shrivelled, burnt down to stumps. Flying was but a memory finely dusted with ash, and she found nothing inside to justify brushing it clean. Past glories dwindled in the distance. Behind her, behind them, behind them all. But her descent was not over. Soon, she knew, she would crawl. And finally slither like a drying worm, writhing ineffectually, making grand gestures that won her nothing. Then would come the stillness of exhaustion.

She must have seen such a worm once. She must have knelt down beside it as children did, to better observe its pathetic struggles. Dragged up from its dark comforting world, by some cruel beak perhaps, and then lost on the fly, striking a hard and unyielding surface—a flagstone, yes—one making up the winding path in the garden. Injured, blind in the blazing sunlight, it could only pray to whatever gods it wanted to exist. The blessing of water, a stream to swim back into the soft soil, a sudden handful of sweet earth descending upon it, or the hand of some merciful godling reaching down, the pluck of salvation.

She had watched it struggle, she was certain she had. But she could not recall if she had done anything other than watch. Children understood at a very young age that doing nothing was an expression of power. Doing nothing was a choice swollen with omnipotence. It was, in fact, godly.

And this, she now realized, was the reason why the gods did nothing. Proof of their omniscience. After all, to act was to announce awful limitations, for it revealed that chance acted first, the accidents were just that—events beyond the will of the gods—and all they could do in answer was to attempt to remedy the consequences, to alter natural ends. To act, then, was an admission of fallibility.

Such ideas were complicated, but they were clean, too. Sharp as the crystals jutting from the ground at her feet. They were decisive in catching the rays of the sun and cutting them into perfect slices, proving that rainbows were not bridges in the sky. And that no salvation was forthcoming. The Snake had become a worm, and the worm was writhing on the hot stone.

Children withheld. Pretending to be gods. Fathers did the same, unblinking when the children begged for food, for water. They knew moments of nostalgia and so did nothing, and there was no food and no water and the sweet cool earth was a memory finely dusted with ash.

Brayderal had said that morning that she had seen tall strangers standing beneath the rising sun, standing, she said, on the ribby snake's tail. But to look in that direction was to go blind. People could either believe Brayderal or not believe her. Badalle chose not to believe her. None of the Quitters had chased after them, even the Fathers were long gone, as were the ribbers and all the eaters of dead and dying meat except for the Shards—who could fly in from leagues away. No, the ribby snake was alone on the Glass Desert, and the gods watched down and did nothing, to show just how powerful they really were.

But she could answer with her own power. That was the delicious truth. She could see them writhing in the sky, shrivelling in the sun. And she chose not to pray to them. She chose to say nothing at all. When she had winged through the heavens, she had sailed close to those gods, fresh and free as a hatchling. She had seen the deep lines bracketing their worried eyes. She had seen the weathered tracks of their growing fear and dismay. But none of these sentiments was a gift to their worshippers. The faces and their expressions were the faces of the self-obsessed. Such knowledge was fire. Feathers ignited. She had spiralled in a half-wild descent, unravelling smoke in her wake. Flashes of pain, truths searing her flesh. She had plunged through clouds of Shards, deafened by the hissing roar of wings. She had seen the ribby snake stretched out across a glittering sea, had seen—with a shock—how short and thin it had grown.

She thought again of the gods now high above her. Those faces were no different from her own face. The gods were as broken as she was broken, inside and out. Like her, they wandered a wasteland with nowhere to go.

The Fathers drove us out. They were done with children. Now she believed the fathers and mothers of the gods had driven them out as well, pushed them out into the empty sky. And all the while and far below the people crawled in their circles and from high up no one could make sense of the patterns. The gods that sought to make sense of them were driven mad.

'Badalle.'

She blinked in an effort to clear her eyes of the cloudy skins that floated in them, but they just swam back. Even the gods, she now knew, were half-blinded by the clouds. 'Rutt.'

His face was an old man's face, cracked lines through caked dust. Held was wrapped tight within the mottled blanket. Rutt's eyes, which had been dull for so long that Badalle thought they had always been so, were suddenly glistening. As if someone had licked them. 'Many died today,' she said. 'We can eat.'

'Badalle.'

She blew at flies. 'I have a poem.'

But he shook his head. 'I—I can't go on.'

> 'Quitters never quit,
> And that is the lie we live with
> Now they walk us
> To the end.
> Eating our tail.
> But we are shadows on glass
> And the sun drags us onward.
> The Quitters have questions
> But we are the eaters
> Of answers.'

He stared at her. 'She was right, then.'

'Brayderal was right. She has threads in her blood. Rutt, she will kill us all if we let her.'

He looked away, and she could see he was about to cry. 'No, Rutt. Don't.'

His face crumpled.

She took him as he sagged, took him and somehow found the strength to hold him up as he shuddered with sobs.

Now he too was broken. But they couldn't let that happen. She couldn't, because if he broke then the Quitters would get them all. 'Rutt. Without you, Held is nothing. Listen. I have flown high—I had wings, like the gods. I went so high I could see how the world curves, like the old women used to tell us, and I saw—Rutt, listen—I saw the end of the Glass Desert.'

But he shook his head.

'And I saw something else. A city, Rutt. A city of glass—we will find it tomorrow. The Quitters won't go there—they are afraid of it. The city, it's a city they know from their legends—but they'd stopped believing those legends. And now it's invisible to them—we can escape them, Rutt.'

'Badalle—' his voice was muffled against the skin and bone of her neck. 'Don't give up on me. If you give up, I won't—I can't—'

She had given up long ago, but she wouldn't tell him that. 'I'm here, Rutt.'

'No. No, I mean'—he pulled back, stared fixedly into her eyes—'don't go mad. Please.'

'Rutt, I can't fly any more. My wings burned off. It's all right.'

'Please. Promise me, Badalle. Promise!'

'I promise, but only if you promise not to give up.'

His nod was shaky. His control, she could see, was thin and cracked as burnt skin. *I won't go mad, Rutt. Don't you see? I have the power to do nothing. I have all the powers of a god.*

This ribby snake will not die. We don't have to do anything at all, just keep going. I have flown to where the sun sets, and I tell you, Rutt, we are marching into fire. Beautiful, perfect fire. 'You'll see,' she said to him.

Beside them stood Saddic, watching, remembering. His enemy was dust.

What is, was. Illusions of change gathered windblown into hollows in hillsides, among stones and the exposed roots of long-dead trees. History swept along as it had always done, and all that is new finds shapes of old. Where stood towering masses of ice now waited scars in the earth. Valleys carried the currents of ghost rivers and the wind wandered paths of heat and cold to deliver the turn of every season.

Such knowledge was agony, like a molten blade thrust to the heart. Birth was but a repetition of what had gone before. Sudden light was a revisitation of the moment of death. The madness of struggle was without beginning and without end.

Awakening to such things loosed a rasping sob from the wretched, rotted figure that clambered out from the roots of a toppled cottonwood tree sprawled across an old oxbow. Lifting itself upright, it looked round, the grey hollows beneath the brow-ridges gathering the grainy details into shapes of meaning. A broad, shallow valley, distant ridges of sage and firebrush. Grey-winged birds darting down the slopes.

The air smelled of smoke and tasted of slaughter. Perhaps a herd had been driven over a bluff. Perhaps heaps of carcasses spawned maggots and flies and this was the source of the dreadful, incessant buzzing sound. Or was this something sweeter? Had the world won the argument? Was she now a ghost returned to mock the rightful failure of her kind? Would she find somewhere nearby the last putrid remnants of her people? She dearly hoped so.

She was named Bitterspring in the language of the Brold clan, Lera Epar, a name she had well earned for the terrible crimes she had committed. She had been the one flower among all the field's flowers whose scent had been deadly. Men had cast away their own women to clutch her as their own. Each time, she had permitted herself to be plucked—seeing in his eyes what she had wanted to see, that he valued her above all others—even and especially the mate he had abandoned—and so their love would be unassailable. Before it went wrong, before it proved the weakest binding of all. And then another man would appear, with that same hungry fire in his eyes, and she would think, *This time, it is different. This time, I am certain, our love is a thing of great power.*

Everyone had agreed that she was the cleverest person in all the clans of the

Brold Gathering. She was not a thing of the shallows, no, her mind plunged unlit depths. She was the delver into life's perils, who spoke of the curse that was the alighting of reason's spark. She found divination not in the fire-cracked shoulder-blades of caribou, but in the watery reflections of faces in pools, springs and gourd bowls—faces she knew well as kin. As kin, yes, and more. Such details as made one distinct from all others, she knew these to be illusions, serving for quick recognition but little else. Beneath those details, she understood, they were all the same. Their needs. Their wants, their fears.

She had been regarded as a formidable seer, a possessor of spirit-gifted power. But the truth was, and this she knew with absolute certainty, there was no magic in her percipience. Reason's spark did not arise spontaneously amidst the dark waters of base emotion. No, and nor was each spark isolated from the others. Bitter-spring understood all too well that the sparks were born of hidden fires—the soul's own array of hearth-fires, each one devoted to simple, immutable truths. One for every need. One for every want. One for every fear.

Once this revelation found her, reading the futures of her kin was an easy task. Reason delivered the illusion of complexity, but behind it all, *we are as simple as bhederin, simple as ay, as ranag. We rut and bare our teeth and expose our throats. Behind our eyes our thoughts can burn bright with love or blacken with jealous rot. We seek company to find our place in it, and unless that place is at the top, all we find dissatisfies us, poisons our hearts.*

In company, we are capable of anything. Murder, betrayal. In company, we invent rituals to quench every spark, to ride the murky tide of emotion, to be once again as unseeing and uncaring as the beasts.

I was hated. I was worshipped. And, in the end, I am sure, I was murdered.

Lera Epar, why are you awake once more? Why have you returned?

I was the dust in the hollows, I was the memories lost.

I did terrible things, once. Now I stand here, ready to do them all again.

She was Bitterspring, of the Brold Imass, and her world of ice and white-furred creatures was gone. She set out, a chert and jawbone mace dangling from one hand, the yellowed skin of the white-furred bear trailing down from her shoulders.

She had been too beautiful, once. But history was never kind.

He rose from the mud ringing the waterhole, shedding black roots, fish scales and misshapen cakes of clay and coarse sand. Mouth open, jaws stretched wide, he howled without sound. He had been running straight for them. Three K'ell Hunters, whose heads turned to regard him. They had been standing over the corpses of his wife, his two children. The bodies would join the gutted carcasses of other beasts brought down on their hunt. An antelope, a mule deer. The mates of the felled beasts had not challenged the slayers. No, they had fled. But this one, this male Imass roaring out his battle-cry and rushing them with spear readied, he was clearly mad. He would give his life for nothing.

The K'ell Hunters did not understand.

They had met his charge with the flat of their blades. They had broken the spear and had then beaten him unconscious. They didn't want his meat, tainted as it was with madness.

Thus ended his first life. In rebirth, he was a man emptied of love. And he had been among the first to step into the embrace of the Ritual of Tellann. To expunge the memories of past lives. Such was the gift, so precious, so perfect.

He had lifted himself from the mud, summoned once more—but this time was different. This time, he *remembered everything.*

Kalt Urmanal of the Orshayn T'lan Imass stood shin-deep in mud, head tilted back, howling without sound.

Rystalle Ev crouched on a mound of damp clay twenty paces from Kalt. Understanding him, understanding all that assailed him. She too had awakened, possessor of all that she had thought long lost, and so she looked upon Kalt, whom she loved and had always loved, even in the times when he walked as would a dead man, the ashes of his loss grey and thick upon his face; and in the times before, when she harboured jealous hatred for his wife, when she prayed to all the spirits for the woman's death.

It was possible that his scream would never cease. It was possible that, as they all rose and gathered in their disbelief at their resurrection—as they sought out the one who so cruelly summoned the Orshayn—she would have to leave him here.

Though his howl was without voice, it deafened her mind. If he did not cease, his madness would infect all the others.

The last time the Orshayn had walked the earth had been in a place far away from this one. With but three broken clans remaining—a mere six hundred and twelve warriors left—and three damaged bonecasters, they had fled the Spires and fallen to dust. That dust had been lifted high on the winds, carried half a world away—there had been no thought of a return to bone and withered flesh— to finally settle in a scattered swath across scores of leagues.

This land, Rystalle Ev knew, was no stranger to the Imass. Nor—and Kalt's torment made this plain—was it unknown to the K'Chain Che'Malle. What were they doing here?

Kalt Urmanal fell to his knees, his cry dying away, leaving a ringing echo in her skull. She straightened, leaning heavily on the solid comfort of her spear's shaft of petrified wood. This return was unconscionable—a judgement she knew she would not have made without her memories—to that time of raw, wondrous mortality replete with its terrible crimes of love and desire. She could feel her own rage, rising like the molten blood of the earth.

Beyond the waterhole she spied three figures approaching. T'lan Imass of the Orshayn. Bonecasters. Perhaps now they would glean some answers.

Brolos Haran had always been a broad man, and even the bones of his frame, so visible beneath the taut, desiccated skin, looked abnormally robust. The clear, almost crystalline blue eyes that gave him his name were, of course, long gone; and in their place were the knotted remnants, gnarled and blackened and lifeless. His red hair drifted like bloodstained cobwebs out over the dun-hued emlava fur riding his shoulders. His lips had peeled back to reveal flat, thick teeth the colour of raw copper.

To his left was Ilm Absinos, her narrow, tall frame sheathed in the grey scales of the enkar'al, her long black hair knotted with snake-skins. The serpent staff in her bony hands seemed to writhe. She walked with a hitched gait, remnant of an injury to her hip.

Ulag Togtil was as wide as Brolos Haran yet taller than Ilm Absinos. He had ever been an outsider among the Orshayn clans. Born as a half-breed among the first tribes of the Trell, he had wandered into the camp of Kebralle Korish, the object of intense curiosity, especially among the women. It was the way of the Imass that strangers could come among them, and, if life was embraced and no violence was stirred awake, such strangers could make for themselves a home among the people, and so cease to be strangers. So it had been with Ulag.

In the wars with the Order of the Red Sash, he had proved the most formidable among all the Orshayn bonecasters. Seeing him now, Rystalle Ev felt comforted, reassured—as if he alone could make things as they once were.

He could not. He was as trapped within the Ritual as was everyone else.

Ulag was the first to speak. 'Rystalle Ev, Kalt Urmanal. I am privileged to find two of my own clan at last.' A huge hand gestured slightly. 'Since dawn I have laboured mightily beneath the assault of these two cloud-dancers—their incessant joy has proved a terrible burden.'

Could she have smiled, Rystalle would have. The image of cloud-dancers was such an absurd fit to these two dour creatures, she might well have laughed. But she had forgotten how. 'Ulag, do you know the truth of this?'

'A most elusive hare. How it leaps and darts, skips free of every slingstone. How it sails over the snares and twitches an ear to every footfall. I have run in enough circles, failing to take the creature into my hands, to feel its pattering heart, its terrified trembling.'

Ilm Absinos spoke. 'Inistral Ovan awaits us. We shall gather more on our return journey. It has not been so long since we last walked. Few, if any, will have lost themselves.'

Brolos Haran seemed to be staring into the south. Now he said, 'The Ritual is broken. Yet we are not released. In this, I smell the foul breath of Olar Ethil.'

'So you have said before,' snapped Ilm Absinos. 'And still, for all your chewing the same words, there remains no proof.'

'We do not know,' sighed Ulag, 'who has summoned us. It is curious, but we are closed to her, or him. As if a wall of power stands between us, one that can only be breached from the other side. The summoner must choose. Until such time, we must simply wait.'

Kalt Urmanal spoke for the first time. 'None of you understand anything. The waters are . . . crowded.'

To this, silence was the only reply.

Kalt snarled, as if impatient with them all. He was still kneeling and it seemed he had little interest in moving. Instead, he pointed. 'There. Another approaches.'

Rystalle and the others turned.

The sudden disquiet was almost palpable.

She wore the yellow and white fur of the brold, the bear of the snows and ice. Her hair was black as pitch, her face wide and flat, the skin stained deep amber. The pits of her eyes were angled, tilted at the outer corners. The talons of some small creature had been threaded through her cheeks.

T'lan Imass, yes. But . . . *not of our clans.*

Three barbed harpoons were strapped to her back. The mace she carried in one hand was fashioned of some animal's thighbone, inset with jagged blades of green rhyolite and white chert.

She halted fifteen paces away.

Ilm Absinos gestured with her staff. 'You are a bonecaster, but I do not know you. How can this be? Our minds were joined at the Ritual. Our blood wove a thousand-upon-a-thousand threads. The Ritual claims you as kin, as T'lan Imass. What is your clan?'

'I am Nom Kala—'

Brolos Haran cut in, 'We do not know those words.'

That very admission was a shock to the Orshayn. It was, in fact, impossible. *Our language is as dead as we are.*

Nom Kala cocked her head, and then said, 'You speak the Old Tongue, the secret language of the bonecasters. I am of the Brold T'lan Imass—'

'There is no clan chief who claimed the name of the brold!'

She seemed to study Brolos for a moment, and then said, 'There was no clan chief bearing the name of the brold. There was, indeed, no clan chief at all. Our people were ruled by the bonecasters. The Brold clans surrendered the Dark War. We Gathered. There was a Ritual—'

'What!' Ilm Absinos lurched forward, almost stumbling until her staff brought her up short. '*Another Ritual of Tellann?*'

'We failed. We were camped beneath a wall of ice, a wall that reached to the very heavens. We were assailed—'

'By the Jaghut?' Brolos asked.

'No—'

'The K'Chain Che'Malle?'

Once more she cocked her head and was silent.

The wind moaned.

A grey fox wandered into their midst, stepping cautiously, nose testing the air. After a moment, it trotted down to the water's edge. Pink tongue unfurled and the sounds of lapping water tickled the air.

Watching the fox, Kalt Urmanal put his hands to his face, covering his eyes. Seeing this, Rystalle turned away.

Nom Kala said, 'No. The dominion of both was long past.' She hesitated, and then added, 'It was held among many of us that the enemy assailing our people were humans—our inheritors, our rivals in the ways of living. We bonecasters— the three of us who remained—knew that to be no more than a half-truth. No, we were assailed by ourselves. By the lies we told each other, by the false comforts of our legends, our stories, our very beliefs.'

'Why, then,' asked Ulag, 'did you attempt the Ritual of Tellann?'

'With but three bonecasters left, how could you have hoped to succeed?' Ilm Absinos demanded, her voice brittle with outrage.

Nom Kala fixed her attention upon Ulag. 'Trell-blood, you are welcome to my eyes. To answer your question: it is said that no memory survives the Ritual. We deemed this just. It is said, as well, that the Ritual delivers the curse of immortality. We saw this, too, as just.'

'Then against whom did you wage war?'

'No one. We were done with fighting, Trell-blood.'

'Then why not simply choose death?'

'We severed all allegiance to the spirits—we had been lying to them for too long.'

The fox lifted its head, eyes suddenly wide, ears pricked. It then trotted in its light-footed way along the rim of the pool. Slipped beneath some firebrush, and vanished inside a den.

How much time passed before another word was spoken? Rystalle could not be certain, but the fox reappeared, a marmot in its jaws, and bounded away, passing so close to Rystalle that she could have brushed its back with her hand. A flock of tiny birds descended to prance along the muddy verge. Somewhere in the shallows ruddered a carp.

Ilm Absinos said, in a whisper, 'The spirits died when we died.'

'A thing that dies to us is not necessarily dead,' Nom Kala replied. 'We do not have that power.'

'What does your name mean?' Ulag asked.

'Knife Drip.'

'How did the ritual fail?'

'The wall of ice fell on us. We were all killed instantly. The Ritual was therefore uncompleted.' She paused, and then added, 'Given the oblivion that followed, failure seemed a safe assumption—were we capable of making assumptions. But now, it appears, we were in error.'

'How long ago?' Ulag asked her. 'Do you know?'

She shrugged. 'The Jaghut were gone a hundred generations. The K'Chain Che'Malle had journeyed to the eastern lands two hundred generations previously. We traded with the Jheck, and then with the Krynan Awl and the colonists of the Empire of Dessimbelackis. We followed the ice in its last retreat.'

'How many of you will return, Knife Drip?'

'The other two bonecasters have awakened and even now approach us. Lid Ger—Sourstone. And Lera Epar—Bitterspring. Of our people, we cannot yet say. Maybe all. Perhaps none.'

'Who summoned us?'

One more time she cocked her head. 'Trell-blood, this is our land. We have heard clear his cry. You cannot? We are summoned, T'lan Imass, by the First Sword. A legend among the Brold that, it seems, was not a lie.'

Ulag was rocked back as if struck a blow. 'Onos T'oolan? But . . . why?'

'He summons us beneath the banner of vengeance,' she replied, 'and in the name of death. My new friends, the T'lan Imass are going to war.'

The birds launched into the air like a tent torn loose of its tethers, leaving upon the soft clays nothing but a scattering of tiny tracks.

Bitterspring walked towards the other T'lan Imass. The emptiness of the land was a suffocating pressure. *When everything goes, it is fitting that we are cursed to return, lifeless as the world we have made. Still . . . am I beyond betrayal? Have I ceased to be a slave to hope? Will I once again tread the old, worn trails?*

Life is done, but the lessons remain. Life is done, but the trap still holds me tight. This is the meaning of legacy. This is the meaning of justice.

What was, is.

The wind was insistent, tugging at worn strips of cloth, the shredded ends of leather straps, loose strands of hair. It moaned as if in search of a voice. But the lifeless thing that was Toc the Younger held its silence, its immutability in the midst of the life surrounding it.

Setoc settled down on aching legs and waited. The two girls and the strange boy had huddled together nearby and were fast asleep.

Their saviour had carried them leagues from the territory of the Senan Barghast, north and east across the undulating prairie. The horse under them had made none of the normal sounds a horse should make. None of the grunting breaths, the snorts. It had not once sawed at the bit or dipped its head seeking a mouthful of grass. Its tattered hide remained dry, not once twitching to the frustrated deerflies, even as its ropy muscles worked steadily and its hoofs drummed the hard ground. Now it stood motionless beneath its motionless rider.

She rubbed at her face. They needed water. They needed food. She didn't know where they were. Close to the Wastelands? Perhaps. She thought she could make out a range of hills or mountains far to the east, a dusty grimace of rock shimmering through the waves of heat. Lolling in the saddle behind Toc, she had been slipping into and out of strange dreams, fragmented visions of a squalid farmstead, the rank sweat of herds and small boys shouting. One boy with a face she thought she knew, but it was twisted with fear, and then hard with sudden resolve. A face that had transformed in an instant to one that awaited death. In one so young, nothing was more horrifying. Dreaming of children, but not these children here, not even Barghast children. At times, she found herself wheeling high above this lone warrior who rode with a girl in front, a girl behind, a girl and a boy in the crooks of his arms. She could smell scorched feathers, and all at once the land far below was a sea of diamonds, cut in two by a thin, wavering line.

She was fevered, or so she concluded now as she sat, mouth dry, eyes stinging with grit. Was this meant to be a rest? Something in her was resisting sleep. They needed water. They needed to eat.

A mound a short distance away caught her eye. Groaning, she stood, dragged herself closer.

A cairn, almost lost in the knee-high grasses. A wedge-shaped stone set atop a thinner slab, and beneath that a mound of angled rocks. The wedge was carved on its sides. Etching the eyes of a wolf. Mouth open with the slab forming the lower jaw, the scratchings of fangs and teeth. Worn down by centuries of wind and rain. She reached out a trembling hand, set her palm against the rough, warm stone.

'We are being hunted.'

The rasping pronouncement drew her round. She saw Toc stringing his bow, heard the wind hum against the taut gut. A new voice in the air. She joined him, gazed westward. A dozen or more riders. 'Akrynnai,' she said. 'They will see our Barghast clothing. They will seek to kill us. Then again,' she added, 'if you ride to them, they may change their minds.'

'And why would that be?' he asked, even as he kicked his horse forward.

She saw the Akrynnai horse-warriors fan out, saw lances being readied.

Toc rode straight for them, an arrow nocked to the bowstring.

As they drew closer, Setoc saw the Akrynnai falter, even as their lances lifted defensively. Moments later the warriors scattered, horses bucking beneath them. Within a few more heartbeats, all were in flight. Toc slowly wheeled his mount and rode back to where she stood.

'It seems you were right.'

'Their horses knew before they did.'

He halted his mount, returned the arrow to its quiver and deftly unstrung the bow.

'Actually, you'll need those,' Setoc said. 'We need food. We need water, too.'

It seemed he'd stopped listening, and his head was turned to the east.

'What is it?' she asked. 'More hunters?'

'She wasn't satisfied,' he muttered. 'Of course not. What can one do better than an army can? Not much. But he won't like it. He never did. In fact, he may turn them all away. Well now, Bonecaster, what would you do about that? If he releases them?'

'I don't know what you're talking about. She? Him? What army?'

His head turned to look past her. She swung round. The boy was on his feet, walking over to the wolf cairn. He sang, 'Blalalalalalala . . .'

'I wish he'd stop doing that,' she said.

'You are not alone in that, Setoc of the Wolves.'

She started, turned back to eye the undead warrior. 'I see you now, Toc Anaster, and it seems you have but one eye—dead as it is. But that first night, I saw—'

'What? What did you see?'

The eye of a wolf. She waved towards the cairn. 'You brought us here.'

'No. I took you away. Tell me, Setoc, are the beasts innocent?'

'Innocent? Of what?'

'Did they deserve their fate?'

'No.'

'Did it matter? Whether they deserved it or not?'

'No.'

'Setoc, what do the Wolves want?'

She knew by his intonation that he meant the god and the goddess—she knew they existed, even if she didn't know their names, or if they even had ones. 'They want us all to go away. To leave them alone. Them and their children.'

'Will we?'

'No.'

'Why not?'

She struggled for an answer.

'Because, Setoc, to live is to wage war. And it just happens that no other thing is as good at waging war as we are.'

'I don't believe you! Wolves don't wage war against anything!'

'A pack marks out its territory and that pack will drive off any other pack that seeks to encroach upon it. The pack defends its claim—to the land, and to the animals it preys upon in that land.'

'But that's not war!'

He shrugged. 'Mostly, it's just the threat of war, until threat alone proves insufficient. Every creature strives for dominance, among its own kind and within its territory. Even a pack of dogs will find its king, its queen, and they will rule by virtue of their strength and the threat their strength implies, until they are usurped by the next in line. What can we make of this? That politics belong to all social creatures? So it would seem. Setoc, could the Wolves kill us humans, every one of us, would they?'

'If they understood it was them or us, yes! Why shouldn't they?'

'I was but asking questions,' Toc replied. 'I once knew a woman who could flatten a city with the arch of a single perfect eyebrow.'

'Did she?' Setoc asked, pleased to be the one asking questions.

'Occasionally. But, not every city, not every time.'

'Why not?'

The undead warrior smiled, the expression chilling her. 'She liked a decent bath every now and then.'

After Toc had set off in search of food, Setoc set about building a hearth with whatever stones she could find. The boy was sitting in front of the cairn, still singing his song. The twins had awakened but neither seemed to have anything to say. Their eyes were glazed and Setoc knew it for shock.

'Toc'll be back soon,' she told them. 'Listen, can you make him stop that babbling? Please? It's making my skin crawl. I mean, has he lost his mind, the little one? Or are they all like that? Barghast children aren't, at least not that I remember. They stay quiet, just like you two are doing right now.'

Neither girl replied. They simply watched her.

The boy suddenly shouted.

At the cry the ground erupted twenty paces beyond the cairn. Stones spat through a cloud of dust.

And something clambered forth.

The twins shrieked. But the boy was laughing. Setoc stared. A huge wolf, long-limbed, with a long, flat head and heavy jaws bristling with fangs, stepped out from the dust, and then paused to shake its matted, tangled coat. The gesture cut away the last threads of fear in Setoc.

From the boy, a new song. '*Ay ay ay ayayayayayayay!*'

At its hunched shoulders, the creature was taller than Setoc. And it had died long, long ago.

Her eyes snapped to the boy. *He summoned it. With that nonsense song, he summoned it.*

Can—can I do the same? What is the boy to me? What is being made here?

One of the twins spoke: 'He needs Toc. At his side. At our brother's side. He needs Tool's only friend. They have to be together.'

And the other girl, her gaze levelled on Setoc, said, 'And *they* need *you*. But we have nothing. Nothing.'

'I don't understand you,' Setoc said, irritated by the stab of irrational guilt she'd felt at the girl's words.

'What will happen,' the girl asked, 'when you raise one of your perfect eyebrows?'

'*What?*'

' "Wherever you walk, someone's stepped before you." Our father used to say that.'

The enormous wolf stood close to the boy. Dust still streamed down its flanks. She had a sudden vision of this beast tearing out the throat of a horse. *I saw these ones, but as ghosts. Ghosts of living things, not all rotted skin and bones. They kept their distance. They were never sure of me. Yet . . . I wept for them.*

I can't level cities.

Can I?

The apparitions rose suddenly, forming a circle around Toc. He slowly straightened from gutting the antelope he'd killed with an arrow to the heart. 'If only Hood's realm was smaller,' he said, 'I might know you all. But it isn't and I don't. What do you want?'

One of the undead Jaghut answered: 'Nothing.'

The thirteen others laughed.

'Nothing from you,' the speaker amended. She had been female, once—when such distinctions meant something.

'Then why have you surrounded me?' Toc asked. 'It can't be that you're hungry—'

More laughter, and weapons rattled back into sheaths and belt-loops. The woman approached. 'A fine shot with that arrow, Herald. All the more remarkable for the lone eye you have left.'

Toc glared at the others. 'Will you stop laughing, for Hood's sake!'

The guffaws redoubled.

'The wrong invocation, Herald,' said the woman. 'I am named Varandas. We do not serve Hood. We did Iskar Jarak a favour, and now we are free to do as we please.'

'And what pleases you?'

Laughter from all sides.

Toc crouched back down, resumed gutting the antelope. Flies spun and buzzed. In the corner of his vision he could see one of the animal's eyes, still liquid, still full, staring out at nothing. *Iskar Jarak, when will you summon me? Soon, I think. It all draws in—but none of that belongs to the Wolves. Their interests lie elsewhere. What will happen? Will I simply tear in half?* He paused, looked up to see the Jaghut still encircling him. 'What are you doing here?'

'Wandering,' Varandas replied.

Another added in a deep voice, 'Looking for something to kill.'

Toc glanced again at the antelope's sightless eye. 'You picked the wrong continent. The T'lan Imass have awakened.'

All at once, the amusement surrounding him seemed to vanish, and a sudden chill gripped the air.

Toc set down his knife and dragged loose the antelope's guts.

'We never faced them,' said Varandas. 'We were dead long before their ritual of eternal un-life.'

A different Jaghut spoke. 'K'Chain Nah'ruk, and now T'lan Imass. Doesn't anyone ever go away?'

After a moment, all began laughing again.

Through the merriment Varandas stepped close to Toc and said, 'Why have you killed this thing? You cannot eat it. And since that is true, I conclude that you must therefore hunt for others. Where are they?'

'Not far,' he replied, 'and none are any threat to you.'

'Too bad.'

'Nah'ruk—were they Iskar Jarak's favour?'

'They were.'

'What were they after?'

'Not "what". Who. But ask nothing more of that—we have discussed the matter and can make no sense of it. The world has lost its simplicity.'

'The world was never simple, Jaghut, and if you believe it was, you're deluding yourself.'

'What would you know of the ancient times?'

He shrugged. 'I only know recent times, but why should the ancient ones be any different? Our memories lie. We call it nostalgia and smile. But every lie has a purpose. And that includes falsifying our sense of the past—'

'And what purpose would that serve, Herald?'

He wiped clean his knife in the grasses. 'You shouldn't need to ask.'

'But I do ask.'

'We lie about our past to make peace with the present. If we accepted the truth of our history, we would find no peace—our consciences would not permit it. Nor would our rage.'

Varandas was clearly amused. 'Are you consumed with anger, Herald? Do you see too clearly with that lonely eye? Strong emotions are ever a barrier to perception, and this must be true of you.'

'Meaning?'

'You failed to detect my mocking tone when I spoke of the world's loss of simplicity.'

'I must have lost its distinction in the midst of the irony suffusing everything else you said. How stupid of me. Now, I am done with this beast.' He sheathed his knife and lifted the carcass to settle it across his shoulders. 'I could wish you all luck in finding something to kill,' he said, 'but you don't need it.'

'Do you think the T'lan Imass will be eager to challenge us, Herald?'

He levered the antelope on to the rump of his horse. The eyes, he saw, now swarmed with flies. Toc set a boot in the stirrup and, lifting wide with his leg to clear the carcass, lowered himself into the saddle. He gathered the reins. 'I knew a T'lan Imass once,' he said. 'I taught him how to make jokes.'

'He needed teaching?'

'More like reminding, I think. Being un-alive for as long as he was will do that to the best of us, I suspect. In any case, I'm sure the T'lan Imass will find you very comforting, in all that dark armour and whatnot, even as they chop you to pieces. Unfortunately, and at the risk of deflating your bloated egos, they're not here for you.'

'Neither were the Nah'ruk. But,' and Varandas cocked her helmed head, 'what do you mean they will find us "comforting"?'

Toc studied her, and then scanned the others. Lifeless faces, so eager to laugh. *Damned Jaghut.* He shrugged, and then said, 'Nostalgia.'

After the Herald and the lifeless antelope had ridden away on the lifeless horse, Varandas turned to her companions. 'What think you, Haut?'

The thick-limbed warrior with the heavy voice shifted, armour clanking and shedding red dust, and then said, 'I think, Captain, we need to make ourselves scarce.'

Suvalas snorted. 'The Imass were pitiful—I doubt even un-living ones could cause us much trouble. Captain, let us find some of them and destroy them. I'd forgotten how much fun killing is.'

Varandas turned to one of her lieutenants. 'Burrugast?'

'A thought has occurred to me, Captain.'

She smiled. 'Go on.'

'If the T'lan Imass who waged war against the Jaghut were as pitiful as Suvalas suggests, why are there no Jaghut left?'

No one arrived at an answer. Moments passed.

'We need to make ourselves scarce,' Haut repeated. And then he laughed.

The others joined in. Even Suvalas.

Captain Varandas nodded. So many things were a delight, weren't they? All these awkward emotions, such as humility, confusion and unease. To feel them again, to laugh at their inherent absurdity, mocking every survival instinct—as if she and her companions still lived. As if they still had something to lose. As if the past was worth recreating here in the present. 'As if,' she added mostly to herself, 'old grudges were worth holding on to.' She grunted, and then said, 'We shall march east.'

'Why east?' Gedoran demanded.

'Because I feel like it, lieutenant. Into the birth of the sun, the shadows on our trail, a new day ever ahead.' She tilted back her head. 'Hah hah hah hah hah!'

Toc the Younger saw the gaunt ay from some distance away. Standing with the boy clinging to one foreleg. If Toc had possessed a living heart, it would have beaten faster. If he could draw breath, it would have quickened. If his eye were swimming in a pool of tears, as living eyes did, he would weep.

Of course, it was not Baaljagg. The giant wolf was not—he realized as he rode closer—even alive. It had been summoned. Not from Hood's Realm, for the souls of such beasts did not reside there. *The Beast Hold, gift of the Wolves. An ay, to walk the mortal world once again, to guard the boy. And their chosen daughter.*

Setoc, was this by your hand?

One-eyed he might be, but he was not blind to the patterns taking shape. Nor, in the dry dust of his mind, was he insensitive to the twisted nuances within those patterns, as if the distant forces of fate took ghastly pleasure in mocking all that he treasured—the memories he held on to as would a drowning man hold on to the last breath in his lungs.

I see you in his face, Tool. As if I could travel back to the times before the Ritual of Tellann, as if I could whisper in like a ghost to that small camp where you were born, and see you at but a few years of age, bundled against the cold, your breath pluming and your cheeks bright red—I had not thought such a journey possible.

But it is. I need only look upon your son, and I see you.

We are broken, you and me. I had to turn you away. I had to deny you what you wanted most. But, what I could not do for you, I will do for your son.

He knew he was a fool to make such vows. He was the Herald of Death. And soon Hood would summon him. He would be torn from the boy's side. *Unless the Wolves want me to stay. But no one can know what they want. They do not think anything like us. I have no control . . . over anything.*

He reached the camp. Setoc had built a small fire. The twins had not moved from where they'd been earlier, but their eyes were fixed on Toc now, as if he could hold all their hopes in his arms. *But I cannot. My life is gone, and what remains does not belong to me.*

I dream I can hold to my vows. I dream I can be Toc the Younger, who knew how to smile, and love. Who knew what it was to desire a woman forever beyond his reach—gods, such delicious anguish! When the self would curl up, when longing overwhelmed with the sweetest flood.

Remember! You once wrote poems! You once crawled into your every thought, your every feeling, to see and touch and dismantle and, in the midst of putting it all back together, feel wonder. Awed, humbled by complexity, assailed by compassion. Uncomprehending in the face of cruelty, of indifference.

Remember how you thought: How can people think this way? How can they be so thoughtless, so vicious, so worshipful of death, so dismissive of suffering and misery?

He stared at the wolf. Baaljagg, not Baaljagg. A mocking reflection, a crafted simulacrum. *A Hairlock.* He met Setoc's slightly wide eyes and saw that she had had nothing to do with this summoning. *The boy. Of course. Tool made me arrows. His son finds me a companion as dead as I am.* 'It is named Baaljagg—'

'Balalalalalalalalala!'

Sceptre Irkullas sat, shoulders hunched, barricaded from the world by his grief. His officers beseeched him, battering at the high walls. The enemy was within reach, the enemy was on the move—an entire people, suddenly on the march. Their outriders had discovered the Akrynnai forces. The giant many-headed beasts were jockeying for position, hackles raised, and soon would snap the jaws, soon the fangs would sink deep, and fate would fill the mouth bitter as iron.

A conviction had burrowed deep into his soul. He was about to tear out the throat of the wrong enemy. But there were no thorns to prick his conscience, nothing to stir to life the trembling dance of reason. Before too long, loved ones would weep. Children would voice cries unanswered. And ripples would spread outward, agitated, in a tumult, and nothing would be the same as it once was.

There were times when history curled into a fist, breaking all it held. He waited for the crushing embrace with all the hunger of a lover. His officers did not understand. When he rose, gesturing for his armour, he saw the relief in their eyes, as if a belligerent stream had once more found its destined path. But he knew they thought nothing of the crimson sea they now rushed towards. Their relief was found in the comfort of the familiar, these studied patterns preceding dread mayhem. They would face the time of blood when it arrived.

Used to be he envied the young. At this moment, as the sun's bright morning light scythed the dust swirling above the restless horses, he looked upon those he could see—weapons flashing like winks from a thousand skulls—and he felt nothing but pity.

Great warleaders were, one and all, insane. They might stand as he was standing, here in the midst of the awakening machine, and see nothing but blades to cut a true path to his or her desire, as if desire alone was a virtue, a thing so pure and so righteous it could not be questioned, could not be challenged. This great warleader could throw a thousand warriors to their deaths and the oily surface of his or her conscience would reveal not the faintest swirl.

He had been a great warleader, once, his mouth full of iron shards, flames licking his fingertips. His chest swollen with unquestioned virtues.

'If we pursue, Sceptre, we can meet them by dusk. Do you think they will want to close then? Or will they wait for next dawn? If we are swift . . .'

'I will clench my jaws one more time,' Irkullas said. 'I will keep them fast and think nothing of the bite, the warm flow. You'd be surprised at what a man can swallow.'

They looked on, uncomprehending.

The Akrynnai army shook loose the camp of the night just past. It lifted itself up, broke into eager streams flowing into the wake of the wounded foe, and spread in a flood quickened to purpose.

The morning lost its gleam. Strange clouds gathered, and across the sky, flights of birds fled into the north. Sceptre Irkullas rode straight-backed on his horse, riding the sweaty palm, as the fist began to close.

'Gatherer of skulls, where is the fool taking us?'

Strahl, Bakal observed, was in the habit of repeating himself, as if his questions were a siege weapon, flinging stones at what he hoped was a weak point in the solid wall of his ignorance. Sooner or later, through the dust and patter of crumbling mortar, he would catch his first glimpse of the answers he sought.

Bakal had no time for such things. If he had questions, he burned them to the ground where they stood, smiling through the drifting ashes. The wall awaiting them all would come toppling down before too long. *To our regret.*

'We've left a bloody trail,' Strahl then added, and Bakal knew the warrior's eyes were fixed upon Hetan's back, as she limped, tottered and stumbled a short distance ahead of them in the column. Early in the day, when the warriors were still fresh, their breaths acrid with the anticipation of battle—perhaps only a day away —one would drag her from the line and take her on the side of the path, with others shouting their encouragement. A dozen times since dawn, this had occurred. Now, everyone walked as slowly as she, and no one had the energy to use her. Of food there was plenty; their lack was water. This wretched land was an old hag, her tits dry and withered. Bakal could almost see her toothless grin through the waves of heat rising above the yellow grasses on all sides, the nubbed horizon with its rotten stumps of bedrock protruding here and there.

The bloody trail Strahl spoke of marked the brutal consolidation of power by Warchief Maral Eb and his two brothers, Sagal and Kashat. And the widow, Sekara the Vile. What a cosy family they made! He turned his head and spat, since he found the mere thought of them fouled the taste on his tongue.

There had been two more attempts on his life. If not for Strahl and the half-dozen other Senan who'd elected themselves his guardians, he would now be as dead as his wife and her would-be lover. A widow walked a few steps behind him. Estaral would have died by her husband's hand if not for Bakal. Yet the truth was, his saving her life had been an accidental by-product of his bloodlust, even though he had told her otherwise. That night of storms had been like a fever coursing through the Barghast people. Such a night had been denied them all when Onos Toolan assumed command after Humbrall Taur's drowning—he had drawn his stone sword before all the gathered clan chiefs and said, '*The first murder this night will be answered by me. Take hold of your wants, your imagined needs, and crush the life from them.'* His will was not tested. As it turned out, too much was held back, and this time everyone had lunged into madness.

'They won't rest until you're dead, you know.'

'Then they'd best be quick,' Bakal replied. 'For tomorrow we do battle with the Akrynnai.'

Strahl grunted. 'It's said they have D'ras with them. And legions of Saphii Spears.'

'Maral Eb will choose the place. That alone can decide the battle. Unlike our enemy, we are denied retreat. Either we win, or we fall.'

'They think to take slaves.'

'The Barghast kneel to no one. The grandmothers will slide knives across the throats of our children, and then sever the taproot of their own hearts.'

'Our gods shall sing and so summon us all through the veil.'

Bakal bared his teeth. 'Our gods would be wise to wear all the armour they own.'

Three paces behind the two warriors, Estaral stared at Bakal, the man who had killed her husband, the man who had saved her life. At times she felt as if she was walking the narrowest bridge over a depthless crevasse, a bridge reeled out behind Bakal. At other moments the world suddenly opened before her, vast as a flooding ocean, and she flailed in panic, even as, in a rush of breathless astonishment, she comprehended the truth of her freedom. Finding herself alone made raw the twin births of fear and excitement, and both sizzled to the touch. Estaral alternated between cursing and blessing the warrior striding before her. He was her shield, yes, behind which she could hide. He also haunted her with the memory of that terrible night when she'd looked into her husband's eyes and saw only contempt—and then the dark desire to murder her.

Had she really been that useless to him? That disgusting? He could not have always seen her so, else he would never have married her—she remembered seeing smiles on his face, years ago now, it was true, but she could have sworn there had been no guile in his eyes. She measured out the seasons since those bright, rushing days, seeking signs of her failure, struggling to find the fatal threshold she had so unwittingly crossed. But the memories swirled round like a vortex, drawing her in, and everything blurred, spun past, and the only thing she could focus on was her recollection of his two faces: the smiling one, the one ugly with malice, flitting back and forth.

She was too old to be desired ever again, and even if she had not been so, it was clear now that she could not keep a man's love alive. Weak, foolish, blind, and now widow to a husband who'd sought to kill her.

Bakal had not hesitated. He'd killed her man as she might wring the neck of a yurt rat. And then he had turned to his wife—she had stood defiant until his first step towards her, and then she had collapsed to her knees, begging for her life. But that night had been the night of Hetan's hobbling. The beast of mercy had been gutted and its bloody skin staked to the ground. She'd begged even as he opened her throat.

Blood flows down. I saw it doing just that. Down their bodies, down and down. I thought he would turn to me then and do the same—I witnessed his shame, his rage. And he knew, if I had been a better wife, my husband would never have fixed his eyes upon his wife. And so, the failure and the crime was mine as well.

I would not have begged.

Instead, he had cleaned his knife and sheathed it. And when he looked upon her, she saw his fury fall away, and his eyes glistened. 'I wish you had not seen this, Estaral.'

'You wish he'd already killed me?'

'No—I came here to stop them doing that.'

That had confused her. 'But I am nothing to you, Bakal.'

'But you are,' he said. 'Without you, I would have no choice but to see this night—to see what I have done here—as black vengeance. As the rage of a jealous man—but you see, I really didn't care. She was welcome to whoever she wanted. But she had no right—nor your husband there—they had no right to kill you.'

'You are the slayer of Onos Toolan.' She still did not know why she had said that then. Had she meant that the night of blood was his and his alone?

He had flinched, and his face had drained. She'd thought then that he regretted sparing her life; indeed, that he might even change his mind. Instead, he turned away and an instant later he was gone.

Did she know that her words would wound him? Why should they? Was he not proud of his glorious deed?

Of course, Bakal had since failed to become the leader of the Barghast. Perhaps he had already seen the power slipping from his grasp, that night. So she followed him now. Had tethered herself to him, all with the intention of taking back her words, and yet not one step she took in pursuit found her any closer. Days now, nights of hovering like a ghost beyond the edge of his hearth-fire. She had witnessed the attempt on him by the first assassin, a Barahn warrior desperate for status—Strahl had cut him down five strides from Bakal. The next time it had been an arrow sent through the darkness, missing Bakal's head by less than a hand's-width. Strahl and three other warriors had rushed off after the archer but they had lost the would-be killer.

Upon returning, Strahl had muttered about Estaral's spectral presence—calling her the Reaper's eyes, wondering if she stayed close in order to witness Bakal's death. It seemed Strahl believed she hated Bakal for killing her husband. But the notion of hate had never even occurred to her, not for him, anyway.

She wanted to speak with Bakal. She wanted to explain and if she could understand her own motivations from that night, why, she would do just that. Salve the wound, perhaps heal it completely. They shared something, the two of them, didn't they? He must have understood, even if Strahl didn't.

But now they spoke of a battle with the Akrynnai, a final clash to decide who would rule this land. Maral Eb would lead the Barghast, warriors in their tens of thousands. It had been one thing for the Akrynnai to strike clan camps—now at last all of the White Face Barghast were assembled and no tribe in the world could defeat such an army. Even so, Bakal might die in the battle—he would be commanding the Senan after all, and it was inconceivable to imagine Maral Eb being so arrogant as not to position the most powerful clan in the line's centre. No, the Senan would form the jagged wedge and it would cut savage and deep.

She should approach him soon, perhaps this very night. *If only to take back my words. He struck them down to save my life, after all. He said so. Even though I was the cause of so much—*

She had missed something, and now Bakal had sent Strahl away and was dropping back to her side. Suddenly her mouth was dry.

'Estaral, I must ask of you a favour.'

Something in his tone whispered darkness. *No more death. Please. If she had other lovers—*

'Hetan,' he said under his breath. 'You are among the women who guard her at night.'

She blinked. 'Not for much longer, Bakal,' she said. 'She is past the time of fleeing. There is nothing in her eyes. She is hobbled. Last night there were but two of us.'

'And tonight there will be one.'

'Perhaps not even that. Warriors will use her, likely through the night.'

'Gods' shit, I didn't think of that!'

'If you want her—'

'I do not. Listen, with the sun's fall, as warriors gather for their meals, can you be the one to feed her?'

'The food just falls from her mouth,' Estaral said. 'We let the children do that—it entertains them, forcing it down as if she was a babe.'

'Not tonight. Take it on yourself.'

'Why?' *I want to speak with you. Take things back. I want to lie with you, Bakal, and take back so much more.*

He fixed his eyes upon her own, searching for something—she quickly glanced away, in case he discovered her thoughts. 'I don't understand,' he said. 'Why are you women so eager to hobble another woman?'

'I had no hand in that.'

'That is not what I asked.'

She had never before considered such a thing. It was what was done. It had always been so. 'Women have claws.'

'I know—I've seen it often enough. I've seen it in battle. But hobbling—that's different. Isn't it?'

She refused to meet his eyes. 'You don't understand. I didn't mean the claws of a warrior. I meant the claws we keep hidden, the ones we use only against other women.'

'But why?'

'You speak now in the way Onos Toolan did—all his questions about the things we've always done. Was it not this that saw him killed, Bakal? He kept questioning things that he had no right to question.'

She saw as he lifted his right hand. He seemed to be studying it.

His knife hand.

'His blood,' he whispered, 'has poisoned me.'

'When we turn on our own,' she said, struggling to put her thoughts into words, 'it is as water in a skin finds a hole. There is so much . . . weight—'

'Pressure.'

'Yes, that is the word. We turn on our own, to ease the pressure. All eyes are on her, not us. All desire—' she stopped then, stifling a gasp.

But he'd caught it—he'd caught it all. 'Are men the reason then? Is that what you're saying?'

She felt a flush of anger, like knuckles rapping up her spine. 'Answer me this, Bakal'—and she met his wide eyes unflinchingly—'how many times was your touch truly tender? Upon your wife? Tell me, how often did you laugh with your friends when you saw a woman emerge from her home with blood crusting her lip, a welt beneath an eye? "Oh, the wild wolf rutted last night!" And then you grin and you laugh—do you think we do not hear? Do you think we do not see? Hobble her! Take her, all of you! And, for as long as she lifts to you, *you leave us alone!*'

Heads had turned at her venomous tone—even if they could not quite make out her words, as she had delivered them low, like the hiss of a dog-snake as it wraps tight the crushed body in its embrace. She saw a few mocking smiles, saw the muted swirls of unheard jests. *'Bound tight in murder, those two, and already they spit at each other!' 'No wonder their mates leapt into each other's arms!'*

Bakal managed to hold her glare a moment longer, as if he could hold back her furious, bitter words, and then he looked ahead once more. A rough sigh escaped him. 'I remember his nonsense—or so I thought it at the time. His tales of the Imass—he said the greatest proof of strength a male warrior could display was found in not once touching his mate with anything but tenderness.'

'And you sneered.'

'I saw women sneer at that, too.'

'And if we hadn't, Bakal? If you'd seen us with something else in our eyes?'

He grimaced and then nodded. 'A night or two of the wild wolf—'

'To beat out such treasonous ideas, yes. You did not understand—none of you did. If you hadn't killed him, he would have changed us all.'

'And women such as Sekara the Vile?'

She curled her lip. 'What of them?'

He grunted. 'Of course. Greed and power are her only lovers—in that, she is no different from us men.'

'What do you want with Hetan?'

'Nothing. Never mind.'

'You no longer trust me. Perhaps you never did. It was only the pool of blood we're both standing in.'

'You follow me. You stand just beyond the firelight every night.'

I am alone. Can't you see that? 'Why did you murder him? I will tell you. It's because you saw him as a threat, and he was surely that, wasn't he?'

'I—I did not—' He halted, shook his head. 'I want to steal her away. I want it to end.'

'It's too late. Hetan is dead inside. Long dead. You took away her husband. You took away her children. And then you—we—took away her body. A flower cut from its root quickly dies.'

'Estaral.'

He was holding on to a secret, she realized.

Bakal glanced at her. '*Cafal.*'

She felt her throat tighten—was it panic? Or the promise of vengeance? Retribution? Even if it meant her own death? *Oh, I see now. We're still falling.*

'He is close,' Bakal went on under his breath. 'He wants her back. He wants me to steal her away. Estaral, I need your help—'

She searched his face. 'You would do this for him? Do you hate him that much, Bakal?'

She might as well have struck him in the face.

'He—he is a shaman, a healer—'

'No Barghast shaman has *ever* healed one of the hobbled.'

'None has tried!'

'Perhaps it is as you say, Bakal. I see that you do not want to wound Cafal. You would do this to give to him what he seeks.'

He nodded once, as if unable to speak.

'I will take her from the children,' Estaral said. 'I will lead her to the west end of the camp. But, Bakal, there will be pickets—we are at the eve of battle—'

'I know. Leave the warriors to me.'

She didn't know why she was doing this. Nor did she understand the man walking at her side. But what difference did knowing make? Just as easy to live in ignorance, scraped clean of expectation, emptied of beliefs and faith, even hopes. *Hetan is hobbled. No different in the end from every other woman suffering the same fate. She's been cut down inside, and the stem lies bruised and lifeless. She was once a great warrior. She was once proud, her wit sharp as a thorn, ever quick to laugh but never with cruelty.* She was indeed a host of virtues, but they had availed her nothing. *No strength of will survives hobbling. Not a single virtue. This is the secret of humiliation: the deadliest weapon the Barghast have.*

She could see Hetan up ahead, her matted hair, her stumbles brought up by the crooked staff the hobbled were permitted when on the march. The daughter of Humbrall Taur was barely recognizable. Did her father's spirit stand witness, there in the Reaper's shadow? Or had he turned away?

No, he rides his last son's soul. That must be what has so maddened Cafal.

Well, to honour Hetan's father, she would do this. When the Barghast came to rest at this day's end. She was tired. She was thirsty. She hoped it would be soon.

———

Kashat pointed. 'See there, brother. The ridge forms half a circle.'

'Not much of a slope,' Sagal muttered.

'Look around,' Kashat said, snorting. 'It's about the best we can manage. This land is pocked, but those pocks are old and worn down. Anyway, that ridge marks the biggest of those pocks—you can see that for yourself. And the slope is rocky— they would lose horses charging up that.'

'So they flank us instead.'

'We make strongpoints at both ends, with crescents of archers positioned behind them to take any riders attempting an encirclement.'

'With the rear barricaded by the wagons.'

'Held by mixed archers and pike-wielders, yes, exactly. Listen, Sagal, by this time tomorrow we'll be picking loot from heaps of corpses. The Akrynnai army will be shattered, their villages undefended—we can march into the heart of their territory and claim it for ourselves.'

'An end to the Warleader, the rise of the first Barghast King.'

Kashat nodded. 'And we shall be princes, and the King shall grant us provinces to rule. Our very own herds. Horses, bhederin, rodara. We shall have Akrynnai slaves, as many of their young women as we want, and we shall live in keeps—do you remember, Sagal? When we were young, our first war, marching down to Capustan—we saw the great stone keeps all in ruin along the river. We shall build ourselves those, one each.'

Sagal grinned at his brother. 'Let us return to the host, and see if our great King is in any better mood than when we left him.'

They turned back, slinging their spears over their shoulders and jogging to rejoin the vanguard of the column. The sun glared through the dust above the glittering forest of barbed iron, transforming the cloud into a penumbra of gold. Vultures rode the deepening sky to either side. Barely two turns of the beaker before dusk arrived—the night ahead promised to be busy.

The half-dozen Akryn scouts rode between the narrow, twisting gullies and out on to the flats where the dust still drifted above the rubbish left behind by the Barghast. They cut across that churned-up trail and cantered southward. The sun had just left the sky, dropping behind a bank of clouds dark as a shadowed cliff-face on the western horizon, and dusk bled into the air.

When the drum of horse hoofs finally faded, Cafal edged out from the deeper of the two gullies. The bastards had held him back too long—the great cauldrons would be steaming in the Barghast camp, the foul reek of six parts animal blood to two parts water and sour wine, and all the uncured meat still rank with the taste of slaughter. Squads would be shaking out, amidst curses that they would have to eat salted strips of smoked bhederin, sharing a skin of warm water on their patrols between the pickets. The Barghast encampment would be seething with activity.

One of Bakal's warriors had found him a short time earlier, delivering the details of the plan. It would probably fail, but Cafal did not care. If he died attempting to steal her back, then this torment would end. For one of them, at least. It was a selfish desire, but selfish desires were all he had left.

I am the last of Father's children, the last not dead or broken. Father, you so struggled to become the great leader of the White Faces. And now I wonder, if you had turned away from the attempt, if you had quenched your ambition, where would you and your children be right now? Spirits reborn, would we even be here, on this cursed continent?

I know for a fact that Onos Toolan wanted a peaceful life, his head down beneath the winds that had once ravaged his soul. He was flesh, he was life—after so long—and what have we done? Did we embrace him? Did the White Face Barghast welcome him as a guest? Were we the honourable hosts we proclaim to be? Ah, such lies we tell ourselves. Our every comfort proves false in the end.

He moved cautiously along the battered trail. Already the glow from the cookfires stained the way ahead. He could not see the picket stations or the patrols—coming in from the west had disadvantaged him, but soon the darkness would paint them as silhouettes against the camp's hearths. In any case, he did not have to draw too close. Bakal would deliver her, or so he claimed.

The face of Setoc rose in his mind, and behind it flashed the horrible scene of her body spinning away from his blow, the looseness of her neck—had he heard a snap? He didn't know. But the way she fell. Her flopping limbs—yes, there was a crack, a sickening sound of bones breaking, a sound driving like a spike into his skull. He had heard it and he'd refused to hear it, but such refusal failed and so its dread echo reverberated through him. He had killed her. How could he face that?

He could not.

Hetan. Think of Hetan. You can save this one. The same hand that killed Setoc can save Hetan. Can you make that be enough, Cafal? Can you?

His contempt for himself was matched only by his contempt for the Barghast gods—he knew they were the cause behind all of this—*another gift by my own hand.* They had despised Onos Toolan. Unable to reach into his foreign blood, his foreign ideas, they had poisoned the hearts of every Barghast warrior against the Warleader. And now they held their mortal children in their hands, and every strange face was an enemy's face, every unfamiliar notion was a deadly threat to the Barghast and their way of life.

But the only people safe from change are the ones lying inside sealed tombs. You drowned your fear in ambition and see where you've brought us? This is the eve of our annihilation.

I have seen the Akrynnai army, and I will voice no warning. I will not rush into the camp and exhort Maral Eb to seek peace. I will do nothing to save any of them, not even Bakal. He knows what comes, if not the details, and he does not flinch.

Remember him, Cafal. He will die true to the pure virtues so quickly abused by those who possess none of them. He will be used as his kind have been used for thousands of years, among thousands of civilizations. He is one among the bloody fodder for empty tyrants and their pathetic wants. Without him, the great scything blade of history sings through nothing but air.

Would that such virtue could face down the tyrants. That the weapon turn in their sweaty hands. Would that the only blood spilled belonged to them and them alone.

Go on, Maral Eb. Walk out on to the plain and cross swords with Irkullas. Kill each other and then the rest of us can just walk away. Swords? Why such formality? Why not just bare hands and teeth? Tear each other to pieces! Like two wolves fighting to rule the pack—whichever one limps away triumphant will be eyed by the next one in line. And on it goes, and really, do any of the rest of us give a fuck? At least wolves don't make other wolves fight their battles for them. No, our tyrants are smarter than wolves, aren't they?

He halted and crouched down. He was in the place he was supposed to be.

The jade talons raked up from the southern horizon, and from the plain to the west a fox loosed an eerie, piercing cry. Night had arrived.

Estaral grasped the girl by her braid and flung her back. They had been trying to force goat shit into Hetan's mouth—her face was smeared from the cheeks down.

Spitting in rage, the girl scrambled to her feet, her cohorts closing round her. Eyes blazed. 'My father will see *you* hobbled for that!'

'I doubt it,' Estaral replied. 'What man wants to take a woman stinking of shit? You'll be lucky to keep your hide, Faranda. Now, all of you, get away from here— I know you all, and I've not yet decided whether to tell your fathers about this.'

They bolted.

Estaral knelt before Hetan, pulling up handfuls of grass to wipe her mouth and chin. 'Even the bad rules are breaking,' she said. 'We keep falling and falling, Hetan. Be glad you cannot see what has become of your people.'

But those words rang false. *Be glad? Be glad they chopped off the fronts of your feet? Be glad they raped you so many times you couldn't feel a damned bhederin pounding into you by now? No. And if the Akrynnai chop off our feet and rape us come tomorrow, who will weep for the White Faces?*

Not Cafal. 'Not you, either, Hetan.' She flung the soiled grasses away and helped Hetan to stand. 'Here, your staff, lean on it.' She grasped a handful of filthy shirt and began guiding the woman through the camp.

'Don't keep her too long!' She glanced back to see a warrior behind them—he had been coming to take her and now stood with a grin that hovered on the edge of something dark and cruel.

'They fed her shit—I'm taking her to get properly cleaned up.'

A flicker of disgust. 'The children? Who were they? A solid beating—'

'They ran before I got close enough. Ask around.'

Estaral tugged Hetan into motion once again.

The warrior did not pursue, but she heard him cursing as he wandered off. She didn't think she'd run into many more like him—everyone was crowding around their clan cookfires, hungry and parched and short-tempered as they jostled and fought for position. There'd be a few flick-blade duels this night, she expected. There always were, night before battle. Stupid, of course. Pointless. But, as Onos

Toolan might say, the real meaning of 'tradition' was . . . what had he called it? *'Stupidity on purpose', that's what he said. I think. I never much listened.*

I should have. We all should have.

They neared the western edge of the camp, where the wagons were already being positioned to form a defensive barricade. Just beyond, drovers were busy slaughtering stock, and the bleating cries of hundreds of animals filled the night. The first bonfires for offal had been lit using rotted cloth, bound rushes, dung and liberal splashes of lamp oil. The flames lit up terrified eyes from within crowded pens. Chaos and horror had come to the beasts and the air was thick with death.

She almost halted. She'd never before seen things in such a way; she'd never before felt the echo of misery and suffering assailing her from all directions— every scene painted into life by the fires was like a vision of madness. *We do this. We do this all the time. To all these creatures who look to us for protection. We do this and think nothing of it.*

We say we are great thinkers, but I think now, that most of what we do each and every day—and night—is in fact thoughtless. We will ourselves empty to numb us to our cruelty. We stiffen our faces and say we have needs. But to be empty is to have no purchase, nothing to grasp on to, and so in the emptiness we slide and we slide.

We fall.

Oh, when will it end?

She pulled Hetan to a position behind a wagon, the plains stretching westward before them. Thirty paces ahead, limned by the deepening remnants of the sunset, three warriors were busy digging a picket. 'Sit down—no, don't lift. Just sit.'

'Listen, Strahl—you have done enough. Leave this night to me.'

'Bakal—'

'Please, old friend. This is all by my hand—I stood alone before Onos Toolan. There must be the hope . . . the hope for balance. In my soul. Leave me this, I beg you.'

Strahl looked away and it was clear to Bakal that his words had been too honest, too raw. The warrior shifted nervously, his discomfort plain to see.

'Go, Strahl. Go lie in your wife's arms this night. Look past everything else— none of it matters. Find the faces of the ones you love. Your children, your wife.'

The man managed a nod, not meeting Bakal's eyes, and then set off.

Bakal watched him leave, and then checked his weapons one last time, before setting off through the camp.

Belligerence was building, sizzling beneath the harsh voices. It lit fires inside the strutting warriors as they bellowed out their oaths among the hearth circles. It bared teeth in the midst of every harsh laugh. War was the face to be stared into, or fled from, but the camp on a night such as this one was a cage, a prison to them all. The darkness hid the ones with skittish eyes and twitching hands; the bold postures and wild glares masked icy terror. Fear and excitement had closed jaws upon each other's throat and neither dared let go.

This was the ancient dance, this ritualized spitting into the eyes of fate, stoking the dark addiction. He had seen elders, warriors too old, too decrepit to do anything but sit or stand crooked over staffs, and he had seen their blazing eyes, had heard their cracking exhortations—but most of all, he had seen in their eyes the pain of their loss, as if they'd been forced to surrender their most precious love. It was no quaint conceit that warriors prayed to the spirits for the privilege of dying in battle. Thoughts of useless years stretching beyond the warrior's life could freeze the heart of the bravest of the brave.

The Barghast were not soldiers, not like the Malazans or the Crimson Guard. A profession could be left behind, a new future found. But for the warrior, war was everything, the very reason to live. It was the maker of heroes and cowards, the one force that tested a soul in ways that could not be bargained round, that could not be corrupted by a handful of silver. War forged bonds closer knit than those of bloodkin. It painted the crypt's wall behind every set of eyes—those of foe and friend both. It was, indeed, the purest, truest cult of all. What need for wonder, then, that so many youths so longed for such a life?

Bakal understood all this, for he was indeed a warrior. He understood, and yet his heart was bitter with disgust. No longer did he dream of inviting his sons and daughters into such a world. Embracing this addiction devoured too much, inside and out.

He—and so many others—had looked into the face of Onos Toolan and had seen his compassion, had seen it so clearly that the only response was to recoil. The Imass had been an eternal warrior. He had fought with the warrior's blessing of immortality, given the gift of battles unending, and then he had willingly surrendered it. How could such a man, even one reborn, find so much of his humanity still alive within him?

I could not have. Even after but three decades of war . . . if I was this moment reborn, I could not find in myself . . . what? A battered tin cup half-filled with compassion, not enough to splash a dozen people closest to me.

Yet . . . yet he was a flood, an unending flood—how can that be?

Who did I kill? Shy from that question if you must, Bakal. But one truth you cannot deny: his compassion took hold of your arm, your knife, and showed you the strength of its will.

His steps slowed. He looked round, blearily. *I am lost. Where am I? I don't understand. Where am I? And what are all these broken things in my hands? Still crashing down—the roar is deafening!* 'Save her,' he muttered. 'Yes. Save her—the only one worth saving. May she live a thousand years, proof to all who see her, proof of who and what the Barghast were. The White Faces.' *We hobble ourselves and call it glory. We lift to meet drooling old men eager to fill us to bursting with their bitter poisons. Old men? No, warleaders and warchiefs. And our precious tradition of senseless self-destruction. Watch it fuck us dry.*

He was railing, but it was in silence. Who would want to hear such things? See what happened to the last one who held out a compassionate hand? He imagined himself walking between heaving rows of his fellow warriors. He walked, trailing the gutted ropes of his messy arguments, and from both sides spit and curses rained down.

Truths bore the frightened mind. Are we bored? Yes! Where is the blood? Where are the flashing knives? Give us the unthinking dance! Charge our jaded hearts, you weeping slave! Piss on your difficult thoughts, your grim recognitions. Lift up your backside, fool, while I seek to pound feeling back into me.

Stand still while I hobble you—let's see you walk now!

Bakal staggered out from the camp's edge. Halting ten paces beyond the wagons, he tugged loose the straps binding the lance to his back. Rolled the shaft into his right hand. His shoulder ached—the tears of tendon and muscle were not yet mended. The pain would wake him up.

Ahead was the banked berm of the picket's trench. Three helmed heads were visible as lumps projecting above the reddish heap of earth.

Bakal broke into a trot, silent on the grasses as he closed the distance.

He launched the lance from twelve paces behind the three warriors. Saw the iron point drive between the shoulders of the one on his left, punching the man's body against the trench wall. As the other two jerked, heads snapping in that direction, he reached the trench—blades in hands—and leapt down between them. His cutlass bit through bronze skull-cap, split half the woman's skull, and jammed there. The knife in his left hand slashed the back of the last warrior's neck—but the man had twisted, enough to save his spinal cord, and spinning, he slammed a dagger deep into Bakal's chest, just under his left arm.

Intimately close with his enemy in the cramped trench, he saw the warrior open his mouth to cry out the alarm. Bakal's back-slash with his knife ripped out the man's throat, even as the dagger sank a second time, the blade snapping as it snagged between two ribs.

Blood rushed up to fill Bakal's throat and he fell against the dying warrior, coughing into the wool of the man's cloak.

He was feeling so very tired now, but there were things still to be done. *Find her. Save her.* He crawled from the trench. He was having trouble breathing. A memory that had been lost for decades returned to him suddenly: the last time he'd been near death—the Drowning Fever had struck him down, his lungs filling up with phlegm. The thick poultices encasing his chest, the eye-stinging smell of ground mustard seeds—his mother's face, a blurred thing, hovering, dread hardening to resignation behind her eyes. *Crypt walls. We all have them, there inside— you don't go there often, do you? It's where you keep your dead. Dead relatives, dead dreams, dead promises. Dead selves, so many of those, so many. When you loot, you only take the best things. The things you can use, the things you can sell. And when you seal it all up again, the darkness remains.*

It remains. Ah, Mother, it remains.

My crypt. My crypt walls.

He thought to regain his feet. Instead, he was lying on the ground, the trench pit almost within reach. *Mother? Are you there? Father? Desorban, my son, oh precious son—I put that sword into your hand. I pretended to be proud, even as fear curled black talons round my heart. Later, when I looked down at your so-still face, when all the others were singing the glory of your brave moments—only moments, yes, all you had—I pretended that the music eased the hurt in my soul. I pretended, because to pretend was to comfort them in turn, for the time when they stood in my place, looking down on the face of their own beloved.*

Son! Are you there?

Crypt walls. Scenes and faces.

In the dark, you can't even see the paint.

Estaral struggled in the gloom to see that distant picket. Had something happened there? She wasn't sure. From the camp behind the row of wagons at her back, she could hear a child shouting, something vicious and eager in the voice. A tremor of unease ran through her and she shot Hetan a glance. Sitting, staring at nothing.

This was taking too long. Warriors would be looking for their hobbled prize. Words would break loose—Estaral had been seen, dragging Hetan through the camp. Westward, yes. Out past the light of the fires.

She reached down and pulled Hetan to her feet. Took up the staff and pushed it into the woman's hands. 'Come!'

Estaral dragged her towards the picket. No movement from there. Something lying on this side, something that hadn't been there earlier. Mouth dry, heart in her throat, she led Hetan closer.

The stench of faeces and urine and blood reached her. That shape—a body, lying still in death.

'Bakal?' she whispered.

Nothing. From the trench itself, a heavy silence. She crouched at the body, pulled it on to its back. She stared down at Bakal's face: the frothy streaks of blood smearing his chin, the expression as of one lost, and finally, his staring, sightless eyes.

Another shout from the camp, closer this time. *That's Faranda—and that one, that's Sekara. Spirits shit on them both!*

Terror rushed through her. She crouched, like a hare with no cover in sight.

Hetan made to sink to her knees. *'No!'* she hissed. *'Stay up, damn you!'* She grasped the woman's shirt again, tugged her stumbling round one end of the trench, out on to the plain.

Jade licked the grasses—a hundred paces ahead the ground rose, showing pieces of a ridge. The column had skirted round that, she recalled. 'Hetan! Listen to me! Walk to that ridge—do you see it? Walk there. Just walk, do you understand? A man waits for you there—he's impatient. He's angry. Hurry to him or you'll regret it. Hurry!' She shoved her forward.

Hetan staggered, righted herself. For one terrible moment she simply stood where she was, and then the hobbled lurched into motion.

Estaral watched her for a dozen heartbeats—to be certain—and then she spun and ran back towards the camp. She could slip in unseen. Yes, she'd cleaned up Hetan's face, and then had simply left her, close to the wagons—the bitch was dead behind the eyes, anyone could see that. She fled out on to the plain? Ridiculous, but if you want to go look, out where the Akrynnai are waiting, go right ahead.

She found shadows between two wagons, squeezed in. Figures were moving in and out of firelight. The shouts had stopped. If she avoided the hearths, she could thread her way back to where Strahl and the others were camped. She would have to tell him of Bakal's death. Who would lead the Senan tomorrow? It would have to be Strahl. He would need to know, so he could ready his mind to command, to the weight of his clan's destiny.

She edged forward.

Thirty paces on, they found her. Six women led by Sekara, with Faranda hovering in the background. Estaral saw them rushing to close and she drew her knife. She knew what they would do to her; she knew they weren't interested in asking questions, weren't interested in explanations. *No, they will do to me what they did to Hetan.* Bakal was gone, her protector was gone. There were, she realized, so many ways to be alone.

They saw her weapon. Avid desire lit their eyes—yes, they wanted blood. '*I killed her!*' Estaral shrieked. '*Bakal was using her—I killed them both!*'

She lunged into their midst.

Blades flickered. Estaral staggered, spun even as she sank to her knees. Gleeful faces on all sides. *Such bright hunger—oh, how alive they feel!* She was bleeding out, four, maybe five wounds, heat leaking out from her body.

So stupid. All of it . . . so stupid. And with that thought she laughed out her last breath.

The massive bank of clouds on the western horizon now filled half the night sky, impenetrable and solid as a wall, building block by block to shut out the stars and the slashes of jade. Wind rustled the grasses, pulled from the east as if the storm was drawing breath. Yet no flashes lit the clouds, and not once had Cafal heard thunder. Despite this, his trepidation grew with every glance at the towering blackness.

Where was Bakal? Where was Hetan?

The bound grip of the hook-blade was slick in his hand. He had begun to shiver as the temperature plummeted.

He could save her. He was certain of it. He would demand the power from the Barghast gods. If they refused him, he vowed he would destroy them. *No games, no bargains. I know it was your lust for blood that led to this. And I will make you pay.*

Cafal dreaded the moment he first saw his sister, this mocking, twisted semblance of the woman he had known all his life. Would she even recognize him? Of course she would. She would lunge into his arms—an end to the torment, the rebirth of hope. Dread, yes, and then he would make it good again, all of it. They would flee west—all the way to Lether—

A faint sound behind him. Cafal whirled round.

The mace clipped him on his left temple. He reeled to the right, attempted to pivot and slash his weapon into the path of his attacker. A punch in the chest lifted him from his feet. He was twisted in the air, hook-blade flying from his hand, and it seemed the fist on his chest followed him down, driving deeper when he landed on his back. Bones grated, splintered.

He saw, uncomprehending, the shaft of the spear, upright as a standard, its head buried in his chest.

Shadowy shapes above him. The gauntleted hands gripping the spear now twisted and pushed down hard.

The point thrust through into the earth beneath him.

He struggled to make sense of things, but everything slipped through his nerveless fingers. Three, now four shapes looming over him, but not a word was spoken.

They watch me die. I've done the same. Why do we do that? Why are we so fascinated by this failure?

Because, I think, we see how easy it is.

The Akrynnai warrior holding the man down with his spear now relaxed. 'He's done,' he said, tugging his weapon loose.

'If he was scouting our camp,' the mace-wielder said, 'why was he facing the wrong way?'

'Barghast,' muttered a third man, and the others nodded. There was no sense to these damned savages.

'Tomorrow,' said the warrior now cleaning his spear, 'we kill the rest of them.'

She stumbled onward, eyes on the black wall facing her, which seemed to lurch close only to recoil again, as if the world pulsed. The wind pushed her along now, solid as a hand at her back, and the thud of the staff's heel thumped on and on.

When four Akrynnai warriors cut across her field of vision, she slowed and then halted, waiting for them to take her. But they didn't. Instead, they made warding gestures and quickly vanished into the gloom. After a time, she set out once more, tottering, her breath coming in thick gasps now. The blisters on her hands broke and made the staff slick.

She walked until the world lost its strength, and then she sat down on the damp grasses beside a lichen-skinned boulder. The wind whipped at her shredded shirt. She stared unseeing, the staff sliding out from her hands. After a time she sank down on to her side, drawing her legs up.

And waited for the blackness to swallow the world.

It was as if night in all its natural order had been stolen away. Strahl watched as the White Faces fed their fires with anything that would burn, crying out to their gods. *See us! Find us! We are your children!* Goats were dragged to makeshift altars and their throats slashed open. Blood splashed and hoofed legs kicked and then fell to feeble trembling. Dogs fled the sudden, inexplicable slash of cutlass blades. Terror and madness whipped like the smoke and sparks and ashes from the bonfires. By dawn, he knew, not a single animal would be left alive.

If dawn ever comes.

He had heard about Estaral's death. He had heard about what she had claimed to have done. None of that made sense. Bakal would not have used Hetan—clearly, Estaral had believed she would be with Bakal, that she would be his wife, and when she saw him with Hetan her insanity had painted the scene with the drenched colours of lust. She had murdered them both in a jealous rage.

Strahl cursed himself. He should have driven the widow away days ago. He should have made it plain that Bakal had no interest in her. Spirits below, if he'd seen even a hint of the mad light in her eyes, he would have killed her outright.

Now command of the Senan in the battle this dawn fell to him. He had been handed his most hidden ambition—when he had in fact already willingly surrendered it to stand in Bakal's shadow. But desire, once it reached the mouth, never tasted as sweet as it did in anticipation. In fact, he was already choking on it.

Bakal had discussed the engagement with him. Had told him what he intended. Strahl had that much at least. And when the Senan gathered at dawn, he would summon the chiefs of the clan, and he would give him Bakal's words as if they were his own. Would they listen?

He would know soon enough.

The sun opened its eye in the east and seemed to flinch in the face of the massive wall of dark clouds devouring half the sky. On the vast plain at the very edge of what had once been the lands of the Awl, two armies stirred. Bestial standards of the Barghast clans lifted like uneasy masts above the wind-flattened grasses, as ash from the enormous bonfires spun and swirled in the air thick as snow. Approaching from the southwest was a vast crescent, warriors mounted and on foot. Pennons snapped above legions of Saphii soldiers marching in phalanx, shields tilted to cut the wind, long spears blazing with the dawn's fires. Companies of D'ras skirmishers and archers filled the gaps and ranged ahead of the main force in loose formations. Mounted archers advanced on the tips of the bhederin's horns, backed by the heavier lancers. The horses were skittish beneath the Akrynnai warriors, and every now and then one reared or bolted and fellow riders would close to help calm the animal.

Along the summit of the ridge, Warleader Maral Eb had positioned the Senan in the centre, framed by the lesser clans. His own Barahn he had divided between his brothers, anchoring the outer flanks.

As the day awakened, the crescent approached the Barghast position, swinging south as scouts rode back to report on the field of battle.

All at once the wind fell off, and in its place frigid cold gripped the air. It was the heart of summer, yet breaths plumed and steam rose from the backs of thousands of horses. Warriors shivered, half with chill and half with sudden dread.

Was this a battle between gods? Were the Akrynnai spirits about to manifest like fangs in snapping jaws? Were the undead ancestor gods of the White Faces only moments from clambering up from the hard, frozen earth, chanting an ancient dirge of blood? Were mortal men and women destined to cower beneath the terrible clash of ascendants? Above them all, the sky was split in two, the brittle light of morning to the east, the unyielding darkness of night in the west. None—not Barghast, not Akrynnai, not Saphii nor D'ras—had ever before seen such a sky. It filled them with terror.

Frost sheathed the grasses and glistened on iron and bronze as icy cold air flowed out from beneath the storm front. Among the two armies, no fierce songs or chants rang out in challenge. An unnatural silence gripped the forces, even at the moment when the two masses of humanity came within sight of each other.

Not a single bird rode the febrile sky.

Yet the Akrynnai army marched closer to its hated enemy; and the enemy stood motionless awaiting them.

A thousand paces west of the Barghast position lay the body of a woman, curled in the frozen grasses with her back against a lichen-skinned boulder. A place to lie down, the last nest of her last night. Frost glittered like diamond scales upon her pale skin.

She had died alone, forty paces from the corpse of her brother. But this death belonged to the flesh. The woman that had been Hetan, wife to Onos Toolan, mother of Absi, Stavi and Storii, had died some time earlier. The body will totter past the dead husk of its soul, sometimes for days, sometimes for years.

She lay on frozen ground, complete in her scene of solitary surrender. Did the sky above blink in witness? Not even once? When a sky blinks, how long does it take between the sweep of darkness and the rebirth of light?

The ghosts, their wings burnt down to black stumps, waited to tell her the answers to those questions.

Saddic, are you still alive? I have dreamed a thing. This thing was a vision, the death of a lizard-wolf lying curled on its side, the danger of bones beneath the sun. Listen to my dream, Saddic, and remember.

Greed is the knife in the sheath of ambition. You see the wicked gleam when you've drawn too close. Too close to get away, and as I told you: greed invites death, and now death takes her twice. This thing was a vision. She died not forty paces from her brother, and above her two armies war in the heavens, and beasts that are brothers are about to lock jaws upon each other's throat. Strange names, strange faces. Painted white like the Quitters. A man with sad eyes whose name is Sceptre Irkullas.

Such a sky, such a sky!

Greed and ambition, Saddic. Greed and treachery. Greed and justice. These are the reasons of fate, and every reason is a lie.

She was dead before dawn. I held her broken soul in my hands. I hold it still. As Rutt holds Held.

I knew a boy.

Absi, where are you?

Saddic listened, and then he said, 'Badalle, I am cold. Tell me again about the fires. The wonderful fires.'

But these fires were burned down to cinders and ash. The cold was the cold of another world.

Saddic, listen. I have seen a door. Opening.

Chapter Eighteen

What feeds you is rent
With the claws of your need.
But needs dwell half in light
And half in darkness.
And virtue folds in the seam.
If the demand of need is life
Then suffering and death hold purpose.
But if we speak of want and petty desire
The seam folds into darkness
And no virtue holds the ground.
Needs and wants make for a grey world.
But nature yields no privilege.
And what is righteous will soon
Feed itself with the claws
Of your need, as life demands.

QUALITIES OF LIFE
SAEGEN

Weak and exhausted, Yan Tovis had followed her brother through the gates and into the dead city of Kharkanas. The secret legends possessed by her bloodline had virtually carved into her soul the details before her. When she'd walked the bridge, the echo of the stones underfoot embraced her, as familiar and steeped in sorrow as a dead grandmother's cloak. Passing beneath the storeyed arch, she felt as if she had returned home—but this home was a forgotten place, as if she had inherited someone else's nostalgia. Her discomfort turned to distress as she emerged from the cool darkness and saw before her a silent, lifeless vista of tall, smoke-stained buildings, smeared towers and disfigured statues. Tiered gardens had grown past weeds and were now thick with twisted trees, the roots of which had burst the retaining walls, snaking down walls and buckling pavestones. Birds nested on ledges above walls painted white in guano. Heaps of wind-blown leaves mouldered in corners, and plants had pushed up between flagstones.

She could feel the ancient magic, like something fluttering at the edge of her vision. The city had survived the eons far better than it rightly should have. And the sorcery still resisted the relentless siege of time. She looked upon a scene that might have been abandoned little more than a generation ago, when in truth it was ancient beyond imagining.

Mothers will hold children close
Until the world itself crumbles

So wrote some poet from this very city, and Yan Tovis understood it well enough. *The child and the home shall never change, if that child's mother has any say over the matter. But explanations make truths mundane. The poet seeks to awaken in the listener all that is known yet unspoken. Words to conjure an absence of words. But children will grow up, and time will drive spears through the thickest walls. And sometimes the walls are breached from within.*

It had always been her habit—and she knew it well enough—to sow uncertainty. In her mind, indecision was a way of life. Her brother, of course, was the very opposite. They stood facing one another in extremity, across a gulf that could not be bridged. When Yedan Derryg stepped beyond challenge, his will was a brutal thing, a terrible force that destroyed lives. When she did not have him facing her—his hands dripping blood and his eyes hard as stone—she came to believe that indecisiveness was the natural order of the world, a state of mind that waited until acted upon, doomed to react and never initiate, a mind that simply held itself in place, passive, resigned to whatever the fates delivered.

They were meant to stand together, meant to fix pressure each upon the other like the counterweights at either end of the bridge, and in that tense balance they might find the wisdom to rule, they might make solid and sure the stones beneath the feet of their people.

He had murdered her witches and warlocks, and it had not been a matter of stepping round her to get to them, for she had proved no obstacle to him. No, she had been frozen in place. *Awaiting the knife of fate. Yedan's knife.*

I forgot. And so I failed. I need him back. I need my Witchslayer.

Behind her trooped the vanguard of her people. Pully and Skwish, plump and rosy as maidens, their faces growing slack as the residual magic bled through their meagre defences. The two officers commanding the Watch's company, Brevity and Pithy, had already begun sending squads on to the side streets, to scout out places to accommodate the refugees. Their calm, drawling instructions were like a farrier's file over the uneven edge of fear and panic.

She could not see Yedan, nor his horse, but ahead, close to the centre of the city, rose a massive edifice, part temple, part palace and keep, from which five towers rose to spear the heavy gloom of the sky. The Citadel. It occupied an island encircled by a gorge that could be crossed by but one bridge, and that bridge was reached by this main avenue.

Yan Tovis glanced back, found Pithy. 'Settle the people as best you can—but don't spread them out too much. Oh, and tell the witches they won't be able to think straight until they've worked a protective circle around themselves.'

At the woman's nod, Yan faced the heart of the city again, and then set out.

He rode to the Citadel. Of course he did. He was Yedan Derryg. *And he wants to see for himself where all the blood was spilled.*

Some enormous concussion had cracked the marble pillars flanking the Great Hall. Fissures gaped, many of the columns bowed or tilted precariously, and a fine scattering of white dust coated the mosaic floor. In places that dust had congealed into muddy stains.

Indifferent to the rubbish, Yedan crossed the vast chamber. He could feel a warmth coursing through him, as if he was about to wade into a battle. Currents of power still drifted in this place, thick with discordant emotions. Horror, grief, black rage and terrible agony. Madness had descended upon this citadel, and blood had drenched the world.

He found a side corridor just beyond the Great Hall, its entranceway ornate with arcane carvings: women marching in solemn procession. Tall, midnight-skinned women. Once within the passage, the images on the walls to either side transformed into carnal scenes, growing ever more elaborate as he proceeded to the far end. After a series of cloisters, the function of which was in no way ambiguous, Yedan entered a domed chamber. The Terondai—was that the word? Who could say how time had twisted it? The sacred eye in the darkness, the witness to all things.

There was a time, the secret legends told, when light did not visit this world, and the darkness was absolute. But only the true children of the Mother could survive in such a realm, and no blood remains for ever pure. More, there were other beings dwelling in Night. Some saw truly, others did not.

Light was what seeped in with the wounding of the Mother—a wounding she chose to permit, a wounding and then the birthing that came of it. *'All children,'* she said, *'must be able to see. We gift the living with light and darkness and shadow. The truth of our natures cannot be found in the absence of that which we are not. Walk from darkness, walk into shadow, walk beyond into light. These are the truths of being. "Without ground, there can be no sky." So spoke the Azathanai in the dust of their quarries.'*

Secret legends, likely little more than nonsense. Words to give meaning to what already existed, to what existed with or without the guiding hand of sentient beings. To this rock, to that river, to the molten fires from below and the frozen rain from above. He wasn't much impressed with things like that.

The Terondai was smeared in ashes and cluttered with dried leaves. Shapeless ridges of white dust were all that remained of bodies left lying where they fell. There was no sign of weapons or jewellery, leading Yedan to surmise that looters had been through the chamber—and everywhere else in the Citadel, he suspected. Odd that his bloodline's secret legends made no mention of those flitting thieves. *Yet, weren't we here at the grisly end? Not wielding weapons. Not making heroic stands. Just . . . what? Watching? Prompting the question: who in the name of the Shore were we? Their damned servants? Their slaves?*

Secret legends, tell us your secret truths.

And what of this ancient claim to some kind of royal bloodline? Rulers of what? The woodshed? The garden island in the river? Yes, he would trot out the righteous assertions that he and his sister were fit to command, if that was what was needed to bend others to his will. They had titles, didn't they? Twilight. The Watch. And Yan Tovis had done much the same, taking upon herself the role of Queen of the Shake. The burden of privilege—*see how we bow beneath its weight.*

Jaws bunched, he scanned the chamber once more, now with greater care.

'You damned fool.'

He twisted round, eyed his sister.

'You're in the temple, idiot—get off the damned horse.'

'There are raised gardens,' he said. 'Find some farmers among your lot and get them to start clearing. I'll send others down to the river—we've got plenty of nets.'

'You want us to occupy the city?'

'Why not?'

She seemed at a loss for words.

Yedan drew his horse round until he faced her. 'Twilight, you took us on to the Road of Gallan. The Blind Man's Road. Now we are in the Realm of Darkness. But the realm is dead. It is preserved in death by sorcery. If this was once our home, we can make it so again. Was that not our destiny?'

'Destiny? Errant's balls, why does speaking that word sound like the unsheathing of a sword? Yedan, perhaps we knew this city once. Perhaps our family line reaches back and every story we learned was true. The glory of Kharkanas. But not one of those stories tells us we *ruled* here. In this city. We were not this realm's master.'

He studied her for a time. 'We move on, then.'

'Yes.'

'To where?'

'The forest beyond the river. Through it and out to the other side. Yedan, we have come this far. Let us make the journey to the place where it started. Our true home. The First Shore.'

'We don't even know what that means.'

'So we find out.'

'The river is still worth a look,' he said. 'We're short of food.'

'Of course. Now, in honour of those who fell here, brother, get off that damned horse!'

Moments after the two had left the chamber, the stillness that had existed for millennia was broken. A stirring of dead leaves, spinning as if lifted by small whirlwinds. Dust hazed the air, and the strange muted gloom—where light itself seemed an unwelcome stranger—suddenly wavered.

And something like a long, drawn breath slowly filled the chamber. It echoed wretched as a sob.

Brevity followed Pithy to the mouth of the alley. They carried lanterns, shadows rocking on walls as they made their way down half the narrow thoroughfare's length.

She halted beside her friend and together they stared down at the bodies.

'Dead?' Brevity asked.

'No, sweetie. In the realm of dreams, the both of them.'

'When did this happen?'

'Couldn't a been too long ago,' Pithy replied. 'I seen the two wander in here to do that ritual or whatever. Little later I chanced to peek in and saw their torches had gone out. So I come for a look.'

Brevity settled into a crouch and set the lantern to one side. She grasped the witch nearest her and pulled the woman over, peering down at the face. 'Pully, I think. They look like twins as it is.'

'Gettin' more so, too,' Pithy noted, 'or so I noticed.'

'Eyelids fluttering like mad.'

'Realm of dreams, didn't I say so?'

Brevity pushed back an eyelid. 'Rolled right up. Maybe the ritual turned on 'em.'

'Could be. What should we do?'

'I'm tempted to bury them.'

'But they ain't dead.'

'I know. But opportunities like this don't come every day.'

'What's broken cannot be mended. You broke us, but that is not all—see what you have done.'

Gallan had been horrified. He could not abide this new world. He wanted a return to darkness and, when he'd done gouging out his own eyes, he found it. Sandalath, her son's tiny hand held tight within her solid grip, stood looking down on the madman, seeing but not registering all the blood on his face and smeared across the floor—the impossibility of it here at the very threshold to the Terondai. He wept, choking on something again and again—yet whatever was in his mouth he would not spit out—and his lips were glistening crimson, his teeth red as cedar chips.

'Mother,' said her son, 'what's happened?'

The world changes. Gallan, you fool. What you've done does not change it back. 'An accident,' she replied. 'We must find someone to help—'

'But why is he eating his eyes?'

'Go now, find a priestess—quickly, Orfantal!'

Gallan choked, trying to swallow his eyeballs only to hack them back into his mouth. The holes in his head wept bloody tears.

Ever the poetic statement, Gallan. The grandiose symbol, artfully positioned at the temple door. You will lie here until someone important comes, and then you'll swallow those damned things down. Even the masterpiece is servant to timing.

Will Mother Dark be struck in the heart by this, Gallan? Or simply disgusted? 'It's done, old man,' she said. 'No going back.'

He clearly misunderstood her, as he began laughing.

She saw one of the eyes in his mouth roll into view, and for one insane moment it seemed to look up at her.

'What's broken cannot be mended. You broke us, but that is not all—see what you have done.'

Sandalath hissed as that echo intruded a second time into her memories. It didn't belong in the scene she had resurrected. It belonged somewhere else, with someone else. *With* someone else, not *to*. Of course that was the horrid thing about it. She heard those words spoken and they indeed came from her, arriving in her own voice, and that voice was from a woman who truly understood what it was to be broken.

And that is the bitter truth. I have not mended. After all this time . . .

'You asleep?' Withal asked from where he lay behind her.

She contemplated the merits of a response, decided against them and remained silent.

'Talking in your sleep again,' he muttered, shifting beneath the furs. 'But what I want to know is, what broke?'

She sat up as if stung by a scorpion. '*What?*'

'Awake after all—'

'*What did you just say?*'

'Whatever it was, it's put my heart in my throat and you poised to tear it out. I suppose you could beat me senseless—'

Snarling, she flung the furs back and rose to her feet. The three Venath demons were, inexplicably, digging a huge hole a short distance down from the road. Mape was in the bottom, heaving enormous boulders into Rind's arms where the demon crouched at the edge. Rind then swung round to transfer the rock to Pule, who pitched it away. *What in Hood's name are they doing? Never mind.* She rubbed at her face.

Talking in my sleep? Not those words. Please, not those words.

She walked some way up the Road, eager to be off. But Withal needed some sleep. Humans were absurdly frail. Their every achievement proved similarly fragile. If there weren't so damned many of them, and if they didn't display the occasional ant-nest frenzy of creativity, why, they'd have died out long ago. *More to the point, if the rest of us hadn't sneered in our idle witnessing of their pathetic efforts—if we'd wised up, in fact, one or all of us would have wiped them out long ago. Tiste Andii, Jaghut, K'Chain Che'Malle, Forkrul Assail. Gods, Tiste Edur, even. Scabandari, you slaughtered the wrong enemy. Even you, Anomander—you play with them as if they're pets. But these pets will turn on you. Sooner or later.*

She knew she was avoiding the scaly beast gnawing at the roots of her mind. Urging her thoughts to wander away, away from the place where kindred blood still glistened. But it was no use. Words had been spoken. Violence had given answer, and the rise and fall of chests faded into eternal stillness. And that beast, well, it had the sharpest teeth.

Sandalath sighed. *Kharkanas.* The city awaited her. Not so far away now, her ancient home, her own private crypt, its confines crammed solid with the worthless keepsakes of a young woman's life.

> *Watch me chase my dreams*
> *In the transit of dust*

Snorting, she swung round, retracing her path to where her husband slept. The demons—*Venath, who'd once been allies of the Jaghut. Who gave of their blood to the Trell—and what a fell mix that turned out to be*—the demons had all vanished into the hole they'd dug. Why had the damned things attached themselves to Withal? He said he'd found them on the island where he'd been imprisoned by the Crippled God. Which suggested that the Crippled God had summoned and bound the demons. But later, the Nachts had abetted Withal's escape and seemed instead to be in league with Mael. *And now . . . they're digging a hole.*

'Never mind,' said Withal, rolling over and sitting up. 'You're worse than a mosquito in a room. If you're in such a hurry, let's just go until we get there. I can rest then.'

'You're exhausted.'

He eyed her. 'It ain't the walking that's exhausting me, beloved.'

'You'd better explain that.'

'I will. But not right now.'

She saw the defiance in his eyes. *I could make him talk. But that look in his eyes . . . it's cute.* 'Gather up your gear then, husband. And while you do, I will explain something to you. We are following the road that leads to the city where I was born. Now, that's stressful enough. But it's something I can handle. Not happily, mind you, but even so. No, there is something else.'

He'd tied up his bedroll and had it tucked under an arm. 'Go on.'

'Imagine a pool of black water. Depthless, hidden within a cave where no air stirs and nothing drips. The pool's surface has not known a single ripple in tens of thousands of years. You've come to kneel beside it—all your life—but what you see never changes.'

'All right.'

'I still see nothing to change that, Withal. But . . . somewhere far below the surface, in depths unimaginable . . . *something moves.*'

'Sounds like we should be running the other way.'

'You're probably right, but I can't.'

'This old life of yours, Sand—you've said you were not a fighter—you knew nothing of weapons or warfare. So, what were you in this city home of yours?'

'There were factions—a power struggle.' She looked away, up the Road. 'It went on for generations—yes, that may be hard to believe. Generations among the Tiste Andii. You'd think that after the centuries they'd be entrenched, and maybe they were, for a time. Even a long time. But then everything changed—in my life, I knew nothing but turmoil. Alliances, betrayals, war pacts, treacheries. You cannot imagine how such things twisted our civilization, our culture.'

'Sand.'

'I was a hostage, Withal. Valued but expendable.'

'But that's a not a life! That's an interruption in a life!'

'Everything was breaking down.' *We were supposed to be sacrosanct. Precious.* 'It doesn't matter now,' she added. 'It's not a career I can pick up again, is it?'

He was staring at her. 'Would you? If you could?'

'A ridiculous question.' *'What's broken cannot be mended. You broke us, but that is not all—see what you have done.'*

'Sand.'

'Of course not. Now, saddle up.'

'But why is he eating his eyes?'

'Once, long ago, my son, there was nothing but darkness. And that nothing, Orfantal, was everything.'

'But why—'

'He is old. He's seen too much.'

'He could have just closed them.'

'Yes, he could have at that.'

'Mother?'

'Yes, Orfantal?'

'Don't eat your eyes.'

'Don't worry. I am like most people. I can keep my eyes and still see nothing.'

Now, woman, you said no such thing. And be thankful for that. The other rule applies. Mouth working, nothing said. And that is the ease we find for ourselves. After all, if we said everything we could say to each other, we'd have all killed each other long ago.

Gallan, you were a poet. You should have swallowed your tongue.

He had hurt someone, once. And he had known he had done so, and knowing led him into feeling bad. But no one enjoys feeling bad. Better to replace the guilt and shame with something turned outward. Something that burned all within reach, something that would harness all his energies and direct them away from himself. Something called *anger*. By the time he was done—by the time his rage had run its course—he found himself surrounded in ashes, and the life he had known was for ever gone.

Introspection was an act of supreme courage, one that few could manage. But when all one had left to stir was a heap of crumbled bones, there was nothing else one could do. Fleeing the scene only prolonged the ordeal. Memories clung to the horrors in his wake, and the only true escape was a plunge into madness—and madness was not a thing he could simply choose for himself. *More's the pity.* No, the sharper the inner landscape, the fiercer the sanity.

He believed that his family name was Veed. He had been a Gral, a warrior and a husband. He had done terrible things. There was blood on his hands, and the salty, bitter taste of lies on his tongue. The stench of scorched cloth still filled his head.

I have slain. In this admission, he had a place to begin.

Then, all these truths assembled themselves into the frame of his future. Leading to his next thought.

I will slay again.

Not one among those he now hunted could hope to stand before him. Their petty kingdom was no more formidable than a termite mound, but to the insects themselves it was majesty and it was permanence and it was these things that made them giants in their own realm. Veed was the boot, the bronze-sheathed toe that sent walls crashing down, delivering utter ruin. *It is what I am made to do.*

His path was unerring. Into the sunken pit and through the entrance, finding himself in a chamber crowded with reptilian corpses that swarmed with orthen and maggots. He crossed the room and halted before the inner portal.

They were somewhere far above—they had seen him, he was sure of it. Watched him from the eyes or mouth of the dragon. They did not know who he was, and so they had no reason to fear him. Even so, he knew that they would be cautious. If he simply lunged into their midst, blades flashing, some might escape. Some might fight back. A lucky swing . . . no, he would need his charm, his ability to put them all at ease. *It is possible that this cannot be rushed. I see that now. But I have shown patience before, haven't I? I have shown a true talent for deceit.*

Empty huts are not my only legacy, after all.

He sheathed his weapons.

Spat into the palms of his hands, and slicked back his hair. Then set off on the long ascent.

He could howl into their faces, and they would hear nothing. He could close invisible hands about their throats and they would not even shrug. *A slayer has come! The one below—I have sailed the storm of his desires—he seeks to murder you all!* His wretched family remained oblivious. Yes, they had seen the stranger. They had seen his deliberate path to the great stone edifice they had claimed as their own. And they had then resumed their mundane activities, as if suffering beneath a geas of careless indifference.

Taxilian, Rautos and Breath followed Sulkit as the K'Chain drone laboured over countless mechanisms. The creature seemed immune to exhaustion, as if the purpose driving it surpassed the needs of the flesh. Not even Taxilian could determine if the drone's efforts yielded any measurable effect. Nothing sprang to sudden life. No hidden gears churned into rumbling action. Darkness still commanded every corridor; feral creatures still scurried in chambers and made nests in the rubbish.

Last and Asane were busy constructing a nest of their own, when they weren't hunting orthen or collecting water from the dripping pipes. Sheb maintained vigil over the empty wastes from a perch that he called the Crown, while Nappet wandered without purpose, muttering under his breath and cursing his ill luck at finding himself in such pathetic company.

Blind fools, every one of them!

The ghost, who once gloried in his omniscience, fled the singular mind of the Gral named Veed and set out to find the ones accompanying Sulkit. The witch Breath was an adept, sensitive to sorcery. If any of them could be reached, awakened to the extremity of his need, it would be her.

He found them in the circular chamber behind Eyes, but the vast domicile of the now-dead Matron was a realm transformed. The ceiling and walls dripped with bitter slime. Viscid pools sheathed the floor beneath the raised dais and the air roiled with pungent vapours. The vast, sprawling bed that had once commanded the dais now looked diseased, twisted as the roots of a toppled tree. Tendrils hung loose, ends dripping, and the atmosphere shrouding the malformed nightmare on the dais was so thick that all within it was blurred, uncertain, as if in that place reality itself was smudged.

Sulkit stood immobile as a statue in front of the dais, its scales streaming fluids—as if it was melting before their eyes—and strange guttural sounds issuing from its throat.

'—awakening behind every wall,' Taxilian was saying. 'I'm sure of it.'

'But nothing like this!' Rautos said, gesturing at Sulkit. 'Gods below, this air— I can barely breathe!'

'You're both fools,' Breath snapped. 'This is a ritual. This is the oldest sorcery of all—the magic of sweat and scent and tears—against this, we're helpless as children! Kill it, I say! Drive a knife into its back—slash open its throat! Before it's too late—'

'No!' retorted Taxilian. 'We must let this happen—I feel it—in what the drone does we will find our salvation.'

'Delusions!'

Rautos had positioned himself between the two, but his expression was taut with fear and confusion. 'There is a pattern,' he said, addressing neither of them. 'Everything the drone has done—everywhere else—it has led to this moment. The pattern—I can almost see it. I want—I want . . .'

But he didn't know what he wanted. The ghost spun wild in the currents of the man's ineffable needs.

'There will be answers,' said Taxilian.

Yes! the ghost cried. *And it comes with knives in its hands! It comes to kill you all!*

Beneath the level of the Womb, Nappet stood beside a strange pipe running the length of the corridor. He had been following alongside it for some time before becoming aware that the waist-high sheath of bronze had begun emanating heat. Dripping sweat, he hesitated. Retrace his route? He might melt before he reached the stairs he had come down. In the gloom ahead, he could make out nothing to indicate side passages. The hot, brittle air burned in his lungs. He was near panic.

Something swirled within the pipe, rushing down its length. A whimper escaped him—he could die here! 'Move, you fool. But which way? Hurry. Think!' Finally, he forced himself forward in a stagger—somewhere ahead, there would be salvation. There had to be. He was sure of it.

The air crackled, sparks arcing from the surface of the pipe. He shrieked, broke into a run. Flashes blinded him as lightning ignited in the corridor. Argent roots snapped out, lanced through him. Agony lit his nerves—his screams punched from his chest, tearing his throat—and he flailed with his hands. Arcs leapt between his fingers. Something was roaring—just ahead—bristling with fire.

The wrong way! I went—

Sudden darkness. Silence.

Nappet halted, gasping. He drew a breath and held it.

Desultory trickling sounds from within the pipe, draining away even as he listened.

He sighed unsteadily.

The air reeked of something strange and bitter, stinging his eyes. What had just happened? He had been convinced that he was going to die, cooked like a lightning-struck dog. He had felt those energies coursing through him, as if acid filled his veins. Sweat cooling on his skin, he shivered.

He heard footsteps and turned. Someone was coming up behind him. No lantern illuminated the corridor. He heard the scrape of iron. 'Sheb? That you? Last? You damned oaf, light a lantern!'

The figure made no reply.

Nappet licked his lips. 'Who is that? Say something!'

The ghost watched in horror as Veed strode up to Nappet. A single-bladed axe swung in a savage arc that bit into Nappet's neck. Spittle flew from the man's mouth as he rocked with the blow. Bone grated and crunched as Veed tugged his weapon free. Blood gouted from the wound and Nappet reached up to press his palm against his neck, his eyes still wide, still filled with disbelief.

The second blow came from the opposite side. His head fell impossibly on its side, rested a moment on his left shoulder, and then rolled off the man's back. The headless body toppled.

'No point in wasting time,' muttered Veed, crouching to clean the blade. Then he rose and faced the ghost. 'Stop screaming. Who do you think summoned me in the first place?'

The ghost recoiled. *I—I did not—*

'Now lead me to the others, Lifestealer.'

The ghost howled, fled from the abomination. He had to warn the others!

Grinning, Veed followed.

Stepping down, he crushed the last cinders of the paltry hearth, feeling the nuggets roll under his heel, and then turned to face the lifeless hag. He glared at her scaled back, as if silent accusation could cut her down where she stood. But what Torrent willed, he knew, was weaker than rain. 'Those are the spires of my people's legends—the fangs of the Wastelands. You stole the stars, witch. You deceived me—'

Olar Ethil snorted, but did not turn round. She was staring south—at least, he thought of it as south, but such certainties, which he had once believed to be unassailable, had now proved as vulnerable to the deathless woman's magic as the very stones she lit aflame every night. As vulnerable as the bundles of dead grass from which she conjured slabs of dripping meat, and the bedrock that bled water with the rap of one bony knuckle.

Torrent scratched at his sparse beard. He'd used up the last of the oils young Awl warriors applied to burn off the bristle until such time that a true beard was possible—he must look a fool, but nothing could be done for it. Not that anyone cared anyway. There were no giggling maidens with veiled eyes, no coy dances from his path as he strutted the length of the village. All those old ways were gone now. So were the futures they had promised him.

He pictured a Letherii soldier standing atop a heap of bones—a mountain of white that was all that remained of Torrent's people. Beneath the rim of his helm, the soldier's face was nothing but bone, leaving a smile that never wavered.

Torrent realized that he had found a lover, and her name was hate. The Letherii details were almost irrelevant—it could be any soldier, any stranger. Any symbol of greed and oppression. The grasping hand, the gleam of avid hunger in the eyes, the spirit that took all it could by virtue of the strength and might it possessed.

Torrent dreamed of destruction. Vast, sweeping, leaving behind nothing but bones.

He glanced again at Olar Ethil. *Why do you want me, witch? What will you give me? This is an age of promises, isn't it? It must be, else I exist without reason.*

'When you find your voice,' she said without turning, 'speak to me, warrior.'

'Why? What will you answer?'

Her laugh was a hollowed-out cackle. 'When I do, mountains shall crumble. The seas shall boil. The air shall thicken with poison. My answer, warrior, shall deafen the heavens.' She spun amidst flapping rags. 'Do you feel it? The gate—it cracks open and the road will welcome what comes through. And such a road!' She laughed again.

'My hate is silent,' Torrent said. 'It has nothing to say.'

'But I have been feeding it nonetheless.'

His eyes widened. 'This fever comes from you, witch?'

'No, it ever lurked in your soul, like a viper in the night. I but awakened it to righteousness.'

'Why?'

'Because it amuses me. Saddle your horse, warrior. We ride to the spires of your legends.'

'Legends that have outlived the people telling them.'

She cocked her head in his direction. 'Not yet. Not yet.' And she laughed again.

'*Where is he?*' Stavi screamed, her small fists lifted, as if moments from striking her.

Setoc held her ground. 'I don't know,' she replied levelly. 'He always returned before.'

'But it's been days and days! Where is he? Where is Toc?'

'He serves more than one master, Stavi. It was a miracle he was able to stay with us as long as he did.'

Stavi's sister looked close to tears, but she'd yet to speak. The boy sat with his back against the lifeless flank of Baaljagg where the huge beast lay as if asleep, nose down between its front paws. Playing with a handful of stones, the boy seemed oblivious to his sisters' distress. She wondered if perhaps he was simple in the head. Sighing, Setoc said, 'He turned us into the east—and so that is the direction we shall take—'

'But there's nothing out there!'

'I know, Stavi. I don't know why he wants us to go there. He wouldn't explain. But, would you go against his wishes?' It was an unfair tactic, she knew, the kind meant to extort compliance from children.

It worked, but as every adult knew, not for long.

Setoc gestured. The ay lifted to its feet and trotted ahead, while Setoc picked up the boy and cajoled the twins into her wake. They set out, leaving behind their measly camp.

She wondered if Toc would ever return. She wondered if he'd any purpose behind his taking care of them, or had it been some residue of guilt or sense of responsibility for the children of his friend? He had left life behind and could not be held to its ways, or the demands it made upon a mortal soul—no, there could be no human motivation to what such a creature did.

And the eye he'd fixed upon her had belonged to a wolf. But even among such beasts, the closeness of the pack was a tense game of submission and dominance. The bliss of brother- and sisterhood hid political machinations and ruthless judgements. Cruelty needed only opportunity. So, he had led this paltry pack of theirs, and his lordship had been uncontested—after all, he could hardly be threatened with death, could he?

She understood, finally, that she could not trust him. And that her relief at his taking command had been the response of a child, a creature eager to cower in the shadow of an adult, praying for protection, willing itself blind to the possibility that the true threat was found in the man—or woman—standing over it. Of course, the twins had lost everything. Their desperate loyalty to a dead man, who had once been their father's friend, was reasonable under the circumstances. Stavi and Storii wanted him back. Of course they did, and they had begun to look upon Setoc with something like resentment, as if she was to blame for his absence.

Nonsense, but the twins saw no salvation in Setoc. They saw no protector in her. They'd rather she had been the one to vanish.

The boy had his giant wolf. Would it protect them as well? Not a notion to rely upon.

And I have power, though I can't yet make out its shape, or even its purpose. Who in their dreams is not omnipotent? If in sleep I grow wings and fly high above the land, it does not mean I will awaken cloaked in feathers. We are gods in our dreams. Disaster strikes when we come to believe the same is true in our real lives.

I wish Torrent was here. I wish he'd never left me. I see him in my mind even now. I see him standing atop a mountain of bones, his eyes dark beneath the rim of his helm.

Torrent, where are you?

'They looked near death,' Yedan Derryg said.

Riding beside her brother, Yan Tovis grimaced. 'They must have awakened something—I told them to protect themselves, now I'm thinking I may have killed them both.'

'They may look and act like two giggling girls, Twilight, but they aren't. You killed no one.'

She twisted in her saddle and looked back down the road. The light of torches and lanterns formed a refulgent island in the midst of buildings at the far end of the city. The light looked like a wound. She faced forward again. Darkness, and yet a darkness through which she could see—every detail precise, every hint of colour and tone looking strangely opaque, solid before her eyes. As if the vision she had possessed all her life—in that now distant, remote world—was in truth a feeble, truncated thing. And yet, this did not feel like a gift—a pressure was building behind her eyes.

'Besides,' Yedan added, 'they're not yet dead.'

They rode on at a canter as the road climbed out of the valley, leaving behind the weed-snarled fields and brush-crowded farm buildings. Ahead was the wall of trees that marked the beginning of the forest called Ashayn. If the tales were true, Ashayn had fallen—every last tree—to the manic industry of the city, and in the leagues beyond that wasteland great fires had destroyed the rest. But the forest had returned, and the boles of blackwood could not be spanned by a dozen men with hands linked. There was no sign of a road or bridle path, but the floor beneath the high canopy was clear of undergrowth.

The gloom thickened once they rode beneath the towering trees. Among the blackwood she could now see other species, equally as massive, smooth-barked down to the serpentine roots. High above, some kind of parasitic plant created islands of moss, serrated leaves and black blossoms, like huge nests, depending from thick tangles of vines. The air was chill, musty, smelling of wet charcoal and sap.

A third of a league, then half, the horses' hoofs thumping, hauberks rustling and clasps clicking, but from the forest itself only silence.

The pressure had sharpened to pain, as if a spike had been driven into her forehead. The motion of the horse was making her nauseated. Gasping, leaning forward, she reined in. A hand to her face revealed bright blood from her nostrils. 'Yedan—'

'I know,' he said in a growl. 'Never mind. Memories return. There's something ahead.'

'I don't think—'

'You said you wanted to see the First Shore.'

'Not if it makes my head explode!'

'Retreat is not possible,' he said, spitting to one side. 'What assails us, Yan, does not come from what awaits us.'

What? She managed to lift her head, looked across at him.

Her brother was weeping blood. He spat again, a bright red gout, and then said, 'Kharkanas . . . the empty darkness'—he met her eyes—'is empty no longer.'

She thought back to the two unconscious witches in the city behind them. *They will not survive this. They cannot. I brought them all this way, only to kill them.* 'I must go back—'

'You cannot. Not yet. Ride that way, Twilight, and you will die.' And he kicked his horse forward.

After a moment she followed.

Goddess of Darkness, have you returned? Are you awakened in rage? Will you slay all you touch?

The black pillars marched past, a cathedral abandoned in some timeless realm, and now they could hear a sound, coming from just beyond the broken black wall ahead. Something like the crashing of waves.

The First Shore.

Where we began—

A glimmer between the boles, flashes of white—

Brother and sister rode clear of the forest. The horses beneath them slowed, halted as the reins grew slack, lifeless.

With red-smeared vision, silence like a wound, they stared, uncomprehending.

The First Shore.

The clouds in the west had blackened and fused into an impenetrable wall. The ground was silver with frost and the grasses crunched and broke underfoot. Hunched beneath furs, Strahl watched the enemy forces forming up on the gentle slope of the valley opposite them. Two hundred paces to his right Maral Eb stood in a vanguard of chosen Barahn warriors, behind him the mixed units of four lesser clans—he had taken command of those warriors who had tasted the humiliation of defeat. A courageous decision, enough to grind away some of the burrs in Strahl's eyes. Some, but not all.

Breaths plumed in white streams. Warriors stamped to jolt feeling back into their feet. Blew on hands gripping weapons. Across the way, horses bucked and reared amidst the ranks of mounted archers and lancers. Pennons hung grey and dull, standards stiff as planed boards.

The iron taste of panic was in the bitter air, and eyes lifted again and again to stare at the terrifying sky—to the west, the black, seething wall; to the east the cerulean blue sparkling with crystals and the sun burnished white as snow and flanked by baleful sun-dogs. Directly above, a ragged seam bound the two. The blackness was winning the battle, Strahl could see, as tendrils snaked out like roots, bleeding into the morning.

Now on the valley floor phalanxes of kite-shielded Saphii held to the centre, their long spears anchored in the hinged sockets at the hip. D'ras skirmishers spilled out around the bristling squares, among them archers with arrows nocked, edging ever closer. The Akrynnai cavalry held to the wings, struggling to keep formation as they advanced at the walk.

Sceptre Irkullas was wasting no time. No personal challenges on the field, no rousing exhortations before his troops. The Akrynnai wanted this battle joined, the slaughter unleashed, as if the chorus of clashing weapons and the screams of the dying and wounded could wrench the world back to its normal state, could right the sky overhead, could send the cold and darkness reeling away.

Blood to pay, blood to appease. Is that what you believe, Akrynnai?

Strahl stirred into motion, stepping forward until he was five paces in front of the Senan line. He swung round, studied the nearest faces.

Belligerence like bruises beneath the sheen of fear. Hard eyes fixing on his, then shifting away, then back again. White-painted faces cracking in the cold. In turn, his officers stung him with their acuity, as if they sought the first sign of uncertainty, the first waver of doubt in his face. He gave them nothing.

Strange crackling from the silvered sky, as of a frozen lake breaking in the first thaw, and warriors ducked as if fearing the descent of shards of ice. But nothing came of the eerie sounds. *The fists of the gods are pounding against the glass of the sky. Cracks craze the scene. It's all moments from shattering. Well may you duck, my friends. As if that will do any good.*

'Bakal,' Strahl said, loudly enough to startle the figures he faced, and he saw how the lone word rippled back through the ranks, stirring them to life. 'And before Bakal, Onos Toolan. Before him, Humbrall Taur. We came in search of an enemy. We came seeking a war.'

He waited, and saw in the nearest faces a host of private wars unleashed. He beheld in those expressions the fiercest battles of will. He saw the spreading stain of shame. And nodded.

'Here we stand, Senan.' Behind him he could hear and feel the sudden thunder of soldiers on the advance, of waves of riders sweeping out from the flanks. 'And I am before you, alone. And I shall speak the words of those before me.' He held high in his right hand his tulwar, and in his left the weapon's scabbard.

'*Not this enemy! Not this war!*'

Strahl sheathed the sword, slamming the weapon hard to lock it and then holding it high with both hands.

Weapons flashed. Iron vanished. Barked commands from the rear and the Senan forces wheeled round.

And now, we leave.

You wanted this, Maral Eb? Then take it.

Someone was shouting, but Maral Eb's eyes remained fixed on the enemy as it advanced. The first arrows hissed through the glittering air—almost unseen in the gathering gloom. The phalanxes were readying for a charge, long spears levelled in the first three ranks. On the outer wings horse-archers were fast closing, moments from loosing arrows and then wheeling to rake the front Barghast lines with subsequent salvos.

Bastards fought like babies. Once those Saphii closed, everything would change—

The shouting was suddenly louder and then a hand gripped his shoulder and yanked him round. He glared into the face of one of his bodyguards—but the man was pointing, spittle flying as he shrieked. What was he saying? The damned idiot—what—

Then he saw the growing gap that was his line's centre.

What? Did they charge—no—I see nothing—but—

'They've withdrawn! Warleader! The Senan!'

'Don't be a fool!' He pushed his way through his milling guards until his view was unobstructed. The Senan were gone. The most powerful of the Barghast White Faces—routed! 'Get them back!' he shrieked. '*Get them back!*'

Sceptre Irkullas reined in, a deep frown knitting his features beneath the helm's flaring rim. What was the centre doing? *Do you invite us to march into that maw? Do you really think that will work? Damned barbarians, have you never before faced a phalanx?* 'Rider! Inform the Saphii commander to be certain to hold their squares—if the Barghast want to bite down on that mouthful of spikes, they're welcome to.' He twisted round until he spotted a second messenger. 'Have the lancers draw in closer to our centre and await my orders to charge. Go!'

Another messenger who had been among the skirmishers rode up, saluting. 'Sceptre! The centre clan is *withdrawing* from battle!'

'It's a feint—'

'My pardon, Sceptre, but their leader was seen facing his warriors—he sheathed his weapon and held it high, sir. And they did the same back, and then turned round and left the line!'

Errant's pull! 'Sound the Saphii advance to close! Before the bastards can plug the hole—ride, soldier! Signallers! To me!'

Sekara the Vile pushed her way through the press for a better look at the treachery. She was in command of the rearguard, the elders, unblooded youths and their mothers, along with eight hundred warriors still recovering from wounds. Their task was to hold the line of wagons should the Akrynnai encircle or pull round to strike for the belly. But with the front centre gone, they would have nothing but enemy at their backs.

She spat out a string of curses at the retreating warriors. 'Cowards! I will wait for you at the Gate, for every one of you!' She ran out a half-dozen strides—the last ranks of the Senan were almost within reach. Not of her claws—that would be too risky—but she could spit as well as any Barghast woman, and now—

Someone moved up beside her. She twisted round, teeth bared.

A gauntleted hand hammered her face. Light exploded behind her eyes. Legs giving out, she collapsed in a heap. Her mouth was full of shards of teeth.

Strahl's voice spoke from directly over her. 'Sekara, wait at the Gate all you want. But remember, your husband's already there. Waiting just for you. The dead will say what they dared not say in life. Oh, don't forget to take your hoard with you.'

She heard his moccasins crunching on the grasses as he set off in the wake of his clan.

My husband? Whenever did he not cower before me! She spat out a mouthful of slimy blood.

We'll stand side by side, Strahl, to welcome you. To tear you to pieces! A curse upon the Senan! Choose what you will, you shall not see the fangs until it is too late!

The ground shook. A shock wave thundered through the Barghast. Screams battered the frozen air. The battle was joined.

Sekara regained her feet, her face already swollen and hot. 'Other side of the wagons!' she shouted. 'Everyone—through! And then form up!'

She saw them lurch into motion.

Yes, hold for a time. Time enough for me to run. Darkness, such a blessing! She staggered towards the wagons.

Another sleet of arrows and Sagal ducked behind his hide shield. Two thuds bit into the thickly matted reeds and he flinched as his forearm was pricked. Warm blood trickled beneath his vambrace. He cursed. His brother had done the best he could in selecting this site, but to deal with these Akrynnai horse-archers most effectively they would have done better to find broken ground. A proper range of hills, plenty of rock, gullies and draws.

Instead, the bastards didn't even have to close—at least for as long as they had arrows—and Barghast were dying without even the honour of clashing blades with the enemy. The rattling pass of the horses continued its deadly sweep.

The next time, Sagal would straighten and lead a charge—right into the path of the riders—*see how you will fare with three thousand White Faces in your midst!*

The descent of arrows fell off and Sagal waited a moment longer—he could still hear those horse hoofs—but sound was doing strange things this morning.

Yet, they seemed . . . heavier than before. He lowered his shield and straightened. Blinking, struggling to make out details in the infernal gloom.

Crazed motion rising up from the valley, the entire hillside trembling—

Three chevrons of lancers had come in behind the screen of archers. There was no time to close ranks, to lift and settle pikes. He stared, furious, and then unsheathed his tulwar. 'They come! They come!'

The Barghast seemed to grunt like some massive beast stirring awake. As thousands of levelled lances churned up the slope, the White Faces answered with a roar, and at the last instant, the mass of Barahn warriors heaved into the iron fangs. The front lines vanished, ducking beneath the lanceheads, heavy blades chopping into horses' forelegs. Beasts shrieked, went down, and all at once the charge ground to a halt against a seething wall of carnage, the points of the chevrons flattening out in wild, vicious maelstrom.

Deluged in the fluids of a gutted horse, Sagal surged back to his feet, howling like a demon. *Time to deliver slaughter! The fools closed—the fools charged! They could have held back all day until the Barahn on this flank were nothing but a heap of arrow-studded meat—but their impatience betrayed them!* Laughing, he hacked at everything in sight. Cut deep into thighs, slashed through wrists, chopped at the stamping legs of the horses.

He could feel the cavalry attempting to withdraw, a giant snagged weapon, its edges nicked and blunted. Bellowing, he pushed deeper into the press, knowing his fellow warriors were all doing the same. They would not let go easily, no, they would not do that.

Half the Free Cities of Genabackis have flung their cavalry at us—and we destroyed them all!

Sceptre Irkullas stared as the heavy lancers fought to extricate themselves from the outer flanks of the Barghast position. Scores of fine warriors and superbly trained mounts were going down with every breath he drew into his aching lungs, but there was no help for it. He needed that retreat as ugly as it could be, slow enough to draw more and more of the enemy down the slope. He needed to see that entire flank committed to the slaughter, before he could command the horse-archers in behind the Barghast, followed quickly by his skirmishers and then a phalanx of Saphii to ensure the entire flank was thoroughly cut off and exposed on the hillside. Then he would send the bulk of his lancers and mounted axe-wielders, the hammer to the Saphii anvil.

The other flank was not going as well, he saw, as the commander there had managed to lock shields and lift pikes to ward off the cavalry charge, and now the horse-archers were resuming their sweeps across the face of the line—this was a game of attrition that served the Akrynnai well enough, but it took longer. How many arrows could the Barghast suffer?

His final regard he fixed on the centre, and a surge of pleasure washed up against the chill of the day. The Saphii phalanxes had driven deep into the gap, effectively bisecting the enemy line. On the far side, the isolated enemy was locked in a bloody, fighting withdrawal back towards the outside flank—those Barghast knew how to fight on foot—better than any other soldiers he'd ever seen, but they were losing cohesion, pitching wayward as Saphii spears drove them back, and back; as the Saphii kaesanderai—the jalak-wielding in-fighters—shot forward into every gap, their curved shortswords slashing and hacking.

Elements of the lead phalanx had pushed into the rearguard, and flames were rising from the wagons—likely fired by the Barghast after they'd broken and fled through the barrier. That phalanx was falling out into a curling line to close any hope of retreat by the far flank.

The savages had found their last day, and they were welcome to it.

Irkullas lifted his gaze and studied the sky. The sight horrified him. Day was dying before his eyes. Ragged black arteries, like slow lightning, had arced through the morning sky until it seemed nothing but fragments of blue remained. *It shatters. The day—it shatters!*

He could see something now, a darkness descending, falling and falling closer still.

What is happening? The air—so cold, so empty—Errant defend us—what—

Kashat reached over his shoulder and tore the arrow loose. Someone cried out behind him, but he had no time for that. 'We hold!' he screamed, then stumbled as fresh blood rushed down his back. His right arm was suddenly useless, hanging at his side, and now the leg it thumped against was growing numb. *Spirits below, it was but a prick—a damned puny arrow—I don't understand.* 'We hold!' The shout filled his mind, but this time it came out weak as a whisper.

The army was split in two. No doubt the Sceptre believed that that would prove the death of the Barghast. The fool was in for a surprise. The White Faces had fought as clans for generations. Even a damned family could stand on its own. The real bloodbath had yet to begin.

He struggled to straighten. 'Stupid arrow. Stupid fuck—'

A second arrow punched through his left cheek, just under the bone and deep into his nasal passage. The impact knocked his head back. Blood filled his vision. Blood poured down his throat. He reached up with his one working hand and tore the bolt from his face. '—ing arrows!' But his voice was a thick, spattering gargle.

He struggled to find cover behind his shield as more arrows hissed down. The ground beneath him was wet with blood—his own—and he stared down at that black pool. The stuff filling his mouth he swallowed down as fast as he could, but he was beginning to choke and his belly felt heavy as a grain sack.

Try another charge, you cowards. We will lock jaws on your throat. We will tear the life from you. We shall stand on a mountain of your bodies.

An arrow caught a warrior's helmet—almost close enough to be within reach—and Kashat saw the bolt shatter as if it was the thinnest sliver of ice. Then he saw the helmet slide in two pieces from the man's head. Reeling, the warrior stared a moment at Kashat—with eyes burst and crazed with frost—before he collapsed.

Arrows were exploding everywhere. The screams of warriors cut short with a suddenness that curled horror round Kashat's soul. Another impact on his shield and the rattan beneath the hide broke like glass.

What is happening? The agony of his wounds had ceased. He felt strangely warm, a sensation that left him elated.

Horses were falling just beyond the line. Bowstrings shivered into sparkling dust, the laminated ribs snapping as glues gave out. He saw Akrynnai soldiers—their faces twisted and blue—tumbling from saddles. The enemy was a mass of confusion.

Charge! We must charge! Kashat forced himself upright. Flinging away the remnants of his shield, he tugged his sword into his left hand. Pushing forward, as if clawing through a deadly current, he raised his weapon.

Behind him, hundreds followed, moving slow as if in a dream.

Maral Eb, a mass of mixed clans behind him, led yet another charge into the bristling wall of Saphii. He could see the terror in their eyes, their disbelief at the sheer ferocity of the White Faces. The shattered stumps of spears marred the entire side, but thus far they had held, pounded and at times close to buckling, as the savagery of the Warleader's assaults drove like a mailed fist into the square.

The air felt inexplicably thick, unyielding, and night was falling—had they been fighting that long? It was possible, yes—see the ranks of dead on all sides! Saphii and Barghast, and there, on the slope, mounds of dead riders and horses—had the Senan returned? They must have!

Such slaughter!

The fierce charge slammed into the wall of flesh, leather, wood and iron. The sound was a meaty crunch beneath snapping spear shafts. Lunging close, tulwar lashing down, Maral Eb saw a dark-skinned face before him, saw the frozen mask of the fool's failed courage, and he laughed as he swung his weapon—

The iron blade struck dead centre on the peaked helm.

Sword, helm and head exploded. Maral Eb staggered as his sword-arm jumped out to the side, impossibly light. His eyes fixed on the stump of his wrist, from which frozen pellets of his blood sprayed like seeds. Something struck his shoulder, careened off, and then two commingled bodies fell on to the ground—the impact had driven them together and Maral Eb stared, uncomprehending, at their fused flesh, the exposed roots of blood and muscle beneath split skin.

He could hear dread groaning on all sides, pierced by brief shrieks.

On his knees, the Warleader sought to rise, but the armoured caps of his greaves were frozen to the ground. Leather buckles broke like twigs. He lifted his head—a reddish mist had swallowed the world. What was this? Sorcery? Some poisonous vapour to steal all their strength?

Spirits, no—the mist is blood—blood from burst bodies, ruptured eyeballs—

He understood. The stump of his wrist, the complete absence of pain—even the breaths he dragged into his lungs—the cold, the darkness—

He had been thrown to the ground. A horse, one foreleg stamping down, the bones shearing just above the fetlock, twin spikes of jagged bone plunging through his hauberk, his chest, and pinning him to the earth. Screaming, the huge beast fell on to its side, flinging the lifeless hulk of its rider from the saddle, the man's body breaking like crockery.

The scything foreleg tossed Sagal a few paces away, and he landed again, feeling his hip crumple as if it were no more than a reed basket. Blinking, he watched the cold burn the hide from the thrashing, blinded beast. He found its confusion amusing at first, but then sadness overwhelmed him—not for the hapless animal— he'd never much liked horses—but for everyone on this hillside. Cheated of this battle, of the glory of a rightful victory, the honour of a noble defeat.

The gods were cruel. But then, he'd always known that.

He settled his head back, stared up at the red-stained darkness. A pressure was descending. He could feel it on his chest, in his skull. The Reaper stood above him, one heel pressing down. Sagal grunted as his ribs snapped, the collapse jerking his limbs.

The slingstone caught the hare and spun it round in the air. My heart was in my throat as I ran, light as a whisper, to the grasses where it had fallen. And I stood, looking down on the creature, its panting chest, the tiny droplets of blood spotting its nose. Its spine had broken and the long back legs were perfectly still. But the front paws, they twitched.

My first kill.

I stood, a giant, a god, watching as the life left the hare. Watching, as the depths in the eyes cleared, revealing themselves to be shallow things.

My mother, walking up, her face showing none of the joy she should have shown, none of the pride. I told her about the shallowness that I had seen.

She said, 'It is easy to believe the well of life is bottomless, and that none but the spirits can see through to the far end of the eyes. To the end that is the soul. Yet we spend all our lives trying to peer through. But we soon discover that when the soul flees the flesh, it takes the depth with it. In that creature, Sagal, you have simply seen the truth. And you will see it again and again. In every beast you slay. In the eyes of every enemy you cut down.'

She'd been poor with words, her voice ever flat and cruel. Poor with most things, in fact, as if everything worth anything in the world wasn't worth talking about. He'd even forgotten she'd spoken that day, or that she'd been his teacher in the ways of the hunt.

He realized that he still didn't understand her.

No matter. The shallowness was coming up to meet him.

Sceptre Irkullas crawled, dragging one leg, from the carcass of his horse. He could bear its shrieks no longer, and so he had opened its throat with his knife. Of course, he should have done that after dismounting, instead of simply leaning over his saddle, but his mind had become fogged, sluggish and stupid.

And now he crawled, with the splintered stub of a thigh bone jutting from the leather of his trouser leg. Painless, at least. *'Brush lips with your blessings', as the saying went. I used to hate sayings. No, I still do, especially when you find how well they fit the occasion.*

But that just reminds us that it's an old track we're walking. And all the newness is just our own personal banner of ignorance. Watch us wave it high as if it glitters with profound revelation. Ha.

The field of battle was almost motionless now. Thousands of warriors frozen in the clinches of murder, as if a mad artist had sought to paint rage, in all its frayed shrouds of senseless destruction. He thought back on that towering host of conceits he had constructed, every one of which had led to this battle. Cracked, grinding, descending in chaotic collapse—he so wanted to laugh, but the breaths weren't coming easy, the air was like a striking serpent in his throat.

He bumped up against another dead horse, and sought to pull himself atop the blistered, brittle beast. One last look, one final sweep of this wretched panorama. The valley locked in its preternatural darkness, the falling sky with its dread weight crushing everything in sight.

Grimacing, he forced himself into a sitting position, one leg held out stiff and dead.

And beheld the scene.

Tens of thousands of bodies, a rotting forest of shapeless stumps, all sheathed in deathly frost. Nothing moved, nothing at all. Flakes of ash were raining down from the starless, impenetrable heavens.

'End it, then,' he croaked. 'They're all gone . . . but me. End it, please, I beg you . . .'

He slid down, no longer able to hold himself up. Closed his eyes.

Was someone coming? The cold collector of souls? Did he hear the crunch of boots, lone steps, drawing closer—a figure, emerging from the darkness in his mind? *My eyes are closed. That must mean something.*

Was something coming? He dared not look.

He had once been a farmer. He was certain of that much, but trouble had befallen him. Debt? Perhaps, but the word was stingless, as far as Last was concerned, suggesting that it was not a haunting presence in his mind, and when memories were as few and as sketchy as were his, that must count for something.

Instead, he had this: the stench of bonfires, that ashy smear of cleared land, everything raw and torn and nothing in its proper place. High branches stacked in chaotic heaps, moss knotted on every twig. Roots dripping in inverted postures. Enormous boles lying flat and stripped down, great swaths of bark prised loose. Red-stained wood and black gritty rocks pulled from the flecked soil.

The earth could heave and make such a mess, but it had not. It had but trembled, and not from any deep stirring or restlessness, but from the toppling of trees, the bellowing of oxen straining at stumps, the footfalls of mindful men.

Shatter all you see. It's what makes you feel. Feel . . . anything.

He remembered his hands deep in the rich warm earth. He remembered closing

his eyes—for just a moment—and feeling that pulse of life, of promise and purpose. They would plant crops, nurture a bounty for their future lives. This was
just. This was righteous. The hand that shapes is the hand that reaps. This, he
told himself, was pure. Sighing, a sure smile curving his lips, he opened his eyes
once more. Smoke, mists here and there amidst the ruination. Still smiling, he
then withdrew his hands from the warm earth.

To find them covered in blood.

He never counted himself a clever man. He knew enough to know that and not
much else. But the world had its layers. To the simple it offered simplicity. To the
wise it offered profundity. And the only measure of courage worth acknowledging
was found in accepting where one stood in that scheme—in hard, unwavering
honesty, no matter how humbling.

He stared down at his hands and knew it for a memory not his own. It was, in
fact, an invention, the blunt, almost clumsy imposition of something profound.
Devoid of subtlety and deliberately so, which then made it more complicated
than it at first seemed.

Even these thoughts were alien. Last was not a thoughtful man.

The heart knows need, and the mind finds reason to justify. It says: destruc-
tion leads to creation, so the world has shown us. But the world shows us more
than that. Sometimes, destruction leads to oblivion. Extinction. But then,
what's so bad about that? If stupidity does not deserve extinction, what does?
The mind is never so clever as to deceive anyone and anything but itself and its
own kind.

Last decided that he was not afraid of justice, and so he stood unmoving, unflinching, as the slayer appeared at the far end of the corridor. Asane's shrieks had
run down to silence. He knew she was dead. All her fears come home at last, and
in oblivion there was, for her, relief. Peace.

Murder could wear such pleasant masks.

The slayer met his eyes and at that final moment they shared their understanding. The necessity of things. And Last fell to the sword without a sound.

There had been blood on his hands. Reason enough. Justice delivered.

Forgive me?

Sheb couldn't remember who he had been. Indebted, a prisoner, a man contemptuous of the law, these things, yes, but where were the details? Everything had
flitted away in his growing panic. He'd heard Asane's death echoing down the
corridor. He knew that a murderer now stalked him. There was no reason for it.
He'd done nothing to deserve this.

Unless, of course, one counted a lifetime of treachery. But he'd always had
good cause for doing the things he did. He was sure of it. Evading imprisonment—
well, who sought the loss of freedom? No one but an idiot, and Sheb was no idiot.
Escaping responsibility? Of course. Bullies earn little sympathy, while the victims are coddled and cooed over at every turn. Better to be the victim than the
bully, provided the mess is over with, all threat of danger past and it's time for

explanations, tales of self-defence and excuses and the truth of it was, none of it mattered and if you could convince yourself with your excuses, all the better. Easy sleeping at night, easier still standing tall atop heaps of righteous indignation. *No one is more pious than the guilty. And I should know.*

And no one is a better liar than the culpable. So he'd done nothing to deserve any of this. He'd only ever done what he needed to do to get by, to slip round and slide through. To go on living, feeding all his habits, all his wants and needs. The killer had no reason!

Gasping, he ran down corridor after corridor, through strange rooms, on to spiralling ascents and descents. He told himself that he was so lost no one would ever find him.

Lost in my maze of excuses—stop! I didn't think that. I never said that. Has he found me? Has the bastard found me?

He'd somehow misplaced his weapons, every one of them—how did that happen? Whimpering, Sheb rushed onward—ahead was a bridge of some sort, crossing a cavernous expanse that seemed to be filling with clouds.

All my life, I tried to keep my head down. I never wanted to be noticed. Just grab what I can and get out, get free, until the next thing I need comes up. It was simple. It made sense. No one should kill me for that.

He had no idea how thinking could be so exhausting. Staggering on to the bridge, iron grating under his boots—what was wrong with damned wood? Coughing in the foul vapours of the clouds, eyes stinging, nose burning, he stumbled to a halt.

He'd gone far enough. Everything he did, he'd done for a reason. As simple as that.

But so many were hurt, Sheb.

'Not my fault they couldn't get out of the way. If they'd any brains they'd have seen me coming.'

The way you lived forced others into lives of misery, Sheb.

'I can't help it if they couldn't do no better!'

They couldn't. They weren't even people.

'What?' He looked up, into the killer's eyes. 'No, it's not fair.'

'That's right, Sheb. It isn't, and it never was.'

The blade lashed out.

The ghost shrieked. Suddenly trapped in the Matron's chamber. Mists roiled. Rautos was on his knees, weeping uncontrollably. Breath was casting her tiles, which were no longer tiles, but coins, glittering and bright—yet every pattern she scanned elicited a snarl from her, and she swept them up yet again—the manic snap and bounce of coins filled the air.

'No answers,' she hissed. 'No answers! No answers!'

Taxilian stood before the enormous throne, muttering under his breath. 'Sulkit transformed it—and now it waits—everything waits. I don't understand.'

Sulkit stood nearby. Its entire body had changed shape, elongating, shoulders hunched, its snout foreshortened and broader, fangs gleaming wet with oils. Grey reptilian eyes held fixed, unblinking—the drone was a drone no longer. Now a J'an Sentinel, he stood facing the ghost.

The unhuman regard was unbearable.

Veed strode into the chamber and halted. Sword blade dripping gore, the front of his studded vest spattered and streaked. His face was lifeless. His eyes were the eyes of a blind man. 'Hello, old friend,' he said. 'Where should I start?'

The ghost recoiled.

Rautos stood facing his wife. Another evening spent in silence, but now there was something raw in the air. She was searching his face and her expression was strange and bleak. 'Have you no pity, husband?'

'Pity,' he'd replied, 'is all I have.'

She'd looked away. 'I see.'

'You surrendered long ago,' he said. 'I never understood that.'

'Not everyone surrenders willingly, Rautos.'

He studied her. 'But where did you find your joy, Eskil? Day after day, night after night, where was your pleasure in living?'

'You stopped looking for that long ago.'

'What do you mean?'

'You found your hobbies. The only time your eyes came alive. My joy, husband, was in you. Until you went away.'

Yes, he remembered this now. One night, one single night. 'That was wrong,' he'd said, his voice hoarse. 'To put all that . . . in someone else.'

Her shrug horrified him. 'Overwhelmed, were you? But Rautos, that's just not so, is it? After all, you can't be overwhelmed by something you don't even bother to notice.'

'I noticed.'

'And so you turned away from me. Until, as you say, here you stand with nothing in your heart but pity. You once said you loved me.'

'I once did.'

'Rautos Hivanar, what are these things you are digging up from the river bank?'

'Mechanisms. I think.'

'What so fascinates you about them?'

'I don't know. I cannot glean their purpose, their function—why are we talking about this?'

'Rautos, listen. They're just pieces. The machine, whatever it was, whatever it did, it's broken.'

'Eskil, go to bed.'

And so she did, ending the last real conversation between them. He remembered sitting down, his hands to his face, outwardly silent and motionless yet inside he was wracked with sobs. Yes, it was broken. He knew that. And not a single piece left made any sense. And all his pity, well, turned out it was all he had for himself, too.

Rautos felt the bite of the blade and in the moment before the pain rushed in, he managed a smile.

Veed stood over the corpse, and then swung his gaze to Taxilian. Held there for a moment, before his attention drifted to Breath. She was on her knees, scraping coins into her hands.

'No solutions. No answers. They should be here, in these! These fix everything—everyone knows that! Where is the magic?'

'Illusions, you mean,' Veed said, grinning.

'The best kind! And now the water's rising—I can't breathe!'

'He should never have accepted you, Feather Witch. You understand that, don't you? Yes, they were all mistakes, all fragments of lives he took inside like so much smoke and dust, but you were the worst of them. The Errant drowned you—and then walked away from your soul. He should not have done that, for you were too potent, too dangerous. *You ate his damned eye.*'

Her head snapped up, a crazed grin smeared across her face. 'Elder blood! I hold his debt!'

Veed glanced at the ghost. 'He sought to do what K'rul did so long ago,' he said, 'but Icarium is not an Elder God.' He regarded Feather Witch again. 'He wanted warrens of his own, enough to trap him in one place, as if it was a web. Trap him in place. Trap him in *time.*'

'The debt is mine!' Feather Witch shrieked.

'Not any more,' said Veed. 'It is now Icarium Lifestealer's.'

'He's broken!'

'Yes.'

'It's not his fault!'

'No, it isn't, and no, it's not fair either. But there is blood on his hands, and terror in his heart. It seems we must all feed him something, doesn't it? Or perhaps it was the other way round. But the ghost is here now, with us. Icarium is here. Time to die, Feather Witch. Taxilian.'

'And you?' Taxilian asked.

Veed smiled. 'Me, too.'

'Why?' Taxilian demanded. 'Why now?'

'Because Lifestealer is where he must be. At this moment, he is in place. And we must all step aside.' And Veed turned to face the ghost. 'The J'an sees only you, Icarium. The Nest is ready, the flavours altered to your . . . tastes.' He gestured and the ghost saw that both Feather Witch and Taxilian had vanished. 'Don't think you are quite rid of us—we're just back inside you, old friend. We're the stains on your soul.'

The ghost looked down and saw grey-green skin, long-fingered, scarred hands. He lifted them to touch his face, fingers brushing the tusks jutting from his lower jaw. 'What must I do?'

But Veed was gone. He was alone in the chamber.

The J'an Sentinel, Sulkit, stood watching him. Waiting.

Icarium faced the throne. A machine. A thing of veins and arteries and bitter oils. A binder of time, the maker of certainty.

The flavours swirled round him. The entire towering city of stone and iron trembled.

I am awake—no. I am . . . reborn.

Icarium Lifestealer walked forward to take his throne.

The shore formed a ragged line, the bleak sweep of darkness manifested in all the natural ways—the sward leading to the bank that then dropped to the beach itself, the sky directly overhead onyx as a starless night yet smeared with pewter clouds—the realm behind them, then, a vast promise of purity at their backs. But the strand glowed, and as Yan Tovis dismounted and walked down her boots sank into the incandescent sand. Reaching down—not yet ready to fix her gaze on what was beyond the shoreline—she scooped up a handful. Cool, surprisingly light—she squinted.

Not crumbled coral. Not stone.

'It's bone,' said Yedan Derryg, standing a few paces to her left. 'See that driftwood? Long bones, mostly. Those cobbles, they're—'

'Yes,' she snapped. 'I know.' She flung away the handful of bone fragments.

'It was easier,' he continued, 'from back there. We're too close—'

'Be quiet, will you?'

Suddenly defiant, she willed herself to look—and reeled back a step, breath hissing from between her teeth.

A sea indeed, yet one that rose like a wall, its waves rolling down to foam at the waterline. She grunted. But this was not water at all. It was . . . *light*.

Behind her, Yedan Derryg said, 'Memories return. When they walked out from the Light, their purity blinded us. We thought that a blessing, when in truth it was an attack. When we shielded our eyes, we freed them to indulge their treacherous ways.'

'Yedan, the story is known to me—'

'Differently.'

She came near to gasping in relief as she turned from the vast falling wall to face her brother. 'What do you mean?'

'The Watch serves the Shore in its own way.'

'Then, in turn, I must possess knowledge that you don't—is that what you're saying, brother?'

'The Queen is Twilight, because she can be no other. She holds the falling of night. She is the first defender against the legions of light that would destroy darkness itself. But we did not ask for this. Mother Dark yielded, and so, to mark that yielding, Twilight relives it.'

'Again and again. For ever.'

Yedan's bearded jaws bunched, his face still stained with blood. Then he shook his head. 'Nothing's for ever, sister.'

'Did we really lack sophistication, Yedan? Back then? Were we really that superstitious, that ignorant?'

His brows lifted.

She gestured at the seething realm behind her. 'This is the true border of Thyrllan. It's that and nothing more. The First Shore is the shore between Darkness and Light. We thought we were born on this shore—right here—but that cannot be true! This shore *destroys*—can you not feel it? Where do you think all these bones came from?'

'This was a gift to no one,' Yedan replied. 'Look into the water, sister. Look deep into it.'

But she would not. She had already seen what he had seen. 'They cannot be drowning—no matter what it looks like—'

'You are wrong. Tell me, why are there so few Liosan? Why is the power that is Light so weak in all the other worlds?'

'If it wasn't we would all die—there'd be no life anywhere at all!'

He shrugged. 'I have no answer to that, sister. But I think that Mother Dark and Father Light, in binding themselves to each other, in turn bound their fates. And when she turned away, so did he. He had no choice—they had become forces intertwined, perfect reflections. Father Light abandoned his children and they became a people lost—and lost they remain.'

She was trembling. Yedan's vision was monstrous. 'It cannot be. The Tiste Andii weren't trapped. They got away.'

'They found a way out, yes.'

'How?'

He cocked his head. 'Us, of course.'

'What are you saying?'

"In Twilight was born Shadow."

'I was told none of this! I don't believe you! What you're saying makes no sense, Yedan. Shadow was the bastard get of Dark and Light—commanded by neither—'

'Twilight, Shadow is everything we have ever known. Indeed, it is everywhere.'

'But it was destroyed!'

'Shattered, yes. Look at the beach. Those bones—they belong to the Shake. We were assailed from both sides—we didn't stand a chance—that any of us survived at all is a miracle. Shadow was first shattered by the legions of Andii and the legions of Liosan. Purity cannot abide imperfection. In the eyes of purity, it becomes an abomination.'

She was shaking her head. 'Shadow was the realm of the *Edur*—it has nothing to do with us, with the Shake.'

Yedan smiled—she could not even recall the last time he had done that and the sight of it jolted her. He nodded. 'Our very own bastard get.'

She sank down to her knees in the bed of crumbled bone. She could hear the sea now, could hear the waves rolling down—and beneath all of that she could hear the deluged voices of the doomed behind the surface. *He turned away when she did. But his children had no way out. We held against them, here. We stood and we died defending our realm.* 'Our blood was royal,' she whispered.

Her brother was beside her now, and one hand rested on her shoulder. 'Scar Bandaris, the last prince of the Edur. King, I suppose, by then. He saw in us the sins not of the father, but of the mother. He left us and took all the Edur with him. He told us to hold, to ensure his escape. He said it was all we deserved, for we were our mother's children, and was she not the seducer and the father the seduced?' He was silent for a moment, and then he grunted and said, 'I wonder if the last of us left set out on his trail with vengeance in mind, or was it because we had nowhere else to go? By then, after all, Shadow had become the battlefield of every Elder force, not just the Tiste—it was being torn apart, with blood-soaked forces dividing every spoil, every territory—what were they called again? Yes, *warrens*. Every world was made an island, isolated in an ocean of chaos.'

Her eyes felt raw, but not a single tear sprang loose. 'We could not have survived that,' she said. 'That assault you described. You called it a miracle that we survived, but I know how—though I never understood its meaning—not until your words today.'

Yedan said, 'The Watch commanded the legions, and we held until we were told to withdraw. It's said there were but a handful of us left by then, elite officers one and all. *They* were the Watch. The Road was open then—we but marched.'

'It was open because of Blind Gallan.'

'Yes.'

'Because,' she looked up at him, 'he was told to save us.'

'Gallan was a poet—'

'And Seneschal of the Court of Mages in Kharkanas.'

He chewed on this for a while, glanced away, studying the swirling wall of light and the ceaseless sweep of figures in the depths, faces stretched in muted screams—an entire civilization trapped in eternal torment—but she saw not a flicker of emotion touch his face. 'A great power, then.'

'Yes.'

'There was civil war. Who could have commanded him to do anything?'

'One possessing the Blood of T'iam, and a prince of Kharkanas.'

She watched his eyes slowly widen, but still he stared at the wall. 'Now why,' he asked, 'would an Andii prince have done that?'

She shook her head. 'It's said he strode down to the First Shore, terribly wounded, sheathed in blood. It's said he looked upon the Shake, at how few of us were left, and at the ruin surrounding us—the death of the forests, the charred wreckage of our homes. He held a broken sword in one hand, a Hust sword, and it was seen to fall from his grip. He left it here.'

'That's all? Then how do you know he commanded Gallan to do anything?'

'When Gallan arrived he told the Twilight—he had torn out his eyes by then and was accompanied by an Andii woman who led him by an arm down from the shattered forest—he came down like a man dying of fever but when he spoke, his voice was clear and pure as music. He said to her these words:

> *"There is no grief in Darkness.*
> *It has taken to the skies.*
> *It leaves a world of ashes and failure.*
> *It sets out to find new worlds, as grief must.*
> *Winged grief commands me:*
> *Make a road for the survivors on the Shore*
> *To walk the paths of sorrow*
> *And charge them the remembrance*
> *Of this broken day*
> *As it shall one day be seen:*
> *As the birth of worlds unending*
> *Where grief waits for us all*
> *In the soul's darkness." '*

She slipped out from the weight of his hand and straightened, brushing bone dust from her knees. 'He was asked, then, who was this Winged Grief? And Gallan said, "There is but one left who would dare command me. One who would not weep and yet had taken into his soul a people's sorrow, a realm's sorrow. His name was Silchas Ruin." '

Yedan scanned the beach. 'What happened to the broken sword?'

She started, recovered. Why, after all this time, could her brother still surprise her? 'The woman with Gallan picked it up and threw it into the sea.'

His head snapped round. 'Why would she do that?'

Yan Tovis held up her hands. 'She never explained.'

Yedan faced the refulgent wall again, as if seeking to pierce its depths, as if looking for the damned sword.

'It was just a broken sword—'

'A Hust sword—you said so.'

'I don't even know what that means, except it's the name for Ruin's weapon.'

He grimaced. 'It should have healed by now,' he muttered, walking out on to the strand, eyes scanning the pallid beach. 'Light would reject it, cast it up.'

She stared after him. Healed? 'Yedan!'

He glanced back. 'What?'

'We cannot live here.'

'No, of course not.'

'But something is happening in Kharkanas—I don't know if I can even go back there.'

'Once she's fully returned,' Yedan said, swinging back, 'the power should ease.'

'She? Who?'

'Don't be obtuse, sister. Mother Dark. Who else arrives like a fist in our skulls?' He resumed his search along the First Shore.

'Errastas,' she whispered, 'whatever will you do now?'

Torrent scowled at the hag. 'Aren't you even listening?'

Olar Ethil straightened, gathering up her rotted cape of furs and scaled hide. 'Such a lovely carpet, such a riot of richness, all those supine colours!'

The withered nut of this witch's brain has finally cracked. 'I said these carriage tracks are fresh, probably not even a day old.'

Olar Ethil had one hand raised, as if about to wave at someone on the horizon. Instead, one taloned finger began inscribing patterns in the air. 'Go round, my friends, slow your steps. Wait for the one to pass, through and out and onward. No point in clashing wills, when none of it has purpose. Such a busy plain! No matter, if anyone has cause to quake it's not me, hah!'

'An enormous carriage,' Torrent resumed, 'burdened. But while that's interesting, it's the fact that the tracks simply begin—as if from nowhere—and look at the way the ground cracked at the start, as if the damned thing had landed from the sky, horses and all. Doesn't any of that make you curious?'

'Eh? Oh, soon enough, soon enough.' She dropped her arm and then pointed the same finger at him. 'The first temple's a mess. Besieged a decade ago, just a burnt-out husk, now. No one was spared. The Matron took weeks to die—it's no easy thing, killing them, you know. We have to move on, find another.'

Snarling, Torrent mounted his horse and collected the reins. 'Any good at running, witch? Too bad.' He kicked his horse into motion, setting out on the carriage's weaving trail. Let the thing's bones clatter into dust in his wake—the best solution to all his ills. Or she could just stand there and stare at every horizon one by one and babble and rant all she wanted—as if the sky ever answered.

A carriage. People. Living people. That's what he needed now. The return of sanity—*hold on, it dropped out of the sky, don't forget. What's so normal about that?*

'Never mind,' he muttered, 'at least they're alive.'

Sandalath made it to the bridge before collapsing. Cursing, Withal knelt at her side and lifted her head until it rested on his lap. Blood was streaming from her nose, ears and the corners of her eyes. Her lips glistened as if painted.

The three Nachts—or whatever they were called in this realm—had vanished, fled, he assumed, from whatever was assailing his wife. As for himself, he felt nothing. This world was desolate, lifeless, probably leagues from any decent body of water—but oh how he wished he could take her and just sail out of this madness.

Instead, it looked as though his wife was dying.

Crimson froth bubbled from her mouth as she began mumbling something— he leaned closer—words, yes, a conversation. Withal leaned back, snorting. When she'd thought him asleep, she'd said the same lines over and over again. As if they were a prayer, or the beginning of one.

'What's broken cannot be mended. You broke us, but that is not all—see what you have done.'

There was the touch of a lament in her tone, but one so emptied of sentiment it cut like a dagger. A lament, yes, but infused with chill hatred, a knuckled core of ice. Complicated, aye, layered—unless he was just imagining things. The truth could be as silly as a childhood song sung to a broken doll, its head lolling impossibly with those stupid eyes underneath the nose and the mouth looking like a wound to the forehead—

Withal shook himself. The oldest memories might be smells, tastes, or isolated images—but rarely all three at once—at least in so far as he knew from his own experience. Crammed into his skull, a crowded mess with everything at the back so tightly pressed all the furniture was crushed, and to reach in was to come up with a few pieces that made no sense at all—

Gods, he was tired. And here she was, dragging him all this way, only to die in his lap and abandon him at the gates of a dead city.

'. . . see what you have done.'

Her breathing had deepened. The blood had stopped trickling down—he wiped her mouth with a grimy cuff. She suddenly sighed. He leaned closer. 'Sand? Can you hear me?'

'Nice pillow . . . but for the smell.'

'You're not going to die?'

'It's over now,' she said, opening her eyes—but only for a moment as she gasped and shut them again. 'Ow, that hurts.'

'I can get some water—from the river here—'

'Yes, do that.'

He shifted her from his lap and settled her down on the road. 'Glad it's over, Sand. Oh, by the way, what's over?'

She sighed. 'Mother Dark, she has returned to Kharkanas.'

'Oh, that's nice.'

As he made his way down the wreckage-cluttered bank, waterskins flopping over one shoulder, Withal allowed himself a savage grimace. 'Oh, hello, Mother Dark, glad you showed up. You and all the rest of you gods and goddesses. Come back to fuck with a thousand million lives all over again, huh? Now, I got an idea for you all, aye, I do.

'Get lost. It's better, you see, when we ain't got you to blame for our mess. Understand me, Mother Dark?' He crouched at the edge of black water and pushed the first skin beneath the surface, listening to the gurgle. 'And as for my wife, hasn't she suffered enough?'

A voice filled his head. *Yes.*

The river swept past, the bubbles streamed from the submerged skin until no bubbles were left. Still, Withal held it down, as if drowning a maimed dog. He wasn't sure he'd ever move again.

The descent of darkness broke frozen bone and flesh across the width of the valley, spilling out beyond the north ridge, devouring the last flickering flames from the burning heaps that had once been Barghast wagons.

The vast battlefield glistened and sparkled as corpses and carcasses shrivelled, losing their last remnants of moisture, and earth buckled, lurching upward in long wedges of stone-hard clay that jostled bodies. Iron steamed and glowed amongst the dead.

The sky above was devoid of all light, but the ashes drifting down were visible, as if each flake was lit from within. The pressure continued pushing everything closer to the ground, until horses and armoured men and women became flattened, rumpled forms. Weapons suddenly exploded, white-hot shards hissing.

The hillsides groaned, visibly contracted as something swirled in the very centre of the valley, a darkness so profound as to be a solid thing.

A hill cracked in half with a thunderous detonation. The air seemed to tear open.

From the swirling miasma a figure emerged, first one boot then the other crunching down on desiccated flesh, hide and bone, striding out from the rent, footfalls heavy as stone.

The darkness seethed, pulsed. The figure paused, held out a gauntleted left hand.

Lightning spanned the blackness, a thousand crashing drums. The air itself howled, and the darkness streamed down. Withered husks that had once been living things spun upright as if reborn, only to pull free of the ground and whirl skyward like rotted autumn leaves.

Shrieking wind, torn banners of darkness spiralling inward, wrapping, twisting, binding. Cold air rushed in like floodwaters through a crumbling dam, and all it swept through burst into dust that roiled wild in its wake.

Hammering concussions shook the hills, sheared away slopes leaving raw cliffs, boulders tumbling and pitching through the remnants of carnage. And still the darkness streamed down, converging, coalescing into an elongated sliver forming at the end of the figure's outstretched hand.

A final report, loud as the snapping of a dragon's spine, and then sudden silence.

A sword, bleeding darkness, dripping cold.

Overhead, late afternoon sunlight burned the sky.

He slowly scanned the ground, even as desiccated fragments of hide and flesh began raining from the heavens, and then he stepped forward, bending down to retrieve a battered scabbard. He slid the sword home.

A sultry wind swept down the length of the valley, gathering streamers of steam.

He stood for a time, studying the scene on all sides.

'Ah, my love. Forgive me.'

He set out, boots crunching on the dead.

Returned to the world.

Draconus.

Book Four

The Path
Forever Walked

When your penance is done
Come find me
When all the judges cloaked in stone
Have faced away
Seek the rill beneath the bowers and strings
Of fine pearls
Down in the fold of sacred hills
Among the elms
Where animals and birds find shelter
Come find me
I am nestled in grasses never trod
By heartbroken
Knights and brothers of kings
Not a single root torn
In the bard's trembling grief
Seek out what is freely given
Come find me
In the wake of winter's dark flight
And take what you will
Of these blossoms
My colours lie in wait for you
And none other

Come Find Me
Fisher

Chapter Nineteen

In the midst of fleeing
the unseen enemy
I heard the hollow horrors
of the wretched caught
We collected our gasps
to make ourselves a song
Let the last steps be a dance!
Before the spears strike
and the swords slash
We'll run with torches
and write the night
with glutted indulgences
Our precious garlands
bold laughter to drown
the slaughter in the stables
of the lame and poor
Entwine hands and pitch skyward!
None will hear the dread
groans of the suffering
nor brush with tips
glistening sorrow'd cheeks
on stilled faces below
Let us flee in mad joy—
the unseen enemy draws near
behind and ahead
and none will muster
to this harbinger call
for as long as we are able
to run these perfect circles
confound the fates
all you clever killers!
I am with you!

UNSEEN ENEMY
EFLIT TARN

Moving like one bludgeoned, Kilmandaros slowly, by degrees, picked herself up from the ground. She leaned to one side and spat red phlegm, and then glanced over to see Errastas lying curled on the dead grasses, motionless as a stillborn calf. Off to one side stood Sechul Lath, arms wrapped tightly about his torso, face bleached of all warmth.

She spat again. 'It's him.'

'A summoning beyond all expectation,' Sechul said. 'Odd, Errastas looks less than pleased at his own efficacy.'

Kilmandaros levered herself upright, stood unsteadily. 'He could be subtle when he wanted,' she said, in some irritation. 'Instead, he made sure to let us know.'

'Not just us,' Sechul replied. 'Nothing so crass,' he added, 'as careless.'

'Is it anger, do you think?'

He rubbed at his face with both hands. 'The last time Draconus was wakened to anger, Mother, nothing survived intact. Nothing.' He hesitated, and then shook his head. 'Not anger, not yet, anyway. He just wanted everyone to know. He wanted to send us all spinning.'

Kilmandaros grunted. 'Rude bastard.'

They stood at the end of a long row of standing stones that had taken them round a broad, sweeping cursus. The avenue opened out in front of them, with scores of lesser stones spiralling the path inward to a flat-topped altar, its surface stained black. Little of this remained in the real world, of course. A few toppled menhirs, rumpled tussocks and ruts made by wandering bhederin. Errastas had drawn them ever closer to a place where time itself dissolved into confusion. Assailed by chaos, straining beneath the threats of oblivion, even the ground underfoot felt porous, at risk of crumbling under their weight.

The builders of this holy shrine were long gone. Resonance remained, however, tingling her skin, but it was an itch she could not scratch away. The sensation further fouled her mood. Glaring down at Errastas, she asked, 'Will he recover? Or will we have to drag him behind us by one foot.'

'A satisfying image,' Sechul conceded, 'but he's already coming round. After the shock, the mind races.' He walked up to where the Errant lay. 'Enough, Errastas. On your feet. We have a task to complete and now more than ever, it needs doing.'

'She took an eye,' rasped the figure lying on the grasses. 'With it, I would have seen—'

'Only what you wanted to see,' Sechul finished. 'Never mind that, now. There is no going back. We won't know what Draconus intends until he shows us—or, Abyss forbid, he finds us.' He shrugged. 'He's thrown his gauntlet down—'

Errastas snorted. 'Gauntlet? That, Setch, was his *fist*.'

'So punch back,' Sechul snapped.

Kilmandaros laughed. 'I've taught him well, haven't I?'

The Errant uncurled, and then sat up. He stared bleakly at the altar stone. 'We cannot just ignore him. Or what his arrival tells us. He is freed. The sword Dragnipur is shattered—there was no other way out. If the sword is shattered, then—'

'Rake is dead,' said Kilmandaros.

Silence for a time. She could see in the faces of the two men sweeping cascades of emotion as they contemplated the raw fact of Anomander Rake's death. Disbelief, denial, wonder, satisfaction and pleasure. And then . . . fear. 'Yes,' she said. 'Great changes, terrible changes.'

'But,' Errastas looked up at her, 'how was it possible? Who could have done such a thing? Has Osserc returned—no, we would have sensed that.' He climbed to his feet. 'Something has gone wrong. I can feel it.'

Sechul faced him. 'Master of the Holds, show us your mastery. You need to look to your own hands, and the power within them.'

'Listen to my son,' said Kilmandaros. 'Seek the truth in the Holds, Errastas. We must know where things stand. Who struck him down? Why? And how did the sword break?'

'There is irony in this,' Sechul said with a wry smile. 'The removal of Anomander Rake is like kicking down a gate—in an instant the path beyond runs straight and clear. Only to have Draconus step into the breach. As deadly as Rake ever was, but a whole lot crueller, that much closer to chaos. His appearance is, I think, a harbinger of the madness to come. Squint that lone eye, Errastas, and tell me you see other than ruination ahead.'

But the Errant was shaking his head. 'I can tell you now who broke Dragnipur. There could be no other. The Warlord.'

Breath hissed from Kilmandaros. 'Brood. Yes, I see that. The weapon he holds—none other. But that only confuses things all the more. Rake would not have willingly surrendered that weapon, not even to Caladan Brood.' She eyed the others. 'We are agreed that the Son of Darkness is dead? Yet his slayer did not take Dragnipur. Can it be that the Warlord killed him?'

Sechul Lath snorted. 'Centuries of speculation—who was the deadlier of the two? Have we our answer? This is absurd—can any of us even imagine a cause that would so divide those two? With the history they shared?'

'Perhaps the cause was Dragnipur itself—'

Kilmandaros grunted. 'Think clearly, Errastas. Brood had to know that shattering the sword would free Draconus, and a thousand other ascendants—' her hands closed into fists—'and Eleint. He would not have done it if he'd had a choice. Nothing could have so fractured that ancient alliance, for it was more than an alliance. It was friendship.' She sighed heavily and looked away. 'We clashed, yes, but even me—no, I would not have murdered Anomander Rake if the possibility was presented to me. I would not. His existence . . . had purpose. He was one you could rely upon, when justice needed a blade's certain edge.' She passed a hand over her eyes. 'The world has lost some of its colour, I think.'

'Wrong,' said Sechul. 'Draconus has returned. But listen to us. We swirl round and round this dread pit of truth. Errastas, will you stand there frozen as a hare? Think you not the Master of the Deck is bleeding from the ears right now? Strike quickly, friend—he will be in no condition to intercept you. Indeed, make him fear we planned this—all of it—make him believe we have fashioned the Consort's escape from Dragnipur.'

Kilmandaros's eyes were wide on her son.

Errastas slowly nodded. 'A detour, of sorts. Fortunately, a modest one. Attend me.'

'I shall remain here,' announced Kilmandaros. At the surprise and suspicion she saw in the Errant's face, she raised her fists. 'There was the danger—so close to the Eleint—that I lose control. Surely,' she added, 'you did not intend me to join you when you walked through that last gate. No, leave me here. Return when it's done.'

Errastas looked round at the shrine's standing stones. 'I would not think this place suited you, Kilmandaros.'

'The fabric is thin. My presence weakens it more—this pleases me.'

'Why such hatred for humans, Kilmandaros?'

Her brows rose. 'Errastas, really. Who among all the races is quickest to claim the right to judgement? Over everyone and everything? Who holds that such right belongs to them and them alone? A woodcutter walks deep into the forest, where he is attacked and eaten by a striped cat—what do his fellows say? They say: "The cat is evil and must be punished. The cat must answer for its crime, and it and all its kind must answer to our hate." Before too long, there are no cats left in that forest. And humans consider that just. Righteous. Could I, Errastas, I would gather all the humans of the world, and I would gift them with *my* justice— and that justice is here, in these two fists.'

Errastas reached up to probe his eye socket, and he managed a faint smile. 'Well answered, Kilmandaros.' He turned to Sechul Lath. 'Arm yourself, friend. The Holds have grown feral.'

'Which one will you seek first?'

'The one under a Jaghut stone, of course.'

She watched as blurry darkness swallowed them. With the Errant's departure, the ephemeral fragility of the ancient shrine slowly dissolved, revealing the stolid ruins of its abandonment. A slew of toppled, shattered stones, pecked facings hacked and chipped—the images obliterated. She walked closer to the altar stone. It had been deliberately chiselled, cut in two. Harsh breaths and sweat-slick muscles, a serious determination to despoil this place.

She knew all about desecration. It was her hobby, after all, an obsessive lure that tugged her again and again, with all the senseless power of a lodestone.

A few thousand years ago, people had gathered to build their shrine. Someone had achieved the glorious rank of tyrant, able to threaten life and soul, and so was able to compel hundreds to his or her bidding. To quarry enormous stones, drag them to this place, tilt them upright like so many damned penises. And who among those followers truly believed that tyrant's calling? Voice of the gods in the sky, the groaning bitches in the earth, the horses of the heavens racing the seasons, the mythologies of identity—all those conceits, all those delusions. People of ancient times were no more fools than those of the present, and ignorance was never a comfortable state of being.

So they had built this temple, work-gangs of clear-eyed cynics sacrificing their labour to the glory of the gods but it wasn't gods basking in that glory—it was the damned tyrant, who needed to show off his power to coerce, who sought to symbolize his power for all eternity.

Kilmandaros could comprehend the collective rage that had destroyed this place. Every tyrant reaches the same cliff-edge, aged into infirmity, or eyeing the strutting of heirs and recognizing the hungry looks in their regard. That edge was death, and with it all glory fell to dust. Even stone cannot withstand the fury of mortals when fuelled by abnegation.

Nature was indifferent to temples, to sacred sites. It did not withhold its gnawing winds and dissolute rains. It devoured such places with the same remorseless will that annihilated palaces and city walls, squalid huts and vast aqueducts. But carve a face into stone and someone is bound to destroy it long before nature works its measured erosion.

She understood that compulsion, the bitter necessity of refuting monumental achievements, whether they be dressed in stone or in the raiment of poetry. Power possessed a thousand faces and one would be hard pressed to find a beautiful one among them. No, they were ugly one and all, and if they managed to create something wondrous, then the memory of its maker must be made to suffer all the more for it.

'For every soul sweeping away the dust,' said a voice behind her, 'there are a thousand scattering it by the handful.'

Kilmandaros did not turn round, but bared her teeth nonetheless. 'I was growing impatient.'

'It's not rained here for some time. Only the roots of the stones still hold moisture. I have followed your journey in the morning mists, in the damp breaths of the beasts.' After a moment, Mael moved up to stand beside her, his eyes settling on the desecrated altar stone. 'Not your handiwork, I see. Feeling cheated?'

'I despise conceit,' she said.

'And so every mortal creation is to be crushed by your fists. Yes, the presumption of all those fools.'

'Do you know where they have gone, Mael?'

He sighed. 'The Holds are not as they once were. Have you considered, they may not return?'

'Errastas is their Master—'

'Was, actually. The Holds have not had a master for tens of thousands of years, Kilmandaros. Do you know, you forced the Errant's retreat from the Holds. He feared you were coming for him, to destroy him and his precious creations.'

'He was right. I was.'

'See how things have turned out. His summoning compelled none of us—you must realize that.'

'That is no matter—'

'Because deceiving him continues to serve your purposes. And now Knuckles walks at his side. Or, more accurately, a step behind. When will the knife strike?'

'My son understands the art of subtlety.'

'It's not an art, Kilmandaros, it's just one among many tactics to get what you want. The best subtlety is when no one even notices what you've done, ever. Can Sechul Lath achieve that?'

'Can you?' she retorted.

Mael smiled. 'I know of only a few capable of such a thing. One is mortal and my closest friend. The other wasn't mortal, but is now dead. And then, of course, there is Draconus.'

She fixed a glare upon him. 'Him? You must be mad!'

Mael shrugged. 'Try this for a consideration. Draconus needed to get something done. And, it now seems, he achieved it. Without lifting a hand. Without anyone even noticing his involvement. Only one man ever defeated him. Only one man could possess Dragnipur but never kneel before it. Only one man could oversee the weapon's destruction—no matter the cost. Only one man could force an end to Mother Dark's denial. And only one man could stand in the face of chaos and not blink.'

Breath gusted from her in a growl. 'And now that man is dead.'

'And Draconus walks free. Draconus has broken Kallor's curse on him. He holds Darkness in a blade of annihilation. No longer chained, no longer on the run, no longer haunted by the terrible error in judgement that was Dragnipur.'

'All this by his hand? I do not believe it, Mael.'

'But that is precisely my point, Kilmandaros. About true subtlety. Will we ever know if what I have just described was all by the Consort's hand? No.'

'Unless he admits it.'

'But who wouldn't?'

'I hate your words, Mael. They gnaw like the waves you love so much.'

'We are all vulnerable, Kilmandaros. Don't think Draconus is about to build a little farm in some mountain valley and spend the rest of his days whittling whistles while birds nest in his hair. He knows we're here. He knows we're up to something. Either he's already figured it out, in which case he will come to find us, or he is even now setting out to pull loose all our secret ambitions.'

'Who killed Anomander Rake?'

'Dessembrae, wielding a sword forged by Rake's own hand.'

She was rocked by that. Her mind raced. '*Vengeance?*'

'None other.'

'That weapon always terrified me,' she said. 'I could never understand why he set it aside.'

'Really? The hand that holds it must be pure in its desire. Kilmandaros, Rake yielded it to his brother because his heart was already broken, while Andarist . . . well, we know that tale.'

As the significance of Mael's words struck home, Kilmandaros found she was trembling. 'Andarist,' she whispered. 'That . . . that . . .' but she had no words to describe her feeling. Instead, her hands rose to her face again. 'He is gone,' she said, voice catching in a sob. 'Anomander Rake is gone!'

Mael spoke, his tone suddenly harsh. 'Leave Dessembrae alone. He was as much a victim as anyone else involved. Worse, he has been cheated, and used, and now his suffering is immeasurable.'

She shook her head, the muscles of her jaws creaking. 'I was not thinking of Dessembrae.'

'Kilmandaros, listen well. My thoughts on Draconus—my musings on his possible culpability—they are unproven. Speculations, nothing more. If you seek a confrontation with Draconus—if you seek vengeance—you will die. And it may well be for naught, for perhaps Draconus is innocent of all charges.'

'You do not believe that.'

'I was but reminding you of the danger he presents to us. How long was he trapped within Dragnipur? What did that do to him? To his mind? Is he even sane any more? One other thing, and think on this carefully, Kilmandaros. Would Rake have willingly freed a mad Draconus? Has he ever shown a thoughtless side to his decisions? Ever?'

Her eyes narrowed. '*He had a purpose.*'

Mael's smile was wry. 'Even though he is dead, we find ourselves holding to faith in him. Extraordinary, isn't it?'

'Mother Dark—'

'No longer faces away, and as with Darkness, so too it is with—'

'Light. Gods below, Mael. What has he forced upon us?'

'A final accounting, I'd wager. An end to the stupid games. He might as well have locked us all in one room—and no one leaves until we settle things once and for all.'

'Bastard!'

'Your grief was rather shortlived, Kilmandaros.'

'Because what you say rings true—yes! Rake would think that way, wouldn't he?'

'Else he could not permit his own death—his removal from the stage. More than just ending Mother Dark's obstreperous pique, he now forces our hands— we are all stirred awake, Elders and children both, mortal and immortal.'

'To what end?' she demanded. 'More blood? A damned ocean's worth?'

'Not if there's a way around it,' Mael replied. 'To what end, you ask. This, I think: he wants us to deal with the Crippled God.'

'That pathetic creature? You cannot be serious, Mael.'

'The wound ever festers, the poison spreads. That alien god's power is anathema. We need to fix it—before we seek anything else. Before we lose K'rul's gift for ever.'

'Errastas had other ideas.'

'So do you and Setch. So does Olar Ethil. And Ardata.'

'And Draconus too, I would think.'

'We cannot know if Anomander Rake and Draconus spoke—was a bargain reached between them within Dragnipur? "*I will free you, Draconus, if . . .*"'

'They could not have spoken,' said Kilmandaros. 'For Rake was killed by *Vengeance.* You said so yourself.'

Mael walked over to sit down on one of the blocks of the altar stone. 'Ah, well. There is more to say on that. Among other things. Tell me, Kilmandaros, what Hold did Errastas choose?'

She blinked. 'Why, the obvious one. Death.'

'Then I will begin with this curious detail—for I wish to know your thoughts on the, uh, implications.' He looked up and something glinted in his eyes. 'Before Rake met Dessembrae, he met Hood. Met him, and killed him. With Dragnipur.'

She stared.

Mael continued: 'Two gods were in attendance, that I know of.'

'Who?' the word came out in a dry rasp.

'Shadowthrone and Cotillion.'

Oh, how she wished for a tall, imposing standing stone—within her reach—a proud pinnacle of conceit—just there, at the very end of her fist as it swung out its path of ferocious destruction.

'*Them!*'

Mael watched her flail and stamp about, watched as she descended on one toppled menhir after another, pounding each one into rubble. He scratched at the bristles on his chin.

Oh, you are indeed clever, Kilmandaros. It all falls home, doesn't it?

It all falls home.

He'd wanted her to consider the implications. *So much for being subtle.*

Suffering could be borne. When the blood was pure, purged of injustices. Brayderal was not like the others, not the same as Rutt, or pernicious Badalle with Saddic ever at her side. She alone possessed the legacy of the Inquisitors, shining bright beneath her almost translucent skin. And among all the others, only Badalle suspected the truth. *I am a child of the Quitters. I am here to complete their work.*

She had finally seen her kin on their trail, and now wondered why they did not simply stride into the midst of the Chal Managal, to take up the last of these pathetic lives.

I want to go home. Back to Estobanse. Please, come and get me, before it's too late.

Suffering could be borne. But even her unhuman flesh was failing. Each morning, she looked upon the survivors of yet another night and trembled with disbelief. She watched them drag the corpses close and she watched them pick the bones clean and then split them to greedily suck at the marrow.

'*Children are quickest to necessity. They can make any world normal. Be careful, daughter, with these humans. To live, they will do anything.*'

She looked upon Rutt's world and saw the truth in her father's words. With Held cradled in his arms, he called the stronger ones to him and examined the floppy bags of human skin they now used to trap Shards whenever a swarm found the ribby snake. These fleshless, de-boned bodies, flung into the air as the locusts descended, drew the creatures as flames drew moths, and when the seething mass struck the ground the children pounced, stuffing locusts into their mouths by the handful. Rutt had found a way to turn the war of attrition, to hunt the hunters of this glass wasteland.

His followers were hardened now, all angles and flat eyes. Badalle's poems had turned cruel, savage. Abandonment honed sure edges; sun and heat and crystal horizons had forged a terrible weapon. Brayderal wanted to scream to her kin, there in the blurred haze of their wake. She wanted to warn them. She wanted to say *Hurry! See these survivors! Hurry! Before it's too late!*

But she dared not slink away—not even in the deepest of night beneath the jade spears. They would find out. Badalle had made certain that she was watched. Badalle knew.

She has to die. I have to kill her. It would be easy. I am so much stronger than them. I could snap her neck. I could unleash my Holy Voice for the first time ever and so force my kin to come to my aid when Rutt and Saddic and all the others close on me. I could end this, all of it.

Yet, the Inquisitors kept their distance. They must have a reason. Any precipitate act by Brayderal could ruin everything. She needed to be patient.

Huddled beneath layers of rags, ever careful to stand in the way that humans stood—so limited, so bound by physical imperfections—she watched as Rutt walked out ahead of the snake's head, the flicking tongue, Badalle would say, before snapping open her mouth and sucking in flies, which she then crunched with obvious relish.

The city that awaited them did not look real. Every glimmering line and angle seemed to bite Brayderal's eyes—she could barely look in that direction, so powerful was her sense of wrongness. Was it in ruin? It did not seem so. Was it lifeless? It must be. There were no farms, no trees, no rivers. The sky above it was clear, dustless, smokeless. Why then this horror and dread?

The humans did not feel as she did. Instead, they eyed the distant towers and open faces of buildings as they would the arrival of a new torment—diamonds and rubies, gems and shards—and she could see the gauging regard in their eyes, as if they silently asked: *Will this attack us? Can we eat it? Is its need greater than ours? Is any need greater than ours?*

Sickened, Brayderal watched Rutt walk ever closer to the faintly raised track encircling the unwalled city.

He has decided. We are going in. And I can do nothing to stop it.

'In knowing,' Badalle whispered, 'I am in knowing, always. See her, Saddic? She hates this. She fears this. We are not as weak as she hopes. Saddic, listen, we have a prisoner in the ribby snake. She is chained to us, even as she pretends her freedom under those rags. See how she holds herself. Her control is failing. The Quitter awakens.'

Kill her then, Saddic pleaded with his eyes.

But Badalle shook her head. 'She would take too many of us down. And the others would help her. Remember how the Quitters command? The voice that can drive a man to his knees? No, leave her to the desert—and the city, yes, the city.' *But is this even true? I could—I could . . .* She had fled the Quitters, made them a thing of her past, and the past was ever dead. It had no hold, no claim upon her. Yet, none of this had proved true. The past stalked them. The past was fast closing in.

Torn fragments floated through her mind, island memories surrounded in the depthless seas of fear. Tall gaunt figures, words of slaying, the screams of slaughter. *Quitters.*

She caught a fly, crunched it down. 'The secret is in his arms,' she said. 'Held. Held is the secret. One day, everyone will understand. Do you think it matters, Saddic? Things will be born, life will catch fire.'

Badalle could see that he did not understand, not yet. But he was like all the others. Their time was coming. *The city called to us. Only those it chooses can find it. Once, giants walked the world. The sun's rays were snared in their eyes. They found this city and made it a temple. Not a place in which to live. It was made to exist for itself.*

She had learned so much. When she'd had wings and had journeyed across the world. Stealing thoughts, snatching ideas. Madness was a gift. Even as memories were a curse. She needed to find power. But all she could find within herself was a knotted host of words. Poems were not swords. Were they?

'Remember temples?' she asked the boy beside her. 'Fathers in robes, the bowls filling with coins no one could eat. And on the walls gems winked like drops of blood. Those temples, they were like giant fists built to batter us down, to take our spirits and chain them to worldly fears. We were supposed to shred the skin from our souls and accept the pain and punishment as just. The temples told us we were flawed and then promised to heal us. All we needed to do was pay and pray. Coin for absolution and calluses on the knees, but remember how splendid those robes were! That's what we paid for.'

And the Quitters came among us, down from the north. They walked like the broken, and when they spoke, souls crumpled like eggshells. They came with white hands and left with red hands.

Words have power.

She lifted a hand and pointed at the city. 'But this temple is different. It was not built for adoration. It was built to warn us. Remember the cities, Saddic? Cities exist to gather the suffering beneath the killer's sword. Swords—more than anyone could even count. So many swords. In the hands of priests and Quitters and merchant houses and noble warriors and slavers and debt-holders and keepers of food and water—so many. Cities are mouths, Saddic, filled with sharp teeth.' She snapped another fly from the air. Chewed. Swallowed.

'Lead them now,' she said to the boy beside her. 'Follow Rutt. And keep an eye on Brayderal. Danger comes. The time of the Quitters has arrived. Go, lead them after Rutt. Begin!'

He looked upon her with alarm, but she waved him away, and set out for the snake's tattered tail.

The Quitters were coming.

To begin the last slaughter.

Inquisitor Sever stood looking down on the body of Brother Beleague, seeing as if for the first time the emaciated travesty of the young man she had once known and loved. On her left was Brother Adroit, breathing fast and shallow, hunched and wracked with tremors. The bones of his spine and shoulders were bowed like an old man's, legacy of this journey's terrible deficiencies. His nose was rotting, a raw wound glistening and crawling with flies.

To her right was Sister Rail, her gaunt face thin as a hatchet, her eyes rimmed in dull, dry red. She had little hair left—that lustrous mane was long gone, and with it the last vestiges of the beauty she had once possessed.

Sister Scorn had collected Beleague's staff and now leant upon it as would a cripple. The joints of her elbows, high-wrists and wrists were inflamed and swollen with fluids, but Sever knew that strength remained within her. Scorn was the last Adjudicator among them.

When they had set out to deliver peace upon the last of the south-dwellers— these children—they had numbered twelve. Among them, three of the original five women still lived, and but one of the seven men. Inquisitor Sever accepted responsibility for this tragic error in judgement. Of course, who could have imagined that thousands of helpless children could march league upon league through this tortured land, bereft of shelter, their hands empty? Outlasting the wild dogs, the cannibal raiders among the last of the surviving adults, and the wretched parasites swarming the ground and the skies above—no, not one Inquisitor could have anticipated this terrible will to survive.

Surrender was the easy choice, the simplest decision of all. They should have given up long ago.

And we would now be home. And my mate could stand before his daughter and feel such pride at her courage and purity—that she chose to walk with the human children, that she chose to guide her kin to the delivery of peace.

And I would not now be standing above the body of my dead son.

It was understood—it had always been understood—that no human was an equal to the Forkrul Assail. Proof was delivered a thousand times a day—and towards the end, ten thousand, as the pacification of the south kingdoms reached its blessed conclusion. Not once had the Shriven refused their submission; not once had a single pathetic human straightened in challenge. The hierarchy was unassailable.

But these children did not accept that righteous truth. In ignorance they found strength. In foolishness they found defiance.

'The city,' said Scorn, her voice a broken thing. 'We cannot permit it.'

Sever nodded. 'The investment is absolute, yes. We cannot hope to storm it.'

Adroit said, 'Its own beauty, yes. To challenge would be suicide.'

The women turned at that and he flinched back a step. 'Deny me? The clarity of my vision?'

Sever sighed, gaze dropping once more to her dead son. 'We cannot. It is absolute. It *shines*.'

'And now the boy with the baby leads them to it,' said Sister Rail. 'Unacceptable.'

'Agreed,' said Sever. 'We may fail to return, but we shall not fail in what we set out to do. Adjudicator, will you lead us into peace?'

'I am ready,' Scorn replied, straightening and holding out the staff. 'Wield this, Inquisitor, my need for it has ended.'

She longed to turn away, to reject Scorn's offer. *My son's weapon. Fashioned by my own hands and then surrendered to him. I should never have touched it again.*

'Honour him,' Scorn said.

'I shall.' She took the iron-shod staff, and then faced the others. 'Gather up the last of your strength. I judge four thousand remain—a long day of slaughter awaits us.'

'They are unarmed,' said Rail. 'Weak.'

'Yes. In the delivering of peace, we will remind them of that truth.'

Scorn set out. Sever and the others fell in behind the Adjudicator. When they drew closer, they would fan out, to make room for the violence they would unleash.

Not one Shriven would ever reach the city. And the boy with the baby would die last. *By my husband's daughter's hand. Because she lives, she still lives.*

Something like panic gripped the children, dragging Brayderal along in a rushing tide. Swearing, she tried to pull loose, but hands reached out, clutched tight, pushed her onwards. She should have been able to defy them all, but she had overestimated her reserves of strength—she was more damaged than she had believed.

She saw Saddic, leading this charge. Plunging after Rutt, who was now almost at the city's threshold. But of Badalle there was no sign. This detail frightened her. *There is something about her. She is transformed, but I do not know how. She is somehow . . . quickened.*

Her kin had finally comprehended the danger. They waited no longer.

Scuffed, tugged and pushed, she waited for the first screams behind her.

Words. I have nothing but words. I cast away many of them, only to have others find me. What can words achieve? Here in this hard, real place? But doubts themselves are nothing but words, a troubled song in my head. When I speak, the snakes listen. Their eyes are wide. But what happens to all I say, once the words slip into them? Alchemies. Sometimes the mixture froths and bubbles. Sometimes it boils. Sometimes, nothing stirs and the potion lies dead, cold and grey as mud. Who can know? Who can predict?

I speak softly when all that I say is a howl. I pound upon bone with my fists, and they hear naught but whispers. Savage words will thud against dead flesh. But the slow drip of blood, ah, then they are content as cats at a stream.

Badalle hurried along, and it seemed the snake parted, as if her passage was ripping it in two. She saw skeletal faces, shining eyes, limbs wrapped in skin dry as leather. She saw thigh bones from ribbers picked up on the trail—held like weapons—but what good would they do against the Quitters?

I have words and nothing else. And, in these words, I have no faith. They cannot topple walls. They cannot crush mountains down to dust. The faces swam past her. She knew them all, and they were nothing but blurs, each one smeared inside tears.

But what else is there? What else can I use against them? They are Quitters. They claim power in their voice. The islands in her mind were drowning.

I too seek power in my words.

Have I learned from them? This is how it seems. Is this how it is?

Stragglers. The sickened, the weakened, and then she was past them all, standing alone on the glass plain. The sun made the world white, bitter with purity. This was the perfection so cherished by the Quitters. *But it was not the Quitters who cut down our world. They only came in answer to the death of our gods— our faith—when the rains stopped, when the last green withered and died. They came in answer to our prayers. Save us! Save us from ourselves!*

Emerging from the heat shimmer, four figures, fast closing. Like wind-rocked puppets, every limb snapped back until broken, wheeling loose, and death surrounded them in whirlwinds. Monstrous, clambering out of her memories. Swirls of power—she saw mouths open—

'*YIELD!*'

The command rushed through Badalle, hammered children to the ground behind her. Voices crying out, helpless with dread. She felt it rage against her will, weakening her knees. She felt a snap, as if a tether had broken, and all at once she lifted free—she saw the ribby snake, the sinuous length stretched out as if in yearning. But, segment by segment, it writhed in pain.

As that command thundered from bone to bone, Badalle found her voice. *Power in the word, but I can answer it.*

> '—to the assault of wonder
> Humility takes you in hand—'

She spun back down to lock herself behind her own eyes. She saw energies whirl away, ignite in flashes.

'*HALT!*'

Cracking like a fist. Lips split, blood threading down. Badalle spat, pushed forward. One step, only one.

> '—in softest silence
> Enfold the creeping doubt—'

She saw her words strike them. Stagger them. Almost close enough, at last, to see their ravaged faces, the disbelief, the bafflement and growing distress. The *indignation*. And yes, that she understood. Games of meaning in evasion. Deceit of intent in sleight of hand.

Badalle took another step.

> '*Yield all these destinations*
> *Unbidden jostle to your bones*
> *Halt in the shadow thrown*
> *Beneath the yoke of dismay—*'

She felt fire in her limbs, saw blinding incandescence erupt from her hands. Truth was such a rare weapon, and all the more deadly for it.

> '*Do not give me your words!*
> *They are dead with the squalor*
> *Of your empty virtues*
> *YIELD to your own lies!*
> *HALT in the breathless moment*
> *Your lungs scream*
> *And silence answers*
> *Your heart drums*
> *Brittle surfaces*
> *BLEED!*'

They staggered back as if blinded. Blue fluids spurted from ruptured joints, gushed down from gaping mouths. Agony twisted their angled faces. One fell, thrashing, kicking on the ground. Another, a woman closer to Badalle than the others, dropped down on to her knees, and their impact with the crystalline ground was marked by two bursts of bluish blood—the Quitter shrieked. The remaining two, a man and a woman, reeling as if buffeted by invisible fists, had begun retreating—stumbling, half-running.

The fires within Badalle flared, and then died.

The Quitters deserved worse—but she did not have it in her to deliver such hard punishment. They had given her but two words. Not enough. *Two words. Obedience to the privilege of dying. Accept your fate. But . . . we will not. We refuse. We have been refusing things for a long time, now. We are believers in refusal.*

They will not come close now. Not for a long time. Maybe, for these ones, never again. I have hurt them. I took their words and made them my own. I made the power turn in their hands and cut them. It will have to do.

She turned round. The ribby snake had begun moving again, strangely mindless, as if beaten by drovers, senseless as a herd of cattle crossing a . . . *a river? But, when have I seen a river?*

She blinked. Licked salty blood from her lips. Flies danced.

The city awaited them.

'It is what we can bear,' she whispered. 'But there is more to life than suffering.' *Now we must find it.*

Darkness passed, and yet it remained. A splinter pure, promising annihilation. Onos T'oolan could sense it, somewhere ahead, a flickering, wavering presence. His stride, unbroken for so long, now faltered. The bitter rage within him seemed to stagger, sapped of all strength. Depression rose like flood waters, engulfing all sense of purpose. The tip of his sword bit the ground.

Vengeance meant nothing, even when the impulse was all-consuming. It was a path that, once started upon, could conceivably stretch on for ever. The culpable could stand in a line reaching past the horizon. An avenger's march was endless. So it had been with the vengeance sought against the Jaghut, and Onos T'oolan had never been blind to the futility of that. Was he nothing but an automaton, stung into motion that would never slow in step?

He felt a sudden pressure wash over him from behind.

Baffled, all at once frightened, his weapon's stone tip carving a furrow in the dry soil, the First Sword slowly swung round.

He could deny. He could refuse. But these choices would not lead him to the knowledge he sought. He had been forced back from the realms of death. The blood ties he had chosen had been severed. No longer a husband, a father, a brother. He had been given vengeance, but what vengeance could he find sifting through a valley heaped with corpses? There were other purposes, other reasons for walking this pathetic world once again. Onos T'oolan had been denied his rightful end— he intended to find out why.

Not one among the thousand or so T'lan Imass approaching him had yet touched his thoughts. They walked enshrouded in silence, ghosts, kin reduced to strangers.

He waited.

Children of the Ritual, yes, but his sense of many of them told him otherwise. There was mystery here. T'lan Imass, and yet . . .

When all the others halted their steps, six bonecasters emerged, continuing their approach.

He knew three. Brolos Haran, Ulag Togtil, Ilm Absinos. Bonecasters of the Orshayn T'lan Imass. The Orshayn had failed to appear at Silverfox's Gathering. Such failure invited presumptions of loss. Extinction. Fates to match those of the Ifayle, the Bentract, the Kerluhm. The presumption had been erroneous.

The remaining three were wrong in other ways. They were clothed in the furs of the white bear—a beast that had come late in the age of the Imass—and their faces were flatter, the underlying structure more delicate than that of true Imass. Their weapons were mostly bone, ivory, tusk or antler, with finely chipped chert and flint insets. Weapons defying the notion of finesse: intricate in their construction and yet the violence they would deliver promised an almost primitive brutality.

Bonecaster Ulag Togtil spoke. 'First Sword. Who knew dust could be so interesting?'

There was a frustrated hiss from Brolos Haran. 'He insists on speaking for us, and yet he never says what we wish him to say. Why we ever acquiesce is a mystery.'

'I have my own paths,' Ulag said easily, 'and I do not imagine the First Sword lacks patience.'

'Not patience,' snapped Brolos, 'but what about tolerance?'

'Bone bends before it breaks, Brolos Haran. Now, I would say more to the First Sword, before we all await the profundity of his words. May I?'

Brolos Haran half-turned to Ilm Absinos, one hand lifting in an odd gesture that baffled Onos T'oolan—for a moment—before he understood.

Helplessness.

'First Sword,' Ulag resumed, 'we do not reach to you in the manner of Tellann, because we make no claim upon you. We are summoned, yes, but it was—we have come to believe—not by your hand. You may refuse us. It is not in our hearts to force ourselves upon the will of another.'

Onos T'oolan said, 'Who are these strangers?'

'Profound indeed,' Ulag said. 'First Sword, they are T'lan Imass of a second Ritual. The descendants of those who sought to follow Kilava Onass when she rejected the first Ritual. It was their failure not to determine beforehand Kilava's attitude to being accompanied. But when there is but one hole in the ice, then all must use it to breathe.'

'My sister invited no one.'

'Alas. And so it comes to this. These three are bonecasters of the Brold T'lan Imass. Lid Ger, Lera Epar and Nom Kala. The Brold number two thousand seven hundred and twelve. The majority of these remain in the dust of our wake. Our own Orshayn number six hundred and twelve—you see them here. If you need us, we shall serve.'

Nom Kala studied the First Sword, this warrior she had once believed was nothing but an invention, a myth. Better, she concluded, had he remained so. His bones were latticed, as if he had been pounded into fragments—and some of those bones were not even his own.

The First Sword was not the giant of the legends. He did not wear a cloak of ice. Caribou antlers did not sprout from his head. He did not possess breath that gave the gift of fire. Nor did he seem the kind of warrior to recount his exploits for three days and four nights to belittle an overly proud hero. She began to suspect few of those ancient tales belonged to this figure at all. Dancing across the sea on the backs of whales? Crossing swords with demon walruses in their underwater towers? The secret seducer of wives left alone at night?

How many children among her clan, generation upon generation, bore some variation of the name Onos, to account for impossible pregnancies?

The sudden shocked gulp that erupted from her drew everyone's attention.

Brolos Haran had been speaking—about what Nom Kala had no idea—and he was not pleased with the interruption. 'Nom Kala, what is it about the Fall at the Red Spires that so amuses you?'

'Nothing,' she replied, 'unless it was meant to. I apologize, Brolos Haran. A stray thought. Well, a few stray thoughts.'

The others waited.

She elected to refrain from elaborating.

The wind moaned, whispered through remnants of fur.

Onos T'oolan spoke. 'Orshayn. Brold. I have forsworn the Jaghut Wars. I seek no battle. I do not invite you to join me, for what I seek is an accounting. Like you, I am summoned from the dust, and it is to dust that I wish to return. But first, I will find the one who has so punished me with resurrection. The bonecaster of the Logros T'lan Imass, Olar Ethil.'

Ulag said, 'Can you be certain it is her, First Sword?'

Onos T'oolan cocked his head. 'Ulag Togtil, after all this time, do you still hold to the virtue of certainty?'

'We fought no war against the Jaghut,' Nom Kala said.

The bonecasters of the Orshayn reacted with a chill wave of disapproval. She ignored it.

Onos T'oolan said, 'Ulag. I see the Orshayn Warleader standing with your kin. Why does Inistral Ovan not come forward?'

'He is shamed, First Sword. The losses at the Red Spire . . .'

'Nom Kala,' Onos then said, 'have you no ruler of the Brold Clan?'

'Only us,' she replied. 'Even the war we fought against the humans was not a war that demanded a warleader. It was clear that we could not defeat them on a field of battle. There were too many.'

'Then how did you fight?'

'By keeping alive our stories, our ways of living. And by hiding, for in hiding, we survived. We persisted. This is itself a victory.'

'And yet,' cut in Ilm Absinos, 'you failed in the end. Else you would not have attempted the Ritual of Tellann.'

'That is true,' she replied. 'We ran out of places to hide.'

Ulag spoke. 'First Sword, we would accompany you nonetheless. Like you, we wish to know the purpose of our return.'

'If you join my quest,' said Onos T'oolan, 'then you bow to Olar Ethil's desires.'

'That perception may lead to carelessness on her part,' Ulag replied.

Standing amidst the other T'lan Imass, Rystalle Ev watched, listened, and imagined a world taut with purpose. It had once been such a world, for her, for all of her kin. But that had vanished long ago. Perhaps the First Sword could bind them all to this quest of his. Perhaps answers could relieve the burden of despair. Reasons to stand, reasons to stand *against*.

But the dust beckoned with its promise of oblivion. The trail to the end of things had been hacked clear, pounded level. She yearned to walk it.

Beside her, Kalt Urmanal said, 'See the sword he carries. See how its tip pins the earth. This Onos T'oolan, he is not one for poses. He never was. I remember when I last saw him. He had defeated his challenger. He had shown such skill that ten thousand Imass stood silent with awe. Yet, he stood as one defeated.'

'Weary,' Rystalle murmured.

'Yes, but not from the fighting. He was weary, Rystalle Ev, of its necessity.'

She considered that, and then nodded.

Kalt then added, 'This warrior I will follow.'

'Yes.'

She sat on a pyramid of three stacked canvas bolts, huddled beneath her night-cloak. The shivering would not go away. She watched the glowing tip of her smoker dancing like a firefly close to her fingers. Atri-Ceda Aranict listened to the muted sounds of the Malazan encampment. Subdued, weary and shaken. She understood that well enough. Soldiers had fallen out from the column, staggering as if reeling from blows. Collapsing senseless, or falling to their knees spitting blood. Panic rippling through the ranks—was this an attack?

Not as such.

Those stricken soldiers had been, one and all, mages. And the enemy, blind and indifferent, had been *power*.

Her nausea was fading. Mind slowly awakening—wandering like a hungover reveller, desultorily sweeping aside the ashes—she thought back to her first meeting with High Mage Ben Adaephon Delat. She had been pathetic. It was bad enough fainting in a heap in front of Commander Brys Beddict; she had barely recovered from that before she was led into Quick Ben's presence.

And now, weeks later, only fragments of the conversation that followed remained with her. He had been a distracted man, but when he had seen the enlivened earth cupped in Aranict's hand, his dark eyes had sharpened, hardened as if transformed into onyx.

He had cursed, and she remembered that curse.

'Hood's frantic balls on the fire.'

She had since discovered that Hood was the god of death, and that if any god deserved its name being uttered in bitter curses, then he was the one. At the time, however, she had taken the High Mage's expostulation somewhat more literally.

Fire, she'd thought. Yes, fire in the earth, heat cupped in my hand.

Her eyes had widened on the High Mage, astonished at his instant percipience, convinced in that moment of his profound genius. She had no place in his company. Her mind moved in a slow crawl at the best of times, especially in the early morning before she'd drawn alive the coal of her first smoker. Quickness of thought (and there, she'd assumed, must be the reason for his name) was in itself a thing of magic, a subtle sorcery, which she could only view with superstitious awe.

Such lofty opinion could persist only in the realm of mystery, however, and mystery rarely survived familiarity. The High Mage had formally requested that she be temporarily attached to his cadre. Since then, she'd heard plenty of curses from Ben Adaephon Delat, and had come to conclude that his quickness was less sorcerous than quixotic.

Oh, he was indeed brilliant. He was also in the habit of muttering to himself in a host of entirely distinct voices, and playing with dolls and lengths of string. And as for the company he kept . . .

She pulled fiercely on her smoker, watching a figure approach—walking like a drunk, his ill-fitting, cheap clothing caked in dust. Bottle's strangely childlike face looked swollen, almost dissolute.

Here we go. Yet another incomprehensible conversation between them. And oh, he doesn't like me being there for it, either. That makes two of us.

'Is he breathing?' the Malazan soldier asked as he halted in front of the tent.

She glanced at the drawn flap to her left. 'He sent me out,' she said.

'He'll want to see me.'

'He wants to know how Fiddler fared.'

Bottle grimaced, looked away briefly, then back down to her, seeming to study her. 'You've got sensitivity, Atri-Ceda. A draught of rum will soothe your nerves.'

'I've already had one.'

He nodded, as if unsurprised. 'Fiddler's still losing what's left of his supper. He'll need a new tent.'

'But he's not even a mage.'

'No, he isn't.'

She fixed her eyes on him. 'Are all you Malazans this cagey?'

He smiled. 'And we're getting worse, Atri-Ceda.'

'Why is that?'

The smile dropped away, like it never really fitted in the first place. 'It's simple enough. The less we know, the less we say. Pretty soon, I expect, we'll be an army of mutes.'

I can't wait. Sighing, she flicked away the smoker, slowly rose.

The stars were returning to the sky in the northeast. At least that was something. *But someone's out there. Holding a weapon . . . gods, such a weapon!* 'Errant's bouncing eye,' she said, 'he's the High Mage. He can't hide for ever.'

Bottle's eyes were wide on her. 'Never heard that curse before,' he said.

'I just made it up.'

'Seems oddly irreverent coming from a Letherii. I'm slightly shocked, in fact.'

'It's all your bad habits, I suppose.' She stepped to the tent-flap and rapped the hide with her knuckles. 'We're coming in.'

'Fine!' came the snapped reply.

The cramped interior was steamy, as scented candles flickered from the floor in a circle surrounding a crosslegged Quick Ben. The High Mage dripped with sweat. 'Bastard's reaching out to me,' he said, voice grating. 'Do I want a conversation? No, I do not. What's to say? Anomander killed Hood, Dassem killed Anomander, Brood shattered Dragnipur, and now Draconus walks free. Burn trembles, the Gate of Starvald Demelain rages with fire, and cruel twisted warrens the like of which we've never before seen now lie in wait—when will they awaken? What will they deliver?

'And there's more. Do you realize that? There's more—stop staring, just listen. Who brokered the whole damned mess? Bottle?'

'Sorry, I was listening, not thinking. How should I know? No, wait—'

'Aye. Shadowthrone and Cotillion. Does the Adjunct really believe she chooses her own path? Our path? She's been driving us hard, ever since we landed—sure, it's all a matter of logistics. It's not like the Akryn traders are happily handing over everything they have, is it? It's not like things won't get worse the further east we march—the Wastelands are well named.'

'Quick Ben—'

'Of course I'm babbling! Listen! There are T'lan Imass out there!' His wild gaze fixed with sudden intensity on Aranict. 'The dust will dance! Who commands them? What do they want? Do you know what I want to do with that dirt? I want to throw it away. Who wants to know? Not me!'

'The T'lan Imass,' said Bottle, 'knelt to the Emperor. He took the First Throne and never relinquished it.'

'Exactly!'

'We're being set up. We need to speak with Tavore. Now.'

But the High Mage was shaking his head. 'It's no use. She's made up her mind.'

'About what?' Bottle demanded, his voice rising.

'She thinks she can cheat them. Did you know she was the pre-eminent scholar of the lives of Kellanved, Dancer and Dassem? You didn't, did you? Before she was made Adjunct. Even before she inherited command of House Paran. A student of war—imperial war. The Conquests—not just tactics on the field, but the motivations of the Emperor and his mad cohorts. The lives of them all. Crust, Toc the Elder, Urko, Ameron, Admiral Nok, Surly, even Tayschrenn—why do you think she keeps Banaschar around? That drunk fool is her potential emissary should Tayschrenn finally decide to do something.'

But Bottle was clearly stuck at Quick Ben's first revelation. 'Cheat them? Cheat the Lords of Shadow? Cheat them of what?'

Quick Ben's bared teeth glimmered like gold in the flickering candlelight. 'I dare not say.'

'You don't trust us to keep our mouths shut?'

'No. Why would I?' He pointed a long finger at Bottle. 'You'd be the first one running for the hills.'

'If it's that bad, why are you still here?'

'Because Draconus changes everything, and I'm the only one who can stand against him.'

Bottle gaped, and then a thin word creaked out: '*You?*'

'But don't think for a moment that I'm doing it for Shadowthrone and Cotillion. And don't think I'm even doing this for the Adjunct. All that time inside Dragnipur—it's changed him. He was never so subtle before—imagine, a gentle invitation to converse—does he think we're idiots? But wait'—and he waved his hands—'it'd only be subtle if it wasn't so obvious! Why didn't we think of that?'

'Because it makes no sense, you damned fool!'

But the High Mage did not react to Bottle's outburst. 'No, he *really* wants to talk! Now that's subtle for you! Well, we can match that, can't we? Talk? Not a chance! No, and let's see what he makes of it, let's just see!'

Aranict ran both hands through the thick hair on her scalp, and then rummaged in her belt-bag for a smoker. She crouched and snatched up one of Quick Ben's candles. As she was lighting up she happened to glance across at the High Mage and saw him staring, his expression frozen.

Bottle grunted a laugh. 'She ain't so shy any more, is she? Good. Now we'll find out the real Atri-Ceda. Just like Brys wanted.'

Behind a veil of swirling smoke, Aranict's gaze narrowed on Quick Ben. She slowly returned the candle to its pool of melted wax on the hide floor. *Brys? Is that what all this is about?*

The High Mage shot Bottle a disdainful look. 'It's ignorance, not bravado.'

'Bravado usually *is* ignorance,' Bottle snapped back.

'I'll grant you that,' Quick Ben conceded. 'And you're right,' he added, sighing, 'we could do with a little more of the unflappable around here.'

Aranict snorted. 'Unflappable? You're not describing me.'

'Maybe not,' the High Mage replied, 'but you manage a convincing pose. That candle you took from the circle of protection—you opened a pathway to Draconus. He sensed it immediately. And yet—'

'He didn't use it,' Bottle said.

'He didn't use it.'

'Subtle.'

'Ha ha, Bottle, but you're more right than you know. The point is, she made us address that so fiercely burning question, didn't she?'

'Unknowingly.'

Quick Ben glanced up at her, curious, thoughtful.

Aranict shrugged. 'I needed the flame.'

The reply seemed to please them both, in rather different ways. She decided to leave it at that. What point was there in explaining that she'd no idea what they'd been talking about. All those names Quick Ben mentioned—even Draconus— they meant nothing to her. Well, almost nothing. *Draconus. He is the one who arrived in darkness, who made a gate that stole half the sky, who holds in his hand a weapon of darkness and cold, of blackest ice.*

And Quick Ben means to stand in his path.

Errant's mangled nuts, I only joined because I'm lusting after Brys Beddict. Me and a thousand other women.

Quick Ben said, 'Atri-Ceda, your commander, Brys—'

She started guiltily. Had he read her thoughts?

'He died once, didn't he?'

'What? Yes, so it is said. I mean, yes, he did.'

The High Mage nodded. 'Best go see him, then—he may have need of you right now.'

'Me? Why?'

'Because Hood is gone,' said Bottle.

'What does that mean to Commander Beddict?' she asked.

She saw Bottle meet Quick Ben's eyes, and then the soldier nodded and said, 'The dead never quite come back all the way, Aranict. Not while there was a god of death. It may be that Brys is now . . . awakened. To everything he once was. He will have things to say to his Atri-Ceda.'

'We'll see you again,' Quick Ben added. 'Or not.'

They dismiss me. Oh well. She turned and exited the tent. Paused in the sultry darkness of the camp. Drew deep on her smoker, and then set out for the distant Letherii encampment.

Brys wants me. What a lovely thought.

Smiles threw herself down by the fire. 'Stupid patrols,' she said. 'There's no one out there. Those Akryn traders—all creaking old or snot-nosed runts.' She glanced at the others sitting round the hearth. 'See that village we passed yesterday? Looked half empty.'

'No warriors,' said Cuttle. 'All off fighting the White Faces. The Akryn can't maintain control of this Kryn Free Trade right now, which also explains all those D'ras traders coming up from the south.'

Tarr grunted. 'Heard from some outriders about a Barghast camp they came on—site of a big battle, and looks like the White Faces got bloodied. Might be they're on the run just like the Akryn are saying.'

'Hard to believe that,' Cuttle countered. 'I've fought Barghast and it's no fun at all, and the White Faces are said to be the toughest of the lot.'

Smiles unstrapped her helm and pulled it off. 'Where's Koryk then?' she asked.

'Wandered off,' Tarr answered, tossing another dung chip on to the fire. 'Again,' he added.

Smiles hissed. 'That fever, it marked him. In the head.'

'Just needs a good scrap,' Cuttle ventured. 'That'll settle him right enough.'

'Could be a long wait,' Tarr said. 'We've got weeks and weeks of travel ahead of us, through mostly empty territory. Aye, we're covering ground awfully fast, but once we're done with the territories of these plains tribes, it'll be the Wastelands. No one can even agree how far across it is, or what's on the other end.' He shrugged. 'An army's deadliest enemy is boredom, and we're under siege these days.'

'Corabb not back yet?' Smiles shook her head. 'He had two heavies with him on the round. They might've got lost.'

'Someone will find 'em,' Cuttle said, climbing to his feet. 'I'll check in on the sergeant again.'

Smiles watched him step out of the firelight. She sighed. 'Ain't had me a knife fight in months. That stay in Letheras made us soft, and them barges was even worse.' She stretched her boots closer to the fire. 'I don't mind the marching, now the blisters are gone. At least we're squads again.'

'We need us a new scam,' Tarr said. 'You see any scorpions?'

'Sure, plenty,' Smile replied, 'but only two kinds. The little nasty ones and the big black ones. Besides, we try that again and people will get suspicious—even if we could find a good cheat.' She mulled on the notion for a time, and then shook her head. 'It's no good, Tarr. The mood's all wrong.'

He squinted across at her. 'Sharp. You're right. It's like we're past all that, and it'll never come again. Amazing, that I should feel nostalgic about Seven Cities and that miserable, useless march. We were raw, aye, but what we were trying to do, it made sense. That's the difference. It made sense.'

Smiles snorted. 'Hood's breath, Tarr.'

'What?'

'Cuttle's right. None of it made sense. Never did, never will. Look at us. We march around and cut up other people, and they do the same to us—if they can. Look at Lether—aye, it's now got a decent King and people can breathe easy and go about their lives—but what's in those lives? Scraping for the next bag of coins, the next meal. Scrubbing bowls, praying to the damned gods for the next catch and calm seas. It ain't for nothing, Tarr, and that's the truth. It ain't for nothing.'

'That fishing village you come from was a real hole, wasn't it?'

'Leave it.'

'I didn't bring it up, soldier. You did.'

'It was no different from anywhere else, that's my point. I bet you wasn't sorry to get out from wherever you come from, either. If it was all you wanted, you wouldn't be here, would you?'

'Some people don't go through their lives searching, Smiles. I'm not looking, because I'm not expecting to find anything. You want meaning? Make it up. You want truth? Invent it. Makes no difference, to anything. Sun comes up, sun goes down. We see one, maybe we don't see the other, but the sun doesn't care, does it?'

'Right,' she said, 'so we're in agreement.'

'Not quite. I'm not saying it's not worth it. I'm saying the opposite. You make worlds, worlds inside your head and worlds outside, but only the one inside counts for anything. It's where you find peace, acceptance. Worth. You, you're just talking about everything being useless. Starting with yourself. That's a bad attitude, Smiles. Worse than Cuttle's.'

'Where are we marching to, then?'

'Fate's got a face, and we're going to meet it eye to eye. The rest I don't care about.'

'So you'll follow the Adjunct. Anywhere. Like a dog on a master's heel.'

'Why not? It's all the same to me.'

'I don't get you.'

'There's nothing to get. I'm a soldier and so are you. What more do you want?'

'I want a damned war!'

'It's coming.'

'What makes you so sure of that?'

'Because we're an army on the march. If the Adjunct didn't need an army, she'd have dissolved the whole thing in Lether.'

'Maybe, maybe not.'

'What do you mean?' he asked.

'I mean, maybe she's just selfish.'

The dung burned down to layered glowing chips. Moths spun round the licking flames. Silence descended on the two soldiers, who had nothing more to say to each other. At least for this night.

Cuttle found his sergeant lying on the floor. A jug of rum lay on its side close by. The confined space reeked of puke with the rum's heady layer settling on it like sweet sap.

'Dammit, Fid, that won't help your gut.'

'I ain't got a gut no more,' Fiddler replied in a slur. 'I tossed it up a bell ago.'

'Come the morning, your skull's gonna crack open.'

'Too late. Go 'way, Cu'll.'

The sapper drew one edge of the cot closer and settled down. 'Who was it, then?'

'Iz all changed, Cu'll. Iz all goin' bad.'

'That's news to me? Listen, this fast march—I've already worn out one pair of boots—but it's got to tell you something. The Adjunct, she's got a nose—she can sniff things out better than you, I think. Ever since the barges, we've been damned near on the run. And even before what happened tonight, you've been a haunted man.' He rubbed at the bristle on his cheeks. 'I'll follow you, Fid, you know that. I've got your back, always.'

'Don' mind me, Cu'll. It's the young ones, y'got to guard their backs, not mine.'

'You're seeing a lot of dead faces, aren't you?'

'I ain't no seer.'

Cuttle grunted. 'It's a precious day, you ain't talking it up. Squad's the thing, you keep tellin' 'em. The soldier at your side, the one whose sweat stink you smell every damned day. We're family, you say. Sergeant, you're making us nervous.'

Fiddler slowly sat up, clutched at his head. 'Fishing,' he said.

'What?'

'There's a demon in the deep. Sly eyes . . . watchin' the bait, y'see? Jus' watchin. Quick Ben, he's got to show himself. Finally. We need 'em, we need 'em all.'

'Fid, you're drunk.'

'Darkness' got an edge. Sharp, the blackest ice—cold like you never imagined. You don't get it. Here we was, all yippin' and dancin', but now the biggest wolf of all has returned. Games are over, Cuttle.'

'What about the Adjunct? Fiddler?'

He looked up with red, bleary eyes. 'She don't stand a chance. Gods below, not a chance.'

'Is that the camp? It's got to be.' Corabb looked at his companions. Three blank faces stared back at him. 'It's all lit up, too big for a caravanserai. Let's go.'

He led the way down the grassy slope, waving as a cloud of midges rose to engulf them. 'We should never have followed that rabbit—this is no place to get lost in, didn't I say that? The land rolls too much. You could hide whole armies in these valleys.'

'Maybe that's what they did,' Saltlick said. 'Hey, Corabb, did you think of that? They's playing a trick on us.'

'The whole Bonehunter army? That's stupid.'

'It was a big rabbit,' said Drawfirst.

'It wasn't a rabbit at all,' Saltlick insisted. 'It was a wolf. Rabbits ain't got glowing eyes and a bloody muzzle and they don't snarl neither.'

'It got a bloody muzzle biting you,' Drawfirst pointed out.

'Passed right by me—who wouldn't jump on it being so close? It's dark out here, you know. But I jumped on rabbits before, and that was no rabbit.'

'Beasts are different here,' Drawfirst said. 'We keep hearing howling, but that could be rabbits, how do we know? Did you see those lizard hides them D'ras was selling? Those lizards was even bigger than the ones we saw from the barge. Those lizards could eat a horse.'

'That's how they catch 'em down south, that's what the trader said. They stick a big hook through a horse and throw it in the river—'

'That won't work unless you tie a rope to the hook.'

'He didn't mention that, but it makes sense.'

They were drawing closer to the sea of campfires—well, Corabb amended, maybe not a sea. More like a big lake. But an awfully big lake. He glanced over at Flashwit, who wasn't saying much, but then she rarely did. All she did was smile and wasn't it a lovely smile? It was.

'If we hooked a rabbit,' said Saltlick, 'we could catch wolves.'

'Hook a horse and we'd get an even bigger wolf, I bet.'

'We got horses, too. That's an idea, Drawfirst, it surely is. Hey, Corabb, we're gonna jump the next big lizard we see. For its skin. You want in?'

'No.'

A distant howl sounded, drifting mournfully through the night.

'Hear that?' Saltlick asked. 'More rabbits—keep an eye out, Drawfirst. You too, Flashwit.'

'That sounded more like a hooked horse,' Drawfirst muttered.

Corabb halted. 'Cut it out, all of you. I'm Fid's heavy, right? I stand just like you do.' He pointed at Flashwit. 'Don't even think of winking. I spent half my life making mistakes about people, and I vowed I'd never do that again. So I keep my peace, but I pay attention, right? I'm a heavy, too. So stop it.'

'We was jus' havin' fun, Corabb,' Saltlick said. 'You could always join in.'

'I don't believe in funny things. Now, come on, we done enough walking.'

They walked a further twenty paces before a sentry in the gloom ahead barked something—in Letherii. 'Hood's breath,' hissed Corabb. 'We done found the other army.'

'Nobody can hide from the Bonehunters,' intoned Drawfirst.

Koryk stood in darkness, a hundred paces out from the nearest picket. He had a memory that might be real or invented—he could not be certain. A dozen youths commandeered to dig a latrine trench for some garrison troop out on manoeuvres. Seti and Seti half-bloods, back when they were young enough to see no difference between the two, no reason yet for contempt, envy and all the rest.

He'd been one of the runts, and so his friends set him against a boulder at the far end of the pit, where he could strain and sweat and fail. Blistered hands struggling with the oversized pick, he had worked the whole morning trying to dislodge that damned boulder—with the others looking over every now and then with jeers and laughter.

Failure wasn't a pleasant notion. It stung. It burned like acid. On that day, he now believed, young Koryk had decided he would never again accept failure. He'd dislodged that boulder in the end, with dusk fast coming on, the other boys long gone and that troop of riders—their little exercise in independence done—riding off in a cloud that hung like a god's mocking breath of gold dust.

That rock had been firmly lodged in place. It had hidden a cache of coins. As twilight crept in, he found himself on his knees at one end of the trench, with a vast treasure cupped in his hands. Mostly silver, a few tiny gold clips, not one recognizable to Koryk's pathetically limited experience—this was a spirit hoard, straight out from Seti legends. 'Under any stone, lad . . . ' Yes, the whores who'd raised him had plenty of tales. Could be the whole memory was just one of those tales. A pathetic story, but . . .

He'd found a treasure, that was the meaning of it. Something precious, wonderful, rare.

And what did he do with his spirit hoard?

Squandered it. Every last fucking coin. Gone, and what was left to show for it?

Whores are warm to the touch, but they hide their souls inside a cold keep. It's when you surrender to that world that you know you are truly lost, you are finally . . . alone.

It's all cold to the touch these days. Everything. And now I spend the rest of my years blaming every damned coin.

But nobody's fooled. Except me. Always me. Forever me.

He longed to draw his sword, to vanish into the mad mayhem of battle. He could then cut in two every face on every coin, howling that it made a difference, that a life wasn't empty if it was filled with detritus. He could scream and curse and see not a single friend—only enemies. Justifying every slice, every lash of blood. At the very least, he vowed, he'd be the last one standing.

Smiles said the fever had scarred him. Perhaps it had. Perhaps it would from now on. It had done one thing for certain: it had shown him the truth of solitude. And that truth was seared into his soul. He listened to Fiddler going on and on about this so-called family of companions, and he believed none of it. Betrayals stalked the future—he felt it in his bones. There was coming a time when everything would cut clear, and he could stand before them all and speak aloud the fullest measure of his distrust. *We are each of us alone. We always were. I am done with all your lies. Now, save yourselves. As I intend to do for myself.*

He wasn't interested in any last stands. The Adjunct asked for faith, loyalty. She asked for honesty, no matter how brutal, how incriminating. She asked for too much. Besides, she gave them nothing in return, did she?

Koryk stood, facing the empty land in the empty night, and contemplated deserting.

Everything they gave me was a lie, a betrayal. It was the spirit hoard, you see. Those coins. Someone put them there to lure me in, to trap me. They poisoned me—not my fault, how could it be?

'Look at him under that boulder! Careful, Koryk, playing under there will get you crushed!'

Too late. *It was all those fucking coins that did me in. You can't fill a boy's hands like that. You just can't.*

It was a memory. Maybe real, maybe not.

The whores, they just wink.

Skanarow's lithe form rippled with shadows as someone outside the tent walked past bearing a lantern. The light coming through the canvas was cool, giving her sleeping form a deathly hue. Chilled by the vision, Ruthan Gudd looked away. He sat up, moving slowly to keep her from waking.

The sweat that had sheathed him earlier was drying on his skin.

He had no interest in revisiting the cause of his extremity—it wasn't the love-making, Hood knew. As pleasing as she was—with that sudden smile of hers that could melt mountains of ice—Skanarow didn't have it in her to send his heart thundering the way it had not long ago. She could delight, she could steal him away from his thoughts, his memories of a grim and eventful life; she could, in bright, stunning flashes, give him back his life.

But this night darkness had opened its flower, with a scent that could freeze a god's soul. *Still alive, Greymane? Did you feel it? I think, your bones could be rotting in the ground right now, old friend, and still you'd have felt it.*

Draconus.

Fuck.

He combed through the damp snarl of his beard.

The world shook. Balls of fire descending, the terrible light filling the sky. Fists hammering the world.

Wish I'd seen it.

But he remembered the Azath's deathcry. He remembered the gnarled trees engulfed in pillars of flames, the bitter heat of the soil he'd clawed through. He remembered staggering free beneath a crazed sky of lurid smoke, lightning and a deluge of ashes. He remembered his first thought, riding that breath of impossible freedom.

Jacuruku, you've changed.

One found loyalty under the strangest circumstances. Penitence and gratitude, arms entwined, a moment's lustful exultation mistaken for worship. His gaze flicked back to Skanarow. The shadows and ill hue were gone. She slept, beauty in repose. Innocence was so precious. *But do not think of me with love, woman. Do not force upon me a moment of confession, the truth of foolish vows uttered a lifetime ago.*

Let us play this game of blissful oblivion a little while longer.

'It's better this way, Draconus.'

'This is Kallor's empire, friend. Will you not reconsider?'

Reconsider. Yes, there is that. 'The shore seems welcoming enough. If I mind my own business . . .'

He'd smiled at that.

And I smiled back.

Draconus returned to that continent—I felt his footfalls, there inside my seemingly eternal prison. He returned to see for himself the madness of Kallor.

You were right, Draconus. I should have minded my own business. For once.

Can you hear me now? Draconus? Are you listening?

I have reconsidered. At long last. And so I give you this. Find me, and one of us will die.

'It's the swirl in the dog's fur.'

Balm stared. 'What?'

Widdershins scowled. 'You want this divination or not?'

'I ain't so sure no more.'

The mage stared down at the mangy creature he held by the scruff of the neck, and then snarled and sent it winging through the air.

Deadsmell and Balm and Throatslitter watched the thing twist smartly in the air and manage in the last possible instant to land splayed out wide on its four paws, whereupon with a flick of its bushy tail it bolted, vanishing into the night.

'Just like a damned cat,' Throatslitter said.

'Wasn't even a dog,' Deadsmell said.

Widdershins threw up a hand in dismissal. 'Dog, fox, what's the difference? Now I'll need to find something else.'

'How about a sheepskin?' Balm asked.

'Is a sheepskin alive? No. Won't work. Needs to be breathing.'

'Because breathing fluffs the swirls,' Balm said, nodding. 'I get it.'

Widdershins cast a helpless look upon Deadsmell, who shrugged and then said, 'This whole thing's a waste of time anyway. Every seer and diviner in the whole damned world's got scrambled brains right now.' He gingerly touched his own neck. 'I swear I felt that sword's bite. What was Hood thinking? It's insane. The whole thing—'

'Never mind Hood,' snapped Widdershins. 'Wasn't him made me wet my trousers.'

Balm stared with huge eyes. 'Did you really? Gods below.'

Throatslitter burst out a sudden, piping laugh. Then ducked. 'Sorry. Just . . . well, never mind.'

Widdershins spat on the ground. 'None of this is funny, Throatslitter. You don't get it. That . . . that *thing*. It didn't show up on the other side of the world. It showed up *here*.'

Balm started, looked round. 'Where? Get me my armour—who—what—'

'Relax, Sergeant,' Deadsmell said. 'He didn't mean "here" as in right here. He meant it as . . . Wid, what did you mean, exactly?'

'What's with the jokes? You're as bad as Throatslitter. I don't know why I'm talking to any of you.'

'We wanted a divination,' said Throatslitter.

'I'm changing my mind. It was a stupid idea. You think Fid's playing with the Deck right now? Not a chance. Forget it, I'm going to bed. Not that I'll get any sleep. In fact—'

Balm stepped up and punched Widdershins. The man fell in a heap.

Throatslitter yelped again. 'Sergeant! What did you do that for?'

Frowning, Balm rubbed at his knuckles. 'He said he wasn't gonna get any sleep. He's asleep now. You two, drag him to his tent. It's time to take charge of things and that's what I'm doing. Once you get him tucked in, why, we can go find Ebron. We'll get a divination tonight if it kills us.'

'I need more corporals,' Hellian announced to the night sky. She'd been sitting by the hearth, staring into the flames. But now she was on her back, beneath spinning stars. The world could change in an instant. Who decided things like that? 'One ain't enough. Ballsgird, you're now a corporal. You too, Probbly.'

'It's Maybe.'

'No, I made up my mind.'

'And Balgrid.'

'Tha's what I said. As soon as the earthquake's over, we'll get right on it. Who am I missing? How many in my squad? Four of ya, right? That last one, he's a corporal now, too. I want four corporals, t'take my orders.'

'What orders?'

'The ones I come up with. Firs' off, you're all my bodyguards—I'm done with Skulldumb—keep him away from me.'

'He's convinced you're royalty, Sergeant.'

'An' I am, Iffy, so you got to do what I say. Where my 'riginal corporal? Touchy Breath? You here?'

'Aye, Sergeant.'

'Yes, Sergeant.'

'I can't be looking at this mess any longer. Take me to my tent—no, quit that, don't help me up, you idiots. Take my feet. Nice an' slow now—ow, who put rocks under me? Corperl Marble, clear them rocks, will ya? Gods, where's my tent? Letheras?'

'We're looking, Sergeant—didn't you put it up?'

'Me? You're my corperl, that was your job.'

'Hold on, Sergeant. Just rest here—we're on it.'

'So I should think. Derliction of duty. Gi'me a wax and a stick, someone, got to write you up. I'm bustin' you down, to . . . to, uh, undercorperl. What's that pounding?'

'Putting the stakes down, Sergeant. Not long now.'

'Hey! Look at those green things! In the sky! Who put those there—get rid of 'em!'

'Wish I could, Sergeant.'

'You're now an unnerunnercorperl—for disobeying unners. Orners. Oars. Udders. Hold on.' She rolled on to her side and was sick, but in a lazy way. 'Orders. Hah. Hey, where you dragging me to? I wasn't done there. Something's in the sky—I saw it—cut right across those greens. Saw it, corperls, you lissinin'? Big wings—I saw . . . oh, whatever. Someone's in turble, but it ain't me. Check that tent now—no spiders allowed—stupid stars, how'd they get in here?'

Gesler brought the lantern close. 'Look at that, will you? One of Bottle's rats did that, I bet. Chewed right through the Hood-damned strap. If I catch 'im, I'm going to twist his tiny head right off.'

'The rat or Bottle?' Stormy asked.

'Either. Both. I knew it was hanging funny, down on one shoulder—'

'Aye,' Stormy said, 'you looked ridiculous. Lopsided. Like some green recruit ain't figured out how to wear the slingwork.'

Gesler glared across at his corporal. 'And you didn't say nothing all day—some friend you are. What if I got snot smeared across half my face—you just going to stand there?'

'Count on it,' Stormy said, 'assuming I can keep a straight face.'

'Next time I see you with bark-hair hanging from your back end, I ain't saying a thing.'

'Pays to check twice—I learned that much. Think we should go find Flashwit? She's way overdue.'

'Send Mayfly and Shortnose.'

'You can't be serious.'

Gesler paused in his tugging loose the chewed-through strap. 'Huh. Right. Off you go, then.'

'Sure you don't need any help there?'

'Naw, you done too much already.'

'That's just it—I'm all wore out, Ges. I'm too old to march the way we're marching right now. I'll be walking on stumpy knees if this goes on much longer.'

'Thus matching your intellectual height. Know what your problem is, Stormy? You've gone all edgy.'

The huge Falari snorted. 'Ges, we just saw a hundred or so squad mages fall out of line, leaking every which way, eyes rolling up inside their skulls, kicking and gagging. And our scary High Mage reeled like a damned drunk and nearly brained himself on a wagon's edge. Fid lost his last five meals.'

'None of that's got anything to do with you going round saying someone's spyin' on us, Stormy.'

'I'm just telling you what I'm feeling, that's all. Like an itch between my shoulder-blades, you know the kind. And it's only got worse since whatever happened . . . happened.'

'Fid said you're just imagining things—'

'No he didn't. He didn't say anything—he wouldn't even meet my eyes—you were there, you saw.'

'Well, maybe he didn't say anything, but then, he didn't have to.'

'I been having strange dreams, Ges.'

'So?'

'Stuff falling out of the sky. I look up and I'm right under it and there's no way to escape. Can't run far enough or fast enough, can't do anything, except watch it come down on me.' He leaned forward and slapped his hand on the ground, making Gesler jump. 'Like that. You'd think I'd wake up then. But I don't. I just lie there, crushed, feeling all that weight. Can't move a muscle, can't even breathe.'

Gesler tossed down his hauberk and harness. 'Stand up, Stormy, you're coming with me.'

'Where?'

'Walk, Corporal, it's an order.'

Gesler led Stormy through the camp, passing cookfires with their huddled, muttering circles of soldiers. They threaded through the cutters' station, where weary healers worked on soldiers suffering blistered feet, ankle sprains and what-not, and then out past the first of the horse corrals. Ahead was a trio of laden wagons, an oversized carriage, and fifteen or so tents.

Gesler called out as they approached. 'Hedge?'

A figure came round one end of the carriage and walked over. 'Gesler? You deserting the Bonehunters? Come to join the Bridgeburners? Smart lads—the legend's right here and nowhere else. I got these soldiers stepping smart, but they could do with your learnin' and that's a fact.'

'Enough of the rubbish,' Gesler said. 'Where's your two beauties?'

'Aw, Gesler, they're beat, honest—'

'Wake 'em up, both of them. Stormy here's got a need.'

'You got a need, you mean—'

'No, both of them for him. By the time I come to collect my corporal, I want this man's rope so stretched it's tangled round his ankles. I want to see bludgeoned bliss in his tiny blue eyes and curly black hairs in his beard. Tell the lovelies I'll pay triple the going rate.'

'Fine, only you got to consider what I said. About deserting, I mean.'

'Capital offence, Hedge.'

'Unofficial transfer, then.'

'Keneb would never allow it.'

'Fine, then just march with my squads for a week or so, alongside like, right? Give 'em advice and stuff—'

'Advice?' Gesler snorted. 'Like what? "Don't die, soldiers." "First hint of trouble, strap on and belt up." "Your weapon's the thing strapped to your web." How's that?'

'That's perfect!'

'Hedge, what in Hood's name are you doing here?'

The sapper glanced round, and then grasped Stormy by an arm. 'See those tents, those big ones there? Go on, Corporal, tell the lasses it's a special order.'

Stormy scowled across at Gesler, who scowled back.

'I never rolled with real fat women before—'

'Nothing like it,' Hedge said. 'Get one under ya and one over ya and it's all pillows. Go on, Stormy, me and Ges got to talk.'

'Pillows, huh?'

'Aye. Nice warm pillows. Step smartly now, Corporal. There you go.'

As the Falari trundled off, Hedge looked round suspiciously once more, and then gestured for Gesler to follow.

'Bottle's using bats,' Hedge muttered as they walked away from the firelight. 'Almost skewered one of his rats, y'see, so now he's gone more cagey.'

'What're you up to that's got him so curious, Hedge?'

'Nothing. Honest.'

'Gods below, you're a bad liar.'

'Just comes from being a legend, Ges, all that fawning and spying. Y'get used to it, so the precautions, they come natural now. All right, this will do.'

They had walked a dozen or so paces past the ornate carriage, out beyond the faint glows from the fires, and then Hedge had led him into a circle of low stones which Gesler assumed was an old tipi ring. They now stood within it.

'Bottle could use anything out here, Hedge—'

'No he can't. I got my company mage to seal this circle. We do this every night, for our staff meetings.'

'Your what?'

'Me, my sergeants, corporals and Bavedict. Daily reports, right? To stay on top of things.'

'What things?'

'Things. Now, listen, you heard anything yet about what happened earlier?'

Gesler shrugged. 'Some. There was a gate and someone came through it. Someone stinking with power.'

Hedge was nodding and then he changed it to shaking his head. 'That's nothing— so some nasty's shown up—that means he's here, in the real world. Anyone here in the real world can die from a damned rotten tooth, or a knife, or whatever. I ain't shaking in my boots, and if I have to, I'll kiss a quarrel's point and whisper the fool's name. A bolt in the eye can fuck up even a god's day. No, what really matters is what happened *before* he showed up.'

'Go on.'

'It's Hood.'

'What about him? Oh, right, you and he are best friends these days—or bitter enemies—how does he take you coming back, anyway?'

'Probably not well, but it don't matter any more. I won.'

'You won what?'

'I won! The Harrower's gone and gotten killed! The God of Death is dead! Head chopped right off! A carcass but no grin, a bouncer down the hill, a roll and wobble and blink, a mouth mover, a hat stand—'

'Hold on, Hedge! What—who—but that doesn't make sense! How—'

'I don't know and I don't care! Details? Squat and shit on 'em! Hood's dead! Gone!'

'But then, who's taking the Throne?'

'Nobody and everybody!'

Gesler's right hand twitched. Gods, how he wanted to punch this grinning fool! But that nose had seen a few dozen breaks already—he doubted Hedge would even notice. 'What,' he said carefully, 'do you mean, Hedge?'

'I mean, there's a whole crew of 'em. Holding the gate. Nothing's shaken out yet. It's all hazy. But one thing I can tell you—and you can ask Fid if you want— he won't say any different unless he lies to you. One thing, Ges. I can *feel* them. I can feel *him*.'

Gesler stared at the man's glittering eyes. 'Who?'

'The Fallen Bridgeburners, Ges. And aye, Whiskeyjack. It's him—I'd know that sour look anywhere, no matter how dark it is around him. He's astride a horse. He's in the Gate, Gesler.'

'Wait. *That's* who stepped through?'

'Naw, never mind that one. That one ain't got a thought that ain't ten thousand years outa touch. Different gate, anyway. I'm talking about Whiskeyjack. Go and die, Ges, and who'd you rather meet at the Gate? Hood or Whiskeyjack?'

'So why ain't you cut your own throat, if you're so excited about it all?'

Hedge frowned. 'No reason t'get all edgy. I was a sapper, remember. Sappers understand the importance of patience.'

Gesler choked back a laugh. From the tents someone squealed. He couldn't tell who.

'Laugh all you want. You'll be thankful enough when it's your head rolling up to that gate.'

'I thought you hated worshipping anyone, Hedge.'

'This is different.'

'If you say so. Now, anything else you wanted to tell me about?'

'Nothing you'd care about either way. You can hand over the coins now, though. Triple the going rate, right? Dig it out, Ges, it's getting late.'

Commander Brys threw on his cloak and fastened the breast clasp. 'I walk through camp before settling in, Atri-Ceda. Join me, if you please.'

'Honoured, my Prince.'

He stepped out of the command tent and she followed. They set out for the nearest row of legionaries' tents. 'That title just won't sit comfortably, Atri-Ceda,' he said after a moment. ' "Commander" or "sir" will do. In fact, when it's just the two of us, "Brys" '.

She wondered if he caught her faint gasp, or noted the momentary wobble in her knees as she moved up alongside him.

'Assuming,' he continued, 'you will permit me to call you Aranict.'

'Of course, sir.' She hesitated, could feel him waiting, and then said, 'Brys.' A wave of lightheadedness followed, as if she'd quaffed a tumbler of brandy. Her mind spun wildly for a moment and she drew a deep breath to calm herself.

This was ridiculous. Embarrassing. Infuriating. She itched to light a smoker, but that would likely breach protocol.

'At ease, Aranict.'

'Sir?'

'Relax. Please—you're starting to make me jumpy. I don't bite.'

Try the right nipple. Oh gods, shut up, woman. 'Sorry.'

'I was hoping your stay with the Malazan High Mage might have calmed you some.'

'Oh, it has, sir. I mean, I'm better.'

'No more fainting?'

'No. Well, almost once.'

'What happened?'

'At day's end, I made the mistake of being in his tent when he pulled off his boots.'

'Ah.' And then he shot her a startled look, his face lighting in a sudden smile. 'Remind me to send you out before I do the same.'

'Oh, sir, I'm sure you don't—uh, that is, it's not the same—'

But he was laughing. She saw soldiers round campfires turn, looking over at the two of them. She saw a few mutter jests and there were grins and nods. Her face burned hot as coals.

'Aranict, I assure you, after a day's fast march as we've been experiencing since the landing, my socks could stun a horse. None of us are any different in such matters.'

'Because you choose to march alongside your soldiers, Brys. When you could ride or even sit in one of the grand carriages, and no one would think ill of you—'

'You would be wrong in that, Aranict. Oh, they might not seem any different, outwardly, saluting as smartly as ever and all the rest. Certain to follow every or-der I give, yes. But somewhere deep inside every one of them, there's a stone of loyalty—when it comes to most of those giving them orders, that stone stays smooth and nothing sticks, it all washes off. And so it would be with me as well, were I to take any other path than the one they happen to be on. But, you see, there may come a time when I must demand of my soldiers something . . . impossible. If the stone was still smooth—if it did not have my name carved deep into it—I could lose them.'

'Sir, they would never mutiny—'

'Not as such. But in asking for the impossible, I would intend that they succeed in achieving it. The impossible is not the same as sending them to their deaths. That I would never do. But if I am to ask more of them than any commander has even the right to ask of his or her soldiers, then I must be with them, and be seen to be with them.

'Tonight,' he continued, 'you must become my Atri-Ceda again for a time, and I your commander. When we speak with our soldiers. When we ask them how they fared on this day. When we endeavour to answer their questions and concerns, as best we can.' He paused, his steps slowing. They were in a gap of relative darkness between two cookfires. 'Especially on this night,' he said, his tone low. 'They are shaken—word's come of the affliction striking the Malazan mages.'

'Yes, Commander. I understand. In fact, High Mage Delat wondered, er, rather, he asked me. About you. Said that you may seem . . . different now . . . sir.'

'And what will you tell him, when next you two meet?'

'I—I am not sure, sir. I think so. Maybe . . .'

'He is a clever man,' Brys said. 'This evening, Aranict, I felt as if . . . well, as if I had awakened, stepped out from a dark, cold place. A place I'd thought was the real world, the honest world—the coldness, I'd thought, was simply what I had never before noticed—before my death and resurrection, I mean. But I understand, now, that the cold and darkness were within me, death's own touch upon my soul.'

She stared at him, adoring, eyes bright. 'And it is gone now, sir?'

His returning smile was all the answer she needed.

'Now, Atri-Ceda, let us speak with our soldiers.'

'Carving the stone, sir.'

'Just that.'

No need to worry about mine. I am yours. That stone, it's all melted, reshaped—Errant save me, it's got your face now. Oh, and about that biting—

As they stepped into the firelight, Brys chanced to glance across at his Atri-Ceda, and what he saw in her expression—quickly veiled but not quickly enough—almost took his breath away.

Lascivious hunger, a half-smile upon her lips, a fancy snared in the reflecting flames in her eyes. For an instant, he was at a loss for words, and could only smile his greeting as the soldiers turned and voiced their heartfelt welcome.

Aranict. I truly was half-dead inside, to have so thoroughly missed what is now so obvious. The question now is, what am I to do about it? About you?

That look, there was a darkness upon it—not cold as I found in myself—but hot as a burning ember. Is it any wonder I so often see you standing inside swirls of smoke?

Atri-Ceda, what am I to do?

But he knew he would have no answer to that question, not until he knew his own feelings. It all seemed so new, so peculiar, so unfamiliar. All at once—and he felt the shift with a grinding lurch—she was the one standing so self-possessed and content inside her own inner world's visions—whatever they happened to be—while he stood awkwardly at her side, flustered, dumbstruck.

Ridiculous. Set it aside for later, Brys.

This soldiering business was getting easier, Sunrise decided. Plenty of marching, and marching fast at that, but the soles of his feet had toughened, he'd got his wind back, and even carrying his armour, shield and weapons wasn't proving so hard any more. They'd even found time for some sword practice. *Duck and stab, duck and stab—hold the shield up, soldier! Hold the line—no one breaks in the Bridgeburners. You stand and take the shock and then you step forward. Stand, take, step—it's like felling a forest, soldiers, tree by tree. Duck and stab!*

Couldn't help but be a bit of a challenge, of course, living up to the legend that was the Bridgeburners, but then they had themselves a real one looking on, all sharp-eyed and stern, and that kept everyone trying and trying hard. High standards, aye, the highest.

The Bridgeburners had singlehandedly won the Blackdog Campaign. Sent the Crimson Guard and the Mott and Genabarii legions reeling in retreat. Kicked in the front gates of a dozen cities from Nathilog to One Eye Cat. And before that, they'd conquered all of Seven Cities. He'd never heard of any of these places but he liked the names. Seven Cities sounded simple and obvious. Place got seven cities? Call it Seven Cities. Straight thinking, that was. And all that Genabackan stuff, well, those names were amazing and exotic. Cities called Pale and Greydog, Tulips and Bulge. And then there were the wonderful beasts in those distant lands. Dragonflies big enough to ride—imagine whizzing through the clouds, looking down on everything! Seeing how beautiful it all was, and then dropping hundreds of bombs on it.

And the Bridgeburners had done all that and, more importantly, they weren't done yet. More adventures were coming. Glories and heroic defences, monsters in the sky and flooded deserts and ghosts with sharp swords and warriors made of dust. Moranth and Barghast and Tiste Andii and Jaghut tyrants and all the rest.

Sunrise couldn't wait, couldn't wait to get to the legendary stuff. It's what he was meant for, what his whole life was heading towards—as if he'd only been waiting for these foreign soldiers to arrive. To sweep him up and carry him along and now he was one of them. And he knew the others felt the same. *We're Bridgeburners now. They'll look to us when things get desperate, too desperate for the others to handle. We'll march forward, shields locked, faces cold and with hearts of iron. We'll prove we're worthy of the legend.*

Wait and see, just wait and see.

Two women stood well away from the fires, waiting for a third.

There was nothing sure in this. In fact, Sinter reminded herself, it was almost guaranteeing trouble. There wasn't much sisterhood among the Dal Honese. Scarce any brotherhood either, come to that. Tribes get left behind, and with them ties of the blood, feuds and all the rest. That was how it should be and mostly they held to it, since to do otherwise could rip a company apart. Squad's the new kin, company's the tribe, army's the people—the kingdom, the damned empire. *What are you, soldier?*

Marine, Fourth Squad, Third Company, Bonehunters, sir.

Not Dal Honese?

No, sir.

Malazan?

No, sir. Bonehunters, sir.

Now, if only she believed all that—there, in that gnarled hard thing at the centre of her being. Step up, aye, and mark it out with all the right attitudes. Diligence, discipline, loyalty. Don't blink at any damned order given, no matter how stupid or pointless. The tribe lived to keep itself alive, and keeping itself alive meant making sure everything was in order and working the way it should. Made sense to her. And it was worthy enough to believe in, especially when there was nothing else in sight looking any better.

So, she'd wanted to believe. For herself and for her wayward, flighty sister. Steady enough for the both of them, aye. Kisswhere was going to stray—she was like that, it was in her nature. People like her needed understanding kin, the kind of kin who'd step in and clean up and set right what needed setting right. And Sinter had always held to that role. *Kisswhere bends, I stand firm. She slips out, I fill the gap. She makes a mess, I clean and set right. She lets people down, I pick them back up.*

Sometimes, however, she chafed under the strictures of being ever reliable, solid and practical. Of being so utterly *capable.* Just once, Kisswhere could take Sinter's cloak and hold fast, and Sinter could snag her sister's and go out and play. Stealing husbands, jilting lovers, signing on, fucking off. Why not? Why did all the expectation have to settle on her shoulders, every damned time?

She was, she realized, still waiting to start living.

Badan Gruk wanted her, loved her. But she . . . she didn't know. If she wanted to be loved, or even chased after. She played it out, aye, as if it was all real. She even spent time telling herself it was the way it looked. But the truth was, she didn't know what she felt, not about him, not about anything. And wasn't that the real joke in all this? Everyone saw her as such a capable person, and all the while she asked herself: *capable of what? Will I ever find out?*

When is it my turn?

She had no idea what this army was doing, and that frightened her. Not that she'd ever give away her true feelings. Sinter saw how the others relied on her. Even the other sergeants. Primly, Badan Gruk, even that cow-eyed fool, Urb. No, she needed to keep playing the unimaginative soldier, biting her tongue and with that solid look in her eyes not once wavering, not for an instant giving away the crazed storm in her head.

She needed help. They were marching into blackness, a future profoundly unknown barring the simple, raw truth that at some point they would all draw their weapons, they would all stand facing an enemy that sought their annihilation. They would be told to fight, to kill. *But will we? Can we? If you could show us a cause, Adjunct. A reason, just a handful of worth, we'd do as you ask. I know we would.*

She glanced across at her sister. Kisswhere stood, a faint smile on her face to mark whatever inner peace and satisfaction she found so easy to indulge, her eyes on the blurry stars in the northern sky. Amused patience and the promise of derision: that was her most favoured expression, there on those deceptively sweet and innocent features. Yes, she was breathtaking in her natural beauty and charm, and there was that wild edge—sticky as honey—that so drew to her otherwise reasonable men. She froze lives and loves in amber, and her hoard was vast indeed.

Could I be like her? Could I live as she does? Look at that half-smile. So contented. Gods, how I wish . . .

There had to be a way out of this, and her sister had better find it soon. Else Kisswhere feared she would go mad. She'd joined the Malazan marines, for Hood's sake, not some renegade army marching up some damned god's ass. She'd joined knowing she could hand it all back to them once boredom forced the situation. Well, not that they'd happily let her go, of course, but disappearing wasn't so hard, not in a civilized land like the Malazan Empire. So many people, so many places to go, so many possible lives to assume. And even in the military itself, who really cared which face was which beneath the rim of the helm? Could be anyone, so long as they took orders and could march in step.

She could have slept her way into some soft posting. In Unta, or Li Heng, or Quon itself. Even Genabackis would have been fine. If only her sister hadn't jammed her nose into things. Always trying to take charge, constantly stepping into Kisswhere's path and causing grief. Complicating everything and that had always been the problem. But Sinter hadn't figured it out yet—Kisswhere had run to the marines to escape her sister's infuriating interference in her life. Among other things.

But she followed, didn't she? She followed and so did Badan Gruk. It's not my choice, not my fault at all. I'm not responsible for them—they're all grown up, aren't they?

So if I want to desert now, before we head into someplace where I can't, well, that's my business, isn't it?

But now Sinter had dragged her out from the cosy fire, and here they were, waiting for one of Urb's soldiers and what was all this about, anyway?

Running. Is that it, finally? I hope so, sister. I hope you've finally come to your senses. This time, I'm with you.

But why this woman we hardly even know? Why not Badan Gruk?

We got to get out, and now. I got to get out. And I don't need anyone's help to do it. Stow away with a D'ras trader. Easy, nothing to it. Two of us could do it, even three. But four? Now that's a stretch. It's logistics, sister, plain and simple. The kind you like so much. Straightforward. Too many and we'll get caught. You'll want Badan, too. And four's too many.

She'd wait, however. She'd see what Sinter had in mind here, with this meeting. She could work on Sinter later, but nothing direct, since that never worked. Sinter was stubborn. She could dig in deeper than anyone Kisswhere knew. No, Kisswhere would have to twist carefully, so that the decision, when it finally went the right way, would seem to be coming from Sinter herself.

It wasn't easy, but then Kisswhere had had a lifetime of practice. She knew she could do it.

Sinter softly grunted and she turned to see a figure approaching from the camp. Swaying hips, and everywhere a whole lot of what men liked. A Dal Honese for sure, which was why Sinter had invited her in the first place. But since when did three Dal Honese women agree about anything?

Madness. Sinter, this won't work. You remember the histories. It's us women who start most of the wars. Snaring the wrong men, using them up, humiliating them. Throwing one against another. Whispering blood vengeance beneath the furs at night. A sly comment here, a look there. We've been in charge a long time, us women of Dal Hon, and we're nothing but trouble.

Masan Gilani was from a savannah tribe. She was tall, making her curvaceous form all the more intimidating. She had the look of a woman who was too much for any man, and should a man get her he'd spend his whole life convinced he could never hold on to her. She was a monster of sensuality, and if she'd stayed in her tribe the whole north half of Dal Hon would be in the midst of a decades-long civil war by now. *Every Dal Honese god and mud spirit tossed in on this one, didn't they? She's got pieces of them all.*

And here I thought I was dangerous.

'Sinter,' she said under her breath, 'you have lost your mind.'

Her sister heard her. 'This one is far on the inside, Kiss, way farther in than anyone we know.'

'What of it?'

Sinter did not reply. Masan Gilani had drawn too close for any exchange now, no matter how muted.

Her elongated eyes flitted between the sisters, curious, and then amused.

Bitch. I hate her already.

'Southerners,' she said. 'I've always liked southerners. Your sweat smells of the jungle. And you're never as gangly and awkward as us northerners. Did you know, I have to special-order all my armour and clothes—I'm no standard fit anywhere, except maybe among the Fenn and that's no good because they're extinct.'

Kisswhere snorted. 'You ain't that big,' and then she looked away, as she realized how petty that sounded.

But Gilani's smile had simply broadened. 'The only real problem with you southerners is that you're barely passable on horseback. I'd not count on you to ride hard as me, ever. So it's a good thing you're marines. Me, I could be either and to be honest, I'd have jumped over to the scouts long ago—'

'So why didn't you?' Kisswhere asked.

She shrugged. 'Scouting's boring. Besides, I'm not interested in always being the one delivering bad news.'

'Expecting bad news?'

'Always.' And her teeth gleamed.

Kisswhere turned away. She was done with this conversation. Sinter was welcome to it.

'So,' Masan Gilani said after a moment, 'Sergeant Sinter. Rumour has it you're a natural, a talent. Tell me if that's true or not, since it's the only thing that brought me out here—the chance that you are, I mean. If you're not, then this meeting is over.'

'Listen to her!' Kisswhere sneered. 'The Empress commands!'

Masan blinked. 'You still here? Thought you went to pick flowers.'

Kisswhere reached for her knife but Sinter's hand snapped out and closed on her wrist. Hissing, Kisswhere yielded, but her eyes remained fixed on Gilani's.

'Oh, it's all so amusing to you, isn't it?'

'Kisswhere, yes? That's your name? I'll say this once. I don't know what's got the stoat in your breeches so riled, since as far as I know I ain't never done anything to cross you. Leaves me no choice but to assume it's just some kind of bizarre bigotry—what happened, lose a lover to a willowy northerner? Well, it wasn't me. So, why not drop the hackles? Here, will this help?' And she drew out a Dal Honese wineskin. 'Not wild grape from our homeland, alas—'

'It ain't that rice piss from Lether, is it?'

'No. It's Bluerose—an Andiian brew, originally, or so the trader claimed.' She shrugged and held out the skin. 'It's drinkable enough.'

Kisswhere accepted the skin. She knew overtures when they arrived, and she knew that Masan had given her a way through without too much damage to her pride, so it'd be stupid not to take that path. She tugged loose the gum stopper and took a mouthful. Swallowed and then gasped. 'That'll do,' she said in a suddenly husky voice.

Sinter finally spoke: 'Everyone's claws retracted? Good. Masan, you want to know if I'm a talent. Well, not in the way of Dal Honese witches. But I've got something, I suppose.'

'All right. So what's that "something" telling you?'

Sinter hesitated, and then reached out to intercept the wineskin. She took two deep draughts. 'Aye, you're a northerner and we're not, but we're all still Dal Honese. So we understand each other, and when I say I'm going to give you something I don't need to add that I expect something back.'

Masan Gilani laughed, but it was not a mocking laugh. Not quite. 'You just did.'

'You been a soldier longer than us,' Sinter countered, 'so I was just reminding you of the ways you've maybe forgotten, or at least not used in a while.'

'Go on, then.'

'I get senses of things about to happen, or maybe could happen—if we don't do something to make sure they don't.'

'You're a seer.'

But Sinter shook her head. 'Not so clear as that.'

'What is about to happen to us, Sergeant?'

'We're about to be abandoned.'

Kisswhere joined Masan Gilani in regarding Sinter with alarm. What was all this? 'Sister,' she said, 'what does that mean? Abandoned? By who? Do you mean just us? Or the Bonehunters?'

'Yes,' answered Sinter. 'Bonehunters. All of us, the Adjunct included.'

Masan Gilani was frowning. 'You're talking about the Burned Tears? The Perish? Or the Letherii escort?'

'I'm not sure. Maybe all of them.'

'So wherever we end up,' Masan said slowly, 'we'll be fighting on our own. No one guarding our backs, no one on our flanks. Like that?'

'I think so.'

Masan rubbed at her neck. When Kisswhere offered her the skin she shook her head. 'Hard to know, Sinter, how much shit should be freezing with that, since nobody has a clue about who we'll be fighting. What if it's some noseplug savages cowering behind a bamboo palisade throwing rocks at us? We'd hardly need help knocking on that door, would we?'

'But you know we're not heading for anything so easy,' Sinter said.

Masan's lovely eyes narrowed. 'This is what you want back from me? You think I've got my ear against the Adjunct's tent?'

'I know you know more than we do.'

'And if I do? What difference would it make to you?'

Kisswhere's breath caught as she saw her sister's hands clench into fists at her sides. 'I need a reason, Masan Gilani. I need to know it's all worth it.'

'And you think what little I know can give you that? You must be desperate—'

'Yes! I am!'

'Why?'

Sinter's mouth shut, her jaw setting.

Masan Gilani looked over at Kisswhere, as if to ask: *What's her problem here? What's so hard to say?*

But Kisswhere had no answers. Well, not satisfying ones. 'My sister,' she said, 'is a very loyal person. But she holds that loyalty in highest regard. She'll give it, I mean—'

'But,' cut in Masan Gilani, 'whatever or whoever she's giving it to had better be worthy of it. Right. I think I'm beginning to understand this. Only, Kisswhere, you should look to your own feelings about that.'

'What do you mean?'

'I mean, you sounded pretty bitter right there. As if loyalty is a curse and not one you want any part of. I'd wager your sister dragged you here as much to convince you of something as to convince me. Sinter, would that be a good guess?'

'That's between me and her,' Sinter replied.

Kisswhere glared at her sister.

'All right,' said Masan Gilani, 'I'll give you what little I know. What Ebron and Bottle and Deadsmell and Widdershins have put together. Maybe it'll help, maybe it won't. That's for you to decide. Here's what we think.' She paused, reached for the skin.

Kisswhere handed it to her.

Masan drank, then squatted before them—taking the pose of the teller of tales, one they knew well—and both sisters followed suit.

'He didn't ask for it. But he's been making trouble ever since. Quick Ben met him face to face. So, we worked out, did that Meckros weaponsmith, Withal. He's poison and he knows it and he can't help it, because he doesn't belong here. There are pieces of him scattered over half the world, but the biggest one is sitting in this place called Kolanse—and it's being . . . used.'

'We're going to kill the Crippled God.'

Kisswhere shot her sister a wild look. 'But who'd want to stop us doing that?'

Sinter shook her head. Her face was wretched with confusion.

Masan was eyeing them and when she spoke her voice was flat, 'You jumped the wrong way, Sinter, like a one-eyed mongoose.' She drank again, sloshed the skin and then scowled. 'Should've brought two. We don't think we're off to kill the Chained One. In fact, it's those chains we're after. Well, the Adjunct, I mean. What she's after.' She lifted her head and fixed on Sinter's eyes, and then Kisswhere's. 'We're going to set the bastard free.'

Kisswhere barked a savage laugh. 'No wonder they'll all abandon us! And I'm the first in line to join them!'

'Be quiet,' Sinter said through the hands she'd lifted to her face. She was trembling, no, shuddering, and Kisswhere saw the glitter of tears trickle to the heels of her sister's palms.

Masan Gilani's face was grave, patient.

Kisswhere rounded on Sinter. 'You cannot! No! This is impossible! What if they're wrong? They must be—even the Adjunct's not that stupid! Every god and ascendant in the world will be coming against us, never mind those idiots in Kolanse! She's lost her mind! Our commander's insane and there's no damned law anywhere says we have to follow her!'

Sinter drew a deep breath and then lowered her hands. Something solid filled her face, as if implacable stone was replacing the soft tissues beneath her onyx skin. The bleakness drained from her eyes as they settled on Kisswhere. 'It will do,' she said. 'I think,' she added, 'nothing else would have.'

'What—'

'It is just, sister. *Just.*'

'They'll all turn on us,' Kisswhere retorted. 'You said so yourself—'

'If we do nothing, yes. They will turn on us. And what little chance we had to succeed will go with them. We need to change their minds.'

'How?' asked Masan Gilani.

'I will tell you how,' said Sinter. 'And it begins with you, Kisswhere.'

'I didn't say I was going to help—'

'You're going to desert.'

'Wha—what?'

'That's how this starts. It's the only way. Now, it's what you want and don't tell me any different. You're deserting the Bonehunters, and you're doing it to-night—on the fastest horse Masan Gilani can find you.'

But Masan Gilani held up a staying hand. 'Hold on. I need to talk this over with—'

'Of course,' cut in Sinter, 'but it changes nothing. Now, you need to hear the rest, because I need you to do the same—'

'Desert? Me?'

Sinter nodded. 'But you'll ride in a different direction, Masan Gilani. Different from Kisswhere. With luck, you'll both return.'

'And get hanged? No thanks, sister—'

'You won't. The Adjunct is cold iron—the coldest there ever was. She'll work it out, fast as lightning, she'll work it out.'

'Then why don't we just go tell her?' asked Masan Gilani. 'We figured it all out but there's a problem, only you got an idea on how to fix it.'

Sinter smiled, and it was a smile that would have fitted well on the Adjunct's own face. 'I will do just that . . . once you two are gone.'

'She might just chase us down anyway.'

'She won't. I said she's quick.'

'So why wait until we leave?'

Sinter rubbed at her face, wiping away the last of the tears. 'You don't get it. She's locked in a room, a prison of her own making. In there, she hears nothing, sees nothing. In there, she is absolutely alone. And holding on with white knuck-les. It's her burden and she won't dump it on anyone else, not even her Fists, not even on her High Mage—though he's probably worked it out by now. She's put herself between us and the truth—but it's killing her.'

'So,' said Masan Gilani, 'you got to show her she ain't alone, and that we're not all fools, that maybe we're ready for that truth. We not only worked it out, we're with her. There to help, whether she asks for it or not.'

'That's it,' said Sinter.

Masan Gilani sighed, and then flashed Kisswhere a grin. 'You won't surprise anyone. Me, that's a different story.'

'The Adjunct will hint something to put your reputation square,' said Sinter. 'Otherwise, you going might tip the balance for a whole mass of wavering soldiers in the ranks. Kisswhere, well, sister, nobody will be much surprised by you, will they?'

'Thank you. So long as people understand I'm no coward—'

Masan Gilani grunted, 'But they'll see it that way. Nothing you can do about it, either, Kisswhere. We're marching to a war, and you went and ran off. Me too. So Sinter and the Adjunct work it out so it sounds like I was sent on some kind of mission—'

'Which is true,' cut in Sinter.

'Which helps, aye. Thing is, people already thinking of maybe deserting might just take it as the perfect push. That's the risk that the Adjunct might find unacceptable, no matter what you say to her, Sinter.'

'I'm no coward,' Kisswhere repeated. 'I'm just not one for this whole family thing. Armies ain't families, no matter how many times you try to tell me different. It's rubbish. It's the lie commanders and kings need so they always got us ready to do shit for them.'

'Right,' snapped Masan Gilani, 'and I guess in that snarly jungle where you grew up you never heard any stories about what happens when armies mutiny. Kill their commanders. Depose their country's ruler. Take over—'

'What's that got to do with the whole "we're family" business?'

'I'm saying some people run things and the rest should just stay out of it. That's all. Just like in a family. Somebody's in charge, not everybody. Usurpers never been anything better, or even different, from whoever they killed. Usually, they make it worse. That whole "family" thing, it's about fighting to survive. You stand fast for kin, not strangers. Don't you get that?'

'And the ones in charge exploit it. Use us up. They ain't interested in being kin to the rest of us, and you know it.'

'You two,' Sinter said, 'could go at this all night. But we don't have the time. Kisswhere, since when did you care what the people you leave behind think of you? Unless, of course, you've found some pride as a Bonehunter—'

'Do you want me to help you or not?'

'All right. Peace, then. The point is, it's only looking like you're deserting. The way Faradan Sort did outside Y'Ghatan.'

'I ride south.'

Sinter nodded.

'I go find the Perish and the Khundryl.'

'Yes.'

'And say what?'

'You convince them not to abandon us.'

'How in Hood's name do I do that?'

Sinter's look was wry. 'Try using your charms, sister.'

Masan Gilani spoke. 'Sergeant, if she's going after both of them, where am I going?'

'That's not so easy to say,' Sinter admitted haltingly.

Masan snorted. 'Work on that answer, Sinter. Meanwhile, let's go steal some horses.'

'Ah, Lieutenant, found you at last.'

'Master Sergeant now, sir.'

'Of course, and where are your charges, Master Sergeant?'

'Dispensed with, sir.'

'Excuse me?'

'Rather, dispersed, sir. Inserted seamlessly into the ranks, not a stitch out of place.'

'Why, that is simply superb, Master Sergeant. You would deserve a commendation if you deserved anything. Alas, having perused the latest roster updates, I have discovered that not a single one of those recruits can be found anywhere in the army.'

'Yes, sir, they are well trained.'

'At what, Master Sergeant? Disappearing?'

'Well now, sir, I am reminded of a story from my youth. May I?'

'Please, do go on.'

'Thank you, sir. Ah, my youth. A sudden zeal afflicted young Aramstos Pores—'

'Aramstos?'

'Yes, sir—'

'That's your other name?'

'It is indeed, sir. May I continue my tale, sir?'

'Proceed.'

'A sudden zeal, sir, to dig me a pond.'

'A pond.'

'Just behind the heap of broken bricks, sir, close to the lot's back wall. I often played there when my parents had gone from fighting with words to fighting with knives, or the hovel caught fire as it was wont to do. On my hands and knees among the broken shards of pots and shattered dog teeth—'

'Dog teeth.'

'My father's failures with pets, but that, sir, is another story, perhaps for another time. A pond, sir, one into which I could transplant the tiny minnows I was rescuing from the fouled river down past the sewage outlets—where we used to swim on cold days, warming up as it were, sir. Minnows, then, into my pond. Imagine my excitement—'

'It is suddenly vivid in my mind's eye, Master Sergeant.'

'Wonderful. And yet, having deposited, oh, fifty of the tiny silver things, just the day before, imagine my horror and bafflement upon returning the very next morning to find not a single minnow in my pond. Why, what had happened to them? Some voracious bird, perhaps? The old woman from down the alley who kept her hair in a net? Are there perchance now glinting minnows adorning her coiffure? Insects? Rats? Unlikely to be either of those two, as they generally made up our nightly repast at the dinner table and so accordingly were scarce round our home. Well, sir, a mystery it was and a mystery it remains. To this very day and, I am certain, for the entirety of the rest of my life. Fifty minnows. Gone. Poof! Hard to believe, sir, and most crushing for that bright-eyed, zealous lad.'

'And now, if I am to understand you, Master Sergeant, once more you find yourself victimized by inexplicable mystery.'

'All those recruits, sir. Dispersed into the ranks. And then . . .'

'Poof.'

'As you say and say well, sir.'

'Whatever happened to your pond, Master Sergeant?'

'Well, my pet water snake thrived for a while longer, until the pond dried up. Children have such grand dreams, don't they?'

'That they do, Master Sergeant. Until it all goes wrong.'

'Indeed, sir.'

'Until we meet again, Master Sergeant Pores.'

'And a good night to you, too, Captain Kindly.'

It was him. I was fooling myself ever thinking otherwise. Who can explain love anyway? She slid the knife back into its sheath and pushed through the loose flaps of the tent, stepping outside and suddenly shivering as something cold slithered through the faint breeze.

The dark north flicks its tongue. Echoes of some unwanted rebirth—glad I'm not a mage. They had nothing to dance about this afternoon.

Lostara moved away from the command tent. The Adjunct sending her away this late at night was unusual—*I was ready for bed, dammit*—but having the guards roust and drive out a drunken Banaschar wasn't just sweet entertainment. It was, on another level, alarming.

What did Quick Ben and Bottle tell you this night, Tavore? Is there any end to your secrets? Any breach in your wall of privacy? What's so satisfying about being alone? Your love is a ghost. The empire you served has betrayed you. Your officers have stopped talking, even to each other.

O serpent of the north, your tongue does not lie. Draw closer. We're barely breathing.

She was forced to halt as Banaschar reeled across her path. Seeing her, he managed to stop, tottering a moment before straightening. 'Captain Yil,' he said genially, taking a deep breath and then letting it loose in the way that drunks did when mustering sodden thoughts. 'Pleasant evening, yes?'

'No. It's cold. I'm tired. I don't know why the Adjunct cleared everyone out—it's not as if she needs the extra room. For what?'

'For what, indeed,' he agreed, smiling as if his purse was full of sweets. 'It's the wardrobe, you see.'

'What?'

He weaved back and forth. 'Wardrobe. Yes, that's the word? I think so. Not makes for easy travel, though. Doesn't, rather. But . . . sometimes . . . where was

I? Oh, sometimes the wardrobe's so big the girl, she just runs away from it, fast and long as she can. Is that what I mean? Did I say it right?'

'Wardrobe.'

Banaschar pointed at her, nodding. 'Precisely.'

'Who runs away from a wardrobe? Girls don't do that—'

'But women do.'

'I don't understand.'

'All those choices, right? What to put on. And when, and when not. If it's this, but not if it's that. What to put on, Captain Yil. Choices. Surrounding you. Closing in. Creeping. Girl's got to run, and let's hope she makes it.'

Sniffing, Lostara stepped round the fool and continued on between the tent rows.

It was him. But you let him go. Maybe you thought he'd come back, or you'd just find him again. You thought you had the time. But the world's always armed and all it takes is a misstep, a wrong decision. And suddenly you're cut, you're bleeding, bleeding right out. Suddenly he's gasping his last breaths and it's time to put him away, just close him up, like a scroll bearing bad news.

What else can you do?

It was him, but he's gone and he's not coming back.

Her pace slowed. She frowned. *Where am I going? Ah, that's right.* 'New whetstone, that's it.'

The world's armed, Adjunct, so be careful. Kick open that wardrobe, girl, and start throwing on that armour. The days of fetes are over, all those nights among the glittering smirks of privilege and entitlement.

'You idiot, Banaschar, there's only one item in her wardrobe. What's to choose?'

She almost heard him reply, '*And still she's running away.*'

No, this conversation wasn't even real, and it made no sense anyway. Resuming her journey to the smiths' compound, she encountered a marine coming up the other way. A quick exchange of salutes, and then past.

A sergeant. Marine. Dal Honese. Where in Hood's name is she going this time of night? Never mind. Whetstone. They keep wearing out. And the sound of the iron licking back and forth, the way it just perfectly echoes the word in my head—amazing. Perfect.

It was him. It was him.

It was him.

Most of the ties and fittings on his armour had loosened or come undone. The heavy dragon-scale breast- and back-plates hung askew from his broad shoulders. The clawed bosses on his knees rested on the ground as he knelt in the wet grasses. He'd pulled off the bone-strip gauntlets to better wipe the tears from his cheeks and the thick smears of snot running from his nose. The massive bone-handled battleaxe rested on the ground beside him.

He'd bawled through half the night, until his throat was raw and his head felt packed solid with sand. Where was everyone? He was alone and it seemed he'd been alone for years now, wandering lost on this empty land. He'd seen old camps, abandoned villages. He'd seen a valley filled with bones and rubble. He'd seen a limping crow that laughed at him only to beg for mercy when he caught it. Stupid! His heart had gone all soft and he foolishly released it, only to have the horrid thing start laughing at him all over again as it limped away. It only stopped laughing when the boulder landed on it. And now he missed that laughing crow and its funny hopping—at least it had been keeping him company. Stupid boulder!

The day had run away and then come back and it wasn't nearly as cold as it'd been earlier. The ghost of Old Hunch Arbat had blown away like dust and was that fair? It wasn't. So he was lost, looking for something but he'd forgotten what it was and he wanted to be home in Letheras, having fun with King Tehol and sexing with Shurq Elalle and breaking the arms of his fellow guards in the palace. Oh, where were all his friends?

His bleary, raw eyes settled on the battleaxe and he scowled. It wasn't even pretty, was it. 'Smash,' he mumbled. 'Crush. Its name is Rilk, but it never says anything. How'd it tell anybody its name? I'm alone. Everybody must be dead. Sorry, crow, you were last other thing left alive! In the whole world! And I killed you!'

'Sorry I missed it,' said a voice behind him.

Ublala Pung climbed to his feet and turned round. 'Life!'

'I share your exultation, friend.'

'It's all cold around you,' Ublala said.

'That will pass.'

'Are you a god?'

'More or less, Toblakai. Does that frighten you?'

Ublala Pung shook his head. 'I've met gods before. They collect chickens.'

'We possess mysterious ways indeed.'

'I know.' Ublala Pung fidgeted and then said, 'I'm supposed to save the world.'

The stranger cocked his head. 'And here I was contemplating killing it.'

'Then I'd be all alone again!' Ublala wailed, tears springing back to his puffy eyes.

'Be at ease, Toblakai. You are reminding me that some things in this world remain worthwhile. If you would save the world, friend, that Draconean armour is fine preparation, as is that weapon at your feet—indeed, I believe I recognize both.'

'I don't know,' Ublala said. 'I don't know where to go to save the world. I don't know anything.'

'Let us journey together, then.'

'Gods make good friends,' nodded Ublala Pung, pleased at this turn of events.

'And spiteful enemies,' the stranger said, 'but we shall not be enemies, so that need not concern us. Wielder of Rilk, Wearer of Dra Alkeleint, what is your name?'

He swelled his chest. He liked being called Wielder and Wearer of things. 'Ublala Pung. Who are you?'

The stranger smiled. 'We will walk east, Ublala Pung. I am named Draconus.'

'Oh, funny.'

'What is?'

'That's the word Old Hunch Arbat's ghost screamed, before the black wind tore him to pieces.'

'You must tell me how you came to be here, Ublala Pung.'

'I'm no good with questions like that, Draconus.'

The god sighed. 'Then we have found something in common, friend. Now, collect up Rilk there and permit me to refasten your straps.'

'Oh, thank you. I don't like knots.'

'No one does, I should think.'

'But not as bad as chains, though.'

The strangers hands hesitated on the fittings, and then resumed. 'True enough, friend.'

Ublala Pung wiped clean his face. He felt light on his feet and the sun was coming up and, he decided, he felt good again.

Everybody needs a friend.

Chapter Twenty

Let the sun warm the day.
If light holds all the colours
then see the union as pure
and free of compromise.
Walk the stone and burden of earth
with its manes like cats lying in wait
as the wind slips silken
and slides round the curl
of your sure vision.

Let the sun warm this day
armoured against all argument,
solid in sanctity to opinion.
The hue does not deceive
and the blur hides no thought
to partake of grey masses in the sky
lowering horizon's rim
where each step is balanced
on the day's birth.

Wake to the warmth of the sun.
It knew other loves past
and stole all the colours
from eternal promises.
The dust only flows to life
in the lost-treasure golds of light.
Hold to nothing new
for even the new is old
and burden-worn.

Let the sun bring forth the day.
You have walked this way before
amid hunters in the grasses
and wheeling lovers of death
crowning every sky.
The armies have pursued anon,
riders risen along the ridge.
Maids and courtiers abide

in future's perfect shadows
until what is lost returns.

LAY OF WOUNDED LOVE
FISHER

It's no simple thing,' he said, frowning as he worked through his thoughts, 'but in the world—among people, that is. Society, culture, nation—in the world, then, there are attackers and there are defenders. Most of us possess within ourselves elements of both, but in a general sense a person falls to one camp or the other, as befits their nature.'

The wind swept round the chiselled stone. What guano remained to stain the dark, pitted surfaces had been rubbed thin and patchy, like faded splashes of old paint. Around them was the smell of heat lifting from rock, caught up, spun and plucked away with each gust of the breeze. But the sun did not relent its battle, and for that, Ryadd Eleis was thankful.

Silchas Ruin's eyes were fixed on something to the northwest, but an outcrop of shaped stone blocked Ryadd's line of sight in that direction. He was curious, but not unduly so. Instead, he waited for Silchas to continue, knowing how the white-skinned Tiste Andii sometimes struggled to speak his mind. When it did come, it often arrived all at once and at length, a reasoned, detailed argument that Ryadd received mostly in silence. There was so much to learn.

'This is not to say that aggression belongs only to those who are attackers,' Silchas resumed. 'Far from it, in fact. In my talent with the sword, for example, I am for the most part a defender. I rely upon timing and counter-attack—I take advantage of the attacker's forward predilections, the singularity of their intent. Counter-attack is, of course, aggression in its own way. Do you see the distinction?'

Ryadd nodded. 'I think so.'

'Aggression takes many forms. Active, passive, direct, indirect. Sudden as a blow, or sustained as a siege of will. Often, it refuses to stand still, but launches upon you from all possible sides. If one tactic fails, another is tried, and so on.'

Smiling, Ryadd said, 'Yes. I played often enough among the Imass children. What you describe every child learns, at the hands of the bully and the rival.'

'Excellent. Of course you are right. But bear in mind, none of this belongs solely within the realm of childhood. It persists and thrives in adult society. What must be understood is this: attackers attack as a form of defence. It is their instinctive response to threat, real or perceived. It may be desperate or it may be habit, or both, when desperation becomes a way of life. Behind the assault hides a fragile person.'

He was silent then, and Ryadd understood that Silchas sought to invite some contemplation of the things just said. Weighing of self-judgement, perhaps. Was he an attacker or a defender? He had done both, he knew, and there had been times when he had attacked when he should have defended, and so too the other way round. *I do not know which of the two I am. Not yet. But, I think, I know this much: when I feel threatened, I attack.*

'Cultures tend to invite the dominance of one over the other, as a means by which an individual succeeds and advances or, conversely, fails and falls. A culture dominated by attackers—and one in which the qualities of attacking are admired, often overtly encouraged—tends to breed people with a thick skin, which nonetheless still serves to protect a most brittle self. Thus the wounds bleed but stay well hidden beneath the surface. Cultures favouring the defender promote thin skin and quickness to take offence—its own kind of aggression, I am sure you see. The culture of attackers seeks submission and demands evidence of that submission as proof of superiority over the subdued. The culture of defenders seeks compliance through conformity, punishing dissenters and so gaining the smug superiority of enforcing silence, and from silence, complicity.'

The pause that followed was a long one and Ryadd was pleased that it was so, for Silchas had given him much to consider. *The Imass? Ah, defenders, I think. Yes. Always exceptions, of course, but he said there would be. Examples of both, but in general . . . yes, defenders. Think of Onrack's fate, his love for Kilava, the crimes that love forced upon him. He defied conformity. He was punished.*

It was more difficult to think of a culture dominated by attackers. *The Letherii? He thought of his father, Udinaas. He defends when in himself. But attacks with derision, yet even then, he does not hide his vulnerability.* 'Is there no third way of being, Silchas?'

The warrior smiled. 'In my long life, Ryadd, I have seen many variations—configurations—of behaviour and attitude, and I have seen a person change from one to the other—when experience has proved damaging enough, or when the inherent weaknesses of one are recognized, leading to a wholesale rejection of it. Though, in turn, weaknesses of different sorts exist in the other, and often these prove fatal pitfalls. We are complex creatures, to be sure. The key, I think, is to hold true to your own aesthetics, that which you value, and yield to no one the power to become the arbiter of your tastes. You must also learn to devise strategies for fending off both attackers and defenders. Exploit aggression, but only in self-defence, the kind of self-defence that announces to all the implacability of your armour, your self-assurance, and affirms the sanctity of your self-esteem. Attack when you must, but not in arrogance. Defend when your values are challenged, but never with the wild fire of anger. Against attackers, your surest defence is cold iron. Against defenders, often the best tactic is to sheathe your weapon and refuse the game. Reserve contempt for those who have truly earned it, but see the contempt you permit yourself to feel not as a weapon, but as armour against their assaults. Finally, be ready to disarm with a smile, even as you cut deep with words.'

'Passive.'

'Of a sort, yes. It is more a matter of warning off potential adversaries. In effect, you are saying: *Be careful how close you tread. You cannot hurt me, but if I am pushed hard enough, I will wound you.* In some things you must never yield, but these things are not eternally changeless or explicitly inflexible; rather, they are yours to decide upon, yours to reshape if you deem it prudent. They are immune to the pressure of others, but not indifferent to their arguments. Weigh and gauge at all times, and decide for yourself value and worth. But when you sense that a line has been crossed by the other person, when you sense that what is under attack is, in fact, your self-esteem, then gird yourself and stand firm.'

Ryadd rubbed at the fine hairs downing his cheeks. 'Would these words of yours have come from my father, had I remained at home?'

'In his own way, yes. Udinaas is a man of great strength—'

'But—'

'Great strength, Ryadd. He is strong enough to stand exposed, revealing all that is vulnerable within him. He is brave enough to invite you ever closer. If you hurt him, he will withdraw, as he must, and that path to him will be thereafter for ever sealed. But he begins with the gift of himself. What the other does with it defines the future of that particular relationship.'

'What of trust?'

The red eyes flicked to his and then away again. 'I kept them safe for a long time,' he said in a low voice. 'Evading the Letherii mages and soldiers. None of that was necessary.'

'My father knew.'

'I believe Fear Sengar did as well.'

'So neither then trusted you.'

'On the contrary. They trusted me to hold to my resolve.'

Now it was Ryadd's turn to look away. 'Did she really have to die?'

'She was never really alive, Ryadd. She was sent forth as potential. I ensured that it was realized. Are seeds filled with hope? We might think so. But in truth hope belongs to the creator of that seed, and to those who choose to plant it.'

'She was still a child to everyone's eyes.'

'The Azath used what it found.'

'Is she still alive then?'

Silchas Ruin shrugged. 'Perhaps more now than ever before. Alive, but young. And very vulnerable.'

'And so now,' Ryadd said, 'my father yearns for the survival of the Azath, and he hopes too for your continued resolve. But maybe "hope" is the wrong word. Instead, it's *trust*.'

'If so, then you have answered your own question.'

But what of my resolve? Do you trust in that, Silchas Ruin?

'They draw nearer,' the Tiste Andii said, rising from his perch on the stone. Then he paused. 'Be wary, Ryadd, she is most formidable, and I cannot predict the outcome of this parley.'

'What will she make of me?' he asked, also straightening.

'That is what we shall discover.'

His horse had stepped on a particularly vicious fist of cactus. Torrent dismounted, cursing under his breath. He went round and lifted the beast's hoof and began plucking spines.

Olar Ethil stood to one side, watching.

It had turned out that escaping the hoary old witch wasn't simply a matter of riding hard and leaving her behind. She kept reappearing in swirls of dust, with that ever-present skull grin that needed no laugh to add sting to its mockery.

Following the heavy wagon tracks, he had ridden past two more dragon towers, both as lifeless and ruined as the first one. And now here they were, approaching yet another. Arcane machinery had spilled out from rents in the stone, lying scattered, spreading outward from the foot of the edifice a hundred or more paces on all sides. Crumpled pieces of armour and broken weapons lay amidst the wreckage, as well as grizzled strips and slabs of scaled hide. The violence committed at this particular tower remained, intrusive as bitter smoke.

Torrent tugged loose the last thorn and, collecting the reins, led the horse forward a few steps. 'Those damned things,' he said, 'were they poisoned?'

'I think not,' Olar Ethil replied. 'Just painful. Local bhederin know to avoid stepping on them.'

'There are no local bhederin,' snapped Torrent. 'These are the Wastelands and well named.'

'Once, long ago, warrior, the spirits of the earth and wind thrived in this place.'

'So what happened?'

Her shrug creaked. 'When it is easy to feed, one grows fat.'

What the fuck does that mean! He faced the tower. 'We'll walk for—' Motion in the sky caught his attention, as two massive shapes lifted from the enormous carved head of the stone dragon. 'Spirits below!'

A pair of dragons—*real ones*. The one on the left was the hue of bone, eyes blazing bright red, and though larger than its companion, it was gaunter, perhaps older. The other dragon was a stunning white deepening to gold along its shoulders and serrated back. Wings snapping, sailing in a curving descent, the two landed directly in their path, halfway between them and the tower. The earth trembled at the twin impacts.

Torrent glanced at Olar Ethil. She was standing still as a statue. *I thought you knew everything, witch, and now I think you thought the same. Look at you, still as a hare under the cat's eyes.*

He looked back in time to see both dragons shimmer, and then blur, as if nothing more than mirages. A moment later, two men stood in place of the giant creatures. Neither moved.

Even at this distance, Torrent could see how the dragons had so perfectly expressed the essences of these two figures. The one on the left was tall, gaunt, his skin the shade of bleached bone; the other was younger by far, thickly muscled yet nearing his companion's height. His hair, hanging loose, was gold and bronze, his skin burnished by the sun, and he stood with the ease of the innocent.

Saying nothing, Olar Ethil set out to meet them, and to Torrent's eyes she was suddenly diminished, the raw primitiveness of her form looking clumsy and rough. The scaled hide of her cloak now looked to be a faintly sordid affectation.

Tugging his skittish horse along behind him, he followed. There was no escaping these warriors, should they desire him harm. If Olar Ethil was prepared to brave it out, then he would follow her lead. *But this day I have seen true power. And now I will look it in the eye.*

I have travelled far from my village. The small world of my people gets smaller still.

As he drew closer, he was surprised to see that the two swords belted to the gaunt, older warrior were both Letherii in design. *Blue steel. I remember seeing a knife once, traded into the chief's hands, and how it sang when struck.* The younger one bore weapons of flaked stone. He was dressed in strange, rough hides.

'You are not welcome, Silchas,' said Olar Ethil. And then she stabbed a gnarled finger at the younger man. 'And this one, who so mocks my own people. This is not his world. Silchas Ruin, have you bargained open the Gate to Starvald Demelain?'

'He is Menandore's son,' replied the white-skinned warrior. 'You know the payment for such a bargain, Olar Ethil. Do you think I am prepared to pay it?'

'I do not know what you are prepared to do, Silchas. I never did.'

'He is named Ryadd Eleis, and he is under my protection.'

She snorted. 'You think too highly of yourself if you think he requires your protection. No,' and she cocked her head, 'I see the truth. You keep him close in order to control him. But, since he is Menandore's spawn, you will fail. Silchas Ruin, you never learn. The blood of Eleint can never flow close to its own. There will be betrayal. There is always betrayal. Why does she possess a hundred heads? It is to mock an impossible concord.' She shifted slightly to face Ryadd Eleis. 'He will strike first if he can. When he sees you surpass him, he will seek to kill you.'

The young golden warrior seemed unperturbed by her warning. 'He will see no such thing, bonecaster.'

She started, and then hissed. 'A bold claim. How can you be so certain?'

'Because,' Ryadd replied, 'I already have.'

All at once everything shifted. Torrent saw Silchas Ruin step away from his companion, both hands stealing closer to the grips of his swords.

Olar Ethil cackled.

'Bonecaster,' Ryadd said, adding a faint bow to the title, 'I know your name. I know you are the Maker of the Ritual of Tellann. That without you all the will of the Imass would have achieved nothing. The One Voice was yours. You took a people and stole from them death itself.'

'You have dwelt among T'lan Imass?'

He shook his head. 'Imass. But I know one who was once a T'lan Imass. Onrack the Broken. And I know his wife, Kilava.'

'Kilava, that sweet bitch. His wife now? She almost undid me. Is she well? Tell her I forgive her. And tell Onrack the Broken of the Logros, I shall not reclaim him. His life is his, now, and for all time.'

'It is well you said so,' Ryadd said. 'For I have vowed that no harm come to them.'

'Ryadd Eleis, I have chosen: I am not your enemy and be glad for that. If I had chosen otherwise, that bold vow would have killed you.'

He shrugged. 'Perhaps between the two of us, you would prevail. But against me and Kilava both, the outcome might prove the opposite.'

'Is she close? No! I sense nothing!'

'She is the oldest true bonecaster of all, Olar Ethil. The others ceased to grow once they surrendered to the Ritual. And look at yourself—the same is true. You are only what you once were, that and nothing more. If Kilava wishes to remain undetected, so it shall be. You do not rule this world, Olar Ethil. You surrendered that privilege long ago, with your very own Ritual.'

Olar Ethil swung to Silchas Ruin. 'See what you have invited into your shadow? You fool! And now, best you beg me for an alliance—quickly!'

But Silchas Ruin let his hands fall away from his weapons. 'It may be that I have kept him close for the reasons you say, Olar Ethil, but there are other reasons—and these are proving far more compelling the more I come to know this son of Menandore. If he has indeed surpassed me, I will yield my leadership of the pair of us. As for an alliance with you, frankly, I'd rather bed an enkar'al.'

Torrent laughed, as much to release the tension and fear building within him as at the notion of this warrior bedding something with the ugly name of enkar'al. The sound, unfortunately, drew everyone's attention.

Ryadd addressed him. 'Warrior, are you indebted to this bonecaster?'

He frowned. 'I'd not thought of that. Possibly, but I do not know the coin, nor its value. I am Torrent of the Awl, but the Awl are no more. Instead, I keep company with bones.'

The youth smiled, as if unexpectedly pleased with the answer.

Silchas said, 'Torrent of the Awl. I grieve for the passing of your people. Their memory rests with you now. Cherish it but do not let it destroy you.'

'An interesting distinction,' Torrent said after a moment's thought. 'But I am past such things, since I now cherish destruction. I would slay my slayers. I would end the lives of those who have ended mine.' He glanced across at Olar Ethil. 'Perhaps this is the coin between me and this undead witch.'

Sorrow tinged Ruin's face but he said nothing.

Ryadd's smile was gone. 'Look around then, warrior. This is the home you would make for your enemies and for yourself. Does it please you?'

'I think it does, Ryadd Eleis.'

The young man's displeasure and disappointment at that answer was plain to see.

A short span of silence, and then Olar Ethil spoke. 'You have waited to spring this ambush, Silchas Ruin. Were the words we have exchanged all you sought, or is there something else?'

'My curiosity is satisfied,' Silchas said to the bonecaster. 'But I will give you this as a gesture, if you will, as evidence that I wish no enmity between us. Two undead dragons are seeking you. I know them of old. They will bow and scrape and swear fealty. But in their hearts they are vile.'

Olar Ethil sniffed. 'I thought I sensed . . . something. On our trail. You say you know them, while I do not. I find that odd, given the world you and I once shared.'

'From when the Eleint were unleashed, out through the Gate, seeking to claim realms to rule amidst the shattered remains of Kurald Emurlahn.' He paused, and then added, 'My own encounter with them was brief, but violent. They are true spawn of T'iam.'

'Yet they travel together. Why has neither one committed treachery upon the other?'

'I believe they are twins, Olar Ethil, hatched from a single egg as it were. Among all the Eleint during the Wars of Shadow, they came closest to victory. It was the last time I stood beside my brother, the last time he held my flank and I his. For a time, then . . .' and his voice fell away, 'we were happy.'

Though Torrent knew nothing of these Wars of Shadow, nor the other players involved, he could not but hear the sorrow in Ruin's voice, and it stung him deep inside. *Fucking regrets. We all have them, don't we. Live long enough and maybe it's all we have, all we keep alive in our minds. Spirits below, what a miserable thought.*

But Olar Ethil had no room in her bag of bones for sentiment. She hacked out a laugh. 'Happy delivering death! Oh, you were all such righteous fools back then! And now among you and your brothers, only you remain, like a thorn no one can dig loose! Tell me the great cause you have espoused for yourself this time, Silchas Ruin. Tell me about all the regrettable but necessary deaths to shore up your grisly road! Do not think I won't cheer you on—nor this mortal beside me either, if one would purchase truth from his words. You are welcome to mayhem, Silchas Ruin! You and this flawed fire of a child at your side, and Kilava too, for that matter!'

At her outburst, Silchas frowned. 'Speak what you are hiding, bonecaster.'

'Gesture for gesture? Very well. Errastas has summoned the Elders. Sechul Lath, Kilmandaros, Mael—and now Draconus—yes! When you hide yourselves so well you yield your touch on this trembling world—you become blind. Your brother is dead, Silchas Ruin. Dragnipur is shattered. Draconus is loose upon the realm, Darkness in his hands—and what does his old lover see now that she sets eyes upon us all once more? Have you greeted your mother yet, Silchas? Have you felt her touch upon your brow? I thought not. She grieves for the son she cherished the most, I think. In whom the black flames of her love burned brightest. She reserves true spite and contempt for—'

Torrent's backhanded swing caught her full in the face, hard enough to knock her from her feet, falling in a clatter of bones. As he loomed over her, he found he'd drawn his sword. 'Spite, witch? Well, you'd know of it better than anyone. Now shut that bony jaw and keep it shut.'

Her black pitted eyes seemed to fix upon his own as if bearing claws, but he did not flinch. *Destruction? You scrawny bitch, I fear only its escape.* He stepped back and shot Silchas a glance.

The man looked so wounded it was a wonder he was still standing. He had wrapped his arms about his own torso, curled in and shrunken. The liquid that leaked down from his eyes traced crimson glints down his hollowed cheeks. Torrent saw Ryadd, his face ravaged with distress, take a step towards his companion, and then he wheeled to advance on Olar Ethil.

Torrent stepped into his path. 'Go back,' he said. 'Now is not the time. Console your friend, Ryadd. I will lead her away from here.'

The young warrior trembled, his eyes incandescent with fury. 'She will not—'

'Heed me? She will. Ryadd, the attacks are over—'

He started, eyes widening. 'Attacks.' Then he nodded. 'Yes, I see. Yes.' He nodded again, and then turned round, ready to give his youthful strength to an old man suddenly broken.

And so he surpasses, and leadership now belongs to him. Simple as that. Torrent sheathed his sword and swung up on to his horse. He gathered the reins, shot one last withering look upon Olar Ethil—who'd yet to move—and then kicked his mount into motion.

On to the trail of the wagon, east and south. He did not look back, but after a time he saw a spinning cloud of dust lift from a nearby rise. She was with him. *I see you, sweet as crotch rot, but will you even admit I probably just saved your sorry sack?*

Didn't think so.

As the sun painted gold the brutal facing of the stone tower, a figure of gold and bronze stood above another who knelt, bowed forward over his thighs with his face in his hands.

Neither moved until long after the sun set and darkness claimed the sky.

There had been an old man among the Barghast, brain-addled and prone to drag on to his shoulders a tattered, mangy wolf hide, and then fall to his hands and knees, as if at last he had found his true self. A beast incapable of speech beyond yips and howls, he would rush in amongst the camp dogs, growling, until he had subdued every bewildered, cowering animal. He had sought to do other things as well, but Setoc found even the memory of those to be too pitiful and painfully pathetic to revisit.

The giant plains wolf, Baaljagg, reminded her of that old man. Hide patched and rotted, in places hanging in mangled strips. Its muzzle was perpetually peeled back, revealing the massive oak-hued teeth and fangs, as if the entire world deserved an eternal challenge. The creature's black pitted eyeholes haunted her, speaking to her in eloquent silence: *I am death*, they said. *I am your fate and the fate of all living things. I am what is left behind. Departed from the world, I leave you only this.*

She wondered what had happened to that old man, to make him want to be a wolf. What wound stuck in his mind made him lose all sense of his true self? And why was there no going back, no finding that lost self? The mind held too many secrets. The brain was a sack of truths and their power, hiding there inside, was absolute. Twist one truth into a lie, and a man became a wolf. His flesh and bones could only follow, straining to reshape themselves. Two legs to four, teeth to fangs: new forms and new purposes to give proof to the falsehood.

But such lies need not be so obvious as that old man with his broken brain, need they? The self could become lost in more subtle ways, could it not? *Today I am this person. Tomorrow I am another. See the truths of me? Not one is tethered. I am bound to no single self, but unleashed into a multitude of selves. Does this make me ill? Broken?*

Is this why I can find no peace?

The twins walked five paces in front of her. They were one split in two. Sharp-eyed round faces peering into the mirror, where nothing could hide. Truths could bend but not twist.

I willingly followed Toc Anaster, even as I resented it. I have my very own addiction and it is called dissatisfaction. And each time it returns, everyone pays. Cafal, I let you down. I cried out my own failure of faith—I forced you to flee me. Where are you now, my soft-eyed priest?

Baaljagg's dead eyes fixed on her again and again as they walked. She lagged behind the twins. The boy's weight was making the muscles of her arms burn. She would have to set him down again, and so their pace would suddenly slow to a crawl. Everyone was hungry—even an undead wolf could find little to chase down out here. The withered grasses of the plains were long behind them now. Soil had given way to stones and hard-packed clay. Thorny shrubs clung here and there, their ancient trunks emerging from beds of cacti. Worn watercourses revealed desiccated pieces of driftwood, mostly no more substantial than the bones of her forearm; but occasionally they came upon something far larger, long and thick as a leg, and though she could not be certain she thought that they showed signs of having been worked. Boreholes large enough to insert a thumb—though of course to do so would invite a spider's bite or a scorpion's sting—and the faint scaly signs of adze marks. But none of these ancient streams could have borne a boat of any kind, not even a skiff or raft. She could make no sense of any of it.

The north horizon hinted at high towers of stone, like mountains gnawed through from every side, leaving the peaks tottering on narrow spires. They made her uneasy, as if warning her of something. *You are in a land that gives nothing. It will devour you, and there is no end to its vast hunger.*

They had made a terrible mistake. No, *she'd* made it. *He was leading us east, so we will go east. Why was he leading us in that direction? Stavi, I have no idea.*

But here is a truth I have found inside myself. All that dissatisfaction? It's not at Toc. It's not at anyone. It's with me. My inability to find peace, to trust it when I do find it, and to hold on to it.

This addiction feeds itself. It may be incurable.

Another rutted watercourse ahead—no . . . Setoc's eyes narrowed. Two ruts, churned up by horse hoofs. A track. The twins had seen the same, for they suddenly ran ahead, halting and looking down. Setoc didn't catch their words but both turned as she arrived, and in their faces they saw a hardening determination.

Storii pointed. 'It goes that way. It goes that way, Setoc.'

'So will we,' Stavi added.

Southeast, but curving ahead, she saw. *Eastward. What is out there? What are we supposed to find?*

'Blablablabla!' cried the boy, his loud voice—so close to one ear—making her flinch.

Baaljagg trotted out to sniff the trail. *Probably just instinct. The damned thing hasn't even got a working nose . . . has it? Maybe it smells different things. Life, or something else.*

When the twins set out on the path, the huge beast followed. The boy twisted in Setoc's arms and she lowered him to the ground. He ran to join his sisters.

Some leader I am.

At the turn she saw skid marks, where the wagon's wheels had spun and juddered out to the side, tearing at the ground. Here, the horse hoofs had gouged deep. But she could see no obstacle that would have forced such a manoeuvre. The way ahead ran straight for a hundred paces before jagging south again, only to twist east and then northeast.

At this Setoc snorted. 'They were out of control,' she said. 'They went where the horses dragged them. This is pointless—'

Stavi spun. 'We don't care where they're going!' she shouted. 'It doesn't matter!'

'But how can they help us if they can't even help themselves?' Setoc asked.

'What's so different about that?'

The bitchy little runt has a point. 'Look at those marks—they were riding wild, crazy fast. How do you expect we'll ever catch them?'

'Because horses get tired.'

They resumed their journey. Tracking the aimless with purpose. *Just like growing up.*

Stones crunched underfoot, the bridling heat making the gnarled stalks of the shrubs tick and creak. They were low on water. The meat of the lizards they'd eaten this morning felt dry and sour in Setoc's stomach. Not a single cloud in the sky to give them a moment's respite. She couldn't recall the last time she'd seen a bird.

Noon passed, the afternoon stretching as listless as the wasteland spreading out on all sides. The track had finally straightened out on an easterly setting. Even the twins were slowing down. All of their shadows had pitched round and were lengthening when Storii cried out and pointed.

A lone horse. South of the trail by two hundred or so paces. Remnants of traces dangled down from its head. It stood on weak legs, nuzzling the lifeless ground, and its ebon flanks were white with crusted lather.

Setoc hesitated, and then said, 'Keep Baaljagg here. I want to see if I can catch it.'

For once the twins had no complaint.

The animal was facing away but it caught some noise or scent when Setoc was still a hundred paces off and it shifted round to regard her. Its eyes, she saw, were strange, as if swallowed in something both lurid and dark. At least the animal didn't bolt.

Ghost wolves, stay away from me now. We need this beast.

Cautiously, she edged closer.

The horse watched. It had been eating cactus, she saw, and scores of spines were embedded in its muzzle, dripping blood.

Hungry. Starving. She spoke in low, soothing tones: 'How long have you been out here, friend? All alone, your companions gone. Do you welcome our company? I'm sure you do. As for those spines, we'll do something about that. I promise.'

And then she was close enough to reach out and touch the animal. But its eyes held her back. They didn't belong to a horse. They looked . . . *demonic.*

It's been eating cactus—how much? She looked to where she had seen it cropping the ground. *Oh, spirits below. If all that is now in your stomach, you are in trouble.* Did it look to be in pain? How could she tell? It was clearly weary, yes, but it drew a steady and deep breath, ears flicking curiously as it in turn studied her. Finally, Setoc slowly reached out to take the frayed leather traces. When she gathered them up the animal lifted its head, as if about to prod her with its wounded muzzle.

Setoc wrapped the reins about her left hand and gingerly took hold of one of the spines. She tugged it loose. The horse flinched. That and nothing more. Sighing, she began plucking.

If she licked the blood from the spines? What would the beast think of that? She decided not to find out. *Oh, but I dearly do want to lick this blood. My mouth yearns for that taste. I can smell its warm life.*

Old man, give me your skin.

When she'd removed the last spine she reached up and settled a hand on its blazoned brow. 'Better? I hope so, friend.'

'Mercy,' said a thin voice in accented trader tongue, 'I'd forgotten about that.'

Setoc stepped round the horse and saw, lying in a careless sprawl on the ground, a corpse. For an instant her breath caught—'Toc?'

'Who? No. Saw him, though, once. Funny eyes.'

'Does nothing dead ever go away around here?' Setoc demanded, fear giving way to anger.

'I don't know, but can you even hope to imagine the anguish people like me feel when seeing one such as you? Young, flush, with such clear and bright eyes. You make me miserable.'

Setoc drew the horse round.

'Wait! Help me up—I'm snagged on something. I don't mind being miserable, so long as I have someone to talk to. Being miserable without anyone to talk to is far worse.'

Really. Setoc walked over. Studied the corpse. 'You have a stake through your chest,' she said.

'A stake? Oh, a spoke, you mean. That explains it.'

'Does it?'

'Well, no. Things got confused. I believe, however, I am lying on a fragment of the hub, with perhaps another fragment of spoke buried deep in the earth. This is what happens when a carriage gets picked up and then dropped back down. I wonder if horses have much memory. Probably not, else this one would still be running. So, beautiful child, will you help me?'

She reached down. 'Take my arm, then—can you manage that much? Good, now hold tight while I try and lift you clear.'

It was easier than she'd expected. *Skin and bones don't weigh much, do they?*

'I am named Cartographer,' said the corpse, ineffectually trying to brush dust from his rags.

'Setoc.'

'So very pleased to meet you.'

'I thought I made you miserable.'

'I delight in misery.'

She grunted. 'You'll fit right in. Come with me.'

'Wonderful, where are you going?'

'We're going after your carriage—tell me, is everyone in it dead like you?'

Cartographer seemed to ponder the question, and then he said, 'Probably. But let's find out, shall we?'

The children of Onos Toolan and Hetan seemed unaffected by the arrival of yet another animated corpse. When Cartographer saw Baaljagg he halted and pointed, but said nothing.

Setoc took the boy's hand and led him close to the horse. She vaulted on to the animal's back and reached down and lifted up the boy.

The twins set out once more on the trail. Baaljagg fell in with them.

'Did you know,' Cartographer said, 'the dead still dream?'

'No,' said Setoc, 'I didn't know that.'

'Sometimes I dream that a dog will find me.'

'A dog?'

'Yes. A big one, as big as that one.'

'Well, it seems your dream has come true.'

'I hope not.'

She glanced down at him as he trudged beside the horse. 'Why?'

'Because, in my dream, the dog buries me.'

Thinking back to her vision of Baaljagg clawing free of the ground, she smiled. 'I don't think you have to worry about that, not with this dog, Cartographer.'

'I hope you are right. I do have one question, however.'

She sighed. *A corpse that won't shut up.* 'Go on.'

'Where are we?'

'The Wastelands.'

'Ah, that explains it, then.'

'Explains what?'

'Why, all this . . . waste.'

'Have you ever heard of the Wastelands, Cartographer?'

'No.'

'So let me ask you something. Where did your carriage come from, and how is it you don't even know the land you were travelling in?'

'Given my name, it is indeed pathetic that I know so little. Of course, this land was once an inland sea, but then one might say that of countless basins on any number of continents. So that hardly amounts to brilliant affirmation of my profession. Alas, since dying, I have been forced to radically reassess all my most cherished notions.'

'Are you ever going to answer my questions?'

'Our arrival was sudden, but Master Quell judged it propitious. The client expressed satisfaction and indeed no small amount of astonishment. Far better this wretched land than the realm within a cursed sword, and I would hardly be one to dispute that, would I? Maps being what they are and such. Naturally, it was inevitable that we let down our guard. Ah, see ahead. Ample evidence of that.'

The tracks seemed to vanish for fifteen or twenty paces. Where they resumed wreckage lay scattered about, including half an axle.

A lost horse and a lost wheel behind them, half an axle here—how had the thing managed to keep going? *And what was it doing in that gap? Flying?*

'Spirits below, Cartographer—' and then she stopped. From her height astride the horse, she could make something out ahead. Daylight was fading, but still . . . 'I see it.'

Two more stretches without tracks, then where they resumed various parts of ornate carriage lay strewn about. She saw one large section of painted wood, possibly from the roof, bearing deep gouges scored through it, as if some massive hand had been tearing the carriage to pieces. Some distance ahead rested the carriage itself, or what was left of it. The humped forms of dead horses lay thrown about to the sides.

'Cartographer—'

'It struck from the sky,' the corpse replied. 'Was it a dragon? It most assuredly was not. An enkar'al? What enkar'al could boldly lift from the ground the entire carriage and all its horses? No, not an enkar'al. Mind you, I was witness only to the first attack—tell me, Setoc, do you see anyone?'

'Not yet,' she replied. 'Stavi, Storii! Hold up there.' She lifted the boy and set him down on the ground. 'I will ride ahead. I know it's getting dark, but keep your eyes on the sky—there's something up there.' *Somewhere. Hopefully not close.*

The horse was nervous beneath her, reluctant to draw nearer to the carriage, but she coaxed it on.

Its fellow beasts had been torn apart, bones splintered, gouges of flesh missing. Everywhere those same thin but deep slashes. Talons. Enormous and deadly sharp.

She found the first corpse, a man. He had wrapped the ends of the traces about his forearms and both arms were horribly dislocated, almost pulled free of the shoulders. Something had slashed through his head diagonally, from above, she judged. Through his skullcap helm, down along one side of the nose and out beneath the jaw, leaving him with half a face. Just beyond him was another man, neatly decapitated—she couldn't see the head anywhere close by.

She halted her mount a few paces from the destroyed carriage. It had been huge, six-wheeled, likely weighing as much as a clan yurt with the entire family shoved inside. The attacker had systematically dismantled it from one flank, as if eager to get within. Blood stained the edges of the gaping hole it had made.

Setoc clambered up to peer inside. No body. But a mass of something was heaped on the side that was now the floor, gleaming wet in the gloom. She waited for her eyes to adjust. Then, in revulsion, she pulled back. Entrails. An occupant had been eviscerated. Where was the rest of the poor victim? She perched herself on the carriage and scanned the area.

There. Half of him, anyway. The upper half.

And then she saw tracks, the ground scuffed, three or four paths converging to form a broader one, and that one led away from the wreckage, eastward. *Survivors. But they must have been on the run, else they would have done more for their dead. Still, a few made it . . . for a little while longer, anyway.*

She descended from the carriage and mounted the horse. 'Sorry, friend, but it looks like you're the last.' Swinging the horse round, she rode back to the others.

'How many bodies?' Cartographer asked when she arrived.

'Three for certain. Tracks lead away.'

'Three, you say?'

'That I saw. Two on the ground, one in the carriage—or, rather, bits of him left in the carriage.'

'A man? A man in the carriage?'

'Yes.'

'Oh, dear. That is very bad indeed.'

Returning to the wreckage, Cartographer moved to stand over each victim, shaking his head and muttering in low tones—possibly a prayer—Setoc wasn't close enough to hear his words. He rejoined her once they were past.

'I find myself in some conflict,' he said. 'On the one hand, I wish I'd been here to witness that dread clash, to see Trake's Mortal Sword truly awakened. To see the Trell's rage rise from the deepness of his soul. On the other hand, witnessing the gruesome deaths of those I had come to know as friends, well, that would have been terrible. As much as it grieves me to say, there are times when getting what one wants yields nothing but confusion. It turns out that what one wants is in fact not at all what one wants. Worse is when you simply don't know what you want. You'd think death would discard such trials. If only it did.'

'There's blood on this trail,' said Setoc.

'I wish that surprised me. Still, they must have succeeded in driving the demon away, in itself an extraordinary feat.'

'How long ago did all this happen?'

'Not long. I was lying on the ground from midmorning. I imagine we'll find them—'

'We already have,' she said. 'They've camped.'

She could see the faint glow of a small fire, and now figures straightening, turning to study them. The sun was almost down behind Setoc and her companions, so she knew the strangers were seeing little more than silhouettes. She raised a hand in greeting, urging her mount forward with a gentle tap of her heels.

Two of the figures were imposing: one broad and bestial, his skin the hue of burnished mahogany, his black braided hair hanging in greasy coils. He was holding a two-handed mace. The other was taller, his skin tattooed in the stripes of a tiger, and as Setoc drew closer, she saw a feline cast to his features, including amber eyes bisected by vertical pupils. The two heavy-bladed swords in his hands matched the barbed patterns of his skin.

Three others were visible, two women and a tall, young man. He was long-jawed and long-necked, with blood-matted hair. A knotted frown marred his high forehead, above dark, angry eyes. He stood slightly apart from all the others.

Setoc's eyes returned to the two women. Both short and plump, neither one much older than Setoc herself. But their eyes looked aged: bleak, dulled with shock.

Two more survivors were lying close to the fire, asleep or unconscious.

The bestial man was the first to speak, addressing Cartographer but not in a language that Setoc recognized. The undead man replied in the same tongue, and then turned to Setoc.

'Mappo Runt welcomes you with a warning. They are being hunted.'

'I know,' she said. 'Cartographer, you seem to have a talent for languages—'

'Hood's gift, for the tasks he set upon me. Mappo addresses me in a Daru dialect, a trader's cant. He does so to enable his companions to understand his words, as they are Genabackan, while he is not.'

'What is he, then?'

'Trell, Setoc—'

'And the striped one—what manner of creature is he?'

'Trake's Mortal Sword—'

'Meaning what?'

'Ah. Trake is the Tiger of Summer, a foreign god. Gruntle is the god's chosen mortal weapon.'

The one Cartographer had named Gruntle now spoke, his eerie eyes fixed upon Setoc. She noted that he had not sheathed his swords, whilst the Trell had set down his mace.

'Setoc,' said Cartographer after Gruntle had finally finished, 'the Mortal Sword names you Destriant of Fanderay and Togg, the Wolves of Winter. You are, in a sense, kin. Another servant of war. Yet, though Trake may view you and your Lady and Lord as mortal enemies, Gruntle does not. Indeed, he says, he holds his own god in no high esteem, nor is he pleased with . . . er, well, he calls it a curse. Accordingly, you are welcome and need not fear him. Conversely,' Cartographer then added, 'if you seek violence then he will oblige your wish.'

Setoc found her heart was pounding hard and rapid in her chest. Her mouth was suddenly dry. *Destriant. Have I heard that word before? Did Toc so name me? Or was it someone else?* 'I am not interested in violence,' she said.

When Cartographer relayed her reply, Gruntle glanced once at the undead

wolf standing between the twins—Baaljagg's bristled back was unmistakable—
and then the Mortal Sword momentarily bared impressive fangs, before nodding
once and sheathing his weapons. And then he froze, as the twins' brother toddled
forward, seemingly heading straight for Gruntle.

'Klavklavklavklav!'

Setoc saw the Trell start at that, turning to study the boy who now stood
directly in front of Gruntle with arms outspread.

'He wants Gruntle to pick him up,' Setoc said.

'I'm sure Gruntle can see that,' said Cartographer. 'A most fearless child. The
word he seeks is Imass. I did not think such things even existed. Imass children,
I mean.'

Gruntle snatched up the boy, who yelped in delight, filling the night air with
laughter.

Setoc heard Baaljagg's low growl and glanced over. Although the undead
beast made no move, the black pits of its eyes were fixed—as much as could be
determined—upon the Mortal Sword and the child he held. 'Getting killed once
wasn't enough?' she asked the giant wolf. 'The pup needs no help.'

The twins had edged closer to Setoc, who now dismounted. 'It's all right,' she
said to them.

'Mother said cats were teeth and claws without brains,' said Storii. She pointed
at Gruntle. 'He looks like his mother slept with a cat.'

'Your brother isn't afraid.'

'Too stupid to be scared,' said Stavi.

'These ones,' said Setoc, 'fought off the sky demon, but they didn't kill it, else
we would have found the carcass. Would we be safer with or without them?'

'I wish Toc was here.'

'So do I, Storii.'

'Where were they going, anyway? There's nothing in the Wastelands.'

At Storii's question Setoc shrugged. 'I can't quite get an answer to that yet, but
I will keep trying.'

The two women had returned to tending their wounded companions. The tall
young man remained off to one side, looking agitated. Setoc stepped closer to
Cartographer. 'What is wrong with that man?'

'It is, I am told, ever a misjudgement to view a Bole of the Mott Irregulars with
contempt. Amby is angry and that anger is slow to fade. His brother is sorely
wounded, near death, in fact.'

'Does he blame Gruntle or Mappo for that?'

'Hardly. Oh, I gather that both of those you speak of fought valiantly against
the sky demon—certainly, the Mortal Sword is made for such encounters. But
neither Gruntle nor Mappo succeeded in driving the creature away. The Boles despise such things as demons and the like. And once awakened to anger, they
prove deadly against such foes. Precious Thimble calls it a fever. But Master Quell
suggested that the Boles themselves are the spawn of sorcery, perhaps a Jaghut
creation gone awry. Would that explain the Boles' extravagant hatred for Jaghut?

Possibly. In any case, it was Amby and Jula Bole who sent the demon fleeing. But the residue of that fury remains in Amby, suggesting that he maintains his readiness should the demon be foolish enough to return.'

Setoc studied the man with renewed interest, and more than a little disbelief. *What did he do to it, bite it with those huge front teeth?*

Cartographer then said, 'Earlier, you mentioned Toc. We here all know him. Indeed, it was Toc who guided us from the realm of Dragnipur. And Gruntle, why, he once got drunk with Toc Anaster—that would be before Toc got himself killed, one presumes.'

The twins were listening to this, and Setoc saw relief in their eyes. *More friends of Toc. Will that do, girls?* Seemed it would.

'Cartographer, what is a Destriant?'

'Ah. Well. A Destriant is one who is chosen from among all mortals to wear the skin of a god.'

'The—the skin?'

'Too poetic? Let me think, then. Look into the eyes of a thousand priests. If there is a Destriant among that thousand, you will find him or her. How? The truth is in their eyes, for you shall, in looking into those eyes, find yourself looking upon the god's own.'

'Toc bears a wolf's eye.'

'Because he is the Herald of War.'

The title chilled her. 'Then why is his other eye not a wolf's eye, too?'

'It was human, I'm sure.'

'Exactly. Why?'

Cartographer made the mistake of scratching his temple, and came away with a swath of crinkled skin impaled on his fingernails. He fluttered his fingers to send it drifting away into the night. 'Because, I imagine, humans are the true heralds of war, don't you think?'

'Maybe.' But she wasn't so sure. 'Toc was leading us into the east. If he's the Herald of War, as you say, then . . .'

Cartographer nodded. 'I should think so, Setoc. He was leading you to a place and a time where you will be needed.'

As Destriant to the Wolves of Winter. To gods of war. She looked over to where Baaljagg stood, just beyond the firelight. Deathly and deathly still, the huge teeth for ever bared, the eyes for ever empty.

The skin of war.

And I am to wear it. Her attention snapped over to Gruntle. 'Cartographer.'

'Yes?'

'He said he holds his god in no high esteem. He said he calls what he is a curse.'

'That is true.'

'I need to talk to him.'

'Of course, Setoc.'

The Mortal Sword had sat down by the fire, with the boy perched on one bouncing knee. The barbed tattoos seemed to have inexplicably faded, as had the feline traits of his features. The man looked almost human now, barring the eyes. There was quiet pleasure in the face.

What would Onos Toolan have made of this? Toc, were you bringing us to these ones? She sighed. *The skin of war. The Wolves want me to wear it.*

But I do not.

'Take me to him, please.'

Mappo glanced over to see the young woman crouching opposite Gruntle, with Cartographer providing translations. No doubt they had much to discuss. An unknown war in the offing, a clash of desperate mortals and, perhaps, desperate gods. *And Icarium? Old friend, you must have no place in what is coming. If thousands needlessly die by your hand, what dire balance would that tip? What cruel fate would that invite? No. I must find you. Take you away. Already, too many have died on your trail.*

He heard a ragged sigh to his left. Angling round, he studied the woman lying on a bedroll. 'You will live, Faint,' he said.

'Then—then—'

'You did not reach him in time. If you had, you would be the one now dead, rather than Master Quell.'

She reached up to her own face, dragged her nails to scrape away the blood crusting the corners of her mouth. 'Better for you if I had. Now we are stranded.'

He might have replied, *But we are now so close. I can feel him—we are almost there.* But that was a selfish thought. Delivering Mappo was but half the task. These poor shareholders needed to find a way home, and now they had lost the one man capable of achieving that. So, to Faint's statement, he had nothing to say.

'My chest hurts,' she said.

'The Che'Malle struck you, its claws scoring deep. I have sewn almost three hundred stitches, from your right shoulder to below your rib cage on the left.'

She seemed to think about that for a moment, and then she said, 'So we've seen the last of Faint's bouncing tits.'

'You did not lose them, if that is what you fear. They will still, er, bounce, if perhaps unevenly.'

'So the gods really do exist. Listen. Precious Thimble—is she still alive?'

'Yes.'

'Then we have a chance.'

Mappo winced. 'She is young, Faint, mostly untutored—'

'There's a chance,' Faint insisted. 'Beru's black nipples, this *hurts*.'

'She will attempt some healing, in a while,' said Mappo. 'It took all of her strength just to keep Jula alive.'

Faint grunted and then gasped. Recovering, she said, 'Guilt will do that.'

Mappo nodded. The Bole brothers had followed Precious Thimble into this Guild, and she had joined on a whim, or, more likely, to see how far her two would-be lovers would go in their pursuit of her. When love turned into a game, people got hurt, and Precious Thimble had finally begun to comprehend the truth of that. *You took them too far, didn't you?*

At the same time without the Boles none of them here would be alive right now. Mappo still found it difficult to believe that a mortal man's fists could do the damage he'd seen from Jula and Amby Bole. They had simply launched themselves on to the winged Che'Malle, and those oversized knuckles had struck with more power than Mappo's own mace. He had heard bones crack beneath those blows, had heard the Che'Malle's gasps of shock and pain. When it lashed out, it had been in frantic self-defence, a blind panic to dislodge its frenzied attackers. The creature's talons, each one as long as a Semk scimitar, had plunged into Jula's back, the four tips erupting from the man's chest. It had flung the man away—and at that moment Amby's lashing fists found the Che'Malle's throat. Those impacts would have crushed the neck of a horse, and they proved damaging enough to force the Che'Malle into the air, wings thundering. A back-handed blow scraped Amby off and then the thing was lifting upward.

Gruntle, who appeared to have been the Che'Malle's original target—carried off in the first attack and presumed by the others to be dead—had then returned, an apparition engulfed in the rage of his god. Veered into the form of an enormous tiger, its shape strangely blurred and indistinct except for the barbs that writhed like tongues of black flame, he had launched himself into the air in an effort to drag down the Che'Malle. But it eluded him and then, wings hammering, it fled skyward.

Mappo subsequently learned from Gruntle—once his fury was past, something like his human form returning—that his first battle with the thing had been a thousand reaches above the Wastelands, and when the Che'Malle failed to slay him, it had simply dropped him earthward. Gruntle had veered into his Soletaken form in mid-air. He now complained of bruised, throbbing joints, but Mappo knew it was a fall that should have killed him. *Trake intervened. No other possible explanation serves.*

He thought again about that horrifying creature, reiterating his own conviction that it was indeed some breed of K'Chain Che'Malle, though not one he had ever seen before, nor even heard of from those more intimate with the ancient race. It was twice the height of a K'ell Hunter, although gaunter. Its wingspan matched that of a middle-aged Eleint, yet where among dragons those wings served to aid speed and direct their manoeuvring in the air—with sorcery in effect carrying the dragon's massive weight—for this Che'Malle all lift was produced by those wings. And its weight was but a fraction of an Eleint's. *Gods, it was fast. And such strength!* In its second attack, after Gruntle was gone, the Che'Malle had simply lifted the entire carriage into the air, horses and all. If the carriage's frame had not splintered in its grip, the beast would have carried them all skyward, until it reached a height from which a fall would be fatal. Simple and effective. The Che'Malle had attempted the tactic a few more times, before finally descending to do battle.

To its regret.

And, it must be admitted, ours as well. Glanno Tarp was dead. So too Reccanto Ilk. And of course Master Quell. When Mappo had reached the carriage to pull Precious Thimble from the interior cabin, she had been hysterical—Quell had interposed himself between her and the attacking Che'Malle, and it had simply eviscerated him. If not for the Boles leaping on to its back, it would have slain her as well. Mappo still bore slashes on his hands and wrists from the woman's blind terror.

The carriage had proved beyond mundane repair. There had been no choice but to continue on foot, carrying away their wounded, with the threat of another attack ever looming over them.

Still, I think the Boles hurt it.

That Che'Malle, it wasn't out here waiting for us. Its attack was opportunistic—what else could it have been? No, the creature has other tasks awaiting it. For all I know, it too is hunting Icarium, a possibility too terrible to consider. In any case, let us hope it has now concluded we're too much trouble.

His eyes strayed to his mace, lying on the ground close to hand. He had managed to strike the Che'Malle one solid blow, enough to rock it back a step. It had felt as if his mace had collided with an iron obelisk. His shoulders still ached. *The eye looks past the target, to where the weapon is intended to reach. When it fails, shock thunders through the body. Every muscle, every bone. I can't even remember the last time it so utterly failed.*

'Who are these strangers?' Faint asked.

Mappo sighed. 'I am not sure. There is an undead ay with them.'

'A what?'

'An ancient wolf, from the age of the Imass. Their bloodline was harvested in the shaping of the Hounds of Shadow . . . but not the Hounds of Darkness. For those, it was the bloodline of a breed of plains bear. *Ty'nath okral*, in the language of the Bentract Imass.'

'An undead wolf?'

'Pardon? Oh, yes, called an *ay* when alive. Now? Perhaps a *maeth ay*, one of rot or decay. Or one could say an *oth ay*, referring to its skeletal state. For myself, I think I prefer *T'ay*—a broken ay, if you will—'

'Mappo, I really don't care what you call it. It's an undead wolf, something to keep Cartographer company—he's back, right? I'm sure I heard him—'

'Yes. He guided these others to us and now interprets.'

'They don't speak Daru? Barbarians.'

'Yet two of them—those twin girls—they possess Daru blood. I am almost certain of it. The boy now clinging to Gruntle, there is Imass in him. More than half, I would judge. Therefore, either his mother or father was probably Barghast. The leader among them—she is named Setoc and proclaimed by Gruntle to be the Destriant of the Wolves—reminds me of a Kanese, though she is not. Some scenes painted on the oldest of tombs on the north coast of Seven Cities display people much like her in appearance, from the time before the tribes came out of the desert, one presumes.'

'You're trying to keep me awake, aren't you?'

'You landed on your head, Faint. For a time there, you spoke in tongues.'

'I did what?'

'Well, it was a mix of languages, sixteen that I could identify, and some others I could not. An extraordinary display, Faint. There is a scholar who states that we possess every language, deep within our minds, and that the potential exists for perhaps ten thousand languages in all. She would have delighted in witnessing your feat. Then there is a *dystigier*, a dissector of human corpses, living in Ehrlitan, who claims that the brain is nothing more than a clumped mass of snarled chains. Most links are fused, but some are not. Some can be prised open and fitted anew. Any major head injury, he says, can result in a link breaking. This is usually permanent, but on rare occasions a new link is forged. Chains, Faint, packed inside our skull.'

'Only they don't look like chains, do they?'

'No, alas, they don't. It is the curse of theory disconnected from physical observation. Of course, Icarium would argue that one should not always test theory solely on the basis of pragmatic observation. Sometimes, he would say, theory needs to be interpreted more poetically, as metaphor, perhaps.'

'I have a metaphor for you, Mappo.'

'Oh?'

'A woman lies on the ground, brain addled, listening to a hairy Trell with tusks discussing possible interpretations of theory. What does this mean?'

'I don't know, but whatever it may be, I doubt it would qualify as a metaphor.'

'I'm sure you're right, since I don't even know what a metaphor is, truth be told. Try this, then. The woman listens to all that, but she knows her brain is addled. So, just how addled is it? Is it so addled that she actually believes she's listening to a hairy Trell spouting philosophy?'

'Ah, perhaps a tautology, then. Or some other manner of unprovable proof. Then again, it might well be something else entirely. Though I am occasionally philosophical, I do not claim to be a philosopher. The distinction is important, I'm sure.'

'If you really want to keep me awake, Mappo, find a new subject.'

'Do you truly believe Precious Thimble is capable of taking you back to Darujhistan?'

'If she isn't we're stuck and it's time to start learning the local tongue from Setoc. But she can't be from here anyway, can she? This land is blasted. Quell says it's used up. Exhausted. No one can live here.'

'The cut of Setoc's clothing is Barghast,' said Mappo. He scratched the bristle on his jaw. 'And since that boy has, I think, Barghast blood . . .' He raised his voice and, in Barghast, called over to Setoc, 'Do we share this language between us, Destriant Setoc?'

At the question all four newcomers looked over. And Setoc said, 'It seems we do.'

'Nice guess,' said Faint.

'Observation and theory,' Mappo replied. 'Now, you can rest for a short time. I mean to get the story of these strangers. I will be back to wake you anon.'

'Can't wait,' Faint muttered.

'If no solution serves,' ventured Shield Anvil Tanakalian, 'then what remains to us? We must proceed on the path we have always known, until some other alternative presents itself.' He held his gaze on the entourage of Queen Abrastal as it slowly drew closer, the dozen or so horses gently cantering across the uneven ground, the pennons above the riders flapping like impaled birds.

Beside him, Mortal Sword Krughava shifted heavily on her saddle. Leather creaked, iron scraped. 'The absence haunts,' she said. 'It gapes at our side, sir.'

'Then choose one, Mortal Sword. Be done with it.'

Her expression darkened beneath the rim of her helm. 'You truly advise this, Shield Anvil? Am I to be so desperate as to be careless? Must I swallow my dissatisfaction? I have done this once already, sir, and I begin to find regret in that.'

Once already? You miserable witch. I took that sour face of yours to be the one you always wear. Now you tell me I was a choice made without confidence. Did that old man talk you into it, then? But between you and me, woman, only I was witness to his bitter dissatisfaction at the very end. So, in your mind he still argues in my favour. Well enough. 'It grieves me, Mortal Sword, to hear you say this. I do not know how I have failed you, nor do I know what reparation remains available to me.'

'My indecision, sir, stings you into impatience. You urge action without contemplation, but if the selection of a new Destriant does not demand contemplation, what possibly can? In your mind, it would seem, these are but titles. Responsibilities one grows into, as it were. But the truth of it is, the title awaits only those who have already grown into a person worthy of the responsibility. From you, I receive all the irritation of a young man convinced of his own rightness, as young men generally are, said conviction leading you into rash impulses and ill-considered advice. Now I ask that you be silent. The Queen arrives.'

Tanakalian struggled against his fury, endeavouring to hold flat his expression in the face of the Bolkando riders. *You strike me in the moment before this parley, to test my self-control. I know all your tactics, Mortal Sword. You shall not best me.*

Queen Abrastal wasted little time. 'We have met with the Saphii emissary, and I am pleased to inform you that resupply is forthcoming—at a reasonable price, I might add. Generous of them, all things considered.'

'Indeed, Highness,' said Krughava.

'Furthermore,' Abrastal continued, 'the Malazan columns have been sighted by the Saphii, almost due north of the Saphii Mountains, approaching the very edge of the Wastelands. They have made good time. Curiously, your allies are with escort— none other than Prince Brys Beddict, in command of a Letherii army.'

'I see,' said Krughava. 'And this Letherii army now marches well beyond Lether's borders, suggesting their role as escort was not precautionary.'

The Queen's eyes sharpened. 'As I said, most curious, Mortal Sword.' She paused, and then said, 'It has become obvious to me that, of all the luminaries involved in this escapade, I alone remain ignorant.'

'Highness?'

'Well, you are all marching *somewhere*, yes? Into the Wastelands, no less. And through them, in fact, into Kolanse. My warnings to you of the grim—no, horrifying—situation in that distant land appear to have gone unheeded.'

'On the contrary, Queen Abrastal,' said Krughava, 'we heed them most assiduously, and hold your concern in the highest regard.'

'Then answer me, do you march to win yourselves an empire? Kolanse, weakened so by internal strife, drought and starvation, must present to you an easy conquest. Surely, you cannot imagine such a beleaguered people to be your deadliest enemy? You've never even been there. If,' she added, 'you were wondering why I am still with you and the Khundryl, so far from my own realm and still weeks to go before our grand parley with the Adjunct, perhaps now you can surmise my reasons.'

'Curiosity?' Krughava asked, brows lifting.

A flash of irritation lit Abrastal's features.

Yes, Queen, I know how you feel.

'A more apt description would be *unease*. As co-ruler of Bolkando, it is my responsibility to hold tight the reins of my people. I am well aware of the human tendency towards chaos and cruelty. The very purpose of rule, as I hold it, is to enforce civility. To achieve this, I must begin with a personal adherence to the same. Does it distress me that I am perhaps aiding a horde of rabid conquerors? Does it sit well with my conscience that I am assisting in the invasion of a distant kingdom?'

'At the earning of vast profits from us,' Krughava said. 'One would conclude that much civility can be purchased for yourself, Highness, and for your people. At no direct cost or burden to you, I might add.'

She was genuinely angry now, Tanakalian could see, this hard, clear-eyed Queen sitting astride her horse in the insignia of a soldier. *A true ruler of her people. A true servant of the same.*

'Mortal Sword, I am speaking of *conscience*.'

'It was my understanding, Highness, that coin in sufficient quantities could salve anything. Is this not the belief dominating Lether and Saphinand, and indeed Bolkando?'

'Then you do in truth seek to descend upon the poor people of Kolanse?'

'If it is so, Highness, should you not be relieved? After all, even without the Malazans, we were at the very walls of your capital. To win ourselves a kingdom . . . well, yours was entirely within our reach. Without need for further marching and all the hardships that entails. As for the Malazans, why, they have just completed a successful conquest of the Empire of Lether. A most opulent nest, were they inclined to settle in it.'

'This is precisely my point!' Abrastal snapped, tugging her helm to loose a cascade of fiery, sweat-strung hair. '*Why Kolanse? What in the Errant's name do you want with Kolanse?*'

'Highness,' said Krughava, unperturbed by the Queen's uncharacteristic out-burst, 'an answer to that question would find you in a difficult situation.'

'Why?'

'Because you speak to me of conscience. By withholding explanation of our purpose, Highness, we leave to you the comfort of the solitary consideration of your own people. You are their Queen, after all, and therein lies the crucial dif-ference between us. We Perish begin and end with responsibility only to our-selves, and to the purpose of our existence. The same is true for Warleader Gall and the Burned Tears. And finally and most importantly, an identical circumstance obtains among the Bonehunters.' She cocked her head a fraction. 'Prince Brys, however, may soon find himself facing a difficult decision—to return to Lether or to continue accompanying the Adjunct and her allies.'

'And so,' retorted Abrastal, 'in serving only yourselves, you are prepared to de-liver misery and suffering upon a broken people?'

'While this is not our desire, Highness, it may well come to that.'

In the shocked silence that followed, Tanakalian saw the Queen's eyes flatten, and then a frown slowly knot her brow. The skittering clouds of uncertainty edged into her expression. When she spoke it was a whisper. 'You will not explain yourself to me, will you, Mortal Sword?'

'You have the truth of that, Highness.'

'You say you serve none but yourselves. The assertion rings false.'

'I am sorry you think so,' Krughava replied.

'In fact,' Abrastal went on, 'I now begin to suspect the very opposite.'

The Mortal Sword said nothing.

You have the truth of it, Tanakalian silently answered, mocking Krughava's own words. *What we do is not in service to ourselves, but to all of you.*

Can anything be more glorious? And if we must fall, if we must fail, as I be-lieve we will, is no end sweeter than that? The grandest failure this world has ever seen.

Yes, we all know the tale of Coltaine's Fall outside Aren. But what we shall find at the end of our days will beggar that tale. We seek to save the world, and the world will do all it can to stop us. Watch us lose. Watch us squeeze the blood from your stony heart!

But no. There shall be none to witness. If existence itself can be said to be po-etic, we stand in that silence, unyielding servants to anonymity. None to see, none to even know. Not a single grave, nor stone lifted to cast shade upon our scattered bones. Neither hill nor tomb. We shall rest in emptiness, not forgotten—for forgetting follows remembrance, and there shall be no remembrance.

His heart thundered with the delicious beauty of it—all of it. *The perfect hero is one whose heroism none sees. The most precious glory is the glory lost on sense-less winds. The highest virtue is the one that remains for ever hidden within one-self. Do you understand that, Mortal Sword? No, you do not.*

He watched, flushed with satisfaction, as Queen Abrastal gathered her reins and pitched her horse about with a vicious twist. The entire entourage hastened to follow. The gentle canter was gone, awkward jostling knotting the troop like a hand twisting cloth, stretching out confused behind their departing Queen.

'Gift me with your wisdom, Shield Anvil.'

Her dry request made him start. The flush of heat in his face suddenly fed darker feelings. 'They will leave us, Mortal Sword. The Bolkando are done with us.'

She snorted. 'How long must I wait?'

'For what, Mortal Sword?'

'For wisdom in my Shield Anvil.'

They were as good as alone, the Perish camp settled behind them. 'It seems I can say nothing that pleases you, Mortal Sword.'

'Queen Abrastal needs to understand what we intend. She cannot let it go. Now, she will maintain her resolve, in the hope that the Adjunct Tavore will provide her with satisfaction.'

'And will she?'

'What do you think, Shield Anvil?'

'I think Queen Abrastal will be a very frustrated woman.'

'Finally. Yes.'

'The Adjunct is selfish,' said Tanakalian.

Krughava's head snapped round. 'Excuse me?'

'She could invite others to share in this glory—this Evertine Legion of the Queen's, it looks to be a formidable army. Well-trained, capable of marching in step with us—unlike the Conquestor Avalt's soldiers. Were they to stand at our side in Kolanse—'

'Sir,' cut in the Mortal Sword, 'if the Adjunct is selfish—for what you clearly imagine to be a glorious achievement—then it may serve you better to consider that selfishness as one of unprecedented mercy.'

'I am aware of the likely outcome of this venture, Mortal Sword. Perhaps more than even you. I know the souls awaiting me—I see their mortal faces every day. I see the hope they settle upon me. Nor am I regretful that what we seek shall be unwitnessed, for with our brothers and sisters, *I* am their witness. When I spoke of the Adjunct's selfishness, I did not mean it as a criticism; rather, I was indicating the privilege I feel in her permitting the Grey Helms to share her fate.'

Krughava's bright blue eyes were fixed on him, calculating, thoughtful. 'I understand, sir. You await the death of the Grey Helms. While you look upon them and see naught but their souls soon to be gifted to you, what do they see in the eyes of their Shield Anvil?'

'I shall honour them all,' Tanakalian replied.

'Will you?'

'Of course. I am Shield Anvil—'

'Will you embrace the soul of every brother and sister? Free of judgement? Unsullied in your love for each and every one of them? And what of our enemies, sir? Will you take them into your arms as well? Will you accept that suffering defies boundaries and that pain carves no line in the sand?'

He was silent. How could he answer her? She would see the lie. Tanakalian looked away. 'I am Shield Anvil to the Perish Grey Helms. I serve the Wolves of Winter. I am the mortal flesh of war, not the sword in its hand.' He glanced back at her. 'Do I crowd your throne, Mortal Sword? Is that what all this is about?'

Her eyes widened. 'You have given me much to consider, Shield Anvil. Leave me now.'

As he walked back into the camp, he drew a deep breath and shakily let it out. She was dangerous, but then he'd always known that. *She actually thinks we can win. Well, I suppose that is the role of the Mortal Sword. She is welcome to the delusion—no doubt it will serve well our brothers and sisters when the Wolves howl. As for me, I cannot be so blind, so wilfully defiant of the truth.*

We can manage this between us, Mortal Sword. I will follow your will in not choosing a Destriant. Why share the glory? Why muddle things at all?

A difficult, searing conversation, but he'd survived it yet. *Yes, now we understand each other.*

It is well.

After the Shield Anvil was gone, the Mortal Sword stood for a time, eyes on the gloom rising skyward in the east. Then she turned and gestured with one gauntleted hand. A runner quickly joined her.

'Send word to Warleader Gall, I will visit him this evening, one bell after supper.'

The soldier bowed and departed.

She studied the eastern horizon once more. The mountains surrounding the kingdom of Saphinand formed a jagged wall to the north, but there in the place of dark's birth, there was no hint of anything but level plain. The Wastelands.

She would suggest to Gall that they march hard now, taking up stores from the Saphii traders as they went. It was imperative that they link up with the Adjunct as soon as possible. This was one of the matters she wished to discuss with Gall. There were others.

A long, sleepless night awaited her.

The Gilk Warchief grinned as he watched Queen Abrastal ride back into the camp. Firehair indeed. Flames were ready to spit out from her, from every place an imaginative man might imagine, and of course he was a most imaginative man. But a woman like that, well, far beyond his reach and more's the pity as far as he was concerned.

Spultatha had emerged from his tent behind him and now edged up on his right. Her eyes, so like her mother's, narrowed as they tracked the woman's approach. 'Trouble,' she said. 'Stay away from her, Spax, for this night at least.'

His grin broadened. 'Afraid I can't do that, wildcat.'

'Then you're a fool.'

'Keep the furs warm,' he said, setting out for the Queen's pavilion. Soldiers of the Evertine Legion watched him stride past their posts, and he was reminded of a pet lion he'd once seen in the camp of another clan. It had had the freedom of the camp and was in the habit of sauntering back and forth in front of the cages crowded with hunting dogs. Those beasts were driven into a frenzy, flinging themselves bloody and stupid against the iron bars. He'd always admired that lion, its perfect insouciant strut, its lolling tongue and the itch that always made it pause directly opposite the cages, for a leisurely scratch and then a broad yawn.

Let the eyes track him, let them glitter beneath the rims of their helms. He knew these soldiers so wanted to test themselves against the White Face Barghast. Against the Gilk, who were the match of any civilized heavy infantry unit anywhere in the world. But they had little chance of ever doing so. The next best thing was to stand beside them, and that was a competition the Gilk well understood.

Now we shall see what will come to pass. Do we all march to a place of battle against an enemy? Who will stand fastest? Evertine, Grey Helms, Khundryl, or the Gilk? Hah. Spax reached the inner cordon and grunted a nod when the last bodyguard outside the pavilion stepped to one side. He strode into the silk-walled corridor with all its pale tones backlit by lanterns, and as always felt he was walking through colour itself, soft and dry and strangely cool, one flavour after another.

One of her trusted lieutenants stood at the last portal. As Spax approached, the lieutenant shook his head. 'Can it not wait, Warchief?'

'No, Gaedis. Why, is she bathing?'

'If she is, the water's long since boiled away.'

What did that iron woman say to Abrastal? 'Brave enough to announce me, Gaedis?'

'It's not bravery that makes me say yes, Warchief, but then stupidity's gotten me this far and I'm a conservative man.'

'The offer still stands,' Spax said.

'I doubt my Queen would take kindly to one of her court lieutenants shucking all this to wear turtle shells and dance naked under the moon.'

Spax smiled. 'Saw that, did you?'

Gaedis nodded.

'It was a show, you understand. Don't you?'

'Warchief?'

'The Queen's clutch of scholars—we made something up to give them something to write about and then ponder its meaning for the rest of their dull, useless lives. Spirits below, a man's grapes get tiny in the cold night—why'd you think we kept jumping over the fire?'

After a moment's gimlet regard, Gaedis turned and slipped through the drapery.

Spax hummed softly to himself.

Gaedis's muffled voice invited him to enter the Royal Presence. *Naked in the bowl?* wondered Spax. *Bah, the gods are never so kind.*

She stood in her underquilting, armour discarded, her long hair still tousled from the ride. The quilting was tight against her curves. 'If eyes were paint,' Abrastal said, 'I'd be dripping right now. Barbaric bastard. What's so important you'd dare my ill humour?'

'Just this, Highness,' Spax replied. 'She struck sparks from you and I want to know how, and why.'

'Ah, you're curious, then.'

'That's it, Firehair.'

'If it wasn't that your rabid warriors might complain, I'd see you strangled with your own entrails and perhaps—just perhaps—that would satisfy my desire in this moment. Arrogance is a strange thing, Spax. It amuses when it cannot reach, then stings to rage when it can. What in the Errant's empty skull convinced you that I'd yield to your shit-fouled curiosity?'

Spax glanced across at Gaedis, saw the man's face and the expression that seemed carved from stone. *Coward.* 'Highness, I am Warchief of the Gilk. Each day I am under siege from the clan leaders, not to mention the bolder of the young warriors—who'd wage war on the wind if they had any chance of winning. They don't complain of the coin, Highness. But they want a fight.'

'Bolkando is at peace,' Abrastal replied. 'At least, it was when you were first hired, and now it is so again. If it was war you wanted, Spax, you should have stayed with the other White Faces, since they went and jumped with both feet on to a hornet's nest.' She faced him and he saw all the places he could put his hands, given the chance. Her expression darkened. 'You are Warchief, as you say. A proud title, one with responsibility, one assumes. You are under siege, Spax? Deal with it.'

'Not many arrows left in my quiver, Highness.'

'Do I look like a fletcher?'

'You look like someone with something on her mind.' Spax spread his broad, scarred hands. 'I don't know these Perish Grey Helms, but I know of the order, Highness—'

'What order?'

'The warrior cult of the Wolves. A chapter of that cult defended at the siege of Capustan. The Grey Swords, they were called.'

Abrastal studied him for a time, and then she sighed. 'Gaedis, open us a jug of wine—but don't even think of pouring yourself one. I'm still annoyed with you for letting this cattle-dog whine his way into my presence.'

The lieutenant saluted and walked to the ornate wooden frame bearing a dozen or so amphorae, drawing a small knife as he scanned the stamps on the dusty necks.

'Cults, Mortal Swords, Shield Anvils and wolf gods,' Abrastal said in a mutter, shaking her head. 'This has the stink of fanaticism—and that well matches my assessment after this evening's parley. Is it simply war they seek, Spax? One where any face will do?'

The Warchief watched as Gaedis selected a jug and then, with an expert hook and twist of his knife, deftly removed the cork. 'Impressive, Lieutenant—you learn that between off-handed swordsmanship and riding backwards?'

'Pay attention to me!' barked Abrastal. 'I asked you a question, you island of fleas!'

Spax tilted his head in something between deference and amused insolence. When he saw the flaring of her eyes he bared his teeth and snapped out, 'As long as you feel inclined to spit out insults, Highness, I will indeed stand as an island. Let the seas crash—the stones will not blink.'

'Errant's shit-hole throne—pour that wine, Gaedis!'

Wine sloshed.

Abrastal walked over to her cot and sat down. She rubbed her eyes with the palms of her hands, and then looked up in time to accept a goblet. She drank deep. 'Another, damn you.' Gaedis managed to get the second goblet into Spax's hand before turning about to retrace his steps. 'Never mind the Perish for now. You say you know these Malazans, Spax. What can you tell me of this Adjunct Tavore?'

'Specifically? Almost nothing, Highness. Never met her, and the Barghast have never crossed her path. No, what I can do is tell you about the cant of the Malazan military—as it took shape at the hands of Dassem Ultor, and the way the command structure changed.'

'It's a start, but first, what does her title mean? Adjunct? To whom? To what?'

'Not sure this time round,' the Warchief admitted after swallowing down a mouthful of wine. 'They're a renegade army, after all. So why hold on to the old title? Because it's what her soldiers are used to, I suppose. Or is there more to it? Highness, the Adjunct—as far as I've gathered—was the weapon-bearing hand of the Empress. Her murderer, if you like. Of rivals inside the empire, enemies outside it. Slayer of sorcerors—she carries an otataral weapon, proof against any and all manner of magic.'

Abrastal remained sitting through this, only to rise once more when he paused. She held out her empty goblet and Gaedis poured again. 'Elite, then, specially chosen—how many of these Adjuncts did this Empress have at any one time?'

Spax frowned. 'I think . . . one.'

The Queen halted. 'And this Malazan Empire—it spans three continents?'

'And more, Highness.'

'Yet Tavore is a renegade. The measure of that betrayal . . .' she slowly shook her head. 'How can one trust this Adjunct? It is impossible. I wonder, did this Tavore attempt to usurp her Empress? Is she even now being pursued? Will the enemy they find be none other than her Malazan hunters?'

Spax shrugged. 'I doubt the Grey Helms would care much either way. It's a war. As you said, any face will serve. As for the Khundryl, well, they're sworn to the Adjunct personally, so they will follow her anywhere.'

'Yes, and why would they do that to a betrayer?'

'Highness, this is none of our concern,' said Spax. 'As much as my warriors lust for a fight, we have put ourselves at a tactical disadvantage—after all, it would have been better to deal with the Khundryl and the Perish back in Bolkando, and then take on the Bonehunters later. Mind you, it's still possible. A secret emissary to the Saphii, a few tens of thousands of coins—we could catch them by surprise—'

'No. After all, Spax, if it truly is none of our concern as you say, why attack them at all?'

'Just my point, Highness. I was simply observing that our opportunity for a tactical advantage is fast disappearing, assuming we had cause, which we haven't.'

'I'm not prepared to make any such assumption, Warchief. Thus my dilemma. It is as you describe. None of the three foreign armies still poses us any threat. They have made plain their desire to vanish into the east. Is it time to dust off our hands and return to our beloved homeland?'

'It might be, Highness.'

'But then,' and her frown deepened. 'Very well,' she said, 'I have sent a daughter eastward, by sea, Spax. A most precious daughter. It seems you and I share the same curse: curiosity. Kolanse has fallen silent. Our trader ships find nothing but empty ports, abandoned villages. The Pelasiar Sea is empty of traffic. Even the great net-ships have vanished. And yet . . . and yet . . . something is there, perhaps deep inland. A power, and it's growing.'

Spax studied the Queen. She was not dissembling. He saw her fear for her daughter (*gods, woman, you got enough of them, what's the loss of one?*) and it was genuine. *Your heiress? Does it work that way in Bolkando? How should I know, when I don't even care?* 'Summon her to return, Highness.'

'Too late, Spax. Too late.'

'Highness,' said the Warchief, 'do you mean to tell me we're going with the foreigners? Across the Wastelands?'

Gaedis had frozen in place, two strides to one side where he had been about to open another jug. The lieutenant's eyes were on his Queen.

'I don't know,' Abrastal said, eventually. 'No, in fact—we are not equipped for such a venture, nor, I imagine, would they even welcome us. Nonetheless . . . I will see this Adjunct.' She fixed Spax with a look that told him her tolerance was at an end, and she said, 'Chew on what you've heard this night, Warchief, and if your stomach still growls, do not bring your complaints to my tent.'

Spax dipped his head and then handed his goblet to Gaedis. 'I hear your maids readying that bath, Highness. A most restorative conclusion to this night, I'm sure. Good night to you, Highness, Lieutenant.'

Once outside, he set out, not back to his clans, but to the encampments of the Burned Tears. It had occurred to him, when envisioning the grand parley to come, that he and Gall would, in all likelihood, be the only men present. An exciting notion. He wasn't sure Gall would see it that way, of course, if the rumours he'd picked up were true, but there was another rumour that, if accurate, could offer a common rug for them both. *Not a drinker of fancy wines, this Gall. No, the man likes his beer, and if manhood has any measure, it's that.*

Just my opinion, mind. Now, let's see, Warleader Gall, if you share it.

Stepping beyond the legion's last row of tents, Spax paused. He spat to get that foul taste from his mouth. *Wine's for women. Gaedis, I bet that trick with the cork has spread a thousand soft thighs. You'll have to teach it to me one day.*

She might as well have tied a cask of ale to her belly. Her lower back was bowed, and every shift of weight made the bones creak. Muscles quivered, others were prostrate with exhaustion. Her breasts, which had never been modest or spry, now sat resting uneasy on the swell of that damned cask. *Everything* was swollen and too big—how was it that she kept forgetting? Of course, amidst all these groans and shuffles and grunts, her thoughts swam through honey. So sweet, this drowning. The world glowed. Life shouted. Sang.

'Hoary witches of old,' she muttered under her breath, 'you've a lot to answer for.' There was no possible position in which to sit in comfort, so Hanavat, wife to Gall, had taken to walking through the camp each night. She was the wandering moon of her people's legends, in the ages before her sister moon's betrayal, when love was still pure and Night lay down in the arms of Darkness—oh, the legends were quaint, if ever tainted with sorrow, that inevitable fall from grace. She wondered if such creations—those tales of times lost—were nothing more than a broken soul's embrace of regret. The fall was in sensibility's wake, too late to do anything about, but this—look around!—this is what it made of us.

The moon had ceased to wander. Snared in the webs of deceit, it could only slide round and round the world it loved—never to touch, doomed to tug at its lover's tears, that and nothing more. Until, in some distant future, love died and with it all the pale fires of its wonder, and at last Night found her lover and in turn Darkness swallowed her whole. And that was the end of all existence.

Hanavat could look up now and see a vision that did not fit with the legend's prophecy. No, the moon had been struck a mortal blow. She was dying. And still the web would not release her, whilst, ever cool, ever faint, her sister moon watched on. Had she murdered her rival? Was she pleased to witness her sister's death throes? Hanavat's gaze strayed southward to the jade lances arcing ever closer. The heavens were indeed at war.

'Tea, Hanavat?'

Her attention, drawn down from the skies, found the shapes of two women seated round a small fire banked against a steaming pot. 'Shelemasa. Rafala.'

Rafala, who'd been the one voicing the offer, now lifted into view a third cup. 'We see you pass each night, Mahib. Your discomfort is plain to our eyes. Will you join us? Rest your feet.'

'I was fleeing the midwives,' Hanavat said. She hesitated, and then waddled over. 'The Seed Wakeners are cruel—what's wrong with just an egg? We could manage one, I think, about the size of a palm nut.'

Shelemasa's laugh was low and wry. 'But not as hard, I'd hope.'

'Or as hairy,' Rafala added.

The two warrior women laughed.

Grunting, moving slowly, Hanavat sat down, forming the third point to this triangle surrounding the fire. She accepted the cup, studied it in the soft light. Pewter. Bolkando. 'So, you didn't sell everything back to them, I see.'

'Only the useless things,' Rafala said. 'They had plenty of those.'

'It's what makes us so different from them,' observed Shelemasa. 'We don't invent useless things, or make up needs that don't exist. If civilization—as they call it—has a true definition, then that must be it. Don't you think, Mahib?'

The ancient honorific for a pregnant woman pleased Hanavat. Though these two were young, they remembered the old ways and all the respect those ways accorded people. 'You may be right in that, Shelemasa. But I wonder, perhaps it's not the objects that so define a civilization—perhaps it's the attitudes that give rise to them, and to the strangely overwrought value attached to them. The privilege of making useless things is the important thing, since it implies wealth and abundance, leisure and all the rest.'

'Wise words,' murmured Rafala.

'The tea is sweet enough,' replied Hanavat.

The younger woman smiled, accepting the faint admonishment with good grace.

'The child kicks,' said Hanavat, 'and so promises me the truth of the years awaiting us. I must have been mad.' She sipped tea. 'What brew is this?'

'Saphii,' answered Shelemasa. 'It's said to calm the stomach, and with the foreign food we've been eating of late, such calm will be a welcome respite.'

'Perhaps,' added Rafala, 'it will soothe the child as well.'

'Or kill it outright. At this point I don't really care which. Heed this miserable Mahib's warning: do this once to know what it means, but leave it at that. Don't let the dream serpents back into your thoughts, whispering to you of pregnancy's bliss. The snake lies to soften your memories. Until there is nothing but clouds and the scent of blossoms in your skull, and before you know it, you've gone and done it again.'

'Why would the serpents lie, Mahib? Are not children women's greatest gift?'

'So we keep telling ourselves, and each other.' She sipped more tea. Her tongue tingled as if she'd licked a bell of pepper. 'But not long ago my husband and I invited our children to a family feast, and my how we did feast. Like starving wolves trying to decide which among us was the stranded bhederin calf. All night our children flung that bloody hide back and forth, each of them cursed to wear it at least once, and finally they all decided to drape the two of us in that foul skin. It was, in short, a most memorable reunion.'

The two younger women said nothing.

'Parents,' resumed Hanavat, 'may choose to have children, but they do not choose their children. Nor can children choose their parents. And so there is love, yes, but there is also war. There is sympathy and there is the poison of envy. There is peace and that peace is the exhausted calm between struggles for power. There is, on rare occasions, true joy, but each time that precious, startling moment then dwindles, and in each face you see a hint of sorrow—as if what was just found will now be for ever remembered as a thing lost. Can you be nostalgic for the instant just past? Oh yes, and it's a bittersweet taste.' She finished her tea.

'That whispering serpent—it's whispered its last lie in me. I strangled the bitch. I tied it neck and tail to two horses. I collected every knuckled bone and crushed it to dust, then blew that dust to contrary winds. I took its skin and made it into a codpiece for the ugliest dog in the camp. I then took that dog—'

Rafala and Shelemasa were laughing, their laughs getting louder with each antic of vengeance Hanavat described.

Other warriors, round other small fires, were all looking over now, smiling to see old pregnant Hanavat regaling two younger women. And among the men there were stirrings of curiosity and perhaps a little unease, for women possessed powerful secrets, and none more powerful than those possessed by a pregnant woman— one need only to look into the face of a mahib to know that. The women, watching on but like their male companions too distant to hear Hanavat's words, also smiled. Was that to soothe the men in their company? Possibly, but if so the expression was instinctive, a dissembling born of habit.

No, they smiled as the urgent whispers of their dream serpents filled their heads. *The child within. Such joy! Such pleasure! Put away the swords, O creature of beauty—instead sing to the Seed Wakeners! Catch his eye and watch him fall in—the darkness beckons and the night is warm!*

Was a scent released upon the air? Did it drift through the entire camp of the Khundryl Burned Tears?

In the Warleader's campaign tent, Gall sat with a bellyful of ale heavy as a cask leaning on his belt, and eyed with gauging regard the tall iron-haired woman pacing in front of him. Off to one side sat the Gilk Barghast, Spax, even drunker than Gall, his own red-shot, bleary gaze tracking the Mortal Sword as she sought to prise from Gall every last detail regarding the Malazans. Where had this sudden uncertainty come from? Had not the Perish sworn to serve the Adjunct? Oh, if Queen Abrastal could witness what he was witnessing! But then she'd be interested in all the unimportant matters, wouldn't she? Eager to determine if the great alliance was weakening . . . and all that.

All the while missing the point, the matters that were truly interesting and so sharply relevant to this scene before him.

The Warleader's wife was nowhere to be seen, and it had already occurred to Spax that he should probably leave. Who knew if or when Krughava would finally take note of the look in Gall's eyes—and what might she do then? Instead, Spax sat sprawled in the leather sling of the three-legged chair, too comfortable to move and, it had to be admitted, too fascinated as she fired question after question into the increasingly senseless arrow butt that was Gall. When would she realize that the man had stopped answering? That while she went on attacking and attacking, he'd stopped defending long ago? He so wanted to see that moment—her expression, yes, one he could take away with him and remember for evermore.

What would it take for her to notice? *If he pulled out his gooseneck and took aim? Would that do it? Or just wrestled his way out of his clothes? Gods below, the drooling's not done it.*

He should leave. But they'd have to drag him out of this tent. *Come on, Krughava, you can do it. I know you can. Take a second look, woman, at the man you're talking to.* No, he wasn't going anywhere.

Ah, but this was a most agitated woman. Something about a weakening resolve, or was it a failure of confidence—a sudden threat from within the ranks of the Grey Helms themselves. Someone missing in the command structure, the necessary balance all awry. A young man of frightening ambitions—oh, swamp spirits be damned! He was too drunk to make sense of any of this!

Why am I sitting here?

What is she saying? Pay attention, Krughava! Never mind him—can't you see this bulge? No one wants the goose to honk, come and strangle it, woman! I'll solve your agitation. Yes, if only you women understood that. Your every answer, right here between my legs.

Half the world's mired in ignorance!

Half the world . . .

Gooseneck.

Chapter Twenty-One

Listen then these are the charms
And will I see your pleasure stretched
An even dozen they crowd the tomb
You can read the dead in twelve faces
And the winter months are long

The shields are hammered into splinters
Beating war's time will never ring true
Fools stir in the crypt counting notches
And the snow settles burying all traces
Crows spill the sky knocked like ink

Babies crawl to the front line
Plump arms shouting proof 'gainst harm
The helms rock askew in pitching tumult
And the brightest blood is the freshest
Round the well charged and spatted

Cadavers cherish company's lonely vigil
The tomb's walls trumpet failures
Dressed as triumphs and glory's trains
And the fallen are bundled lying under foot
Each year Spring dies still newborn

Listen then these are the charms
History is written for the crows
By children with red lips and eyes blinking
On the cocked ends of their tongues
And it seems summer will never end

> HAIL THE SEASON OF WAR
> GALLAN

C*ity of darkness, see how that darkness hides your ugly face.*

They were on the bridge. She was leaning heavily on her husband's shoulder, both relieved and irritated by his stolid strength. 'But you don't see, do you?'

'Sand?'

She shook her head. 'Doesn't matter. The air is alive. Can you feel that? Withal, can you feel that much at least?'

'Your goddess,' he said. 'Alive, aye, alive with tears.'

That was true. Mother Dark had returned with sorrow knotted into grief. Darkness made helpless fists, like a widow trying to hold on to all she had lost. *Lost, yes, something has been lost. She is no longer turned away, but in mourning. Her eyes are averted, downcast. She is here, yet behind a veil. Mother, you make this a most bitter gift.*

Her strength was slow in returning. Memories like wolves, snapping on all sides. *Kharkanas.* Sandalath clutched Withal's right arm, feeling the thick muscles, the cables of his will. He was one of those men who were like a finely made sword, sheathed in a hard skin, hiding a core that could bend when it had to. She didn't deserve him. That was brutally clear. *Take me hostage, husband. That much I will understand. That much I know how to live with. Even though it too will break in the end—no, stop thinking that way. It's a memory no one here deserves.*

'There are fires in the city.'

'Yes. It is . . . occupied.'

'Savages in the ruins?'

'Of course not. These are the Shake. We've found them.'

'So they made it, then.'

She nodded.

He drew her to a halt ten steps from the bridge's end. 'Sand. Tell me again why you wanted to find them. You wanted to warn them, isn't that right? Against what?'

'Too late for that. Gallan sent them out, and now his ghost pulls them back. He cursed them. He said they could leave, but then he made them remember enough—just enough—to force them to return.'

Withal sighed, his expression showing he was unconvinced. 'People need to know where they came from, Sand. Especially if they've lived generations not knowing. They were a restless people, weren't they? What do you think made them restless?'

'Then we're all restless, Withal, because at the very heart, none of us know where we came from. Or where we're going.'

He made a face. 'Mostly, nobody much cares. Very well, have it your way. These Shake were cursed. You didn't reach them in time. Now what?'

'I don't know. But whatever Andii blood remains within them is all but drowned in human blood. You will find in them close company, and that is something.'

'I have all the company I need in you, Sand.'

She snorted. 'Sweet, but nonsense. See it this way, then. I am of the land—this land. You are of the sea—a distant sea. And the Shake? They are of the Shore. And look at us here, now, standing on a bridge.' She paused and then grimaced. 'I can almost see the blind poet's face. I can almost see him nodding. When grief was too much, Withal, we were in the habit of tearing out our own eyes. What kind of people would do such a thing?'

He shrugged. 'I'm not following you, Sand. You need simpler thoughts.'

'The Shake are home, and yet more lost than they ever have been. Does Mother Dark forgive them? Will she give them her city? Will she grant them the legacy of the Tiste Andii?'

'Then perhaps you have a purpose being here, after all, Sand.'

She searched his eyes, was stung by his compassion. 'What do you mean?'

'You need to convince Mother Dark to do all those things. For the Shake.'

Oh, husband. I was a hostage, nothing more. And then, and then, I lost even that. 'Mother Dark has no time for the likes of me.'

'Tell me, what was the purpose of being a hostage?'

He'd caught her thoughts. She looked away, studied the wreckage-cluttered river sliding under the bridge. *Dark waters . . .* 'The First Families sparred. Power was a wayward tide. We were the coins they exchanged. So long as we were never spent, so long as we'—*remained unsullied*—'remained as we were, the battles saw little blood. We became the currency of power.' *But gold does not feel. Gold does not dream. Gold does not long for a man's hand closing about it. You can win us, you can lose us, but you can't eat us. You can hide us away. You can polish us bright and hang us from a chain round your neck. You can bury us, you can even carve a likeness of your face into us, but in the next season of fire all sign of you vanishes.*

You can't eat us, and you can't fuck us. No, you can't do that.

'Sand?'

'What?'

'Were hostages ever killed?'

She shook her head. 'Not until the end. When everything . . . fell apart. All it needs,' she said, memories clouding her mind, 'is the breaking of one rule, one law. A breaking that no one then calls to account. Once that happens, once the shock passes, every law shatters. Every rule of conduct, of proper behaviour, it all vanishes. Then the hounds inside each and every one of us are unleashed. At that moment, Withal'—she met his eyes, defiant against the anguish she saw in them—'we all show our true selves. We are not beasts—we are something far worse. There, deep inside us. You see it—the emptiness in the eyes, as horror upon horror is committed, and no one feels—no one feels a thing.'

She was trembling in his arms now and he held her tight—to keep her from sinking to her knees. Sandalath pressed her face into the curve of his shoulder and neck. Her words muffled, she said, 'She should have stayed turned away. I will tell her—go away—we weren't worth it then, we're not worth it now. I will tell you—her—'

'Sand—'

'No, I will beg her. Turn away. I'm begging you, my love, *turn away*.'

'Sand. The Shake—'

The bridge beneath them seemed to be swaying. She held him as hard as she could.

'The Shake, my love. They've found us.'

Her eyes closed. *I know. I know.*

'Well?'

Brevity adjusted her sword belt. 'Well what?'

'Should we go and talk to 'em, love?'

'No, let's just stand here. Maybe they'll go away.'

Snorting, Pithy set out. 'Dark dark dark,' she muttered, 'it's all dark. I'm sick of dark. I'm gonna torch the forest, or maybe a few buildings. Fire, that's the solution. And lanterns. Giant lanterns. Torches. Oil lamps. White paint.'

'You going to go on like that all the way to 'em?' Brevity asked, keeping pace a step behind her.

'That woman looks like she walked outa one of them wall paintings in the temple.'

'Maybe she did.'

'Then what? Got lost? Our lookout watched 'em coming up the road. Nah, the point is, her people built this city. She's got more claim to it than the Shake. And that's a problem.'

'Y'saying she won't like the new neighbours? Too bad. She's only got that one man. Besides, she looks sick.'

Their conversation ended as they drew closer to the two strangers.

The man's eyes were on them, even as he continued to support the woman in his arms. 'Hello,' he said.

Trader tongue. Pithy nodded. 'And the same. Meckros?'

'Good guess,' he replied. 'I am named Withal. You're Letherii, not Shake.'

'Good guess,' Pithy responded. 'We're the Queen's Honour Guard. I'm Captain Pithy, and this is Captain Brevity. Is your mate sick?'

'She is Tiste Andii,' he said. 'She was born in this city.'

'Oh,' said Pithy, and she shot her friend a look that asked: *Now what?*

Brevity cleared her throat. 'Well then, if it's a homecoming, we'd best bring her in.'

At that the woman finally looked up.

Pithy's breath caught, and beside her Brevity started.

'Thank you,' said the Tiste Andii. Tears had streaked her face.

'Need another shoulder to lean on?' Pithy asked.

'No.' And she disengaged herself from Withal's arms. Straightening, she faced the gate. 'I'm ready.'

Pithy and Brevity let her and Withal take the lead, at a pace of their choosing.

As soon as they'd moved a half-dozen strides ahead, Brevity turned and plucked Pithy's sleeve.

'See her face?' she whispered.

Pithy nodded.

'She ain't just like them in the wall paintings, Pithy. She *is* one of 'em! I'd swear it!'

'Side room, first one on the left just inside the altar room—the only one without stone beds. She's in there. Her and maybe ten others. They got manacles on their wrists.'

'That's right! One of them!'

No wonder she ain't happy about coming home. Pithy said, 'Once we're in, you go get the witches and bring 'em over. Unless Tovis or Yedan have come back, in which case get them.'

'That'd be a better choice,' Brevity replied. 'Them witches are still drunk—'

'They ain't drunk for real.'

'You know what I mean. Eel-eyed. Horny. The kinda drunk that makes a woman ashamed of being a woman.'

'They ain't drunk. I told you. So get 'em, all right?'

'All right, but we should a buried 'em when we had the chance.'

The deeper shadow of the gate's arch slipped over them like a shawl. Sandalath slowly released her breath. Mother Dark's pervasive presence filled the city, and she felt her weariness drain away as the goddess's power touched her, but the benediction felt . . . indifferent. The grief was still there, appallingly fresh—a reopened wound, or something else? She could not be sure. *So . . . sorrow does not end. And if you cannot let it go, Mother, what hope do I have?*

Something brushed her mind. An acknowledgement, a momentary recognition. Sympathy? She sighed. 'Withal, will you walk with me?'

'Of course—as I am doing right now, Sandalath.'

'No. The temple, the Terondai.' She met his eyes. 'Kurald Galain. To the very foot of Mother Dark.'

'What is it you seek?' he asked, searching her face.

She turned back to the two Letherii women standing a few paces behind. 'You spoke of a Queen,' she said.

'Twilight,' said Pithy. 'Yan Tovis.'

'And her brother,' added Brevity. 'Yedan Derryg, the Watch.'

'I must go to the temple,' Sandalath said.

'We heard.'

'But I would speak with her.'

'They left us a while back,' Pithy said. 'Went into the forest. When the witches finally come round they said the two of 'em, Tovis and her brother, probably rode to the First Shore. That was after they was in the temple—the Queen and the Prince, I mean. The witches won't go anywhere near it, the temple, I mean.'

Sandalath cocked her head. 'Why do I make you so nervous, Captain?'

'You ain't changed much,' blurted Brevity.

'I—what? Oh. In the Skeral—the Chamber of Hostages.'

Pithy nodded. 'Only, the witches said this city's been dead a long, long time.'

'No,' said Brevity, 'a *long* time.'

'I said that,' Pithy retorted, scowling at her companion.

'You didn't say it right, is all. Long. *Long*.'

Sandalath faced her husband again. 'This world is born anew,' she said. 'Mother Dark has returned and now faces us. The Shake have returned as well. Who remains missing? The Tiste Andii. My people. I want to know why.'

'And do you think she'll answer you?' Withal asked, but it was a question without much behind it, and that made Sandalath curious.

'Husband. Has she spoken to you?'

He grimaced. Then reluctantly nodded.

But not to me. Mother Dark, am I so flawed in your eyes now?

There was no silent reply to that. The presence remained unperturbed, as if deaf to Sandalath, deaf and wilfully blind. *Not fair. Not fair!*

'Sand?'

She hissed under her breath. 'The Terondai, *now*.'

Beyond the scores of buildings now occupied by the Shake and refugee islanders, Kharkanas remained a place of ghosts. The witches decided they liked that. They had found an estate situated on a terrace overlooking an overgrown park. The outer wall's main gate had been burned down, leaving ancient soot smears on the marble frame and deep heat cracks latticing the lintel stone. The garden flanking the formal approach was now a snarl of stunted trees on both sides, their roots tilting the flagstones of the path.

Atop four broad steps double doors marked the entrance to the residence. These had been shattered from the inside. Bronze statues reared on either side of the staircase, each standing on an ornate marble pedestal. If they had been fashioned in the likeness of living creatures, decided Pully, then the world was a stranger place than she had ever imagined. Towering, the statues were of warriors, human from the shoulders down, whilst their necks and heads belonged to a hound. Both sentinels bore weapons. A double-bladed axe for the one on the left, a two-handed sword for the one on the right. Verdigris marred the details of the beastly visages, but there was enough to see that the two were not identical. The sword-wielder was terribly scarred, a slash that had cleaved through one eye, deep enough to bite bone.

Humming under her breath, Pully set one knee on this particular statue's horizontal penis, and pulled herself up for a closer look at that face. 'Now them's big teeth, an' precious so.'

Skwish had already gone inside, likely painting a thick red line down the middle, staking her half of the estate. Pully had forgotten how competitive the cow had been in her youth, but now it was all coming back. *Wrinkles gone, bitch returns! An what was I sayin? Right, bitter's a habit, Skwish. Bitter's a habit.* No matter. Skwish could have her half of the estate and half of every room. But then half of everything was half of nothing. They could live here, yes, but they couldn't own the place.

She clambered down from the statue, brushed the dust from her hands, and then ascended the steps and strode inside. Eight paces opposite her was a wall bearing a carved crest of some sort, arcane heraldry announcing the family that had claimed this place, or so she supposed. Even so, one sniff told her there was sorcery in that sigil, latent, possibly a ward but too old to manage much. She could hear Skwish rummaging about in a room down the corridor on the right. *Tripped nothing. Dead ward, or as good as. Did you even notice, sister?*

One thing was impossible not to notice. Ever since they'd crawled out of that deathly sleep, they'd felt the presence of the goddess. Mother Dark had looked upon them both, had gathered up their souls like a pair of knuckled dice. A rattle or two, curious fingertips exploring every nuance, every pit and crack. Then the cast. Dismissive, all interest lost. Damned insulting, yes. Infuriating. Who did the hag think she was, anyway? Pully snorted, eyes still on the marble crest. Something about it made her uneasy. 'Never mind,' she muttered, and then raised her voice: 'Skwish!'

'Wha?'

'We ain't welcome here.'

Skwish reappeared, stood in the corridor's gloom. 'The Queen will take the palace. Her and Witchslayer. We don't want t'be anywhere close to 'em. There's power here, Pully. We can use it, we can feed on it—'

'Risky. It ain't as quiet as I'd like.'

'It's memories is all.'

'What do you mean?'

Skwish rolled her eyes, approached. She halted directly in front of the crest. 'Old symbols,' she said. She pointed. 'See that? That's the Terondai, and there, that's the sigil of Mother Dark herself.'

'Empty throne! This ain't a Royal House, is it?'

'Not quite, but as good as. See that mark? The one in the centre. That's the Consort—you never was interested in studying the Oldings. So, this house, it belonged to a man lover to some princess or maybe even the queen herself. See, that's his name, the one there.'

'What was it?'

'Daraconus, something like that.'

They heard someone in the courtyard and turned in time to see Captain Brevity climbing the steps.

'What?' demanded Pully, her harsh voice startling the Letherii.

'Was looking for you,' Brevity said, slightly out of breath.

'What for?' Skwish asked.

'Visitors.'

'From where?'

'Best come with me, you two. There's a woman. Tiste Andii.'

'Bluerose?'

'What? No. She was born here.'

Pully and Skwish exchanged glances. And then Pully scowled. *Bad news. Competition. Rival.* 'But she's not alone?'

'Got a man with her. A Meckros.'

'Where'd they come from, then? They ain't always been here—we'd a sensed that. The city was empty—'

'Up the road, Pully,' said Brevity, 'same as us.'

'We got here first,' Skwish growled.

Brevity blinked. 'It's a big city, witch. Now, you coming?'

'Where is she?' Pully asked.

'The temple.'

Bad news. The worst. 'Fine then,' she snapped.

Yedan Derryg had walked a thousand or more paces along the ethereal First Shore, but now at last he was returning. And in one hand, Yan Tovis saw, he held a sword. The weapon flashed green in the incandescent fall of liquid light. The blade was long as a man's leg yet thinner than the width of a hand. A wire basket hilt shielded the grip. As he came up to where she stood, something lit his eyes.

'A Hust sword, sister.'

'And it's healed.'

'Yes.'

'But how can a broken sword grow back?'

'Quenched in dragon's blood,' he replied. 'Hust weapons are immortal, immune to all decay. They can shear other blades in two.' He held up the sword. 'This is a five-blade sword—tested against five, cut through them all. Twilight, there is no higher calibre of sword than the one you see here. It was the possession of a Hustas, a Master of the House itself—only children of the Forge could own such weapons.'

'And the woman threw it away.'

'It is a mystery,' Yedan Derryg said.

'She was Gallan's escort—'

'Not that. The matter of how a five-blade Hust sword broke in the first place.'

'Ah. I see your point.'

He looked round. 'Time dissolves here, this close to the Sea of Light. We have been away from our people too long—'

'Not my fault,' she said.

'True. Mine. No matter. It is time to go back.'

Yan Tovis sighed. 'What am I to do?' she asked. 'Find the palace, sink down on to whatever throne I find?'

The muscles of his jaws knotted beneath his beard and he glanced away. 'We have things to organize,' he eventually said. 'Staff for the palace, officers for the guard. Work teams. Is the river rich with fish? If not, we are in trouble—our stores are depleted. Will crops grow here? Darkness seems to somehow feed the trees and such, but even then, we face a hungry season before anything matures.'

The list alone exhausted her.

'Leave all that to me,' Yedan said.

'Indolence for the Queen—I will go mad with boredom.'

'You must visit the temple again, sister. It is no longer empty. It must be sanctified once more.'

'I am no priestess.'

'Royal blood will suffice.'

She shot him a look. 'Indeed. How much?'

Yedan shrugged. 'Depends.'

'On what?'

'On how thirsty she is.'

'If she drains me dry . . .'

'The threat of boredom will prove unfounded.'

The bastard was finding himself again. Wit dry as a dead oasis, withered palm leaves rustling like the laughter of locusts. Damned Hust sword and the illusion of coming home. Brother. Prince. Witchslayer. He'd been waiting for this all his life. When she had not. *I'd believed nothing. Even in my desperation, I walked cold as a ghost doomed to repeat a lifetime's path to failure. And my blood— gods below—my blood. This realm demands too much of me.*

Yedan faced her again. 'Sister, we have little time.'

She started. 'What do you mean?'

'The Shake—the very impulse that drove you to set us on the Road of Gallan— it was all meant to bring us here. Kharkanas, the First Shore. We must find out why. We must discover what the goddess wants of us.'

Horror rippled through Yan Tovis. *No.* Her eyes lifted past Yedan to the First Shore, to that tumultuous wall of light—and the innumerable vague figures behind the veil. *No, please. Not again.*

'Mount up, sister. It is time to return.'

Given enough time, some ghastly concatenation of ages, lifetimes compressed, crushed down layer upon layer. Details smoothed into the indefinite. Deeds hollowed out like bubbles in pumice. Dreams flattened into gradients of coloured sands that crumbled to the touch. Looking back was unpleasant, and the vaster that field of sediment, the grislier the vista. Sechul Lath had once chosen a bowed, twisted frame to carry the legacies of his interminable existence. Beauty and handsome repose—after all that he had done—was, as far as he was concerned, too hypocritical to bear. No, in form he would seek justice, the physicality of punishment. And this was what had so galled Errastas.

Sechul was tempted to find for himself that bent body once again. The world took those flat sediments and twisted them into tortured shapes. He understood that. He favoured such pressures and the scarred visages they made in stone and flesh.

The sky was blood red and cloudless, the rocky barren soil suffused with streaks of orange and yellow minerals tracking the landscape. Wind-sculpted mesas girdled the horizon, encircling the plain. This warren possessed no name—none that he knew, at any rate. No matter, it had been scoured clean long ago.

Kilmandaros strode at his side in a half-hitching gait, lest she leave him and Errastas far behind. She had assumed her favoured form, bestial and hulking, towering over her two companions. He could hear her sliding breath as it rolled in and out of four lungs, the rhythm so discordant with his own that he felt strangely breathless. Mother or not, she was never a comforting presence. She wore violence like a fur cloak riding her shoulders, a billowing emanation that brushed him again and again.

She was a singular force of balance, Sechul knew—had always known. Creation was her personal anathema, and the destruction in her hands was its answer. She saw no value in order, at least the kind that was imposed by a sentient will. Such efforts were an affront.

Kilmandaros was worshipped still, in countless cultures, but there was nothing benign in that sensibility. She bore a thousand names, a thousand faces, and each and every one was a source of mortal dread. Destroyer, annihilator, devourer. Her fists spoke in the cruel forces of nature, in sundered mountains and drowning floods, in the ground cracking open and in rivers of molten lava. Her skies were ever dark, seething and swollen. Her rain was the rain of ash and cinders. Her shadow destroyed lives.

The Forkrulian joints of her limbs and their impossible articulations were often seen as physical proof of nature gone awry. Broken bones that nonetheless descended with vast, implacable power. A body that could twist like madness. Among the believers, she personified the loosing of rage, the surrendering of reason and the rejection of control. Her cult was written in spilled blood, disfigurement and the virtue of violence.

Dear mother, what lessons do you have for your son?

Errastas walked ahead, a man convinced he knew where he was going. The worlds awaited his guiding hand, that nudge that all too often invited Kilmandaros into her swath of mindless destruction. Yet between them was Sechul Lath, Lord of Chance and Mischance, Caster of Knuckles. He could smile the mockery of mercy, or he could spit and turn away. He could shape every moment of his mother's violence. Who lives, who dies? The decision was his.

His was the purest worship of them all. So it had always been and so it would always remain. No matter what god or goddess a mortal fool prayed to, Sechul Lath was the arbiter of all they sought. *'Save me.' 'Save us.' 'Make us rich.' 'Make us fruitful.'* The gods never even heard such supplications from their followers. The need, the desire, snared each prayer, spun them swirling into Sechul's domain.

He could open himself, even now, to the cries of mortals beyond counting, each and every one begging for an instant of his time, his regard. His blessing.

But he'd stopped listening long ago. He'd spawned the Twins and left them to inherit the pathetic game. How could one not grow weary of that litany of prayers? Each and every desire, so heartfelt, invariably reduced to a knot of sordidness. To gain for oneself, someone else must lose. Joy was purchased in reams of sorrow. Triumphs stood tall on heaps of bones. Save my child? Another must die. *Balance! All must balance! Can existence be any crueller than that? Can justice be any emptier? To bless you with chance, I must curse another with mischance. To this law even the gods must bow. Creation, destruction, life, death—no, I am done with it! Done with it all!*

Leave it to my Oponnai. The Twins must ever face one another, lest existence unravel. They are welcome to it.

No, he'd had his fill of mortal blood.

But *immortal* blood, ah, that was another matter. With it, he could . . . he could . . . what? *I can break the fulcrum. I can send the scales crashing down. It's all pointless anyway—the Che'Malle saw to that. We rise and we fall, but each and every time the cycle renews, our rise is never as high as the last time, and the fall in turn takes us farther down. Mortals are blind to this spiral. All will end. Energies will lose their grip, and all will fade away.*

I have seen it. I know what's coming.

Errastas sought a resurrection but what he sought was impossible. Each generation of gods was weaker—oh, they strode forth blazing with power, but that was the glow of youth and it quickly dissipated. And the mortal worshippers, they too, in their tiny, foreshortened lives, slid into cynical indifference, and those among them who held any faith at all soon backed into corners, teeth bared in their zeal, their blind fanaticism—where blindness was a virtue and time could be dragged to a halt, and then pulled backward. Madness. Stupidity.

None of us can go back. Errastas, what you seek will only precipitate your final fall, and good riddance. Still, lead on, old friend. To the place where I will do what must be done. Where I will end . . . everything.

Ahead, Errastas halted, turning to await them. His lone eye studied them, flicking back and forth. 'We are close,' he said. 'We hover directly above the portal we seek.'

'She is chained below?' Kilmandaros asked.

'She is.'

Sechul Lath rubbed the back of his neck, looked away. The distant range of stone fangs showed their unnatural regularity. Among them could be seen stumps where entire mountains had been uprooted, plucked from the solid earth. *They built them here. They were done with this world. They'd devoured every living thing by then. Such bold . . . confidence.* He glanced back at Errastas. 'There will be wards.'

'Demelain wards, yes,' Errastas said.

At that, Kilmandaros growled.

Speak then, Errastas, of dragons. She is ready. She is ever ready.

'We must be prepared,' Errastas continued. 'Kilmandaros, you must exercise restraint. It will do us no good to have you break her wards and then simply kill her.'

'If we knew why they imprisoned her in the first place,' Sechul said, 'we might have what we will need to bargain with her.'

Errastas's shrug was careless. 'That should be obvious, Knuckles. She was uncontrollable. She was the poison in their midst.'

She was the balance, the counter-weight to them all. Chaos within, is this wise? 'Perhaps there's another way.'

Errastas scowled. 'Let's hear it, then,' he said, crossing his arms.

'K'rul must have participated. He must have played a role in this chaining—after all, he had the most to lose. She was the poison as you say, but if she was so to her kin that was incidental. Her true poison was when she was loose in K'rul's blood—in his warrens. He needed her chained. Negated.' He paused, cocked his head. 'Don't you think it curious that the Crippled God has now taken her place? That he is the one now poisoning K'rul?'

'The diseases are not related,' Errastas said. 'You spoke of another way. I'm still waiting to hear it, Knuckles.'

'I don't have one. But this could prove a fatal error on our part, Errastas.'

He gestured dismissively. 'If she will not cooperate, then Kilmandaros can do what she does best. Kill the bitch, here and now. You still think me a fool? I have thought this through, Sechul. The three of us are enough, here and now, to do whatever is necessary. We shall offer her freedom—do you truly imagine she will reject that?'

'What makes you so certain she will honour whatever bargain she agrees to?'

Errastas smiled. 'I have no worries in that regard. You will have to trust me, Knuckles. Now, I have been patient long enough. Shall we proceed? Yes, I believe we shall.'

He stepped back and Kilmandaros lumbered forward.

'Here?' she asked.

'That will do, yes.'

Her fists hammered down on to the ground. Hollow thunder rumbled beneath the plain, the reverberation trembling through Sechul's bones. The fists began their incessant descent, pounding with immortal strength, as dust slowly lifted to obscure the horizons. The stone beneath the hardened ash was not sedimentary; it was the indurated foam of pumice. Ageless, trapped in the memory of a single moment of destruction. It knew nothing of eternities.

Sechul Lath lowered himself into a squat. This could take some time. *Sister, can you hear us? We come a-knocking . . .*

'What?' Torrent demanded. 'What did you just say?'

The haggard witch's shrug grated bones. 'I tired of the illusion.'

He looked round once more. The wagon's track was gone. Vanished. Even the trail behind them had disappeared. 'But I was following—I saw—'

'Stop being so stupid,' Olar Ethil snapped. 'I stole into your mind, made you see things that weren't there. You were going the wrong way—who cares about a damned Trygalle carriage? They're probably all dead by now.' She gestured ahead. 'I turned you from that trail, that's all. Because what we seek is right *there.*'

'If I could kill you, I'd do it,' said Torrent.

'Stupid as only the young can be,' she replied with a snort. 'The only thing young people are capable of learning is regret. That's why so many of them end up dead, to the eternal regret of their parents. Now, if you've finished the histrionics, can we continue on?'

'I am not a child.'

'That's what children always say, sooner or later.' With that, she set out, trudging past Torrent, whose horse shied away as soon as the bonecaster drew too close.

He steadied the animal, glaring at Olar Ethil's scaled back.

'—*what we seek is right there.*' His gaze lifted. Another one of those damned dragon towers, rising forlorn on the plain. The bonecaster was marching towards it as if she could topple it with a single kick. *No one is more relentless than a dead woman. With all the living ones I've known, I shouldn't be surprised by that.* The desolate tower was still a league or more away. He wasn't looking forward to visiting it, not least because of Olar Ethil's inexplicable interest in this one in particular; but also because of its scale. A city of stone, built upward instead of outward—what was the point of that?

Well. Self defence. But we've already seen how that didn't work. And what if some lower section caught fire? There'd be no escape for everyone trapped above. No, these were the constructs of idiots, and he wanted nothing to do with them. *What's wrong with a hut? A hooped tent of hides—you can pick it up and carry it anywhere you want to go. Leaving nothing behind. Rest lightly on the soil—so the elders always said.*

But why did they say that? Because it made running away easier. Until we ran out of places to run. If we'd built cities, just like the Letherii, why, they would have had to respect us and our claim to the lands we lived on. We would have had rights. But with those huts, with all that resting lightly, they never had to take us seriously, and that made killing us all that much easier.

Kicking his horse into motion, he squinted at that ragged tower. Maybe cities weren't just to live in. Maybe they were all about claiming the right to live somewhere. The right to take from the surrounding land all they needed to stay alive. *Like a giant tick, head burrowed deep, sucking all the blood it can. Before it cuts loose and sets off for a fresh sweep of skin. And another claim of its right to drink deep of the land.*

The best way he'd found to kill a tick was with his thumbnail, slicing the insect in half on a flat rock. He remembered a dog trying to eat one once. It had had to spit it out. Ticks tasted foul—too foul even for dogs, which he'd not thought possible. Cities probably tasted even worse.

Listen to me. I'm losing my mind. Damned witch—are you still here? Inside my skull? Making my thoughts go round and round with all these useless ideas?

He rode up beside her. 'Leave me alone.'

'You were never that interesting in the first place,' she replied.

'Funny, I'd decided that about you long ago,' said Torrent, 'but you're still here.'

She halted and turned round. 'That will do, then. We're about to have company, warrior.'

He twisted in his saddle and studied the cloudless sky. 'The ones Silchas Ruin spoke of? I see nothing—'

'They come.'

'To fight?'

'No. They were fools once, but one must assume that dying has taught them a lesson.' She paused, and then added, 'Or not.'

Motion in the wiry grasses caught his eye. A lizard—no—'Witch, what is *that*?'

Two skeletal creatures—birds?—edged into view, heads ducking, long tails flicking. They stood on their hind legs, barely taller than the grasses. Leather and gut bindings held the bones in place.

When the first one spoke, the voice formed words in his head. 'Great One, we are abject. We grovel in servitude—'

The other cut in, 'Does she believe all that? Keep trying!'

'Be quiet, Telorast! How can I concentrate on lying with you barging in all the time! Now shhh! Oh, never mind, it's too late—look at them, they can both hear us. You, especially.'

The creature named Telorast had crept closer to Olar Ethil, almost on all fours. 'Servitude! As my sister said. Not a real lie. Just a . . . a . . . a temporary truth! Allegiance of convenience, so long as it's convenient. What could be more honest?'

Olar Ethil grunted and then said, 'I have no need of allies among the Eleint.'

'Not true!' cried Telorast.

'Calm down,' hissed the other one. 'This is called *bargaining*. She says we're useless. We say we don't really need her help. She says—well, something. Let's wait to hear what she says, and then we say something back. Eventually, we strike a deal. You see? It's simple.'

'I can't think!' complained Telorast. 'I'm too terrified! Curdle, take over—before my bones fall apart!'

The one named Curdle snapped its head back and forth, as if seeking somewhere to hide.

'You don't fool me,' said Olar Ethil. 'You two almost won the Throne of Shadow. You killed a dozen of your kin to get there. Who stopped you? Was it Anomander Rake? Edgewalker? Kilmandaros?'

At each name the two skeletons cringed.

'What is it you seek now?' the bonecaster asked.

'Power,' said Telorast.

'Wealth,' said Curdle.

'Survival,' said Telorast.

Curdle nodded, head bobbing. 'Terrible times. Things will die.'

'Lots of things,' added Telorast. 'But it will be safe in your shadow, Great One.'

'Yes,' said Curdle. 'Safe!'

'In turn, we will guard your back.'

'Yes! That's it exactly!'

'Until,' said Olar Ethil, 'you find it expedient to betray me. You see my dilemma. You guard my back from other threats, but who will guard my back from you two?'

'Curdle can't be trusted,' said Telorast. 'I'll protect you from her, I swear it!'

'As will I from my sister!' Curdle spun to face Telorast and snapped her tiny jaws. *Clack clack clack!*

Telorast hissed in reply.

Olar Ethil turned to Torrent. 'Eleint,' she said.

Eleint? Dragons? These two? 'I always imagined they'd be bigger.'

'Soletaken,' said Olar Ethil, and then she regarded the two creatures once more. 'Or, I think, *D'ivers*, yes? Born as Tiste Andii, one woman, but *two* dragons.'

'Nonsense!'

'Insane!'

'Ridiculous!'

'Impossible!'

'Impossible,' conceded Olar Ethil, 'for most—even among the Andii. Yet, you found a way, didn't you? How? The blood of the Eleint resists the fever of D'ivers. A ritual would have been necessary. But what kind? Not Kurald Galain, nor Kurald Emurlahn. No, you have made me curious. I will have the answer—this is the bargain I offer. Tell me your secret, and you shall have my protection. Betray me, and I will destroy you both.'

Curdle turned to her companion. 'If we tell her, we are undone!'

'We're already undone, you idiot. We were never meant to be Soletaken. It just happened that way!'

'But we were true Eleint—'

'Be quiet!'

Olar Ethil suddenly stepped forward. 'True Eleint? But that makes no sense! Two who become one? Soletaken? A Tiste Andii Soletaken? No, you twist every truth—I cannot believe a thing you say!'

'Look what you did, Curdle! Now we—aagh!'

Telorast's cry came when Olar Ethil's bony hand snapped out, snaring the skeleton. It writhed and strained in her grip. She held it close, as if about to bite its head off.

'Tell her!' Telorast shrieked. 'Curdle! Tell her everything!'

'I will I will! I promise! Elder One! Listen! I will speak the truth!'

'Go on,' said Olar Ethil. Telorast now hung limp in her hand, as if lifeless, but Torrent could see the tip of its tail twitching every few moments.

Curdle leapt to a clear patch of dusty earth. With one talon it inscribed a circle round where it stood. 'We were chained, Elder, terribly, cruelly chained. In a fragment of Emurlahn. Eternal imprisonment stretched before us—you could not imagine the torment, the torture of that. So close! To our precious prize! But then, the three stood before us, between us and the throne. The bitch with her fists. The bastard with his dread sword. Edgewalker gave us a choice. Kilmandaros and the chains, or Anomander and Dragnipur. Dragnipur! We knew what

Draconus had done, you see! We knew what that sword's bite would do. Swallow our souls! No,' the skeleton visibly shivered, 'we chose Kilmandaros.'

'Two Eleint,' said Olar Ethil.

'Yes! Sisters—'

'Or lovers,' said Telorast, still lying as if dead.

'Or that, yes. We don't remember. Too long ago, too many centuries in chains—the madness! Such madness! But then a stranger found us.'

'Who?' barked Olar Ethil.

'Dessimbelackis,' said Curdle. 'He held Chaos in his hands. He told us its secret—what he had made of it. He was desperate. His people—humans—were making a mess of things. They stood as if separate from all the animals of the world. They imagined they were the rulers of nature. And cruel their tyranny, so cruel. Slaughtering the animals, making the lands barren deserts, the skies empty but for vultures.'

'Soletaken,' said Olar Ethil. 'D'ivers. He created a ritual out of chaos—to bind humans to the beasts, to force upon them their animal natures. He sought to teach them a lesson. About themselves.'

'Yes, Elder. Yes to all of that. He brought the ritual to his people—oh, it was an old ritual, much older than Dessimbelackis, much older than this world. He forced it upon his subjects.'

'This tale I know well,' said Olar Ethil. 'I was there, when we gave answer to that. The swords of the T'lan Imass dripped for days. But, there were no dragons, not there, not then.'

'You'd begun the slaughter,' said Curdle. 'He'd fled even before then, taking his D'ivers form—'

'The Deragoth.'

'Yes. He knew you were hunting him. He needed allies. But we were chained, and he could not break those chains. So he offered to take our souls—and he brought us a corpse. A woman. Tiste Andii.'

'Where did he come by it?' Olar Ethil asked. 'Who was she?'

'He never told us. But when he bound our souls to her, we stood—unchained. We thought we were free. We vowed to serve him.'

'But you did not, did you?'

Curdle hesitated.

'You betrayed him.'

'No! It wasn't like that! Each time we sought to semble into our true selves, the chains returned! Each time, we found ourselves back within Emurlahn! We were useless to him, don't you see?'

'Yet,' said Olar Ethil, 'now, you can find your true selves—'

'Not for long. Never for long,' said Curdle. 'If we hold to our Eleint selves, the chains find us. They steal us back. These bones you see here—we can do this much. We can take a body, one or two, and exist within them. But that is all. If we could reach the throne, we could break our bindings! We could escape our prison!'

'You will never win that throne,' said Olar Ethil. 'And, as you are, well, that is useless to me.'

'Great Elder! You could break those chains!'

'I could,' she replied. 'But I have no reason to. After all, why risk the enmity of Edgewalker? Or Kilmandaros? No, they chained you two for a reason. Had you not sought the throne, you would have lived free.'

'Eternal punishment—who deserves that?' Curdle demanded.

Olar Ethil laughed. 'I have walked with the T'lan Imass. Do not speak to me of eternal punishment.'

Torrent was startled by that. He faced her, his mouth twisting. 'You did that to them, bonecaster. And now you call it a punishment? Those Imass. What had they done to you, to punish them for all eternity?'

She turned her back on him.

He stared. 'Spirits of the earth! It *was* punishment! Olar Ethil—that Ritual— *you were cursing them!* Look at you—'

She spun round. 'Yes! Look at me! Do I not choose to wear that curse? My own body, my own flesh! What more can I do—'

'But wear your remorse?' He studied her in horror. 'You miserable, pathetic thing. What was it? Some offhand insult? A jilted love? Did your man sleep with some other woman? Why did you curse them for all eternity, Olar Ethil? Why?'

'You don't understand—'

Telorast chose this moment to thrash loose from her grip, landing lightly on the ground then darting a half-dozen paces away, where Curdle scrambled to join her. Olar Ethil stared at the two creatures for a moment—or so it seemed.

'Why don't you let it go?' Torrent asked. 'Bonecaster. Let them all go.'

'No! I have no choice in this—none! You mortals are such fools—you just don't see it, you don't see anything!'

'What am I supposed to see?' Torrent shouted back.

'*I am trying to save your pathetic lives! All of you!*'

He was silent for a long moment. Her gnarled hands had closed into fists. Then he said, 'If to save us, Olar Ethil, means holding prisoner the souls of the T'lan Imass, then, as a pathetic mortal, I tell you: it's too much. Free them. Leave us to die.'

She snorted—but he could sense his words had shaken her—'You would speak for all humanity, Torrent, last of the Awl? You, who dream only of an end?'

'Make it meaningful and I will not complain.'

'So wish we all,' she said in a rasp.

'Besides,' Torrent said, 'it's not their fight. Not their responsibility. Not yours, either. You seek redemption, bonecaster? Find another way. One that doesn't devour souls. One that doesn't close chains about an entire people.'

'You know so little,' she said, her tone filled with contempt. 'The T'lan Imass— *my* T'lan Imass—do you even know what they are?'

'Not really. But I've put enough together. All your conversations with strangers, and when you speak to the darkness at night—thinking me asleep. You command an army, and they are not far away from us. They are trapped in this Ritual of yours, Olar Ethil. You treat them as slaves.'

'I need them.'

'They don't need you, though, do they?'

'I summoned them! Without me they would be dust and nothing more!'

'Maybe that's how they want it,' he replied.

'Not yet. Not yet!'

Torrent gathered his reins. 'You two,' he called to the skeletons, 'here's *my* offer. No one, no matter how venal, deserves an eternity of punishment. I will seek a way to free your souls. In return, you guard my back.'

Curdle hopped forward. 'Against whom?'

He glared across at Olar Ethil. 'Her, for a start.'

'We can do that!' Telorast cried. 'We're stronger than she thinks!'

Curdle pranced up alongside Torrent's horse. 'Where are we going, Master?'

'Call me Torrent, and I am not your Master. I make no claim to own you. We are, it seems, riding to that tower.'

'Rooted!' crowed Telorast, 'but which one is it? Curdle? Which one is it?'

'How should I know? Never been here.'

'Liar!'

'So are you!'

The bickering continued as Torrent urged his mount forward. A short time later he glanced back to see Olar Ethil trudging after him. *Unbreakable, and yet . . . broken. You sour old woman. Let it go.*

Kebralle Korish led a clan of four men and three women, all that remained of the B'ehn Aralack Orshayn T'lan Imass. Once, not long ago, the Copper Ashes Clan had numbered three thousand one hundred and sixteen. There were memories of living, and then there were the memories of death, such as remained to those of the Ritual. In her memories of death, the final battle with the Order of the Red Spires hung blazing in her mind, a frozen scream, the abrupt howl of annihilation. She had stood upon the edge of the Abyss, longing to join her fallen kin but held back by the duty of her title. She was Clan Chief, and so long as will remained to her, she would be the last of the Copper Ashes to fall.

That time had not yet come, and the wake of the Red Spires was stretched out behind her, lifeless, desolate, the echoes of her scream like a bony hand at her back.

The First Sword had, perversely, elected to retain his corporeal form, walking with the weight of stone across this ravaged land, his long-bladed weapon dragging a careless furrow. The warriors of the Orshayn and the Brold had in turn surrendered the bliss of dust and now strode in a ragged, colourless mass behind him. She walked among them, her seven warriors arrayed around her. They were battered, permanently scarred by the sorcery of the Three. The tattered remnants of skin and tendon that remained were blackened, scorched. The sections of exposed bone were burnt white, webbed with cracks. The flint weapons they held had lost their sepia hue, the reddish brown replaced by mottled mauves and bluegreys. Furs, leather and hides were gone.

Among all in her clan, Kebralle Korish alone had succeeded in drawing close enough to the Three to swing her blade. She remembered, with vivid clarity, the shock upon the face of the Bearded One, when her curved weapon's edge had bit deep, scoring the flesh deep and wide across his chest. Blood, the gleam of notched ribs, rings of mail scattering against the stones of the parapet. He had staggered in retreat but she was in no mood to relent—

His companions had driven her back, a concatenation of magics hammering her from the ledge. Engulfed in raging sorcery, she had tumbled to the foot of the wall. It should have ended there, but Kebralle was Clan Chief. She had just witnessed the slaughter of almost her entire clan. No, she would not yield to oblivion. When she had risen, shrugging off the terrible chaotic flames, she had looked up to see two of the Three—they were in turn peering down at her. In their faces, disbelief, the stirrings of fear—

Inistral Ovan had sounded the withdrawal then. She could have defied him, but she had obeyed. For the seven who remained standing. For the last of her kin.

Yet even now, her memory of the bite of her blade's edge was the sweetest nectar in the hollowed husk of her soul. *Kebralle Korish stood on the wall of the Fastness. She delivered a wound upon one of the Three, the only T'lan Imass to have done so. Had he stood alone, she would have killed him. The Bearded One would have fallen, the first breach in the defences of the Three. Kebralle Korish, who had made the curved blade she held, naming it Brol—Cold Eye—and see the stain of his blood? Running black as night. In the moment the war turned, she was recalled.*

The Copper Ashes had fallen for nothing. No gaining of ground, no victory. They had been flung away, and one day she would make Inistral Ovan pay for that.

Enough reason to persist, this secret vow. The First Sword could have his war, his search for answers, his demand for an accounting with Olar Ethil. Kebralle Korish had her own reasons for continuing on. Olar Ethil—who had summoned them all—was welcome to her secret motives. Kebralle did not care. Besides, Olar Ethil had given her another chance, and for that alone Kebralle would do as she asked. Until such time that the opportunity for vengeance presented itself.

Inistral Ovan bore the shame of defeat, and he did so without dissembling. But it was not good enough. Not even close. *I will punish him. I will find for him an eternity of suffering. Upon the lost lives of my kin, this I do vow.*

It wasn't smell—he was not capable of picking up a scent—but something that nevertheless reached into his mind, pungent, redolent of memories Kalt Urmanal weathered as would an ice spire a blizzard's wind. He was annealed in madness, polished bright with insanity. All conflict within him had been smoothed away, until he was nothing more than the purity of purpose.

The K'Chain Che'Malle were upon this land. The slayers of his wife, his children. Their vile oils had soaked this dusty soil; their scales had whispered through the dry air. They were *close.*

Hatred died with the Ritual of Tellann. So it was held, so it was believed by every T'lan Imass. Even the war against the Jaghut had been a cold, unfeeling prosecution. Kalt Urmanal's soul trembled with the realization that hatred was alive within him. Blistering hatred. He felt as if all his bones were massed, knotted into a single fist, hard as stone, a fist that but awaited its victim.

He would find them.

Nothing else mattered. The First Sword had not bound his kin—a dread error, for Kalt knew that wars raged within each and every one of them. He could feel as much, swirls of conflicting desires, awakened hungers and needs. An army must kneel before a single master. Without that obeisance, each warrior stood alone, tethers loose, and at the first instant of conflict each would seek his or her own path. The First Sword, in his refusal to command, had lost his army.

He was a fool. He had forgotten what it meant to rule. Whatever he sought, whatever he found, he would discover that he was alone.

First Sword. What did the title mean? Skill with his weapon—none would deny that Onos T'oolan possessed that, else he would never have earned the title. But surely there was more to it. The strength to impose his will. The qualities of true leadership. The arrogance of command and the expectation that such commands would be followed unquestioningly. Onos T'oolan possessed none of these traits. He had failed the first time, had he not? And now, he would fail again.

Kalt Urmanal would trail in the wake of the First Sword, but he would not follow him.

The Jaghut played games with us. They painted themselves in the guises of gods. It amused them. Our indignation stung to life became a rage of unrelenting determination. But it was misplaced. In our awakening to their games, they had no choice but to withdraw. The secret laid bare ended the game. The wars were not necessary. Our pursuit acquired the mien of true madness, and in assuming it we lost ourselves . . . for all time.

The Jaghut were the wrong enemy. The Ritual should have been enacted in the name of a war against the K'Chain Che'Malle. They were the ones who hunted us. For food. For sport. They were the ones who saw us as nothing more than meat. They would descend upon our camps sleek with the oils of cruel, senseless slaughter, and loved ones died.

Indignation? The word is too weak for what I feel. For all of us who were victims of the K'Chain Che'Malle.

First Sword, you lead us nowhere—we are all done with the Jaghut. We no longer care. Our cause is dead, its useless bones revealed to each and every one of us. We have kicked through them and now the path stretches clear—but these paths we do not share with our kin.

So, why do we follow you here and now? Why do we step in time with you? You tell us nothing. You do not even acknowledge our existence. You are worse than the Jaghut.

He knew of Olar Ethil, the bonecaster who had cursed them into eternal suffering. For her, he felt nothing. She was as stupid as the rest. As blind, as mistaken as all the other bonecasters who folded their power into the Ritual. *Will you fight her, First Sword? If so, then you will do it alone. We are nothing to you, and so you are nothing to us.*

Do not let the eyes deceive. We are no army.
We are no army.

Nom Kala found the bonecaster Ulag Togtil at her side. He was, without question, the biggest warrior among the Imass she had ever seen. Trell blood. She wondered what he had looked like in the flesh. Frightening, no doubt, broad-mouthed and tusked, his eyes small as an ice boar's. She had few memories of Trell—they were all but gone in her time, among the first to be driven from the face of the earth by the humans. Indeed, she was not even certain her memories were true ones, rather than something bled into her by the Orshayn.

Sour blood, that. A deluge of vicious sentiments, confused desires, depthless despair and pointless rage. She felt under assault—these Orshayn were truly tortured, spiritually destroyed. But neither she nor her kin had acquired any skill in fending off this incessant flood. They had never before experienced the like.

From the First Sword himself, however, there was nothing. Not a single wisp of thought escaped him, not a hint of emotion. Was he simply lifeless, there in his soul? Or was his self-command so absolute that even her most determined assaults upon his thoughts simply slid off, weak as rain on stone? The mystery that was Onos T'oolan dogged her.

'A measure of mercy,' Ulag said, intruding upon her thoughts.

'What is, Bonecaster?'

'You bleed as well, Nom Kala. We are all wayward. Bone trembles, darkness spins in what remains of our eyes. We believe we are the creators of our thoughts, our feelings, but I think otherwise.'

'Do you?'

He nodded. 'We roil in his wake. All this violence, this fury. It devours us, each one, and is shaped by what it eats. And so we believe each of us stands alone in our intent. Most troubling, Nom Kala. How soon before we turn upon one another?'

'Then there is no measure of mercy,' she replied.

'That depends.'

'On what?'

'On how subtle is Onos T'oolan.'

'Please, explain.'

'Nom Kala, he has said he will not compel us to obedience. He will not be as a T'lan Imass. This is significant. Is he aware of the havoc wrought in his wake? I believe he is.'

'Then, what purpose?'

'We will see.'

'Only if you are correct, and if the First Sword is then able to draw us to him—before it is too late. What you describe holds great risk, and the longer he waits, the less likely he will be able to gather us.'

'That is true,' he rumbled in reply.

'You believe in him, don't you?'

'Faith is a strange thing—among the T'lan Imass, it is little more than a pale ghost of memory. Perhaps, Nom Kala, the First Sword seeks to awaken it in us once more. To make us more than T'lan Imass. Thus, he does not compel us. Instead, he shows us the freedom of mortality, which we'd all thought long lost. How do the living command their kin? How can a mortal army truly function, given the chaos within each soldier, these disparate desires?'

'What value in showing us such things?' Nom Kala asked. 'We are not mortal. We are T'lan Imass.'

He shrugged. 'I have no answer to that, yet. But, I think, he will show us.'

'He had better not wait too long, Bonecaster.'

'Nom Kala,' Ulag was regarding her, 'I believe you were beautiful once.'

'Yes. Once.'

'Would that I had seen you then.'

But she shook her head. 'Imagine the pain now, had you done so.'

'Ah, there is that. I am sorry.'

'As am I, Bonecaster.'

'Are we there yet? My feet hurt.'

Draconus halted, turned to observe the half-blood Toblakai. 'Yes, perhaps we can rest for a time. Are you hungry?'

Ublala nodded. 'And sleepy. And this armour chafes my shoulders. And the axe is heavy. And I miss my friends.'

'There is a harness ring for your axe,' Draconus said. 'You don't have to carry it at the ready. As you can see, no one can come upon us without our seeing them from some distance away.'

'But if I see a rabbit or a chicken, I can run it down and then we can eat.'

'That won't be necessary—you have already seen that I am able to conjure food, and water.'

Ublala scowled. 'I want to do my part.'

'I see. I am sure you will, before too long.'

'You see something?' Ublala straightened, looked round. 'Rabbit? Cow? Those two women over there?'

Draconus started, and then searched until he found the two figures, walking now towards them but still three hundred or so paces away. Coming up from the south, both on foot. 'We shall await them,' he said after a moment. 'But, Ublala, there is no need to fight.'

'No, sex is better. When it comes to women, I mean. I never touched that mule. That's sick and I don't care what they said. Can we eat now?'

'Build us a fire,' Draconus said. 'Use the wood we gathered yesterday.'

'All right. Where is it?'

Draconus gestured and a modest stack of broken branches appeared almost at Ublala's feet.

'Oh, there it is! Never mind, Draconus, I found the wood.'

The woman in the lead was young, her garb distinctly barbaric. Her eyes shone from a band of black paint that possibly denoted grief, while the rest of her face was painted white in the pattern of a skull. She was well-muscled, her long braided hair the colour of rust. Three steps behind her staggered an old woman, barefoot, her hide tunic smeared with filth. Rings glittered on blackened fingers, a jarring detail in the midst of her dishevelled state.

The two stopped ten paces from Draconus and Ublala. The younger one spoke.

Ublala looked up from the fire he'd just sparked to life. 'Trader tongue—I understand you. Draconus, they're hungry and thirsty.'

'I know, Ublala. You will find food in that satchel. And a jug of ale.'

'Really? What satchel—oh, never mind. Tell the pretty one I want to have sex with her, but say it more nicely—'

'Ublala, you and I speak the same trader tongue, more often than not. As we are doing now.' He stepped forward. 'Welcome, then, we will share with you.'

The younger woman, whose right hand had closed on a dagger at her belt as soon as Ublala made his desire plain, now shifted her attention back to Draconus. 'I am Ralata, a Skincut of the Ahkrata White Face Barghast.'

'You are a long way from home, Ralata.'

'Yes.'

Draconus looked past her to the old woman. 'And your companion?'

'I found her, wandering alone. She is Sekara, a highborn among the White Faces. Her mind is mostly gone.'

'She has gangrenous fingers,' Draconus observed. 'They must be removed, lest the infection spread.'

'I know,' said Ralata, 'but she refuses my attentions. It's the rings, I think. Her last claim to wealth.' The Skincut hesitated, and then said, 'My people are gone. Dead. The White Face Barghast are no more. My clan. Sekara's. Everyone. I do not know what happened—'

'Dead!' shrieked Sekara, holding up her rotted hands. 'Frozen! Frozen dead!'

Ublala, who'd jumped at the old woman's cries, now edged closer to Draconus. 'That one smells bad,' he said. 'And those fingers don't work—someone's going to have to feed her. Not me. She says awful things.'

Ralata resumed: 'She tells me this a hundred times a day. I do not doubt her—I cannot—I see slaughter in her eyes. And in my heart, I know that we are alone.'

'The infection has found her brain,' said Draconus. 'Best if you killed her, Ralata.'

'Leaving me the last of the White Faces? I do not have the courage to do that.'

'You give me leave to do so?' Draconus asked.

Ralata flinched.

'Ralata,' said Draconus, 'you two are not the last of your people. Others still live.'

Her eyes narrowed. 'How do you know that?'

'I saw them. At a distance, dressed little different from you. The same weapons. They numbered some five or six thousand, perhaps more.'

'Where, when?'

Draconus glanced over at Ublala. 'Before I found my Toblakai friend here. Six, seven days ago, I believe—my sense of time is not what it used to be. The very change of light still startles me. Day, night, there is so much that I had forgotten.' He passed a hand over his face and then sighed. 'Ralata, do you give me leave? It will be an act of mercy, and I will be quick. She will not suffer.'

The old woman was still staring at her blackened hands, as if willing them to move, but the swollen digits were curled into lifeless hooks. Her face twisted in frustration.

'Will you help me raise her cairn?'

'Of course.'

Ralata finally nodded.

Draconus walked up to Sekara. He gently lowered the woman's hands, and then set his own to either side of her face. Her manic eyes darted and then suddenly fixed on his. At the last instant, he saw in them something like recognition. Terror, her mouth opening—

A swift snap to one side broke the neck. The woman slumped, still gaping, eyes holding on his even as he slowly lowered her to the ground. A few breaths later and the life left that accusing, horror-filled stare. Straightening, he stepped back, faced the others. 'It is done.'

'I'll go find some stones,' said Ublala. 'I'm good at graves and stuff. And then, Ralata, I will show you the horse and you'll be so happy.'

The woman frowned. 'Horse? What horse?'

'What Stooply the Whore calls it, the thing between my legs. My bucking horse. The one-eyed river eel. The Smart Woman's Dream, what Shurq Elalle calls it. Women give it all sorts of names, but they all smile when they say them. You can give it any name you want and you'll be smiling, too. You'll see.'

Ralata stared after the Toblakai as he set off in search of stones, and then she turned to Draconus. 'He's but a child—'

'Only in his thoughts,' Draconus said. 'I have seen him stripped down.'

'If he tries—if either of you tries to rape me, I'll kill you.'

'He won't. Nor will I. You are welcome to journey with us—we are travelling east—the same direction as the Barghast I saw. Perhaps indeed we will catch up to them, or at least cross their trail once more.'

'What is that meat on the fire?' she asked, drawing closer.

'Bhederin.'

'There are none in the Wastelands.'

Draconus shrugged.

Still she hesitated, and then she said, 'I am hunting a demon. Winged. It murdered my friends.'

'How are you able to track this winged demon, Ralata?'

'It kills everything in its path. That's a trail I can follow.'

'I have seen no such signs.'

'Nor I of late,' she admitted. 'Not for the past two days, since I found Sekara, in fact. But the path seems to be eastward, so I will go in that direction. If I find these other Barghast, all the better. If not, my hunt continues.'

'Understood,' he replied. 'Now, will you join me in some ale?'

She spoke behind him as he crouched to pour the amber liquid into two pewter tankards. 'I mean to bury her with those rings, Draconus.'

'We are not thieves,' he replied.

'Good.'

She accepted the tankard he lifted to her.

Ublala returned with an armload of boulders.

'Ublala,' said Draconus, 'save showing your horse for later.'

The huge man's face fell, and then he brightened again. 'All right. It's more exciting in the dark anyway.'

Strahl had never desired to be Warleader of the Senan. It had been easier feeding himself ambitions he had believed for ever beyond reach, a simple and mostly harmless bolstering of his own ego, giving him a place alongside the other warriors opposed to Onos T'oolan, just one among a powerful, influential cadre of ranking Barghast. He had enjoyed that power and all the privileges it delivered. He had especially revelled in his hoard of hatred, a currency of endless value, and to spend it cost him nothing, no matter how profligate he was. Such a warrior was swollen, well protected behind a shield of contempt. And when shields locked, the wall was impregnable.

But now he was alone. His hoard had vanished—he'd not even seen the scores of hands reaching in behind his back. A warleader's only wealth was the value of his or her word. Lies sucked the colour from gold. Truth was the hardest and purest and rarest metal of all.

There had been an instant, a single, blinding instant, when he'd stood before his tribe, raising high that truth, forged by hands grown cold. He had claimed it for his own, and in turn his kin had met his eyes, and they had answered in kind. But even then, in his mouth there had been the taste of ashes. Was he nothing more than the voice of the dead? Of fallen warriors who each in turn had been greater than Strahl could ever hope to be? He could voice their desire—and he had done precisely that—but he could not think their thoughts, and so they could not help him, not here, not now. He was left with the paltry confusions of his own mind, and it was not enough.

It had not taken long for his warriors to discover that. After all, where could he lead them? The people of the settled lands behind them sought their blood. The way ahead was ravaged, lifeless. And, as bold as the gesture had been, the Senan had fled a battle, leaving their allies to die. No one wanted the guilt of that. They gave it all to Strahl. Had he not commanded them? Had he not ordered their withdrawal?

He could not argue the point. He could not defend himself against the truths they spoke. *This belongs to me. This is my crime. The others died to give it to me, because they stood where I now stand. Their courage was purer. They led. I can only follow. If it had been any other way, I could have been their match.*

He squatted, facing away from the few remaining fires of the camp stretched out in a disorganized sprawl behind him. Stars spread a remote vista across the jade-soaked sky. The Talons themselves seemed much closer, as if moments from cleaving the heavens and slashing down to the earth itself. No clearer omen could be imagined. *Death comes. An age ends, and with it so end the White Face Barghast, and then their gods, who were freed only to be abandoned, given life only to die. Well, you bastards, now you know how it feels.*

They were almost out of food. The shouldermen and witches had exhausted themselves drawing water from this parched land. Soon the effort would begin killing them, one by one. The retreat had already claimed the eldest and weakest among the Senan. *We march east. Why? No enemy awaits us out there. The war we sought is not the one we found, and now glory has eluded us.*

Wherever that one true battle is, the White Faces should be there. Cutting destiny off at the knees. So sought Humbrall Taur. So sought Onos Toolan. But the great alliance is no more. Only the Senan remain. And we falter and soon will fade. Flesh to wood, wood to dust. Bone to stone, stone to dust. The Barghast shall become a desert—only then will we finally find a land on which to settle. These Wastelands, perhaps. When the wind stirs us awake with each dawn.

Before long, he knew, he would be cut down. Sometimes, after all, guilt must be excised with a knife. He would not resist. Of course, as the last surviving Senan staggered and fell, the final curse on their lips would be his name. *Strahl, who stole from us our glory.* Not much of a glory, to be sure. Maral Eb had been a fool and Strahl could shrug off most of the venom when it came to that fiasco. *Still, we could have died with weapons in our hands. That would have been something. Like spitting to clear the taste. Maybe the next watery mouthful of misery won't be as bad. Like that. Just that one gesture.*

Eastward then. Each step slowing.

Suicide was such an ugly word. But one could choose it for oneself. When it came to an entire people . . . well, that was different. Or was it? *I will lead us, until someone else does. I will ask for nothing. We march to our deaths. But then, it is all we ever do.* This last thought pleased him. In the ghoulish darkness, he smiled. Against futility, guilt did not stand a chance.

Life is a desert, but, dear friends, between my legs you will find the sweetest oasis. Being dead, I can say this with not a hint of irony. If you were me, you'd understand.

'You have a curious expression on that painted face, Captain. What are you thinking?'

Shurq Elalle pulled her gaze from the desolate sweep of sullen grey waves and glanced over at Felash, fourteenth daughter of King Tarkulf and Queen Abrastal of Bolkando. 'My First Mate was complaining, Princess, a short time ago.'

'This has been a pleasant enough journey thus far, if somewhat tedious. What cause has he to complain?'

'He is a noseless, one-eyed, one-handed, one-legged half-deaf man with terrible breath, but I agree with you, Princess. No matter how bad things can appear to be, they can always get worse. Such is life.'

'You speak with something like longing, Captain.'

Shurq Elalle shrugged. 'You may be young, but you are not easily deceived, Princess. I trust you comprehend my unique circumstances.'

Felash pursed her plump lips, fluttering her fingers dismissively. 'It took some time, to be honest. Indeed, it was my handmaiden who first broached the possibility. You do well in disguising your situation, Captain, a most admirable achievement.'

'Thank you, Highness.'

'Still, I wonder what so consumed your thoughts. Skorgen Kaban, I have learned, has no end of gripes, not least the plague of superstitions ever haunting him.'

'He has not been at his best,' Shurq admitted. 'Ever since you purchased this extension, in fact. A thousand rumours have drifted from Kolanse, not one of them pleasing. The crew are miserable, and to the First Mate, that misery feeds his every fear.'

'It is well understood, I trust,' said Felash, 'that most of the Perish fleet has preceded us. Have we seen any indication that disaster befell them?'

'That depends,' Shurq replied. 'The absence of evidence of any sort is ominous enough, especially for sailors—'

'Then they can never be satisfied, can they?'

'Absolutely true, which is why I adore them so.'

'Captain?'

She smiled at the princess. 'Neither can I. You wondered what I was thinking, and that is my answer.'

'I see.'

No, little girl, you do not. But never mind. Give it time.

Felash continued: 'How frustrated you must be!'

'If it is frustration, it is a most delicious kind.'

'I find you fascinating, Captain.'

The plump princess was wearing a fur-lined cloak, the hood drawn up against the sharp offshore wind. Her round, heavily made-up face looked dusted and flawless. She clearly worked very hard at appearing older than she in truth was, but the effect reminded Shurq of those porcelain dolls the Shake used to find washed up on the beaches, the ones they traded away as if the things were cursed. Inhuman in perfection, but in truth hinting at deeper flaws. 'And you in turn interest me, Highness. Is it the simple privilege of royalty that permits you to commandeer a foreign ship, captain and crew, and set out on a whim into the unknown?'

'Privilege, Captain? Dear me, no. Burden, in fact. Knowledge is essential. The gathering of intelligence is what ensures the kingdom's continued survival. We are not a great military power, such as the Letherii who can hold their insensitive bullying as if it was a virtue of forthright uncomplexity. Attitudes of false provincialism serve a well-honed suspicion of others. "Deal me straight and true and I am your friend. Deal me wrong and I will destroy you." So goes the diplomat's theme of discourse. Of course, one quickly learns that all those poses of righteous honesty are but a screen for self-serving avarice.'

'I take it,' Shurq said, 'the children of the Bolkando King and Queen are well schooled in such theories of diplomacy.'

'Almost from birth, Captain.'

Shurq smiled at the exaggeration. 'It seems your sense of Lether is somewhat antiquated, if I dare venture an opinion on the matter.'

But Felash shook her head. 'King Tehol is perhaps more subtle than his predecessors. The disarming charm hides a most devious mind.'

'Devious? Oh yes, Highness. Absolutely.'

'Naturally,' Felash went on, 'one would be a fool to trust him. Or believe anything he says. I would wager his Queen is precisely the same.'

'Indeed? Consider this, if you will, Princess: you see two rulers of a vast empire who just so happen to despise virtually every trait that empire possesses. The inequity, the cruel expression of privilege and the oppression of the dispossessed. The sheer idiocy of a value system that raises useless metals and meaningless writs above that of humanity and plain decency. Consider two rulers who are trapped in that world—yes, they would dismantle all of it, if they could. But how? Imagine the resistance. All those elites so comfortable with their elevated positions of power. Do you truly believe such people would willingly relinquish that?' Shurq leaned on the rail and regarded Felash, whose eyes were wide.

'Well, Highness? Imagine, in fact, if they delivered upon you and your people a diplomatic onslaught of emancipation. The end of the nobility and all the inherited rank and privilege—you and your entire family, Princess, out on your asses. The end of money and its false strictures. Gold? Pretty rings and baubles, oh yes, but beyond that? Might as well hoard polished stones from a shoreline. Wealth as proof of superiority? Nonsense. Proof only of the power to deliver violence. I see by your shocked expression, Highness, that you begin to comprehend, and so I will leave it there.'

'But that is madness!'

Shurq shrugged. 'Burdens, you said, Princess.'

'Are you saying Tehol and his wife revile their own claim to power?'

'Probably.'

'Meaning, in turn, they hold people like me in similar contempt?'

'Personally? I doubt it. Rather, they likely question your right to dictate the lives of your kingdom's people. Clearly, your family asserts such a right, and you possess the military might to enforce such a claim. I will not speak for Tehol or Janath with any certitude, Highness, but I suspect they deal with you and every other dignitary from every other kingdom and whatnot, with an identical forbearance. The system is what it is—'

'*Someone* needs to rule!'

'And, alas, most of the rules rulers impose are the ones that make certain it's *them* doing the ruling from now on, and they'll co-opt and exploit an entire nation of people to keep it that way. Generation upon generation and for evermore. Anyway, Highness, should you ever return to Letheras by all means debate it with Tehol or Janath. They delight in such things. As for me, I can only answer as a ship's captain—'

'Exactly! No ship can function without a hierarchy!'

'So very true. I was but conveying to you an interpretation of Tehol and Janath's position contrary to the one you have been taught to believe. Such complicated philosophies are well beyond me. Besides, do I really care any more? I work within this system because that is an agreeable option, a means, in fact, of avoiding boredom. I am also able to help make my crew wealthier than they might otherwise be, and this pleases me. For myself, of course, I cannot even tell you if I believe in anything—anything at all. Why should I? What would such beliefs grant me? Peace of mind? My mind is at peace. A secure future? Since when is the future *ever* secure? Worthy goals? Who decides what's worthy? What's "worth" all about anyway? Highness, believe me, I am not the one for this discussion.'

'Errant look away, Captain, you have shocked me to the core. I feel positively faint, assailed from so many directions my mind spins.'

'Shall I summon your handmaiden, Highness?'

'Dear me, no. Her seasickness refuses to abate, the poor thing.'

'There are medicines—'

'Not one of which do a thing for her. Why do you think I am up here with you, Captain? I cannot abide her moaning. Even more deplorable, before long when we are both in the cabin it is I who must attend to her, rather than the other way round. The impropriety of that is intolerable.'

Shurq Elalle nodded. 'Impropriety, yes, I see. You should have brought the matter to me long ago, Highness. I am happy to assign a member of my crew to look after your handmaiden. Perhaps indeed we can have her transferred to another berth—'

'No no, none of that, Captain. Though I do thank you for the generous offer. My frustration is ever shortlived. Besides, what better means of reminding myself that privileges of rank are but false constructs? When humanity and simple decency demand the relinquishing of such things?'

'Well said, Highness.'

Felash fluttered her fingers. 'And on that thought, best I return below, to see how the wretched child fares.' She smiled up at Shurq with her doll's smile. 'Thank you for a most invigorating discussion, Captain.'

'I too enjoyed it, Princess.'

Felash strode away, admirably sure-footed on the pitching deck. Shurq settled her forearms down on the rail and scanned the distant coastline to port. Jungle had given way to brown hills a few days past. The only trees she'd seen since had been uprooted boles crowding the thin line of beach. Enormous trees. Who tore up thousand-year-old trees so indiscriminately as to leave them to waste? *Kolanse, what have you been up to?*

We'll find out soon enough.

Felash entered the cabin. 'Well?'

Her handmaid looked up from where she sat crosslegged before the small brazier of coals. 'It is as we feared, Highness. A vast emptiness awaits us. Desolation beyond measure. Upon landing, we shall have to travel north—far north, all the way to Estobanse Province.'

'Prepare my bowl,' Felash said, shrugging off her cloak and letting it fall. She sank down on to a heap of pillows. 'They can go nowhere else, can they?'

The bigger woman rose and stepped over to the low table where sat an ornate, silver-inlaid, glass hookah. She measured out a cup of spiced wine and slowly filled the bulb, then drew out the silver tray, tapping out the old ashes into a small pewter plate. 'If you mean the Perish, Highness, that is a fair assumption.'

Felash reached under her silk blouse and loosened the bindings of her undershirt. 'My eldest sister did this too much,' she said, 'and now her tits rest down on her belly like a trader's bladders riding a mule's rump. Curse these things. Why couldn't I be more like Hethry?'

'There are herbs—'

'Then they'd not fix their eyes there, would they? No, these damned things are my first gifts of diplomacy. Just seeing those dilated pupils is a victory.'

The handmaid brought over the hookah. She'd already drawn it alight and aromatic smoke spread out through the cabin. She had been doing this for her mistress for four years now. Each time, it preceded an extended period of intense discussion between her and the princess. Plans were created, tested, every detail hammered into place with the steady tap-tap-tap of rounding a copper bowl.

'Hethry views you with great envy, Highness.'

'She's an idiot so that's no surprise. Have we heard from Mother's cedas?'

'Still nothing. The Wastelands seethe with terrible powers, Highness, and it is clear that the Queen intends to remain there—like us, she seeks answers.'

'Then we are both fools. All of this is so far beyond Bolkando's borders that we would be hard pressed to extend any legitimate reasons to pursue the course we're on. What did Kolanse contribute to our kingdom?'

'Black honey, hardwoods, fine linens, parchment and paper—'

'In the past five years?' Felash's eyes glittered in a veil of smoke.

'Nothing.'

'Precisely. My question was in fact rhetorical. Contact has ceased. We acquired nothing essential from them in any case. As for the Wastelands and the motley armies crawling about on them, well, they too have left our environs. We dog them at our peril, I believe.'

'The Queen marches beside some of those armies, Highness. We must assume she has discovered something, providing a compelling reason for remaining in their company.'

'They march to Kolanse.'

'Indeed.'

'And we don't know why.'

The handmaid said nothing.

Felash sent a stream of smoke ceilingward. 'Tell me again of the undead in the Wastelands.'

'Which ones, Highness?'

'The ones who move as dust on the winds.'

The handmaid frowned. 'At first I thought that they alone were responsible for the impenetrable cloud defying my efforts. They number in the thousands, after all, and the one who leads them emanates such blinding power that I dare not look too long upon it. But now . . . Highness, there are others. Not dead to be sure. Even so. One of darkness and cold. One of golden fire high in the sky. Another at his side, a winged knot of grief harder and crueller than the sharpest cut diamond. Still others, hiding in the howl of wolves—'

'Wolves?' Felash cut in. 'Do you mean the Perish?'

'No and yes, Highness. I can be no clearer than that.'

'Wonderful. Go on.'

'Yet another, fiercer and wilder than all the others. It hides inside stone. It swims in a sea thick with the pungent flavours of serpents. It waits for the moment, and grows in its power, and facing it . . . Highness, whatever it faces is more dreadful than I can bear.'

'This clash—will it occur on the Wastelands?'

'I believe so, yes.'

'Do you think my mother knows?'

The handmaid hesitated, and then said, 'Highness, I cannot imagine her cedas to be anything but utterly blind and thus ignorant of that threat. It is only because I am able to see from this distance, from the outside, as it were, that I have gleaned as much as I have.'

'Then she is in trouble.'

'Yes. I think so, Highness.'

'You must find a way,' said Felash, 'to reach through to her.'

'Highness. There is one way, but it risks much.'

'Who will bear that risk?'

'Everyone aboard this ship.'

Felash pulled on her mouthpiece, blew rings that floated, wavered and slowly flattened out, drifting to form a chain in the air. Her eyes widened upon seeing it.

The handmaid simply nodded. 'He is close, yes. My mind has spoken his name.'

'And this omen here before us?'

'Highness, one bargains with an Elder God at great peril. We must pay in blood.'

'Whose blood?'

The handmaid shook her head.

Felash tapped the amber tube against her teeth, thinking. 'Why is the sea so thirsty?'

Again, there was no possible answer to that question. 'Highness?'

'Has the damned thing a name? Do you know it?'

'Many names, of course. When the colonists from the First Empire set forth, they made sacrifice to the salty seas in the name of Jhistal. The Tiste Edur in their great war canoes opened veins to feed the foam, and this red froth they called Bloodmane—in the Edur language that word was *Mael*. The Jheck who live upon the ice call the dark waters beneath that ice the Lady of Patience, *Barutalan*. The Shake speak of *Neral*, the Swallower.'

'And on.'

'And on, Highness.'

Felash sighed. 'Summon him, and we shall see what cost this bargain.'

'As you command, Highness.'

On the foredeck, Shurq Elalle straightened as the lookout cried out. She faced out to sea. *That's a squall. Looks to be a bad one. Where in the Errant's bung-hole did that come from?* 'Pretty!'

Skorgen Kaban clumped into view from amidships. 'Seen it, Cap'n!'

'Swing her out, Pretty. If it's gonna bite, best we lock jaws with it.' The thought of the storm throwing *Undying Gratitude* on to that treefall shore wasn't a pleasant one, not in the least.

The black wire-wool cloud seemed to be coming straight for them.

'Piss in the boot, this dance won't be fun.'

Chapter Twenty-Two

This is ancient patience
belly down on the muds
lining the liana shore.
Everyone must cross
rivers in high flood.
Bright blossoms float
past on the way down
to the snake mangroves
harbouring the warm sea.
But nothing slides smooth
into the swirling waters
hunting their bold beauty.
We mill uneasy on the verge
awaiting necessity's
paroxysms—the sudden rush
to cross into the future.
Rivers in high flood
dream of red passages
and the lizards will feed
as they have always done.
We bank on numbers,
the chaotic tumult,
the frenzied path on the backs
of loved ones, fathers and
mothers, the quill-lickers
inscribing lists of lives:
this solid stand, that
slippage of desire.
Ancient patience swells
the tongue, all the names
written in tooth-row jaws—
we surge, we clamber eyes
rolling and the distant shore
calls to us, that ribbed future
holds us a place in waiting.
But the river scrolls down
high in its hungry season
and the lizards wallow fat

in the late afternoon sun.
See me now in the fleck
of their lazy regard—and
now I wait with them,
for the coming rains

THE SEASON OF HIGH FLOOD
GAMAS ENICTEDON

Children will wander. they will walk as if the future did not exist. Among adults, the years behind one force focus upon what waits ahead, but with children this is not so. The past was a blur of befuddled sensations, the future was white as the face of the sun. Knowing this yielded no comfort. Badalle was still a child, should one imagine her of a certain age, but she walked like a crone, tottering, hobbling. Even her voice belonged to an old woman. And the dull, fused thing behind her eyes could not be shaken awake.

She had a vague recollection, a memory or an invention, of looking upon an ancient woman, a grandmother perhaps, or a great aunt. Lying shrunken on a bed, swaddled in wool blankets. Still breathing, still blinking, still listening. And yet those eyes, in their steady watching, their grainy observation, showed nothing. The stare of a dying person. Eyes spanning a gulf, slowly losing grip on the living side of the chasm, soon to release and slide to the side of death. Did those eyes feed thoughts? Or had things reduced to mere impressions, blobs of colour, blurred motions—as if in the closing of death one simply returned to the way things had been for a newborn? She could think of a babe's eyes, in the moments and days after arriving in the world. Seeing but not seeing, a face of false smiles, the innocence of not-knowing.

She had knelt beside a nameless boy, there on the very edge of the Crystal City, and had stared into his eyes, knowing he saw her, but knowing nothing else. He was beyond expression (oh, the horror of that, to see a human face beyond expression, to wonder who was trapped inside, and why they'd given up getting out). He'd studied her in turn—she could see that much—and held her gaze, as if he'd wanted company in his last moments of life. She would not have turned away, not for anything. The gift was small for her, but all she had, and for him, perhaps it was everything.

Was it as simple as that? In dying, did he offer, there in his eyes, a blank slate? Upon which she could scribble anything she liked, anything and everything that eased her own torment?

She'd find those answers when her death drew close. And she knew she too would remain silent, watchful, revealing nothing. And her eyes would look both beyond and within, and in looking within she would find her private truths. Truths that belonged to her and no one else. Who cared to be generous in those final moments? She'd be past easing anyone else's pain.

And this was Badalle's deepest fear. To be so selfish with the act of dying.

She'd not even seen when the life left the boy's eyes. Somehow, that moment was itself a most private revelation. Recognition was slow, uncertainty growing leaden as she slowly comprehended that the eyes she stared into gave back not a single glimmer of light. *Gone. He is gone.* Sunlight cut paths through the prisms of crystal walls, giving his still face a rainbow mask.

He had probably been no more than ten years old. He'd come so far, only to fail at the very threshold of salvation. *What do we living know about true irony?* His face was leather skin pulled taut over bones. The huge eyes belonged to someone else. He'd lost his eyelashes, his eyebrows.

Had he been remembering those times before this march? That other world? She doubted it. She was older and she remembered very little. Patchy images, wrought dreams crowded with impossible things. Thick green leaves—a garden? Amphorae with glistening flanks, something wonderful in her mouth. A tongue free of sores, lips devoid of splits, a flashing smile—were any of these things real? Or did they belong to her fantastic dreams that haunted her now day and night?

I grow wings. I fly across the world, across many worlds. I fly into paradise and leave desolation in my wake, because I feed on all that I see. I devour it whole. I am discoverer and destroyer both. Somewhere awaits the great tomb, the final home of my soul. I will find it yet. Tomb, palace, when you're dead what's the difference? There I will reside for ever, embraced by my insatiable hunger.

She'd dreamed of children. Looking down from a great height. Watching them march in their tens of thousands. They had cattle, mules and oxen. Many rode horses. They glittered blindingly in the hard sunlight, as if they bore the treasures of the world on their backs. Children, but not *her* children.

And then the day ended and darkness bled to the earth, and she dreamed that it was at last time to descend, spiralling, moaning through the air. She would strike swiftly, and if possible unseen by any. There were magics below, in that vast multi-limbed camp. She had to avoid brushing those. If need be, she would kill to silence, but this was not her true task.

She dreamed her eyes—and she had more of those than she should, no matter—fixed upon the two burning spots she sought. Bright golden hearth-flames—she had been tracking them for a long time now, in service to the commands she had been given.

She was descending upon the children.

To steal *fire*.

Strange dreams, yes, but it seemed they existed for a reason. The deeds done within them had purpose, and this was more than anything real could manage.

The Quitters had been driven away. By song, by poems, by words. Brayderal, the betrayer among them, had vanished into the city. Rutt oversaw the ribby survivors, and everyone slept in cool rooms in buildings facing on to a broad fountain in the centre of which stood a crystal statue weeping the sweetest water. It was never quite enough—not for them all—and the basin of the surrounding pool was fissured with cracks that drank with endless thirst. But they were all managing to drink just enough to stay alive.

Behind a glittering building they'd found an orchard, the trees of a type none had seen before. Fruits massed on the branches, each one long and sheathed in a thick skin the colour of dirt. The pulp within was soft and impossibly succulent. It filled the stomach with no pangs. They'd quickly eaten them all, but the next day Saddic had found another orchard, bigger than the first one, and then yet another. Starvation had been eluded. For now.

Of course, they continued to eat those children who for whatever reason still died—no one could think of wasting anything. Never again.

Badalle walked the empty streets closer to the city's heart. A palace occupied the centre, the only structure in the city that had been systematically destroyed, smashed down as if with giant mallets and hammers. From the mounds of shattered crystals Badalle had selected a shard as long as her forearm. Having wrapped rags around one end she now held a makeshift weapon.

Brayderal was still alive. Brayderal still wanted to see them all dead. Badalle meant to find her first, find her and kill her.

As she walked, she whispered her special poem. Brayderal's poem. Her poem of killing.

> 'Where is my child of justice?
> I have a knife that will speak true
> To the very heart
> Where is my child of justice?
> Spat out so righteously
> On a world meant to kneel
> In slavery
> Where is my child of justice?
> I want to read your proof
> Of what you say you deserve
> I will see your knife
> Where is my child of justice?
> Let us lock blades
> You claim whatever you please
> I claim no right but you'

She had sailed down in her dreams. She had stolen fire. No blood had been shed, no magics were awakened. The children slept on, seeing nothing, peaceful in ignorance. When they awoke, they would face the rising sun, and begin the day's march.

By this detail alone she knew that these children were indeed strangers.

She'd looked upon the boy until life left him. Then, with Rutt and Saddic and two dozen others, she had eaten him. Chewing on the stringy, bloody meat, she thought back to that look in his eyes. Knowing, calm, revealing nothing.

An empty gaze cannot accuse. But the emptiness was itself an accusation. Wasn't it?

When Saddic looked upon the city they'd found in the heart of the Glass Desert, he believed he was seeing the structure of his very own mind, a pattern writ on a colossal scale, but in its crystalline form it was nevertheless the same as that which was encased in his own skull. Seeking proof of this notion, he'd left the others behind, even Badalle, and set out to explore, not from street to street, but downward.

He soon discovered that most of the city was below ground. The crystals had settled deep roots, and whatever light was trapped within prismatic walls up above sent down deeper, softer hues that flowed like water. The air was cool, tasteless, neither dry nor damp. He felt as if he walked a world between breaths, moving through that momentary pause that hovered, motionless on all sides, and not even the muted slap of his bare feet could break this sense of eternal hesitation.

Vast caverns waited at the very base, a dozen or more levels down from the surface. Crystal walls and domed ceilings, and as Saddic edged into the first of these, he understood the secret purpose of this city. It wasn't enough to build a place in which to live, a place with the comforting crowds of one's own kind. It wasn't even enough to fashion things of beauty out of mundane necessity—the pretty fountains, the perfect orchards with their perfect rows of ancient trees, the rooms of startling light as the sun's glow was trapped and given new flavours, the tall statues of tusked demons with their stern yet resolved expressions and the magical way the sun made vertical pupils in those glittering eyes—as if the statues watched still, alive inside the precise angles of translucent stone. None of these were sufficient reason for building this city. The revelation of the true secret was down here, locked away and destined to survive until oblivion itself came to devour the sun.

Above on the surface, the buildings, the domes and spires and tilted towers; the rooms and the plazas and spiral staircases: they each marked the perfect placement of a single, enormous machine. A machine of light and colours. But not just light, not just colours.

Saddic walked into the cavern, breathless with wonder.

Each day, each moment he could manage, Saddic listened to the words of Badalle. He listened and he watched and all that he heard and all that he saw passed through his surface, shifted and bounced, curled and bent until reaching the caverns of his memory, where they re-formed, precise and exact, destined to live on, secure in perfection—for as long as Saddic himself remained alive.

But this city had defeated mortality and, he realized, it had defeated time as well.

Far above, the sun's light fed the city's memories—all the life it had once held within its chambers and halls, on its streets and in the squares with their fountains.

The chaotic angles of the walls around him flowed with scenes, murky and ghostly—not of Rutt and the children now dwelling above, but of the inhabitants of long, long ago, persisting here for all eternity.

They were tall, with skin the colour of lichen. Their lower jaws bore tusks that rose up to frame the thin-lipped mouths. Men and women both wore long, loose clothing, dyed in deep but vibrant colours. They wore braided belts of grey leather, weaponless, and nowhere could Saddic see armour. This was a city of peace, and everywhere there was water. Flowing down building walls, swirling in pools surrounding fountains. Blossom-filled gardens bled their riotous colours into rooms and down colonnaded hallways.

Saddic walked through cavern after cavern, seeing all that had once been, but nowhere could he find those moments that must have preceded the city's death—or, rather, the fall of the tusked people and their rich culture. Invaders? Desert savages? He could find nothing but the succession of seemingly endless days of perfection and tranquillity.

The scenes seemed to seep into his mind, as if impressing themselves upon his own crystalline brain, and he began to comprehend details of things he had no way of knowing. He came to discover the city's name. He saw the likeness in the statues and realized that they all belonged to the same individual, and that variations arose solely from the eyes of the sculptors and their skill as artists. And, as he drew closer to what he knew was the centre of the city, to its most cherished heart, he now saw other creatures. In what seemed peaceful co-existence, huge two-legged reptiles began appearing in scenes.

These were the ones Badalle had spoken about. The ones who had found the city, but Saddic now knew more than she did. They'd found it, yes, but it had not been empty. In finding it, they found the ones who dwelt in it, who called it their home.

They were called Jaghut. Returned to this way of living, in the cities they had abandoned long before. They were drawn to a humble man, a half-blood. They were drawn to his great machine of memories, this place he made by his own hand. What he did not possess within him, he built around him. To trap all that he was.

The city is called Icarias.

He left a cavern, walked down a twisting passage murky with dark hues, and came upon the buried heart of the city.

Saddic cried out.

Before him, in a chamber more massive than any of the others . . . *Darkness. Destruction.* The roots were dead, unfed by light from above. Fissures split the crystals.

Broken. His heart is broken.

Brayderal sat, knees drawn up and arms wrapped tightly round them, in the corner of a small room on the fourth level of a tower. She had escaped her captors, leaving her alone with her grief and torment. She had drawn her kin to their deaths. She should have killed Badalle long ago, the first moment she sensed the power of the girl.

Badalle had shattered the Inquisitors. She had taken their own words and thrown them back, and precious blood had spilled on to the shard-studded ground. At least two of them had died, the other two retreating with grievous wounds. If they still breathed, somewhere out there, it would not be for much longer. They had no food, no water and no shelter, and each day the sun lit the sky on fire.

Badalle needed to die. Brayderal had raided an orchard not yet found by the others. She could feel her strength returning, her belly full for the first time in months. But guilt and loneliness had stolen all her will. Worse yet, this city itself assailed her. Whatever force still lingered here was inimical to the Forkrul Assail. A despiser of justice—she could almost taste its contempt for her.

Were the others hunting her? She believed they were. And if they found her they would kill her. They would rend her flesh from her bones and eat until their stomachs were swollen. Perhaps that was fitting. Perhaps, indeed, it served a kind of justice, the kind that recognized the price of failure.

Still, could she kill Badalle . . . Rutt alone was not enough to oppose her. Saddic was nothing more than Badalle's pet. Standing over Badalle's cold corpse, Brayderal could command the others to obedience. Yield, kneel . . . die. Wasn't it what they wanted? The purest peace of all.

She stiffened, breath catching, as she heard sounds from somewhere outside. Rising into a crouch, Brayderal edged out of the corner and approached the window overlooking the ruins of the palace. She peered out.

Badalle. Wielding a crystal sword—but not just any fragment, no, this was from the palace. It blazed in the girl's hand, blinding enough to make Brayderal snatch her head back in pain. The palace was destroyed, yet somehow it lived on.

She hated this city.

And now it is Badalle who hunts me. She will drive that shard into my chest, and it will drink deep.

She needed to hide.

Badalle turned at a scuffing sound from one of the towers, catching a glimpse of a face pulling back from a small window halfway up. Was it time, then? So soon?

She could unleash the power of her voice. She could, she knew, compel Brayderal to come to her. She had been able to overwhelm four adult Quitters. One of their children, weak and alone, would be unable to defend herself.

But she wanted this death to be a silent one. After all, the battle between these two forces of righteousness had already been decided. The peace that was death had been rejected. *But of course we have been fighting that war since the very beginning. Fighting, and now we have won. It's over.*

Would they live here for ever then? Could the orchards sustain them? What would they do? Was simple survival enough reason to go on living? What of dreams? Desires? What kind of society would they shape?

No, this is not enough. We cannot stay here. It's not enough.

Killing Brayderal will achieve nothing. No. I have a better answer.

She raised her voice. 'Child of justice! This city is not for you! You are banished! Return to your kind, if you can. *GO!*'

She heard a weak cry from the tower. The Quitters had driven them from their homes, from their families. It was fitting, then, that she now drive from her home a Quitter. *My home, my family. Not hers, it was never hers. This family, it is mine. And wherever they are, they are my home.*

They were done with Brayderal.

Badalle set off to return to Rutt and Held and Saddic. There were things to discuss. A new purpose to find. Something beyond just surviving. *Something we deserve. For we have earned the freedom to choose.*

She glanced down at her makeshift sword. It seemed unaccountably bright, as if gathering all the light it could drink. Golden flames seemed to glitter in its heart. It was beautiful, yes, but there was something else there. Something of power . . . a terrible power.

She remembered, from somewhere, tales about weapons, and those weapons were given names. Thus. She would name hers *Fire*.

Fuck! Fiddler spun away from the three worried faces, the sets of frightened eyes, the twitches of incipient panic. He scanned the ground. 'Stay where you are,' he told the heavies. 'No, wait. Shortnose, go and get Bottle. Flashwit, you and Mayfly enforce a cordon round here, especially their tent. No one gets in, understood?'

Solemn nods from the soldiers, and then Shortnose set off at a lumbering run.

On all sides, the camp was breaking, tents dropping down, stakes rocked loose from the hard stony soil. Soldiers shouted, complained and bickered. The smell of spicy food from the kitchen tents wafted in the cool morning air. Closer by, two other squads were looking over, uneasy, bereft of answers. They'd slept sound, they said. Heard nothing.

Fiddler's gaze drew back to the tent. Slashed to ribbons. Inside—what was left of inside—the cots bore rumpled bedding. But no blood. *Fuck. Fuck and fire.* His breath slowly hissed as he resumed studying the ground, seeking tracks, signs of a scuffle, anything. Nothing caught his eyes. *Too scared to concentrate. Where in Hood's name is Bottle!*

Flashwit had come to him half a bell earlier. He'd barely crawled out from his tent to find her standing in front of him, a look of dread on her broad face.

'They're gone, Sergeant.'

'What! Who's gone!'

'Their tent's all cut up, but no bodies—'

'Flashwit, what are you talking about! Whose tent! Who's gone!'

'Our sergeant and corporal. Gone.'

'Gesler! Stormy!'

'Their tent's all cut up.'

Not cut up, he discovered, after following Flashwit back to the Fifth Squad's camp. *Slashed*. The thick canvas was rent from all sides, with what must have been frenzied zeal. And of Gesler and Stormy there was no sign. Their weapons and armour were gone as well. *And the heavies were in tents to either side— barely room to walk between them, and in the dark with all the guy ropes and stakes . . . no, this doesn't make sense.*

He turned to see Shortnose and Bottle jogging up to where stood Mayfly—who held out thick arms as if to bar their passage.

'Let 'em through, Mayfly—but no one else. Not yet, anyway. Bottle, get over here.'

'What's this I hear about Gesler and Stormy deserting?'

Fiddler almost cuffed the man. Instead, he hissed, 'Ain't nobody's deserted— but now *that* rumour's on its way, isn't it? Idiot.'

'Sorry, Sergeant—it's too damned early in the morning for me to be thinking straight.'

'Better wake up fast,' Fiddler snapped. He pointed at the tent. 'Look for signs, all round it. Someone had to walk in to get that close. And if you find a single drop of blood let me know—but quietly, understood?'

Licking his lips as he eyed the ravaged tent, Bottle nodded, and then edged past his sergeant.

Fiddler unstrapped and drew off his helm. He wiped sweat from his brow. Glared across at the nearby squads. 'Wake up your sergeants and all of you make sure we got a full cordon!' The soldiers jumped. Fiddler knew that news of his sickness had gone through the ranks—he'd been down for days, stinking with fever. Standing close to Anomander Rake had been miserable enough, he recalled, but nothing compared to *this*. He didn't need the Deck of Dragons to know what he knew. Besides, nowhere in the Deck would he find a card called the Consort of Darkness. At least, not that he knew of, though sometimes powers were of such magnitude, such insistence, that they could bleed the paint off a minor card and usurp it. Maybe that had happened with his Deck—but he wasn't about to shuffle through for a look. In any case, his being down had scared people— damned unfair, but there it was, nothing Fiddler could do about it. And now that he was back on his feet, well, he could see far too much undisguised relief in too many eyes.

The older he got, he realized, the more sensitive his talent—if it could be called talent. He preferred *curse*.

Now Rake went and got himself killed. Unbelievable. Insane. Dragnipur is in pieces. Oh sure, Rake and Hood made sure most of the monsters chained within it were wiped out—nice deal, that. Chained souls and Hood's own menagerie of scary malcontents, all fed into Chaos. 'The dead will sleep, and sleep for ever-more.' Amen.

He clawed at his beard. Barely three days on foot again—he still felt wobbly— and now this. *They've been snatched. Right out from the middle of a whole damned army. Gesler. Stormy. Why them? Oh don't be obtuse, Fid. They were an-nealed in the Forge of Thyrllan. Ascendants both.*

So think about that. Gesler—he can throw a punch heavy enough to stagger a god. Stormy can swing a sword through three bodies if he's mad enough. But . . . not a drop of blood—

'Found a drop of blood, Sergeant.'

Bottle was suddenly at his side, head lowered, voice barely a whisper.

'Just one?'

'Well, maybe two drops together. A dollop? It's thick and it stinks.'

Fiddler scowled at the man. 'Stinks?'

'Not human blood.'

'Oh, great. Demonic?'

'More like . . . rhizan.'

Rhizan? 'This ain't the time for jokes, Bottle—'

'I'm not. Listen. There's not a trace, not a single footprint beyond the kind soldiers make—and we both know it wasn't no soldiers jumped the tent and the two men inside it. Unless they had talons long as swords, and it was talons that did in that tent. But the hands they belonged to were *huge*. It gets stranger, Sergeant—'

'Hold on. Let me think a moment.' *Rhizan? Flit around at night, eating insects, small bats . . . winged. They got fucking wings!* 'It came down out of the sky. Of course, it's bloody obvious now. That's why there's no tracks. It just dropped straight down on to the tent—'

'Then someone should've heard it—at the very least, Ges and Stormy would've been screaming.'

'Aye, that part still doesn't scry.'

'Let me examine the tent, Sergeant—pick it apart, I mean.'

'Go ahead.' Fiddler walked over to Shortnose. 'Another trip for you. Find Captain Faradan Sort, and maybe Fist Keneb. And Quick Ben—aye, get Quick Ben first and send him here. And listen, Shortnose, don't say nothing about desertions—we already got enough of those. Gesler and Stormy didn't desert—they were kidnapped.'

Shortnose shook his head. 'We ain't seen or heard nothing, Sergeant—and I'm a light sleeper. Stupid light, in fact.'

'I'm guessing some kind of sorcery silenced the whole thing. And the demon was winged. It just picked them both up and flew off into the night. Now, go on, Shortnose.'

'All right. Quick Ben, Sort and then Keneb.'

'Right.' Turning back, he saw Bottle on his hands and knees, lifting up shreds of canvas. The soldier looked up, nodded him over.

Fiddler joined him, crouching at his side. 'What is it?'

'Everything stinks, Sergeant. Feel this cloth—it's oily.'

'That's what keeps 'em waterproof—'

'Not this stuff. This stuff smells like a lizard's armpit.'

Fiddler stared at Bottle, wondering when the fool last jammed his nose into a lizard's armpit, then decided that some questions just should never be asked. 'Enkar'al? Could be, but it would have had to have been a big one, old, probably female. And somehow it got its hands round both their mouths, or round their necks.'

'Then Ges and Stormy are dead,' whispered Bottle.

'Quiet, I'm still working through this. I can't recall ever seeing an enkar'al big enough to fly carrying two full-grown men. So, Locqui Wyval? Draconic lapdogs? Not a chance. A bull enkar'al masses more than a wyval. But then, wyval fly in packs—in *clouds*, I think it's called—so if a dozen came down, striking fast . . . maybe. But all those wing-beats . . . no, somebody'd hear the ruckus for certain. So, not wyval and probably not an enkar'al. What's that leave us with?'

Bottle stared at him. 'Dragon.'

'Do dragons smell like rhizan armpits?'

'How the Hood would I know?' Bottle demanded.

'Calm down, sorry I asked.'

'But it doesn't work anyway,' said Bottle after a moment. 'The slashed tent—the rents aren't big enough for a dragon's talons, or teeth. And if a dragon did swoop down, wouldn't it just pick up the whole thing? Tent, people, cots, the whole works?'

'Good point. So, we're back to a giant rhizan?'

'I was just saying what it smelled like, Sergeant. I didn't mean a real rhizan, or even one of those slightly bigger ones we got round here.'

'If it wasn't for the wings,' muttered Fiddler, 'I might think K'Chain Che'Malle.'

'They died out a hundred thousand years ago, Sergeant. Maybe even longer. Even the ones Hedge went up against at Black Coral—they were undead, so probably stinking of crypts, not oil.'

Quick Ben arrived, pushing through the crowd that had gathered. 'Shortnose said something about—shit, they have a cat fight or something?'

'Snatched,' said Fiddler. 'Something with wings. Big enough to shut them both up—not a sound, Quick. Smells like magic—'

'Like lizards, you mean,' cut in Bottle. 'Look at this, High Mage.'

Quick Ben held out a hand and Bottle gave him the strip of canvas. 'Lizards, Bottle?'

'Feel the oil?'

'This is K'Chain Che'Malle.'

'They ain't got wings,' objected Fiddler.

But Quick Ben was squinting skyward. Under his breath he said, 'Some do.'

'But no one heard a damned thing, Quick.'

'The oil is like the breath of a dragon, Fid. Just not as virulent. It came down, sprayed the tent, took off again. The stuff soaked through, filled the air in the tent, and inside you could have knocked their heads together and neither one would've woken up. So it came back down, sliced through the tent to keep all the guys and stakes in place, and took them both.'

'You can't know all this—' Bottle began but stopped at a look from Fiddler.

Quick Ben. You snake-eyed shifty know-it-all bastard from the bung-hole of

Seven Cities. I never liked you. Never trusted you, even when I had to. The things you know about, why I—

Bottle blurted, 'Quick! The strings you tied! They weren't snapped? Then they're still alive, right? You tied strings to them—to Gesler and Stormy—you did, didn't you?'

'Got lazy,' Quick Ben said with a slow blink. 'Had too many. It was hard concentrating, so I cut down on them, Bottle. Didn't even think about Ges and Stormy.'

'You're lying.'

'Head back to the squad, Bottle,' said Fiddler. 'Help Tarr get us ready to march.'

'Sergeant—'

'Get out of here, soldier.'

Bottle hesitated, and then, jabbing a warning finger at Quick Ben, he stalked off.

'Strings still humming, Quick?'

'Listen, Fid. I cut 'em, just like I told Bottle—'

'Don't even try.'

'Yeah, well, you ain't Whiskeyjack, are you? I don't have to answer to you. I'm High Mage now and that means—'

'It means do I have to talk to the Adjunct directly? Or are you gonna keep spinning round on that flagpole? How long can you keep up the puckered butt, Quick?'

'All right. They're alive. I know that much.'

'Close by?'

'No. A Shi'gal Assassin can fly two hundred leagues in a single night.'

A what? Never mind. 'Why those two?'

'No idea—'

'I hear the Adjunct's a damned dragon herself these days—'

'Fine. I figure someone needed them.'

'A shigral assassin K'Chain Che'Malle *needed* Gesler and Stormy?'

'Shi'gal. But they don't go rogue, not this way, anyway. Meaning it was sent. To find them.'

'Sent by who?'

Quick Ben licked his lips, looked away and then shrugged. 'A Matron, obviously.'

'A Matron? A *K'Chain Che'Malle* Matron? A *real live breathing* K'Chain Che'Malle Matron?'

'Keep it down, will you? People are looking. We can—'

Fiddler's helm caught the High Mage flush on the side of his head. Watching the wizard fall in a heap was, for Fiddler, the most satisfying experience he'd known in years.

He stepped back, glared round. 'High Mage Quick Ben needs to commune with his gods. Now, all of you, finish breaking your camps—we march in half a bell! Go!'

Fiddler stood, waiting for the captain and Fist Keneb. His threats about the Adjunct had come back to sink fangs deep into his backside. They'd need to talk to her. With Quick Ben up and awake and cornered with nowhere to hide. She could take over wresting answers from the smug bastard. For himself . . . he glanced down at the unconscious wizard . . . he'd had enough.

Never liked him. Need him, count on him, pray for him, love him, aye. But like him? Not a chance. Goatsticker, dollmaker, souleater. Probably Soletaken or D'ivers, too, if I'm any judge of things.

Whiskeyjack, did you hear the sound it made hitting his head? This old helm of mine? Did it stir the dead all around you? Did you all sit up, rush to the Gate? You looking in on us right now, Sarge? Hey, all you Bridgeburners. How'd I do?

Fist Keneb had ridden out alone just before dawn, passing through bleary-eyed pickets and cantering eastward until the sun broke the distant horizon. He reined in on a slight rise and sat slumped in the saddle, steam rising from his horse, low mists scudding over the broken ground as the air slowly warmed.

The Wastelands stretched before him. To his right and now slightly behind him, the vague smudge of the Saphii Mountains rumpled the southern skyline. He was exhausted, but insomnia plagued Keneb. He had been more or less running the Bonehunters since leaving Lether. Fist Blistig had done his best to evade the responsibilities of command—he was in the habit of wandering among his soldiers in the evenings, eager to tell tales of the Chain of Dogs and the Fall at Aren, as if no one had heard them a dozen times before. He'd drink with them and laugh overloud and play at being a comrade of no special rank. As a consequence, he was viewed with amused contempt by his soldiers. They had enough friends. They didn't need their Fist spreading his hams on a crate at the fire, passing a jug. Such nights should be rare events, on the eve of battle, perhaps, but even then no one should ever be permitted to forget an officer's position.

Blistig wanted to be one of the lads. But he was a Fist by rank, and that meant standing apart from his soldiers. Staying watchful, aye, but ever ready to command and expecting that command to be followed. He was supposed to *lead*, damn him. At the morning briefing sessions Blistig sat scowling, hungover, thick-tongued and bored. He ventured no ideas and looked upon every suggestion with something between disbelief and outright derision.

We need better than that. I need better than that.

The Adjunct had the right to expect that her Fists could manage the army on this march. She had other issues to chew on, whatever they were—and Keneb was nowhere near close enough to even imagine what they might be; in fact, no one was, not even Lostara Yil.

There were two sub-Fists, each commanding regulars—foot, skirmishers, scouts and archers—and Keneb found he was growing far too dependent on them with the logistical demands. They had enough of their own concerns to deal with, after all. But both were veteran officers, seasoned campaigners, and Keneb drew heavily on their experience—though he often felt as he once had when he'd been a young captain under the stubbled wing of a sergeant. Neither Hobble nor Kellant likely had much good to say about him behind his back.

Aye, that's the truth of it. I just managed as a captain. I'm far past my level of competence here, and it's showing.

The Wastelands looked forbidding. Perhaps even more lifeless than the worst stretches of Seven Cities—between Aren and Raraku, or that northwest push to the walls of Y'Ghatan. He'd managed to acquire an honest list of warlocks and witches among the ranks, those possessing magics that could conjure forth edible plants, small mammals, insects and such from even the most miserable of lands. And water, as well. To stretch out the supplies they carried, he had them hard at work supplementing daily rations allotted each squad.

But the complaints had already begun. 'These Wastelands, Fist, are well named. Damn near sucked lifeless underfoot. Finding stuff is starting to hurt.'

Do what you can. It's all I can ask.

A more useless response from an officer was beyond his imagining, and what soured the most were his own recollections of receiving such inane replies from his commanders all those years ago. At last he understood the helplessness they often suffered, when attempting to deal with something that couldn't be dealt with; with things and forces beyond any hope of control. *Just say what you can, and look confident and reassuring when saying it. Nobody buys it, and both sides know that fact, so what's really being acknowledged is the motions we both go through.*

Indeed, he was beginning to truly understand the burdens of command, a phrase he used to scoff at and mock derisively. *Burden, sir? Try carrying this kit pack on your shoulders all day, up and down hills and worse. What do you know about burdens? Shut that whining, sir, before I slide my knife across your scrawny throat.*

What did Blistig know about the Whirlwind? He'd been cosy behind the walls of Aren, commanding a bored garrison. *But I was in the middle of it. Half-dead of wounds before Kalam Mekhar showed up. Sister, where are you now? Was turning your back on him worth it?* Keneb shook his head. His thoughts were wandering, exhaustion pulling loose the tethers. *What haunts me now? Yes, now I remember. The army.*

Without hate, what army could function? Unquestionably, other things were needed: respect, duty, the slippery notions of honour and courage, and above all of those, the comradeship between soldiers and all the responsibilities that created. But hate had a role, didn't it? Useless officers, unreasonable orders, the pervasive conviction that the ones in overall command were all incompetent idiots. *But then, all of that means we're all in this together—we're all trapped in this insane bloated family where every rule of behaviour strains near to snapping.*

And we're a family bred to answer everything with violence. Is it any wonder we're all so badly messed up?

He heard the pounding of horse hoofs and twisted round in his saddle to see a soldier from his staff quickly approaching.

Now what?

But then, he didn't really want to know. Any more desertions, real or otherwise, and he'd start to hear the spine cracking, and he dreaded that sound more
than anything else, because it would mean that he had truly failed. The Adjunct
set this one task upon him, and he'd proved unequal to it, and as a consequence
the entire Bonehunters army was falling apart.

Blistig needed to be pushed aside. He could think of a number of officers sharp
enough to take on the role of Fist. Faradan Sort, Raband, Ruthan Gudd. Kindly.
*Kindly, now there's an idea. Has seniority. Instils a healthy dose of terror in his
soldiers. Brilliantly unreasonable. Aye, Kindly. Now, all I need to do is convince
the Adjunct—*

The rider reined in. 'Fist, the Adjunct requests your presence in the sub-camp
of the Fifth Squad, Ninth Company, Eighth Legion. There has been an incident.'

'What kind of incident?'

'I don't know, sir. Captain Yil didn't say.'

Keneb glanced back at the rising sun, and then the stretch below it. *Wastelands. Even the name leaves a sick feeling in my gut.* 'Let's go then, Bulge. On
the way, you can amuse me with another story about Master Sergeant Pores.'

The scarred man's round, pocked face split into a smile. 'Aye, sir. Got plenty.'

They set out at a brisk canter.

After relaying Fiddler's orders to the squad, Bottle returned to the Fifth Squad's
camp. He found a solid cordon round it and was forced to use his sergeant's name
to push his way through. The three heavies were sitting close to a weak dung fire,
looking morose. Fiddler stood close to the motionless, prostrate body of Quick
Ben. Alarmed, Bottle hurried over.

'What happened? He try a quest?'

'You back again? I sent you away, soldier—'

'Not a good idea, Sergeant. You shouldn't have let Quick try anything—'

'Why?'

Bottle pointed down. 'That's why. He's still alive, isn't he? He'd better be.'

'Aye. Now what's this about avoiding any magics, Bottle?'

'Small stuff is fine. Food, water, all that. But I wouldn't even think of doing anything bigger. First off, the Wastelands might as well be dusted in otataral. Attempting sorcery here is like pulling teeth. Most places, that is. But there's other, uh,
places, where it's the damned opposite.'

'Back up, soldier. You're saying there's areas out there where magic comes easy?
Why didn't you mention this before? Our warlocks and witches are half-dead right
now—'

'No no, it's not like that, Sergeant. It's not areas, it's *people*. Or, more accurately,
things. Ascendants, stinking with power.' Bottle waved one hand eastward. 'Out
there, just . . . I don't know, just walking around. And they bleed, uh, energies.
Sure, we could feed on them, Sergeant, but that would mean getting close to them,
and close is probably a bad idea.'

Quick Ben groaned.

Bottle frowned down at the High Mage. 'Is that a welt on the side of his head?'

'How close to us is the nearest *thing*, Bottle?'

'I know the smell of one of them. T'lan Imass.'

'Really.' The word was flat, dangerous.

'Still far away,' Bottle hastily added. 'There's nothing within twenty leagues of us. That I know of—some ascendants are good at hiding—'

'You winging out there, Bottle? How often?'

'Hardly at all, Sergeant. It's scary out there. In the dark, I mean.' Bottle was beginning to regret coming back here. *What's with me, anyway? Sticking my nose into every damned thing, and if it stinks real bad what do I do? I go find something else to stick my nose in. And they all stink—you'd imagine, wouldn't you, I might quit the habit. But no, of course not. Gods, Bottle, listen to yourself—*

Quick Ben sat up, cradling his head. 'What?' he asked. 'What?'

'Took a fall there, High Mage,' said Fiddler.

'A fall?'

'Aye, I'm thinking you was struck with a thought.'

Quick Ben spat, gingerly probing the side of his head. 'Must have been some thought,' he muttered. 'Hit so hard I can't even remember it.'

'Happens,' said Fiddler. 'Listen, Bottle. Wasn't a T'lan Imass who kidnapped Gesler and Stormy. It was what we talked about before: K'Chain Che'Malle.'

'Wait,' said Quick Ben. 'Who said anything about T'lan Imass?'

'I did,' Bottle replied. 'You were the one talking about winged K'Chain Che'Malle.'

Fiddler snorted. 'No doubt the Adjunct will talk to us about the fucking Forkrul Assail. Who's left? Oh, the Jaghut—'

'Still days away—' said Bottle and Quick Ben in unison, and then glared at each other.

Fiddler's face reddened. 'You bastards,' he hissed under his breath. 'Both of you! We've got a Jaghut tracking us?'

'Not one,' admitted Bottle. 'I counted fourteen. Each one a walking armoury. But I don't think they're actually following us, Sergeant—unless our High Mage knows more about it, which is possible.'

Fiddler had buried the fingers of one hand in his beard and looked ready to start tearing loose handfuls. 'You reporting all this to the Adjunct, Quick?'

The High Mage scowled and looked away. 'I've given up. Nothing surprises her, Fid. It's as if she already knows.'

'Bottle, any hint of K'Chain Che'Malle? Your nightly explorations go out how far?'

'Depends on how crowded it is out there,' Bottle admitted. 'But, thinking on it, there's plenty of agitation going on, especially among the winged stuff—the rhinazan, the capemoths. The scaled rats keep massing and setting off on wild paths, as if trying to follow something. Oh, and I've caught the occasional scent on the winds, but I took those to be draconic. I don't even know what a K'Chain Che'Malle smells like.'

Quick Ben flung the scrap of canvas at Bottle. 'Yes you do.'

It dropped at Bottle's feet. 'Right,' he said, looking down at it. 'Oily lizards.'

'Draconic,' said Fiddler. 'Forgot about those. Anyone we know, Quick?'

'You're asking me? Bottle's the one smelling them.'

'I am. Well?'

The wizard hesitated, and then said, 'Aye, we bloodied him at Letheras.'

'Can't keep a fly from buzzing your shit,' said Bottle, earning hard looks from both men. 'Look, the Wastelands may be all wastes, but they ain't empty, Sergeant. I'm wagering the High Mage here suspects why it's so crowded. In fact,' he added, 'I think you know too, Sergeant. That pig of a reading you did—and then what hit you a few days back—someone showed up, and you probably know who—'

'Bottle,' cut in Fiddler. 'Just how much do you really want to know? I told you to keep your head down, didn't I? Now here you are, and here comes the Adjunct and Yil. I sent you back to the squad for a reason, soldier. You should've listened. Now it's too late.'

Keneb sent Bulge off to finish striking his command tent and rode through the breaking camps of the Ninth Company. Soldiers stopped talking to watch him ride past. There was none of the usual banter, suggesting to Keneb that the tale of the 'incident' at Gesler's camp had bled out among the ranks. Whatever had happened, it looked bad.

It'd be nice to get some good news. For a change. 'The High Mage has opened us a warren that'll take us right to wherever it is the Adjunct wants us. A lovely warren, rolling fields of flowers and gambolling deer that fall dead at our feet whenever we get hungry. Water? No, the rivers are rivers of wine. Ground's soft as pillows every night, too. It's great! Oh, and when we get there, the enemy take one look at us and drop their weapons and send for wagons loaded with the booty of a king's vault. And the women! Why—'

'Keneb!'

He turned in his saddle to see Blistig riding up from a side avenue. The man fell in alongside him.

'The morning's turned into Hood's hole, Keneb. What else did you hear?'

'About what? Got called to the Ninth, Fifth Squad. That's all I know.'

'Gesler and Stormy have deserted.' There was a glint in Blistig's eyes.

'Ridiculous.'

'The word's gone out, right out—the whole damned army knows it now. She's losing it, Keneb, and none too soon as far as I'm concerned. We ain't gonna hold for this march across the Wastelands. She'll have to disband us. I liked the look of Letheras—how about you?'

'Gesler and Stormy have not deserted, Blistig.'

'You said you knew nothing—'

'I don't have to. I know those two. They're solid as mountains.'

'They're gone, Keneb. Simple as that—'

'You were summoned to this meeting?'

'Not officially. But it sounds to be army's business.'

'It concerns a squad in one of my companies, Blistig. Do me a favour, ride the fuck back to your Legion and get them in order. If new commands are going to come down, leave it to the Adjunct's staff. If she wanted you she'd have invited you.'

The man's face darkened. 'You've turned into a real shit, Keneb. Don't settle in Letheras—the city ain't big enough for both of us.'

'Go away, Blistig.'

'Once we're disbanded, I'm coming looking for you, Keneb.'

'The day that happens, Blistig, you won't make it out of your Legion's camp. They'll cut you down not two steps from your tent.'

'Shows what you know. I got rapport. They'll be at my back when I go for you.'

Keneb glanced over, brows lifting. 'Rapport? You're a joke, Blistig. You're *their* joke. Now get out of my face—'

'Not a chance. I'm off to talk with the Adjunct.'

'Talk? About what?'

'My business.'

They drew closer to a cordon of soldiers. That ring parted as they rode in.

Within the circle waited an ominous gathering. Keneb saw Tavore and Yil along with Quick Ben, Fiddler and Bottle. His gaze then found the destroyed tent. *That doesn't look good.* He reined in, dismounted. A soldier from the Eighteenth Squad came forward and took the reins. 'Thank you, Corporal Rib.' Keneb paused. 'Think we still need this cordon?'

'Only the inner ring's doing that, Fist,' Rib replied. 'The rest are just gawking.'

'Get me your sergeant,' Keneb said.

'Aye, sir.'

Smirking, Blistig moved past, heading for the Adjunct.

The Eighteenth's sergeant pushed through. 'Fist. Bad news, this.'

'So I hear, Gaunt-Eye. Now, round up the other sergeants all these soldiers belong to. I want them out of here. I want them all getting ready for the day's march. Tell them if I look up in a hundred heartbeats and still see this mob, Hood's heel is coming down. Am I understood, Sergeant?'

The Genabackan blinked. 'Aye, Fist.' He saluted and then plunged back into the crowd. Almost at once, he started barking orders.

Corporal Rib grinned. 'He don't need the other sergeants, Fist. I ain't never known a meaner sergeant.'

'Carry on, Corporal.'

'Aye, Fist.'

Keneb walked over to the motley gathering—these damned all-too-familiar faces, the miserable expressions, the Adjunct's flat eyes and thin, straight mouth as she stood listening to whatever Blistig was saying. As Keneb reached them Tavore lifted a gauntleted hand, cutting Blistig off.

'Fist Blistig,' she said, 'is this the time to petition for an increase in the rum ration?'

'Adjunct, the Eighth Legion may be about to crumble. I'm just wanting to make sure my own legion—'

'That will be enough, Blistig. Return to your legion immediately.'

'Very well, Adjunct. Still, who'd have thought those two would desert.' He saluted and was forced to hold it while Tavore stood motionless, her regard level and lifeless. As the moment grew uncomfortable, the Adjunct returned the salute, converting it into a dismissive gesture—as if brushing lint from her cloak.

Face paling, Blistig wheeled and marched back to his horse, only to find that the animal had wandered off—no one had taken the reins from him.

As he hesitated, Keneb grunted and said, 'Rapport, aye.'

'Not my legion,' he snapped. 'You might want a word or two about courtesy with your soldiers, Keneb.'

'The Malazan military demands courtesy first and expects respect to follow. Lose respect and the courtesy usually goes with it.'

'Remember, I'll be looking for you.'

'Best find your horse first, Blistig.'

The Adjunct gestured Keneb over.

'Fist. Our camp security seems to have been breached.'

'They are truly missing, Adjunct?'

She nodded.

'I cannot see how anyone managed to penetrate this deep into our camp,' Keneb said. 'Unless they were our own—but then, where are the bodies? I don't understand this, Adjunct.'

'The High Mage suggests the attacker was a Shi'gal K'Chain Che'Malle.'

'A what?'

'Sometimes,' Quick Ben said, 'those ones grow wings. They're the Matron's own assassins, Fist. And one dropped down out of the night and stole them both.'

'To do what with them? Eat them? Why did neither man make a sound?'

'They were selected,' said the High Mage, 'and no, I have no idea why.'

Keneb struggled to make sense of all this. He glanced at Fiddler. The sergeant looked miserable. *Well, nothing new there.* 'Gesler and Stormy,' he slowly ventured, 'were anything but average marines.'

'As close to ascendants,' said Quick Ben, 'as anyone in this army.'

'Will this winged assassin come back for more of us?' Keneb asked, offering the question to any one of the five soldiers standing opposite him.

Fiddler grunted. 'Damn, that's the first time the question's come up—you got a point. Why stop with just them?'

'The problem is,' said Quick Ben, 'we have no idea what the Che'Malle want with Gesler and Stormy.'

'And no real way to find out,' added Bottle.

'I see,' said Keneb. 'Well, how can we defend against such future attacks? High Mage?'

'I'll see what I can think up, Fist.'

'One squad member with a crossbow stays awake at all times at night,' said Keneb. 'Maybe that won't help, but it's a start. Adjunct, if the soldiers begin thinking people can go missing at any time and we can do nothing about it, we'll end up facing a mutiny.'

'You are correct, Fist. I will see to it that the order goes out.' She turned. 'Captain Yil, ride to the Letherii camp and report our losses—you need hold nothing back from Commander Brys Beddict. Include in your report our conjectures.'

As Lostara made to leave, Quick Ben said, 'Captain, be sure that Atri-Ceda Aranict is present.'

She nodded and then departed.

The Adjunct stepped close to Keneb. 'Fist. We have suffered a wound here. It may prove deeper and more serious than any of us presently believe. You may be assured that I will do all that is in my power to find and retrieve Gesler and Stormy—but understand, we must continue the march. We must hold this army together.'

'Aye, Adjunct. To that end, we have another problem. He was just here, in fact.'

She held his gaze. 'I am aware of that, Fist. I am also aware of the additional burdens you have been forced to carry as a consequence. I will deal with this matter shortly. In the meantime, we need to make certain that the rumour of Gesler and Stormy deserting is laid to rest. The truth is unpleasant enough in its own right that none will think us dissembling. Summon your officers, Fist.' She then turned to her High Mage. 'Do what you can to protect us.'

'I will, Adjunct.'

'And find them, Quick Ben.'

'Again, whatever I can do, I will do it.'

'We cannot lose any more veterans.'

She did not need to add that without them the chains of this army would snap at the first moment of trouble. *Even now, one more gust of ill wind could do us all in.*

Gesler and Stormy, you damned idiots. Probably tossing dice in that rank tent you shared—or stitching a solid wall down the middle to close another spat. As bad as brothers, you two were. And now you're gone and there's a huge hole in my company of marines, one I can't hope to see filled.

The Adjunct and the High Mage had left. Fiddler and Bottle drew close to their Fist.

'Fire, sir.'

Keneb frowned at Fiddler. 'Excuse me?'

'It's the fire. The one they went through. Thinking on it, I doubt that winged lizard will be back. I can't be sure, but my feeling is we've seen the last of it. And the last of them.'

'You said this to the Adjunct?'

'Just a feeling, sir. I'm sending Bottle out tonight, to see what he can find.'

Bottle looked thrilled at the prospect.

'Let me know what he discovers, Sergeant. Immediately—don't wait until morning. I'm not sleeping anyway.'

'I know the feeling, sir. As soon as we get something, then.'

'Good. Go on, now. I'll see to dispersing Gesler's squad—hold on, why not take one now? Take your pick, Fid.'

'Shortnose will do. He's hiding a brain behind all that gnarly bone and what-not.'

'Are you sure?' Keneb asked.

'I sent him to collect four people in a specific sequence. I didn't need to repeat myself, sir.'

'And he's a heavy?'

'Aye, sometimes things ain't what they seem, you know?'

'I'll have to think about that, Fiddler. All right, take him and get going.'

Outrider Henar Vygulf walked up the main avenue between the ordered rows of the Letherii camp. Though a horseman, the ground trembled slightly with each step he took, and there was little debate as to who was the tallest, biggest soldier in Brys's army. He drew curious stares as he made his way to HQ. He wasn't astride his huge horse, after all, and not riding at a torrid pitch making people scatter as was his habit; thus, seeing him on foot was shocking in itself, quite apart from the fact that he was striding into the heart of the encampment. Henar Vygulf hated crowds. He probably hated people. Could be he hated the world.

Trailing two steps behind him was Lance Corporal Odenid, who was attached to the commander's staff as a message-bearer. This was his sole task these days: finding soldiers and dragging them back to Brys Beddict. The commander was conducting intensive and extensive interviews, right through the whole army. Odenid had heard that for the most part Brys was asking about the Wastelands, collecting rumours, old tales, wispy legends. The most extraordinary thing of all, when it came to these interviews, was Brys Beddict's uncanny ability to remember names and faces. At day's end he would call in a scribe and recount for her a complete and detailed list of those soldiers and support staff he'd spoken with that day. He would give ages, places of birth, military history, even family details such as he had gleaned, and he would add notes on whatever each soldier knew or thought they knew about the Wastelands.

The Beddict brothers, Odenid concluded, were probably not even human. Probably both god-touched. Hadn't Brys returned from the dead? And hadn't he been the only one—until that Tarthenal—to have defeated the Emperor of a Thousand Deaths?

Henar Vygulf had been summoned for an interview, but this time there was more to it, or so Odenid suspected. An officer from the Bonehunters had ridden into camp early this morning. Something had happened. Odenid didn't rank high enough to be able to lounge around in the HQ tent, and the commander's inner circle were a close-mouthed lot one and all. Whatever the news had been, it had stalled the march, probably until noon. And the Malazan was still there, in a private meeting with Brys and his Ceda—Odenid had seen them himself when he'd been summoned in and told to head to the outriders and bring back Henar Vygulf. 'Or,' had said Brys, '*I think he is so named. The tall one, the one with Bluerose ancestry. Has in his train about ten specially bred horses strong enough to carry him—a family of horse-breeders, I seem to recall . . .'*

And the man slept on his right and pissed standing on one leg, yes, that's him all right.

The added thought made Odenid smile. God-touched. Brys hadn't even interviewed Henar yet.

They reached the front entrance to the command tent. Henar halted, ignoring the lone guard standing beside the flap as he turned to Odenid. 'Do you announce me?'

'No. Just go in, Outrider.'

Henar had to duck, something that never put him in a good mood. There were reasons for living out in the open, good ones, and even these flimsy walls of canvas and now silk seemed to push in on him. He was forced to deepen his breathing, struggling to beat down the panic rising within him.

Two other aides waved him through to the inner chambers. He tried not to see them once the gestures were made. Walls were miserable enough; people crowded inside the tight spaces they made, with Henar trapped in there with them, was even worse. They were breathing his air. It was all he could do not to snap both their necks.

That was the problem with armies. Too many people. Even the relatively open camp with its berms and corner fortlets and widely spaced tent rows could instil in him a wild desperation. When he delivered dispatches into such camps, he rode like a madman, just to push through and deliver the message and then get the damned out as quickly as possible.

He made his way down a too-narrow passage and stepped through a cloying slit in the silks to find himself in a larger room, the ceiling peaked and morning sunlight making the air glow. Commander Brys sat in a folding chair, the Atri-Ceda Aranict standing on his left. Seated in another chair was the Malazan officer, her legs folded showing him a solid, muscled thigh—his eyes followed the sweeping curve of its underside and all at once his breathing steadied. A moment later his gaze lifted to her face.

Brys waited for the huge man's attention to return to him. It didn't. Henar Vygulf was staring at Lostara Yil as if he'd never before seen a woman—granted, a beautiful woman in this instance. Even so . . . he cleared his throat. 'Outrider Henar Vygulf, thank you for coming.'

The man's eyes flicked to Brys and then back again. 'As ordered, sir.'

'If I could have your attention? Good. You were attached to the Drene Garrison during the Awl Campaign, correct?'

'Yes, sir.'

'Liaising with the Bluerose Lancers, the company to which you once belonged.'

'Yes, sir.'

Brys frowned. 'Well, this isn't working. Outrider, may I introduce to you Captain Lostara Yil, adjutant to the Adjunct Tavore of the Bonehunters. Captain, this is Outrider Henar Vygulf.'

In the manner of Bluerose court etiquette, Henar lowered himself on to one knee and bowed his head. 'Captain, it is a pleasure.'

Yil glanced over at Brys with raised brows.

He shook his head, equally baffled. As far as he knew, the captain wasn't nobleborn, and certainly not royalty.

She hesitated, clearly uncomfortable, and then said, 'Please rise, Henar. Next time, a salute will suffice.'

He straightened. 'As you command, sir.'

'Now,' said Brys, 'might we resume?'

Henar pulled his eyes from Lostara with obvious effort and then nodded. 'Of course, sir.'

'During the most recent campaign, a renegade Awl named Redmask infiltrated Drene. Blood was shed, and in the pursuit that followed, garrison soldiers were ambushed. Is this accurate so far?'

'Yes, sir.'

'There followed reports of two demonic creatures serving as bodyguards to this Redmask.'

'Yes, sir. Lizards, running on two legs, fast as a horse, sir. They were sighted and reported on in the campaign itself. The Atri-Preda included descriptions in her dispatches up to and including the first major battle. Thereafter, no messengers managed to make it back.'

'Do you happen to know a soldier named Pride?'

'No, sir.'

'An Awl by birth, but raised by a family in Drene. He was old enough when taken to still remember a number of Awl legends regarding an ancient war for the land with an army of demons of similar description. The Awl were not victorious, but the war ended when the demons migrated east into the Wastelands. Once enemies, then allies? It is possible. Do we know what happened to Redmask? Does he still live?'

'Sir, it's assumed he's dead, since the Awl are no more.'

'But no direct proof.'

'No, sir.'

'Thank you, Henar Vygulf. You are dismissed.'

The outrider saluted, looked once more upon Lostara Yil, and then departed.

The Malazan captain blew out a breath. 'Well.'

'Please accept my apologies,' said Brys. 'There are somewhat fewer women in my army than there are in yours—certainly not by policy, but Letherii women seem more inclined to pursue other professions. It may be that Henar has not—'

'I take your point, Commander, if you'll forgive the interruption. Besides, it must be said that he is a most impressive man, so there is no need for you to apologize.' She uncrossed her legs and rose. 'In any case, sir, the lizards he mentioned certainly seem to fit with descriptions of K'Chain Che'Malle. These were living specimens? Not undead?'

'There was no evidence to suggest that they were anything but alive. In the first battle, they took wounds.'

Lostara nodded. 'Then Quick Ben is probably right.'

'He is.' Brys leaned back, regarded the tall woman for a moment, and then said, 'There was a god once . . . I know its name but that isn't particularly relevant now. What is relevant is where it dwelt: in the lands we now call the Wastelands. It lived there and it died there. Its life was stolen from it by a force, a power coming from the K'Chain Che'Malle—a civilization, by the way, that I'd never heard of, but in that god's memories there are the name itself and scattered . . . images.' He shook his head, and after a moment continued, 'It may be that this power'—and he glanced over at Aranict for a moment—'is one of these warrens you Malazans have brought to us. Or it could have been a ritual of some sort. Its name was Ahkrast Korvalain. What it did, Captain, was steal the life-force of the land itself. In fact, it may well have *created* the Wastelands, and in so doing it killed the spirits and gods dwelling there, and with them, their worshippers.'

'Interesting. The Adjunct needs to hear all of this.'

'Yes, we must pool our knowledge as best we can. Please, Captain, can you ride to the Adjunct and inform her that we will be paying her a visit.'

'At once, Commander. How soon?'

'Let us make it the midday meal.'

'I had best go, then, sir.' And she saluted.

Brys smiled. 'No need for that in here, Captain. Oh, on your way out, could you please tell one of my aides to get in here.'

'Of course. Until noon then, Commander.'

After she had left the chamber, Brys gestured to the now empty chair. 'Sit down, Atri-Ceda. You look a little pale.'

She hesitated, and then relented. He watched her settle nervously on the chair's edge. *Well, it's a start.*

There was a scuffing sound at the room's flap and then Corporal Ginast entered and stood at attention.

'Corporal, attach Henar Vygulf to my staff. Furthermore, he is to accompany my entourage when I attend a lunch today at the Malazan camp. Issue him the appropriate cloak and inform him he is now a lance corporal.'

'Er, excuse me, Commander, but isn't Vygulf Bluerose?'

'He is. What of it?'

'Well, military regulations state that no Bluerose-born soldier is eligible for any officer's rank in the regular Letherii forces, sir. Only among the Bluerose Lancers can a Bluerose-born soldier ascend in rank, and even there only to that of lieutenant. It was written into the capitulation agreement following the conquest of Bluerose, sir.'

'The same agreement that demanded horses and stirrups from the Bluerose, not to mention the creation of the Lancers themselves?'

'Yes, sir.'

'And the stirrups they sent us were rubbish, weren't they?'

'A nasty trick, sir, that one. I'm surprised the King has not insisted on proper reparations.'

'You are most welcome to your surprise, Ginast, but not to your disapproving tone. As far as those stirrups are concerned, I admit to applauding the Bluerose in their deviousness. Revenge most deserved. As for the ceiling on advancement in the Letherii army, I have this to say: from now on, any and every soldier in the Letherii army, no matter where they originally come from, has equal opportunity for advancement based on merit and exemplary service to the kingdom. Bring in a scribe and we'll get that written up immediately. As for you, Ginast, best hurry since you need to track Henar down in time for him to return here, mounted and ready as my escort, understood?'

'Sir, the highborn officers will not like—'

'I understand the Malazan Empress conducted a campaign that scoured her armies of those ranks bought by privilege and station. Do you know how she went about it, corporal? She arrested the officers and either executed them or sent them to work in mines for the rest of their lives. A most charming solution, I think, and should the nobleborn in my forces prove at all troublesome, I might well advise my brother to adopt something similar. Now, you are dismissed.'

The aide saluted and then fled.

Brys glanced over to see shock on Aranict's face. 'Oh come now, Atri-Ceda, you don't really think I'd suggest such a thing, do you?'

'Sir? No, of course not. I mean, it wasn't that. Well, sorry, sir. Sorry.'

Brys cocked his head and regarded her for a moment. 'What then? Ah, you are perhaps surprised that I'd indulge in a little matchmaking, Atri-Ceda?'

'Yes, sir. A little.'

'That was the first hint of life I've seen in Captain Yil's face since I first met her. As for Henar, why, he seems man enough for her, don't you think?'

'Oh yes, sir! I mean—'

'He clearly has a taste for the exotic. Do you think he stands a chance?'

'Sir, I wouldn't know.'

'As a woman, rather, what think you?'

Her eyes were darting, her colour high. 'She saw him admiring her legs, sir.'

'And made no move to cover up.'

'I'd noticed that, sir.'

'Me too.'

There was silence then in the chamber, as Brys studied Aranict while she in turn endeavoured to look everywhere but at her commander.

'For the Errant's sake, Atri-Ceda, make use of the rest of that chair, will you? Sit back.'

'Yes, sir.'

Throatslitter's high-pitched laugh cut across from behind the captain's tent. Again. Wincing, Cuttle leaned over and dragged close his studded hauberk. No point in crawling into the thing until they were finally ready to march. But it was getting patchy, needing some grease. 'Where's the rend pail?'

'Here,' said Tarr, collecting the small bucket and passing it over. 'Don't take too much, we're getting low and now that Pores is in charge of the quartermaster's—'

'The bastard ain't in charge of nothing,' Cuttle snapped. 'He's just set himself up as a middleman, and we all choke our way through him to get anything. Quartermaster's happy since so few requests ever reach 'im, and between the two of 'em they're hoarding and worse. Someone should tell Sort, so she can tell Kindly, so he can—'

'Kindly's got nothing to do with Pores any more, Cuttle.'

'So who does?'

'Nobody, s'far as I can tell.'

Smiles and Koryk trudged back into the camp—which wasn't much of a camp any more, just a smouldering hearth and a ring of kit packs and gear. 'First bell after noon,' said Smiles, 'and no sooner.'

'Any other word on Ges and Stormy?' Cuttle asked her.

'Fid can say what he wants,' said Koryk, 'and same for the others. They probably bolted.'

'Don't be an idiot,' retorted Cuttle. 'Veterans don't walk. That's what makes them veterans.'

'Until they decide they've had enough.'

'Go ask Bottle,' said Tarr, his face darkening as he glared at Koryk, 'and he'll tell you the same. They got snatched.'

'Fine, they got snatched. Point is, they're gone. Probably dead by now. Who's next?'

'With luck,' said Smiles, slumping down to lean against her pack, 'you, Koryk.' She looked over to Tarr. 'His brain is burnt out—Koryk ain't the Koryk I once knew, and I bet you're all thinking the same.' She was on her feet again. 'Piss on this, I'm going for a walk.'

'Take your time,' said Koryk.

Another piping laugh from Throatslitter. Cuttle scowled. 'What's so fucking funny?'

Corabb had been sleeping, or pretending to sleep, and now he sat up. 'I'll go find out, Cuttle. It's getting on my nerves too.'

'If he's being a bastard, Corabb, punch his face in.'

'Aye, Cuttle, count on it.'

Cuttle paused to watch him tramp off. He grinned over at Tarr. 'Catch all that?'

'I'm sitting right here.'

'He ain't on the outside of us no more, is he. He's our heavy. That's good.'

'So he is and so it is,' said Tarr.

'I'm this squad's heavy,' said Koryk.

Tarr resumed lacing his boots. Cuttle looked away and ran a hand through what was left of his hair, and then realized that the hand was thick with grease. 'Hood's breath!'

Tarr looked over and snorted. 'Won't keep it from cracking,' he said.

'What?'

'Your skull.'

'Funny.'

Koryk stood as if he didn't know where to go, as if he no longer belonged anywhere. After a moment he walked off, in a direction opposite to the one Smiles had taken.

Cuttle resumed rubbing down his hauberk. When he needed more grease he collected it from the top of his head. 'He might, you know.'

'He won't,' Tarr replied.

'Gesler and Stormy, they're his excuse. That and Kisswhere.'

'Kisswhere didn't care about anybody but Kisswhere.'

'And Koryk does? Used to, maybe, but now he's all inside his own head, and in there it's as Smiles says, burnt up, nothing but cinders.'

'He won't run.'

'Why are you so sure, Tarr?'

'Because, somewhere inside, in all those ashes, something remains. He still has something to prove. Not to himself—he can convince himself of anything—but to all of us. Like it or not, admit it or not, he's stuck.'

'We'll see, I guess.'

Tarr reached over and collected some grease from Cuttle's temple. He started rubbing down his boots.

'Funny,' said Cuttle.

Corabb walked round the command tent to find Throatslitter, Widdershins and Deadsmell crouched in a huddle just beyond the latrine trench. He made his way over. 'Stop that laughing, Throatslitter, or I'll have to bash your face in.'

The three men looked over guiltily. Scowling, Throatslitter said, 'Like to see you try, soldier.'

'No you wouldn't. What are you doing?'

'Playing with scaled rats, what's it to you?'

Corabb edged closer and peered down. Three of the scrawny things were struggling in the grass, their tails tied together. 'That's not a nice thing to do.'

'Idiot,' said Widdershins, 'we're going to eat them for lunch. We're just making sure they don't go nowhere.'

'You're torturing them.'

'Go away, Corabb,' said Throatslitter.

'Not until you either untie their tails or snap their necks.'

Throatslitter sighed. 'Explain it to him, Deadsmell.'

'They ain't got brains, Corabb. Just ooze, like pus, in those tiny skulls. They're like termites, or ants. They can only do any thinking if there's lots of them. Looks like three ain't enough. Besides, they stink of something. Like magic, only oilier. Me and Wid, we're trying to figure it out, so leave us alone, will you?'

'We're eating greasy magic?' Corabb asked. 'That sounds bad. I'm not eating those things any more.'

'Then pretty soon you're gonna go hungry,' Widdershins said, reaching down to flip one of the scaled rats on to its back. The other two attempted to drag it away, but chose opposite directions. 'There's millions of these things out here, Hood knows what they live on. We saw a swarm of 'em this morning, like a glittering river. Killed about fifty before the rest took off.' The flipped-over rat managed to right itself and once more the three were all pulling in different directions. 'More and more of them, every day. Like maybe they're following us.'

The notion chilled Corabb, though he wasn't sure why. It wasn't as though the rats could do anything. They didn't even seem to be going for their food supplies. 'I heard they got a nasty bite.'

'If you let 'em, aye,' said Deadsmell.

'So, Throatslitter, they stopped being funny?'

'Aye, now go.'

'Cos if I hear another laugh, I ain't coming back to talk.'

'It's just a laugh, Corabb. People got 'em, right? All kinds—'

'But yours makes the skin crawl.'

'Good, since it's how I sound when I slit some bastard's useless throat.'

Corabb stepped between Widdershins and Deadsmell, reached down and snatched up the three rats. In quick succession he broke their necks. Then dropped the tangled bodies between the three men.

'Next time you hear me laugh . . .' growled Throatslitter.

'Fine,' Corabb replied, 'only I don't need a single breath to cut off your damned head, Throatslitter, so that laugh will be your last.'

He headed off. This was getting ugly. Whatever ever happened to glory? Used to be this army, for all its miseries, had some dignity. Made being a Bonehunter mean something, something worthwhile. But lately it was just a mob of bored bullies and thugs.

'Corabb.'

He looked up, found Faradan Sort blocking his path. 'Captain?'

'Fiddler back with you yet?'

'Don't think so. He wasn't there a quarter bell ago.'

'Where's your squad?'

'They ain't moved, sir.' He jerked a thumb backward. 'Just over there.'

'Then where are you going?'

'Somewhere, nowhere, sir.'

Frowning, she marched past him. He wondered if she expected him to follow— she was heading to his squad mates, after all. But since she didn't say anything and just continued on, he shrugged and resumed his aimless wandering. *Maybe find the heavies again. Throw some bones. But then, why? I always lose. Corabb's famous luck don't run to dice. Typical. Never the important stuff.* He rested his hand on the pommel of his new Letherii sword, just to confirm he still had it. *And I ain't gonna lose it neither. Not this one. It's my sword and I'm gonna use it from now on.*

He'd been thinking about Leoman lately. No real reason, as far as he could tell, except maybe it was the way Leoman had managed to lead soldiers, turn them into fanatical followers, in fact. He'd once believed that was a gift, a talent. But now he was no longer so sure. In some ways, that gift was the kind that made a man dangerous. Being a follower was risky. Especially when the truth showed up, that truth being that the one doing the leading didn't really care a whit for any of them. Leoman and people like him collected fanatics the way a rich merchant collected coins, and then he spent them without a moment's thought.

No, the Adjunct was better, no matter what everyone said. They talked as if they wanted a Leoman, but Corabb knew how that was. They didn't. If they got a Leoman, every one of them would end up getting killed. He believed the Adjunct cared about them, maybe even too much. But between the two, he'd stay with her every time.

Dissatisfaction was a disease. It had ignited the Whirlwind and hundreds of thousands had died. Standing over grave pits, who was satisfied? Nobody. It had launched the Malazans into eating their own, and if every Wickan was now dead, who'd be so foolish as to believe the new land the settlers staked out for themselves wouldn't exact its vengeance? Sooner or later, it would turn them into dust and the wind would just blow them away.

Even here, in this camp, among the Bonehunters, dissatisfaction spread like an infection. No reason but boredom and not-knowing. What was so bad about that? Boredom meant nobody was getting chopped up. Not-knowing was the truth of life itself. His heart could burst in the next step, or a runaway horse could trample him down at the intersection just ahead. A blood vessel in his skull could explode. A rock could come down out of the sky. Everything was about not-knowing, the whole future, and who could even make sense enough of the past to think they really knew everything and so, knowing everything, know everything to come?

Dissatisfied? See if this punch in the face makes you feel any better. Aye, Cuttle was a sour one, but Corabb was starting to like him. Maybe he complained a lot, but that wasn't the same as being dissatisfied. Clearly, Cuttle *liked* being able to complain. He'd be lost without it. That was why, no matter what, he looked comfortable. Rubbing grease into boiled leather, honing his short sword and the heads of his crossbow bolts. Counting and counting again his small collection of sharpers and smokers, his one cracker, his eyes straying to Fid's pack in which was hidden at least one cusser. The man was happy. You could tell by his scowl.

I like Cuttle. I know what to expect with him. He ain't hot iron, he ain't cold iron. He's bitter iron. Me too. Bitter and getting bitterer. Just try me, Throatslitter.

Captain Kindly ran a hand through the last few threads of hair on his head and leaned back in his folding chair. 'Skanarow, what can I do for you?'

'It's Ruthan.'

'Of course it is. Hardly a secret, Skanarow.'

'Not that, well, some of that. Thing is, he's not what I think he is.'

'Early days, isn't it?'

'I don't think he's using his real name.'

'Who is? Look at me. I earned mine over years of diligent deliberation. Now, even "Skanarow" isn't what most people think, is it? Archaic Kanese for a female hill-dog, I believe.'

'Not like that, Kindly. He's hiding something—oh, his story works out, at least on the surface. I mean, his timeline makes sense—'

'Excuse me, his what?'

'Well, when he did what and where he did it. A proper course of events, but I figure that just means he's worked it out to sound plausible.'

'Or it sounds plausible because it is in fact his history.'

'I don't think so. That's just it, Kindly. I think he's lying.'

'Skanarow, even if he is, that's hardly a crime in the Malazan military, is it?'

'It is if there's a price on his head. If, say, the Claw get wet dreams thinking about killing him, or the Empress has a thousand spies out there looking for him.'

'For Ruthan Gudd?'

'For whoever he really is.'

'And if they are? Does it even matter now, Skanarow? We're all renegades these days.'

'The Claw has a long memory.'

'What's left of them, after Malaz City. I think they'd save all their venom for the Adjunct and all of us traitorous officers of significance. Heroic veterans such as myself, not to mention the Fists, barring perhaps Blistig. Presumably,' he continued, 'you are thinking in the long term. The two of you settling down somewhere, a house overlooking the Kanese beaches, perhaps, with smoke rising from the chimney and a brood of bearded offspring playing with fire-ants and whatnot. For what it is worth, Skanarow, I believe you will face no challenge in sleeping peacefully at night.'

'I'm beginning to understand how Lieutenant Pores felt when serving under you, Kindly. It all slides past, doesn't it?'

'I'm not sure I know what you mean.'

'Right,' she drawled. 'Consider this. Ruthan's getting nervous. And it's getting worse. He's just about combed his beard off his chin. He has troubled dreams. He speaks in his sleep, in languages I've never heard before.'

'Most curious.'

'For example, have you ever heard of Ahkrast Korvalain?'

Kindly frowned. 'Can't say I have, but it sounds Tiste. For example, the Elder Warrens of Kurald Galain and Emurlahn. Similar construction, I'd wager. You might mention it to the High Mage.'

She sighed, looked away. 'Right. Well, I'd best get back to my squads. The loss of Gesler and Stormy, so soon after Masan lit out—and that other one—well, things are fragile at the moment.'

'That they are, Skanarow. On your way out, have Corporal Thews bring in my collection.'

'Your collection?'

'Combs, Skanarow, combs.'

Master Sergeant Pores sat up, wiping the blood from his nose. Strange motes still floated and drifted in front of his eyes, but he could see that his personal wagon of stores had been ransacked. The two oxen harnessed to it were watching him as they gnawed on their bits. He wondered, briefly, if it was possible to train oxen as guard dogs, but the image of the beasts baring giant square teeth and moaning in a threatening fashion struck him as not quite frightening enough.

As he was picking himself up, brushing dirt and grass from his clothes, the sound of approaching footsteps made him flinch and then straighten, raising his hands defensively.

But there was no need. The newcomers didn't look particularly threatening. Hedge, and behind him four of his Bridgeburners. 'What happened to you?' Hedge asked.

'Not sure, I'm afraid. Someone came by with a requisition I was, er, unable to fill.'

'Wrong wax seal on the request?'

'Something like that.'

Hedge eyed the wagon. 'Looks like he went and took what he wanted anyway.'

'Capital offence,' said one of Hedge's corporals, shaking his head and frowning as if in disbelief. 'You Bonehunters lack discipline, Master Sergeant.'

Pores stared at the scrawny Letherii. 'You know, I was just thinking the same thing, Corporal. It's anarchy here. I truly feel under siege, a lone island of reason and order in a storm of rapacious chaos.' He gestured behind him and said to Hedge, 'If you're here to request anything, as you can see you will have to wait until I reorganize things. Besides, my own supplies are not, strictly speaking, available for official restitution. I can, however, provide you with a writ giving you an audience with the Quartermaster.'

'Kind of you,' said Hedge. 'Only we already been there.'

'Without a writ? You had no joy, did you?'

'No, funny that. Seems the only writs he's looking at are the ones from you.'

'Of course,' said Pores. 'As you might imagine, Commander—it is "commander", isn't it? As you might imagine, in the midst of the very chaos your corporal so sharply observed, it has been necessary to take it upon myself to enforce some measure of control on our dwindling supplies.'

Hedge was nodding, eyes still on the wagon. 'Thing is, Master Sergeant, what we're hearing is that most of the chaos is due to the fact that everyone has to go through you. Now, I'm wondering if Fist Keneb is fully aware of the situation. As a commander, you see, I can just go straight and talk to him, as equals, I mean. None of your cronies to try to get through—aye, I marked 'em in that unofficial cordon round the HQ camp. Quite the organization you put together, Master Sergeant. Makes me wonder who got through to rearrange your nose like that.'

'If I had memory of the incident, Commander, I'd tell you who—at least, after I'd hunted him down and crucified him for looting.'

'Well,' said Hedge, 'I caught a rumour not fifty paces from here. It's fresh as that dung behind them oxen.'

'Splendid.' Pores waited.

'About that writ,' Hedge said.

'Coming right up—let me just find a spare wax tablet—'

'Not using parchment? No, of course not. Parchment doesn't melt, does it? Wax does. Evidence? What evidence? Clever, Master Sergeant.'

Pores found a tablet and a stylus from his small portable desk close to the toppled-over folding chair where he'd—presumably—been sitting when the fist said hello. He quickly scratched his symbol and then looked up expectantly. 'What is it you want, specifically?'

'Specifically? Whatever we decide we need.'

'Right. Excellent. I'll write that right here.'

'Make it legible and all.'

'Naturally.'

Pores handed the tablet over, waited while Hedge squinted at it.

Finally, the bastard looked up and smiled. 'Rumour is, it was Neffarias Bredd who done cracked you one.'

'Ah, him. Who else would it be? How silly of me. I don't suppose you know what he looks like?'

Hedge shrugged. 'Big, I heard. Got a brow like a rock shelf, a hamster's eyes, a nose spread from here to Malaz Island and he can crush rocks with his teeth. More hair than a bull bhederin's dangly sack. Knuckles that can bust a Master Sergeant's nose—'

'You can stop there,' said Pores. 'I have an amazingly precise picture in my head now, thank you.'

'Mayfly says that's all wrong, though,' Hedge added. 'Bredd's tall but skinny, says Mayfly, and his whole face is tiny, like the bud of a flower. With sweet and pleasant eyes and pouty lips—'

'And Mayfly dreams about him every night, aye. Well, this has been a wonderful conversation, Commander. Is our business finished? As you can see, I have some work to do here.'

'So you do, so you do.'

He and the oxen watched them leave. Then he sighed. 'Gods, they really are Bridgeburners.' He glared at the oxen. 'Chew on that some, you useless oafs.'

Skulldeath, last surviving prince of some Seven Cities desert tribe and the most frightening melee killer Sergeant Sinter had ever seen, was plaiting Ruffle's hair. The style was markedly different from anything the Dal Hon tribes favoured, but on Ruffle's round and somewhat small head the effect was, to Sinter's eyes, somewhere between functional and terrifying.

'Lickeet at,' muttered Nep Furrow, his blotched brow wrinkling into folds that reminded her of turtle skin, 'Dasgusting!'

'I don't know,' interjected Primly. 'Those curls will be all the padding she needs under her helm. Should keep her a lot cooler than the rest of us.'

'Nabit, furl! Skeendath, rap izzee, a gurl?'

'Nice rhyme,' offered Shoaly from where he lounged, legs stretched out and boots edging the still smouldering coals of the hearth. The heavy's hands were laced behind his head and his eyes were closed.

Sinter and the other half-dozen soldiers seated close by occasionally glanced over to check on progress. Through a flurry of hand signals bets had been laid on when Shoaly would finally notice he was cooking his feet. Corporal Rim was doing the ten-count and he'd already reached sixty.

Ruffle's now ubiquitous pipe was puffing smoke into Skulldeath's eyes and he had to keep wiping them as he worked his wooden plug and bone hook.

Strange, mused Sinter, how it was misfits always found each other in any crowd or, in this case, wilderness. Like those savannah grass-spiders that dangled finger-long feelers out in front of them in the mating season. Catching herself thinking about spiders again, for perhaps the fifth time since the morning, she looked over at the recumbent, motionless form of Sergeant Hellian, who'd stumbled into their camp thinking it belonged to her own squad. She was so drunk Rim kept her from getting too close to the fire, lest the air round her should ignite. She'd been running from the spiders. What spiders? Hellian didn't explain. Instead, she'd toppled.

Skulldeath had looked her over for a time, stroking her hair and making sure none of her limbs were pinned at odd angles, and when at last he fell asleep, it was curled up against her. *The mother he never had. Or the mother he never left. Well, all those lost princes in fairy tales ain't nearly as lost as Skulldeath here. What a sad—if confused—story he'd make, our sweet little boy.*

Sinter rubbed at her face. She wasn't feeling much different from Hellian, though she'd had nothing but weak ale to drink the night before. Her mind felt bludgeoned, bruised into numbness. Her haunting sensitivities had vanished, making her feel half deaf. *I think I am . . . overwhelmed.*

By something. It's close. It's getting closer. Is that what this is?

She wondered where her sister was by now—how far away were the Perish and Khundryl anyway? They were overdue, weren't they?

Sinter thought back to her fateful audience with the Adjunct. She remembered Masan Gilani's fierce expression the moment before the Adjunct sent her off. There had been no hesitation in Tavore's response to what Sinter said what was needed, and not a single objection to any one of her suggestions. The only visible reaction had preceded all that. *Betrayal. Yes, that word hurt her. It's the one thing she cannot face. The one thing, I think, that devours her courage. What happened to you, Tavore Paran? Was it something in your childhood, some terrible rejection, a betrayal that stabbed to the deepest core of you, of the innocent child you once were?*

When does it happen? All those wounds that ended up making us the adults we are? A child starved never grows tall or strong. A child unloved can never find love or give it when grown. A child that does not laugh will become someone who can find nothing in the world to laugh at. And a child hurt deeply enough will spend a lifetime trying to scab that wound—even as they ceaselessly pick at it. She thought of all the careless acts and indifferent, impatient gestures she'd seen among parents in civilized places, as if they had no time for their own children. Too busy, too full of themselves, and all of that was simply passed on to the next generation, over and over again.

Among the Dal Honese, in the villages of both the north and the south, patience was the gift returned to the child who was itself a gift. Patience, the full weight of regard, the willingness to listen and the readiness to teach—were these not the responsibilities of parenthood? And what of a civilization that could thrive only by systematically destroying that precious relationship? *Time to spend with your children? No time. Work to feed them, yes, that is your responsibility. But your loyalty and your strength and your energy, they belong to us.*

And we, who are we? We are the despoilers of the world. Whose world? Yours. Hers—the Adjunct's, aye. And even Skulldeath's. Poor, lost Skulldeath. And Hellian, ever bathed in the hot embrace of alcohol. You and that wandering ex-priest with his smirk and broken eyes. Your armies, your kings and queens, your gods, and, most of all, your children.

We kill their world before they even inherit it. We kill it before they grow old enough to know what it is.

She rubbed at her face again. *The Adjunct was so alone, aye. But I tried. I think I did, anyway. You're not quite as alone as you think, Tavore Paran. Did I leave you with that much? When I was gone, when you stood there in your tent, in the silence—when Lostara Yil left and not one set of eyes was upon you . . . what did you do? What did you free from chains inside yourself?*

If Bottle watched through the eyes of one of his rats, what did he see? There in your face?

Anything? Anything at all?

'What's burning?'

'You are, Shoaly.'

The heavy made no move. His boots were now peeling off black threads of smoke. 'Am I done yet, Primly?'

'Crispy bacon, I'd wager.'

'Gods, I love bacon.'

'You gonna move your feet, Shoaly?' Mulvan Dreader demanded.

'Got bids, all you bastards?'

'Of course,' said Pravalak Rim.

'Who's counting tens?'

'I am,' said Rim. 'Got an order, doing rounds. We got ten in all, counting Skulldeath and Ruffle, though they ain't counted in personally, being busy and all.'

'Sinter bet?'

'Aye,' said Sinter.

'What number?'

'Seven.'

'Rim, where you at now?'

'Three.'

'Out loud.'

'Five, six, se—'

Shoaly pulled his feet from the fire and sat up.

'Now that's loyalty,' Sinter said, grinning.

'De ain feer! De ain feer! I eed farv! Farv! Erim, de ain feer!'

'It's Shoaly's feet,' said Mulvan, 'he can do what he wants with them. Sinter wins the pot, cos she's so pretty, right, Shoaly?'

The man smiled. 'Right. Now, Sint, you like me?'

'By half,' she replied.

'I'll need it. Nep Furrow, what'll a quick heal cost me?'

'Ha! Yar half! Yar half! Ha ha!'

'Half of my half—'

'Nad! Nad!'

'It's either that or the sergeant orders you to heal me and you get nothing.'

'Good point,' said Sinter, glancing over to Badan Gruk. 'Got need for your healer, Badan, you all right with that?'

'Of course,' he replied.

'This was all a set-up,' Primly muttered. 'I'm smelling more than bacon right now.'

'Arf ad yar arf! Shably! Arf ad yar arf!'

'Be kind to him, Shoaly, so he does you a good job.'

'Aye, Sergeant Sinter. Half of half. Agreed. Where's the kitty?'

'Everybody spill now,' said Rim, collecting a helm. 'In here, pass it around.'

'Scam,' said Drawfirst. 'Lookback, we all been taken.'

'What's new about that? Marines never play fair—'

'They just play to win,' Drawfirst finished, scowling at the old Bridgeburner adage.

Sinter rose and walked from the camp. Numb and restless at the same time, what kind of state was that to be in? After a few strides she realized she had company and glanced over to see Badan Gruk.

'Sinter, you look . . . different. Sick? Listen, Kisswhere—'

'Never mind my sister, Badan. I know her best, remember.'

'Exactly. She was going to run, we all knew it. You must've known it too. What I don't get is that she didn't try to get us to go with her.'

Sinter glanced at him. 'Would she have convinced you, Badan?'

'Maybe.'

'And then the two of you would have ganged up on me, until I relented.'

'Could be like that, aye. Point is, it didn't happen. And now she's somewhere and we're stuck here.'

'I'm not deserting, Badan.'

'Ain't you thought about it, though? Going after Kisswhere?'

'No.'

'Really?'

'She's all grown up now. I should have seen that long ago, don't you think? I don't have to take care of her any more. Wish I'd realized that the day she joined up.'

He grimaced. 'You ain't the only one, Sinter.'

Ah, Badan, what am I to do with you? You keep breaking my heart. But pity and love don't live together, do they?

Was it pity? She just didn't know. Instead, she took his hand as they walked.

The soft wind on his face woke him. Groggy, thick-tongued and parched, Gesler blinked open his eyes. Blue sky, empty of birds, empty of everything. He groaned, struggling to work out the last thing he remembered. Camp, aye, some damned argument with Stormy. The bastard had been dreaming again, some demonic fist coming down out of the dark sky. He'd had the eyes of a hunted hare.

Did they drink? Smoke something? Or just fall back to sleep, him on one side of the tent, Stormy on the other—one side neat and ordered, the other a stinking mess. Had he been complaining about that? He couldn't remember a damned thing.

No matter. The camp wasn't moving for some reason—and it was strangely quiet, too, and what was he doing outside? He slowly sat up. 'Gods below, they left us behind.' A stretch of broken ground, odd low mounds in the distance—had they been there last night? And where were the hearths, the makeshift berms? He heard a scuffing sound behind him and twisted round—the motion rocking the brain in his skull fierce enough to make him gasp.

A woman he'd never seen before was crouched at a small fire. Just to her right was Stormy, still asleep. Weapons and their gear were stacked just beyond him.

Gesler squinted at the stranger. Dressed like some damned savage, all colourless gum-gnawed deerhide and bhederin leather. She wasn't a young thing either. Maybe forty, but it was never easy to tell with plainsfolk, for that she surely was, like an old-fashioned Seti. Her features were regular enough; she'd probably been good-looking once, but the years had been hard since then. When his assessing gaze finally lifted to her dark brown eyes he found her studying him with something like sorrow.

'Better start talking,' Gesler said. He saw a waterskin and pointed at it.

She nodded.

Gesler reached over, tugged loose the stopper and drank down three quick mouthfuls. An odd flavour came off his lips and his head spun momentarily. 'Hood's knocker, what did I do last night?' He glared at the woman. 'You understanding me?'

'Trader tongue,' she said.

It was a moment before he comprehended her words. Her accent was one he'd never heard before. 'Good, there's that at least. Where am I? Who are you? Where's my damned army?'

She gestured. *Gone.* And then said, 'You are for me, with me. By me?' She shook her head, clearly frustrated with her limited knowledge of the language. 'Kalyth my name.' Her eyes shifted away. 'Destriant Kalyth.'

'Destriant? That's not a title people just throw around. If it doesn't belong to you, you and your whole damned line are cursed. For ever more. You don't use titles like that—Destriant, to what god?'

'God no. No god. K'Chain Che'Malle. Acyl Nest, Matron Gunth'an Acyl. Kalyth me, Elan—'

He raised a hand. 'Hold it, hold it, I'm not understanding much of that. K'Chain Che'Malle, aye. You're a Destriant to the K'Chain Che'Malle. But that can't be. You got it wrong—'

'Wrong no. I wish, yes.' She shifted slightly and pointed at Stormy. 'He Shield Anvil.' Then she pointed at Gesler. 'You Mortal Sword.'

'We ain't . . .' and Gesler trailed off, gaze straying over to Stormy. 'Someone called him Shield Anvil, once. I think. Can't recall who it was, though. Actually, maybe it was Mortal Sword, come to that.' He glared at her. 'Whoever it was, though, it wasn't no K'Chain Che'Malle.'

She shrugged. 'There is war. You lead. Him and you. Gunth'an Acyl send me to find you. I find you. You are *fire*. Gu'Rull see you, fill my head with you. Burning. Beacons, you and him. Blinding. Gu'Rull collect you.'

Collect? Gesler abruptly stood, earning yet another gasp as his head reeled. 'You snatched us!'

'Me not—not me. Gu'Rull.'

'Who is Gu'Rull? Where is the bastard? I got to cut his throat and maybe yours too. Then we can try to find the army—'

'Gone. Your army, many leagues away. Gu'Rull fly all night. With you. All night. You must lead K'Chain Che'Malle army. Eight Furies, coming now. Close. There is war.'

Gesler walked over and kicked Stormy.

The big man grunted, and then clutched the sides of his head. 'Go piss yourself, Ges,' he mumbled. 'It ain't morning yet.'

'Really?' Stormy had spoken in Falari and so Gesler did the same.

'Bugle wakes me every time, you know that. Miserable sh—'

'Open your eyes, soldier! On your damned feet!'

Stormy lashed out with one bare foot, forcing Gesler back a step. He'd felt those kicks before. But Stormy then sat, eyes open and widening as he looked around. 'What did you do to me, Ges? Where's . . . where's *everything*?'

'We got ourselves kidnapped last night, Stormy.'

Stormy's bright blue eyes fixed on Kalyth. 'Her? She's stronger than she looks—'

'Fener's sake, Stormy, she had help. Someone named Gu'Rull, and whoever he is, he's got wings. And he's strong enough to have carried us away, all night.'

Stormy's eyes flashed. 'What did I tell you, Gesler! My dreams! I saw—'

'What you said you saw made no sense. Still doesn't! The point is, this woman here calls herself the Destriant to the K'Chain Che'Malle, and if that's not dumb enough, she's calling me the Mortal Sword and you the Shield Anvil.'

Stormy flinched, hands up covering his face. He spoke behind his palms. 'Where's my sword? Where's my boots? Where the fuck is breakfast?'

'Didn't you hear me?'

'I heard you, Gesler. Dreams. It was those damned scaled rats. Every time I saw one on the trail I got the shivers.'

'Rats ain't K'Chain Che'Malle. You know, if you had even half a brain maybe you could've figured out your dreams, and maybe we wouldn't be in this mess!'

Stormy dropped his hands, swung his shaggy head to regard Kalyth. 'Look at her,' he muttered.

'What about her?'

'Reminds me of my mother.'

Gesler's hands twitched, closed into fists. 'Don't even think it, Stormy.'

'Can't help it. She does—'

'No, she doesn't. Your mother had red hair—'

'Not the point. Around her eyes, see it? You should know, Ges, you went and bedded her enough times—'

'That was an accident—'

'A what?'

'I mean, how did I know she went around seducing your friends?'

'She didn't. Just you.'

'But you said—'

'So I lied! I was just trying to make you feel better! No, fuck that, I was trying to make you feel that you're nobody important—your head's swelled up bad enough as it is. Anyway, it don't matter any more, does it? Forget it. I forgave you, remember—'

'You were drunk and we'd just trashed an alley trying to kill each other—'

'Then I forgave you. Forget it, I said.'

'I wish I could! Now you go and say this one looks like—'

'But she does!'

'*I know she does! Now just shut the fuck up! We ain't—we ain't—*'

'Yes, we are. You know it, Ges. You don't like it, but you know it. We been cut loose. We got us a destiny. Right here. Right now. She's Destriant and you're Shield Anvil and I'm Mortal Sword—'

'Wrong way round,' Gesler snarled. 'I'm the Mortal Sword—'

'Good. Glad we got that settled. Now get her to cook us something—'

'Oh, is that what Destriants do, then? Cook for us?'

'I'm hungry and I got no food!'

'Then ask her. Politely.'

Stormy scowled at Kalyth.

'Trader tongue,' Gesler said.

Instead, Stormy pointed at his mouth and then patted his stomach.

Kalyth said, 'You eat.'

'Hungry, aye.'

'Food,' she said, nodding, and then pointed to a small leather satchel to one side.

Gesler laughed.

Kalyth then rose. 'They come.'

'Who come?' Gesler asked.

'K'Chain Che'Malle. Army. Soon . . . war.'

At that moment Gesler felt the trembling ground underfoot. Stormy did the same and as one they both turned to face north.

Fener's holy crotch.

Chapter Twenty-Three

I am the face you would not own
Though you carve your place
Hidden in the crowd

Mine are the features you never saw
As you stack your thin days
In the tick of tonight's straw

My legion is the unexpected
A forest turned to masts
Grass blades to swords

And this is the face you would not own
A brother with bad news
Hiding in the crowd

HARBINGER
FISHER

She'd had an uncle, a prince high on the rungs but, alas, the wrong ladder. He had attempted a coup, only to find that all his agents were someone else's agents. Was it this conceit that had led to his death? Which choice made it all inevitable? Queen Abrastal had thought many times on the man's fate. The curious thing was, he'd actually made his escape, out from the city, all the way to the eastern border, in fact. But on the morning of his last ride, a farmer had woken with crippling rheumatism in his legs. This man was fifty-seven years old and, for thirty-odd years, each month through the summers and autumns he had taken the harvest of his own family's plot up to the village a league and a half away. And he had done this by pulling a two-wheeled cart.

He must have awoken that morning in the turgid miasma of his own mortality. Wearing down, wearing out. And studying the mists wreathing the low hills and glades edging the fields, he must have held a silence in his hands, and in his heart. We pass on. All that was effortless becomes an ordeal, yet the mind remains lucid, trapped inside a failing body. Though the morning promised a fine day, night's cold darkness remained lodged within him.

He had three sons but all were in the levy and off fighting somewhere. Rumours of some uprising; the old man knew little about it and cared even less. Except for the fact that his sons were not with him. In motions stiff with pain he had hitched up the mule to a rickety flatbed wagon. He could as easily have chosen the cart, but the one mule he owned that wasn't too old or lame was a strangely long-bodied specimen, too long for the cart's yoke and spar.

The efforts of preparation, concluding with loading the flatbed, had taken most of the morning, even with his half-blind wife's help. And when he set out on the road, quirting the beast along, the mists had burned off and the sun was high and strong. The stony track leading to the section road was more suited to a cart than a wagon, and so the going was slow, and upon reaching the section track and drawing close to the high road, he had the sun in his eyes.

On this day, in a heap of stones in the corner of a field just next to the high road, a civil war was erupting in a wild beehive. And only a few moments before the farmer arrived, the hive swarmed.

The old man, half-dozing, had been listening to the rapid approach of a rider, but there was room on the road—it had been built for moving armies to and from the border, after all—and so he was not particularly concerned as those drumming hoofs drew ever closer. Yes, the rider was coming fast. Likely some garrison messenger carrying bad news and all such news was bad, as far as the farmer was concerned. He'd had a moment of worry over his sons, and then the swarm lifted from the side of the road and spun in a frenzied cloud to engulf his mule.

The creature panicked, bolting forward with a bleat. Such was its strength, born of terror, that the old man was flung backward over the low seat back, losing his grip on the traces. The wagon jumped under him and then slewed to one side, spilling him from it. He struck the road in a cloud of dust and crazed bees.

The rider, on his third horse since fleeing the city, arrived at this precise moment. Skill and instinct led him round the mule and wagon, but the sudden appearance of the farmer, directly in the horse's path, occurred so swiftly, so unexpectedly, that neither he nor his mount had the time to react. Forelegs clipped the farmer, breaking a collar bone and striking the man's head with stunning impact. The horse stumbled, slammed down on to its chest, and its rider was thrown forward.

Her uncle had removed his helm some time that day—the heat was fierce, after all—and while it was debatable whether that made any difference, Abrastal suspected—or, perhaps, chose to believe—that if he'd been wearing it, he might well have survived the fall. As it was, his neck was snapped clean.

She had studied those events with almost fanatic obsession. Her agents had travelled out to that remote region of the kingdom. Interviews with sons and relatives and indeed, the old farmer himself—who had miraculously survived, though now prone to the falling sickness—all seeking to map out, with precision, the sequence of events.

In truth, she'd cared neither way for the fate of her uncle. The man had been a fool. No, what fascinated and indeed haunted her was that such a convergence of chance events could so perfectly conspire to take a man's life. From this one example, Abrastal quickly comprehended that such patterns existed everywhere, and could be assembled for virtually every accidental death.

People spoke of ill luck. Mischance. They spoke of unruly spirits and vengeful gods. And some spoke of the most terrible truth of all—that the world and all life in it was nothing but a blind concatenation of random occurrences. Cause and effect did nothing but map out the absurdity of things, before which even the gods were helpless.

Some truths could haunt, colder, crueller than any ghost. Some truths were shaped by a mouth open in horror.

When she stumbled from her tent, guards and aides swarming round her, there had been no time for musings, no time for thoughts on past obsessions. There had been nothing but the moment itself, red as blood in the eyes, loud as a howl trapped inside a skull.

Her daughter had found her. Felash, lost somewhere inside a savage storm at sea, had bargained with a god, and as the echoes of cries from drowning sailors sounded faint and hollow beneath the shrieking winds, the god had opened a path. Ancient, appalling, brutal as a rape. In the tears swimming before Abrastal's eyes, her fourteenth daughter's face found shape, as if rising from unfathomable depths; and Abrastal had tasted the salt sea on her tongue, had felt the numbing cold of its immortal hunger.

Mother. Remember the tale of your uncle. The wagon crawls, the mule's head nods. Thunder in the distance. Remember the tale as you told it to me, as you live it each and every day. Mother, the high road is the Wastelands. And I can hear the swarm—I can hear it!

Elder Gods were reluctant, belligerent oracles. In the grip of such a power, no mortal could speak in freedom. Clarity was defied, precision denied. Only twisted words and images could come forth. Only misdirection played true.

But Felash was clever, the cleverest of all her beloved daughters. And so Abrastal understood. She comprehended the warning.

The moment vanished, but the pain of that assault remained. Weeping blood-clouded tears, she struggled and pushed her way through panicked staff and body-guards, stumbled outside, naked above the hips, her fiery hair snarled and matted with sweat. On her skin the salt already rimed and she stank as would a body pulled up from the sea bottom.

Arms held out to keep everyone away, she stood, gasping, head hanging down, struggling to recover her breath. And, finally, she managed to speak.

'Spax. Get me Spax. *Now.*'

Gilk warriors gathered in their kin groups, checking weapons and gear. Warchief Spax stood watching, scratching his beard, the sour ale from the cask the night before swirling ominously in his belly. Or maybe it was the goat shank, or that fist-sized brick of bitter chocolate—something he'd never seen nor tasted before arriving in Bolkando, but if the good gods shat it was surely chocolate.

He saw Firehair's runner long before the man arrived. One of those scrawny court mice, all red-faced from the exertion, his quivering lip visible from ten paces away. His own scouts had informed him that they were perhaps a day away from the Bonehunters—they'd made good time, damn near impoverishing Saphinand's traders in the process, and for all his bravado Spax was forced to admit that both the Khundryl Burned Tears and the Perish were as tough as a cactuseater's tongue. Almost as tough as his own Barghast. Common opinion had it that armies with trains were slow beasts even on the most level ground, but clearly neither Gall of the Burned Tears nor Krughava of the Perish paid any heed to common opinion.

Glancing at his own warriors one more time before the runner arrived, he saw that they were showing fatigue. Not enough to worry him, of course. One more day, after all, and then Abrastal could have her parley with the Malazans and they could all turn round and head home at a far more reasonable pace.

'Warchief!'

'What's got her excited now?' Spax asked, ever pleased to bait these fops, but this time the young man did not react to the overfamiliarity with the usual expression of shock. In fact, he continued as if he'd not heard Spax.

'The Queen demands your presence. At once.'

Normally, even this command would have elicited a sarcastic comment or two, but Spax finally registered the runner's fear. 'Lead on then,' he replied in a growl.

Dressed now in armour, Queen Abrastal was in no mood for banter, and she'd already said enough to the Gilk Warchief to keep him silent as he rode at her side towards the Perish camp. The morning's light was clawing details down the furrowed scape of the mountains to the west. Dust hung over the raw tracks leading to and from the Saphinand border, and already lines of wagons and carriages were streaming out from the three camps, beds empty barring chests of coin, merchant guards and prostitutes. They would be back out here and waiting, she knew, for the return of the Evertine Legion.

They might have a long wait.

She had told Spax of the sending, had registered with little surprise his scowl. The Barghast knew enough to have no doubt about such things. He had even commented that his own warlocks and witches had been complaining of weakness and blindness—as if the Barghast gods had been driven away, or did not possess the strength to manifest in the Wastelands.

As the horses were being readied, he'd spoken of the belief in convergence, and she had been impressed to discover that behind his white skull paint and turtle-shelled armour, this barbarian knew of the world beyond his own tribe and his own people. The notion of power drawing power, however, did not seem to draw close to her sense of what was coming.

'You say that such forces are fated to meet, Spax. But . . . this is not the same.'

'How do you mean, Highness?'

'Is chance the weapon of fate? One might say so, I imagine, but what is drawing close before us, Spax, is something crueller. Random, unpredictable. Stupid, in fact. It is the curse of being in the wrong place at the wrong time.'

He'd chewed on that for a moment, and then he said, 'Will you seek to turn them away? Firehair, this Krughava is rooted like a mountain. Her path is the river of its melting crown. You will fail, I think.'

'I know, Spax. And this forces upon me a dire decision, doesn't it?'

But he would not see it that way, and he didn't—she was certain of it, though he'd said nothing, and now the horses were brought forward and they mounted up and kicked the beasts into a quick canter, and then, once beyond the Evertine pickets, into a gallop. Such a pace did not invite conversation beyond a few terse words at best. Neither bothered.

Perish pickets marked them and the banner rising from the socket on Abrastal's saddle. They quickly and efficiently cleared a path straight to the camp's centre. As they rode into the main avenue between officer tents, Abrastal and Spax found themselves the subject of growing interest, as soldiers formed lines to either side to watch them pass. Certain moments, fraught and crowded, could spread a chilling fever.

A short time later they reined in at the headquarters of the Grey Helms. The Mortal Sword Krughava and Shield Anvil Tanakalian stood awaiting them, kitted in full armour as was their habit.

Abrastal was the first to slip down from her winded horse. The Gilk followed a moment later.

Krughava bowed with a tilt of her head. 'Queen, you are welcome among the Perish—'

'Forget the formal shit,' Abrastal cut in. 'Your command tent, if you please.'

A flicker of something in the woman's hard eyes, and then she gestured to the tent behind her.

Spax said, 'Might want to summon Gall.'

'Already done,' Tanakalian replied with a half-smile that did not belong to this moment. 'It should not be long.'

Abrastal frowned at the Shield Anvil, and then swept past him and the Mortal Sword, trailed a step behind by Spax. A few moments later the four were in the tent's main chamber. Krughava ushered her aides away and then sent the guards to the tent's outer perimeter.

Drawing off her gauntlets, the Mortal Sword faced Abrastal. 'Highness, the agenda is yours. Will you await Warleader Gall before beginning?'

'No. He's a smart man. He'll work it out. Mortal Sword, we find ourselves in a storm that can only be seen from the outside. We ourselves as yet sense nothing, for we are close to its heart.' She glanced to the Shield Anvil, and then back to Krughava. 'Your priests and priestesses are in difficulty, do you deny it?'

'I do not,' Krughava replied.

'Good. Your allies are but a day away—'

'Half a day if necessary,' Krughava said.

'As you say.' Abrastal hesitated.

At that moment Warleader Gall arrived, sweeping through the curtains of the doorway. He was breathing hard, broad face beaded with sweat.

'You intend to leave us this day,' Tanakalian said, glaring at the Queen.

Abrastal frowned. 'I have said no such thing, Shield Anvil.'

'Forgive my brother,' said Krughava. 'He is precipitate. Highness, what would you warn us against?'

'I shall use the term Spax has given me—one you will understand at once, or so I am led to believe. The word is *convergence*.'

Something came alight in Krughava's eyes, and Abrastal could almost see the woman straightening, swelling as if to meet this moment. 'So be it—'

'A moment!' Tanakalian said, his eyes widening. 'Highness, this is not the place—rather, you must be wrong. That time is yet to arrive—it is far away, in fact. I cannot see how—'

'That will be enough,' Krughava interrupted, her face darkening. 'Unless, sir, you can speak plainly of knowledge you alone possess. We await you.'

'You don't understand—'

'Correct.'

The man looked half-panicked. Abrastal's unease regarding Tanakalian— which she had first discovered outside the tent—now deepened. What hid within this young soldier-priest? He seemed somehow knocked awry.

The Shield Anvil drew a breath, and then said, 'My vision is no clearer than anyone else's, not here in this place. But all that I sense of the coming convergence tells me that it does not await us in the Wastelands.'

Krughava seemed to be bristling with anger—the first time Abrastal had seen such a thing in the Mortal Sword. 'Brother Tanakalian, you are not the arbiter of destiny, no matter the vast breadth of your ambition. On this day, and in the matter before us, you would do best to witness. We are without a Destriant—we cannot help but be blind to our future.' She faced Abrastal. 'The Grey Helms shall strike for the Bonehunters. We shall find them this day. It may be that they will need our help. It may be that we will need theirs. After all, to stand in the heart of a storm is, as you say, to be blind to all dangers yet safe from none.'

Gall spoke for the first time. 'The Khundryl shall ride as the tip of the spear, Mortal Sword. We shall send Swifts out ahead, and so be the first to sight our allies. If they be in dire need, word shall wing back.'

'That is well and I thank you, Warleader,' said Krughava. 'Highness, thank you for your warning—'

'We are coming with you.'

Spax turned, his face expressing shock.

But the Mortal Sword nodded. 'The glory that is within you, Highness, refutes all disguise. Yet, I humbly suggest that you change your mind, that you heed the objections your Gilk commander is so eager to voice. This is not your destiny, after all. It belongs to the Bonehunters and to the Khundryl and to the Perish Grey Helms.'

'The Gilk,' Abrastal replied, 'are under my command. I believe you have mis-apprehended Warchief Spax. He is surprised, yes, but so long as he and his Barghast bed themselves in my coin, they are mine to lead.'

'It is so,' said Spax. 'Mortal Sword, you have indeed misapprehended me. The Gilk are without fear. We are the fist of the White Face Barghast—'

'And if that fist drives into a wasps' nest?' Tanakalian asked.

Abrastal started.

Spax bared his teeth. 'We are not children who die at the sting, Shield Anvil. If we should stir awake such a nest, look to your own.'

'This is wrong—'

'Enough!' snapped Krughava. 'Shield Anvil, prepare to embrace all who may come to fall this day. That is your task, your responsibility. If you so cherish the gleam of politics then you should have stayed in the kingdom shores of Perish. We who are here refused those games. We left our homes, our place of birth. We left our families and our loved ones. We left the intrigue and the deceit and the court dances of death. Will you now presume to broach that bitter wine? Go, sir, harness your strength.'

Face pale, Tanakalian bowed to Abrastal, Spax and Gall, and then left.

'Highness,' Krughava said, 'you risk too much.'

'I know,' she replied.

'And yet?'

She nodded. 'And yet.'

Damned women! It's all women!

She reined in her mount atop a low hill, eyes scanning the south. Was there dust on the horizon? Possibly. Kisswhere arched to ease the ache in her lower back. Her thighs were on fire, as if dipped in acid. She was low on water, and the horse beneath her was half-dead.

Fucking Adjunct. Lostara Yil. That bitch of a sister—it's not fair! She had been undecided, but no longer. Oh, she'd find the fools, the pompous Perish and the rutting Khundryl who'd weep at a broken pot. She'd deliver all the useless pleas for help to Krughava—another Hood-damned woman—and then she'd be done with it. *I'm not going back. I've deserted, right? I'm riding right through them. Saphinand. I can get lost there, it's ringed in with mountains. I don't care how squalid it is, it'll do.*

What else did they expect from her? Some heroic return at the head of two armies? Riding to the rescue, snatching them all back from the very gates of Hood? That kind of rubbish belonged to Sinter, or even Masan Gilani, who was riding to find an ally that might not even exist—yes, leave the legend to that northern slut, she had all the necessary traits, after all.

Kisswhere was carved from softer stuff. Not bronze. More like wax. And the world was heating up. They'd saluted her on her way. They'd decided to put all their trust and faith in her. *And I will find them. That is a dust-cloud. I can see* it now. *I can reach them, say whatever I need to say. The Adjunct says, O Mortal Sword, that betrayal does not suit the Perish. Nor the Khundryl. Come to her, she asks.*

The Adjunct says the sword's for wearing and wielding, not sitting on. It's a weapon, it's not courage, no matter how straight up it holds you. The Adjunct says there is a betrayer among you, and by that betrayer's words, you doom the Bonehunters. The Adjunct says the blood is on your hands, you frigid cow.

Find whatever means, Sinter had said. Use whatever you need to use. Shame them, shit on them, spit on them. Or turn sly and build up the fires until their boots burn. Blind them by reflecting the blazing sun of their own egos. Beg, plead, drop to your knees and suck them dry. *Use your wiles, Kisswhere, it's what you do best.*

Gods, she hated them all. That knowing look in their eyes, that acceptance of everything that wasn't good within her. Yes, they knew she'd not come back. And they didn't care. She was expendable, whipped like an arrow and once it struck, why, it was spent, a shattered thing lying on the ground.

So, a broken arrow she would be. Fine. Why not? They expected nothing more, did they?

Kisswhere kicked her horse into motion. It answered reluctantly. 'Not much further,' she said as she worked it into a loose canter. 'See those riders? Khundryl. Almost there.' *I don't need to convince them of anything—they're on their way already. I just need to add a few spurs to their boots. Who knows, maybe it's what Krughava goes for anyway. She has that look about her, I think.*

Here, sweetie, I bring spikes and whips—

The riders of the Vedith Swift drawing towards the lone soldier were commanded by Rafala, who held sharp eyes on the stranger. A Malazan to be sure, she could see. On a tired horse. She tasted the excitement, proof that something was happening, yet another clench of history's jaws, and no struggle could pull one free. Gall had sent them out ahead, riding hard. Find the Bonehunters. Ride into their column and speak to the Adjunct. Tell her to wait, or indeed to angle her march southward.

The terrible gods were gathering—she could see it in the high clouds building to the southwest, tumbling down off the mountains. The armies must come together and so stand as one, facing down those gods. Such a moment awaited them! Adjunct Tavore, commander of the Bonehunters; Gall, Warleader of the Khundryl Burned Tears; Krughava, Mortal Sword of the Wolves; and Abrastal, Queen of Bolkando and commander of the Evertine Legion. *Oh, and the Gilk, too. Those Barghast know how to roll in the furs, don't they just. I won't cringe with them on one flank, that's for certain.*

What sought them in the Wastelands? Some pathetic tribe, no doubt—not much else could survive out here. No secret kingdom or empire, that was obvious. The land was dead, after all. Well, they would crush whoever the fools were, and then march on, seeking whatever fate the Adjunct knew awaited them all in distant Kolanse. Rafala only hoped she'd get the chance to bloody her blade.

The Malazan soldier was slowing her exhausted mount, as if content to let the Khundryl horses do most of the work. Well enough. The Dal Honese did not look very comfortable on that saddle. For decades the Malazans had been clever in building their armies. They used horse-tribes to create their cavalry, mountain-dwellers for their scouts and skirmishers, and farmers for their infantry. City folk for sappers and coastal folk for marines and sailors. But things had since grown confused. The Dal Honese did not belong on horses.

No matter. I remember the Wickans. I'd barely a month of bleeding then, but I saw them. They humbled us all.

And now it is the Khundryls' turn to do the same.

She gestured to slow the riders behind her and continued ahead to rein in before the Malazan. 'I am Rafala—'

'Happy for you,' the woman cut in. 'Just take me to Gall and Krughava—and switch me to a fresher horse, this one's done.'

'How many days away?' Rafala asked as one of her corporals took charge of switching mounts.

The Malazan dropped down from her horse with some difficulty. 'Who? Oh, not far, I should think. I got lost the first night—thought I could see the mountains on my right. Turned out those were clouds. I've been riding south and west for two days now. Is that fool ready yet?'

Rafala scowled. 'He gives you his finest battle-horse, soldier.'

'Well, I ain't paying.' Wincing, the woman climbed into the saddle. 'Gods, couldn't you do with some decent padding? I'm sitting on bones here.'

'Not my fault,' drawled Rafala, 'if you let your muscles get too soft. Let's ride then, soldier.' *And see if you can keep up with me.* To her Swift she said, 'Continue on. I will provide her escort and then return to you.'

And then they were off. The Swift resumed riding northward; Rafala and the Malazan struck southward, and, trailing at ever greater distance behind them, the lone corporal followed on the spent horse.

Well, thought Kisswhere as she and Rafala approached the vanguard, *this will make it easy.* A forest of banners marked the presence of a clash—an old Malaz Island joke—of commanders. She could say what needed saying once and then be done with it.

It was obvious to her that disaster awaited them all. *Too many women holding skillets here.* She'd always preferred men to women. As friends, as lovers, as officers. Men liked to keep things simple. None of that absurd oversensitivity, reacting to every damned expression or glance or gesture. None of that stewing over some careless passing comment. And, most importantly, none of that vicious backstabbing and poison cups so smilingly given. No, she'd long since learned all the nasty lessons of her own gender; she'd seen enough eyes crawling up and down her body and judging the clothes she wore, the cut of her hair, the man at her side. She'd seen women carving up others when those ones weren't looking, eyes like blades—*snip slice snip*.

And wasn't it true—beyond all challenge—that women who preferred the company of men were the most hated women of all?

Too many commanders with tits in this mob. *Look at Gall, he's under siege behind those tattooed tears. And that Barghast, no wonder he's hiding his face behind all that paint.*

'You can go back now, Rafala,' Kisswhere said. 'I won't get lost.'

'I need your horse, Malazan.'

'So I am to walk from now on?'

The young Khundryl looked surprised. 'Walk where?'

Kisswhere scowled.

They rode through the scattered line of outriders and drew up before the vanguard—the mounted commanders made no concession to their arrival, continuing on at a steady trot, forcing Rafala and Kisswhere to swing round and fall in step beside them. That attitude annoyed Kisswhere—when was the last time they'd even seen each other?

Rafala spoke: 'Warleader Gall, I bring you a Malazan messenger.' And then she said to Kisswhere, 'I will go and find you another horse.'

'Good. Don't take too long.'

With a flat look, Rafala pulled her mount round and headed into the trailing columns.

A red-haired woman Kisswhere had never seen before was the first to address her, in the trader tongue. 'Malazan, where are your kin?'

'My kin?'

'Your fellow soldiers.'

'Not far, I think. You should reach them today, especially at this pace.'

'Marine,' said Krughava, 'what word do you bring us?'

Kisswhere glanced about, noting the various staff officers clumped round the commanders. 'Can we get a little more private here, Mortal Sword? You and Warleader Gall, I mean—'

'Queen Abrastal of Bolkando and Warchief Spax of the Gilk White Faces have allied their forces with our own, sir. This said, I will send our staffs a short distance away.' She faced the Queen. 'Acceptable, Highness?'

Abrastal's face registered distaste. 'Oh yes, they're worse than flies. Go! All of you!'

Twenty or more riders pulled away from the vanguard, leaving only Krughava, Tanakalian, Gall, the Queen and Spax.

'Better?' Krughava asked.

Kisswhere drew a deep breath. She was too tired to have to work at this. 'Among the seers serving the Adjunct . . . Mortal Sword, I can say this no other way. The threat of betrayal was judged to be very real. I was sent to confirm the alliance.'

The Mortal Sword went deathly pale. Kisswhere saw the foreign Queen cast a sharp look at the young Shield Anvil, Tanakalian.

What? Fuck, they know more of this than I do. Seems the threat is real after all. Sister, you have eyes that see what others do not. No wonder I'm always running away from you.

Warleader Gall was the first to respond. 'What is your name, soldier?'

'Kisswhere. Tenth Squad, Third Company, Eighth Legion.'

'Kisswhere—spirits know, how you Malazans can make a name an invitation never ceases to delight me—I will answer the Adjunct's fear as the Khundryl must. We shall advance ahead and ride with you with all haste, and so rejoin the Bonehunters as soon as possible.'

'Sir,' said Krughava, 'there will be no betrayal from the Perish. See the pace of our march. We are apprised of imminent danger, and so hasten to reach the Adjunct's army. It is our added fortune that the Bolkando Queen leads her Evertine Legion and the Gilk and has vowed to give us whatever aid we may require. Tell me, are the Bonehunters beset? What enemy has appeared out of the Wastelands to so assail them?'

You get around to asking this now? 'As of two days past, Mortal Sword, our only enemy was clouds of biting flies,' Kisswhere replied.

'Yet you were dispatched to find us,' Krughava observed.

'I was.'

'Therefore,' the Mortal Sword continued, 'some apprehension of danger—beyond that of possible betrayal—must exist to justify such urgency.'

Kisswhere shrugged. 'There is little more I can tell you, Mortal Sword.'

'You ride all this way seeking nothing but reassurance?'

At Gall's question, Kisswhere glanced away for a moment. 'Yes, it must seem odd to you. All of you. I have no answer. The alliance was perceived to be in jeopardy—that is all I know of the matter.'

No one seemed satisfied. *Too bad. What can I say? My sister's got a bad feeling. Fid keeps throwing up and the only high priest on Tavore's staff has been drunk ever since Letheras. And those flies got a vicious bite.*

Rafala returned leading a saddled horse, a bay mare with a witless look to her. She led the beast up alongside Kisswhere. 'Climb over, if you can.'

Scowling, Kisswhere kicked her boots free of the stirrups and drew her right leg over. Rafala pulled the mare a step ahead and the Malazan set her right foot into the stirrup, rose, reaching for the Seven Cities saddle horn, and then pulled herself astride the broad-backed beast.

The transfer was smooth and Rafala's lips tightened, as if the notion of a compliment threatened nausea. She dropped back to come up behind Kisswhere, taking the reins of her warrior's battle-horse. Moments later she was leading that mount away.

Kisswhere looked over to see Gall grinning. 'I know just the place,' he said.

The Barghast barked a laugh.

'Ride with the Khundryl then,' Krughava said to her. 'Lead them to the Bonehunters.'

Gods below—how to get out of this? 'I fear I would only slow them, Mortal Sword. While this mount is fresh I, alas, am not.'

'Ever slept between two horses?' Gall asked.

'Excuse me?'

'A slung hammock, Kisswhere, with tent poles to keep the beasts apart. This is how we carry wounded whilst on the move.'

All these women, looking at her. Knowing, seeing what the men did not. *Showing all your sharp little teeth, are you? So delighted to see me trapped.* To Gall she said, 'If it comes to that need, Warleader, I will tell you.'

'Very good,' the warrior replied. 'Then, let us ride to my Burned Tears. Highness, Mortal Sword, when next we meet it shall be in the Adjunct's command tent. Until then, travel well and may the gods be blinded by your dust.'

Kisswhere set off with the Warleader and they cut eastward and slightly arrears to where the main mass of the horse-warriors rode in loose formations. Once clear of the vanguard, Gall said, 'My apologies, soldier. I see that you have discarded your uniform, and the last place you want to go is back to where you came from. But the Mortal Sword is a stern woman. Not one Perish Grey Helm has ever deserted, and should one ever try, I doubt they'd manage to live long. She would have acted on the Adjunct's behalf, no matter the consequences. In every army imaginable, the Bonehunters included I'm sure, desertion is a death sentence.'

Not stupid after all. 'I was commanded to give nothing away whilst riding alone, Warleader, and so I wore nothing that could be construed to be a uniform.'

'Ah, I see. Then I must apologize a second time, Kisswhere.'

She shrugged. 'My sister walks in that column, Warleader. How could I not seek to return as quickly as possible?'

'Of course. I understand now.'

He fell into something like an amiable silence as they approached the Burned Tears. She wondered if he'd been fooled. True, simple wasn't necessarily the same as stupid, after all. She'd given reasonable answers, with only a hint of affront. *Aye, a little dignity before the insult, as my mother used to say, makes a fine weapon.*

'She will be delighted to see you again, I am sure.'

Kisswhere shot the man a searching look, but said nothing.

Columnar clouds heaped the western horizon ahead, and Masan Gilani could feel a cool breeze freshening against her face. She had taken to spelling her horse every three or so leagues, but the animal was wearying nonetheless. It was this detail that killed most deserters, she knew. The pursuing troop would be leading spare mounts, whilst the fool on the fly generally had nothing but the lone beast he or she was riding.

Of course, no one was chasing her, which, oddly enough, did nothing to assuage her guilt. She belonged with her squad, sharing mouthfuls of the same dust, cursing at the same whining flies. And, if things were as bad as people had intimated, she wanted to be there, right beside her friends, to face whatever arrived. Instead, here she was, hunting for . . . for what? For the tenth time this day she reached to brush her hand against the small leather pouch tied to her belt, confirming it was still there. Lose it, she knew, and this whole mission was a failure.

It probably already is, anyway. I can't find what I can't see, pouch or no pouch.

She could see the rain ahead and not much else, grey-blue sheets angling down on the sliding wind, the curtains sweeping across the land. More misery to add to this overflowing kitty. *This is pointless. I'm looking for ghosts. Real ghosts? Maybe. Maybe not. Maybe just the ghosts living in the Adjunct's head, those old hoary hags of lost allegiances and forgotten promises. Tavore, you expect too much. You always did.*

Rain spat into her face, swarmed the ground until it seemed the dust danced like crazed ants. In moments all visibility beyond a few dozen paces vanished. She was now more blinded to what she was looking for than at any other time.

The world mocked.

Pointless. I'm going back—

Five figures stood before her, grey as the rain, dull as the muddy dust, sudden as a dream. Cursing, she reined in, fought with her panicking horse. Gravel skittered. The beast snorted, hoofs stamping in the sluicing streams and puddles.

'We are who you seek.'

She could not tell which one the voice came from. She grasped the pouch containing the seething dirt, gift of the Atri-Ceda Aranict, and gasped at its sudden heat.

They were corpses one and all. T'lan Imass. Battered, broken, limbs missing, weapons dangling from seemingly senseless hands of bone wrapped in blackened skin. Long hair, dirty blond and rust red, was plastered down round their desiccated faces, where rainwater ran like eternal tears.

Breathing hard, Masan Gilani studied them for a time, and then she said, 'Just five of you? No others?'

'We are who remain.'

She thought the one speaking was the one standing closest to her, but could not be certain. The rain was a roar around them all, the wind moaning as if trapped in an enormous cave. 'There should be . . . more,' she insisted. 'There was a vision—'

'We are the ones you seek.'

'Are you summoned then?'

'We are.' And the lead T'lan Imass pointed to the pouch at her hip. 'Thenik is incomplete.'

'Which one of you is Thenik?'

The creature on the outside right stepped forward. Every bone looked to be shattered, with splinters and chips missing. A crazed web of cracks broke up its face beneath a helm made from the skull of some unknown beast.

Fumbling with the ties, Masan finally managed to pull free the pouch. She tossed it over. Thenik made no move to catch it. The pouch landed at its feet, sank into a puddle.

'Thenik thanks you,' said the speaker. 'I am Urugal the Woven. With me is

Thenik the Shattered, Beroke Soft Voice, Kahlb the Silent Hunter and Halad the Giant. We are the Unbound, who once numbered seven. Now we are five. Soon we shall be seven again—there are fallen kin in this land. Some refuse the enemy. Some will not follow the one who leads nowhere.'

Frowning, Masan Gilani shook her head. 'You've lost me. No matter. I was sent to find you. Now we must return to the Bonehunters—my army—it's where—'

'Yes, she is the hunter of bones indeed,' Urugal said. 'Her hunt is soon complete. Ride on your beast. We shall follow.'

She wiped water from her eyes. 'Thought there'd be more of you,' she muttered, gathering her reins and dragging her horse round. 'Can you keep up?' she asked over one shoulder.

'You are the banner before us, mortal.'

Masan Gilani's frown deepened. She'd heard something like that before . . . somewhere.

Four leagues to the northwest, Onos T'oolan suddenly halted, the first time in days. Something not far away had brushed his senses, but now it was gone. *T'lan Imass. Strangers*. He hesitated, as the more distant and altogether different wave of compulsion returned, insistent, desperate. He knew its flavour, had known its flavour for weeks now. This was what Toc the Younger had sought, what he had demanded of the First Sword.

But he was no longer the friend Toc once knew, just as Toc was no longer the friend Tool himself remembered. The past was both dead and alive, but between them it was simply dead.

The summons was Malazan. It was the claim of alliance as had been forged long ago, between the Emperor and the Logros T'lan Imass. Somewhere to the east, a Malazan force waited. Danger approached, and the T'lan Imass must stand with allies of old. Such was duty. Such was the ink of honour, written so deep as to stain the immortal soul.

He defied the command. Duty was dead. Honour was a lie—see what the Senan had done to his wife, his children. Mortality was the realm of deceit; the sordid room of horror hid in the house of the living, its walls crusted and streaked, dark stains on the warped floor. Dust crowded the corners, dust made of skin flakes and snarls of hair, nail clippings and clots of phlegm. Every house had its secret room, where memories howled in the thick silence.

He had once been of the Logros. He was no longer. He had one duty now and it was truly lifeless. Nothing would turn him aside, not the wishes of Toc the Younger, not the mad aspirations of Olar Ethil—oh yes, he knew she was close, far too clever to come within his reach, knowing well that he would kill her, destroy her utterly. Demands and expectations descended like that distant rain to the southwest, but it all washed from him and left no trace.

There had been a time when Onos Toolan had chosen to stand close to mortal humans; when he had turned his back upon his own kind, and in so doing he had

rediscovered the wonders of gentler emotions, the sensual pleasures of camaraderie and friendship. The gifts of humour and love. And then, at last, he had
achieved the rebirth of his life—a true life.

That man had taken that life, for reasons even he could barely understand—
a flush of empathy, the fullest cost of humanity paid out in the blade pushing
into his chest. Strength fell away, in some other direction than the one taken
by his sagging body. He had looked out on the world until all meaning drained
of colour.

They had done unspeakable things to his corpse. Desecration was the wound
delivered upon the dead, and the living did so with careless conceit—no, *they*
would never lie motionless on the ground. They would never rise from cold meat
and bones to witness all that was done to the body that been the only home they
had ever known. It did not even occur to them that the soul could suffer from
phantom agony, the body like a severed hand.

And his adopted kin had simply looked on, stone-eyed. Telling themselves
that Tool's soul was gone from that mangled thing being dismembered on the
bloody grasses; that the laughter and mockery could not reach unseen ears.

Could they even have guessed that love alone was of such power that Tool's
soul had also witnessed the hobbling of his wife and the rapes that followed?
That, unable to find his children, he had at last set out for the underworld—to
find his beloved Hetan, his family, to escape with finality the cruel spikes of the
mortal realm?

And you turned me away. Toc. My friend. You turned me back . . . to this.

He was not that man, not any more. He was not the First Sword either. He
was not a warrior of the Logros. He was none of these things.

He was a weapon.

Onos T'oolan resumed his march. The summons meant nothing. Nothing to
him, at any rate. Besides, in a very short time it would cease. For evermore.

There was no road leading them through the Wastelands; no road to take them to
their destiny, whatever destiny that happened to be. Accordingly, the companies
marched in loose units of six squads, and each company was separated from the
others yet close enough to those of their own legion to link if need demanded.
Groups of six squads were arranged as befitted their function: marines at the
core, the mixed units of heavies next, and outside of them the medium regular
infantry, with skirmishers forming the outermost curtain.

The massive column that was the supply train forged its own route, hundreds of
ox-drawn wagons and bawling herds of goats, sheep, cattle and rodara that would
soon begin to starve in this lifeless land. Herd dogs loped round their charges and
beyond them the riders entrusted with driving the beasts kept a watchful eye for
any strays that might elude the dogs—although none did.

Flanking wings of lancers and mounted archers protected the sides of the column; units of scouts rode well ahead of the vanguard while others ranged on the
south flank and arrears, but not to the north, where marched the legions and

brigades under command of Brys Beddict. His columns were arranged in tighter formation, replete with its own supply train—almost as big as the Malazan one. Bluerose cavalry rode in wide flank, sending scouts deep into the wastes in a constant cycle of riders and horses.

Mounted, Commander Brys Beddict rode to the inside of his column, close to its head. Off to his right at a distance of about two hundred paces were the Malazans. Riding beside him on his left was Aranict, and they were in turn trailed by a half-dozen messengers. The heat was savage, and the water-wagons were fast being drained of their stores. The Letherii herds of myrid and rodara could manage this land better than sheep and cattle, but before long even they would begin to suffer. The meals at the beginning of this trek across the Wastelands would be heavy on meat, Brys knew, but then things would change.

What lay beyond this forbidding stretch of dead ground? From what he could glean—and rumours served in place of any direct knowledge—there was a desert of some sort, yet one known to possess caravan tracks, and beyond that the plains of the Elan people, a possible offshoot of the Awl. The Elan Plains bordered on the east the kingdoms and city-states of Kolanse and the Pelasiar Confederacy.

The notion of taking an army across first the Wastelands and then a desert struck Brys as sheer madness. Yet, somehow, the very impossibility of it perversely appealed to him, and had they been at war with those distant kingdoms, it would have signified a bold invasion sure to achieve legendary status. Of course, as far as he knew, there was no war and no cause for war. There was nothing but ominous silence from Kolanse. Perhaps indeed this was an invasion, but if so, it was not a just one. No known atrocities demanding retribution, nor a declaration of hostilities from an advancing empire to be answered. *We know nothing.*

What happens to the soul of a soldier who knows he or she is in the wrong? That they are the aggressors, the bringers of savagery and violence? The notion worried Brys, for the answers that arrived were grim ones. *Something breaks inside. Something howls. Something dreams of suicide.* And, as commander, he would be to blame. As much as his brother, Tehol. For they were the leaders, the ones in charge, the ones using the lives of thousands of people as mere playing pieces on some stained board.

It is one thing to lead soldiers into war. And it is one thing to send them into a war. But it is, it seems to me, wholly another to lead and send them into a war that is itself a crime. Are we to be so indifferent to the suffering we will inflict on our own people and upon innocent victims in unknown lands?

In his heart dwelt the names of countless lost gods. Many had broken the souls of their worshippers. Many others had been broken by the mortal madness of senseless wars, of slaughter and pointless annihilation. Of the two, the former suffered a torment of breathtaking proportions. There was, in the very end—there *must be*—judgement. Not upon the fallen, not upon the victims, but upon those who had orchestrated their fates.

Of course, he did not know if such a thing was true. Yes, he could sense the suffering among those gods whose names he held within him, but perhaps it was his own knowledge that engendered such anguish, and that anguish belonged to his own soul, cursed to writhe in an empathic trap. Perhaps he was doing nothing more than forcing his own sense of righteous punishment upon those long-dead gods. And if so, by what right could he do such a thing?

Troubling notions. Yet onward his legions marched. Seeking answers to questions the Adjunct alone knew. This went beyond trust, beyond even faith. This was a sharing of insanity, and in its maelstrom they were all snared, no matter what fate awaited them.

I should be better than this. Shouldn't I? I lead, but can I truly protect? When I do not know what awaits us?

'Commander.'

Startled from his dark thoughts, he straightened in his saddle and looked over to his Atri-Ceda. 'My apologies, were you speaking?'

Aranict wiped sweat from an oddly pale face, hesitated.

'I believe you are struck with heat. Dismount, and I will send for—'

'No, sir.'

'Atri-Ceda—'

He saw the wash of terror and panic rise into her face. 'We are in the wrong place! Commander! Brys! We have to get out of here! We have to—*we are in the wrong place!*'

At that moment, thunder hammered through the earth, a drum roll that went on, and on—

Dust storm or an army? Keneb squinted in the bright glare. 'Corporal.'

'Sir.'

'Ride to the vanguard. I think we've sighted the Khundryl and Perish.'

'Yes, sir!'

As the rider cantered off, Keneb glanced to his left. Brys's columns had edged slightly ahead—the Malazans had been anything but spry this day. Moods were dark, foul, discipline was crumbling. Knots of acid in his stomach had awakened him this morning, painful enough to start tears in his eyes. The worst of it had passed, but he knew he had to find a capable healer soon.

A sudden wind gusted into his face, smelling of something bitter.

He saw Blistig riding out from his legion, angling towards him. Now what?

Head pounding, Banaschar trudged alongside a heavily laden wagon. He was parched inside, as parched as this wretched land. He held his gaze on the train of oxen labouring in their yokes, the flicking tails, the swarming flies, the fine coat of dust rising up their haunches and flanks. Hoofs thumped on the hard ground.

Hearing some muttering from the troop marching a few paces to his right, he lifted his eyes. The sky had suddenly acquired a sickly hue. Wind buffeted him, tasting of grit, stinging his eyes.

Damned dust storm. She'll have to call a halt. She'll have to—

No, that colour was wrong. Mouth dry as stone, he felt a tightening in his throat, a pain in his chest.

Gods no. That wind is the breath of a warren. It's—oh, Worm of Autumn, no.

He staggered as convulsions took him. Half-blinded in pain, he fell on to his knees.

Sergeant Sunrise dropped his kit bag and hurried over to the fallen priest's side. 'Rumjugs! Get Bavedict! He's looking bad here—'

'He's a drunk,' snapped Sweetlard.

'No—looks worse than that. Rumjugs—'

'I'm going—'

Thunder shook the ground beneath them. Cries rose from countless beasts. Something seemed to ripple through the ranks of soldiery, an unease, an instant of uncertainty stung awake. Voices shouted questions but no answers came back, and the confusion rose yet higher.

Sweetlard stumbled against Sunrise, almost knocking him over as he crouched beside the priest. He could hear the old man mumbling, saw his head rock as if buffeted by unseen blows. Something spattered the back of Sunrise's left hand and he looked down to see drops of blood. 'Errant's push! Who stabbed him? I didn't see—'

'Someone knifed him?' Sweetlard demanded.

'I don't—I ain't—here, help me get him round—'

The thunder redoubled. Oxen lowed. Wheels rocked side to side with alarming creaks. Sunrise looked skyward, saw nothing but a solid golden veil of dust. 'We got us a damned storm—where's Bavedict? Sweet—go find 'em, will ya?'

'Thought you wanted my help?'

'Wait—get Hedge—get the commander—this guy's sweating blood all over his skin! Right out through the pores! Hurry!'

'Something's happening,' Sweetlard said, now standing directly over him.

Her tone chilled Sunrise to the core.

Captain Ruthan Gudd drew a ragged breath, savagely pushing the nausea away, and the terror that flooded through him in its wake had him reaching for his sword. *Roots of the Azath, what was that?* But he could see nothing—the dust had slung an ochre canopy across the sky, and on all sides soldiers were suddenly milling, as if they had lost their way—but nothing lay ahead, just empty stretches of land. Teeth bared, Ruthan Gudd kicked his skittish horse forward, rising in his stirrups. His sword was in his hand, steam whirling from its white, strangely translucent blade.

He caught sight of it from the corner of his eye. '*Hood's fist!*' The skeins of sorcery that had disguised the weapon—in layers thick and tangled with centuries of magic—had been torn away. Deathly cold burned his hand. *She answers. She answers . . . what?*

He pulled free of the column.

A seething line had appeared along a ridge of hills to the southeast.

The thunder rolled on, drawing ever closer. Iron glittered as if tipped with diamond shards, like teeth gnawing through the summits of those hills. The swarming motion pained his eyes.

He saw riders peeling out from the vanguard. Parley flags whipping from up-ended spears. Closer to hand, foot-soldiers staring at him and his damned weapon, others stumbling from the bitter cold streaming in his wake. His own armour-clad thighs and the back of his horse were rimed in frost.

She answers—as she has never answered before. Gods below, spawn of the Azath—I smell—oh, gods no—

'Form up! Marines form up! First line on the ridge—skirmishers! Get out of there, withdraw!' Fiddler wasn't waiting, not for anything. He couldn't see the captain but it didn't matter. He felt as if he'd swallowed a hundred caltrops. The air stank. Pushing past a confused Koryk and then a white-faced Smiles, he caught sight of the squad directly ahead.

'Balm! Deadsmell—awaken your warrens! Same for Widdershins—where's Cord, get Ebron—'

'Sergeant!'

He twisted back, saw Faradan Sort forcing her horse through the milling soldiers.

'What are you doing?' she demanded. 'It's some foreign army out there—we've sent emissaries. You're panicking the soldiers—'

Fiddler caught Tarr's level gaze. 'See they're formed up—toss the word out fast as it can go, you understand, Corporal?'

'Aye sir—'

'Sergeant!'

Fiddler pushed his way to the captain, reached up and dragged her down from the saddle. Cursing, she flailed, unbalanced. As her full weight caught him, Fiddler staggered and then went down, Sort on top of him. In her ear he said, '*Get the fuck off that horse and stay off it. Those emissaries are already dead, even if they don't know it. We need to dig in, Captain, and we need to do it now.*'

She lifted herself up, face dark with anger, and then glared into his eyes. Whatever she saw in them was hard and sharp as a slap. Sort rolled to one side and rose. 'Someone get this horse out of here. Where's our signaller? Flags up: prepare for battle. Ridge defence. Foot to dig in, munitions spread second trench—get on it, damn you!'

Most of the damned soldiers were doing nothing but get in the way. Snarling and cursing, Bottle forced through the press until he reached the closest supply wagon.

He scrambled on to it, pulling himself by the rope netting until he was atop the heaped bales. Then he stood.

A half-dozen of the Adjunct's emissaries were cantering towards that distant army.

The sky above the strangers swarmed with . . . birds? No. *Rhinazan . . . and some bigger things. Bigger . . . enkar'al? Wyval?* He felt sick enough to void his bowels. He knew that smell. It had soaked into his brain ever since he'd crawled through a shredded tent. *That army isn't human. Adjunct, your emissaries—*

Something blinding arced out from the foremost line of one of the distant phalanxes. It cut a ragged path above the ground until it struck the mounted emissaries. Bodies burst into flames. Burning horses reeled and collapsed in clouds of ash.

Bottle stared. *Hood's holy shit.*

Sinter ran as fast as she could, cutting between ranks of soldiers. They were finally digging in, while the supply train—the wagons herded like enormous beasts between mounted archers and lancers—had swung northward, forcing, she saw, the Letherii forces to divide almost in half to permit the retreating column through their ranks.

That wasn't good. She could see the chaos rippling out as the huge wagons plunged into the narrow avenue. Pikes pitched and wavered to either side, the press making figures stumble and fall.

Not her problem. She looked ahead once again, saw the vanguard, saw the Adjunct, Captain Yil, Fists Blistig and Keneb and a score or so honour guard and mounted staff. Tavore was issuing commands and riders were winging out to various units. There wasn't much time. The distant hills had been swallowed by marching phalanxes, a dozen in sight and more coming—and each formation looked massive. Five thousand? Six? The thunder was the measure of their strides, steady, unceasing. The sky behind them was the colour of bile, winged creatures swarming above the rising dust.

Those soldiers. They aren't people. They aren't human—gods below, they are huge.

She reached the vanguard. 'Adjunct!'

Tavore's helmed head snapped round.

'Adjunct, we must retreat! This is wrong! This isn't—'

'Sergeant,' Tavore's voice cut through like a blade's edge. 'There is no time. Furthermore, our obvious avenue of retreat happens to be blocked by the Letherii legions—'

'Send a rider to Brys—'

'We have done so, Sergeant—'

'*They aren't human!*'

Flat eyes regarded her. 'No, they are not. K'Chain—'

'*They don't want us! We're just in their fucking way!*'

Expressionless, the Adjunct said, 'It is clear they intend to engage us, Sergeant.'

Wildly, Sinter turned to Keneb. 'Fist, please! You need to explain—'

'Sinter,' said Tavore, 'K'Chain *Nah'ruk*.'

Keneb's face had taken on the colour of the sickly sky. 'Return to your squad, Sergeant.'

Quick Ben stood wrapped in his leather cloak, thirty paces on from the Malazan vanguard. He was alone. Three hundred paces behind him the Letherii companies were wheeling to form a bristling defensive line along the ridge on which the column had been marching. They had joined their supply train and herds to the Bonehunters' and it seemed an entire city and all its livestock was wheeling northward in desperate flight. Brys intended to defend that retreat. The High Mage understood the logic of that. It marked, perhaps, the last rational moment of this day.

Ill luck. Stupid, pathetic, miserable mischance. It was absurd. It was sickening beyond all belief. Which gods had clutched together to spin this madness? He had told the Adjunct all he knew. As soon as the warren's mouth had spread wide, as soon as the earth trembled to the first heavy footfall of the first marching phalanx. *We saw their sky keeps. We knew they weren't gone. We knew they were gathering.*

But that was so far away, and so long ago now.

The reek of their oils was heavy on the wind that still poured out from the warren. Beyond the ochre veil he could see a deepness, a darkness that did not belong.

They have come here, to the Wastelands.

They have been this way before.

Ambitions and desires spun like ash from a pyre. All at once, it was clear that nothing was important, nothing beyond this moment and what was about to begin. Could anyone have predicted this? Could anyone have pierced the solid unknown of the future, carving through to this scene?

There were times, he knew, when even the gods staggered back, reeled with bloodied faces. *No, the gods didn't manage this. They could not guess the Adjunct's heart, that wellspring so full with all she would reveal to none. We were ever the shaved knuckle, but in whose hand would we be found? None knew. None could even dream . . .*

He stood alone, warrens awake and seething within him. He would do what he could, for as long as he was able. And then he would fall, and there would be no one left but a score of squad mages and the Atri-Ceda.

On this day, we shall witness the death of friends. On this day, we may well join them.

The High Mage Adaephon Ben Delat drew from a pouch a handful of acorns and flung them to the ground. He squinted once more at the deepness beyond the veil, and then down to the Nah'ruk legions. Monstrous in their implacability— *steal one away and it's damned near mindless. Gather them in their thousands,*

*and their will becomes one . . . and that will is . . . gods below . . . it is so very
cold . . .*

The Nah'ruk were half again as tall as a man and perhaps twice the weight. Little
of their upper bodies could be seen, even as they drew to within two hundred
paces, for they were clad in sheaths of enamel or boiled-leather armour extending
out to their upper arms and reaching down to protect their forward-thrusting
thighs. The stubs of their tails bore similar armour, but in finer scales. Wide
helms enclosed their heads, short snouts emerging between ornate cheek-guards.
Those in the front lines held arcane clubs of some sort, blunt-ended and wrapped
in bundles of what looked like wire. For each dozen or so, one warrior walked
burdened beneath a massive ceramic pack that sat high on its shoulders.

Behind this first line of warriors the other ranks carried short-handled halberds
or falchions, held vertically. Each phalanx presented a breadth of at least a hundred
warriors, all marching in perfect time, upper bodies leaning forward above their
muscled, reptilian legs. There were no standards, no banners, and no obvious vanguard of commanders. As far as Ruthan Gudd could determine, there was nothing
to distinguish one from another, barring those wearing the strange kit bags.

Frost glistened from his entire body now, and ice had spread thick as armour to
encase the horse beneath him. It was already dead, he knew, but the ice knew to
answer his commands. He rode a dozen paces ahead of the front line of Malazans,
knowing that countless eyes were upon him, knowing they were struggling to understand what they were seeing—not just this alien army so clearly intent on
their annihilation, but Ruthan Gudd himself, out here astride a horse sheathed in
ice, the ice murky with hints of the form it had engulfed.

He held the Stormrider sword as if it was an extension of his forearm—ice had
crept up to his shoulder, gleaming yet flowing as would water.

Eyeing the Nah'ruk, he muttered under his breath. '*Yes, you see me. You
mark me. Send your fury my way. First and last, strike me . . .*'

Behind him, from haphazard trenches, an ominous hush. The Bonehunters
crouched as if pinned to the ground, caught unawares, so rocked by the unexpected
impossibility of this that not a single defiant shout sounded, not a single weapon
hammered the rim of a shield. Though he did not turn round, he knew that all motion had ceased. No more orders to be given. None were, truth be told, necessary.

By his rough count, over forty thousand Nah'ruk were advancing upon
them. He almost caught an echo of the cacophony only moments away, as if the
future's walls were about to be shattered, flinging horror back into the past—to
this moment, to ring deafeningly in his skull.

'Too bad,' he muttered. 'It was such a pretty day.'

'Hood's breath, who is that?'

Adjunct Tavore's eyes narrowed. 'Captain Ruthan Gudd.'

'That's what I thought,' Lostara Yil replied. 'What's happened to him?'

In answer the Adjunct could only shake her head.

Lostara shifted on her horse, free hand drifting to the knife at her belt, and then twitching away. *Sword, you idiot. Not the knife. The stupid sword.* A face drifted into her mind. Henar Vygulf. He would be with Brys right now, ready to set off with orders. The Letherii were set back, forming two distinct outside flanks, like the outer bends of a bow. They would witness the collision of the front lines, and then, she hoped, they'd quickly see the suicidal insanity of standing against these damned lizards, and Brys would deliberately rout his army. *Get the Hood out of here—leave all the gear behind—just flee. Don't die like us, don't stand just because we're standing. Just get out, Brys—Henar—I pray you. I beg you.*

She heard horse hoofs and glanced over to see Fist Keneb riding down the length of the humped berm, passing the ranks of his dug-in soldiers. *What's he doing?*

He was riding for Captain Ruthan Gudd.

Tavore spoke. 'Sound horn, signaller—order Fist Keneb to personally withdraw.'

A blast of wails lifted into the air.

'He's ignoring it,' Lostara said. 'The fool!'

Quick Ben caught sight of Ruthan Gudd and he grunted. *I'll be damned. A Mael-bit Nerruse-whore-spawn Stormrider. Who knew?*

But what was he doing out front like that? After a moment, the High Mage swore under his breath. *You want 'em to take you first. You want to draw them to you. You're giving the Bonehunters a dozen heartbeats to realize what they have to deal with. Captain Ruthan Gudd, or whoever you are . . . gods, what can I possibly say? Go well, Captain.*

Go well.

Swearing, Keneb savagely drove his spurs into the flanks of his mount. That was Ruthan Gudd, and if the fool wasn't what he pretended to be, then the Malazans needed him more than ever. *The man could be a damned god but single-handedly charging those things will still see him chopped to pieces. Ruthan! We need you— whoever and whatever you are—we need you alive!*

Could he reach him in time?

Captain Skanarow kicked at one of her soldiers, pushing the idiot back into the shallow trench. 'Keep digging!' she snarled, and then returned her attention to that gleaming figure riding out towards the lizards. *You stupid lying bastard! A Stormrider? Impossible—they live in the damned seas.*

Ruthan, please, what are you doing?

Seeing the first line of the nearest phalanx level their bizarre clubs, Ruthan Gudd gritted his teeth. *This Stormrider crap had better work. But gods below, it does hurt to wear.* He wheeled his mount to face the Nah'ruk, and then raised high his sword.

Sunlight flashed through the ice.

A rider was coming up from behind and to his left. *Poor bastard. That's what you get for taking orders.* Without a backward glance, he drove his spurs into the flanks of his mount. Sparks flashed from the ice. The beast lunged forward.

You sorry Malazans. Watch me, and then ask yourself: How deep can you dig?

Fiddler cocked his crossbow, carefully inserted a sharper-headed quarrel. Now that it was happening, he felt fine. Nothing more to be done, was there? Everything was alight, cut clear, the colours of the world suddenly saturated, beautiful beyond belief. He could taste it. He could taste it all. 'Everybody loaded?'

Grunts and nods from his squad, all of them crouched down in the trench.

'Keep your heads right down,' Fiddler told them again. 'We'll hear the charge, count on it. Nobody pokes up for a look until my say so, understood?'

He saw, a few squads down, Balgrid edging up for a look. The healer shouted, 'Gudd's charging them!'

Along the entire line of marines, helmed heads sprung up like mushrooms.

Fuck!

Crump was on his hands and knees, a clutch of sharpers set like black-turtle eggs in a shallow pit pushed into the stony floor of the trench.

Ebron stared in horror. 'Have you lost your mind? Spread 'em down the line, you idiot!'

Crump looked up, eyes widening. 'Can't do that, mage. They're mine! All I got left!'

'Someone could step on them!'

But Crump was shaking his head. 'I'm protecting them, mage!'

Ebron swung round. 'Cord! Sergeant! It's Crump! He's—'

The wire-bound clubs in the front line seemed to ignite like torches. Lightning arced from the blunt heads, two serpentine tendrils snaking into the air. From each weapon, one of the bolts twisted and spun to sink into one of the strange ceramic packs—a dozen such arcs for each pack. The second crackling tongue of white fire seemed to throb for an instant, and then as one they lashed out, a score or more converging on the charging, ice-clad rider and horse.

The detonation engulfed Ruthan Gudd and his mount, tore gouts of earth and stone from the ground in a broad, ragged crater.

An instant before the explosion, other front lines had awakened their own weapons, and even as the flash erupted, hundreds of bolts snapped out to strike the front trench.

On his way back to the squad, Bottle was thrown down into the trench, the impact punching the breath from his lungs. Gaping, his head tilted to one side, he saw a row of bodies lifted into the air along the entire length of the berm—all those who had climbed up to watch Ruthan's charge. Marines, most of them headless or missing everything above their rib cages, twisted amidst dirt and rocks and pieces of armour and weapons.

Still unable to breathe, he saw a second wave of the sorcery lance directly over his trench. The ground shook as ranks behind him were struck. The blue of the sky vanished behind thick clouds. Bodies sailed in and out of those churning clouds.

Bottle writhed, deaf, his lungs howling. He felt the muted impacts of sharpers, too close, too random—

A hand reached down out of the sudden gloom and closed on his chest harness. He was dragged out from the slumped side of the collapsed trench.

Bottle coughed out a mouthful of earth, hacked agonizing breaths, his throat afire. Tarr's spattered face was above him, shouting—but Bottle could hear nothing. No matter, he pushed Tarr back, nodding. *I'm all right. No, honest. I'm fine— where's my crossbow?*

Keneb had come too close. The detonation caught him and his horse and literally ripped them both to pieces. Chunks of flesh sprayed outward. Ebron, leaning hard over the berm, saw part of the Fist's upper torso—a shoulder, a stub of the arm and a few splayed ribs—cartwheel skyward, lifted on a column of dirt.

Even as the mage stared, disbelieving, a sorcerous bolt caught him dead centre on his sternum. It tore through him, disintegrating his upper chest, shoulders and head.

Limp howled as one of Ebron's arms flopped down across his thighs.

But no one heard him.

They had seen Quick Ben, but had elected to ignore him. He flinched as the first waves of lightning ploughed into the defences along the ridge. Thunder rattled the ground and the entire facing side of the Bonehunter army vanished inside churning clouds of dirt, stone, and dismembered bodies.

He saw the nodes recharging on the shoulders of the drones. How long? 'No idea,' he whispered. 'Little acorns, listen. Go for the drones—the ones with the packs. Forget the rest . . . for now.'

Then he set out, walking down towards the nearest phalanx.

The Nah'ruk front was less than a hundred paces away.

They had seen him and now they took note. Lightning blistered all along the front line.

Horse clambering drunkenly from the crater, Ruthan Gudd shook his head, readying his blazing weapon. Dirt streamed down his back beneath his smeared, steaming armour. He spat grit.

That wasn't so bad now.

Directly in front of him, twenty paces away, looming huge, the front line. Their eyes glittered like diamonds within the shadows beneath the rims of their ornate helms. The fangs lining their snouts glistened like shards of iron.

He had an inkling that they had not expected to see him again. He rode over to say hello.

'Crossbows at the ready!' Fiddler yelled. 'Go for the nodes!'

'The what?'

'The lumpy ones! That's where the magic's coming from!'

Koryk scrambled to crouch beside Fiddler. The man was sheathed in bloody mud. 'Who pops up for a look, Fid?'

'I will,' said Corabb, surging upward and clawing up the berm. 'Gods below! That captain's still alive! He's in their ranks—'

As Corabb made to clamber out of the trench—clearly intending to join Gudd and charge the whole damned phalanx, Tarr reached out and dragged the fool back down.

'Stay where you are, soldier! Get that crossbow—no, that one there! Load the fucker!'

'Range, Corabb?' Fiddler asked.

'Forty and slowed, Sergeant—that captain's carving right through 'em!'

'Won't matter much. I don't care if he's got Oponn's poker up his ass, he's only one man.'

'We should help him!'

'We can't, Corabb,' Fiddler said. 'Besides, that's the last thing he'd want—why d'you think he went out there on his own? Leave him, soldier. We got our own trouble come knocking. Koryk, you take the next look, count of ten. Nine, eight, seven—'

'I ain't getting my head blasted off!'

Fiddler swung his crossbow round to point at Koryk's chest. 'Four, three, two, one—up you go!'

Snarling, Koryk scrambled upward. Then was back down almost instantly. 'Shit. Twenty-five and picking up speed!'

Fiddler raised his voice. 'Everyone ready! The nodes! Hold it—hold it—*NOW!*'

Hedge led his Bridgeburners just to the rear of the last trenches. 'I don't care what Quick thinks, he's always had backup, he never went it alone. Ever. So that's us, soldiers—keep up there, Sweetlard! Look at Rumjugs, she ain't even breathing hard—'

'She's forgotten how!' Sweetlard gasped.

'Remember what I said,' Hedge reminded them, 'Bridgeburners have faced worse than a bunch of stubby lizards. This ain't nothing, right?'

'We gonna win, Commander?'

Hedge glanced over at Sunrise. And grinned. 'Count on it, Sergeant. Now, everyone, check your munitions, and remember to aim for the lumpy ones. We're about to pull into the open—'

A concussion shook the very air, but it came from the Nah'ruk lines. A billowing black cloud rose like a stain of spilled ink.

'Gods, what was that?'

Hedge's grin broadened. 'That, soldiers, was Quick Ben.'

Lightning arced out from hundreds of clubs, from multiple phalanxes to either side of the one he had attacked. The bolts snapped towards him, then slanted off as Quick Ben flung them aside. *And I ain't Tayschrenn and this ain't Pale. Got no one behind me, so keep throwing them my way, y'damned geckos. Use it all up!*

The first dozen or so ranks of the phalanx he'd struck were down, a few writhing or feebly struggling to rise with crushed limbs and snapped bones. Most were motionless, their bodies boiled from the inside out. As he walked towards those who remained, he saw them regrouping, forming a line to face him once more.

The huge falchions and halberds lifted in readiness.

Quick Ben extended his senses, until he could feel the very air around the creatures, could follow currents of that air as they slipped through gills into reptilian lungs. He reached out to encompass as many of them as possible.

And then he set the air on fire.

Lightning shunted from the High Mage, careened off into the sky and out to the sides.

Sergeant Sunrise shrieked as one bolt twisted and spun straight for Hedge. He flung himself forward, three paces that seemed to tear every muscle in his back and legs. He was a Bridgeburner. He was the man he had always wanted to be; he'd never stood taller, never walked straighter.

And all because of Hedge.

See me? Sunrise—

He was smiling as he flung himself into the lightning's path.

Hedge's sergeant erupted, blinding white, and then where he had been was nothing but swirling ashes. His soldiers were screaming behind him. Spinning,

Hedge shouted, 'Everyone down to the ground! We'll wait it out—we wait it out!'

Fuck you, Quick—this ain't Pale, you know! And you ain't Tayschrenn!

Ruthan Gudd slashed down to either side, but the damned things were pressing in—they'd halted his forward progress. Heavy iron blades cracked and skittered against his horse, his thighs. The armour was showing cracks, but after each blow those fissures healed. His sword cut through helms and skulls, necks and limbs, but the Nah'ruk did not relent, closing tighter and tighter about him.

He heard concussions somewhere to his left, caught the stench of howling warrens being forced to do unspeakable things—*Quick Ben, how much longer can you hide?* Well, Ruthan knew he'd not be around to witness any revelations. They were taking him down with their sheer weight. His horse staggered, head thrashing and flinching with every savage downward strike of falchions.

The rest of the phalanx had moved past the knot trapping him, were ascending the ridge, only moments from reaching the first trench. He caught flashes of other phalanxes marching past.

Four blades struck him simultaneously, lifting him from the saddle with a splintering explosion of ice shards. Cursing, he twisted, lashing out even as he plunged into the maelstrom of reptilian limbs and iron weapons. And then taloned feet, slashing, stamping down. A blow to the face stunned him. White, and then blessed darkness.

Twelve paces. The surviving marines rose as one from the foremost trench. Crossbows thudded. Sharpers cracked and burners ignited. Directly before Fiddler, he saw his bolt glance off a node and then explode immediately behind the lizard's head. The helm went spinning, whipping fragments of brain and bone in a wild cavorting tail of gore. The node blackened, and then exploded.

The concussion threw Fiddler back, down into the trench. Pieces of hide and meat rained down.

Half-winded, he struggled to reload his lobber. One last cusser—*gotta get rid of it, before it goes up like those sharpers down the line—gods, we've been chewed up—*

Shadows swept over the trench.

He looked up.

The Nah'ruk had arrived.

Corabb had managed to reload. Lifting his head, he saw a giant lizard rising above the berm, maw tilting down as if grinning at him.

His quarrel vanished into its soft throat, punched out through the back of its skull. The creature wobbled. Flinging away the crossbow, Corabb drew his sword and scrambled to his feet. He swung at the nearest shin. The impact nearly broke his wrist and the weapon's edge bit deep into bone and jammed there.

Still the creature stood, twitches rippling through its massive body.

Corabb struggled to pull loose his sword.

To either side, Nah'ruk clambered over the berm, leapt down into the trench.

The backswing lifted Sergeant Primly into the air, and he rode the iron blade, his blood spilling down as if from a bucket. Shrieking, Neller flung himself on to the lizard's left arm, pulled himself higher and then forced the sharper down between the enamel chest-plate and the greasy hide. Jaws snapped, closed on his face. Phlegm like acid splashed his eyes and skin. Howling, Neller tightened his grip on the sharper and then drove the fist of his other hand against the armour, directly opposite the munition.

Mulvan Dreader, driving a spear into the lizard's belly, caught the blast as the creature's chest exploded. Ceramic shrapnel shredded Mulvan's neck, punching red gore into the air behind him. Neller was flung back, his right arm gone, his face a slashed, melting horror.

Primly's corpse landed five paces away, a flopping thing painted crimson.

The lizard toppled.

Two more appeared behind it, falchions lifting.

Stumbling, Drawfirst set her shield and readied her sword. As Skulldeath leapt past her, landing in between the two Nah'ruk.

A bolt sizzled close to her horse's head. Its muzzle and mane burst into flame. Skin peeled and cracked from mouth to shoulders. The animal collapsed. Lostara Yil managed to roll clear. The heat had flashed against her face and she could smell the stench of scorched hair. Staggering to her feet, she looked over to see a dozen staff riders down, roasted in their armour. The Adjunct was lifting herself from the carnage, her otataral sword in one hand.

'Get me Keneb—'

'Keneb's dead, Adjunct,' Lostara replied, staggering over. The world spun and then steadied.

Tavore straightened. 'Where—'

Lostara reached the woman, pulled her down to the ground. 'You shouldn't even be alive, Tavore. Stay here—you're in shock. Stay here—I'll find help—'

'Quick Ben—the High Mage—'

'Aye.' Lostara stood over the Adjunct, who was sitting as would a child. The captain looked over to where she'd last seen Quick Ben.

He'd annihilated an entire phalanx, and where it had been the fires of super-heated flesh, hide and bone still raged in an inferno. She saw him marching towards another phalanx, above him the sky convulsing, blackening like a bruise.

Sorcery erupted from the High Mage, struck the phalanx. Burning corpses lifted into the air.

'I see him. Adjunct—I can't—'

From the darkness in the sky a sudden glow, blinding, and then an enormous spear of lightning descended. She saw the High Mage look up, saw him raise his arms—and then the bolt struck. The explosion could have levelled a tenement block. Even the Nah'ruk in the phalanx thirty or more paces away were flattened like sheaves of wheat. Flanking units buckled on the facing sides.

The shock wave staggered Lostara, stole her breath, deafened her. Hands to her face, she slumped down, struck the ground hard.

Pearl?

Skanarow threw herself down into the second trench where the heavies were waiting. 'The marines are overrun! Sound the fall-back—and make room for the survivors—let 'em through! Get ready to hold this trench!'

She saw a messenger, unhorsed, crouching behind the headless corpse of a heavy. 'You—find Captain Kindly. I just saw the vanguard go down—and I don't know where Blistig is, so as far as I'm concerned Kindly's now in command. Tell him, we need to begin a retreat—we can't hold. Understood?'

The young man nodded.

'Go.'

Brys flinched as the Nah'ruk lines struck the Malazan defences. He saw the heavy falchions descending. Barely slowing, the lizards swarmed over the first trench and began closing on the next one.

'Aranict—'

'I think she lives, Commander.'

Brys swung round in his saddle, caught the eyes of his outriders. 'We need to retrieve the Adjunct. Volunteers only.'

One rider pushed through the others. Henar Vygulf.

Brys nodded. 'Get your spare horses, Lieutenant.'

The huge Bluerose saluted.

'When you have them,' Brys said before the man turned away, 'ride for the supply train.'

The soldier frowned.

Brys gritted his teeth. 'I will not stand here watching this slaughter. We will close with the enemy.'

They saw the impossibly thick bolt of lightning tear down from the dark stain ahead. As the shockwaves drummed through the ground, Warleader Gall raised an arm to signal a halt. He faced Kisswhere, his face ashen. 'I am sending you to the Mortal Sword Krughava—tell her the Malazans are assailed, and that the Khundryl ride to their succour.'

She stared at the man. 'Warleader—'

'Ride, soldier—you are not Khundryl—you do not understand what it is to fight from a horse. Tell Krughava the gods were cruel this day, for she will not reach the Malazans in time.'

'Who is their enemy?' Kisswhere demanded. 'Your shamans—'

'Are blind. We know less than you. Ride, Kisswhere.'

She swung her horse round.

Gall rose in his stirrups and faced his warriors. He drew his tulwar and held it high. And said nothing.

In answer, six thousand weapons were freed and lifted skyward.

Gall pulled his horse round. 'Ride ahead, Rafala, until you sight the enemy.'

The woman kicked her mount into a gallop.

After a moment, Gall led his army after her, at a quick canter, and the sound of thunder grew louder, and the yellow sky deepened to brown in which flashes bloomed like wounds.

He wondered what his wife was doing.

Worse than chopping down trees. Fiddler gave up trying to hack through legs and began hamstringing the bastards, ducking the slashes of notched weapons, dodging the downward swings. The surviving Malazans had been driven from the first trench, were now struggling to hold a fighting withdrawal across the ten paces to the heavies' trench.

Crossbow quarrels and arrows spat out from the troops arrayed behind the heavies, winging at heights mercifully above the heads of the soldiers in their desperate retreat. Most missiles shattered against enamel, but a few were punching through, finding gaps in the Nah'ruk's armour. Beasts were toppling here and there.

But not enough. The phalanx was a machine, devouring everything in its path.

Fiddler had lost his cusser and lobber in the first trench. The shortsword felt puny as a thorn in his hand. A glancing blow had sent his helm flying and blood streamed down the right side of his head.

He saw Koryk pushing his sword through a Nah'ruk's neck; saw another lizard step in behind the man, halberd lifting high. Bolts punched into both armpits. The creature fell forward, burying Koryk. Smiles rushed over, diving and rolling to evade a lashing falchion.

Cuttle stumbled up against Fiddler. 'Retreat's sounded!'

'I heard—'

'Quick Ben's been Rannalled, Fid—that giant strike—'

'I know. Forget him—help me get the squad back—the heavies will hold, enough so we can regroup. Go on, I ain't seen Corabb or Bottle—'

Nah'ruk and human corpses half-buried Bottle, but he was in no hurry to move. He saw more of the lizards marching past on all sides.

We never even slowed them.

Quick, whatever happened to subtlety?

He could see a sliver of sky, could see the wyval wheeling round up there, eager to descend and feed. *Grandma, you always said don't reach too far. Close your dead eyes now, and remember, I loved you so.*

He left his body, winged skyward.

Corabb yanked hard and dragged his sword from the Nah'ruk's left eye socket, then he reached down to take up again Shoaly's ankle—but the man had stopped screaming and as he looked he saw in the heavy's face a slackness, a dullness to the staring eyes.

A line of Nah'ruk was closing, only a few paces away. Swearing, Corabb released his grip and turned to run.

The trench of the heavy infantry was just ahead. He saw helmed faces, weapons readied. Arrows and quarrels hissed over them and the thud and snap of their impacts was torrential behind him. Corabb hurried over.

Cuttle fell in beside him. 'Seen Tarr?'

'Seen him go down.'

'Bottle?'

Corabb shook his head. 'Smiles? Koryk?'

'Fid's got 'em.'

'Fiddler! He's—'

The first trench directly behind the two marines erupted. Nah'ruk ranks simply vanished in blue clouds.

'What—'

'Some bastard stepped on a cusser!' Cuttle said. 'Serves 'em right! C'mon!'

Deathly pale faces beneath helm rims—but the heavies were standing, ready. Two parted and let the marines through.

One shouted over at Cuttle. 'Those clubs—'

'Got 'em, soldier!' Cuttle yelled back. 'Now it's just iron.'

At once a shout rose from the length of the trench. '*HAIL THE MARINES!*'

And the faces around Corabb suddenly darkened, teeth baring. The instant transformation took his breath away. *Iron, aye, you know all about iron.*

The Nah'ruk were five steps behind them.

The heavies rose to meet them.

Hedge watched as the lizards clambered from the enormous crater where Quick Ben had been, watched as they re-formed their ranks and resumed their advance. Twisting from where he was lying, he then looked back to study the Letherii legions drawing up at a steady half-trot, pikes set and slowly angling in overlapping layers.

Hedge grunted. *Good weapons for this.*

'Bridgeburners! Listen up! Never mind the High Mage. He's ashes on the wind. We're going to soften up the lizards for the Letherii. Ready your munitions.

One salvo when I say so and then we retreat and if the Letherii are sharp, they'll make room for us! If they don't, then swing to the right—to the right, got it? And run like Hood himself is on your heels!'

'Commander!' someone cried out.

'What?'

'Who's Hood?'

Gods below. 'He's just the guy you don't want on your heels, right?'

'Oh. Right.'

Hedge lifted his head. *Shit, these ones got clubs and nodes.* 'Check your munitions! Switch to Blue. You hear me? *Blues!* And aim for that front line! Nodes, lads and lasses, those white lumps!'

'Commander!'

'Hood's the—'

'I hear horses! Coming from the southeast—I think—is that horses?'

Hedge rose slightly higher. He saw two lizard phalanxes smartly wheeling. *Oh gods . . .*

Rolling into a charge, Gall leaned forward on his horse. Just like the Malazans to find the ugliest foes the whole damned world had to offer. And the scariest. But those squares had no pikes to fend off a cavalry charge—and they would pay for that.

When he'd led his army up to where Rafala had reined in, he'd seen—in the first dozen heartbeats—all he'd needed to see.

The enemy was devouring the Malazan army, driving them back, cutting down hundreds of soldiers if they were no more than children. This was slaughter, and barely a third of the phalanxes had actually closed with the Bonehunters.

He saw the Letherii moving up on both flanks, forming bristling pike walls in a saw-tooth presentation, but they'd yet to meet the enemy. Out to the far flanks mounted troops mustered, yet held far back—unaccountably so, as far as Gall was concerned.

Directly ahead of the Khundryl charge, two phalanxes were closing up to present a solid defensive line, denying the Burned Tears the opportunity to drive between the squares, winging arrows on both sides. Gall needed make no gestures or call out commands—his lead warriors knew to draw up upon loosing their arrows; they knew their lanes, through which the heavier lancers would pass to drive deep into the wounded front ranks of the enemy—drive in, and then withdraw. There would be no chance of shattering these phalanxes—the demons were too big, too heavily armoured. They would not break before a charge.

This is the last day of the Khundryl Burned Tears. My children, do you ride with me? I know you do. My children, be brave this day. See your father, and know that he is proud of you all.

The foremost line of demons began preparing strange clubs.

Hedge saw the lightning erupt from the Nah'ruk line, saw the jagged bolts tear into the mass of Khundryl warriors. The charge seemed to disintegrate inside a horrific cloud of red mist.

Sickened, he twisted on to his back, stared up at the sky. Didn't look like sky at all. 'Bridgeburners, get ready! Munitions in hand! One, two, three—*UP*!'

Brys had thought the bodies lying on the ground ahead were corpses. They suddenly rose, forty or fifty in all, and flung objects at the front line of Nah'ruk. The small dark grenados splashed as they struck the enemy warriors. An instant later, the Nah'ruk who had been struck began writhing as the liquid ate through their armour, and then their hides.

One of the nodes exploded, flinging bodies back. Then another and another. All at once the front ranks of the phalanx were a chaotic mess.

Brys turned to his signaller. 'Sound the charge! Sound the charge!'

Horns blared.

The legions broke into a dog-trot, pikes levelled.

The sappers were running, swinging to the left and out from the gap between the two forces. They might just make it clear in time.

At six paces, the Letherii ranks surged forward, voices lifting in a savage roar.

The teeth of the saw bit deep, one, three rows, four. The Nah'ruk phalanx buckled. And then the two forces ground to a halt. Pikes were held in place, infighters armed with axes and stabbing swords pushing between the front line to begin their vicious close work. Falchions flashed high, and then descended.

Brys gestured. Another messenger came up alongside him.

'The onager and arbalest units are to draw up on the hill to the east. Begin enfilade. Cavalry to provide initial screen until they commence firing.'

The man saluted and rode off.

Brys looked southeastward. Miraculously, some remnant of the mounted horse-warriors had survived the sorcerous salvos—he could see riders emerging from the dust and smoke, hammering wildly into the front ranks of the Nah'ruk. They struck with inhuman ferocity and Brys was not surprised—to have come through that would have stripped the sanity of any warrior.

He breathed a soft prayer for them in the name of a dozen long-lost gods.

A messenger reined in on his right. 'Commander! The west legions have engaged the enemy.'

'And?'

The man wiped the sweat from his face. 'Knocked 'em back a step or two, but now . . .'

Seeing that he could not go on, seeing that he was near tears, Brys simply nodded. He turned to study what he could see of the Malazan position.

Nothing but armoured lizards, weapons lifting and descending, blood rising in a mist.

But, as he stared, he noticed something.

The Nah'ruk were no longer advancing.

You stopped them? Blood of the gods, what manner of soldiers are you?

The heavy infantry stood. The heavy infantry held the trench. Even as they died, they backed not a single step. The Nah'ruk clawed for purchase on the blood-soaked mud of the berm. Iron chewed into them. Halberds slammed down, rebounded from shields. Reptilian bodies reeled back, blocking the advance of rear ranks. Arrows and quarrels poured into the foe from positions behind the trench.

And from above, Locqui Wyval descended by the score, in a frenzy, to tear and rend the helmed heads of the lizard warriors. Others quickly closed to do battle with their kin, and the sky rained blood.

Bottle's soul leapt from body to body, grasped tight the souls of Locqui Wyval, and flung them down upon the Nah'ruk. As each one was pulled down to the slaughter, he tore himself free to enslave yet another. He had reached out, taking as many as he could—dozens of the creatures—the stench of blood and all that they saw had driven them mad. He needed only crush the tatters of their restraint, loose them upon the nearest beasts that were not wyval.

When kin attacked, he did not resist—*the more dead and dying wyval, the better.*

But he felt himself being torn apart. He felt his mind shredding away. He could not do much more of this. Yet Bottle did not relent.

Tarr stumbled into a knot of marines. Glared round. 'Limp—where's your—'

'Dead,' Limp said. 'Just me an' Crump—'

'Ruffle?'

The round-faced woman shook her head. 'Got separated. Saw Skim die, that's all—'

'So what are you doing sitting here? On your feet, marine—those heavies are dying where they stand. And we're going to join them. You, Reliko! Pull Vastly on his feet there—you're all coming with me!'

Silent, without a single word of protest, the marines clambered to their feet. They were bleeding. They were exhausted.

They gathered up their weapons, and, Tarr in the lead, set out for the trench.

Nearby, Urb plucked away the shattered fragments of his shield. Hellian crouched beside him, breathing hard, her face streaked with blood and puke, with more of both drenching her chest. She'd said she didn't know whose blood it was. Glancing at her, he saw her hard eyes, her hard expression. Other soldiers were drawn up behind them.

Urb turned. 'We do what Tarr says, soldiers. Back into it. Now.'

Hellian almost pushed past him on the way to the trench.

Henar Vygulf reined in beneath the hill—he could see fallen horses and sprawled, scorched bodies where the Adjunct's command post had been. He slipped down from his horse, drew his two swords and jogged up the slope.

Reaching the summit, he saw four Nah'ruk arriving on the opposite ridge.

Lostara Yil and the Adjunct were lying almost side by side. Likely dead, but he needed to make sure. If he could.

He charged forward.

The clash of iron woke her. Blinking, Lostara stared into the sky, trying to recall what had happened. Her head ached and she could feel dried blood crusting her nostrils, crackling in her ears. She turned her head, saw the Adjunct lying beside her.

Chest slowly rising and falling.

Ah, good.

Someone grunted as if in pain.

She sat up. In time to see Henar Vygulf stagger back, blood spraying from a chest wound. Three Nah'ruk closed.

Henar fell on to his back almost at Lostara's feet.

She rose, drawing her blades.

He saw her, and the anguish in his eyes took her breath away.

'I'm sorry—'

'You're going to live,' she told him, stepping past. 'Prop yourself up, man—that's an order!'

He managed to lift himself on one elbow. 'Captain—'

She glanced at the Nah'ruk. Almost upon her, slowed by wounds. Behind them, a dozen more appeared. 'Just remember, Henar, I don't do this for just anybody!'

'Do what?'

She stepped forward, blades lifting. '*Dance.*'

The old forms returned, as if they had but been awaiting her, awaiting this one moment when at last she awoke—possibly one last time—no matter. *For you, Henar. For you.*

The Shadow Dance belonged to this.

Here.

Now.

Henar watched her, and his eyes slowly widened.

———

A league to the southeast, Kisswhere dragged herself from her fallen horse. A badger burrow, the den mouth of a fox, something. Her horse thrashed, front legs shattered, its screams shrill in the air.

Kisswhere's left leg was bent in four places. The stub of bone thrust through her leggings. She drew a knife and twisted round to study the horse, eyes fixing on a pulsing artery in its neck.

Didn't matter. They were all dead. Even if she could have reached the Mortal Sword and that mad red-haired Queen, it wouldn't have mattered.

She glanced up. The sky was flesh, and that flesh was rotting before her eyes. *Sinter. Badan.*

Bonehunters—Adjunct, are you happy? You killed them all.

You killed us all.

Chapter Twenty-Four

On this dawn they lined the banks of the ancient river, a whole city turned out, near a hundred thousand, as the sun lifted east of the mouth that opened to the deep bay. What had brought them there? What ever brings the multitudes to a moment, a place, an instant when a hundred thousand bodies become one body?

As the red waters spilled into the bay's salty tears, they stood, saying little, and the great ship pyre took hold of the fires and the wind took hold of the soaked sails, and the sky took hold of the black column of smoke.

Ehrlitan's great king was dead, the last of the Dessimb line, and the future was blowing sands, the storm's whisper was but a roar of strife made mercifully distant, a thing of promise drawing ever closer.

They came to weep. They came seeking salvation, for in the end, even grief masks a selfish indulgence. We weep in our lives for the things lost to us, the worlds done. A great man was dead, but we cannot follow him—we dare not, for to each of us death finds a new path.

An age was dead. The new age belonged to generations still to come. In the stalls of the market rounds the potters stacked bowls bearing the face of the dead king, with scenes of his past glories circling round and round, for ever outside of time, and this was the true wish of the multitudes.

Stop. Stop now. Pray this day never ends. Pray the ashes drift for ever. Pray tomorrow never becomes. It is a natural desire, an honest wish.

The tale dies, but this death will take some time. It is said the king lingered, there in the half breath. And people gathered each day at the palace gates, to weep, to dream of other ends, of fates denied.

The tale dies, but this death will take some time.

And the river's red tongue flows without end. And the spirit of the king said: *I see you. I see you all.* Can you not hear him? Hear him still?

DEATH OF THE GOLDEN AGE
THENYS BULE

Nom Kala stood with the others, a silent mass of warriors who had forgotten what it was to live, as the wind pulled at rotted furs, strips of hide and dry tangles of hair. Dull, pitted weapons hung like afterthoughts from twisted hands. Air pitched into the bowls of eye sockets and moaned back out. They could be statues, gnawed by age, withering where they stood facing the endless winds, the senseless rains, the pointless waves of heat and cold.

There was nothing useful in this, and she knew she was not alone in her disquiet. Onos T'oolan, the First Sword, crouched down on one knee ten paces ahead of them, hands wrapped round the grip of his flint sword, the weapon's point buried in the stony ground. His head was lowered, as if he made obeisance before a master, but this master was invisible, little more than a smear of obligations swept aside, but the stain of what had been held him in place—a stain only Onos T'oolan could see. He had not moved in some time.

Patience was no trial, but she could sense the chaos in her kin, the pitch and cant of terrible desires, the rocking rebuffs of vengeance waiting. It was only a matter of time before the first of them broke away, defying this servitude, this claim of righteous command. He would not reach for them. He had yet to do so, why imagine he would change—

The First Sword rose, faced them. 'I am Onos T'oolan. I am the First Sword of Tellann. I reject your need.'

The wind moaned on, like the flow of sorrow.

'You shall, however, bow to mine.'

She felt buffeted by those words. *This is what it means, then, to yield before a First Sword. We cannot deny him, cannot defy him.* She could feel his will, closing like a fist about her. *We had our chance—before this. We could have drifted away. He gave us that.* But not one T'lan Imass had done any such thing. *Instead, we fell inside ourselves, ever deeper, that endless eating and spitting out and eating all we spat out—this is the seductive sustenance of hatred and spite, of rage and vengeance.*

He could have led us off a cliff and we would not have noticed.

The three Orshayn bonecasters stepped forward. Ulag Togtil spoke. 'First Sword, we await your command.'

Onos T'oolan slowly faced south, where the sky above the horizon seemed to boil like pitch. And then he swung north, where a distant cloud caught the sun's dying light. 'We go no farther,' the First Sword said. 'We shall be dust.'

And what of our dark dreams, First Sword?

Such was his power that he heard her thought and so turned to her. 'Nom Kala, hold fast to your dreams. There will be an answer. T'lan Imass, we are upon a time of killing.'

The statues shifted. Some straightened. Some hunched down as if beneath terrible burdens. The statues—*my kin. My sisters, my brothers. There are none to look upon us now, none to see us, none to wonder at who we once were, at who shaped us with such . . . loving hands.* As she watched, they began, one by one, falling into dust.

None to witness. Dust of dreams, dust of all that we never achieved. Dust of what we might have been and what we cannot help but be.

Statues are never mute. Their silence is a roar of words. Will you hear? Will you listen?

She was the last, alone with Onos T'oolan himself.

'You possess no rage, Nom Kala.'

'No, First Sword, I do not.'

'What might you find to serve in its place?'

'I do not know. The humans defeated us. They were better than we were, it is as simple as that. I feel only grief, First Sword.'

'And is there no anger in grief, Nom Kala?'

Yes. It may be that there is. But if I must search for it—

'There is time,' said Onos T'oolan.

She bowed to him, and released herself.

Onos T'oolan watched as Nom Kala fell in a gusting cloud. In his mind a figure was approaching, hands held out as if beseeching. He knew that harrowed face, that lone glittering eye. What could he say to this stranger he had once known? He too was a stranger, after all. Yes, they had once known each other. *But now look at us, both so intimate with dust.*

Nom Kala's anguish returned to him. Her thoughts had bled with dread power— she was young. She was, he realized, what the Imass might have become, had the Ritual not taken them, had it not stolen their future. *A future of pathos. Sordid surrender. The loss of dignity, a slow, slow death.*

No, Toc the Younger. I give you nothing but silence. And its torrid roar.

Will you hear? Will you listen?

Any of you?

She had dwelt like a parasite deep in its entrails. She had seen, all around her, the broken remnants of some long abandoned promise, the broken clutter, the spilled fluids. But there had been heat, and a pulsing presence as if the very stone was alive—she should have understood the significance of such things, but her mind had been wallowing in its own darkness, a lifeless place of pointless regrets.

Standing not six paces from the two gold-skinned foreigners, she had turned and, like them, looked with wonder, disbelieving.

Ampelas Rooted.

Ampelas Uprooted. The entire city, its massive, mountainous bulk, filled the northern sky. Its underside was a forest of twisted metal roots, from which drained rainbow rain as if even in pain it could bleed nothing but gifts. Yet, Kalyth could see its agony. It was canted to one side. It was surrounded by smoke and dust. Fissures rose from its base, like the broken knuckles of a god only moments from once again hammering the earth.

She could feel . . . something, a bristling core of will knotted in breathless pain. The Matron's? Could it be anyone else? Her blood flowed through the rock. Her lungs howled, winds shrieking between caverns. Her sweat glistened and ran like tears. She bled in a thousand places, bones splintering to vast, ever growing pressures.

The Matron, yes, but . . . there was no mind left inside that nightmare of oozing flesh.

Uprooted, this long-dead thing. *Uprooted*, a thousand upon a thousand generations of belief, faith, the solid iron of once immutable laws.

She defies every truth. She wills life into a corpse, and now it staggers across the sky.

'A sky keep,' said the one named Gesler. 'Moon's Spawn—'

'But this one is bigger,' said Stormy, clawing at his beard. 'If Tayschrenn could see this—'

'If Rake had been commanding one of these—'

Stormy grunted. 'Aye. He'd have flattened the High Mage like a cockroach under a thumb. And then he'd have done the same to the whole Hood-damned Malazan Empire.'

'But look,' said Gesler. 'It's in rough shape—not as ugly as Rake's rock, but it looks like it could come down at any time.'

Kalyth could now see the Furies marching beneath the Dragon Tower—*the sky keep, yes, that is well named.* Ve'Gath Soldiers in their thousands. K'ell Hunters well in advance of the legions and ranging out to the sides in looser formations. Behind the ranks of the Furies, drones struggled to pull enormous wagons groaning beneath towering loads.

'Look at the big ones,' Gesler said. 'The heavies—gods below, one of those could rip a Kenyll'rah demon in half.'

Kalyth spoke. 'Mortal Sword, they are Ve'Gath, the soldiers of the K'Chain Che'Malle. No Matron has ever birthed so many. A hundred was deemed sufficient. Gunth'an Acyl has birthed more than fifteen thousand.'

The man's amber eyes fixed on her. 'If Matrons could do that, why didn't they? They could be ruling this world right now.'

'There was terrible . . . pain.' She hesitated, and then said. 'Sanity was lost.'

'Soldiers like those,' Stormy muttered, 'what ruler needs to be sane?'

Kalyth grimaced. These two men were irreverent. They seemed to be fearless. *They are the ones. But nothing insisted I must like them, or even understand them. No, they frighten me as much as the K'Chain Che'Malle do.* 'She is dying.'

Gesler rubbed at his face. 'No heir?'

'Yes. One waits.' She pointed. 'There, the two now drawing close. Gunth Mach, the One Daughter. Sag'Churok, her K'ell guardian.' Then her breath caught as she saw the one trailing them, its motions smooth as oil. 'The one beyond, that is Bre'nigan, the Matron's own J'an Sentinel—something is wrong—he should not be here, he should be at her side.'

'What about those Assassins?' Stormy asked, squinting skyward. 'Why ain't they showed—the one that snatched us—'

'I do not know, Shield Anvil.' *Something is wrong.*

The two foreigners—they called themselves *Malazans*—backed away as Gunth Mach and Sag'Churok drew closer. 'Ges, what if they don't like the look of us?'

'What do you think?' Gesler snapped. 'We're dead, that's what.'

'There is no danger,' Kalyth assured them. *Of course, I am sure Redmask believed the same.*

Sag'Churok spoke in her mind. *'Destriant. The Matron is chained.'*

What?

'The two Shi'gal who remained in the Nest forged an alliance. They have eaten her forebrain and now command what remains of her. Through her body, they have uprooted Ampelas. But her flesh weakens—soon Ampelas will fail. We must find the enemy. We must find our war.'

Kalyth looked to Gunth Mach. 'Is she safe?'

'She is.'

'But . . . why?'

'The Shi'gal see no future. The battle is the end. No future. The One Daughter is irrelevant.'

'And Gu'Rull?'

'Outlawed. Missing. Possibly dead—he sought to return, sought to defy, but was driven away. Bearing wounds.'

Gesler cut in: 'You're speaking with this thing, aren't you?'

'Yes. I am sorry. There are powers awake in me . . . flavours. The One Daughter . . . it is a gift.'

Stormy said, 'If we're to lead this army of elephant-rapers—'

'Stormy—hold on!' Gesler advanced on his companion, falling into their foreign language as he continued with a barrage of protestations.

Kalyth did not need to understand the words, as Stormy visibly set his heels, face flushing as if in deadly warning. This was a stubborn man, she could see, far more so than the Mortal Sword. Gesler railed at his friend, but nothing he said altered Stormy's stance. *He said he had dreams. He has accepted this.* 'She will share the flavours,' Kalyth said to them. 'It is necessary—'

Stormy faced her. 'Those Ve'Gath, how fast are they? How smart? Can they answer to commands? Discipline? What sort of signalling do they heed? And who in Hood's name is the enemy?'

To these questions, Kalyth shook her head. 'I have no answers. No knowledge. I can say nothing.'

'Who can?'

'Damn you, Stormy!'

The big red-bearded man wheeled on his companion. 'Aye! You're the Mortal Sword—these are the questions you need to be asking, not me! Who's going to command here? You are, you stupid lump of dhenrabi shit! So stop lapdogging me and get on with it!'

Gesler's hands closed into fists and he took a half-step closer to Stormy. 'That's it,' he growled. 'I'm going to crush your fat head, Stormy, and then I'm going to walk away—'

Stormy bared his teeth, squaring himself to await Gesler's charge.

Sag'Churok thumped between the two men, sword blades straightening out to the sides, the motion forcing the men apart, lest those notched edges find them. Snarling, Gesler spun round and marched off a dozen or so paces.

Grinning, Stormy straightened. 'Give me those flavours, lizard. We got to talk.'

'Not that one,' Kalyth said. 'Gunth Mach is the one without swords. There—not the J'an, this one. Go to her.'

'Fine, and then what?'

'Then . . . nothing. You will see.'

He walked up to stand directly in front of Gunth Mach. *Brave or stupid—I think I know which way Gesler would say.* But she saw that Gesler, arms crossed, had turned to watch.

'Well? Gods, she stinks—' He suddenly recoiled. 'Sorry, lizard,' he mumbled, 'I didn't mean it.' He wiped at his face, then held out his hand, scowling. 'I'm covered in something.'

'Flavour,' Kalyth said.

Gesler snorted. 'The lizard in your head now, Stormy? I don't believe it—if she'd done that she'd be running for the nearest cliff.'

'I ain't the one staying deliberately stupid, Ges.'

Gesler glared over at the approaching legions. 'Fine, tell me what they can do.'

'No. Find out for yourself.'

'I ain't being nobody's Mortal Sword.'

'Whatever. You just going to stand there, Ges?'

Swearing something under his breath, the soldier walked over to Gunth Mach. 'Fine, do your sweat thing, it's not like I just had a swim or nothing—' As soon as he drew close he snapped his head back, and then rubbed at his eyes. 'Ow.'

Kalyth sensed a presence at her side.

Bre'nigan. The J'an Sentinel's milky eyes caught the deepening blue of the day's end. *'Against two Shi'gal, I could do nothing.'*

The voice in her head shocked her. This ancient Che'Malle had seemed beyond any acknowledgement of her whatsoever. The voice trembled.

'I have failed.'

As you said, you could do nothing against two Shi'gal, Bre'nigan.

'The Matron is no more.'

That has been true for some time.

'Destriant, the wisdom in your words is bitter, but I cannot deny what you say. Tell me, these two humans—they seem . . . wayward. But then, I know little of your kind.'

'Wayward? Yes. I know nothing of these Malazans—I have never heard of any tribe by that name. They are . . . reckless.'

'It does not matter. The battle shall be final.'

'Then you think we are lost, too. If that is so, why fight at all?' *Why force me and these two men to our deaths. Let us go!*

'We cannot. You, Destriant, and the Mortal Sword and the Shield Anvil, you are what remains of Gunth'an Acyl's will. You are the legacy of her mind. Even now, how can we say she was wrong?'

'You put too much upon us.'

'Yes.'

She heard Gesler and Stormy arguing again, in their foreign tongue. The Furies were drawing closer, and now two Ve'Gath loped out ahead of the others. Their backs were strangely shaped. 'There,' said Kalyth, drawing the attention of the two Malazans. 'Your mounts.'

'We're going to ride *those*?'

'Yes, Mortal Sword. They were bred for you and for the Shield Anvil.'

'The one for Stormy's got the saddle around the wrong way. How's he going to stick his head up the Ve'Gath's ass, where he'll feel at home?'

Kalyth's eyes widened.

Stormy laughed. 'With you in charge, Ges, I'll hide anywhere. You barely managed a measly squad. Now you got thirty thousand lizards expectin' you to take charge.'

Gesler looked sick. 'Got any spare room up that butt hole, Stormy?'

'I'll let you know, but just so you're clear on this, when I shut the door it stays shut.'

'You always were a selfish bastard. Can't figure why we ever ended up friends.'

The Ve'Gath lumbered up to them.

Gesler glanced at Stormy and spoke in Falari. 'All right, I guess this is it.'

'I can taste their thoughts—all of them,' said Stormy. 'Even these two.'

'Aye.'

'Gesler, these Ve'Gath—they ain't nasty-looking horses—they're smart. We're the beasts of burden here.'

'And we're supposed to be commanding them. The Matron got it all wrong, didn't she.'

Stormy shook his head. 'No point in arguing, though. The One Daughter told me—'

'Aye, me too. A bloody coup. I imagine those Assassins figured out—and rightly so—just how redundant we are. Kalyth too. Stormy, I can reach out to them all. I can see through the eyes of any one of them. Except Gunth Mach.'

'Aye, she's built thick walls. I wonder why. Listen, Ges, I really have no idea what it is a Shield Anvil's supposed to do.'

'You're a giant pit everybody bleeds into, Stormy. Funny your dreams didn't mention that bit. But for this battle, I need you to command the Ve'Gath directly—'

'Me? What about you?'

'The K'ell Hunters. They're fast, they can get in and out and with their speed they will be the deadliest force on the field.'

'Ges, this is a stupid war, you know. The world's not big enough for Long-Tails and Short-Tails both? Stupid. There's barely any left as it is. Like the last two scorpions busy killing each other, when the desert covers a whole damned continent.'

'The slaves are loose,' Gesler replied. 'With a few hundred generations of re-pressed hate to feed off. They won't be satisfied until the last Che'Malle is a chopped-up carcass.'

'And then?'

Gesler met the man's eyes. 'That's what scares me.'

'We're next, you mean.'

'Why not? What's to stop them? They fucking breed like ants. They're laying waste to warrens. Gods below, they're hunting down and killing *dragons*. Listen, Stormy, this is our chance. We've got to stop the Nah'ruk. Not for the Che'Malle—I don't care a whit for the Che'Malle—but for everyone else.'

Stormy glanced over at the Che'Malle. 'They don't expect to survive this battle.'

'Aye, bad attitude.'

'So fix it.'

Gesler glared, and then looked away.

The two Ve'Gath waited. Their backs were malformed, the bones twisted and lifted taut beneath the hide to form high saddles. Something like elongated fingers—or the stretched wings of a bat—slung down the beast's flanks, the finger-ends and talons curling to form stirrups. Plates of armour ridged the shoulders. Lobster-tail scales encased the forward-thrusting necks. Their helms wrapped about the flattened skulls, leaving only the snouts free. They could look down upon a Toblakai. The damned things were grinning at their riders.

Gesler faced Gunth Mach. 'One Daughter. The last Assassin—the one that escaped—I need him.'

Kalyth said, 'We do not know if Gu'Rull even lives—'

Gesler's eyes remained on Gunth Mach. 'She knows. One Daughter, I ain't going to fight a battle I can't win. If you want us leading you, well, one thing us humans don't understand, and that's *giving up*. We fight when the fight's been thumped out of us. We rebel when all we got left that's not in chains is inside our skulls. We defy when the only defiance we got left is up and dying. Aye, I seen people bow their heads, waiting for the axe. I seen people standing in a row in front of fifty crossbows, and doing nothing. But they've all made dying their weapon, the last one left, and they are nightmare's soldiers for ever afterwards. Is this getting through to you? I'm not one for inspiring crap. I need that Assassin, Gunth Mach, because I need his *eyes*. Up there, high overhead. With those eyes, I can win this battle.

'You say Matrons never produce more than a hundred Ve'Gath. But your mother made fifteen thousand. Do you really think the Nah'ruk have any idea of what they're getting into? You've filled my head with scenes of past battles—all your pathetic losses—and it's no wonder you're all ready to give up. But you're wrong. The Matron—was she insane? Maybe. Aye. Insane enough to think she could *win*. And to *plan* for it. Mad? Mad genius, I'd say. Gunth Mach, One Daughter, summon your Shi'gal—he *is* yours now, isn't he? Not ready to give up, not ready to surrender to the fatalism of his brothers. Summon him.'

Silence.

Gesler stared up into the Che'Malle's eyes. *Like staring into a crocodile's. It's the game of seeing all but reacting to nothing. Until necessity forces the issue. It's the game of cold thoughts, if thoughts there are. It's what makes a man's balls crawl up looking for somewhere to hide.*

She spoke in his mind. *'Mortal Sword. Your words have been heard. By all. We shall obey.'*

'Gods below,' Stormy muttered.

Kalyth stepped close to Gesler. Her eyes were wide. 'A darkness lifts from the K'Chain Che'Malle.' But in those eyes, beyond the wonder, he saw a flittering fear. *She sees me sowing false hope. Gods, woman, what do you think a commander does?* He walked up to one of the Ve'Gath, gripped what passed for a saddle horn, set one boot into a stirrup that suddenly clasped tight round his foot, and then swung himself astride the enormous beast.

'Get ready to march,' he said, knowing his words were heard by all. 'We're not waiting for the Nah'ruk to come to us. We're heading straight for them, and straight down their damned throats. Kalyth! Does anyone know—will that sky keep follow? Will they fight?'

'We don't know, Mortal Sword. We think so. What else is left?'

Stormy was struggling to climb on to his beast. 'Trying to crush my damned foot!'

'Relax into it,' Gesler advised.

The One Daughter spoke in his mind. *'The Shi'gal comes.'*

'Good. Let's get this mess started.'

Gu'Rull tilted his wings, swept close round the towering cliff-face of Ampelas Uprooted. There was but one Shi'gal left inside—he'd managed to deliver fatal wounds to the other before he'd been driven from the Nest, and then the city. Deep slashes wept thick blood down his chest, but none of these threatened his life. Already he had begun to heal.

Before him on the plain the massed Furies had resumed their ground-eating march. Thousands of K'ell Hunters spread out to form a vast screen in a crescent as they struck southward, where dark clouds boiled on the horizon, slowly disappearing as the sun finally sank beneath the western hills. The Nah'ruk had fed this day, but the quarry had proved deadlier than they could have anticipated.

This Mortal Sword and his words impressed Gu'Rull, in so far as these soft humans could do so; but then, neither the one named Gesler nor the one named Stormy were truly human. Not any more. The aura of their presence was almost blinding to the Shi'gal's eyes. Ancient fires had forged them. Thyrllan, Tellann, perhaps even the breath and blood of the Eleint.

The K'Chain Che'Malle did not bow in worship, but when it came to the Eleint, this abhorrence weakened. *Children of the Eleint. But we are nothing of the sort. We simply claim the honour. But then, is this not what all mortals do? In grasping their gods, in carving the vicious rules of worship and obedience? Children of the Eleint. We name our cities for the First Born Dragons, those who once sailed the skies of this world.*

As if they cared.

As if they even noticed.

This Mortal Sword spoke of a refusal, a defiance of the fate awaiting them. He possessed courage, and stubborn will. Laudable conceits. *I answer his summons. I give him my eyes, for as long as I remain in the skies. I do not warn him that such time shall not long survive the commencement of battle. The Nah'ruk will see to that.*

Even so. In Gunth'an Acyl's memory, I shall abide.

Doubts swirled round the red-bearded one, the Shield Anvil. His heart was vast, it was true. He was a thing of sentimentality and compassion, so contrary to his bestial appearance, his simian fire. But such creatures were vulnerable. Their hearts bled too freely, and the scars never knitted true. It was madness to embrace the pain and suffering of the K'Chain Che'Malle—not even a Matron would yield to such a thing. The mind would howl. The mind would die.

No matter, he was but one mortal, a human at that. He would take what he could, and then fail. Falchions would descend, an instant of purest mercy—

'*Enough of that—and I don't give a flying fuck for all your miserable thoughts. Assassin, I am Gesler. Your Mortal Sword. On the morning to come, on the dawn of battle, you will be my eyes. You will not flee. I don't care how nasty it gets up there. If you ain't looking like a pigeon that's gone through a windmill by the time we're all done, you'll have failed me—and your kin, too. So don't even think—*'

I hear your words, Mortal Sword. You shall have my eyes, more's the pity.

'*So long as we're understood. Now, what should I be expecting when we sight the Nah'ruk?*'

And so Gu'Rull told him. The human interrupted again and again with sharp, percipient questions. And, as the shock of his power—which had so easily torn through his defences to plunder Gu'Rull's mind—slowly faded to a welt of indignation, the Shi'gal's esteem for the Mortal Sword grew, grudgingly, half in disbelief, half in resentment. The Assassin would not permit himself the delusion of hope. But, this man was a warrior in the truest sense.

And what is that true sense? Why, it is the insanity of belief. And now you make us believe. With you. In you. And in your madness, which you so insist upon sharing.

You taste bitter, human. You taste of your world.

Cursing, Stormy forced his mount up alongside Gesler. 'I'm picking up a stink of something. It's hiding in back thoughts, at the bottom of deep pools—'

'What in Hood's name are you talking about?' Gesler demanded. 'And be quick, that Assassin's even now winging towards the enemy—they're camped, I can see them—there are fires and one big one—lots of smoke. Gods, my head's ready to explode—'

'You ain't listening,' Stormy said. 'That stink—they know something. Gunth Mach—she knows something and she's hiding it from us. I got this—'

Gesler snapped out a hand, and Stormy could see a distant look in his friend's battered face, and as he watched, he saw horror filling the man's eyes. 'Beru fend . . . Stormy. I'm seeing wreckage—heaps of armour and weapons. Stormy—'

'Those Nah'ruk—they—'

'The Bonehunters—they found 'em, they . . . gods, there's piles of bones! *They fucking ate them!*' As Gesler reeled Stormy reached out to steady him.

'Ges! Just tell me what you're seeing!'

'What do you think I'm doing! Gods below!'

But all at once words dried up, and Gesler could only stare downward as the Assassin wheeled over the battlefield, the massive encampment, a crater that could swallow a palace, and the vast stain of what looked like coals amidst flame-licked tree-stumps—no, not stumps. Limbs. Scorched Nah'ruk, still burning. Was it magic that hit them? Gesler could not believe that. A single release of a warren, torching thousands? *And that crater—a hundred cussers maybe . . . but we didn't have a hundred cussers.*

He could hear Stormy shouting at him, but the voice seemed impossibly distant, too far away to be of any concern. Trenches ribboned a ridge, some of them filled with shattered armour and weapons. Lesser craters pocked the summit, crowded with bones. Off to one side, hundreds of Nah'ruk were moving through the carcasses of horses and blackened bodies. Heavy wagons trailed them, slabs of meat heaped on their beds. Dozens of Nah'ruk were harnessed to them, straining in their yokes.

That was a Khundryl charge. Wiped out. At least some of the allies arrived in time—in time for what? Dying. Gods, this was the Lord's cruellest push. They weren't looking for a fight—not with damned lizards, anyway. Not here in the useless Wastelands.

The Shi'gal Assassin's voice intruded. *'Your kin have damaged the Nah'ruk. This harvest was paid for, Mortal Sword. At least three Furies have been destroyed.'*

Those were my friends. This wasn't their fight.

'They were brave. They did not surrender.'

Gesler frowned. *Was surrender possible?*

'I do not know. I doubt it. The matter is irrelevant. Against us, tomorrow, there will be no quarter.'

'You got that right,' Gesler said in a growl.

'Gesler!'

Blinking, the scene spinning away from his mind, he turned to Stormy. Wiping his eyes, he said, 'It's bad. Bad as it can get. The Nah'ruk were marching to meet these K'Chain Che'Malle. They slammed like a fist right into the Bonehunters. Stormy, there was slaughter, but only one army remains—'

Gu'Rull spoke once again in his mind. *I have found a trail, Mortal Sword. Signs of retreat. Shall we pursue it? The Nah'ruk can feel our approach—our Ve'Gath are as thunder in the earth. They prepare to march to meet us—the sky is a place of no light, there are alien winds—I cannot—'*

Lightning flashed to the south, cracking through the night. Gesler grunted as the concussion reverberated through his skull. *Assassin? Where are you? Answer me—what's happened?*

But he could not reach out to the winged lizard; he could not find Gu'Rull anywhere. *Shit.*

'Is that a damned storm cloud up ahead, Gesler? Is that blood on your face? Tell me what the Hood's going on!'

'You really that curious?' Gesler said, baring his teeth. He then spat. 'The Nah'ruk have dropped everything. They're coming for us. We're on our own.'

'And the Bonehunters?'

'We're on our own.'

The scouts emerged from the unforgiving darkness. On this night the Slashes had vanished, taking the stars and the jade glow with them. Even the swollen haze that was the moon did not dare the sky. Shivering in the sudden chill, Warleader Strahl waited for the scouts to reach him.

The two Senan warriors were hunched over, as if fearful, or perhaps wounded. When they halted before him, both knelt. They were exhausted, he saw, their chests heaving.

Look at them. Look at this darkness. Has the world ended this night?

He would not rush them, demanding words they would struggle to feed. The dread was thick enough in their harsh breaths.

Behind the Warleader the Senan Barghast waited. Some slept, but for most sleep would not come. Hunger. Thirst. The famine of loss, a song of soft weeping. He could feel scores of eyes fixed upon him, seeing, he knew, little more than a vague, smudged silhouette. Seeing the truth of him, and before them he had nowhere to hide.

One of the scouts had recovered his wind. 'Warleader. Two armies on the plain.'

'The Malazans—'

'No, Warleader—these are demons—'

The other hissed, 'There are thousands!'

'Two armies, you said.'

'They march towards each other—through the night—we are almost between them! Warleader, we must retreat—we must flee from here!'

'Go into the camp, both of you. Rest. Leave me. Say nothing.'

Once they'd staggered off, he drew his furs closer about his shoulders. This dusk, they'd sighted a Moon's Spawn, but one of hard angles and planes—his sharper-eyed warriors claimed it was carved in the shape of a dragon. *Two demon armies—what better place to clash than on the Wastelands? Kill each other. Yours is not our war. We mean to find the Malazans . . . do we not? Our old enemy, a worthy one.*

Did they not betray the alliance at Coral? Did they not try to cheat Caladan Brood and steal that city in the name of the cursed Empress? If not for Anomander Rake, they would have succeeded. These Bonehunters claim to be renegades, but then, did not Dujek Onearm say the same? No, this is the usual nest of lies. Whatever they seek, whatever they conquer, they will claim for the Empress.

Onos Toolan, what other enemy existed? Who else could you hope to find? Who else as worthy as the Malazans, conquerors, devourers of history? You said you once served them. But you left them. You came to lead the White Faces. You knew this enemy—you told us so much that we now need—we were fools, that we did not see.

But now I do.

The demons were welcome to their battle.

Yes, they would retreat from this. He swung round.

Dust spun in the Senan camp, silver as moonlight, in spirals rising on all sides. Someone shrieked.

Ghostly warriors—the gleam of bone, rippling blades of chert and flint—

Strahl stared, struggling to comprehend. Screams erupted—the terrible weapons lashed out, tore through mortal flesh and bone. Barghast war-cries sounded, iron rang against stone. Rotted faces, black-pitted eyes.

A hulking figure appeared directly in front of Strahl. The Warleader's eyes widened—as in the firelight he saw the sword gripped in the creature's bony hands. *No. No!* 'We avenged you! Onos Toolan, we avenged them all! Do not— you cannot—'

The sword hissed a diagonal slash that cut through both of Strahl's legs, from his right hip to below his left knee. He slid down with that blade, found himself lying on the ground. Above him, only darkness. Sickly cold rushed through him. *We did all we could. Our shame. Our guilt. Warleader, please. There are children, there are innocents—*

The downward chop shattered his skull.

The Senan died. The White Face Barghast died. Nom Kala stood apart from the slaughter. The T'lan Imass were relentless, and had she a heart, it would have recoiled before this remorseless horror.

The slayers of his wife, his children, were paid in kind. Cut down with implacable efficiency. She heard mothers plead for the lives of their children. She heard their death-cries. She heard tiny wailing voices fall suddenly silent.

This was a crime that would poison every soul. She could almost feel the earth crack and bleed beneath them, as if spirits writhed, as if gods stumbled.

The rage emanating from Onos T'oolan was darker than the sky, thicker than any cloud. It gusted outward in waves of his own horrified recognition—he knew, he could see himself, as if torn loose and flung outside his own body—he saw, and the very sight of what he was doing was driving him mad.

And us all. Oh, give me dust. Give me a morning born in oblivion, born in eternal, blessed oblivion.

There were thousands, and scores were fleeing into the night, but so many were already dead. *This is what was, once. Terrible armies of T'lan Imass. We hunted down the Jaghut. We gave them what I see here. By all the spirits, is this our only voice?* A terrible moaning was rising in the foul wake of the last few death-blows, a moaning that seemed to spin and swirl, coming from the T'lan Imass, from each warrior splashed in gore, dripping weapons in their hands. It was a sound that cut through Nom Kala. She staggered before it in retreat, as if begging the darkness to swallow her whole.

Onos T'oolan. Your vengeance—you delivered it . . . upon us, upon your pathetic followers. We followed your lead. We did as you did. We broke our own chains. We unleashed ourselves—how many millennia of this anger within us? Lashed loose, lashed into life.

Now, we are become slayers of children. We have stepped into the world, again, after all this time spent so . . . so free from its crimes. Onos T'oolan, do you see? Do you understand?

Now, once more, we are born into history.

If this is what a Shield Anvil feels, then I don't want it. Do you hear me? I don't want it! He knew Gesler, knew what the man's refusal meant. Through that damned rhizan's eyes he'd seen the corpses. The slaughtered remains of the Bonehunters and the Letherii. Only two days ago they'd been marching with them—all those faces he knew, all those soldiers he liked to swear at—now gone. Dead.

This was all wrong. He and Ges should have died with them, died fighting at their sides. Brotherhood and sisterhood only found true meaning in the wash of death, in the falling one after another, the darkness and then the shuddering awake before Hood's Gate. *Aye, we're family when fighting to the last, but the real family is among the fallen. Why else do we stagger half-blind after every battle? Why else do we look upon dead kin and feel so abandoned? They left without us, that's why.*

A soldier knows this. A soldier saying different is a Hood-damned liar.

Dawn was not far off. The last day was close. *But this ain't the family I knew. It ain't the one I wanted. All I got is Gesler. We been through it all, true, so at least we can die together. At least that makes sense. Been through it all. Falar—gods we were young! Damned fools, aye. Running off, swearing ourselves into the Fener cult—it was the rumours of the orgies that did us in. What rutting lad wouldn't jump at the thought?*

Damned orgies, oh yes. But we should've worked it out for ourselves. S'damned god of war, right? Orgies, oh indeed, orgies of slaughter, not sex. Think-

ing with the wrong brains, is what we did. But, at that age, isn't it how it's supposed to be?

Only we never got out, never got wise, did we? We found ourselves in a cesspool and then spent the next twenty years telling each other the smell ain't so bad. Sweet as rain, in fact.

The K'Chain Che'Malle were going to die. They were going to pour their blood into him, souls crowding for his embrace, whatever that meant. The Matron who wanted all this was dead, but then . . . ain't dying the first and most obvious path into ascendancy, into godhood?

Though eating the front of her skull, that's just sick. She'll make 'em pay for that, now that she's a goddess or whatever.

Well, he'd keep the door barred until the last moment—he had an army to order around, after all. A mob of heavies who'd wheel on a horse-hair with an instant's thought. Imagine what Coltaine could've done with these legions. If he'd had 'em, Korbolo Dom wouldn't be wiggling his finger up Laseen's backside right now. In fact—

'Hood's breath, Stormy, you're leaking the sickest things.'

'So get outa my head!'

'I said "leaking," you oaf. I ain't in your head. Listen, stop thinking we're all vulture shit, all right? I don't know if these things got anything like morale, but if they do you've just beaten it into a pulpy mess.'

'Those were my thoughts!'

'So figure out a way of keeping them inside. Just picture your thick skull—it's got holes, right. Out the eyes, the nose, whatever. So, picture blocking 'em all up. Now you're safe. Now you can think all the stupid things you like to think about.'

'Is that why I ain't getting anything from you?'

'No. Right now, I'm too witless to think. Sky's lightening—look at that cloud to the south. It's not a cloud. It's a hole in the sky. It's a warren ripped wide open. Just looking at it makes my skin crawl like a leech under a rock.'

'Ges, these legions—'

'Furies.'

'They ain't presented for battle, unless you plan on us just marching right up to 'em. Like the Quon used to do.'

'You're right. The Quon had badly trained troops, but they had a lot of them. Who needs tactics?'

'We do.'

'Right. So, see if we can get 'em sawtooth—' He stopped suddenly.

In the same instant something rushed through Stormy and he grunted, twisting round.

The massive baggage train had halted. Drones—smaller creatures, not much taller than a human—swarmed the beds, unshipping rectangular slabs of iron. 'Gesler—are those shields?'

Gesler had halted and wheeled his mount. 'Aye, I think so. I was wondering at those hand-and-a-half axes the Ve'Gath carried. So, these really are heavies—'

'I couldn't pick up one of those shields, let alone hang it from one arm. The Nah'ruk got missile weapons?'

'Unplug your skull,' said Gesler, 'and you'll get your answer. Another innovation from the Matron. She must have been something, I think.'

'She was a big fat lizard.'

'She also broke ten thousand years of changing nothing—and the Che'Malle claim they never had a religion.'

Grunting—and not quite understanding what Gesler had meant—Stormy cast about to find the Destriant.

Twenty paces to the west, Kalyth was astride the back of Sag'Churok, but she was not watching the smooth distribution of the huge shields through the Ve'Gath ranks. Instead, she was squinting south. Stormy followed her gaze.

'Ges, I see 'em. A line of legions—'

'Furies,' said Gesler.

'Five across making the facing. And what, three deep? Hood's breath, they look to outnumber us badly. I'm thinking three teeth each legion, ranks no more than thirty deep. We can reach that high ground just ahead, shield-lock there.'

'You'll screen my K'ell, then, Stormy. Show your teeth and let the Nah'ruk close jaws on 'em. How long you think you can hold that ridge?'

'How long do you need?'

'I want most of the enemy Furies committed to pushing you off that ridge. I want you to savage them, enough to get them ducking their heads and thinking about nothing but the next step forward. I don't want 'em looking right or left.'

'What's Ampelas Uprooted going to be doing during all this?' Stormy demanded.

'Unplug your skull.'

'No, this is better.'

Kalyth had ridden closer. 'There is sorcery—defences, weapons.'

Stormy wasn't understanding something. He knew he would if he knocked down the walls he'd raised around his thoughts, but he didn't want to do that. Ampelas Uprooted—Gesler wasn't factoring it into his tactics at all. Why not? *No matter.* 'Ges, when holding isn't what we need to do any more, what do you want from us?'

'Single wedge, advance at the walk. Cut the bastards in half, Stormy. One wing will be healthier than the other. That one needs blocking—we annihilate the weaker wing. Then we can wheel and take down the other half.'

'Ges, these Ve'Gath never fought this way before. The K'Chain Che'Malle had no tactics at all, from what I can see in my head.'

'That's why they need us humans,' Kalyth said. 'She understood. You two—' she shook her head. 'The Che'Malle—they drink down your confidence. They are sated. They hear you, discussing the battle to come, and they are awestruck with wonder. And . . . faith.'

Stormy scowled. *Woman, if you could read me right now, you'd run screaming. Of course we say we're doing this and then that and then this other thing and it's all so perfect and so logical. We know it's all a joke. We know that once the battle is engaged, it all turns into Hood's hoary picnic basket.*

Me and Ges, we're just amateurs. Dujek was damned good at this, but Dassem Ultor, ah, he was the best of them all. He could stand there in front of ten thousand soldiers, and he'd take 'em all through every sword-stroke in the battle to come. By the end of all that wheeling here, driving there, breaking through there, we'd all be nodding half bored and ready to get on with it. It was a done deal to us, and the First Sword, why, he'd just take us all in with his eyes and give back one single nod.

Then the day went out and mayhem was a field of flowers and by dusk the enemy was dead or on the run.

Aye, Gesler, I hear you echoing him. I see you taking on his matter-of-fact tone and that face of sun-warmed iron that we all knew would turn to ice when the time came. I'll give you this, friend, you're stealing from the best of 'em all, and doing good.

He clawed through his beard. 'Anyone got a cask of ale? I can't remember the last time I went into a battle not belching sour brew.' He studied Kalyth for a moment, and then sighed. 'Never mind. Go on, Ges, go hide your K'ell, I got it here.'

'See you when it's done, Shield Anvil.'

'Aye, Mortal Sword.'

Heat was building beneath Kalyth. Sag'Churok was flooded with flavours of violence. But she sat hunched, chilled, her very bones feeling like sticks trapped in lakeshore ice. These two soldiers appalled her. Their confidence was insane. The ease with which they took command—and the mockery with which they exchanged their titles moments before separating—left her reeling.

Her people had met with traders from Kolanse. She had seen armoured caravan guards, looking bored as the merchants haggled with the Elan elders. Children had drawn close to them, eyes shining, but none drew close enough to touch, as much as they might have wanted to. Killers were lodestones. Their silence and their flat eyes fed something in the young boys and girls, and Kalyth could see their childlike longing, the whispering romance of the horizons these warriors had seen. Such scenes had frightened her, and she had prayed to the spirits for the strangers to leave, to take their dangerous temptations with them.

Looking into Gesler's eyes moments ago, she had seen the same terrible promise. The world was ever too small for him. The horizon chained him and that chain's pull was relentless. He didn't care what he left in his wake. His kind never did.

Yet I knew. Gu'Rull saw true. These were the ones I was seeking. These two men are the answer to Gunth'an Acyl's vision. A future alive with hope.

But they don't care. They will lead us in this battle, and if we all die they will either flee at the last moment, or they will fall—it's no matter to them. They are no different from Redmask.

Those caravan guards still squatting in her memory, they were dead and they knew it. This knowledge was the one lover every warrior and every soldier shared, a whore of monstrous proportions. Paid in blood, pimped by kings and generals and fanatic prophets. *And it's all twisted round. It's the whore who does the raping.*

You couldn't catch her in a thousand years.

One time, two young braves had vanished after a caravan's departure. The elders and parents met to discuss whether or not to set out after them, to drag them back to the village. In the end, the elders wandered off, and the mothers wept softly with their husbands looking on.

They put chains on and called it freedom. The whore stole them.

She wanted Gesler and Stormy to die. She wanted it with all her heart. There was no reason for it. They'd done nothing wrong. In fact, they were about to do precisely what they were meant to do. And they would not shrink from their destiny. *They are not to blame for my hate and my fear.*

But I want a world without soldiers. I want to see them all kill each other. I want to see kings and generals standing alone—not a single soul within reach of their grasping claws. No weapon to back their will, no blade to sing their threats. I want to see them revealed for the weak, miserable creatures they truly are.

What can bring this about? How do I make such a world?

Spirits bless my ancestors, I wish I knew.

She'd lost her Mahybe, her clay vessel awaiting her soul. For her, death was a nightmare she knew was coming. She had no reason to dream of any future. In this, was she not like those caravan guards? Was she not the same as Gesler and Stormy? What did they see in *her* eyes?

I am Destriant. And yet I dream of betrayal. When she looked upon the Ve'Gath, the echoes of their agony of birth returned to her, the terrors of the Womb. They did not deserve what was coming, and yet they longed for it. Could she steal them away from this day of dying, she would. She'd lead them, instead, against her own kind. A holy war against the soldiers of the world and their masters.

Leaving only herders and farmers and fisherfolk. Artists and tanners and potters. Story-tellers and poets and musicians. *A world for them and them alone. A world of peace.*

The Nah'ruk Furies seemed to devour the broken plain as they advanced. The east was bright with the sun's birth, but the sky above the enemy legions was a vast stain, a bruise, a maw from which wind howled.

Stormy drew his sword. He could see the front ranks of the foe preparing clubs—weapons of sorcery: the visions or stolen memories flashed scenes of devastating magic through his mind. *Ready your shields, and pray the iron holds.*

He glared over a shoulder to Ampelas Uprooted. A veil of white smoke enwreathed the sky keep. Clouds? Scowling, Stormy turned his attention to his Ve'Gath. They were arrayed upon the ridge as if painted from his own mind—they knew his thoughts now that he'd knocked down his mental walls. They knew what he wanted, what he needed. *And they will never break. Never flee—unless panic takes me, and Hood knows, for all the shit I been through, it ain't happened yet. And it won't today neither.*

'So, we stand, lizards. We stand.'

A sudden rustling through the ranks as heads lifted.

Stormy swung round.

From the gaping hole in the morning sky shapes were emerging. Towering, black, pushing out from the maelstrom foaming out from the warren.

Sky keeps. None as huge as the one behind him, massing perhaps two-thirds, and none were carved beyond angled plains of black stone. And yet . . .

Three . . . five . . . eight—

'Beru fend!'

Ampelas Uprooted ignited like a star behind him.

The deafening, blinding salvo of sorcery ripped across the sky. Enormous chunks of gouged, burning stone erupted from the nearest three Nah'ruk sky keeps. Streaming churning smoke and rubble, shattered fragments the size of tenement blocks plunged earthward, slamming into the ground in the midst of the rearmost ranks of the Nah'ruk.

Ears numbed by the concussion, Gesler rose high on his stirrups—Ampelas Uprooted had drawn closer, looming almost directly overhead. 'Hood's breath! Ke'll Hunters—flee the shadow! Get out from under it! East and west—*run!*'

He charged forward on his Ve'Gath. *Stormy! Fuck the stand—charge 'em! You hear? Charge and close!*

He'd heard the stories of the Siege of Pale. Moon's Spawn's rain of wreckage into the city had broken the backs of the defenders. This deadly rain of rubble could shatter his entire army.

More Nah'ruk sky keeps emerged from the wound.

Lightning crackled, arced savagely out from a half-dozen sky keeps, converging on Ampelas Uprooted.

The detonations thundered. And the rain of slaughter began.

The huge wagons and their scrambling drones vanished beneath an avalanche that lifted nearby K'ell Hunters into the air, tails lashing for balance as they flailed about. Dust rolled out thick as a tidal wave to swallow the spreading horror as massive chunks of stone descended from the battered Uprooted.

Through the torrential, billowing smoke and rubble, Ampelas lashed back.

The saw-tooth line of Ve'Gath lifted as if heaved forward by the ridge itself, and all at once the huge warriors were pouring down the slope, straight for the lines of Nah'ruk.

Sorcery arced out from the wired clubs, crashed into a shield-locked wall of iron. The Ve'Gath staggered, but not one fell.

There was no time for a second salvo.

The Ve'Gath toothed line hammered into the Nah'ruk. The impact of the charge flattened two, then three ranks of the Short-Tails. Weapons lashed down as the Ve'Gath trampled the fallen enemy, closing with the deeper lines still reeling from the impact.

Stormy was at the very heart of the attack. He'd swung his sword twice, and both times his blade had bitten deep into armour—but his targets were in the act of dying anyway, for they had come within reach of his mount. He couldn't close with anything worth hacking apart. He roared in frustration.

The Nah'ruk warriors were outmatched. They bore no shields. The Ve'Gath simply chewed through them.

Lightning ripped down from the sky, ploughed a bloody, burning swath through the rearmost Ve'Gath ranks, slaying hundreds in an instant.

Stormy snarled, battered by those sudden, terrible deaths. *Break formation! Close with the enemy!*

Another lash of sorcery scythed down hundreds more.

Close!

Ampelas Rooted burned from a dozen gaping fissures. Massive pieces had shorn clear, revealing exposed innards from which poured black smoke. The sky keep shuddered as attack after attack pounded into it. The edifice's forward progress had halted, and now it was being buffeted backward. Still it spat its own fury, and Gesler could see one of the Nah'ruk keeps leaning far to one side, billowing flames and smoke, and from this one no lightning winged out.

But there were too many of the damned things. Three had drifted out to the east, and were now angling to draw up behind Ampelas Rooted—where the thick iron plates armouring that side of its flank had been removed to fashion shields for the Ve'Gath. In moments, they would strike a soft target.

And that'll kill her. Like a knife to the back.

When she's finished, those keeps will turn on us here below. If they can.

But I won't let them.

'K'ell Hunters! Flanking charge from both sides. Cut in behind the contact—hollow out those engaged legions! Don't piss around, damn you all! Charge!'

The three Nah'ruk sky keeps loosed raging arcs of lightning. Kalyth stared in horror as the lower half of Ampelas Rooted seemed to bulge, limed in red glow. The concussion of the detonation threw Sag'Churok and Gunth Mach down. Kalyth tumbled clear of the thrashing beasts, rocks lacerating her shoulder and face. She rolled on to her back. The sky was burning, and flaming stones rained down.

She cried out, covering her eyes.

———

At the rush of hot wind, Stormy twisted round. The lower third of Ampelas Rooted was simply gone, and what remained was spilling its guts, everything burning as the wreckage plunged earthward. The impact was driving the keep on to its side—or back—exposing the destroyed maw of its base.

He swore as Ampelas Rooted somehow managed to return fire, two serpents of lightning writhing out behind it.

They must have struck, though he could not see past the Che'Malle keep, but the thunder of impacts trembled the earth—and then he saw one of the Nah'ruk keeps rising behind Ampelas Rooted, climbing on streamers of smoke.

His eyes widened to see the huge thing gaining speed as it shot still higher. With smoke swarming down its flanks, damaged beyond hope of control, the keep seemed to lunge as it shot into the sky—and kept going.

The remaining two ignited in another sorcerous strike.

Light engulfed Ampelas Uprooted—

The K'ell Hunters plunged into the buckling flanks of the Nah'ruk Furies that were locked jaw to jaw with the Ve'Gath. Their massive blades hacked bloody paths into the press. The Nah'ruk could not match their speed, their reach, and they seemed to melt before the attack.

In his mind, Gesler was shouting the same words over and over, a mantra of desperation. *Close close close in—close—they won't fire if—*

Two sky keeps, hovering directly above the battle, sent down writhing spears. Nah'ruk, Ve'Gath and K'ell bodies lifted into the air, blackened, iron shattering.

You pieces of shit!

It was lost. All of it. He realized that in this instant.

The keeps would sterilize the plain below them, if that was what it took—

Off to the west, two more sky keeps were swinging round to approach the battle.

Gesler glared at them.

And then both exploded.

My flesh is stone. My blood rages hot as molten iron. I have a thousand eyes. A thousand swords. And one mind.

I have heard the death-cry. Was she kin? She said as much, when first she touched me. We were upon the ground. Far from each other, and yet of a kind.

I heard her die.

And so I came to mourn her, I came to find her body, her silent tomb.

But she dies still. I do not understand. She dies still—and there are strangers. Cruel strangers. I knew them once. I know them now. I know, too, that they will not yield.

Who am I?

What am I?

But I know the answers to these questions. I believe, at last, that I do.

Strangers, you bring pain. You bring suffering. You bring to so many dreams the dust of death.

But, strangers, I am Icarium.

And I bring far worse.

Kalyth's eyes flickered open, on a scene jostled and chaotic with smoke. She was in Gunth Mach's clutches, gripped as would be a child. The One Daughter was flanked on the right by Sag'Churok and by Bre'nigan on the left, the three of them running at a steady trot across the valley floor.

The battle raged just beyond the J'an Sentinel. The K'ell Hunters had cut through to the foremost ranks of the Ve'Gath, but now the enemy had begun an encirclement.

Lightning lashed down from the keeps directly above the field, tearing ragged paths of destruction through the press.

Huge drums were pounding the air to her right and she twisted round to look in that direction. Two Nah'ruk keeps were breaking apart, the fires in their cores burning so hot she saw stone melting like wax, falling away from iron bones. The one to the north was descending earthward as if sinking through water. Multiple explosions racked them both.

Rising from behind them, shouldering through thick pillars of black smoke, another Uprooted.

What? Who? Sag'Churok—

'Kalse Uprooted, Destriant. But there is no Matron within it. The one who commands . . . it has been a long time since he last walked among the K'Chain Che'Malle and Nah'ruk.'

Sorcery swarmed round Kalse, green, blue and white—a kind she had never before seen—and then suddenly pulsed out in a seething wave. The magic cut through the two dying keeps and Kalyth gasped to see ice explode out from fissures in the ravaged black stone. As the wave burst through the struck keeps, the one to the south simply split in half, the lower section dropping like a mountain, the upper end lifting and spinning inside swirling streams of smoke, rubble and shards of ice. The other one's upper third disintegrated in a white cloud moments before it struck the ground.

The concussions of the two impacts shook the earth. The hills to the west were crushed flat. The remnants of the keeps blew apart in vast clouds of dust and rock.

At this same moment the wave passed directly over Kalyth and the three K'Chain Che'Malle, carrying with it air so cold it stunned her lungs. Gasping, agony convulsing her chest, she did not see the wave strike the three sky keeps above the battlefield. The explosions deafened her—darkness rushed in, even as Gunth Mach staggered.

The arrival of a second Che'Malle keep filled the sky with a storm of violence. Above them, Gesler could see nothing but churning clouds and deathly flashes— even the bulks of the keeps had vanished. It seemed as if the sky itself burned, raining white-hot stones that snapped as they shot down through bitterly cold air. Impossibly, snow swirled down amidst ashes and rubble.

Nah'ruk keeps crowded the warren's gate, as if seeking to break through to bring succour to those dying before the stranger's onslaught, but wave after wave slammed into them, and the unknown Uprooted was bulling ever closer, as if to drive down the very throat of the warren. Lightning lashed into it, tore huge gashes in its flanks. Death poured down from the sky.

Gesler's mount towered amidst the K'ell Hunters crowded in on all sides—he knew the K'ell were providing a cordon around them—though nothing could defend any of them against the deadly deluge from above. He could see the rear Nah'ruk Furies committing to the battle—they had been and were still being decimated by falling wreckage. Even so, sheer numbers alone were beginning to tell. Stormy's Ve'Gath had ceased their advance, but Gesler could see his friend, the battle lust upon him, his face red as his hair, his eyes blazing with madness.

'Stormy! *Stormy! Androjan Redarr, you brainless bastard!*'

The head swung round. The man smiled.

Gods below, Stormy. 'We're encircled!'

'And we're cutting 'em to pieces!'

'We need to break out—the sky's killing us!'

'Withdraw your K'ell! Regroup and set up a charge!'

'Which side?'

'Whatever's *behind* Kalse!'

Kalse. I ain't been paying attention. 'And you?'

'Back-to-back wedges—we're driving out to the fucking sides! You watch 'em pour into the gap and then you charge 'em! We about face and close the vice!'

Stormy, you Hood-damned genius. 'Agreed!'

The pain was overwhelming. He bled from wounds sheathing his body. Blow after blow hammered into him. Blind, deafened, he struck back, not even knowing if his sorcery found the enemy. He felt himself tearing loose, moments from being ripped from his flesh of cracked stone, his bones of tortured iron.

I shall become a ghost again. Lost. Where are my children? You have aban-doned me—there are too many of them, they close like wolves—my children— help me—

'You must close the gate.'

Breath?

'Yes. Feather Witch. The Errant drowned me. I took his eye, he took my life. Never bargain with gods. His eye—I give it to you, Lifestealer. The gate—do you see it? You are drawing nearer—Lifestealer, do not stop—'

Another voice spoke. '*They killed a dragon for this power, Icarium.*'

Taxilian!

'*Its blood burned this hole—if you fail, the sky shall fill with the enemy machines—and the Nah'ruk will triumph this day. See the K'Chain Che'Malle, Icarium! They can win this—if you stop the Gath'ran Citadels, if you stop them from entering this realm. Seal the gate!*'

He could see it now. He held in his hand the eye of an Elder God. Slick, soft, smeared with blood.

The wound between the realms was vast—even Kalse Uprooted could not—

'*You must build a wall—*'

'*A prison!*'

Feather Witch hissed, '*Root and Blueiron, Lifestealer! Ice Haunt is not enough! You must awaken the warrens within you! Root to the rock and earth. Blueiron to hold life in your machines. Command the breach!*'

'*I cannot hold. I am dying.*'

'*There are children in the world, Icarium.*'

'*Asane? You do not understand. You are not enough—*'

'*There are children in the world. The warrens you have made from your own blood—*'

Feather Witch snarled. '*Our blood!*'

'*And ours, yes. The warrens, Icarium—did you imagine they belonged to you and none other? It is too late for that. This day is the day of fire, Icarium. The children wait. The children hear.*'

In his mind, even as it crumbled on all sides, he could hear a new voice, a sweet voice, one he had never heard before.

> '*I dream we are three*
> *Rutt who is not Rutt and Held*
> *Who cannot be held—*
> *The girl knows silence*
> *Is a game*
> *The boy knows the kiss*
> *Of the Eres'al*
> *The mother of wheeling stars*
> *Who seeds all time*
> *Through me they hear your need*
> *I am the voice of the unborn*
> *In crystal I see fire and I see smoke*
> *I see lizards and Fathers*
> *In crystal I see the boy and the girl.*
> *Heal the wound, God,*
> *Your children are close—*'

Rautos whispered—the last words Icarium would remember. '*Icarium, in the name of a blessed wife . . . have faith.*'

Faith. He took hold of that word.

His hand closed about the eye and he heard the shriek of an Elder God, as he transformed the eye into what he needed. For Root.

A seed.

A Finnest.

Kalyth saw Kalse Uprooted plunge into the maw, and then halt as a storm of lightning tore into it. The very sky seemed to tremble, and then the ground began to shake, and as she stared, she saw stone burst upward from the plain, directly beneath Kalse. The bedrock lifted like gnarled arms, as if an enormous upended tree was flinging roots into the air.

Those roots rose yet higher, touched the base of Kalse Uprooted, and then spread in a frenzy outward. Branches of rock twisted, crowded against the edges of the gate, where fires flared only to vanish. The Wastelands seemed to grow ashen on all sides, as if the very last drops of its lifeblood were being drawn into this savage growth.

The four surviving Nah'ruk sky keeps on this side of the portal unleashed a frenzied assault upon Kalse. Stone exploded. Massive fissures ripped through, spewing molten rock—the entire city was moments from bursting apart.

The stranger fails—but, such glory! To see this! To witness such courage!

The stone tree—if that was what it was—did not cease its mad growth, and she saw roots curl into the wounds in the city's flanks. Where the lightning struck the writhing stone, the sound of the impacts boomed deeper than any thunder, but everywhere that wounds broke open stone swarmed in to heal the damage.

All at once the attacks ceased. Sudden heat washed down upon Kalyth and she cried out in pain.

The four Nah'ruk sky keeps were engulfed in flames, reeling away from the gate. The fires brightened, and then, in a flash, burst incandescent white at their cores. As she watched, in horror, in wonder, the keeps seemed to be vaporizing before her eyes. Churning, the towering pillars of fire pitched eastward, beneath them the ground blackening with scorching heat.

Gunth Mach spoke in her mind. *'Destriant. See through my eyes. Do you see?'*

'Yes,' she whispered.

Two figures stood upon a torn, ruined ridge to the northwest. Sorcery poured from them in terrible waves.

A boy.

A girl.

He didn't care. The world could be moments from being swallowed by the Abyss itself, Stormy was finally in the midst of war's sharpest truths and nothing else—nothing—mattered. Laughing, he slashed and hacked at the Nah'ruk as they pressed in, as the dead-eyed lizards sought to clamber over the Ve'Gath, sought by numbers alone to overwhelm this savage wall of denial.

Gesler's charge down the pocket had pierced the bastards like a boar-sticker, forcing them into the narrow spaces between the frenzied K'ell and the shield-locked Ve'Gath. They fought with appalling ferocity, and died in chilling silence.

His mount was wounded. His mount was probably dying—who could tell? All these lizards fought until their last breath. But its defences had slowed, weakened. There was blood everywhere and he could feel its chest heaving with shuddering cadence.

A short-snouted maw lunged at his face.

Cursing, he pitched back to avoid the snapping dagger teeth, struggled to draw close his short-handled axe—but the damned Nah'ruk surged still closer, clawing its way up the Ve'Gath's shoulder. His mount staggered—

He chopped with his axe, but the range was too tight, and though the edge bit into the side of the lizard's head the wound it delivered was not enough to sway the creature. The jaws opened wide. The head snapped forward—

Something snarling struck the Nah'ruk, a knotted mass of mottled, scar-seamed hide and muscle, savage canines sinking deep into the lizard's neck.

Disbelieving, Stormy kicked his boots free of the stirrups to roll further back—

A fucking dog!

Bent!

That you!

Oh, but it surely was.

Greenish blood spilled from the Nah'ruk's mouth. The eyes dulled, and a heartbeat later dog and lizard pitched down from the Ve'Gath.

At that moment, Stormy saw the burning sky keeps.

And the storm was gone, the thunder vanished, the world filling with sounds of iron, flesh and bone. The song of ten thousand battles, made eerily surreal by there being not a single scream, not a single cry of agony or shriek begging mercy.

The Nah'ruk were falling.

Battle halted. Slaughter commenced.

No song lives upon a single note.

But to a soldier, who had faced death for an eternity since the dawn, this grisly music was the sweetest music of all.

Slaughter! For my brave Ve'Gath! Slaughter! For Gesler and his K'ell! Slaughter, for the Bonehunters—my friends—SLAUGHTER!

As if some fulcrum had been irrevocably destroyed, Ampelas Uprooted slowly rolled upside down. The entire edifice was burning now, spilling sheets of flaming oil that splashed bright upon rubble, corpses and wounded drones directly below.

Gesler knew it was now dead, a lifeless hulk slowly tumbling in the sky.

Two sky keeps still raged in death-throes behind it, leaning like drunks, moments from colliding with one another. The smoke column from a third was shredding apart to high winds, but of the keep itself there was no sign. The rest were but ashes on the black wind.

Before them rose a mountain of gnarled rock, enclosing the wreckage that had once been Kalse Uprooted, holding it up as if it was a gem, or a giant shattered eye. Something about the stone was familiar, but for the moment, he could not place it. The manifestation reached stunningly high, piercing through the dust and smoke.

Stormy's hunt for the last fleeing Nah'ruk had taken him and a thousand or so Ve'Gath beyond the hills to the southeast.

Exhausted, numbed beyond all reason, Gesler leaned back in the strange saddle. Some damned dog was yapping at his mount's ankles.

He saw Kalyth, Sag'Churok, Gunth Mach and the J'an Sentinel, and beyond them, approaching at a careless walk, two children.

Grub. Sinn.

Gesler leaned forward and glared down at the yapping dog. 'Gods below, Roach,' he said in a hoarse voice, 'you returning the favour?' He drew a shuddering breath. 'Listen, rat, cos I'm only going to say this once—I guarantee it. But right now, your voice is the prettiest sound I've ever heard.'

The miserable thing snarled up at him.

It had never learned how to smile.

Slipping down from the Ve'Gath, Gesler sagged on aching legs. Kalyth was kneeling, facing the direction from which Sinn and Grub were approaching. 'Get up, Destriant,' he said, finding himself leaning against the Ve'Gath's hip. 'Those two got heads so swelled it's a wonder a mortal woman pushed 'em out.'

She looked over and he saw the muddy streaks of tears on her cheeks. 'She had . . . faith. In us humans.' The woman shook her head. 'I did not.'

The two children walked up.

Gesler scowled. 'Stop looking so smug, Sinn. You two are in a lot of trouble.'

'Bent and Roach found us,' said Grub, scratching in the wild thatch of hair on his head. It looked as though neither of them had bathed in months. 'We were safe, Sergeant Gesler.'

'Happy for you,' he said in a growl. 'But they needed you—both of you. The Bonehunters were in the Nah'ruk's path—what do you think happened to them?'

Grub's eyes widened.

Sinn walked up to the Ve'Gath and set a hand on its flank. 'I want one for myself,' she said.

'Didn't you hear me, Sinn? Your brother—'

'Is probably dead. We were in the warrens—the new warrens. We were on the path, we could taste the blood—so fresh, so strong.' She looked up at Gesler with bleak eyes. 'The Azath has sealed the wound.'

'The Azath?'

She shrugged, facing the tree of rock, its lone knot gripping Kalse Uprooted. She bared her teeth in something that might have been a smile.

'Who is in there, Sinn?'

'He's gone.'

'Dead stone can't seal a gate—not for long—even an Azath needs a life force, a living soul—'

She shot him a quick look. 'That's true.'

'So what seals it—if he's gone—'

'An eye.'

'A what?'

Kalyth spoke in the trader tongue. 'Mortal Sword, the One Daughter is now the Matron of Mach Nest. Bre'nigan stands as her J'an Sentinel. Sag'Churok is the bearer of the seed. She will speak to you now.'

He turned to face the K'Chain Che'Malle.

'Mortal Sword. The Shield Anvil returns. Shall we await him?'

Don't bother, Matron, it's not like he's smart or anything.

'I can, even from this distance, breach the defences he has raised.'

Do that. He deserves the headache.

'Mortal Sword. Shield Anvil. Destriant. You three stand, you three are the mortal truths of my mother's faith. New beliefs are born. What is an eternity spent in sleep? What is this morning of our first awakening? We honour the blood of our kin spilled this day. We honour too the fallen Nah'ruk and pray that one day they will know the gift of forgiveness.'

You must have seen it for yourself, Matron, Gesler said, *that those Nah'ruk are bred down, past any hope of independent thought. Those sky keeps were old. They can repair, but they cannot make anything new. They are the walking dead, Matron. You can see it in their eyes.*

Kalyth said, 'I believed I saw the same in your eyes, Mortal Sword.'

He grunted and then sighed. *Too tired for this. I have grieving to do.* 'You might have been right, Destriant. But we shed things like that like snake skin. You wear what you need to get through, that's all.'

'Then perhaps we can hope for the Nah'ruk.'

'Hope all you like. Sinn—can they burn another gate through?'

'Not for a long time,' she replied, reaching down to collect up Roach. She cradled the foul thing in her arms, scratching it behind the ears.

The ugly rat's pink tongue slid in and out as it panted. Its eyes were demonic with witless malice.

Gesler shivered.

The Matron spoke: *'We are without a Nest. But the need must wait. Wounds must heal, flesh must be harvested. Mortal Sword, we now pledge ourselves to you. We now serve. Among your friends, there will be survivors. We shall find them.'*

Gesler shook his head. 'We led your army, Matron. We had our battle, but it's over now. You don't owe us anything. And whatever your mother believed, she never asked us, did she? Me and Stormy, we're not priests. We're soldiers and nothing more. Those titles you gave us—well, we're shedding that skin too.'

Stormy's voice rumbled through his mind, *'Same for me, Matron. We can find our friends on our own—you need a city to build, or maybe some other Rooted* you can find. Besides, we got Grub and Sinn, and Bent here—gods, he's almost wagging that stub of a tail and I ain't never seen that before. Must be all the gore on his face.'

Kalyth laughed, even as tears streamed down her lined cheeks. 'You two—you cannot shed your titles. They are branded upon your souls—will you just leave me here?'

'You're welcome to come with us,' said Gesler.

'Where?'

'East, I think.'

The woman flinched.

'You're from there, aren't you? Kalyth?'

'Yes,' she whispered. 'Elan. But the Elan are no more. I am the last. Mortal Sword, you must not choose that direction. You will die—all of you.' She pointed at Grub and Sinn. 'Even them.'

The Matron said, *'Then we see the path before us. We shall guard you all. Ve'Gath. K'ell. J'an. Gu'Rull who still lives, still serves. We shall be your guardians. It is the new way our mother foresaw. The path of our rebirth.*

'Humans, welcome us. The K'Chain Che'Malle have returned to the world.'

Sulkit heard her words and something stirred within her. She had been a J'an Sentinel in the time of her master's need, but her master was gone, and now she was a Matron in her own right.

The time had not yet come when she would make herself known. Old seeds grew within her: the first born would be weak, but that could not be helped. In time, vigour would return.

Her master was gone. The throne was empty, barring a lone eye, embedded in the headrest. She was alone within Kalse.

Life was bleeding into the Rooted's stone. Strange, alien life. Its flesh and bone was rock. Its mind and soul was the singular imposition of belief. *But then, what else are any of us?* She would think on this matter.

He was gone. She was alone. But all was well.

'I have lost him. Again. We were so close, but now . . . gone.'

With these words the trek staggered to a halt, as if in Mappo's private loss all other desires had withered, blown away.

The twins had closed on the undead wolf. Faint had a fear that death had somehow addicted them to its hoary promise. They spoke of Toc. They closed small fingers tight in the ratty fur of Baaljagg. The boy slept in Gruntle's arms—now who could have predicted that bond? No matter, there was something in that huge man that made her think he should have been a father a hundred times by now—to the world's regret, since he was not anything of the sort.

No, Gruntle had broken loves behind him. Hardly unique, of course, but in that man the loss belonged to everyone.

Ah, I think I just yearn for his shadow. Me and half the lasses here. Oh well. Silly Faint.

Setoc, who had been conversing with Cartographer, now walked over.

'The storm to the south's not getting any closer—we have that, at least.'

Faint rubbed the back of her neck and winced at the pressure. 'Could have done with the rain.'

'If there was rain.'

She glanced at the girl. 'Saw you meet Gruntle's eyes a while back. A look passed between you when we were talking about that storm. So, out with it.'

'It was a battle, not a storm. Sorcery, and worse. But now it's over.'

'Who was fighting, Setoc?'

She shook her head. 'It's far away. We don't have to go there.'

'Seems like we're not going anywhere right now.'

'We will. For now, let's leave him be,' she said, eyes on Mappo, who stood a short distance away, motionless as a statue—as he had been for some time.

Amby had been walking alongside the horse-drawn travois carrying his brother—Jula was still close to death. Precious Thimble's healing was a paltry thing. The Wastelands could not feed her magic, she said. There was still the chance that Jula would die. Amby knelt, shading his brother's face with one hand. He suddenly looked very young.

Setoc walked back to the horse.

Sighing, Faint looked around.

And saw a rider approaching. 'Company,' she said, loud enough to catch everyone's attention. All but Mappo reacted, turning or rising and following her gaze.

From Setoc: 'I know him! That's Torrent!'

More lost souls to this pathetic party. Welcome.

A single flickering fire marked the camp, and occasionally a figure passed in front of it. The wind carried no sound from those gathered there. Among the travellers, sorrow and joy, grief and the soft warmth of newborn love. So few mortals, and yet all of life was there, ringing the fire.

Faint jade light limned the broken ground, as if darkness itself could be painted into a mockery of life. The rider who sat upon a motionless, unbreathing horse, was silent, feeling like a creature too vast to approach any shore—he could look on with one dead eye or the other dead eye. He could remember what it was like to be a living thing among other living things.

The heat, the promise, the uncertainties and all the hopes to sweeten the bitterest seas.

But that shore was for ever beyond him now.

They could feel the warmth of that fire. He could not. And never again.

The figure that rose from the dust beside him said nothing for a time, and when she spoke it was in the spirit language—her voice beyond the ears of the living. 'We all do as we must, Herald.'

'What *you* have done, Olar Ethil . . .'

'It is too easy to forget.'

'Forget what?'

'The truth of the T'lan Imass. Did you know, a fool once wept for them?'

'I was there. I saw the man's barrow—the gifts . . .'

'The most horrid of creatures—human and otherwise—are so easily, so carelessly recast. Mad murderers become heroes. The insane wear the crown of geniuses. Fools flower in endless fields, Herald, where history once walked.'

'What is your point, bonecaster?'

'The T'lan Imass. Slayers of Children from the very beginning. Too easy to forget. Even the Imass themselves, the First Sword himself, needed reminding. You all needed reminding.'

'To what end?'

'Why do you not go to them, Toc the Younger?'

'I cannot.'

'No,' she nodded, 'you cannot. The pain is too great. The *loss* you feel.'

'Yes,' he whispered.

'Nor should they yield love to you, should they? Any of them. The children . . .'

'They should not, no.'

'Because, Toc the Younger, you are the brother of Onos T'oolan. His true brother now. And for all the mercy that once dwelt in your mortal heart, only ghosts remain. They must not love you. They must not believe in you. For you are not the man you once were.'

'Did you think I needed reminding, too, Olar Ethil?'

'I think . . . yes.'

She was right. He felt inside for the pain he'd thought—he'd believed—he had lived with for so long. As if *lived* was even the right word. When he found it, he saw at last its terrible truth. *A ghost. A memory. I but wore its guise.*

The dead have found me.

I have found the dead.

And we are the same.

'Where will you go now, Toc the Younger?'

He gathered the reins of his horse and looked back at the distant fire. It was a spark. It would not last the night. 'Away.'

Snow drifted down, the sky was at peace.

The figure on the throne had been frozen, lifeless, for a long, long time.

A fine shedding of dust from the corpse marked that something had changed. Ice then crackled. Steam rose from flesh slowly thickening with life. The hands, gripping the arms of the throne, suddenly twitched, fingers uncurling.

Light flickered in its pitted eyes.

And, looking out from mortal flesh once more, Hood, who had once been the Lord of Death, found arrayed before him fourteen Jaghut warriors. They stood in the midst of frozen corpses, weapons out but lowered or resting across shoulders.

One spoke. 'What was that war again?'

The others laughed.

The first one continued, 'Who was that enemy?'

The laughter this time was louder, longer.

'Who was our commander?'

Heads rocked back and the thirteen roared with mirth.

The first speaker shouted, 'Does he live? Do we?'

Hood slowly rose from the throne, melted ice streaming down his blackened hide. He stood, and eventually the laughter fell away. He took one step forward, and then another.

The fourteen warriors did not move.

Hood lowered to one knee, head bowing. 'I seek . . . penance.'

A warrior far to the right said, 'Gathras, he seeks penance. Do you hear that?'

The first speaker replied. 'I do, Sanad.'

'Shall we give it, Gathras?' another asked.

'Varandas, I believe we shall.'

'Gathras.'

'Yes, Haut?'

'What was that war again?'

The Jaghut howled.

The Errant was lying on wet stone, on his back, unconscious, the socket of one eye a pool of blood.

Kilmandaros, breathing hard, stepped close to look down upon him. 'Will he live?'

Sechul Lath was silent for a moment, and then he sighed. '*Live* is such a strange word. We know nothing else, after all. Not truly. Not . . . intimately.'

'But will he?'

Sechul turned away. 'I suppose so.' He halted suddenly, cocked his head and then snorted. 'Just what he always wanted.'

'What do you mean?'

'He's got an eye on a Gate.'

Her laughter rumbled in the cavern, and when it faded she turned to Sechul and said, 'I am ready to free the bitch. Beloved son, is it time to end the world?'

Face hidden from her view, Sechul Lath closed his eyes. Then said, 'Why not?'

This ends the Ninth Tale
of The Malazan
Book of the Fallen